Hannaford Prep

J Bree

The Mounts Bay Saga/J Bree – 1st ed.
ISBN-13 - 9798692157874

For Raine Florence and River Frances

.

Just Drop Out

Hannaford Prep Year One

Pre-Hannaford

LIPS

The meeting is being held at the strip club that the Jackal owns.

It's disgusting and I'm sure he's doing it as some sort of game for me, some new set of hoops for me to jump through for his enjoyment, so I keep my face carefully blank.

His eyes never leave me.

It's pretty obvious that he's obsessed with me and every other member can see it clearly. The Crow is watching him as closely as he's watching me. I had noticed it during the Game, this weird dynamic between the two of them.

Great.

Looks like I'm caught in the middle of some bullshit turf war I have no interest in.

Luca helps me into a seat like I'm some dainty princess and I give him a glare. He shrugs back, his usual flirty grins gone thanks to the Jackal's careful eye.

I have to remind myself that all of this is the only way out.

The Jackal may be watching me even closer now but he can't actually touch me, not without risking the wrath of the rest of the Twelve. There are rules he has the abide by and one look at the Crow tells me he's ready to throw down with the Jackal over fucking *anything*.

If only he looked a little less terrifying, I might have gone to him for help.

Nope, no thanks.

I'll figure it out on my own.

The Coyote takes a seat next to me. He's the closest to me in age, a few years younger than the Jackal. He smirks at me, making a show of looking me over but it doesn't feel lecherous... more assessing.

"Damn, girl. If I hadn't seen you take Xav out myself I would believe a pint-size like you could do it."

I shrug.

No one ever believes I could do it.

"It is nice to get some fresh puss at the table."

I don't even have to look up to know it's the Vulture talking. He's the worst of the worst, and all throughout the Game he'd made comments about me. I'm fourteen years out and yet he's ready to 'break me in'.

Disgusting.

The Crow seems to think so as well, the look he gives him is severe. "The Wolf is a member of the Twelve now. You'll show her the same respect you do any other member."

The Jackal scoffs. "Which is fucking nothing. If you don't keep your pimps out of my parties I will start sending you their body parts in trash bags, Vulture. If you fuck with my business, I'll take yours out."

Right.

It's then I learn that the meetings are a whole lot of arguing about business and turf. Who owns what.

The Lynx doesn't seem to want another female in the Twelve, she spits little comments and jabs at me the whole meeting but I ignore it entirely. The Tiger and the Fox both ignore me. The Boar keeps glancing at me, like he's unsure of me which I get.

I'm a kid after all.

I look like one at least.

Once the meeting finally comes to an end, the Boar stands and approaches me. Fuck.

"I heard you're planning on doing hits. Are you already trained for it?"

That's a fucking weird question. "Of course. Why, do you have a job?"

He frowns but nods. "Yeah, kid. I've got someone I need gone."

And that's how I get my very first diamond.

Killing some rouge biker.

Prologue

The forest at the edge of Mounts Bay, California, city limits are well known for being haunted.

The kids at the local high school have spent generations whispering about the bodies buried in shallow graves, waiting for the wolves to scent them and dig them up for food. There're even more legends about the souls that walk amongst the towering redwoods. It's quiet, not silent, but compared to the ever-present sounds of traffic and humanity.

It's eerie and adds to the haunted feel.

While I don't believe in ghosts, I can feel the souls that linger here.

It's probably just my guilty conscience giving me the heebie-jeebies as I look over the corpse of my opponent. His blood is still fresh on my hands, cold and congealed, and I wipe them uselessly down my jeans. My clothes are just as stained as my hands, even my face is spattered with the red stains of his life ending. I look like something out of a horror movie, which is about right considering I've just bashed a man's skull in with a rock while a whole crowd of people looked on in sick fascination. There isn't a person watching that dares to make a noise. The vise-like grip of the Club holds their tongues.

I'm not afraid of being caught.

I'm small for my age. Years of food insecurity have taken their toll, and I was the youngest contender in the Game this season. None of that matters though; I've won. I've beaten thirty men and teenage boys to take the victory and the spoils of this war.

I stumble toward the men at the perimeter of the fighting ring. They're all cloaked in black, hard looks on their faces and black ink etched over their cheeks. My hands tremble at the thought of wearing those same marks. The marks of the Twelve. But I've earned them. I've earned the right to stand with them and be one of them.

To be free.

"Congratulations, you've won the Game," the Jackal speaks, and I shiver at the cold tone of his voice, so unlike the warmth he usually extends to me.

I nod my head. I want this over with. I want a hot meal and an even hotter shower.

"Welcome to the Twelve. You're replacing the Hawk. Who do you choose to be?"

Free. I guess a hawk is a good embodiment of freedom, but it feels strange to take a dead man's name, like climbing into his bed with the sheets still warm. I look around at the other men that make up the Twelve. Their names are what they're known as on the streets, what their gangs cover themselves with as protection and a warning. I could have that too. I could make myself a queen of my own empire. I could rule the streets and never go hungry again.

I could escape the cycle of poverty my mother has left me in.

My eyes land back on the Jackal, and I lift my chin until I no longer feel like I'm looking up at him.

"I am the Wolf."

Chapter One

The boy on the stand is so gorgeous, it's hard to look directly at his face.

Instead, I look at his hands as they clench tightly where they rest on his lap. There are dozens of other teenagers in the room, but I can't look away from him for long before I am drawn back to him, a moth to a stunning flame. He has broad shoulders and big arms, like he works out more than regularly. His hands are big and strong. I like the look of those hands. The more I look at them, the more I imagine what they would feel like on my skin. I imagine them stroking over my arms, my neck, cupping my face and pulling me in against his chest, tilting my head back. A flush settles over my skin. Who is this guy? How has the mere sight of him turned me into a babbling mess?

I can look as far as his neck without breaking out in a sweat, and as the trial drags on, I manage to make out the script tattoo on his neck. The words *'honor before blood'* are tucked under his chin, the black ink stark against his pale skin. He has to be a gangster, but that doesn't suit his fair looks at all. He looks as though he has never done a hard day's work in his life. His sandy hair is messed artfully, and his nose is straight and unmarred. The tattoo tucked under his jaw is the only suggestion that he's not a pampered model. When the judge reads out his case, he says the guy is my age, and no boy of fifteen gets ink like that unless they're already out on the streets.

When I spot the Rolex on his wrist, I realize he must be a drug dealer. It's like a cold bucket of ice over my lustful body. Drug dealers are scum, and I do not want to admire him anymore. I am doing everything in my power to get away from drugs and the people that peddle them. It doesn't matter how drawn I feel to this guy. I look away and resist the pull of his stunning looks.

The courthouse we are trapped in is a converted historic building that had been built by convicts. The district of Mounts Bay is small enough that court proceedings are held twice a week. All children's cases are held here in the morning, and then the adults are brought through in the afternoon. My case was supposed to start half an hour ago, but the beautiful dealer is arguing belligerently with the judge and taking up more than his allocated time slot.

What a dick.

His rap sheet isn't great, but it also isn't violent, which makes me feel slightly better about ogling him.

Car theft. Breaking and entering. Violating a work order.

Clearly it isn't his first time in this building. I glance up at him again, I can't help myself, and I can see how bored and unaffected his eyes are, like this is all such an inconvenience to him and his time. I want to roll my eyes, but once again I'm transfixed.

"You ready, kid?" My social worker interrupts my staring and I startle. She's looking at me like I'm fragile again, and I don't know how to tell her that I'm easily the strongest person in this room. You don't survive what I have without becoming bulletproof. I have five pins holding one of my legs together to prove it.

I'm the Wolf of Mounts Bay, and I can survive anything.

The gangster kid steps down from the stand, and it's my turn.

As he walks down the stairs, we cross paths. I force myself to look up at him. His face is a mask of disinterest and apathy, but my breath catches in my throat when I see his eyes. The icy blue depths pull me in, and I feel like I'm drowning. He's angry. He's hiding it well, but he looks at me and I can see the burning pits of hell in his eyes. This guy is one step away from being a killer. I shiver. I should not find that attractive or exciting. But, fuck me, I do. It's my curse for being a loyal supporter of the Jackal.

He doesn't seem to notice me the way I notice him, and it makes sense. I'm not stunning. I'm not the most gorgeous girl in the room. I'm just trying to get by, skate under the radar and make it through to adulthood. I take the stand.

Unlike him, I'm not here to defend myself from my own mistakes.

If I were, I'd probably be locked up. The things I've done to get here, to have a chance at freedom, they will follow me for the rest of my life. But that doesn't matter. Act by act, brick by brick, I've built my way here and now I'll get what I've sacrificed so much for.

I'm claiming my freedom.

It's time to put away the empty, cold shell I had to become to survive. I don't know who the new version of myself will be, but I'm ready to find out.

TWO MONTHS LATER

"This is your last chance to make any requests of the state before you are officially emancipated and on your own."

Heather has her eyebrow cocked at me like I'm being dense for not having anything to say, but honestly, I'm torn between being afraid of saying goodbye to her and wanting her to leave so I can start my new life.

We're standing outside Hannaford Preparatory Academy, and the building looms over us like a ghoul. It looks more like a castle than a school, and there are honest-to-god turrets and an incomplete moat surrounding the building. There's a bronzed statue of a light-horseman in the gardens. The school was built in the 1800s and boasts many presidents and political savants as alumni. The extracurricular roster includes an equestrian program and an Olympic-level swim team. It has a near perfect college acceptance rate from the students who have walked these halls, and the waiting list to get in is the stuff of legends. Looking at the building alone makes me feel so intimidated that I consider getting back in the car.

A tingle runs down my spine at the thought of going back to my old school, and I turn back to my social worker. Huh, ex-social worker now. The tingle turns into a shiver and takes over me, despite the warmth still in the air.

"I'm fine. I understand all of my rights, I've done the mandatory counseling, and I'm ready to be a big girl out in the world."

She snorts, then hands me my case files and the enrollment forms for the head office. She's a brusque sort of woman, not maternal at all, and I think that's why we get along so well. It's weird to think I won't see her again. I've gotten used to listening to the comforting Southern tones of her voice.

"You ain't ready for shit, kid. I've left your emergency line on a card in your files if you get into trouble, but you're off my roster now. Try to do well at your fancy school and stay off the streets."

What a glowing statement of confidence. I think about giving her a hug but decide against it, and instead I give her a small wave. She gets back in the car and I watch as she drives away. For a second I feel a flare of panic in my chest, but I quickly push that away. It doesn't matter that I'm alone now. I don't need anyone but myself. If my life so far has proven anything to me, it is that I am strong enough to survive anything.

Once the car is no longer in view, I grab the small satchel that holds all my belongings and head up the cobblestone path toward the main building. It's like a fairy tale here, and if I believed in such things, it probably would have felt like a good omen.

There are students everywhere. The entire grounds are teeming with teenagers, and I'm getting a ton of curious looks. I try not to let it get to me as I walk up to the office. When I make it, huffing and puffing under the weight of my bag, the door is being held open by a group of teenagers and it's clear they're closely related. They're all dark-haired, blue-eyed, and their facial features look as though they were carved from marble by a master artist. The older boy is smirking at the front desk, and the other two, a boy and a girl, are looking at him despondently, glassy-eyed and utterly bored. None of them spare me so much as a glance.

"Yvette, I really don't care what your policies are, I'm not sharing with Ash. Put Avery in with him. They're attached at the hip anyway."

The receptionist, a lush woman who is at the very least in her forties, gives him a firm look, but he clearly doesn't care. His shoulders are broad and tight under his blazer. He looks like he's poised and ready to strike. I press my back against the wall out of habit, a lesson learned years ago. When there's danger in the room, you don't leave your back unguarded.

"Mr. Beaumont, as you well know, it is against school policy for there to be co-ed rooms, even amongst siblings."

He sneers at her and spits out, "I am not sharing. Who do I have to write the check out to? You will give me a single room."

I scoff at that, but then Yvette is pulling out a ledger and he's handing over a shiny black credit card. This is my first clue at how truly messed up this school's moral code is.

"And who, exactly, are you?" the girl, Avery, says and I startle when I realize she's talking to me.

"Lips. Lips Anderson. I'm a freshman."

A smile dances around the edge of her painted lips, but her eyes aren't amused.

"What sort of degenerate names their child *Lips*?" the boy drawls and, weirdly, it makes me feel kind of boneless. He turns to face me, and I'm struck dumb by the sight of him. That is until I see the disgust on his face. He looks at me like I'm a venereal disease. I choose not to answer him and push away from the wall. I brush past the group to pile all my paperwork up on the desk, feigning confidence, even though I'm kind of shaky. Is the whole school full of gorgeous, rich assholes? The older sibling looks down his nose at me as well before he turns on his heel and stalks out, presumably to go find his new single room. The receptionist ignores me and turns soft eyes onto the remaining boy.

"I'm so sorry. I assumed you would want to share with your brother, Ash. Do you want a single too? I have a spare in the boys' dorms."

He smiles, and his whole face changes. My breath catches in my chest and I take note. This boy can use his looks as a weapon, and he very clearly knows it.

"Actually, I'd rather share with Mr. Arbour and Mr. Morrison, if that's possible? I know there's some triple rooms, and we're probably the best candidates in our year to bunk together."

Yvette blushes and stumbles over her words. She's quick to take his bait, and it's hard not to roll my eyes.

"Oh, the triple rooms aren't for boys of your breeding or stature. They're for the lower families."

Lower families? Sweet lord, here we go. I assume with just how low my family is, I'll be in the damn basement. That suits me just fine.

"I insist. I need to keep a close eye on them both and make sure there isn't a repeat of last year." He winks, and Yvette nearly swoons.

I glance over and see Avery watching the entire exchange with molten fury in her eyes. I think for a minute that she's pissed at her brother, and then she reaches out gently and clasps his hand. He doesn't look back at his sister, but he gives her hand a quick squeeze. She doesn't like that he's being forced to flirt with this woman; she's protective of him.

"Are there singles available in the girls' dorms?" His voice is back to the drawl. Yvette checks some papers in front of her and smiles.

"Avery is already in one of the singles. There's two available, and I popped her straight in it. Your twin called me earlier and...expressed her desires."

Her hesitation seems totally out of place, and when she looks at Avery there's fear in her eyes. I make a note of that too and file the information away.

"Lovely. Thank you, Yvette."

The twins leave with another look my way, and then Yvette turns to give me a once-over.

"I'm assuming you're the scholarship student?" Jeez, if only I looked like Ash, I might have gotten a better welcome. I smile despite her tone and offer her my hand to shake.

"Eclipse Anderson. I prefer Lips, though."

She ignores my hand, gives me a hard look, and takes my paperwork.

"Scholarship students are a handful already, and now we have an emancipated student? I'll warn you that this school is held to the highest standard of morals, and you will be expected to behave in an exemplary manner," she says, like she wasn't just getting hot and heavy over a teenage boy.

I make sure my face is a mask of polite obedience and nod along with her. You don't survive foster care as well as I have without being able to lie a little.

"You are also being put in a single. There was some upset about your lodging amongst the other students."

"Upset?" I raise my eyebrows at her tone.

"These are girls of very prestigious families, and they have some serious concerns about sharing with a girl with your…reputation."

What the hell? "What exactly is my reputation?"

"We've had a few run-ins with Mounts Bay High girls before, which has led to strict rules about how our students spend their time outside of Hannaford. There are concerns for the safety of the students and their property."

I flush scarlet and clench my teeth together so hard I might crack them. I'm about to tell this woman where to shove her opinions when the door to the principal's office opens and Mr. Trevelen steps out. His eyes light up when he spots me, and he lets out a long exhale.

Mr. Trevelen was responsible for awarding scholarships, and he personally interviewed me at the end of my last school year. He had sat in the care house I was stuck in, and listened to my entire life story like he actually gave a damn about helping me. Even with my great marks, I had been turned down for other scholarships because of my living situation and family history, so I knew he had gone out on a limb for me.

"Miss Anderson, what a relief you've made it here safely! I had some concerns after the Academy car was declined by your guardian."

I smile and readjust the bag strap on my shoulder.

"I think she just wanted to be nosey and see the school up close."

An extravagant fence surrounds the entire school property, and the ornate gate is electric. I'd been given a keycard to get in, which I now hand back to Mr. Trevelen.

"I won't hold it against her," he says with a wink, "I have cleared some time from my schedule this morning to walk you to your dorm, and then show you around a little. Most of your peers will already know where to go, as they have completed an orientation week here during the spring. I wouldn't want you to get lost."

Yvette gives me another look, but I smile at her sweetly and grab my bags to follow the principal out the door.

At least I have someone on my side.

My room is tiny.

It's at the end of the hall in the girls' dorm. I had to walk past all the other large and luxurious suites to get to it, so I know it must be a converted closet. Some of the other girls are lounging around the common areas and sniggering behind their hands as I walk past, like it's so funny I've got this room.

It's the first time in my life I've got a room to myself.

These spoiled brats have no clue what I've survived and having a room that barely fits my bed in it is not hard. The bed is a double, which is another first, and there's a small closet that would still fit ten times the clothes I own. I can feel a silly smile tugging at my lips, and I fight the urge to squeal.

I have my own room at the best school in the country.

I am going to nail this year, and then every other year until I graduate. I'm going to go to an Ivy League college on another scholarship, and then I'm going to become… actually, I haven't figured that out yet. I'm still researching what the highest paid industry is and whether I could work there for forty years without wanting to kill myself.

I unpack and stash my bags away. I get down on my hands and knees and tap away quietly until I find a suitable wooden board to pull up. It's easy enough work with my knife, and once it's out, I slide the tiny safe I've brought with me into the gap. I use some old shirts to stuff the space and hide the hollow crevice from others who would think to tap around, then I slide the wood back over it. What the safe holds is worth more than my life.

I've got a text waiting on my phone, and I don't have to look at it to see it's Matteo. He's the only person who has my number and, really, he's the last piece of my old life I have left. The same icy fingers of fear crawl up my spine as I read his text.

This town doesn't feel the same without you. Come home soon.

I snort, but there isn't much I can say to him without some sort of consequences.

Matteo D'Ardo was another foster kid, and four years older than me. We met at school, and he had taken me under his wing even before my mom died and I wound up in the system. He was dangerous. More dangerous than any of these rich kids could ever be. They play pretend in their safe little bubble, but Matteo was the Jackal. He owned more than my home city; he owned the entire state. In a lot of ways, he owned me too.

Keep me in the loop. I'll be back for the party and trials next summer.

When the scholarship offer had arrived at the care home I was living in, I had made the decision to put aside my life in Mounts Bay, California, and to take a chance on a better life. The public school I had left behind had a reputation for churning out drug dealers, gangsters, and single mothers. If I didn't make it at Hannaford Prep, my options were limited. I didn't want to follow Matteo. I didn't want to settle for a desperate life.

I shove the phone into my back pocket and head down to the dining hall. The whispers follow me and it's creepy as fuck. It's pretty clear that not only am I not welcome but the other students actively resent me being here. I wonder what exactly the other Mounts Bay students have done to leave this kind of impression.

The dining hall is a long room that resembles a wide corridor. It's in the center of the building, so there're no windows and the room is lit only by massive chandeliers. There's only room for a single, stretched wooden table that could easily seat two hundred people. Hannaford is very exclusive, but I know there must be more students attending than that. At the far end there are teachers already eating, but there's gaps everywhere. I only spare the logistics of mealtimes a moment's thought before I go to stand in line. I get to hear more of the crap that's being said about me. One girl even says I slept with Mr. Trevelen to get the scholarship, and I turn to give her a proper glare. The arrogance in this room is astounding. I need to build up a shield to it all. I need to become immune, so I can make it through my time here.

The food looks incredible, and I heap it onto my plate. I'm way too skinny, the type of skinny that only happens after years of food scarcity, and I'm licking my lips at the thought of eating three big meals a day.

Once my tray is full, I start to look for a seat that isn't surrounded by glaring students. I end up at the far end, close to the teachers, with no other students within ten chairs of me. It's actually perfect.

Until the far door opens and they walk in.

The twins are flanked by a guy so gorgeous I'm stunned, and it takes me a second to realize it's the guy from the courthouse last month. He looks absolutely devastating in his uniform, and there are girls frothing left, right and center over both him and Ash. Avery is looking down her nose at them all. I notice again that the teachers all eye her like she's a ticking time bomb with their name on it. *Interesting.*

I watch them discreetly as I eat, the subtle art of surveillance being something I picked up from my time with the Jackal. Ash is holding two plates, and as Avery picks out food, he's filling one up for her. It's kind of sweet how close they are, how effortlessly they're taking care of each other. The other boy is laughing and joking with them both, but his laugh is dark and twisted, like he's making fun of everything around him.

When they're done, they head to the table and a hush falls over the room. I can practically see students praying they decide to sit with them, like it'll somehow boost their social status. This school is so weird.

Avery leads the boys to sit across the table and a few seats down from me. The stunning guy pulls out a chair for her. I know they have no intention of speaking to me, so it makes it easier to duck my head and eat, listening to the scraps of conversations around me.

"Morrison is going to start mid-semester; he's still in Europe doing his thing."

"Lucky us, we get a reprieve from all of the little shit's revelers. If I have to find one more pair of lacy panties stuffed in his door frame, I will retire on the spot."

The explicit language from a teacher makes me smile, but I don't look to see which one said it. What kind of a school is this? I shake my head and try to focus on my dinner. I've never eaten such delicious food in my life, and I'm looking forward to the next four years for that alone.

"I can see the hole from across the table. I'm ordering you a new one, so swallow your useless pride," Avery says, and even with the harshness of the words, her voice is much nicer when it's not directed at me.

"I don't fucking need a new one. It's a design statement. Leave it be, Floss," the other boy says, and even though he's swearing at her I can hear the affection. I can also *feel* Avery seething.

"Don't call me that here. And the only statement you're making is 'too poor to care'. Do you want a repeat of last year?"

That's the second reference to something happening last year I've heard, and now I'm interested to find out what they're going on about. I glance up and make eye contact with the hot boy by accident. I hold it for a second, and then glance away because I don't want to look like I'm scared of his attention, even though I'm beginning to sweat in his general proximity. *Get ahold of yourself.*

"Who's the new kid?"

"Lips." Avery stretches my name out, and it sounds so juvenile coming from her. Both boys snigger, and I roll my eyes where they can't see. Ash sums up the opinion of me that the whole room has already come to.

"Who gives a fuck, she's Mounty trash."

If only that were true.

Chapter Two

If you're in the top classes at Hannaford, they start at 7 a.m., which seems to be cruel and unusual torture to me. Why punish the high achievers?

I sleep like the dead, and still I want to pitch my alarm at the wall.

I manage to get up and look human in my crisp uniform. I even squeeze in the time to put on a little makeup to try and hide the dark marks under my eyes. I don't need to give the other kids any more ammo.

My scholarship pays for exactly three daily uniforms, two sets of sporting tracksuits, and a formal uniform for representing the school at social functions. This means I have to be very mindful of what happens to these clothes, because the school skirt alone costs more than a month's worth of groceries.

The dining hall is basically empty, so I get to sit close to the door and stuff my breakfast into my mouth. I wish I had the time to savor the fluffy scrambled eggs and crispy bacon, but I'm on a serious time crunch. I hoover it down, and then grab an apple on the way out.

My first class is history, and I'm relieved to see a seating plan posted on the door. I'm at the back and sharing with a male student, Harley Arbour. Avery is at the desk in front of us, and Ash isn't in the class, which is great because I don't want to be called trash this early in the morning. It's harder to rein my temper in.

It's like a gut punch when I realize the super hot guy's name is Harley, and I now have to share a desk with him three times a week. He smells incredible, like bergamot and cloves, and I find myself angry at him for it. I have never really taken much notice of guys. I'm not interested in being knocked up and abandoned like my mom was. It was easy enough in Mounts Bay. All the guys in my grade had that air of desperation that comes with teenage hormones and poverty. Everyone at that school was living below the poverty line, and everyone was going hungry. I couldn't look at any guy without getting the distinct feeling they just wanted an escape from the bleak hole that was their life. Plus, they all knew I was associated with Matteo. They all steered clear of me.

None of the boys at Hannaford are desperate. They all have the means to be here, they've never struggled for anything, and I quickly learned that with money comes looks. I'm not saying that only rich people are attractive, I know that's not the case, but they can all afford to take care of themselves and show their best side every day. There isn't a single girl I've seen yet that doesn't look plucked, primped, and plumped to within an inch of their life, and all the guys are sporting Rolexes, coiffed hair, and expensive cologne.

Harley winces when he sees me at the desk, but he sits and methodically empties his bag. His handwriting is much neater than mine, and he already has notes from the textbook we were assigned. All of this conflicts with the gangster image I had in my head, and my eyebrows are raised as I take it all in. He might just be the person to beat in the class.

"Your name is Eclipse?" His voice drips with venom. Fucking rich boys.

"What can I say, my parents were hippies." That's not even close to true, but it's an easy lie I've told a hundred times. It's much easier than saying my mom had a conversation with the moon one night and decided to dedicate her unborn child's name to it. That kind of story comes with blank stares, or worse, they figure out she must have been high. I wonder how many kids can say they spent the first three weeks of their lives detoxing from heroin in a NICU? Lucky me.

"Whatever, Mounty. Don't cheat off my notes. I can see you eyeing them. I don't share, I don't want to work as a team, I'm not fucking helping you."

A laugh rips out of my chest in shock. He doesn't look at me; his eyes stay glued to the front of the classroom.

"I don't need your help. Why would I need help from some gangster kid? Steal any cars recently? What the hell are you doing at this school?" I say, and the words come out harsher than I intended.

Shock flits across his face, but it's gone as quickly as it was there. He turns and looks at me with such intense loathing, I swallow. My survival instincts have clearly been misplaced since I arrived here. Who would have thought a school full of rich assholes could be just as volatile as Mounts Bay High? I have to remember I'm not the Wolf here. I'm at the bottom of the ladder with no friends, no allies, no hope.

"What the fuck are you talking about?" Of course, he didn't recognize me, why would he remember seeing me there? I only remember him because he's, well, utterly drool-worthy.

"I was at the courthouse getting my emancipation last month. I had to sit and hear all about your summer activities."

He shoves away from the desk roughly and turns on me. I notice immediately that he's much bigger than me. His shoulders are wide and filled out, like he knows his way around a gym. The words tattooed under his jaw flick as his muscles clench tightly in rage.

"Listen here, you little bitch—"

"Harley. I will deal with it. Focus on your schoolwork." My head snaps around at Avery's voice, but she hasn't even bothered to look at us. What the hell? Deal with *it*, like I'm not even a person?

Harley hesitates, like he'd rather rip my head off himself, but then the teacher is stepping into the room and he gets situated back at the desk. I glance around to see wide eyes in every direction.

Great.

I'd just pissed off one of the alpha males at the school.

Ms. Aurelia introduces herself, and then hands out a pop quiz to each student.

"I like to start out the year knowing what my students already know, so we don't accidentally cover old subjects. Anyone who does not get 80 percent or higher will be moved into the lower classes, as we won't have the time to cover older subjects."

At least a half-dozen students groan. I glance through the pages and I'm relieved to find I know all the answers. My biggest concern with coming to Hannaford was that I'd be behind thanks to my public school education. I'd spent the entire summer break reading all of my textbooks.

I have all three pages filled out in under three minutes. Harley glares at me as I put down my pen, but he finishes up less than a minute later.

Ms. Aurelia collects our papers and grades them while we wait on the rest of the class. Harley flicks through his notes like he's grading himself from memory, and I'm forced to stare around the classroom in silence. It's pretty clear that at least four of the students are going to be lucky to stay in the class, the panic easy to read in their posture as they slouch over their work.

"Oh dear, Mr. Arbour," says Ms. Aurelia, and Harley's head snaps up to look at her. His eyes are wide.

"You got 99 percent, with only one question wrong. A very good score."

He exhales, and then his eyes narrow. "What's wrong with that?"

"I know you enjoy being the top of the class. Miss Anderson got 100 percent. I don't think you've ever been beaten in my class before, so I hope you're up for a challenge."

If I thought he had looked angry when I'd called him a gangster, it was nothing compared to his face now. Avery turns to smile at me, but it's the smile of a predator who has identified their prey. Dread leaves a trail of ice down my spine.

Maybe I have made a mistake coming to Hannaford.

Lunch is a hellish experience, and I desperately wish I could eat out in the sunshine on the grass.

My stomach rumbles loudly at all the delicious smells coming from the buffet tables, and once again I fill my plate to the brim. The long table is bustling and overflowing with students, and I have no choice but to take the first empty seat I can find. The girl to my left gives me a hard look and turns her back on me. The boy on my right leers at me and tries to peer down my shirt. I elbow him, hard, and then start in on my food. The noise in the room is raucous and deafening, so when it suddenly dies down to whispers, I look up.

The guy from the office, the older Beaumont kid, is standing in front of a group of freshmen kids seated at the end of the table, not too far away from where I'm sitting. He's flanked by four other students who are all smirking.

"Move."

The freshmen look at each other, and then one of them, a guy I haven't seen before, says, "We haven't finished yet. You have to wait."

All of the whispers stop.

You could hear a pin drop in the room; even the kitchen staff are silent.

"Get. Up," he says again, but the guy stares at him blankly. The flush on his face betrays him.

"Let me explain to you how this works. I'm a Beaumont. My family is old money, so old it will never run dry. In fact, I wipe my ass with more money than your pathetic little family has ever made, and I have the connections to not only ruin your life, but to end it. If I tell you to move, *you move.*"

All the freshmen stand at once and move. The guy who spoke grabs his tray and manages one step away before Beaumont slaps the tray and covers him in his lunch. He hisses as the hot soup splashes on his face and down his uniform.

"There is a clear hierarchy in this school, and you are at the bottom. Don't fucking forget it."

No one moves to help the guy, and I can see angry tears welling up in his eyes. The kitchen staff starts motioning for the kids in the line to move along, ignoring the situation happening before them.

Fucking rich kids.

I focus on my food again, except now I can hear the older kids talking because they're sitting so close to me.

"How are the twins settling in? I'm thinking about fucking your brother, by the way. I like the scowl on his face. It'll be like fucking an angry, miniature you."

"You're such a slut, Harlow. Make sure he pays you well."

The girl just laughs, like she enjoys this pompous dick speaking about her like she's nothing.

"Maybe I'll do him right after I do you, just to see who fucks better."

The group laughs again, and they start a terrible game of comparing their conquests, loudly and in detail. I chew faster to get out of the room. I don't want to attract their attention. I can't help but listen to them, though.

"I want to fuck Morrison, just to say I've had him. Joey, get your sister to get me in with him. I've heard she's the gatekeeper to all three of those boys."

Joey, who is the older Beaumont sibling, scoffs.

"She's a little cunt, just like Mom was. You have no chance there; I've always assumed she's fucking them all. I'm expecting her to get knocked up by Ash and them to have a three-headed, incestuous baby. Father would be so proud."

They cackle again and I get up with my plate, too sick to keep eating. What a great guy to have as a brother. I mean, the twins didn't exactly seem like upstanding human beings, but no one deserves a sibling who speaks so badly of them, and in such a public way.

I leave the dining hall to walk to my next class, and I try to ignore the looks and whispers.

The girls' dorms don't have individual private bathrooms, so you have to use a giant communal bathroom.

It's worse than being in the group home.

I manage to get in and out of the shower before any of the other girls come into the bathroom, and I tuck my toiletries bag under my arm as I walk back to my room. I'm dressed in old boxer shorts and an old band tee that I love.

Every girl in my dorm stops and watches me walk past.

I don't get what their problems are with me. Surely being on a scholarship doesn't mean I'm the enemy, and yet I haven't had a single student try and talk nicely to me. It's exhausting.

As I open my door, I hear Avery's voice, and I pause for a second.

"Fucking pathetic."

I whip my head around to stare at her. She's leaning against her own doorframe across the hall from my room. I can see her room is at least four times bigger than mine and furnished luxuriously. I can't help but feel jealous, even as her eyes are fixed on my shirt. I glance down, but there are no holes or stains in it. What does she have against band tees?

"If you think that will get his attention, you're an even more stupid Mounty slut than I thought."

"Whose attention? These are my pajamas; I don't want to show them to a guy."

She stares at me for a second before smirking. She is strikingly beautiful, but with her lips twisted into a sneer, I think she looks older than fifteen.

"You're totally clueless. Even better."

I see a flash and blink owlishly. She's taken a photo of me on her phone and then retreated into her room, locking the door behind her.

These rich kids are going to do me in.

After I'm safely behind my own locked door, I collapse onto my bed and groan. I had better end up with an amazing career for putting up with this school.

I check my phone and see Matteo has texted me again.

Are you raising hell yet?

I bite my lip. While I've always been academically driven, and always the top of my classes, I had a reputation for being a bitch at my last school. Not that I was a bully, I just had a lot of anger because of my home life.

My mom was addicted to drugs and, because of that, neglected me.

It's hard to admit that out loud. It makes me feel like she mustn't have loved me very much if she was willing to spend all our food money on heroin, coke, meth, pills, whatever she could get her hands on really. I didn't ever want to admit how much easier my life had become after she died. I must be the worst child in the world to think that, and yet it's true. In foster care, I never had to worry about if there was going to be food on the table at night.

Granted, the food was shit and never quite enough.

My mom told me that my dad had been sent to prison in a different state for drug trafficking, which meant I had basically been left to raise myself. I think I'd done a great job of not turning into a hopeless asshole, and someday I would be a doctor or an engineer or some other career that paid ridiculous money. Then I would never have to worry about food ever again.

So, I was known for having a smart mouth and being angry all the time. It had worked out in my favor with Matteo.

I'm definitely not in Kansas anymore, Toto.

I smile as I hit send. Matteo had sent the same message to me the day after he had moved out of the group care home. Back then, I'd wished so hard that I could move out of there with him. He was like a security blanket to me in the group home. Something safe to go home to. He'd told me when I'd accepted the scholarship that I would have to go back to him when I was done with school, and that I wasn't allowed to grow apart from him. It made me feel wanted, in a dark, twisted way.

I've never felt that before.

Come home then, kid. I'll take good care of you.

I smiled and rubbed my thumb over the screen. How I wished life was that simple. How I wished he hadn't become a monster.

I have to make a life for myself, we can't all be the Jackal.

The Jackal. His name on the streets. I knew he was involved in all sorts of trouble, and I tried not to think too hard about it.

This Jackal just wants his Wolf safe and by his side. Don't forget that while you're at this big posh school.

A shudder ran down my spine. Why did that always sound more like a threat than a promise?

Chapter Three

The first time I get a real break from Avery and Harley is during study hall. It is the one required unit that's flexible about the location, and I choose to go to the library.

The library is huge and looks vaguely Victorian. The fiction section is a third of the size of the non-fiction and referencing sections, and the librarians are all matronly women with tight gray buns perched on their heads. I feel most out of place at this school in this room. It makes me feel like a grubby child to walk through the doors, and I still cringe after weeks of doing it.

I don't have a laptop to use quietly in my room, and the library has a selection of computers to use, the only modern luxury. I get there early and choose a desk toward the back of the room. One of the librarian's nods at me in acknowledgment but doesn't offer any help as I struggle with the technology. My last school only had one computer in the library, and it was a glorified typewriter. Internet access was limited, and students generally didn't bother using it. The computers here are high-tech, complicated, and in my opinion, high maintenance. I guess they fit in well with the student population.

The bell tolls, and the room begins to fill with students. A girl I recognize from my biology class approaches my desk and smiles sweetly before taking a seat across from me. Once the rest of the seats at the other tables are taken by students, a group of freshmen reluctantly fill the remaining seats at my table. I don't even spare them a glance and instead focus on my assignment.

I'm focusing on my research at the computer when a piece of paper slides toward me.

I saw your argument with Harley in history. You shouldn't piss Avery and the boys off. The rest of us learned that lesson in middle school.

I look up at her, and then at the rest of the table, but no one is paying us any attention. I scribble a reply and slide it back.

If I always did what I was supposed to do, I wouldn't be at this school.

She smiles and scrabbles back. The library isn't exactly quiet, students are talking all around us, so I'm not sure why we're doing this with notes, but I'll play along for now.

My name is Lauren. If they hadn't put a ban on the rest of us speaking to you, I would've already approached you. I know what it's like to be the new girl at school.

How the hell do they ban other students from talking to people? Who the hell do they think they are? I'm angry enough that I grip my pencil so hard my hand shakes.

What happens to you if you speak to me?

She bites her lip before sliding the paper back.

Then they add me to the list, and they will do to me what they're going to do to you. I'm sorry, I'm terrified of Avery.

The list? Was that metaphorical, or did that psycho Avery actually organize her reign of terror that methodically? I let out a deep sigh and nod my head at Lauren. I guess I didn't blame her, or any of the others in our class. I'd seen what Joseph had done to the other freshmen. I was fine on my own, but sometimes it was hard to see the other students walking around, chatting and laughing together, and not wish I had someone to talk to.

I give her a nod and scrunch the note up in my hand, a clear sign of conversation over. She gives me a sad smile and gets back to work on her own homework.

I try to focus back on my own work, but I'm all hot and cranky. I hate this sort of bullying. I'd rather they just come at me with fists so I could fight back properly. Whispers and intrigue are annoying, but then I think about life back home and Matteo. Maybe learning this political shit isn't such a terrible idea.

It might help me survive the Jackal someday.

As the first few weeks pass, I learn something very important.

Harley and Avery are in every single one of my classes except choir, and they, along with Ash, have a lot of influence on our classmates.

News had spread quickly of my argument with Harley, and it has made me even more of a pariah than my scholarship status ever has. No one tries to speak to me, not during classes or meals. I think they are trying to make me feel shitty enough to leave, but little do they know I am enjoying the quiet.

At the beginning of the year, I had signed up for a bunch of extracurricular duties to get class credits and plump up my applications for college. The one I am looking forward to the least is tutoring especially now that I've pissed off Harley. It takes three weeks before I get an email from the school's admin to let me know I have had someone sign up and to meet the student in the library during three of my study halls. I groan but go along to it. When I see who the student is, I begin to think it's a trap.

Ash Beaumont.

Clearly, I've pissed someone off in a past life.

He's waiting at the assigned desk in the library, his books and supplies spread out around him. He's so classically good looking, like he's a Grecian fantasy, and I have to remind myself that he is a dick before I sit down with him. The sneer he gives me helps to calm my hormones down. I can admire him from a distance, but the vitriol he spits at me on a daily basis, proves just how badly I need to keep him at arm's length.

"Oh, goody. I get to spend three hours a week with trash," he drawls, and I grit my teeth.

"If you want the help with your assignments, then yeah, you're stuck with the trash."

He grins at me, and it's not a nice thing.

I pull out my own schoolwork and get the utter joy of his criticism on what seems like every aspect of my life. I do my best to ignore it, but I'm not the most patient person.

"Your handwriting is atrocious. Why do you bite your nails? They make you look like a boy? You shouldn't slouch; you might actually have a decent rack, and no one will notice it if you're all hunched over— "

"Can you shut the fuck up and tell me what you need help with?" I hiss at him. He smirks like he knows he's got a direct hit. Fuck, I wish I'd met him at Mounts Bay. I'd have destroyed him with calculated calm and a grin on my face. I would have Matteo at my back and be able to end him in creative and devious ways. We could have made a real game of it. But instead I'm at Hannaford, and I've already pissed one of Avery's boys off so far. I can't push it until I know the lay of the land. I need to hold my cards close to my chest until I know the best way to play them.

He shows me his math homework, and then starts to work through the problems quietly. I watch him while he works, and I realize straightaway that something is off. I can't quite put my finger on it, but the way he looks at the paper, he's not really trying to work out the answers. It's infuriating.

"Can you at least do a better job of pretending to try? If you're not going to take this seriously, I'll use the time to study instead."

He gives me a look. His eyes are penetrating, like he's trying to get a good look at what's happening under my skin. I'm used to being looked at like this, but it's disconcerting getting it from a rich kid at Hannaford. Why would he need to know anything about me? In four years, I'll cease to exist in his life, and he'll take over his family's billion-dollar empire. Yeah, I looked up the Beaumonts. Billionaires. It made me queasy to think about that sort of money.

"You only get the credit if you do it properly. I'll let the office staff know how little you care about helping other students."

"Why should I help you if you won't try?"

He leans back in his chair and folds his arms. He's leaner than Harley but he's still much bigger than me. I shiver. God, I'm broken.

"Because you're Mounty trash and you need the credits. I could never work a day in my life and I'll still out-earn you exponentially."

I clench my teeth. I hate him. Even if he is gorgeous.

We continue to bicker and fight our way through all his homework. He tells me he needs help with every subject, and as the hour dwindles down, I can taste my freedom. The library door swings open and Avery walks in, making a beeline for our table.

Great.

I brace myself, assuming she's here for me, but she doesn't even glance my way. Her eyes are glued on Ash.

"What's this about you starting fights with Joey?"

She's softer with Ash than anyone else, like he's some precious thing that needs to be handled with care. He doesn't look that way to me, especially as he looks at her with a glare. It's clearly not aimed at her. He treats her with the same unflinching care.

"Fuck Joey. He knows Harley is off-limits, and yet, he still keeps coming for him. I'll fucking end him, Floss."

Her eyes flick at me when he calls her that, but she doesn't pull him up. She has her hands on her hips and she's looking at him like he's a naughty child she needs to discipline.

"Can you please contain yourself? It's a lot harder to minimize damage here than it was in the lower grades. I have a lot on my plate as it is."

"He's the one being a dick. I couldn't exactly sit around with my thumb up my ass while they started in on Harley, could I? I don't know why they seem to think that they'll be able to beat us. We've been handing them their own asses since middle school."

He goes back to his homework, but if he thinks she's going to let it go, he is sorely disappointed.

"I wasn't saying you should! Next time, call me." She tucks a perfect black curl behind her ear with long, slender fingers. She makes me feel so damn unrefined and clumsy. I stop looking at her altogether.

"So, I should just make you fight all our battles, then? I should hide behind your skirt when our big, bad brother zeros in on us? That's not how this works." Some of his cool demeanor slips, revealing the rage burning in his eyes.

"No, let me deal with it so I have less to do. Once you let him get to you, it turns into a bigger problem, and then I spend weeks cleaning it up. Do you really want to put more on my plate, Ash?" she pleads.

"Fuck him. Don't clean it up, I'll burn him and everyone who decides they're on his side." He starts packing up, and I follow his lead. Family politics are not my thing, and I want to get out of here before Avery remembers I'm sitting here listening to them.

"I can't wait for Morrison to get back. I need a sane ally in this place," Avery moans, and Ash scoffs at her, stepping around the table to sling an arm over her shoulders.

"If you think he's sane, then you're not as smart as you think you are, Floss."

They walk out together. He doesn't even bother to thank me for helping him.

Fucking rich dicks.

My first clue that something isn't right is the hush that falls all around me as I walk to my room.

I've just finished up with Ash in the library, and I need to change before dinner. The hallway that leads to my room is so quiet I can hear my stomach rumble. I try to ignore it, to walk in carefully measured steps like none of this is bothering me, but I just want to snarl something snarky at the lot of them.

I make it to my door and find Avery standing in her doorway, smirking over at me, her entire body screaming with smugness.

The second I crack the door open I can smell it. The eye-watering stench of piss. There is urine on everything in my room.

Every. Single. Thing.

I gag as the door swings fully open, and that's when I hear the laughter start. It isn't just Avery. All the girls on our floor are laughing. They have all been in on this disgusting prank. I take a deep breath, through my mouth so I don't pass out from the stink, and then close myself inside my room.

I find gloves stashed in my first-aid kit and then I get to work stripping my bedding off and piling all the clothing I can salvage. My sneakers can be saved, but the three books I brought with me are ruined. Luckily, I had taken all my textbooks with me to my tutoring, just in case I needed them, because they were easily more expensive than everything else in the room combined.

I drag all the piss-soaked linens to the small laundry room and completely ignore the gaping looks from the girls.

It's clear they thought this would rattle me, maybe even break me. No chance of that.

After all five washing machines are running, I sit on the floor in the laundry room to start on my own homework. There's no way I'm going to leave my things out in the open, and now I need to invest in some serious hardware for my door.

Fuck these little rich kids, throwing tantrums and acting like animals. Never in all my time in foster care did anyone play with their own piss. I try hard not to think about which diseases are transmitted through urine and try to remember these kids have access to care, so they should be clean.

Should be.

I've finished two classes' worth of homework when Avery walks in, carrying a single sheet of paper. She stands over me with contempt in her eyes and a sneer on her painted lips.

"Finished yet?"

I know she's not talking about my sheets swirling in the washing machine. I turn back to my homework.

"Nope." I pop the 'p' obnoxiously and don't even look at her. She drops the paper, and it lands at my feet. I read the title and scoff at her.

"I'm not leaving. You think your little prank can run me out of here? All it shows is that you're disgusting and desperate."

She laughs like tinkling bells, but all I hear are the shards of glass she'll wield to stab me with.

"I've never been desperate in my life, Mounty. I don't have to be. You are, though. And if you don't leave, I'll see just how desperate I can make you."

What the hell was this girl's problem? What had I done to her that would make her act like this? Did rich people really hate the poor that much?

I pick up the paper, and then I maintain icy eye contact with her as I tear it in half.

"Feel free to fuck off, Beaumont."

The smirk doesn't leave her face as she prances out of the room, her kitten heels clicking on the hardwood floors. I can feel the creeping fingers of a migraine at the corners of my brain. How was it that I made it through a drug addict mom, absent dad, foster care, public school in a bad district, and now I'm rewarded for my efforts with Avery Beaumont?

A deep, dark voice whispers to me: *it's punishment for the Wolf.* I give myself a little shake and get back to work.

It takes two hours to get my room back to normal. The piss had soaked through the floorboards, and I had to scrub my little safe clean as well. I have to go ask the cleaning staff for bleach and air purifiers, because the smell lingers, but eventually I can't smell it anymore and I manage to fall asleep around midnight.

Chapter Four

I'm cranky as hell the next day from lack of sleep. I'd kill for a hot coffee.

The boys all hear about the piss prank, and the whispering that follows me makes me grit my teeth. I'm so distracted by it all that I don't notice the extra attention the juniors have begun to give me.

Turns out I've caught all three sets of Beaumont eyes.

Lucky. Fucking. Me.

I'm at my locker swapping over textbooks—why does this school love hardbacks that weigh more than I do? —when I get approached by one of Joseph's flunkies. I recognize him from the dining hall, and I eye him warily.

"Hey there, Mounty. Do you have a name? Everyone just calls you Mounty or trash, so I wasn't sure your family could afford a name."

Kill me now and just put me out of my misery. I level him with my most deadly glare. I don't like the feel of his eyes on my skin, it makes me feel as though I need to scrub myself raw.

"Do you need something? Your winning personality isn't exactly doing anything for me, and I have a class to get to."

He smirks at me, and then makes a big show of working his eyes over my body lasciviously. I fight the urge to either cross my arms over my chest or smack him in the nose.

"So, I've always wanted to fuck a Mounty. I hear you poor folk are wild in bed, and I'm willing to give it a go. When are you free this week for a quick fuck?"

I see red, and then my vision whites out, and then I think I'm having a full rage blackout. I'm a little concerned that when I come to, this dickhead will be dead. I hear his laugh and then, without meaning to, my hand shoots out and jabs him in the throat. The noise he makes is magnificent, and he sprawls back into the lockers like I've shot him. Sometimes my survival instincts are a goddamned blessing.

The hallway goes quiet, and I grin down at him maliciously. I speak quietly, but I know everyone can hear me. All eyes are on us.

"I wouldn't fuck you if you were the only rich dick left in this building. I wouldn't touch your disgusting cock for a million dollars."

He manages to straighten himself, and then throws me a haughty look.

"We'll see about that," he rasps, and then turns on his heel to stride off.

I glance around as the whispers start up again, then roll my eyes. This place is exhausting. Surviving four years here may be harder than I thought. I start walking to my next class and try not to let the dread creep in.

Hannaford requires either a sport or some form of music as subjects and picking between them was like choosing a method to die. I physically could not do anything that required strenuous use of my legs. I have five pins and two plates holding one of my legs together, which is a violent and dark story for another time, which means unless I could've done basketball sitting down, I couldn't pick gym. Music was a very different beast. I can't play any instruments, but I can sing. Actually, I can fucking *sing*. But I haven't been able to hear the sound of my own singing for years without my PTSD kicking my ass all over the shop.

I've managed to only open my mouth during group numbers and warm-ups so far, but I have a copy of the class syllabus, and I know my project is a solo. I need to ace this class to keep my score up, but it feels impossible to me right now. My past is royally screwing me over.

I have one last class before choir, and I round the corner to get to chemistry when everything changes.

My entire worldview changes.

The door in front of me opens, and out walks Blaise *fucking* Morrison.

Blaise. Fucking. Morrison.

Never in my wildest dreams did I ever think I would be at school with Blaise Morrison. I knew that he went to an ultra-exclusive private school and that he had dozens of privacy orders in place to make sure he could go to school like any other teenager, but I couldn't have ever hoped that I would see him in the flesh, let alone breathe the same air as him.

I should probably explain why my entire existence is melting at this boy's appearance.

Blaise Morrison, Blaise *fucking* Morrison, is the lead singer and guitarist for Vanth Falling, which is my favorite band and, not to be too dramatic, is also my entire reason for existence. I first heard of Morrison when he was still solo and uploading covers of his favorite songs. I was completely struck by the fact he was my age and doing what I could only dream of doing. I have every song he has ever sung, even his earlier less-great stuff, and I sleep in one of the band's shirts every night. I have followed his entire career—of two years, but that is irrelevant—and I'm basically a walking encyclopedia on all Vanth Falling knowledge.

He is perfection. A living god.

My obsession for him is for his lyricism and his range. He is so talented, and a modern poet, and I respect him so much as an artist. Now, seeing him up close, I can also say with absolute confidence that he is panty-dropping hot.

His hair is spiked up like he's run his hand through it a hundred times already today, and his glowing green eyes are dancing. He's tall and leanly muscled, he fills out his uniform in a mouth-watering way, and I want to rip it off him.

My knees are weak just looking at him, and I'm sure I look like a deer in the headlights. My brain finally catches up with my body, and I move out of his way.

He doesn't notice my meltdown, thank god, and he swaggers down the hall with an air of confidence that would be so obnoxious on any of these other rich dicks, but on him I am swooning.

Swooning.

Lord save me, because I may die from the very presence of this guy.

I duck behind something random, a potted plant, to stay out of his sight line because honestly, I'm making a complete fool of myself and my heart stutters just a little when I see him grin. Sweet lord, there's his dimples.

Then he throws his arms around Ash *fucking* Beaumont's neck, and they grin at each other like they're in love. Then Harley pops around the corner and joins in on the group hug and then, fuck me, Avery squeals and piles on too.

This school is ruining every aspect of my life.

Why couldn't I keep Blaise? It is so unfair, and I feel like this might be the thing that breaks me.

Why! Ugh.

Suddenly I remember all the conversations I've been listening to about 'the Morrison kid'. The teachers had talked about his door being stuffed with panties, and Avery had told Ash she couldn't wait for him to get here. Fuck.

Because the world hasn't actually finished shitting on me, I have to sit next to Harley in chemistry, and Avery is sitting in front of us once again. The whole seat assignment by surname is really a pain in my ass, and I consider a name change to get away from him.

I'm sweating and shaking like mad when I sit down, but Blaise isn't in this class, so maybe my brain will kick in at some point. I can feel Harley's eyes on me as I empty out my bag with trembling hands.

"What's your problem?" he says in a haughty tone.

I give a shrug because, well, we're not friends and I don't owe him an answer. He grunts at me, and then grabs my wrist to turn my hand over. My knuckles are red and a little puffy. I must have hit that dickhead harder than I thought.

"Fighting isn't tolerated on campus," he drawls.

I give him a look, and he surprises me by grinning. The teacher walks in and starts to take attendance. Harley leans over to whisper in my ear.

"I would have paid good money to watch you punch that asshole."

The corners of my mouth tug up into a grin. Who would have thought the way to civility with Avery's boys was by acts of violence toward Joey's group?

The positive of sitting next to Harley is that he doesn't speak at all during classes. He just sits and soaks in information, like the hottest sponge you've ever laid eyes on. Watching him helps distract me from the throbbing pain in my knuckles. I'm going to have to start packing instant ice packs into my school bag.

I watch as Harley writes neatly spaced notes flawlessly. Unlike every other rich boy, I've ever had to sit next to, he doesn't spread out obnoxiously onto my side of the desk. If he wasn't tied to the devil that is Avery Beaumont, I might fall for him.

But I only have to remember the stink of urine on all of my belongings to shudder and swear off him.

When we are dismissed from chemistry, I have to take a minute before I can get up and head to choir. Harley looks at me curiously, and then falls into step with me. I shoot him a look of my own, but I don't say anything. Avery ignores me completely and tucks her arm into Harley's.

I make it three steps out of the room before another random junior I've never seen asks me out. He words it better than the last guy, but it's still pretty obvious he's after sex. Avery's giggle is infuriating, but I manage not to hit this guy. I just tell him I'm not interested. Four more steps, and I see another junior make a beeline towards me.

"Fuck, am I going to have to elbow my way to class?" I mutter, and Harley grins at me.

"Such popularity! Maybe you should try and move up to the junior class instead of slumming it with us, Mounty," says Avery as she breezes forward, tugging Harley with her. He grumbles at her. "If she flattens another guy, I want to see it. If she does it to Joey, I will wank over it for the rest of my life."

I blush, and then I curse myself for it.

"If she hits Joey, she'll be dead before the week is out." Avery's tone is no-nonsense, monotone, and dark. I shiver.

The Beaumonts are not the type of people to fuck with without serious consideration. I need a plan.

Blaise Morrison is in my choir and voice development class.

I avoid him like the plague. It's easy because he stays attached to Avery, and I was already trying to stay as far away from that girl as possible. They're such close friends, it's easy to see in the way they banter with each other and their casual touches.

I had been planning on speaking to Miss Umber about doing my solo privately but, embarrassingly, I find I can't even speak in Blaise's presence. It's humiliating and humbling, and I consider leaving the school for the very first time since arriving in the hellhole.

How can he affect me so much?

But I know the answer to that already. He's every single one of my fantasies come to life and walking the halls of Hannaford with me. I can't look at him without thinking about all the times I've listened to his crooning or sung along at the top of my voice. I used to listen to him and imagine what my life would be like if I were brave enough to start a band and run away from all my troubles. But I'm not brave. Not that type of brave, anyway.

We make it through warm-ups without a hitch, and then Miss Umber breaks us up into groups to work through the vocal exercises. I'm with Lauren, who smiles at me shyly, and two other girls I don't really know. It's easy enough to distract the other girls and not actually do any singing myself. Lauren is good, but not as good as I am, and the other two can harmonize well. I'm kind of shocked to realize how much fun I'm having. I wish so badly that I could sing, but the loss hurts less when I can laugh with the other girls.

"Oh god, he's about to sing!" Dahlia says. Well, squeals is more accurate.

I glance over, and Avery is grinning up at Blaise as he starts with his vocal work. I try not to show on my face what his voice is doing to me because honestly, I've never been so turned on in my life. It's wildly unfair and cruel.

All the other groups have stopped to listen to him as well, and Miss Umber is *blushing* at Blaise as she watches him over her glasses. She's looking at him like she'd eat him right up. Are all the teachers at this school predatory, or is that just the intense allure of Avery's guys?

Speaking of Avery, she is enjoying being in the thick of it. Her hand is curled around his arm possessively. I roll my eyes at her, and Lauren giggles next to me. She's a sweet kid. I wish she were a bit braver, and we could actually be friends.

"Any other songs you'd like, Claire?" he says to Miss Umber with a flirty wink.

I could just die.

If he ever does that in my direction, I *will* expire.

"O-oh, no, that's quite alright! How was your touring during the break? Did you get to spend some time at home with your family?" She blushes her way through her questions, and then sits down with his group. The room stays quiet. He's the focus of everyone's attention, and he grins easily.

"It was great! I did a lot of Europe and a little bit of Asia. We focused on smaller, more intimate venues, so I could look into the crowd and see people rather than just a giant, writhing mass. My parents came out to me, so I did get to see them. It's hard being young and still going to school. I have to try and fit a lot into my year."

Miss Umber nods along with him, her eyes affectionate.

"I'm ready to be here, though. I missed my friends and I need a rest."

"Only you would see school as a rest," Avery scolds him, smiling like a Cheshire cat.

"Well, I'm expecting to sleep at least ten hours a night, and my liver is going to have a chance to empty out a bit, so yeah, it's a break. You never realize how precious sleeping on a stationary bed is until you're trapped on a bus for months," he says with another wink at Miss Umber. I'm starting to worry the poor woman's heart wouldn't be able to cope with all the blushing she's doing.

"Trapped, like you don't love every second of it! Last year you were the worst to be around because you'd been home for too long. I give it a week and you'll be planning your next move."

He laughs, and his whole face lights up when he looks at Avery. I've never been so jealous in all my life.

"I'd kill for a boy to look at me like that," whispers Lauren, and I smile at her. Dahlia nods frantically, and Jessie hums in agreement. At least I'm not the only girl feeling this way.

Chapter Five

I've decided I'm going to try every breakfast option at least once, so I'm sure I'm eating the best while I'm here. I'm sitting in the dining hall enjoying a giant stack of pancakes when Joseph Beaumont sits down beside me. I stiffen up, but I try not to make it obvious. I fail.

"Relax, Mounty. I'm here to chat," he says, and his voice is like dark malt liquor. Rich, seductive, dangerous.

"Is there something I can help you with?" I put down my cutlery and stare across the table at him. He's attractive like his brother, but his features are sharper, like you could cut yourself on him and bleed out in seconds.

"I've heard that you've been getting some unwanted attention."

Right. I'd been propositioned by eleven juniors this week, and it was only Wednesday.

Eleven.

So far, I've only had to punch that one guy, but I'd had a few more close calls. It was beginning to make the short walks between classes unbearable.

My eyes narrow at him. "Do you know why this is happening to me?"

He laughs and leans back in his chair, crossing his arms. He's so similar to his brother that it's jarring. I had been tutoring Ash for long enough that I could pick out his mannerisms, his little ticks, so seeing them on Joseph was weird. I glance over his head to see the twins and the other two boys walk into the room. Avery frowns deeply when she sees Joseph sitting with me, and Harley looks like he wants to come over and interrupt. The students around us are quickly finishing up their breakfast and moving away.

"I know that it's going to stop. I've made it clear to the boys that if you were interested in a quick fuck, you would have taken one of them up on the offer by now. You won't be bothered by them again." It's a nice thing to do, and so I'm instantly wary. He's sitting there casually, like he owns the school. Fuck, maybe his family does own it.

"What do I owe you for that favor?"

His smile is all teeth. I'm sure he thinks he's terrifying, but I've befriended the Jackal. I'm sure Joey is a kitten by comparison. "I'd like you to come to a party next week. I'm hosting. It's unusual for anyone to miss my parties, and yet you haven't been to any of them yet."

I have no interest in getting drunk with spoiled brats and bullies. Still, if it takes one night of hanging around these idiots so I can walk to class alone, it's worth it, right? I hope so.

"Okay, sure. Why not."

"Great. Do let me know if you have any more troubles with students. I know my sister can be a little cunt when she's forced to share her toys."

I glance over at Avery and find the whole lot of them are watching our every move. This sibling rivalry was dangerous; best to steer clear of it. "I'm fine. It takes a lot to bother me."

Joseph smiles again and stands up.

"Oh, I'm counting on it," he says with a wink, then leaves me alone.

What a dramatic asshole, I think as I tuck back into my food.

He's true to his word. I can feel the eyes of the other students on me, but no one approaches me for the rest of the day.

I'm not looking forward to my tutoring session with Ash after my conversation with his brother. I still meet with him three times a week for an hour, though I have no idea how much I'm actually helping him. He's an infuriating student. We go around and around in circles, and when I'm ready to strangle the life from him, he writes out the answers perfectly, as if he's known all along.

I arrive early to set up, like I always do, but this time Ash has beaten me there. He's brooding, all dark and frowning, and when he sees me coming, he crosses his arms and glares at me.

"If you're going to be like this the whole hour, I'm just going to go study in my room."

"If you think my brother wants to be your friend, then you are a dense Mounty slut," he snaps at me.

Oh, the ways I would break this boy if I didn't desperately need my scholarship. I sit, because I also need the credits I get for these sessions, and then I fold my own arms to mirror him.

"It is such a joy to spend this time with you. Rest assured that I don't trust a single hair on the heads of any human bearing the name Beaumont."

His eyes narrow, and he leans in toward me. "Then why did you agree to go to his party?"

I roll my eyes at him and start setting up my books. I have assignments due in every damn class, so I don't have the time to explain myself to this ass. "What do you need help with today? I know you must have the same economics stuff due, so let's work on that."

"Fuck economics, why did you agree?"

He is the single most infuriating human I have ever met. Even Avery is easier to deal with, all smiles and knives in the back. How do you inform the privileged that you're just trying to survive when they can't see the danger from their vantage point? I want to kick him under the table.

"Maybe I don't enjoy having guys follow me around all day begging me for sex. Maybe I'm starting to get worried I'll have to fight one of them off who won't take no for an answer. Maybe it's easier to go to a party than be on my guard all the fucking time. Now, do you want to do the assignment or not?"

We were starting to attract the attention of the other students around us. I'd rather not be at the center of another Hannaford scandal, but Ash is oblivious. "Go to the school staff, then. Go tell your student advisor. Do anything else."

"Why do you care? Your sister has been my biggest torturer, so why are you telling me to stay away from Joseph and not Avery?" I hiss at him, all my patience gone.

The glare he levels at me is his best yet. A shiver runs down my spine, but I refuse to back down. "Don't *ever* compare them."

"Why not? She's just as cruel as he is."

He snaps forward in his chair and grabs my tie to yank me forward. Our faces are so close together, I can feel his breath on my lips, and I fight the urge to lick them. Or lick his lips. God, I need some serious therapy. I wonder if my scholarship covers that.

"My sister is perfect. She is selfless, smart, and the kindest person I know. Joey is a sociopath. Don't you ever forget it," he whispers, and I feel the words on my skin.

He doesn't let me go. If anything, he pulls me closer, and I can feel the heat of his lips on my own. My face flushes. My legs are trembling, and he smells unbelievably good. Maybe all my time spent with the Jackal has damaged me permanently, because lusting after a guy who despises me so deeply must mean I'm irreparably broken.

"Don't go to the party, Mounty."

I roll my eyes, and he lets me go suddenly. I slump back into my seat like a rag doll and try not to think about how hard my nipples are underneath my thin blouse. I straighten up and roll my shoulders. I glance over to see the librarians eyeing us both, but they don't approach. How easy life must be with Beaumont as your last name.

Ash looks completely unaffected and just opens his textbooks. He's starting with history, because he's a pompous brat, who won't do anything I ask him to. He's pulling out his notes when I finally snap. "You know he tells people you're fucking Avery. He's told half the school that you four are having some big orgy every night, and someday he'll be an uncle to a deformed, incestuous child."

Ash stops and grins. I think it's the first true smile I've ever seen on him. Clearly, he has a twisted sense of humor if he finds that funny.

"And you believe him? Are you asking me if I'm fucking my own sister?" His voice is sultry and seductive and promises dark things. I swear he can see how hard my nipples are, and he's messing with me.

"No. I just thought you should know."

Ash doesn't look up from his notes. "I'm well aware of the depths of Joey's depravity. I do have to live with him occasionally."

It's hard to choose between the Beaumont boys. Which devil should I trust? Neither of them is the obvious answer, but I have to make a decision on whether or not to go to the party. What's the worst that can happen to me there? A lot of things, but how many of those could actually break me? Very little.

I feel like no matter what I choose, I'm going to get burned.

The rest of the week is so blissfully quiet that I should have known something was up.

Harley doesn't speak to me in class, Ash is quiet and studious during our library sessions, I barely see Avery, and I manage to completely avoid seeing Blaise altogether. If I could keep this up, I would have a great year.

I eat dinner by myself, reading the *Iliad* for Lit while I chew. I can zone the entire room out that way and get ahead with my homework for the weekend. I might even be able to take a day off and sleep for the whole day.

That would be incredible.

I make it to my room with no interruptions, and I grab my pajamas to head in to have a shower before bed. The group bathroom is empty, and I feel as though I've won the lottery. I take my time, washing my hair and shaving every inch of unwanted hair until I'm feeling like a smooth goddess. When I still lived with my mom, we never had hot water, so showers were rare and quick. During winter I'd only really shower at school after gym. It was gross to think about now, but it was all I could do at the time. Once I got moved to the group house, showers were hot but on timers, so the water would shut off after two minutes. Still, it felt like a luxury to me to have those two minutes every day.

Most of the girls in my dorm shower twice a day and can easily spend twenty minutes under the hot spray. I find it shocking and wasteful, but none of them even realize the small luxuries they have.

After the fourth passover with the soap, I know I'm just lingering to enjoy the warmth soaking through my skin into my bones. I'm as clean as I'm ever going to get. I reach for my towel and find it's not in the stall with me. I frown because I'm pretty sure I brought it in with me, but I open the door anyway.

My bag is gone.

I have no towel, no clothes, absolutely nothing to dry myself with or to cover my naked body.

Fucking Avery, I think, but there's nothing I can do about it. I start to shiver now that I'm out of the heat of the water. This is bad.

I can feel tears prickling at the corners of my eyes, but I refuse to cry. Losing my clothes and having to walk back to my room naked isn't great, but I've survived worse. I can feel the panic start in my chest, and I count backwards from a hundred. In French, just to really keep my mind busy.

This isn't so bad. Foster care meant I was forced to shower around other girls all the time. It's practically the same thing, except the other girls will probably be standing around laughing. Oh god.

Cent, quatre-vingt-dix-neuf, quatre-vingt-dix-huit...

I'm not ashamed or embarrassed by my body. I used to be scrawny, too thin and lanky for my frame, but the months here at Hannaford have put some meat on my bones. I have boobs for the first time in my life too, nice ones and big enough that they hide the scars on the left side. I didn't need Avery seeing that and digging around in my past. I am more than a little shy about how many scars I have. My leg is mottled with red and white raised skin after all the operations to put it back together. I have a burn on my hip that I can't think about without triggering my PTSD, and then there's the two perfect circles on my shoulder. Bullet in, bullet out. Would these girls know what a healed bullet wound looks like? Would they question me about it?

Could I handle them asking without lashing out?

When I'm sure I won't cry or scream at these rich bitches, I open the bathroom door and start walking back to my room. It's maybe thirty steps, and I force myself not to run.

The giggling starts the second the door opens.

I don't look down at myself, I don't look over at the giggling to see which girls are watching, don't cross my arms over my boobs.

Head held high, looking straight ahead, fuck the lot of them.

The giggles sputter out. I'm not doing what they expect me too . I'm not crying or breaking down. I'm not screaming at them.

I make it to my door and find my bag sitting on the floor. I bend down to pick it up, and then I catch Avery's eye as I straighten. She's not laughing or smiling. She's just watching me. Her eyes are cold on mine, and I think about how Ash described her.

She doesn't seem very kind to me.

I lock my door behind me and throw my clothes on with trembling hands. It takes me a minute to realize Avery must have had the opportunity to case my room while I was in the shower, if she had my bag and my key, and I rip the loose board up to check my safe is still there untouched. Once I'm sure it hasn't been tampered with, I spend two hours pulling everything else apart in my room until I'm sure there isn't anything missing, or a hidden camera planted. That's all I need, that girl having video of me drooling in my sleep. Or dancing around with my headphones in, listening to Blaise's crooning. I shudder at the thought.

When I finally put my room back together, I climb between my sheets and text Matteo. I need something, anything, from someone who cares about me and, in his own twisted way, Matteo does.

Do you remember when I drank for the first time and you told me I was too good for that kind of thing? I think I'm going to go out next week, and I think I may end up in a fight.

If I see Avery while I'm drinking, she may not walk out of it alive.

You could call in a favor. There are many people that would take care of your problems for you.

I could.

But I won't.

Chapter Six

By the time I make it to breakfast on Monday, the photos—yes, *photos*—of my naked walk have been seen by the entire school.

The first guy to approach me about it gets ignored, but the second guy gets a bloody nose. He made the mistake of telling me how much he wanted to watch my tits bounce while he fucked me, and I take note of his name when his friend calls out to him while he slinks away. Spencer Hillsong is a dick.

I don't get approached after that. I eat breakfast in my usual spot, and there's a three-chair buffer on every side of me, like no one is willing to risk my violence.

That is until Joseph Beaumont sits across from me again.

"I hope you're not embarrassed, Mounty. I'm actually impressed with what you've got going on under the uniform. I didn't realize your rack was so big."

I don't even glance up at him. I'm reading the last book I need to for Lit for the year, having spent the entire weekend studying like a fiend to keep myself distracted. I hadn't gone to the dining hall to eat, so I'm starving, and my plate is overflowing with eggs and bacon.

"Aww, don't be like that, Mounty. Nudes are an everyday thing here at Hannaford. I can show you mine, if you want. I'm quite the photographer."

I would rather gouge my eyeballs out than see Joey's dick. I think about telling him that, but it's more appealing to ignore him until he fucks off.

"Cold shoulder, and I'm trying so hard. You're a hard girl to befriend. I could deal with Avery for you, you know. Would that win me your trust?" he coos at me.

"No." I look up at his cold, blue eyes. The color and shape are identical to his siblings, but they don't feel the same. Looking into Joseph Beaumont's eyes was like staring into a void.

I get the impression that this boy tortures his siblings for the simple pleasure of it, and I have no interest in being dragged into it. Besides, I was starting to get ideas of what I would do to Avery senior year when graduation came closer and my chances of being expelled were drastically reduced.

I'd destroy that girl.

But I'd do it myself. I wouldn't hide behind her evil brother.

"She speaks! Are we talking now, or are you insisting on freezing me out?"

"What exactly would you like to talk about, Joseph?" I put down my book and fold my arms. His eyes trace over my chest, and I clench my jaw because I know he's thinking about the damned photos.

"Call me Joey; my father is Joseph. Let's talk about my party. We're going to the edge of the school boundaries, there's a small woodland area that I've made my own. I'll pick you up after curfew and personally walk you down there, so you don't run into any trouble."

I didn't want to go to the damned party at all. How many of the guys would proposition me there? Would Avery and the boys be there, and would I get drunk and confront her? It was a recipe for disaster. I open my mouth to say so when Harley sits down next to me.

I glance around, but he's alone.

"What the fuck do you want, degenerate?" Joey sneers at him. Harley looks at him the same way you would look at dog shit you've just stepped in. His uniform is crisp and new, so I guess Avery finally wore him down enough for him to replace his older one. He looks hot, but then he always does.

"Lips and I have a chemistry assignment to discuss." True, but we had already finished the assignment. Neither of us leave things to the last minute.

"Well, fuck off and talk to her about it later. We're busy."

A slow smile works its way across Harley's face, and he starts to eat his eggs. His plate is even bigger than mine. He's a solid guy, but I get the impression it's all muscle, so he must spend serious time in the gym. The image of him in a tank and gym shorts flits into my head, and I lock the image down fast. I do not need to get turned on surrounded by these assholes.

"I'm good here. Lips and I are regular desk buddies. She enjoys my company, you know. I don't have to taunt her to get her to speak to me."

Joey scowls at him, but I refuse to speak to either of them. Instead I pick my book back up and zone their bullshit out. Joey finally gets up and storms off. Harley doesn't say a word, just eats his eggs and smells delicious.

"I don't need rescuing." I say as I turn the page.

He snorts at me.

"Everyone needs rescuing from Joey Beaumont. You shouldn't be speaking to him. If he sits here again, get up and walk away."

"Oh yeah, and what should I do if Avery sits here?"

Harley pauses and then puts his fork down. I watch as his face does a complicated dance before settling into what I think is an attempt at a sincere look.

"I know you won't believe me, but Avery didn't set you up, and she definitely didn't take the photos."

It's my turn to snort. I give up on my eggs and start in on my apple instead. I kind of want to vomit thinking about how many people were looking and laughing at the photos. It's bad enough that I have to put down the apple too.

"Think about it. Plus, I haven't looked at them. If Joey actually gave a shit about your feelings, he wouldn't have looked at them either. He's a snake in the grass."

No, he's not in the grass. He's a snake that's wrapped around your throat. "You expect me to believe you care about my feelings?"

He pauses shoveling his food into his mouth and says, "Nah. I just don't find naked photos all that great without consent. I have enough sent to me from willing partners that I don't feel the need to look at yours."

That's...really decent. Like, a really human and empathetic thing to say. I have to fight back tears. This place is making me soft.

I sniff and say, "You're not missing much. I'm just a scrawny Mounty."

He laughs, but it's not as cruel as it usually sounds.

My go-to reaction to the gossip and whispers from other students is to stare at them like they're stupid until they get uncomfortable and leave me alone.

It works well, and by the time I get to the library for my tutoring, I've used this against a decent enough amount of people that now everywhere I walk, the other students clear a path. I think they're waiting for me to snap. I kind of am too.

I sit at my usual table and get started on my assignments. I'm now five weeks ahead of schedule in every class except choir.

Ash walks in ten minutes later and joins me, sitting at his usual seat across from me. He doesn't speak while he gets out his textbooks and notes.

"Do you need help today?" I say without looking up.

"I'll ask if I do," he replies, and I give him a curt nod.

We work in silence, and I enjoy the time to just focus on what I need to get done. For once it doesn't feel hostile; more companionable. When the bell goes, I stay put, since I'm only halfway through a math worksheet—and to my surprise, Ash does too. The rest of the library starts to empty and a girl from our year comes to lean against the table, twirling a strand of her long russet hair around her finger. She's gorgeous, but she was also present for my walk, so I throw her a filthy look before turning back to my work.

"Hey. You didn't come out last night, I was waiting for you," the girl—no idea what her name is—says in a seductive tone. I try not to gag. Ash doesn't look very impressed. I try not to feel pleased about that, but I fail miserably.

"I'm sure you found an adequate replacement."

Oooh, *burn*. I smile down at my equations so the girl doesn't notice. Ash's eyes flick to my face, before he zeros back in on the girl.

She tosses her hair over her shoulder and pouts at him. "That's a bit harsh. I was forced to when you didn't show. What, am I supposed to just wait around at your beck and call? Your dick isn't that great."

The smile he gives her is dangerous. It's the type he would give me, not a potential fuck.

"We both know that isn't true. You're gagging for it."

Sweet lord. He doesn't sound like he's flirting, but maybe I'm just bad at reading the signs. I have no experience to fall back on, so it's entirely possible. "If you two are going to fuck right here at my study table, please tell me so I can make other arrangements," I say as I tap formulas into my calculator. I don't look up, because I don't want to see if Ash is into her and they're just gearing up for a hate-fuck.

"Fuck off, then, Mounty," she says, and I sigh as I go to grab my books. Ash puts his hand over mine and stops me. It's the first time he's ever touched me, and I feel flutters in my stomach.

"Allow me to paraphrase for you, Mounty, I wouldn't fuck Harlow if she were the last piece of pussy left at this school. Stay. I need help with my equations when you've finished yours."

The girl, Harlow, glares down at us both. She snaps, "I thought you and Avery hated the Mounty bitch."

"I hate my brother more. Tell me, how did his dick feel up your ass last night?"

"Sweet lord," I murmur and try not to laugh. This just gets worse and worse.

Maybe I should just leave and study in my room?

"At least he isn't a frigid little bitch like you. It's your own fault you lost me to him," she hisses back at him.

Ash throws his head back and laughs.

The chair next to me pulls back, and I look up to see Blaise *fucking* Morrison slinging his bag down. He drapes himself into the chair so casually and gracefully, like the god he is. Ugh, one look at him and I'm a dripping mess.

"Is this seat taken?" Lord help me, his voice even sounds amazing when he's just talking.

How the hell do I get out of this?

I've been preparing myself for weeks for this moment.

I knew at some point I'd be faced with Blaise, and I'd have to speak to him. We share a class, I'm kind of on speaking terms with two of his best friends, and from what I'd observed from a safe distance, he's a pretty social guy. Too social for my liking.

I gesture vaguely in his general direction, and then start to move my textbooks so he has somewhere to put his stuff. He grins at me, oh *god*, and then opens his bag.

Ash and Harlow are still hissing jabs at each other, but I can't find it in myself to care now that Blaise is here. It's taking all my energy not to pass out.

"I've signed up for your tutoring. I haven't been given a time slot yet, but I'm hoping to just tag into Ash's. Do you think you could do us both at once?"

I nearly faint.

He must be doing this on purpose.

"That's fine. I can—I can do that. What do you need help with?"

He grins, and I decide that the only way to get through this is to just avoid looking at him until I'm desensitized, like I did with Harley. I barely notice he's the epitome of panty-dropping gorgeousness anymore. Okay, I do notice, but I can look past it.

"Great! Are you guys working on math right now? Because I may fail math, and if I do my old man will have a stroke."

I try to smile reassuringly, but I'm sure it looks like *I'm* having a stroke. He gets out his worksheets, and I see he's in the lower math class, so I learned this stuff two years ago. I focus on the sums and walk him through the first set. Harlow finally stomps off, and Ash now looks like he wants to bathe in her blood.

"I need a drink," he says as he loosens his tie with a sharp yank.

"Oh, have you two finished arguing over which brother has the biggest dick?" Blaise grins at Ash wickedly, and I keep my eyes firmly on the page in front of me.

"We both know I win that one. She's a lousy, backstabbing whore. She sold herself to him in the hopes it'll give her a leg up in the social hierarchy."

I move back to my own worksheet while they gossip. It's not like I can tell them to get back to work. The tutoring session has ended, and I can't even look Blaise in the eye yet.

"What were you expecting, loyalty and devotion? She's a Roqueford. They're widely known to be double-dealing sluts. Her father has more bastards than legitimate children, and he has six of those."

"I wasn't expecting her to be so open about it. Floss woke me up this morning with the picture, so forgive me if I'm not in the greatest mood."

So Avery was sharing around more than just my photo? Great. *What a kind girl*, I think with no small amount of sarcasm. Ash glances over at me like he's forgotten I was here. His face is flushed, and he looks less like the perfect Grecian statue than I've ever seen him. He looks approachable and hot. Why did I hate him so much?

"Are you enjoying your infamy?" There it is. He always knows just what to say to make me feel like an insignificant fleck of dirt. I clench my teeth.

"Fuck you, Beaumont." There's no heat behind my words, but I still mean them. I snatch his worksheet up and start marking it. He's gotten most of the equations right, but I enjoy the small amount of red ink I get to use. When I shove the page back at him, he's still watching me, his eyes unreadable.

"I told you not to trust Joey." He shrugs at me like this is all justified.

I snort at him. Blaise watches us both with captive interest, twirling his pen between his long fingers. I wonder how they became friends.

"Your sister did this to me. Now the entire fucking school has photos of me naked, and I get to enjoy the *privilege* of being looked at by you lot, like I'm a piece of meat. Like I actually want your rich dicks, when really I'd rather fucking die."

Ash rolls his eyes at me. "Avery doesn't use naked photos against people. She does have a line, you know."

"Sure. Piss on all my belongings, but she draws the line at naked photos. I definitely believe you."

Blaise's nose wrinkles, and it's goddamn adorable. I turn away from him, so I don't humiliate myself by blushing at him or drooling.

I am in real danger of drooling.

"You don't mean actual piss, do you? I cannot imagine Floss ever handling piss."

"Yeah, actual urine. It took me hours to fucking clean, all because I'm a scholarship student and I pissed Harley off by accident."

Ash groans and runs his hands through his hair. He shares a look with Blaise, and then turns to me again. "Avery is very protective, and you managed to get on the bad side of one of the three humans she gives a shit about. She won't let that go, and sometimes she goes to great lengths to keep us safe."

"Right. Which is why I don't believe you about the photos. Doesn't matter anyway, a few pictures of my tits aren't going to break me."

Ash's eyes dip down to my chest and then back to my face. It doesn't feel lecherous at all, nothing like Joey's looks. More curious. "There isn't a whole lot to see though, right? I've been sent the photos eight times and deleted them without looking."

I raise my eyebrow at him. Blaise knocks my elbow gently with his, and I flinch away from him hard. "Whoa, sorry! I was just going to say that we are pretty anti-revenge porn in our group. There was… an incident. No one has looked at it. I'm not saying we're friends, and Avery still wants you taken out, but you have at least four people who haven't seen your nudes."

"Three. Avery was there when the photos were taken," I grumble, and start to pack my bag. I'm so done with this for the night. I don't want to think about the weird, twisted triangle that is the Beaumont siblings and their friends.

Blaise scratches the back of his neck and grabs his papers.

"So, tomorrow we can meet up, right? I really do need help with my math."

I sigh and sling my bag over my shoulder. I brace myself, and then look right at his gorgeous and alluring face. Damn, his eyes are such a beautiful, clear green that I could just lose myself in them.

"Sure. I meet with Ash during the study period. If you're here, I'll help you too."

Chapter Seven

The one free study hall I have for the week without tutoring the boys is my haven.

Seeing Joey sitting at my desk is enough to piss me off. Seeing him sitting there with his boots on the table makes my blood boil. Of all the pompous, dickhead things to do, this guy just takes the cake.

His uniform is hanging on his frame a little loosely, like he's lost some weight in the last few months. His eyes are as manic and calculating as ever.

He smirks and waves an arm at me, like a king entertaining the petty whims of a peasant. I want to punch him. In the dick.

I manage to contain myself, but it's a close call.

"Mounty! I thought I'd find you here. I'm starting to think you're a bit of a nerd." His smile would be called flirty by lesser folk. I saw it for what it was: a baring of teeth, like a lion would do to its prey.

"What can I do for you, Beaumont? I have homework to get to."

He drops his feet back to the floor and then leans forward towards me as I empty out my bag. He doesn't have any of his own class work with him, so I'm hoping he'll disappear once he has what he wants. "What's your poison? I'm having some supplies sent in, and I don't know what you like to drink. Any party favors you like? I can get whatever you'd like, on me as my guest."

Party favors.

He's asking me if I want him to buy me drugs. I give him what I hope is a bored look. His smile doesn't falter.

"I don't need anything. I'll drink whatever, I'm not a rich dick with fussy taste," I say in an airy tone.

Joey grabs one of my pens and twirls it in his fingers. I wonder how many girls he's done this with, this casual dance to lure in a victim. He's attractive, but all I see when I look at him is the evil in his eyes when he looks at his siblings. All I can see is the guy who talks down to everyone around him, the guy who calls girls he's slept with sluts.

He's waiting me out. He wants to see if I'll tell him to leave or try to get him to talk to me. I choose to ignore him instead. I've spent years learning to study no matter where I am or who is around me. I focus on the Lit assignment in front of me, and I'm jolted out of my study by another voice.

"Chatting up the Mounty? I thought she was off limits." I look up and see a familiar junior. It takes me a minute, and then I realize it's the dickhead I punched in the throat, the one who told me he would schedule me in for a fuck. Guys like this are the type to rape a woman and then tell his friends she was gagging for it. The type of guy who thinks he's a gift to the world and everyone should get on their knees for him.

I fucking hate him.

Joey is watching me with this sly look on his face, like he knows what I'm thinking. The other guy doesn't notice at all. "I don't really think that's fair-"

"Fuck fair. If you don't leave now, I'll have to make an example of you, Devon."

A single bead of sweat appears on Devon's brow and rolls down his face. It's not that warm in the library. I can see the tremble on his lip. The tiny flick of the muscle in his cheek.

Joseph Beaumont Jr. doesn't have friends.

He has victims, plebs, and pawns.

Better to be a pleb, out of his eye line and safe, than to be a pawn in his game. I don't think I have that option anymore. I think he's toying with me, testing me, until he knows whether I will have any use to him.

I fucking hate him, too.

Devon leaves without another word, and I get back to my studying, intent on just blocking him out. I can study under any circumstances, so it's nothing for me to shut him out and get back to work. "What if I want to buy you something? I've invited you there as my guest, it would be rude not to."

I grit my teeth. I don't want him to think I owe him anything. "I'm not interested, thanks. If there's not going to be some sort of drinks table, I'll just go and dance. Not a big deal."

He blows out a breath like he's frustrated. I don't think he's ever really known that emotion. "Suit yourself. You sure do make it hard to impress you, Mounty. I've had girls start Fight Clubs over who got to have me for the night. I'm a little put out."

"No, you're not. You'll forget I exist the second you leave this room."

He laughs, and then finally he does leave. I try to ignore the sinking feeling in my stomach. I don't like the way Joey speaks about me, like I'm a thing to possess. It takes me a minute to realize why it feels so wrong, but so familiar.

That's exactly how Matteo talks about me.

One of the perks, or drawbacks depending on how you look at it, of sitting next to Harley, in the majority of my classes is that we are always paired up for assignments.

Hannaford is big on joint assignments, as they like to foster working relationships. I know this is because the other students all come from their own dynasties, and they'll all be dealing with one another once they take over the family businesses. I'll never have to worry about that shit. The best I can hope for is to be accepted into a pre-med college course.

Harley is an exemplary student, we are neck-and-neck for the top of every class but working with him can be a major pain in my ass. He likes things done his way, to the point that compromise is a dirty word to him. He will look at the syllabus and just cut the assessment down the middle, the exact middle, and in the same way every time. I'll be handed one half, and he will do the other half.

After my first experience with him, I'd made the decision to just roll with his shitty attitude, but that means that it is difficult to get ahead in my classes without knowing how he is going to split the assignment up. So I do what only an insane person would do.

I do the entire assignment, and then give him whichever half he deems to be mine.

This has become a truly joyful experience for me.

The highlight of my week, even.

Every time he tells me what I need to do, I open my bag and hand him the half I am required to do. The first time, he had scoffed at me but took the papers anyway. After reading my work, he was incredulous and pissed off. After I've done this to him in five different classes, he is now used to lagging behind me, eating my academic dust.

"How far ahead are you, really?" He's holding my half of our French Revolution assignment. I am particularly proud of this one and tempted to give Harley the other half. If I thought he would take it, I totally would, just to know how highly the teacher would mark it.

We're sitting in our history class, and we're supposed to be plotting out how we plan to do the assignment. Harley is reading through my half with raised eyebrows and a little frown on his face. I'm reveling in that look. I'm gloating. I'm feeling fan-fucking-tastic.

"I could catch a plague and be out for three months and still be the top of the class." I'm so damn smug. I can't help but be.

He shakes his head at me, but he drops my work into his binder and snaps it shut. Avery is whispering furiously at the girl she's partnered with, and I feel sorry for the poor soul. Dealing with the devil is never pleasant.

"I heard you're going to Joey's party tomorrow night." A statement, not a question. I give him a look.

"I promised I would, so I am. If I say I'm going to do something, I always follow through."

He blows out a breath, and then leans forward on his elbows toward me. I can see his brain working, the cogs moving and mice running on the wheel. He's not happy about something.

"Look, I get that I've been a dick to you. I get that Avery has been full-on, and you have no reason to trust me, but you should not go tomorrow night. Joey is up to something, and when he's scheming, it never turns out good. Things have gone really bad in the past before, like *permanent-damage-and-death* bad. You should just pretend you've gotten sick."

How do I explain to this gorgeous, infuriating rich prick that there is no way Joey Beaumont could break me? That I'm friends with the Jackal and I survived becoming the Wolf? He wouldn't even understand what any of that means, that I'd been put to the test by the most dangerous underground criminal organization, and I hadn't just survived. I'd won.

There is no way to say it without risking more questions, so I shrug at him vaguely.

"Seriously. What do you hope to gain by going to the party with him? He's not going to date you."

I snort and give Harley an incredulous look. "You think I want to date anyone at this pompous school? None of you lot know a damn thing about real life. None of you will ever have to live in it! You'll all graduate and then live in the perfect little worlds your parents have already carved out for you, and then you'll go on to have kids and set them up into your billion-dollar empires, while I scrape to make sure I can afford to eat and keep the lights on each month. Fuck you and fuck your assumptions. I'm just here to graduate and get scholarships for college."

He looks at me like I'm a piece of shit, which is so damn confusing.

"Yeah, well, fuck you and your assumptions about me."

Because my week hasn't been bad enough, I have to sit through another choir class watching Ms. Umber fawn over Blaise.

Choir and voice development is the only class I hate going to, and I sometimes fantasize about faking a recurring head cold to get out of it. I tell myself I hate it so much because she's a teacher and at least thirty years older than him, but I think I might be a little jealous that he smiles at her and jokes along with her. It's fucking pathetic of me. We break up into our groups to run through our warm-ups, and Avery slips into the class. Her lips look pouty and bruised, like she's been making out for hours and only just come up for breath, and she smirks at Blaise. He gives her a look in return, and if I had to guess, I'd say he was pissed off. Ugh, he is probably in love with her, and I'll have to deal with them getting together and running off into the sunset and having beautiful, talented, rich babies.

I need a drink.

Maybe going to this party won't be the worst idea I've ever had.

Lauren is nice enough to take the lead in the warm-up, and I can fake my way through. Dahlia is too busy watching Blaise to contribute much, but I don't blame her. The second I hear his voice, my skin prickles with goose bumps and I mentally weep over my misfortune at going to school with him.

"Ash is going to murder Rory. Well, if Rory is lucky it'll be Ash. Otherwise Harley will do it, and Rory will *actually* die," Lauren whispers to Dahlia, and they giggle together.

"Who the hell is Rory?" I ask. Ms. Umber is busy teaching one of Avery's flunkies proper breathing techniques, so I'm not worried about my class marks.

"He's Avery's new boyfriend. He's in our grade, but he's—well, not as bright as you, so you wouldn't have any classes with him. He plays football."

A jock. Of course, she would date a football player. I glance over at Avery and find Blaise frowning at her and talking in quiet tones. I can clearly read the disapproval in the tense lines of his shoulders.

"Why will they kill her boyfriend? That's pretty misogynistic; they all date too."

Dahlia and Lauren share a look, and then lean in toward me.

"First of all, the guys don't date, they sleep around. And Avery is the center of her brother's life. He does not cope with any sort of sharing unless it's Harley and Blaise. Last year she kissed one of the upperclassmen at the end-of-year party, and Ash broke the poor fool's jaw. *Broke it.*"

He did not seem like the type to rule over his sister. It was jarring to think of him like that. My face must give my thoughts away, because Lauren gives me a half-smile. "Cillian is a dickhead. He told his friends he would bag her and her fortune, and it got back to Ash. He was already pissed about the kiss, and when he heard that, he took Cillian out. When Cillian came back to school this year, Harley had a… chat with him, and then Cillian changed schools."

Fucking rich people.

I shake my head at them in disbelief. Imagine the arrogance, to be able to affect another kid's whole life just because they hurt your sister's feelings. The things that had happened to me without any sort of justice were staggering. My mom's neglect. Her death, beatings in foster care, seeing the Game as the only way out. I look over at the perfect princess Avery, and I've never hated the girl more.

"Don't look at her like that unless you want to die, Lips!" Lauren whispers urgently. I school my features into something more placid, and we start taking notes from Ms. Umber again.

When the class finally wraps up and I'm packing up, I hear a gasp behind me right as another body slams into my own.

My bag spills out onto the floor. I glance behind me to see who the hell knocked me and find Harlow, the girl who stood up to Ash.

"Get out of the way, Mounty trash! Bottom-feeding scum like you should bow at the feet of the elite students who actually matter."

It takes every ounce of willpower, but I don't react to her at all. After a full minute of me just staring at her, like she's the piece of shit she is, Harlow makes a noise low in her throat and flounces off. The room empties out while I pick up my books and move on to my next class.

Nothing seems amiss, right up until I get back to my room to change out for dinner.

My stomach hollows out when I see my keys sitting in the lock on my door. I know I didn't leave them there. Someone has once again had access to my room.

It takes until the early hours of the morning before I'm confident nothing has been taken or left in my room.

I hate this fucking school.

Chapter Eight

Picking an outfit for a party I don't want to go to with rich kids I hate to be around is its own special form of torture. I'm not going to wear a dress on a cold night in the woods, though I'm sure I'll be the only girl who doesn't, and my selection of jeans is tiny. Finally, I go with a dark, distressed denim, and I pair them with a lacy top, Doc Martens, and I throw my hair into a high ponytail. I do a smokey eye and nude lip color because despite my Mounty status at the school, I can make myself look great if I need to. I give myself a once-over in my mirror and try not to let the dread creep in. Going to Joey's party is a dangerous idea. I have no real friends, or even allies. I don't have Matteo there to keep an eye on me, which is a first. I've never gone out drinking without him. He'd bought me my first-ever bottle of vodka when I'd moved into the group home, and then he'd held my hair while I'd puked my guts up for hours after finishing it. One thing was certain—I would not be getting drunk tonight. As a final precaution, I slip my Matriarch serrated knife into my pocket. It's easily the most expensive thing I own, and it's gotten me out of trouble more than once.

Joey arrives at my door a little after our 10 p.m. curfew, dressed in a crisp white shirt and pressed black slacks. I try not to flinch away from his eyes as he slowly inspects every inch of my body, like I belong to him.

"Wow. I thought after seeing your nudes I'd seen everything you had on offer, but you clean up good, Mounty."

"Gee, thanks." I make sure my tone is dry as fuck, and he laughs.

"Come on now, I didn't mean anything by it! I'm just giving you a compliment, jeez. Let's head down, the underclassmen should have it all set up by now."

He holds out his arm, and I reluctantly slip my own into it. He smells like something expensive and sinful, but it does nothing for me. I can't be in his presence without seeing him slapping that kid's tray and covering him in scalding soup.

We walk out of the girls' dorms and even though I know he practically owns the school; it still shocks me that the teachers we bump into just turn on their heels and walk away without a word. It should be an instant expulsion for him setting foot up here, but he's untouchable.

There's a crowd already forming, flowing down and out of the building, a mass exodus into the woodlands and toward the free booze. I'm sure I'm the only one who really cares about the free part. It's colder than I thought it would be, and I curse myself for not throwing on a jacket. I don't recognize any of the faces around me because there aren't a whole lot of freshmen here. I do see quite a few of the junior boys that have approached me for sex, and my face sets like concrete into an icy look.

"Don't worry about them, Mounty, let's get you a drink to loosen you up a bit. You can't dance if you're that pissed off." Joey's tone is thick and smooth, and I'm sure it did wonders on that bitch Harlow. He tugs me over to the small clearing and begins to pour drinks from a loaded table. He does a pathetic job at it. Truly terrible. I could have wiped the floor with him at any bar in the state. I glance around and see a sound system pumping out shitty pop music that makes me grit my teeth, but there's already drunk girls dancing in tiny skirts. I was right about the dress code. Joey hands me a cocktail that's some godforsaken mashup of a daiquiri and a mojito, and I down the whole thing in two gulps.

"Atta' girl! Another?"

"Fuck no. You may be rich, but you're shit at this." I push him out of the way as he roars with laughter. I swipe a bottle of whiskey and drink it straight. I hear the tinkling of laughter that says Joey's friends have arrived and they're enjoying watching the poor girl drink. He steps away to greet them, and the sinking sensation of unease pools in my stomach, but I drown it with another swig straight from the bottle. I need to have enough of a buzz to survive this, but I'll have to ride the line carefully. I can't lose my head, or I might lose something else.

Joey walks back over to me and says, "Dance with me." It's not a request. He holds out his hand expectantly.

I'd rather choke, but I take it anyway and let him lead me to where the other students are grinding on each other in time with the beat. I take the whiskey with me, and Joey grabs the bottle to have a swig of his own. I don't want to drink from the same bottle as him, but when he lifts the rim to my lips, I have no choice but to take it. His arms drop to my waist and he pulls me in tight against him. I hate every single thing about this, but I go along with it.

I can feel the haze of alcohol start to dig in and my limbs grow warm and loose. Joey twirls me in his arms, and as I turn, I see the girls around us staring, glaring at me. They all want to be where I am. They all want Joseph Beaumont.

Rich kids have nothing on the parties at Mounts Bay.

There's music and dancing, I've seen two blowjobs and one girl bent over a fallen tree with a guy pumping away behind her, but overall, it's pretty tame. I'm enjoying my buzz, and I'm surprised to find I'm enjoying the eyes that follow me around the party. Being here with Joey means no other guys approach me, but that doesn't mean they don't watch me dance. I've always loved jumping around and swaying and gyrating to music, and it's even better with whiskey coursing through my veins.

When the bottle has been passed between us and is finally empty, Joey pulls away and whispers in my ear, "I need something a bit stronger."

I hate the feeling of his breath on my neck, but I smile and nod like a good guest. He leaves, bumping shoulders with his friends, and they take off into the denser section of the woods. I twirl and spin until the song finishes, and then I stumble over to a lawn chair set up near the drinks table.

I can't see where Joey has disappeared to and I'm starting to get suspicious that his 'something stronger' is drugs. I need to find a discreet way of leaving this party before he gets back, because there is no way in hell I'm going to be around drugs. My mother was a hard lesson to learn, but boy, did I learn it.

I'm pooling the energy to get up and leave when Harlow and three other girls sit down around me. They're all in tiny dresses, high shoes, and shivering like crazy. I groan and level her with a look. "Well, you're clearly better at this than we originally gave you credit! Bagging Joey as your first Hannaford fuck."

Harlow is a tall girl, she has a good foot on me, and I know she enjoys playing basketball, but I'm sure that even with half a bottle of spirits under my belt I could beat her in a fight.

"I'm not fucking him."

The tinkling sounds of their giggles makes me clench my jaw. It's so fake and grates on me something wicked. "We all know he brought you here. He wouldn't do that unless he wanted something in return."

"He can want all he likes. That doesn't mean I'm going to sleep with him."

One of the girls, a platinum blonde with fire-engine red lips, leans in toward me, and I can smell the whiskey on her breath. "His family is richer than god. Why wouldn't you fuck him? Maybe your Mounty cunt will bewitch him, and you'll never have to worry about who's paying for your clothes and shoes again."

Clothes and shoes. Yep, that's my biggest concern. I roll my eyes at her and stand up. Harlow's hand shoots out, and she grabs my wrist hard. I freeze and look down my nose at her.

"Don't fall for him, Mounty. Don't you even try and get your claws into him." Her voice is dark as she stakes her claim on him. I shake her off, and then walk off in the direction of the school to the sounds of their tittering. I don't see Joey, but that suits me just fine. I'd be able to tell him I got cold and bailed tomorrow.

I can hear the sounds of students having sex as I stumble out of the clearing. It's such a cliché, these kids could sneak into each other's rooms, but instead they're out here freezing their asses off to get laid instead. I try not to look at any of them closely, since I have no interest in anyone's sex life, but as I get to the edge of the woods, I look up… and make eye contact with Harley.

He's leaning against a tree.

There's a girl kneeling at his feet, her head bobbing as she sucks his dick.

I freeze. I can't look away, and Harley doesn't break eye contact either. He doesn't look shocked to see me or embarrassed. He looks blissed out and smug as the girl goes to town on him. I can't see who it is, and I'm glad. My skin feels all hot and prickly. I'm jealous.

I guess I really am broken.

Harley quirks an eyebrow at me, but he doesn't call out to me or wave me off. He just stares at me. I can feel my face heating up and beads of sweat forming on my forehead despite the brisk breeze. Why can't I leave? I shouldn't be standing here watching this! But my traitorous body won't move. I begin to pant as a loud moan rips out of Harley's chest, and then he shudders as he starts to come. His hand digs into the girl's hair and he pulls her head back. I can see the thick white streams of his come as it coats her face. He finally shuts his eyes, and I can move away.

I bolt for the school.

I get as far as the light-horseman statue at the front of the school before I hear Joey call out to me. I curse under my breath as I turn around, and I'm still shaking from watching Harley…finish. *Jesus fucking wept.*

"Hey! The party has barely started. Don't bail on me now, Mounty!" Joey's voice is strange, hyper and excited like I've never heard it before. His sleeves are pushed up around his elbows so I can check for track marks, and I'm relieved to see none. It doesn't mean he's not smoking something, but at least he wasn't injecting heroin. The relief lasts for a second before I remember that my mom used to inject between her toes so her boss wouldn't find out, and then I'm looking at his shoes to see if they look messed with. I don't care about him at all, I just hate drugs so much that I need to know if he's using. If he is, I'm going to stop playing this little game of ours and freeze him out completely.

He catches up to me and throws his arm around my waist, pulling me into his body, and I smell it.

Cocaine.

The good shit too, all sweet and floral and none of the chemical scent that comes with poor product. I'm sure anyone else smelling him would brush it off, but my mom spent a summer dating a cocaine dealer and he would pack his little Ziplock baggies in our living room in the morning before I would head off to school. The second I smell it on Joey, I'm back in that tiny goddamned living room getting yelled at by my mom. I freeze and Joey pulls me into his body tightly. "Come back to my room, we can party there instead," he murmurs.

I'm going to scrub my neck when I get back to my room, because he just keeps breathing on me. I can feel the tremble in his arms, and I know he's high. I'd never been hugged by my mom without feeling that vibration under her skin. I should leave him, walk off and enjoy my buzz in my room by myself, but stupidly, I feel like I should see him to the safety of his room. I know he would never do the same for me, but that didn't mean I had to stoop to his level, right? One last kind deed for this dickhead, and then I'll never speak to him again.

"Lead the way."

I feel him chuckle as the wind drowns out any sound of it. He begins to babble incessantly, but I ignore him.

My mom's addiction made some sort of sense. She had been a foster kid after my grandparents died in a house fire. She herself had only made it out of the blaze in the nick of time, and half her body was covered in thick scars. She had never been smart or motivated like I am, and she dropped out of school at fourteen. She had worked as a waitress, a dockworker, in the factories, anything she could do to eat and keep some sort of roof over her head. Then she got knocked up and found drugs. I'd never known her sober. The woman I knew was a shaking, cackling, retching, screaming banshee that would beat you if the demons in her head told her to.

Joey's addiction stemmed from boredom, and that made me so angry. All the privilege in the world, and he decides to snort cocaine instead of making something of himself. Do the twins know what their brother is getting himself into. Is this why they're so afraid of him? Cocaine usually made people ecstatic and happy, not the deep and cruel violence of other narcotics, but that didn't mean he was a good person to be around.

We arrive at the boys' dorms and climb to the juniors' floor. I wonder if Ash is downstairs or if he, too, was in the woods getting off with some girl. I shake my head at myself. Pathetic. It doesn't matter what any of those boys are doing. I don't let myself think about Blaise. Seeing Harley was bad enough.

We stop outside the end room, and Joey shoves the door open. No lock. I'm guessing the other guys know exactly what will happen to them if they dare to enter this room. I push Joey's arm off my waist, and his hand latches over my wrist.

"Come in, little Mounty girl."

I pull against his grip, but his fingers tighten like a vice. He's easily twice the size of me.

He shuts the door behind us, closing me into his room.

Chapter Nine

Joseph Beaumont's room is easily the size of the house I used to share with my mom.

It has a kitchen, a sitting area, a giant Cal King bed, and he has a private bathroom, which is the only thing I'm truly jealous of. Joey drags me toward the bed, and I go with him begrudgingly. I'm waiting for him to let my wrist go, and then I'll make a run for the door. I size Joey up and I know, without a doubt in my mind, that he would have no problem sexually assaulting me. His drug use makes him a bit of a wild card, so I don't know how hard he would fight me if I tried to shake him off. I could scream, but I don't think that would work all that well. The walls in the dorms are pretty thick, the other boys are probably at the party, and even if someone heard me, it's likely they wouldn't want to take on the psychotic Beaumont sibling for a poor scholarship student.

I'm on my own.

Joey sits and pulls me down next to him. His eyes are still dancing wildly around the room, bouncing off everything they touch. "Have you ever been fucked on a mattress that costs more than a Bentley?"

I jerk away from him when his lips touch my ear. What a dumb question. I'd never tell him I am a virgin. I won't hazard a guess about what he'd do if he found out. I decide to just be honest with him, and if he attacks me, I'll have to take my chances with my knife.

"I'm not fucking you."

He chuckles and kisses my neck. I cringe away from the feeling. His fingers are still tight on my wrist, tight enough that I can feel the bones grinding together and I know it's pretty close to snapping. My fingers start tingling. Writing assignments will be a bitch if he breaks it. I slip my fingers into my pocket and grip my knife, but I don't pull it out just yet. I give it one last try.

"Joey. I'm not having sex with you. Let me go."

He grunts and rips my arm until I sprawl backwards onto the bed and covers me with his own body. The hand I have wrapped around the handle of my knife is trapped between our bodies, and I can feel his erection digging into my thigh. Instinct tells me to scream, but I choke it back. I put the scared fifteen-year-old girl into a box, and I let the Wolf take over. The Wolf is calm and patient and can wait for the right moment to go for his throat.

"Just lay still. You might find you have less trouble at this school once you've been fucked by me." His lips crush into mine, and I can feel his tongue come out and force its way into my mouth.

I've never been kissed before.

It's disgusting.

I might never kiss a guy again, if it's always like this.

I arch my back deliberately and he purrs at me, obviously thinking I'm melting for him. It gives me just enough room to pull the knife out of my pocket and press it against his groin. I'm aiming for his femoral artery, but I know he's more worried about his dick when he pulls away and gapes down at me. There's a comical look on his face, and I know it's only there because the cocaine has taken hold.

"Get off me." I say softly. The vein in his neck is flicking, his blood pumping like crazy. He's frozen for a second, just staring down at the knife pressed against the hard line of his dick.

He finally releases my wrist and stumbles back. I can see the high is really setting in, and for once in my life I'm glad he's taken cocaine. I don't want to think about how he would fight back if he were lucid. He runs a hand over his face and laughs.

"Fuck it. It's not like I need the money, I was just hoping for the bragging rights."

Money? Bragging rights? What the hell was he going on about? I shoot him a glare and raise the knife toward him as I edge around him toward the door. Maybe Ash had been right, maybe I should have taken his warnings a little more seriously. Clearly, Joey is more than a psychopath. He's also deranged. "What the hell are you going on about? I wasn't going to give you money."

He laughs again, and I flinch at the cruel edge to it. "My family earns more money in a minute than your worthless bloodline ever has, so clearly I didn't mean your money. If you fuck me, I'll win the sweep."

"What fucking sweep?"

He smirks and stands up. His pants have a clean cut in them from my knife, and I can clearly see the outline of his erection in his dark boxers. A dark thrill of panic shoots through my blood, and I look back up at his face quickly.

"First to fuck you gets the sweep. There's currently a hundred and forty grand on the line, and it's climbing daily. I thought it would be worth a quick fuck even if you are Mounty trash."

A hundred and forty grand?! That's more than four times the amount my mom used to earn in an entire year at the docks, and these pompous dicks are throwing it around on a stupid bet? I see red. I see so much red that I think about slapping his handsome, cruel face. I think about stabbing him too, but then I count down slowly from five until my vision clears. This boy is way too dangerous for a scholarship girl to mess with without a plan. If I want to end him, I'll have to be more subtle about it.

And now.

Now I want to end him.

The walk back to the girls' dorm is much more tense now that I don't have a rich dickhead to clear the path from teachers. I have to duck and weave, and I find myself thankful that Hannaford is a big, old, castle-like building with lots of alcoves and statues to hide behind. I sigh with relief when I make it and sneaking past the other freshman rooms is easy. I get to the sitting area across from my room when I see Avery straddling some guy and making out with him like she's starving for oxygen, and he's the best option she's got.

I don't have the problem I did with Harley, and I sprint to my room. Once I'm safely locked inside, I give myself a minute to freak out about Joey and how close

I came to something terrible happening. When the minute is up, I change into my pajamas and climb into my bed.

I don't sleep.

I think about skipping classes the day after the party because it's the last day before fall break, but I don't want to ruin my perfect attendance record. I spend double my usual time on my makeup, because you can see every sleepless minute carved into my face. I finally give up and head straight to class, skipping breakfast. My stomach is rolling with the memories of the whiskey last night, and I'm sure if I touch food, I'll hurl. I'm early enough that I've even beaten the teacher to history, so I enjoy the quiet.

I collapse into my desk and rest my head against my textbooks. I'm sure I look hungover, but I can't summon enough energy to care. I hear the teacher arrive and I give her a little wave without looking up. She doesn't seem to be concerned that I'm expiring at my desk. Then I feel the chair next to mine pull out and Harley drops into his seat. I glance up at him and he looks too healthy, too happy, just too much, and I give him a glare.

"Did someone have a big night?" he says, too loud and far too cheery. I want to hurt him.

"Feel free to choke," I reply, and he grins at me. Avery is already at her spot in front of us and she looks down her nose at me with a smirk. The class starts, and she flips her hair at me. I spare her a second of my time, just long enough to wonder if she has anything else planned for me, before I push her out of my mind.

I manage to pull myself together enough to get through the class. My stomach gurgles toward the end, and Harley keeps slipping me these looks until I'm squirming in my chair.

"Enjoy the show?" He doesn't look at me when he says this, and I know it's on purpose. He's taking notes for the homework we're supposed to get done over the break. It takes me a second to remember what I saw last night in the woods. I can't think about any of it without thinking about Joey's dick pressing into me and his body pressing me into the bed. My wrist is still aching, and I'm a little worried he's sprained it.

"Not particularly. Though if you need my opinion, I'd suggest you start using protection. The girls at this school get around even more than Mounties do, and you don't want to catch something that makes your dick fall off."

He smirks at me, and then leans in toward me. He smells amazing, and usually I'd secretly love feeling the heat from his torso against mine, but I'm just not in the mood for his shit today.

"That's why she was sucking me off."

I lean away from him and shoot him a glare. I don't find his banter amusing. I don't want to high-five him, except maybe slapping him would be cathartic. I decide to change tactics instead.

"Did you know there's a price on me? Did you know that's why I'm being stalked by guys at this shitty school?"

Harley's smirk falters on his lips for a second, and then it's as strong as ever.

"Everyone knows about it. They all know Joey staked his claim on you as well."

Staked his claim, like I'm a slab of fucking meat. I feel the grips of that white-hot rage taking me again. Harley must see it too, because his face splits into a grin. "Like I said, Mounty, if you hit Joey, I will take that memory to bed for the rest of my life."

"Fuck hitting him," I whisper back, and Avery turns to glare at us both. It must kill her that I'm next to Harley in nearly all our classes. She can't contain him or control him if she's not right beside him.

The bell tolls. I shove my books away and pull out the required homework for the fall break. I enjoy the feeling of all the students' eyes on me as I hand it over to the teacher. She takes it with a shocked look, and then scans over the page.

"Well done, Miss Anderson. Enjoy your fall break."

Harley is the only student who knows how far ahead I am, so he's the only student not gaping at me when I arrive at every class for the day with all the assignments already complete. Even Avery is hissing at me by the end. I'm smug as fuck, knowing they'll all be at home with their families and slaving over classwork, and I'll be running around Hannaford doing whatever the hell I want to do.

I refuse to go down to the dining hall for dinner. I don't want to see Joey or be approached by any of his raucous group. I don't know if he's now lifted his ban and I'll be propositioned in the halls again, so I settle into my bed and try to ignore the rumbling of my stomach. By tomorrow afternoon I'll have the building to myself, and I'll be able to eat all I want.

Fall break is the best week of my life so far.

I sleep in. I shower at odd times of the day. I eat whenever I feel even the slightest bit peckish. I watch movies on my phone and dance around my room in my underwear while listening to good music. I do whatever the hell I want, and I do it in my own time. I feel free.

I should know by now that nothing good in my life lasts.

I'm enjoying my last day of quiet in the sitting area when I hear my phone ping. I very rarely get texts, and there's only one person with my contact details. My heart sinks as I pick it up and see Matteo's text.

I've been asked to contact you about a job.

A job. That could mean anything from tailing someone's girlfriend to killing an errant informant. Coming to Hannaford Prep has been an attempt to close the door on my old life in Mounts Bay and to start a new, legitimate life. I had done things at Matteo's command that I wanted to leave firmly in the past. The trouble was Matteo had no intention of letting me go. I would always belong to him.

I'm not leaving Hannaford until summer break. The food is free and good. Sorry.

I chew on my lip for a minute, and then I dig out my emergency bottle of whiskey while I wait for his reply. I'd smuggled it in on the first day but hadn't felt the need to drink it until now.

I owe a lot to Matteo. He's the reason I'm alive today. I could just have easily stayed with him in Mounts Bay and dropped out. He had encouraged me to, he wanted to bring me into his organization and have me run it with him. If I hadn't gotten the scholarship, I would have been stuck in the Bay with him and playing a game that is impossible for me to win. I'm not a fool, I know he's the head of a gang. I know he sells drugs.

I know he kills people.

I try to think about those years in foster care as a story, something that happened to some other girl. It's easier to do now that I'm here in the sheltered halls of Hannaford. I have a real buzz going on before I finally take that trip down memory lane.

Once upon a time, a young girl finds herself orphaned and at a group house. Another kid takes her under his wing. He protects her and cares for her for an entire year. She is lost and hungry, but she thinks someday she will know what it means to be happy.

And then one day he tells her he's named her in the Game. She doesn't know what that means, but he tells her it's the only way she will ever be safe and free. So, she learns. She learns how to fight. She learns how to disappear. She learns how to make others disappear. And then she competes. She is broken beyond repair. She will never run again. She is covered in scars. She can't sleep at night, she can't bear the sound of her own voice, she sleeps with a knife, she startles at every sound, she's scared of what hides in the shadows, she can't breathe—

She wins.

She is crowned the Wolf.

She could become a leader. Have a gang of her own, make millions, live an untouchable life. She goes to school instead. Gets a scholarship. Disappears. Tries to forget all the things she did to get to where she is. She does forget, most of the time. She forgets until the Jackal calls her home.

It's the Boar. He'll pay cash or a favor. Whichever you prefer. The job is small enough. It can wait until summer break.

Despite what the spoiled kids here think, I don't actually need the money. The favor makes it tempting. I'm owed a lot of favors, and I like having them up my sleeve. I could have Joey taken out of my life as permanently as I wanted. It amuses me that Ash and Harley warn me about him.

If only they knew who I really was.

Chapter Ten

"Joey wants to see you in the chapel after the assembly," Harlow says to me with a smug look on her pretty face.

I'm sitting in the dining hall on the first day back after the break, lamenting all the noisy students after my week of peace. I also have a teensy bit of a hangover after finishing off the whiskey, and I'm not in the mood to deal with Joey's bullshit. I stare Harlow down until she finally gets the picture and stomps off. I cradle my piping hot, black coffee and try to absorb the superpowers of the caffeine. The school doesn't serve hot coffee, but I have a small stash in my room for emergencies.

Today is an emergency.

I'm having a moment when I hear Blaise's voice down the table from me. I'm proud to say I can now listen to it without wanting to die, but I still can't look him in the damn face. I glance over and see he's only a couple of seats away, surrounded by other students in our grade. I can't help but listen in.

"My parents are pissed at my scores. Father wants me to spend more time at home, and Mother is backing him up for once. I think she's still pissed I went on a tour to Europe without asking her first."

The group around him laughs, and I can hear the fake tones from where I sit. How awful it must be to have to entertain all these kids who are just trying to gain social status by sitting with you. I'd feel bad for him, but he's a rock god with millions in the bank and an established career. He doesn't need my sympathy.

"Father wants to get me on track to take over Kora from him. I have no interest in technology and manufacturing. I'm not going to pull my grades up just for his dreams," he continues. His eyes are guarded and sharp, and I can't look at them for longer than a second. Kora is his family's business. His dad became a billionaire in his twenties by manufacturing computer parts during the first big technology wave.

"At least you're doing better than me in math. Maybe you should study more and mess around on your guitar less."

A wounded look darts across Blaise's face, but he covers it with a smirk effortlessly and the girl who spoke doesn't seem to notice. The lyrics I've listened to and sung over the years that he wrote come to me all at once. Living a lie, wearing a mask, walking alone. None of these kids understand him. No one here really knows what it feels like to have melodies creep into your subconscious while you sleep and steal your soul. None of them have listened to the same words over, and over again, until they're burned into their being. None of them understand what it means to be Blaise fucking Morrison. If you had told me two years ago that I'd be listening to Blaise have this conversation at school one day, I wouldn't believe you.

"Never mind. Obviously, you'll do what your father wants."

Blaise gives the girl a look, and I realize I recognize her. She's the girl I saw in the woods that night with Harley. A blush begins to crawl along my cheeks as I think about the white streaks that painted her pretty face. She's stroking Blaise's bicep possessively. He doesn't pull away from her, even though he's obviously pissed. "Why would I give up my music, Annabelle? I'm already successful, I've made my own money independently. Why would I give that up for the stuffy, corporate life?"

Annabelle laughs again and the muscle in Blaise's jaw ticks, but he still doesn't move away. Is she his girlfriend? Is she cheating on him with one of his best friends? I can't imagine Harley doing that. Maybe I don't know him at all.

"Your parents are worth *billions*. You don't give up money like that for some singing and dancing."

I snort. I can't help myself; it just happens. Breakfast has wound down enough that Annabelle clearly hears it and looks over at me. I've never noticed her before, but she knows all about me. Everyone at the school knows about the Mounty trash amongst them.

"This is a private conversation. Inferior students aren't welcome." Her voice is sweet and her face a mask of placid joy. If I've learned nothing else about the human race, it is that the quiet ones are usually the worst. Best to nip this in the bud.

"Inferior? You've both just said you're flunking the lower math class, and you're not in any of the other top classes with me. Clearly *I'm* not the inferior student."

Annabelle doesn't flinch. She just flips her long, mousy brown hair over her shoulder and looks at me like I'm nothing. I consider slamming her pretty face into the table, but then I rein myself in. I don't need another rich kid hating on me. I need to learn to shut my mouth and keep my head down.

I need to stop feeling all these emotions for gorgeous rich boys.

Blaise is sitting there surrounded by people he's probably known his whole life, and yet none of them understand how badly he needs his music. None of them have looked past his handsome face and his bank balance to see the real guy underneath it all. I'm not stupid, I know he isn't just his musical talent, but I'm certain that I know more about him than this Annabelle girl does.

She's vapid, shallow, and hungry for the immense wealth that being with Blaise would give her access to. "You could be the smartest girl on Earth, and you'll still never be someone worth our time." She laughs and looks around at the others they're sitting with to make sure they're laughing too.

I do not need the trouble opening my mouth will bring me. But I do it anyway. My temper is going to get me killed someday; Matteo says it to me all the time. I should really listen to him. He's killed people for dishing out less honesty than I am. "I'd rather be poor and smart than rich and brainless. You can't even tell how pissed off you've made Morrison."

I don't look away from my breakfast, but I can see her eyes narrow at me from the corner of my eye. Blaise doesn't say a word, and I wonder again if she's his girlfriend. She lets him go and turns on me, but I snort at her derisively and tuck back into my breakfast. "Well, that just shows you're a stalker and he should start sleeping with one eye open at night. I did hear you're obsessed with him. Don't you sleep in one of his band tees?"

I try not to blush, but I fail. Avery fucking Beaumont and that damned photo she took of me in my pajamas. Of course she's shared it around. I glue my eyes to Annabelle so my traitorous eyes can't flit over to Blaise. "Actually, it shows I like his music, and not his reputation or his face. But what am I saying? At this school, all the girls just like how much money a guy has."

She rolls her eyes at me, and I clench my fists at her. "Sure you don't. It doesn't matter anyway; he would never fuck trash. No guy with any self-respect at this school would."

I know I need to work on my poker face now that I'm not channeling the Wolf every day, but I manage to stare the little bitch down as I clear up my breakfast. I accidentally glance toward Blaise and see the look he's giving me, like I've just shocked the shit out of him. I pick up my tray and leave the dining hall without looking back. I tell myself I'm not going to hate Annabelle just because she's sleeping with two of the hottest guys in our grade, but I've never been good at lying to myself.

I'm still feeling hot and irritable with embarrassment when I take a seat at the assembly.

Blaise is sitting two rows in front of me, and Harley is with him. They're both laughing and nudging each other boisterously. The twins are nowhere in sight.

I look around to find Annabelle sitting among Avery's flunkies. She's gazing at the two boys with appreciative and possessive eyes. She could be sleeping with them both and hiding it. They could be sharing her. *I wish they'd share me,* I think, and then I shut that part of my brain down tight. I am Mounty trash to them. I need to get over my little crushes. They will never want someone like me, and the sooner I accept that, the better.

Mr. Trevelen stands on the small stage, and the chatter around me ceases. The twins still haven't appeared, and Harley looks around, concern clear on his face. Blaise joins in and he looks back at me. I feel a jolt of lightning in my blood as his eyes meet mine, and I look away quickly. I hate that I have somehow gained his attention, and I definitely shouldn't have come to his defense in the dining hall. He didn't need my help with anything but his studies. He certainly didn't thank me for interfering.

As the principal's speech starts and he drones on, Harley becomes more and more agitated. He's practically vibrating in his chair, his leg bouncing so hard I can feel it two rows back, and his hand keeps running through the hair at the back on his head until it's all mussed up. His concern worries me. I glance around and I see Joey isn't here either. Harlow and that idiot Devon are both present. I pick out all of Joey's cronies. Not a good sign. I have a sinking feeling that the violence Joey unleashes on his siblings is kept behind closed doors.

No wonder Harley and Blaise are antsy.

Harley makes as if to stand, and Blaise shoots out an arm to keep him seated. I can't hear what they're whispering, but they're getting more and more heated. The other students around them are starting to take notice.

"Trouble in paradise?" Lauren murmurs. She's been getting braver about talking to me outside of our choir class. I give her a sidelong look and grin, and she wiggles her eyebrows in response. I don't question myself before I ask, "Hey, do you know anything about that Annabelle girl? The brunette over there?"

Lauren doesn't have to look to where I gesture.

"Yeah. Her family is old money, but not like Beaumont's. Her great-grandfather was loaded, something to do with oil, but then her grandfather made a lot of bad business moves. They nearly lost it all. Her father married her mom to pay back debts, and now they're stable enough. She struts around like she's royalty, when really her father is constantly skating on ice to keep them millionaires."

Huh. Calling me inferior when she's pretending her family isn't struggling? What an idiot. Especially if it's common knowledge. I guess that's what they call fake it 'til you make it.

"She's obsessed with Avery's boys. She drapes herself over them at every opportunity. Avery only allows it because she's discreet about whether she's actually banging them."

My eyebrows shoot up. "Them? As in…"

Lauren nods and eyes the back of Blaise's head with pure lust. "She's totally doing them all. Her room is next to mine, and her roommate is constantly getting kicked out because one of them shows up."

Yep. I hate her. I think I might even hate her as much as I hate Joey. Damn my hormones. This must all show on my face, because Lauren grins at me again and nods, her own jealousy clear to see.

Mr. Trevelen starts handing out awards, and I try to focus again. I know I'm going to get one of the academic trophies, and I'm sure Harley will too. As students begin to take the stage and accept their framed accolades, I see Harley slip away. Blaise doesn't move, and when my name is finally called, I catch a glimpse of his face as I walk past.

He's livid.

His eyes are glowing green orbs and his jaw is clenched so tight, I'm worried his teeth will crack.

I take my award and stand on the stage to have my photo taken. Harley's name is called out, and when he doesn't come up, Mr. Trevelen grumbles into the microphone. I look down at Blaise again and I feel the dread start to take hold in my stomach.

I look around to see Harlow smirking at me. I'm not afraid of her summoning me to face Joey at all. I'm only really worried about what he's doing to the twins. I'm clearly crazy, because Avery is trying her best to get me out of the school and Ash insults me every opportunity he has.

Yet I'm still having trouble breathing.

When I arrived at the abandoned warehouse to complete the last round of the Game, I had been faced with the remaining members of the Twelve. There were only eleven men present, plus myself and the two other contenders for the spot. The Coyote and the Fox both looked at me like I was a raw piece of meat. It didn't rattle me; I'd spent weeks being put to the test, and I had gotten used to being the untried liability of the group. Only the Jackal looked at me like I was someone worth backing.

I wasn't afraid of Geordie. He was the bigger of the two other contenders, but he only really had his size to use to try and win. He wasn't bright, or cunning, he didn't know how to blend in, or take someone by surprise. He didn't have the skills required to seduce someone into taking a drink without sniffing it first, or to get out of handcuffs or an exemplary sailor's knot. He didn't know how to survive in the underground criminal world.

Xavier did. He only looked at me when he absolutely had to but when he did, I felt the piercing slice of his eyes on every inch of my soul. If I lost to him, he would take pleasure in what he did to me. Every cut his blade made would be savored, every ounce of blood would be intentional.

I know exactly what it means to look into the soul of a killer.

When I arrive at Hannaford Prep's chapel, the grin on Joey's face chills me to my core.

He's not pretending to be a decent person anymore. There's no fake civility. All I see is the evil that lives under his skin. An echo of Xavier rings out in my mind and the inventory of what it took to disable him. I can't believe I'd thought he looked like Ash and Avery. The differences in the siblings are so clear to me now that I struggle to see their similarities. I am no longer blinded by the good looks.

The girl I had put away to come to this school, the one that lived inside a box in my mind—her job wasn't quite done yet.

"Thank you for joining us, Mounty." His tone is conversational and jovial. I want to hit him so badly; I clench my fists to stop myself from lunging at him. "I thought we should all get to know you a little better. I took the liberty of looking into your records so we could get a better idea of who Eclipse Anderson *really* is."

My records, *fuck*. I manage to keep my breathing even. They can't know about Matteo or the Wolf. There's no written evidence of my position within the Club, or as one of the Twelve. I'd never been caught or implicated in any of my jobs. There's nothing he could have that would break me.

I wasn't wrong.

He doesn't break me.

But fuck it if I don't bend a little.

Chapter Eveler

I'm the only kid in my class who walks to and from school without a parent or older sibling. The area I live in isn't safe, not by a long shot, but my mom doesn't care if I make it home alive. She would probably rather I disappeared, so she didn't have to feed me.

The holes in my jeans aren't artfully placed or fashionable. The shirt I'm wearing has bloodstains from the last time my mom's boyfriend smacked me so hard my nose shattered. I still have the lump to remind me not to breathe too loudly around a guy so high on meth, he thinks his skin is crawling with insects and the walls are bleeding. My mom had told me it was my own fault as she threw a dirty rag at me to wipe up. I didn't have any respect for her left to lose.

My teacher had pulled me to the front of the class to sing happy birthday to me. I was embarrassed, and I didn't want to admit it was the first time I'd ever been sung to. What kid wants to admit their mom never remembers the day they were born? I only knew when my birthday was because of my enrollment at school and the teachers adding my name to the class birthday tree each year.

I hear sirens in the distance as I approach the front steps of our house. It's barely a step up from sleeping on the streets. It's ancient and decrepit and it belongs to my mom's dealer. He arrives twice a week to take his payment from her, and she makes me sit outside while she gives it to him. I can still hear them.

The door is locked, but I don't need a key. I jiggle the door handle until the lock springs free and the door opens. The room is dark as I enter, but that's nothing out of the ordinary. I kick my shoes off and sling my bag to the floor, wincing as I feel the straps pull. It's threadbare and ratty, like everything else I own. I've had to use duct tape to fill in a hole, and I know I'm a few short weeks away from having to find a replacement. I have no money and no way of making money. Well, there are ways I could make money, but the thought of getting down onto my knees in the bathroom of the gas station on the corner and doing… that stuff is inconceivable to me. I know girls my age who are doing it to eat at night. I'd rather starve.

I do starve.

I start toward the kitchen, and as soon as the door cracks open, the smell hits me. I gag and step back. It smells like vomit and shit and rotting meat. There had been a heatwave happening in Cali for weeks, and the temperature had gone over a hundred degrees every day that week. We didn't have air conditioning or even a fan. I'd learned to just sweat it out. It helped that I was skin and bone.

I know now that the heat had accelerated my mother's decomposition.

She had overdosed. Vomited and shat herself while she convulsed on the dirty kitchen floor. I might have even been home that morning when it happened and not noticed. Her eyes are bloodshot and milky. Her hands are rigid and twisted like claws, and one of her fingernails is ripped out at the nail bed from where she clawed at the floor in her dying moments. Her hair is lank and matted. Her lips are blue and stretched over what is left of her rotting teeth. I can see the burn scars that cover her arms and belly, the gray hue of her skin distorting the look until I'm sure she's made of wax and this is all a nightmare.

It takes me a while to realize I'm screaming.

The smell has crawled up through my nose and down into my lungs and I think I'll never be able to get it out of my body again. I'm rooted to the ground. I can't move my arms or my legs, every fiber of my being has turned to stone. I just stand and stare and bear witness to the demise my mother had been crawling toward my entire life.

I'm only nine years old.

Eventually, long after the sun has set and the traffic has picked up on the road out front, I shake myself out of the trance I'm in. I need help. I need to call someone to get her and take her away. I just want someone to take her away.

There's no landline. I don't have a cell phone, but my mom has one. I do a quick check of the house with shaking knees. There're only really three rooms to check, so I'm quick about it. Then I realize, with a stuttering heart that just won't pump the way it's supposed to, that I can see the outline of the cell in her pocket.

I have to touch her to get it out.

I sit and hug my knees. I let myself cry for the first time, but I hate the feel of the fat, hot tears sliding down my cheeks. I think the smell has dissipated, but really, I've just grown accustomed to it. My body has absorbed the unthinkable stench of death, and now I'm immune.

The feel of my mother's skin slipping from her bones as I wiggle the cell out of her pocket will stay with me forever. If I ever need to vomit on command, that is the memory I recall. I open the back door to vomit on the rickety wooden steps.

My hands shake as I dial 911.

I pause before I hit call. I'm a smart kid. I know what will happen if I call emergency services. There are girls in my class being abused by their foster dads. I could just run away. I could leave and let the neighbors call it in when the smell finally hits them. It's tempting, but then I think about the girls kneeling in the gas station restroom, and I finally hit the call button.

My voice shakes.

I am only nine years old.

As the recording of my 911 call plays over the PA system, I have two choices. I can give in to the chaos of my trauma, or I can retreat into the dark and survive. It's not really a choice. *I can never lose myself again.* I had climbed out of the pit of Mounts Bay tooth and nail. I would never be forced back into the desperate form I'd once been.

I let the calm wash over me instead.

I let everything drop away from me. Everything that is destroying the little scraps that remain of my soul slips away and, instead, I open the box in my mind, and I let my senses out to play. I'd honed these senses for two years under the watchful eye of the Jackal. I'd learned how to walk in and out of a building without a single eye touching me. I'd learned how to endure extreme, bone-shattering pain without screaming out. I'd learned how to kill a man. I'd left all this behind me when I'd arrived at Hannaford, but now I let it all out.

I'm surrounded. There are two exits, the door I just came through and one on the far side of the room. I see a familiar flash of blond hair, but I put that aside. I don't need to be distracted by gorgeous, intelligent, ruthless boys. There're wooden bench seats in neat rows, littered with students gaping at the scene playing out before them. Joey has chosen the spot with careful consideration to maximize the audience and my humiliation. I don't have any allies in this room, I don't have my knife, and there isn't much I can do to stop the recording. The damage is done.

Joey is smirking at me, and he's flanked by his usual group of guys. Every last one of them has approached me for sex, every single one has tried to win the bet. I look at each one of them long enough to commit their faces to my memory. I will never forget their willing participation in this. The girls who flock them are all laughing behind sly hands, fanned out. If they try to attack me, I know exactly what to do. I may not have my knife, but I don't truly need it. As long as my busted leg holds together, I know I have a chance of getting out of the room. I doubt the girls have ever raised a fist in their lives, and the guys... well, I doubt they've ever had to fight for their lives. I don't make the first move. I don't need to. One of Joey's flunkies grabs my arm, in an attempt to stop me from leaving.

Big mistake.

My body is in survival mode. Not private school, I'm-so-sad survival mode, but true life-or-death survival mode. The type of survival you need when your back is against the wall and a guy three times the size of you is coming at you for blood. The type you need to survive your leg being smashed to pieces and someone looming over you with a knife. The type of thing none of these rich kids could ever understand. My eyes lock with Harley. He's standing at the end of the chapel, and he's the only one not laughing. He's the only one who can read the cold, dead calm in my eyes. He doesn't call out to help the girl who has touched me. He just stands witness.

Good.

Let him watch.

I swing the textbook that's in my arms and listen to the satisfying crunch as Harlow Roqueford's nose breaks, shatters completely under the sheer force of my swing.

Her blood goes flying, I'm spattered in it, and the room explodes with her screams. She drops to her knees and cradles her face with both of her hands. I get a fist full of her hair, and her hands scramble at me pathetically. I tighten my grip until she squeals, and her hands drop to her side. Her eyes meet mine and they're wide, petrified. Devon lurches toward us, but he stops when I jerk her body closer to mine. The PA system is still playing the 911 call, it's on repeat, and I can hear the nine-year-old version of me screaming, but the fifteen-year-old me, standing here covered in blood with a fist full of some rich bitch's hair—she is hollow. She is carved out until there is nothing but cold, dead calm.

She is the Wolf.

"Let her go. You can't take us all." Devon tries to command, but his voice trembles. Pathetic. My eyes stay on Harley. He's watching me with such a grim satisfaction that I wonder what this group has been doing to him. I wonder what torture Joey had been putting him through. I wonder what he did to the twins today. I answer Devon without bothering to glance at him.

"Are you sure?" My voice doesn't tremble. It does, however, push them all back. Everyone except Joey takes a step away from me. He holds his arms out and grins at me.

"Looks like you're out, Mounty. This school is a zero-tolerance establishment. The principal has no choice but to throw you out like the trash you are." His words should inspire some sort of dread in me, but nothing can penetrate my frozen walls. I pull Harlow up to stand by her auburn hair, and her whimpers fail to incite any sort of remorse on my part. She's crying. Fat tears are rolling down her face and mixing with the blood pouring from her nose. I think about pushing her, bending her and seeing how quickly she breaks. I doubt it would take much. Her eyes are pleading on mine. Truly pathetic. She would never survive the Jackal. She's a child playing at a game she has no real place in.

"Run," I whisper, and then I let go. Harlow flings herself into Devon's arms and he pulls her out of the chapel. The other students part, and some follow them out. I see that the crowd is dispersing, and then I hear why.

"Miss Anderson. My office. Now."

The principal has arrived.

Joey looks at me, and the sick pleasure I see in his eyes melts the ice I've encased myself in a little. He thinks he's untouchable. Maybe. Maybe he just hasn't found the right opponent yet.

Chapter Twelve

Mr. Trevelen leaves me in his office to go and check on Harlow.

He's not happy with me, but he also hasn't expelled me yet. Joey didn't just play the recording in the chapel. I have to face the fact that the entire school has now heard the call. They all know about the worst thing that has happened to me.

Or so they think.

I wait for two whole minutes before I reach out and take the phone on Trevelen's desk. I punch in Matteo's number and I wait for him to answer. My eyes dance around and focus in on the watercolor painting of lilies over the bookshelf. It's pretty, but bland. There's no real passion in the strokes, just like every kid at this school. Pretty, vapid, empty, useless.

"How did you get access to the principal's landline?" he answers, and I wonder again if he has eyes in the school.

"They're going to expel me. I broke a girl's nose." My voice is flat, emotionless. My eyes trace to the blood drying on my hands with detached interest.

Matteo chuckles, but he stops when I don't join him. I can hear the chatter in the background. He's at his house, I can tell by the sounds of the ocean and the low tones of the shitty jazz rap he listens to when he's plotting. I recognize all the voices as the henchmen he likes to surround himself with. A show of muscle to distract from the fact that Matteo is always the most dangerous man in the room. "What's happened, my Wolf?"

I'm not his. I will never be his. I will fight tooth and nail, with everything I have, to not be his girl. It doesn't matter, though. I can never tell him that; only bide my time until I can make an escape.

"I need your help. I'm willing to call in a favor."

I can hear him moving around and closing a door. His voice is gentle, soothing, but I'm not falling for his games anymore. I'm not the scared little girl on that 911 call anymore. I just need him to fix this for me, I need him to have my back again. "No favor necessary. Tell me what you need."

I twirl the phone's cord around my finger and stare at it with glassy eyes. I need to hold onto this calm apathy as long as I possibly can. "I cannot be expelled. I'm going to destroy the kid who is doing this to me."

"What is he doing? I can remove his piece from the board, if you want me to." The calm offer to kill Joey for me is tempting. I'm definitely going to hell, because it takes me a full minute before I can reply.

"No. I'm going to destroy him at his own game. It's not satisfying if I can't do it myself."

"That's my girl. I'll fix it for you. No favor required, but I will ask that you make it to the Club meeting in the summer."

He's so intent on getting me to the meeting, so I take note, filing it away for inspection at a later date, when I can think clearly. I hear the principal coming back, so I agree and hang up. By the time I've straightened myself back into my chair, Mr. Trevelen strides back into his office. He sits down and begins to fidget with his shirt cuffs. He seems so nervous, and I feel bad for putting him in this situation. He believed in me enough to offer me the scholarship despite my emancipation. He'd had to fight with the school board for them to let me in. Now I'd just proved them all right. I'm just an angry girl from Mounts Bay who can't fit in with the polished, upper-society teenagers. I've failed him. *Don't lose it now,* I tell myself as I blink back the hot tears.

He finally clears his throat and opens his mouth. The phone rings. He frowns but holds up a finger to signal that I must wait. I nod, and he picks up the phone.

"Yvette, I'm sure I just asked you to hold calls."

He pauses, and then he turns ghostly pale.

"Put him through."

Sometimes I'm amazed at the reach Matteo has managed to achieve. I doubt he even knew Hannaford existed before I told him I was applying here. I also know the moment I got my scholarship; he would have started to reach out and find all the secrets he would need to use to manipulate these people. I wondered what Trevelen had done. I wonder what skeletons he was hiding that Matteo threatened to shine a light on. From the look on his face, it wasn't good. He looked like he wanted to vomit his breakfast all over his lovely oak desk.

After a terse 'of course,' Mr. Trevelen hangs up and then he looks at me like he's never seen me before. He looks at me like he's let a monster into his school.

He has.

"I'm going to let you off with a warning this time, Miss Anderson, in light of... new information. Harlow will also be receiving a warning for her prank on you. I will not be so lenient on you if you choose to retaliate." I stare him down. I'm sure he would turn a blind eye on anything I choose to do from here on out, now that he's been threatened by the Jackal. I nod obediently and stand.

"I'm going to go get cleaned up. I'll skip my next class, but I'll be in my Health Ed."

He nods and motions for me to leave as he drags a silk handkerchief over his sweaty forehead. I'm tempted to call Matteo back and ask what his buttons were, but sometimes, ignorance is bliss. I'd rather not find out the depths of evil this man has stooped to.

Yvette stares at me as I walk out free and clear. Classes have resumed, so I don't see anyone all the way up to the girls' dorms. I head into the bathroom to shower and clean Harlow's blood off me. I take my bag into the stall with me, and I don't let it out of my sight as I wash down. The shaking starts when I dry off. It takes twice as long as it should to redress, thanks to the trembling. I will finish today with my head held high, and then tomorrow I will let myself crumble.

As I walk into the classroom, all the eyes in the room turn towards me.

No one expected me to last the day, and yet here I was, taking my seat in Health Ed and ignoring the lot of them. I would not cry. I wouldn't let them enjoy my tears. I'd survived my body being put through hell, but this sort of psychological torture grated against me. The Wolf has retreated, and I'm back to the little girl who cries and has crushes and wants to be liked. I kind of hate her. I can't wait to graduate and leave all this behind. So much for my new start.

I unpack my bag and set everything out onto my desk in clear lines as the whispers get louder. I can't have any sort of control anywhere else but in my pencils right now, so I measure everything out with my fingertips. When that doesn't calm my racing heart, I start to count backwards from a hundred in French, my go-to for panic reduction. The overcomplicated number system keeps enough of my brain occupied that I can usually fight back the panic.

As the bell begins to toll, Avery, Ash, Harley, and Blaise walk in and sit in their usual spot behind me. It's the only class we all share, and I'm pissed I have it today of all days. Thankfully, I don't have to sit next to Harley. I hear Avery snort out a laugh that doesn't suit her manicured appearance. She's the epitome of grace and beauty. When you think about the beauty that wealth can create, she's exactly what you would picture.

She murmurs, "Stupid Mounties," and then opens her books. She seems pissed about all of this, but I'm sure it's because she wanted to be the one to break me.

"Your brother really fucked up everyone's chances of winning the sweep." Harley isn't even trying to be discreet; I think he's enjoying my downfall more than anyone else. The guy who bore witness to the retribution I wrought isn't in this room at all, so I'm left with the pompous asshole instead. There's something in his eyes when he looks back at the sound of his voice, a recognition that tells me he's still trying to figure me out. Well, good luck.

"She still looks at Blaise like she would enjoy a ride on his dick. Looks like the money is yours, man," Ash drawls, and I want to kick his perfect face in.

I turn to give him a scathing look, but they're all enjoying every second of this torture. Harley is looking at me the same way he was in the chapel. I try not to shiver at the intensity. Blaise looks over at me, and for the first time he actually *looks*. I squirm in my seat as his eyes trail over my scuffed shoes, nails chewed to the quick, and the mess of black ringlets that is my hair. I know I look nothing like any of the girls at Hannaford, and for the first time since I started here, I feel pissed off about it. I've never felt so out of place as in this school with all of these obscenely privileged kids.

"I don't fuck fans."

They all howl with laughter, and even Avery manages a smug look in my direction. I turn back to the front of the class and ignore the comments all around me as the other students snicker and join in. Only Lauren, who's still sitting as far away from me as she can to not be targeted by association, is silent.

I decide on the spot that I'm going to burn my Vanth Falling t-shirt and sleep in the nude from now on. I will never listen to his beautiful voice again. I'd rather die than admire this guy anymore.

After class, I go to the library and email in all my classwork for the week, my obsessive need to be ahead working in my favor once again. I tell each of my teachers I'm feeling unwell and will not be able to go to any classes in the foreseeable future. Then I go to the dining hall and grab a box of protein bars.

I don't leave my room for a week.

Chapter Thirteen

After my self-imposed sabbatical from my classes, I make an important decision: I'm going to unleash the Wolf on these wealthy assholes and show them some real-life consequences for their terrible behavior. Things the rest of us had to learn as children, things I had learnt the hardest way imaginable.

Sneaking around the dorms during classes is not the easiest thing to do. Technically, all the guys who live here should be in classes but there's the chance someone else is playing hooky or genuinely sick and hanging around. What I'm about to do cannot have any witnesses, so I'm extra cautious and I take my time.

The ballet flats I'm wearing are the softest soles I could find in shoes, and I've worn them enough to know exactly how to position my feet to go unnoticed. They are silent on the old oak floorboards. My black tights and tee are closely fitted and don't rustle either. There're surgical gloves on my hands from my first-aid kit, and my hair is swept under my biggest knit cap. I've become the living shadow I've had to be hundreds of times before.

I remember the path to Joey's room, and I slip through the unlocked door easily. This will teach him to lock the damn thing.

I wait until I'm sure he's not here, and then I begin the slow and careful process of checking for security cameras. There're no obvious lenses, but I'm sure he's more imaginative than that. The living areas and the bathroom are clear, but I find a small camera that faces the bed.

Typical. Fucking. Rapist.

Collecting trophies is the usual predator MO, but I'm still pissed to see it. Did he still have the footage of him trying to force himself on me? Was he planning on sharing around the video of the assault as proof he'd won the bet? He had told me that nudes were so common at this school that no one really cared about them, but what about sex tapes? Would the other students care about seeing a rape, or would someone be willing to report Joey? I already knew the answer to that.

I swipe it, tucking it into my bra. I'm sure I'll find something abhorrent on it that will come in handy later, but I'm here for one thing.

His stash.

I walk back to the front door and start a meticulous search for his drugs. He's certainly not shy about all of the contraband in his room. There's alcohol everywhere, whiskey and rum mostly, and there's even glasses half-full still in the sink, like he was interrupted before classes this morning. I wonder if he's ever truly sober. He must be a high-functioning addict to be getting away with it. Hiding the scent alone is tricky, and to sit tests while buzzed must be an experience. I've never smelled it on his breath, but there's ways around that.

The bathroom turns up dozens of bottles of prescription medications. I snap photos of all the labels in case there's anything of interest there. But still no drugs. They have to be here somewhere. I'm getting antsy and frustrated at how long it's taking to find something worth finding. I should have hours before Joey is due back, but he doesn't come across as someone who cares about the rules at Hannaford. I begin to pace the rooms as I think.

On my third trip around the living room, I finally hear it.

There's a loose floorboard in the sitting area in front of the luxurious leather couch. I drop down to my hands and knees to run my fingers along the edges of the wooden plank. The gap is razor-fine, just barely registering on my fingertips, but it's there. I have to use a knife from the kitchen to pry it open, but when it does, I could crow with happiness.

Inside a small recess there's a tiny box, no bigger than the palm of my hand but a little longer. I open it carefully and find three bags of coke, a fake ID, and a stack of crisp hundred-dollar bills. I flick through the cash and make a quick estimate of ten grand. Pocket change to this guy, but enough to buy a lot of drugs for one person. I take a photo of the ID to check it later. I try not to touch the bags at all, but as I move the box, I hear the tinkling sort of rustle of something else sliding around. I use the flashlight on my phone to look for the culprit.

There's a small, heart-shaped locket. It's obviously pricey, I'd guess the stones on the front are real diamonds, but it's nothing special when you consider the Beaumonts are billionaires. My fingers catch on the raised edges of the back, and I flip it over. There's a delicate, tiny inscription on the back.

You before my blood,
My soul, my life,
My heart. Iris Arbour.

Arbour. Joey has taken this from Harley, probably earlier in the year when Avery was in damage control and Ash told her to let them fight it out. I stare at the words. They are lover's words, something private and sacred. I would guess that Iris was his mother. Had she died, and this was something he has left to remember her? Joey is the kind of heartless psychopath to enjoy taking something of that sort of value.

I slip the necklace around my neck. I don't have any pockets, and I'm afraid I won't feel it if it slips out of my bra. The metal feels cold against my skin.

I slip the box back into the gap and take photos of the placement. As I slip out of the room and head back to my room, the necklace swings against the hollow of my neck in an unfamiliar way. It feels like a win against Joey already.

When I arrive at the second-period class I share with Harley, he frowns at me as he moves his books from my desk. I know I'm radiating my smugness out for everyone to see. I'm using it as my armor for the day, so I don't feel any of the barbs being thrown at me. I've already had two teachers pull me aside and offer counseling because of the 911 call. The students are less kind about it. I've had to watch a couple of juniors do a dramatic reenactment in the dining hall over my early breakfast. They both looked at me, baiting me to hit them and risk another run-in with the principal, but the Wolf doesn't make rash decisions, and today I am the Wolf. I just watched them with a blank face and then gave them a slow, deeply ironic clap that echoed through the dining hall. Their bravado quickly dried up, and I got to watch them gulp and run away.

"Where were you this morning?" Harley says as he gives me a sidelong look. I watch him out of the corner of my eye, but I don't give him any extra attention. My mind is on bigger things today. "Are you still in a bloodthirsty rage, or have you mellowed enough to talk to me?"

"I have nothing to say to you or your little friends," I reply, and then I tune him out completely. He gives up trying pretty quickly.

The class drags, but only because I'm waiting for the big reveal I know is coming. When the bell finally goes, I shove everything into my bag as quickly as I can. Harley notices and does the same, his eyebrows drawn in tight as he stares at me.

"If you enjoy watching Joey get what he deserves, you should probably follow me," I murmur, just to get to see the look on his face. It doesn't disappoint.

"What did you—fuck it, lead the way, Mounty." He gestures with his arm, and I take the lead. He falls in step with me and he's got his phone out, texting with one hand. We get some looks as we walk together, the other students aware of the animosity between us.

"The twins might have a heart attack if they see this, so you might not want to tell them," I say as we approach the crowd that is slowly building in the front courtyard. Harley gives me this sort of dazed look, but he shakes his head and shoves his phone back in his pocket. I push through the crowd, and when I finally get to the front, I school my face into a blank look, so the shit-eating grin doesn't accidentally pop out.

Joseph Beaumont Jr. is in handcuffs.

The crowd is full of gasps and whispers already, and all the voices are laced with a reverent kind of fear. To see the self-appointed king of the school subjected to something so pedestrian, so scandalous, as being put in handcuffs. There're three police officers, and while one holds Joey's wrists, another is talking to him quietly. The third one, a tall imposing man, is talking to the principal in a heated discussion. I'm sure this is a first for Hannaford.

"What. The. Fuck," I hear Blaise say behind me. I glance behind me and see he's standing with an arm slung casually over Ash's shoulder. They're both dressed for the gym, the track team if I remember correctly. Ash's face is ghostly white, and his eyes are haunted as he takes in the scene. Harley nudges me and leans in to whisper in my ear, his breath dancing over my throat.

"Please explain to me what the fuck you did?"

"Did you know he's an addict? Cocaine was found in his room this morning. It seems the police were called in without Trevelen's knowledge, what a shame Joey couldn't talk his way out of it before law enforcement arrived."

Harley swears under his breath and leans away from me quickly as Avery arrives, with Rory close behind her. Harley shoots him a dark look full of loathing, but he doesn't say anything, and Avery doesn't notice. She doesn't have the same haunted look Ash does. Instead, she stares at the police officers reading Joey his rights with calculating eyes. Joey doesn't struggle or make any sort of scene; he just nods along amicably. I suppose he knows his dad will bail him out the second his ass hits the bench at the station, so why bother putting up a fight? Avery looks over at me, and she really looks at me for the first time. She's trying to read me, get some insight on my involvement. I wonder how much Harley put in the text message to her.

"If this was your doing, you'd better hope he never finds out," she says, and I shrug. I know they're all looking at me again, but this time I feel powerful. I've made my own move on the board, and now I have to wait to see what Joey does next.

Mr. Trevelen finally notices the huge crowd and starts to order us all to disperse. Avery tugs Harley away. He's hesitant to go, like he'd rather watch Joey be dragged away until the image is burned into his corneas for life. My eyes trace the tattoo that curves along his jaw: *Honor before Blood.* The necklace is in my pocket. I think about giving it to him now, but there are too many people watching. It feels wrong to keep it.

I wait until the crowd has thinned right down and Joey looks over to catch my eye. He doesn't look upset or surprised, he tips his head at me and grins. It's his maniac grin, the one that lets me know he will never be a good or kind person. I tip my own head back just a little and let him see the challenge I'm setting him. Let him come for me.

By dinner, the entire school knows about Joey's arrest and subsequent suspension from Hannaford.

I fill my tray with all the meats and vegetables I can fit—I'm starving and a little worried about possible scurvy after my week of surviving on protein bars—and then I find a seat at the long table. No one spares me a second glance, which I'm smug about. I get to listen to the rumors already circulating about what Joey has done to land himself in handcuffs. My personal favorites were prostitution, money laundering from street fighting, and involvement in his family's business.

Avery and the guys are also at the table, and Harley is staring my way. He's not trying to be discreet, just openly glaring my way as he chews on his meal. Avery is chatting to Blaise and, though their tones are light, I can see the strain in her shoulders. Ash is scowling at his plate. No amount of cajoling by Avery will get him to talk. I'm busy observing them, so I miss Harlow arriving at the dining hall. She doesn't miss me.

"Move, idiot," she snaps at the guy sitting across from me. He startles and glances between us both. I get my first real look at the damage I'd done to her face as he scrambles up and away from us, leaving his tray behind. Both her eyes are black and swollen, her nose has been taped and braced, and her cheeks are mottled with bruises. None of her pretty features are visible anymore. She looks horrific, like she's been the victim of a violent crime, and the smile I give her is all teeth.

"Is there something you want, Roqueford? I'm busy." A hush falls over the dining hall. Even the teachers further down the table have stopped to watch our confrontation. I wonder if they've been warned off from me as well.

"You're dead. The minute Joey gets back, he's going to fucking kill you, Mounty scum." She spits at me, literally spits; I feel it land on my cheek. I fight the urge to wipe it away.

"Why would he bother with me? He's already extracted his revenge for me turning him down." I laugh at her, and she flinches back at the icy sound.

"He's not stupid. Obviously, it was you who snitched on him." Her knuckles are white as she grips the chair. I let my eyes roam over her face again with pride. I really do feel proud of what I did to her. There's only the strong and the weak in this world, and it didn't matter what Joey and his fucked-up flunkies did to me. I'd always be stronger than them.

"How about you prove it?" I whisper and smile at her again. She curses at me again and turns on her heel to storm out. The room seems to hold its breath for a second, and then the conversations resume, quietly at first and then with some gusto.

I enjoy my dinner and I don't waste another second thinking about Joey Beaumont.

He's out of my hair for a few weeks.

Chapter Fourteen

I get a week's reprieve from Avery and her minions. I don't know if I've rattled her, or if she's still recovering from whatever it was that happened between her and her siblings, but I enjoy the silence. I throw myself back into my studies and focus on my vocal work for choir. I have worked out that if I wear earplugs, I can go through the exercises Miss Umber has assigned us, but that means I have no idea how I sound. If the class didn't directly affect my overall grade, I wouldn't care whatsoever about it, but my scholarship required a near-perfect GPA to stay eligible. There was no way I was letting my PTSD lose my chances at a decent future.

During my training with the Jackal, I'd been subjected to torture. There was no other word for it, no pretty little name that changed what happened into a useful lesson. I'd been taught how to withstand extreme levels of pain without screaming. The side effect of that training was that now I couldn't hear my own voice, screaming or singing, without the bone-deep fear of the consequences the Jackal had set for me. I had the scars to show for the punishment I was dealt, and the thought of going through that again made my brain switch firmly into fight-or-flight mode.

It was one of many reasons I had run away from Mounts Bay, and why I could never love Matteo the way he loved me.

Sometimes, when I didn't keep myself busy or on high alert, those memories would creep into my mind unbidden and I'd find myself shaky and nervous, twitchy even.

I was in one of those moods when I sat in the library for my usual study session with Ash.

He'd blown off our other session for that week, so I had no real expectations for him showing up today. If anything, I hoped he wouldn't show up. I didn't want him questioning the tremor in my fingers as I answered the math equations in my workbook.

I get fifteen minutes of peace before Blaise arrives. He looks around the library as if he is looking for someone else to help him, and then sighs and sits down in the seat Ash usually uses. I don't look up or acknowledge him as he empties his bag and gets settled in his seat. Once he's set up, he clears his throat to get my attention. I look up and focus my eyes at the tip of his nose instead of staring into those gorgeous green eyes. He shifts in his seat, and I think about feeling sorry for him. Then I remember his cold words when he'd publicly humiliated me on the worst day of my time at Hannaford so far—*I don't fuck fans*—and I give him the tiniest glare instead. God, I am pathetic.

"I'm going to fail math if you can't perform a miracle on me."

I take the paper he slides across to me and see the mess he's made of his own workbook. It's bad. It's not completely hopeless, but he's definitely going to fail if he hands this in. I start to mark it and jot down observations in silence, trying to ignore the slight tremble of my fingers. I can help this arrogant, gorgeous, talented, swoon-worthy asshole without having to look or speak to him. I am just that good.

He squirms in his seat.

"Look, if you don't want to help me, then I can find someone else."

I snort at him derisively without stopping my methodical work. "Harley is on par with me in math. Why don't you ask him to help you? Then you wouldn't have to ever look at me. I could continue to stay as far away from you as possible, and you could forget I even go here."

He clears his throat again and looks around the room. His tie is off, and his shirt is unbuttoned enough that I can see his tattoos peeking out. I try my best not to think about them and finish marking the page, sliding it back across the table to him. When I pick up my own work again, he finally answers me.

"Harley is really impatient. He used to try and help me, but we would end up at each other's throats. He doesn't understand how I don't get it. It's all so easy to him that he's removed from the work the rest of us have to do to understand."

It's an honest statement. Something revealing and raw. I nod at him, and then I sigh, looking up to walk him through the work verbally until I'm sure he's got a decent understanding of the formulas. He's obviously smart, but it takes a few tries to find the right explanations to help him get a good grasp on the sums. It's pleasant, much nicer than the antagonistic banter with Ash, and I find myself enjoying him being there. We get the workbook in a solid A condition, and I even help him develop a great page of notes for the upcoming tests.

"So, how did you first hear Vanth?" he asks as I do a last read-through.

The question throws me, and I just barely manage to keep hold of my pen. I glance up to see his eyes fucking twinkling at me, and I choke on my tongue.

"I heard your early covers and I bought the albums." I don't mention what I had to do to get the money to buy them. I don't know how well he'd take me gambling with my body in the fighting scenes of Mounts Bay middle school.

He groans and rubs a hand over his face.

"How did you find the covers? They're terrible! You must be a very dedicated fan to go looking for them."

I know logically that he's joking around with me, but he hits a nerve. The same nerve he'd struck uttering those words to me in Health Ed. My face flames, and I slowly put my pen down with a glare at him. His face drops, the smile sliding right off his features.

"I didn't go looking for them. I'm not a fucking stalker. I meant that I heard them when you released them. I'd been listening to your shit from the beginning, and I followed your career from there to Vanth. But don't worry about going to school with a fan, I'm certainly not one now. I've fucking burned the shirt and deleted your shit from my phone. I have no interest in listening to music from a stuck-up, spoiled, rich brat. I'll listen to music from people who are real and write lyrics from the heart."

I've managed to strike a nerve with him too. I know all about his insecurities, how he didn't want to use his parents' money to prop up the band in their early years or use their connection to get a record deal. I know exactly what to say to piss him off, and that's what I've done.

He leveled me with a look so dark, my mind flashes to Ash sitting across from me. I take in every inch of his fire and give him back my own. I may never be able to speak to him again, but at least I've told him exactly what I think of him, exactly what his dismissal of me did to me.

Now Avery might actually kill me. But fuck him and fuck her.

Two things cross my mind when I get back to my room after dinner the next night: Avery Beaumont works fast; and where the hell could I get some locks that would keep the bitch out of my room?

I thought the urine was the worst thing they could throw around my room, and I guess it was a stinking biohazard. However, piss could be washed out. You could splash enough bleach around to disinfect and clean the damage done to the room.

You can't wash out pure, industrial-strength black paint.

When I open the door and switch on my light, the blackness eats it up so much, for a second I think the light has blown. There isn't a single inch of the room or contents that isn't now black. My clothes and shoes, my books, my fucking pillow. I take a step forward and I feel the tackiness of the floor. The paint isn't even dry yet. They must have barely finished before I got here. I can hear the tittering of their laughter, a sound that will probably haunt me for life once I've left this damned place behind, but I don't look back to see who it is. I know that no matter who held the tin and brushes, Avery is behind this. I'm grateful that I've made copies of all my classwork, so at least I don't lose that work, but I now have nothing. I'll have to spend some of my stash of funds to replace my uniforms and my clothing. I've lost every damn thing I own. Well, not everything. My safe hidden under the floorboards is fine.

I have no choice but to call the administration office and report the damage thanks to the black walls and floor.

While I wait for help to arrive, I pick through my destroyed belongings and start a mental list of what I'm going to have to replace, the bare minimum I'll need to survive. It's frustrating that Avery knows exactly where to hit to cause the most damage to my life. While Joey uses big, sweeping acts to attempt to break me, Avery knows the small pressure points that chip away at me. The bet and the guys chasing me for sex is annoying, but manageable. Even Joey trying to fuck me against my will was something I could deal with; a knife to the dick is pretty persuasive. The 911 call was closer to the mark, but he underestimated my mental walls.

The exhaustion of cleaning out my room constantly, of checking for cameras, of showering as quickly as I can, of replacing everything I own—that was all much more likely to get me to quit this school, and honestly, if my only other option wasn't returning to the Jackal, I might've walked away by now. But I know the second I go back to him; I will never get out. I'll be stuck as his second-in-command in his gang, and probably even his girlfriend. I'll be his to own and control. I can't ever belong to him again.

Avery's face is the perfect picture of innocence when Mr. Trevelen arrives. I don't have any evidence to say it was her, but there isn't a doubt in my mind that she's responsible. I'm escorted down to the sick bay in the nurse's office to sleep for the night, and Mr. Trevelen informs me I'll be reimbursed for the items lost. I don't kick up a fuss, there's no point, and when I lay my head down, I sleep like the dead.

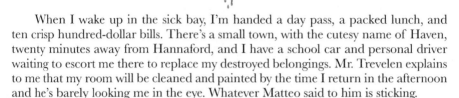

When I wake up in the sick bay, I'm handed a day pass, a packed lunch, and ten crisp hundred-dollar bills. There's a small town, with the cutesy name of Haven, twenty minutes away from Hannaford, and I have a school car and personal driver waiting to escort me there to replace my destroyed belongings. Mr. Trevelen explains to me that my room will be cleaned and painted by the time I return in the afternoon and he's barely looking me in the eye. Whatever Matteo said to him is sticking.

During the drive, I tap out a quick text to Matteo and ask him for some recommendations on pick-proof locks. I'm willing to pay big bucks to keep the other girls out of my shit from here on out. His reply is immediate and coddling, but I take it. He'll send me what I need.

It's a Saturday, so the town is full of students. I've never seen the appeal in venturing outside the school. I don't want to spend money or run into one of Matteo's men out here, but the town is one of those cookie-cutter-perfect places with cafés and boutique stores, and I have to admit it's nice. There isn't a big box chain store in sight. Giant trees line the brick streets, and they're all decorated with hundreds of white, blinking fairy lights. It's magical looking, even for my jaded heart, and I let myself stare out the window at it all a little wistfully.

A thousand dollars isn't enough to replace what I need if I stick to these higher-end stores, I'd be lucky to find a single item of clothing for that price, so I ask the driver to drive around for a while until I spot what I'm looking for. Tucked away off the main street in a tiny alleyway, I find a thrift store. I ask the driver to wait, and he informs me with a curt smile that he's mine for the day and to take my time. Rich kid perks, I guess.

The store is teeming with designer labels I care nothing about, and I dig through the shoes until I hit a jackpot. A pair of cherry red Docs that hit me mid-calf. They're a touch too big, but with thick socks they're perfect, and my spirits are instantly lifted. I trawl through the jeans until I find three pairs that work for me, and then I look for some booty shorts.

An hour later, I leave the store with more bags than I've ever carried out of anywhere before, and the driver has to pop the trunk and help me pile my haul in. It's still early enough in the afternoon, so I decide to stop to get a coffee. I shouldn't be wasting money on something as frivolous as coffee, but I think of it as a reward for all my hard work and perfect marks at Hannaford so far.

I choose one of the smaller shops, because the bigger ones are overrun with Hannaford uniforms and I do not want to be accosted by one of the Beaumonts or their loyal followers. I order it to go, eager to get back to my room and get my life back in order. I chat to the barista, Emily, and I enjoy just being a teenager for a moment. She doesn't know anything about me except that I go to Hannaford, and the shock that I'm speaking to her at all is evident on her face. I find out the other students have a reputation in this town for being assholes. What a shock. When she hands me the coffee, I thank her warmly, and then slip back out to the alleyway.

I should have ignored the sounds coming from the tiny back parking lot.

I knew what I was hearing, I'd heard it a million times before, but curiosity killed the cat and it may someday kill me too. I move slowly and try to be silent, which is hard in the kitten heels I'm forced to wear as part of the Hannaford Prep uniform. As I round the corner, I get the disgusting view of Rory's bare ass as his hips swing. He's got Avery bent over his garishly orange Lamborghini Huracan. I can't see her face, only the skirt pushed up over her hips and twisted in Rory's fists as he pumps away at her. He's grunting and swearing under his breath, and I startle at the sharp crack of his palm hitting her ass.

Why would they be fucking out here instead of just doing it in the dorms? The zero-tolerance bullshit Trevelen spouts means nothing to any of these rich assholes, so why risk public sex? Maybe they're exhibitionists and Rory needs the thrill to get his dick hard. I smother the snort I have at the thought. I'm tempted to take a photo and send it out, give her a taste of her own medicine, but I won't stoop to her level. Plus, the guys all told me it wasn't her and, while I don't believe them, I prefer to extract the right forms of punishment. Just as I turn to leave them to it, Rory grunts and pulls Avery up by her hair so roughly, I wince. It doesn't look sexy at all, more controlling and dominative in a shitty, misogynistic way. He turns them both so he can sit on the car and she can straddle him reverse cowgirl to finish the job. Her head is down, but I don't need to see the face to know that's not Avery riding his dick. The hair isn't the perfect black curls of the devil that's torturing me.

It's Harlow Roqueford.

She tips her head back, and I see her nose is still taped, but the bruises have all faded enough to be covered by makeup. She's moaning loudly, seemingly uncaring of being caught, and she's bouncing on him with gusto. I'm shocked enough to freeze for a second, gaping at the sight of them both, but after a heartbeat I get my wits about me. I get my phone out and snap a photo, not to share around, but if I decide to tell Avery, she won't believe me without some proof. I take a short video for good measure, and then I sneak back down the alleyway and out to the waiting car. I flick through the photos and smile as I sip my coffee and the driver pulls back onto the highway.

Chapter Fifteen

My room is now freshly painted, white and crisp, and the new bed I've been supplied is even more comfortable than the last one. The sheets and pillows are also brand new, and the thread count must be higher than my postcode. I feel like I should send Avery a thank-you note. I grin to myself at the mental image of her reading all about her little prank backfiring. I'm also in love with my new boots, and I spent hours trying them on with all my new clothes to see what I like best. Hannaford is quickly teaching me to take the good with the bad.

True to form, the lock Matteo had promised me was already installed by the time I arrived back at Hannaford, and the single key is on a chain around my neck. If anyone wants access to this room, they will have to pry it from my cold, dead body. I'm sure nothing would give Joey more pleasure.

My great mood lasts until choir, and then I'm overcome with nerves. I arrive early, having sprinted down the halls and shoving other students out of my way, so I can corner Miss Umber and persuade her to take pity on me. Our class assignment is to sing a solo in front of the class, and there is no way on this earth that I'll be able to do it. I've been practicing at every available opportunity and I've become decent at distracting myself, but the second my concentration wavers, I get the shakes and lose my stomach contents. If I perform in front of the class, Avery will not only have photos of my disgrace, she will also have a new weakness of mine to exploit. Now that I've managed to lock down any access to my room, I'm not looking at giving her a new avenue to explore.

Miss Umber looks right through me. There's this puzzled look on her face, like she's trying to place my face, and I grumble under my breath. Such is life when you share a class with the fabled lead singer and guitarist of Vanth Falling. I'm not sure she remembers any of my classmates, only the shining god that joins us each lesson. It doesn't matter to me if she doesn't remember me. All that matters is convincing her to let me have a private assessment. It's not an easy sell.

"Part of the mark is your ability to perform to a crowd. I alone am not a crowd, Miss…er-And-Anderson." I ignore the stumble over my name. I've already had to tell her what it is twice.

"I understand that, but I'm currently undertaking extensive therapy to be able to do so, and my health care professionals aren't comfortable with me stepping out on stage to more than a few people." Lie-lie-lie, I don't care. I'll keep spewing out falsehoods until I get what I want, and if she asks for proof, I'll call in a favor. Fuck, I'll call in ten favors. Whatever it takes, I'm not getting on that stage.

"Oh. Yes, okay. That's a different case. We wouldn't want to upset your parents and have them in here, would we? You can come after the winter break, and I'll assess you privately. Now, take a seat and start your warm-ups! Mr. Morrison should be here soon, and then we can start."

I thank her and slump onto my usual chair, relief coursing through my veins. I'm still feeling prickly with irritation and relief when the rest of the students arrive. Avery has her hand tucked into Blaise's, and they're chatting happily with their adoring fans. I nod to Lauren when she joins me, but my mind is on Avery. What is the best way to get back at her for everything she's been doing to me without becoming a bully myself? If I get caught, I'll lose my scholarship, but it's more than that.

I've never done anything out of spite. I've hurt people, I've stolen, I've lied. I've beaten someone until the life left them. But never have I done anything with the intent of hurting someone purely to get back at them. I'd only ever acted in self-preservation or defense. That was the moral high ground I clung to, so I didn't lose my mind about all the wrong I'd done. What am I willing to do to Avery as revenge?

"Oh, Lord. You're staring at Avery again. Should I be worried? Is another Beaumont about to be taken out in handcuffs?" whispers Lauren, breaking my chain of thought. I give her a sidelong look, and she grins at me. I don't know how she guessed about my involvement in Joey's arrest. Maybe the whole school has already guessed.

"What do you think of our oh-so-benevolent overlord?" I reply. Lauren is nice enough. If she thinks Avery is the devil, then maybe I could be spiteful just this once. Lauren glances over to her, and we both watch as she plays around on her phone, not a care for the teacher and lesson going on around her at all.

"I think she's lonely. I think she comes from a fucked-up family and her brother is so scared of anything happening to her that she's now isolated. Did you hear that Rory and Blaise got into a fight over dinner last night? Rory came back from his football game and Blaise said, in front of the whole dining hall, that the pussy he could smell on him had better not be Avery's." Lauren giggles at the shocked look on my face. "I think he was just saying it to bait Rory into spilling about their sex life. Ash was there too, and everyone knows he'll murder Rory if he touches her."

"But why? If any of the rumors are true, they're all fucking half the damn school between them. Pretty damn sexist to say she can't sleep around if she wants to." I did not want to think about any of the whispers I've heard. Or about Annabelle. Ugh, fuck Annabelle.

"I know. It's an old money thing. My parents would also have a lot to say if I started dating, and I'd murder my little sister if I found her hanging around someone like Rory." Lauren shrugs and settles back in her chair.

Ash Beaumont is lying to me.

I'm not stupid, and it's starting to be really obvious. He doesn't need my tutoring at all. I watch as he follows my explanations on his physics assignment, and he's not even listening to me. He knows every damn thing I'm saying to him.

Why the hell is he torturing me by being here, then? He's more distracted today than he usually is, so I test out my theory by purposefully explaining the theory wrong, and then I watch him answer the questions. He gets them all correct. What the hell is his problem?

"I told you during our first session that if you're not here to learn, then you shouldn't come," I say, my temper rising. It doesn't really matter if he's learning or not, I get the credits just for being here, but I feel duped. Like he's just here to push all my buttons, or to find ways for Avery to torture me.

"And I told you, if you want the credits, you'll sit and teach me." He doesn't look up from his work as he speaks, which is probably for the best. I'm seething even as I survey his stunning eyelashes. It's a crime that he has naturally sooty eyelashes that curl beautifully. I wonder how many girls have stared at them enviously before me. He looks like he's wearing eyeliner, a dark frame around the cerulean blue irises.

"If you're not actually learning anything, then we could just sit and study together in silence. I could get my work done, and you could… do whatever it is that you're here for, without me having to ramble on uselessly."

He glances up and catches me ogling him. I refuse to blush; I tell myself I'm staring because I'm pissed. He gives me a slow smirk and leans back in his chair, cocky as he crosses his arms over his chest. I forget sometimes that he's built. The uniform hides the physique of the male students far better than the legs and curves of the females. Sexist bullshit. If the guys get to see whether, or not I've shaved my legs this week, I think I should be able to see who bench presses my bodyweight on the regular.

"Enjoying the eye fuck?" he drawls. Oh, no. That self-flagellating tone will just not do. I need to take him down a notch.

"I'm assessing your weak spots, so I'm confident in my aim when I have to take you out." He doesn't back down. If anything, my words egg him on. His smirk turns into an entirely too-confident flirty grin. I haven't been this close to swooning since Blaise's appearance at the school. This guy is devil spawn.

"Sure, you are, Mounty. And will you be aiming for my eyes, then?"

I nod and attempt a glare. "Blinding you gives me a much better chance at survival. You're twice the size of me, so unless you're well trained at fighting in the dark, that should even the playing field nicely."

He chuckles and lets his eyes roam over my chest and down my legs. I hate people looking at my legs. The scars may have faded a little but they're still plain to see. I can't wait until I'm a junior and I can wear thigh-high socks. Cute, and a satisfactory cover up. His gaze is heated, I think he's flirting with me, but with no prior experience I don't want to jump to conclusions. I might be mistaking things because of how badly I want Ash. He's such an asshole but, fuck, I'm attracted to him.

"Don't sleep with any of the boys." I look up to see Ash looking at me with such intensity, my knees think about shaking.

"What the fuck?!" I splutter out, more at my reaction than his words.

"I know it probably goes against your Mounty nature, but you'll just dig a bigger hole for yourself if you fuck any of them." How do I find him so attractive when he's such a dick to me?

"My Mounty nature? I'm not some sexual fucking deviant! Why is every boy in this damn school so far up their own asses?"

He smirks at me and shrugs. I don't know what to do with him or how to reply, so I drop my eyes back to the assignment in front of me and get back to marking it. It's all correct, because of course it is, he's fucking with me by being here.

"Joey has decided he's going to fuck you. That's why he started the bet in the first place. He likes to prove how powerful he is. Every year he picks some big, elaborate goal, and then we all get to sit back and watch while he crushes, breaks, and mutilates everyone around him to achieve it. This year it's you." I think I've stopped breathing. This should be over. He can't possibly be saying I'm still going to be a target for Joey to *rape*. "If you fuck any other guy, Joey will probably kill you both."

It's become so commonplace to use the word 'kill' flippantly. They'd kill for those shoes, they'd kill you if you tell on them, they'd love nothing more than to kill that person. Ash isn't saying the word kill like that. He's saying it like he's seen his brother choke the life out of another human being. I give him a curt nod. It's not like I had any plans to date at this place. I'd always planned on waiting until college to lose my cherry, so what difference did it make if Joey had a say in it too?

A fucking big difference.

Now I wanted to fuck half the school just to spite him. Well, not really. I wanted him to think I had, because I didn't want my celibacy to look like I was bowing to him and his whims.

"What do your parents think of Joey and his actions?"

It's the wrong thing to say. I watch as Ash's face sets and a thunderous look rolls in. I shouldn't have asked. The gossip mill here at Hannaford is active enough that I could have just asked around instead. I was bolstered by his kindness in warning me, and I forgot myself. I forgot for a second that, to this man, I will always be trash.

"How about I'll answer that when you answer something for me. Did it hurt? When you found your mom, did it cripple you, even though you always knew it was going to end that way?"

My chest collapses in on itself like a vice is squeezing the life out of me. I should know by now that Ash always goes for the low blow in a fight. It did cripple me, but I'm not that girl anymore. I think about my life as the me before, the one who had to fight for food but had a mom, and there's the me now. I don't have to fight for food anymore, and I have a safe place to sleep every night. I'm at the best school in the country. I already have the attention of several of the top colleges in the state, and I have plans to start reaching out to others further away from home. I did a lot of bad things to get to where I am today, my hands are filthy with it. I don't feel any better now than I did before.

I am truly alone.

"One of these days, I am going to show this school what it takes to survive at Mounts Bay High and foster care." My voice shakes, and he smirks at me.

"I'll take that as a yes."

He turns his attention back to his homework, and I grit my teeth. Why, oh why, did I have to do this for extra credits? I finish my page of sums in seconds, my affinity with numbers making this all child's play, and then I crack open the required reading for my literature class while I wait for him to catch up.

"Hey, man! Just in time, as per usual," Ash calls out, and I cringe. I know what that sarcastic tone of voice means. My other student has arrived.

Blaise looks like he would rather be anywhere but here. I've lost the fire within me that had enabled me to speak to him callously, so I stare at his ear lobe again and wait for him to sit down.

"I need help with my Lit assignment, and no one else has been able to help me like you did with the math shit. Can you please help me?" he grinds out from between his clenched teeth, like the words are hurting him. Ash watches us both with raised eyebrows and a half smile.

"Sure. Sit down and show me what you need." The cool tone replaces the snarky one I was using, and he gets even more curious.

"What the fuck went down with you two?"

Blaise ignores him, slumping in his chair, and I consider doing the same. Ash throws a pen at me, and I sigh. "I informed Blaise that I burned my Vanth shirt because I don't listen to music written and performed by assholes, and he ran off to tattle to the spawn-of-Satan you shared a womb with, and she destroyed my room to avenge his hurt feelings."

"I didn't fucking tattle! She asked me why I was pissy, and I answered," Blaise hisses back at me. Ash's mouth drops open as he watches us.

I snort. "So, you're put out that I don't fucking worship you like you think you deserve, and in return I lose every single thing I own at the hands of Avery's minions? Fair trade. Fair fucking trade."

Ash leans back in his chair, the glee at our spat shining in his icy eyes. "Everything you own is here at Hannaford?"

"I'm emancipated. Of course it is. No, was. I have nothing now, until the summer break when I can go back to Mounts Bay. Happy now, Morrison? Got your revenge? Great. Show me your assignment and let me fix it so you can tell your billionaire daddy how fucking great you're doing at this hellhole."

Blaise is gaping at me like I've just kicked him in the balls and asked for his gratitude for doing so. I raise my eyebrows at him until he hands over the assignment, and I start in on it.

The evidence of Rory's unfaithful ways is burning a hole in my consciousness. I want to get the shit off my phone and out of my mind as quickly as possible. Plus, I caught Avery making out with him on the couch in the girls' dorms again. If he's cheating on her, if they're not in some weird polygamist relationship like the guys are, then I hate the idea of him getting away with it.

I can't email her the video. There're too many risks of the school administration finding out about it. I know for a fact that all our study and interactions online are monitored. Texting it to her is another option. The only way I can get Avery's phone number is by either breaking into the administration office or asking around for it. Neither are good options.

I end up in the library printing off copies of the photos. I feel gross even looking at them, and I'm twitchy about being caught. I did not want to explain all of this to Matteo if Mr. Trevelen catches wind of this. He'd probably insist on using the photos as blackmail against Rory and Harlow, and while I did enjoy the thought of them sweating it out at the hands of the Jackal, it would complicate my life.

I don't want to think about Matteo anymore. I'm so confused about him. His gentle tones on the phone when I called him for help made my chest ache. I used to love him. Back when I first went into foster care, he was the cool kid. Someone in my corner who loved me back. I truly thought he loved me too. Now I know that he sees me as a valuable pawn on the chessboard. Nothing more. But I still feel guilty for having certain feelings about Ash. And Blaise and, fuck, Harley. I can't forget the feelings I have for Harley.

I get back to my room and deliberate over my note to Avery. Fuck, I should be so happy to be able to crush her with this, but it feels so underhanded. I don't want to break her with a guy. I want to outsmart her. Outplay her. I want to survive everything she throws at me, and then dish it back twice as bad.

I'm not Joey. I don't enjoy cutting people where it stings the most. I'm not cruel. I'm no angel, but every rotten thing I've done has been to survive. Someday I'll be able to shed all of this and just be kind.

I slip the photos and the note under Avery's door before I head down for dinner. All the other students will be leaving for winter break in the morning, and I need her to know before she goes.

Taken three days ago. Dump him.

Chapter Sixteen

The entire school is empty for winter break.

At least that's what I think, until day three when I spot Harley sitting in the dining hall eating a massive pile of eggs by himself. He freezes when he hears the door, and then glares over at me. I pile my own plate full of pancakes, fruit, syrup, and ice cream, and then sit as far away from him as possible.

I wasn't expecting to see anyone, so I'm wearing tiny shorts, an old, torn shirt, and thigh-high socks. I'd been sliding my way around the school and squealing like a toddler all morning. There was only a skeleton staff still at the school, so I hadn't felt any shame in doing it. I now cringe at the thought of Harley catching me.

It was uncomfortable eating in silence, knowing he was at the other end of the table. A few times I thought I could feel his eyes on me, but when I glanced up, he was scrolling through his phone. He was probably texting the others about how ridiculous I look. I sigh into my fruit and prepare for how much shit I'll get from Avery when the break is over.

I'm contemplating my future doom when Harley gets up and leaves the hall. As he walks past my chair, I meet his eyes and keep my face blank. He sneers down at me, and I roll my eyes.

Stupid rich kids.

When I'm finished, I head back to my room and start the colossal pile of homework I have. It's not the fun winter break I think the rest of Hannaford students are having. I think back to when my mom was still alive and it was Christmas time, but we never actually did anything. Too broke for presents, too sad for a tree or good food. My only really good memories from then were watching the Christmas specials on TV by myself while my mum got high and walked the streets. Fuck, if that's where my brain was going, I was going to have a miserable break.

I have a scholarship to keep and not much else to do, so homework it is.

The most pressing is to do my vocal work.

I can't practice in my room when the other girls are here. I'm too nervous that they can hear me and even with my headphones on, the anxiety triggers my PTSD. I've picked my song, having ditched the Vanth Falling song for good now that I've met Blaise, and I just need to practice it enough that I can zone completely out while I perform.

I will never admit this to another living soul, but I pick *Pompeii* by Bastille because of Blaise's cover of it. It sucks that so much of my own musical story is intertwined with his because of my past obsession with him, but I need something I've sung a thousand times before to get through the assignment. No one will ever have to know it's all because of him.

I'd rather die.

I decide to skip lunch to keep practicing, and then finally my stomach drags me to the dining hall for dinner. The menu is very festive, and it takes me a second to realize it's Christmas Eve. I feel bad for the kitchen staff who have to be there to feed me, a scholarship student, and then I remember Harley and the giant mountain of money his family would have paid to send him here, and I feel a bit better.

I fill my plate with such a feast I feel bad for the kids back home, and then I sit and tuck in.

Harley is in his usual seat, so I situate myself at the other end of the table again. Not long after I sit down, I hear him get up, and to my utter shock he sits down across from me. His plate is only half-empty, and he gets back to eating as soon as he's sat down.

"Rumor has it you're emancipated," he says without looking up at me, so I have to do more than nod.

My voice is barely more than a croak. "Yeah."

"How the fuck did you manage that?"

I can't figure out his angle. Is he fishing for information to use against me, or is he just curious, bored, feeling the Christmas spirit?

"I was already in foster care and I proved I could provide for myself, so it was one less kid the state had to take care of. Took me a year, but I just kept trying."

He grunts and leans back in his chair to study my face. I try desperately not to flush scarlet under his gorgeous stare.

"How the fuck can a Mounty provide for herself? You have a sugar daddy or some shit?" He doesn't speak like the other rich kids. It jars me, because he may look like the most heavenly being I've ever seen but he speaks like a roughneck kid from the streets. He sounds like me. It's comforting, even while he's all smirks and asshole nature.

"I'm not selling myself to anything except my scholarship."

He scoffs. "That's vague."

"Why do you want to know? Mommy and Daddy pissing you off? Why aren't you home celebrating the holidays with them?"

His eyes narrow to a glare, and he clenches his teeth. I could apologize or change the subject, but he started it. He looks away from me and I can see his brain at work. I give him a minute of silence before I prod him again. "I answered you honestly. Is there no honor among rich kids?"

He gives me a dark look, and I tuck back into my dinner while I wait.

"My dad's dead. My mom is locked up. I'm thinking about applying for emancipation, too. My caseworker won't say a word to me about it, she just tells me it's not for me. So, I'm offering you a meal of peace for the information. I know you're smart, you wouldn't be here if you weren't, so I'll take you at your word."

Huh. He was an orphan like me. So why does he treat me so badly? And why does Avery protect him so fiercely?

"Are you on a scholarship too?"

"Fuck no." Like it's something to be ashamed of, like I didn't spend half my life working to be here instead of paying my way in. I give him my own dark look, which he promptly ignores.

"Then you must have the means to provide for yourself. It should be an easy process for you."

He stabs around at his plate violently. I almost feel sorry for the beans.

"I don't have access to any of the money my dad left for me. Or… well, any of the money that's rightfully mine. So, no, it won't be."

I shrug at him. "If you have an estate that pays for you, then that will count too."

"Don't have one of those either," he grumbles.

I set my fork down and fold my arms over my chest. He watches me, and then mirrors my movement. Is he fucking with me? "Who pays for your school tuition, then?"

"Avery."

Holy fuck. "Is she in love with you? I see her tongue down that dickhead Rory's neck all the time, so I wouldn't have guessed it."

He snorts and looks at me incredulously. When I stare at him blankly, he shakes his head. "We're cousins. Our moms were sisters. Avery takes that shit very seriously, so I'm here with her and Ash because she couldn't bear the thought of me going to a public school back home."

Cousins! They look nothing alike. Harley is a golden god, and Ash is like a dark prince, with all that dark hair and brooding. I look at him closer and think maybe around the nose there's a hint of similarity, but nothing obvious.

"Well, fuck. I don't know how to advise you with only half your story. So, either tell me it all, or go spend weeks researching it online like I had to."

He looks at me again, and then sighs, rubbing his hands over his face like he wanted to scrub years off it. His biceps flex invitingly with the action and I resist the urge to reach out and squeeze them. "Fuck it. I have a large inheritance from my parents, but to get it, I'd have to fulfill certain… obligations that I refuse to do. I won't lose my soul for the money. My mom has nothing. Avery pays for all my shit. How do I get emancipated?"

I push my tray away, the meat now cold and unappealing. Every time I'm interrupted by one of these guys, I end up missing out on good food. The kitchen staff had put out an amazing spread for only two students, and now I'm not even going to finish my plate. So damn wasteful.

"You would have to have enough money to cover all of your expenses for the next three years in a bank account, and a plan on how you would use them. Detailed, like an itemized list, down to how much soap you use in a year. Can Avery give you that?"

He doesn't answer, he just grits his teeth again and picks up his tray. I huff out a breath, feeling dismissed, and then he calls out to me as he leaves, "Thanks, Mounty."

I grab my own tray and head back up to bed.

I don't get out until Christmas Day is over.

Boxing Day is not a good day for me.

I decide to go down and eat breakfast, and Harley pours me a cup of juice as he passes by my chair. I stupidly think it's a nice gesture after how much information I gave him at our last meeting. I should know better by now.

He'd put laxatives in it.

I could not leave the girls' dorms for the rest of the day.

I am so angry about the juice that I throw caution so far into the wind, it ends up in fucking Kansas.

I know Harley is on the swim team because it's the only class we don't share, and I've heard Blaise and Avery talking about it in our choir and voice development classes. I also know that being as unbelievably gorgeous as he is, he must be very attached to his looks and, especially, his immaculately coiffed golden-blond hair. You can't be *that* hot without also being vain.

I have no access to any beauty stores, but I'm an inventive sort of girl. The kitchen staff are very happy to help me out with my science project and armed with two bottles of food-grade dye, I find his shampoo and conditioner and pour an entire bottle in each. I'm not sure Harley is the type to pull off the Smurf look, but *good god* am I ready to find out.

Being the only two students in the school gives me an extra dose of bravery, like I'm untouchable over the holidays, when really I know that Harley will tell his friends, and then I'll have to face whatever it is they decide to retaliate with. Avery had already proven herself to be an unconscionable bully, and that was without me ever fighting back. It was a sobering thought of what she would do once she finds out. But for now, I'm going to enjoy the sport of beating this gorgeous guy at his own game. It's nice to be able to mess with him in such a low-level way.

I get to dinner early and sit at the far end of the table in the exact chair that he usually sits. I enjoy ten minutes of silence and steak before showtime. When the door at the far end of the dining hall swings open, I don't look up, and it's a struggle not to smirk. I can hear him filling his plate and then the sound of him walking toward me. I roll my eyes that he would insist on sitting at his chair even in an empty hall, and I prepare to stare him down but then he pulls out the chair across from me and sits. I glance up and snort.

Between the bright blue tones and the tattoo, he looks like he belongs in an eighties punk band. The shocking part is that his eyes are twinkling with laughter rather than the malice I expected.

"Good shower?" I prod at him.

"Great. Just what I needed. How's your bowels?"

"Lovely and cleared, thanks for asking."

He snorts with laughter and digs into his plate. It's weird to sit with him, but I can't move away without seeming weak or bitchy. Plus, he's just as alluring as the first time I saw him, so hot it hurts to look right at him.

"Which dictator did you pick for history? I'm going to wipe the floor with you." His eyes are still twinkling, and it makes me feel lightheaded. Is he flirting? He can't be. I clear my throat.

"Avery Beaumont, but Ms. Aurelia said I can't choose someone still in power, so I went with Mao Zedong. Who did you pick?"

He smirks and shows off his perfect teeth.

"Like I'd tell you." He gives his juice a sniff before shrugging and drinking from it. I regret not messing with it. He sees me watching him and says, "I'm sure you've thought of something worse, but if you have spiked it, I needed some fiber anyway."

I smile and hope that not knowing drives him a little crazy.

"I bet you've picked Hitler like every other student ever. Predictable. Boring," I taunt him, but he just smiles. Even his smile is deadly. I can feel it slicing into my soul.

"Have you finished yet? Is it printed out and ready to be handed in?" His voice is soft and sweet, and fuck if it doesn't make me nervous. And a little turned on, but mostly nervous.

"My breakfast, my assignment, or fucking with you?"

He leans back in his chair and crosses his arms.

"I don't expect you to ever stop fucking with me. You came to this school swinging, like we wouldn't swing back. I meant your assignment."

My eyes narrow. This is a trap. He is far too smug right now.

"It's a shame about the computers," he says innocently. "Sounds like they'll be out for the whole week."

Fucking *bastard*.

"Seriously? That's all you've got?" I say with confidence that I'm not feeling, and I stand up with my tray. I walk out of the hall to the sound of his raucous laughter.

It takes two seconds in the library to discover that he has in fact messed with all the IT systems in the school. My completed assignment is stuck on the little USB stick I'd been forced to buy. There's a chance the computers will be fixed before classes resume, but I'm not really one for taking chances. It's such a rich kid thing to assume that he's won because I can't access the computers, and yet the school has a bigger and better stocked library than my home town does, so I pull a dozen books and spend the day rewriting my assignment before he decides to burn the library down instead.

After six hours of intensive work, Harley shows up with a smug look that only falters on his face for a second when he spots me in my fortress of books. I give him my own smug look and finish off my attempts at perfect penmanship, though I can never completely disguise my scratchings successfully.

"I didn't expect to see you here. I thought you were so out of touch from the library that you wouldn't know where to find it."

He grins wolfishly at me, and my breath catches. Goddamn it, why is he so hot!

"I know the library well." He pulls a chair out across from me and straddles it. "I've fucked quite a few girls in the stacks."

A shiver runs up my spine. I should feel disgusted, like I had at every other boy who's said that kind of thing to me, but all I can think is how much I want him to take me into the stacks. How sick is that?

Maybe foster care messed me up more than I thought.

A slow grin spread across his face.

"Don't worry, Mounty, I don't want to fuck you. There's at least three guys in this school who don't want you."

Himself, Ash and Blaise. My stomach drops, and I want to scream at myself. Why the hell do I want them so much, when they are the ones torturing me? Some secret part of my brain whispers to me that the last few days hadn't felt like torture. They've been the most fun I'd had since I'd come to this pretentious school.

"What a relief. I suppose none of you need the money."

His eyes tighten like he's taken a hit. I open my mouth to ask him why, but he cuts me off.

"Not enough to fuck trash, no."

I would have given anything to be able to stop myself from blushing, but I couldn't. I tell myself it's a flush of anger, but its shame burning in my gut.

"You might want to bury your nerves a bit deeper, Mounty. Putting them on display like that just gives us all a target."

He winks at me, *fucking winks*, and then leaves me.

I tell myself I'm not gutted.

But I am.

The students all arrive back Sunday night.

By Monday morning, Harley's head is shaved, and he looks at me like I'm nothing again.

Chapter Seventeen

Miss Umber is late to my choir assessment by twenty minutes, which is coincidentally just long enough for me to start sweating bullets at the thought of singing for her. The choir room looks so much bigger without the other students milling about. I'm glad she agreed to do it here, and not at the chapel. Standing on the stage there, where I'd heard my 911 call, I would've lost my mind. And my lunch.

"Right. You. Yes, of course. Which song did you pick?" Miss Umber sounds flustered as she drops her bag onto the tiny desk. She's far too old to be a Miss, she should have at least switched out to be a Ms. by now. Her startlingly white hair is chopped off into a severe-looking bob with bangs, and her glasses are too large for her face. On a teeny runway model, it would have looked fashionable, but on the aging teacher it looks unflattering. I'd much rather sit here and pick apart her appearance than start my assessment. When Miss Umber turns to give me a look, I snap to it.

"*Pompeii*. By Bastille," I croak. Not a good sign of my vocal abilities for the day.

"Good choice! Do you need music, or are you going to play an instrument?"

I hold up my phone to show her the instrumental song I have prepared. I had learned a handful of songs on guitar, this one included, but I didn't want to tempt fate by putting too much pressure on myself. I run through the warm-ups under her watchful eye, and I realize this is the most amount of attention she's ever given me. This is definitely the first time she's ever heard my voice, because I always hide among the other students in class.

Once I have the phone set up and the music starts, I slip my noise-cancelling headphones in, and then I sing.

My eyes slip shut and I forget Miss Umber is even in the room. For the first time I can focus on the feeling of singing, the rush of my body working hard at something that isn't entirely physical, and I lose myself in it. I sway and swing my arms for emphasis, the way I've watched Blaise do a thousand times before. I can hear myself, but the headphones tone it down just enough that I can immerse myself fully into the act of singing rather than the sound.

It's incredible.

I feel like a piece of me that I lost years ago has come back. It's a relief to think that the damage done to me at the hands of the Jackal and the Game could be healed. I can someday be a whole person again. Tears prickle at the back of my eyes, and I know the second I open them, they will fall. If I can stay at this school and survive everything being torn down around me, I can pull myself up and out of the world I was born into. I can make something of myself through sheer will and perseverance alone.

When the last word slips out from my lips, my chest is heaving and my heart pounds wildly in my chest. I give myself a second before I open my eyes, just a moment to collect myself so I don't fall to my knees and sob like a child. When I pull the earbuds out, I hear clapping and I grin at Miss Umber. She's looking at me the exact same way she looks at Blaise when he sings, like I've exceeded all her expectations and dreams as a teacher.

"Miss Anderson! I've never—you are a rare talent!" She grips my hand tightly in hers and tugs me into a hug. I try not to freeze or flail awkwardly, but I'm not hugged often enough to be comfortable. I can't actually remember the last time I was hugged. As she lets me go, I turn and see Avery standing in the doorway, her jaw damn near hitting the ground.

She's heard me sing.

I feel exposed. Worse than even my 911 call, I feel like she can see inside me. I'd given up singing so long ago that not even Matteo has heard me. Only my dead mom, and she took the memories of my singing to the grave with her.

I break away from her slack-jawed stare and turn back to our teacher, a flush staining my cheeks. I don't know what to do with myself, and I nod along dumbly as Miss Umber gushes to me.

"I can't believe I've missed your voice so far this year! Your range rivals Mr. Morrison's. Has he heard you sing?"

Oh, God. There is no way I want him to ever hear me.

"I don't think so. It's not… I'm not interested in performing. I'd rather stick to the group sessions."

Once she's finished marking my rubric, I take the page and flee the room.

Avery hasn't moved from the doorway, and I have to brush past her to leave. She doesn't move to let me pass, and when I look down at her fist, I see the pages I'd slipped under her door crumpled in her hands.

Hannaford prides itself on 'encouraging' its students to excel by posting all grades publicly. It's never bothered me because I've always had top spot, or occasionally second spot if Harley beats me. I would feel bad for the other students here who land closer to the bottom if I didn't already know they were going to be millionaires the moment they turn eighteen and get their trust funds.

The first time I decide I hate this system is when the choir marks are posted. That's when I learn Blaise has never come second in that class in his life.

I've beaten him by a teeny-tiny margin.

I take my usual seat with Lauren, Jessie, and Dahlia, and I try to ignore the eyes that are on me. Lauren leans toward me and then stops dead as Avery and Blaise walk in. I had expected Avery to have told Blaise about my singing, but one look at him tells me she didn't.

"What. The. Fuck."

He whips around to look at me, and I glue my eyes to Miss Umber so I can keep blanking him. The students around us start to murmur and gasp, but I don't let my gaze waver. Miss Umber claims first place in my list of favorite teachers by starting the lesson before Blaise can confront me.

"Mr. Morrison, Miss Beaumont, if you could both take your seats so we can begin! Please start our usual warm-ups, and then we can start discussing what each student can be working on to improve before our next assignments."

There is no way I want to discuss my singing with the whole class, but short of faking an illness, there is nothing I can do to get out of it. And then Miss Umber tumbles back down to the bottom of the list by ruining my life.

"Miss Anderson, can you please swap groups? I'd like you and Mr. Morrison together, where I can monitor your progress accordingly."

Every eye in the room is on me.

I flush scarlet and pray that a stroke takes me out. There is no justice in the world, because my heart continues to beat, and I'm forced to collect my bag and move across the room. Miss Umber holds out a seat for me, and then I'm sitting right next to the devil herself. Blaise is still trying to catch my eye, but I will not play his game.

Once the warm-ups are finished, my hands are trembling, and my stomach is a roiling pit. I can't half-ass it now. I'm stuck under Miss Umber's eye and Avery is watching my every move. I sit on my hands so she can't see how badly I'm shaking. The moment Miss Umber starts to write out notes during her explanation of the correct breathing methods we should be using, depending on application, Blaise leans over Avery so far, he's practically in her lap.

"Since when can you fucking sing?"

I take out my notebook and ignore him. I never take notes in choir, but it's a good excuse to ignore him. He's not an easy guy to get away from. "Mounty, how did you get a higher mark than me? Are you fucking the teacher?"

I snort and keep writing. I don't spare him a glance as I reply. "If anyone is fucking Miss Umber, it's you. Why would I take choir if I can't sing? I told you I liked Vanth for your voice. Did you not think I was telling the truth? It was one singer admiring the talent of another, that's it. Get over it."

Avery pushes Blaise back into his own seat and off her lap. I'm a little wary that she seems to be helping me, but I know there'll be an ulterior motive. Blaise is mumbling under his breath and Avery slips her hand into his, and that's when I know I'm in trouble. I'm about to be tormented by them again. Avery Beaumont is always the calm before the storm. While her brother and his friends get angry and loud about it, Avery is silent as she efficiently makes her moves to destroy me.

I shake my head at her and go back to my notes.

When the class finishes, I leave without looking at Blaise again. Classes are done for the day, and when I round the corner to walk back into the main building, I hear the footsteps right behind me.

They're both following me.

It's taco night and I've had to miss the last two taco nights because of Beaumont bullshit, so I head straight to the dining hall for an early dinner. I give them both a warning look when they sit across from me at the long table. Neither of them have bothered to grab anything to eat, so we sit in silence as I start to eat my tacos. They're good, but I can't enjoy them with my hostile audience watching my every move.

I break the silence.

"What are you planning on doing to me just because I got a better mark than your little friend?"

Blaise's eyes narrow at me, and then he hesitantly glances at Avery. She's staring at me, down her nose like Ash does, and it sends my blood boiling. I've grown accustomed to being the poor little foster kid. Even at Mounts Bay I had people looking down at me for my drug addict mom, but no one makes me feel more shit about it than the Beaumonts do.

"Did you take the photos of Rory and Harlow together?" she says, completely monotone, like she's not discussing her cheating boyfriend.

I nod and drink my juice. I'm distracted enough by the conversation that I don't think twice about it. Blaise is staring at her, his eyes slits of rage, and his cheeks have deep red patches. I've assumed this far that they're all so close they don't keep secrets, but now I see I was wrong. He runs a hand over the back of his neck and blows out a frustrated breath. I wonder how long it will take before Ash is publicly beating the life out of Rory. Or will it be Harley this time?

"Why didn't you send them out to everyone? You're convinced I sent out your nudes. Wouldn't that be the best revenge for you?"

It's a trap, but I know no matter what, she'll hate me. Why not tell the truth? "I believed Ash when he said you didn't have anything to do with that. It doesn't matter, though. Even if you did, I wouldn't have sent them out. I don't do that shit. If I want revenge, I go straight to the source and do it properly. I'm not good at this social hierarchy stuff. I'm at this school to make a better life for myself. Whatever you guys do to me, it's nothing compared to what's waiting for me at Mounts Bay."

"That doesn't answer my question."

I blow out an exasperated breath. Why does this girl rile me up so badly? I'm giving her answers, and she still wants more. I should tell her to go fuck herself. I should tell her to choke, to jump off a cliff, to go and hide among the beautiful boys she hangs around and leave me the hell alone. I don't.

"Rory is a fucking scumbag. I'm not one of these brainwashed bimbos who thinks it's funny when other girls are treated like shit by guys. I think he's a dick, and I think you deserve to know *where* he's sticking his dick. Plus, I didn't see a condom in use so, you know. He's probably caught something truly heinous from that bitch, and you should get tested to make sure he hasn't passed it on to you."

As I lift my juice to my lips, I see a flash of regret pass over her face. I've never seen that sort of human emotion out of her before, and it makes me feel another pang of sympathy for her. We were both born into cages. Mine was poverty, drugs, the threat of gangs and violence. Hers is a gilded cage, but the bars work just the same. She's trapped by her blood and her name. I wonder, not for the first time, what her parents are like. Are they as beautiful as their children? Are they loyal and caring like the twins, or did Joey come by his cruelty honestly? I should really take a closer look into them, maybe get Matteo to dig around for me.

"For the record, none of this is because of what you did to Harley. It's not an eye for an eye anymore. If you stay here, Joey will kill you. He likes to break things. You're not shattering the way he likes; you're proving to be too strong. He doesn't let strong things survive." She's warning me. What has she put in place, what will I have to survive this time? I swallow.

"It's okay. I'll survive it. Whatever it is you've done, and then I'll survive your brother, too. I have no choice but to survive."

She nods sharply and bumps Blaise to get him moving. He's not happy. He's watched our entire exchange with that frown on his face, and I do something entirely out of left field.

I smile at him.

Just a tiny, sad lifting of the corners of my lips, but he stares at me with heartbreak in those stunning green eyes of his.

He's in on whatever she's done, and he's torn about it. He had probably convinced himself to help because I was a stalker fan in their eyes, and then I'd gotten that higher mark.

The last thing I remember thinking is that he wears heartbreak so fucking well.

And then my mind knows nothing.

Chapter Eighteen

The blackout is so overwhelming that I have no memory of what happened that night.

I ate dinner with Avery and Blaise, and then I'm waking up in one of the seniors' bathrooms. I only know that for sure because I'd accidentally used it on my first day and had been bitched out by one of Joey's flunkies. The large, ornate mirrors are a dead giveaway. The door is locked from the inside, so I know I've done that myself, and I'm freezing. My whole body is shivering uncontrollably. It may be the temperature, or it could be the aftereffects of whatever it is Avery drugged me with.

I swear under my breath at my own idiocy. It must have been slipped in the juice. I'd forgotten the number-one rule of being around these assholes: never accept a drink from them.

I push myself up to stand on my shaking legs and look in the large mirror. I still have all my clothes on, which is a relief, and my bag is on the floor by the door but there's vomit all down my shirt and splattered on my legs. My hair is a mess and there are deep, black circles under my eyes. I can't see any new bruises or scratches, and I hope that Avery's moral code includes making sure I wasn't assaulted while I was out of it. I look as though I've been out drinking all night, and I'm sure that's the end game here. Underage drinking by paying students is frowned upon and will result in a warning, but I'm held to a different standard here at Hannaford. I'll lose my scholarship if I'm caught and breathalyzed.

I pull my phone out of my bag and thank whatever guiding hand led me to this bathroom while I was out of it. I take a deep breath before hitting call. I know Matteo has the resources to help me. How else had he gotten me out of breaking Harlow's nose? He answers right away, and I don't even bother with pleasantries, I just dive right into an explanation of what has happened. He listens intently.

"It's bad, Matteo. I'm going to get kicked out if you can't help me."

"Maybe you should come home, kid." His cool tones do nothing to soothe my nerves.

"Fuck that. I'm not going to get run out of this place by spoiled rich kids. Please, just… help me."

He sighs at me, like I'm being unreasonable. I know he's getting pissed at me for not just leveling the damn building and being done with it, but if I have to, I can start calling in favors.

"Give me ten minutes."

I hang up and slump down on the wall again. The vomit on my shirt is still wet, it's cold, and the smell is truly horrendous. I can't wait for a hot shower and my bed. Fuck these rich dicks. I wipe down my shirt and my legs as best I can to clear away the vomit. Tacos have now been ruined for me forever. Thanks, Avery. I stare at the wall and I must zone out, because when my phone pings again, it makes me jump.

All sorted. Just walk back to your room. Call me if you need anything else. M.

I exhale and open the door. There are students standing around in the hall, and I can see Avery's little flunkies with their phones out. I step into the hall and I can hear them whispering and giggling among themselves. I keep my head high as I start to head back to the dorms. I get as far as the main staircase before I'm faced with Avery, Ash, and Blaise. Avery looks victorious, but the boys both look a little sick at the sight of me. Clearly, they're not fans of girls covered in vomit, which is mildly reassuring. There's a teacher I don't recognize standing with them, wearing gym clothes.

"Mr. Embley? I found Miss Anderson. She's a little worse for wear, and I think I can smell alcohol." Avery's voice is saccharine, and I could vomit again at the sound of it. Mr. Embley steps out from his office, and I try not to cringe. Did Matteo know I'd be facing this teacher? How did he think I'd be getting out of this? Fuck, I'm doomed. Before I can spiral any further into a panic, Mr. Embley ushers me forward.

"Miss Beaumont, please let Miss Anderson pass. She doesn't look well."

I sigh in relief. I shouldn't ever doubt Matteo. His reach is unparalleled, and he makes Avery look like the child she is. He may be infinitely more dangerous, but at least he's the devil I know. I start back up the stairs as the whispers get louder and more insistent.

"Mr. Embley, aren't you going to breath test her? I saw her drinking last night." Avery's voice changed back to the sharp edge she always reserved for people she thought were lesser than her. It was the first time I'd heard her use it on a teacher.

I level her with a look as I go to pass her. I feel like we've come to some sort of an agreement where she'll dish out punishments, and I'll take them just the same. Ash steps in front of me so I'm forced to stop. I think about stepping into him and getting my vomit on him but stop myself. He's looking at me, at my face and the bruises under my eyes. For a second it looks like he's checking to make sure I'm okay. He seems uneasy about what his sister has done to me.

"Let her pass. She needs some rest. Do you need the nurse, Miss Anderson? No? Then head straight to your room, please. The Jackal sends his regards."

Ash's eyes widen slightly, like he's never heard anyone disobey his sister before, and Blaise crosses his arms. I smirk at them both. The moment would feel a lot more victorious if I wasn't cold and disgusting.

"Looks like you're not the only one with connections, Floss," I whisper so only they can hear me.

Ash finally moves, and I walk back to my room, slowly and with my head held high. As I round the corner to the girls' dorm I see Lauren and Jessie studying in the sitting area. They look up and see me, their jaws drop. Lauren scrambles to get up, but then she glances around the room to check and see who else is watching. I clench my jaw and give her a quick shake of my head. I'm frustrated at how afraid she is, how easily she bows down to the whims of the more popular students.

I make it to my room, and I grab my shower bag. I make it four steps away from my door when Harley steps out of one of the other girls' rooms and directly in my path. Annabelle steps out after him. I had no idea she lived two doors down from me, that the guys had been fucking her two doors down from me, and as irrational as it may seem, it pisses me off to know how close I am to that.

If looks could kill, Annabelle would be buried by now.

Harley glances at me, and then levels her with a glare so dark I'd be worried if I were in her shoes. She ignores him completely. The smirk she gives me only lasts as long as it takes me to flip her the bird as I shove past them both and into the bathroom to shower.

I remember to take everything into the shower stall with me this time.

"Out."

Harley's voice bounces off the bathroom tiles. I've stripped out of my dirty uniform, and I've barely got the shower running. I think for a second he's talking to me, and then I hear the other girls leave and the door to the communal shower close and lock.

"I'd rather not be locked in here with you," I say, my voice still raw as I wrap a towel around my naked body. I don't know if I think he'll burst in here with me or what, but it feels too intimate to be naked with only the stall door between us.

"Just have your shower. We'll talk once you're clean."

I wait a minute, and when he doesn't go on, I drop the towel and get under the spray. The heat from the water pierces my skin and soaks straight through my bones until I'm left tingling. I just stand there and try and get warm for a moment before I start scrubbing my skin to wash away the vomit and grime. The smell at first is vile, but after my second pass over the washcloth, I'm able to just enjoy the shower. Once I'm happy with the state of my body, I brush my teeth, and then again for good measure.

My mind keeps skipping back over to Harley being in here with me. He can't see me, at least I hope he can't, but there's something intimate about me washing myself with him in the room. I begrudgingly admit to myself that I like the feeling. He's probably hating every second of standing here and waiting for me, but my mind is still too foggy. I really couldn't give a damn about what he's thinking.

When I shut off the water and wrap myself back up in the towel, I wait for the steam to dissipate enough to start dressing. It's a Saturday, so there's no classes for me to get to, only extracurriculars, and I'm not going down to the dining hall after last night. I may never eat down there again.

Once I've pulled my pajamas on, I look down at myself and see the bruises that have formed over my arms. There're two perfect handprints, one on each arm, like I've been grabbed roughly. I place one of my own hands over the prints, and it fits near perfectly. A girl has put them on me. No guy at this school has hands as small as mine. It was probably Avery. She would have grabbed me and shoved me into the bathroom so I was safe enough until I came to and she could get me expelled for drinking. That girl is an evil psycho, but I grin at the thought. Maybe it is stupid of me, but I've started admiring her work. She has a good understanding of the school rules, and she's working hard to exploit them and get me out of here.

I open the stall door and step out into the bathroom with my bag slung over my shoulder. Harley is propped up on the sinks, and he's glaring at his phone. He glances up at me and shoves the phone into his back pocket like it's offended him. His eyes roam over me, like Ash's had down at the staircase, like he's looking for injuries, and it makes me fucking livid.

"Is there something specific you need, because *I* really need a nap," I croak out, my throat still sore. I need water and something to eat. I need ten hours of sleep.

"What happened to you? What the fuck did Joey do this time?"

I laugh at him. Was he the only one who wasn't in on it? Why had Avery left him out? "I'm fine. I'm still standing. Go back to Annabelle and enjoy your weekend."

I make to move around him, and Harley's hands shoot out to grab me. They land right on the bruises, and I grunt at the sharp sting of pain. His eyes widen and he loosens his grip on me as he pulls me into his chest. It's not a hug, not even close, but now I'm pressed up against him and I can feel every inch of his rock-hard torso pressing against me until I want to melt into him. Danger, Will Robinson. Big fucking danger.

"Fuck Annabelle, she's in on this. Did Avery do it?" His eyes dance around my face, and I think he's judging how willing I am to kiss him. A shot of fear shoots through my blood. I can't kiss him. For one, I have no idea how to even kiss someone. My experience so far is just the forced kiss from Joey, and I mostly just laid there for that. For another, if he kisses me now and then leaves this room and goes back to hating me, I will break. I want him too much. So instead of facing my fears head-on, I focus on the tattoo on his jaw like a coward. It's moving as he clenches his jaw, and I think of the little heart pendant I have back in my room that belongs to him.

You before my blood. If I tell him what Avery had done, would he put me before his blood? Did I want him to? Now that I had started to question Avery's motives, I wasn't sure I wanted to drive a wedge between them.

The longer I stay silent, the more agitated Harley becomes, until his chest is heaving, and his hands begin to shake where he holds me.

"Fuck, can you just stay alive? Can you just leave and keep breathing? Is that too much to ask?" he ground out.

"Afraid your cousin is going to get life for my murder? I'm sure he can buy his way out of it. I'd rather risk death than leave here. Do you hear me? I'd rather die here than go back to Mounts Bay and become what's waiting for me there."

He stares down at me, his eyes burning into my skull, and then he shoves me away from his body with a vicious curse under his breath. When he rubs the back of his head, he glances over at me with a calculating look. I don't like it; I don't like feeling that he's assessing me and found me wanting.

"Don't worry about today. I'll live to die another day, and it won't be at your cousins' hands. Go back to your friends."

He doesn't fight me as I swing the door open. We find Annabelle waiting on the other side, close, like she's been eavesdropping on us both. I ignore her, walking straight out and toward my room as she begins to yell at Harley. I intend to ignore their lover's spat altogether, but then I hear the slap of her palm across his cheek and I glance over my shoulder at them both. She's crying, and he's looking at her with a bored expression that doesn't gel with the tightness in his shoulders. She takes another swing at him, and he catches her wrist.

"It's pretty fucking simple. I don't take orders from my cousins. You've just proved that you do, so you can kiss my ass goodbye."

He drops her wrist and turns to leave. Annabelle grabs his arm and screams at him again.

"Over the fucking Mounty? Maybe Ash is right, maybe you are soft over her."

Harley whips around and, using his chest alone, he backs her up against the wall so quickly that the other girls watching scatter. Again, no one steps up to help her. No one cares if he does turn out to be violent. My eyes collide with his for a second before he leans down to her. I think he's going to kiss her, and if he does, I'm going to vomit all over again.

"If you think I'm the soft one, then you're dumber than I thought."

And then he leaves her. Annabelle is panting, tears are streaming down her face, and the crowd is lapping up her humiliation. She's always enjoyed the attention she's had for being shared by them, but I don't think she'll enjoy being dumped so publicly by him.

Chapter Nineteen

I wake on Monday to the news that Avery has dumped Rory.

There isn't a single freshman that will look at or speak to him, or Harlow for that matter. Neither seems to care all that much, but Rory is now walking the halls of Hannaford like he's got a target on his back. From the looks he's getting from Ash and Harley, it's obvious they're the ones that have put it there.

I watch the entire spectacle of Rory trying to find a seat at lunch with a grin on my face. I must look like a lunatic, but there's something incredibly satisfying about seeing his football team turn their backs on him. After a cold glare over at Avery, he ends up sitting with Harlow and Joey's flunkies. Ash glances over and sees my glee, and we share a moment. He knows I gave Avery the photos and, angry at Rory as he is, he's fucking ecstatic about the way this is all panning out. *Join the club, Beaumont.* It feels weird to be on the same side for once.

My joy quickly evaporates when the dining hall doors open and Joey walks through, his suspension finally lifted.

He's looking much healthier than the last time I saw him. There's meat on his bones, and the dark circles that were ever-present have faded. I wonder if he's been in rehab. He's been gone long enough to have finished a twelve-step process, but I snort at the very thought of him sitting around a facility and making nice with people there. Still, it would explain his appearance. Maybe the suspension was really the school covering for him at his parents' request. I'm sure Mr. Trevelen is on their payroll; he's certainly on Avery's.

He doesn't bother to grab a tray. After giving his siblings a sarcastic little wave, he joins his flunkies and gives Rory a once-over.

"Weren't you fucking my sister? Have you lot let a spy into my house?" His arrogant tone cuts through the rest of the chatter at the table.

"He got caught sticking his dick in someone else's hole, so now he's sitting with us. You always said anyone who fucks with the twins is welcome here," is Harlow's dripping reply. She doesn't mention that she was the hole. She's still open for Joey's business, first and foremost.

Joey tips his head back and laughs too loud for the echoes in the room. Ash gets up to leave, and he tugs Avery along beside him. He's practically vibrating with rage but, aside from her ashen face, Avery looks unaffected by their behavior. Blaise leans back in his chair and stares Joey down. I wonder whether new money would win over the old if those two had it out.

I'd bet on Blaise in the physical fight any day of the week. His shoulders were easily broader and more defined than Joey, and I knew from concert photos he was ripped. I'd also heard the rumors of the fights he'd won here over the years. The boys' dorm is basically a fight club half the time, fighting over girls and money. None of those three ever lost.

The problem was the old adage that the Jackal had told me over and over again: new money can't become old money without getting dirty first. Amongst the Twelve, it was crucial to our domination and survival. If you can find a family close to turning and get in with them, become indispensable, then you can amass power as quickly as money. Matteo had done it dozens of times, and now he was the most powerful man in the state.

The Beaumonts were old and dirty. The Morrisons were unparalleled in their wealth, but squeaky clean. If Blaise took on Joey for what he's doing to his friends, then his hands wouldn't stay clean for long.

From the look on his face, I'd guess he didn't want them to.

"And how fares my little Mounty love?" Joey calls out to me, breaking my train of thought. I've been staring at Blaise for too long. Instead of being embarrassed about it, I just flip Joey the bird.

Gasps ring out around me. People begin to get up and move out of the way, desperate not to be noticed by Joey. I take a bite out of my apple and chew slowly, sending a glare down the table at the teachers hearing all of this and ignoring it completely. What a bunch of pussies.

When the bell tolls its warning, I get up and walk out of the dining hall calmly. As I push out of the dining hall, I feel the heat of Joey's gaze on my back, so I turn to look at him.

The little smile on his face is manic, feral, and edged with insanity.

He's not sober.

The time away has given him the chance to get a grip on himself and hide the addiction better, but the dancing flames in his eyes tell me all I need to know about what's running through his veins right now. He winks at me, and I let the door swing shut behind me.

Joey's return to Hannaford means I have trouble sleeping again.

It doesn't matter that I have the best lock system money can buy now, thanks to Matteo. Every time I shut my eyes, I see that raging psycho's face as he pinned me to his bed, and that fucking wink in the dining hall. I've slipped my knife into the pocket in the hoodie I'm wearing like a safety blanket but sleep still evades me.

Usually, I fight my insomnia by throwing myself headfirst into my studies, but I've just about finished all my assignments for the entire school year. I could go over my notes for my upcoming tests and the end-of-year exams, but I know that I already know everything, that I've already crammed it all into my head and it's stuck. I could also start on the reading required for next year, but nothing is holding my interest at the moment.

I feel restless. Like my skin is crawling and my mind is climbing the walls of my skull and trying to get out. I can't stop moving or jiggling my legs. My mind is currently torturing me with images of Matteo doing to me what Joey tried to do. I know someday his patience will wear thin, and he'll want to take what he thinks he's owed. It's why I have to do well here at Hannaford, so that someday I can disappear somewhere even the Jackal cannot reach.

I'm thinking the Caribbean.

I have no idea what job I'll do there but fuck it if I'm not resourceful. Everywhere needs doctors, so my original career path works. I'll just have to figure out how to go to med school there. I can figure this out if I put my mind to it.

I'm two hours into a deep internet research spiral when a door slams in the hallway.

I glance over and see it's three in the morning, so not the usual time for loud noises in the girls' dorm. It's possible someone has gotten up to pee or is even sneaking a guy into their room, but my mind is currently a vortex of spiraling anxiety and what-ifs. I carefully roll out of bed; thankful the creaking mattress has been replaced and I can be silent as I sneak my door open.

My stomach bottoms out.

Joey is sitting against Avery's door, his phone in his hand and his face lit up in the dark as he texts someone. He's wearing dark slacks and a polo shirt, loafers on his feet, like he's just left some elitist gentleman's club. He doesn't notice me watching him, and I think about calling the student helpline to report him being up here to get him out. I reach into my pocket, and grip my knife. If he spots me and rushes toward me, I'll only need one good swing to take him out. I will use his momentum as he rushes to let the knife sink deep into his throat. It's a smaller target than his belly, but more effective at getting him taken out fast. I'd seen guys stabbed in the gut go on to run through the streets for hours during the Game. It was a good lesson on picking out the weakest spot and aiming true.

I don't know how long I sit there and watch him. My ass goes numb and my fingers ache from where I'm gripping the knife handle so tight. I can't look away from him, even for a second; my eyes refuse to blink. I jump when the door opens, and Joey pushes himself off the ground to face Avery.

I've never seen the two of them interact. It's weird to think we've been at the same school for months, eating meals together and passing each other in the halls, and yet I've never seen them so much as look at each other.

"Dad's not happy you called the cops on me, Floss," he says in a sing-song voice. Avery's eyes are cool, even as her shoulders tremble.

"Don't call me that. Is that all you have to say? Because we both know it wasn't me that called them."

The clock was ticking. Joey was going to make his next move on me soon. "Nevertheless. Just telling you what dear old Dad thinks. He asked me to pass this on to you."

Joey's hand cracks across her cheek so hard, she bounces back against her door. Her head makes a sickening thud, and I open my door up wide, the light from my room cutting through the darkness. Joey doesn't look up at me, but Avery's eyes grow wide.

"Goodnight," he says in that same tone, and he walks off.

I take a step toward Avery, and she pegs me with a look of such loathing I stop dead in my tracks. She tucks back into her room and shuts her door quietly, and I'm left with my own thoughts again.

My head is pounding with an intense headache from lack of sleep the next day. Aside from preparing myself for Joey's next tantrum at me, I've put his little visit with Avery out of my head completely. She didn't want my help when it happened right there in front of me, so I assumed she still wanted me to stay the fuck away from her—so it was a surprise to arrive at history and find her leaning against my desk.

Harley has a habit of getting to all his classes mere seconds before they begin, so he wasn't the reason for her visit. I give her a cool look as I take my seat and gather my supplies.

"Something has been bothering me, Mounty, and I want some answers. I own the teachers at this school. I have since middle school, so how is it a lowly little scholarship student could override my instructions, hm? I've had a chat with Mr. Embley, and he nearly went into heart failure at my questions. It seems you're now scarier than I am."

She's deflecting. She's running interference so I don't question her on her brother or her fucked-up family dynamics. I play along with her little game in the hopes that she'll leave me alone so I can focus on Joey instead. "Did you know that money isn't the only thing that can influence people? Some people have other buttons, and all you need to know is where they are."

She smiles slowly at me and Harley walks into the classroom. He frowns when he sees Avery speaking to me and hurries over to us both. "I'm well acquainted with manipulation. What I'm asking is how you did it."

I drop my gaze down to the assignment I'm due to hand in today and I give it a once-over, even though I know it's perfect. Harley drops his bag onto the floor at my feet and stands over me with his hands on his hips, frowning. I look up and find Avery still staring at me with an expectant look fixed on her features.

"That is absolutely none of your business, but a word of warning: you should think twice about who you target at this school."

Avery glances between Harley and me, and then smirks and takes her own seat. The teacher arrives and starts calling for quiet, and Harley drops down into his chair.

"The fuck was that about?" he whispers at me, leaning in so I'm drowning in his delicious smell. Would it kill the guy to be average for once and not smell like living ambrosia? Ugh.

"Just discussing tactics, nothing to worry yourself with. Your cousin is fine," I whisper back as I breathe him in. I hope it's not too obvious that I'm turning to putty over him again.

He shakes his head at me and takes his seat, a small frown creasing his brow.

He doesn't ask me again.

I think that will be the end of the confrontation with Avery, but once again, I've underestimated her. It's another hard lesson to learn.

I walk into the sitting room in the girls' dorms after dinner and stop dead when I see Avery holding my bag. Gritting my teeth, I curse under my breath at her. I should have known this was coming. I had seen too much and gotten too close to the Beaumont family once again. No good deed at this school goes unpunished.

She holds the lighter up, and I cringe.

It's replaceable. I did the sums once, I can do them again, but they're due tomorrow and I'd slaved away at the workbook for weeks. It's the culmination of months of learning, and it's worth seventy percent of my overall class mark. I'll have to pull an all-nighter to have a chance of getting them done in time.

"I'm quickly learning that personal humiliation isn't the way to get you out of here. I'm tempted to look into what happened to you at your Mounty school to make you so resilient, but who has the time for that, hm? You need a 3.75 GPA or higher to stay here, right? How low do you think flunking math will drop it?"

I shut my eyes and take a deep breath. When I open them again, she can see the resolution I've come to.

"Burn it, then."

The flames eat the paper ravenously. Avery drops in into the bin, and soon the whole thing is engulfed in flames. The smile she gives me as she walks away is infuriating, but I give her my best serene face in return. There are things I know better than most about myself and the ways of the world. A night of no sleep won't kill me. A week without food won't kill me. Finding my mother's dead body rotting on my kitchen floor won't kill me. A bullet to the shoulder won't kill me. The bullying at Hannaford Prep *won't kill me.*

Chapter Twenty

Lunch is the only meal of the day that is at a set time for me. Since my drugging episode, I had started skipping breakfast and eating dinner at 10 p.m., right before the dining hall closes, and I am usually only ever joined by teachers. Still a risk, as I know Avery has most of the school staff under her impressive thumb, but there were only so many protein bars I could eat and meals I could skip. The small amount of weight I had put on is quickly disappearing off my body, and I miss my boobs already. I also miss the French toast with syrup and strawberries that are only served at breakfast. Ugh.

For lunch each day I select a sealed drink, usually a bottle of water, and a couple of apples and bananas. It's barely enough to stop the intense hunger pangs in my empty stomach, and I still have to listen to the rumbling for most of the afternoon. To every other student, it looks like I've gone on a strict diet, which is common among the girls here. I know for a fact there are at least five girls I share the bathroom with that are vomiting after their meals in an effort to be supermodel thin. One of them even confronted me and asked my secret to being so small. When I answered poverty with a blank face, she snarled at me like a rabid dog. Calorie deprivation can turn even the nicest girls into bitches.

My phone pings as I sit, and I'm careful to keep my eyes on my food while I fish around in my bag to grab it and see what Matteo needs from me.

You never call to chat anymore.

I stare at the screen for a second while the other students around me eat and talk and laugh like normal teenagers. What I wouldn't give to be one of them. To be worried about what my parents think about my grades, or what I'm going to wear to the next party I attend. Instead, here I am trying to decipher obscure text messages from gangster kingpins while planning my next move against billionaire sociopaths.

I need to catch a break.

I wonder what it is about me that appeals to these types of guys. Matteo had handpicked me out of hundreds of foster kids at age nine to train to someday become the Wolf. Joey had taken one look at me when I arrived at Hannaford and decided I would make a good game. If I knew what it was that beckoned to them, I could try and snuff it out, or at least conceal it. Instead, I'm stuck dealing with the ramifications of their desires.

I shove my tray aside and tap out a reply. I can use this opening if I'm smart about it; I want to try and clear my summer break from any Club business. I need some downtime.

I'm fielding a lot at the moment. I'm making some good connections. A lot of future leaders in my classes.

I pick up an apple. I like the wholeness of it. I can see if anyone has tampered with it, so now I'm surviving on fruit. Lauren sits down across from me and gives me a little half-smile. I return it with a sigh.

I've heard some disturbing things about you, Starbright.

Ugh, I hate it when he calls me that. I'm sure he is one of the last people on this Earth that knows my middle name. He enjoys teasing me with it. Nothing makes my blood boil quicker than hearing the name my doped-up mother assigned me. Eclipse Starbright Anderson. The second I turn eighteen, I'm changing my name to Claire, or Kylie, or fucking Frances. Anything normal, anything that people just write down without making a smart-ass comment about.

I'm acing my classes and I'm finally looking like a girl instead of a skinned rat. What's so disturbing about that?

Avery and the guys walk in and line up for food. Harley is back to laughing and joking with them all, my drugged night of vomit clearly forgotten. Avery looks dimmed from her usual smiling overlord shine. I watch them all out of the corner of my eye, and I don't miss the looks Ash sends me. Curious.

Why does Joey Beaumont want you dead?

My stomach drops. So Joey is running his mouth about me so much that now even Matteo has heard it all the way back at Mounts Bay? Rationally I know the Jackal has eyes here as well, and any of them could have passed the information on, but it still makes a shiver run up my spine. I know how badly Matteo wants to own me, mind and body, so this at least I can work to my favor.

He wants to fuck me. He's made a game out of it. I have no intention of fucking any guy here, and when I expressed that to him, he tried to rape me. He was unsuccessful and doesn't take kindly to the word no.

I think Matteo gets a kick out of the idea of me being untouched. I think he fantasizes about being the one and only person to be inside me someday. I know this is the best card to play. Maybe I am learning how to play the political game.

I will pay little Joey a visit. Do not argue with me on this.

I glance over to watch Joey as he presses over his group of flunkies like he's their king, and smile. Occasionally, it's a good thing to keep Matteo's dreams about me alive.

I wouldn't dream of arguing with you, Jackal.

As I grab my tray to head back out of the dining hall, I see Joey frowning down at his phone, and it feels like a victory to me.

"You should talk Avery into taking some self-defense lessons."

Ash stares over the library table at me like I've lost my goddamn mind. Maybe I have, but I've also lost the ability to give a fuck at this place anymore. I decide it's sleep deprivation. I only got twenty minutes of sleep after finishing the re-do on my math workbook, but I'm confident I'll get at least an A-minus on it, so it was worth it.

"And why do you think I should do that?" He speaks slowly, dragging out the words like I'm very simple.

"Maybe next time your sociopath brother takes a swing at her, she can plant him on his ass like he deserves."

His eyebrows show the exact toll my words have taken on him. He's fucking devastated, and my heart drops to see it. I guess she didn't tell him about Joey's homecoming. I feel weirdly guilty, like somehow, it's my fault his twin was hurt.

"When did you see that?" His voice is as raw as his face. I look down at the page in front of him, and I realize he's shaking. Fucking Joey, he ruins everything he touches. Even his siblings have been broken by him.

"Last week. I tried to speak to her about it and she freaked. She should at least learn enough to make him think twice about touching her."

Ash groans and scrubs a hand over his face, all long tan fingers I try not to stare at. It's jarring to see real emotions on his face this close. He's usually so reserved, so cut off, that I never see his face without a sneer in my direction. It's oddly comforting.

"I've tried. She said if she fights back, it'll only make him more violent toward her. We always make sure she has one of us with her." He groans again and cradles his head in his hands.

There're so many questions I want to ask him, but I don't want to break the spell that has him opening up to me. Does his father hit them both, or was Joey lying? What does their mother think about this? How much time are they forced to spend with Joey outside the school year? How does Avery have access to enough money to pay Harley's tuition, which I know for a fact is over eighty thousand dollars a year?

Why does Ash lie about needing help with his classwork?

I'm still deciding if I'm brave enough to try and ask him any of these questions when Blaise arrives. We've been studying for twenty minutes already, so I give him a look. He's still doing his best to not look at me at all, so he doesn't see it. My temper flares.

"How kind of you to grace us with your presence." Sarcasm drips from my words. Blaise ignores me, but Ash chuckles from where his head is still pressed into his palms.

"He does what he can for his people."

"Yes, yes, you're both so fucking amusing. I had to re-sit a test for history, because apparently Mr. Smithton gets hard over ruining my life. He called my dad, so now I'm truly fucked. Why can't I just drop out and make music and fuck groupies and get fucking blind drunk every night? Why do I have to learn inane bullshit about dead people? Why?"

"Ah, good. The dramatics have started, Mounty, settle in. We're going to be here for hours while he gets this out of his system."

Blaise slumps into his chair theatrically, and I scoff at him. He looks like a poor little rock star, forced to be a scholar. He groans and tugs at his hair roughly, so it stands up everywhere. He has sex hair at the best of times, but now it's bordering on obscene. I can't tear my eyes away from it no matter how hard I try.

"I hate this place and I hate my dad's business and I hate the expectations he has for me."

Ash drops his hands and looks over at his friend with fake sympathy, nodding at him.

"Yes, so unfair to be the sole heir to a billion-dollar empire that your father sold his soul to be able to create. So sad. Do you want a drink, Mounty? May as well drown this tirade out while we have the chance."

Ash starts snapping his fingers, like a bartender is going to appear out of nowhere. I smother a laugh in my blazer sleeve. My chest aches at being so close to their friendship and playful banter, my favorite blend of sarcasm and fondness. The world is a cruel place to put this so close to me, but so wildly out of my reach.

"You know what, fuck capitalism. If we could be happy with what we have instead of constantly striving to be at the top, I wouldn't be in this mess. Let's be fucking hippies instead. Let's make music and throw away all of our worldly possessions and ask the moon what it thinks about our problems."

That strikes a familiar chord in my chest. My mom used to get high and talk like that all the time. It's how I got my name, for God's sake.

"No, no, I won't be growing a beard and smoking joints out of a van like a fucking pedophile. Get it all out, though. Bottling it up will only make it worse."

I tune out their banter, as amusing as it is, to look over Blaise's classwork. He's started bringing in bigger and bigger piles, and it's clear to me just how far behind he really is. How he managed to convince his parents and the faculty that he could afford to miss the first few weeks of the year is beyond me. I'm good, but I'm not sure even I can work this miracle, given how little time we actually interact.

I'm about to interrupt the pity party to suggest we start in on the mountain of work when I feel someone walk up behind me. I tense, expecting it to be Joey, and a dark, hidden part of my mind expects him to have a knife. Ash and Blaise fall silent as the chair next to mine pulls back and a student I don't recognize sits down. He's blond and broad, but with none of the grace or stunning features that Harley has.

"Can I help you?" I say, aiming for a light tone.

"Sure you can. I wanted to discuss the sweep Joey started."

For fuck's sake. I cut him an icy glare, but he just smiles in return. His teeth are too straight, a fake white row that makes him look like an android. Everything about him makes my teeth clench so hard my jaw aches.

"Look, it's admirable that you're taking a stand and refusing to fuck anyone for the sake of the money. It shows you have more integrity than the average Mounty. At some point, someone is going to fuck you and get the money. Why not give Joey a taste of his own medicine and let me fuck you for it? I'll even give you a percentage of the sweep for your troubles."

A percentage. For my troubles. I silently weigh up my options. There're three librarians, and two are within eyesight of our table. If I slam his face into the desk and break his pompous nose, there'll be too many witnesses. If I ignore him, he might go away, or maybe he'll start stalking me instead. I could call the Jackal and have him murdered in his sleep.

The guy, who still hasn't even told me his name, slings an arm over my shoulders and his hand ends up hovering over my chest. I have what can only be described as a full rage blackout.

One minute he's laughing and touching me, and the next he's howling and clutching his now-broken hand to his chest like it's a baby bird. I'm much faster than he is, and while he's flailing, I slap a hand over his mouth, so the librarians don't assume he's being murdered and come over here to stop me. He could push me off, but he's too busy losing his shit over his mangled hand.

"What's your name, asshole?" I whisper. He's swearing and sweating too much to answer, so Blaise surprises me by doing it for him.

"Mounty, this is Samuel Hanson. He's a sophomore and he's at risk of being kicked out by his parents because he's been caught gambling away his trust fund. Is that why you need the money, Sammy-boy? Run out of funds to feed your addiction?"

Samuel manages to stop screaming, so I let my hand drop away from his face. He's panting and his eyes keep rolling back into his head. It's pathetic.

"Your pain tolerance is worse than a child's," I hiss at him, and Ash snickers, but I don't spare him a glance. I need to make a point with this guy. It's been too long since I hurt someone for propositioning me, and they've forgotten what I can do.

"I won't fuck you. I won't fuck anyone at this school, not for a hundred grand."

"The pot is sitting around the seven hundred grand mark now, Mounty," Ash drawls. I don't let the shock show on my face. These fucking wealthy bastards.

"Well, I won't fuck you for that either, even if my *percentage* was a hundred percent. If you so much as look in my direction again, I will *bury* you. Do those rumors make their way up here about us Mounties too? About how easily I can and will kill you for insulting me?"

He's managed to pull himself together enough to kick back into obnoxious rich-kid mode. "I will report you, and you'll be out for this, you little cunt."

I. Hate. That. Word.

My mom's boyfriends all used to call her that, or me, or they'd tell me all about my mom's gaping cunt. I was six the first time I realized what they were talking about. It still sends me to a crazy place in my head to hear it uttered.

"No, you'll walk your ass out of here, and you'll do exactly what she said," Blaise says, and I've never heard him so angry. "See, you're encroaching on my study time, and she's the best tutor I've ever had, so if I have to beat you senseless myself to keep her here and teaching me, then I will, Hanson. Are you ready to bleed by me again?" Blaise cracks his knuckles to drive home the point, and Samuel stands. The chair falls as he lurches out of the room and out of my life.

"Is your crisis over now? Can we get started on the important stuff?" I say as I shake out my hand. The force required to break bones is less substantial when you know exactly where to strike, but that didn't mean I wasn't paying for it.

Blaise finally glances at me and nods like he didn't just defend me.

None of us talk about how exactly it is that I know how to break someone's hand using only two fingers.

Chapter Twenty-One

Hannaford is a writhing snake pit of gossips.

I didn't even make it to my room after my tutoring session with Ash and Blaise without being asked about Samuel. It was late by the time we finished up, and I'd been forced to skip dinner.

My stomach wakes me at 5 a.m. and I know for certain I can't skip breakfast. Harley will be pissed if he has to listen to the grumbling of my stomach all through our classes. The dining hall opens at 5:30 a.m. and I reason with myself that I'll be safe to eat at that time. What other students would be willing to eat that early?

I'm pissed to find that there are a heap of students waiting at the door for the dining hall to open. It turns out the swim team, track, and the row team all meet at 6 a.m. to torture themselves. It's all elbows and swearing to get to the front of the line, so I hang back and survey the crowd. Harley is on the swim team but he's not here. The room he shares with Ash and Blaise probably has a fully-stocked kitchen and a personal chef, for all I know. Yes, I'll admit I'm hungry and bitter. I need to come up with a better system to keep me from turning into a hangry bitch.

My mouth waters when I see the French toast, and I decide to risk a second roofie episode. I pile on the cream and strawberries, drizzle so much syrup it drips everywhere, and I'm a sticky mess.

I'm a happy, sticky mess.

When I've literally licked my plate clean, I dump my tray onto the pile by the door and start back toward the girls' dorm for a quick shower before classes. My belly is full, and I even catch myself humming cheerfully under my breath. The perfect morning.

Rough hands grab me and pull me into an empty classroom.

I shove at them, but I have a six-foot guy on each side of me, neither of whom I have spoken to before. They're upperclassmen for sure. I grunt and pull at their arms, only to have their hands tighten around my biceps. Avery isn't the only person who is swift in their retribution. I'm sure this is Samuel's doing. I'm convincing myself to stay still and meek when a third student steps into the classroom.

Spencer Hillsong.

He's the guy who approached me after the naked photos of me were sent out. I'd forgotten he even exists, but he hasn't forgotten me.

Now that I know how much money is on the line for having sex with me, I'm sure that's what he's here for. Even rich kids must be tempted by seven hundred thousand, especially those who don't have unlimited access to their parents' wallets.

"My sweet mother would be so disappointed," he says as he steps toward me. He's smiling cruelly, but he's got nothing on Joey or Matteo. Still, he could rape me for the cash all the same.

"That you'd forced yourself on a girl? I should hope so."

He laughs right in my face. I swear to myself that I'll start carrying my knife with me from now on. It was stupid of me to believe I wasn't in danger of this now that I'd dealt with Joey. I'd only really dealt with him, not all of his blind followers.

"I would never put my dick in trash. Lord knows what commoner diseases you have. No, I'm going to show you what happens to girls who don't do what they're told."

The crack of his hand across my face leaves me dazed. He's certainly not holding back on account of my gender. I weigh up my options while he looks at me with glee. I could attempt to fight them off. Three to one, not great odds but doable. They're big guys, I can feel the muscular frames on the two holding me, so my chances of success aren't great. I tug my arms a little to gauge the reaction and their grips tighten. So they're both committed to playing their part, neither of them seeming to care about me suggesting they were here to sexually assault me.

Spencer seems to be the only one interested in actually hitting me. When he punches me in the stomach, I feel the guy on my left flinch even as my breakfast roils in my belly. So, if I stand there and take the beating, I'll only be hit by one guy. If I pretended to be more hurt than I actually am, I might be able to minimize the damage.

I moan when he punches me again. It feels strange after having spent so much time learning how to stay silent, but I lay it on thick. When he lands another blow to my head, this time behind my ear, where my hair will cover the bruise because he's a sneaky fuck, I see stars and swear roughly. I could vomit, and I swear under my breath at the thought of wasting that beautiful, fluffy toast.

"You should think twice about messing with Joey. He owns this school. If he says jump, then the whole damn building moves."

How utterly pathetic. Spencer is just openly admitting he's Joey bitch. And for what? Doesn't he realize Joey doesn't have the capacity to make friends? There's no loyalty in him at all. Spencer is just another child playing a man's game.

I don't have to fake the grunt that's pushed out of me as I feel my ribs snap. It hurts like a bitch, and I'm forced to pant instead of taking deep breaths.

"Fuck, c'mon, Spence. The bitch is done. If you keep going, we'll get caught for sure."

Spencer is panting and sweating from using my body as a punching bag. I don't know how many hits I've taken, only that I've got a concussion and broken ribs.

"Don't be a pussy, Kyle, she can take a bit more. I'm sure she's been slapped around before and fucking loves it."

He pulls his arm back for one last hit, but the guy on my left drops me. I lurch to the ground, and the guy on my right gives up on holding me too. I manage to put my arms out to catch myself, but the intense roaring pain has them collapse, and I face plant onto the carpet.

Every breath feels like I'm drawing glass into my chest cavity and inviting it to shred my lungs to nothing. I think I have at least two broken ribs, and I have to remember to baby them a bit, so I don't puncture a damn lung. I know the score, I've done this all before, but I dream about the day that I never have to worry about being beaten again.

It takes everything in me to get dressed for the day and then make it back down the stairs to start the school day. When I arrive at my history class, Harley is already present, and he watches me ease myself into my chair with knowing eyes. The rest of the class filters in behind me, and the teacher shuts the door firmly as she starts the class. I grunt as I lean down to empty my bag, but he doesn't offer me any help. Only after I've completely set myself up does he speak to me.

"Who did that to you?" His voice is so soft, I know Avery hasn't heard him. Whether he's afraid to attract her attention or he thinks the answer is she's responsible, I can't even begin to guess.

"A junior. Joey's getting desperate," I murmur back. I don't want his help, but I can't afford to have him say anything to Avery and get me in the shit with her again. I physically could not fight her off right now.

"Which junior?" He's still whispering, but the words are distorted, like he's barely squeezing them out. I swivel in my chair to look at him, though it pains me. He's not looking at me, he's taking notes in his beautiful, even handwriting, and no one would guess that he was taking any notice of me. I shake my head at him and try to ignore the pain and focus on the teacher's words.

The teacher announces a pop quiz in our next lesson, and the class erupts with groans and whining from the other students. Harley uses the distraction to lean in to me, to whisper into my ear. My body is still firmly in defensive mode, so I startle, grunting at the white-hot pain that threatens to take my vision, sucking air into my ravaged lungs too quickly. As I cough and hack into my palm, I can taste the coppery tang on my tongue, and I know the wet spot on my palm is blood. Harley's hand wraps around my wrist carefully but firmly, like he knows I'll try and pull away from his touch. Even with my whole body lit up with intense pain, my skin tingles underneath his touch as he looks down at the evidence of my internal bleeding.

"Tell me who the fuck did that to you, or I'll tell the teacher you're spreading Mounty diseases by leaking blood everywhere."

Typical Harley. He can't even be sympathetic about my beating without acting like an ass. I tilt my head back to meet his eyes. I don't know what to do with what I see on his face.

He's staring at me how he looks at Avery, like I'm something precious, and my mind scrambles to figure out why. I gape at him and try to find my voice.

"Why would you care who did this to me?" I croak.

His eyes quickly shutter and his jaw twitches. From the corner of my eye, I see Avery turn to stare at us both. Great. Now I'm going to be attacked on my way to the toilet at midnight and I'll probably rack up some medical bills I can't afford to sort out.

"Spencer Hillsong. He had a couple of friends, but I didn't recognize them."

Harley gives me a curt nod, and then I nearly fall off my damn chair as he stoops down to pick up my bag for me and starts to pack away my books. Avery is still watching us, and while she's not outright glaring, I wouldn't call it a friendly sort of stare.

"Harley, you shouldn't—"

He cuts her off with a sharp tone. "Shut it, Floss. Messing with her shit is one thing, beating her bloody is fucking disgusting. I'll *end* that dickhead."

I snort at him and take my now-full bag, slinging it gingerly over the shoulder that isn't bruised. He gives me another look and then gently takes my elbow to steer me out of the class. I'm shocked enough to let him, and I can feel eyes following us both down the hall. Avery falls into step with him, but she doesn't glance my way again.

We round the corner to get to our shared chemistry lab when we run right into Ash and Blaise. I cringe and try to pull away from Harley, but his grip only tightens. Blaise looks shocked to see me, but when he recovers, he is back to refusing to look at me. It's like yesterday didn't happen at all. That works for me. I'm doing my best to forget he exists. Ash is more curious about my appearance; his eyes take me in, inch by painstaking inch. It was possibly the worst time to start coughing up blood again. It becomes clear to me that if Harley wasn't holding me up, I would collapse from the pain radiating around my chest, and my vision blurs threateningly again. Why did I even try to make it through today? I'm losing my edge at this school. At Mounts Bay, I always knew my limits. I need to regroup before it gets me killed.

"I told you to stay away from Joey. All of this is his doing. Honestly, you have no one but yourself to blame for this," says Ash as he grabs my other arm. I grit my teeth, but I'm not sure if it's because of his words or if I'm trying to take control of my body once again. The edges of my vision start to black out, and I can't even choke out a retort.

"It wasn't Joey, it was Hillsong, and he's a fucking dead man walking," snaps Harley.

I shut my eyes as we walk. There's no point in fighting them, I barely have the energy to stay conscious. My mind is hazy. Not a great sign; I'm going to end up in the nurse's office.

"Do you really think he's acting without Joey's influence? Ash is right, she should have stayed away from him," says Avery. She doesn't sound happy at all.

It takes me a minute for my mind to catch up with our movements and to realize we're still walking. Our lab is only a few yards away, so it makes no sense. Panic claws up my spine, and I jerk my arms to try and get free. *They're dragging me somewhere secluded to finish the job, Harley hates me, there's no way he would care about some junior beating me!* I plant my feet and try to stop them from moving forward, but Harley and Ash are too strong for me.

"Calm the fuck down, Mounty. We're going to take you back to your room so you can die somewhere more comfortable than the lab," says Ash, and I can hear the laughter in his voice.

"Don't be a dick, Ash. She's probably suspicious we're helping her. Twice in a week, I'd be suspicious too," says Blaise, and I jerk my head around to see that he's trailing behind us. He still won't meet my eyes.

"Why are we helping her, again?" drawls Avery, not even bothering to look up from her phone. Her arm is linked with Ash's, and he's directing her as much as he's helping me.

We arrive at my room, and it takes me three attempts to fumble the key out from around my neck and into the door. When I pause, Ash finally drops my arm and lets Avery tug him away from me. She's probably scared he's developing a soft spot for me, but I could set her straight about that. There's no way the guy who snarls at me over the table in the library would ever feel anything but contempt for me. I have to admit, this rescue is pretty confusing for me. I'm struggling with my own feelings for all three of the guys, and their kind and gentle touches are just making this all the more difficult for me. It is not normal for a girl to be crushing on three guys this hard at the same damn time. I don't want one of them, I want all three, even after everything they've done to me. I need to clear my head. I need some space, and I need it now.

Harley won't move. I attempt a pointed look at him, but he just raises his eyebrows at me in return. When it's clear neither of us are willing to back down, Blaise groans at us both and then pushes between us to grab the key and open the door. When his arm brushes mine, I flinch away from him so hard I hit the doorframe and grunt in pain. My body is going to pay dearly for that move.

"Why the fuck does she flinch like that when you touch her?" Harley snaps, and Blaise backs up quickly like his ass is on fire. I shuffle into the room and drop my bag on the floor.

"How the fuck should I know? I've never touched her!"

I flinch again. I know that if I ever do touch him, and if he touched me back, I'd be ruined for life. It doesn't matter how angry I am at him, how badly he's humiliated me, how much he loathes me. He could destroy me, and I would ask for more. I turn and grab the door, mostly to keep myself upright. I'm so pathetic. Thank God the Jackal can't see me right now.

"I don't want him running off to your little shared fuck and telling her I'm stalking him or acting inappropriately. The last thing I need is that bitch starting a vendetta on me. I'd say thanks for the help up here, but I'm sure you'll find a way to make me pay for it later."

I enjoy the twin looks of shock on their faces as I slam the door on them both.

Chapter Twenty-Two

It takes two days to be able to go back to class.

I still can't breathe without being able to feel exactly which ribs are broken, but my concussion has eased. For those two days, I can't sit up for longer than ten minutes without a migraine splitting open my skull and rummaging around in my brain matter. I'm once again saved by the fact that I'm so far ahead in all my classes.

When I take my seat in math class and I see that I got a solid A for my workbook re-do, I'm so relieved I could slump in my chair. I remember at the last second that the action would hurt me dearly, and I smile instead. It feels strange on my face. I've only winced and grimaced for days.

Only Harley beat me, a defeat I'll take gracefully thanks to him carrying me back to my room. He's smug about it, and I keep my mouth shut about Avery's little pyromaniac episode. Another boon I'm granting. I'm practically a saint.

At the end of our class, he waits for me to pack up. Avery doesn't share our math class, so I don't have to worry about the repercussions of Harley speaking to me. I look at him curiously, and when he gives me a slow smile, I fight the blush that's creeping up my neck.

"Let's take a walk, Mounty," he says with a voice full of honey, rich and thick.

We walk in silence as I let him lead me through the school. I forget sometimes how big this place is when I'm sprinting from class to class. I get jostled a few times by passing students, and I push out my elbow to try and force them around me instead. Being so damn short is a pain in the ass sometimes.

"Kyle and Nicky have both been expelled."

Harley doesn't look down at me as he says this. They must be the guys that held me while Spencer whaled on me. The pace he has set is brutal on my ribs, and I'm panting so hard to keep up with his ridiculously long legs. His sculpted, swimmer's legs. *Dammit, stop thinking about his legs!*

"What did you get them for?" I ask. I'm not sure if he'll give me a straight answer or not. I certainly didn't give him one when I'd led him out to watch Joey get arrested. Harley grins savagely.

"Kyle got done for doping. He was on the track team, and there are students on the fast-track to the Olympics. They don't take kindly to their teammates taking banned supplements. Nicky… well, little Nicky Bianchi has some strange sexual adventures, and he likes to take pictures of himself doing what it is he does. Half of the classrooms in the school are closed for cleaning today."

I wrinkle my nose. Guys are disgusting. If I've touched that guy's DNA matter just because he's a fucking deviant, I'll be pissed.

"So what do you have planned for Hillsong, then? What skeletons hide in his closet?"

If anything, the grin on Harley's face gets even more savage. He looks imposing, vicious in the best possible way. The kind of darkness my heart reaches out for because it recognizes it. I swear to God my panties damn near disintegrate at the look of him right now.

"No explosion for Spencer. I told you, I'm going to end him."

A shiver takes over me. This could get out of hand fast, but that only makes it more exciting. "Give me details. I need to know what I'm signing up for."

I'm running through lists in my head, equations and formulas on how I can help. Minimize the witnesses, something to transport the body, cleanup crew so no evidence is left behind, a deep grave somewhere remote and unrelated to either of us. It's a lot to figure out on the fly but fuck it. I'm all in. I didn't become the Wolf because I'm afraid of getting my hands dirty.

"I'm going to beat him bloody until he needs a tube to breathe. Anything less and he's getting away too lightly. It'll be hard, but I'll stop myself from taking him out. I'm not sure you'll be able to keep your scholarship if you're aiding and abetting a murderer."

"The Beaumonts want me out anyway, what a way to go," I mutter. Harley either ignores me or he doesn't hear me as he steps into the rose-colored light streaming down in the chapel. A senior who is even bigger than Harley shuts the door behind us and slides the bolt into place. My hand slips into my pocket and grips my knife. I feel the urge to put my back against the wall. After everything that's happened to me in this room, I guess it's to be expected.

Spencer Hillsong is already there, bare-chested, frowning over at us both.

"Why the fuck did you bring the Mounty? You know the rules. No girls."

The rules. Harley has challenged him to one of their little fight club matches. Spencer has no clue what he's in for. My heart surges in my chest as I watch them both circle each other.

"Fuck the rules and fuck you, Hillsong. You've already shown everyone what a coward you really are. You need your friends to hold a girl down while you hit her. That's fucking pathetic."

Spencer scans the crowd, but he doesn't find what he's looking for. I'd bet it was Joey. He's hoping the puppet master would leap to his rescue. What a dumb ass. Joey only saves himself.

Harley shrugs out of his blazer, and for a single heart-stopping second, I think he's going to take his shirt off too. Disappointment burns me when he rolls up his sleeves instead. Shouldn't he be worried about getting blood on his crisp white shirt? God, I'm such a pervert.

Harley glances down at me and gestures to one of the pews, right at the front where I'll get the perfect view of what's about to go down. When I'm comfortable, he dumps his bag next to me and then surveys the room. There're about fifteen guys all standing around, and the air is thick with their eager bloodlust. None of them spare me a glance as they watch Harley with greedy eyes.

"Anyone touches her or asks her for sex from here on out will get the same as

Hillsong. You can film it and spread it around, for all I fucking care, but that's how it's going to be. We clear?"

There're nods, grunting, and a few phones make an appearance. Spencer laughs and puts his hands on his hips like he's preening under Harley's judgment. It's gross.

"And what about your cousin? Joey is the whole reason this started, are you going to beat him up? I'm not afraid of you, Arbour. You think getting a face tat makes you so fucking tough? You're just a pussy with a deadbeat dad and a fucked-up mom who's riding on your cousins' coattails."

Harley leans down to drop his blazer on his bag and I see the flames burning in his eyes. Spencer is a dead man.

"I can organize a cleanup crew if you want to kill him," I whisper, a smile playing at the corners of my mouth. Harley smirks at me and straightens.

"We can talk about how you have access to one of those later, Mounty."

He turns and steps into the proverbial ring.

I don't know who calls the ambulance, but I do enjoy watching them wheel Spencer Hillsong away. Harley grabs his shit and leaves the chapel without looking at me, so I guess his charitable mood has up and left him. His hands are a mess and there's blood all over him. Any teacher who comes across him would have to be on Avery's books to not call the cops. It's a good thing they all are.

I manage to convince the kitchen staff I'm an overworked, flailing mess, and they scrape together a tub of roast pork and sides smothered in gravy for me to take to my room to eat. I don't know why I didn't think of trying it before, and I'm thrilled when I sit on my bed and dig in. I mess around on my phone and try to tell myself I'm googling Vanth Falling news to keep tabs on my bully, and because I'm bored.

I didn't burn the shirt.

I did stuff it in the bottom of my bag to try and forget about it, but old habits, and devotion die hard, so I'm back to wearing it, and a tiny pair of sparkly booty shorts, when there's a knock at my door.

I panic.

It's embarrassing as fuck to think about any girl in this place seeing me wearing it after my tantrum at Blaise over it, so I scramble to find something else to throw on over it quickly.

"Mounty, for fuck's sake, I can hear you rummaging around in there. Open the door."

It's Harley. Oh *God*, I cannot open this door wearing the shirt. I will lose any credibility I've managed to gain with Blaise if he tells him. "I'm- ah- naked. Give me a second."

I find one of the new sweaters I bought from the thrift store in Haven—it's clearly a man's sweater, and it's three times the size of me—and I throw it over my head.

When I'm sure he won't be able to see the Vanth shirt, I throw open the door to his deep frown. His eyes trail down my body, and when they reach my bare legs, he starts to look around my room, his scowl deepening.

"Can I help you?" I say, breathless. He curses at me under his breath and brushes past me into my room. Rude.

"Please come in," I say sweetly and shut the door behind him before I can think better of it. He may still have it out for me academically, but I'm not afraid of being around him. I snort at myself. I've just watched him pummel another student to the point the kid had to be intubated before he was scraped off the chapel floor by the EMT's, and yet, that had proved to me that I had nothing to be afraid of. Funny old world.

"Is there a guy in here?" he says as he peers into my closet. My jaw drops.

"What—why would there be a guy in here?"

"You said you were naked. It's five o'clock, you haven't just showered, and you're wearing someone else's clothes. Who did you let win the bet?" He's damn near hissing at me. I look down at myself, sigh, and then rub at my face.

"I lied. I wasn't naked, I'm wearing a shirt and shorts under this. I just—it doesn't matter. This is my sweater. I'm not a wannabe model like the other girls here, and I like being comfortable. No guy. Not interested in seeing any guys here at Hannaford naked, thanks."

Blatant lie. I'd be interested in him. Or either of his friends, really. I try not to think about the time I saw him come all over Annabelle's face in the woods, but then it's all I'm thinking of and my face heats up. Harley squints at me like he's trying to decide if I'm lying. I roll my eyes at him.

"This place is a literal closet. Check under my bed and see for yourself that there's no one here." He actually bends down and does check. My blood heats, and not with desire. "What exactly gives you the right to police who I fuck, anyway?"

He smirks at me and shows me his knuckles. They're a mess; he hasn't cleaned them at all. From the look of him he's just thrown different clothes on, no shower. I should feel grossed out by that, but I lick my lips at the thought of the sweat that's still on him. He still smells fantastic—totally unfair, because I know for a fact that I smell putrid after that much exercise. I duck under my bed, pull out my first-aid kit, and grab out some antiseptic wipes. He drops onto my bed like he owns the place, and I start to clean up his wounds.

"I've just cleared your social calendar for you, I wouldn't want that to be for nothing."

I chuckle as I carefully wipe away the blood that's already dried, and he doesn't flinch. His knuckles are covered in raised white scars, crisscrossing and gouging into his skin. It looks more extreme than what a prep school fight club would warrant. I make yet another mental note to look into him and his past. He clears his throat to get my attention.

"So, which cleanup crew would you have called? Manning's?"

I snort. "Only if I wanted to be blackmailed with it later. Amateurs call Manning."

He smiles at me, a real one, and I have to focus to breathe. He's magnificent this close. I survive sitting next to him all day in our classes by not looking at him, but now I let myself just take him in. I tape some gauze over the parts of his hands that are still bleeding, and he lets me, watching me as much as I'm watching him.

"So, who then? Who would a Mounty call to get rid of a body?"

I can't really answer him. It would give too much away. I'd call the Jackal or the Bear. I wouldn't have to pay them a cent for their services, either. I'd call in a favor or make a deal with them on the spot, and then my problems would just vanish.

"That should hold if you don't shower until tomorrow. Or just get one of your friends to do it again for you. I'm assuming you have a kit of your own?"

He nods and watches me pack everything away. I feel his eyes on my legs as I bend to shove the kit back under my bed, but when I stand and face him, he's got his phone out. When he lifts it to his ear, I frown down at him.

"Nothing is wrong, Floss. Can't I call you to be social?"

I cross my arms and take a step away from him. I guess this is where I pay for making him bleed for me. Nothing ever comes for free, not here at Hannaford and certainly not back home.

"Okay, you're right I do need something. I need you to leave Lips alone. Stop trying to get her kicked out... No, I'm not joking... I'm not telling you to be her friend, I'm saying stop fucking with her on my behalf. I'm over it. I'm done...I don't like her, I owe her, and I hate owing people shit. Just drop it... if Joey wants her dead and she's too stubborn to leave to save her skin, then that's not our problem. You don't owe him a cleanup, Aves."

My stomach hollows out as I listen to him negotiate a ceasefire with Avery for me. He said he owes me; what did I do for him? I think back, but I can't remember anything I've done. Well, the necklace, but I haven't even told him I have it yet. I wince guiltily.

He hangs up and meets my eyes again. I wait for him to explain, to get up and leave, to tell me what I now owe him for this. I wait for him to tell me it's all a joke and I'm still trash to him. I guess he did tell Avery he doesn't like me, but he's not acting like that. When he just stares at me, nervousness bubbles up until I speak, just to break the intensity of his gaze.

"Why do you owe me? I don't remember helping you."

He grumbles and stands up. He looks almost bashful; it's charming as fuck.

"Joey set his eyes on you because of me. He heard me raging at Avery about you, and it caught his interest. Whatever, you should leave Hannaford. You're stupid if you think you can take on Joey and survive."

I scoff at him. "Of course you do. What could a poor Mounty do against a billionaire sociopath?"

He shrugs at me and flexes his fingers. I can't stop thinking about the damn necklace, until finally I sigh and walk over to where I've dropped my bag. I've been carrying it around for weeks, trying to pluck up the courage to give it back to him.

"Don't ask me how I got this, and please don't start shit with me over it, just take it and forget this ever happened," I ramble. He quirks an eyebrow, but he reaches for me. I drop the little gold chain into his outstretched hand, and he freezes. The look on his face breaks my heart. He's so reverent, so gentle as he cradles the little heart pendant in his big, bandaged palm. When he looks up at me, his eyes are red-rimmed and glassy. I feel like scum for carrying it around for so long.

"I'm sorry I didn't give it to you sooner. I don't even have a reason, I just didn't. Like I said, please just forget I ever had it."

"Lips, this is... I've been trying to get this back for *years*."

I blink away tears of my own as I turn away from him. I wish so much that we had met under different circumstances and we could be friends. The fierce, protective nature of him draws me in like nothing else. I want him, but I want to be in his circle more.

I hear him moving behind me, but I don't want to look back at him. I should have slipped the necklace into his bag while he wasn't looking or given it to Ash to pass along instead. I feel the heat of his body press up along my back as his scent envelopes me. I freeze, and my heart stutters in my chest. It takes me a second to realize he's not attacking me, he's not trying to hurt me or get some sort of revenge, he's just close to me. I clear my throat like I'm going to speak, but I don't know what I would say to him. He's everything I wish I had, and it pains me to have him this close and to know it's only going to last for a second.

He leans down and brushes his lips to my cheek softly. My eyes fall shut, and I struggle to stop myself from leaning back into his warmth.

"Thank you," he whispers into my ear, and then he disappears, closing my door quietly behind him and taking his heat and delicious smell with him.

I feel gutted.

Chapter Twenty-Three

My whole world has shifted on its axis a little after Harley's visit to my room.

I don't see him for the entire spring break, even though I eat every meal in the dining hall. I barely sleep, because I'm too busy freaking out about how much I actually like him. Like, not just wanting to ogle him or even consider making out with him, but to actually keep him. It's disturbing. I hate crushes so much, because they really do *crush* you.

When class goes back after the break, I make the perilous decision to trust him at his word, and I go down to the dining hall for breakfast. The lure of the incredible French toast is strong enough to let me test him out. I notice the difference the second I leave the safety of my room.

There's no whispering.

I've grown so accustomed to the constant gossiping that happened around me, because of me, that it's jarring to have the other students ignore me.

Avery Beaumont really is an evil dictator.

The dining hall is teeming with students, and I have to use my elbows as weapons to get a seat. I ignore the looks from the girls around me at the size of my plate—six pieces of French toast, thank you very much—and dig in like it's my last meal on death row. I'm starting my third slice when Blaise sits down across from me and actually looks at me. In the face. I wipe my chin in case there's syrup or cream splattered all over me, and I swallow roughly, trying to not lose what I've just eaten.

"Did you know that for the first time in my academic career here at Hannaford, I am sitting on a solid C in math? My dad called me yesterday and offered to buy me the Ferrari of my dreams if I get a B by the end of the year."

It takes me two tries to speak to him. It's far easier to speak when he's not grinning at me and being charming. "So you want my help to get the Ferrari?"

He smirks and makes a slashing motion with his hand. "Fuck the Ferrari. I can buy my own if I want one. I negotiated with him, and if I get a B-plus he's going to let me take three weeks away during the summer holidays to record my next album. I need a B-plus, Mounty. My career and my very soul need to get away from all of my parents' bullshit."

I nod sagely and sip at my drink, feigning a nonchalance I definitely don't feel. He looks at me expectantly, and when I don't fall over myself to offer my services to him, he sighs.

"What's it going to cost me to get you to help me?"

A favor, Matteo's voice says in my mind. What would I even ask of him, though? I put down my cutlery and push my plate away, giving my food a mournful look. I can never eat around these guys, and the look on Blaise's face has butterflies dive-bombing deep in my gut.

"No cost. You need to ask for extra credit though; you don't have enough time left to bring your grade up without it. You'll need to come to every study session, on time, for the rest of the year, and you'll have to ask Ash very nicely if he can stop pretending he needs my help so I can focus on helping you."

"Done." Blaise grins at me and then starts eating his breakfast. I don't know what to do with myself. I'm debating if I should get up and leave when Harley steps into the dining hall with Avery's arm tucked firmly into his. He sees us immediately and he frowns, his eyes darting between us both. I give him what I hope is a reassuring smile, but it only makes his frown deepen. Avery rolls her eyes, grabs a tray, and shoves it into his chest. I watch, curiously, as he fills it up for them both. I've never seen him dote on her like this. Usually Ash is the one who carries her things, but he's nowhere to be seen.

They walk past us, and Avery only pauses long enough to kiss Blaise's cheek and murmur a *good morning* to him as she passes. She doesn't bother to look my way. Once Harley has Avery all set up and their food is portioned out, he stalks back over to us. Avery glares and shakes her head at him as he sidles up beside me.

As I glance up, the light from the chandeliers catches on the necklace around his neck, and I swallow. I don't know why I'm shocked that he's wearing it. If it means so much to him that he'd gotten choked up, then it makes sense he would want to keep it close. I can't pull my eyes away from it until he speaks and breaks the spell.

"What are you two doing eating breakfast together? People will talk."

Blaise leans back in his chair and looks every inch the rock star he is. He usually hides it well, like he puts away '*Blaise Morrison: Lead Vocalist for Vanth Falling*' when he arrives in the gates of Hannaford and becomes the spoiled rich kid everyone expects him to be. I've only ever seen the brash musician when he's around his friends. I get the feeling that this is the mask he wears to survive, that he protects himself and his music from this place, the way Avery protects those she loves.

"The Mounty has just offered to be my own personal tutor for the rest of the year. We're going to be practically inseparable; doesn't that sound fun?"

My cheeks flush, and I give him a look. A *don't-fuck-with-me-after-I've-agreed-to-help-you* look. The cocky grin I get in return is something poets could write sonnets about. It's stunning and terrible and hot and heartbreaking.

"I could've helped you. Why didn't you ask?" Harley grumbles. I look up at him, and he looks away from me quickly, like he didn't want me to catch him staring. He is the most confusing guy I've ever met.

"No, you really can't. What's the problem, man? Avery's lifted the speaking ban. Any other reason I should be staying away from the Mounty?" His voice is too smug, and the smirk he levels at Harley makes my heart stutter. It's almost as if…they can't be fighting over me. They both have made their feelings toward me perfectly clear this year. Harley shrugs coolly—aiming, I think, to look unaffected—but I can see his fists clenching. He puts his elbows on the chair next to me and leans forward like he's going to whisper at Blaise. He's loud enough that the students around him here every.

Goddamn. Word.

"Just thought you'd be more afraid of spending that much time alone with your stalker."

The blood drains from my head until I'm left feeling dizzy. There it is. There's the reason I shouldn't ever speak to Blaise without classwork in front of us. The sounds of sniggering and laughter start up around us from the students shamelessly eavesdropping. I stand up abruptly and grab my bag. Harley chuckles under his breath at me, but I refuse to look at him. He was right all those months ago. I need to bury my nerves better when it comes to him and Blaise. And Ash. *Goddammit.*

"Just get the extra credit work. I'll help you during the tutoring sessions, but don't talk to me otherwise."

I stomp out of the dining hall to the sound of Harley's roaring laughter and Blaise swearing up a storm at him.

I decided to arrive at our study group late.

Well, I actually decide to skip the tutoring sessions altogether, but then I think about my college submissions and I cave. I don't want to have to face Blaise again so soon. His opinion of me shouldn't matter. I'm the Wolf, for fuck's sake, but hot shame washes over me whenever I think about him. He really does think I'm a sad little groupie. Not an awesome, sexy groupie. I've met girls like that before, I've been to gigs and seen girls that are so powerful with how they hold themselves up and live their truths.

My truth is I'm an inexperienced, blushing idiot with responsibilities no student at Hannaford would ever understand.

I wish I hadn't stayed quite so far away from guys back at Mounts Bay. Not that I wish I'd had sex with anyone, but if I'd dated guys or, fuck, kissed anyone before coming here, maybe I wouldn't be so awkward about this. Maybe Joey's little sweep wouldn't have been such a big deal. I can't think of a single girl in my last school who wouldn't jump at the chance to fuck a Hannaford guy, and maybe even get some cash for her troubles.

Ash and Blaise are already at our table when I get to the library. There's no laughing or joking going on this time, and Ash is taking stacks of paper from Blaise and flicking through them. My eyes narrow. It's all just more evidence that he's been lying about needing my help.

Blaise looks up at me with stark relief, and I take the chair next to him without a word, unpacking the bare essentials from my bag. "Thank God, Mounty, I thought—"

"I'd rather not have this conversation. Give me everything you have from the math class, and I'll work out a plan of attack." I hold out my hand and focus my eyes on a speck of dust on the tabletop.

Ash raises an eyebrow and hands me the stack. Blaise is twitching in his chair, but neither of them try and make conversation. We sit in total silence until I've flicked through everything he's given me. I glance up to see they're having a conversation entirely with their eyebrows. I'm oddly impressed.

"Here. Do this page so I can see where you're up to." I slide the page across to Blaise, and he murmurs a quiet, *sure* under his breath. I start to write out notes for him to study at night and to use during tests. I have to focus to keep my scrawling handwriting neat enough to be read by mere mortals.

Not that I think Blaise is mortal.

Or mere.

He gets straight to work. He's quiet, subdued from his usual flirty manner, and I give myself a second to breathe. It's hard to do, because I can feel Ash's calculating eyes on me. I wonder how much Blaise told him while they were waiting for me to show. I've always arrived at the sessions at least ten minutes early, so I would think Ash would have made a smart comment about my tardiness.

Ash begins to tap his pen in his hand as he says, "You should have asked Blaise to pay you for your tutoring. *He's* a millionaire and, someday, he's going to be the sole recipient of a billion-dollar empire. You're an orphan, Mounty, who has lost everything. There's only a few weeks left of the school year. Charge him, say, a grand a week. That's literally *nothing* to us."

I pause long enough to glare at him, but he just waves me off. "I'm not being an arrogant asshole, I'm just stating facts. Avery dropped more cash on hair products this week than what I'm suggesting he pay you. It's a business transaction. A legitimate one. You can replace all of your shit, and Blaise can stop moping around like a kicked fucking puppy because you're being nice to him for no reason."

Ash grunts as Blaise's foot connects with his shin. I think about it for about three seconds. I could increase my bank balance by thousands of dollars for doing something I've already committed to. I'm not going to lie, it's tempting. Then I think of something better. This is my moment to prove a point.

I set my pen down and fold my hands together, letting my face drop into a serene mask before I speak. "You're going to be a man of business someday, Beaumont, and I'm here to help Blaise out with numbers. So, let's look at some *real world* facts." Ash tilts his head at me and motions me on. "I have a full ride scholarship that covers food, shelter, and clothing for thirty-six weeks of my year, which leaves me with sixteen weeks to have to financially provide for myself. I have a hundred grand in the bank. At my current rate of spending, by the time I graduate Hannaford and move on to college, I'll still have more than seventy grand in the bank. I will get a scholarship for college, full ride just like this one because we all know I'm that good, so that money is going to keep sitting in the bank. When I start out in the career of my choice, I'm going to hit the ground running."

I pause. Ash is staring at me, rubbing his chin absently, and so I continue. "I know that to you that amount of money may sound pathetic, but to me, and to most people, I'm set. Major, catastrophic disasters would have to happen for me to have to touch the money I've got. So, I don't. Want. Your. Fucking. Money."

I pick up my pen, expecting the conversation to be over. Blaise certainly thinks it is. He's frowning down at the numbers like he's waiting for them to give up all their secrets. Ash snatches the pen out of my hand.

"Inheritance?" he says.

I shake my head.

"Gambling? Are you a secret poker savant?"

"Nope."

"Shame. I could have used the pointers." Ash lets out a little gasp and leans in. His torso is long enough that he easily covers the distance between us. "Did you steal it, Mounty?"

I smirk and lean in to him. Once my chest is pressed against the table and my lips brush his earlobe, I whisper, "I earned it from a dead man."

I lean back and see that he's staring down the front of my blouse, where the small amount of cleavage I have is pushing up lusciously.

"Why, Mounty, I didn't think you were the type," he drawls, and I don't know if he means my chest or my money-making methods. There's this little grin on his face that makes me want to scream. I think he enjoys the push-pull banter we slide into the moment we're near each other. I have no idea how to flirt, but I think this might be it.

I open my mouth, unsure of what I'd even reply, when we hear a scream.

I jerk around in my seat to look toward the sound at the back of the stacks. Students start moving en masse, but the librarians are nowhere to be seen.

"Avery?" says Blaise urgently, and Ash replies, "Harley took her down to her ballet class."

There's another shriek and I'm up and out of my chair, pushing past students to find the source. I have a sinking feeling as I make it through the crowd, Ash and Blaise pushing through behind me, and I stop dead.

Joey is standing over another student.

A dead student.

Chapter Twenty-Four

Joey's chest is heaving.

There's a sheen of sweat on his forehead and his eyes are glassy, bouncing around the room like he can't focus on anything. I spare him a second before I grab Ash's arm and haul him over to the dead student. Joey begins to laugh. It's an awful sound, too loud and hyper, and tears stream down his face as he clutches at his chest.

I've learned a lot of important, life-saving shit while in Mounts Bay, but I don't know if there's a damn thing I can do for this guy. He's a freshman—I recognize him from my French class—with mousy brown hair and a dimpled chin that makes him look younger.

"Call 911, Ash," I say firmly. Ash startles away from me. He's watching Joey's every move like he's waiting for him to strike again, but he fumbles his phone out of his pocket and makes the call. Only seconds have passed since we got to the kid, but I know exactly how critical time is. I check his airways, clear, then his breathing... nothing. His throat is already looking mottled.

Joey has strangled him.

Ash starts talking down the line to the operator, and I start CPR. I'm focused entirely on the kid, counting compressions and singing the stupid song in my head to keep time. When I stop to do the breaths, Ash switches his phone onto speaker and takes over the compressions.

"Like this?" he asks, and I start to sing *Staying Alive* by the Bee Gees softly, just loud enough for him to catch the rhythm. I hear a scuffle behind us, but I ignore it. No, I trust Blaise to keep Ash and I safe while we try and help the kid.

No other students step forward to help.

I lose any respect for them, any shred that I had, because only a monster would step away from this without helping out.

He's just a fucking kid.

The 911 operator tells us the ambulance is at the gates, and I bark at the crowd to send someone down to lead them up. The scuffle gets louder, swearing and spitting and wood snapping, and then a palm touches my shoulder blade. I flinch and look up to see the EMTs have arrived. I slide away from the kid and Ash stops the compressions. As his hands leave his chest, I hear a wet, sucking, gurgling noise, and then a moan.

He's alive.

I scramble away and Ash catches me by the elbow, lifting me off the ground. I can't take my eyes off the EMTs while they load him up and start working on him.

"What's his name?" I say, and Ash pants back, "Matthew. Matthew Steiner."

When they're wheeling him away, I finally look over to where Joey was standing. Blaise and Harley have him pinned to the ground, but just barely. Blaise is bleeding profusely from a deep gouge in his forehead. Avery is standing over them, scanning the crowd with a keen eye. She's making her assessment, planning out the damage control required to minimize her brother's attempt at murder. I see red—seething, maniacal, bleeding red—and I step forward only to be stopped by the vise grip of Ash's hand around my wrist. He doesn't look down at me, but he gives it a little squeeze.

A warning.

"Anyone get it on tape?" Avery even sounds like her usual icy self.

Two girls step forward and hand over their phones. Avery taps away at them, her phone pings, and then she hands them back. I watch the crowd. I want to memorize the faces, so I know who the truly weak and apathetic students are. As easy as breathing, I start to notice the behaviors. There are three students, all guys, who are digging their phones deeper in their pockets subconsciously, like they're trying to push them out of Avery's reach.

I do not trust Avery.

But Ash just stepped up to the plate. He's earned my respect where a whole group of kids just failed. I now have some level of trust in him.

"There's others who have the footage." Ash looks down at me, and then when I point them out, he starts calling names, sharp and authoritative. The guys lurch forward at his command. Avery arches an eyebrow at them while they fumble over themselves to make excuses. She takes a copy of their footage and wipes the phones.

There're other ways to do it. Software and coding that can be done to hack into the phones and get whatever you need out of them. I might suggest it to Ash later, an extra sweep to make sure this stays buried.

I still don't know *why* we are burying it.

"Go, Mounty. You don't need your name attached to this." Ash lets my wrist go reluctantly and gives me a gentle push toward the door. It occurs to me that there are still no teachers or librarians here, and that Avery and Harley made it, but no adults have yet. If I hadn't rushed forward, that kid could have died. I mean, he might still die or have a brain injury, but at least we gave him a chance.

I glance back at Joey one last time before I leave. He's stopped thrashing about, but he's hissing at Harley instead. He's not looking at his face, his eyes are lower, his neck—

The necklace.

He's spotted the necklace I stole from his room the day I called the cops and had him arrested. I turn and walk away, shoving past the crowd, not giving a damn who I hurt with my bony elbows. I only stop at the table long enough to grab my bag and throw my supplies back in it.

I get to the far side of the school, where the staircases to the girls' dorms are, before I see Mr. Trevelen and the librarians rush past. Too little and far too late, thanks to the interference Avery ran.

I lock my door, check it's secure, and then collapse back onto my bed.

So I now have two lists I'm compiling.

One is an ongoing list of everything the Beaumonts can get away with, which now includes murder.

And the second is a to-do list.

I'm going to need to call in a favor.

"A phone call, Starbright? Is the school burning down? Have you castrated a young, enamored boy? Are you finally coming home?" Matteo's voice settles into my skin like a throbbing wound. I feel like I need to scrub my skin the second I get off the phone, regardless of the fact that I only just showered. The banter didn't feel fun anymore; it hasn't felt fun in a long time. Now all I can hear is the possession in his dulcet tones. He's speaking to someone he thinks he owns.

I won't ever let him own me.

"I need to call in a favor," I say sweetly. It sounds fake because it is. I'm not sweet. I'm fucking tired.

"Tch, kid, this is getting out of hand. You know, you wouldn't have to keep running to me for help if you did some recruiting of your own. There are dozens of suitable candidates, all clamoring to sign up under the infamous Wolf. I could move some of my crew around for you. As a member of the Twelve, you have to have people behind you. This is why you need to come to some meetings."

I roll my eyes. He wants to give me some people to start a gang with. His people, so he can always have loyal eyes on my back. In his mind, it'll make it easier for when he claims me and have the two gangs amalgamate to become one super criminal organization.

It's much easier to lie to him on the phone. "I've been giving it some thought, and I've got a few leads. I'm looking for very specific skill sets, and if I'm going to do this, I'm doing it right. I gave you my word I'd be at the next meeting over the summer, didn't I? Is my word not good enough anymore?" I finish with a teasing tone. Some might even call it flirty, but I just call it a necessity.

I hear him cover the mouthpiece and bark out orders. If you're with the Jackal, you're always at war or starting a new one. When I was just a kid and Matteo had first taken notice of me at the group home, he'd told me he looked up to Alexander the Great. All he wanted to do was build an empire. He enjoys the thrill of the chase, the outsmarting, and the kill.

I think I caught his interest because I was strong.

I think I've kept it because I won't give in.

"We can talk about your leads at the meeting. I'm interested to know who you have your eye on." The censure in his voice is clear to me. Great, something else I need to think about and plan for. "Let's get back on topic, I have someone waiting for me. Someone…went on an unsanctioned holiday and needs to be reminded of their duties. What do you need?"

He has a defector in his office, tied to a chair, listening in on our every word. They can listen because they will be dead by morning. I have seen Matteo work so many times, I don't even need to shut my eyes to see it. I know which knife he will reach for first, I know where he keeps his blowtorch, I know which hand he will wipe clean first.

"Joey Beaumont is deteriorating quickly. I need all the information you can give me about him, his family, their businesses, and their history. I need to know how I can safely neutralize him, because I'm going to have too. Soon."

I hear the knife at Matteo's waist slip out of its sheath. I do not want to have to try and sleep after listening to the defector scream. *Hurry up, asshole.*

"I'll send Diarmuid up with a copy of my files. He'll be happy to come visit; he has a nephew who goes to school with you."

My eyebrows shoot up.

Diarmuid O'Cronin was the son of an old Irish mobster. Forty years ago, the O'Cronin family had held a large territory. They'd exclusively run the docks and controlled the importation of drugs and weapons into Cali. Then the institution of the Twelve started and the family had lost members, lost loyalties, lost three-quarters of their territory, and rumor had it the patriarch of the family, Liam O'Cronin, had started to lose a grip on reality. Diarmuid had defected and became a gun for hire ten years ago. He is an unparalleled assassin, a terrifying driver, and he has a shitty attitude. I like him. The Jackal is one of the very few who can afford his price, so I have spent some time with him over the years.

"Who is his nephew? I can't imagine an Irish mobster going to Hannaford."

I hear the swing of Matteo's knife in the air and his grunt as he impales the poor idiot's leg. He doesn't scream, he just lets out a grunt of his own. *Buddy, you want to scream. If you don't, he'll only get more creative.*

"Kid goes by his mom's name. Arbour. Blond and blue-eyed like her, too. Apparently, he looks fuck-all like the O'Cronins."

My heart stops.

Harley.

Harley is the mobster's son.

'Honor before Blood'

Holy.

Fucking.

Shit.

"Diarmuid will pop in and see him, and then drop off the file. Does that work for you, Starbright?" I hear fabric ripping, grunts of pain, and Matteo's labored breathing. I hope to God he's just carving the guy up and not…doing anything worse. I don't want to think about it.

"Yeah, thanks. You'll only owe me two favors now."

Matteo agrees, which comes as a little bit of a shock. He'd been so adamant that he was just being nice and doing things for me this year that I thought I'd have to fight him. "I'll send you the diamond back with Diarmuid, if you trust him with that."

Oh, did I mention I have millions of dollars' worth of cut diamonds, all of the favors I'm owed, hidden in the safe under my floorboards?

Yeah.

My life is too complicated.

I sit in my doorway, pretend to read a book and eat a protein bar for an hour. I've changed into my old man sweater, a pair of shorts, and thigh-high socks. I like to cover the scars on my leg, and it's already too warm for pants. I'm getting impatient waiting for

Avery to appear. Every minute that goes by is a minute closer to Harley being ambushed by his uncle, and it's all my fault. Not that I can tell him it's my fault. I can't tell him I'm getting information on the Beaumonts without starting another war. My stomach turns. I have to tell them something.

When Avery finally arrives and breaks my spiraling thoughts, she's being escorted back to her room by Ash. It's a pain in the ass, because I was hoping it was still Harley's turn to babysit her. Now I'd have to actually come up with some excuse for them to get Harley up here.

"Too poor for a chair, Mounty?" drawls Ash, Avery's ballet bag slung over his shoulder. I've told him about my stash, so I know he's baiting me. It's the next step in our push-pull game.

"I was waiting for you guys to get back." I haul myself up off the floor and prop my hands on my hips.

Avery doesn't acknowledge me; she just grabs her bag and saunters into her room. Ash smirks at me, but I can see something has changed in his eyes. There's a soft edge in them that wasn't there before. It's like every one of our interactions so far has chipped away a little at him, and he's opening up. I shiver and rub my arms uselessly. I'm not cold. Someone should tell my pebbled nipples that fact too.

"I can't give you any answers, Mounty. But I can say thanks for helping out and shutting up about it." He leans back into the doorframe, and I run my gaze down the long line of his legs. Focus, Lips, fuck.

"Look, it's not about Joey. I need to speak to Harley urgently. Can you text him to come here? Or meet me somewhere else on campus?"

A frown appears on his brow, and he straightens. Whatever expression I have on my face is concerning him. He slides his hand into his pocket, but then Avery pokes her head out of the door again.

"Stay the fuck away from my cousin." It's the first time I've ever heard her swear. Cousin. I forgot about that; the Beaumonts have a mobster for a cousin. This is a fucking mess. I'm in too deep and I need to get out.

Deep breath.

There's no way out. Only through it.

I dart across the hallway and grab Avery's arm. She freezes and so does Ash, the tense lines of him pressed against my chest where he's trapped between us. I make sure my grip is gentle, so she can't screech at me and he can't attack me over touching his beloved sister. I don't need to be rough, though; I have their attention.

"Does the name Diarmuid O'Cronin mean anything to you?" I whisper, and then I watch as they both turn to stone. "He's on his way here to speak to his dear nephew."

Ash breaks first, cursing long and hard under his breath in creative and colorful ways. I nod curtly and let Avery go.

"Fucking call him. Now."

Chapter Twenty-Five

Avery's room is utterly ridiculous, and I am jealous as all hell about it.

It is fitted out perfectly not only for her, but for the three guys in case they all wanted to have a big freaking sleepover there every night. There're rollout beds under her giant Cal King and a day bed built into the window. Everything is in tasteful shades of cream and gray, pillows and throw rugs on every surface. How have I never noticed them coming and going from her room? I glance around while we wait.

The kitchen is fully stocked, I have no idea why she bothers with the overcrowded dining hall, and her closet is the size of my entire room. I only ever see her wearing her uniform. Why the hell does she need this much space? And there, in the corner, is a private bathroom. That's the thing I'm most jealous of. To be able to lock the bedroom door and shower in your own bathroom. Avery is living the dream four fucking steps from the closet I sleep in. I take some deep, deep breaths, and I tell myself I'll have this someday. Better even, because I'll have earned it myself and I'll appreciate it.

Avery paces in the kitchen area, running her hands along the surfaces like she's looking for dust, but it doesn't exist, and Ash sits stiffly on the couch. I perch on the edge on one of the armchairs and roll my eyes at Avery's dirty look.

"Is there somewhere I can sit, then? Or are you afraid I'll sully your fucking furniture?" I snap at her, and she rolls her eyes.

"That's Harley's seat. Blaise usually just camps on the floor like a three-year-old so maybe sit in his chair, the other armchair. I don't want Harley getting ideas." I open my mouth to retort 'what ideas' when Ash snaps at us both.

"She can sit wherever the fuck she wants, just tell us what's going on? How the fuck, do you know Diarmuid?"

Avery starts wiping down the kitchen counters. Huh, I did not expect her to know how to clean. I shake the thought out of my head and reply to Ash, "I'm not repeating myself; it'll only piss us all off. How far away are they? We're on a time crunch here."

"We're here." Harley opens the door, and he and Blaise stroll in. There's no tenseness to him at all, just curiosity. I sigh. Avery didn't tell him what this was all about, then.

Harley spots me on his chair, and before I can get up, he slings himself down the couch so he's closest to me. Avery scoffs and scrubs harder. Blaise does exactly what she said he would and just collapses on the floor with an obscene groan. His shirt rides up, and I look away from his colorfully patterned skin before I get caught looking. I have to remember I'm surrounded by sharks. I need to keep my head, or I'll lose it.

Harley watches Avery's manic scrubbing for a second, then says, "Fuck, Avery's cleaning. What's wrong? What's this about?"

I take a deep breath, and then just blurt out. "I have a connection to an underground criminal organization. The connection is not up for discussion. But he has a package for me. He tells me he's sending one of his hired guns to bring it here. The guy offered because he has a nephew who goes to the school. I was unaware that you're an O'Cronin."

Harley's face shuts down so fast, I'm surprised he doesn't get whiplash. Avery stops cleaning to cock her hip, and says to me with a glare, "So it's your fault he's coming here, then? You've called him in?"

Fuck. "I didn't call him in. He heard the name Hannaford and decided to come up. I am not at fault here. I could have just let him come and ambush Harley, but I chose not to. Do not make me regret that."

Harley is a blank slate. I can see the deep programming from a mile away—I mean, I have it too. It lives in your brain, and even when you've changed your life and you're living like a civilian, all it takes is hitting that trip line and the training will fall into place. I take a deep breath and cover his hand with mine. "I will stay with you. It'll put a stop to… whatever it is you think he's going to do to you. My connection means immunity."

He doesn't react. He doesn't move at all. I have to focus on the base of his throat to see he's still breathing. I don't tell him that I'll be risking my own skin to help him. If word about Harley gets back to the Jackal… I don't think Matteo will like just how breathtaking Harley is.

I meet Ash's eyes across the room and find he's scowling at me. Their fear sends a shiver down my spine, and I tentatively ask, "What are you afraid he's going to do? I can call ahead and stop it. Believe it or not."

There's silence while they all look at one another. No one offers up an explanation.

"Do you fuck gangsters and mobsters, Mounty? Is that why you won't fuck any of the upstanding students here? Does your pussy belong to a monster?" Blaise drawls from the floor. "Do you need the violence to get wet?"

I slowly take my hand off Harley's and stand. Blaise always knows just what to say to eviscerate me. It's his super-fucking-power.

I make it to the door when Avery calls out, "You can't leave, we don't have a plan. I need to make a plan." I turn to ask her what the hell she's going on about and I find Harley standing behind me. He can be just as silent on his feet as I can. His eyes are blank. I hate that I can't read them, that there's none of his usual fire and wit to be found. He's a shell, the mindless soldier they have trained him to be. I hate it.

His voice is as empty as his eyes. "The plan is to keep you three out of my family's hands. That's it. I'll call when it's… done."

I take Harley into my room, and I make him face the wall as I dig out the safe hidden under my floorboards and lift the tiny box out. The diamonds all shift around and make that distinctive clinking sound.

Each of the twelve had a color assigned to them. If you were willing to pay another member in a favor, you had to have the cash to buy and hand over a diamond in the color you're assigned. I have at least three in every color except my own.

I have never given out a favor.

I can't afford to give out favors.

My color was the deep dark blue, the same color as my eyes, as close to black as blue can get. The Jackal had walked me into a ritzy jewelry store and pointed one out to me that was set in a stunning ring, just so I'd know what I needed to get if the time ever came. The last time I priced a single blue diamond out, and fuck was it hard to find, it came in just under the half-million-dollar mark.

I rummage around until I find the three little red diamonds I'd been given by the Jackal. They are the rarest diamonds, and how he found and purchased three is beyond me. These are the only favors he's ever given out and I know it's because in his mind, it's safe to give them to me. I'll just give them back to him the moment he orders me to, when he owns me.

I slip the smallest of the three into a velvet bag and then into my bra, where I can feel it against my skin. After I've hidden the safe once again, I follow Harley back downstairs and out to the front foyer. He doesn't ask me what I collected. I don't know how much time he's spent around these sorts of people, but it's enough that he doesn't ask stupid questions. At the roar of a motorbike, I roll my eyes.

Subtle isn't Diarmuid's specialty.

His specialty is blood.

Harley notices my exasperation and finally speaks. "You've met him before?"

I nod, then hesitate before asking, "Have you?"

Harley shakes his head, and I frown.

"Why are you so worried then?"

He chews on his bottom lip, the first sign of anxiousness I've ever seen in him. "It's a double-edged sword. He might kill me because he left the family and I'm next in line to take over. A big fuck you to my grandfather if he does that, and if anything I've heard about him is true, then I think that's how this will go. If Diarmuid doesn't kill me, it could get back to my grandfather that we're meeting up, and then the family will kill me. Either way, I'm fucked."

Fuck.

Mobster family politics.

I'm not stupid or brash, but I follow my gut, always. Ultimately, this guy took out three guys for beating me. He made Avery cut her shit out. He's made his decision not to hate me, and then he followed through with it. How can I not offer him the same loyalty? My gut tells me he's worth saving, and I'm quickly discovering we're cut from the same cloth.

"Are you going to take over the family business?" I say, curious.

He glares down at me. "I'd rather fucking die. I *will* die when my grandfather figures out I won't change my mind. I've made peace with that."

He can't die, I won't let him. I have a fairly reckless plan, and a prayer that it will work. "Do you trust me, Arbour?" I wipe my sweaty palms down my legs and meet his eyes. Something is inching back into his baby blues, and I never want to see it leave again.

"Enough to be standing here," he rasps back.

"Then keep your mouth shut, and I'll keep you alive. I mean it. Not a single word."

Diarmuid is an O'Cronin through and through.

Dark, shaggy hair that falls over his green eyes as he pulls the helmet off his head. His face splits into a grin when he spots me, and he waves me over to crush my body into a hug, while he's still straddling the bike. When he speaks, it's with a delightful Irish accent that has prevailed even though as the youngest child, he'd been born in the States.

"Jesus, Mary, and fuckin' Joseph, you're growin' up, kid!" I tug away from his arms and give him a small smile. His fingers press down on the perfect circle scar I have on my shoulder, like he always does. Even fully clothed, drunk, and blind, he can find it. It is his reminder and his penance.

From the time he shot me.

The bastard.

I digress. He hands me a thick envelope, and I tuck it into the waistband of my shorts, flipping the sweater over it and concealing it perfectly. He's still grinning like an idiot when Harley takes a step forward and silently demands his attention. The grin dries up, and he pushes me away from his body enough to swing his leg over and perch on the bike's seat. He digs around in his pocket and lights up a cigarette. I wrinkle my nose and step back until my arm brushes Harley's again.

"You're the fuckin' image of Iris. It's disturbing to see her standing there as a boy. There any of your da in you at all, *buachaill beag*?" He takes a long drag and then blows the smoke directly up in the air, the wind catching it and letting it dance away into nothing.

Harley doesn't say a word, he just folds his arms across his chest and stares at his uncle.

Diarmuid looks back at me and says, "Can you give us a minute, kid? I need to talk some business. Family business."

I meet his gaze and slowly shake my head. "I'm afraid not. It's come to my attention just how sought-after Arbour is." He quirks an eyebrow at me, and I grin, forcing the bravado I don't feel into it. "I'm a fickle sort of girl. It brings me great joy to be able to keep Harley from those who want him. I think I'll keep him."

Diarmuid blanches for a second, and then tips his head back and roars with laughter. He rubs his hands together with a vicious glint to his eye. "You bring my little nephew back to Mounts Bay and our mutual friend gets an eyeful of him? Blood and pain, little girl. Blood and pain."

I don't need to be reminded of that at all, and I certainly don't need Harley hearing it. I reach into my bra and pull out the little velvet bag. Diarmuid's eyes catch on it, and I hold it out to him. When he lets the little blood diamond fall onto his palm, he sucks in a breath. "It's a thing of beauty, this. You know what it is, *buachaill beag*?" He waits until Harley finally shakes his head. "It's a million dollars and a priceless fuckin' favor."

"Tell him I'm buying Harley's life with it, too. The envelope alone isn't worth that, and he well knows it. Tell him I've picked my first inductee, and when he has questions, he can call me."

Diarmuid sobers and looks down his nose at me. "My da will come for you both. He'll kill him for standing here and listening in on this conversation alone."

I take a deep breath. I know the cliff I'm about to go over, and it's a scary thing to do. Harley will know more than I'd ever wanted anyone outside of Mounts Bay to know. I need this conversation over. Now. "Liam O'Cronin can't do shit to me. He knows it, I know it, and you should know it too."

Diarmuid grins at me again and tucks the diamond into his jeans. "Oh, I know it. I'm just making sure my little nephew knows it too. He looks a little green around the gills, is all." He steps forward and slaps Harley's shoulder. "I came here to have a little heart-to-heart with you about decisions you need to make, but I see you've already made them. It all comes down to this: if you don't kill the old man someday for what he did to your ma and da, then I will. And if I don't succeed, then your little Wolf here will do it for us both. She's got one hell of a steady hand."

He swoops down and smacks a kiss onto my cheek. As he climbs on his bike and starts the engine, he calls out to us one last time. "Call me when your tits fill in, kid, and I'll show you how real men fuck."

I roll my eyes and watch his taillights until they disappear completely. Then I turn and start to make my way back up to the dorms without looking to see if Harley is following. He's going to rat me out to his friends. He's going to hate me for interfering with his family's business. There're a hundred different things he's going to do.

I didn't bet on him pushing me through my bedroom door and then kissing me.

It's raw and dark and it's fucking perfect. He's not gentle about it at all. He pushes and sucks at my lips, but it's nothing like the one Joey had forced on me. I moan when his tongue touches mine and take fistfuls of his shirt to pull his body into mine. His hands tangle in my hair and pulls until he's got the perfect angle to deepen our kiss and steal my breath away. I feel it all the way down to my toes.

This is how my first kiss should have been.

I break away from him as my mind spins, and I try to catch up with where he's at. He shuts his eyes and rests his forehead against mine. It's a tender moment, more intimate than even his kiss.

"Are you a member of a gang?" he croaks, and I shake my head. "Did you just tell him you recruited me to your friend's gang?" I shake my head again. I pull away so I can catch my breath because I can't breathe in his arms. When he touches me, I don't want oxygen. I just want to consume him.

"I just bought your freedom until our graduation. I'm out the second the diploma touches my hand, so you need to get a plan in place for then. I can help, but I'm letting you know this favor has an expiry date. Until then, you're… mine." It feels strange to say that to him, and I can't look at him as the words slip from my lips.

"This is seriously fucking insane, Lips. You've got to give me something. Where did you get the diamond, and how many more do you have? Why are they favors? Why is your protection greater than the O'Cronin family business? Fuck, give me anything, Lips!"

As his voice raises to a shout, I press my hands into his lips and try to calm him down. *He said my name.* I can't answer any of his questions without knowing he's all in. And why would he be all in for a scrawny little Mounty? Tears prick at my eyes, but I don't regret my hasty actions. My gut had gotten me to where I was today. It will get me through this, too.

I slip the envelope out of my shorts, and I drop it on the bed. Then I tug down the collar of the sweater until Harley can see the perfectly healed circle.

"I got that diamond by taking a bullet for the man whose favor it represented. I saved his life, and I also won him the trust of his favorite gun for hire."

Harley's fingers rub at the raised skin, pressing the same way his uncle had. My skin tingles deliciously. "Diarmuid did this?"

I nod, and then shrug. "I think... I think I have Diarmuid's trust over... the other person. I just can't afford his fees," I whisper, never having allowed myself to even think that before.

It was something else to file away for later.

Harley swallows, and then pulls away from me. His hands are shaking. I have to face the facts that the kiss was just his adrenaline needing an out.

"I won't tell the others. I don't know how the fuck I'd explain it, anyway."

And then he walks out.

Once again, I'm gutted as I close the door behind him.

I've got to stop letting him in my room.

Chapter Twenty-Six

I almost forget about the envelope that Diarmuid had delivered while I am wallowing over my kiss with Harley. His protection of me with Avery stays intact, but he no longer speaks to me. None of them speak to me. At first, I'm worried because I think he's told the rest of them what I did, but I can feel Avery's eyes bore holes into my back whenever she's in my proximity. It's like I'm a bomb about to go off, and she doesn't know the range of potential casualties. I make it through a few weeks of being ignored by them all and tutoring Blaise like crazy. It's only after I bump into Joey in the library punching one of his friends for not laughing at his jokes that I decide to get back to work on taking him out. I'm not sure what I was expecting to get from the envelope, but the information is brutal and sobering.

I was wrong. Joseph Campbell Fedor Beaumont, or Joey, isn't a killer *in the making*. He's already got three deaths under his belt.

Not that the file says that outright, but it's clear what's been going on. There's a nanny, a maid, and a groundsman who have all turned up dead on the property. Newspapers have declared the house haunted since the police ruled the deaths accidental. There are pages and pages of evidence that any prosecutor worth their wage would be able to convict Joey with, but it's all been swept under the rug. The autopsies are unpleasant, to say the least. The things he's done, especially to the maid, are truly horrifying. Biting, burning, stabbing. Evidence of sexual assault.

He was eleven.

It dawns on me just how lucky I was that night of the party. Had he been sober, or at a different stage of his high, if I hadn't had my knife. If, if, if. So many things had worked in my favor that I didn't know about.

At the very back of the file, there's a single page of information on the twins.

Alexander Asher William Beaumont. Born three minutes before his sister, former state swimming champion, now retired, allergic to mangoes, presented at the emergency department seventy-six times in his lifetime, which is an average of five times a year. I grimace. There's a list of the injuries too. Broken wrist, fractured skull, internal bleeding, concussions, every rib in him must have been broken at least twice. Child protection services have been contacted multiple times, but no one ever checks on the family, which tells me his father is paying bribes. Frequent and expensive bribes.

Then, finally, there's Avery Aspen Waverley Beaumont. Only daughter, interests include ballet, violin, and the war strategy game of Go. No known allergies, though she refuses to eat mangoes thanks to Ash's allergy. One trip to the emergency department for Avery. Last year she was DOA and resuscitated. Clear signs of strangulation, another call to child protection services, but again no follow-up.

That explains the escort she gets from the guys everywhere she goes. It also explains why they're so protective. She wasn't just attacked; she was killed. My chest hurts as I think about how Ash would have felt, knowing she had stopped breathing. Knowing she was gone, even for the few minutes she was, must have destroyed him. The day Joey strangled Matthew in the library Ash didn't hesitate for a second to help me. After so much trauma, he is stronger than I would have ever thought. I've always looked at him and seen the spoiled rich brat he puts on. Even the anger and the flinches in his brother's directions didn't clue me in to how bad Joey really is.

I'm going to have to deal with Joey.

I've done a lot in life, but I've never actually planned a murder. I'm not quite sure that's what I'm doing now, but I'm going to have to start taking Joey and the warnings about him seriously. Loose cannons and unpredictable drug addicts are dangerous people to have around you, especially if you carry as many secrets as I do.

I flip the last page to make sure I haven't missed anything and there is a small, handwritten note in the back. It's not Matteo's handwriting, so it would have to be from Diarmuid.

Do not let Joseph Beaumont Sr. know you're looking into his son. His hands are bloodier than mine.

Fuck. A complicated web to unravel.

Now that I'm not being whispered about or having my food spiked, I begin to use the study areas that are everywhere at Hannaford. All my assignments have been handed in for the school year, and now I'm focusing on my last-minute revision for the upcoming exams. I'm an expert at keeping well-organized notes, and so I drag a giant file around with me everywhere I go, so I can read and cram at every opportunity. I'm confident I'll be the top in all my classes, but the perfectionist in me compels me to study until every second of every day until the exams are over.

I'm enjoying the quiet of one particular study nook, when Joey slips into the chair beside me. I tense and slip my hand into my blazer pocket to clutch at my knife. There is no one close by. I'm aware that has never stopped Joey in the past, but I'd prefer to never be alone with him again. The images of his maid's autopsy flash into my mind and I focus to keep my breathing even.

"It's been such a long time since we last spoke, Mounty. I've missed you," he drawls, as he flicks my colored pens so they roll around the desk.

"Is there something you want, Beaumont?" I try to keep my tone civil but uninviting. I watch him from the corners of my eyes, assessing just how high he is.

"There are so many things I want, but I've just been told I can't have one of them. Tell me, how is it you know the Jackal? I received a personal phone call from him."

I shrug and look back down at my notes. I knew this was coming. When I don't answer he continues.

"I've met quite a lot of his, shall we say, associates. I enjoy his products. They're much more pure than the crap you get out here or in the city. So, I do a pickup with my usual supplier, and he tells me his boss needs a word with me. I'm thinking I'm going to get a frequent shopper card, or a job offer, and instead I'm given an order. Stay away from one, Eclipse Anderson."

I set my pen down and turn in my chair to look at him. His eyes are clearer than they were in the library, but he is still having trouble tracking. His cheek has a little tick as he talks, and his brow is furrowed like I'm confusing him. I decide it's safe enough to speak calmly to him.

"He's a friend of mine. It came up in conversation that you were interested in me, and he was concerned that I'm too young for such a thing, so he told me he would have a friendly chat. That's all this is." That is not even close to what this is.

"He told me you belong to him. He told me if even a single Hannaford boy touches your pussy, he's going to come here and deal with it personally."

I clench my jaw so the words I want to say don't come flying out of my mouth. When I have myself under control, I say, "So you're going to leave me alone, then?"

He tips his head back and laughs.

I can't stand the manic sound of it, so I grab my books and leave.

Chapter Twenty-Seven

I arrived at my last tutoring session in the library early and set up the table. I've written pages and pages of notes for Blaise's final math test, and if he nails this one, he's got the B-plus. He's still being a dick to me at every opportunity, but I'm letting everything just bounce off me. He can believe whatever he wants about me; I know who I am. Plus, I'm doing all of this, so I have a new Vanth album to listen to. I want to know what he's going to write now that I've actually met him. Not that I think I'm going to affect his writing at all, I'm nothing to him, but the rock star Blaise and the Hannaford Blaise still don't completely gel together in my mind yet.

When neither of the guys arrive on time, I'm pissed. When they're both twenty minutes late, I'm starting to get worried. Ash always comes to our tutoring sessions, and he's always on time. There's a chance they had both been held up in their last class, they shared biology, but there's also a chance Joey has escalated. I'm about to pack up and leave when Ash walks in, without his bag, and sits down across the table from me.

Something is wrong.

The softness I'd once seen in Ash's eyes is gone. He's looking at me the same way he did back when I first started tutoring him and he wanted to get rid of me. I don't know what's happened. I feel like we were close to being… friends? Or friendly, at least.

"You know, the very first week we got to Hannaford, I set up a camera to watch Joey's door. We all try to keep tabs on his movements," he says without a greeting. "I've got footage of you sneaking in, and then back out again, on the day he was arrested for drugs." He's glaring at me. This is not what I was expecting at all.

I speak carefully. "So you're going to tell Joey you have proof it was me, then?"

Ash doesn't move. He doesn't lean back in his chair and cross his arms with a cocky grin. He doesn't lean forward to whisper at me. He doesn't move an inch as he says, "Joey has told his friends you're off limits."

I close my textbook. I should have known this was coming. Matteo had told me he was going to step in now that he knows Joey wants to rape me. Not that Matteo gives a shit about rapists; he just doesn't want anyone breaking his toys. I feel sick at the thought.

"I'm going to send Trevelen the videos. I'm going to tell him if he doesn't expel you, I'll go to my father."

I look up at him. Ash is staring at me with his face carefully blank. There's no conflict in his eyes. He's called me names and laughed at everything that's happened to me, but he's never actually tried to get me out. He's never actively campaigned against me like Avery and Joey have, but I have never doubted that he was capable of doing whatever he deemed necessary to get what he wants.

If he wants me out, then telling his father will make that happen.

Whatever the dirt Matteo has on Trevelen, I doubt it would trump the hell that billionaire Joseph Beaumont Sr. could unleash. Plus, the warning from Matteo's file rings in my head. If Ash tells his father, I will have his attention. I've been very careful about the things I've done in my life, but that doesn't mean he won't be able to uncover something and destroy me. He could also just hire someone to take me out. Diarmuid comes to mind. But there is something I'm missing about the Beaumonts, a piece to this puzzle that I haven't quite placed yet—but I can feel the answer dancing just out of my grasp. Why do the twins protect him?

"So your brother finally leaves me alone, and you're just going to take his place? Is there a standard number of fucked-up Beaumonts that must bully me at any one time?" My voice is level even as my heart thuds violently in my chest.

"Joey didn't just warn them off for his own enjoyment. He told them you were permanently off limits." I nod. I already know this but it's nice to have it confirmed. I might start getting some sleep if I didn't have to worry about being killed during lunch.

"Harley told me you were dangerous, but I didn't believe him until now. You're out of this school by Friday." He moves as if to stand up and leave me. I shoot out a hand and grab him by the wrist, and he freezes. His eyes are the color of a summer storm, seething rage. It makes no sense. I've been moving the pieces on the board to get away from this sort of hatred.

"If you've chosen to take Joey's side, then I'm getting you out. I can't have you sleeping across the hall from Avery." My fingers loosen a fraction, and he rips his arm out from my grasp. I'm gaping at him; I don't even try to hide it. He shakes out his arm like he's trying to shake off the feel of my touch. I'm just Mounty trash to him.

"I would never take Joey's side. The guy is a serial killer in the making."

Ash laughs derisively and pegs me with a look.

"I wonder what it was you offered him, what someone like you could offer him, to get his protection. I know exactly what the other girls here do. I guess it was only a matter of time before you gave it up to him, too."

That final jab hurt far more than it should.

Possibly the biggest problem of being expelled is dealing with Harley.

Word will have already reached the O'Cronin family. I can't rescind my protection; he'll be killed the second he walks out of this school if I do. I could call Diarmuid and tell him the problem, but then I'll have to admit why I told him I was keeping him in the first place, and he'll have leverage over me. Leverage the Jackal will pay him big money for.

I can't leave Harley here without some sort of warning, either. There's a whole list of people that would kill him to prove a point with me and, again, the Jackal is at the top of that list.

My only chance at stopping Ash is to talk to Harley and try to make him understand that I don't want anything to do with Joey. He's in a better position than anyone to believe me, knowing what he does about the world I'm from.

It's the weekend, so I have to search the entire school to find him. When I can't find him in the main building, I'm forced to look through the outbuildings and sports facilities. I'm about to give up and walk right into the boys' dorms when I find him.

My jaw drops, and I think I destroy my panties instantaneously.

The school has a boxing ring in the gym. I've never been down here, and I'm suddenly pissed I didn't pick gym instead of choir. In the ring, sparring, are Harley and Blaise.

Shirtless.

Teeny, tiny black shorts.

Legs, tattoos, muscles, sweat, oh my god I've fucking died and gone to the one place I know I'm not going to end up.

They don't notice me come in, thank god, so I have a minute to collect my brains from where they've spilled out onto the floor. My legs are shaking so badly, I have to give myself a stern talking-to about how serious my current situation is. I don't have time to turn into a puddle at boys' feet. Even if they are *ridiculously* attractive.

Blaise is covered in colorful tattoos. They stretch from his collarbones down both arms and his chest. One of his legs is covered, and the other has a few on his thighs, obviously a work in progress. It's shocking to see, because with his uniform on, you can't see any of them. He looks like every other polished rich kid.

Harley has a chest piece, wings and a crowned heart like a bastardized claddagh ring, all in black and white and shades of gray. It makes his chest look even wider and more impressive. I can't breathe.

I get all the way to the ropes before they notice me. Blaise's eyes flick to mine, and Harley uses the opportunity to smack him in the ribs, and then wrestle him to the ground. It's all just a writhing pile of bulging biceps, defined legs, and sweaty chests.

It's basically better than porn.

Resisting the urge to get my phone out and film this for, ahem, later and more intensive viewing, I call out to them instead. "Sorry to interrupt. Harley, can I speak to you for a minute, please?"

He releases Blaise, who stays panting on the floor, and gets up to walk over to me. He's not panting or red. The only sign of his exertion is the sheen on his chest. He unwinds the strapping on his hands and tightens it casually, like he's done it a million times before. He won't look me in the eye. Unease begins to pool in my gut.

"What do you want, Mounty? We're busy."

Yes, you are. My eyes flick over to Blaise, who's still lying on the ground, but his head has turned so he can watch us both intently. I choose my words carefully. "Are you aware of Ash's intention to get me kicked out of Hannaford?"

Harley smirks and nods, his eyes still focused over my shoulder. Not what I'm expecting. I wasn't expecting him to bitch out his cousin and best friends, but I was kind of hoping after everything I've done for him, he could at least *care* that my life was about to be ruined.

"Do you really want to discuss this with him here?" he drawls, jerking his head at Blaise.

"Will you make him leave?" I snap back.

"Nope."

I grit my teeth and smile, so it looks like I'm baring them, "I guess I have no choice then, do I? If Ash gets me kicked out, then we have some things to discuss."

"Oh yeah? Like what."

"Like the fact that you'll need to be very careful without me being here to keep an eye on you. Like there are teachers here who are on the payroll for someone other than the Beaumonts, and he's looking for an opportunity to remove you from my protection. Like you need my contact details so if something does happen, I can fix it."

Blaise's eyes have narrowed, and he has that look on his face I've seen far too much lately. The one he pulls right before he runs his mouth to try and piss me off or embarrass me. "How would you be able to protect Harley? You can't even protect yourself."

They both snigger at each other for a second, and I lose my cool. "Do you really not give a shit about whether or not your grandfather can come for you? Have you become suicidal in the last few weeks without me noticing? You should have told me that before I paid such a high price to keep you alive."

Harley's eyes turn into slits. It's the first time he's looked me in the eye since our kiss. I lift my chin and stare him down. I don't really give a shit about the favor, but I have very little to work here with them. Blaise shoots a lopsided grin at me and says, nonchalantly, "Leave, Mounty. You don't belong at this school or around people like us. You're a groupie, you fuck gangsters and serial killers, and you're playing in a world you don't belong in. No one wants you here."

Chapter Twenty-Eight

I wander through my classes on the last day of freshman year in a daze.

Ash hasn't made his move yet, but I know it'll have to be today or tomorrow. There's a closing assembly tomorrow for each school year to give out the usual awards and praises, parents are invited, so I'm sure I'm going to come face-to-face with Joseph Sr. and have to face his wrath. I think it'll happen then. Ash will tell his dad right before the awards, and I'll be dragged out of the building and thrown out of the school grounds. I'll be forced to go home to Mounts Bay and back to the Jackal.

I need a new plan.

I'm scowling so much; students are darting away from me as I walk through the school halls. Some of the guys in the upper grades flinch as I walk past, and that cheers me up a little. Punch a guy in the throat for hitting on you and they'll all learn to fall into line. When classes end, I duck into the bathroom on the lower floors to wash my hands before I have an early dinner. I'm planning on savoring the last of the good food I'll probably ever have. It's a depressing thought.

I open the bathroom door, and I can hear breathing.

A grunt. Scuffing of shoes. A slap of a hand against bare skin.

I know those sounds. Growing up in the public school system in a shitty area means I've gone into more than one bathroom to find students fucking. I think the majority of my education of what happens between two people came from these sorts of encounters, which is probably why I have avoided relationships so far. I roll my eyes and I'm about to leave when I hear a boy curse.

"Fuck you, hold still."

That doesn't sound…consensual. Without hesitation, I creep forward, just a quick peek to make sure the girl is okay, and my eyes connect with Avery Beaumont.

She's fucking terrified.

Rory has her bent over the sink awkwardly, one hand over her mouth and his body pinning her arms behind her back while he fumbles with his pants. Her panties are torn and on the floor. She's bleeding from her head, her nose looks swollen, her phone is in pieces on the floor, and that fucking dick Rory is about to rape her.

I don't even take a second to think.

I lurch forward and take Rory by surprise. As my shoulder connects with his chest, his breath is knocked out of him and he falls backwards against the cold tiles.

Avery scrambles away from him and behind me. I expect her to leave, to run away and leave me to deal with this horny rapist whose dick is just bobbing in the breeze, but she doesn't. She looks at me like she's looking at a ghost, and then she croaks, "Help."

Rory recovers and staggers at us both. He's easily twice my size and a football player, so naturally stacked with muscle. Someone you don't want to fight without a plan. He may have the advantage, but I was raised in nothing and I fought my way to where I am. I duck and kick his knee, ignoring the shooting pain from the pins holding my leg together, and then I slam my knee into his stomach until he drops. I want to kick him right in the dick, I want him to piss blood for a week, but he's hunching so I can't get to it. He manages to get a fistful of my hair on his way down and flings my head around until I smash my face into the mirror, but then Avery gives him a quick jab to his ribs, and he goes down, groaning. She swears and shakes out her hand, shifting her weight like it will help. She's obviously never had to punch someone before, and she's tucked her thumb in. Silly girl. I'm feeling a little dazed as I think to myself, *I should really teach that girl to punch properly*.

I pick up one of my textbooks, the history tome that's a hardcover and weighs more than a brick, and then I use every ounce of strength in me to slam it into his face.

He's knocked clean out.

I'm heaving like I've run a marathon, and Avery isn't much better. Her shirt is ripped open and she looks down, clutching at the halves to hold them together. She's clearly in shock, and I know I must be as well. My brain feels like a ball in a pinball machine, like it's been shot around my skull a few dozen times. I can't think of anything to say or what to do now.

"He fractured his ribs during a football game last week. It was a lucky guess they were still sore," she says, looking down at him. He's breathing, but I'm not sure I'm happy about it.

"Fucking lucky. Piece of shit."

She hums in agreement and then steps forward to stomp on Rory's phone that's landed on the floor. I hiss at her, worried he'll come to with all the noise, but she turns a baleful look at me.

"He has photos of me."

Then we stop to look at each other.

The queen and the pauper.

There's blood dripping down her nose, her eyebrow is cut open, and I can see the fleshy muscle that lies underneath. It will scar. I wonder for a minute if it will diminish her incredibly good looks, and then I remember that she can afford a plastic surgeon to fix it.

"Why did you help me?" she says abruptly, and I have to wipe my own bleeding nose on my sleeve.

"He's a dick and a rapist, so why wouldn't I?"

"Oh, I don't know, maybe because I've spent the whole year torturing you, turning everyone against you, helping my brother and his friends turn your whole life to shit? Give me a good reason why."

This girl is *unbelievable*. I just saved her, and she's standing there, demanding answers from me!

"The appropriate thing to say is thank you," I hiss at her instead.

I turn to walk away, and she grabs my arm. Her hand is shaking so badly I can feel the tremble up my arm. We stare at each other in silence for a minute. I can't tell what she's thinking, she's as unreadable as ever, even with the shakes. Rory starts to groan on the floor and Avery flinches, then she stomps on his phone one last time and bends over to grab the chip out of it.

"I have a guy that can get the photos out. I don't need anyone getting their hands on them; I have enough problems in my life as it is," she explains as she tucks it into her bra.

She tugs me out of the room by my elbow, and we set a brisk pace back to the dorms. I wince as my leg begins to protest the speed we're going, but I don't slow down. When we get back, she stands and waits for me to unlock the door to my room and follows me in.

I have never been ashamed of how little I have until suddenly there's *this* girl, who has the whole world at her feet, looking around curiously. Her room is a palace in comparison. My cheeks flush, and I shake myself. What does it matter what she thinks? Three more years until I am free from all this shit. Avery turns, and I know the look on her face. It was the exact one she always used to clean up after her family's exploits.

"I don't know what agreement you and Harley came to, but I will pay you to keep this quiet," she starts, and I snort at her. She raises a perfect eyebrow at me. "I know you need the money. Name a price and I'll pay it."

"Fuck your money. Just because I have nothing, doesn't mean I need to be paid for being a decent fucking person. That's what's wrong with you lot. You're all so busy stabbing each other in the back that you've forgotten how to be human." I start to rummage around under my bed until I find my first-aid kit. After the year I've had, it's in dire need of a top-up, but I crack two of the instant ice packs and wait until they're cold. Avery takes one gingerly, like she's never seen one, and then copies my movements to press it against her head. I'm starting to worry she has a concussion.

"Well, what do you want, then? Everyone wants something. Name your price."

"I don't want anything! You being nice to me just because I helped you means nothing to me!"

She looks at me like I've grown another head. I sigh and slump back onto my bed, glancing down at myself to take stock of the damage. My stockings have holes in them now, and I wince because they're my last pair. I'll have to get through the rest of the week with them and just deal with the taunts from the other students. There's blood on my white shirt, but I think I can get that out. I have a fair bit of practice with blood removal.

My arms and legs are starting to ache; I can feel the pins holding my leg together and the bone throbs around them. I realize how regularly I'm having to fight people and put my body on the line here. So much for this school being a better place.

Avery sighs and turns to the door to let herself out, but she hovers for a minute in the doorway. Her eyes are dry, but her mouth is turned down in a little miserable frown.

"If you're willing to do that for your enemy, then what you do for your friends must be really special."

It's… a genuinely nice thing to say, and my eyes well up despite it. I'm struck again by how much I wish I had what she has. I wish I had people who love me and watch out for me. I wish I had real friends. I wish my life wasn't empty.

"I wouldn't know, I've never really had any."

She gives a sharp nod and closes the door tightly after herself. I get up and lock it, and then I crawl under my covers and try to ignore the pain I'm in.

When I open the door the next morning, there is a brand-new uniform hanging from my door handle, stockings and all.

It fits me perfectly.

I'm not so naive to think that the universe will suddenly stop shitting on me just because of my good deed.

I make it to the chapel for the full school presentation of awards, and I find that seating is assigned. I'm between Avery and Harley, and that is when I decided that karma cannot be a real thing, because how did I deserve that torture? Avery had probably recovered well enough from the assault and would have something to say about my uniform. Would Harley tease me for taking it? Or will he just continue to ignore me for dragging him into my twisted, bullshit world? I'm still walking with a limp after using my bad leg to kick Rory.

Ugh. Rich dicks.

I take my seat, and Avery isn't there. I should feel relieved, but my stomach drops like a stone. Is she okay? What if she did have a concussion? Fuck, I should have walked her to the nurse.

After a minute of stewing by myself, Harley takes his seat and he looks at my bandage with calculating eyes. "Who the fuck beat you up this time?" he says, frustrated and angry, which throws me. He must have not heard from Avery yet. I can't tell him, not with this many students around us. Even if we were alone, I didn't think I could tell him. Is there a girl code about this kind of thing? Did it count if the girl loathed your very existence?

Fuck.

I don't know.

"Doesn't matter. I'll survive," I reply. His eyebrows tug into a little frown, but then the lights are dimming, and the stage is lighting up. I think that will be the end of it, but he slumps down in his chair until he can whisper in my ear. "It does fucking matter. I've made it clear no one's allowed to touch you, and I'm *yours* now, aren't I?"

He says it sarcastically, and I flush. There it is; the resentment for what I did to protect him. I should feel angry at him for blaming me, but mostly I just feel guilty and miserable. Okay, I'm a little angry that he didn't care about being 'mine' when I confronted him about Ash getting me thrown out of school. Fuck, I need some time to clear my head. I need a plan for next year.

I swallow and whisper back, "That just means no one outside these walls can touch you. You don't owe me anything."

He scoffs at me. "Thank God, because I sure as hell can't afford the diamonds your favors cost."

His leg is pressed against mine, so I feel it when his phone buzzes. He ignores it until it stops. Then it buzzes again. And again. And again.

He curses under his breath and discreetly slides the phone out of his pocket. I look away because I have no interest in snooping. Okay, I do, but I'm also afraid it'll be a girl texting him and I don't need any more pain from this guy right now. He nudges me gently and turns the screen so I can read it.

Courtyard after the assembly. Bring the Mounty.

It's from Ash.

I suck in a breath. This is it; he's going to make his move and get me kicked out. He's probably already done it, but Mr. Trevelen wouldn't pause an assembly just to kick me out. I'm going to walk out there and face the humiliation of my expulsion.

I screw my eyes shut and try to fight the panic that's squeezing my chest so hard, I think my heart might explode. I start to count in French, and I miss every word Mr. Trevelen says in his speech. I clap robotically when everyone around me does, and then when Harley stands, he looks down at me with cold eyes.

I have no choice but to follow him out to face Ash.

Chapter Twenty-Nine

Ash is furious.

He's standing with Blaise in the middle of the courtyard, surrounded by groups of students who are all eyeing him nervously. Harley frowns when he sees him and then moves quickly to stand with him, so I'm faced with all three of them at once. I stare at Ash, refusing to even glance at the other two, and he looks at me like I'm worse than nothing.

"How the fuck did a little Mounty manage to hack my accounts and clear all of the video files? I'll have your fucking head for this. There's no way you can talk your way out of this with the principal," he snarls at me.

I have no clue what he is talking about. He's right, it is outside of my abilities, and I didn't do it. I squint up at him, and I must look like the dense Mounty they all think I am before it hits me.

Avery.

She wouldn't even need to hack in. She had all his account details and passwords. It was the only way his data could have been wiped so thoroughly. It was a steep price she was paying for my help, and if Ash found out, he would be crushed by her betrayal.

I *could* just tell him. I could tell him every intimate detail of his sister's assault; just how close she had come to being raped. But when I open my mouth nothing comes out.

After years in the foster care system I have seen so many kids who had been molested, and it was truly horrifying. How far away from my humanity would I fall if I use this against Avery? They may all be monsters, and I know I am too, but I don't want to be. Someday I will be a fully-fledged adult out in the world, and I refuse to let this school turn me the way it has every other student.

"Get fucked, Beaumont."

Silence. The entire area holds its breath.

Ash opens his mouth to rip me to shreds, but then it snaps shut. His face shutters closed, the anger dissolving. His eyes dart to my left and narrow, but not in the same vicious way he'd been directing it at me.

Blaise crosses his arms over his broad chest, and Harley straightens. I realize Avery must have arrived, because no one else gets the boys' attention so completely.

She steps up beside me, and her fingers wrap around my wrist gently, using her body as a shield so no one else can see. Her hand is cold and clammy, but her voice is firm.

"Lips didn't clear your accounts. I did."

Gasps ring out across the courtyard. I look around and see we have the attention of the entire class. The gaggle of girls that usually follow Avery around are darting quick glances between the twins, unwilling to get on Ash's bad side, and I want to snap at them. Gutless. I know in my heart she's right, none of them would have rushed in to help her. They would have let Rory rape her and then gossiped about it later.

"Avery, what—" Ash starts forward, his eyes haunted, and I glance over to see the white bandages over his sister's face. They look professionally applied, nothing like the amateur job I did with my scraps. Ash doesn't care about the accounts at all now that he's faced with his injured twin. It would be totally sweet, if he hadn't just been on the edge of ending my school career and my opportunity at a decent life.

"You would know if you had answered your phone, but you didn't, so now you can deal with the consequences. Lips, is mine."

Blaise's eyes dart between us, and my face begins to flush. Someday I will be able to handle his eyes on me, but clearly today is not that day.

"What the actual fuck?!" Harley sputters out, and I try not to laugh at the sound. I had never heard any of them sound unsure, and yet all three of the boys were gaping at us both.

"Okay, I get it. I should have answered. You don't need to take on trash just to get back at me, Floss," Ash says gently, aiming to placate her. His hands are outstretched toward her, like he wants to pull her in to him and hold her in the safety of his arms. My angry shield cracks a little at the sight.

Avery's eyes narrow when he uses her nickname, and instead of answering, she slips her arm fully into mine where everyone can see. I try not to flinch, because if I push her away now, it will only make things worse for me. She doesn't get the chance to destroy him, though, as the far door leading into the courtyard opens and Rory walks out.

Ash does a double take when he spots the scratches down his cheeks and the black eye. He looks back, and I watch as he takes inventory of all the marks on Avery, and then, as if an afterthought, the ones on me. I watch as everything clicks into place in his head. It's clear to everyone what has happened. Harley's face turns thunderous. Blaise's cool and unaffected mask finally drops, and his jaw clenches.

I watch as Ash's entire body begins to shake, the need to *break* and *smash* and *destroy* whoever has touched his sister so strong that the other students begin to back away slowly, and Blaise steps up to join him, his eyes dark swirling pits. Harley calls out to Rory, and when he turns fearful eyes on them, he signs his own death warrant. The guilt is written on every fiber of his being.

"Where did you get those from, dickhead?" Harley says, gesturing at the scratches. He has always hated Rory, but now his voice is dark and taunting. There is blood in the water and sharks are beginning to circle.

"We had a misunderstanding. It's not a big deal." Rory sounds arrogant, even with the quaking look on his face, and it makes me see red.

"I hope your broken ribs puncture your lungs and you drown in your own blood," I hiss at him. I would say more, but Avery starts tugging me away. She doesn't want to watch her brother mete out his physical punishments and I'm honestly not sure if

Rory will make it out alive.

"I told you, I don't want your protection," I murmur. I can't be too loud about it in case any of the students hear and it gets back to Ash.

"This isn't payment, it's a white flag. And an olive branch. I want to be your friend."

I stop dead in my tracks. I can hear screaming and yelling starting in the chapel, and I flinch. Memories of my time in the Game surface, and I shove them away. I don't have time to deal with my own issues right now.

"What?"

"I don't have friends either. I want one, and I want one as fierce as you."

"You can't just—Blaise is your friend."

She shakes her head dismissively, and I roll my eyes at her. Had she not just seen their reactions to her injuries? I'd kill to have them defend me like that, to have my back and expect nothing but friendship in return.

"No, he's Ash's friend, and he both loves and respects me well enough, but he will always defer back to him. I want a real friend that's mine."

"You can't just claim me. I'm not property," I sputter, and my voice is louder than I intend on being. I glance around, but the halls have deserted. Everyone wants to watch Rory die. I kind of do, too. Mostly because there's something about watching justice being served that makes my dark heart sing. Plus, the boys were hot at the best of times. Watching their fists fly and beat Rory bloody? Um, yes, please. I just need a pair of earplugs to drown out the yelling, and I'm good to watch the whole damn thing.

Avery huffs and pulls me into the study den. There's a group of students packing up, and at her sharp look, they hightail it out of there.

"I know you don't trust me, and I deserve that. I'm going to give you something as insurance, so we know we're both in this for the right reasons. That is, if you want a friend?"

I do. Desperately really, but how can I trust this girl that looks like an angel but is really a crossroads demon, bargaining and making deals with mere mortals for their souls? She can be just as twisted as Joey; they are siblings, after all. I know in my heart she isn't a sociopath like him, but she could be just as ruthless. *She could survive the Wolf,* my mind whispers unbidden. She's probably the only girl I'd ever met who could.

"Why did Joey call a ceasefire?" she asks with a raised brow. It's a test, one last hurdle to leap before we can be friends. Could I do it? Could I take the leap?

"We have a… mutual acquaintance. Joey thought this person was under his thumb, but he was wrong. He was told that under no uncertain circumstances could he harm me again."

Avery leans forward and whispers in my ear, "The Jackal?" and I nod. A smile flits at the corners of her mouth.

She hands me an envelope. I open it and, after leafing through the papers for a second, I scrunch it up hurriedly. I'm holding the missing piece of the puzzle. I'm holding the records of the Beaumonts' mother's death. Alice Beaumont, nee Arbour, was murdered.

"Why the hell—"

"That's your insurance. It would destroy both me and my brother if that got out. I've spent years keeping that out of people's hands. Everything I do is to keep Ash and the boys safe. Everything I did to you was to keep us safe." She doesn't look sorry at all, like my year of torture was reasonable. I don't know what to do with that, or with the envelope in my hand.

"I want a friend I can trust to have my back completely, and no girl has ever looked at me as anything other than competition or a way to get in with my brothers. You took everything I threw at you, and you're still here. Unbroken. Are you in, or not?"

God help me, but I was so in. My hands begin to shake.

"I don't want you to speak to them for me. The boys."

"Well, I don't want to speak to them at all, so you're safe there. I promise I won't tell them to be nice, but if we're friends, then I'm on your side from here out."

I bite my lip. I want this so bad, and the envelope in my hand makes me believe this is legit. I might regret it later, but I nod.

"Friends it is, then."

"*Best* friends. Now, how do you feel about helping me destroy Rory's entire existence for what he did to me? I'd love your input."

I smile and tuck the papers into my satchel. I can hear the sounds of teachers breaking up the beating, and Avery's eyes have that wicked glint in them. A shot of excitement shoots through my blood. This could be fun.

"I have a few ideas, actually."

"Let's just agree that from here on out, we only ever tell each other the truth. If we can't discuss something, then we come out and say so."

I'm sitting in Avery's room and watching while she packs. It took me three minutes to pack my entire room up, and Avery had moaned about how jealous she was I was finished. I was kind enough to point out that, she actually has the opportunity to own things, which is something I'm more than jealous of. It's utterly ridiculous how quickly we've fallen into a relaxed hangout.

There are boxes everywhere, suitcases full of clothes, stacks of boxed-up shoes that are taller than we are, and still Avery is shoving random items into bubble wrap. I expected her to pay someone else to do this.

"I guess I can handle that," I say, shoving a fistful of popcorn into my mouth and flicking through her record collection. It's mostly classical music and scores from ballet recitals, but she also has every single Vanth Falling record, first editions and signed, and I'm trying not to tuck them under my arm and make a run for it. I put one on, and she cackles at me from the bathroom where she's trying to pack the equivalent of an entire Sephora store's worth of makeup and hair care products. Ash wasn't wrong; she has a lot of stuff.

Avery arches an eyebrow at me and grins, "I don't expect you to tell me all of your secrets tonight. I was thinking while we're on break, we can text each other one secret a day. When school starts again in the fall, we can do the same each morning. It'll be a fun little bonding experience."

I shrug in return as I tap my fingers along with the song. Some things can't be sent digitally; texts and emails can be hacked. I'm sure I don't have to explain this to her, and I guess it's a way to ease into things. "I'm not sure you'll ever know it all. There's stuff I've done… I'm a dangerous person to be around. You need to know that from the get-go, so you can tap out now if you need to."

She flops back on her bed dramatically. Her face is no longer the blank mask I've seen every day; it's open, and a little vulnerable. "My cousin is a mobster's son. My brother is a sociopathic murderer. My father is… my father is true evil. Whatever you have following you, we can sort out together, the same way I've worked at sorting everything out for Harley. I'm all in, Lips."

I sigh and crawl up to sit on the bed beside her. Maybe we will get there. Maybe I'll offer her the same protection as I've given Harley. Ugh, thinking about him makes my chest ache and leaves me with too many questions. Seeing as this is my first opportunity to get some answers, I ask her, "Where does Harley go during the summer break?"

It's Avery's turn to sigh. "He goes back to his grandfather's place for two weeks each year. It's part of a seedy deal the old crook cut with a dirty judge. Then he either stays with Blaise, touring or whatever, or I get him a hotel. He can't come to our house; my father would never allow it."

"Wouldn't he know you're helping him, though? Where else do you get your money?"

She laughs and pulls out a black nail polish from the box she was just packing, tugging my hand until I let her paint my nails.

"My mother and Harley's mom were twins; did you know that? Twins run pretty strongly in our family. They were heiresses themselves. If you trace our family line back far enough, you hit Russian royalty. My grandparents disowned Aunt Iris when she ran off with Éibhear O'Cronin; they were horrified their blue-blooded daughter had been seduced by the handsome degenerate." She fluttered her eyes and pretended to faint, and I giggle for probably the first time in my life. "So my mother was the sole heir. Now my father, the asshole, had a prenup to say that all finances were to stay separate, because her hundreds of millions were nothing compared to his billions. When my mother died, her will said the money was to be split and shared three ways."

"So you and your brothers each have a share of the millions and no parental supervision on how you use it? Fuck, you are the luckiest kid in this school."

She grins and tips her head back. "My mother left her money to Ash, me… and Harley."

My jaw drops.

Avery grins and nods. "Best day of my life was seeing that murderer's face when he realized he was getting nothing."

"So then why doesn't Harley have the money?"

"His grandfather stole it. Sort of. His grandfather had custody of Harley when my mother died, so he had it put in trusts and bonds and offshore accounts, then told Harley he could have it the moment he swore in. He's using the money as leverage to get Harley to join the family business."

Liam O'Cronin is not the brightest man.

One of the very first lessons you're taught as a sponsored candidate for the Twelve is that loyalty can only be given freely. Yes, you can hire someone, but there's always the risk someone will offer them more money. You can torture and break someone, bend them to only serve you, but there are limits to what a broken person can do. Blackmailing Harley into the family would only succeed in letting a bomb tick in your organization.

Fucking dumb.

"Harley can't go to his grandfather's house anymore."

Avery looks up from where she's blowing on my nails to dry them. "Oh? Is this part of your little agreement? His grandfather will kill him if he doesn't."

I don't want to talk about the mess I've made to protect Harley. I need some time and space to figure it out before I discuss it with her. Now that I know a little more about the situation, I can make a plan. So, instead I say, "He can't kill him. I've tied the old fuck's hands for the moment. Now that I have a little more information, I'll see what I can do about getting Harley out of there permanently."

Avery swallows, and her eyes grow glassy. "I started to come around to the idea of being friends when you started messing with Joey. No one, has even been brave enough to take him on. When Harley showed up with his mom's necklace and told me we were done messing with you, I knew you would fit in with us."

"I think Ash would disagree with you strongly there," I mumble. I'm still smarting over his dismissal of me, and how easily he believed I was sleeping with Joey.

"Ash will get over his issues. He's angry with himself more than anything. He thinks he's responsible for taking care of me, and he's pissed that he failed."

I cock my head at her. "Are you pissed?"

She shakes her head with a little frown. "I'm only upset that he doesn't trust my judgment of you. He's hell-bent on you being in league with Joey, and it's clouding his decisions."

I don't think he's upset. I think he's decided I'm evil, and I'm going to spend the rest of my time at Hannaford fielding both of Avery's brothers and their desires to get rid of me. At least Ash doesn't want to kill me. I groan, and Avery smiles ruefully.

I shake my head to clear it. "Back to Harley, I'll pay for a hotel for him for the entire summer break. He's my responsibility."

She raises her eyebrows at me with the shadow of a smile on her face. "The bill for the hotel he stays at comes in at seventy thousand dollars if he stays for the entire break. Then I give him a credit card with a fifty-thousand-dollar limit, and he uses that to cover food and boy stuff. He usually uses about ten grand of it. Do you have a spare eighty grand lying around to fund his summer holiday?"

"Fucking rich people. Who spends *seventy thousand dollars* on a hotel?!" I sputter.

Avery throws herself back on the bed and laughs so hard, tears stream down her face. I'm laughing too, but it's more of an angry sound. "I'd pay ten times that if he'd let me pick where he stays. The hotel is on the coast, right on a cliff, so he can be moody and watch the waves and mope. That's all these boys are good for, really."

I groan and grab my phone. This is my mess; I need to be the one to clean it up. "Does he have a bank account? Give me the details, and I'll transfer the cash across. I'll do eighty-five so he has a buffer. Fucking boys."

Avery's head snaps around so she's scowling at me. "You have money? You have enough money to pay for that?"

I let a smug little grin creep onto my face. "I do. I'm going to be working over summer break, so I'll just take an extra job to cover his break."

"Take an extra—*what the hell is happening right now?*"

Chapter Thirty

I call a taxi to pick me up from Hannaford by 8 a.m. the next morning.

I'm the only student who doesn't have a car of their own or parents who send a chauffeur to collect them, but it's not at all surprising to me. What is surprising is that Avery helps to carry my pathetically small amount of belongings down to the school entrance. I carry the bag with the safe tucked in it.

We had spent two hours in her room last night getting to know each other. The switch from bully to best friend had flipped so suddenly and completely that I felt like I had whiplash. She is actually really funny, and smart, too. Before I went to my own room for bed, she had put her number in my phone and made sure I could text her.

Now, standing together by the gate, we laugh about the shocked looks from the other students. "They should know by now that I do what I say I will. You should find next year much easier to tolerate."

I laugh, and she grins at me.

"Avery." Ash steps up beside us, and I flinch. I can't hear his voice without thinking of how he wanted to destroy my life. Avery stiffens, and then turns to him with sharp eyes.

"Please stop ignoring me. Whatever happened, I can help you fix it."

She laughs, and it sounds like the one she had always used with me; cruel and lacking in humor. "Lips fixed it and wanted nothing in return, so don't concern yourself."

"Floss—"

"Don't you *dare*."

She had told me last night about how much she loved Ash and how she had spent years fixing his entire life. She wouldn't be angry at him forever, but it would be a while before she got over him ignoring her call.

"I beat him for you. I'll fucking kill him, if that's what it takes to get you to stop looking at me like that."

My taxi rolls in. She shakes her head at Ash and walks up to drop my bags in the trunk. I move to follow her, and his hand shoots out to grab me.

"Whatever you've done to get her on your side, I will fucking end you for it. You think my brother is bad? You have no idea what I will do to you next year."

"Why don't you want her to have friends?"

The glare he leveled at me was so dark, a shiver ran up my spine.

"She can have friends, just not Mounty trash," he sneers at me, his eyes icy blue.

And in that moment, I don't care if I am signing up for another year of hell. I give him my own dark glare.

"Fuck you." I pull my arm out of his grip, and I give Avery a quick hug before I drop into the taxi. Ash glares at me as Avery waves cheerfully, and then the taxi takes off down the driveway and out of the huge, ornate school gates. My grin is plastered to my face. I survived Hannaford, and I made a friend.

The ride back to Mounts Bay is over an hour, and I enjoy watching the scenery as it changes from the lush, sprawling, reticulated green to the urban coastal wasteland. It feels like coming home. I'm going back to where I belong, and where I'm running from, even if I do feel nostalgic looking at it all.

I'm lost in thought when my phone buzzes in my pocket.

Club party next week. Be there.

I roll my eyes, as the taxi stops outside the dingy apartment I rented for summer break. It's an absolute hole, but it was cheap and wouldn't be too much of a drain on my dwindling stash of cash. Originally, I'd planned to rent a tiny townhouse in a gated community that cost four times what this place does, but now that I have a pampered rich guy I have to fund, I am on a budget. I didn't tell Avery, but part of why I have to pay for Harley is to make my protection legitimate. If Matteo starts to look into his life and his financials, and he sees Harley being supported by someone else, he will kill him and tell me he was a snitch. I am just going to have to go to the Club party next week, like Matteo wants me to, and pick up some extra jobs.

My phone pings again. I smile down at Avery's text.

Ash is a nightmare, Harley is pouting, and Blaise is pleading with me to seek therapy. I'm going to enjoy taking these boys down a notch or two. I'll text you tomorrow x

I went against my better judgment to trust this girl, but I do not regret it.

And I can't wait for school to start back.

Just Drop Out

Exclusive Excerpt

ASH

"I've signed you up for tutoring."

I don't look up from my plate. "And why would you do that?"

Avery fusses with her plate, just little things that no one else would notice but I know she's feeling out of control, that something has happened.

"Tell me what it is and I'll fix it."

She sighs. "The Mounty's background check came up with nothing so I don't have anything to use against her. I went through the scholarship records and every last student has dropped out for either failing to keep up with the curriculum, being caught with drugs, or lewd behavior."

I put my fork down and raise an eyebrow at her until she huffs. "She's smarter than *Harley*. She's not going to be left behind and she's practically a monk. She barely leaves her room."

I smirk at her. "You want me to fuck the Mounty to get her out? I distinctly remember you telling me to take up celibacy this year to lighten your workload."

The smile she gives me is sweet and full of sharp teeth. "I'm not asking you to have sex with trash, I'm asking you to get more information from her, like who she is having sex with. No Mounty goes without for this long and I need some evidence. She's caught Joey's eye, Ash. If he gets involved... no, we need her out. Get some dirt on her *without* getting your dick out. Please."

The please is through gritted teeth and I think about saying no, I have no interest in spending time with some slut from the slums, but the cleanup if Joey does take an interest and kills her... I don't want that for Avery this year. My knuckles are still a mess from beating one of his pathetic little flunkies last night at fight club and I'm surprised Avery hasn't bitched me out for it yet.

Maybe the gossiping bitches here have kept their mouths shut for once.

"Fine. I'll go pretend I'm dense and get her out for you."

My phone pings and I roll my eyes at Annabelle's name. She's getting fucking desperate and I have no interest in her brand of easy today.

"Stop being distracted by that *slut*. Your tutoring is during your study period. So… it starts in ten minutes. You can skip the first one if-"

"Why would I skip it? This is nothing, Floss. Give me a week, maybe two, and she'll be out."

I arrive at the library before the Mounty and sit at the table assigned. Pretending to need help is less than ideal but better me than Morrison.

He'd probably fall in love with her.

He has terrible taste, always wanting things he can't have, and I'm not sure there's much that would piss his father off more than him bringing home some gold-digging Mounty.

I know she's arrived without looking up because the whispers precede her. The little stories and gossip that must be chipping away at her self-esteem and will to live, I'm oddly impressed she lasted the week.

"She's fucking Trevelen, that's how she got in."

"He hand picked her. She must really know how to suck dick."

"They teach a class on it at Mounts Bay High, I heard she was the top of the class."

"Fuck maybe I should try her out then, just to say I know what an expert feels like."

"The whore would love it and beg for more."

Her steps don't falter. She has more backbone than half the girls here, but that doesn't mean she should stay. Getting her out is a kindness really.

I glance up and find her staring at me, the big blue eyes of hers striking. That pisses me off.

"Oh, goody, I get to spend three hours a week with trash."

After ignoring far worse insults, she looks at me like she's taken a hit. *Interesting.*

"If you want the help with your assignments, then yeah, you're stuck with the trash." She says through her gritted teeth.

I grin. This will be far more fun than I originally thought. She pulls out her books and pens, all of them brand new but already they look worn, like she's spent months using them and obsessing over her lessons. Her workbook is entirely filled in, it's not even due until after winter break. I know this because Harley has been a fucking nightmare over all of the classes he's been taking.

I decide to see just how far I can push the Mounty, to see just how much my words hurt her.

She doesn't disappoint.

"Can you just shut the fuck up and tell me what you need help with?" She hisses, and when I smirk back at her she gives me a look that promises she'd slit my throat if given the chance. It's kind of cute on such a petite little thing like her. There's no way she could ever get that close to me but choose not to say that to her, instead I slide my homework over to her and get to work.

She sees through me instantly. Too quickly for my liking.

"Can you at least do a better job of pretending to try? If you're not going to take this seriously, I'll use the time to study instead."

I stare her down, relishing in her obvious discomfort as she takes me in. I almost think I've broken her, forced her into ducking her head and giving in like every other girl here, but then she snaps back at me.

Interesting.

By the time Avery comes to find me and bitch me out, I'm ready to put on a show for the gossiping little bitches all watching us fight like we're the best damn thing they've ever seen. I ignore them, choosing not to put them in their place because it will only help the Mounty and I'm discovering I like her on edge.

I enjoy the fire in her, all the more fun to destroy.

It must show on my face, because when I escort Avery out of the library she gives me her sternest, most scathing look.

"If you fuck the Mounty I will *murder* you in your sleep, Ash." She hisses, and I grin.

Maybe I will.

But I'll see how far I can push her first.

Make Your Move

Hannaford Prep Year Two

Prologue

ALEXANDER

My arm is sore.

My fingers have pins and needles shooting down them and my shoulder aches where the sling digs into my skin. Mommy is packing a bag in my room and I don't know where we're going. She's crying. She does that a lot but this time her face isn't sad, she looks angry even with tears streaming down her face. My sister is holding a little bag under her arm and she's already wearing a coat and polished shoes. Her eyes are wide but she isn't crying.

We don't cry anymore.

"Listen, Ash, we need to go. Leon is getting the car and bringing it around. Is there anything you need me to pack? I have your blanket," Mommy says and she's whispering like it's a secret. It doesn't make any sense to me but I shake my head anyway. She never calls me Ash while we're in the manor. Father hates it, the last time he heard her call me Ash he slapped her. I'm scared he's heard her say it now and he's going to hit her again. My good hand shakes.

"We've got to leave now. Ash, Floss hold Mommy's hands."

Mommy tugs us both out of my room and down the hall. When we get to the stairs she looks around and then quietly opens the hidden door behind the big ugly painting. I bite my lip and look at Floss. She's so white that she looks sick. Her eyes are round and frightened.

We are *never* allowed to use the servants' stairs.

Once the door is firmly but quietly shut behind us Mommy pulls us both down the stairs, much faster than we were moving before. She's sobbing, even her lips clamped shut can't hold them in.

I'm scared. Mommy doesn't cry like that, even when Father hits her or calls her terrible things, she never ever makes noises like that.

We make it to the kitchen. I've never stepped foot in the kitchen before, our meals are all served to us at the table in the formal dining room. I don't even know where in the manor the kitchen is. Mommy pulls us through the room, the staff all avert their eyes and ignore us, and we get to the side door when I hear his voice.

"Where are you going, Mommy?"

I hear those words over and over again, long after my mother has been buried.

Chapter One

Joey is missing.

The air around me throbs as I'm jostled by the mass of bodies writhing to the shitty electronica music. I stare down at my phone for a second and then I look over to the bar where Joseph Beaumont Jr. is standing, doing lines of cocaine off of the dirty barrels that are a makeshift bar. He's here alone. He paid a lower level Club member a whole wad of hundred dollar bills to get in and now he's in my fucking town, getting high and groping unimpressed Mounty girls. Strobe lights dance along the warehouse walls and there must be five hundred people dancing and sweating and getting high in here right now.

It's the last day of summer break. Well, it's 3am so in four short hours I'm getting into an Uber and heading back to Hannaford. I'm just waiting on the Vulture to arrive to make the pickup of the package I've got for him and then I'm getting out of here. I picked up eight jobs over the summer break and now I'm flush with cash. Okay, not flush but I've got Harley's tuition paid through to graduation and most of his housing costs covered. Better yet, I have a plan to get him out of my checkbook and paying for his own shit.

I'm so tired and ready for the break to be over. Too tired to be dealing with Joey's bullshit. I text Avery the address of the warehouse the party is being held.

He's here. I've got eyes on him. Are you close by?

I flag down two of the Jackal's bigger henchmen and push through the crowd towards the bar. Joey doesn't notice me. He's too far gone to notice anything other than his high. I point him out and then watch as one of them knock him out with a sharp punch to the face. No one around him flinches. Club parties always have someone disappearing with no witnesses. So many eyes refusing to see a damn thing.

Ten minutes ETA. Blaise is driving and the other two are pissed about the location.

I roll my eyes as I move towards the exit. Just what I need, the guys giving me shit even though I'm helping them out. I nod at the doorman and he lets me through, the cold slap of the night air harsh against all of the skin I'm showing. I had to blend into the crowd to get the information the Vulture needed which means I am basically naked. I have a matching two piece set on, shorts that barely cover my ass and a strappy bralette. The fabric it's made out of is black with metallic thread running through it and I shimmer as I move. I had found a new pair of black calf-length Doc's at the thrift store last week that completes the look. With glitter across both cheeks and a high ponytail I am just another party girl here to lose control. It's all so exhausting. I check my phone, again, to see where the hell the Vulture is. Nothing. I let out a frustrated sigh and look out into the darkness of the early morning.

The docks look abandoned.

No one is allowed to leave the party before dawn so the only people outside of the warehouse are the Jackal's men. I sidle up to Luca and he grins at me, gesturing at the bags at his feet. My bags. "Kept them safe, princess. Are you taking out the trash for the Jackal before you go?"

I glance back at Joey's unconscious form slung over the other guy's shoulder. What a funny choice of words Luca had chosen. Joey would be pissed to hear my Hannaford nickname being thrown at him. "I called in for a collection of this one. Can you let DeMarco know to expect a car?"

Luca nods and lifts his radio to his face. He pauses as my phone rings.

"We're here but the guy at the gate won't let us through." Avery sounds pissed and I smile.

"Give him the phone."

Luca grins at me and tucks the radio back onto his belt. I hear Avery argue with DeMarco and then his asshole voice barks down the phone at me, "Listen here, kid, we don't let extra in after the open hour. Now you need to tell these little rich fucks to get on out of here-"

"DeMarco." I can actually hear the snap of his teeth slamming shut at the sound of my voice. I'm not ashamed to say I enjoy the hell out of the power I have in Mounts Bay. "That car is here for me. Let them through and apologize to the little rich fucks."

"Sorry. I didn't know they were with you. If they had've just said I would've-" I hang up on his rambling and then I flick a text to the Vulture again.

You're late. I have places I need to be.

"Who are these friends of yours?" Luca nudges me with his elbow. I tense a little. I know he's asking as a friend, or as close as a friend as I can have under the Jackal's watchful eye, but I'm hesitant to say much. I don't need to create any issues for myself.

"Kids from school. Too much money and far too much ego. Makes it fun to play with them." I wiggle my eyebrows at him and he shoots me another grin as the car rolls up to a stop before us.

They pull up in a Maserati.

No wonder DeMarco was such a dick to them. They couldn't look more out of place down here if they tried. I wave an arm at the guy holding Joey and he walks him over to the car. Harley jumps out and helps shove his cousin in. I saunter over as Avery puts her window down and I lean in to talk to her.

"Having fun?" she smirks at me, her eyes trailing over my outfit. She's wearing a silk robe over a delicate lacy nightgown, well put together even in her pajamas. Yep, still jealous.

"Don't get me started, I need a shower and twelve hours of sleep. Try not to lose him again, I'm heading out soon."

Blaise is watching the group of the Jackal's men like he thinks they're going to attack his car. Ash is struggling in the back trying to get Joey's seatbelt on and Harley is still standing with the car door open. I look up and meet his eyes. He looks angry, clearly he's not a fan of being dragged out of bed for a pick up.

"What the hell are you doing here?" he hisses at me and I narrow my eyes. He's pissy at *me*!

"Watch your fucking tone, we are not at school." His head snaps back at my warning. He glances over his shoulder and sure enough, the entire group of men are watching him. They all know he's the guy I've recruited and they're sizing him up. I don't think they've heard what he said to me, thank God, and Harley straightens up. He shuts the car door and walks around to me. Avery swears under her breath but I keep my eyes on Harley. If he isn't smart about this I'm going to have to knock him out before the Jackal catches wind of what's happening on his turf.

"What are you doing here? Dressed like *that?*" he whispers and I'm glad we have an audience. I might have kicked him in the balls if there weren't one. He thinks I'm selling myself. I guess I am, but he thinks I'm selling my *body* when I'm really just selling my skills.

Does anyone ever think about anything other than sex?

"Do not suggest that I'm a prostitute. I'm here for a job and as soon as I get paid I'm leaving." Harley nods reluctantly and his eyes never leave the group of guys behind us. I wait for a minute but he doesn't move or speak. I'm about to snap when the lights of another car hit us and Harley is trying to shove me behind him. I jab him in the kidney with a closed fist, enjoying the little grunt I get out of him.

"That would be my payment. You guys need to leave." Avery is watching the car with anxious eyes and I rub her shoulder. She has no idea just how bad the guy in there really is.

"We're not leaving without you," Harley says and he crosses his arms. I can't argue with him, I don't have time as the car parks and three guys dressed like sleazy bodyguards get out, guns in clear view at their hips. They look around the empty car park and then assess us all one by one. I'm not at all happy with the way they look at Avery and I step in front of her again. After a minute of this scrutiny the Vulture steps out of the car.

The very sight of him turns my stomach.

He grins at me and I fight to keep my lips from curling up in disgust at him. He's wearing a cheap suit and the little hair he has left is slicked back into a shiny cap. I can see the bulge of his gun at his hip and, unfortunately, I can also see the bulge of his erection. I've never been in his presence without him being hard.

"Hello, puss."

The Vulture's tone of voice is so utterly sleazy and disgusting. I feel bile creep up the back of my throat. I hate that he calls me that. He's nicknamed me after the body part he loves to sell and the only thing of worth he ever sees in a woman. It's vile. Harley tenses and I just know he's spotted the tent that's happening in the putrid man's pants. I hear an argument start up in the car and I glance down to see Blaise has his seatbelt off and a hand on his door handle. Avery is chewing him out and Ash is fighting to keep Joey's airways open. He's so high he's slumping and choking on his own tongue. Idiot.

"Wire my money through and I'll give you the package."

The Vulture smiles at me and waves a hand. One of his men pops the trunk of the car and lugs two bags out. Motherfuckers. He's paying me in cash.

"Seriously? I told you I only deal in transfers," I snap at him and Harley is doing his best not to gape. I'm not sure how much experience he has around large quantities of cash but the twitching of his jaw tells me he's doing some quick math. There's a hundred grand in those bags.

It's going to be a nightmare to launder.

"Sorry, puss. I didn't get the chance to pop this into the bank before they closed."

You know how it is. How 'bout you walk that sweet ass of yours over here and get your money?"

"Like fuck," Harley spits at him and the Vulture looks at him for the first time. His eyes take in the tattoo, the piercing eyes, the build, and I know he's working out how much he could make from selling Harley at one of his hellish auctions. The quirk of his lips tells me the fee would be *astronomical*.

"How about I double the payment and you give me him, puss?" I roll my eyes at him.

"How about you get one of your little friends to bring me my money and I'll hand him the package so we can all get out of here, hmm?"

The Vulture laughs and waves his guys forward. The guy hands Harley the bags and I can smell the body odor wafting from him. Harley sneers at him and I shove the USB into his hands to get him away from us.

"Pleasure doing business with you, puss."

I stare him down until he grins and leaves. We don't move until the car is out of the parking lot completely. I turn and hold my hand out for my giant bags of cash but Harley turns on his heel and marches to the trunk. He taps it gently and Blaise pops it open for him to shove them inside.

"What are you doing?"

He straightens and gives me a fiery look back. "I told you. I'm not leaving without you."

My stomach does a little flip and I have to tell it to calm the hell down. "Fuck. Fine, leave it open. I have the rest of my stuff here too."

Harley nods and walks over to where Luca is guarding my shit. Luca takes a step forward, over the bags, and crosses his arms. Harley smirks at him, throwing down a silent challenge and I know Luca will accept it in a heartbeat. Luca is the tiniest bit taller than Harley but Harley is easier broader, more muscular. I've seen Luca take out three guys bigger than Harley at the same damn time though so really, all bets are off on who would win. I don't have time to deal with them. I need to get out of here. I need to get Harley out of here.

The Jackal *cannot* see him.

Not after the warning he issued me at the meeting. I give myself a little shake to try and shift the ghosts.

"Luca, it's fine. My feet hurt and I need a bath," I say sweetly with a little pout. He's one of the decent guys on the Jackal's payroll, a rare breed. Luca leans down and brushes a kiss against my cheek without breaking eye contact with Harley. Harley stares down at him like he's going to gut him if given the chance. Finally, I step around them both to grab my bags and then I shove one into Harley's chest to get him moving.

"I'm going to miss that ass while you're gone, princess," Luca calls as I load my bag into the car. Harley glares back at him but I laugh his words off.

"You get more ass than the average Mounty street girl on a Saturday night, Luca. I'm sure you'll survive without mine." He grabs his chest like I've wounded him and grins back at me. Harley opens the door to the backseat and I realize I'm about to be sandwiched in with him and the Beaumont brothers. Fuck. No.

I dart around and climb in with Avery instead. I've lost all of the weight I'd managed to gain last year and we easily fit in the sleek seat together. Blaise arches an eyebrow and then takes off, fast enough that my body is pressed back in the seat and the tires squeal.

"So. How much money is in this car right now?" whispers Avery and I giggle at her.

"How should I know, do you guys all carry cash?" I whisper back and she laughs out loud at me.

"Where should I drop you off, Mounty? Feel free to tip me for my services," drawls Blaise and I shudder. Avery snorts at me. Traitor.

"She's coming back to the hotel with us," grumbles Harley.

"Why?" snaps Ash and I'm reminded of his newfound hate for me.

"Thank you Lips for finding my coked up brother and getting him out of danger before he got himself stabbed by an angry Mounty girl for not keeping his hands to himself," I say in my most sarcastic tone. Avery gives my hand a squeeze and I smile at her.

"Thank you Mounty for traipsing around the docks dressed like a slut and tripping over Joey. Do all your clients pay you in large bags of dirty money? Is your *puss* really that good?"

"Ash, *shut your mouth.*" Avery turns in her seat to glare at him. I don't even care.

Harley ignores his cousin completely and leans forward in his seat. "Who was the guy with your bags?"

"Luca. He's... he works for the same guy your uncle does. We've known each other forever."

"Have you fucked him?" he asks. *Sweet lord.* Here we go.

"How is that any of your business?"

Blaise tips his head back and laughs. He changes gears smoothly but he takes corners way too fast considering I'm sharing a seat with no belt on. "How many of those Mounty guys have you fucked?"

"Why do either of you care?" Avery says sweetly and they both finally shut up.

Chapter Two

Avery secures us a shared room with a private bathroom and an *honest-to-God* coffee machine. I am going to bathe in coffee this year. I can, because the bathroom has a tub. The room is bigger than Avery's single was last year and my two bags feel pathetic as I look around at all of the space I now have to fill.

"Look on the bright side, you won't have to worry about anyone sneaking in and messing with your stuff now that you're roomed with me."

I scoff at her and I wave the lock I've brought with me. There's no way I'm trusting anyone here this year, other than Avery. She laughs and then watches me struggle to screw the damn thing in place. When she ducks into the bathroom to make a phone call, I wriggle under my bed to hide my safe. I trust Avery but some things will take time.

I'm excited to share a room with her. I'm actually shocked at how excited I am to have her as a friend. It feels kind of pathetic how relieved I am to have someone on my side but then I remind myself of exactly how hard I worked for it last year.

When we woke up at the hotel Avery and the guys were all staying at, a meager two hours after we had gone to sleep, we had ordered room service for breakfast and gossiped about our summer breaks. I had never stayed in a hotel, or eaten food delivered to me by a guy in a suit, and Avery kept giggling at how awkward I was about it all. I was shocked to see she eats as much as I do when given the chance and at my raised eyebrow she'd told me, "Ballet is hardcore. I eat more than Ash does during the recital season."

It was refreshing.

After breakfast Avery had a heated argument with Ash about our travel arrangements, he did *not* want me to join them, and it ended with us girls tucked in the back of one of the Beaumont's luxurious chauffeur driven Bentley's. I squirmed in the seat for about thirty seconds before Avery told me to get over Ash's shitty attitude. "He's been a nightmare the entire break. I'm looking forward to getting back to school and finding new ways to avoid him."

I still feel guilty about it. I can't help it.

So, after spending the two minutes it takes me to unpack I perch on my bed and glare down at the bags of cash I now have to get sorted. The movies make it look so easy, just get a fake business and funnel the money through, but in reality without asking for the Jackal's help I am going to struggle to get the funds clean. I need a second option amongst the Twelve to get shit done. I'll add that to my never-ending list of things I need to think about.

"You never told me how much is in there," says Avery as she unpacks her millionth box of shoes. I think she could wear a different pair every day for the rest of her life and still have some left over. I have three pairs. And I love the shit out of them.

"A hundred grand. It's a pain in my ass and I don't want to leave it here tomorrow during classes."

She snorts and pokes her head out of the closet to give me a look. "Anyone at Hannaford wouldn't need your dirty cash, Lips."

I give her a sidelong look. "It's not just that. Having bags full of hundred dollar bills raises questions I don't want to answer. There's enough people here who think I'm a whore," I grumble. I'm just a little bit sour over the guys' reactions last night.

Avery comes over to drop down onto the bed next to me and she props her chin up in her palm as we both stare at the bags like they'll give us some answers. "I know someone who could help. It's a risk but he's always been discreet. And kind to me. I could play the dumb damsel in distress and get him to sort it for us. He probably wouldn't even ask for a cut."

I glance at her, curiously. We've gotten to know each other much better thanks to her texting truths game. I had been skeptical when she had suggested it but it had really helped me to understand her. I know just enough about her father's business and associates to realize just how much of a criminal he really is.

The Jackal would love to know Joseph Beaumont Sr.

Avery sighs and grabs one of the bags, slinging it over her shoulder. "Let's hide them in the closet for now and we can mull over the cleaning options. Have you picked your secret for today?"

I had and I was damned nervous about saying it. I'd woken to a text from the Jackal, telling me how much he would miss me while I was gone, and I'd decided then I'd have to start telling Avery about him. I didn't speak until we had tucked the bags securely behind the mountain of boxes Avery had that I find out have her scarves in them. Scarves, for Christ's sake.

Scarves.

"What's yours?" I chicken out and ask. Avery smiles and lets me avoid it for a minute, bless her.

"The guy I can ask to process the money is from a family I wouldn't ever trust, the Crawfords." She walks over to the kitchen and starts rummaging around for cleaning supplies. The girl could not stop cleaning the room. I was a little nervous about pissing her off by, you know, *existing* in the same room full time. "His father is my father's best friend. When I was a child my mother would gossip with her friends about how she wanted me to marry one of his sons. I hate the whole damn lot of them, except for Atticus."

"Atticus? Wow."

Avery rolls her eyes. "His mother named all three of her sons after notable literary figures. Atticus is the youngest and his mother had been hoping for a girl. His father is big on the old adage of 'an heir and a spare' so he has no use for a third son. The older boys are absolute assholes because they know just how powerful they are going to be when their father passes the business on. Atticus gets nothing and has been told to forge his own path."

I nod along. I'm starting to get used to the bizarre and cruel ways of the super rich parents of Hannaford. Then again my own mother picked a gram of heroin over me every day of the week so I can't really judge. Avery looks up from where she's wiping down the fridge. I can honestly say I've never even thought about wiping a fridge down in my life. "Atticus started his own business in his final year here at Hannaford. He's now independently wealthy and very vague about how he makes his money. He claims it's because he doesn't want his brothers snooping around his business dealings but I once asked him if I could do an internship with him during the summer break, for college applications and to get away from Joey, and he told me his business is not appropriate for a young lady. He's not a chauvinistic kind of guy and he's never said anything like that to me before. So, I'm thinking it's either illegal or sexual."

Hmm. Either would work to clean the cash. I wouldn't mind him taking a cut as long as it was a reasonable amount and he keeps his mouth shut.

Avery moves on to scrub the coffee table in our little lounge area, complete with a massive TV on the wall and an honest-to-God fireplace, and she blushes a little as she clears her throat. "The truth here is that I used to have a crush on him. A big one, I would follow him around like a lost puppy but then he hit high school and started avoiding me. I think Joey's violence scared him off."

It's honestly weird to see her blush. I stare at it for a second before I can speak. "If he avoids you, how will you get him to clean the cash?"

"Oh we still see each other at society functions and galas. He's nice to me, just distant. I've given up on my feelings for him." Her tone says otherwise. I wonder how Ash feels about this and then I remember he's a dick and I don't care what he thinks.

I can't avoid my truth forever so I take a deep breath and just blurt it out. "The Jackal told Joey not to touch me because he thinks he owns me. He's going to take me someday, lock me in a room, and force me to be with him. He'll rape and torture me until I submit to him. If I don't make some very careful moves in the next three years I'm going to be trapped by him. Any guy who touches me is in danger if it gets back to him."

Avery stops scrubbing and straightens up sharply. Her eyes narrow and she looks the exact same as when I met her a year ago, cold and stunning and calculating.

"Well, we need to plan some moves then, don't we?"

It's only the first fucking day back to class and I'm already facing Harley and Blaise's bullshit.

I've come down for an early breakfast, knowing Avery had to deal with some issue involving the student council, and I've saved her a seat. Even though the ban on speaking to me has clearly lifted now I'm friends with Avery, the other students still give me a wide berth.

It's fine.

I like the quiet.

And it *is* quiet.

Right up until the moment Harley and Blaise drop themselves down across from me at the table with full plates of food and wary looks in their eyes. I haven't seen hide nor hair of either of them since Ash stormed off at the hotel and I'm not feeling much warmth towards them now. Okay, that's a lie, I'm feeling pissy but turned on at the very sight of them. Sue me.

"Seriously. I'm not dealing with either of you this fucking early in the morning unless it's a life or death situation. Is someone bleeding?" Harley snorts at me and offers me a glass of juice. I give him a truly dark glare, one of my very best, and I shake my head.

"I'd rather not start my week off with the runs, thanks, asshole."

He cackles at the curious look Blaise gives us both. I try not to blush at having the rock god's eyes touch me. Maybe this will be the year I get over my obsession for him and his music. I can only live in hope.

"Don't ask, man. We had a great winter break last year. I like to think that was when we became friends."

I point my knife in his direction. "We are not friends. I'm Avery's friend and you two are firmly Team Ash." Blaise gives me another look and I grumble into my eggs. I'd love to tell him to fuck off but I can't imagine saying those words to his face. Harley watches us both, watches how I react to Blaise, and I think I see a hint of jealousy in his eyes. I roll my own at him. I'm no threat to their bromance, I doubt Blaise even remembered my name before Avery and I became friends. I Joey Beaumont saunters into the dining hall flanked by his usual group of simpering flunkies. He meets my eye and tips his head at me with a challenge. Great.

"Look, it's only a matter of time before Aves wears Ash down and then we'll all be one big happy fucking family. So stop fighting it. We're friends by association," says Harley.

"Fuck off," I mumble around my food because I can say it to Harley, I have said it to him a hundred times before. I also do not care if I look like a savage. Fuck these boys and their heartbreakingly good looks. Fuck them.

Actually, I wouldn't mind—*nope*. Not going there.

"God, are you going to be a grumpy ass like Harley all the time? There's only so much of that shit I can take." Blaise's eyes goddamn twinkle and I want to claw mine out rather than look at him. Harley elbows him and they both laugh. They are so clearly the best of friends that I'm a little jealous. Then I remember I have Avery now and I smile to myself instead. That girl and her fierce loyalty is worth a hundred gorgeous boys.

Harley clears his throat and pegs me with a *look*. I try not to squirm. It is too damn early to be dealing with him at such intensity. "Listen, I'm not Ash. Avery can't throw pretty words around and fool me. I know exactly what scratches down a cheek fucking mean. I need you to tell me exactly what happened between her and Rory. I've spent the whole break fucking stewing on it and I need an answer."

My spine snaps until I'm sitting straight and rigid. Both boys have stopped eating and they're staring at me like I'm the most fascinating thing in the damn room. I've been working on my poker face and I know Harley is pissed he can't get a thing out of me. "If Avery has chosen not to tell you herself then you will never get it out of me. End of story."

Harley's eyes narrow but it's not really a glare. He's looking at me like he wants to crack my head open and sort through everything inside my brain.

"Good. I'm glad you're a decent friend to her. She's never had one of those. But I need to know if I need to kill Rory. No, not beat him bloody or start a social campaign against him. I need to know if I need to end his life and fucking bury him somewhere. Because if that piece of shit raped my cousin, if he did that to her, I will end his life. I'm not asking for details, just tell me if he has to die."

He's serious. I've met enough killers in my life to know what it looks like when a man is going to follow through with his threat. Clearly there is more of his father's blood in his veins than he'd like to admit. I think about saying that to him, riling him up more to get him to forget about Avery's assault, but I don't actually want him to hate me. Fuck, I don't want him to hate me at all. When did all of this become so complicated? I move my eggs around my plate for a minute while I think. The tension in our little bubble at the table soars. When I look up at Harley he's barely containing his anger and his shoulders have begun to shake.

"Fine, no details. If I were ten seconds later than what I was, you would be burying that dickhead. But I got there in time."

Harley lets out a breath and nods. He doesn't look relieved, just like he can put off the killing for a later date. Just because Rory didn't rape her didn't mean he was a decent guy, it just meant I got in his way. Harley is definitely on the same page as I am. Rory cannot stay at this school with Avery. He's a danger to her and to every other girl here.

"Color me impressed. Rory's a linebacker, you're what, five-two? How the hell did you stop him?" Blaise asks, his eyes moving over my tiny frame leaving behind a trail of fire.

I snort at him and drop my cutlery onto my half-eaten plate. I can't eat now that I'm thinking about this shit. My digestion has always been at the mercy of my brain. The moment I'm thinking too much, agitated, nervous, any strong emotion, I can't stomach a thing.

"I'm a Mounty. I'm a foster kid. I was a child of neglect before that. Last year I was the target of a game that had most of the male population of this school following me around bugging me for sex every day. I've had to threaten Harley's psycho cousin with a knife to the dick. You think I don't have experience fighting off rapists? Please. Go back to your privileged, gilded fucking towers and leave me the hell alone."

Blaise's face drops. He looks like he's going to question me so I stand up and grab my bag instead, my heart thundering in my chest dangerously. As I shove away from the table, Avery struts in like she owns the whole damn school and a smile tugs at my lips. She grins back at me and then levels Harley and Blaise with a *look*. I meet her in the line and she tucks her arm into mine.

"They giving you shit?" She's wearing a vibrant shade of red lipstick and I'm jealous that I could never pull off such a polished look. I'll always be rough around my edges.

"Nah. They want to be one big happy family."

Avery snorts and grabs a banana and an iced coffee. I grab a drink as well and we duck out of the dining hall. We share our first class with Harley. I share nearly every class with the gorgeous asshole.

"Ash will be livid. He's still gunning for you."

"Let him. I'm not scared."

Avery laughs.

This year is going to be a fucking blast.

Chapter Three

A quick glance at the listing on the door of our math class confirms we're still being seated alphabetically by surname. Another year of working with Harley, sitting next to him, and being drowned in the scent of him. Okay, that sounds creepy but he really does smell incredible.

Avery is directly in front of us once again. She's sitting next to some guy I don't recognize and she's pissed off about it. She doesn't frown or snap at him but the smile she gives him is pure ice. I almost feel sorry for him. I wonder how long it will take before Ash is challenging him in one of the guys' dorms fight club sessions at her order.

Harley walks in seconds before the teacher and drapes himself in his chair. He doesn't look at me or acknowledge me which pisses me off considering not even an hour ago he was declaring us friends over plates of eggs. I should know by now not to trust a single word out of his mouth.

"Can we just agree now on how we're going to halve all of our joint assessments this year so I can save myself some work?" I whisper at him as the teacher starts to take attendance. Harley smirks at me without looking up from his notes. He's always so prepared for his classes. I mean, I am too but it's still a surprise to me.

"Nope. I'd rather keep you busy studying than running around the school getting jumped. Besides, you just said we're not friends. I don't help people that aren't my friends," he drawls. The teacher starts handing out worksheets and I roll my eyes at Harley. He refuses to look at me.

"I'm not going to get beaten up. I'm pretty sure we sorted that out last year."

Harley shrugs and we fall into silence again as the class gets into full swing. I focus on the numbers and formulas and I let myself forget about everything else for a minute. I don't want to admit to myself just how much I'm enjoying being back at school. It's good to focus on something I'm good at.

When the class finally wraps up and I have the syllabus firmly tucked into my bag I follow Harley out and to our next class. Avery is still giving him icy looks but he just grins at her, his charm doing nothing for her and everything to me.

"By the way, Mounty, I meant getting jumped for the sweep."

My stomach hollows out. He can't be serious? How could it still be going?

"It's now well over the million dollar mark and there have already been…ideas thrown around about how to get you into bed. Or against a hard surface really, they don't care about the particulars."

Avery scoffs and links her arm in mine so I can stop her from falling while she focuses on her phone. I've seen her do it with the guys a thousand times and I smile at her effortless trust in me. Harley shrugs and leads us to our next class. Biology.

"As long as none of the ideas involve rape then I really don't want to hear about it. I'm not fucking a Hannaford boy."

Tension forms in his shoulders but he doesn't turn to face me. Avery chuckles under her breath and I glance over to see she's watching him, her phone gone.

"Got your fill of Mounty guys over the break?" he snaps and Avery's chuckle turns into what can only be described as an evil cackle. He cuts her a glare and she ignores it entirely.

"What do you have against Mounty guys, Harls? That big guy the other night, Luca was it? He was pretty hot. I'd fuck him." Avery teases and I groan at her. The fastest route to pissing the guys off is the very thought of any guys touching their sweet Floss.

"I wouldn't ever let you near him. He's… a good guy but he's… very loyal to a bad guy."

Harley sneers at me. "Like you are?"

I grit my teeth and ignore him. It takes serious fucking willpower. Our conversation about the Jackal is still fresh in Avery's mind and she kicks him in the shin, her polished school heels nicely pointed. "She's as loyal to him as you are to Liam O'Cronin so don't be a dick."

"Difference is I can't help the family I was born into," he grumbles under his breath.

Her eyes are pure ice. "Neither can she."

I sign up to tutor students again and I'm sure I'm going to be as popular as last year.

I arrive to the library early and find a guy sitting at the table I've come to call my own. I feel the prickle of irritation and then grumble at myself to stop being so stupid. As I move past the table to stake out one of the others the guy calls out, "Aren't you Eclipse Anderson?"

I grimace and then turn back to him. I don't recognize him at all but he doesn't look old enough to be an upperclassman. "I go by Lips."

He smiles at me and I'm struck by the *niceness* of it. Not that I'm attracted to him, thank God because I have enough trouble containing my hormones, but he doesn't look like he's aiming for anything. He's just smiling.

"I'm Lance. I've signed up for your tutoring, the librarian told me this was your table."

I let out the breath I was holding and pull out my chair instead. He watches me, still smiling, and I glance at the work spread out in front of him. I recognize the assignments straight away. He's a freshman.

"I'm the new scholarship student. I thought it would be nice to meet the first kid to make it past freshman year since they started handing out these scholarships and see if you have any pointers?" he says and still he's fucking smiling. I'm starting to get creeped out. Guys don't smile at me like that.

I give him a stern look and say, "Get as far ahead in your classwork as possible, don't accept drinks from anyone, and stay away from the Beaumonts."

The smile finally falters and he grimaces as I pull out my own textbooks and supplies. "So they roofie drinks at parties here, do they? Typical rich brats."

I look up to answer him as the library door opens again and in strides Ash and Blaise. I swear under my breath and silently pray they're here for something else.

The universe does not listen.

"Mounty! Lovely to see you again, though I'm a little disappointed you're not in your party clothes. Such a shame," says Blaise as he drops down into the chair beside me. I roll my eyes in his general direction. He doesn't mention our meeting at breakfast earlier in the week, which makes me think he hasn't told his best friend about it.

Ash glares at Lance as he stands over him with a malicious look. "Move. You're in my seat."

Lance plasters on that friendly smile again and moves across while Blaise chuckles under his breath at Ash's shitty attitude.

"Is there a reason you've signed up for another year of pointless tutoring?" I raise an eyebrow at the arrogant dick and he just stares me down. Lance's eyes dart between us both and then he breaks the heated silence.

"I'm Lance. Nice to meet you both."

Neither of the guys even bother to look at him so I sigh and say, "This is Blaise Morrison. Don't insult his music or beat him in choir or he'll get pissy and you'll be miserable for the rest of the year. And this is Ash Beaumont."

"Ah. A member of the family I should stay away from?"

Blaise's face has this little smile on it that makes me want to scream. I keep my focus on Lance as I answer. "Yes. His older brother is insane and his sister would destroy your will to live without breaking a sweat. Ash, here, could beat the life out of you and then run a marathon for shits and giggles. Or just pay someone else to bury you, he's richer than God," I say in my most monotone voice, while I sort through Blaise's assignments. We're only two weeks into the year and he's already behind, I feel like *this* is his true skill in life. Which is saying something because he's a musical genius.

I manage to corral them all into working on their assignments quietly for the hour, which I count in the top five hardest things I've ever done. Ash is moody and petulant and he looks at me with obvious suspicion. I try not to let it get to me but I feel his moody gaze on my skin like a scouring pad.

"How do you stay away from them if you're tutoring him?" Lance says as he packs away his work. Ash glowers at him and Blaise is watching them both with that dark gluttonous need they all have, like he's feeding on the inevitability of blood being spilled.

"I don't. Avery is my best friend and roommate. I tutor Ash even though he hates me. Joey is hell-bent on murdering me. I'm saying you should stay away from them if you want to survive the year."

"You think you're tougher than me?" He grins at me and I get the feeling he's trying to flirt with me. I don't need any more guys following me around, especially not a fellow Mounty. How the hell do I discourage this kind of thing without violence? Fuck.

"Have you ever broken the bones in a guy's hand in half a second one-handed?" Ash drawls. I forgot I even did that. Lance frowns at him and shakes his head. "Then she's tougher than you."

Lance blinks at me.

"Are you here to study or to try to get into the Mounty girl's panties because you should be warned, she only fucks crime lords," Blaise laughs and I shove his math workbook into his chest to shut him up. Lance recovers from his shock to look down his nose at him.

"You think you're cool because your daddy bought your shitty punk band a record deal? Write another pathetic song about your feelings, dickhead, and stay out of my business."

My jaw drops and Blaise turns to stone beside me. Ash bursts out laughing, so loud that the students around us stop and stare.

"They're not going to find enough of your corpse left to get an ID by the time we're done with you."

I scrub my face with my hands and then peg Lance with a look. "You didn't want to take my advice at all then?"

"Mounties stick together. I don't like the way they talk to you."

I scoff at him and shove my textbooks and supplies back into my bag. Ash looks between us both with a cold eyes but I ignore him as I walk out. I do not need the complication of another Mounty at this school.

"I'm going to get a background check on him. I can't believe he said that to Blaise."

I groan, slumping onto my back, and Avery swats my leg from where she's painting my toenails. I swear I've had eight different colors since school started back. Avery only ever wears nude polish but her collection of colors is insane. I'm a kind enough friend to let her paint my nails whenever she feels the need. Such a sacrifice.

"I don't recognize him. He's probably from a middle class area and he has no clue of what he's dealing with here."

She hums under her breath and studies her handiwork. We're lying on her bed and trying to figure out what to do about Lance. Blaise followed me up to the girls' dorms to rant passionately at Avery while I showered. She managed to calm him down enough to leave before I got out and then we decided to cook dinner ourselves and just hang out. The dining hall is always crazy on Friday taco night and I'm still adverse after vomiting them over myself last year. I still give Avery shit for that every chance I get.

"Do you always avenge the guys when people insult them? It puts a lot of work on your plate." I ask. I'm genuinely curious.

She screws the bottle of polish shut and puts it back into the shelving unit she has hung on the wall. I find it funny that I was so worried about pissing her off by being messy when we first moved in. Her belongings are slowly migrating onto my half of the room purely by need because she has so damn much. I think she has a shopping compulsion, last week she misplaced some of her dance gear and the next day I woke up to find dozens of boxes being delivered to replace it all.

"People stay in power by being proactive. If I let the Mounty boy insult Blaise without consequence then what's to stop one of the privileged kids from doing it? It keeps me busy and the sheep where they belong."

My head tilts as I consider her words. It sounds like something the Jackal would say and it's exactly why I'm terrible at this type of politics. I just don't care about the social hierarchy. But Avery does so I'll have to help out. I'm not saying I'm going to actively terrorize the guy but I'm interested in seeing Avery work.

I shrug. "So what do we do?"

She gives me a look and sighs. "I'll look into his background and find his weak spots. Blaise will beat the crap out of him and I'll turn him into a pariah. He's not a priority at the moment so I'll just make it known that we don't like him and the lower students will start it off for us."

I hum under my breath for a minute while I think. I'm lost in my head when Avery pokes me. "What's your truth today, Mounty?" she continues with a smirk.

I groan and scrub a hand over my face. "I don't know how to flirt."

She laughs at me and says, "That's not a truth. That's a sad revelation. We need to get out of this school and find some hot, random guys to play with."

That doesn't appeal to me at all. I don't want random hot guys. I want a mobster's son with the face of an angel and the rap sheet of a street kid. I want the singer with a soft heart wrapped in barbs and trip wires of devastating wit to keep it safe. I want the billionaire's unwanted son with eyes of ice and an endless love for his sister.

I can't tell Avery that truth.

She gives me a little smile but her eyes are sad. She doesn't look like a Beaumont right now. She looks like a teenage girl who needs a hug. It's weird. "I think I'm going to start dating again. I think it's time to wash away Rory and what he did to me."

I exhale sharply. "If you think the guys are protective of you, you have another thing coming. I'm vetting anyone that comes near you and they're going to answer to me. I'm also going to teach you how to castrate a guy properly. I mean it, I'm going to teach you how to cut a dick off."

Avery laughs all over again and the haunted look fades from her eyes.

Chapter Four

"There's a party tonight, out in the old groundskeeper's cottage. I think we should go."

What the hell is with rich kids and partying on school nights? Avery manages to shovel pancakes into her mouth and still look like a delicate, refined lady. I'm sure I look something like Cookie Monster as I tear into my muesli. I'm trying to get more variety in my breakfast because I've gorged on French toast for weeks. Not great nutritionally but it's done wonders for my boobs. Namely, I have some now.

Avery decided to take the higher math class this year but she's relaxed some of her other subjects so we have less overlap. When I asked her why she shrugged and said she likes to piss her father off in low-risk situations. I decide not to push the subject.

"Is there a specific reason why or are we enjoying our youth?" I say and she scoffs at me.

She pokes her knife at me as she replies. "We don't ever do things for fun, Lips. We're just not wired that way."

I shrug but she has a point. I can't remember the last time I did anything for fun. Avery arches her eyebrow at me with a little smile, fusses with her phone, and then hands it to me. There's a photo of Joey with his arm around a woman who is definitely not a student at Hannaford. She must be at least twenty-five and she's dressed in a sharp pantsuit and heels, a sleek bob haircut and minimal makeup. She's attractive enough in an understated way, nothing like the girls I've seen that flock around him.

"This charming lady is one of our guidance counselors. She's supposed to be advising Joey on how to best achieve his career goals and instead she's sucking his dick in her office every Tuesday and Friday during their scheduled meetings."

I pull a face as she swipes her thumb across the screen and I see the photo evidence. "For future reference, I'll take your word on shit like that."

Avery hums under her breath and pulls the phone back to pocket it. She looks around the busy dining hall in a way that makes her look haughty. I used to think she was looking down at everyone but now I know this is her plotting action. She's planning and making connections in her head, the students milling around her have no idea of the scale of manipulation going on while they eat.

"I need to get some photos of him at the party, ideally with girls and blow, so I can send her a nice little slideshow ending with the photo of her on her knees. She needs to know how far out of her league she really is with him."

"Why not call the cops?" I'm curious for her answer as I'm sure it will show me more of her family dynamics.

"He's eighteen so it's not illegal. I could send the photos to the school board but then my father will get involved and he will just make her disappear." Her voice becomes clipped towards the end and she clears her throat uncomfortably.

"Pay off or burial?"

She looks up at me and I see the hesitation. "Usually it's a threat. Senior doesn't part with his money for any woman. If she doesn't take him seriously then he sends chaos."

Chaos.

There are many things I could send someone's way if I wanted to send a message so I can only imagine what the billionaire Joseph Beaumont could do. I nod and wipe my hands thoughtfully, mulling over her plan. Finally, I shrug and say, "We'll go. I can get the photos you need. Information collection is my specialty."

Avery changes into a sleek, gorgeous navy dress and a pair of stiletto heels that make my own feet cringe in sympathy. She rages for a half hour about her favorite Louboutins being missing, one of a kind and irreplaceable, and I bitch her out for being too rich to take care of her shit. She lets her hair down and wears only a little makeup. The look doesn't scream high school party to me, she looks like she's twenty-one and heading out clubbing at some exclusive rooftop nightclub in New York.

I decide not to tempt fate with a skirt. After Harley's warning about the money still up for grabs I'm wary about how tonight is going to pan out but it's still too hot to wear jeans and a jacket. I go with a black playsuit with a halter top that just manages to cover my ass and I put on the thickest cotton underwear I own. I'm not planning on drinking because peeing in a romper is a bitch. Plus if there are no working toilets at this cottage I'm not getting naked in the woods to pee. I lace up my black Docs and wiggle my toes in sheer joy.

Avery grimaces at the sight of my shoes and I give her a playful nudge. We'll see who's laughing when we stumble home at the end of this stupid party.

I follow Avery's lead out of the girls' dorms and through the school grounds. We purposefully decided to arrive two hours after the party got underway so Joey would be drunk and high before he has a chance to see us. My hand keeps slipping into my pocket and gripping my knife like a security blanket. I gave Avery a can of mace back in our room and she had tucked it into her bra like a pro.

"Does Ash come to these parties?" I ask as we trudge through the wooded boundaries in the school campus.

"Yeah, and the other two. They all get wasted and pick fights over girls." Avery rolls her eyes and manages to look superior even as she's wobbling in her heels in the dirt.

"I bumped into Harley last year at Joey's party." I blush at the memory. God, I really don't want to find him like that again.

Avery snorts when she sees my face and links her arm in mine. "Let me guess, Annabelle was bent over a table."

"On her knees actually." Avery's nose wrinkles and she shakes her head. I want to ask her what part she's grossed out about but then I see the lights and I realize that low throbbing sound means we're coming up on the party.

I can feel the music in my chest as we walk into the groundskeeper's cottage.

Cottage is a terrible word for the building. It's huge but old and dilapidated. I find myself cringing the further we get in, like that will somehow save me when the ceiling caves in. It's definitely going to collapse and the pulsing beat coming from the speakers seems to be teasing the cracked plaster, coaxing it into giving up.

Avery doesn't seem concerned about being crushed to death as she struts into the party and heads straight for the drinks table. There's a couple of guys playing bartenders and the drunk girls ordering drinks are paying them in kisses, which are getting more and more explicit as we stand there waiting. When Avery reaches for a bottle of snobby bubbly the guy raises his eyebrows at her and she gives him a ball-shriveling smirk. He looks away pretty quickly and focuses on me instead.

"Mounty! What's your poison? It'll only cost you a quick fuck. Just lay back and think of the Queen."

He's pretty cocky with a table between us but I'm limber when I need to be and I could jump it to smack him out. Avery watches the plans form in my brain and laughs as she grabs a bottle of whiskey. "Such a glowing review of your skills, Rafe, but rest assured, you couldn't handle Mounty pussy."

I cannot believe the word pussy just came out of Avery Beaumont's silver-spooned mouth. I snatch the whiskey from her and take a few big gulps straight from the bottle, just enough to take the edge off and make this clusterfuck bearable.

"Let's dance for a while. We should be able to find Joey while we do." Avery shouts over the music and I give her a sharp nod.

The dance floor takes up the entire bottom floor of the cottage and the only people who aren't dancing in someway are those waiting to grab drinks. The DJ is at the bottom of the staircase and he has a joint dangling from his lips precariously. Avery throws her head back to sip at the bubbly as she sways and grinds to the music. I'm too distracted by the pressing crowd and my own surveillance to really get into it but it's still fun to dance with her.

It takes three songs to spot Joey and he's practically skipping up the stairs with two barely dressed girls under his arms. I'm sure they're holding him up more than anything.

I signal to Avery and we move towards the staircase.

The music is so loud there that I'm sure my eardrums are going to start bleeding and I hurry to flee upstairs. I manage two steps before Avery's hand clamps around my wrist and I look back to see Blaise standing over her with a frown. He's fucking gorgeous in tight jeans, biker boots, and a band tee. His eyes are glazed and he's all sweaty from dancing. I force myself to look away from him before I embarrass myself.

Avery taps a message on her phone and then turns it to me.

He's wasted. He said he'll call Ash if I go upstairs because it's practically an orgy up there.

I take the phone and reply.

Stay here and dance. I'll get what we came for.

Avery purses her lips at me and gives a curt nod. I try to smile reassuringly but she's glaring at Blaise and misses it. I wait until she tugs him back into the crowd and then I start back up the stairs.

Upstairs is definitely not one big orgy.

It's six different orgies, spread throughout the rooms.

I get some raised brows at the landing and one guy tries to coax me into the bathroom once he recognizes me. I raise a fist with a warning look and he backs off pretty quickly. He is completely naked so he probably thought I was going to punch him directly in his dick.

It was definitely my intended target.

I move slowly and quietly from room to room while I look for Joey. No one involved in the group sex notices me, thank God, because it's much easier to be impartial when you're not making eye contact with the girl who sits in front of you in Health Ed while she's being eaten out by her blonde, cutesy best friend.

I make it to the ensuite bathroom at the very end of the hall before I find Joey.

He's sprawled out on the floor making out with a girl and twisting her bare nipples while the second girl rides his dick. The girl he's kissing keeps flinching away from his hands and I know she is not enjoying the pain he's causing her but she's kissing him all the same.

I take a few photos and a little video before I leave them to it.

Avery has finished the bubbly and is letting off some serious steam on the dance floor. As I make it over to her Blaise throws his head back and roars with laughter at something she says to him, though the music is too loud for me to hear it. He's drunk. He's fucking plastered and when I spot the bottle of whiskey Avery had snatched for me I see he's finished it off. Fuck. He'll be lucky to survive the night without choking on his own vomit.

Avery grins when she sees me and then I join them both for a few songs, dancing and twirling and sweating my heart out. I could stay there all night with them both but then Blaise turns green and lurches away, stumbling outside to puke on the steps.

Charming. But my infatuation with him doesn't falter. I need therapy.

Avery tucks herself under one of his arms and starts to lead him back to the school but she struggles underneath his weight when he stumbles. His eyes are closed and he's mumbling incoherently under his breath, a shiver running through him as the night air hits the sweat on his skin. I watch her take two steps before I sigh and duck under the other arm to help out. I breathe through my mouth, absolutely determined to not drown in his scent, and Avery shoots me a grateful look. She can guess at how much I do not want to touch him.

It's fine. I can feel his muscular arm across my shoulder and his chest is half draped over my back and I feel like I'm dying but it's fine. Totally fine. I'm fine.

We make it to the tree line uninterrupted. My leg is starting to protest the extra weight and I make a note to take something to stop the inevitable swelling before I pass out. I'm busy keeping my brain preoccupied so I don't notice Annabelle until Avery abruptly stops.

I glance up at her and curse viciously under my breath.

"Move, Summers," Avery snaps.

Annabelle's face is flushed and her eyes are hazy. She's wearing a red bandage dress and absolutely ridiculous heels. Honestly, I'm surprised her ankles haven't snapped yet.

"Give him here. We came together and we'll leave together."

Avery huffs and adjusts her hold around Blaise's waist so he doesn't fall. He's gently rocking on his feet and making us both rock with him. I'm glad I didn't drink much because it's already making my stomach protest. I can tell Avery is about to lose her cool and go full Beaumont on the bitch's ass.

"He's done for the night. We'll see him back safely," I say and Blaise chooses that moment to tuck his face into my neck and mumble nonsense into skin. The greatest achievement of my life so far is suppressing the shiver that threatens to take me over.

Annabelle looks at me like she didn't even notice I was there to begin with. "You? Fuck no, if he goes home with you he'll be tied to a fucking bed and forced to play out all of your stalker fantasies."

"If he goes home with you, he'll wake up naked and an expectant father. Now fuck off." Avery hisses at her and starts to walk again. Blaise's legs stumble, like he's startled that we're on the move again, and when Annabelle starts screaming at us he lifts his head and yells out to her, "I told you to leave me the fuck alone, Summers." Then he tucks his face back into my neck and sighs.

My leg is shaking as we enter the school building and by the second flight of stairs Avery declares that she's going to gift the school an elevator. Blaise is snoring and his feet are dragging along behind us as I fumble to get our door open. Avery is looking sweaty and disheveled. When I grin at her she pokes her tongue out at me.

Blaise is dropped unceremoniously onto the couch and Avery flings a thin blanket over him.

"Fucking rich kids," I say and Avery laughs all the way to the bathroom.

When I was living in the group foster home there was a girl there who had been forcibly removed from her home by child services because her stepbrother had been molesting her. She was older than me, seventeen and on her way to aging out of the system, and her stepbrother was the same age. He'd convinced her, as a fourteen year old, that they were married like their parents were and that she belonged to him. She was forced to cater to his every whim and he would get violent with her if she disobeyed him.

One night we were woken up by the sound of him trying to kick in the door. It was locked, bolted, and had a safety bar across it so it didn't budge but we had to sit and listen to the enraged asshole kick it and shove it with his body while we waited for the police to arrive.

Three hours after we passed out from the party, I wake to the sound of a different but equally enraged asshole attempting to kick our door in.

I shoot out of bed and grip my knife. Avery slaps her hand out to turn her bedside lamp on and reaches for her phone. The biggest shock is Blaise's reaction.

For a guy who couldn't even stay conscious long enough to carry his own body weight back to our room he's pretty quick to leap to our defense. He's up and charging for the door before I realize he's awake and Avery yells out to stop him but he ignores her completely.

He rips open the door to find Joey, raving and deadly, with his leg raised to kick out again and Blaise jumps on him, taking him to the ground. Joey's movement becomes even more frenzied and he bucks wildly to try to flip Blaise off but the rocker is a better fighter, even drunk off his ass.

Blaise smashes his fists into Joey's face, over and over, and I scramble to watch. If Joey brought some of his flunkies I'll need to step in and help. I hear Avery snarl orders down her phone so backup must be on its way.

Joey's arms finally fall down to his sides and Blaise shuffles until his legs pin them to his body. Doors have started opening down the hallway and there are girls poking their heads out to see what's going on. I cross my arms and glare at them until the doors all shut again. No one wants to deal with Joey when he's high and destructive. I know I don't.

Blaise stops hitting Joey and his chest heaves, his lungs probably screaming for air.

"Mounty, I'm gonna fucking puke." He croaks and I scramble to find him a bucket. I shove a large bowl under his chin just in time to save Joey's face from the whiskey bile. Blaise retches into it again and I take pity on him. I find a washcloth and wet it to scrub over his sweaty face. He looks pretty pathetic by the time Ash and Harley arrive.

"What the fuck, Morrison?" snaps Harley while I'm tentatively rubbing Blaise's back. Avery is emptying the bowl down the toilet and gagging at the vile smell.

"This is what death must feel like." Blaise moans and I scoff at him. Oh joy. Here comes the signature Morrison dramatics.

Ash glares at us both as he grabs Blaise under the arms and pulls him off of Joey's unconscious form. Avery appears in the doorframe, her robe tucked tight around her body, and uses a clean washcloth to wipe Blaise's face with the efficiency of a seasoned mother. "If Blaise wasn't here Joey would have gotten in. Lips would have had to stab the asshole."

I mutter under my breath at her, "I fucking would've, too."

Harley's glare hasn't eased off at all. He gives Avery a quick hug and then he grabs Joey's legs to start dragging him down the hall. He holds them with the same enthusiasm you'd grab a pile of shit with bare hands. I watch with satisfaction as Joey's head slams into every bump and chair leg on the way. I swear Harley is picking the most damaging path. I like his style.

"I'll stay here with you." Ash mumbles into Avery's hair as he hugs her tight. Blaise is still slumped on the ground, taking deep breaths that make me think he's gearing up for round two of emptying his gut.

"There's no need. Go help Harls and we'll make sure Blaise doesn't have liver poisoning."

Blaise moans, "I do. I definitely feel poisoned. Someone put me out of my fucking misery."

I roll my eyes at him and help him up, stumbling and lurching back into our room. I give him a gentle push towards the couch but he stumbles towards the beds instead. I glance away quickly when he starts to strip right down to his boxers. Thank fuck he wasn't commando. I may have *died*.

Our beautiful, ornate bay window is already showing signs of the sunrise, destroying any chances of me getting back to sleep. I turn the coffee machine on and start fussing with cups. I need an IV line of caffeine at this point. Today is going to suck.

"I'm too fucked for this shit," Blaise moans and crawls into Avery's bed. He pulls a pathetic looking face and she scoffs at him as she locks the door behind Ash. I pour out our drinks while Avery scrubs the bowl and her hands until I'm afraid she's going to scour away her skin to the bone.

I hand her a cup and then we both sit on the couches, listening to Blaise snore as he sleeps away his hangover. My mind wanders for a minute while I process the night we've had.

"What did you mean about him waking up an expectant father?"

Avery's eyes narrow, flashing dangerously, and she blows into her coffee while she seethes. "Last year she told Blaise and Ash that she was on the pill and that they didn't have to use condoms anymore. Didn't say it to Harley though. That makes it pretty obvious she's lying and wants a rich baby daddy."

I grimace. That's something I've heard heaps of Mounty girls do to get out of care homes and away from abusive families. "They didn't, did they?"

"Lord no! Those three don't trust any girls they've ever fucked. Besides, they all talk to each other and when they figured out she'd left Harley out they knew what she was after. So obvious considering he was her favorite. If she wanted to have more *intimate* sex she would want it with him more than the other two."

Right. So his declaration of stopping their...arrangement last year had nothing to do with me. My stomach sinks and I get angry at myself over it. I clear my throat and try to pull myself out of the little pity party that's threatening to start in my head. "Was Harley into her as well?"

Avery laughs and shakes her head. "Annabelle was easy. She was so eager to have the guys' attention that she didn't care that they weren't after a relationship. If they wanted to chase someone they'd go out, if they just wanted to fuck they'd go see her."

I screw my nose up at her and drink my coffee. I shouldn't be enjoying hearing this but, fuck me, I am. Annabelle was always so smug about being with them and I know most of the girls assumed they were offering her some sort of commitment.

The bitch wouldn't want to call me a stalker again.

I make it through my morning classes but only because I'm used to withstanding and overcoming pure, unadulterated torture.

Avery looks polished and perfect, and I look like someone backed over my dead body with a semi and then resuscitated me to force me to class. I tell her that at lunch and she smirks into her grilled salmon like a bitch. She's lucky I've decided to love her.

Ash joins us and sneers at me the entire time. I ignore his shitty attitude, which only makes it worse. Avery tells him about her classes, her plans for Lance, the pose she's perfecting in her ballet class, and he treats her like she's the center of his universe. It's sweet. She gives me an apologetic look and I brush her off. I know how much she hates the distance he's put between them because of me.

I drop Avery off to her literature class on the way to my own. I turn into the hall and find myself shoved into an empty storage room. I'm about to start swinging when Ash snaps, "Calm down, I just want a word with you."

For fuck's sake.

I turn on my heel to glare at him. "We just ate together, you didn't have to hurt me to speak to me."

He darts his gaze down to where I'm rubbing at my shoulder and he winces, slightly. "I didn't think I'd pushed that hard."

He hadn't. It was an old injury. I'm a walking mess of scar tissue, crookedly healed bones, and nerve damage. I just do my best not to let anyone know that. "Whatever. What did you want to speak to me about?"

He straightens, his shoulders rolling back which made his chest double in width, and the look in his eye is the same one he's given me every day when he sees me with Avery. He loathes me and he'll cut me out of her life the second I prove my disloyalty.

"Stay the fuck away from Blaise and Harley. I don't need you poisoning them with the same shit you've fed Avery. You're a Mounty slut with an agenda and I'm not falling for your little act."

Wow. I don't know why I'm so shocked but my mind is stuck on the words *Mounty slut*. "I'm not trying anything with them. I'm actually actively avoiding them both. And don't you ever call me a slut again, I think the *ongoing* bet proves I'm not."

He scoffs at me and crosses his arms. "That's why you sit with Harley in every class? And Blaise was in your room last night? You really are working overtime to get them. Just because you're picky about the dick you want doesn't make you any better than any other Mounty."

I squint up at him and wonder if he's had some sort of break from reality. Maybe Joey's hit him too hard too many times and his brain has finally decided to tap out.

"Seating in all of our classes is assigned. He's Arbour, I'm Anderson, we can't change that unless he decides to go back to being an O'Cronin and I think we both know that isn't happening. As for Blaise, I helped your sister carry him back last night. Then I helped him out while he spewed. Should I have handed him over to Annabelle instead? Are you okay with your friends being raped while they sleep by gold digging tramps? Or is it okay for her to fuck you all, even if you're not conscious and consenting, because her family has money?"

Ash's eyes have become scathing but he doesn't answer me. I wait a minute before I scoff at him and storm out of the storage room right as Harley strides past. He frowns at me and then when Ash steps out after me he scowls. He opens his mouth to snarl at me and I cut him off. "You need to keep him the fuck away from me until he decides to get his head out of his ass."

Ash scoffs, marching down the hall away from us both, and calls out over his shoulder, "Stay the fuck away from my friends, Mounty."

I seethe during the rest of my classes. Harley doesn't speak to me and he only looks at me when he thinks I won't notice. My skin itches and crawls with irritation and I'm going to have to throat punch someone to calm the fuck down.

Mounty slut.

How fucking dare that womanizing, man-whore call me that.

I'm a fucking virgin! I've only kissed two guys and only one of them by choice. Fuck him!

When classes end Harley follows me to the stairs that lead to the dorms, completely silent like he knows I'm one word away from homicide. Avery is waiting at the bottom with Ash and when he sees me with Harley he turns on me.

"What the fuck do you not understand about staying away from him?"

I step up to poke his chest with my finger. "I don't answer to you, asshole. You ever speak to me like this again and I'll bury you."

Avery puts a gentle hand on Ash's chest as Harley tugs me back by the arm. I wrench my arm out of his grip and glare at him. He ignores me.

"Ash, you need to calm down and think about this." Avery murmurs and when he looks at her he's gutted, betrayed.

"She just said she'd bury me and you're taking her side? Nice, Floss. Proves my point."

Avery flings her arms around his neck and hugs him. "She wouldn't actually do anything to hurt you. She saved me last year. If she hadn't helped me Rory would've raped and beaten me. He might've killed me, Ash. Please just trust me and trust that I know what I'm doing being her friend."

His arms slowly rise to hold her and I look away from them both to Harley.

He's watching them with something close to envy but it's not a bad emotion. Like he loves them both so much and wishes he was their twin, too. When he looks down at me he whispers, "We need a plan for Rory. I'm done sharing the halls with him."

"Agreed."

Avery wipes at her dry eyes like she's worried the other students might see some sort of emotion from her and then we leave the guys there.

When we get back to our room we find Annabelle outside the door screaming at a very tired looking Blaise who is propped up on the doorframe, eyes bloodshot and bleary. When she finally stops to take a breath he snaps at her, vitriol and fire in his tone.

"Can you just fuck off? You had everything you wanted and then you fucked it all up. That's it."

A sob bursts out of her. "Please, Blaise! It's not what you think!"

"What else would it be?" He shouts back. The hallway is teeming with girls and there's more than a few phones recording. I wait for Avery to start collecting them and get onto damage control but she's smiling her evil little smile instead.

"I thought I was doing the right thing, I thought that's what you guys would want. I was going to talk to Harley about it as well! You only think that I was being dishonest because of Avery, she's become so jealous since she's become friends with the Mounty. The stalker has turned you all against me!"

Fucking lying bitch. Avery arches an eyebrow at me and we both push past the lover's quarrel to get into our own room. I think about shoving Blaise through the door and slamming it on him but then he answers Annabelle.

"The Mounty you hate so much has never betrayed my trust like that. She's kept promises when she should have told me to fuck off because I was an absolute dick to her. I even offered to pay her for tutoring me last year and she told me to shove my money up my ass. So, who's the manipulative slut here? If you want a baby daddy to fund the life you want, go find one dumb enough to believe your lies."

Okay, I've reached my threshold of being called a slut today. I've hit the limit and I'm going to start stabbing people. Avery's super senses must pick up on this and she joins Blaise to get Annabelle to leave. I lock myself in the bathroom to try and scrub the anger out of my skin.

By the time I get out, Avery is packing her ballet bag and Blaise is grumbling as he prepares to walk her down to her class.

"Better?" she says and I plaster a fake smile on.

"I won't ever bury your brother but if he calls me a slut ever again I will castrate him. Like I said, it's in my skill set and I can actually do it. If you ever want to be an aunty someday you should probably warn him."

Avery bursts out laughing while Blaise looks at me with horror, one hand subconsciously covering his groin. I'm so proud of myself as I wink at him and when my phone pings in my pocket I don't even think as I grab it.

Have you forgotten about me, little Starbright?

My blood turns to ice. It's a good way of stopping my attraction from becoming obvious. Avery watches my face carefully and when I slump onto my bed to figure out how the fuck to answer Matteo without causing more trouble she ushers Blaise out of the room.

Never. I could never forget you.

Chapter Six

I'm woken by a quiet knock at the door.

I glance at my phone and see it's two in the morning. Not happy. Avery is still asleep, breathing slow and even, and it takes me a second to realize what has woken me up. As I slide out of my bed, the knock repeats, louder and more insistent. I check the peephole to find Ash standing there. I glance back to Avery but she still hasn't woken up. It's been two weeks since our confrontation and I've managed to avoid him completely. I don't want to see him now.

With a sigh, I open the door.

It's only after it's open that I realize I've never seen so much as a bare ankle on Ash before. He's always wearing a full uniform, pressed to perfection and spotless, which only leaves his hands and above his neck uncovered.

And now he's standing in front of me in boxers and a loose tank top, the armholes so big I can see his nipples peeking out.

Sweet lord. Jesus have mercy.
Fuck me, my soul has left my body.
They're some damn good nipples.

"Yes?" I manage to squeak out. I force my gaze to stay firmly above his shoulders, which isn't much better on my poor libido. His hair is rumpled and adorable, he'd give Blaise's sex hair a run for its money. He raises an eyebrow at me, his cold eyes. The look calms the chaos of my hormones a bit. I remember that he's an utter dick and I glare back at him.

"I'm not here for you," he snaps and pushes past me. I let him go and then swing the door shut behind him. After I've gotten all of the extra bolts in place I head back to my own bed. Ash climbs onto Avery's bed and wakes her. She looks cranky for a second and then she softens. Ash glares over his shoulder at me until I get the point and slip my headphones on. I roll away from them so he can talk to her in peace.

I pray I don't snore and then I slip back to sleep.

When my alarm wakes me again at six, I find Ash asleep on one of the couches. My breath catches in my throat looking at him with his head pillowed on his bicep. There's a blanket tangled up in his legs and he's frowning even in his sleep. Avery is sitting up in her bed and tapping away on her phone. She glances up at me and grimaces.

"Joey." she whispers, "He's been telling Senior a load of crap about Ash and now Father is sending all sorts of lovely messages to Ash. He's under so much pressure from them both, I'm really worried."

I swing my legs out of bed and pad quietly over to sit on her bed so we don't wake Ash. "Is your dad…like Joey?" I ask hesitantly. We haven't covered this with our truths yet. Avery sighs and nods.

Great.

I scrub a hand over my face and then I smile at her. "We'll add that to the list of things we need to sort out then."

Avery scoffs as I head into the bathroom. "There's no sorting Senior out, Lips. There's only surviving him."

I had always thought that about the Jackal too. But I have some ideas and plans in the pipeline. Now I have the desire to get us out of this mess alive and relatively unscathed. All of us, even Ash. He might be an asshole to me right now but he loves his sister and, before Joey fucked things up, we'd been close to being…friends? On friendly terms at the very least.

I shower and dress for the day. When I walk back into the kitchen to grab a coffee and some fruit for breakfast Ash is gone and Avery is still in her bed on her phone. I have no idea who she would even call in to help with this. I sit on my bed to face her.

"When you're ready, we should talk about your father. I can't help if I don't have the full scope of the problem," I say, trying to sound gentle. I don't know if I succeed.

Avery looks up and her eyes are wet. It's the closest to crying I've ever seen her and I panic a little. Avery Beaumont doesn't cry. Just like Lips Anderson doesn't do girl talk. It's fucking weird.

She clears her throat. "I don't see how you can help. On the surface, Senior is a well-respected businessman. He was born filthy rich and will die that way. He has three beloved children he's raised on his own since his beautiful wife died under tragic circumstances. He's on the board for multiple charities and he's a highly sought after bachelor."

She stops and takes a deep breath. "His legitimate businesses are all a front for the illegal ones. He has a lot of say on what happens in politics, there are senators that answer to him, and he makes sure that legislation that helps his business and crushes others is pushed through. He enjoys hurting women and beat my mother every day when she was alive. He's in a gentleman's club and they bet on awful, depraved things I can't speak about."

I nod and blow out a breath as I think. "He knows Joey kills people for fun and he covers for him. He knows he's hurting Ash, too. He knows Joey killed you and he covered for him then as well. I'm guessing Joey is his favorite?"

Avery drops her phone.

Fuck.

I forgot we hadn't talked about any of that. The Jackal had given me that information when I was trying to sort Joey out after he'd attacked another student.

"How-how did you know that?" Avery whispers. She looks beyond shocked, haunted, and terrified.

I grimace. Not a good way to prove I'm trustworthy. "Last year I did some digging into your family. I was trying to figure out how much of a danger Joey really was. I should have told you, I'm sorry."

Avery stares at me, her face unblinking, and I start to really think I've fucked up. She recovers and swoops down to grab her phone. "Ash will lose his mind if he finds out you know."

Typical Avery, always protecting her brother first. I speak carefully, measuring my words, "I found all of this out last year when you were trying to get me to drop out. If I wanted to spread it, I would've done it then."

Avery nods, then whispers, "We haven't even told Harley or Blaise. Ash doesn't want anyone to know."

Holy fuck.

I start to chew my nails, a habit I've kicked but unless I can find some whiskey it'll have to do. "I'll take it to my grave, Avery. I swear to you, I will never tell a soul. But I need more information so we can get you both out of there." She nods reluctantly and I go on, "Why doesn't Ash stop him? He's bigger and he wins all of his fights in the boys dorms."

Avery traces the stitching in her pillow with one of her long, manicured fingers as she refuses to meet my eye. "It's because of me. Joey told him he'd kill me if he fights back. The summer before freshman year Ash lost his temper with him and punched him back. Broke his jaw with one punch. That night Joey strangled me. Ash had to call Harley to get us and get me to the hospital."

"How did you explain it to Harley?"

"Ash told him what had happened. He just didn't tell him it's been going on for years."

I decide then and there that I'm going to stop being shit at girl talk and learn how to do this whole best friend thing properly. I get up and hug Avery.

She startles, because she knows just how hug-adverse I am, but she hugs me back tightly. I hook my chin onto her shoulder and say, "There are a few things I can do. Let me help you."

She nods.

I'm going to have to take out both Joseph Beaumonts one way or another.

911. Coffee. Ballet.

Right. I'm not sure why bringing a coffee to Avery at her ballet class is being considered an emergency but I'm scrambling to do it anyway. I'm still pretty jittery after our long conversation about her fucked up father and my mind immediately goes into overdrive. I'm picturing Joey attacking her or an assassin, maybe a kidnapping.

Is our room bugged?

I need to do a full intensive search the second I can. I'd been studying in my pajamas so I had to throw a sweater over my Vanth shirt while the coffee machine worked its magic.

I dodge curious looks and leering seniors as I sprint to the dance gym, my hand steady on the reusable, glass coffee cup Avery had personalized with 'Dictator in Power' after I'd told her about my sniping with Harley about our history class last year. I can't look at it without bursting out laughing.

Someday, when I tell her who I am, I want one with a wolf on it. Two very different, but very deadly, predators.

When I make it to the gym I expect to find a crowd or a dead body or something and instead Avery is sitting on the bench by the doors scowling at her phone. I slump down next to her and hand her the coffee.

"Harlow Roqueford is a dirty, pathetic bitch who needs a reality check. She's going on my planner for next week. You in?"

On her planner. That's Avery's way of saying she's going to start a campaign. Currently, we have Joey, Rory, Lance, and Annabelle on her planner and I feel like we're getting nowhere with all of them. Well, why the fuck not?

I lean back and say, "Definitely. What do you want me to do?"

"How about you take your dirty, trash self back to where you belong? In the slums."

Great. I look up to see the woman of the hour standing over us with her hands on her hips. She was wearing a sports bra and leggings that are so tight I could see not only her lack of underwear but also the fact that she has a landing strip. Pass the bleach, I want to die.

Avery's eyes drop thirty degrees in temperature and she becomes a marble statue, cold, and hard. "Harlow, if you're going to speak to us can you please put on some underwear? I can see your gaping vagina trailing down your thighs from here."

Sweet merciful lord, I nearly choke.

Harlow doesn't flinch. She flicks her hair over her shoulder and shrugs at Avery. "You think you're untouchable because you're a Beaumont, well guess what? Your own brother wants you dead."

I roll my eyes and Avery chuckles, her voice as sweet and kind as shards of broken glass. "I am well aware of Joey's thoughts on me. I do live with him, you know."

Harlow's eyes flick to me. "You call in your little guard dog? How much are you paying the trash to watch your back?"

Avery takes a long sip of her coffee. Long enough that Harlow begins to twitch. She wants Avery's full attention. She wants to scare her and knock her off of the top of the social ladder.

She's so stupid.

"Are you trying to win Joey's affection by attacking me? Because that would make you brain dead and pathetic. Joey doesn't have affections, he just wants to get high and fuck as many different girls as he can. You'll never keep him. It baffles me to think of a reason why you would want to keep him." The door to the dance rooms opens and students pour out. We get a few curious looks and Jessie gives me a shy wave. I smile at her.

Harlow's mouth slides into a smug, over-the-top smirk that makes her look deranged and simple. "He's rich, hot, and he has a huge dick. What more could a girl want?"

I gag. I can't help it, it happens before I can lock it down. Avery pats me gently on the back like it's totally normal and her mouth quirks upwards.

Annabelle steps up besides Harlow and I tense. She's wearing a pale pink leotard and tights, her legs look like they go on forever. I can see the appeal. "Well, Harlow. If I gave a damn about you in any way I would tell you I think you've picked the wrong Beaumont brother on all of those accounts."

Avery sighs. We share a look as Harlow scoffs and turns on Annabelle, "Why pick the boy when you can have the man?"

Annabelle laughs right in her face. I've fallen down the rabbit hole and now I'm stuck in Wonderland watching two evil queens battle it out. It's surreal and highly entertaining.

"Oh, Harlow. Joey has to ask Senior for everything; Ash doesn't. Joey is a tweaking, sinewy mess with his little habit; Ash isn't. And I know for a fact that Ash has a good three inches on his brother."

I'm kind of horrified at myself but I'm stuck between being jealous and curious at what Annabelle is saying. I also feel a nervous giggle starting in my chest and I need to shut that shit right down. Avery has scrunched her nose up in disgust. Right, talk of your brothers' dicks must be gross. Poor Aves.

"You'd know all about that, wouldn't you, Easy A?"

Annabelle shakes her head at Harlow with a smile. "Sweetheart, I have seen more photos of you on a dick than any other girl at this school. Don't mistake which one of us is the whore."

I stand up and tug Avery to her feet. This is getting monotonous and I don't want to hear anything else about Ash's sex life. Or the other two. Avery slips her arm into mine and we head back to our room. When we stop so Avery can unlock our door Annabelle calls out to us. Avery scoffs and rolls her eyes. I'm tempted to ignore her but she's on Avery's planner and we might be able to use whatever she's here about to destroy her.

I meet her eye and give her a curt nod.

Avery ignores her completely in favor of heating up some of the weird soup with kale and fish she's currently obsessed with. I pull a face at the smell and grab a tub of ice cream out to soften. Annabelle looks around curiously. It occurs to me that Avery never lets anyone but the boys into the room.

"Where did Blaise sleep when he was here?" says Annabelle, eyeing my bed like it carries diseases. I snort at her and Avery laughs.

"Summers, he slept wherever the hell he wanted to like he always does. What's it to you, anyway?"

Annabelle crosses her arms and looks down her nose at me. "I'm here to ask you two to stop interfering in my relationships. It's none of your business who I'm dating."

I grab a spoon and share a look with Avery. She's got her phone out and she's got someone on the line but Annabelle can't see it from where she's standing. "What my family does is very much my business and I'm not having an illegitimate child born to some gold digging, teenage girl who wants to spread her legs and spend someone else's money."

Annabelle sighs and rubs her arms. She doesn't look like the pretty, confident girl I'd first seen with Blaise. She's tired, angry, and desperate.

"Whatever. Let me have Blaise. His parents like me because I don't encourage his stupid music and he's not your family. Get the Mounty bitch to stop tutoring him and I'll leave Harley and Ash alone."

Avery tuts at her. "I thought you loved Harley? Didn't you tell him that?"

"I do but my family are going under, as you well know, and I don't want to end up on the streets. If he had access to his inheritance then I'd be fighting for him. I can't wait around while he figures out how to get the money back."

I shove a huge spoonful of ice cream into my mouth so I don't cuss the bitch out. There are a thousand good reasons to pick a guy. I can think of plenty of reasons why I would pick Blaise, Harley, or Ash, even while they hated me. But picking one over the other because of money is disgusting. Saying Harley isn't a worthy choice makes me sick.

Avery sets down her soup and glides past Annabelle to open the door for her, a clear dismissal. When Annabelle doesn't move Avery gives her a predatory smile.

"I don't make promises to anyone but my family. Get out of my room and just remember who you're speaking to."

When the door is locked behind Annabelle and Avery is back sitting with her soup I arch an eyebrow at her.

"Ash, Harley and Blaise are all my family. You're my family. That's it. I'll be damned if that bitch touches any of them again."

Chapter Seven

I spend all day on Saturday trying to get in front with my classwork. Avery spends the day with Ash and Harley in Haven and she surprises me with a gorgeous pair of boots. They're black leather, soft as a baby's butt, with chains and studs. The top of the boot has a tiny sheath that I can keep my knife in. I'm speechless and amazed. She laughs at me and brushes off my thanks. I refuse to look up how much they cost and I tell her to stop spending money on me which only makes her laugh harder.

We eat the sushi she's brought home and then I get back to work while she jumps into the shower to start her nighttime routine. She takes forever.

The knock at the door startles me out of my studying. I sigh, frustrated at the distraction, and fling open the door to find Blaise propped up on the doorframe with a lazy smirk. I grit my teeth and attempt a smile.

"Avery is in the shower. You're welcome to hang out on the couch until she's out."

The smirk grows wider and way too cocky for my liking. "I'm here for you, Mounty."

I let my eyes take him in, every detail from head to toe. He's wearing a pair of dark gray, fitted jeans with a band tee. I know the band, Malice Unfolding, but I'm surprised he does too. His smirk grows wider but then I give him one back and say, "No thanks."

He is so shocked at my dismissal that he barely manages to stop me from shutting the door in his face. "Mounty, for fuck's sake. Hear me out. Please." Urgh. It's the please that gets me. I'm also curious to see if this is about Annabelle's appearance here the night before.

I let him push the door open again and give him an expectant look.

"Right." Blaise stops and clears his throat. I already know I'm going to hate whatever comes out of his mouth next. It's either going to be insulting or endearing and I don't want to deal with either of those things. "I've made another deal with my dad. If I graduate senior year with a 3.0 GPA or higher, he's going to let me take a gap year without pitching a fit. I want to fit in a world tour and a new album. I also want to use that time to convince my parents that college isn't for me."

I sigh and motion him into the room. Avery is still in the shower and the coffee machine starts beeping to say the sweet, sweet nectar of the gods is ready to be consumed in bucket-like quantities to get me through an all-nighter. I head towards the machine. "You didn't need to come here, I already tutor you. We can go through all of your syllabi and get a plan together on how we're going to make it work."

I pour myself a cup and then, after hesitating for a second, I pour one for Blaise too. I know exactly how he takes his coffee but there's no torture method on the planet that would get me to admit that so I slide the sugar and creamer to him.

"Lance is taking up too much of your time. Ash would back off and let you work with me in peace but the little Mounty fuck wouldn't."

I cut him a look. Fuck knows why I'm defending Lance, probably the venom in Blaise's voice as he spits out Mounty. I'm waiting for him to say something about the pickup at the docks and the dirty money I had with me.

He grimaces under my stare and then speaks carefully, "I don't want *Lance* to know how much trouble I have with my classes. He's an arrogant asshole and I'd rather not have to beat the shit out of him if he runs his mouth. If Avery finds out, it'll be the next Mounty hunt."

Is Blaise fucking Morrison, lead singer and guitarist of Vanth Falling, rock god and literal idol of my heart, embarrassed? Fuck me, that's worse than an insult or sweetness. I'm doomed to pander to his every fucking whim.

I scrub a hand over my face and try to look stern, to hide just how whipped I am for this guy who still thinks I'm trash.

Look, I'm not saying I'm going to fall at his feet. I have self-respect and I'm perfectly aware of just how much he loathes me.

But the fleeting pink tinge to his cheeks and the way he's chewing on his lip is enough to make me jump through some academic hoops with him. Sue me. Plus, he's not actually dumb. He's really smart but he doesn't process information the same way as the other students do so the teachers just assume he's slacking off. Now I've figured him out, I've cut his study time in half, which is why he insists on it being me who helps him. Fuck.

I hold up three fingers and his eyes light up, goddammit. "Three rules."

He nods.

"One: you'll come to every study session on time and with the agreed work done before. If I'm going to put in the time and effort you will too. I don't care if it's wrong and we have to redo it, you have to give everything a go."

"Agreed. Next?"

"Rule two: you'll show me respect while we study. We can do it here, Avery has ballet and dance most nights so we can pick a few nights a week and we'll be left to it but I'm not having you get pissy and tearing into me for no reason. Save that for the dining hall or parties or some shit."

He has the decency to look sheepish, but not quite enough to apologize. "Yep. Next?"

"Rule three is simple: don't tell Ash."

This gets me a frown and a stern eye. "Why? He wouldn't give a shit."

I scoff at him and move to rinse out my now empty cup. "He lost his mind over you sleeping here after the party. He cornered me and told me to stay the fuck away from you and Harley. He's practically pissed on your leg to assert his ownership of you."

Blaise's frown deepens and he chews on those damn lips of his again. "Alright. But I'm going to have a chat to him about you." I'm shaking my head before he even finishes the sentence.

"I don't need your help. He'll figure it out on his own."

I sound way more confident than I am but, hey, I'm faking it until I make it.

Harley laughs at me when I hand him my completed half of our history assignment. I glare back at him but it only makes him laugh harder.

When he finally settles down he hands me his completed half and I groan at him. "Can you just tell me which half you're doing for the rest of them? I have a lot more on my plate this year helping Avery and tutoring."

Harley just grins and shakes his head. He is absolutely breathtaking. Literally, I can't breathe if I look at him for longer than a second. But I'm seriously tempted to scratch his eyes out right then.

He reads this on my face and his grin grows wider. Asshole. "I forgot to tell you. I've dealt with our Rory issue. Take him off Aves' planner."

I straighten, surprised. "What did you do?"

Avery and I had been torn on the best way to get rid of him. I wanted something permanent, like death or severe mutilation. I daydream sometimes about carving the word rapist into his face so every woman he encounters from then onwards would know the type of guy he really is. Avery enjoys public humiliation better. She's been digging around in his emails, texts, social media, anything she can to find something to destroy him with. Nothing so far.

Harley waves the teacher over to hand him our completed assignment. He's damn near preening as the entire class glares at us both. "Have you ever been to a football game at Hannaford? The hotdogs are pretty good."

My eyes narrow. "Not yet. Is there one coming up? I do like hotdogs."

I love the smug look on his face, it's laced with a dark, malicious glee that I know all too well. "Friday night. Everyone leaves for the fall break when it finishes. Bring Aves and we'll make a night of it."

I nod and smile back at him, happy and relieved it's been taken care of. Harley's grin slips a little and he glances away from me. I try really hard to not be offended that he doesn't like the look of my smiling face. I know I'm not ugly. I'm still on the scrawny side but the food at Hannaford and Avery's constant supply of coffee and ice cream means I'm filling in and I have some cleavage. Not a lot but enough to no longer look like a twelve-year-old boy. My ass is also nicely rounded, which was a bit of a surprise to me. I've honestly never eaten enough to have any sort of an ass and my mom had always been the sort of skinny only drug addicts can be. Avery tells me it's a good look in my booty shorts that I love so much so I know I'm not hideous.

I focus on my classwork, and not my wounded ego, and he doesn't try to speak to me again. When the class finishes I head straight to the library for my tutoring sessions so I can take a minute to pick my brain up off the floor and remember why I don't ever get involved with guys.

Why am I not a lesbian?

By the time Ash arrives I'm mostly settled. He gives me a curt nod and hands over a pile of assignments for me to look through. Lance arrives as I hand it all back. He smiles at me like I'm his long lost lover and I'm pissed off that I'll have to try and manage this crush he seems to have. The whispers from the other students don't seem to be affecting him at all. The fight with Blaise hasn't even been enough to get him to drop out of my tutoring sessions. He's got a much thicker skin than I expected and that only pisses me off more.

Half an hour in, it becomes clear Blaise isn't coming to the session. I know the reason why but the frown on Ash's face tells me Blaise didn't warn him he'd dropped out.

"Scared the crappy singer off?" Lance laughs and I don't even try to pretend to find it funny. He keeps looking at me through his eyelashes and I'm cringing away from him.

"You'll need to come up with better insults than that. The guy sings like a fucking audible orgasm."

That throws him off. Lance blanches and gapes at me. "Audible...orgasm?"

Ash squints at me like he's waiting for the insult to come out and I ignore him. "Yep. I've been listening to his music for years and I love every fucking second of it so pick something else to insult him about. Like his shitty attitude or his man-whoring ways."

Ash snorts and then slaps a hand over his mouth like he's just been caught cavorting with the enemy. I roll my eyes at him and get back to work. Lance sulks pathetically. I swear the guys at this school are all moody, temperamental shits.

When the hour is up Lance leaves with barely a goodbye. I pack up my stuff but Ash just stares at me. I wait him out.

"No longer embarrassed about your obsession?" Ash sneers at me, but it really looks like he's forcing it. Like he doesn't want me to know he is interested in the answer but I'm now a fucking expert in Beaumont Bullshitting. I see right through him.

"Nope. Avery is obsessed with Ed Sheeran and she's choreographed her entire ballet performance piece this year to one of his songs. Does that mean she wants to fuck the ginger? No. Last year I got flustered around Blaise because I was completely unaware that he went here and I'd be facing someone I'd spent years listening to. I admire his vocal talent. Does not mean I want to fuck him or stalk him or... any of the other things you've accused me of. So, get over it."

Ash folds his arms and leans back in his seat. "Hypothetically, if Morrison wanted to fuck you—"

I cut him off. "I'm not fucking any guy from Hannaford, hypothetically or otherwise. No one. Not a single one. No one will win the damn bet."

I mean every word.

He doesn't have to know it's not exactly by choice.

I get back to the dorms and pass Avery in the hall. She's dressed for her contemporary dance class and her bag is slung over her shoulder. She quirks an eyebrow at me and pulls me into a hug. I startle but then she whispers, "There's a rock star waiting in our rooms for his tutor."

Crap. I'd forgotten to tell Avery.

I pull back and scrunch my nose up at her. She just laughs and heads to dance class with a wave. I have eight steps left to get myself together and then I'm opening the door to find Blaise sprawled out on the floor with pizza boxes. Where the hell he found the pizza is beyond me but the smell is practically orgasmic to my empty stomach.

"You're late, Mounty." He teases and I lock the door behind me. I roll my eyes at him because I'm three minutes late and he's being an ass about it even though he's never made it on time before.

"Just let me get changed and then we can start."

He nods and shoves another slice into his mouth. I flick the coffee machine on as I head into the bathroom and quickly pull on some yoga pants and a sweater. I look like a toddler wearing her dad's clothes but it also feels a little like armor. I know I look like crap so it's totally okay if Blaise thinks I do too. I wonder if I could convince the teachers to let me wear it to class as well?

I sit down and hand Blaise a cup. He pushes a box closer to me and when I open it I find a chicken, bacon, and mushroom pizza. My favorite. My eyes narrow.

"Did you ask Avery to get us dinner?" I ask as I gulp down some coffee. I'm exhausted and by the looks of the piles of assignments Blaise isn't planning on having a slack evening.

"Nah, I drove into Haven to get it. She told me what you'd eat though. You didn't tell her I was studying here?" He scratches his chest and I can't help but admire the tattoos peeking out from the collar of his Henley shirt.

"I forgot. I'm busier this year and there's more to do now that I'm keeping Avery safe."

Blaise stares at me for a second then he chews his bottom lip. "Is she safe?"

Fuck I hope so. "As safe as I can get her. Look, I've had a rough day. I appreciate you grabbing us dinner, I wouldn't have eaten otherwise. Can we get into this so I can try to get a few hours of sleep?"

He nods and we fall into a quiet studying session, the hour passing quickly. Avery texts to say Ash is walking her back from dance and I start to pack Blaise up to avoid a fight.

When we both stand Blaise holds out an iPod. It's an old one, nothing special, and it's scuffed and scratched. I take it hesitantly.

"What's this?"

"A playlist. If we're going to be friends then I'm taking advantage of your good taste in music. Give it a listen and let me know what you like. I'll grab it next week so wipe it and make me a list."

My heart flutters and I silently tell it to calm the fuck down. He wants to swap music with me? That's an irresistible move and I'm sure he knows it, too. What the hell is he playing at?

"How do you know I have good taste?"

Blaise grins at me and then sucks on his bottom lip, rolling it between his teeth. I force myself not to watch the action because I may drool.

"Well, you like Vanth. I'm assuming your taste must be decent."

Then he leaves. I stare at the cushions he was sitting on, stunned, and then with a smile I put the headphones on and listen to the little piece of his soul he's gifted me.

Chapter Eight

I wake up on Friday filled with nervous, excitable energy.

Avery laughs at me as I jitter my way around the kitchen and bathroom and she tries to cut off my caffeine supply. A solid deathly glare fixes that.

"We'll meet at the library after class to sort out your biology notes. We can leave there together to go to the football game," I say as I wash out my cup. Avery is fussing with her hair in the bathroom with the door open so she can snark at me. She's less than ecstatic about Harley asking us to go to the football game, she hates every single thing about the sport. Only the lure of watching Rory's downfall manages to convince her.

Harley notices my energy but doesn't comment until our last class for the day. He gives me a little grin, evil twinkling in his stunning blue eyes, and says, "See you there, Mounty."

I take a second to remember that oxygen is something I need and then I head off to meet Avery. She beats me there and is sitting at my tutoring desk, already working on the notes.

I sit and try not to fidget.

"What's your truth for the day?" I say. I'd woken up determined to tell Avery who I really was and how we're going to use that to sort Joey out. Now that Rory was off the list and Annabelle was, apparently, on limited time we had to focus on the real danger in the school. The only problem is I'm shitting myself about telling her. I'm actually happy for the first time in my life. I have a best friend, I have two other sort-of friends, and I'm hopeful Ash will come around. Avery already knows I have some involvement in the Twelve and the shady, criminal world that comes with it but knowing I am a member? Knowing what I do for money? That might be a deal breaker. I should have told her sooner.

Avery surveys the room with a cold look. Students scurry away from our table and she smirks at me. "Hmm. When I was nine I failed a spelling test. My mother had just died and I didn't care about anything. I wanted to die as well but I was afraid of leaving Ash. Anyway, the teacher said she would have to call my father and tell him about it. I knew what he would do to me if he found out and instead of being scared, I got angry. I'd heard all about this teacher from my mother's book club, which was basically a front for day drinking and gossiping. I knew she was married to a doctor and lived a really great life. I also knew that the man that picked her up for lunch every day was not her husband. I'd seen her lipstick on his neck and made the deduction that he wasn't her brother. I told her that I was going home to tell my father about it. I told her I didn't want to be taught by such an immoral woman. She decided not to call him and I ruled supreme in her class for the rest of the year."

It's like the magician had pulled back the curtain and I was finally seeing just how Avery Beaumont had become the force of nature that she was. Why am I not surprised she started her campaigns as a primary school child?

"It was a pivotal turning point in my life when I realized I could manipulate adults even more than I could my peers. I also realized I take in more than other people do. I spot things that my brothers don't."

I nod, thoughtfully. Avery sets down her pen and folds her hands in her lap. I know without looking that her ankles are crossed and her head tilts a fraction to the right. I call this the 'Avery power pose'. She makes it when she's plotting.

I clear my throat to bring her back to our conversation. "What's the one thing you want to know about me? If you could ask for a truth, what would it be?"

She doesn't hesitate or think about her answer. "Where exactly does a foster child orphaned by drug users find herself a hundred thousand dollars? Not the money you need laundered, I mean the money you had to pay for Harley's hotel."

I nod and blow out a breath. I clear my throat again and pick at my nails. "Have you ever heard of the Game that's held by the Twelve?"

Avery freezes and stares at me like I've just grown another head. She gives the slightest nod of her head.

"I survived Mounts Bay because the Jackal took an interest in me. When I was thirteen he sponsored me and I won the Game. I was untouchable after that. I still am I guess, outside of these walls. There are people in the city that would not take kindly to how your brothers treat me."

Avery's jaw drops and she gapes at me. I fidget and sweat with nerves. When she still doesn't speak I continue, "I chose to work alone because I don't want to start a gang or an empire. Instead, I collect information from places no one else can and sometimes... I take people out. Outside of Hannaford I'm known as the Wolf."

Avery finally comes out of her stupor and squeals with such zeal that the librarian rushes towards us expecting a dire injury. Blaise dashes out of one of the stacks with his shirt untucked and lipstick smeared down his neck. To my horror, Annabelle *freaking* Summers follows him out of the stacks with a savage but smug look on her face and her bra in full view. I level a glare at Blaise, which he promptly ignores to lean over Avery.

"Hey, what's happened? Are you okay?" his voice sounds wrong, all throaty and raspy from the making out he's clearly been doing. I try not to let jealousy consume me but, really, *Annabelle*?! Is he mentally compromised or something?

The look Avery gives him is probably the worst I've ever seen. "I'm fine, thank you, Morrison. Go back to your dirty public fuck."

Avery swearing is basically DEFCON 1. Blaise glares at Annabelle and when he turns back to Avery he actually looks a little embarrassed. "I had a momentary lapse in judgment."

Then he pulls out a chair next to me and all but collapses into it to sit with us. Annabelle glares at us and tries to pull the chair out next to him. He stops her and refuses to look at her. It is so awkward I want to *die*.

"Blaise—"

He rubs his face with a rough hand and groans at her, "Go away. I'm not going there with you again. I told you that last night when you showed up at my room, I told you again this morning when you text me, and I told you for the last time ten minutes ago when you stripped in the stacks. I'm not saying it again. Please just…fuck off."

Avery and I share a look. I almost laugh when I realize we're talking to each other with our eyebrows, something I'd seen her and the boys do a hundred times but a skill I didn't think I had.

As Annabelle turns away from him, he adds, "And give me back my Vanth shirt. It was the first one and irreplaceable."

"I told you I don't have the ugly thing." she snaps and finally stomps off, gritting her teeth so hard I hear her jaw crack. Blaise doesn't lift his head from where he's cradling it in his hands.

"So, what you're saying she molested you in the stacks?" Avery snipes. I start to grab my stuff to leave them to it but she shakes her head at me. Great. I don't want to hear this and after my confession I'm a little jumpy. I stay put.

"No. I'm saying I was in a shitty mood. I was working on my literature paper and she ambushed me in the stacks with her shirt unbuttoned and no underwear on."

"And you thought you'd give her one last fuck for old times' sake?"

Blaise grits his teeth and takes a deep breath like he's trying not to rip her head off. Thank God Ash isn't here to see it. "No. I told her I wasn't interested and she wrapped herself around me and started kissing my neck. I told her to get off of me and she refused."

She frowns at him, her anger softening. "How is that a lapse in judgment? You made it sound like you caved."

"I didn't shove her the fuck off of me. She kept talking about shit we've done together and I felt bad for her. I forgot that she's a manipulative bitch. If I hadn't heard you scream I would've just stood there like an idiot." He groans again and Avery shoots me a look.

"I'll have her sorted by the time we get back from fall break. Let's get a move on and meet the others."

Ash and Harley are waiting for us in the bleachers.

They both eye Blaise with something close to hostility until Avery snaps at them and tells them about Annabelle. Blaise looks ashamed for about three seconds before Ash's smirks piss him off enough to snark back at him. I sit between Avery and Harley, and Blaise sits on the end with Ash. Harley hands me a hotdog and I look at his shoulder to choke out a thank you. His eyes are too intense for me after the day I've had.

Avery is watching me now too.

She hasn't said a word about my confession. She still tucked her arm into mine as we walked here and she teased me with Blaise about my utter ignorance of all things football. I'm not sure if that means she's cool with me, or if she's waiting until we get back to our room before she kicks me out of her life.

I tell myself I'll be fine either way.

I'm lying.

Well, not *lying*. I'd survive it. I survive everything like a damn cockroach. But it would suck and probably hurt worse than having my leg smashed to pieces so I'm really hoping that squeal she let out in the library was a good one.

"We're not going to have to sit through the whole thing, are we?" Avery gripes. She's cringing at Harley and I as we eat our hotdogs. Ash looks absolutely disgusted at us both and Blaise is too busy trying to fight the breeze to light a blunt to notice what we're doing. I frown at him and Harley nudges me gently.

"Relax. No one here gives a shit, Mounty."

Whatever.

I don't want to be a stick in the mud but I'd watched my mother use every single drug she could get her hands on and it made me deeply, intensely wary of any type of high that isn't liquor. I shrug and look out over the crowd.

The stands are awash with the deep blood red and charcoal gray of Hannaford's colors. The away team is another private school from a city three hours away so their crowd is much smaller and far less festive. The cheerleaders from both schools are busy flipping, twirling, dancing, and shaking. The uniforms look like they were stolen from a porn set and I can pick out the dirty, old men that would happily risk a lengthy jail sentence to lift those skirts. I shudder and look away.

Avery is still cursing Harley's name and Ash tucks her under his arm to keep her warm and safe. The crowd is on the rowdy side and Harley's massive frame is the only thing stopping me from being jostled about. He turns to glare at the guys behind us and when they get a good look at who they're bumping they settle the fuck down.

"We'll be gone by quarter time, Floss. Just get a hotdog and enjoy the show."

He waves his food in her face and she gags dramatically. Blaise hands the blunt to Ash and when he takes a drag he offers it to Harley. He hesitates and then waves them off. I grumble at him, "Don't turn it down because I don't like it."

He shoves the last of the hotdog into his mouth and grabs the uneaten half of my hotdog I've abandoned on my lap thanks to my nervous stomach. With an eyebrow quirk he says, "I want to remember every second of this and I need a clear head."

Of course. Why would he do anything for me? My face heats and I nod as the players march out onto the field. Blaise starts critiquing their movements like he knows something about what's going on and Ash ignores everyone for his phone. Avery reads his texts and they murmur to each other quietly.

I try to keep my eye on the field but three minutes in I want to throw myself head first onto the concrete beneath the bleachers to get out of this torture. Instead, I discreetly watch Harley as he fixates on the game. He's wearing his uniform, a Hannaford requirement to attend the game, but he's taken his tie off and put a coat on. I can tell it's one Avery's bought for him because it's perfectly tailored to fit his broad shoulders like a glove. He's still wearing his mother's necklace but he's swapped the gold chain for a thin leather rope.

He notices me looking and says, "A senior tried to get it back for Joey during a fight. The leather won't break like the chain did."

I scowl and cross my arms, shivering in the cold night air with only a skirt on. "I hope you made him bleed."

Harley shrugs his coat off and drapes it to cover Avery's bare legs and then he tucks the other end under my thigh to cover me as well. I thank him quietly and he shrugs without looking away from the game. Ash watches him and shakes his head at me like I'm to blame for his kindness. Avery nudges him and draws his attention back to his phone.

"Fuck Aves, this is it."

I look up just in time to see a player go down hard, three opposition players piling on. It just looks like a tackle to me but Blaise curses under his breath and the crowd falls silent. Harley's eyes are fixated on Rory's prone form, greedily drinking in the scene as the coaching team and medics race out onto the field.

Blaise whistles and murmurs, "He'll be lucky to walk again."

Harley chuckles and leans in to whisper to me, "I paid enough to make sure he won't."

I smile. Avery tucks her arm into mine and gives me her trademark smug smile. Something eases in my chest and I can breathe again.

Rory never returns to Hannaford Prep.

Chapter Nine

Avery wakes me at five in the morning with a gentle shake.

She's dressed already and her phone is tucked away in her coat pocket, buzzing incessantly with incoming messages. She's stern looking and I push myself up to sit and face her. She had left the football game with Ash and returned to our room after I'd fallen asleep.

"I was going to wait until after the break to speak to you but I know you're freaking out about what you told me. I've thought a lot about how to say this and I think it's best if I just say it."

I try to swallow around the lump in my throat but I'm so dry it hurts. Avery waits for me to nod before she continues.

"You saved Harley's life and offered him protection even when we all hated you. You used those same connections to neutralize Joey without just killing him. If I know you at all then I also know you're planning on using your status as the Wolf to take care of Senior and Joey. If anything, I trust you even more now than I did before. When we became friends, I told you that I'm an all or nothing person. You're my family and nothing about this changes that."

Fuck me.

Fuck me, I actually tear up a little and then I have to blink like crazy to stop myself from bawling my eyes out, which is so not me. This whole girl talk shit is messing with me. I'm the Wolf, dammit! Avery reaches over and squeezes my hand before getting up. She struts out of the door with a casual 'Bye!' thrown over her shoulder.

I smile and drag myself to the shower even though it's too early and I have no obligations. I'm going to use the break to sort Joey and Harlow out and get them both off of the planner.

I wait until I'm sure the school has emptied out for fall break. I go down to the dining hall for dinner in case Harley is down there and lonely but he's a no show. Once the sun sets and the whole building is scary quiet I change into a pair of Avery's black yoga pants, a long sleeve black shirt, and my flats. The yoga pants have pockets, which is why I borrowed them. I slip my tools into them and then lock the door on the way out. You can never be too careful.

Harlow's room, a single because she's filthy rich, is on the opposite end of the girls' dorms and her lock has also been upgraded. I take it as a good sign for my hunt.

I've never met a lock I couldn't pick and thirty seconds later I'm quietly closing her door behind me.

I choke on my own spit.

Holy fuck.

Harlow Roqueford is a hoarder. The room is only slightly smaller than the one I share with Avery but I instantly feel that type of claustrophobic you get when you think stacks of crap are going to fall on you and you'll die of starvation before the rescue teams can dig you out. It's all luxury shit but piled up like this I feel like I'm in a shady discount warehouse. I can't tell what color the walls are or what furniture she has. I couldn't even say if she has a private bathroom because all I can see are the piles of clothes and shoes. There has to be an obscene amount of money sitting in this room in luxury items.

I start to sweat.

Avery would have an aneurysm.

I'm smarter this time, having been burned from my break in at Joey's room last year, and I use the Spy Finder device I use on jobs as the Wolf to scan for cameras. It's not foolproof but it gives me a better chance of finding hidden security measures and with the mess this place is in I need all the help I can get. Once it's clear, I take a few photos of the mess, though I'm not sure how we could use this against her. I dig through some of the clothing but there's nothing suspicious about it, she's obviously got a shopping addiction that far exceeds Avery's.

There's no loose floorboards, no drugs, no incriminating photos, nothing that is any use. I'm frustrated but undeterred. I'll call Avery and let her know.

I turn to leave and then I spot them.

Sitting innocuously on the bedside table are Avery's missing Louboutins. I don't even have to check with her to know that they're it. She has shown me pictures of them dozens of times, lamenting their loss, and snarling that the packing company must have stolen them. She's been watching auction sites for weeks to see if they show up. They were worth more than a year's tuition at Hannaford and there is only one pair in existence.

Harlow's stolen them.

I look around the room with a far more critical eye. The clothing is in different sizes and styles. Some of the dresses are so tiny there is no way Harlow could fit in them and there's monogrammed blazers and robes, none have HR on them. In her cupboard I find suitcases stacked and some of those have tags with other girls names on them. Under the bed I find the other item I'm really looking for.

Blaise's missing Vanth shirt.

One of a kind and I'm just the type of fan to know it from a mile away.

He's been raging about Annabelle stealing it for weeks. Avery had mentioned it to me as a possible issue because if she offered to give it back she could lure him into her room, he'd cave for the shirt any day of the week. She wasn't lying about it.

Harlow Roqueford is a hoarding kleptomaniac.

And she likes to take priceless, one-of-a-kind items.

I take the shirt and the shoes. There's no way I'm leaving them behind in this cave of stolen treasures and when I slip back into our room I video call Avery. She picks up immediately and smirks at me, one finger on her mouth to silence me.

I nod and watch her move through the rooms of her father's mansion. Ash stalks behind her but I don't think he sees me.

"Miss me already, Mounty?"

I'm so smug I swear it beams through the phone to her. I don't even say a word and she knows.

"Harlow, Annabelle, or Joey?"

I hold up her shoes and she squeals. Ash ducks into view, scowling, and then he glances at Avery. I cut in before he can insult me by suggesting I've stolen them.

"Can you forward a picture onto Morrison for me? I've recovered his missing shirt."

Avery shoulders Ash away. "Of course. Who had them?"

I text through the photos of the shirt and the shots I took of the room. Avery shudders and frowns when they come through. "Who lives in that cesspit?"

"Harlow. She's stealing and hoarding from other students. Should I call the student hotline or will you deal with the bitch?"

Avery smiles the same way I imagine an executioner does as he sharpens his guillotine blade.

"I'll do it."

After I hang up I shower and dig out the file the Jackal sent me last year with Joey's information in it. I've read it a hundred times but I keep going back to it like I'll spot something that will get him out of our lives. The problem is I don't know if Avery wants him relocated, locked up, or dead. She's always so damn cagey when I bring it up and I haven't pushed her on it.

My phone pings and I grab it, distracted by the images of Joey's victims.

Mounty, I'm sending you something as a thank you for finding my shirt.

Sweet fucking lord. Avery has given him my number. My hands shake and a little nervous giggle bubbles in my chest. Is there a Wikihow on texting a hot, thankful rock star who is also your semi-reformed bully and tutoring pupil? What the hell do I even say?

My phone pings again and I gulp before I look.

She shouldn't be sneaking into other student's rooms without backup. The shirt isn't worth that much. Wait until we're back, Mounty.

That one is from Harley and it dawns on me that it's a group text. Avery's added me to their group chat. My stomach drops when I see Ash is on it too and now he'll be able to insult me at all hours of the day. I'm not sure why I'm so pissed off about him calling me a slut. I mean, he did it last year and I didn't give a shit.

Don't get Avery involved when Harlow finds out you were in there. She doesn't need to be cleaning up your mess.

Hmm. Not so bad, I can deal with grumpy Ash.

Welcome to the madhouse Mounty. Now your phone will blow up all day long and you'll hate me for adding you when they start talking about who has the nicest tits or who fucked which girl first.

I cannot think of anything worse than seeing them talk about that. I choose sarcasm as my shield and climb into bed.

Can't wait.

I'm just about asleep when the last text comes through from Blaise.

Seeing as we're all banned from Annabelle and Harley's apparently taken a vow of celibacy there will probably be more complaints of blue balls than anything else.

A box arrives on Friday morning addressed to The Mounty.

I don't open it. Mostly because I'm dealing with a major crush and my hormones can't handle knowing what he's sent me. Also, Ash and Harley have taken up texting me all day guessing what the present will be. Avery messaged me privately to laugh at them because she thinks they're being so obvious. I'm too tired from studying to ask her what the hell she means by that.

She arrives back to school Sunday night.

"Tell me I'm your favorite," Avery says with an obnoxiously smug tone.

I roll my eyes at her without looking up from the assignments I have spread over my bed. I'm only five weeks ahead and I'm getting twitchy because of it. Damn Blaise and all of his tutoring. He's a damn distraction of the hottest kind.

"Of course you're my favorite. You're my favorite human on the planet, it's not fucking hard to figure out."

She perches on my bed delicately so she doesn't disturb my work, bless her. "Aw, you're the best. I also rank you in my top four. It's a constantly revolving list, you guys should really take more care to battle it out for my affection."

I smirk at her. "I'm winning. When do those assholes ever make time to plan out the maiming and torture of fellow students with you? Hmm? When was the last time they walked into a literal orgy to take photos for you? Do I need to remind you of that time I brought you a coffee after ballet because you were going to rip Harlow's slutty face off? I walked into a cesspit to recover your shoes."

She tilts her head like she's considering it. "Point taken. You've definitely spent longer in the top spot than the others this year. Anyway, you should check your bank balance."

I frown and grab my phone. I hadn't noticed she'd grabbed the bags of dirty cash from the closet. Sure enough, there's an extra hundred grand now safely deposited into my offshore accounts. Yep, I'm that much of a badass criminal that I can't even bank locally. Lucky fucking me.

"Thanks. Atticus didn't want a cut?"

Avery shakes her head. "He had some questions. I told him it was dirty money and I was so worried about my father finding it. He practically fell over himself to launder it for me. He asked if I'm going to the High Society Charity Ball this year."

There's a blush on her cheeks and the nervous fluttering of her fingers tells me she's not even close to getting over her crush on this guy. I should really look him up. We do not need another Rory in our lives, especially so soon after we got rid of the last one.

"A charity ball, how exciting!" I say with so much sarcasm that Avery groans and walks over to put the coffee machine on. She grabs me a cup without asking and fusses with my coffee until it's perfect. Again, I adore this girl so fiercely I wish I were a lesbian and I could lock this shit down.

Alas, I like dick.

Well, I think I do. I like it enough to wish I could have it occasionally, but not enough to risk the Jackal. I wonder where exactly that puts me on the spectrum?

"You're tempting me to go and drag you along! I told him I was too busy with school and he agreed to take me next year instead. He was… kinder this year. Hmm, no, not *kinder*. Maybe… more interested in speaking to me."

Uh oh. I get up and follow her into the kitchen. She hands me my cup and I try to figure out how the hell to talk to her about this kind of thing.

"So. You're…into him…again?"

Avery snorts at me, the most unrefined thing I've ever seen her do. "You really are hopeless at girl talk. Yes, I'm once again thinking about him way too much. He's just so…perfect. I can't go to the ball this year because if he doesn't kiss me at the end of the night I may climb into my bed and refuse to get out. He's gorgeous. Absolutely stunning and such a gentleman, I'm a mess around him. Ugh, he said he's going to come to my ballet recital that's coming up and I'm freaking out about it."

I nod and sip. When the silence stretches out Avery huffs at me, "This is where you tell me to stop being so pathetic."

I sigh at her. "I can't. I'm even more pathetic than you when it comes to guys and I try my best not to be a hypocrite."

"I highly doubt it. Explain your boy troubles to me so we can compare."

Hell *fucking* no. I try not to ever lie to Avery so instead I give her a half-truth. "Oh, you know. The Jackal means I can't ever date or hook up without fearing for my life."

She winces and scrunches her nose up. "At some point we need to tell the guys about that you know."

Nope. No thank you. Why would they need to know? I shake my head and sit at the bench. Avery fusses with her cup and then ducks down to grab her bucket of cleaning supplies.

Uh oh.

"Is something wrong?"

She pulls on a pair of gloves and starts to scrub the stovetop. It's already clean from the last time she scrubbed it but I don't argue with this brand of crazy.

"Shit, Aves. What's happened?"

She huffs and scrubs harder. "Harlow's parents were called about her little habit. They paid off one of the laundry staff to take the fall. All of the items have been returned and she's still here. As you're the only student that was here during the break, and the shoes and shirt were missing, it'll be pretty obvious it was you. She's already gone to Joey about it."

I shrug. I'm not afraid of Harlow and Joey getting involved might work in our favor. I need to draw him away from his siblings so I can deal with him once and for all.

Avery clears her throat. "Are you going to tell me what Blaise sent you? Harley is also *dying* to know."

The box is sitting on my bed. Avery can see it's unopened and she's baiting me. I arch an eyebrow at her.

"I don't accept bribes from rich playboys. Only favors."

She grins at me, savage and beautiful.

Chapter Ten

I'm woken by no less than thirty text messages.

My phone may crap out and die if this keeps up. I'm used to, like, three phone calls a year when I'm not the Wolf in Mounts Bay. Even then the most I get is one or two calls a week. When I complain at Avery she shakes her head at me in pity.

Breakfast at the dining hall. Stop avoiding us just because Ash is a dick.

Harley has taken to openly calling Ash out on my behalf. I'm pretty sure it'll only make things worse but I have zero control over this shit. Plus I get this warm feeling in my chest when I read it. I get warm in other places too, places that are entirely inappropriate when I have Harley's cousin sitting next to me eating a fruit salad and yogurt.

Ash sits on Avery's other side and staunchly pretends I don't exist. Harley sits across from me, and Blaise lounges next to him. When the freshman kid next to me bumps me and then offers to let me blow him as an apology Harley threatens to stab him with the butter knife. I've never seen a guy piss himself over breakfast cutlery so quickly.

Ash leans forward in his chair to add in, "You don't win the sweep for getting your dick sucked anyway, Javier. You'd have to be able to get it up *and* slip it in, and we all know you have problems with that."

The kid leaves the table to the sounds of Avery's tinkling laughter and the guys all sniggering like five year olds over fart jokes. I try to focus on my breakfast.

Blaise, who has been watching Harley like a hawk all morning, pours me another glass of juice. "Did you like your present, Mounty?"

Avery grins down at her phone. "She hasn't even opened it, Morrison."

The smirk falls off of his face. "Why not?"

I sigh and push my plate away. "I don't want to have things bought for me."

Blaise frowns and hurt flashes in his eyes. "It was a thank you, Mounty. Jesus, I wasn't bribing you."

I shrug and take a bite of my apple. "Most people say thank you with words. I don't want your money."

Blaise's gaze grows even more intense on my face. Avery flicks a grape at him to get his attention. "She threw a tantrum at me last week for buying new sheets for her bed because I hated the color of the other ones. She's as weird about money as Harley is."

Her cousin doesn't look up at any of us. He's texting under the table as he eats his toast, his tattoo flexing over his jaw looking lickable.

Wow. Mind out of the gutter, Anderson.

I turn back towards Avery to snark at her but I catch the bruise peeking out of her shirt. I stare at it for long enough that she notices and then I meet her knowing eyes. Her face has shut down. The smile gone and, in its place, the shield of ice and cruelty is back.

I won't be deterred.

"Junior or Senior?" I murmur. Harley looks up and scowls at us.

Avery looks over to where her brother is holding court with his little flunkies. Harlow is stroking his leg under the table while making fuck-me eyes. Well, I hope it's his leg. Gross.

"Senior."

I grit my teeth. The bruises are fingerprints circling the base of her throat like a necklace. Seems Joey got his infatuation with choking from his father. Avery must have been terrified. After the near miss from Joey this would have been fucking terrifying.

Ash stands abruptly and tugs Avery to her feet. "I'll walk you to class."

I rub my eyes and plan. I have always worked best under pressure.

Avery and Ash can never go home to that man again.

I'm calling in a favor.

My hand shakes even as I hit send. I've hesitated over this for weeks and, now Avery's been attacked by her father, I need to stop being Lips and remember who I really am.

I wondered if you'd ever call.

I read the words and my mind even conjures up his voice to take my terror up a notch. Great. Wonderful. What this situation needs is more fear for sure.

Meet me tonight at Hannaford Prep. I'll give you the details.

I hear the door swing open and a gaggle of girls walk into the toilets talking about what an asshole Mr. Trevelen is and where Joey's next party is being held. Fuck I wish sometimes that my problems were that small.

I'm well known at Hannaford. Meet me at the park in Haven. Green bench by the swings. Midnight.

Fucking hell, really?! That's going to be near impossible to make happen but what choice do I have?

See you there.

I stand and tuck my phone away, flushing the toilet so the other girls don't question me. My mind works overtime as I walk to history and slip into my seat. Harley is already there, reading notes, and he frowns at the look on my face.

"What now?"

I unpack my bag on autopilot, grabbing the assignment that's due and handing it to the teacher as he walks past. I chew on my nails and think. Harley gets so agitated he's practically vibrating in his seat. When the teacher finally turns his back on the class and starts droning on about 18thth century France Harley leans down to whisper in my ear, "Tell me what *the fuck* is wrong with you. Now."

I roll my eyes at his bossy, entitled words but I answer him anyway, "I need to be in Haven at midnight. I need to figure out how to get there and I don't want to tell Avery about it before I go. She'll either insist on coming with me or she'll try to talk me out of it."

He frowns and shifts his focus back to the teacher, dismissing me the same way he always has. My chest tightens. I wasn't expecting his help but I thought he'd take a little more interest than that.

When the class ends and we pack away our supplies he grabs a set of keys out of his bag and drops them into mine. "Blaise's car is in the staff parking. Same one we picked you up in at the docks. The gate will automatically open when you drive up because Avery got him a sensor. I'll square it with him, just don't fucking scratch it."

My jaw drops and I snap my mouth shut before he notices how much of an idiot I look like. I can't find words until we get to our next class and sit together.

"Thanks. I'd tell you why but it's better if you don't know."

He shrugs at me, his face nonchalant but his hands are curled into fists. "I know it's for Ash and Avery. I saw your face when you saw the bruises. I'm guessing you're using your connections to try and help them. Ash's bruises are worse, by the way. I don't know how he's still walking."

I curse under my breath and push my luck with his charitable mood. "Can you distract Avery for me? Keep her in your room all night?"

He nods and we fall quiet, focusing on the class and taking notes.

When classes are over for the day and I get to our room, Avery texts to say Harley caught Blaise talking to Annabelle again and she has to go tear him apart. She asks to borrow my knife to hammer home the message and I start to wonder what Harley told him to get him to risk the fury of Avery to distract her for me.

I eat a sandwich for dinner and try to focus for long enough to do some work on my pile of assignments. At ten, Avery texts to say she's sleeping in the boys room and I slip into the shower to get ready.

I'm preparing myself, putting Lips away and letting out the Wolf.

I almost forget to grab the diamond payment. I slip it into the pocket of my jeans, I picked the tightest pair I own so I can feel the hard stone pressing into my thigh at all times. I'm paranoid as hell about losing it.

Slipping out of my room, I walk on silent feet out of the building. I make it, unseen, all the way to the staff parking lot only to find Ash leaning against the Maserati.

Fuck.

Of all the fucking students in this school.

Fuck.

I freeze and stare at him. I'm still clutching the keys in my frozen fingers like they'll save me from the pissy fit Ash is about to throw. How did he know I was here? I mean, there's only one way but surely-

"Harley sent me."

Fuck. What the hell?!

I could fucking scream I'm that angry. "You can't stop me, I have to go. I'll explain later."

I'm not telling him a goddamn thing but I need him out of my way right now. He pulls another set of keys out of his pocket and unlocks the car.

"I'll drive."

What the actual fuck? No glare, no questions, no argument. I'm going to have to break the news to Avery that aliens have taken over her beloved brother's body.

With that lovely image in my mind I get in and slam the door shut. Ash slides in, casual and fucking calm, and starts the car. He doesn't look at me as he drives and I direct him to the meeting place. I settle into the seat and breathe until I can speak civilly to him again.

"You have to stay in the car. I'm just going to talk to someone about a job. You can't be seen with me."

He ignores me until he parks the car. Haven looks even more picturesque at night. The fairy lights strung up in the trees twinkling in the slight breeze like glow bugs dancing. I do a quick scan of the area and find the street is empty except for a black Escalade.

He's beaten me here.

I unbuckle my seatbelt. When I reach for the door handle, Ash stops me with a firm hand wrapped around my wrist. "You can't have my father or my brother killed. Harley seems to think that's what's about to happen. You can't."

I stare him down and take in every shard of ice his eyes are throwing at me. Why they both protect Joey is just beyond me. I'm looking forward to the day I know every last one of Avery's secrets and I can plan without worrying about hurting her or pissing her off.

"I'm not ordering a hit."

I wrench my arm out of his hold and get out of the car. I wait a second to make sure he's staying put and then I walk up the small incline to the green bench. It takes serious effort, but I manage to control the tremble that's threatening to take over my whole body.

He's already sitting there, his back to the car and Ash, and I sit down next to him.

I don't look at him. It's like every cop show, where the informant and the cop stare ahead and pretend they're not there to pass along information. I don't want to look at him because he scares the crap out of me and I'm not sure my shields are still up thanks to Ash hijacking the trip over here. Asshole.

"It must be serious if you're coming to me, little Wolf."

I nod and stare at the swings for a minute longer. I hope my voice is as hollow and lifeless as his is when I say, "Thank you for meeting me on such short notice, Crow."

He places his hands in his lap. "A favor is binding. I would never go back on my bond."

Right. Well, I guess I should just dive right in. "You have some dealings with Joseph Beaumont, correct?"

He turns to look at me, and the steely gray of his eyes cut me to ribbons. He's a handsome man. His hair is only a shade or two lighter than Avery's and it's short on the sides with some length on top, making him look like a distinguished, clean-cut businessman. Cleanly shaven, straight nose, and cheekbones for days. His tattoos swirls across the skin of his chest that his v neck shirt shows and look faintly like feathers and claws. Tall and broad but completely self-assured in the way he carries himself. He looks older than twenty-two. His entire demeanor screams wealth, enough that I keep questioning myself on who he is when he's not the Crow. Only the desperate enter the Game to become a member of the Twelve.

"I find it wise to avoid the man. I'd suggest you do the same."

I reach into my pocket and pull out the velvet bag that holds his black diamond. His eyes drop to it and grow hungry. He wants the diamond back and favor over with. I can only imagine how heavy the weight of an owed favor must be.

"I need to make sure he's busy. I need him to disappear during the school breaks, all of them, until I graduate. I don't care how, I don't need details."

The Crow takes the bag and pockets it. He doesn't check the contents like Diarmuid did, that would be a grave insult to me. Even the Crow is cautious of what I can do.

"You should tell the Jackal to stay away from Joseph Beaumont as well. Whatever it is he's making you do in that house, it's not worth the wrath of that man."

I measure my words very carefully before I speak. I need to start distancing myself from the Jackal and everything he does but to say that outright would risk him coming to Hannaford for me.

"This favor is my own. I have people I need to protect, people who are no concern of any other member of the Twelve, and I am well aware of the extent of that man's wrath."

His eyes flash. His face slips just enough that I see concern. I've never been close to him, I've only really seen him at meetings, so I don't know why he's worried about me.

"You're protecting his children. They go to school with you, don't they?"

"They're not up for discussion. I'm asking you to ensure that man never steps foot in a room with the twins again. Do you require any further information?"

I slip into protocol to end this little meeting. I don't want him digging into this and drawing more eyes to my back.

"Done. I'll call if anything comes up."

I give him a curt nod and walk back to the car, slow and steady like I'm used to meetings at midnight with crime lords and no backup. Ash looks grim in the front seat his eyes never falter from the silhouette of the Crow. Only when I'm safely buckled into the Maserati does he glance away. My hands shake and I lace them together on my lap to hide it.

Ash doesn't speak to me as we drive back. He walks me back to my room and once I'm inside he grabs Harley's keys off of me. He hesitates by the door.

"Whatever you've done, if he finds out—"

"He won't. He won't the same way Harley's grandfather can't come after him. I'm not going to explain it, you'll just have to trust that it's taken care of."

That's the problem. Ash doesn't trust anyone but his friends and I am not his friend. I can see him fighting with himself, the war waging in his mind clearly visible on his face, and I must be tired because I feel so fucking bad for him. How many times has he gone home from school to be beaten by his father? How long has he been abused by the other men in his family? Is that why he can't trust anyone? How deep is the damage?

"Go get some sleep, Ash. Just forget tonight ever happened."

Chapter Eleven

I text Harley the next morning and tell him he's a treacherous asshole.

I know he has training for his swim team so I'm not expecting a text back, just the cold shoulder he'll give me all day in our classes. As I rush out the door, late because Avery wasn't around to make coffee and snark with, my phone pings.

I check it while I lock the door.

I'm helping Ash get his head out of his ass. I see how much you're doing for us. I see how much Avery means to you. I see that you're one of us. He needs to open his eyes and see it too. Fuck, even Morrison sees it and he's usually too far up his own ass jotting down morbid love poems to see anything.

My heart does a weird little flip.

I don't know how to answer it. Shrug it off, make a joke, or give him the same honesty? It's a private chat, not the group one, so I take a risk.

I'll do whatever it takes to get us all out of here alive and together.

He doesn't text back.

When I arrive late to our first class he doesn't say a word, he just tips his chin to acknowledge me when I sit down. We work in silence but it's soothing to me now, I don't feel any hostility from him at all. When it's time for lunch he grabs me by the elbow and directs me to the dining hall with him. Usually I eat an apple in the library and work on assignments or hang out in the dance rooms while Avery practices.

He grabs a tray and fills it with food. I know he's grabbing for me as well because he hates mushrooms and he's grabbed the mushroom risotto I like. I grab us both iced coffees and we sit together.

My stomach does not want to eat under his intense scrutiny but I also can't turn him down like that. We don't speak while we eat and after a few minutes Ash takes a seat next to me. I put down my cutlery with a sigh.

Harley sees the look on my face and says, "Just eat, Mounty. He's here for lunch not war."

I eat my banana.

Harley and Ash start up a random conversation about cars they're interested in, though Harley seems to be more reserved. Ash doesn't look at me or try to speak to me and I focus on eating my lunch. I'm busy texting Avery about our plans to go to Haven together when Joey takes a seat next to Harley. I don't acknowledge him and I finish the text. I'm not going to show this evil dickhead any respect or fear. Fuck him.

"Does the Jackal know you've made some friends, Mounty?"

I hit send and then I lean back in my chair. Ash's leg has tensed where it's pressed against mine under the table. Harley is glaring at Joey and the nerve in his jaw is ticking. "I don't answer to him, or you, Joey. Where have you been hiding this year? I've barely seen you."

His eyes slide around the room in an awful liquid way, like he's something not quite human, and his grin is nothing short of psychotic. "Oh, have you missed me, my little Mounty love?"

I force myself to swallow the bile creeping up my throat. "I don't think anyone misses you, Joey. I don't think anyone could ever like you enough to miss you. What are you here for?"

He picks up Harley's steak knife and begins to play with it. Harley watches him carefully and, knowing what family he belongs to, I'm fairly confident he can defend himself if Joey takes a swing with it. However, Ash turns ghostly pale and looks like he's going to vomit. If he has to stop Joey then he knows it will be Avery that pays. I don't know why but I put a hand on his knee under the table and squeeze gently. He takes a deep breath.

"The twins and Morrison are going to the recital next week in the city and I'm celebrating in their absence. Come to my party. I've missed hanging out with you and I think you should have a drink with me. I'll make sure they have your favorite whiskey."

I glance at Harley to see a little frown on his face but his eyes still follow the knife.

"Sure, why not. Arbour will come with me and we can make a night of it."

Joey grins and moves as if he's going to put the knife down. He stares into his brother's eyes obsessively, straight into the soul of his favorite victim, and then swings his hand down to impale the knife through Ash's hand and into the table below.

Well, that's what he tries to do except my reflexes are quicker and I shoot out to catch his wrist. Harley gets a hold of his arm a fraction of a second later and the tip of the knife stops millimeters away from Ash's skin. Joey pants like he's getting off on this. He licks his lips and grins at us. It's disgusting.

I lean forward and whisper, "You may have tied his hands but you haven't tied mine. Push me and I'll show you that being a Beaumont only gets you so far in this world."

Ash and Harley have a raging argument about the party and I duck away from them both to head to my choir class. I have to go to the party, I need to know what Joey is planning and if Harley doesn't want to come with me then I'll go by myself. I only offered to take Harley because I thought he'd insist.

Avery is laughing along with Blaise when I take my seat and I smile at Lauren, Jessie, and Dahlia. They all look at me with that awe-struck fear they direct at Avery and it's pretty fucking weird to have it directed at me as well.

"Stop being nice to the sheep." Avery teases and I cut her a look.

"Your green-eyed monster is showing, Aves. You know you're my favorite."

She giggles and bumps my shoulder with hers. "The only green-eyed monster around here is Morrison and he's too hungover to be any trouble."

Blaise rolls his eyes and I notice how bloodshot they are. "Drinking on a school night? How very rock star of you."

He groans and slumps down. "I had no choice. Ash borrowed my car to go fuck a Haven chick and Avery cornered me about my own *evening activities* so I tried to drown her out with bourbon. I think I'm going to join Harley in celibacy because I haven't found a pussy yet that's worth dealing with Avery's lectures."

Avery makes a gagging noise at him and I stare at him, stunned. I do not have anything to say. Miss Umber starting the class saves me, thank Christ.

"I have some exciting changes in your syllabus to announce! Usually your final assignment for choir is to perform in front of the class but this year we're joining forces with the music students and holding a concert for the entire school!" She claps her hands like an excited toddler while she's casually ruining my life. This woman... this fucking woman and her 'good ideas'.

"What the fuck is Miss Umber's obsession with individual performances?" I hiss at Avery the moment the teacher's back is turned.

Avery hums under her breath at me, lifting her shoulder in a nonchalant way, and my palms begin to sweat. I'll just have to talk to her again and get out of it somehow.

Miss Umber hands out worksheets, designed to help us pick which song we will sing, and then giggles when Blaise smiles at her. Avery scoffs and rolls her eyes, which only makes him turn up the charm. I don't know how the older lady's heart survives it, I am sweating.

"The concert will be held at the end of the school year, choir students will sing in front of the entire school. Then the musicians will perform. So I hope you all take this very seriously, as always the majority of your mark will be determined by your performance. No exceptions. If you're not there, you're not passing this class."

Oh, God.

I was no longer sweating at Blaise's hotness. There is no way I can do this. No way. Next year I'm risking my fucking leg and doing track or something. Maybe I should join Harley on the swim team? Ash would probably have an aneurysm over it but whatever. Is it too late to switch out now? I'm spiraling, I know I am and I have to grit my teeth to pull myself out.

Miss Umber starts directing the warm ups and I don't even try to pretend to join in. Once her back is turned again, I lean into Avery.

"911." I hiss and she startles to look back at me. Blaise casts us both a curious look but he doesn't miss a single note in his warm up.

"Singing for a group is a 911?" she murmurs and I nod emphatically. She frowns at me, and then nods.

I don't join in for the rest of the class. When Miss Umber questions me about it, Blaise cuts her off and flirts mercilessly with her until she forgets why she ever walked over to our group. Instead of thanking him, I hand him the iPod and he nods.

We communicate better with lyrics than with words.

Later that night, when Blaise has left from our tutoring session and Avery is freshly showered, I explain our confrontation with Joey at lunch.

"He's up to something."

Avery rolls her eyes at me. "He's always up to something. The question is what's changed? He's stayed away from you because of the Jackal's warning so he must have found something out if he's playing with you again."

I nod and take a seat at the bench while she fusses with the stove. "Ash wasn't too keen on Harley joining me. He thinks we're walking into a trap. I mean, we are, but what choice do I have?"

Avery cocks her head as she stirs her cocoa. "I'll try and put some feelers out, see if there's any gossip about what he's planning."

I nod and sigh, scrubbing a hand over my face. Who would think high school politics would be as complicated as this?

"So? Are you going to tell me why singing is a 911?" Avery shoves a spoon into a tub of ice cream and slides it across the bench at me. It's cherry flavored, I've never told Avery it's my favorite and yet the sneaky bitch knows. I swear to God she's going to take over the country some day. Or she'll put a puppet in power and she'll pull all the strings and make the whole damn world dance for her. The secret, darkest parts of my soul whispers to me about how much I love it.

"Have you ever heard of the NTT? Naval Torture Technique?"

Avery shakes her head and sips her cocoa.

"It's a way to increase your pain tolerance. It's a long process where the degree of pain inflicted onto you is upped slowly until you're able to stay silent and function even when you've been shot or have multiple broken bones."

Avery looks a little green. She's put down her cup while I was talking and now her chin is propped up on her fist as she watches me.

"I can't hear the sound of my own raised voice, not yelling or singing, without triggering my PTSD from my training."

She rubs her eyes with her fists like she's trying to scrub the shock and horror out of them too. "Right. Who did this...training to you?"

"The Jackal."

Avery nods and drops her hands away from her face.

"I should have known. Can you switch out to do a sport instead?"

I raise my leg up so she can see the thick scars that run from thigh to ankle. "Nope. I'll be in agony for days after any major activity."

"You really are broken, aren't you?" she says with a smile. I think if anyone else said it to me I'd lose my mind at them but there's this kindness in her eyes when I look at her. Like she knows exactly what it's like to be shattered into a million pieces and taped back together in the wrong order. Fuck, we're both a hot mess.

I shrug and eat some ice cream. I wash up the dishes and Avery roots around in the bathroom. I think she's doing her bedtime routine but then she hands me a pack of earplugs, saying, "Put those in," and then drags me over to her record player.

If there is anything in this room that I'm truly jealous of it's Avery's record player and collection of vinyl. It was her mom's and Blaise adds to it constantly, his own music and anything he thinks she'll like.

"What are we doing?" I slip one of the earplugs in.

Avery messes around with the record player for a minute and then whirls around to me. "We're fixing you. I heard you sing to Miss Umber so we know that you can do it, we just need to practice. We're going to do this over and over again until it's perfect."

I hesitate as she hits play and 'High Hopes' by Panic at the Disco starts. The sneaky bitch must have looked at my worksheet. I sigh and slip the other earplug in just before I need to sing.

I make it through the whole song. I remember the lyrics, having listened to this song a hundred times, and after the first chorus I'm calm enough to open my eyes. Avery watches me with rapture, sitting on her bed with her head propped up by her fists. When the song ends I give myself a second to breathe and then I take the earplugs out.

"We need to fix you because you need to sing, Lips. I can't even—there aren't words for how you sound. Blaise is going to *lose* his *mind* when he hears you."

I blush and shrug. I don't see myself getting over the PTSD. I'm going to do this because I need my scholarship but I'm never going to be able to just sing along with the radio or hold concerts in my shower. It's just not possible.

She starts the song over and I go again.

Chapter Twelve

Avery leaves for her recital at lunchtime on Saturday.

There's no word of what Joey has planned but I refuse to let it bother me. I can handle whatever he throws at me.

I spend the afternoon on my assignments and practicing my singing. I heat up some leftovers for dinner and tuck in when my phone pings.

Swim training finishes in an hour. I'll come shower and get ready in your room after that.

I gulp. Harley showering in my bathroom. Harley getting naked in my bathroom. Harley naked.

Sweet lord.

I scramble to get showered and ready before he gets here. I grab jeans, a lacy tank top and then throw a hoodie on over it all. I'm not trying to impress anyone, I just need to be comfortable and warm. I keep telling myself that even as I do my makeup and hair. When Harley knocks at the door I'm pretty happy with how I look.

"Where's the shorts and bra? I thought that's what you wear to parties?" Harley smirks at me but his eyes roam over me appreciatively and I mentally fist bump myself. Sometimes it's nice to know I'm not a complete ogre.

"I don't need frostbite on my nipples. Come to a party in the summer with me and I'll wear the other outfit again." Wait, what? What am I saying? I've lost my damn mind.

Harley strides into the room and heads straight to the bathroom. "I'm holding you to that, Mounty."

The door swings shut behind him but he doesn't lock it. I don't let my mind fixate on that fact and instead I sprawl out on my bed and text Avery.

Good luck, wish I was there to see you dance. Tell Morrison to send me a video.

I chew my nails for a minute while I listen to the shower.

Thank you. It's weird, my father isn't here. He always shows up to these things so he can monitor what Ash and I are doing. I'm so relieved. Blaise isn't so lucky, his father is on the warpath. I'm expecting I'll have to play nursemaid to him later while he gives himself liver poisoning. Text me when you get back from the party safely, Harley promised me he'd have your back all night x

I frown down at the screen. Blaise has been doing so well in his classes, our tutoring sessions and his dedication has paid off impressively. He's easily on top of all of his classes now and he's been asked to move into the higher classes in a few subjects. What could his dad possibly be pissy at him for? Fuck it. I text him.

Send me a video of Avery's dance please. Let me know if you need anything

I curse at myself under my breath. What would he need from *me*? He has two of his best friends with him and I'm barely a person in his life. The shower shuts off and I start to sweat. My phone pings again and I cringe before I look down at it.

Avery has already threatened me if I don't. Thanks. If you could send me bourbon and a blowjob that would be great.

I cackle as Harley comes out of the bathroom and raises an eyebrow at me.

"Morrison wants me to send him booze and sexual favors to help him get through the night with his parents. Should I send him a Mounty hooker?"

Harley laughs, a proper laugh, and I blush at the sight of it. I jump up off the bed and try to discreetly check him out. His dark jeans are just fitted enough that I can appreciate his ass but not his dick. I'll take it as a win. He has a dark gray shirt on with a deep v neckline so I can see his mother's necklace and the edges of his tattoo peeking out. He throws a jacket on and we leave together.

He leans against the wall as I lock the door and he's so close to me that I can feel the heat of his body and smell him. I swear he's like fucking ambrosia to me. My body melts the second I get a whiff of him. I hear him curse softly under his breath and look up.

Annabelle scowls at me, standing before us in a lacy transparent nightgown-thing. Teddy? I've never owned one so fuck knows what it's called. There's no reason other than sex that a woman would wear one is what I'm saying.

"It's bad enough I have to watch Blaise leave here most nights now you're here with her, too? Come on, Harley, what are you thinking?"

I move to walk past her but Harley grabs my hand and tugs me to his side. Oh fuck. I'm about to be thrown in the middle of relationship drama. Avery's going to be *pissed*.

"We're heading out to Joey's party. Have a great night with whatever dumbass you're all dressed up for, Summers."

Annabelle pouts at him but there's real hurt in her eyes. Avery did say Harley was her favorite. "I haven't broken the rules Harley. I haven't had anyone else and I won't. I know you'll get bored of slumming it with Mounty pussy and come back to me."

Harley chuckles under his breath and takes a step forward, pulls me with him. "I was born in the same city as Lips. I spend all of my summer breaks there. We have friends in the same circles. When I leave Hannaford, I'm going back there. I'm as much a Mounty as she is. Give up, Summers. I'm never touching you again. I never should've touched you in the first place."

The tears start as we walk past her. I can't find it in myself to feel bad for her.

The party is in the same clearing as last year.

We have to walk past the same tree I watched Annabelle blow Harley on and I think about pointing it out to him but his mood is fucking woeful after our run in with her. He hasn't let go of my hand. I tried to tug it back and he glared down at me like I was wounding him. Fucking guys.

When we make it to the drinks table Harley swipes a bottle of whiskey, holding it up until I nod then he drops my hand to open it and hands it to me. As I take a swig I see Joey's usual group of flunkies approach us. I roll my eyes at Harley and pass him back the bottle.

"Joey's waiting for you."

Harley slings his arm over my shoulders and sneers at Devon. "And he can keep waiting. We're busy."

I tell myself I'm not going to enjoy being this close to Harley all night and I also tell myself that I'm shamelessly lying. Harlow looks between the two of us and sneers at me. When she opens her mouth I tug Harley towards the makeshift dance floor and grab the bottle back from him.

"How long should we let the asshole wait for us?" Harley whispers and I smile and pull away from him to dance.

"At least four songs. I haven't danced in weeks and I don't have to keep an eye on Avery."

He grins and pulls my hips back so we're dancing together and I let the warmth spreading through my limbs turn me into something pliable and fluid. I let go of everything, all the stresses and worries, all the planning and manipulating, everything that I spend every waking moment thinking about. He's watching my back and I'm protecting his. Harley is surprisingly good at dancing. He manages to walk that fine line between dirty sexy grinding and mindless dry humping. I'm panting like a whore in no time. It would be mortifying but Harley is just as worked up as I am.

By the third song we'd drunk enough of the bottle that I tug Harley away from the music. We need to have enough brains about us to handle Joey but I'm not really worried. Harley is a seasoned drinker and I'm no lightweight, despite my size.

"Let's get this over with."

Harley nods and I take the lead further into the woods where I know Joey goes to get high. There's groups of students already out to play, moaning and grunting following us as we make our way over to Joey's group. I don't look around; I don't want to know who's doing who.

When we reach the fence line I see two very familiar figures leaning against the wrought iron latticework. Two of the Jackal's underlings are doing lines with Joey. I freeze before they spot me and Harley steps up to press himself against my back.

"Friends of yours?" he whispers into my ear.

Joey has seriously misjudged who I am.

He looks up and grins at me, all baring teeth and threats. The two Mounts Bay locals notice his attention is elsewhere and look up to me as well. Daniel damn near pisses himself as he scrambles away from Joey but Trenton manages to keep his cool. He meets my eye and dips his head, a sign of respect. His eyes dart over my shoulder and he does the same to Harley. I stare at him with a blank face and I hope Harley follows my lead but I can't glance back and check. Joey frowns at him and then back at me.

I arch an eyebrow at him but I don't say a word. He wanted to out me as a gangster, either a whore or a drug dealer. Well, asshole, you guessed wrong.

"This guy bothering you?" Trenton says, jerking a thumb at Joey. His other hand slips behind him and I know he's gripping a gun shoved into the waistband of his jeans. One word and the eldest Beaumont child catches a bullet between his eyes.

I look at Joey and raise an eyebrow at him. His lip curls into a snarl when he realizes his little reveal has backfired so superbly on him. I don't think he's noticed Trenton's movements but the tension in Harley's body tells me he has.

"He's just a guy with too much money and too little respect for how things are done in the real world, boys," I say and Harley grips my elbow.

Trenton nods as he looks down at his toes. "What'll it be then? You need me to take care of him?"

Harlow frowns at me and her lip quivers as she takes a step away from Joey. Hmm. She's more observant than I thought. I stare Joey down even though his eyes burn my skin with their manic fixation.

"I'm here to go to school, not start a war. Head home, boys. Hannaford isn't the place for you."

Daniel takes off from the clearing, damn near running towards his car. Trenton hesitates before shaking Harley's hand and bowing his head at me, respectfully. The entire crowd of students watch in silence as they walk away. When the car starts and peels away Joey speaks.

"Who the fuck are you, Mounty?"

I grin and lift the bottle of whiskey to my lips, "Maybe you should watch yourself until you know, Beaumont. I did warn you."

Harley sniggers behind me and, after I've taken a sip, he grabs the bottle and takes a swig. "Come dance, Mounty. Let's enjoy the rest of the night."

"I'm sleeping in Avery's bed tonight. If Joey comes up here again, I don't want you alone."

My hands fumble with the keys but I manage to unlock the door and get us into the room. Harley slips his jacket off and hangs it over the armchair he's claimed. He's still clutching the bottle of whiskey. When he notices I'm frozen by the door, he takes a sip, his eyes burning my skin. He offers me the bottle and I snap out of my trance to walk over and take it. It's nearly empty so I finish the last of it, feeling the warmth spread through my limbs.

"Do you have pajamas here or do we need to go back to——" my voice dries up as Harley reaches behind his head to pull his shirt off.

Holy.

Fuck.

His eyes stay fixed on mine as he reaches down to unbutton his jeans and my entire body spontaneously combusts. There's too much whiskey coursing in my blood to stop myself from moaning when he smirks and drops the jeans to the floor, kicking them away so all he is left wearing are his boxers. There is too much skin on display for my brain to process. I'm shaking, my body trembling with the intimacy and intensity of the moment. It's like everything has ceased to exist except for us and this moment.

I want him so fucking bad.

"Are you just going to stare, Mounty, or are you gonna do something?" he taunts and I shiver. I think I'm going to do something. Wait, I know I'm going to do something.

I strip off, with the same efficiency he has, until I'm standing before him in my bra and panties. Thank God I bothered to wear nice ones, matching black with a tiny bit of lace. His eyes never drop down to my body but his throat works as he swallows roughly. I know I'm covered in scars but I don't feel ashamed of them when he looks at me the way he is. He waits for a second, like he's making sure I'm with him, and then he pounces.

He grabs me by the backs of my thighs and lifts me up into his body like I weigh nothing. I wrap my legs around his waist to hold on and my arms wind around his neck as he claims my lips. I know that's exactly what he's doing, he's claiming me. I open my mouth to his and groan as his tongue sweeps in and I melt.

He is so unbelievably hot, his skin pressing against me burning me until I'm sweating and shaking. I tug at his bottom lip with my teeth and his hands move to my ass and squeeze. I wriggle and he breaks away from the kiss to murmur, "Bed?"

I'm not thinking, I don't want to think ever again, so I nod and kiss him once more.

He sits on my bed and holds me over him until I can tuck myself into his lap comfortably, straddling him. We pause for a second, panting and staring at each other before Harley cups my face gently. His eyes are soft, something I've never seen on him before, my breath hitches in my throat but before I can think he pulls me back into his lips.

He kisses me like I'm a drug he's desperate for and I kiss him back like he's the only air I'll ever need to breathe.

I move my hips until I feel the rigid length of his dick pressing against my panties. Good lord, his dick is so fucking hard and I gulp at the size. I do not want to be torn in half for my first time and I'm about to pull away but then he sucks the skin just below my ear and my hips rock in response and then nothing else matters except what his lips are doing to me. I grind down onto him and savor every grunt and moan he gives me. He's only wearing his boxers so there are two thin layers of fabric separating us and my eyes roll back into my head at the thought. I can feel how wet I am, soaking through my panties and leaving a wet spot on Harley's boxers. I tug at his hair and moan softly.

"Fuck," he mumbles as he drags his lips away from my shoulder. "This isn't how I wanted to do this. You've had too much to drink."

Whether it's the alcohol or his mouth, the jury is out, I don't feel drunk until he says that, and now I feel lightheaded and rejected. I pull away from him sharply, snatching my arms back from where they're pressed into his chest, but he keeps his hands circling my waist. He pulls his knees up to push me back into his chest and moves a hand to gently stroke the hair away from my face while he scowls at me.

"Don't freak out. I'm just saying I don't think we should be doing anything more than making out when we've finished a bottle of whiskey between us."

Dammit. Damn him to hell, he's being fucking reasonable. How can I argue with that?! I don't want to take this further, not really, because he doesn't do commitment and I don't want casual for my first time. I don't want to be another Mounty girl used and thrown away. Urgh. Why?!

"You're right. We should stop."

Harley cradles my face in his hands again and kisses me slowly until I can't breathe. Well, if he isn't the most confusing guy *on the freaking planet* I don't know who is, but my mind turns off again and I lose myself in his lips. I shift my weight, rocking my hips just a fraction, and he pulls away.

"Nope. No. We'll stop. If you can't kiss me without grinding on my dick like that we have to stop."

I groan at him and collapse on the bed beside him. Rude. "You're the one that stripped off."

He scoffs at me and I swear he mumbles, "I had to get your attention somehow."

But that doesn't make any sense to my whiskey-soaked brain so I brush it off. Clearly he isn't taking his celibacy very seriously. I wonder why he's even doing it. He could easily find a replacement for Annabelle. Maybe he wants me to be his regular casual hookup. I mean, I room with his cousin so he has access to me without drawing suspicion from the other girls. My eyes drift shut while I hypothesize Harley's sex life.

I feel the blankets being pulled up around me, and a hand brushing my hair back from my face.

"I can't fuck a Hannaford boy." I remind myself and then I pass out.

Chapter Thirteen

I wake up hungover, in my underwear, and alone.

I take some time to reassess my life choices because, boy, did I make some life choices last night. When I finally drag my ass out of bed and into the shower I'm in full sulk mode. Not Morrison levels of sulk but enough that I'm not leaving my room. Avery has different plans for me.

Stop being a hermit and join us for dinner. Harley said you haven't come out all day and I can't be bothered cooking.

Dinner? I glance at the clock and, fuck me, it's after five. I've slept and moped the whole day away.

I think about texting her back some bullshit excuse but she'll tell Harley and he'll rat me out so I throw an oversized sweater and Avery's yoga pants on and trudge down to the dining hall like I'm heading to the executioner's block. When I open the door I find Harley scowling down at his phone waiting for me. I open my mouth, not that I know what the fuck I'm going to say, but he turns away and grabs a tray. "Risotto or salmon? There's pizza too but it's shit."

I stumble behind him as he grabs us both food. It's chivalrous and sweet but he won't look at me and his jaw is clenched. I'm embarrassed about making out with him last night but he looks *pissed* and I have no fucking clue what I've done to warrant that so I keep my mouth shut and watch him from the corner of my eye instead. The twins are already eating in their usual seats and Blaise is nowhere to be seen.

When we take our seats Avery tucks her arm into mine and Ash does a double take when he sees my face. Fuck, do I have toothpaste on my chin or something? He stands and takes off without a word. What the fuck is going on?

"Why do your lips look all red and pouty?" says Avery to me with narrowed eyes. I refuse to blush. I refuse but my body doesn't listen. Fuck. "Is that a hickey?"

I clear my throat but I can't think of an answer so I grab my plate and tuck in. The risotto tastes like ash because of my anxiety and just once I'd like to enjoy my food. Just once.

Harley arches an eyebrow at me and I don't know what the hell to say because he's acting so weird.

"Did you forget your morals for a second and mess around with a Hannaford guy?" he sneers and I want to stab him with my fork. I didn't ask him to get naked and kiss me! He has no right to be a dick to me!

Avery looks between the two of us and then snaps at Harley, "This is about safety not morals."

He frowns at her and I butt in before she says too much. "I went to the party to see about Joey's threats. I drank too much and made out with someone. I forgot myself for a second, don't worry. I won't do it again."

Avery purses her lips and glances at Harley. I can see her measure out her words before she speaks them. "I just need you to be safe, Lips. I don't want you to get carried away and risk something happening to you."

Harley pins me with a searing look like he's trying to pry my brain open with his eyes and learn all of my secrets. I ignore him and steer the conversation onto safer topics.

After we finish eating Harley insists on walking us back to our room. Avery tucks herself under his arm and tells him all about her recital. I've already watched her entire performance thanks to Blaise's recording. When we make it back, I find clean piles of folded clothing waiting outside our door and I grab piles, noting a complete lack of underwear yet again. Every pair I've sent down to be cleaned have gone missing and I'm running out! Avery lets us into the room and Harley holds the door open for me.

"Remind me tomorrow that I need to talk to the laundry personnel, my underwear is missing again." I grumble quietly as I pack away my clothes.

Harley, of course, overhears me and snorts out a laugh. "You sure you don't have some pervert stalking you?"

I shudder. I certainly do have a sociopath stalking me I guess. Avery grabs her pajamas and heads to the bathroom. "Ask Harlow, maybe she's moved onto stealing lacy unmentionables instead of my fucking shoes."

I cringe at her swearing and I don't notice I've been left alone with Harley until it's too late.

"Why is your safety a concern for what we did last night?"

Fuck. Here we go. "Why?"

"What?" He frowns at me.

"Why do you care? You were just sick of your celibacy, right? You were just drinking and made a mistake because Annabelle is off the cards. So what does it matter?" I'm snippy at him but his attitude is grating on me.

Harley stalks over to me and grabs the shirts I'm holding and throws them on my bed. "Maybe it matters because I'm fucking worried about you. Maybe it matters because if someone is threatening you I want to know about it. Maybe I take this friendship pretty fucking seriously. You gave up a diamond for me."

I groan and scrub a hand over my face. "You don't owe me for that. I made a decision and the cost of that lands with me."

Harley's hands wrap around my elbows and squeeze firmly. "When I beat Hillsong for you last year, called Avery off, told all of the guys they couldn't approach you, I did all of that because I wanted to be your friend. So let me in. Tell me why you don't want to get involved with someone who goes here."

I squirm under the intensity of his eyes and I try to tug away from him but he won't let me go. Fuck. I have to tell him something. "It's not about whether or not I want to, it's just not a good idea for me to get involved with someone from Hannaford. I don't want to talk about it."

He glares down at me before blowing out a breath and stepping back. "One day you're going to trust me to have your back, Mounty."

Avery uses my missing underwear as an excuse to get a day pass from our classes to go into Haven together the following day. I can't believe it's as easy as that, but then again she's a Beaumont.

She wears a dress, stockings, and heels with her hair curled and perfect makeup. I throw on jeans and a jacket, a messy bun and a touch of mascara. We couldn't look more different but Avery tucks her arm in mine like there's no question we're best friends and then cackles at the looks we get from other students. I laugh because, I mean, what else can I do?

A town car drops us off in front of the small cafe I went to last year and I smile at the waitress Emily as we take a seat in one of the booths. Avery rolls her eyes at me, thoroughly bemused by my insistence on being friendly to people, and we each order our drinks. I know it's coming before she speaks so I've already resigned myself to spilling my guts to her.

"Are you going to tell me who you kissed or am I going to have to pry the information out of you?"

I sigh. "It was Harley."

"I fucking knew it." She's smug and I think about pinching or slapping her or something. She knows she's treading a fine line and sticks her tongue out in an entirely non-Avery way and I roll my eyes.

"We went to the party, had our little showdown with Joey, shared a bottle of whiskey and danced, came back to the room, and then made out."

"No sex?"

"No." My cheeks probably look sunburnt, for Christ's sake.

"I'm glad you showed some self-control. I mean, he wouldn't have claimed the sweep but you guys couldn't keep that a secret."

I can't look her in the eye. I know who had the self-control that night and it certainly was not me. I had the raging hormones and the soaked panties. I had taut nipples and gyrating hips but I definitely did not have any sort of restraint.

"Can we just forget about it? Harley has and I'd like to."

Avery narrows her eyes at me and shrugs. "Sure. Tell me about the henchmen Joey had there?"

I wait until Emily has brought us our drinks and then I smirk. "You should have seen his face, he was so pissed his little surprise backfired."

Avery laughs and I go on, "They were both bottom rung guys, you know, like the lowest on the ladder. I've met Trenton before a few times. He's done some work for Luca and I've seen him around. The other guy knew who I was but I've never met him. He shit himself, I'm surprised Harley didn't ask me about his reaction."

She nods and props her chin up on the table with her fist. "I think he's made some assumptions about who you are. Every time he gets close to figuring you out you throw him a new secret and he has to start all over."

I shrug. "His family runs in a lot of the same circles as the Jackal and others. The only Twelve members who stay out of the lower society dealings are the Crow, the Tiger, and the Lynx."

Avery looks around but I've already done a sweep of the room. No one can hear us from where we're sitting and I can see who's coming in and out of the cafe. I raise an eyebrow at her and she clears her throat before whispering, "Can you tell me more about them? What they each do?"

"The Crow deals in information. The type of information you deal in, I've always guessed that he's the bastard son of a big player or a governor or something. The Tiger is a lawyer. He's actually a decent guy, dirty as they come but he makes bank by digging people out of shit. He's married, got kids, lives a white picket life while being a member of a criminal institution. It's fucking weird."

"The Lynx?" Avery takes a gulp of her drink and I remember I have mine to drink as well.

"She's a mafia princess. Well, queen I guess, she's in her fifties. Her family has always had a member in the Twelve and when her father died, both her brothers were locked up and couldn't enter into the Game so she did. She was the first woman to win it. Her brothers both despise that she's their representative. They can't touch her because of her power and they have to run all of their business decisions past her. It's hilarious."

Avery chuckles and rearranges sugar packets absently. "So, who are the others then? What do they do?"

"The Boar runs the imports and exports, the Viper is a bookie, the Bear does cleanups and party drugs, the Fox runs parties of all kinds, the Ox runs protection and enforcing, the Coyote is the tech guy, and the Vulture sells skin."

"Is that the guy who paid you with a raging boner down at the docks?" She shudders delicately.

"Yeah. He's... fucking disgusting. He offered to double my money for Harley. Dickhead move, I could get at least five hundred grand for him in the right circles."

Avery chokes on her coffee and fixes her watery eyes on me. "Excuse me?"

I laugh. "Aves, he's hot. He's built, pretty, tattooed, and he's not at all lacking in the dick department. I'd get half a mil easy."

Avery slams her cup back on the table and glares at me. "Firstly, how the hell do you know what his dick length is if you didn't have sex with him and, secondly, but *most importantly*, he is my cousin and I never, *ever* want to talk about his dick with you. Ever."

I blush and fidget in my seat. "We only kissed but I got close enough to him to know what he's working with."

"Ugh, hand me some fucking brain bleach," she snarls and picks up her phone.

"What the fuck are you doing?" I hiss and try to snatch the phone out of her hands. She glares and turns away from me.

"I'm letting him know that you're off limits. Jokes! I'm joking, I'm congratulating him on his dick."

I could fucking die. "Avery, we're no longer friends. If you hit send, I'm leaving you."

"Yeah right, I'm your favorite, remember?" she says, cackling like the evil witch she is.

I grumble under my breath as we get up and head out of the cafe.

Avery directs us both to a tiny boutique store that sells ridiculous underwear that is basically scraps of lace for hundreds of dollars. When I say this to Avery she glares at me and throws me a basket, demanding I fill it up. I put three pairs in and refuse to get anymore. She makes a joke about showing them off to Harley and I pray the ground will swallow me whole. When we're finished and safely buckled back into the town car, Avery grabs my hand.

"You know, you didn't tell me what you and the Jackal do."

I bite my lip. I don't want to answer this question at all but I've trusted her with everything so far and she's never let me down. "The Jackal does everything. Drugs, guns, extortion, kidnapping, fucking everything. He's a gang leader, through and through. And the Wolf… is invisible. Collects things. Does things no one else wants to do and the stuff no one else *can* do. I'm good at not being seen."

She squeezes my hand. "I think you're good at being underestimated. Joey's proved that over and over again."

Chapter Fourteen

Harley starts sitting with Avery and me at breakfast in the dining hall before classes. He still doesn't really speak to me, which is fine, but he laughs and jokes with Avery again and she's so ecstatic about it that I'm once again feeling guilty about how much I've changed her relationships with the guys. When I say this to her, she smirks at me and tells me they all deserve to grovel at her feet for her affection. I laugh because, well, it's such a Beaumont thing to say.

I wake up to Ash sleeping on our couch more often than not. When I ask Avery about it she sighs and admits Joey is sending them both threatening texts once more and he's worried Joey is going to show up at our door again. Ash is still moody and scowling at me but he doesn't try to speak to me. I take it as a win.

My tutoring sessions with Blaise have become one of the best parts of my day.

He starts to bring me more than just our playlists. He slips me partial lyrics he's working on and little scratchy sketches drawn in the margins of his workbooks. They're all little pieces of the real Blaise Morrison, the person he is onstage and away from the toxic wealth of Hannaford, and I'm totally enamored by it. He stops smirking and gives me these heartbreakingly cocky little grins instead. Our time studying alone together leaves me with an ache deep in my chest that won't go away. I also frequently require a cold shower afterwards to calm my hormones the fuck down. I do not want to be making the same mistakes with him that I have with Harley but I'm starting to forget that he used to hate me. We work together so well as I help get him to the GPA he needs.

We spread out on the floor because Blaise works best when he's comfortable and he likes the cushions in front of the TV best. He kicks his shoes off at the door and leaves his blazer draped over the couch. He only does this when Avery isn't here. I think she's threatened him for it before. His shirt is unbuttoned and his tattoos are peeking out. I can't take my eyes off of that little patch of exposed skin, not even when Blaise looks up and catches me staring.

"Fuck, Mounty, don't make this even harder for me than it already is," he groans and I look up, licking my bottom lip.

"What's hard?" I croak, the desire in my voice so clear and foreign to me. I sound like a sexed up harlot. *Sweet lord.*

Blaise exhales and tips his head back to blink at the ceiling like I'm testing him.

Oh. Right. My mind kicks back online and I realize I'm drooling all over him and he's just trying to study. He's so beyond not interested that he's actually repelled by me. Fuck.

"Sorry," I mumble and I turn away from him, focusing my eyes back onto the assignment in front of me and trying not to vomit in shame. I'm fucking pathetic.

Blaise doesn't speak again. I mark everything he's finished and we put together a page of notes for an upcoming test. I manage to calm down and focus on the work enough that I almost forget about how humiliating my reaction to him was. When my phone pings with a text from Avery to say she's heading back from ballet class I'm shocked the hour is already up. I put away my supplies as Blaise watches me. I avoid his eyes.

He clears his throat and when I refuse to look at him he raises up to his knees before me. I startle, my head jerking up to finally meet his eyes, and then he pushes me back into the cushions until he's lying on top of me. His eyes on my face are molten, fierce and smoldering, and I can't breathe as he slowly lowers his lips to mine.

It's soft and languid for a second, just the barest of touches, like he's worried I'll run away. When I kiss him back, opening my mouth and tasting him, he groans and kisses me harder until I think I'm going to pass out. His chest is a solid weight on top of me. My nipples are hard as they push up against him and I try not to instinctually rock my hips in time with the thrust of his tongue in my mouth. His lips are hungry as they consume me until I'm a shaking mess in his arms. I'm so fucking wet for him with just one kiss. My legs part so he can settle between them and he breaks away from me, panting.

"Is that better?"

A bucket of ice over my head would have been less devastating than those words.

I scramble out from under him and onto my feet. My hands are shaking and I curse myself under my breath. Blaise scowls at me and I'm so deeply ashamed of myself. I want to crawl under my bed and die.

"Avery is going to be back soon. I need to get ready for bed." I keep my eyes glued to the floor as he packs his bag and leaves. I want to apologize to him but I can't find the words. I don't move or speak until I hear the door shut behind him.

Then I climb into bed and try not to lose myself.

My alarm wakes me. I turn it off and try to go back to sleep.

Last night I pretended to be asleep already when Avery got home and she pretended to believe me which was very kind of her. She's too smart sometimes, too intuitive, and it's a blessing and a curse. I listen as she gets up and showers, then when she pours us both a coffee each and starts to make pancakes, without uttering a word to me, I break exactly how she knows I will. Evil dictator.

"Blaise kissed me."

She lets out a little yelp that is so not an Avery Beaumont noise. I hear something drop and smash in the kitchen. My eyes squeeze shut and tears build up but I refuse to let them fall. I was kind of hoping this would roll off her back and be no big deal but the universe conspires against me. Great, now I'm just as dramatic as Blaise is. Fuck.

"He did *what*?! When? Did you kiss him back? Was it a peck or a proper kiss?

Jesus Christ, what did you do?" Avery screeches as she storms back over to my bed. I don't look at her. I just can't.

"We were studying and he was just being nice to me. When he packed up as we finished he pushed me back onto the cushions and he kissed me."

Avery sinks down onto the bed. I still can't look at her. "Wow. I did *not* think he would do that."

Fuck, my stomach roils all over again. "He only did it because he feels like he owes me for helping him study. I'm that fucking pathetic that he felt like he had to."

Avery clears her throat and says, "Did he say that?"

"He may as well have."

Her eyes narrow at me. "Tell me exactly what he did say."

I groan and sit up. Avery looks worried, like really fucking concerned and now I feel like I attacked her friend. I know he kissed me but if I made him so uncomfortable that he felt forced to do it then it's still me in the wrong, right? Fuck, I have a headache. This just proves I should stay away from guys.

"He said I was making it harder for him while I was watching him study. I apologized then he kissed me. Then he pulled away and said 'is that better'."

Avery frowns at me and then down at her phone.

"I'm staying in bed today. I'm going to be a coward and just fucking hide here. He's coming back to study tonight and I need to figure out how to help him while I'm crawling with shame."

Avery starts typing a message even as she scowls at me. "He kissed you, that's on him. Why should you be feeling shame?"

"Because he doesn't even like me. He was only kissing me so I'd keep tutoring him. Fuck, I'm so fucking stupid. Now Ash is going to lose his goddamn mind and Harley is going to get pissy at me for meddling in their shit again and Blaise is going to tell everyone I'm a pathetic stalker."

She stands up and pulls back the blankets so I'm hit with the chill of the morning air. "Get up and go to class. I'll fix it."

I groan and scrub at my face like it will change how awful I'm feeling. "Aves-"

"No, Lips. I will fix it. You have a test in Biology and I'm not sitting through choir and Harlow's crap without you. Shower and eat, I'm going down to eat with the boys and fix this."

I sigh and do what she says.

I make it through choir without looking at Blaise. He pointedly doesn't look at me either which makes it both easier and more gut wrenching. Avery watches us both with keen interest, like she's waiting to have to pry us apart when we try to kill each other. I feel like I should tell her that I don't want to kill him but I do want to die.

I flee the class the second I can and when I sit down next to Harley in our literature class I give myself the pep talk of a lifetime. I've been stabbed, shot, burned, snapped, chained, broken, and beaten. I need to get some perspective and get over the embarrassment of that pity kiss. I get close to believing myself.

Ms. Lucia had assigned 'A Brave New World' to the class as a reading over the winter break and we're given a pop quiz the moment she arrives. I love the book, having read it in middle school, and I could have done the quiz in my sleep. I'm finished with twenty minutes to spare and I grab my notes for Biology to make absolutely sure I'm going to ace the test in the next class. Harley finishes up five minutes after me and he pulls out his own notes, immaculately written and so much better than mine. Ms. Lucia smiles at us both and then promptly ignores us as she marks our quizzes.

Harley waits until her attention is away from us and then whispers, "Why was Avery threatening Blaise this morning at breakfast?"

I keep my gaze on my notes. Harley doesn't sound happy and my eyes will give me away.

"I don't know. This is the first I'm hearing of it."

He grunts at me and says, "She told him that she'd end him if he tried to touch you again. When did he touch you?"

Fuck. Fuck fuck fuck. Avery, lord help me, why couldn't you have been just a little more discreet?! Did Ash know? I'll be hauled into another supply closet and called a slut in no time! I hope my face isn't showing any of the panic I'm feeling right down to my soul.

"I was helping him with an assignment. Avery is worried about me because Ash is on the warpath about you guys and she doesn't want to cause any issues. Nothing to worry about, forget it."

He leans in closer and whispers, "She made it sound like he'd tried to kiss you. He was pretty ashamed when she started in on him."

Hot shame slides over my skin and my cheeks flush. I raise my hand and when Ms. Lucia calls on me I ask to go to the nurse for a migraine. Harley watches me as I pack up and his eyes follow me out the door.

I don't make it to Biology.

Blaise arrives at our room with a black eye and a shitty attitude.

Avery makes herself comfortable on her bed and starts her own assignments. She'd told her ballet teacher she had cramps and then told me she was going to make sure Blaise wasn't inappropriate with me. I'd argued with her, I was the one who was inappropriate, but she wouldn't budge.

We sit on the floor like we always do, though I'm a little uncomfortable about it now. Blaise sullenly hands over all of his completed work and I hand him a pile of notes to work on while I mark. We settle into a mildly uncomfortable silence as we work.

It's not until Avery gets a phone call and ducks into the bathroom for privacy that Blaise finally speaks to me.

"You're such a hypocrite. You ran straight to Avery."

I blush and nod my head. I just need to get this out and be done with it. "I know. I told her exactly how embarrassed I was with my actions and I owe you an apology."

Blaise frowns at me and I fumble on, praying I can clear the air enough so we can get back to studying as friends. "Look, I'm sorry I was staring and making you uncomfortable. I was tired and not thinking straight. I'm also sorry Avery yelled at you for the whole…thing, I was embarrassed that you had pity kissed me and I moped to her about it. You know how she gets when she's in protect mode. Can we just forget it and move on?"

I force myself to look him in the eye. He's still frowning and now he's chewing on his bottom lip. If he didn't look so serious I'd think he was teasing me.

"That's not what I was expecting you to say," he murmurs.

I shrug because I don't have an answer to that either. When he opens his mouth again, Avery walks out of the bathroom and pegs him with a *look*. He arches an eyebrow at her like he's trying to provoke her into a fight. I get a bad feeling about the two of them circling each other.

"Where did you get that lovely black eye from, Morrison?" Avery croons. She struts into the kitchen and begins to make us each a hot cocoa. She doesn't get a cup for Blaise.

He watches her as he leans back, his attitude melting back into the cocky rock star he really is. "Arbour was defending his love. He thinks I'm trying to steal his girl out from under him and he can be a jealous shit."

My stomach drops and the small amount of peace I'd managed to find with my apology disappears into thin air. Harley has a girlfriend? Blaise is trying to steal her? I don't like the sound of either of those things. Blaise is pity kissing me and then out hunting his best friend's girlfriend. Wow. Why do I like this asshole so much? At least now I'm not feeling so bad about my actions.

"I didn't know he had a girl," snipes Avery, filling my cup with marshmallows and drizzling the entire drink in chocolate syrup. It's like a heart attack in a cup and I'm so fucking ready for it.

Blaise grins and packs away his textbooks and notes. "Try telling him that. Have a good night, girls. I'll see you both tomorrow."

Chapter Fifteen

Lance the Mounty, because I can't remember the little fuck's last name to save my damn life, is becoming a problem.

He gets to our tutoring sessions before me without fail so I don't even get a minute to myself to set up. When Ash realizes this, he starts coming earlier as well so when I arrive ten minutes before the start time they're both already there and being openly hostile towards each other. I do my best to ignore it but, fuck me, Lance will not stop flirting and Ash gets snarky at him the second he starts. I stay polite but I lose my friendly demeanor quickly. I have enough problems in my life without adding an obsessed little Mounty boy to the list. He does not get the hint. If anything, it makes him work harder.

It does work to my advantage in the week leading up to winter break. As we finish the session I quickly pack up to try and flee before he can ask to walk me back to the dorms when he starts in on his latest attempt to befriend me.

"I'm the school photographer. I've got a good shot of you at a football game a few weeks ago. It's the only one I've seen you at."

Ash sneers at him. "You sound like a fucking stalker. Lay off a bit or she'll realize how desperate you really are."

I clench my teeth. I hate that he is defending me because I honestly don't know what the fuck I'd say to Lance if Ash weren't here. He's too much and I feel fucking smothered.

Lance ignores Ash and hands me his iPad with the photo he's talking about. It's great, but I'm not the only one in it. Harley and I are eating hotdogs and laughing with each other. Avery is tucked under Ash's arm and they're both smiling at Blaise who is talking about something and gesturing with his hands. It's the perfect moment in time for all five of us and I instantly know Avery will adore it. I mean, I love it too, but I feel weird about it because Ash hates me, Blaise only tolerates me because I help him with his studies, and, well, I guess Harley is my friend. It's the perfect gift for Avery and I've been struggling to find her something.

"I need a copy of this. Can you email me one? The highest definition you have please," I say and Lance smiles at me like I've complimented him. His hand brushes mine when he takes the iPad back and he runs a finger over my hand. I force myself not to shudder but I move away from him quickly and Ash sees him do it.

"Don't be a creepy fuck." He snaps but Lance just smirks at him.

"You're the one watching her like an obsessed boyfriend. Maybe she should be worried about you."

Ash's face morphs into his icy mask and I groan. Great. I'm going to be scraping Mounty innards off of my bag for the rest of the evening.

"Run along, Mounty. I'll see you back at the dorms."

Finally, Lance gulps and leaves. I quirk an eyebrow at Ash but he ignores me and I shove textbooks into my bag. As I pack, I check my phone and spot a text from Avery. I manage to hold in my groan and say to Ash, "Avery wants us both to meet her for dinner in the dining hall."

He nods and waits for me, frowning and distracted. He motions to Lance's empty seat and says, "Did you really have to encourage him? You obviously aren't interested."

I sigh and we walk out of the library. "How did I encourage him? I never flirt back."

He grabs my elbow to pull me closer when a group of rowdy seniors pass us but he doesn't let go when we're past them. "You asked for a copy of the photo and you don't snap at him like you do when I speak to you."

It sounds like he's whining about sharing me but his tone is aggravated. I roll my eyes at him. "I snap at you because you piss me off. You get under my skin, you hurt me, you say stupid shit to me all the fucking time to get a rise out of me. But you don't creep me out. I'm never worried about you taking things too far."

Ash's spine snaps straight and he drops his hand away from my elbow. I roll my eyes all over again. "Settle down, Beaumont, I'm just saying you're a decent human being when you're not being an asshole to me."

He clears his throat and I swear there's color on his cheeks that wasn't there before.

"Are you blushing right now? What exactly has you swooning? The word asshole?"

He glares at me and rolls his eyes. "Shut up, Mounty, I'm not fucking swooning. No one has ever called me decent before and my reaction is one of shock. It doesn't happen often so you wouldn't have seen it before and don't expect to see it again."

I stop and grab his elbow, the same way he'd taken mine. "You are decent, Ash. You're loyal to your friends and you protect Avery fiercely. You even protect me when you think I'm in danger even though you don't trust me. You lost your mind over the thought of your brother hurting me. Being related to Joey, and your father, doesn't make you bad."

He shrugs and pulls his arm away. I'm glad because for a second there I thought I was going to have to offer to hug him and the thought of being pressed against him like that makes me sweat. The image of his nipples pops into my head and I have to shake it out before I melt into a fucking puddle. When we get to the dining hall he stares at me for a second and then grabs a tray. When I move to grab one for myself he snaps, "Don't be dense, Mounty, what do you want for dinner?"

Well, okay then.

Blaise texts after classes finish to say he's skipping our tutoring session to watch Harley swim in the trials that are being held at Hannaford. I'm actually really glad because I need the space to sort my head out and work on my own assignments. I get twenty minutes to myself before Avery storms into our room and runs for the bathroom.

"What are you doing, we're going to be late! You can't attend the trials unless you're in uniform so change back!" she calls out to me before ducking into the bathroom to change out of her ballet clothes and freshen up. She leaves the bathroom door open because apparently she knows I'm going to argue.

"I'm not going. Harley didn't even tell me they were on," I say but I'm up and getting dressed as I say it. I know Avery won't accept my answer.

"We're being supportive, get your butt moving."

I roll my eyes at her but I speed up anyway. When she's ready I grab my blazer and head for the door, grumbling, "He's your cousin, why do I have to be supportive?"

Avery rolls her eyes at me and waves her phone in my face as we start to walk down to the pool. "He's been obsessively texting me about who is threatening you. Face it, you guys are friends now and you have to support him. Plus, I know you think he's hot and he's going to be walking around in speedos, dripping wet for three hours. *You're welcome.*"

I choke on my own tongue. *Jesus fucking Christ.*

The pool is Olympic-sized with enough seating for the entire school to watch the trials but with the parents and families that came to watch we struggle to find a decent spot. Blaise ends up sweet talking someone's sister and we get close enough that I can see the droplets of water sliding down Harley's abs. Avery laughs hysterically at me, the bitch, but Ash and Blaise just look at her like she's crazy.

"What are the trials for?" I ask as we watch Harley approach the starting blocks. Fuck me, he does look pretty fucking good. I look away before I publicly shame myself.

"A spot on the state team. Harley wins it every year and then when they offer it to him he turns them down." Avery murmurs, sipping her coffee.

"Why?"

She shrugs. "He enjoys winning but doesn't want to take it further. I told him he should do it for scholarships for college but, until you got here, he assumed he'd be dead by then."

I cringe and nod. Harsh but true, without me and the protection I've bought him he would be dead. I let my thoughts spiral as I go through my exit plan for the two of us. Harley steps onto his starting block and gets into position. I quietly admire the muscles in his back and the length of his legs. He's broader and more defined than the other swimmers. I'd have guessed he'd be slower because of the extra weight in muscle he's carrying.

My daydreaming is interrupted when Harlow sits down next to me.

Avery straightens and jabs Ash in the ribs when she sees her but I ignore the bitch, keeping my attention on Harley as the starting gun fires and he dives into the water in a graceful arc.

"How the fuck do you know Joey's dealers?" she murmurs and I turn to look at her.

Her fingers are trembling where she's holding her phone and her eyes are having trouble tracking. Great. She's on something, too.

"His dealers or yours?" I say and Avery snorts, muttering "Typical," under her breath.

Harlow flicks her hair over her shoulder and says, blithely, "Does it matter? They sell the best and they're rough guys. Joey's concerned at having his baby sister rooming with the wrong sort of girl."

Ash throws his head back and roars with laughter like Blaise usually does but the rock star just glares at Harlow like she's a ticking bomb.

"You better not be here at Joey's request because I've already warned him twice about provoking me. If he does it again I'm not going to play games with him, I'm going for his throat."

Avery tucks her arm into mine and holds my hand where Harlow can see it, a clear statement of loyalty. "Run along, Roqueford. Go snort your lines somewhere else so I can enjoy watching my cousin wipe the floor with your brother. Oh, wait, you did know Andrew Wakes was your bastard brother, didn't you? Everyone knows you come by your slutty nature from your father. I hope you use condoms a bit more than he does or you'll have your own horde of bastards in no time."

Harlow curses viciously under her breath as she leaves and I turn back to the race just in time to see Harley touch the wall first, a full body length in front of his competitors.

"He really should join the state team," I say and Avery hums her agreement.

Blaise clears his throat. "Are either of you going to explain what the hell she was talking about?"

I look over at him, startled. "Didn't Harley tell you?"

Ash gives me an incredulous look. "He doesn't tell us anything that involves you."

Huh. I guess he thinks that comes with being 'mine' which is probably wise. I sigh. "Joey brought some of his dealers to the school and thought he'd be able to out me as a gang member or dealer or whatever. As I am none of those things, he was pissed when they left at my request."

They both blink at me then Ash says, "You asked his dealers to leave and they did?"

I shrug. "I asked nicely."

Avery giggles and distracts the guys away from the topic.

When Harley wins his last race of the night Avery ushers me out, telling the guys she's too tired to watch the medals ceremony and we walk back to our room.

The next morning Avery leaves for winter break and I roll out of my bed to say goodbye, though I'm clearly not quite human before I've had my coffee.

"Be good while I'm gone." Avery smirks and kisses my cheek. I laugh and hand over the wrapped gift I've had stashed under my bed. She gasps.

"You said no presents!"

I laugh. "I know you've ignored me and there's something in your closet for me. Don't peek until Christmas."

She laughs and tweaks my nose.

Chapter Sixteen

I refuse to leave my room for winter break. Harley checks in every day but he mostly leaves me alone when I tell him I need to catch up on my assignments while I don't have to tutor anyone else. I text Avery every day and I'm relieved to find the Crow has fulfilled his favor and kept Senior away from home.

On Christmas Eve I go to bed with the same plan I have every year.

I won't exist again until Christmas is over.

Someone is in the kitchen.

I crack one eye open and turn my head just far enough to see who's fumbling around in Avery's cooking supplies.

Harley.

He's standing there in a gray sweatshirt and sweatpants, mixing something in a bowl while a pan heats up on the stove. The coffee machine is beeping and he's turned the TV onto some random channel with Christmas carols.

I groan and shut my eyes.

"I'm making French toast. Aves said it's your favorite, consider it a peace offering. I'm only good at breakfast so you're going to have to figure something out for us to have for dinner."

Why is he here? Why is he making me food and forcing me to function? I just want to wallow between my sheets and forget about this stupid day. I huff and roll over. I'm not getting up, fuck him.

"I get you don't do Christmas but this is the first chance I've had to spend the day with someone since my da died. I've been trapped in boarding schools ever since and teachers really don't give a crap about orphaned mobster kids."

I groan again and sit up, frowning at him. He's got his back to me as he drops the soaked bread into the pan. I can't kick him out. He's being sweet and kind, and, fuck it, if I don't want him spending another Christmas alone. I cannot function on my birthday but I could force myself today if it means this much to him. Clearly, I'm getting soft.

So I get up.

I pull an oversized sweater on and then accept a giant cup of coffee from Harley while I rummage around in the cupboards for syrup and sprinkles. It's Christmas, we deserve some fucking sprinkles.

Harley tries to sit at the counter but I push him into sitting on the floor in front of the TV instead. I put Nightmare Before Christmas on instead of the bullshit carols and then we argue for the entire movie. Let's just say one of us thinks the movie is a Christmas movie and the other person is wrong. The French toast is the best I've ever had.

I stand up to clear our plates and Harley's gaze catches on my bare legs. That's when I realize I'm only wearing underwear and the sweater. My cheeks turn scarlet and I rush to find some pants. Harley chuckles at me like we're friends and I startle when I realize we are. Fuck, how did that happen?

When I return from the closet, Harley has grabbed a bottle of whiskey from Avery's stash and is sitting cross-legged on the floor where I usually study with Blaise. I'm a little worried about drinking with him again because last time I couldn't control myself and I hate how awkward I felt around him afterwards. I don't know how he found Avery's hiding spot but when he grins and holds up a shooter glass I can't help but cave. I roll my eyes and I grab the shot, downing it as I join him. He throws one back and chases it with a beer. Gross.

"Aves told me you guys swap truths. I want to give that a go."

I arch an eyebrow at him and rub my palms on my yoga pants. "We also choose our own truths. I'm assuming you want to ask me questions?"

He nods as he refills the glasses. "We take turns asking. If you want to pass, take the shot."

I'd have liver poisoning in under an hour but we've had such a good day I don't want to spoil it by refusing. If I made it past ten shots I'll bow out. I nod and he smirks at me, wolfishly.

"Ladies first."

I snort. "There are no ladies here, just you and the Mounty trash. But fine." I blow out a breath. There's plenty I want to ask him. The problem is, if I go straight to the deep stuff he may pass or he could do the same and I'll have to quit the game. I need to stick to lighthearted stuff. "First kiss?" I tease.

He flicks the lid from his beer at me. "Lame. Some chick in fifth grade. I can't tell you her name, I honestly don't remember. Yours?"

Fuck. I didn't think that through at all. I take a shot.

"You've got to be kidding me? How is that classified information, Mounty?"

"It's my turn to ask a question." I refill my shot glass so I don't have to look at him.

"I'll give you a freebie. You can insist I answer something if you answer this one."

Hmm. Tempting. I could lie but now I've made a big deal out of it, he'll guess. Maybe I'm becoming a lightweight with my booze because my stomach is warming my blood already. I give in.

"You. Well, one before you but I don't count it because…well, I just don't. Just you because I also don't count Blaise's pity kiss."

It's pretty clear Harley was expecting any answer except that. I want to cringe away from the shocked intensity in his eyes but my stubborn pride makes me sit and endure it. I'm trapped there until he breaks the spell, grabbing the bottle of whiskey and taking a big gulp. Then he leans back against the coffee table and smirks at me, cocky again.

I clear my throat. "My turn. Why get a face tattoo? I know you have the chest piece but most people fill up their arms and even their necks before getting one on their face."

He doesn't speak. The playful look on his face slides right off and he's glaring down at his shot glass.

Fuck. I thought that was a pretty safe question.

We're going to be at each other's throats before the end of the bottle at this rate.

"I didn't choose the tattoo. Or the placement."

I blink at him. I open my mouth to ask him more but he cuts in, "That's your answer. You want another question, wait your turn." There's an edge to his voice that wasn't there before. I nod and wave a hand at him to take his turn.

"Worst memory?"

"Pass." I take a shot.

He rolls his eyes. "Worst memory you're willing to tell me?"

Breaking the rules already and after he's just quoted them to me, typical. I sigh and scour my brain for something. He already knows about my mom's overdose. I can't talk about my life with the Jackal.

"What's yours?" I whisper. He looks at me and tips back the bottle of beer, draining it.

"My da being killed. My grandfather shot him, point blank, right between the eyes. If I close my eyes I can still feel the heat of his blood hitting my face."

I swallow.

Maybe I feel so safe with him because he's broken, too.

Be brave, Lips, if he can do it then you can.

"I'm pretty good at getting into places no one else can. I was given a job to take something from a well-known marksman. Gun for hire. Assassin. Whatever you want to call him, he was the best of the best. I was terrified but I was also hungry. Lonely. Depressed and lost. I snuck in, got what I was paid to get, and I made it to the back door before he woke up. I sprinted to the gate but my leg had only been put back together for a few months at that point and I wasn't quick anymore. Diarmuid pointed a gun at me and told me to give up my employer or he'd shoot. I turned and stared him in the eye. I thought maybe seeing how young I was would be enough to stop him but he stared at me with steady, cold eyes. So I turned and ran, and he shot me. I had to run for two miles with a fresh bullet wound, then I got sewn back together with no pain relief by some nurse turned crackhead. It got infected and I nearly died."

I was being nice and telling him two truths at once; a bad memory and why his uncle had shot me. I knew he'd ask me at some point so why not just tell him? Harley nods and rubs at his chin, a fine dusting of stubble growing where he hasn't bothered to shave. I can't stop looking at it. It's a little darker than the gold waves on his head. I want to rub my cheek on it or even feel the burn of him rubbing his cheek on me. God, I need to get my thoughts out of the gutter.

"Who forced the tattoo on you?"

He doesn't flinch away or get pissy this time, he's expecting me to dig for more information. He runs a finger over the rim of his shot glass like he's going to pass. I'm surprised when he speaks. "My uncle. My da was the oldest in the family. He had nine siblings, four full blood and the rest were from my grandfather's second marriage. Domhnall was the next boy born and he's set to take over now that I'm out." He doesn't look up at me, his eyes just stay on the amber liquid in the glass. "There was a threat made against me and Ma. My grandfather didn't give a shit. He said casualties were the price they paid for being in the business they were in and Da should just deal with it. Da didn't trust his gut and Ma was taken. She was left outside my grandfather's house a week later but the damage was done. She now lives in an institution for the mentally ill. It broke Da and he left, took off and left me with my grandfather. When he came back to get me, he told the family he was out. They killed him. Then, they held me down and tattooed me. The family creed is actually '*Blood, Honor, Faith*'. They said that Da had put Ma before his blood, which he did. It's not something he was ashamed of but they tattooed me to try and shame me for what he did."

He takes another swig from his beer, draining the bottle. "I found out later that my grandfather was the one who took Ma. My uncles all helped…torture her. They kept saying Da put his honor, his pride, before his blood. They're fucking crazy. The tattoo was shit, looked awful because I was only nine when they did it, and I was screaming and trying to get them to stop. When I grew it got even worse, stretched and faded out. Two years ago, Ash and Blaise dragged me to a parlor and we had it redone. None of us have good families, blood doesn't mean shit, but we chose the family we have now. So, when I got mine they both got our new creed tattooed too. Avery keeps saying she's going to get it done as well but she's an absolute fucking sissy about needles so I'm not holding my breath. I don't need her to get it anyway, I know she's one of us."

I let his words soak in but one thing is clear to me.

Liam and Domhnall O'Cronin are going to die.

Fuck it, I'm going to wipe every last O'Cronin out of the state, barring Harley and maybe Diarmuid.

My fingers actually tremble from the rage I'm trying to contain. I'm glad he's still staring at the floor because my face is all Wolf right now. *Fucking Liam O'Cronin!* I'm going to shame that miserable old bastard and then I'm going to kill him. Or help Harley do it. I'm cool either way.

"How did you go from being shot by Diarmuid to being friends? He hugged you like…like he had a right to. I'd swear that you'd slept with him if he hadn't made that stupid comment about your tits."

Why is he so damned fixated on my sex life? Or lack thereof, not that he knew that. "Our mutual acquaintance put him on the books. We met in friendlier circumstances and he kept asking how I'd gotten through his security. When I finally realized he was impressed not pissy I told him and then he started acting like we were best friends. I haven't slept with him, and I won't ever in the future. Even if my tits do fill in."

Harley scoffs and opens another beer. "Your tits don't need to fill in, they're fine. Da used to go on and on about how good of a shot Diarmuid was. I wanted to learn from him. I wanted to be just like him."

I try to ignore him calling my tits 'fine' because I don't know if he's insulting me or reassuring me. I feel like he's opened the door to talking about relationships and romantic interests so I ask the question that's been keeping me up for weeks, trying valiantly not to blush or look too interested in the answer.

"Who are you dating? She seems to be causing waves in your tight-knit family."

"I'm not dating anyone. Who told you that?" The warmth has leached out of his voice and his eyes are guarded again. Great. Why is he allowed to ask if I'm sleeping with his uncle but I can't ask this without a mood swing?

"Blaise. Avery asked about his black eye and he said he'd been making a move on your girl. No, wait, he said you accused him of moving in on your girl."

He blows out a breath and looks up at the ceiling. I'm getting a fair bit of that out of these guys and I don't know what the hell it means. I need to ask Avery.

"I gave him the black eye in the ring. He was mouthing off and I got pissy. We usually don't aim for the head but I lost my cool and cracked him."

I fight the shit-eating grin tugging at the corners of my mouth. "Oh. So, no girl?"

He gives me a sly look. "Not yet."

Huh. That sounded like there was going to be one soon, as if he's chasing some girl. That's probably who he's been texting throughout the day. Fuck. "Let me know. I'm running background checks on everyone we get involved with from now on. I do not want another Annabelle or Rory getting close ever again."

He nods and puts the rim of the beer bottle up to his lips. I try so hard not to watch but he's like a magnet, drawing me in until I'm stuck drooling over him. I watch his throat work and I have to squeeze my thighs together at the sensations running through me. Right, mind out of the gutter Lips. Mind *out* of the gutter. He's so unbelievably hot, it is cruel to sit so close to him.

"I'm fairly observant, I think sometimes you underestimate that," he says, his voice warm and dripping like honey, as he pours another shot. I have to clear my throat twice to find my voice.

"Oh yeah?"

"You're a virgin, aren't you?"

Excuse me?

What the fuuuuuuuuuuck?

Was it that obvious? Was our little make out session that bad? Oh my fucking god, I'm a fumbling idiotic virgin and he spotted it. No wonder he wanted to stop. When I stare at him, jaw clenched and eyes narrowed, he fixes his stunning blue-eyed gaze onto mine. "Yep. I'm observant enough to realize that Joey had to be your first kiss. You told me and Blaise at breakfast on the first day back after summer break, you said you held a knife to his dick. Now you've just told me I was your first real kiss and that the other one didn't count. So, unless you're out fucking guys like the chick in *Pretty Woman* then I'd guess you've never had sex before."

"How have you seen *Pretty Woman?*" I'm grasping at straws, trying to buy my brain some time to recalibrate.

He rolls his eyes at me. "When Aves sulks over guys she watches three movies; *Pretty Woman*, *Dirty Dancing*, and *Ghost*. I dunno, it has something to do with Aunt Alice. Stop avoiding the question. Answer it or take the shot."

I still hesitate. It's not like I'm ashamed about it, other than my lack of skills. I'm actually proud, considering where I grew up and the six years I spent in foster care. It's just that everyone at this school seem to bed hop and while I don't want to do that I also don't want news of my untouched status getting out and the damned bet getting out of control.

Harley misreads my indecision and curses viciously. "If Joey touched you, I'm driving to his place tonight and I'm setting it on fire. I will burn that fuck alive."

A shiver runs down my spine and pools between my thighs. Not for the first time, I think about how damaged I must be to find him irresistible when he talks so casually about enacting blood-soaked revenge for me.

"No, it's—he didn't. He tried but I've found a sharp knife nestled against a guy's dick is usually a good deterrent. I'm more worried about the bet. How much bigger do you think the payout will be if they find out I'm a virgin?"

Harley groans and rubs his eyes. "I forgot about that stupid fucking bet. So you spent your first year here being accosted by horny guys trying to talk you into a quick fuck for money and every single one of them assumed you were up for it because you're a Mounty girl."

I was tempted to point out how often he and his friends called me a slut and accused me of using sex to get my way but he's actually being really sweet so I let it go. When his hands lower he looks a little embarrassed so I think he realized it all on his own.

We fall back into silence, only the sounds of us drinking to be heard. My phone pings and I ignore it. I don't want the Jackal sullying this moment.

"You should get that. Avery is freaked out that you haven't texted her back."

Crap.

I WILL DRIVE BACK THERE IF YOU DON'T ANSWER ME SOON ECLIPSE ANDERSON. Also, what is your middle name? I need to know it because apparently you pull the kind of shit that requires a full name sort of reaction.

Well, shit.

I scroll back to find out what I'm supposed to be answering. Fifteen from Avery on our private chat. Twenty-two in our group message. Fuck.

Merry Christmas

Thank you for the gift, you're too sweet.

Mounty, where did you get the photo? It's so perfect, I cried.

Well, no I didn't because I'm not the crying sort. But I thought about crying which is basically the same.

Senior isn't home. First Christmas I've been able to relax.

Has Harley joined you for brunch?

Lips, I'm starting to get worried that you've been murdered.

Okay Harley just texted to say you've taken to your bed. I told him to make French toast.

Look, I know you've got your demons about today but please get out of bed and text me.

Ash said Senior not being here is your present to both of us for Christmas. Call me with an explanation please.

I text Harley. How is it he can text me back while eating but you can't? I'm feeling very unloved.

Are you pissed at me or something?

So help me, Mounty, I will set Ash on you.

That's a lie. I wouldn't do that to you. Please text me.

Fine. Merry Christmas, you scrooge.

I hit call and wince at the ice she breathes down the phone at me.

"Is this the reanimated corpse of Eclipse unknown-middle-name Anderson?"

The wince turns into a full-blown cringe and Harley takes one look at me and roars with laughter.

What an asshole.

Chapter Seventeen

Avery puts the photo I gave her in the kitchen so she can look at it while she cooks. While she was home, she had the photo blown up and put on a canvas and she hangs that one on the wall between our beds. My heart does little flutters every time I look at it until I force myself to stop looking at it so I don't have a heart attack.

I know Joey must have been awful over the break because Ash sleeps in our room for a full week when they get back. By Friday, Avery is sick of sharing her bed with him and kicks him onto the couch. I try to move around quietly when I get ready for class because his start later and he prefers to sleep until the very last second he can.

I open my drawers to find one pair of underwear. One. So with the pair I just took off that means I have two freaking pairs of underwear left and, like, twenty pairs missing. What. The. Fuck.

I stomp over to the bathroom and wake Ash up with my raging. He cusses me out without even opening his eyes and I snap back at him, "Sleep on your own fucking couch then!" and slam the door behind me.

The hot water mellows me out a little and by the time I exit the bathroom, I'm level enough to apologize to Ash as he heads in for a shower. Avery hands me a plate of toast and a cup of coffee, and I slump onto the couch to mope.

"I'll have some more delivered today and we can go see the ladies in the laundry to find out where they're disappearing from."

I nod and eat my food. Ash joins us for breakfast and when he's finished he grabs Avery's laptop and sits next to me on the couch. When I see the website he's on I blush. He smirks back at me. "What? I don't know where Mounties shop. Is there a slum version of Agent Provocateur?"

I elbow him in the ribs but he doesn't take notice. "I can buy my own underwear, thank you very much."

He shrugs. "You can but after waking me up you'll be nice and let me do it. It's one of my true skills in life."

Avery narrows her eyes at him over the rim of her coffee cup. "What would you know about choosing lingerie?"

Ash smirks back at her. "More than you. You've bought it for one body, I've seen it on—"

"Do *not* give me a number right now Alexander Asher William Beaumont, I will smother you in your sleep. No sister wants to hear how many sluts her brother has gone through. Which reminds me, when were you last tested for STI's? Annabelle probably gave you herpes."

He ignores her and continues to add items. I choke on my toast and try to snatch the laptop away from him when I see what exactly he's picking. "I do not fucking need corsets, suspender belts, or a crotchless bodysuit!"

Ash raises an eyebrow at me. "How very vanilla of you. All cotton granny panties then?"

I cross my arms and seethe at him. No answer I give him will save me so silence it is. Avery comes over to perch on the armrest and point out pieces she likes.

"Why are you doing this? You don't even like me," I say finally, after I hand over my card details and find myself *thousands* of dollars poorer. I'm so glad I risked my life for such a tiny amount of lace and boning. Corset boning, not even the supposedly fun type. Avery pats my head and heads to the coffee machine for round two.

"I know you're going to fuck us over at some point, I figure why not have some fun until then?" Ash replies, nonchalant.

I glare at him and Avery calls out from the kitchen in a sing-song voice, "Baby steps!"

I groan and pack my bag for the day. Ash watches me and I try not to squirm under the intensity of his gaze.

"What?!" I snap when I can't take it anymore.

"Who do you think is stealing your underwear?"

I groan. "If I knew, it wouldn't be happening anymore. I'm fucking sick of replacing it. Whoever it is, they're taking them when I send them out to be washed."

Ash grimaces but doesn't say anything so I continue, "Avery thinks it's a prank and someone in the laundry is in on it. I think it's Harlow being a snotty bitch because I found Avery's shoes."

Ash frowns at me. "They're taking underwear you've already worn. It sounds like a desperate guy taking them to sniff."

My stomach roils, I hadn't thought of that. For fuck's sake. "Guys are disgusting. Seriously. I'm putting a fucking camera on the door and I'm washing my own shit from now on. Fuck this!"

I storm out and head to my classes in a foul mood.

What next?

Avery texts me during classes to say she's having our clothes sent out of the school for cleaning for the foreseeable future. I'll have to order two more uniforms to get through the week but it's cheaper than buying more of the underwear Ash selected.

When I get back to our rooms and find a package waiting for me I empty it straight into my drawers without looking through it. I'm too pissed to enjoy my new things.

Thankfully Ash sleeps in his own room so the next morning I don't have to deal with his commentary while I pick out what I'm going to wear. I blush profusely when it finally hits me that he's picked every piece of lace I now own. Fuck. He didn't just buy underwear either, no, he bought matching bras for every pair. I didn't give him my size and yet they fit perfectly. He's a fucking wizard.

I pick out a black set and once they're on it's clear he's picked out the most risqué underwear possible. They're completely transparent and sexy as fuck. I blush but I also feel feminine and attractive. Yep, a fucking wizard. I wonder if he'll pick out all of my underwear from now on if I ask?

Avery ducks into the bathroom behind me and slaps my ass with a giggle. I scowl at her playfully and pull on some jeans and a shirt.

"I need your help with something today, if you're not too busy?" she says as she brushes her hair. I frown and nod as I brush my teeth.

"A senior, called Yasmin Gilliam, started a gossip website last year. It's stupid and childish and I've barely given it any attention up until now. Someone has made an anonymous account and is posting classified documents on there. Documents from businesses and organizations owned by Hannaford families."

I finish up and lean on the sink, my arms folded, as I listen. Avery gives me a sidelong look. "None of it affects us but it's only a matter of time. If something about Senior's business gets posted, or Harley's parents, we're in for a rough ride through hell. Yasmin plays basketball and the team has training now. If we leave soon we can meet her in the locker rooms and I can sort this out."

I nod. "What do you have on her?"

Avery sighs. "Not enough to get it taken down. I can have it disabled but she can just start it up again. I'm hoping threats are enough. If not she goes on the planner and we destroy her."

I head out of the bathroom and grab my knife, slipping it into my jeans pocket.

Avery adjusts her dress, and again, and again. I frown at her. "What aren't you telling me?"

She bites her lip, a nervous tick I've never seen her do before. "There's dozens of posts about Rory and what he did to me. Girls are commenting about how I was leading him on and how I was only getting what I deserved. All anonymous of course but the idiots don't realize I can trace them. I've got a very long list of bitches on my planner."

I'm disgusted but not surprised. We don't have time to deal with any more spoilt little girls, too privileged and naive to understand real world consequences.

"We'll work something out, Aves. Let's just talk to this girl and go from there. Whatever happens, we're in it together."

Avery smiles and tucks her arm into mine. "I know. I'm just…a little nervous about it. When Ash sees it, he's going to lose his mind and then we'll have to do damage control for him as well. Like I said, it's going to spiral."

I hum my agreement and lock our door behind us.

Avery is silent but determined as we walk down to the gym. Basketball practice is still underway but only the juniors and seniors are still out on the court. Avery leads me into the locker room and, fucking hell, it's practically a day spa.

The only locker room I've been in before is the one at Mounts Bay Middle School and it was a damp, rotting nightmare. This room is a palace of white marble and Egyptian cotton towels. Avery laughs at the look on my face and I give her a lopsided grin in return. Fucking rich kids.

Yasmin blanches when she sees us and Avery easily corners her. I lean against the wall by the door so I can keep an eye on the other girls. Not that I want to, they're mostly walking around in their underwear and giving me dirty looks. I smile back sweetly and flip them off.

Harlow is naked and rubbing her shoulder down with oil. I'm totally horrified but no one else seems to care so I stare at my toes instead. The smell of mint hits my nose and I hear Harlow grunting as she massages the oil into her skin. She must have an old injury, I've used Wintergreen oil on my leg when it's flared up before. I store that knowledge away because it's good to know where her weaknesses are.

I'm still staring at the floor when a hand wraps around my mouth and I'm jerked flush against a hard, naked chest. I don't recognize the scent of the shampoo the guy uses and I tense up. He's twice the size of me and easily drags me out of the girls' locker room and into the guys'.

Chapter Eighteen

I don't bother fighting or struggling.

Whoever it is, they're not Joey so I doubt this is life threatening but I wedge my hand into my jeans pocket to get a hold of my knife anyway. The arm around my chest is like a steel band so I'll have to wait until the asshole eases up on the pressure. Then, I'll stab the fucker.

"Not so tough now, are you Mounty?" Ugh. It's Devon, Joey's favorite flunky, the one with a crush on Harlow. I wonder if he got an eyeful of her rubbing the Wintergreen oil into her shoulder before he grabbed me? Gross.

He marches me over to a little alcove behind the showers and slams me into the wall. I grunt as the air is knocked out of my lungs and he presses himself against me. He's standing there in a pair of silk boxers and flip-flops. For the love of God, I'm going to have to stab him. I meet his gaze and see the glazed look of his eyes. Open too wide and bouncing around my face like he can't stop them. He's taking drugs, too. I bet every last one of Joey's flunkies are snorting coke between classes. I want to scream.

Devon keeps one hand pressed over my mouth and he leans in too closely as he speaks. "I'll let Joey know I caught you. He can come down and finish the bet. We can forget you even exist, Mounty."

My eyes narrow at him. Joey will never forget me now I have his interest. Devon ignores the warning look I'm giving him and moves so his hand wraps around my throat, squeezing just little.

His eyes may be manic but I'm not worried about him choking me. He's too much of a pompous rich boy, he doesn't have the fire required to kill someone, even as high as he is. He starts rambling on like his mouth is running away from him. "Why couldn't you just spread these legs and let Joey win, huh? You're a frigid fucking slut. Why did you just have to become a problem we all have to deal with? Well, I'm going to finish this."

I jerk the knife out of my pocket and press it to his gut. I still prefer the groin but I can't reach it with how he has me pinned. The hand on my throat spasms as he glances down and sees the blade pressing into his skin, a line of blood already starting to well up.

His eyes are wide and when he opens his mouth to start on his next tirade of crap he doesn't get a single word out because his body is thrown away from mine by naked, but far more colorful, body slamming into the side of him. It takes me a second to see who it is, because he's so fucking fast to lay into Devon, but Blaise is beating the shit out of the tweaking asshole. Devon tries to put his hands up but Blaise just keeps on punch until Devon falls limp with a pathetic groan.

I take a deep breath, and then another, and then Avery slips her body in next to mine and watches Blaise pulverize Devon.

"I turned and you were gone," she whispers.

I shrug. "He grabbed me from behind, I had it under control."

When it's clear Devon is unconscious I call out, "He's done, Morrison."

Blaise grunts and punches him in the face one last time. When he stands he's panting and his fists are covered in blood. I finally notice he's only wearing a pair of boxer shorts and he's still wet from the shower. He turns to walk towards us and I can't breathe.

"Sweet lord." I mumble and Avery snorts at me, incredulously. I elbow her gently in the ribs because, seriously, how the fuck is she immune to him?

Blaise stops in front of me and reaches up to push the stray strands of my hair out of my face. "You okay, Mounty?" he rasps.

I clear my throat. "I'm fine. I had it under control but thanks for, uh, stepping in."

He smirks at me. "Yeah, I saw that. I think we're better off with me punching him than you gutting him."

I blush and slip my knife back into my pocket. Avery rolls her eyes at me. "Get dressed, Morrison. You can walk us back to our room so we don't get jumped on the way back."

Avery is on her phone all the way back to our room so I shouldn't be surprised to find Ash waiting for us, leaning on the wall and scowling at his phone. There's a lot of activity in the hall while the other girls swan around in the smallest amount of clothing possible to try and tempt him into their rooms. Avery rolls her eyes and marches through them and I chuckle under my breath at the way they all scatter away from her. She's totally right, they're all sheep.

Blaise sticks to my side and when Ash looks up to see us his eyes dart over my body, looking for injuries.

"I'm fine," I say and he snorts, following Avery into our room.

"She *is* fine but Devon is out. I just sent a copy of his latest urine sample to his father. He'd paid off the school nurse to keep it under wraps but his father won't stand for a drug addict in the family. Not after his brother OD-ed," says Avery, walking straight the kitchen.

I exhale deeply and slump down on my bed to take my Docs off. One less asshole to worry about.

Blaise moves to shut the door and is shoved out of the way by an enraged Harley. "What the fuck happened!?"

Avery huffs and starts wiping down the counter.

Blaise holds up hand and stops Harley in his tracks. "When I got out of the shower I heard Devon threatening someone. Then I heard him mention Joey and the bet I realized he was talking to the Mounty and I came out to find him pinning her to a wall by her throat."

"What?! He hand his hand around your throat? I'll gut him," spits Harley and Blaise smirks at him.

"Oh, don't you worry, the Mounty was going to. Pretty sure he'll end up with a nasty scar. Really, I saved his life with the beating I gave him."

Ash startles and jerks around to look at me. I raise an eyebrow at him. "What? He's twice the size of me and grabbed me from behind like a little bitch. He deserves to lose his intestines."

Avery starts to straighten up the coffee mugs even though you could already take a tape measure to them without finding a fault. "I think I should get one of those knives too."

I nod emphatically. "I'll get you one and teach you how to use it."

Ash grabs her hand to distract her away from her ritual. "Agreed."

She smiles at him. "Stay for the day? I'll cook something for dinner later and we can watch something Blaise picks so he doesn't whine at us. Like old times, but better because Lips will side with me when we pick snacks."

Blaise huffs. "I don't whine, you guys just have shit taste."

Harley kicks his shoes off and ignores the daggers Avery's eyes send his way. "If he's picking I'm going to need a beer."

Ash starts opening cupboard doors in the kitchen and says, "Fuck it, I need something stronger than beer to get through this. Where are you hiding the good stuff, Floss?"

I take the couch knowing Harley likes the armchair on the left, Ash likes the one on the right, and Blaise likes the floor. Avery hands me a coffee and a bowl of popcorn before tucking herself into my side so we're huddled up together. Harley grabs enough beer to survive the apocalypse and then sits on the other side of me so I'm wedged between the cousins. Avery leans forward to give him a look but Harley ignores her.

Blaise starts the movie and messes with the thermostat until the room turns into a freezer. I sigh and nudge Harley.

"Can you grab me the blanket you're sitting on? My nipples can cut glass at this point and I'm not ruining my new bras."

Avery giggles at me and Harley scoffs but he hands me the blanket. Ash watches him tuck it under my leg and then gives me a sly look. "Which ones are you wearing today?"

I choke on my coffee. "Uh no, my underwear choices are not going to be a daily conversation starter."

Ash shrugs. "Might help me like you."

"Hard pass." I snipe back and I try to ignore the hard look Harley is giving me. Ash and his big, meddling mouth!

"They say women pick their colors according to their moods, so which is it Mounty. Red? Are you feeling feisty today?"

I throw a pillow at his head. "Black, now fuck off."

"Depressed or horny?"

Avery groans and buries her face in her hands. I gape at him but, surprisingly it's Blaise who comes to my rescue. "Lay off, man. She's not here so you can poke and prod at her for your own enjoyment."

Ash shrugs and drinks his bourbon. Harley glares at him. "Why are you asking her about her underwear?"

Ash smirks at him and I decide that I'm going back to a single room next year. Sorry, Avery, I can't deal with this crap. "We picked out her entire collection together this week. Why do you care?"

Harley tenses and I nudge him with my shoulder. "He decided our path to friendship is going to be paved in lace. I decided he's a perv and it's easier to let him go than fight it."

"Crap, we haven't gone down to the laundry yet to ask about the thief." Avery mumbles but she doesn't look up from her phone.

Blaise looks up from the floor at us. "Someone is stealing your underwear?"

"Her *used* underwear," says Ash.

Harley looks at me incredulously. "Are you a magnet for fucked up shit and psychos?"

Avery laughs. "Why yes, Arbour, she is."

Fuck me with a rusty spoon, can I please catch a break?

Chapter Nineteen

The phone buzzing silently in my pocket doesn't mean much to me. It's only when I see that everyone in my history class has received a text at the same time that I know there is trouble at Hannaford.

Harley frowns as he looks around and then raises an eyebrow at me. I nod and he slips his phone out of his pocket discreetly. I don't attempt to look at his screen because that will definitely attract the teacher's attention but I shouldn't have worried about discretion.

"Fuck!" Harley shouts and leaps out of his chair. When the teacher scowls at him he grabs his bag and snaps at her, "Lips and I have to go. Family emergency."

He waves a hand at me and I shove my books away too.

The teacher stutters out, "You're not related." But Harley ignores her, throws my bag over his shoulder with his, and then shoves me out of the room.

"I can't just leave my classes, I'm not invincible here like you are." I grumble as he takes my hand and drags me.

"Avery will square it, come on."

I follow him, though I have to run to keep up with his ridiculously long legs, and he propels us back to the girls' dorms. He taps his foot, agitated, as I unlock the door, then drops our bags just inside the door. The room is empty and quiet, no sign of Avery. I grab my phone to try and figure out what the fuck is going on.

There's a text of a link from an unknown number. Harley starts to pace, scrubbing his hands over his face like he can scrub away whatever is eating him, and I click the link. I find myself of the stupid gossip website and I glance up at Harley.

"Is it you or the twins?" I say and he stops to stare at me.

"Neither. It's Morrison."

I frown at him and put my phone down. "What about him? I thought his family was clean."

I hear a key slot into the door and Avery bursts in, Ash hobbling behind her carrying an absolutely trashed Blaise.

"Sit him on the couch! I'll grab the bed out and then I'll deal with this." Avery snaps and I wave her off, rolling the spare bed out from under her bed and setting it up myself. Avery collapses on her bed and starts furiously texting.

"Can someone please explain to me what the fuck is going on?"

Harley shoves a bucket under Blaise's nose as he starts to heave and Ash sits beside him, an arm slung around his shoulders casually.

"Didn't you read it? See the photos?" Ash snaps and I glare at him.

"Obviously not. If it's personal then I'm not fucking looking."

Blaise groans and vomits. Avery gags and stalks over to hide in the bathroom while she furiously sends text messages. Harley grabs a bottle of water out of the fridge and presses it into the back of Blaise's neck.

"It's Annabelle right? It has to be, she's the only one who's been in our room. Dammit Morrison, I told you not to let her in there! She's a fucking snake." Harley says as he starts to pace again.

Ash groans, "Drop it. It's out now, all we can do is deal with the fallout."

A shrill ringing starts and everyone stops to look at Blaise. He loses the little color he had in his face and looks like a corpse instead.

"Just leave it, you can speak to him tomorrow," says Ash, in a tone he usually only uses at Avery. A knot forms in my stomach.

"I'll get it out of the way now. No use putting it off." mumbles Blaise and he answers the call.

To give him some privacy I grab the bucket from him to empty and Harley follows me to the kitchen.

"Annabelle found a stash of letters from Blaise's dad. He writes to him weekly and for some stupid fucking reason Blaise keeps them. She took photos and now the dumb bitch has posted all of them on the gossip site." Harley clears his throat and continues, "She also had photos of him and she's posted them as well. The letters… aren't good and he's drinking and smoking in the photos, which, to his parents, is worse than nudes. His dad is going to fucking kill him."

I stop scrubbing and cut him a look. "As in be very angry or actual murder? Do I need to adopt him, too?"

Harley smirks and shakes his head. The smirk slowly slides off his face as he watches Blaise over my shoulder. "He shouldn't go home. His parents are fucked. Not like the Beaumonts but just fucking shitty humans who shouldn't be trusted with a kid. How fucked is it when I'm the only one with good parents and they're mobsters. Decent and loving, dead or fucking gone."

I swallow roughly at the emotion in his voice and then whisper, "I'm not going to look at the site. He didn't look at my naked photos and I'm not looking at… whatever this is. Is there anything I need to know? To keep him safe?"

Harley hesitates before answering and Avery stomps out of the bathroom. When she spots Blaise on the phone she moves towards us instead.

"I got the photos taken down and a trace on who posted them. It's Annabelle, which we know, but the dumb slut is saying she was hacked. I pointed out to her that she didn't just trip over the letters and they certainly didn't take selfies!"

Harley snorts and Avery nods at him, "Blaise is officially moving in here until we're sure he's not going to try and kill himself over this."

I jerk away from the sink in shock. "Is that a real concern?"

Avery grimaces. "He's jumped off a bridge while drunk and morose before. And the last scandal his dad caught wind of ended with him having his stomach pumped because he tried to drink himself to death. The boys' dorm isn't as secure as ours and everyone has extracurriculars except you. If you can get out of your tutoring session with the Mounty boy then you can make sure he's safe here."

There's a sharp crack noise and I find myself shoved against the sink by Avery's body as Harley pushes us both behind him. Avery squeals and shoves him out of the way. "It's his phone! He's thrown it against the wall, it's not a terrorist attack, for God's sake!"

I meet Harley's eyes and see the shadows there. I lean in to whisper to Avery, "Some things are ingrained. Some things are unavoidable."

I let Blaise spend all of Thursday drunk because I'm a fucking saint like that. Friday he wakes up so unbelievably hungover that I hide every drop of alcohol in our room. When he breaks into Avery's closet to find it while I'm in the toilet I call Harley to come pick it up.

By Saturday, he's climbing the walls and I consider killing him to get some peace.

"Fuck this. Let's go out," he snaps while I cook.

"No. Drink your coffee."

"Fuck coffee, haven't you ever heard of the hair of the dog? I need tequila."

I shake my head and Blaise flicks a pen at me like the spoilt brat he is. When the others get back from their extracurriculars I'm ready to throw Blaise out of the room and Ash smirks when he sees the look on my face.

"How is suicide watch going? Have you hidden the bed sheets from him yet? Why are you still using real forks? You should switch out to plastic until he's come down from the ledge."

Harley walks in with arms full of Blaise's crap I've asked him to bring to try and keep him busy. He drops it on the rollout bed and then waves me over to him.

"He's better. He spent all morning whining before I left so progress is being made." snipes Avery.

Blaise rolls his eyes at them both and slumps back on the couch. "I wouldn't be whining if you let me fucking drink. The Mounty is practically a fucking AA sponsor and she needs to lighten the hell up. Let's go to the bar in Haven, they do the best cheese fries."

I glare at him as Harley hands over the notes he's made me for our classes. I rummage around in my bag and give him all of my assignments. "Drinking is making it worse. Harley brought your guitar, write a song and chill the fuck out. Eat ice cream. Watch your shitty movies. Do homework. Do *not* drink and do *not* get high."

Blaise kicks the coffee table and Avery cusses him out. He'll be dead by dawn it he keeps it up. She marches over to him and jabs him in the chest sharply. "Just so you know, you ungrateful little shit, I've had the posts taken down and I've contacted your agent to release a statement on your behalf claiming the entire thing was a slanderous hoax concocted by a jilted ex. He doesn't give a shit about the photos and the press is lapping it up. You've even had a spike in sales! I've also burned the letters and sent your father a gift basket with a lovely note telling him to choke on the fucking pretzels. Ash and Harley will now be opening, reading, and destroying any correspondence from that man before you see it. So get up. Eat something substantial, have a shower, do your homework. No one fucking cares that your dear old daddy is scum. I don't, Ash and Harley don't, and, if she were honest, Lips would tell you to tuck your vagina back into your jeans and get over it."

On Sunday morning Avery leaves for ballet practice and I force Blaise into the shower. I threaten to drag him and then scrub him myself but I'm lying through my teeth because there is no way I'd survive a shower with him. No way. My panties would disintegrate. Eventually we come to an agreement where I'll let him smoke a joint if he takes the damn shower. While he's busy, I open every window to get our room to stop smelling like a bar.

I cook him pancakes and when he's finished eating I hand him a coffee and a bowl of ice cream. He pulls a face but takes them. I sit with him at the kitchen counter and enjoy my own cup quietly until he breaks the silence.

"What's your earliest memory, Mounty? No wait, don't answer that. It's probably really fucking bad and I'll feel like a pussy for comparing."

I chuckle at him and shove the bowl of ice cream at him. He lights his joint and sucks on it like it's the answer to all his problems, blowing the smoke out the window. The smell of it sparks the memory he's asking for.

"My mom rolling joints on the back steps to our house. It was too hot to move and I kept crying and pissing her off so she filled a bucket with water and dumped me in it. I think she was trying to be cruel but it was the best feeling ever."

Blaise smiles and huffs out a breath. "My father's office. A modernist nightmare of cold steel and crisp white boxes. I've fallen asleep on his weird couch, that doesn't even have cushions, under his suit jacket. I wake up but I keep my eyes shut because even at five years old I know that when my parents talk in that hushed secret way they're talking about me. My mom is telling my dad that 'normal' children can't read by age five and to lower his expectations. My father says he's sure I'm actually retarded. His ethics board would shit themselves if they knew how he speaks to me. He has a whole list of words he likes to use in my direction because he was born with an IQ of 190 and I'm…so fucking average. I remember I cried and he looked so disgusted at me. Said I'd probably turn out to be a faggot too. Imagine every derogatory word in the book and that man has thrown it at me and the worst part…the fucking stupidest thing is I still care. I *still* hate that I don't measure up."

I finally see the damage. I always knew he was a lonely sort of guy, his lyrics make your chest ache in a way that can only come from heartbreak, but I didn't understand how he fit in with Harley and the twins until now. His life may not have been in danger but his soul was. I want to add his dad to the planner. I want to hunt that man down and say hi with my knife but the longing in Blaise's voice is an echo of my own. It's the echo of a little kid praying that someday their parents will love them enough to stop hurting them.

My mom didn't stop hurting me until she stopped breathing. I have a feeling his dad will be the same.

"Eat your fucking ice cream, Morrison. Do we need to hug? It's not really my thing but I'll give it a go for you."

He bursts out laughing and finally lifts his spoon. I can breathe again because I have a feeling he's finally taken a step away from the ledge. When he finishes he slings an arm around my shoulder and whispers in my ear, "How about a song, Mounty? Sing me something with that voice of yours that's so good you can beat me in choir."

Ain't that a bucket of ice over my head? I gulp. "Ah, sorry. I have severe stage fright. Avery and I are working on it."

He groans and pulls away from me. I try not to crawl after him pathetically but really. When he grabs his guitar and his lyric book I stop breathing altogether.

"I'll have to give you a private concert then, Mounty. I've been working on some songs, tell me what you think."

Be still my fucking heart.

Chapter Twenty

Blaise's sabbatical ends on Monday and I've never been so fucking happy to go to classes. I'm still twitchy from being locked up with him for so long. Not that he was a problem, it's just hard to contain your hormones when a sinfully hot guy is lounging over all of your furniture with too much skin on display. He sleeps in boxer shorts and nothing else. I'd wake up, see the tattoos and the abs, and have to flee to take the coldest showers possible.

My teachers all ask if I'm feeling better and I play along with Avery's lies like a pro. It helps that I'm the top of every class, except choir, and I'm still managing to keep six weeks ahead in all my assignments.

After class I have tutoring with Ash and Lance in the library and my good mood fizzles out a little when I see the cheerful smile on the other Mounty's face. Ash is nowhere to be seen, thank God, because Lance has brought me flowers. No, not just flowers, he's bought me fucking roses. He holds them out to me and I shake my head at him.

"I'm not taking these. We're not friends, I don't want anything more, don't buy me flowers."

Lance's smile doesn't falter as he drops the roses on top of his bag on the floor. "I didn't think you'd like them but I thought I was worth a try. I have a proposal for you! I'm glad your scowling friend isn't here so we can talk just between us Mounties."

My skin crawls. I don't know what it is about him that creeps me out so much but I find myself looking around for Ash. Of all the days for him to skip tutoring! I send him an irritated text, which he ignores. Fuck him.

"I've heard about the little bet you're at the center of. I thought it was all in good fun but then I heard about how much money is in the pot and, well, I think we should come to an agreement."

I lean back in my chair as I grit my teeth. An agreement? Should we sign a contract before he sticks his dick in me? I've changed my mind, I want to stab him. He's not a good guy, he's a *nice guy*—the type that expect sex for basic human decency. Well, you little asshole, you picked the wrong fucking tree to bark up.

"Fuck no. Are we going to study or can I leave?"

He leans his chest over the table towards me and I have to fight off a full body twitch at the sickening smell of his cologne. Jesus, did he bathe in it?! The smile stays plastered on his face. "Sex between friends. We can have some fun and get a million dollars each out of it."

"I'm choosing to take the high road and not break your arm for suggesting we fuck for money," I snap and I stand up because fuck tutoring him, he can struggle through math by himself.

I make it three steps away from the desk before he calls out to me, loud enough for the entire library to hear, "I looked you up, you know. I know you're from the south side of the city, near the docks. What's one more cock when you've already serviced hundreds? I'd risk a quick fuck for a ticket out of here."

I hear a snort of laughter and death glare the little rich dick at the next table over. When I'm sure my voice will be level, I turn back to him and say, "You're going to regret that."

He just keeps fucking smiling and I walk, with a calm I don't feel, back to the girls dorms.

It takes me three tries to get the key to work and once I'm into our room I let my rage out. I fling my bag on my bed and kick out of my shoes so they go flying while cursing up a storm. I rip my blazer off and when my hands grip the bottom of my shirt, ready to yank it off, buttons be-fucking-damned, I hear a throat clearing and find Avery and all three guys sitting at the kitchen bench. Avery arches an eyebrow at me with a little smile but the guys are all gaping at my temper tantrum. Fuck this. I need a shower.

"Fuck today, fuck this school, and fuck every fucking knuckle-scraping, chest-beating, egotistical piece of shit guy in this fucking hellhole!" I yell and slam the bathroom door. I tear the rest of my clothes off and get into the shower, screaming a little like the dramatic petal I am today. Fuck, maybe the dramatics are contagious and Blaise fucking infected me? What a dick.

I'm scrubbing my skin like a psycho when Avery pops into the room. She didn't knock but I also didn't lock the door. She crosses her arms and leans against the bathroom cabinet.

"Tell me what's happened so I can go set the guys on whichever loser pissed you off."

I groan and duck under the stream of water to try and cool my head off. Avery taps a foot and I glare at her with no real heat. "Lance tried to convince me to fuck him for the money. Told me it was our tickets out of here and he'd make it good for me. When I said no he told me he knew I was from the slums and he wasn't exactly thrilled at having to fuck a well used gash but he'd push through."

Avery cocks her head. "And that's pissed you off? This badly? Ash has probably said worse to you and Blaise *definitely* has."

I grunt and turn the water off. When she arches an eyebrow at me I huff back at her. "Maybe I'm just PMS-ing."

She side-eyes me as I dry off. I grit my teeth, "Fine. It bothers me because he's so…nice. He's never said a word wrong to me all year and now suddenly he's trying to cut a deal to fuck me. Ash and Blaise have always been honest. If they hate me, they say it. If they think I'm fucking half of Mounts Bay, they say it. They don't buy me red fucking roses like it'll get them a pass into my fucking panties."

Avery cackles and shakes her head. "Roses? Seriously? He's as clueless as the rest of the boys trying to court you."

I pause as I pull my booty shorts on. "Who the fuck is trying to court me?"

"Exactly." Avery says, pointing at me. "They're so clueless you've missed their attempts. What would it take for you to even notice a guy?"

I blush all the way down to my *freaking* toes. Harley's voice pops into my head and provides me with his little one liner, *I had to get your attention somehow.*

I decline a plate of the curry Avery ordered in and go straight for a tub of ice cream, no bowl just a spoon. Harley watches me carefully as I take a seat next to Avery and wallow in my rage.

"You gonna share with the class whose fault it is you're pissy or just attempt a diabetic coma?"

I shove a spoonful of ice cream in my mouth and flip him off. Ash snorts at me and I glare at him. "Thanks for skipping, by the way. I had to deal with the little creep by myself," I say around my mouthful.

Ash smirks at me. "I didn't realize you needed backup, I thought your knife was enough."

I seethe. I seethe and eat ice cream, licking my spoon like it has the answers to this shit.

"Stop tongue fucking the spoon. Some of us are going through a dry spell." Harley grumbles and I flick a cherry at him, ignoring his little jab.

Avery tucks her arm into mine and says, sweetly, "Lance offered his services to end the bet. When Lips declined his offer he took it upon himself to try and persuade her. Alas, the great and complex mind of Eclipse unknown-middle-name Anderson remains an unsolvable puzzle to mere mortal men."

Blaise takes a swig of the beer, the first he's been allowed, and moans, obscenely. "What a dick. Maybe you *should* just fuck someone and get it over with. Might lighten your mood."

Harley's eyes narrow dangerously at him and when he opens his mouth I give him my most severe look. I don't need the epic piles of bullshit I'll have to face if he blabs about my fucking virtue.

He grits his teeth and changes tactics, looking around the table at everyone. "We decided Lips is in, right? Avery and I vouched for her, Blaise has come around, and Ash may still be a stubborn dick but we all know she's in. So, are we going to accept some dickhead chasing her tail, begging for sex, or are we going to remind the sheep of where they belong?"

My chest tightens and I fix my eyes on the pristine white surface of the kitchen counter. Avery squeezes my arm but I'm shocked when it's Ash that speaks. "We've gone from three people on the planner to pure fucking bedlam. Joey, Harlow, Annabelle, Lance, dozens of little bitches from the stupid fucking website. We need to get on the same page and decide what our priorities are. Is Lance going to be an issue?"

I clear my throat. "No. I'm pissed but I'm not in any real danger."

Blaise opens another beer and points the bottle at me with a slow, dirty smirk. "I'll beat the disrespectful little fuck for you."

Harley scoffs. "Only if you get to him first."

Avery laughs and leans in to whisper to me, "Better than roses, right?"

I scrub a hand over my face to try and hide the blush. Like I need Avery teasing me about my stupid crush…well, crushes. I think I'd like roses if they came from one of these three. No, that's a lie. Flowers are stupid, but I'd appreciate the effort. Nope, still a lie. I wish I were the type of girl that wants flowers because then maybe I'd be the type of girl Harley, Blaise, or, dammit, Ash would want to have for more than sex. Ugh. I'm going to kill Blaise for turning me into a whining bitch.

"Joey?" Blaise asks and when Ash opens his mouth I cut him off sharply. I have a plan.

"I'm on it. Next?"

"Harlow?"

Avery hums softly and says, "She'll dig her own grave eventually. Same goes with Devon. The real problem is Annabelle."

All eyes are on Blaise as he fidgets with the bottle cap from his beer. When no one speaks I think, fuck it, and dive in.

"Do we need her to disappear? I…can make that happen."

I refuse to look at anyone except Avery. She doesn't blink or flinch, her face doesn't show even the tiniest bit of fear or disgust, as she looks at me with cool calculation because she really is deciding if Annabelle Summer's needs to be removed from the board.

"So you really do have gangster connections then?" Blaise grumbles and I flinch before I can rein it in.

Harley punches him in the arm and he groans. "Fuck, I didn't mean it like that, Mounty, just…I know nothing about where you come from. I guess Avery does and Harley obviously knows something but I'm trying to figure out how the fuck a sixteen-year-old girl can calmly, casually, offer to end someone's life. Fuck, it's not even the killing. It's the mundane tone, like you've killed a bunch of other girls for pissing in your Cheerios."

I swallow roughly. "I know a lot of people from all different walks of life. Some of them are gangsters. I am not a member of any gangs, I do not fuck members of any gangs, and I do not owe loyalty in any manner to any gangs."

Harley scrubs his hand over the back of his neck. "Whatever, it doesn't matter. We can't *kill* her. She's a dumb, manipulative bitch but she's not Joey. If we're killing anyone it's him."

"No one is killing Joey," Ash snaps and I guess that's the end of that.

Harley is running late for his swimming practice and Avery leaves for ballet soon at the same time, Ash slings a casual arm over her shoulder to walk her down.

Blaise asks for help with his assignments and I've calmed down enough to help him out. After a full hour of work, I stretch out my shoulders and risk asking him the one question that's been bothering me since his dad's letters were leaked.

"When did Annabelle get the documents? Avery said they had to be recent photos because they were dated right up until the day they were released."

Blaise cringes and I frown at him. "Really? Really?! It's almost like you want to be sixteen and pregnant. Will you take the baby on tour?" I snark and instantly regret it when his face falls.

"I didn't have sex with her! I just let her in the room so she could cry on the couch. I didn't know what to do, I'm not good at saying no to crying girls! I've been…

frustrated lately. I made a shit decision because of it. I'm not exactly known for my clear head."

I snort at him and keep writing. He fidgets with his pen, his fingers twitchy and his face is drawn. "If you can't settle down and focus we can leave this for the night. Your assignment is done and we're making good progress on the workbooks. The couple of days we took off won't affect your GPA."

He nods but his eyes stay on the door. I sigh and sit back in my chair.

"What is it? Just spit it out."

He grunts and rubs his hands over his face. "I want something. I can't have it. I'm not good at not getting what I want. I know you're going to bitch me out for being a spoiled rich kid but it's the truth."

I could do that. It's obvious he's been given everything on a silver platter his entire life and you could say this is finally karma happening for his shitty treatment of me. But I like talking to him, I like that he's opening up to me so I choose to be empathetic. I know a lot about not getting what I want. Plus, knowing his home life is actually pretty similar to mine growing up has given us a weird thing to bond over.

"That sucks. I'm sorry."

He blinks at me and then groans. "I was kind of hoping you would bitch me out. Then I'd have a distraction."

I shrug and say, "I can if you want but wouldn't you rather talk about it?"

"I'd rather get fucking drunk and play my guitar. Harley's banned me from playing in our room because he's sick of my, quote, sulky tantrum whining. Apparently, I should be over this by now."

I chuckle at that and pack up his papers and supplies. "Go grab your guitar and you can crash on the couch tonight. Avery moved the booze to the cupboard on top of the fridge. I'll have a shower and mix cocktails when I'm out if you want."

His face lights up and then falls in an instant. He stands and slings his bag over his shoulder and scuffs his boot along the floor. "Fuck, Mounty. I would. I fucking would."

I sigh and nod slowly, taking his hand to stand. "But Ash would be pissed if he found out you were still sleeping here?"

"I'm making a lot of my decisions based on what my friends would think at the moment," he mumbles.

Chapter Twenty-One

"I already hate everything about this."

I don't bother turning around. I know the exact expression that will be on Avery's face as she looks around the gym. I'd explained my plans to Harley during our math class and he'd handed his set of keys over to me without a word, so now we have the entire gym to ourselves. Avery has been putting me off for weeks but I've finally cornered her.

In the center of the room, the boxing ring that I found Harley and Blaise in last year is still set up and I refuse to look at it because I do not need Avery questioning the blush that will absolutely color my cheeks if I do.

I'm dressed in a pair of Avery's yoga pants and a loose hoodie. I've slipped my shoes off but left my socks on because the polished wooden floor is freezing. Avery came here straight from ballet so she looks like a freaking cast member of The Nutcracker. I think. I mean, I have no idea what a ballerina in the nutcracker would wear but I'm confident Avery would fit in.

"I'm not going to teach you how to fight. I wouldn't be good at that anyway because I don't get into fights. I defend myself and I make calculated moves to overcome whoever I need to despite my size. That's what I'm going to teach you."

The door opens and closes but I put it out of my mind while I focus on the lesson. Avery groans and moans her way through the first part. I teach her not to tuck her damn thumb in when she makes a fist. I show her how to center her weight so she's more stable on her feet. I teach her how to breathe when you're afraid so your brain receives the optimal amount of oxygen. I teach her the best points to strike at and what parts of her body she should use to strike them.

After an hour of this Avery is panting and, wonder of wonders, sweating. She looks at least slightly unkempt and I'm grinning like an idiot over it. When we stop to grab water I realize we've been joined by 'The Three Stooges'.

"Do they teach this in Mounty school?" drawls Blaise but there's a flush to his cheeks.

Ash looks conflicted and Avery trots over to talk quietly to him. I know he hates that she's being forced to learn this but I honestly think she should've done this years ago. I drain the water bottle and Harley grabs it from me with an offer to refill it.

I smile at him and then call out, "We still have more to cover, Aves, so get your back over here."

She groans and drags her feet. "I'm not strong like you, Lips. I can't do this."

I sigh and perch against the boxing ring, crossing my arms so she knows I mean business. "You think that because you've always had Ash or Harley or Blaise around to protect you but you're wrong. You exercise six days a week. Some days you do three sessions. You've never broken a bone, no nerve damage, and when you froze at what Rory was doing it was fear not PTSD. Physically, you are stronger than me. What I am teaching you is the basics of self defense but the most important, the most *valuable* thing you need is something you already have."

She huffs and crosses her arms but I keep going. "You're observant and intuitive. You can look at a student and make a quick assessment of what weaknesses they have and how to exploit them to take them out. So far you've used that strength to socially ruin the sheep but you can easily switch to reading body language and defending yourself. You're better at it than anyone I've met, you're as good as I am. You may end up better than me at it."

I glance behind her to see the guys have settled back into their seats and are fixated on us. I quirk an eyebrow at Avery in question but she waves me off. "I don't care that they're here. But I need you to show me something real. Walk me through a situation and explain how knowledge will be better than strength or size. I need you to prove it to me so I can stop second guessing myself."

Hmm. It's a good idea and I'm a little pissy I didn't think of it myself. I cringe a little at the scenario that pops into my head but the more I think about it the better it fits.

I sigh and grab a stack of training mats. I pile them up until they're bed height, then I slip my hoodie off and hand it over to Avery. She takes it hesitantly and pulls it over her head. She looks ridiculous and Ash snorts as he takes a photo of her in it. I dig around in my bag until I find my knife and then I slip that into the hoodie pocket.

I chew on my bottom lip and then address our audience. "Look, you guys have to stay quiet. If she's going to learn how to defend herself you need to let me walk her through this. If you can't hack it then please leave."

They all nod, somewhat hesitantly, and then I push them out of my mind. I grab Avery's wrist, hard enough to bruise. She jumps and frowns at me.

"The party that Joey insisted I go to first year. He told all of the juniors he was going to fuck me, one way or another. He found me walking back to the dorms and I knew he was high but I also knew he could outrun me. He's not as big as Rory or Ash or most of the guys at this school because of his habit but drug addicts are unpredictable. I couldn't just run."

There's a deep furrow on Avery's brow and her lips are turned down at the corners. I've never offered her this truth before. I had put it out of my mind months before we became friends.

I hold up her wrist. "He held my wrist harder than this. I could feel my bones bending under his fingers and pulling away meant fighting him off with a broken wrist. So…what do you do? Knowing him, reading the situation you're in, what do you do?"

Avery swallows. "Play along. Get him talking and distract him."

I nod and tug her over to the mats. Once we're both sitting on them I wait a minute and then continue. "Now he tells you he can fuck you by force or you can lie back an enjoy it. He kisses you. What do you do?"

Her lip quivers but her eyes stay dry. "Play along. I have no choice, he's still got my wrist."

"Good." I shove her back and cover her body with my own, careful not to crowd her or hurt her. Explosive swearing erupts behind us and a chair crashes against the floor but I keep my focus on the lesson. "Now what?"

She frowns and takes stock of what's going on. She tugs a little at her wrist that's still pinned above her head and then wriggles a little. "Oh. The knife is in my pocket."

I smile and nod. She reaches in to grab it and I lower myself on her to pin her. "I grabbed it before he pushed me down so my hand was trapped. What do you do?"

She sighs. "Gross. You can't wrestle your arm out because he'd notice so you have to play along. What a pathetic piece of shit."

I snort but I'm glad she has her fire back. "Yep. Arch your back and moan a little and he'll ease up because he wants you rubbing on him."

"Right." She arches and pulls the knife out but leaves the blade covered. Then, without further instruction, she presses it to my groin. The grin I beam down at her is savage and wild.

"Avery Beaumont, you just saved yourself. No white knight required."

We run through a few more scenarios and Avery's confidence blooms. When we finish up Ash is nowhere to be seen and Harley sends Blaise off to find him then walks us to our room. I don't think about what happened in the training session until there's a knock at the door and I open it to find a fucking wasted Ash, swaying on his feet as he tries to stay upright.

I shove him towards the couch, mumbling under my breath as I lock the door, "My life is now babysitting drunk, spoiled rich kids."

I sigh and rub my face. "Avery is in the shower, if you need to puke please tell me now so I can get you a bucket."

He frowns at me and, fuck, drunk Ash is adorable. My body is in danger of melting into a puddle so I step away from him only to have him snatch my wrist and tug me down onto the couch beside him. "I'm not here for Floss."

His voice isn't slurred and he doesn't look like he's going to lose his stomach contents so I settle back into the couch. "What's wrong? What do I need to fix now?"

"Did my brother rape you?" he blurts out, zero tact as always. I frown at him and he rubs his eyes. "I know you walked her through it but I need to hear from you, that you got away from him. I need to know that he didn't get away with it."

"He tried but I got away from him. Don't worry about it, I'm not losing sleep over it."

He groans and leans forward, his elbows on his knees and his face cradled in his hands. I'm not sure what this crisis is and I find myself praying Avery will hurry up and rescue me.

"Fuck, how can you even stand to look at me? I look just like that fucking monster. We're all the spitting fucking image of our father." He laughs but there's no humor in his tone. "Harley looks like my mom. He gets to look like the only good we ever had in our lives and I get to stare in the mirror at the demons who own us. Fuck, now I sound like Morrison. Someone get me another fucking drink before I start singing."

I stare at my own hands for a beat before answering him. "I don't think you look like Joey. I think you look like Avery and she's one of the very best humans on this earth. So yeah, looking like your mom, like Harley, would have been great but looking like Avery is pretty fucking good, too. Stop having a meltdown over shit that doesn't matter."

The frown is back and the adorable is only increasing in intensity. I can't fucking breathe. He mumbles at me, "Where the fuck did you come from?"

I snort and pat his leg the way Avery does when she thinks I'm being simple. "A drug addict. Or a meth lab, depending on which specific you were looking for."

Chapter Twenty-Two

I drag myself through another week of classes and our class loads are so stacked that we're forced to eat dinner in the dining hall every night. I've gotten used to eating alone with Avery and talking about whatever fucking crisis we're facing without having to censor myself, and I'm grouchy about having to be around the masses of spoilt assholes.

We arrive before the guys do and I fill a tray with food while Avery grumbles at her phone. As I reach for a pitcher of the juice Avery likes my shoulder is shoved out of the way and Harlow jams herself into the line in front of me.

"Oh, sorry Mounty, but students who actually pay to be here shouldn't have to wait behind charity cases." She says sweetly and I take a deep breath so I don't slam her head into a wall.

Avery doesn't even look up from her phone as she casually says, "Wipe your nose, Roquefort, you're wasting my brother's best blow on your face instead of in your blood. With any luck the next line will burst your brain."

Harlow sneers at her and shoves the pitcher of juice at us. "Run along and take your pet Mounty slut with you."

I grit my teeth and direct Avery over to our seats. The group of girls sitting there move before I can even open my mouth which is nice. If only Harlow could be trained the same way. The guys all arrive as we sit and they jostle each other as they line up for food. When Blaise throws his head back to laugh at something Harley has said I find myself grinning over at them. Ash catches my eye and sneers at me. I groan because what I really need after a hard week of study is to be snarked at by that asshole.

"Be gentle with him today, Lips." Avery murmurs and I frown at her, the grin just melting right off my face. "Harley had to peel Joey off him last night. The psycho is getting worse now his time at Hannaford is coming to an end. Next year he'll have to find someone else to torment while we're gone."

Fuck that. "What does Joey like? That's the quickest way to figure out how to get back at him. We need to stop being reactive and start being proactive."

Avery's lips quirk up at me as she starts to empty the plates off of the tray. "Nothing but himself and cocaine. And money, I guess, but we can't touch that without it affecting Ash and me."

Cocaine. Unfortunately, I had some experience with the shit and I'd give anything to be able to wipe it from the surface of the Earth.

"Okay, I think I can work with that. Give me some time with it."

She nods and the guys all arrive and take their seats. Ash is moving a little hesitantly and I share a look with Harley. Avery puts her phone away and rolls her eyes at some stupid joke Blaise is telling her. I don't listen to any of them while I plan.

I grab my iced coffee from the tray then I pour out a glass of juice for Avery. There's a filmy residue on the glass as I pass it to her. It feels slick on my fingers but not soapy. It's more of an oily texture. I think about wiping my fingers on my skirt but I get that pulling feeling in my gut. I've completely zoned out the conversation around me and I don't even hear Blaise start to tease me about smelling my fingers. It smells minty. It's smells like…

My hand shoots out and knocks the cup out of Avery's hand as she raises it to her lips and directly into Ash's lap. Avery gasps and lurches backwards and Ash snaps at me, "What the fuck is wrong with you, Mounty?"

"The glass is oily. Smell it. It smells like Harlow does after gym class. She rubs down with Wintergreen oil." Harley's eyebrows shoot up but the others look at me with blank faces. "It's a type of natural aspirin and she's put it in your juice. She's fucking *poisoned your drink*, Aves."

Silence.

Stunned, no one speaks or moves until finally Ash lifts the glass out of his sopping wet lap and smells it. A storm rolls in over his eyes.

"That. Fucking. Cunt."

I stand abruptly and look around the dining hall. Blaise gets up to look as well and Harley starts drilling Avery for answers.

"Did you drink any? Are you sure it was her? I need to know I'm fucking killing the right bitch." Harlow is nowhere to be seen. Ash's face is starting to crack, the perfect mask he puts on every day shattering and leaving behind only the ruthless protector. I see the same fire burning there that I've seen in Joey dozens of times and it sends a shiver through me. I have to admit to myself that it's not a bad shiver.

"I'll handle this. Avery, go back to our room and get cleaned up. You guys need to walk her up and stay with her until I get back," I say and then I slip away from the table. I get three steps before Ash's hand wraps around my elbow and wrenches me around to face him.

"Mounty——" I cut him off, all of the anger and hurt bubbling out of me without a care at who was watching. I'm angry that he's been hurt again and now Avery's had another close call. I can't help but direct it at him.

"How could you ever think I was in on this? How could you think I wanted to hurt her? You've spent the last year watching us together, do you really think I'd try to *kill* her?"

His eyes flash and then, finally, the soft edge creeps back in. "I don't. I… fuck, you're in. You're family now. I'm coming with you and I'm helping you take Harlow out."

The girls' dorm is a hive of activity and Ash's presence only makes it worse. I duck into my room to grab my lock picking kit and then I break into Harlow's room, unconcerned by the whispering audience. She's had the locks changed and upgraded but nothing could keep me out, not in the fucking rage I'm in now. Ash watches me carefully, his glacial mask dropping so I can see how impressed he is. Once we're in I find a much cleaner room but there's still stolen shit everywhere. I scoff and poke around for a second.

"What's the plan?" says Ash as he grimaces at the clutter. I bet he's a neat freak like Avery.

"I'll deal with her. I'm just checking to make sure the psycho bitch isn't the one stealing my panties."

Ash grunts in acknowledgment and starts moving piles of clothes around but we both come up empty handed. Dammit. I find one of our assigned textbooks for history, a huge hardback, and grin as I heft it into my arms. Ash eyes it warily.

"What do you want me to do? I don't hit girls but I will help with anything else." He doesn't look at me as he talks but the sincerity is clear in his tone.

"Go sweet talk Chastity next door and get her to turn her music up loud enough that no one will hear what happens."

Ash nods and then hesitates. "Don't accidentally kill her…and don't get caught."

If I kill her it won't be an accident but I nod and he leaves, shutting the door quietly behind him.

He's much faster than I expected. Less than a minute later the throbbing bass line of the shitty electronica Chastity insists on listening to starts vibrating the walls. I grimace but it'll do the job.

I stand behind the door facing the mirror. There's a chance she'll see me in it before she steps through properly but that'll make her Ash's problem. I'm betting on her being complacent. No one has been attacking her in her room. Everything we've done so far has been about exposing her malicious actions. I'm done with that. I raise the textbook in my arms and focus.

I don't have to wait long.

Harlow's gaze connects with mine as the door swings shut behind her. There's a flash of fear in them just as the textbook slams into her nose and breaks it for the second time. She collapses to the ground and I grab a fist full of her hair.

I can't hear the screaming, thank God, and this time instead of holding her still I drag her over to her bed and lay her out. She's sobbing, great heaving breaths bursting out of her chest, and her hands are covering the mess that is her nose. I pull my knife out and show her the blade.

She freezes.

I lean down to speak into her ear so she can hear me over the music. "I thought about slitting your throat for what you did. I thought about gutting you, nice and slow, just like you deserve. I could bleed you out and then call in an old friend to make you disappear, and you would disappear Harlow. No one would ever find you. But instead, I'm going to remind you that you're not invincible just because you bow to Joey Beaumont. You're pathetic and someday soon he'll run out of uses for you. You'll be his next victim and no amount of loyalty you show him will stop that."

I hack away at her hair until half her scalp is bared. I need her afraid. I need her so fucking terrified that she will never think about hurting Avery again because if she does I'm going to have to take her out.

"Now, I know you're going to want to run off to the principal or Joey to tattle on me but remember this: Avery Beaumont runs the cleanups at Hannaford. Joey's too fucking high to manage anything and Trevelen is bought and paid for. He belongs to us. You'll wear this warning and you'll swallow your pride because if you don't, next time I'll take your head instead of just your hair."

I throw the fistful of locks on her chest and I walk out without looking back. Ash takes one look at me and follows me as I stalk out of the girls' dorms.

I pull my phone out and text Avery the details.

My arms are shaking.

The dark part of my heart, the inky black stain that lets me become the Wolf, grows and becomes something wild. I've never used it to keep someone else safe like this before. It's the first time I haven't felt dirty for using it. Avery Beaumont will wake up tomorrow because I'm suspicious and have the gut instinct of a seasoned FBI agent. I've never been so relieved to be so damaged.

I stumble and Ash grabs my arm to steady me. He looks down at me with unreadable eyes and I just stare back at him, open and honest about what I've done. I mean, I'm covered in blood. There's no hiding that.

"Come to my room. You can clean up there before you see Avery," He says, his voice low and raspy. I nod and let him lead me to the boys' dorms. There's a lot of eyes on me as I walk one step behind Ash. At first I think it's the blood, that would make any normal person curious, but then as we make it into the dorms I spot Lance and his frown. My chest tightens like a vise. Of course none of these rich assholes care about some blood. They're all pissy because they think I'm about to fuck Ash and let him win the goddamn sweep.

I should have gone back to my own room.

"Take a photo of her right now, Smithson, and you'll never walk again. Do you think your father will still love you if you're not on the State Track team?" sneers Ash and suddenly the room is moving and no one is looking my way. I can breathe again.

We stop outside a door at the end of the hall while Ash unlocks it. He has the same lock system as Avery and I. She must've organized it. Then he steps aside to beckon me into the room.

It's fucking surreal.

The room is the exact same layout as the one Avery and I share but with an extra Cal King. There isn't a doubt in my mind over who sleeps where. Ash's bed is immaculately made, dark bedding, his nightstand only holding a phone charger and a pair of glasses.

Harley's bed is also perfectly made but he has a patchwork blanket on the end and books overflowing from the nightstand. At the foot of his bed there's a bookshelf with even more books.

And then there's the messy nest that Blaise sleeps in. Everything looks clean enough but I can still see the exact position he must've woken up in etched into the pillows and blankets. There's a guitar hanging over his bed and picks everywhere. Tantalizing, there's an open notebook on the pillow and I can see his writing and little pictures all over the pages. His lyric book. Fuck me. He's been sharing little snippets with me for months but it's still tempting as fuck to look.

I do a double take when I see the photo I gave Avery for Christmas on the wall in their kitchen, framed and placed where they'd all see it every day. My heart does a weird little flip in my chest and I have to look away.

"I'll grab you something to change into, the towels are under the sink. Use whatever you need." Ash says as he moves around the room. He doesn't look at me and I'm worried he's regretting bringing me here.

"I can go. Aves seen me worse than this, she's fine."

He snorts and flicks the coffee machine on. My stomach rumbles. I missed out on dinner and caffeine sounds perfect.

"Just take a shower, Mounty."

So I do.

The bathroom looks more like I'd expect from three guys living here. Piles of dirty laundry and towels are in the overflowing basket and there's shaving cream still in the sink. I strip off and, with little options, I throw my clothes into their washing pile. Avery can get them back for me and I make a note to ask her. The water is cranked and blisteringly hot. I'm weak so I use a little bit of each of their soaps and shampoos. I like them all but I love the smell of all three mixed together more.

Once I'm out and wrapped in a towel Ash knocks and hands me a pile of clothes without looking at me which actually is exactly what I need because I'm a bumbling, blushing idiot only covered by the towel. Then I slip my underwear back on and the yoga pants he's handed me. They're Avery's, I've seen her in them before, so it's a decent fit and I don't have to think about which girl left them behind in his room. The shirt is one of his, a black v-neck that's softer than cashmere and hangs off of my small frame.

I dry my hair and once it's tied up I take a deep, calming breath to walk out.

There's a cup of coffee on the bench, and Ash has one of his own, so I grab it and take a big gulp, praying the heat soaks into me and the caffeine gives me the energy to get through whatever bullshit Ash is going to throw at me.

"Why did Joey call the juniors off last year? The real reason." He still doesn't look at me from where he sits on his bed, his long legs braced against the floor and his big hands cradling the coffee cup.

"Someone from Mounts Bay found out about the bet. He's Joey's dealer. Actually, he's the top of the drug dealing food chain. This guy didn't like the idea of me being a bet so he warned Joey off."

Ash hums and takes another sip of his coffee before putting it down. "Why didn't Joey just find a new supplier?"

"The guy owns all of the dealers. Everyone in the state leads back to him so he told Joey that he'd never touch an ounce of anything again if he didn't back off."

Ash nods again and I tip back the last of my drink. I want to fidget but I force myself to stay still. When Ash doesn't say anything else I start to move towards the door, giving him space seems like the right thing to do right now.

His fingers curl around my wrist to stop me. His eyes stay trained on the floor, unblinking, and I take a step towards him. My heart is thumping, I don't know why but I feel like something has shifted in him and finally the gaping chasm between us is going to disappear. He tugs me into him and moves his free hand to the back of my neck, gently cradling the nape of my neck and rubbing the silky curls there.

With his height and the height of the bed, I still have to tilt my head up to look at him. Standing between his legs, looking up into his icy blue eyes, he's surrounding me until all I can see, all I can feel, is him. I take a shuddering breath and the sound of it breaks the dam of his control and he pulls me into his kiss.

His lips are hot and demanding, he swallows my gasp and pushes me for more until all I can do is give in to him. I'm less nervous about kissing now, thank God. I want to give him everything I can and he grunts as my teeth tug on his bottom lip. His hands move to fit over the curve of my waist, his fingers stroking and teasing me. He groans and lifts me up against his chest, my feet dangling and his strong arms banding around me, holding my weight like it's nothing.

I can't think. The world around us is spinning and turning until I'm laid out on his perfect bed and he's hovering over me, our bodies only touching at his searing kiss. I want more. I want him pressing me into the bed, I want him grinding against me, I want him to touch every inch of my skin.

I want him to own me.

And it's that thought that slams reality back into my mind and I break away from his lips. He's running on a high from saving his sister. He's cut Annabelle loose. If I let this continue, he doesn't even know he's risking his life for a quick fuck. And, as crushing as it is to even think, that's exactly what I am to him. Another notch on the post of his ridiculously comfortable and luxurious bed. Seriously, where do rich people get their sheets? I squeeze my eyes shut for a second, just to feel and enjoy having him so close for a little longer, and when I finally open them I see he's doing the same. He's probably cursing himself out for being stuck here with the frigid Mounty.

"I can't," I croak at him and he nods, his eyes still shut.

Neither of us move. I just stare up at his heartbreakingly handsome face until he finally lets out a shuddering breath and rolls off of me.

Chapter Twenty-Three

I decide that all guys are the devil and I need to stay the fuck away from them. I can't hide from Harley or Blaise but I can stay the hell away from Ash if I'm careful. I figure out pretty quickly that Ash is trying to avoid me as much as I am him. It stings more than it should and I might be hypocritical for feeling that way but when Avery starts getting suspicious of his behavior I pretend I have no clue of what's she's talking about. I don't think I've fooled her at all and, if anything, I think I make her even more suspicious.

I can't tell her about the kiss.

She was accepting of Harley kissing me and pissed about Blaise. I can't imagine her reaction to hearing I've also had a try of her beloved twin brother. Sweet lord, for a virgin I am managing to get around.

Avery obviously decides she's done with our shit because she sends out a group text the Friday after the kiss with Ash.

Dinner in our room. Attendance is compulsory, this means you Ash.

I frown down at my phone and Harley smirks at me. "We used to have dinner together once a week. Clearly Avery is sick of her brother's sulking too."

I text her back privately.

You shouldn't cook, we have too much class work to waste time on that.

Her reply is instant because she knows I'm avoiding them all like the fucking plague.

I've ordered in. Blaise is going to grab it on the way up from his boxing session. No excuses, we're getting back to normal programming.

I groan and slump down in my chair.

I try to hide in the library, switching my phone off so I can pretend it's died and I got sidetracked. Unfortunately, Avery has fucking superpowers and finds me before I'm even technically late. She sits across the table from me and places a takeaway coffee on my math workbook, forcing me to stop working on the equations.

"Before the cup is empty, you'll tell me why you keep staring at me like you've stabbed my puppy."

Straight for the throat, there's the dictator I call my best friend.

I sigh and take some deep, deep gulps of the coffee. She raises an eyebrow at me and I fucking cave like a bitch. "I kissed Ash. Well, I think he kissed me but I didn't stop him."

Avery's face stays completely void of any emotion as she cocks her head for me to continue. "I did eventually tell him I couldn't continue. I'm so fucking weak and stupid. Why do I keep ending up in these situations? I can't do anything about it with the Jackal's eyes on me and I'm not a casual type of person. I'm sorry I didn't tell you and I'm sorry I've now made out with all three of your...people."

Avery nods and drums her fingers on the table. "Do you want a non-casual... relationship with my brother? Or one of the other two?"

I blush and clear my throat. "It's not an option. I won't even think about it because it's not what they're interested in. Any of them."

Avery squints at me a little and I try not to squirm. Whatever she's looking for, she doesn't find it in my face and with a sigh, she stands up.

"Don't be dense, Mounty. Kiss whoever the hell you want to but you need to tell them *all* about the Jackal."

I notice the tension in the air the second we walk into our room. Ash is sitting on Avery's bed death glaring at his phone like it has mortally offended him and Harley...well, Harley is standing in the kitchen, braced against the kitchen counter, with murder in his eyes. Avery frowns at them and then gives me a sidelong look but I shrug. Blaise walks in behind us, carrying bags of Thai takeout, and he's stomping around as well.

"What's Joey done now?" Avery snaps.

Blaise won't look at me as he brushes past us to get into the kitchen. Avery waits another second before snapping, "Well?!"

"It's not Joey. Harley's got some emotions he would like to express but he has to work through them first," says Ash, so condescendingly I cringe for Harley but he doesn't flinch. In fact, he acts like he hasn't heard a word Ash has said. He's the only guy in the room who is looking at me, while the other two are pointedly looking elsewhere. I know for a fact I'm PMS-ing and my nerves are fucking wearing thin so I keep my mouth shut. If I open it I may verbally eviscerate the lot of them and I'm sure Avery doesn't want to spend her evening scrubbing their innards off the walls.

Blaise sets out everyone's food and continues to ignore me, even after I thank him. Avery glares at him, then Ash, before finally settling her ire on her cousin who is still staring at me like I stabbed a baby.

He makes it through the world's most awkward and silent dinner before drawling at me, "I didn't peg you for a liar."

Ash laughs and throws a napkin at him. "Of course she's a liar. If you chose to believe anything she's said that's your own fucking insanity."

I set my knife and fork down onto the table carefully and fold my hands. I pull myself into Avery's signature power pose, ankle fucking crossed and everything, before I sweetly say, "What is up your ass now, Arbour?"

"You. You lied about being in danger, you lied about hating the other Mounty, and now you've gone and fucked him. I hope the money was worth it."

Avery meets my gaze from across the table. What the actual hell is he talking about and how widespread is this pile of lies? Her eyebrows ask the same questions and we both slide into damage control. "Uh no, I didn't. He threw himself at me and

I said no," I state, calmly, though my knees start to grow restless.

Harley snorts at me, pushes out of his chair, and stalks over to the fridge to grab a beer. Avery stands to start cleaning up our dishes and snaps, "What does it matter to you if she did fuck him?"

He shrugs casually but the sneer stays fixed to his face. "You said you didn't want to fuck any guy at Hannaford but you made an exception for him."

Ash is watching Avery with narrowed eyes. He knows something is up, something more than what we're saying. If Harley wasn't so pissy he'd notice the cleaning, too.

"I didn't fuck him. I kind of thought you'd believed me over the gossiping bitches but clearly I was wrong," I grit out, the muscles in my jaw twitching.

Harley slams the beer bottle on the bench and moves to stand over me. I don't back away like everyone else does because I'm not afraid of him. His mobster roots and overbearing size don't mean shit to me. I know what type of guy he really is. I do hate that I have to tip my head back to look at him right now and the fury in his eyes cuts me worse than his words.

"He handed in proof. He's been declared the winner and he gets the sweep. All two million dollars of it."

My stomach drops. My vision blurs, my ears ring, and I think my heart has exploded in my chest cavity.

Fuck.

I'm dead.

Chapter Twenty-Four

"Right. This is bad." Avery's voice is thready and mine would sound the same if I could choke some words out.

"So some asshole Mounty guy ends up with the money, what does it matter? With the bet over with Lips won't be followed around anymore. We should have a word with him about the money. He should really split it with you," Blaise says, sounding completely at ease even though he's still refusing to look at me.

"She didn't fuck him! Get your heads out of your fucking asses and believe us both. We're fucked because of that asshole's lie!" Avery screeches.

I can't think clearly. If they're still talking I don't hear it, nothing exists to me anymore except the sheer, blinding terror. The panic clawing at my chest has become so overwhelming that it consumes everything until I'm at its mercy. I think I'm going to pass out. My legs give way and I collapse down on the ground. My arms shake. When I still can't breathe I lie down and begin to count backwards from a hundred in French.

"What are we missing here?" Ash asks, carefully, and I look over to find them all staring at me. Harley looks haunted, his eyes so wide I can see the whites all the way around his irises. Nope. I can't do this. I shut my eyes and get back to counting, out loud so I'm forced to focus. I try to block out the memories of all the things the Jackal will do to me.

"I'm telling them, Lips. We need their help to fix this, that little fuck Lance needs a beating and we all know I can't throw a punch to save my life," says Avery and I jerk my head to form some sort of nod. "Okay. If word gets back to Mounts Bay that Lips has fucked Lance her life is in danger. The Jackal will kill Lance, no question, and he deserves it so *fuck him*. But there's a good chance he'll also kidnap, torture, and rape Lips."

"What?! Why?" snaps Ash as Harley starts cursing up a storm behind him.

"Because he's a sadistic egomaniac who thinks he owns her. He threatened Joey away from her because he doesn't like to share his toys. He's waiting her out, playing a game that he thinks he'll win, and if anyone messes with it he takes them out. *If we don't fix this he's going to rape and kill her.*"

I think about throwing up but I'm paralyzed by the liquid terror coursing through my veins. I let it take me. I give over to the fear and let it consume me for a minute so it will burn off enough that I can tamp it down again. The truth is I'm not ever fearless, I've just learned to live and work through it.

When I can see again, I risk another glance at the others to find Avery trembling in Ash's arms and Harley staring down at me. I take my first deep breath when he looks at me, like the fire in his eyes thaws something in me and the spark in my soul starts up again. I have survived everything that's been thrown at me so far. I will survive this, too.

Harley gives me a nod and turns back to his friends. "We need to fix this and we need to do it now. Ideas?"

There's a stunned silence and then, surprisingly, Blaise pipes up, "The bet says proof has to be either a photo or a video. We get our hands on it and prove it's a fake. No one wants Lance to get the money so it'll be an easy sell if we can find something."

Ash snorts derisively, his voice a twisted snarl, "How exactly would that be good proof if no one here has fucked the Mounty before? Who could vouch it's her?"

"Besides the obvious that her face would have to be in it? The photos last year," says Harley.

I sit up sharply. The photos from my fucked up walk of shame last year. After I'd had my clothes stolen while showering I'd been made to walk back to my room naked by Harlow, who had also taken photos and shared them around. Fucking bitch. I want to go back to her room and slit her throat.

"We need to get the photos and pray. Lance is taking photography and advanced digital design. I'm sure he's got the fake photos damn near perfect," I say, my voice stronger now. I rub my face with shaking hands and consider texting Diarmuid for a hit. Would Avery spot me the fee? I glance at her and the thunder on her face tells me she would pay the son of a bitch ten times over.

"Give me twenty minutes. I know who'll have them," Blaise says and he ducks out of the room.

I stay on the floor until Avery finally drags me up and pushes me into the shower. I try to tell her I'd just had one but she starts on with her 'hot water heals all' philosophy and I just give in. I throw my pajamas on and when I walk back out I don't even care that I'm wearing my Vanth shirt. Avery hands me a bowl of ice cream and I slouch on the couch to eat it. Avery sits with me and chews on her lips as she scrolls aimlessly on her phone. Ash and Harley sit at the bench and talk quietly together, their eyes on me more often than not. I'm scrubbing the bowl clean in the sink by the time the door opens again and Blaise is back.

He startles a little at my shirt then ushers us all to sit at the bench. He hands out a pile of photos so we're each holding a copy of the three photos Lance has produced as his proof. I can't look down at them. Not until I'm able to do it with a clinical eye. Instead, I watch Avery as she begins to sift through them next to me.

"Fuck, Avery, don't look at them," snaps Ash as he tries to pry them out of her hands. She rolls her eyes and turns away from him.

"I've seen nudes before Ash. I'm not happy about being forced to look at that little fuck's dick but I'm the only person here that's seen Lips naked besides Lips herself so I'm the best person to be looking."

Blaise's eyes flash and he purses his lips like he's trying to seal them shut. Harley notices and punches him in the arm but he only shrugs with a wry grin. "I'm not even sorry, I can't help it."

Eh? "Can't help what?"

Avery answers as she holds one of the photos so close to her face that she must be searching it pixel but pixel for inaccuracy. "He's being gross about how I've seen you naked. Boys always are." Then she grins at Blaise and swipes her tongue over her bottom lip. "I've seen her naked, dripping wet in the shower, in every piece of skimpy lace Ash picked out for her, and all sweaty and panting after a long, hard workout. Oh, I've also seen her in yoga poses that would make a monk weep."

I swear I hear all three of them gulp. Huh.

Ash clears his throat. "How exactly does this relate to what we're doing?"

Harley butts in before Avery can answer. "So, about this sex ban the Jackal has you on. Is that the real reason you won't fuck a Hannaford guy?"

I grit my teeth and try to force myself to look down at the photos while I'm distracted by the conversation. Nope. Can't do it. "Yes. If there's a chance it could get back to him that I'm with someone then I can't do it. Hannaford is a pit of snakes and no one gets laid here without the entire school hearing about it. Just not worth the risk."

Avery chuckles under her breath. "Besides, the majority of males at this school don't know how to make it good for girls. Why risk torture and death if you're not even going to come?"

I snort with unexpected laughter at her. "Better off doing it myself, right?"

Avery cackles and I glance up again to find three sets of smoldering eyes glaring at me with a challenge. A blush starts creeping along my cheeks and I'm struck for the first time with the realization that I've kissed all three of them. *Sweet Lord.* Not only that, each kiss had been so fucking hot I had no reason to doubt their...skills.

I hold my hands up in a placating gesture. "Woah, settle down. I'm sure you guys are...great or whatever. You must be if Annabelle is mourning your dicks like she's missed out on the second coming of Christ."

"She's mourning the potential for a wealthy husband not their dicks," murmurs Avery, in no way helping me with calming them the fuck down. I shrug and finally force my eyes down onto the photos in front of me.

I feel lightheaded.

Avery yells, startling us all, "*Ha!* There! Lips, we've got him."

My gaze stays glued on the first photo. It's so fucking disturbing to see your own face on a body that clearly isn't yours. Yeah, he Photoshopped my scars on it but the knees are wrong. The fingers are longer than mine and I've *never* managed to get my nails to that length. The tits are way bigger and the nipples are much darker than mine are. I really, really don't want to have to flash my nipples to get out of this.

I finally look over to the one Avery is waving at me and that photo is even more obscene. Lance has the girl flipped over and is doing her from behind. He's leaning back and the photo has been taken with a nice close up of his dick in her, the fleshy globes of her ass spread by his hand. I immediately see what Avery is talking about.

"Snap, motherfucker," I mutter and Avery tucks her arm into mine.

"Let's go end that Mounty fuck."

Harley texts the bet keeper, some senior named Thomas Darcy, to tell him to hold payment until the next day so I don't have to charge into the boys' dorms at midnight in my booty shorts to kill Lance. He arranges to meet after classes in the chapel. At this point, I never want to step foot in that fucking room again but I grin and bear it. I messaged the Jackal last night to cover my ass and buy time, I told him about the fake photos and my plan to deal with Lance.

Send me the photos. I'll deal with him.

He wants proof they're not real. I text him and tell him I can handle it on my own but I get the digital copy from Blaise and send it to him. He has people on his payroll that can confirm they're a Photoshop. Now Lance owes me a life-debt. The little fuck.

Avery marches into the chapel like she's a general in a war and she's thirsty for they're blood. I trail behind her and the guys are grumbling together behind me. I had woken up with my period and am now bloated and moody as fuck. I've already snapped at Harley during classes so I think he's warned the other two away from me. Lord help Lance if he is a mouthy dick to me today.

Lance is already there, laughing and joking with Darcy, and when I walk in he bites his lip and makes a big show of leering at my body like he knows what's hiding underneath my clothes. My hands curl into fists and I take a second to fantasize about feeling the bones in his cheek break when I punch him. Harley cracks his knuckles behind me.

Darcy saunters over to us and smirks despite the thunderous look on my face.

"You can't be pissy just because you finally caved, Mounty. You still have the moral high ground, you fucked one of your own." Every word out of Darcy's mouth makes me want to grab him by the balls and twist until they pop.

"It's a decent Photoshop, I'll give the kid that, but he's picked the wrong position."

Darcy laughs and Lance, the little fuck, smirks at me. I manage to keep my breathing nice and even, and I hold my composure. Harley doesn't, Blaise has to body check him to keep him from throttling the Mounty boy.

"You're claiming it's a fake because you don't fuck doggy style? That's not good enough, babe."

Rage. Blackout.

I regain control of my body to find myself kneeling on Darcy's not-so-smug-anymore body, one leg on his chest and the other cutting off his airway. I really enjoy the terrified look in his eyes as I press in close to him so I can whisper to him. "Don't you *ever* call me babe again. I'll gut you for that alone. Now, the photo shows the chick's entire lower back. I'm willing to show you mine, here and now, and you'll fucking know that it's not me getting reamed. The Mounty faked them."

Darcy nods his head a fraction and I climb off him. Lance is staring at me in horror, seeing for himself just how much he's underestimated me, and I look back at him like he's a steaming pile of shit. A spade's a spade.

Avery slaps a blown up version of Lance's fake-ass photo down onto the table in front of Darcy. He doesn't look her in the eye at all, just nods along while he tries to suck deep lungfuls of air through his damaged throat. I shrug off my jacket, handing it to Avery, and then pull my crisp white shirt out from where it's tucked neatly into my skirt. I turn on my heel to face the guys and show off my lower back to Darcy and Lance instead.

"What the fuck happened to you?" hisses Darcy and my face heats up. I shove the shirt back down and then spin back to him.

"There's your fucking proof. Are you satisfied?" I snap. Darcy stares at me for a second and then with a glance at the guys behind me he nods and shoots a glare at

Lance, who's backing away from us all like he can get away. Fat chance, dickhead.

"No hard feelings, Mounty. I'm still up for it if you want to end this thing for real," drawls Darcy and I stomp out of the room, livid at this whole miserable day.

I need alcohol, a nap, a shower, a week away from my life, and a whole list of other shit I'll never get.

Avery skips to catch up with me and hooks her arm in mine. "I told the guys to destroy him. I'll get a video of it if you want to enjoy it later."

I force a laugh and the side-eye she gives me says she sees right through me.

"Let's eat a whole tub of ice cream and plot world domination for a few hours. That always cheers you up."

"I need all of the chocolate in this damn building, Avery."

She side-eyes me again and then pets my arm in a way that should have been condescending but instead is affectionate. "I hear drinking the blood of your enemies helps with PMS. I'll ask Ash to bring us a gallon."

I'm wrapped up in bed with a heating pad, Blaise's iPod, and a half-eaten tub of ice cream when Avery opens the door to Harley. He glances over to me as he talks to her but the music in my ears drowns him out and I let my eyes close. This week's playlist makes my heart ache in the best/worst way, all dark and sweet with longing. I'd started putting together a list of songs to give back to him and I knew my list was an answer to his. Whoever it is that Harley is hoping to date, she has done a number on Blaise. I hate her intensely. I keep trying to imagine what she looks like. She must be stunning to have caught both their eyes.

I'm startled out of my thoughts by my bed dipping as Harley sits. I blush and wince as I sit up, the pain in my abdomen intensifying. I pull out my earphones and glance over to where Avery is perched on her bed, watching us both closely.

"What? What's happened?" I croak.

Harley holds an envelope out to me and inside I find dozens of photos. Every single one is of me. They've been taken throughout the day at Hannaford and there's even a few from the trip to Haven I took with Avery. Lance, because I'm sure it's the work of that little fuck, has been stalking me for months. I feel sick.

"Ash and Morrison are trashing his room as we speak and looking for anything else he might have. He stays on the planner," Harley says and I glance back up at his fiercely beautiful face. He's hesitating. I look over at Avery.

"Harley found your underwear on him when he beat him. He was carrying it around like some sick pervert. He said he took it as extra proof for the bet but we all know there has been dozens of pairs taken."

Holy shit.

The creepy little fuck.

Seriously, *am I* some sort of magnet to disgusting rapists and stalkers?! I give myself three seconds of shock and then I get angry. I get fucking livid. I'm not a victim, I'm not some helpless girl he can covet and jerk off to.

I'm the fucking Wolf of Mounts Bay and I'm going to *end* him.

Harley smirks at me when he sees the fire that's been lit behind my eyes. He watches me the same as he did when I attacked Harlow, like he's standing witness to the dark stain inside me and admiring it.

"Give me two days to sort my uterus out and then I'll deal with him myself."

He snorts with laughter but Avery's eyes narrow. "I can hand all of this over to the school board and get him expelled, you don't have to be involved in this."

I don't need her concern, I'm not afraid of that pathetic piece of shit. I shake my head. "This sort of disrespect needs to be punished, Aves."

She picks up on my wording and gives me a curt nod. He's from the Bay and I can't send him home without giving him a message. Harley grabs the photos back and shoves them into Avery's drawer. I slump back and seethe.

I don't want to call the Jackal. I'm still trying to distance myself from him so he doesn't have the chance to manipulate me. I could call him right now and Lance would be dead by sunrise. I could kill him myself but cleanup would be near impossible without Avery pulling some serious strings. Besides, I don't want him dead. I want him afraid. I want him watching every shadow for the rest of his life and wondering if it's me come to kill him. Well, that settles it.

I have a plan.

I slip my earphones back into my ears and fall asleep.

When I wake up in the early hours of the morning to pee I find Harley sleeping on the floor between the two King Cal's on the pullout. Ash is tucked up in Avery's bed, frowning even in his sleep, and Blaise is tangled up in a blanket on the couch. I stare around at them before my bladder forces me to move.

They're gone before I wake in the morning.

Chapter Twenty-Five

Harley refuses to let me out of his sight. He tells Avery that he's going to sleep on the roll out bed in our room until Lance has been dealt with. I immediately make the call that Blaise sleeping in our room for three nights was torturous enough and I'll never willingly put myself through that again. Blaise at least made jokes and played his guitar for me, Harley would sit and stare at me for hours trying to read the secrets written under my skin. So I go with my gut and I throw caution into the wind for the day.

The Jackal sends me a copy of the original photos and I gag when I realize what the Photoshop has covered. He also sends me through a little background information on Lance but it's nothing Avery hasn't dug up already. No, it's the photo that tells me exactly what I need to know and drives home the last nail in Lance's fucking coffin.

I'm careful about my planning because I need to get him alone. Avery shrugs and jots down a list of places to consider, and it only takes a quick glance to know where it has to take place. The photography classroom is the perfect place to have a little chat with my creepy fucking stalker. It's where he's been developing the photos he's been taking of me and there's a black light in the classroom for creating special effects in photos. Perfect.

The problem is Harley follows me down there when I check the space out. When I confront him over it at breakfast he doesn't even pretend to look remorseful about messing with my plans.

"I'm not doubting you're skilled with your knife, I'm just saying any guy at this school is twice as big as you and Lance is clearly fucking deranged."

Ash glances between the two of us and then shrugs at his cousin. "She took down Rory. Don't baby her like we do Avery, she doesn't need it."

Harley stares him down. "She had the element of surprise with Rory and he had his dick out. She's inviting Lance somewhere and I doubt she's going to get him in such a compromising position."

I shudder and pretend to gag. "I've seen more of him then I ever wanted to. If it means that much to you then you can keep watch for me but you're not coming into the classroom. I've got something very specific in mind for the little fuck."

I'm leaning against a desk when Lance saunters in, though he's clutching at his ribs I'm sure Harley broke for him. His jaw is mottled and bruised as well and his split lip looks pretty painful but it doesn't seem to be affecting his mood. The smile is still a mile wide on his face and he gives me this stupid little wave. I just stare at him until he stands before me.

"Changed your mind? I'm still up for the real thing, Lips."

I clasp my hands in front of me and take in every detail of his body, slowly dragging my eyes over him. He mistakes my interest, which is my exact intention, and he adjusts his pants suggestively.

"You ever fuck a member of the Twelve before, Lance?"

He blanches and stutters, "Wh-what?"

I lean forward. "I know you're happy enough to fuck *with* a member of the Twelve but I don't know if you've ever dropped your pants for one."

He frowns and takes a faltering step away from me. I nod at him, slowly, humming under my breath.

"Listen Lance, you've got my attention. I've done my research and I know all about you now. I know where you live when you're not here. I know you grew up in the 'burbs, you have two loving parents and a little sister. I read your application for the scholarship. It was pretty decent, not as good as mine. I know your taste for girls runs on the damaged side. You want them broken so when you're finished with them no one will believe them when they say nice guy Lance Michael Owens would ever stalk, beat, dehumanize, and rape a girl. I know that the money was a good incentive but that's not why you wanted me. You thought I was just your type, a little foster girl with a tragic backstory. But Lance, I'm telling you now, you thought wrong."

His chest rattles as he begins to wheeze. I nod again like we've come to an agreement.

"You're going to drop out and go home to the Bay. You're going to keep your head down and never, ever say my name again. You're going to take a vow of celibacy. You're going to go to bed every night and pray to fucking God that I don't come looking for you. You're going to watch the shadows and remember that I'm watching you. Because I am watching you, Lance. You've gotten my attention and, fuck me, you have no idea how bad that really is for you."

The stupid smile on his face is gone. I'm sure his erection is too but I don't break eye contact for a single second. I wait until the words have sunk in.

"The mistake you made was thinking the guys who beat you are the predators."

I flick the lights off and the black light glows. Lance's eyes widen and he scrambles to get away from me, falling straight onto his ass as he gapes up at me with horror. The whispers in the Bay precede me and tell a hundred stories in the silence between us.

It's only in black light that you can see the ink that covers me. The skeletal structure I've had tattooed to my skin, the jaw opening wide etched in my cheeks with vicious teeth. Every inch of my body is covered in the whorls and arches that imitate the pelt. The black light shows that underneath the human facade I wear the truth of who I am.

The Wolf.

Harley smirks at me when I step out of the photography classroom and straighten my blazer.

"If I asked you what you did would you tell me?" he drawls and I smile back at him.

"Who says I even did anything? We had a chat."

Harley snort and pulls out his phone, turning the screen so I can watch the video he's recorded of Lance bolting from the classroom like the devil himself is on his ass. I bite my lip to stop the smug smirk from forming.

"A chat did that?"

I nod and, without thinking, tuck my arm into his like I do with Avery. It's as close to a hug as I ever get to giving out. He looks down at our linked arms and when I blush and try to move, he grabs my hand and tugs me along with him, our fingers laced together.

"Uhm—"

"Get over it, Mounty, we're friends now, remember?"

I sigh and let him drag me back up to the girls' dorm. I drop his hand before we walk through the halls because all I need is a photo of the two of us of the ridiculous fucking gossip website to finish off this week. Avery is waiting for us, and Blaise is cackling over the video that Harley sent them all. I smile at her and then laugh when Harley starts making up stupid stories about how I did it. By the time I get out of the shower Blaise calls out to me, "Did you really slice one of his balls off and crush it under your heel?"

I stare at them, all three guys now Ash has showed up, and just quirk an eyebrow.

"Did you know there are quite a few different ways to castrate someone? Lips has talked me through four different methods. If she took her knife to him he would have lost more than a single testicle," Avery snipes and they all turn a little green. She looks over at me with a smile and says, "Lance dropped out. Packed everything and called his parents to come get him today. Mr. Trevelen questioned him and he said he doesn't belong here. The administration tried to talk him into finishing out the year and he said he needs to leave immediately."

I make a gesture like I'm ticking a box and say, "Off the planner you go, Mounty fuck."

I sit next to Avery and pull out my notes for history, ready to ignore the TV and the conversations around me. She murmurs into my ear quietly, "Is he definitely out for good?"

I nod. "He understands he is being watched by the Wolf and that is not a position he is happy to find himself in. I think he actually pissed himself."

Harley notices us whispering and looks like he wants to push me for more but then Avery flings a leg over his lap and tells him to rub her feet. He scoffs at her and then, to my absolute shock, he pulls her shoe off and gets to work. I love Avery, I really do.

But right this very second, I would bathe in her blood to take her place.

Chapter Twenty-Six

Lance's departure from Hannaford makes the gossip website and Avery reads every comment out to me while I cook us both pancakes for breakfast. Some of the theories are disgustingly close to the truth and I know Avery is quietly stewing in her own curiosity at how I've actually managed to scare him. I haven't told her about my tattoos yet; I'm saving that truth to mess with her later. For shits and giggles.

Spring break arrives and Harley decides to go home with Blaise as moral support. I think he's hoping Blaise's dad will run his mouth in front of him so he can deal with him. Blaise gives me his iPod before he leaves with a wink and when I listen to it I realize it's all his new unreleased songs.

I have to take a minute to lie down.

Of course, Ash decides to walk in midway through my fangirling and he snorts at me. I glare back and snap, "What time are you leaving?"

"Avery didn't tell you? Our father has been called away on business and he told us to stay here. You're stuck with all three Beaumonts this week, Mounty."

He watches me carefully for a reaction and I shrug. Putting the earphone back into my ear, I try not to shiver lustfully at the heavenly sounds of Blaise's crooning.

Ash tugs it back out and says, "I haven't seen my father since you had your mysterious little midnight meeting in Haven. How long should I be expecting this separation to continue?"

I sit up and find Avery staring at me from the bathroom door, a toothbrush hanging from her mouth. "If I had anything to do with your father's busy schedule, I would think that after graduation you and Avery would both be free of him anyway and the...interference would no longer be necessary."

Avery nods, wide-eyed, and ducks back into the bathroom. Ash stares at me until he finally scoffs and walks away.

I spend the rest of the week studying and avoiding Ash. Avery does her best to keep him busy and away from me but he sleeps on the roll out bed every night, just in case his brother comes out to find us.

The day before the students return from spring break I bite the bullet and text the Jackal. I've put it off for too long and I'm only endangering Avery and Ash with my fear.

I'm calling in a favor.

I roll the diamond between my fingers absently while I wait for the reply. Avery watching the little stone move with something predatory in her eyes. She looks at the diamond the way I imagine I look at Harley, Blaise, and Ash. I hope to God they never notice. I think she's honestly turned on by it. I start to feel weird about playing with it so I sigh and hold it out for her. She lunges for it like a crack addict.

My phone rings.

"What happened to calling me for help, Wolf?"

I flinch at his tone. I don't need the memories that flood me when I hear the dark rage I have pushed the Jackal into. Avery notices and hesitates before tucking her arm in mine.

"I don't want to be a burden to you anymore. I need to stand on my own two feet."

Dead silence. He must be sitting in his bedroom or maybe in the vault, counting his money. I wait him out. I won't break protocol but he might.

"Should we meet somewhere to discuss your requirements?" He spits out from his clenched teeth. Fuck. If I meet him I think I'll be kidnapped and my body never found again.

"Over the phone is more than adequate. You have a customer and I would like him cut off. Permanently and from everything you offer."

He grunts and then says, calmer, "Your little friend just dropped by to see me. I'll do as you ask but he has enough to last him a few weeks already."

I take a deep breath. "I have another favor to discuss with you. I'll see you at the meeting in the summer."

He pauses and then says, smooth and warm as he tries to trap me once again, "That's your last favor little Wolf. I hope it's worth the cost."

I hang up because my voice wouldn't be level if I tried to answer him. Avery leans her head on my shoulder as she rolls the diamond obsessively like one of her routines.

"What's your next favor?"

I pluck the diamond out of her hands and roll it back into the little velvet bag, ready to send back to Mounts Bay with whatever thug the Jackal sends to collect it. "I've got a plan. A huge, expensive, utterly terrifying plan but I think it's going to save Harley's life so it's going to be worth it."

Avery tucks her hand into mine and says, "Those idiot boys have no idea how fiercely the Wolf of Mounts Bay guards them."

Chapter Twenty-Seven

You know that old saying 'when it rains, it pours'? Well, some bastard was out there with a fire hose aimed right the fuck at me.

The shrill sound of Avery's phone wakes me. She mumbles out a string of curses as she answers it and a quick check of my own phone tells me it's two. We've barely managed to get an hour of sleep. Fuck. I flick the light on and glance over at Avery. She has her Joey face on. Fucking great. I get up and start throwing clothes on.

"We'll be there shortly. Keep a set of eyes on him until then." She hangs up, immediately starts a new call, and slides out of bed with the phone pressed to her ear.

When she speaks again she looks at me. "Joey's at the bar in Haven. Ria said he's cooked, we've got to go now."

I nod as I slip my knife into my pocket and fumble around for my Docs. "Ash coming?"

Avery slips an elegant, tailored coat over her lacy nightgown and instantly looks like she's dressed to meet some high profile governor. I roll my eyes at her as she smirks at me. "Blaise and Harley are back, too. Blaise will drive us there."

I throw my hair into a messy high pony and then we're out the door.

The guys arrive at the stairs as we do and, surprisingly, Ash gives me a respecting nod. I'm thrown a little. Then he tucks Avery under his arm and we head out to the staff car park where Blaise's Maserati is sitting. "Fucking rich kids." I mumble and Avery cackles at me.

I end up in the backseat between Ash and Harley, trying my best not to touch either of them. Blaise makes the trip in half the time the school's town cars do, thank God, and we pull up outside the quaint town's only bar.

"Park around the back, Ria will let us in the service entrance. She's lost sight of him, we need to get in and out fast," Avery says with her phone at her ear. I think I'm going to suggest getting a Bluetooth earpiece to her at some point. Her brothers ensure she's glued to the damn thing.

Once Blaise parks we pile out and wait by the door. A heavily tattooed woman in her forties opens it and scowls at us all. "It really gonna take five o' you to git him outta here?"

I raise my eyebrows and expect some fire to spill out of the twins but then Blaise swaggers forward and I nearly choke on my tongue at the smooth, honey tones of his voice. "When have we ever turned down the chance to spend the evening with you, Ria?"

I cast a sidelong look at Harley to find him rolling his eyes so hard for a second I think he's having a stroke.

The woman sputters and then moves to let us all through. We have to walk through a teeming stock room with boxes of booze precariously stacked floor to ceiling then through a bustling kitchen, a single chef pumping out wings and barking orders at the glassy-eyed waitresses. When we get through to the bar area my eyes have to adjust to the darkness of the room, lit only by fairy lights strung up here and there. During the day it would probably look as charming as the rest of the town but now, in the early morning hours, it was a workplace hazard if I've ever seen one.

There are people everywhere and most of them are already wasted. We have to move in single file. Harley takes the lead, Ash pushes Avery in front of him so she's caged in by them both. I find Blaise doing the same to me and I give him a quick look over my shoulder as we start moving through the hazy room. I feel Blaise's breath on my neck as he speaks right into my ear. "Two Hannaford girls were assaulted here last year."

Great. Doesn't matter where the hell you are, there's always some dickhead predator looking to destroy someone's life.

We search the ground floor and then head upstairs. The music is louder up here and there are less people but they're dancing and making it even harder to stick together. Blaise wraps an arm around my waist and hauls me in tight to his body. Thank fuck it's dark and he can't see the exact shade my cheeks have turned. He's a wall of solid muscle. I try not to melt into him.

We lose Harley for five minutes and I start to panic that Joey's stabbed him or something. Ash gestures us over to the restrooms and Blaise finally lets me go. Avery grabs my hand and gives it a squeeze, I squeeze back to reassure her. Ash is glaring out at the room of writhing bodies when the door to the disability restroom opens and Harley's head pops out.

"Mounty, I need you to look at this," he snaps out and I rush forward, ducking behind him and he starts to argue with Avery as he blocks the others from following me.

Joey is unconscious on the dirty floor, surrounded by his own vomit. He's foaming at the mouth and he's going to choke to death on his back like that.

I'm so fucking tempted to leave him.

"Don't judge me for asking this but I am supposed to try and save him or are we waiting this out then calling it in for a clean up?"

Harley grunts as Ash punches him in the gut and shoves his way into the room. He's wild-eyed and pale as he looks down at Joey then back to me.

"I die if he does," he croaks and my body starts moving before my mind does.

I know for sure that he doesn't mean it like he'd be so torn up or furious if his brother died. He loathes him. This is the real reason Avery guards Joey's life with such intensity. Someone is threatening Ash. *Christ.*

I roll Joey to his side and wince as I clear out his mouth. His hacking breath starts to even out and I prop his head up to help his breathing stay steady.

"I can call a doctor. What does he need to reverse this?" Avery asks and I hear the door close and lock behind them. Harley kneels down next to me, right in a puddle of puke, and helps to support Joey's twitching body. Ash starts rummaging through Joey's pockets and finds the little clear baggies, so damn familiar to me with their grinning Jackal stamps on them, with a little of the white powder residue still visible.

"There is no drug to reverse a cocaine overdose. They just treat the symptoms."

"Fuck. Okay." Avery is starting to panic and I look up to meet her eyes.

"He needs an ambulance and 24 hour care until he gets through. Look, it's not too bad." I lie. I feel his pulse and it's not great but Avery's eyes are like saucers and I can't bear to stress her out anymore. The bubbling around his mouth and the jerking also make me wonder if he was having a seizure before we arrived. Harley meets my eyes and he reads me better than Avery can in her state.

"Is there anything we can do while we wait?" His voice is low and calm.

"Recovery position and we need to make sure he doesn't choke on his own tongue. That's it about all we can do in this restroom. We should call an ambulance."

Avery and Ash stare at each other and I start to believe they have some mystical twin connection that lets their minds talk. I can feel their conversation hanging in the air around us. If Ash's life is in danger then we can't sweep this under the rug, we need a professional.

"I'm not waiting for an ambulance, we need to move him now."

I cut a look at Harley and gesture for him to follow me out of the room. Ash and Blaise kneel to take our places besides Joey to keep him where he needs to be. Harley doesn't speak as we descend the stairs, his protective arm around me, and it's not until I point to the black van on the curb out front that he raises an eyebrow at me.

"Boost it. We'll drive him in and dump it at the hospital." I text Avery to get them moving down to us.

"And why do you think I know how to do that?"

I grin at him and wag my finger in his face. "I was at your court hearing last year, remember? You're quite proficient in the ol' grand theft auto. Come on, impress me, Arbour."

My challenge lights a flame in his eyes. His grin is savage and beautiful and he has the van unlocked, motor running and ready to move in less than a minute. It's like watching a pro and I must be seriously damaged because it excites me more than sweet words would. Avery slides into the front seat with him and I help the other two load Joey into the back. Ash drops him with such disgust that I think he'll have a concussion but that will be the least of his concerns if he ever wakes up. We arrange his body so he won't suffocate on his own tongue and then sit around him.

"So, we're criminals now? We just take things whenever we want them? I'm not sure I have enough black in my wardrobe for this, someone should have pre-warned me," drawls Blaise as he wipes his hands on his jeans.

"We were always a little criminal, Morrison," says Ash and I try to ignore their banter. I don't need their input right now.

"Lips, if we can't take him to the hospital is there somewhere else we can take him?" Avery asks, her voice finally losing the authoritative tone and she sounds like the scared sixteen-year-old girl she really is.

"How the fuck would she know?" Ash snaps and we both ignore him.

I glance down at Joey. His condition hasn't gotten any worse. I think he'll make it to Mounts Bay.

"Yeah. Head to the Bay. I'll give you directions once we hit the city."

Harley nods and then we all fall silent.

I'm jostled around by the movement of the van since we're just sitting in the back without proper chairs or seat belts. The guys are both fine, they're big enough that they're stable, but I'm a scrawny Mounty girl and every corner, every pothole, has me lurching and slamming into the sharp metal interior. Finally, after ten minutes of collecting new bruises, Ash rolls his eyes and grunts at Blaise, digging his elbow into him. Then, I'm dragged over by them both to be wedged between their giant frames, their hands landing all over me and gripping firmly. I panic a little but then at the next corner I'm held steady by the hands on my hips and legs.

I clear my throat, "Thanks."

Ash shrugs and Blaise nods, a little distracted.

"What, no smart ass comment?"

Ash stares back at me and then shakes his head slowly. "No. I don't have anything left to say."

I don't know how to answer that so I don't. I let my eyes fall shut and I start to plan out the rest of our evening. Get to Doc's, lose the van, find a hotel to stash the rich kids, keep Harley out of sight as much as possible, get Blaise's Maserati to the hotel to get us back to Hannaford, find clothing because at least three of us are covered in Joey's vomit, the list goes on and on, endless and exhausting. I check Joey's pulse again. Still alive.

As we get to the city limits Harley breaks the silence.

"How much will this cost?"

I shrug. "Nothing, I'll call in a favor."

Harley snarls and rips his body around to snap at me, "*Fuck no.* You're not using up a favor for this fucking murderer. It's bad enough you spent one on me. Get a price and we'll pay it."

Fuck. I forgot he knows about the diamonds. "Not one of those favors. The Doc owes me for some work I did for him last year. It'll be fine."

Avery looks between us both and then raises an eyebrow at me. I nod sharply. I'm going to have to sit them both down soon and tell both of them... as close to everything as I'll ever get. Then Avery won't have to guess at how much Harley knows and he can protect himself from what being mine entails.

We pull up in front of a quiet suburban house in a shitty neighborhood. The house is the nicest on the street, the grass green and trimmed to perfection. I tell them to wait as I scramble out the back door and up to the house. The front door opens before I can knock. A short, elderly Vietnamese man frowns at me as he takes me in.

"Aren't you off at school, my girl?"

I grin at him and nod. "I've got a patient for you. It's really important that he lives, Doc."

He sighs and waves me in. I motion at the van to get the others to join us. Ash and Blaise carry Joey across the grass and into the medical room Doc has set up. It's well-stocked, sterile, and ready for massacre victims at all times.

Doc gets straight to work on his patient and I step out to wash my hands. Ash follows me and stands at the kitchen sink scrubbing the bile from his skin with me. I finally take a shaky breath. If anyone can fix Joey it'll be Doc.

When we get back to the room Harley is glaring at Doc like he's planning to stab him and Avery is tucked up in Blaise's arms. Her shoulders are shaking but her eyes are dry, this is pure panic at the thought of losing Ash.

"Friend of yours?" murmurs Doc.

I don't ever lie to this man, he can smell it. "No."

Doc raises an eyebrow at me but his hands don't falter as he puts an IV line into Joey and starts him on some fluids. "Why bother bringing him in then? Just dig a hole."

Ash stares at Doc like he's a bug he'd like to squash. I try to keep the old man busy instead. "He's worth saving. How's Maria and the kids?" Maria is Doc's granddaughter, his pride and joy. She's eighteen and has three kids already, a typical Mounty girl. She's sweet enough and good to the old man so I always check in with her when I'm in town.

"She's pregnant." He says with a sigh. He moves to start taking down Joey's temperate, heart rate, lord knows what else, to try and assess how bad the repercussions of this episode will be. This is not my first OD rodeo.

"Fuck," I reply and he gives me a dry look.

"I've tried to get her on the stick but she insists on taking the pill then forgets to half the time. I'll be building an extension on the house by the end of the year."

"Maybe tell her to stay away from cocks for a while instead," I say with a grin and he roars with laughter at me. I've seen him carve up a guy's face with a scalpel for saying less but I guess I'm just special like that. Doc knows I say it with love and experience. I know exactly what life is like around here for poor Mounty girls. The conversation is a good distraction for everyone. I can see Avery is slowly collecting herself, the unaffected, cool mask slowly sliding back into place.

Doc starts to hook Joey up to all sorts of noisy machines. "You know, if she finally has a girl I'm going to get her to name it after you. You're a good girl, we need some of that in this house."

I blanch and then sputter out, "Fuck no! Don't traumatize the poor spawn. It'll be bad enough not knowing who the daddy is."

Doc grimaces. "Oh, I know who the daddy is. Maria will be lucky to get to keep the baby."

"Why? Who knocked her up?"

Doc surveys the room before he speaks. "Matteo."

My stomach drops.

Fuck.

That's really, really bad.

"Doc. Doc, do not let her tell him. Fuck, send her away."

"I've tried, she won't go. She's got it in her head that they're in love."

I grab his wrist and give him a shake. "I'll give you the money. I'll pay to get her away, Doc."

"I'm not stupid. I know she's going to be forced to abort the baby."

She's going to be killed. It won't matter that's she's Doc's family. The Jackal will plunge a knife through her heart and then he'll bury her somewhere she'll never be found again. Doc will lose her too.

I can't argue with him without privacy so I shake my head and try to figure out how to help Maria. Poor, stupid, gullible Maria. Taken in by the Jackal's handsome face.

After another tense minute of silence Doc looks up and smiles at me. "He'll be ready to go by midday. Stop worrying about my problems and go get some sleep, my girl."

Avery books us into the same hotel as the last time we were here.

When Harley pulls into the parking I wait until the others are out and then try to get Harley out too.

"I'll help you ditch it."

I scowl at him. "I don't want to get you into any trouble. Just go with the others and I'll be back in an hour."

He stares me down until I give in. I direct him from the passenger seat until we pull up into a chop shop owned by the Bear. Gordon, the guy running it, takes one look at me through the window and waves us through into the garage. "Not a single word." I whisper in what I hope is an authoritative tone to Harley. He just nods and we get out.

"Price?" says Gordon.

I look over the van and glance back to him. "I need it gone and I need a ride back to a hotel. Nothing else."

Gordon grunts and flicks a hand out at one of the guys who darts off to get us a ride. Then he gives Harley a good, long stare. "I'll get the boss to call if there's anything he's got questions about."

Fucking perfect. I nod and then follow Gordon out to the awaiting car at the curb. Harley goes to get in the back and I discreetly push him to the front. Protocol, that he knows *nothing* about, says he gets in the front. I'm supposed to be safely stashed in the back. He eyes me and gives me a tiny nod, opening my door and shutting it behind me. I hope it's enough.

The car ride is mostly quiet. Harley tells the guy the address and I text Avery to tell her we're on our way back. The guy seems nervous, he's practically shaking, and his eyes keep darting to the rearview mirror to watch me. Harley crosses his arms and glowers at him.

"A lot of interest about you, man," The guy says and I tense.

Harley shrugs and plays along. "I'm sure there is."

"My boss said he never thought he'd ever see the day she accepted someone. A lot of people want to know what's so special about you. Can't just be the pretty face or who your old man was."

Nope. Not going to let this go on.

I lean forward and put a hand on the guys arm. He nearly runs us off the road before looking back at me. "Are you trying to dig for information on me?"

"Oh, no! Absolutely not! I was just curious, I would never—"

"Then shut up."

He nods and then drives in silence, sweat dripping from his face and his hands are slick on the wheel. When we pull up, I wait for Harley to get out and open my door. I don't say a word to him or the trembling driver. The tires squeal as the car takes off and the guy flees from us.

"Is there anyone in this city that isn't afraid of you?" Harley drawls and I shrug at him. "Are you ever going to tell me how it is a little Mounty girl can get grown men to fucking shake in their boots with barely a word?"

I start walking to our rooms and say, "You've gotta be all in to know and you're not all in."

Harley grunts and walks ahead of me. I stop at the door of the suite and pull out my phone to text the Jackal. If he hears about me being here without checking in with him he'll get suspicious and start looking into my life at Hannaford. No way I'm letting that happen.

In the Bay. Had to get Joey patched up.

I fidget while I wait for his reply. My head is pounding and I'd kill for ten hours of sleep right now. My phone pings.

Stop off and see me. We can discuss your favor and I can meet the O'Cronin boy.

Fuck no. My hand trembles as I reply.

No time, school tomorrow. I'll bring Harley to a meeting over the summer break.

I can picture the Jackal's face so clearly in my mind as he reads the message. I know he's twitching to punish me, to bend me to him and force me to obey his every command. If I weren't a member of the Twelve I think he would be finding me tonight. I'm not sure how much longer being the Wolf will keep me safe.

I will see you both soon.

I let out my breath and head into the suite.

The shower is running, Harley must be cleaning the vomit off of his legs, and Avery is in one of the rooms talking in a stern tone down her phone. Clean up for the evil Beaumont child is well underway. The other two are out on the balcony. Blaise is smoking a blunt and Ash has a glass with whiskey over ice. I step out and join them. I don't want to be alone with the swirling panic in my mind. They're talking shit about some sporting thing I have no idea about and even less interest in learning. I just sit and stare blankly out at the city I'd do anything to get away from.

I can't think about anything but all the evil that's creeping up on us. The Jackal wants Harley dead. He's knocked up Doc's little Maria and now she's going to die. Ash's head is on the damn chopping block and his life depends on Joey breathing. Fuck.

Eventually Blaise gets up and walks back into the room, hesitating before squeezing my shoulder as he moves past me.

"Drink?" Ash says as he holds out the bottle to me. I take it a drink straight out of it, fuck glasses, and he quirks an eyebrow at me.

"I need a hell of a lot more than a glass can hold right now."

"Not happy to be home?"

I scoff at him. "Cut me some slack. I just found out Doc's grandkid is going to be brutally murdered just because she can't remember to take a damn pill." I groan and hang my head. It's an utter waste and a fucking tragedy and I can't do a thing about it.

"This Matteo will kill her instead of just getting rid of the baby?"

He'd kill her just for the fun of listening to her beg for mercy. "He doesn't exactly value life, in any form."

Ash nods and looks back out over the city. "I'll pay. Get her out and I'll pay for the costs."

I stare at him in shock. He gives me a sidelong look and takes Blaise's blunt from the ashtray. He offers it to me but I wave him away. "I'm not a fan of domestic violence or women being killed. Besides, you just saved Joey. I owe you."

I take another swig, long enough that I can feel the heat of the liquor pooling in my stomach nicely. I'd like to get drunk. I'd like to get absolutely fucked up but now's not the time. "Thanks. I'll reach out to her."

I hand him back the bottle and he shrugs, drinking straight from it then his tongue darts out to swipe across his lips. My stomach heats for an entirely different reason. He's just licked the taste of me off of his lips. I wonder if he remembers the taste of me as clearly as I remember the taste of him. Doubtful.

I stand up and as I step back through the door I turn to look at him. "You don't owe me. I did it for Avery and if you'd just stop hating me, I'd do it for you, too."

His eyes don't waiver from the lights of the city but he nods at me.

I don't know if we've made any progress but I go to sleep easier that night.

Chapter Twenty-Eight

I find myself, terrifyingly, only one week ahead in my studies.

We're down to the last month of the school year and yet with all of the tutoring, singing practice, babysitting, scheming, self-defense lessons, and family dinners I'm now behind. Well, okay, not behind but if I get the flu now I'm fucked academically. Avery rolls her eyes at me and tells me she would never let me lose my scholarship or my place at Hannaford which is reassuring but it doesn't stop me from turning into a crazed insomniac hell-bent on finishing every assignment I have left in three days or less.

I take refuge in the library, texting everyone to tell them I'm skipping dinner, and I slip Blaise's iPod into my ears to block out what little noise there is. I plow through all of my history, literature, biology, and math like my life depends on it. I wince at my now stone cold coffee, completely forgotten about and now I'm mourning its loss.

When I stop to glance at the clock and stretch my arms and fingers out I find it's almost nine and the library is empty. I only have a few minutes before I'll be kicked out and the curfew is only thirty minutes after that. Not that the curfew means anything to me, teachers now turn and run if they see me in the same way they do if they see Avery. It's hilarious.

I'm shoving my textbooks into my bag and yawning when the earphones are yanked out of my ears with enough force that the iPod goes flying. I clench my fists but I recognize the perfume. Annabelle freaking Summers.

"Does Blaise know you've stolen his music? He'll drop you if he finds out you've got this, you dumb Mounty slut," she hisses and I stand up, slinging my bag over my shoulder. When I bend to pick the iPod up she snatches it up first.

"Hand it over or I'll break every finger on your hand. One warning, that's all you're getting," I say, holding up a finger and giving her a menacing look. She's sneering back at me and looking nothing like the stunning girl I first met last year, draped around Blaise and giggling prettily. I do a full assessment of her while her lip curls at my slow perusal. Nothing seems out of place except her roots are showing, a cardinal sin amongst the affluent, bratty girls here. Ah, her nails aren't done either. Her eyelashes are thinner, lighter, and her eyebrows look good but not perfect.

Her parents have cut her off. Whether they've run out of funds themselves or she's pissed them off, I don't know but I also don't care. I think she'd fuck *me* for money at this point, the desperation is seeping from her pores.

I hold out my hand for the iPod and raise an eyebrow at her.

"I'm not fucking giving it back to you. He doesn't even let Ash touch it! I'll be walking it back up to his room and telling him—"

"That you've stolen my iPod from my friend? That you're a jealous, desperate mess and instead of doing your own work you want to trap me and leach off of me? That you're hung up on Harley and hoping you'll be able to get him back into your bed once you've secured eighteen years of child support from me?"

Annabelle's lips drop and her eyes are peeled and wild as she whirls to find Blaise glaring at her, dressed in his sweatpants and an old band tee. He doesn't pause in his scathing rant.

"How about you tell me all about how you manipulated your way into my room to steal my fathers letters and post them for the whole fucking world to see? Or how you're still posting daily about Rory trying to rape Avery? How about you tell me and the Mounty about how you helped that sick freak Lance steal her underwear and you tried to break into her room to let him mess with her shit?"

"Blaise, I—"

"Hand Lips my iPod. I gave it to her." She smacks it into my hand and steps toward him, tears streaming down her face and I decide to get the sweet fresh hell out of the library and away from the drama. I'm allergic to this shit and yet I keep finding myself in the middle of it. Blaise slings an arm around my waist as I try to move past him.

"I'm here to walk you back to your room, don't run off without me," he murmurs into my hair as he drapes himself over me. I will not blush. I will not crumble; I'm not some desperate groupie. If I keep telling myself this maybe it'll miraculously come true.

"You know she spent the night with Harley while you were at Avery's recital. You blame me for loving all three of you but it's okay for her play you all off of each other!" Annabelle wails at us.

I tense up but when I try to shift away Blaise just holds me closer. I swear I can feel the ridges of his abs where I'm pressed against him. Sweet lord.

"Nice try, Summers, but we all know what's going on. Harley has not been discreet and, like you said, I don't give my music away to anyone. C'mon, Mounty. Avery will have my balls if I don't get you back soon."

Annabelle calls out to him but he ignores her, grabbing the iPod from me and handing me one of the earphones. When the music starts I don't know if he's picked the song, 'Iris' by the Goo Goo Dolls, or if he hit shuffle but it's an old favorite of mine and my chest always aches when I hear it.

When the song ends he plays it again and I smile down at our feet, mine still covered by the uncomfortable kitten heels girls are required to wear and his only covered by the skulls he has tattooed on him. The bright yellow carnations trapped in the teeth of the skull seem to glow against the shades of black and gray depicting the bone. The same skulls were on his first EP and I loved the artwork so much. The ink only makes me grin harder.

"Don't ask about the tattoos, it'll only push me to drink." He groans and wiggles his toes as we arrive to the door.

I shrug. "I'll take a stab at it and say your dad. Yellow carnations aren't exactly the norm to find on album covers so I looked them up. Disappointment and rejection.

Didn't make sense to me back then but now I know what a dick your dad is I get it."

I fish out my keys but Blaise grabs my hands and leans down until our noses brush one another. I stop breathing.

"Stop me now, Mounty, or I'm going to kiss you. No pity, no ulterior motives, just a kiss because I can't stop myself."

My brain just ceases to exist and I tilt my head up to meet his lips halfway. This kiss is nothing like the last one, no hesitance in either of us, and when I suck his bottom lip between my teeth he grunts and slams me into the wall next to my door, his hand cradling the back of my head, preventing the concussion I'm positive that move would've given me. Thank fuck Hannaford is built out of solid stone and Avery can't hear us thumping around out here as I drag him closer, hands fisted in his shirt, and groaning into his mouth. He parts my legs with his knee and presses against me until I see fucking stars. I'm so fucking wet that I'm sure he can feel it and I'm desperate for him to touch me.

He breaks away and I take a second to let go of his shirt.

I clear my throat. "I can't."

He nods and presses his forehead against mine. I feel his answers brush across my lips. "I know. I'm being a selfish dick. Just do me a favor and don't tell Avery?"

I nod. I don't need to tell him that I'm not talking about the Jackal's threats. I'm talking about my stupid heart that I need to protect as fiercely as he protects his because when I had nothing at all in this world I still had myself. I can't afford to give pieces of me away to spoiled rich boys looking for distraction.

I can't think about Blaise or the kiss.

I can't think about anything except the massive workload I have in all of my classes and the concert I'll be singing at that's creeping up on me. When summer break starts, I'll take a few weeks to figure out what the actual fuck is going on with Harley, Ash, and Blaise so I can start my junior year without boy drama.

I tell myself this over and over again to get through my classes and it works. I'm sitting in math when my phone vibrates in my pocket and I secret it out to see what Avery needs. My stomach drops.

It's done. I'll collect my diamond when you get home.

I try to shake off the unease that settles deep in my gut but it takes root. He's getting more and more short with me. I've pissed Matteo off and now he's addressing me only as the Jackal. Old fears creep up my spine and bury themselves into my brain like shards of glass. I remind myself that this is necessary, that separating myself from the Jackal is the first step to finding freedom and safety, but it's like losing my security blanket at the same time as ridding myself of the monster under the bed. He's evil, he's twisted and psychotic, and he's the only family I have left. He's cared for me since I was nine years old. He's abused me, broken me, snapped bones and destroyed me. He's had my back in every single situation I've been in as the Wolf. I can't think of Matteo without thinking about the Jackal.

I sigh and then startle when I feel a hand tuck into mine. The teacher is still droning on and on about the interpretation of exponential models. Harley hasn't looked away once, his pen moving rapidly as he takes notes, and yet he's noticed I'm freaking the hell out. He's holding my hand, rubbing his thumb over my skin gently and threading his fingers through mine. I squeeze gently and he squeezes back before I move my hand and get back to taking my own notes. Fuck, maybe I am as bad as Annabelle say. Kissing Blaise one night then swooning over Harley holding my hand the next.

When the class finishes, I clear my throat and say, "We need to eat all of our meals in the dining hall together today. All of us. I've…had something taken care of and we need to be there to see it."

Harley just nods and grabs his phone out. When my phone pings I know he's told the others to join us.

I don't know how to act now that he's casually, discreetly, touching me. When we head to the dining hall he moves me to walk in front of him, so I don't get bowled over by the stream of students bustling around us, and rests his hand on my lower back. The heat of his palm burns through my blazer and shirt, and it feels like a brand.

He grabs us both lunch and then scares off the juniors in our seats with a single look. Before I take my seat I look up and down the table to find that Joey isn't here yet. Good. I want Avery to see his reaction.

Ash arrives next and he leaves a seat between us for Avery. He quirks an eyebrow at Harley who only shrugs in response. I dig into my food so I won't be forced to speak to them. Avery and Blaise come in together, laughing and joking, and when they sit with us Avery murmurs quietly into my ear, "Today?"

I nod and she seems to pull herself to sit straighter and more regally. Ash watches us both but doesn't comment. We're nearly finished when the door flings open with such force that it bounces off the wall.

I don't look up. I know who it is and what's eating his ass.

Avery's leg tenses against mine and she hisses, "Fuck, here he comes. He looks fucking murderous, Lips. He looks like Father does right before he backhands me, fuck."

Swearing is never a good sign from Avery. Her eyes are wide and I can see the tremble in her fingers as she picks up her knife and fork from where she's dropped them. I try to set a good example and I start in on my own plate of pasta, steady and sure. They taste like ash on my tongue but I need to look convincing for her.

"Remember what I said. He's effectively neutered. Don't engage with him."

Harley and Blaise share a look. Ash gives me a hard look of his own and hisses under his breath at me, "What the fuck does that even mean?"

He's panicking. I feel bad that I didn't give him more warning and I don't have time to answer him now. Joey slams his palms onto the table in front of me so hard the china and silverware rattles dangerously. Silence falls over the dining hall. Some of the freshmen around us begin to collect their things and leave, eager to get away from Joey's wrathful presence. There isn't a person in the school who doesn't know what he's capable of.

"Who the fuck do you think you are?" Acid drips from his words but I'm not afraid of this asshole, I've survived worse than him. I am worse than him in all the ways that count and now I have him on a very short leash. I slowly put down my knife and fork and then I cross my arms over my chest. When I meet his gaze the manic in his eyes is wildly present. His tight control has slipped and now the drug addict is clearly visible for the world to see.

"Let me tell you how this is going to go from here onwards, Joseph. You will not speak to me, your siblings, your cousin, or Morrison. You will not speak about us. You won't plot, or scheme, or belittle. You will not raise a hand. You're going to pretend we don't exist. If you come across one of us in the halls you will avert your gaze and walk the fuck away. Am I clear?"

Joey's breath is heaving out of his chest like he's running a marathon and his eyes are wild and darting around the room. Withdrawals are a bitch. I'd watched my mom go through this a hundred times so I know just how much his skin is crawling. I know just how frayed his nerves are. Fuck him. I hope it burns.

"The Jackal sends his regards," I say and I make sure my tone is even, low, placid. Then I pick my fork back up and dig back into my breakfast.

The room is holding its breath.

Joey roars and turns on his heel. He shoves a couple of juniors on his way out and whispers start up all around us.

"What the fuck just happened?" Blaise says, and I look up to see all three boys gaping at me. Avery looks smug as fuck but I know she's dying to spill to them how I did it. I give them the watered down version.

"Joey likes three things. I couldn't touch his money that will take more time than we have. I couldn't kill him without risking Ash. That left his addiction."

"Holy shit. You cut him off. You cut him off?!" Blaise yells.

"There isn't a dealer in the state that will sell to him now."

Ash and Harley share a look while Blaise gapes at me.

"How the fuck does a Mounty have that much pull?"

I smirk at them but Harley's mind is already working. He's too smart. He's book smart and street smart, common sense and imaginative thinking all in one devastating package. "Fuck. You used a favor."

I nod slowly, staring straight into his eyes and ignoring the looks around us. He lets out the breath he was holding and rubs his neck.

I pitch my voice low so no one around us can hear. "I used one to save you. One to get Senior out of the way until graduation. Now I've used another to cut Joey off. I don't regret it and I'd do it again. We're all getting out of this alive, even if I have to call in every favor I have. That's why I have them."

Avery's hand slips into mine. Ash is blinking at me like I've sprouted fucking wings and Blaise is frowning at us.

I tuck back into my food, ignoring them until they're forced to find something else to talk about.

Chapter Twenty-Nine

The last week of classes before exams is so hectic I forget about Joey completely.

My bad leg has a flare up from how hard I push myself, and my lack of sleep. Every morning I wake up with it feeling worse than before. I see the nurse but she refuses to give me anything stronger than aspirin for it.

My tutoring sessions with Blaise become a free-for-all with everyone showing up and Avery ordering take-out so we don't have to stop to cook.

Harley insists on walking me back to the room every night and sitting next to me as we study, even though Ash is technically my tutoring student and Harley is on par with me. When I question him he looks at me like I'm mentally compromised so I drop it and give in without any further questioning.

I focus myself entirely on my exams because if I think about my choir performance I lose my stomach contents, which Blaise learns the hard way by asking me which song I've picked only to have me spew in the bathroom sink. Avery throws a textbook at his head and cusses him out. No one talks about choir after that.

I practice with Avery and she tells me over and over again how good I am. I know that should be enough to calm my insane nerves but I go to sleep each night with a sense of dread.

I'm picking swimming next year.

I wake up on the morning of our choir performances with dread lying heavy in my gut. The same amount of dread I imagine a person on death row would feel the morning of their execution. Avery nearly strains her eyes she rolls them that hard at me when I tell her.

The flare up in my leg only gets worse and I find myself walking gingerly to each of my classes. Harley watches me carefully and starts to snap at any other students walking around us if they get too close to me. It's sweet and I find myself very glad he's decided we're friends.

I refuse to eat all day and instead drink eight cups of coffee until finally Harley notices the tremors in my hands and narks on me. Avery hides the coffee and stalks me so I can't have anymore. What a bunch of assholes.

The tremble is a full body case of the shakes by the time I get to the chapel. It's full of students and various bored-looking teachers trying to corral them into some semblance of quiet and calm. I spot Harley and Ash straight away because they've cleared the bench around them for us to join them as we finish. I must look miserable because Avery tucks her arm in mine and Blaise slings a casual arm over my shoulders. I don't even have the mental capacity to enjoy the feeling. I could definitely vomit on my shoes right now and I wouldn't even care, it would not bother me in the least.

Because Miss Umber hates me, truly despises me I'm sure of it, she saves me for last. Avery goes first and sounds great. She's got a decent range, clear tones, and hits the notes she needs to. I clap with everyone else even though we're behind the curtain and she won't see. Blaise is third so he finds us a quiet spot to sit and then keeps me tucked under his arm until he has to move. When Miss Umber calls him he gives me a little squeeze and then heads out.

He's amazing.

The girls behind the curtain swoon and pant after him. I crawl out of my miserable fog for long enough to glare at them a bit, not that I blame them. I hope Avery has taken a video of it for me to enjoy later because I'm too fucking nervous to function right now. I breathe and center myself until all of my chaos is contained inside my head and not plastered over my face for everyone to see.

I watch as, one by one, the girls all disappear until Miss Umber is calling my name.

If my scholarship didn't ride on this assignment I would leave.

Fuck.

I slip one of the earplugs into my ears as I walk up to the microphone on stage. I don't look at the crowd. I don't even look at Avery. I wait until they start the song, to count myself in, before I slip the other earplug in and the silence in only broken by the thumping of my own heart. I fix my eyes onto the rose colored glass on the far wall and then I sing.

Weeks and weeks of practice.

So many sleepless nights stressing about this moment.

I fucking love it.

I lose myself in the mechanics of singing and I give it everything I've got. I pour sixteen years of anger, frustration, longing, and loneliness into my voice and when I feel the tears pick at the back of my eyes I don't even care that I'm on a stage for the entire school to see.

I push my luck and reach up to loosen one earplug just a fraction so I can hear just a little of my song. I'm fucking incredible. My hand shakes a little but I push through and finish the damn song, hearing every word I'm singing. I feel invincible.

I know in my broken and bent bones I'll sing without fear someday.

I step away from the microphone and duck my head so I don't have to look at anyone while I'm feeling so exposed. I feel raw, like my soul has been torn open and splayed out for all of Hannaford to see.

I faintly hear the applause as I move to the side of the stage and I pop out the earplugs. Avery is yelling, "Yes bitch!" at me like a lunatic and I let out a weak chuckle. Stepping down from the stage, I walk over to sit beside her on jelly legs, adrenaline riding me hard. She looks so elated that I've managed to sing the whole song without shitting myself and I grin back at her. All three boys gape at me, mirror images of shock.

"That was perfect. You should have seen how Blaise looked when you opened your mouth," Avery whispers in my ear. I fight the blush that threatens to bloom over my entire body.

I exhale and settle into my chair to watch as the first of the band students walks out with a cello and sets up. It's quiet for a second and then Blaise and Harley start bickering.

"Move," says Blaise.

"Fuck off. You've just decided to do something about it because she passed your little singing test?"

"Don't be a jealous dick and move. I need to tell her-"

"You'd have to climb over my dead fucking body and we both know I could take you. Now shut up before you get us in the shit."

What the hell? Avery is grinning so hard her face might split open when I look past her to the others. Ash has his arm linked with hers and he's staring ahead like he can't hear the war happening next to him but I can see the nerve twitching in his cheek. Harley's face is flushed with anger and he looks over at me. I don't recognize the emotion in his eyes and I'm worried he's pissed off at me again. I've just barely managed to negotiate a ceasefire with Ash, I don't want something else to start up in its place.

I fidget my way through the rest of the performances and when Mr. Trevelen finally dismisses us I'm feeling the effects of skipping food all day. When my stomach rumbles Avery sighs at me then turns to the guys. "I'm making dinner, are you coming up to eat with us or are you hitting the dining hall?"

They agree to come up and nervous flutters start deep in my stomach. My leg is still aching and when we all stand to leave my knee buckles and gives way. I manage to catch myself on the bench and when I stand again Avery wraps a hand under my elbow to support me.

"You know how I tell you not to buy me shit? If a new leg is on the table, I'll take it," I say through clenched teeth. Avery rubs my back with a little smile and helps me to hobble out of the auditorium. I must look pathetic because Ash wraps a strong arm around my waist and pulls me into his body tightly. It takes me a second to remember exactly how to breathe when I feel the hard lines of his body against mine. I hear Harley begin to grumble behind us.

"What happened?" Ash murmurs.

"My leg just likes to remind me that violence is never the answer."

Ash chuckles under his breath and my legs start to wobble for an entirely different reason. He looks down at me and the concern is easy to see. I'm so fucking confused.

"I'll be fine, I just need to get off my feet for a few days."

He nods and Harley pries Avery off of my elbow so he can support the other side of my body until I'm pretty much being carried by the two of them. Avery stares at each of the guys, one by one, like she's going to stage an intervention. When she opens her mouth Blaise tucks her under his arm and pulls her to lead the way. What the sweet fresh hell is going on?

When we get to the girls' dorms I feel every single set of eyes in the hallway follow me from where I'm wedged between Ash and Harley. Annabelle takes two steps towards us before Ash shuts her down with a single look. She hovers just outside her room and watches Harley pass with devastated eyes. He doesn't spare her so much as a glance. Mentally, I flip her the bird like a smug-ass bitch. How much does his lack of trust fund matter now, you gold digging bitch?

Avery unlocks the door and I get deposited gently on my bed. I'm too busy easing my shoes and socks off my aching leg, wincing and trying not to whimper pathetically, to realize an argument is starting around me. I only take notice when Harley's temper erupts and he yells, "Fuck you, Morrison! You and Ash are as bad as each other."

My head snaps up to see Avery standing in the middle of all three guys. Harley has his back to me but Blaise is flushed and glaring, and while Ash's face looks blank, his fists are clenched and his shoulders are rigid.

Avery glares at Harley and then pokes him on his heaving chest with a finger. "Calm the hell down. I'm not having you break my room because you're in a mood."

Harley doesn't register her words, he just widens his stance and stares down his two best friends like they're going to be brawling in under a minute.

Jesus fuck.

Clearly, I've missed something vital.

Avery thinks so, too.

"One of you idiots had better start explaining what the fuck is going on. *Now*. I've never seen you fight like this before!"

No one moves or says a word. Then, the three guys all turn and look at me.

Oh. They don't want an audience for this and clearly they still don't trust me. It's stings, it fucking stings a whole lot because I think I've proven myself to each of them a hundred times over this year, but I try not to show it. I slide off my bed and mumble something about having a shower to give them some privacy.

When Blaise takes a step towards me to help me as I hobble past them pathetically Harley honest-to-fucking-God *growls* at him and Avery steps up to take my arm.

"I need a fucking drink after this," she murmurs to me as she ferries me into the bathroom.

I take as long as I possibly can to shower, dress, and dry my hair. I brush my teeth. Floss them meticulously. I even pluck a few stray eyebrow hairs just to ensure they've finished their little chat.

I take a deep breath and exit the bathroom. Harley and Ash are already eating the Seafood Carbonara Avery has made. Blaise is doing dishes and Avery is standing at the bench grinning at me like a maniac. Like the Joker and the Cheshire Cat had a secret love child and named her Avery fucking Beaumont.

"Why are you so happy? Did Annabelle choke on a dick or something?" I ask and she gives me her best witchy cackle.

"Better. So much better. We'll talk tomorrow, just eat some dinner and rest your leg for now."

"We could talk about it now," Harley grumbles into his plate but Avery's crazy grin shifts into a glare.

"Eat your damn pasta, Arbour."

I give her a puzzled look and grab a plate. Avery helps me sit on the couch and then tries to talk me into taking some of the other pain pills her private and, I believe, shady doctor gave her. I refuse and try to focus on the TV instead of the tension in the room.

It's a weird night.

Chapter Thirty

The next morning I'm in the shower before classes when I hear a knock and Avery's head pokes in the room.

"Can I come in? I need to pee."

I nod and she shuts and locks the door behind her. She doesn't move to the toilet, instead she props herself up against the counter and gives me a smug-as-fuck look. I raise my eyebrows at her as I wash my hair out. I love the smell of this shampoo and I close my eyes as I take in deep lungfuls of it. I never want to know how much Avery spends on it.

"The boys are here for you. All three of them. They want to walk you down to breakfast," she whispers and I startle out of my daydreaming, looking over at her quickly. She grins and wiggles her eyebrows at me. *Sweet Lord.* I move a bit faster as I wash out my hair. I don't know if I can take much more of their arguing and strange behavior.

"Are you going to tell me what the hell was going on yesterday?"

The next-level, maniacal grin is back on her face. "They were bickering over your performance. Then Ash pulled you into his arms to get you back up here and all hell broke loose. Harley lost it, he already wants to kill Blaise because he's got his eye on you. Even more so because you look at him like he's dinner and you're *starving*. Now he has to contend with Ash too and he snapped."

I shut the water off and try to process what Avery is saying. Blaise has his eye on me? Harley is pissed? What the damned hell?! I grab a towel and step out of the stall. I can't find any words, but Avery doesn't seem to need my input.

"It's *killing* Harley that you look at Blaise like that. I think at this point he would give up his entire inheritance all over again to get you to look at him with those eyes instead. They we're about to throw down last night and I told them I would speak to you. I didn't want our room being destroyed when you picked which one you want. This way you can text them or something and they can throw their pity party elsewhere and my good china will be safe."

I can hear my heart pounding in my ears. I'm a little lightheaded and woozy. This is too much. I can't exist like this. There's still a week left before we leave Hannaford for the summer break and I'll have to lock myself in our room until then. It occurs to me that I've spent the entire time I've been at Hannaford lusting after these guys, hating any girl I've spotted them with, and now I apparently have their attention I want to crawl under my covers and die. I'm not equipped for casual hookups, even without the Jackal looming over me, and I know for a fact they don't do commitment. I am not the girl for them.

I need to call in reinforcements.

"Can you—can you do something for me?"

Avery's answer is instant and whispered.

"Of course. Anything."

I smile. I know she means it, too. That's how this friendship thing works. Ride or die. "I need you to talk to them. All three of them. And, like, make it so they won't give me shit about what I'm about to say because I have no fucking idea how to say this to any of them without pissing them off and starting a whole new war."

"Easy. Done," she says and the little lines between her eyebrows appear, the ones that mean she's in cleanup mode. *Good luck cleaning this up*, I want to say but I manage to reel myself in.

"Right. I had to desensitize myself from Harley. I had to spend weeks looking at abstract parts of him until I could look at him front on, in the face, without passing out."

I'm blushing so hard I think the whole room is heating up from it. Avery is clearly trying her best not to dissolve into a fit of laughter and God do I love her for it. She even manages to smother her snort into a polite cough.

"I almost had the same problem with Ash but he has always distracted me with his attitude so I can forget how… yeah. I'm still having a hard time with Blaise because I spent so long before I met him being obsessed with his songs. I used to listen to him all the time to escape from the group home and everything with the Twelve. It means that he's tied up with that whole part of my life and I can't look at him without feeling… safe. So please explain that to them all so they don't think I'm some crazed psycho fan and just let them know I'm dealing with it. I want to be their friend and not look at him like he's…dinner. I don't want to ruin their friendships or ours just for a quick fuck."

Avery gives me this look, with her brows arched up and her eyes squinted up a little, like she's trying to figure out just how dense I am. I try not to squirm.

"You know all three of them are bordering on obsessed with you, right? Ash is freaking the hell out because he can't figure out when his loathing of you turned into admiration, affection, and lust. Blaise damn near died when he heard you sing because he'd been trying to put you in the little 'do-not-touch' box in his head because of Harley and then your voice burnt the box right down to the ground and, well, we all know how Harley feels. This is not about sex. Well, I'm sure they would be *very* interested in having sex with you but it's more than that."

Panic rises in my chest, bubbling and frothing until I think I might choke on it. My voice comes out thready as I say, "No, I didn't know. I know nothing. This is all very new information for me."

"Jesus H. Christ, Lips. I thought you were refusing to start anything with any of them because you were pissed about last year and wanted to string them along a bit. I was kind of assuming the hot/cold thing you have with them all was foreplay!"

I crumble onto the floor in a heap, oblivious to the fact I am only half wrapped in a towel and I am probably showing off a whole heap of skin to Avery. She sighs and cracks the door open an inch. I blush again, remembering that all three of the guys are waiting in our room for us to come out. I take a deep breath and try not to expire right there on the floor. They can't see me with Avery's body blocking me. Can I look them in the eye after this? God, this is worse than fighting my way through the Game. Give me a target to take out and I'm golden, give me three guys who like me and I'm dying inside. What the hell am I going to do?

"We'll meet you guys down at the dining hall...no, we're fine... Ash, I have cramps and I need a minute to get myself together and I'd rather not have you lot out there listening to me change out tampons... well, if you listened to me the first time I wouldn't have to supply you with the details... no, Lips is still getting dressed... we're girls, she isn't worried about my period, she has her own to deal with. Bye!"

She closes the door and smirks at me.

"You've clearly scarred your brother for life," I choke out but I'm smiling, her joy is infectious.

"I had to go to great lengths to get them the hell out. Harley did not flinch, by the way, he was totally prepared to deal with a blood-soaked Armageddon to stay here and walk you down. The other two manhandled him out."

I flip onto my back and groan. Avery finally breaks and laughs hysterically. When she finally calms down, wiping tears from her cheeks, she pegs me with a look though it's a gentle one.

"We've never actually talked about this so I'm requesting this as your truth for the day. Are you a virgin?"

I groan. "As if you can't tell from my absolute meltdown. Yes, I am. I'm attracted to guys but I've always stayed the hell away from them. The risks with the Jackal were just too much to even try to get my head around it."

Avery hands me my underwear and then she fluffs her hair and checks her makeup while I dress.

"I am too. I've always wanted a boy who loves me like the boys do and Rory was the first guy I thought came close. And, well, you know what happened with Atticus. Clearly I'm terrible at judging a man's character."

I blow out a breath and button my blouse. White-hot rage courses through me every time the name Rory comes out of Avery's mouth.

"Don't beat yourself up. I thought he was obsessed with you too. I just didn't realize he saw you as an object rather than a person."

She shrugs and gives me a sad smile in the mirror. "We can't fix my love life so let's sort yours out. Which one do you like the best? No judgment."

I stop and sit on the closed toilet seat. Which one? Fuck. I think about Ash's face when we did CPR on that kid last year. I think about Blaise's staunch defense when Devon cornered me in the boys' locker room. I think about Harley's eyes when he watched me break Harlow's nose. My body is taken over by a shiver.

"I don't know. I like them all."

Avery pauses then a slow smile spreads across her face as she scoots my shoes towards me. She's basically dressing me, helping me through my breakdown. "I can work with that. I did tell those guys the only way they would ever have a relationship that worked is if were with the same girl."

A hot wave of lust throbs through my body even as I gasp and sputter at her. "The same girl? You think they'll all want to date me together? Avery!"

She cackles and shoves open the bathroom door. I hesitantly peek out to make sure the room is in fact empty.

"They love each other too much to truly let this come between them. But I also think they all might like you too much to let you go. I've *never* seen them fight over a girl before and the bickering that happens when you're not around is getting extreme."

I blanch. How would that even work? I'm a virgin and not exactly ready for a gang bang! Holy fucking shit. Avery pulls out her phone and starts tapping out a text. I wring my hands for a minute until she notices and gives me a smirk.

"I can see you melting down over this. Don't panic. I'm just saying Harley has never wanted to date someone. Ever. Blaise burned the dating bridge years ago after something happened. Ash… doesn't ever let people in. That's the real reason he pushed back about us being friends and now he can't stand the idea of going home at the end of the week and not seeing you for summer break. He's already bugging me about finding a way to escape from Joey and stay with you and Harley in the Bay. Just trust that we can work something out that makes everyone happy."

"What about you? Wouldn't it be weird to have all of us together like that?" I tuck my arm into hers as we start down the hall towards breakfast.

"Not really. It actually makes my life easier. I trust you. I trust you with my brother. I trust you with Harley and Blaise. I'm not worried about you stabbing us all in the back. This is the best idea I've ever had."

We arrive at the dining hall to find it very nearly empty. With the stress of exams at an all time high most students just didn't care about coming down and eating a formal breakfast so the boys were only joined by a small handful of freshmen, so terrified of them that they're sitting at the opposite end of the table. My stomach roils at the sight of them.

"Breathe kid," Avery says with a smile as she squeezes my arm that's tucked in close to her own.

I don't look over at the table because I'm barely keeping my aching leg in line as it is, I can't afford to go weak at the knees. Avery grabs a tray but I doubt I'll be able to eat while I'm thinking about my potential polyandrous relationship. Or the ramifications of said relationship if the Jackal finds out. *Sweet lord.* I grab a glass of juice and an apple and ignore Avery's sharp look.

"You're skin and bones as it is. I'm getting you some French toast."

I *do* love the French toast they serve here. I give her a tiny nod and she directs me to the table. I can feel all three of the boys watching us and I want to scream. Avery must feel my arm tense and she drops her tray with more force than necessary and their attention snaps away from me. She sits and arches an eyebrow at them while she sets out our food.

"Don't start. Lips can't eat when she's stressed."

Great. Now I feel pathetic. I cringe and nudge the plate away from me.

"If Harley is bothering you—"

Avery cuts Blaise off. "I said, *don't start.*" she hisses. I glance up just in time to see Harley elbow Blaise in the stomach while Ash watches me intently.

"I'm never going to eat again. Goodbye boobs, it was nice having you," I mutter and Avery cackles.

"That will shut them up! The boobs are in danger."

Harley snorts and shoves the French toast back at me. "Save the boobs, Mounty."

I flush and start eating while they all laugh around me. I refuse to look up from my plate. By not meeting any of their eyes my stomach settles enough that I can begin to eat.

"So! Plans for summer break?" Avery says brightly and is met with a chorus of groans.

"I'm getting dragged to New York by my father to see what's new with the Kora branch there. I'm looking forward to exactly none of it and I'm pissed off I won't be touring," says Blaise and he pours me another glass of juice. I manage to thank him without stuttering and I'm so damn proud of myself.

Harley scratches the back of his head and chips in, "Two weeks on the coast to see my mom. Then Mounts Bay." He says it like a promise. The other two give him a look and I glance away from them all.

"We'll be going to Amsterdam to celebrate Joey's graduation. He chose the city and Father agreed because he'll want to spend some time in the red light district I imagine. Hopefully he catches something terminal. Or at the very least something that makes his dick rot and fall off. Lips?" says Ash.

I snort at his optimism. I push my now empty plate aside and wipe my mouth with one of the linen napkins Hannaford supplies, like this is a fancy restaurant not a high school dining hall. Harley is watching me with his usual intensity but now I see it for what it is. He *likes* me. *Sweet lord.*

"I have a couple of jobs lined up. Oh, and some Club events to go to," I say mildly. Avery watches me with interest but she doesn't question me. I know she's waiting to see just how much I'm willing to say in front of the boys. "I have some… plans in the pipeline that I'm working on. Lots of groundwork and carefully thought out moves."

Avery hums and pulls out her phone like I've reminded her of her own plans. I'm hit in the chest at how much I'm going to miss talking to her over the break. Texting just isn't the same and I've gotten used to bouncing ideas off of her. It sucks.

Ash clears his throat and he asks, tentatively, "You're going back to the Jackal, then?"

All or nothing. If I'm not honest with them about this then I can't date… any of them. They have to know the real risks. I glance around but we're still alone. "No, I'm not going back to him. Do you guys know what the Club is? Who the Twelve are?"

Only Blaise looks unsure. "They're like gang leaders, right?"

I wince. Not a good start. "Not quite. Some are, the Jackal included. He deals drugs, runs firearms, dabbles in extortion when the payoff is high enough. But really, each member of the Twelve have their own set of skills and they build on that." They all nod along and I give myself one last inhale before I blurt it out.

"I was thirteen when the Hawk died and a spot opened up in the Twelve. They ran the Game, which should really have it's name changed to 'brutal torture sessions'. The Jackal sponsored me. I went up against thirty men and I won."

Avery's hand slips into mine and she squeezes, lending her support even though she doesn't look up from her phone. I try not to hold my breath as I wait. It takes a second and then they all speak at once.

"You won?"

"Thirty men?"

"What the fuck?!"

Avery scoffs at them all and looks up from the screen. "All hail the Wolf of

Mounts Bay."

"The Wolf?!" sputters Harley. Oh, *crap*. He's heard about me. His eyes roam all over my face and my arms then he ducks down and looks under the table at my legs. Avery kicks him in the shin sharply. "We're wearing skirts, idiot!"

He doesn't look fazed as he faces me again, my cheeks on fire, and says, "You took out one of my distant cousins in the Game. His dad was fucking livid and went after you with a blowtorch."

Avery's hand does a sort of spasm in mine. She's seen that particular scar a few times though I've never told her how I got it. It's the one I had to show Darcy to prove Lance was lying about fucking me.

"Yeah. Sorry about that."

Harley stares at me for another second and then tips his head back to roar with laughter. "I can't believe we were all worried about Joey killing you. If only he knew everything you've done. Why didn't you just sneak into his room and slit his throat while he slept?"

I want the ground to open up and swallow me. He knows. He knows exactly what skill set I have that is so highly sought after. I feel dizzy. Maybe I'm not ready for the two separate lives I live to merge. Fuck.

"Shut up, asshole, you're freaking her out," growls Blaise. He *growls* it, just like he growls into his microphone on the stage but I'm too anxious to enjoy the sound of it. I fix my gaze on my cutlery, still sticky with the syrup from my breakfast, until the pounding in my ears stops.

I take a deep breath before I look back up at them. I know I'm going to see disgust and fear and even hatred on their faces. How could anyone hear about what I've done without thinking about just how dirty my hands are? All this time the guys had all been talking about how much of a sociopath Joey is but the truth is...

The truth is my hands are bloodier than his.

Harley looks gutted, all the amusement wiped clean from his face. Blaise looks pissed. Ash is, well, he's got his cold detached mask fixed carefully over his features.

"I'm at Hannaford to get as far away from that life as I can. I wasn't a willing participant. I had two choices: play the Game or die at the Jackal's hands. Everything I've done has been to keep myself alive."

"I didn't mean—" Harley says but Avery cuts him off.

"Lips, you should head to class. I'll meet you there, I need to have a chat with the guys."

I nod and stoop down to grab my bag. I can hear them start to bicker and pointedly don't look back as I hobble out of the dining hall.

I was so close to having something I really want and once again my past has ruined it for me.

Chapter Thirty-One

My leg gives out halfway to my first class and I'm forced to grit my teeth and hobble back to my room. When the pain of my leg hits I can always feel exactly where the pins are holding the bones together. It's like they're pulsing under my skin and muscles, and I get queasy if I think about it too much. I shoot Avery a quick text to let her know where I am then climb back into the shower to try and ease some of the pain in my aching bones with the scalding water.

It takes me ten minutes to get dry and dressed while hopping on one leg and I'm in so much pain I finally cave and take some of the pain medication Avery found for me.

As predicted, the second they kick in I'm high as a kite.

The benefits of having a low drug tolerance is I am no longer worried about the guys' reaction over breakfast. My brain is soup and I'm giggling over nothing for hours, rolling around on my bed and just cackling to myself. I can kind of see why my mom was so hell bent in staying in this state of euphoria. The sheets feel amazing on my bare skin.

There's a knock at the door sometime later but I can't make my legs work to get up and answer it. I'm not sure I even manage to call out but the person stomps away and leaves me to my delirium.

Then there's the sound of keys and only Avery has those so I leave my eyes shut and keep stroking the soft sheets on my bed. Avery bought me these sheets. She's so nice. I think about telling her that.

"You're not thinking anything, you're speaking. How fucking high are you?"

My eyes pop open. That's not Avery's voice.

"No shit. She's still got exams so I came up to check that you're okay. She told me to force the pills down your throat but it looks like you've got that under control."

Nope. I squeeze my eyes shut again. I cannot have Blaise in this room while I'm off my tits. Bad idea. I can't have him around until I'm back... on my tits. Or whatever the opposite of this is.

"Stop saying tits. Look, I can't leave you here like this. Fuck knows what you could end up doing to yourself. Stop stroking the sheets, it's... kinda hot and I'm feeling like a perv watching you. Just get in the bed. In, Lips. Get in bed. Fucking hell, here."

His hands touch me as he guides me under the sheets and I shiver. I clamp my mouth shut, I even slap a hand over it for good measure, and then, Lord help me, his breath tickles the nape of my neck as he huffs out a laugh. The bed dips as the blankets are pulled up around my chin.

I open my eyes and find Blaise sitting with his back against my headboard, his legs stretched out and pressed against me, with his phone out and a smirk on his face. He's on top on the blankets so I'm trapped. He's not wearing his uniform, he has an old Vanth shirt on that I would steal from him in a heartbeat and some sweatpants that look like regular ones but probably cost more than a months rent in LA. He hits the dial button and then he's talking too loud and way too smug.

"Have you ever seen Lips high before? It's adorable...she's fine but I'm not leaving her... she's in bed...I've finished my exams, I'll email the rest of my classes for the day and tell them I have a migraine or whatever... I swear to you, she's fine, she's just off her tits. Her words, not mine... okay, bye."

He tosses his phone onto my nightstand and then shuffles down until his head is on my pillow and he turns to lay on his side, facing me. When I turn my head to look at him we're so close that the back of my hand, still clamped tightly over my mouth, brushes against his lips. I feel him smile and I snatch my hand away quickly.

I will not leave this room with my dignity intact.

"What's wrong, little Nightingale?" Blaise murmurs and his hand brushes my hair away from my face. I think my cheeks would be on fire if I wasn't so out of it. My eyes roam over his face in a way I've never let myself before. I take in his jawline, the dusting of light freckles over his nose I've never noticed before, the eerie clear depths of his eyes.

"This is going to go very badly and then you're never going to speak to me again. After all my work this year to get you guys to trust me and now I've fucked it." It takes a ton of focus to get the words out and my voice is still all weird and floaty. Floaty is a strange word.

"Right, it is a strange word but let's stay on topic." Shit, I'm saying stuff without realizing it again. "Yes, you are. You haven't fucked anything. Harley wasn't pissed this morning, he was impressed. Then he was awkward and embarrassed because he upset you."

Huh.

I try to file that away in my brain for later but I think I've lost the filing cabinet. I think the office is closed for maintenance. I hope they repaint.

"Fuck, we need to get you stoned. I need to see you on THC."

Nope. Whiskey or nothing. Vodka in emergencies. Possibly tequila but sometimes I get mouthy and fight...-y on tequila.

"Duly noted. Your phone keeps buzzing. Want me to get it?"

I nod and then when Blaise leans away from me I take a second to try and breathe while he's out of my space. When he comes back I still feel like there's not enough oxygen in my blood. Or my damn brain.

He hands me my phone but I can't get my eyes to focus, they just dance away from the screen and back onto the little dip in the middle of Blaise's clavicle. It's a nice dip.

"Here. It's from Matteo, who's that? He says he can't wait to see you tomorrow. He calls you Starbright, what the hell does that mean?"

I struggle to sit up out of my cocoon and Blaise has to prop me up. I think whatever my face is doing worries him enough to help me out. I grab his biceps and give him a little shake. "Don't ever tell anyone. That's the Jackal. He's bad. You can't tell anyone his name. He wants me to go to see him but I'm going to put him off. I don't like him and I definitely don't want to fuck him."

I'm shockingly coherent for a second. Blaise nods and runs his hand up and down my spine, soothing me like I'm a skittish toddler. Well, I guess I am at the moment. Sweet Lord, I am never taking any medication from Avery again. I take a deep breath and focus myself for another moment.

"Most importantly, don't ever tell anyone my middle name is Starbright."

I watch the acrobatics his eyebrows and mouth go through as he struggles to stop himself from laughing at me. I'm too fucked to appreciate it fully. When his stunning green eyes finally meet my own he speaks with such sincerity that I know he means every word.

"I will take your secret to the grave, Mounty."

I wake up slowly, hazy and disorientated.

The room is dark, illuminated only by the dancing colored lights from the TV. I'm not lying straight on the bed how I fell asleep, my back is curved and my pillow is pressed into my spine. There's a weight over my hips holding me still. I wriggle a little and I hear a groan behind me.

"For the love of god, Mounty, don't move like that. Avery has already threatened to castrate me twice tonight," whispers Harley and I struggle to sit up with a gasp.

My lower half is draped over his lap, legs bare and my ass barely covered in my teeny pajama shorts. My upper half, Jesus *fucking Christ*, is tucked in Blaise's lap. He grins down at me and I notice his hands are tangled in my hair, like he's been playing with it while I slept.

I scoot off of them both and my ass lands between them.

"What the—"

"Chill. You were thrashing about in your sleep and it took all three of us to settle you back down," Avery chips in from the kitchen where she's brewing her usual cup of chamomile tea. She's wiping down every surface as she goes with a calm hand and that relaxes something in my chest.

I refuse to look at either of the guys as I wriggle back to sit between them against the headboard. Blaise huffs a laugh at me and I blush. "You must be feeling better, there's color on your cheeks again."

The flush on my cheeks gets worse and I clear my throat. "Thank you for checking on me. And letting me word vomit for hours on end. Please leave me to die of shame with what little dignity I have left."

Harley scoffs and pulls out his phone, bringing up a video and handing it over to me. There I am, sitting on Blaise's lap, giggling like a mad woman and stroking his chest like I had spent hours doing to the sheets. I can see he's filming us both and with the smug look on his face it's clear he sent this to Harley to piss him off.

I elbow him but it's like elbowing a freaking wall.

"Hey, they asked me why I called you adorable. I figured a video was better than any explanation I could come up with."

"I am never taking those pills again. I'll white knuckle it through the pain next time," I declare and they all, Avery included, laugh their asses off at me. I can't remember much from the day. I know Blaise has been here the longest but my brain feels like it's full of fog when I try to think about what happened. Not great.

There's a knock at the door and Avery opens it to find Ash standing there in his track uniform and a gym bag slung over his shoulder. Sweaty, flushed, and utterly delectable. I'm sandwiched between two insanely hot guys and I'm still managing to drool over a third. What the hell is wrong with me?

"Mr. Embley is a demon. I'm not doing track next year, fuck him and his shitty attitude," he sulks as he strides in. Avery scrunches her nose up at him and shoves him towards the bathroom.

"Go shower, you're not sleeping here covered in sweat."

I mean, I'd let him sleep in my bed covered in sweat except there is literally no room left with the other two lounging on it.

It's then that I remember my conversation with Blaise. We'd been in the bathroom after my leg had given out on my way to the toilet. For a single horrifying second I can't remember if he was there while I peed but then the memory clears. He stepped out and waited for me to yell for him. *Sweet merciful lord*, this is bad.

He'd held me up while I washed my hands and told me about how they decided to share me. They sat at the freaking dining hall table and came to an agreement to *share me*. All of the blood in my head drains out and I feel floaty all over again.

I scramble onto my hands and knees again and slide straight off the bed, wincing as my leg protests. I don't look back to see the guys reactions and Avery giggles at me as I tug her into the closet by the sleeve of her Chanel robe.

"What happened to discreet?" I croak and she gives me a side-eye.

"I was discreet. Then they decided to woo you as a group and as a result we're having to deal with them all here at once. Now that you're awake and Ash is here we're going to watch some bullshit thriller movie Blaise insists on and then they'll sleep here."

Woo me? Christ. I do not like the look on Avery's face at all. It's glee mixed with her usual dose of evil and I'm really getting worried that she's about to throw me under the bus. Not anything mean or dangerous, just embarrass the utter crap out of me for her own sick pleasure. There's a reason we've ended up best friends.

"Why are the two of you whispering in the closet?"

I squeak and turn to find Ash standing in the doorway, rubbing his hair with one of Avery's fluffy white towels. He has one of those damn tank tops on again and I *refuse* to look at his nipples.

"Secret girls business," says Avery in her most innocent voice.

He rolls his eyes at her. "With the two of you that could be anything from pairing the correct shoes with an outfit to plotting the murder of a filthy rich senator for your own gain."

I scoff at him and cross my arms but he makes a good point. Avery pats him on the chest and says, "Lips is freaking out about where everyone is sleeping. The drugs have scrambled her brain and she's woken up in her ideal fantasy orgy."

Nope.

I spin on my heel and charge towards the bathroom to lock myself away from his raucous laughter at Avery's words. I've never heard him laugh like that before. He calls out to me as I pass him, "You'll have to pause those dirty thoughts, Mounty, Avery has already threatened our dicks if we so much as kiss your cheek in front of her."

They all laugh and I close the door firmly, flicking the lock.

I cannot survive this.

The movie is terrible but the popcorn is good.

Ash kicks Blaise off of my bed and he sprawls onto the floor so he's closer to the TV. Avery gives up on watching it twenty minutes in and falls asleep, perfectly comfortable in her Cal King bed by herself.

It takes me most of the movie to stop twitching and settle down enough to get tired. Ash and Harley don't try to touch me at all, true to their word to Avery, and it's only after Blaise turns the TV off and settles himself on the couch that I realize they're not planning on leaving the bed.

I've never shared a bed before and it makes me panic for a bit in the dark. What if I'm annoying in my sleep? What if I thrash around or snore or drool? What if all of the sexy, irresistible testosterone in the room gives me a sex dream and I moan in my sleep? Christ.

I can tell by his breathing when Harley falls asleep and then when Blaise passes out he's gently snoring. It's a cute sound and I smile. I relax back into the mattress and sigh.

I'm almost asleep when I feel a hand on my hip and then Ash is turning me to face away from him and he's tucking me into his chest. Once he's got me where he wants me, a leg between mine and my head pillowed on his bicep, he strokes the bare skin of my leg gently. It's not a sexual touch, just a light comforting stroke until I doze off too.

I've never been so comfortable.

Chapter Thirty-Two

I'm too warm.

There's a thumb tracing the seam of my lips, stroking the soft skin rhythmically, and when I shift the arm around my waist tightens. I open my eyes to find Harley staring at me in the darkness, the blue of his eyes barely visible in the shadows. Ash's breathing is still deep and steady on my neck so I know he's still asleep and Blaise's gentle snores are still the only noise in the room.

Harley moves to brush his fingers over my cheek and my heart does a little dance in my chest. I want to know what time it is but I don't want to speak or move in case we wake the others. This little moment is just for us.

His eyebrows do that thing where he's asking me a question. I'm not entirely fluent in the language yet but I nod. Whatever he wants right now I'm ready to give him.

His lips pull into a slow, lascivious smirk and then he presses a finger to them to tell me to stay silent. I nod, just a little so Ash doesn't wake up, and then he shifts forward to cup my face in his hands and he kisses me.

It starts out sweet, all light touches and gentle sweeps of his tongue on mine, but he's been hungry for me for a long time and I've been starving for him for longer. He pushes and pushes until he's pressed up against me, pressing me back into his sleeping cousin, and I'm shaking. I hold his wrists just so I have an anchor because I'm drunk on his mouth and rapidly forgetting that we're supposed to be quiet. His thumbs stroke my cheeks reverently even as his mouth is a hot, demanding brand on my own.

"Avery is going to fucking murder you," whispers Ash and I startle away from Harley's lips.

Oh God.

I know they said they were going to share me but I don't know if this was what they were intending. I'm tangled in Ash's limbs and making out with Harley like his lips are an oxygen tank and I'm fucking drowning. My entire body flushes scarlet and I squirm with shame. Harley leans forward and breathes, "Shh…" onto my lips as he kisses me again. I wriggle to pull away from him but then Ash's lips graze my neck and his arm across my waist tightens to keep me where I am. Harley swallows my sigh and Ash grins against my skin before sucking and biting the soft curve where my neck meets my shoulder. As he pulls my shirt collar to find more skin he mumbles, "I'm blaming you if she catches us."

Harley only pulls away from me long enough to whisper back, "Fucking worth it," and then he's sucking my bottom lip into his mouth and dragging his hands down my throat possessively. It's a move that would send me spiraling if any other person were to do it but with Harley it sets my blood on fire and I start to squirm all over again. Ash grunts and plants a hand on my hip to stop my movement and Harley pulls away again, panting.

"Fuck. I'm going to be late for training. I was supposed to be at the pool ten minutes ago," he says, scowling and staring at my lips. I lick them without thinking and he groans.

"That sound had better be an oh-i-hate-waking-up sort of sound and not a my-dick-is-so-hard kind of sound, Harley Éibhear Arbour," Avery snaps.

I am mortified.

The two idiots in my bed are not.

Harley rolls out and when Avery screeches at him and throws a pillow at him he stalks to the bathroom laughing. "I can't help having morning wood, Aves. Better get used to it because me and my blue balls will be here all week."

Avery levels Ash with a vicious glare and his face shifts into an innocent mask. I snort at his attempt to placate her.

"Don't you *dare* get out of that bed until you have your dick under control or I will cut it the *fuck* off. I know how, Lips taught me," she hisses and then throws herself out of bed and stomps to the coffee machine.

"Good morning, my beloved sister, I hope you've slept well. I'd love a coffee, thank you for asking."

Avery starts slamming cups onto the bench and cursing us all out. I choose to plead the fifth and keep my mouth shut. Harley emerges from the bathroom dressed in his sports gear and kisses Avery's cheek with a grin. She cusses him out too but hands him one of her reusable takeaway cups to take down to the pool. He ducks back to the bed and pecks me on the cheek too, with a wink, and then he's out the door.

"What time is it and why the fuck are we awake? It's the weekend, for fuck's sake," Blaise grumbles.

"How is your dick this morning, Morrison?" Avery says as she stomps into the bathroom and slams the door.

Blaise blinks and then turns to face us. "It's too fucking early for this shit."

He rolls off the couch and stumbles over to the bed, slipping into the side Harley just climbed out of.

"Getting in here is just going to piss her off more," I say but I'm secretly swooning. Ash scoffs at me and kisses my neck again before untangling his limbs from mine and sliding out of the bed. He starts rummaging through Avery's drawers and pulls out a pair of his jeans to pull on. It must be nice to have so many clothes you can just leave them everywhere, just in case you may need them. Sigh. Rich kids.

"I'll walk her to ballet and then we can all meet for a late breakfast in the dining hall. Morrison, you have one hour. Use it wisely."

Blaise is already snoring.

I laugh at him and stretch out like a cat in the sun. I'm content. I'm nervous as all fuck about…dating, I guess…three guys, the three hottest guys at Hannaford, but I'm still so happy I could scream.

I get up and drink my coffee, even though it's on the colder side. Avery squeezes my hand as she passes with a little grin, which I return. I know she's being a tyrant about the guys so they take things slow with me. She may be the master manipulator but I'm getting pretty good at spotting her work.

Blaise is still asleep when I'm out of the shower and ready to eat. If I were bold I'd go climb on top of him and wake him with a kiss. Or more.

I'm still pathetically nervous about this.

So I stomp around the room like a herd of elephants only to find that Blaise could sleep through the apocalypse if need be. Great. I send a message to the group text to confirm the time we're heading down and he doesn't wake for his phone either. Fuck's sake!

I pull my big girl panties on and give him a little shake. He moans obscenely and I blush. He's made that noise for me before but I was sucking on his tongue at the time.

"If you want to join us all for breakfast you need to get up now."

He cracks one eye open and squints at me. His voice is rough and delicious. "Why can't we eat here? In four hours like normal people?"

"I want French toast. Avery will have fruit and yogurt, Ash will get pancakes and you and Harley will have mountains of scrambled eggs and bacon. I'm not cooking four different breakfasts and Avery will stab you if you ask her to. Come on, we only have a week left of catered breakfasts."

He pushes himself up and I have to squash the urge to run my hands through his hair. His arms flex invitingly as he leans back to look at me. He grins and jerks his head at me.

"Get over here. I want a good morning kiss, then I'll get up."

I scoff at him and arch an eyebrow but his grin just gets wider. I lean down to give him a quick peck on the cheek and he snaps his hands out to jerk me into his lap. I'm not at all proud of the squeal that comes out of me but I manage to tamp down my reflexes so I don't punch him in the throat.

I should probably warn them all about that.

"A proper kiss, little Nightingale, don't cheat me."

We're going to be late for breakfast.

Blaise tucks me under his arm as we walk down to the dining hall and I decide I'm never going to get used to being that close to him. He didn't shower, just threw a pair of jeans on like Ash did, and yet he smells incredible. I kind of thought guys were supposed to be dirty and smelly but these three, *my three*, were obviously the unicorns of the species. Lucky freaking me. No, seriously.

We find Avery and Ash waiting outside the dining hall for us and when we slip into the line Harley texts to say he's on his way. Ash grabs food for Avery, Harley, and himself and Blaise organizes ours. Again, it's something I've seen them do for each other a hundred times and finding myself included is jarring but in the best way.

Avery scares the shit out of some freshmen sitting in our usual seats and we sit. By the time we have the plates set out Harley arrives, his hair dripping and his eyes a little red from all the chlorine.

"How are the blue balls?" Avery says sweetly and I groan, burying my face in

319

my hands.

Harley gives her a haughty look. "I'll worry about my own balls thanks, Floss."

I abandon my French toast and grab my apple. Ash's eyes narrow at me and he pushes the plate back in front of me. Great. More food police.

"Well, my balls aren't blue. Harley will just have to learn to jerk off a bit more often," Blaise drawls and Ash snorts at him.

Avery's eyes reach subzero temperatures. "Not in my shower he won't. Keep those activities in your room."

Blaise grins and hands me his iPod. I have a mouthful so I nod in thanks and scroll through the playlist. He's titled it 'Starlight, Starbright', the cheeky asshole, and I kinda wanna throat punch him. He laughs at the face I pull and says to Avery, "It's fine, we'll just tempt Lips into our room for the rest of the week."

Lord have mercy on my fucking soul.

I tense and Harley, who's watching me carefully, kicks Blaise in the shin so hard his chair scrapes back. Blaise grunts and curses Harley with such vehemence that the students around us take notice. Ash joins Harley to glare at him.

"Are you fucking dense? We're surrounded, there's an ongoing bet, and Lips is still being watched," hisses Ash, while Avery laughs so no one around us can hear him.

Blaise cringes and looks at me apologetically. I take pity on him because, well, I did let him walk me down here with his arm around me and we haven't exactly talked about what we're doing and the risks.

"Don't bother. Lips has no interest in fucking a guy from Hannaford, she's said it a million times. Find someone who's actually up for it," Harley says, loud enough that the students eating around us can hear and start whispering amongst themselves.

I shoot him a thankful look. Avery takes over and starts talking about her dance recital that we're all going to on Monday.

When the room empties out a bit and we have a little more privacy I decide to address the elephant in the room, the third…wait, no, fifth wheel in our relationship. Fuck.

"I feel like we should be talking about the dangers of doing this. I mean, we can't even sit here and have a conversation without my…baggage coming into it."

Avery clears her throat, kisses my cheek, and then walks off with her phone. I was kind of hoping for her support and input but I guess this is technically a relationship conversation.

"We're not in this for the bet and until you get the Jackal situation under control we'll just be more… discreet about what's going on. Our only other option is to wait until he's not a problem anymore and I don't want to do that. " Harley crosses his arms and stares across the table at me.

Ash hums under his breath, watching over Avery as she takes a call on the far side of the room. "Is there a plan to get him to back off? Do we have any idea of how long it will take?"

I shrug and push my empty plate away. "There is a plan but it's not underway yet. It hasn't been my focus. I've been working on more pressing issues."

The guys all share a look and then Ash says, "I think it's now the most pressing issue."

I blush but I don't let myself break eye contact with him. "I understand that it's important but there's still other things that need to be dealt with. Joey, Senior, the

O'Cronin family, all of them are important to take care of as well."

Harley shakes his head but Blaise answers for them all, "No, top priority is now dealing with the Jackal. Your life is the one at stake and the other situations are… survivable."

Only because I've been working on them but I don't mention it so instead I nod and try to blink back the tears prickling my eyes.

Avery having my back all year has been a totally foreign concept, even if I have loved every second of it but this is almost too much for me. These three have all just agreed that I'm the priority, that my safety trumps every other issue we have going on. My welfare and safety has never been a priority to anyone other than myself. It's a terrifying, amazing thing.

Every night for the last week of school I go to sleep with at least one other person in my bed. There's no more kissing because the guys all seem worried about Avery's self-confessed castration skills but it helps me to settle into being close to them. I mean, they're too fucking hot and I can't think about them agreeing to *share me* without ruining my panties but I no longer blush at their mere proximity.

On Wednesday there's an argument over dinner about who has to take the couch and Avery kicks them all out. I wake in the morning with my face smooshed into Harley's chest and Avery yelling at him for breaking in. She rants at him all day until he finally admits he swiped her keys on the way out and then used them to get back in when he knew she'd be asleep. Sneaky little shit.

On Friday, Avery is getting ready for her end-of-year ballet party and tells the guys they have to clean out all of their clothes they've left behind. I'm sitting on my bed and stressing about leaving Hannaford tomorrow. I don't know how to be in a relationship at all and now I'm trying to navigate a secret plural relationship long distance, with a mobster's son, a murderous billionaire's son, and a rock star. I try to be subtle about asking what the hell we're doing but I'm not exactly a subtle kind of girl. Harley laughs at my attempts.

"Where are you staying in Mounts Bay? Like I said, I'm taking two weeks to visit Ma and then I'm staying in the Bay. I can get a hotel or stay with you, your choice."

He's folding shirts Avery left in a pile on her bed for him and shoving them in a bag while she throws things into her dance bag. Ash is digging through her closet and Blaise is raiding the fridge for beer. I take a breath and just drive in. "Look, Avery's informed me that there's going to be… wooing."

"What the actual fuck is *wooing?*" Harley sounds appropriately disgusted. Blaise roars with laughter, the type that makes him throw his head back and clutch his stomach. It's a good look. He hands Harley a beer and lounges on my bed as he drinks his own.

Ash sounds smug as he calls out, "Avery is secretly eighty years old and thinks that wooing is the current terminology for——"

"For what, Ash?" Avery cuts in sweetly. He pauses and she knows she's got him trapped. It's hilarious and anxiety inducing. Then he shocks the shit out us both by smiling at her and just laying it out there. "For starting something important."

Right. I tug on the front of Blaise's Vanth shirt to get his attention. It's not the one I got back from Harlow for him but it's still super rare. "I really don't care what we're calling it. I'm taking this shirt. I'm also taking that black one of Ash's, and Harley's gray sweatshirt. I'll give them back after the break."

Blaise stares at me, stunned, and then sits up to reach over his head with one arm and pull the shirt off in the typical hot guy way. When he hands it to me the fabric still warm from his skin. I'm getting better at containing my swooning but *sweet lord*. Fuck. Me.

No, seriously.

Fuck. Me.

He's all golden skin, colorful tattoos, and toned muscles. I struggle to focus anywhere other than his naked torso. I'm not sure what I was expecting to happen when I literally told him I wanted the shirt from his back but it sure as shit wasn't this.

"Thank you," I squeak and he fucking winks at me before rooting around in his bag to pull on another one.

Avery side-eyes the shit out of me and then she grins. "How long have you wanted that Vanth shirt?"

I shrug. "Oh, you know, all my life. I'm totally lying, he'll have to pry this from my cold, dead hands. I know at least eight Mounty girls that would gut me for it so I'm going to wear it to the next party I have to go to."

I see the glimmer in Harley's eyes as he laughs with Avery and for a second I'm afraid he's jealous. When he tugs his sweatshirt over my head I instinctively inhale and take in a big lungful of his heady scent. He watches me and the glimmer turns into something predatory. I love it.

Avery waves at us all and then heads out for her party. Ash wanders back over from the closet with an armful of his clothes.

"You're taking our shit so you can smell us while we're gone? That's horribly sappy, Mounty," Ash drawls but he hands over the black shirt I requested and then neatly piles his clothes into a box.

"I'm weird. I wear guys' shirts and sweaters with booty shorts and skirts. I listen to the same three albums on repeat. I like French toast, coffee, and cherry anything. I don't function my birthday or Christmas. I can kill a grown man eight different ways with nothing but my bare hands. I'm never going to be normal."

Ash grabs my chin and stares down at me, the blank mask gone and in its place a smoldering intensity. I can't look away.

"If you're trying to warn us off it's not going to work. We've never agreed to anything as quickly as when we agreed to share you. I'm not planning on *wooing* you, I'm planning on doing whatever I need to do to get to keep you."

I swallow and he licks his lips.

"I want *us* to keep you. I don't want you all to myself, I want to share you with my best friends and I want you to love every fucking second of it."

There isn't a lie in his eyes, only plain truth and desire. I nod and he eases up a little with a smirk.

"I won't get out of bed before the coffee machine is on. I hate blues music and listen to Vanth as religiously as you do. I run track because it makes me feel like I'm dying and sometimes I need to feel like that. I miss my mom and I hate my father. My brother is trying to kill me and my father is taking bets on how long it'll take him to succeed. Finding Joey standing over Avery's lifeless body broke something in me that I don't think I'll ever be able to fix. I'm a bigger monster than you because I don't give a fuck who you've killed or why you did it. In fact, from here out I'm helping you bury the bodies."

It's totally ridiculous but I fixate on probably the least important thing he's said. "I cannot believe you're a Vanth super fan and you've given me all that shit about it. You're a real piece of work, Beaumont."

Blaise sniggers behind me like it's some big fucking secret they've been keeping from me and Ash smirks as he says, "I told Blaise he should get you to sing on his next album. I'll listen to that on repeat, too."

My heart stops beating.

That is the best, worst idea ever and you know what? I'm all fucking in.

"I'll write you a song, Mounty. While you and Arbour are shacked up and loving every second of the break, I'll mope around New York with my parents and write you love songs." Blaise sulks and Harley throws an empty coat hanger at him. I pass him the iPod and he flashes me a gorgeous grin.

"I'll video chat you guys. Harley can stay with me and if you guys can get away to the Bay you can stay, too."

Chapter Thirty-Three

Harley arrives at our door first.

Avery groans when she opens the door and he shoves his way into the room, a single duffel bag slung over his broad shoulder. "This is my life now, isn't it? You lot showing up at my door every hour of the day to make eyes at my best friend."

Harley grabs a beer out of our fridge and drinks half of it in two big gulps. "Get single rooms next year. Be a fuck load easier for us if you're not watching our every move."

Avery slaps his arm and then shoves a box into his chest, directing him to start packing up her glut of belongings. "I'm looking out for my Mounty. I don't want you lot corrupting her."

Harley snorts at her and I try not to be too insulted. My bags are all packed, everything except my safe. I wriggle myself under my bed and use the light on my phone to see as I start to wrench the floorboards loose with my knife.

There's a knock at the door while I'm grunting at the effort to uncover my most valuable possessions. Then I hear the other two guys talking and joking around. I might slow my work down a bit to give myself time to stop blushing.

"Great view," Blaise says and then he grunts as someone hits him. "What? I'm allowed to appreciate my girl's ass, especially in those shorts. What are you doing, Mounty?"

His girl. *Sweet lord.* I don't think I have it in me to get used to that. "Construction work." I tease and then Avery ducks down to have a look at what I'm doing.

"That's where you hid that!"

"Hid what?"

"Her stash," says Harley and he's so smug. He loves knowing more about me than the others.

I wriggle back out and drag the safe with me. Avery does her gimme hands at me and I chuckle. "I'm not sure I can trust you with these, Beaumont."

She bites her lips and stares at the metal box with lusty eyes. "I solemnly swear I'm up to no good."

"Nerd." But I open the safe and hand over the velvet box.

Avery moans as she cracks the lid and Ash looks so fucking mortified that we all get to have a laugh at his expense. "Sex toys? You can't fit a pair of Louboutins in a box that small and I can't think of anything else that gets Floss that excited," he grumbles.

"Better. So much better. Diamonds!" Avery squeals and then she starts pawing through them. Harley's eyebrows shoot up and damn near disappear into his hairline as he looks over her shoulder.

"How many of them do you have?"

Forty-eight. I shrug. "I'm good at what I do and I'm stockpiling so we can get clear of our shit after graduation."

Harley's eyes flash possessively. Avery rolls one of the blood diamonds in her fingers and I swear she's panting. Harley clears his throat at her. "Put them back, Floss. Make Morrison buy you one for your birthday."

Blaise is too busy staring, gaping, at the contents of the box to snap out a comeback. Avery pouts as she carefully packs the diamonds back into the safe. "I don't want boring old diamonds. I want priceless, blood soaked, favor diamonds."

"Someone needs to start explaining what the hell is going on," Ash grumbles.

Avery is still pouting as I bury the safe in my duffle bag and cover it with my clothes so it's obscured and nestled nicely. She answers Ash for me. "The Twelve trade each other favors in times of need. Diamonds are used as a physical representation of the favors and Lips has dozens of them. Dozens!"

"Why? Why not use them and become rich? Why come to school here and put up with us?" Ash asks.

I shrug, entirely uncomfortable talking about them. "I nearly died for most of those. I've only ever used two favors and that was for situations that were life threatening. I won't use them for less than that."

My phone pings and I try not to cringe. Avery shoots me a look because she knows who it must be. Only one person outside of this room has my number.

The building is bigger than I thought it would be. I hope your inductee packs light, I've brought the BMW to bring you both home.

Fuck.

Fuck, this is bad. Bad. Baaaaaaaad.

I glance away from the Jackal's text to find Harley laughing and moving boxes for Avery. He looks so damn happy and I'm going to ruin that by telling him his life is in serious danger. I should have worked harder on getting out from the Jackal. I should have focused on my GPA a little less and stopped avoiding the bigger issue.

I know my face must show every ounce of my fear because one look at it has Avery and Harley both dropping the boxes and bolting to me.

"Lips, what—"

"Fuck, babe—"

I sink to the bed and give myself ten seconds to freak out. Ten seconds and then I'm going to pull myself back together and get through this.

"The Jackal is here. He's picking us up," I croak.

Joey is waiting for us at the bottom of the stairs. His gaze bounces over each of us until he lands back on me.

"How the fuck do you know the Jackal? He's here for you."

I arch an eyebrow and step around him. Harley follows, exactly how I told him to, and my heart flutters in my chest. Joey moves like he's going to stalk after us but then Ash hisses at him, "Do you want to fucking die?"

I can't look back at them to see the answer.

The Jackal is here.

I can't see him yet but every student, every parent, every teacher, they're all turned towards the same man, terror and horror hangs thick in the air. Enough people recognize him and they're all waiting for the killing to start.

I take one last deep breath.

I push down Lips Anderson in my mind. I put her in the little box and I forget about her. I forget about the breakfasts with Avery and dancing to old records together, I forget about planning our futures and world domination. I forget about my GPA and the panic of my choir performance. I forget about the itch of my skirt and the crisp lines of my blazer.

I fucking bury every thought of the three guys I'm on the edge of falling in love with.

And then, all I am, is the Wolf.

"There you are."

I loathe the sound of his voice.

He's brought Luca and Diarmuid and they're standing either side of him. I take note that all three of them are carrying guns, Diarmuid even has a thigh holster with a ten-inch knife strapped in. I knew they would be but it doesn't help with the nerves that are trying to worm their way into my mind. Diarmuid grins and sweeps me into a big hug. I laugh joylessly and give him a little pat on his back. He whispers in my ear, barely more than a breath, "I came to keep our boy safe," and then he drops me back onto my feet and sweeps behind me to hug Harley. I really want to know how Harley reacts to that but I can't risk looking at him.

Luca steps forward and takes my bag from me with a smile I return easily. His eyes are intense and locked behind me as he stoops down to kiss my cheek.

Lord save me from the pissing contest this is going to turn into.

Once Luca steps away I turn to the real monster in the room. The Jackal is tall, well-muscled, and attractive in his crisp navy suit. His Italian roots are easily distinguishable. His deep brown hair falls in waves around his face and his eyes are the same color, dark pools looking out from his olive skin. Even with the thick black lines of his tattoos dancing across the skin of his cheeks he's a handsome man but not to me. All I see is the evil living inside of him.

I meet his eyes and fake a little smile, one I've given him a thousand times before. He looks over every inch of me like he'll be able to see all of the lies I'm telling him etched into my skin. I breathe in deeply and force my heart to slow down while I wait him out.

Finally, he says, "Where's my hug, little Starbright?"

I roll my eyes and step forward into his arms. He presses himself into me fully, chest to thigh, and I focus on where I can feel his weapons so I don't have to think about this public claiming he's hell-bent on.

I pull away from him and he tucks my body under his arm, flicking out a hand to get Harley and his men to follow us.

"We have so much to talk about, my Wolf. Or do you belong to someone else now?" he murmurs into my ear.

Fuck.

He knows about Harley.

Fuck.

Make Your Move

Exclusive Excerpt

HARLEY

I lean on the wall as Lips locks up, angling my body into her and enjoying the sight of her shivering at how close I am. Fuck, I want her. I want her so fucking bad, it's kind of pathetic. I mean, I know it's pathetic already but Ash doesn't let me forget it either.

He shuts up real fucking quick when I point out how obsessively he watches her too.

The thought of her picking him or Morrison over me… fuck.

I need to make a move on her tonight but she's so fucking… jumpy. Literally, if she watches me for too long she startles like a rabbit caught in headlights and scurries away. Floss won't tell me a thing about her, nothing to give me a clue to why she's like this, but at least the blushes and shudders let me know she's into me too.

Something catches my eye and I curse under my breath.

I don't want to fucking deal with Annabelle's bullshit right now. I'm pissed at myself for ever touching her in the first place and now she won't fucking leave me alone.

"It's bad enough I have to watch Blaise leave here most nights now you're here with her too? Come on, Harley, what are you thinking?"

My skin crawls at the sound of her voice.

The attitude is just as bad, I know she doesn't give a fuck about Morrison. He's nothing but dollar signs in her mind and that alone has my teeth clenching.

Lips stalking away, ready to just bail on me over this has me fucking livid at the slut.

I grab the Mounty's hand and tug her back over to me side. There's no way I'm having her doubt me, not over this bitch. Not over anything, I've never been so sure of anything in my life as I am about her. Whatever it takes, she's going to be mine.

you're all dressed up for, Summers." I say, scathing sarcasm dripping from every word.

Annabelle's bottom lip drops and she looks like a fucking child, none of the integrity or backbone of the Mounty. Not a fucking inch of it.

She simpers at me, reading me out a list of shit that she thinks will get her back under me but but the second she puts Lips down, the second she starts to throw shit at her, what little restraint I had for this clueless cunt snaps.

"I was born in the same city as Lips. I spend all of my summer breaks there. We have friends in the same circles. When I leave Hannaford, I'm going back there. I'm as much a Mounty as she is. Give up, Summers. I'm never touching you again. I never should've touched you in the first place."

I keep a firm hold of there Mounty's hand as we walk off, even when she tries to tug it away, never once looking back at Annabelle. Lips finally relaxes when we make it down the stairs, still alert but the tension in her body has eased.

I'm still fucking furious at what the cunt said about her so I'm sure I look positively murderous.

The party is always held in the clearing, Joey likes his shit in the same place because he's a creature of many habits, and I grab whiskey for us to share.

She drinks it without a single flinch and fuck me, it's the hottest fucking thing.

The eye rolls at Joey's friends is even fucking hotter.

She deals with them like they're *nothing*, something even Floss struggles with, and then we move on to dance together and actually enjoy a little of this night together.

There aren't many perks to growing up in Mounts Bay.

Knowing how to dance with her is definitely one of them.

Fuck me, that ass of her grinding back into me... it takes all my fucking self control not to just say 'fuck it' and bend her over right the fuck here. The grins and gasps that come out of her are like nothing I've ever heard before. I'm addicted to it, filing them away to think about and obsess over once the night is over.

If I don't have her by the end of the night these memories might just hold me over while I figure something else out.

She's fucking killing me here.

Finally she spins in my arms, her chest pushing up into mine so I'm panting, and says, "Let's get this over with."

For a second I think she's on the same page as I am, ready to leave this party and find the closest surface to fuck, but then her words actually filter into my brain and nope, we're dealing with Joey.

Fuck him and his psychopath plans.

I nod and we weave our way through the other students dancing, none of them with half the skill or grace that we have, and further into the forest. There's couples fucking everywhere, a few of them definitely cheating and I make a note to tell Floss about them. It's always good to have ammo on the other students.

Lips comes to an abrupt holt and I plant myself behind her, the widening of her stance telling me a whole fucking heap about this situation.

It's the same stance she had down at the docks.

So as much as it kills me, I stay behind her, just for now. The second Joey so much as flinches in her direction I'll get around her and beat the living fuck out of the dickhead.

"This guy bothering you?"

Who the fuck is that guy? His hand slips behind his back. Fuck me, he's offering to kill Joey for Lips?

What the actual fuck?

Every time I think I know what the actual fuck is going on with her something like this happens and I'm back to square fucking one with no idea of who the fuck she is.

"He's just a guy with too much money and too little respect for how things are done in the real world, boys." Lips says, her voice strong and confident. She sounds cold and calculating though, none of the girl I know showing through.

The second guy is shitting himself. He's sitting there like he needs to climb out of his own skin to get away and his eyes are anywhere but Lips.

"What'll it be then? You need me to take care of him?"

Fuck, I wish we could say yes. I almost hope Lips does say yes but Floss and Ash would never forgive her. The twisted mess of a web that their family is in would give a saint a fucking headache.

"I'm here to go to school, not start a war. Head home, boys. Hannaford isn't the place for you."

They leave immediately, not a single question for her once she's given them the order. The guy who was doing the talking comes over and shakes my hand. I frown at him but, fuck, I guess this is what happens when I *belong* to the Mounty.

Once the car is gone, peeling away from the back parking lot with squealing tires, Joey turns back to us, completely fucking clueless to how close he's just come to his brains being blown the fuck out.

"Who the fuck are you, Mounty?"

Isn't that the million dollar fucking question.

Play The Game

Hannaford Prep Year Three

Prologue

HARLEY

I'm forced to walk behind the sick fuck who is holding Lips at his side, pressing her into him until they're moving as one.

Every eye at Hannaford is on us, the building is holding its breath as we walk out to the waiting car. It's a statement, a public claiming, and when we return to school for our junior year Lips will be treated with a whole new level of suspicious reverence. I'm going to fucking hate it, but maybe it'll keep her safe.

The BMW waiting for us is the same type my grandfather owns. It looks fucking showy, but it's the unseen elements that make it worth well over the mil mark. Bulletproof, flame retardant, and supposedly able to withstand a bombing, it's not a status symbol.

It's a vehicle built for war.

Diarmuid drops his arm from where it's slung around my shoulders to open the door and usher me in. Lips warned me about protocol and I know this is a clear move from my uncle, telling the Jackal I'm a protected player. I hate it; I hate what my life is costing everyone, but if it keeps Lips safe too, then I'll play along.

He climbs in beside me and we sit in the rearward facing seats. It's risky because I'll be facing Lips and there's no way I can look at her while the Jackal watches us both.

He watches her like he fucking owns her. He watches her like he's picking out the inches of her skin that he's going to brand with his mark to keep her chained by his side.

I fucking hate it.

The rage that grows inside my chest expands until I can't breathe and it's only the echo of her words, the rules she told me back in her room, bouncing around inside my skull that stops me from reaching forward and choking him the fuck out. My uncle sits beside me, grinning like a fucking idiot, and I try not to look back at the posturing dickhead that keeps kissing and touching my Mounty. I know he's just trying to get a rise out of me, but you know what? He's succeeding. I keep my eyes on my own hands or on the Jackal's hands.

He's gripping her knee hard enough that it has to be hurting her. It's her bad leg, and she's just gotten over the flare up. She ignores him, doesn't attempt to brush him off, and I know she's trying not to provoke the sick fuck. I want to kill him.

When, finally, the barren, gray wasteland of Mounts Bay looms over us, he breaks the silence in the car.

"Where are you staying this year, little Wolf? I'll check your security and make sure you are safe," he murmurs and I clench my fists. Diarmuid nudges me discreetly. I take a deep breath and force myself to unclench.

Lips hums under her breath, a habit she's picked up from Floss, and says, "Take us to the docks, Luca."

"Anything for you, princess," the dickhead says and Lips scoffs at him.

"Where are you staying?" the Jackal asks again, his voice harder. I roll my shoulders back, ready to grab the fuck if he goes for a weapon.

Lips shrugs. "Arbour is heading back up the coast and I have a few jobs lined up. I'm meeting with a friend at the docks to discuss the terms of my acceptance. You know I only take certain jobs."

He speaks through his gritted teeth. "I'm not asking what you're doing in the Bay, I'm asking where you're staying."

She pauses and then with a flat voice she says, "And I'm choosing not to provide you with that information. I told you months ago, I'm learning to stand on my own two feet. I appreciate the ride, but I'm on my own. It's me and Arbour, and any other person I choose to induct. If you wanted me to be one of yours, you should have inducted me instead of sponsoring me."

"I tried. You told me you'd rather die," he snaps.

That's news to me. I look up and meet her eyes.

I know why Floss warned me not to look at her around the Jackal; I can't keep the longing and the worship out of my face, and only Lips has been blind to it. I can't help but look at her now and the clenching on the Jackal's jaw lets me know he sees it for what it is.

Lips stares at me as she replies to him, "I will never be owned, and certainly not by you. I'm the Wolf."

I'm fucking flirting with danger, I know it deep in my bones, but I grin at her with the savage joy that her words rip through me. She tips her head back and laughs like a lunatic, and that's when I know she does feel fear. She's just as affected by this as I am.

The car pulls into the docks and the Jackal's hand tightens on her knee until she grunts. I lurch forward and grab his wrist, ready to choke the fucker out if I have to, and he reaches for his gun with his free hand. At the click of a gun to my right, I tense up.

"You're hurting the little girlie, Jackal. Best you let her go," Diarmuid croons.

Luca parks the car and flings the door open, presumably to help his boss now he has a loaded gun pointed at him, but there's a beat of silence before he says, "Boss. You'd better get out of the car."

The Jackal is sneering at Diarmuid as he wrenches his wrist out of my hand. "Pointing a gun at me? You're a fucking dead man, O'Cronin."

Diarmuid clucks at him. "Hurting a fellow member of the Twelve? You wouldn't want that getting back to the meetings, now would you? Think of what the Crow would do to you, he's been waiting a long time to take you out."

"She's mine!" he roars, grabbing her arm, and the door on his side of the car is ripped open with such force I think it will tear right off the hinges.

"Get your fucking hands off her, D'Ardo!" roars the newcomer. My eyes stay glued on the Jackal until he drops her arm. He looks out the door, grimacing, and finally his face shifts into something close to wary.

I blow out a breath and yank Lips into my arms, shoving us both out of the door on the other side of the car. She's not shaking, no racing heart in her chest or shallow breathing, but I can't say I'm as unaffected by the little spat. Once we're out, and I've run my hands over her to be sure he didn't fucking knife her without me noticing, I glance up only to find the fucking Butcher of the Bay staring back at me.

I gape back at him like an idiot. He winks at me.

Fuck me.

What the hell have I gotten myself into?

"I told you, I called for reinforcements. Illi's a good guy, the best," the Mounty whispers in my ear and then pulls away from me, stepping back into her role as the Wolf.

A good guy.

He's a cage fighter, a trained killer, his weapons of choice are his fists or a fucking meat cleaver, he shows no mercy and has no conscience, and, according to my crazy hot girlfriend, he's a good guy.

I think I'm going to have a fucking stroke.

Chapter One

Spying on clients for the Tiger is my favorite type of work.

I'm picky about what I'll do for him. I've made it pretty fucking clear to him that I will not take out innocent witnesses just to keep his dirty clients out of prison and he's good about finding me work that is okay with my morals.

Which is how I find myself dressed like a Mounty street girl at three in the morning outside a bar fending off sleazy, drunk assholes.

Leaning my overheated, sticky back against the brick wall while I'm staring at my phone should be a big enough indicator that I'm not currently selling but three broken fingers later and I'm still having to tell guys to fuck off. Not that I'm selling at all, it's just the best spot to find the information I'm after without attracting too much attention.

My phone vibrates silently in my hand and I cringe before opening the new text.

Right. Where the fuck are you? If you don't tell me I'm texting the group message and you can explain this shit to Avery.

Ugh. I'd told Harley not to come down until after ten in the morning. I wanted to finish up the job and sneak in three hours of sleep before I had to deal with the fallout of our 'chat' with the Jackal, but in typical Harley style he drove down to the Bay from his hotel on the coast early. I'd called the POA and gotten him into the townhouse in the gated community I've rented, but the barrage of text messages has only gotten worse as the night wears on.

I'll come back to the house now. I'll be 30mins.

I am not going to go back right this second and I order an Uber to arrive in twenty minutes. I'm sure I could persuade Harley to believe there were traffic delays. The mark the Tiger had paid me fifty grand to get photos of is loitering in the gardens across the road. I know he's there for drugs, I just have to wait the dickhead out.

I'm already in the car.

Bossy fucking boys. I send him the name of the bar and glare down at all the skin I'm showing. He's either going to be a total fucking dick over it or I'll get a hot make-out session in the car. I wonder if he's boosted the car? My thighs rub together because I'm fucking damaged and get hot for that shit.

I keep my head ducked like I'm staring at my phone even as my gaze follows my mark. He's coming down from whatever high he's been riding and his body language is becoming more and more agitated as the night wears on. I need him to act before

Harley gets here. If he makes a scene, my cover is blown and I will have to find a new vantage point and then spend another night out here following the idiot around.

The roaring of the engine reaches me first and then shouting and whistling pierces the air. I groan under my breath. When the Mustang pulls up in front of me, I already know who the hell it will be, and now I have the attention of the entire damn street. It's a *fucking* nice car, a vintage muscle car that rumbles like a beast even as it idles at the curb. Matte black and silver trimmings, even to me the car looks like a wet fucking dream.

I pull my lips into my best Mounty street girl smile and trot around to the driver window. Wasted guys outside the bar start catcalling me and the other street girls start talking shit. I ignore them all for the guy smoldering in the driver's seat.

Harley is pissed.

"I'm working so unless you want me out here again you should play the fuck along," I croon because I have to make it look like I'm giving him the sales pitch of his life.

Harley grunts but a fake smirk plasters itself across his lips and he grits out, "I can see the outline of your fucking pussy in those shorts, Mounty."

I take a shaky breath and glance down to double check that he's just being moody. Okay, I have a teeny tiny bit of a camel toe but nothing so dramatic that it's indecent or anything.

"Look, I can't leave until I get this done. This is my ninth job and I've worked my ass off since I got back so I wouldn't have to work once you got here. Please, just leave me to get this done."

He quirks an eyebrow at me and shifts in his seat to grab his wallet. The girls behind me yell out to him, trying to get his attention and cut me out of the deal. Harley curls his lip in their direction and they quieten down.

He pulls out a fifty-dollar bill and waves it at me obnoxiously. I've snapped bones tonight for less. "This gets me an hour, right? Let me take you around the corner, you can pick which one, and I can keep an eye on you while you work."

I chew on my lip for a second and then bend down to lean into the car and kiss him, dirty and raw like the street girls do.

Harley grunts as I bite his lip and he slips the money into my bra, careful not to touch me. He doesn't want to touch me like this, not when I'm dressed up to work and hating every second. It's fucking sweet. I have to remind myself of our audience and keep the kiss outrageously sexual.

It's ridiculous that I know how to do that just from growing up here.

I pull away from him and trot around the car like I'm giving him a preview of what I have to offer him. His eyes stay glued to mine.

I have to do a weird slide to get into the car because my shorts are so tight, and the smell of the warm leather seats hits me as I shut the door. I direct Harley to a good spot and he parks up, cranking the air conditioning up, a blissfully cool breeze on my overheated skin.

"Information or a hit?" Harley asks.

"Photos. Nothing too dangerous really." That's a partial truth. The mark isn't a concern, but if the dealer sees me, there will be serious fallout.

"How much?" Harley murmurs, watching me as I watch my mark.

"Fifty grand. It's the smallest job, so I left it until last."

He nods and settles back in his seat, his eyes closing as he grabs my hand. I blush and try to keep my focus on the drug addict. Harley traces his thumb along my knuckles absently.

"Can we talk or will that distract you?" he murmurs, his eyes still shut.

Ugh, fuck. I sigh. "Is this about Illi or the Jackal?"

"Both of them. I know who you are. I know enough about this world to know it's not fair of me to ask you to stay the fuck away from the Jackal, but seeing him touch you and knowing how much he scares you was fucking *bad*, Mounty."

I swallow around the lump at the back of my throat. "I know. I'm… I'm taking care of it. Illi is part of that."

I grab my phone as the dealer finally shows up. The mark is directly in front of the car, across the street, but the photos I get are clear enough to show what's going down. The guy isn't subtle, but the outrageous price I'm being paid is because of how high the risk of being caught is, not because of how hard it is to find the mark scoring his dope. He's so far gone he would buy it in front of his own mother.

"How did you meet the Butcher?"

I wince. "I hate that name for him."

Harley grunts at me. "That's who he is; he fucking mutilates people."

I cut him a glare. "He also saved both our asses. He's… the same as I am. He came into this life unintentionally, but with a set of highly sought-after skills. When I told him I'd applied to Hannaford, he helped me get out, he helped me remove myself from Mounts Bay, and then he cut off all contact with me so I'd have a fucking chance at getting clear. He's a good guy."

Harley looks at me like I'm challenging his very moral system, then his eyes slide away from me and he snaps, "Fuck. We're made."

I dart my gaze over to find the dealer, one of the Jackal's men I know and who most *definitely* knows me, is now stalking over to the car, and I move without really thinking it through. I lean forward to grab the release on Harley's seat to push it back. He inhales sharply as I climb over to kneel on the floor between his knees and crouch awkwardly under the steering wheel. His eyes widen and he swears viciously as I fumble to get his belt unbuckled and his pants undone. I can feel his dick getting hard as my hand brushes against him even as he protests.

"Mounty—" he hisses, and I cut him a look.

"I'm not going to fucking suck your dick to get out of this, but I *am* going to pretend. How are your acting skills?" I whisper and before he can answer there's a knock at the window.

I blanch a little—because, *really*, am I going to bob my head and fake this properly?—and Harley, thankfully noticing me hesitate, twists my hair around his wrist and grabs a fistful of my hair before winding the window down a few inches.

"I paid good fucking green for this slut. How about you fuck off and let me enjoy my money's worth before I get angry, dickhead?" Harley drawls, becoming the arrogant asshole from school once again.

I can't move with the grip he has on my hair, thank God. I can smell the cigarettes and weed on Reggie from where I'm crouched. He's a fucking creep and I have to hold in a repulsed shiver at his close proximity. Thankfully, the steering wheel hides most of the skin I'm showing, and he won't be able to see or recognize the scars.

"What's a guy like you doing down here, anyway? If you can afford the '67 Rector, you can afford better pussy than what the slum girls have on offer."

Harley chuckles under his breath and replies, "More expensive doesn't mean better. No one sucks like the slum girls."

Reggie waits a second and then laughs. "You can smack them around if they don't. High class girls cry if you're rough with them. Enjoy your time with her. I'll find her myself later, see if that mouth is as good as you say."

Harley grunts and rolls the window up. His tight grip loosens a little, but when I glance up at his face, he's watching Reggie leave. His hand doesn't drop away until Reggie is back in his own car and driving away. He looks fucking pissed so I try to distract him.

"You might be disappointed with this Mounty pussy. I haven't exactly been broken in like the others and I might be a shit lay."

Harley's eyes flash as he hauls me up and into his lap, awkwardly, thanks to the steering wheel. "Don't fucking compare yourself to them and, to be real fucking clear, I haven't ever been disappointed with you. I'm not gonna be either."

He sounds even more like a street kid away from Hannaford and I grin back at him even as I blush. "We'll see."

He smirks lasciviously at me. "Fuck yeah, we will."

I'm starving by the time we get back to the townhouse.

Harley grumbles about the weight I've lost and immediately rummages through the fridge. I hate spending money on food when I know how little I need to get by and when I stupidly mention this to Harley he snarls at me, "Well, you're fucking eating now I'm here."

With a sigh, I shove a beer at him while I make us both burgers. Harley ducks out to the car to grab his bags and dumps them unceremoniously into the living room. The place is tiny; perfect for what I need. The kitchen, dining, and living room are all one space and the two bedrooms are connected by the bathroom. The downstairs area is made up entirely by the garage which can hold two cars.

"Whose car is the 'Stang?" I ask, as I drop the plates on the table and grab more beer for us both. I'm not a fan of beer but I need something to soften my edges tonight. I'm still the Wolf, Lips having been put away for the summer break.

Harley takes a huge bite and groans before saying, "You need to cook more when we get back to school. Avery never makes burgers and Morrison puts fucking pineapple in them when he makes them."

I gape at him in horror, then text Blaise to express my disgust at him, forgetting it's nearly five in the morning. He sends me a little sketch he's done of a wolf in return, simple and in blue ink. I love it.

"It's Morrison's. My da had one and my grandfather had it scrapped after he killed him to piss me off. There's only like ten of those out there, and when I found that one Morrison bought it. I told him someday I'll buy it from him but he's a stubborn dick and transferred it into my name, anyway. So, I guess technically it's mine. Won't feel like mine until I pay for it."

Okay, now I regret waking Blaise up.

I nod and try not to think about my plans for his inheritance. It'll only give me a tension headache because of how fucking tired I am. "What are you going to do after school? I've never actually asked you."

"I never thought I'd get there. I dunno. I'll go wherever everyone else does.

Avery and Ash both want to go into business or some bullshit. I'll find something to do at whichever college they pick. Ma wanted to be a doctor before she met Da so maybe I'll do that for her."

I sip my beer and wince. "Doctors make bank, you'll own that car in no time."

Harley smirks at me as he takes a drink. "They don't make fifty grand in a night."

I blush. "Surgeons can, asshole. Besides, *this* is not my career path. This is making do until then."

He slings a casual arm across the back of my chair, pulling me into his side. I've forgotten what it's like to have him so close to me and I have to take a deep breath to relax. It's like in the weeks we've been away from each other, all the familiarity he'd managed to form that last week of school sharing my bed has been wiped away. Fuck it if I'm not the most damaged fucking option, why the hell did they pick me?

"What are you doing after school? You're coming with us, right?" he murmurs.

I clear my throat. "I'm going to conquer the world with Avery. Haven't been able to find the right college course for that just yet but we're exploring options."

I don't really want to tell him, because I still haven't told him I'm financially supporting him now, but the money I've earned during the break is being sent to Avery and put into investments so I can afford to pay for everything Harley and I need for the next two years.

Avery is a fucking genius in the stock market, so good that the inheritance she and Ash received from their mother has doubled since she gained control of the money. When she told me I immediately asked her to teach me and now, we're investing my dirty money. I'll finally have a legitimate income.

Avery is also now sending me college brochures and course ideas daily. She refuses to pick a school without my input and when I told her I'd pick whatever school gave me the best scholarship, she said she'd apply to that school with me then. No amount of arguing had managed to convince her to leave me behind and fuck it if I didn't love her more for it.

Her father had been called away for business at the last minute before their trip to Amsterdam for Joey's birthday, so they had enjoyed their trip with their father's staff instead. Avery had paid off two of the bodyguards to keep Joey away from Ash, and the twins had enjoyed the break. They had arrived back in the states two days ago and were already packing to move into the townhouse here in the Bay.

Only Blaise is stuck away from us all until school goes back in two weeks.

I am fucking worried about the cocky asshole but I have no clue about how to deal with rich, emotionally fucked, dickhead parents.

I yawn and rub my eyes. Harley kisses my temple and says, "C'mon, I'll get this cleaned up and we can go to bed."

I freeze and he scoffs at me, like my reactions are so fucking amusing.

"I've already told you, I don't have to sleep in your bed with you," he huffs at me and grabs my plate. I argue with him over the dishes until he snaps at me, "You cooked so I clean, get the fuck over it."

I move to sit at the bench, and fidget while I watch him clean. He doesn't look at me but he has extra senses or some shit because after I've agonized over the bed situation for ten minutes and find myself jittery, he says, "Look, I get you're probably gonna have issues—"

"Why I am gonna have issues?" I snap.

He cuts me a stern look. "You've been living under the threat of rape for years and from multiple fucking sources. I'm sure that would make anyone jumpy. I'm not in a rush. The other two will take it slow, especially if you tell them why. Calm the fuck down."

I squirm and bite my nails while he washes the dishes. "I'm not scared."

"I didn't say you were. Pretty sure I said *jumpy*."

I roll my eyes at him. "It wasn't just the Jackal that stopped me. I'm not interested in casual, never have been and never will be. I didn't want to just fuck guys."

Harley scrubs the pots in silence and I watch him while I try to figure out how the fuck to say it. When he moves on to wipe down the bench, with such thoroughness I know he's been trained well by Avery, he says, "Are you asking me if I think this is casual? Because, fuck Mounty, I'm kind of hoping you already know how serious we're all taking this."

I swallow. "Knowing something in your head is very different to letting… letting yourself really believe it. I guess, I still kind of think this is all going to blow up in my face."

Harley nods and wipes his hands before walking around the bench and gently prying my legs open to stand between them. He waits for a moment until the tension melts out of me, then I shiver as he leans down and cups my face gently, breathing the words onto my lips as he speaks. "I'm keeping you forever. I don't do this shit for anything but keeps." And then he swallows my answering sigh.

I missed this. I missed the feeling of his lips on mine and his hands holding my face like I'm everything to him and that alone breaks the hold of the Wolf on me. I wrap my legs around his hips and pull him closer; he never fucking gets close enough to me. I wonder if I'll still feel that way when we do have sex. I shiver at the thought and moan into the kiss, sucking on his tongue for more.

Harley breaks away and groans at me, "You kiss me like you want to fucking *consume* me."

"Maybe I will." I tease, smiling and rubbing myself against his chest in a very non-Lips manner. When he groans again and pulls my hips flush with his, grinding his dick into me, I mentally high-five myself for the move. Another yawn takes over me and he chuckles.

He hooks his arms under my legs to cup my ass in his big hands, squeezing as he lifts me up and presses me against his chest. "I'll tuck you into bed, babe. I'll go take a cold shower."

I clear my throat but it doesn't stop my voice from coming out as a rasp. "Sleep in my… our bed. The other one is for Avery. We can figure out the specifics when the others get here."

Chapter Two

Waking up to Harley's hands stroking over my body is possibly the best fucking feeling in the world. The sun is streaming through the cracks in the blinds and it must be at least midday. I stretch out my back and Harley mumbles under his breath appreciatively as the move pushes my ass up towards his hand.

He strokes down my spine and gets so close to cupping my ass then moves away to start back up between my shoulders again. I grunt and open my eyes to glare at him. "Don't be a tease."

He smirks. "I'm going slow, Mounty, don't be greedy."

It might be the work of his hands, or maybe it's the decent sleep I've finally had after weeks of shit, but I turn my face into his chest and bite him. Not hard, but enough to get his attention.

"Fuck me, Mounty, you start biting me and I will bite you the fuck back." His voice rumbles and I grin at him.

He shakes his head at me. "Last night you were looking at me like you'd rather jump out of the window than touch me, and now you're grinning at me like you want to spend the day naked in this bed with me. I don't know what the fuck to do with you. I've wanted you for so fucking long, and I'm not messing this up by pushing you."

I cringe and pull away from him. "I don't mean to look at you like that. It's hard to switch between Lips and the Wolf. I don't… touch easy. This is new to me. Fuck, it took me weeks of being around Avery before I got used to her touching me all the time. The first time she hugged me I nearly jumped out of my skin. And… I don't want to talk about it, I don't want to piss you off, but before Hannaford, I was only ever touched when people were hurting me." I clear my throat to shift the lump there. Fuck me, I've caught the self-pity bug again. I change topics to try to clear the stain my confession has left in the air.

"Why didn't you tell me? If you had been wanting me for as long as you say you have, then why not just tell me?"

He groans at me and rubs his face with one of his big palms. He gives me a look from the corner of his eye and then sighs. It's weird to see him unsure of himself.

"I've never had a girlfriend or asked someone out."

I snort at him, graceful as ever. "Fuck off. I've seen you blow a load on Annabelle's face, don't start bullshitting me now, Arbour."

He smirks at me probably remembering the intense eye contact in the woodland area while he'd gotten off. "I'm not saying I've never fucked girls before, I'm saying I've never wanted a girl as a… permanent thing."

A permanent thing. What an eloquent way to describe what we all have now. I stare at him until he groans again and continues.

"Look, I was fucking terrified of how I felt about you. I still am, if I'm honest. My circle is small for a reason; I don't trust people and I don't like them. And then you walked into that fucking school with your head high and mouth running, and I just… I love it. I love everything you do, you draw me in and I can't get my eyes off of you. I didn't know how to talk to you without you thinking I was like every other dickhead there trying to win that fucking bet."

I nod. I've spent the weeks we've been apart stewing on this… relationship we now have, and I'm both excited and terrified by it. I like being a part of the 'family'. I don't want jealousy and relationship drama to ruin what we have. "I just don't understand how you went from wanting to rip Blaise's and Ash's heads off to not giving a shit about… sharing me."

He blows out a breath and scrubs his hand over his face. "It wasn't about them being with you. It was about whether *I* would get to have you."

He pulls away and sits on the edge of the bed, like he doesn't want to look at me while he speaks. I hesitate for a second and then tuck myself against his back, my arms and legs wrapped around him. He traces the scar on my ruined leg with a finger idly.

"I thought you would only pick one of us and I couldn't deal with it not being me. We're not normal. The three of us are so fucking messed up from everything we've had to deal with and we're never going to be normal. Sharing you isn't even in the top five of weird shit we've done." He chuckles under his breath and I squeeze him.

I get the feeling this is his little declaration, like the one I made to Ash before we left school. This is him telling me he's not whole and being with him is not the easy option.

He has no reason to worry.

I don't *do* easy.

"I think it'll take all three of us to keep you safe, keep you alive. Fuck, the three of us and Floss, and maybe even then this fucking world you rule could take you out. I can't let that happen, Mounty. Sitting in that car with the Jackal proved to me that we need to get you out of here. Being stuck up the coast without you has been fucking hell."

We fall quiet while we both think about the consequences of what happened. He'd only planned to stay up there for two weeks to see his mom but I'd called his hotel to extend his stay and keep him the hell away from the Jackal. He'd fought me on it and I was forced to call Avery to talk some sense into him. Once he finally agreed, I'd sent Illi up there to watch his back. Something I will never tell Harley because it would piss him the fuck off. I know for a fact these guys have no idea of the hell that has just arrived on our doorstep. Fuck me.

Harley gets up and promises me French toast if I get some more sleep, claiming the dark circles under my eyes are still there and he won't let me out of bed until they're gone. Bossy, irresistible asshole. He takes the 'Stang to the grocery store and I'm a little worried about how much food he'll bring home.

I wake an hour later to my phone pinging and I search the sheets to find it. I groan at the text. It's from Harley to the new group text that doesn't include Avery. The 'joint relationship' group. *Sweet fucking lord.* He's just fucking broadcasted my untouched status to the other two without asking me because he's an utter dick.

The sound of tumblers of the front door unlock drifts to the bedroom followed by the rustling of the grocery bags. Then my phone pings with Ash's reply.

Explain. Now.

"You asshole," I yell out to him as I try to figure out how the fuck to explain this without tearing their arrogant heads off. Fucking lord.

Any guy within the Jackal's world knows they're risking death if they touch me. I haven't left Mounts Bay for anything other than school. I haven't fucked anyone at Hannaford. Is that a good enough explanation?

I swallow and punch my pillow. I hear Harley rummaging around, putting things away and getting out supplies for my breakfast. This had better be the best fucking French toast of my *life*. His phone pings out in the kitchen as mine buzzes in my hand.

So you two haven't fucked yet? How are those blue balls of yours, Arbour?

I roll my eyes at Blaise and Harley replies.

My balls are fine, how are yours, dickhead? Just thought I'd let you both know because the Mounty is jumpy as hell about it.

That's it, I'm killing the fucker.

Ash please get Avery to start building my alibi. I'm stabbing your cousin.

Harley snorts at me, loud enough that I hear it, and calls out, "Your knife is out here, what else would you do it with?"

"I'm pretty fucking innovative when I need to be, Arbour!"

I have to hold onto the photos for the Tiger for two days before I can deliver them to him in person. He's vigilant to the point of madness and refuses to use even the most secure electronic file sharing options for the work I do for him. I'm forced to load them onto an USB and text him a meetup point at the docks. The Fox is hosting his usual summer party with live music, booze, drugs, and every Mounty under the age of fifty will be there. There's nothing over the summer in the Bay bigger than this party.

I tell Harley I'll just pop in to drop the USB off and he looks at me like I've got a brain injury. So, I guess we're going to the party together. Bad idea, it will be teeming with the Jackal's men but there's no talking him out of it.

Which is how I find myself glaring at the bathroom mirror at eleven at night.

The playsuit I've got on is one of my absolute favorites. It's backless, and the top is a flowy halter-neck with a deep v. Like, so deep that you can see my belly button. The bottom half is short enough that I have to wear a thong so my underwear doesn't peek out as I move. It's sexy without showing too much ass or tits, just little glimpses. Compared to the other Mounty girls I'll look like a freaking Amish girl. The problem with the outfit is that, with my new-and-improved boobs, I have to wear some stupid fucking adhesive bra and then tape the front of the playsuit down so I'm not going to have my tits out in the warehouse.

I think Harley would have an aneurysm.

I snap a photo and send it through to Avery. She answers immediately.

Where the hell do you find these outfits? Is there a Chanel version? Also, I'm texting Harley and telling him to feed you more.

I snort at her and send her a photo of my back for good measure. She video calls me back.

"Where are you going? Has Harley seen that yet?"

I shrug. "I'm finishing my last job. Harley knows the score, you can't go to the docks without showing some skin."

Avery smirks at me and still manages to look like an evil queen while wearing her fluffy Chanel robe. "Oh, I'm sure he's positively thrilled about it. Ash just took a call from him and they're gossiping like housewives for their book club."

I snort at her and twirl to get a feel of how much movement I still have.

She cackles down the phone. "I just saw a nipple so unless you want Harley ripping that off of you before you make it out the door you will need more tape."

I grimace and end the call, with Avery still sounding far too amused at my expense.

Once I've taped what feels like every-fucking-thing down, I flounce out of the bathroom and stand in front of the full-length mirror in the living room. I dance around and shake my butt to make sure it's secure, I even throw in a slut drop for good measure.

I hear a strangled sort of noise and then a choking cough behind me.

Harley is sitting at the bench looking fucking devastating in his dark jeans and tight white shirt. My breath catches in my chest for a second before I see the look in his eyes as he watches me. His laptop is still on the table but the screen has been turned around so Ash and Blaise can see my outfit. Ah. They've just been watching me dance Mounty-style. Oops. I give them a little awkward wave.

"Fuck. Pick something else to wear." chokes out Blaise and Ash snorts at him.

"She can wear whatever the fuck she wants. Don't be a dick."

Harley rubs the back of his neck and grumbles, "I'd prefer it if you wore a bra though. Fuck me, I'm going to be fucking busy tonight. One of you two will pay my bail, right?"

Ash nods and waves a hand at me. "Do another one of those squat things. Slowly."

I blush and laugh at him. I go back to the bedroom and grab my phone, flicking through the songs until I find something with a decent beat to dance to. When I come back out Harley looks up at me and smirks when I start the song. He was born and bred in the Bay so he knows what's coming. The other two have no clue how Mounties party.

"No filming." I warn him sternly and he holds up his hands in a mock surrender.

It feels kind of strange to dance by myself, with three sets of eyes on me, but I've spent every summer in a party of some kind working and music lives in my soul. I shut my eyes and just let myself move with the music, not trying to be sexy or seductive, but knowing that to prim rich kids the Mounty-style will look fucking erotic.

When the song finishes, I glance up and Harley is fucking sweating.

Damn, does that make me feel good.

Blaise is gaping at me and Ash looks ready to drive the fuck down here. I shiver, and only the thick silicone of the bra stops my hard nipples from being on display. Harley's eyes darken dangerously as my thighs rub together.

The knock at the door freezes me in place.

Harley glances away from me to frown at the sound and Ash swears viciously. I bend at the waist and motion for the two on the video call to stay silent, then I check the peephole. There's a giant mass of tattooed muscle and silvery-blond hair standing on the doorstep.

Sweet fucking lord.

Harley is going to have a fucking aneurysm.

I sigh and unlock the door. Before I open it, I meet Harley's gaze over my shoulder and say, as calmly as I can, "I know you disagree with me, but I swear to you, he's a good guy. I trust him. Just stay calm and hear him out. It must be important if he's here."

And then Johnny Illium, the Butcher of the Bay, or just plain Illi to me, sweeps me into a bone-crushing hug. I *do not* care that he's the most notorious cage fighter and enforcer-for-hire amongst the Twelve; I don't *do* hugs.

"Get the fuck off me, I'm not a hugger!" I gasp out and he grunts at me.

"Neither am I. That's from Odie. She told me to tell you to fucking call her, she misses listening to you bitch her out for doing things normal people do." He drops me to the floor and kicks the door shut, flicking the lock like it's his house to keep safe. Harley, honest to god, looks like he's going to kill me and then himself.

"This place is better than last year. You trying to impress your *boyfriend?*" Illi says, teasing like the ass he is, and sprawls himself down into one of the dining chairs like he's a regular visitor to the townhouse. He wiggles his eyebrows at me in a way I'm sure he's hoping will piss said boyfriend off.

Harley does look fucking livid, and a little like he's going to vomit. I wince. If the Wolf is whispered about on the streets of Mounts Bay, then the Butcher is the man screamed about at parties and bars when people want to instill fear on their audience of choice.

"I thought I'd stop by to be properly introduced to the boy the Jackal is willing to risk everything to kill." He shrugs out of his leather jacket and hangs it over another seat. He sees the laptop and the open chat room and gives the guys a little mocking wave before snapping it shut. Ash is going to lose his mind.

I groan at him. "Really, Illi? You couldn't just call me? Or warn me you were coming? We are just about to head out."

He nods along with me. "Cool. Where are we going?"

"Like fuck am I letting her go anywhere with *you*." snaps Harley and I give him what I hope is a stern look. He ignores it, and me, completely.

Illi smirks at him. "You're adorable. The Wolf doesn't need a fucking keeper, so cut your shit. I came here to tell you the Jackal offered to *triple* whatever sum you paid me. He's put a hit out on the O'Cronin kid."

I snort. "He can't. Not without answering to the Twelve."

Illi cocks his head at me. "He's put it out amongst the underlings he knows will risk the wrath it'll bring and he can easily pin the whole idea on. Not many took it up, because they know it goes against you, but there are a few who accepted."

"And you?" snarls Harley, "Are you here to kill me?"

"I turned him down." Illi says with a shrug. Well, I assume he was trying to shrug, the thick ropes of muscles that band across his shoulders make it look a little ridiculous. His fingers twitch. He's itching for a cigarette. I never let him smoke around me.

I know exactly what statement Illi has just made but Harley has no real experience in our world, and he's still eyeing Illi like he's an atomic bomb about to level the city. "And what is that going to cost us?" he snaps.

Illi quirks his eyebrow and swings around to give me an incredulous look. I snort and roll my eyes at him. "I'm not his *keeper* either. He can speak to you however he wants and, well, if it pisses you off, I'll only step in if I think you'll kill him. *No* killing him, Illi."

Illi glares a warning at Harley and then swings back to me. "That's not all I'm here for, I'm afraid. The meeting will be postponed. You'll need to come back down during the fall break. I thought I'd warn you before the Crow reaches out to you."

My spine snaps straight. Meetings don't get canceled. Illi eyes Harley again, and I grit my teeth. Fucking boys!

"This is the part where I'm asking for something fucking big from you, little Wolf." Illi grimaces and stares at Harley for a beat longer.

I wave my hand at him and say, "Harley's mine. Whatever it is, won't leave this room."

Harley's eyebrows raise but he gives Illi a curt nod.

"The Vulture is dead."

Fuck.

Oh, sweet lord *fuck*.

I meet Illi's gaze and nod slowly. "So, you're mine now, too."

Harley blanches but we both ignore him. Illi scrubs a hand over his face. "I didn't intend on asking but when the Jackal approached me about your boy, he brought up Odie... I can't leave her open to anything hurting her. *Again*."

I'm nodding before he finishes. "I know. You're mine, both of you. Between us, we'll keep her safe."

Harley looks between us and grinds out, "How does the death of that sick fuck suddenly mean you're inducting him? I thought you wanted to stay away from this world, how does taking on the Butcher keep you free?"

Illi cracks his knuckles absently but Harley watches the move carefully. "The Vulture sold my wife. Twice. I told little Wolf years ago that his death would be mine."

Harley bursts out of his chair. It's a testament to how confident Illi is of his abilities he doesn't so much as flinch. "You've killed a member of the Twelve and now you want to risk Lips by having her take you in?! Fuck. That."

I hold up a hand. "Illi and Odie are in. I should have done it years ago when you asked. I might've been able to get away from the Jackal sooner if I had."

Harley rocks back on his heels. "You've asked her before?"

If these two don't get along my life will get fucking complicated and fast. I can't even think about how much Ash and Blaise would both hate this.

Illi pauses for a second, and then sighs. "My Odie is alive because of the Wolf. If anything happened to her, there is no reason for me to continue breathing. I've asked Lips to induct me before, and I told her that even if she didn't accept, I would answer any call to arms from her."

And he had. One phone call to him back at Hannaford and he'd met us at the docks ready to throw down with the Jackal, whatever the cost. I run through the specifics of inducting him in my head and wince. "I can't pay you yet, I'm—"

"I'm a rich man. Induct me, and I'll give you a cut of my work."

I shake my head. "I'm not taking your money."

Illi stretches his legs out in front of him and laces his fingers behind his head. The move makes him look even bigger and Harley watches him warily. Illi grins at him and then fucking blows him a kiss like an ass. *Fucking hell.*

"I get it, you don't want to take on an empire. But that's why I'll offer myself to you and no one else. You won't use me. You won't betray me. You won't grow so fucking conceited that you turn into a cunt like Matteo did. You've protected Odie from the moment you met her. Offering myself to you and giving you a cut of my work is fucking *nothing* compared to what I owe you. Induct me. I will protect you and the boy, whatever the cost."

Resigned, I nod and exhale sharply. "It's forever, Illi. Just remember that this is forever."

He smiles, and it doesn't soften his fierce face at all. "So is Odie. I owe you a life-debt."

I take another deep breath. "One last thing. It's not just Harley that I'm protecting. I'm protecting my family. My best friend and… the *three* guys I'm… seeing."

Illium blinks at me and then at Harley. Then he fucking roars with laughter.

"Good! *Fuck yes!* No more abiding by Matteo's shitty fucking agendas. Done, little Wolf. Send me their details and I'll stay in touch. We'll get you the fuck away from Matteo."

Chapter Three

The Vulture's death means the Twelve go on lockdown.

The Tiger refuses to meet at the party, texting instead to request a daytime meeting at a deli on the Main Street the following afternoon. Lots of witnesses and places to take cover. The news of Illi and Odie's inductions travels fast and I think having the Butcher answer to me makes the Tiger extra fucking twitchy.

I slip out of bed without waking Harley and leave him a note. We'd argued after Illi had left and I'd stomped off to bed to video call Avery, seething and ignoring the texts and calls from the other two. Harley had abandoned the beer he'd been drinking before Illi's surprise visit, and found my emergency bottle of whiskey. He didn't stumble to bed until he'd finished the damn thing, and I'd spent half the night positive he was going to die of liver poisoning. I should've known he'd be fine, he drinks like a freaking fish, but I'd barely managed to get any sleep.

The drop-off runs smoothly. The Tiger doesn't question me about Illi, although his usual crass jokes are absent and he keeps looking over my shoulder. There are only two members of the Twelve without inductees left and, as one of them, I'm sure that the Tiger never feels more alone than when there is a murder amongst our ranks.

It's not until I go to leave that he says quietly, "Protecting a killer isn't a smart move, Wolf."

I raise an eyebrow at him, forcing bravado I *do not* feel. "The Vulture sold skin. It's not the type of business that cultivates admiration and respect. There are thousands of people who wanted him dead. I hope you're not making assumptions, Tiger?"

He eyes me carefully before giving me a respectful nod and leaving.

I stop at a liquor store that's protected and used by the Bear to launder his dirty cash. The guy behind the counter takes one look at me and waves me on, refusing to take my money. I grab more beer and two new emergency bottles of whiskey.

I groan to myself when I think of the hungover mess in my bed. How the actual fuck do I make him understand this? Ugh.

My phone pings and I cringe as I juggle the bottles to check it.

I'm in the Bay. Can you send through your address?

I stare down at Blaise's text. I'm excited to see him, thrilled actually, but he's supposed to be in New York with his parents. His texts had been coming less frequently and sounding a lot less like him as the break goes on. I chew my lip as I send him the address and then pause for a second before texting him again.

I've just finished a job. Can you pick me up before you head there?

I find a bench to sit on and send him the details of where I am. He must have been only a block over because two minutes later he pulls up.

The Maserati draws eyes. Too many eyes and I know this will get back to the Jackal.

I scramble over to the car and load the bottles into the back seat before climbing in. Once I get my seatbelt on I turn to greet Blaise and the words dry up in my throat. It's hard, but I do my best not to gape at him. He's got his nose piercing back in, now we're out of Hannaford, and his hair is freshly cut. He smells amazing, like he got straight into the car after his shower to come see me. The only thing wrong is the expression on his face.

He's a void.

There's no sign of my cheeky, vicious, passionate, dark rock star. Just a blank, empty vessel, even as he pulls the car back onto the road and drives us back to the townhouse. What the ever-loving *fuck* has happened? I wait him out, but he says nothing.

"How can I fix this?" I say when I can't stand the silence any longer.

He glances over at me and his eyes are dull. "You can't. No one can."

I nod and hesitate before resting my hand on his thigh, too low to be overtly sexual, but high enough that it's more than a friendly gesture.

When we arrive at the gates I pass him the spare sensor to open them. He doesn't move to roll down his window, just stares down at the little plastic sphere like it's the answer to all of his problems. I stay quiet. Sometimes you just have to be patient and wait these things out.

"My mom's pregnant."

Huh.

Not what I expected.

"My father told me they've given up on me ever growing up. He said that they'd thought my shitty grades were a rebellion or a sign I was too spoilt and lazy to have drive, but now they know I'm just *retarded*. His exact words, not mine. They even went to a fertility specialist to make sure they would have another boy to replace me. The second he's born my father is writing me out of his estate."

The monotone sound of his voice and the complete lack of cussing has me worried. Also, I can't fix this at all. How fucked is it that we've all managed to have shitty families? Where are the decent people of the world?

"I don't even care about the money. I'm fine, I have enough of my own and I never wanted to run the business. But they're already talking about keeping my *bad influence* away from the baby. I'm going to have a brother that I'm not allowed to know because I'm too *fucking stupid* to be who my father wants me to be."

Yeah, I can't listen to this.

Not at all. Not from the guy who gave up parties and fun so he could study three nights a week to get his grades up for his miserable excuse of a father. The guy stands with his friends even if it risks his reputation and his career. The guy who goes toe to toe with Joey when he threatens someone he loves. Not the guy who charmed me, apologized to me, with playlists, poems, sketches, and sweet words. Not the guy who saved my life with his songs years before we even met.

I grab his hand until our fingers are curled together around the sensor. "Listen to me, there is plenty we can do to fix this. Not your parents or their shitty fucking attitudes, but we can make it impossible for them to keep you away from your brother.

Don't even think about it anymore, I will fix it. You're not stupid. I'm the best person to judge that, I've spent hours doing assignments with you. You're not what he wants but that doesn't make you *less* than him. I've met a lot of shitty people, Blaise, I've had to deal with a fuck ton of stupid, cruel, self-absorbed people and you're worth so much more than what he wants from you. You don't owe them *anything*."

His hand shakes a little in mine and then he gives me the tiniest of nods.

"No spending blood diamonds on me, Mounty. I'm not worth it."

I swallow past the lump lodged in my throat. "You're worth more than my diamonds. I'm planning on spending every single one of them on us. On our family, the one that actually counts. Even if… even if this is all a temporary thing for you guys, it's still worth it for me."

His head snaps over to me so quickly I would have startled if I weren't firmly wearing the skin of the Wolf. His eyes are wild and fierce. "This is not fucking temporary. Not for me, not for Ash or Harley, and not for you. I know we have a hell of a lot to make up for, but I'm going to do whatever it takes to do that. Don't *ever* say that shit again."

How the fuck am I supposed to walk straight after that?!

Fuck me.

Harley is asleep on the lounge chair when we get back. I help Blaise carry his bags in and we take them to *our* room, stepping over Harley's bags and dumping them in a messy pile on the floor. There isn't a whole lot of room left in the bedroom and once Ash gets here we will be in danger of bursting at the seams.

Blaise looks a little less void-like but he's still fucking morose. I give up trying to cheer him up and instead I start cooking dinner. Harley doesn't wake up with all our noise and I check to make sure the asshole hasn't choked on his own tongue.

I make Mac'n'Cheese because Blaise needs some damn comfort food and when I suggest it his lips twitch like he's thinking about smiling. I put a plate in the fridge for Harley and then I drag the blanket off our bed to wrap Blaise and I up in while we sit on the couch together and eat. Granted, I have to drop the thermostat down to ridiculous temperatures, but it's worth it when Blaise finally slings an arm around me as we eat and watch the fucking awful movie he's put on.

"What's wrong with him?" Blaise mumbles, after he's inhaled the pasta like a starving man.

I eye Harley as I grimace. "We had an argument about… a friend of mine and then he drank himself to sleep. We need to call Ash and Aves so I can tell you all at once about it. It's… about my position as the Wolf."

Blaise nods, and pulls me in closer to his body. His fingers dance over the strip of skin bared between my tank top and booty shorts. "You don't seem jumpy to me. Did Harley try to get you naked the second he got down here? I wouldn't have thought he'd be such an idiot, we all know you're good with knives."

I blush. Fucking boys. "No, he already knew, and I'm not fucking jumpy. I just needed a little time to get back to being the Mounty again and not the Wolf. This place does things to me."

Blaise nods again and dips down to kiss my throat, on the soft skin, right under my jaw. I shiver when his tongue and teeth join the mix, his lips moving slowly down until he's nibbling on my shoulder. My head falls back as I sigh.

"Let's leave Harley out here and go to bed. We can video call the twins and you can tell us what the fuck has happened now."

I have to clear my throat twice to get the words out. "I don't want you angry at me too. Can we just go to bed and I'll face this tomorrow?"

He relents and then takes me to bed, kissing me slow and sweet, until I can't keep my eyes open anymore. I'm so fucking glad he's here and I'm not going to let the morose fucker out of my sight until I'm sure he's okay.

Sometime after midnight Harley joins us and grunts when his shins hit Blaise's bags. When he slides into the bed I roll over in Blaise's arms to face him, the glow of the alarm clock on the bedside table illuminating him enough to see the frown.

"The fuck is he doing here?" he whispers and I shrug.

"His dad's a shitty human. Are you still angry? I can't sleep with rage in the air, it gives me heartburn."

Harley grumbles under his breath then kisses me, tasting minty and clean. I kiss him back for a second before I break away. I won't let him distract me with his tongue, talented as it is. "I'm getting away from the Jackal, but I can't stop being the Wolf. It's for life. If you can't handle—"

"I can handle it, *don't* freak out on me again. I can't help that, I want to keep you safe, and let's be real, the Butcher is a demon. I'm going fucking crazy thinking about how shitty things must have been for you if you've met him. If you've become *friends* with him. But I trust you. I'm all in."

I squint at him in the dark. I wonder if these boys even know how to pronounce the word sorry, if it's ever passed their lips. Hmm. No, I've heard it once from Blaise and Harley's apologized to Avery in front of me, but I guess this is the best I'll get.

I kiss him again, just a quick peck, and fall asleep, tucked snugly between them both.

Playing house with Harley and Blaise is ridiculous and a danger to my health.

The twins have to wait another week before they can join us. Ash rages down the phone at me for an hour before I send smoke signals to Avery to get him to shut the fuck up.

Blaise is smug as fuck, and Harley thinks it's hil-fucking-arious and stops taking his calls to piss him off even more.

They make a game of taunting Ash with random photos and videos of me in compromising positions. Half of them are stupid and the other half make me blush furiously and lock myself in the bathroom. I lose my cool with Blaise after he steals my phone to send fake sexts, and I break his phone against a wall in retaliation. He's fucking loaded so he barely even shrugs about the loss.

When I video call Ash later that night, he snarks at me, "Well, I didn't think you'd be texting me about your greedy, dripping pussy aching for my cock."

I gulp.

Well, maybe I'm not going to text that *now*, but I wouldn't write it off for later.

I make both of the assholes sleep on the fucking couches.

Even with the fun of hanging out and just being 'normal' for a week, I can feel the dread starting to build deep in my gut as my seventeenth birthday approaches.

No amount of fun and games is going to stop the anguish from swallowing me whole.

I warn them both about what to expect, my complete inability to function, but Harley assumes he has superpowers and will be able to get me to move.

He doesn't.

I don't.

Harley holds me to his chest and promises me French toast if I get up. When that doesn't work he promises me a private Vanth Falling concert in the bedroom if I sit up and eat something. Finally, he promises me the world if I'll open my eyes.

I can't.

Not even for him.

Eventually, he gets out of bed and snaps at Blaise to watch me. The bed dips as Blaise sits down and begins to stroke my back. I want to thank him, I want to crack a joke about role reversal and me being finally being the morbid one. I can't. There's nothing left of me.

Blaise doesn't try to speak to me, just touches me gently like I'm so fucking breakable. Fuck, I guess right now I am. Then Harley's voice starts up again.

"She won't move or speak, I'm freaking the fuck out... yes, Floss... yes, come now...I don't care, just get in the fucking car and come now."

Then he stops talking. Blaise strokes the hair away from my face. Eventually he leaves me too, and I can wallow in the silence by myself.

I become aware again to the sound of Avery's sharp tones as she breathes pure ice at her cousin.

"I told you, she doesn't do birthdays at all. She functioned for Christmas because it meant something to you. She *will not* do her birthday, not even for us. Just let her have her fucking space and stop trying to fix her." I feel her lips brush my cheek.

There's murmuring by the door and then cool air washes over my body as the blankets lift and someone climbs in next to me. I don't move or speak. If the heady smell of his skin didn't tip me off, the fingers tracing patterns on my thighs are a dead giveaway that it's Ash. It's fucking hard work, but I manage to sigh.

"Shh, Mounty. We're not functioning today. Avery is going to babysit the other two and keep them busy. You and me will be nothing in here together."

I don't know how long I take, but I slowly move until my head hits his chest, and he takes it as the request it is to bundle me into his arms. I can't open my eyes or speak, but he doesn't seem to care.

"When you're feeling better tomorrow, can you shake that perfect ass of yours for me again? I've been thinking about it non-stop and, fuck, I can't go another fucking day without seeing it in the flesh. The way your hips move, I can't wait to see how you move on my cock."

A shiver runs down my spine and he hums under his breath. "Good to know you're still alive, Mounty. Do you want to hear all about what I'm going to do to you when you're back in the land of the living? All of the things we have to look forward to?"

Chapter Four

Nobody on this earth can make my coffee as well as Avery can.

To my utter surprise and delight, she loves the townhouse. I was sure she'd hate how tiny it is, especially since she brought more bags than the guys combined, and we're all tripping over her shit, but having us all in one spot is all she really needs. We only get one last week together before our classes start.

We both wake up hours before the guys do so we can drink coffee and sift through the mess we're in without their pissy comments. It's fucking bliss.

"What's going to happen now the Vulture is dead?" Avery sips her coffee and nibbles delicately on her breakfast.

I eat mine like an animal, zero fucks given. "They'll run the Game again. It'll take eight or nine months before we have a new member. A lot of palms have to be greased before they can start, and the Vulture's empire needs to be assessed, divided, and dismantled."

Avery cocks her head at me. "How does that work? Who decides that?"

I sigh. "The Crow and the Jackal will go head-to-head for it, I guess. No one else has any interest in selling skin and it'll be another full-time operation to take on. The Jackal would love nothing more than adding skin to his empire. The Crow… I don't know. He'll want to take it on just so the Jackal doesn't get bigger than him but I don't see him keeping it. He's not… how do I say this… he's ruthless. He's cold, clinical, and he won't hesitate. It's what's made his empire the only rival to the Jackal, but he's not a predator. I've seen what the Jackal does to girls, I know what he'll do if he takes over the Vulture's work. I can't see the Crow selling unwilling skin. Running willing girls, hell yeah, but importing kidnapped teenagers to drug and sell off? Nope."

Avery shudders. "I wonder how much money my father has spent at those auctions."

I grimace. I don't want to think about it either, I don't want to be reminded of how much work I still have to do on the Beaumont front. I've only really made strides with the O'Cronin bunch. Having Illi around may become a blessing beyond his ability to kill.

"How's the bed sharing going? I haven't been woken in the middle of the night to the sounds of moaning so I'm assuming you haven't jumped straight into group sex."

I choke so hard on my coffee that it comes out of my fucking nose. Avery screeches with laughter and I decide I'm breaking up with *her*.

When I've mopped up the mess I croak, "Harley decided to tell the others I'm inexperienced so they've become fucking teases."

And, *fuck me*, were they good at it.

Blaise refuses to wear a shirt inside the house during the morning and I'm fucking dying over it. Ash saw it as a challenge, to melt my brain and my damned panties, and he has taken to going for his morning run in the tiniest pair of fucking shorts I have ever seen on a man. I now fantasize about those shorts on that ass in the shower. I tell Avery to order fifty fucking pairs of them and she gags at me dramatically. Harley enjoys watching me; his eyes smoldering and intense, undressing me and fucking me with one damn look, and then when I approach him he backs off.

I think they want me to beg.

I also think I'm going to.

Avery cocks an eyebrow at me. "Well, if you want to break Ash just put on some of the lace he picked out for you. I still can't believe you didn't realize how much he wanted you back then. He insisted on picking out your damn *panties*, for Christ's sake."

I shake my head at her.

She's been giving me shit about it since the day she joined me in the bathroom and laid it all out for me. I consider it for a second and then smirk at her.

"Wanna help me get back at them? Beat them at their own game?"

She quirks an eyebrow at me over the rim of her cup. "Always, Mounty."

I lied. I'm never letting this evil queen go.

On our last night at the townhouse, Avery declares that she's made reservations for us all to eat at a restaurant on the nice side of the city and then shepherds me into her room to get ready. It's barely three in the afternoon so I have no idea why it would take us three hours to get ready. I grumble this at her.

She clutches her stomach as she laughs at me.

It takes even longer.

Avery treats me like her own freaking doll to play with, and I just shut my eyes and let her. She tames and curls my hair into stunning, gentle waves. My makeup is simple, but with a bright red lipstick that makes my pout look lush and sexy. The black dress Avery pulls out of her wardrobe for me is sleek, stunning, and I tell her to *never* let it slip how much it cost her. It has a high neckline and from the front it looks modest, even with the skirt landing just above my knee. The show-stopper is the back, where the cutout dips low and ruches up over my ass so it looks rounded and pert. The neckline buttons at the top to look like a choker, and fuck, even I get a little excited at the look.

Avery cackles.

"Is this what you were thinking when you asked for my help?" She gloats.

I shake my ass at her and she laughs even harder. "This is better. I didn't know my ass could look this good."

There's a thump at the door and Harley grumbles at us both. "Are we going to dinner or a fucking fashion parade? I'm hungry, and if Morrison smokes anymore he's going to be useless."

I swing the door open, to find Blaise and chew him out, and Harley takes a step back at the sight of me. I smirk, even though I am having some trouble breathing at the sight of him in black slacks and a white button-up shirt.

"Jesus Christ, you're both drooling." Avery grouses as she sidles past me.

Harley smirks and steps forward to tug me into his arms. "You look like a *lady*. It's fucking weird."

I scoff at him and I'd be insulted if he wasn't looking at me like he wanted to rip the dress the fuck off of me. He hasn't even seen the best part yet. "I'm assuming Avery is taking us to some uppity place, and I can't wear a band tee and Docs there."

Harley smirks. "Blaise is still going to try."

Avery's screeching cuts through the air and we both laugh at Blaise's pissy reply. Harley's hands smooth over my ass as he leans down to kiss me. I think he was only planning for it to be a quick peck, but I open my lips to his the second they touch and I swallow his groan. Footsteps in the living room pull us apart.

"Are we still going to dinner, or are the two of you just going to fuck in the hallway?" Ash snarks and I smirk back at him.

"I'm not wasting my dress. Let's go." I pull away from Harley, and walk to the door without looking back. I hear gasps and curses, and I smile like an idiot. Avery's smug face tells me everything I need to know about their reaction to the back of my dress.

"Pretty sure you could get any of them to bend you over something right now if you wanted."

I smirk back at the guys. Blaise has joined them, and has paused in buttoning up his dress shirt to stare at me, his eyes ravenous.

"I'm hungry. Let's go eat."

Take that, assholes.

Blaise drives us in the Maserati and I sit between Ash and Harley in the back. Harley tucks his hand into mine and lets his head drop back against the headrest with his eyes closed. Ash scowls out of the window and traces patterns into the exposed skin on my thigh. When I shift in my seat he looks over at me and smirks.

"Black?" he whispers and I know exactly what he's asking.

"Nothing. I didn't want there to be lines."

Ash sucks in a breath and Harley's hand spasms in mine. I grin at Avery when she glances back at me, satisfied I've finally one-upped them in their own game.

The restaurant is ridiculously ritzy, the type of place I imagine Ash and Avery frequent because they fit right in. Blaise is at ease, but looks around with thinly veiled disgust. Harley is the only one who shares my outraged looks when we see the prices of the dishes.

"Is the lobster going to serve itself to me for that fucking price? I haven't spent that much on *groceries* for the entire fucking break."

Avery smirks at me, but Ash looks confused. "How much do groceries cost in the slums?"

Blaise cackles like a madman at the look I throw at the spoiled asshole. "I'm no longer feeding you. Also, you're on the couch tonight."

"Snap, motherfucker," Avery murmurs under her breath, mocking me the way only she can get away with.

Ash glares at her and Harley slings a smug arm around the back of my chair. I'm tempted to order the mango chicken, as a threat to Ash because I know he's allergic, but I decide not to play with fire and order a pasta dish to eat my feelings. Plus, it's the only dish under a hundred dollars on the menu that *isn't* a salad.

"So, how are we all feeling about Hannaford tomorrow?" Avery asks sweetly, and Blaise throws a linen napkin at her.

"I'm glad we don't have to worry about Joey breaking down your door," Ash says, and drinks his bourbon. Yep, the spoiled, seventeen-year-old asshole ordered a bourbon and no one questioned him.

"I'm going to join the state team for swimming. I'm going to apply for some scholarships for college, see if that gives me a better chance," Harley mutters. Avery meets my gaze and I give her a tiny shake of my head. I haven't told him my plans yet and I'm not going to.

"I'm getting my neck tattooed. And my hands. Oh, and I've signed up for the highest classes this year because I'm clearly fucking insane, but the Mounty has promised me she'll get me through it. If she succeeds in getting me to follow you lot to college, I'll have to get the marks to get in," Blaise says, cheerfully.

I smile at him, but the other three all stare at him with various degrees of shock on their faces. Ash recovers first. "Your father will disown you if you tattoo your hands and neck."

Oh. So, he hasn't told them all yet. Shit.

Blaise clears his throat. "Too late, he already has. Family announcement; my mom's pregnant. It's a boy. I've been cut out of the family now there's a replacement son on the way. Oh look, dinner's here."

The stunned silence continues until the waiters have left. Blaise and I tuck into our dinner happily, but it takes the others a minute to start in on theirs.

"Congrats, I guess?" Harley says, and Ash snorts at him.

"He's not the one who's fucking pregnant, and who the hell said that this is a good thing?"

Avery cocks her head. "Did your dad definitely disown you? Can I start ruining his life now?"

I smirk at her. "*We*, Aves, can *we* start ruining his life now? I have some *very* creative plans for Mr. Blaine Morrison."

Blaise looks between us. "What plans?"

"I'm going to royally, and viciously, fuck that man up."

Harley and Ash both whoop with excitement and Blaise looks vaguely concerned. Avery continues to eat her salmon delicately, pausing to say, "Are they going to name the baby Blaise, too? Just completely replace you?"

It sounds harsh as fuck, but the scorn isn't directed at Blaise. He scratches the back of his neck awkwardly. "Blaire. They're naming him Blaire."

I cringe for him. "At least it's not Eclipse?"

Chapter Five

Driving through the gates at Hannaford feels different this year.

Granted, I'm in the front seat of the Maserati, earplugs in and singing along to the new and unreleased Vanth record like a total fucking groupie, and Blaise keeps biting his lip as he shoots me these little awed looks. Harley and the twins are in the 'Stang behind us and when both cars pull into the staff parking Blaise leaves the car idling until the song finishes.

When we finally get out, Avery is there with her phone, grinning at me and when the boys' phones all ping at the same time I know she's fucking recorded my singing through the open car window.

"Ash threatened me, Lips, I was forced," she purrs and I don't believe her for a hot second.

Harley slings my bag across his shoulder and I give him a little nod. My safe and the diamonds are in there. I trust him implicitly so I don't mind him taking it, but I want him aware they're there. Fuck it, I'll probably get them to help me pick the hiding spot this year.

Blaise and Ash bicker happily while I tuck myself under Blaise's arm, still nervous about being so open about touching them. I mean, the Jackal knows about Harley and I've made it clear I'm not interested in submitting to him, but it's still fucking nerve wracking to do this. What if I paint a target on them too? *Fuck.*

Blaise notices my hesitation and curls around me protectively. I swallow roughly at the lump that forms in my throat. I'm never going to get used to being protected and cared for.

We get the same room as last year, thanks to Avery, and she pitches a fit to get the guys to leave us alone. It's nice to get settled by ourselves. School starts tomorrow and we all have to adjust to being back amongst the snakes we share the halls with.

By the time I've helped Avery unpack her shit, I already miss the little bubble we'd been in at the townhouse.

Avery shoves a tub of ice cream at me and when I grumble about it she waves her own at me. We watch *Ghost* together after she finds out I've never seen it, and we mope about being stuck here for another two years. Okay, I mope, Avery plots on her phone and snarks at my shitty attitude.

I wake up just as pissy as I went to bed and it's only as I get dressed into my uniform that I finally remember I have something to be fucking thrilled about this year.

Three words: Thigh. High. Socks.

Junior year is going to be the fucking *best* year at the shitty snake-pit known as

Hannaford Preparatory Academy. Avery laughs her ass off at me when she sees me twirling around our room in my uniform, squealing like a child at the socks pulled right up my leg.

Fuck yes!

Now if only I could convince the school board to ditch the kitten heels and let me wear my Docs, I'd be fucking set. Avery winces at me when I suggest it to her. Traitor.

"What class do we have first? I've barely looked at my schedule," I grumble as I finally tug the kitten heels on.

Avery hums under her breath as she fusses with her already perfect hair. "We have a full school assembly first. It's a late addition, I've messaged Mr. Trevelen and the head of the school board, but haven't heard back from either of them to say what it's for."

I frown.

I'm not a fan of surprises and life just keeps throwing them my way.

The sound of our door unlocking startles me and I shoot Avery a look. She rolls her eyes. "Ash insisted on having a copy. He says it's for emergency use only and *apparently* having a locked door between him and his Mounty this morning counts as an emergency."

Ash strides into the room, Harley and Blaise following closely behind him. They all look fucking devastating in their uniforms and I swear I ruin my panties.

Ash smirks at me and calls out to his sister, "Avery, do we *really* have to have another conversation about your attitude towards my relationship with the Mounty?"

She shrugs sweetly. "If I come back here one day and find you with your dick out, I'll destroy you. Slowly, and with great pleasure."

Right.

I move away from the escalating Beaumont Bullshit and sling my bag over my shoulder. Blaise grins at me and gives me a quick kiss, no tongue because he's a little worried now I've armed Avery with the same type of knife I carry at all times. He's seen first-hand how sharp it is and, despite what his asshole father thinks, he's not stupid.

Harley bites his lip at the sight of my socks and hauls me into his arms, a hand cupping my face as he kisses me, walking us both to the door without breaking the kiss. It's fucking stupid, but I swoon.

He breaks away with a grin and Blaise cackles at one of Avery's snipes to her brother, trailing behind us as we head out.

Four steps.

We make it four fucking steps into the hallway before Annabelle *freaking* Summers accosts us.

"You're all fucking the Mounty *slut* now?" she spits and I clench my jaw at her.

Harley snorts at her and keeps walking, ignoring her completely. I glance back at Blaise only to find she's thrown herself at him. He's trying to, carefully, pry her arms off of him and she starts to sob dramatically. I could fucking vomit at the sight of her.

Harley drops his arm from me, ready for one of us to go deal with her, but there's no need.

Avery dumps a full cup of piping hot coffee over her head.

Annabelle screeches, scrambling away from Blaise and her pathetically fake sobs turn into gut-wrenching real ones. All of the girls in the hall freeze and gape at Avery. I mean, I kind of do too.

She stares down at Annabelle and then surveys the other girls with a detached look. Ash steps up behind her, backing her in every sense of the word.

"I'm done asking nicely. Anyone who interferes with my family from this moment onwards will be dealt with immediately and with force. I will no longer hold back and there is *nothing* I could do to any of you little bitches that I couldn't make disappear from the records. Remember that," Avery says, her voice is glacial and I smile at her like she's my fucking soulmate. "Ash, Harley, and Blaise are off limits to you sluts. This is the only warning you're all getting."

Harley scoffs and whispers in my ear, "Stop looking at her like you want to fuck her, you'll give us all a complex."

I quirk an eyebrow at him. "If we both swung that way, we'd be fucking married by now. I would have wifed her ass last year."

He roars with laughter.

Mr Trevelen starts his welcome speech and I zone the fuck out.

The chapel is still my least favorite place at Hannaford. It's slightly more bearable to be in here now that I am firmly wedged between Avery and Ash, his fingers tracing patterns into my thighs in a delicious way that makes me want to squirm. Thanks to his dirty mouth on my birthday, I now associate those patterns with the filthy things he'd whispered to me.

I was fucking starving and these bastards were parading around like French toast topped with cherry ice cream served with freshly brewed coffee.

I'm gonna break.

My attention snaps back to the stage as a woman in her late twenties walks across, her heels far too high to be a teacher. She's attractive; curvy and seductive, blonde hair with a slash of red lipstick finishing off the Monroe look. She caresses Mr. Trevelen's arm as she passes him and his feet stumble. The row of sophomores in front of us start whispering and shifting in their seats. Avery and I share a look.

The fingers on my thighs don't falter.

"Thank you for that glowing introduction, Richard. Good morning, students. As your principal has just informed you, my name is Ms. Vivienne Turner. I expect I will enjoy meeting you individually throughout this first week and teaching you all history."

Avery and I share another look before her phone comes out. Blaise angles his body so the teacher at the end of our aisle can't see what she's doing. Mr. Embley is on the Jackal's payroll and we've already discussed keeping a low profile with him until we can flush out his other eyes in the school.

Ms. Turner leaves the stage, swaying her hips like she's trying to fuck the air, and Trevelen steps back up to drone on and on about his plans for the school and I let my mind wander away from his continued naivety. I need to get ahead in my studies early this year. I need to be more prepared than I was last year because there is a lot more on my plate. I have three boyfriends, I'm protecting the man who killed the Vulture, the Jackal wants Harley dead, I haven't sorted out the O'Cronins yet, the Beaumonts, and now there's the Morrisons. *Sweet lord fuck*, I may be in over my head.

When the assembly finally finishes, we leave for our morning classes together.

Avery slips her arm into mine and murmurs quietly into my ear, "I just heard back from the school board. Annabelle is here on the scholarship."

I cut her a look. A freshman nudges past us and the snarl Blaise throws at him is orgasm-inducing. "Why would they give it to her? She's barely scraping through her classes."

Avery snorts. "She wrote to them over the break and made her case to them. Told them she wanted the right education to resurrect her family business."

I roll my eyes. "Sure. She's *definitely* here for education and not for dick."

When we arrive to class for the day, having skipped the first two sessions thanks to the assembly, Blaise sulks when he finds himself on the other side of the room thanks to the alphabetical seating arrangement.

I'm at the back of our history class with Harley and the twins are directly in front of us. I don't know the girl that's seated with Blaise and that worries me. I make a note to see who the hell she is and find out what her grade average is. With all of the joint assignments we're forced to do, I need to know that she's not going to be a dead-weight.

Harley sees me eyeing her and hands me the syllabus; Avery must have gotten it early for him. He's already marked the joint assignments and where we'll split them. I smile sweetly at him. I'm sure it looks fucking stupid on my face, but he grins back.

"I have plenty of shit to keep you busy with this year," he jokes and I snort at him.

He cackles back at me and says, "We can split the children up, work out study plans and keep everyone on top. If you show me how to teach Morrison, I'll try not to rip his throat out when he's a dick to me."

I roll my eyes at him. "Maybe if you didn't talk to him like *that* he wouldn't be a dick back."

Harley shrugs. "He's always going to be a dick, Mounty; it's in every fiber of his being."

I open my mouth to snark at him, fuck knows why I'm defending Blaise because he is a total *dick*, but the door opens and our new teacher walks in like she's a stripper walking up to the pole. Christ, give me the fucking strength I need to get through this.

She smiles coyly at the male students, one by one like she's sizing them all up. Avery glances back at me with a murder in her eyes when Ms. Turner zeros in on Harley. I have two thoughts; I fucking adore that girl, and the new teacher is walking a dangerous line.

"Good morning! You all get the absolute *pleasure* of being the first students to enjoy me this year."

Blaise's snort is so loud we hear it across the room and Avery giggles at him. Ms. Turner ignores it and starts to write on the board.

"I prefer to be addressed as Ms. Vivienne. Ms. Turner sounds too old and matronly for someone of my charms."

I share another look with Avery. She sounds like a bitch in heat and it's fucking gross.

She prattles on about the *joys* and *wonders* of history in a breathy tone. I zone her the fuck out and look over the syllabus instead. I'm planning out what I'm going to tackle first when she starts handing out a pop quiz, bending low for each of the guys in the room. Ash snatches the paper out of her hand and sneers at her. When she blinks at him, shocked that he isn't panting like every other dick in the room, he hands us each a quiz.

Harley cackles. "Thanks, man."

I finish the pop quiz first, which is no surprise, but what is surprising is that

Ash finishes his before Harley. I raise my brows at him and he smirks at me. The lying asshole, I knew he was smarter than he ever let on! Harley glares at him and I suddenly realize a whole new headache I'm going to be dealing with this year.

Ms. *Vivienne* walks around the room to look over the quizzes, one by one, and I'm relieved when she smiles at Blaise and gives him a B. Thank fuck.

When she gets to our desk she rests her hip on it and crosses her arms under her tits, pushing them up so they're about to spill out of her shirt and over Harley.

Who the fuck is this bitch?

Harley stares at the whiteboard, his eyes don't even flick in her direction, and once I realize she's nothing but a fucking cradle-snatching predator on the prowl, I stare ahead as well. No point giving the bitch the attention she wants. Harley smirks and tucks his hand into mine under the desk. Avery is the only one still watching her and I know exactly what's going through her mind.

Assess.

Plan.

Destroy.

When Ms. Vivienne realizes she hasn't caught Harley's attention at all she leans across to the desk next to ours, pushing her ass into his arm. The guys across from us groan lustfully, but Harley's hand clenches in mine.

He's not like Ash.

He might not want to hurt a woman, but he's not morally against it either. If a bitch threatens him or his family, he's not going to find a peaceful resolution. He's going to deal with the fucking problem.

He wants to deal with *this* problem.

I lean into him and whisper, "Do you want me to take her out?"

Harley smirks back. "Stop flirting with me, Mounty."

When the class finally fucking ends, Ms. Vivienne calls out as we pack up. "Mr. Arbour, if you could please stay behind after the class ends. I have something to discuss with you."

My gaze snaps up to her face. Avery and Harley glare towards Ms. Vivienne, and she smiles seductively back at Harley.

Fuck that.

I lean in to make a show of whispering to him, "I'll slit her throat and watch her bleed out if she touches you."

Harley smirks back at me. "I'll warn her."

We survive the day without me having to kill anyone, but I don't get the chance to ask Harley what the hell the bitch wanted. I mention it to Avery when we get back to our room for dinner.

She sighs and flicks the coffee machine on for me. "She's a ghost. Her file is full, but it's all clean. I had someone trawl through her entire existence online and *nothing*. I thought she had to have a statutory rape hiding somewhere."

I groan as I pull my shoes off, my feet aching from the stupid heels after weeks of my comfortable Docs. Avery starts fussing with pots and pans in the kitchen, not cooking, but scrubbing maniacally. I understand her rage completely.

Which reminds me.

"The word slut is officially off-limits. If any-fucking-one calls me a Mounty slut again, I'm pulling their fingernails out with pliers," I grumble and Avery raises an eyebrow at me.

"Is that a hypothetical or is it in your skill set?"

I cut her a look. "It's in my skill set."

She tilts her head and hums under her breath. We've never discussed the specifics of what I *can* and *have* done before. I wait a minute, but when she doesn't reply I say, "Problem?"

She smirks. "Of course not, I'm just filing that information away in case a situation arises. It's good to know all the tools we have at our disposal."

I laugh at her and grab the cup of coffee she holds out to me.

Chapter Six

Harley texts us to meet him in the dining hall for breakfast the next morning.

Avery makes us both coffees to go. She doesn't look up from her phone the whole way down, trusting me to lead her there safely with her arm tucked tight in mine. I'm so distracted by my own thoughts and worries of what the fuck the history teacher wanted with him that I don't notice the guy that steps into our path until I slam into him.

I grunt at the sharp pain that shoots up my leg and Avery, thankfully, manages to keep a firm grip of my arm to keep me upright. Her eyes make a quick assessment of whoever the fuck we've hit and then her fingers fly across the screen of her phone.

I glance up to see Darcy.

Now, I know it's not Thomas Darcy, because he was a senior last year and this guy is a good foot shorter than him, but the likeness is striking.

I mentally nickname him little Darcy.

"What can I do for you, asshole?" I snap and Avery giggles at my attitude, lapping it up.

He smirks at me and rubs his chest where I'd bumped into him. "I've been looking for you everywhere, Mounty! My brother did warn me that you're a hard girl to catch."

I roll my eyes and take a step around him, holding in the wince. Just what I need, my leg to act up.

"I just wanted to make sure you haven't been whoring over the summer break? I know that's the common occupation for girls like you and I need to know you didn't have to earn the roof over your head. I've taken over Thomas's position as bet keeper."

For. Fuck's. Sake.

I'm rendered speechless for a second over his disgusting arrogance. No matter, Avery has my back and speaks for me.

"Joey's graduated, there is no bet. Move, Darcy, before I make you disappear in a permanent sort of way," she says, sweet and dangerous.

Little Darcy has no survival instincts and his mouth just keeps running. "Just because Joey isn't here anymore, doesn't mean the bet isn't ongoing. I'm happy to clear the cobwebs out, Mounty! Maybe the time away from cock has tightened that pussy up a bit."

Deep breath in. Deep breath out…

Is what a normal person would do. Me? I break the fucker's nose with the heel of my palm and then punch him so hard in the dick I think his fucking ancestors feel it.

The squealing sound that comes out of him is magical.

Avery giggles and records the entire thing on her phone. I think about telling her to put it the fuck away because I'm going to gut the creepy fuck, but then I hear a bag drop to the floor and see the blur of dark hair and solid muscle fly past us to pin little Darcy against the wall.

"Say it again, Darcy. Proposition my girlfriend again, I want to hear it for myself before I put you in a fucking *coma*."

I swear to god, my heart stops.

The room stops too, all of the students stop moving and talking and fucking *breathing* now there's an enraged Beaumont snarling in their presence. I have to remind my body that the Jackal doesn't own me and I can be with whoever the fuck I want, but there's still a little panic in me at Ash's words.

I just wanted more time to ourselves without the fucking gossips, and the threat of the Jackal hanging over all three of them. Fuck.

"I didn't know she was yours!" sputters little Darcy, literally sputters because there's blood pouring out of his nose and his mouth. Avery cringes away from them, tugging my arm, but I want to see this. I want to know how Ash is going to play this.

"She's mine. She's Arbour's, and she's Morrison's, and if I find out a single dickhead has propositioned her, I will take them out. Gone. *No fucking more*." He speaks loud enough that the students watching all hear his words and I blush at the looks I'm now getting.

There are quite a few girls dumb enough to glare at me and Avery starts taking note on her phone. I roll my eyes at her. I don't have time to deal with petty teenage bullshit. Let them be jealous, fuck, I was writhing with it when I thought Annabelle had what I now do.

Ash moves a hand to grip little Darcy's throat, squeezing enough that his eyes get panicked. "My beloved sister is going to pass along the Mounty's bank details and you're going to deposit the sweep in there. It's her fucking money. If I catch you within ten feet of her again... gone, Darcy. *Gone*."

Little Darcy's phone pings and Avery gives him a sarcastic little wave. Ash drops his hands and takes a step back, swooping down to grab his bag and then he glares around the room until the captive audience scurries away.

"I had it under control." I grouse, and he snorts at me.

"Just let me defend you for once, Mounty, for Christ's sake. Besides, we needed to get word out somehow that you're our girlfriend and not just a random fuck. No better way than making someone bleed."

Avery gives him a look. "You had better not be fucking her."

Ash watches me take one wobbling step and then sighs, slinging an arm around my waist to mold me into his side. Avery tucks her arm into his on the other side but the stern look stays on her face.

"Avery, please. At some point Lips is going to want to fuck me."

Nope.

I try to pull away from him but he laughs at me, the dick, and tightens his arm.

"Lips, I'm firmly team Morrison on the v card debate," Avery says, her voice too fucking loud as we walk through the halls teeming with students.

Why? *Why*?! What have I done to deserve this?!

"You're my sister, you're supposed to be on my side!" Ash hisses back at her, pissy at her supposed betrayal.

Avery giggles and shakes her head at him like he's simple. It's nice to see it directed somewhere other than at me. "We've discussed this. It's a Battle Royale for my affections. Lips is in the lead; massively, you should really start focusing on me more. Morrison is next. Then, you and Harley are joint losers."

"What the fuck has Morrison done to get ahead?"

Avery smirks at him and I decide that death is preferable to this conversation. "You keep arguing with me over Lips, and Harley keeps shoving his tongue down her throat in my presence. Morrison at least *attempts* some form of discretion."

The news of my three-way relationship hits the dining hall before we do.

Blaise is slouched over, held up only by the wall, and Harley is frowning down at his phone as we arrive. He glances up and does a quick once over of me before sneering at Ash, "A public claiming, really? Like she doesn't already have enough on her fucking plate."

Ash's eyes grow glacial and I groan. "I've just *removed* things from her plate. Now there isn't a guy at this school that will touch her because I will personally beat the life out of them."

I shiver and pull away from him so he doesn't give me shit for reacting like he's given me flowers or some other shit normal girls like.

Blaise pushes off from the wall and tucks me under his arm. "Whatever, it's done now. Can we eat so this day can start? I already need it to fucking end."

We move into the dining hall without waiting for their answers, Blaise rubbing his cheek on the top of my head as he yawns like a damn cat.

Every eye turns to watch us.

I tense and only Blaise's arm around me stops me from pulling away from him. Avery steps up to my side and slips her arm into mine, glaring around the room until the other students avert their gaze.

"Just ignore them, Star." Blaise mumbles, and that snaps me out of my awkward nervousness. I give him my best impression of Avery's icy glare.

"What the hell kind of nickname is that?" Avery mocks and Blaise's eyes fucking twinkle. I think about thumbing them the fuck *out.*

"It's an inside joke, you wouldn't get it." He smirks and grabs a tray to fill.

Once we're seated and digging into our breakfasts, Harley's eyes flick to the door and groans. I glance over my shoulder to find *Ms. Vivienne* sauntering in. Blaise snickers under his breath and I jab him in the ribs.

"She offered to write up a *personal* recommendation letter to three different scholarship programs for me if I join her gifted students study group." Harley says, watching her warily.

"She offered that to you and not Lips? She beats you in every class, except choir where she's beating Morrison." Ash, very helpfully, but also very dickishly, supplies.

Harley doesn't take the bait, he just raises a brow and says, "I'm aware of that, but the Mounty doesn't have a dick so I don't think she's the slut's type."

Avery holds up a palm. "I think I should warn you all. Lips has declared the word *slut* off limits. If you like your fingernails where they are, I'd choose a new word."

They all look at me and I shrug. "Pliers hurt like a bitch."

Harley smirks at me. "Is that how you're going to make her bleed over my honor, Mounty?"

I throw a napkin at his smug face. "What honor? You should take her up on it."

Avery cuts me a sharp look and I shrug. "We have nothing on her. Best case scenario she tries to touch him, and after he breaks her *fucking* hand, we own her. Worst case scenario, he has an in for scholarships."

I'm not happy about it, but I'm also not going to be possessive and pathetic about this. Either I trust him or I don't, and I wouldn't have told him I was the Wolf if I didn't trust him. Besides, she's a desperate, attention-seeking cougar. What do we have to be worried about?

Avery looks impressed. "*Ruthless.* I love it."

Harley's eyes narrow. "You're not worried about me?"

"You gonna fuck her? No? Then I'm not worried. If she gets handsy I'm confident you'll be able to figure it out. Just don't accept any drinks from the bitch."

Blaise roars with laughter over the face Harley pulls, but Avery steers the conversation into a safer direction.

Chapter Seven

We agree to all meet back at our room on Friday to have an early dinner together.

I barely get to see Harley outside of class now he has his extra workload and practice with the swim team. I can tell he's starting to get twitchy about it, and after the first few weeks of being forced away from me, I find myself being backed into the bathroom for a blistering kiss. He only stops because Avery throws a serving spoon at his head. I blush profusely, but no one seems to care about my mortification. The routine is soothing for Avery, and I find it great to just hang out after another hectic week in hell.

After dinner is over and the kitchen is clean, Ash, Avery, and Harley all head off to their training sessions, and Blaise and I pull an extra study session together.

We always study until Avery gets back and death glares him into leaving with a quick kiss, which is why I'm shocked to find him lounging on my bed as I come out of the bathroom from changing out of my uniform.

I quirk an eyebrow at him and he grins at me, patting the bed playfully.

"Come on, Mounty, I've been good," he practically fucking purrs at me.

My traitorous knees tremble, but I tell them to quit. I do not need a repeat of last year, playing catch up and wading through piles of assignments last minute with him, so I prop my hands on my hips and give him my best impression of Avery's stern looks.

I'm so fucking ready to chew him out for putting the work off, but then he leans forward to strip his blazer off, popping two buttons on his shirt and letting the color of his tattoos peek out.

Sweet lord.

I cave.

I cave so fucking quickly, climbing up to lay beside him and he covers me with the hard lines of his body the second I do, like he's as desperate as I am. He stares down at me for a second and whatever it is he's looking for he finds, grinning and swooping down to take my lips.

As we kiss, deep and dirty, I slide my hands into the open collar to rub at the vibrant colors of his skin and his answering groan is *obscene*. I fucking love kissing him. The way he uses his whole body, like he needs to move against me because it's too fucking hard to stay still.

He pulls my hips flush into his and my heart stutters in my chest. I'm so fucking worked up and ready for *something* to happen. He moves his lips to kiss down my neck and I can't think anymore.

I'm fucking horny.

That's what's happening here.

They've all been teasing me and working me into a frenzy and, goddammit, someone had better fucking do something about it, or I'm going to have to deal with the problem myself.

When I tell Blaise this, groaning out the words while he sucks on the soft skin below my ear, he grinds his hips into me harder.

There's laughter in his voice as he says, "I can do something about it, Star. What do you want?"

I blanch.

Well fuck, I don't know!

He chuckles under his breath at me and I give him a glare. "If you're going to be a dick about me being a clueless virgin I'm going to go have a cold shower instead."

I move to try to pull away, but he doesn't let go of my hips and the movement makes me rub against his dick. I cannot think about how big or hard he is without gulping and blushing like an idiot.

He groans at me, "Fuck, I'm not being an asshole; I'm trying to go slow. Pick something you've already done."

I blush and glare at him some more.

I watch as it clicks in his brain. He reels back. "You're not serious?"

Miraculously, my face somehow gets even hotter. I snap, "Yes, I'm fucking serious! You know I'm a virgin."

Blaise blows out a breath and reaches for his phone, his body curving over me and pressing me into the bed in an entirely too distracting type of way. "Being a virgin doesn't mean you've never fooled around before. You've never made out with a guy and gotten each other off?"

My mind flashes to the fucking insanely erotic feeling of grinding down on Harley's dick and I cough to hide my reaction. "No. I've barely done anything. Thanks for taking that so well, Jesus. Who are you calling? If you're going to fucking *tattle*—"

He presses a hand over my mouth and slides down onto the bed, maneuvering us around until my back is pressed against his chest. He pulls me until my head drops back onto his shoulder and my throat is bared, as if he's going to slit me ear to ear. It definitely should not be a turn on, but I think we all know I'm not in the ballpark of normal.

He breathes into my ear, a shiver running down my spine, "I want to make you come so fucking hard the Jackal hears you screaming my name from his little fortress. I want you so fucking wet that your come runs down my arm and I can smell you on my skin for days. You're gonna let me touch you, aren't you, Star? I want to watch you come."

Sweet merciful lord.

Who fucking taught him to talk like *that*?!

He doesn't move his hand away from my mouth so I'm forced to nod to answer him.

He mumbles happily into my shoulder as he licks and sucks his way along the skin there, tracing the little scars I have with his tongue until I'm squirming. I pant desperately through my nose when his free hand edges under my shirt and finds nothing but skin.

I decide I'm never fucking wearing a bra again.

His hand cups one of my boobs and squeezes, his groan smothered in the back of my neck sending ripples of pleasure down my spine. Thank the good lord I've been eating again and there's something for him to hold onto because I think I could come just from this.

"Fuck me," he groans, rolling my nipples between his calloused fingertips.

He grunts again when I grind my ass into his dick, and he moves the hand from my mouth for long enough to get the shirt off of me and flip me onto my back, then he keeps me quiet by kissing me like he's dying.

Fuck. Me.

I barely notice him tear my pants off. I'm too busy trying to get his stupid shirt off without just ripping the buttons off and eventually he takes pity on me. He takes off his pants as well, leaving only his boxers, and my mouth waters at the sight of him.

Fuuuuuuck.

I'm struck dumb for a minute and when my brain decides to work again I'm smug that he seems just as affected. He runs his hands up my stomach and over my tits.

"Where the fuck have you been hiding these?" He groans and I scoff at him.

"They come and go."

He leans down to bite my earlobe and growls, "Well don't fucking let them go again."

Bossy asshole but, fuck, that's hot.

I can't think of a witty retort and he kisses me again, biting at my lips and sucking until I'm fucking gone for him. His hands work their way lower and lower until they hit my panties.

My heart stutters, but I'm still so fucking desperate that I don't think twice about moaning into his kiss.

His fingers curve over the lace of my panties and he grunts when he can feel how wet I am already. He pulls away and mumbles something into the skin of my neck as he sucks on the skin there, but there is no way I can focus enough to grasp the words, not when he's marking up the skin on my neck and sliding his fingers through the mess I've already made.

He's barely even started.

I decide that I can't wait another damn second and I rip my own panties off so he'll hurry the hell up.

Works like a charm.

His fingers are sliding over my slick skin and rubbing my clit before my panties hit the floor. Jesus fucking Christ. I do not want to think about the number of girls he must have been with to find my clit that easily.

I'm going to come so fucking quick, the *weeks* of foreplay priming me to just cream for him. He's still a fucking tease, and when my legs start to tremble and thrash on the bed he moves from my pulsing clit to slip a finger in, hooking it up to rub over my G spot. I nearly jolt off the damn bed.

"Fuck, Mounty. Do you want to come?"

I nod and whimper like a whore. He grins at me, pumping his finger into me before adding a second, groaning at the tight fit. It doesn't hurt, but I'm probably going to knee him in the ribs if he tries for a third.

When I start to tremble, from sheer frustration at the orgasm that's *just* out of reach, he finally moves to rub my clit again, tight, maddening circles and I fucking shatter.

I come so hard I feel it run down his hand and my thighs, my head thrown back, his name ripped out of my chest in a gasp.

When I finally blink the stars out of my eyes I find Blaise grinning at me like the cat that got the cream.

Well, he certainly got mine.

It takes me two tries to find some words. "I don't think I can move."

He laughs at me and if I could move, I'd shove a pillow over his smug face. He moves like he's going to get off the bed and I grab his arm.

"Mounty, I'm just gonna go jerk off in your bathroom. After *that* it's not going to take me long."

I blush like an idiot but I tug him closer. "Do it here. I wanna watch."

He quirks an eyebrow up at me like he wasn't expecting that at all and, honestly, I wasn't expecting to say it either, but I don't want him to leave.

He kisses me again, so I miss his hand sliding into his boxers, but when he grunts against my lips I break away to rest my forehead on his chest and look down.

Holy fucking shit.

Okay, I'm now a little nervous about having sex with any of them because Blaise is probably the same size as Harley and, sweet fucking lord, how the hell is that going to fit in me? My mind wanders to Ash, because he's the only one I haven't gotten this close to yet, but Annabelle's taunts stick in my head about the extra inches he has. *Fuck.*

Blaise's eyes are glued somewhere between my nipples and the wet mess on my thighs so he misses the little moment of panic I have as he grunts and comes all over his fist.

Fuck.

That's a good look.

Blaise recovers a bit quicker than me, his face flushed and sweaty and fucking *stunning*, and he wipes his hand on his discarded shirt. I wrinkle my nose at him and he laughs at me, rolling off the bed to throw it in our laundry basket and wash his hands.

I still can't move.

It only makes him laugh harder, but I grin back at him, happy to finally see him without the gloom wrapped around him he's been carrying since he showed up in the Bay.

He helps me back into my shirt and then tucks us both into bed, switching the light off. I settle onto his chest, surprised to find myself close to sleep already. My eyes drift shut and he rubs circles on my back.

"Promise me you won't let Avery cut my dick off."

I blink at him, but it's too dark to really see if he's being serious. "What?"

"I sent her a text so she would stay back at our room with Ash and Harley, and we could have the room to ourselves all night. She's just messaged to say she knew I'd be the one to christen her knife. Mounty, I can't live without my dick."

I smother my laugh in his chest and fall asleep.

I wake to the smell of coffee, and open my eyes to find Avery wafting a cup under my nose.

I hum happily, grabbing the cup, and when I start to gulp down the sweet, sweet life-giving liquid Avery says, so sweetly, "And anything for your bedfellow this morning?"

Bedfellow?

Oh.

Fuck.

I almost forget the cup of piping hot coffee in my hand as I sit up. Thank fuck we put at least a little clothing back on last night before we fell asleep. My cheeks are burning as I brave a look at Avery. She smirks at me.

"I think he'd rather sleep in." I croak and shift around to try to get out of the bed without her noticing my bare ass.

"Exhausted, is he? Big night?" She coos and I give up, swinging my legs out and preparing to run for the bathroom, bare ass be damned! I need a minute for my brain to unscramble.

"You know he's not a morning person, Aves." I mumble and scurry off to the bathroom. I take my time getting clean, letting the water calm me down. Fuck. What the hell am I going to say to Harley or Ash about this? This is the real fucking test of whether or not they can share.

When I finally emerge Blaise is still snoring. Avery is cooking a mountain of pancakes and Ash is drinking a coffee like his life depends on it. When he hears the door, he turns to offer me a cup, no hesitation or judgment. I let out a breath.

"Harley's coming up when he's finished at the pool and we can study together. Avery is getting twitchy about biology already." He smirks and I join him at the bench. Pancakes aren't my favorite, but I could eat fifty of them I'm that hungry.

Avery snarks over her shoulder at him, "Why do we always have to cut up dead things? It's disgusting."

Ash snorts. "Too bad you're not paired with the Mounty, Harley told me word on the street says her hand is the steadiest."

I elbow him in the ribs while Avery laughs. We get set up on the table, pancakes and assignments spread out around us, and eat while we wait for Harley. I refuse to wake Blaise and I don't mention that it's because I know the real torture will start the moment he does. Avery is distracted, her mind on her phone more than her breakfast. When she looks up I quirk an eyebrow at her.

"Joey has moved to my father's estate in Washington. He has a new dealer and he's already causing problems there."

I pull a face at her. "Problems like a trail of dead bodies?"

Ash snorts. "Senior is not enjoying being on Joey babysitting duty. It was easier for him to leave it to us. He's already stabbed two of my father's men when they tried to stop him from going out."

I nod slowly. I have the opportunity to finally ask why the hell Ash's life depends on Joey breathing but I'm not sure now is the right time, with Blaise snoring and Harley on his way back. Avery sees the indecision on my face and cuts a careful look at Ash.

"Senior has made his *disappointment* very clear that Joey is the only one of his progeny to have inherited his taste for violence."

Right.

Gross.

Harley unlocks the door, for *fuck's sake* they all must have keys, and wanders in. He scoffs at Blaise's snoring form and throws a pillow at him. Blaise doesn't so much as twitch. Harley pulls up a chair next to mine and, though his eyes are intense as he looks me over, he kisses my cheek sweetly and his wet hair tickles the side of my face. I try, and fail, not to start to blush but I'm so fucking relieved.

I clear my throat. "Your dad's pissed because the two of you are ruthless dictators, but also manage to have morals? Jesus fucking wept. I don't want to meet the guy. Knowing and dealing with Liam O'Cronin is enough, thanks."

Ash snorts again and says, "Please tell me you're going to record yourself slitting that cretin's throat so we can all enjoy it."

"It's on my list."

Harley's hand squeezes my thigh, not missing a beat in the conversation he's walked into. "Can we pretend for one second that you're not the most secretive person on the fucking planet and can you tell us what's on the list?"

I blow out a breath and share a look with Avery. "We should wait until Blaise is up so I don't have to repeat myself."

Avery gives me a sly look and I brace myself for the shit I know she's about to grab a spoon and start stirring. "Ash, go shake the asshole awake. Ask him what he'd like for his last meal on Earth because I'm going to gut him for kicking me out of my own room just so he could get his dick out. Mounty, I hope he was gentle with you."

Kill me.

Just fucking *kill me* now.

I tip my head back and stare at the ceiling for a second, blushing furiously and avoiding any of the eyes that are now glued on me. Blaise decides that *this* is the moment he will return to the land of the living, sitting up sharply, and I'm sure the look he gives Avery will earn him a knife to the kidneys from Ash or Harley.

"Leave her the *fuck* alone."

The look Avery gives him is so fucking cold the temperature in the room changes. "She's my best friend. I can ask her if I need to *kill you* if I want to."

Blaise heaves himself out of bed, looking rumpled and fucking delicious, before stalking over to us. He kisses my head sweetly, cradling my cheek, and snaps back at her, "Don't be a bitch about it. Ask her that shit when we're not around, don't make her feel like shit by putting her on blast. This isn't a fucking game."

I don't know if it's just the ice Avery is throwing, but the whole room freezes. I'm too damn worried to look at Ash or Harley right now so my focus stays glued on Avery. Her eyes narrow at Blaise but he doesn't back down, and I start to sweat at the thought of the brawl that's about to happen. This is exactly what I was afraid would happen, dammit! I open my mouth, ready to try and diffuse the fight, when a slow smile stretches across her face.

"I'm glad you're taking your relationship seriously. Morrison is still second. You two need to step up," she decrees, shooting me a smug look.

Blaise scoffs at her, kisses my head again, and then stomps his way to the bathroom.

Ash gives Avery a hard look. "How? I look in her direction and you have a fucking episode at me."

Avery stands to clear plates away. "I'm not explaining myself to you, Ash. I'm doing whatever I have to do to keep our family safe and happy, even if that means gutting one of you for Lips."

Harley moves to sling his arm over my shoulders and I take my first deep breath since I woke up. His eyes are possessive on me while he says to Avery in a tone haughty, "So we're all being tested by you to make sure our intentions are pure? I'm not fucking worried. I'm sleeping here tonight. I'm fucking sick of spending all of my time with that skank of a teacher."

Chapter Eight

I'm sitting in math class, keeping a careful eye on Blaise's blushing desk buddy from across the room, when my phone vibrates silently against my leg. Harley feels it and glances around then frowns at me when it's clear the text has come from outside our little family.

I shrug and wait for the teacher to turn his back before checking the text.

I'm coming to your stuck-up school, little Wolf. Big news, the kind that needs to be delivered personally. The O'Cronin kid can get you into the pool, right? Meet me there at 11pm.

I groan. Just what I need. Harley quirks an eyebrow at me and I flash him the screen to show him Illi's text. His frown deepens and he nods his head a fraction.

I try to get my focus back on the sums in front of me, but the swirling pit of my stomach makes it impossible, so instead I glare at the back of the blushing girl's head.

Harley bumps me gently to get my attention, and asks me what the hell my problem is using just his eyebrows. Yep, I'm fluent now. I know exactly what the golden god who's taken over my bed is saying. Only my bed, he won't take over my body with Avery's watchful eyes around and with all of the extra classes he's barely making it to our room before midnight on the nights he comes to me. I'm sort of hoping Ms. Vivienne will hurry up and make a move on him so the whole thing can be done with, even if it does make me twitchy to think of her touching him.

I'm not sure I can get my eyebrows to say what I need them to in return so I shrug instead.

After class Avery laughs at me as I eyeball the fuck out of the blushing girl. I tuck my arm into hers and stomp to the dining hall for lunch, ignoring the guys as they gloat at each other over last night's fight club.

I already know Ash won.

If the bruised and split skin on his knuckles didn't give it away then the looks of respect and sheer terror he gets from the other students would have clued me in. I hear Blaise joking about sending Harley the video of a particularly brutal fight with one of Joey's ex-flunkies and I make a note to get a copy myself.

For research purposes.

Ahem.

Avery grimaces at her phone before murmuring, "I don't know why you're glaring at that poor little sheep. It's not like he even noticed her, and she was too shy to even speak to him."

I roll my eyes at her. "Exactly. So if he needs help with his workbook she's not going to be able to do shit if she can't even speak to him. She didn't take a single note the entire class."

Avery chuckles. "Neither did you."

"Difference is, the Mounty has already finished the entire Algebra unit and is now working on the Geometry workbook that the class won't move to for another *eight* weeks. She's so far ahead even Harley's *extra special tutoring* can't get close to her," Ash interrupts, and Avery cuts me a look.

"Are you sleeping at night? How much coffee are you drinking? Do I need to give up ballet and start stalking you to make sure you're taking care of yourself?" she hisses and I laugh at her.

We push into the dining hall and I try to ignore the looks I get. At least I don't have to listen to the whispers while I'm surrounded by the others. The students here seem to think they're the dangerous ones.

Fucking rich idiots.

I grab a tray for myself and Avery, ignoring three sets of glares at my independent move. I make it two steps before Ash wrestles it from me. Chivalrous dickhead. "I'm sleeping just fine. Things are calmer this year, at school at least. I'm not worried about Joey choking you or Harlow fucking poisoning you. I'm not stressing about hot assholes sitting on my couch glaring at me all day." Avery gags at me dramatically and I smirk back. "I'm just getting ahead before everything turns to shit like it always does."

Famous last words.

Harley arrives at our door at ten.

He lets himself in and I frown, confused about his early appearance. Avery stomps out of the bathroom, wrapped in a fluffy towel, and snarks at him, "The keys are for an emergency! If you don't stop letting yourself in I'm going to start walking around naked!"

Harley snorts at her. "You'll only be risking Morrison's life. I don't wanna see my cousin's tits, but it's not going to scar me for life. Morrison's the one who'll get stabbed for looking at you."

Avery loosens the hold on her towel so it slips a little to call his bluff.

I groan and slap a hand over my face as the two of them glare each other down like some sort of fucked up game of chicken.

I clear my throat to try to interrupt them. "Can we just go, Harley? Please? Or do you want me to put a movie on while we wait?"

He reluctantly looks away and Avery crows in victory. "Grab a bathing suit, we can go for a swim before the Butcher gets here."

I blanch. "I'm shit at swimming."

"Well, I'm not. I'll keep you afloat."

I'm not proud to admit it, but the deciding factor is the very thought of being pressed up against his wet, naked chest.

Yes *fucking* please.

One small problem.

"I don't have a bathing suit."

Harley quirks an eyebrow at me. "You're from the Bay, how do you not have a suit?"

Avery tugs me into her closet and pulls her bathrobe on, rummaging through her drawers until she finds a tiny scrap of fabric and passes it to me.

There is no way it will cover even my small tits.

I cut her a look and she smirks at me. "That asshole should be kissing my feet for giving you that. Try it on."

It's obscene. It's truly fucking obscene.

My entire body flushes as Avery looks me over, clinically approving like I'm her own personal model, and somehow it's so much worse than being naked. It's technically a bandage-style one-piece, but I've seen micro bikinis have more coverage over the important parts. I have underboob cleavage in this thing, for fucks sake! I turn around in the mirror and, oh look, there's eighty-five percent of my butt-cheeks.

"Let me find you something to cover up with for the walk down there," Avery mutters, as she moves to a different drawer.

Harley lets out an exasperated sigh and calls out, "We're not going to get the chance to swim if you turn this into a fashion parade, Floss. Just grab a sweater to wear once our... *friend* gets here."

Avery ignores him and winds a silky, shimmery wrap dress around me, tying and buttoning and tucking me in until I'm positive Harley is going to have to bundle me back into it when we're finished. When she nudges me out of the closet she snarks at him, "If you run into anyone on the way down and she wasn't covered up, you'd stab them. *You're welcome, cousin dearest.*"

Harley rolls his eyes at her, then kisses her cheek sweetly and tucks me under his arm to walk down to the pool. I wait until we're in the hall before I burrow into the solid warmth of his chest. The rumbling noise of contentment he makes is loud against my ear.

He uses his own set of keys to get us into the building and he disarms the alarm with practiced ease. When he catches my questioning look he shrugs. "Coach knows I come here when I can't sleep. He gets an alert saying someone has disabled the alarm and when he sees it's my code he ignores it."

Huh.

I didn't know that this was soothing for him. They all have little rituals, every one of them. Avery cleans obsessively and puts things in meticulous order, Ash runs until he can't breathe, and Blaise messes around with lyrics and drawings in his notebook. They have all learned how to cope with the dark reality of our world.

I take to my bed and cease existing two days a year.

I'm busy musing over our broken little family when Harley does that move of his and pulls his shirt off one-handed. He grins at me, the absolute asshole because he *knows* he has my attention now, and he pushes his jeans down his legs until he's left in a pair of swim shorts.

Sweet merciful lord.

I would like to climb that boy like a freaking *tree.*

It occurs to me that I can now. *Jesus fucking wept.*

His grin stays in place while he waits for my soul to return to my body and it only falters when I start to fumble with the dress, gritting my teeth at the stupid thing until finally the fabric floats to the ground and I'm left in the sparse black suit.

"Holy fuck," Harley croaks, and I barely manage to blink before he's hauling me up into his arms and my legs wrap around him instinctively, like they were made to be. Maybe they were; I'm not questioning it. I couldn't right now if I tried.

He holds me up with one arm under my ass, *holy fucking hotness*, and uses the other to gently grip the back of my neck, pulling my lips into his. Just before they touch he whispers, "We are not having sex for the first time in a pool, but fuck me, it's tempting. That suit is the work of the devil, and she's trying to fucking kill me. I need some frigid water to calm my dick down."

I huff out a laugh, but before I can tease him he tugs me into his kiss. I wriggle in his arms a little, just enough that I slide down his body a fraction and feel that, yep, he really does like what he sees. I wriggle a little more, moaning into the kiss and grinding against him, so distracted by his groans that I barely take note that we're moving. It's only when he steps down into the water, slowly descending the concrete steps, that I break away and prepare to be submerged.

"Don't look so scared, babe. I won't drop you," he teases, nipping at my neck.

I don't want to tell him that I'd once been held underwater until my vision blacked out, and doing this with him is using a level of trust I didn't know I was capable of. Not just going for a swim with him, but being this close to him in the water. I clear my throat, and try to chase the ghosts away.

The water is colder than I expect a pool custom built for spoiled brats to be and a little gasp rips out of my mouth before I can bite it back when the water hits my shoulders. Harley smirks at me and pulls me flush against his chest again, grunting when my hard nipples rub against his chest. He walks us deeper and deeper, until he's swimming to keep us both afloat. I try to think weightless thoughts as the tension eases out of his face the further we drift out.

He looks so fucking relaxed.

I don't want Illi to come and ruin this moment.

"I've missed you. I hate being back at school," I say, trying to swallow the lump in my throat at my admission. I try to duck my head away, but Harley cups my cheek and forces me to look at him.

"I miss you too. I fucking hate that dumb slu—*fuck*—skank for picking me. I was supposed to finally spend the year with you and instead I'm dodging hands."

I pull back from him and fix a stern gaze on him, ready to climb out of the pool and hunt the bitch down, but he shrugs it off. "She keeps stroking my arm and my shoulder. It's not enough to get her under Floss's thumb, but it pisses me the fuck off. Fuck, I don't want to talk about her. Grind on my dick some more, that'll distract me."

He gives me this *wolfish* grin and I cackle at him, so blissfully smug that he wants me just as much as I'm dying for him. I wriggle against his chest again and lean forward to swallow his groan. I'm still not confident in much more than kissing, but his reactions to everything I'm doing spurs me on, like maybe my enthusiasm is enough to get me through this without looking like an inexperienced fool.

Harley swims us over to one side of the pool and perches my ass on a little ledge so he can settle between my legs without me dragging him under the water. He moves to kiss my neck, sucking on the skin below my ear, and I try to grind my hips into his but he holds me still with one hand and a firm grip. Fuck it, I need more.

"No sex or nothing but kissing?" I whisper and he jolts away from my neck. My cheeks are on fire, but the stunned look on his face makes it worth pushing past my nerves.

He stares at me for a second and then says, his voice nothing more than a rasp,

"Fuck."

Right.

I was kind of expecting more than that, but before I can *die* of pure mortification, he's kissing me again and grinding his dick into me like he's on a mission. I'm one hundred percent on-fucking-board, and I suck on his tongue until he's panting and groaning, pulling my hips closer until I'm a shaking mess. His fingers dance along the seam of the swimsuit and I nod, trying not to break away from his lips, but good lord, if he doesn't touch me right now I'm going to die.

The bathing suit is so skimpy he can hook it with one finger and tug it aside, he's groaning again as his fingers slide reverently through my slick pussy lips, stroking me like he's savoring the feeling. My breath catches in my throat and the smoldering look he gives me only makes it harder to breathe.

"We can stop," he whispers, stroking the hair away from face with the hand he isn't cupping my pussy with.

I think about inflicting violence on him out of sheer frustration and grit out from my clenched teeth, "If you do, I'm going to stab you."

He smirks at me then grinds the heel of his palm into my clit, pushing a finger into me, and his hips jerk forward when I clench around the digit. He pumps his finger into me, curving it to rake over my G spot, and my head drops back as I moan. He adds another and moves to rub my clit with his other hand, tight, maddening circles until my hips are jerking and twisting wildly. The water seems to heat up around us, like the heat we're throwing off our bodies is changing the temperature of the pool. I can't think straight, and my whole existence is centered around what he's doing to me, and I think I'm going to die if I don't come soon.

"Fuck, you're going to make me come in my shorts like this is the first pussy I've ever touched." His voice is nothing but need and fire, and I shiver, catching his lips with mine to suck on his bottom lip again. I'm so fucking addicted to the taste of him.

It shouldn't be a compliment, but I'm fucking *preening* at his words, even through the haze of my own impending climax. The only problem is, I don't want him to come in his shorts; I want to make him feel as good as his fingers being buried in my pussy make me feel. It can't be that hard, right?

I gulp.

Then I remind myself that I'm not afraid of anything, let alone a *dick*. Even if it is way bigger than I thought I'd be handling and attached to one of the hottest guys to ever walk the Earth. *Deep breath.* I slip my hand down his incredible abs and into the waistband of his shorts. He groans like a dying man as I wrap my fingers around his dick and, sweet merciful lord, I will take that sound to the grave. He wasn't lying, he's throbbing and searingly hot in my hand like he's a few firm pumps away from coming. I'm going to give it a shot.

I manage one stroke before my ringtone cuts through the air and *ruins everything*.

It can only be Illi and we can't ignore him, even for a few minutes because fuck knows what sort of trouble he could get into at Hannaford if left to his own devices. Harley groans into my mouth, and when I break away he curses viciously. "Is the whole fucking universe cock-blocking me?"

I manage something vaguely resembling a laugh but inside, I'm dying over the interruption.

Harley *can't* get me back into the dress and tugs his shirt over my head instead.

My legs are both restless and wobbling, a dangerous mix, and Harley scoffs at my attempts to walk. "Just sit down and I'll go let him in. Fuck, cross your damn legs! I don't want him seeing that perfect wet pussy."

I blush and do what he says, even though I know Illi has no interest in looking at me. His eyes belong to someone else and I feel a pang in my chest when I think of Odie.

I hope the Jackal hasn't gone after her.

Harley digs around in his swim bag and pulls on his team sweatpants and jacket, zipping it halfway so his tattoo is still clearly visible. I've never seen him in them before and his shoulders look so broad and defined I'm hot for him all over again.

Okay, new rule: no fooling around right before we meet up with Illi to exchange important, possibly life-threatening, information. My hormones are raging and my brain is no longer functioning.

I take a second to try to breathe, before the scuffing sound of Harley walking back pulls my attention back to where it needs to be.

Illi couldn't look more out of place if he tried.

Harley scowls at him, leading him over to the bench I'm perched on. I can smell the acrid scent of tobacco and the twitching of Illi's fingers tell me he wishes he was allowed to light up again. Illi smirks back at Harley, blowing him a kiss and tugging on his leather jacket with a tattooed, scarred hand. I shake my head at him.

"I need you two to get along, Illi, please stop provoking him."

Illi strides over to me, his feet eerily silent in his biker boots, and drapes a casual arm over my shoulders as he sits down. "Anything for you, little Wolf. How's school treating you? The uniform is fucking weird here, you look like a dirty-old-man's wet dream."

Harley was glaring at Illi's arm, but at his little comment his spine snaps straight and he steps forward to snarl, "*Fuck. Off.*"

Illi holds his hands up in mock surrender. "Look at you, assuming I'm a dirty old man! I've skinned people for less, little mobster."

I roll my eyes at them both and give Illi a not-so-gentle shove away from me. I trust him, with more than just my life, but I don't want him sitting so close to me when I'm barely covered. He cackles and scoots along, giving me more than enough space to breathe. That does more for Harley's temper than words ever could, and he takes up watch on my other side. I slip my hand into his, giving him a little squeeze to try to remind him to stay calm. I doubt it'll work, but I'm freaking trying.

"Right, well, I've had my fun. I was trying to lighten the mood a bit before I break the news to you. We're in a world of shit, kid. I hope you've got something fucking big up your sleeve because we're going to need it."

Fuck.

I'm not sure I have *anything* up my sleeve, let alone something big. I give him a nod and mutter, "What's happened now?"

"I asked around about your little crew to see if there's any word in our corner of the world about any of them, like we discussed. Make sure we're on top of anything that might threaten us. Got a hit back from out of state. Morningstar was approached by Matteo to take out O'Cronin."

"It's Arbour," I croak, as I squeeze my eyes shut and take a second to steady myself.

Illi flicks out a dismissive hand gesture. "Right. So, he was contacted about *Arbour*, but I was expecting that. I wasn't expecting him to also be liaising with the senior Joseph Beaumont about your twins."

My eyes snap to him.

What. The. Fuck.

There's silence for a minute while I try to stop my heart from exploding inside my chest cavity. Illi watches the water and nods to himself slowly, like he's agreeing with some internal monologue he has going on.

"Who the fuck is Morningstar?" Harley snaps when he's finally had enough of waiting for answers.

"The Devil," I whisper, and Illi gives me a chagrined smile.

He flicks his eyes over to Harley's and for once he doesn't try to provoke him. He just lays out the facts of exactly how bad this is. "He once walked into the biggest MC clubhouse in the country by himself and painted the fucking walls with biker innards. Not a metaphor; the city had to provide crisis counseling to the first responders because it was the stuff out of nightmares. When the cops ran forensics there were fourteen different strains of DNA, but no bodies were ever found and it's still '*unsolved*'. He's a sociopath. He feels nothing. If he goes after you, we're fucked. If he goes after your cousins, *we're fucked*. If he leaves his state, and wanders the hell into Mounts Bay, *we're fucked*."

Harley groans under his breath and scrubs his face with both his hands. "Why is there *always* someone worse? I thought *you* were the fucking worst there was."

That breaks the somber mood a little and Illi smiles like Harley's just called him pretty. "So sweet of you to say, but there *is* always someone worse. I for one never want to meet whoever the fuck is worse than Morningstar. Any idea on why that fuck Beaumont wants his own kids dead? I thought you said they were good people? I've never known you to put up with dickheads. Well, other than that cock D'Ardo."

I grimace and shrug. "They're the best people. I know some of why their family is messed up, but I'll get the rest of the details and we can work this out. *Fuck*."

Illi cuts me another look. "Kid, there's no dealing with the devil. This isn't a story from old; you can't cut a deal. If he takes the job from Beaumont… they're gone. All of them."

I swallow roughly. There's no way I'm letting that happen. No. Fucking. Way. "Reach out to everyone and tell them the twins are mine. Morrison too."

Illi blows out a breath and rubs his jaw, his skull rings catching the light and grinning at me ominously. "You inducting them?"

Harley watches me closely, but I shake my head. "I haven't asked them, just put it out there that they're under my protection. I don't care how you word it, just make sure it's well known that if anyone touches them they answer to me. If Morningstar takes the job… I'll start calling in favors."

Harley glares at the ground, his fists clenched dangerously. Illi stares at him and then says, softly, like he's testing his grit, "It'll be war, kid."

Harley shrugs. "They're richer than God, if we need to we'll get them out of the country. I hear Antarctica is nice this time of the year. Ash will fucking love that."

Chapter Nine

Harley agrees to keep the bad news to himself until I get the chance to speak to Ash alone about it. I don't want to tell Avery until we have a plan on how to deal with her father and I can't make a plan without knowing what the fuck is wrong with the man.

Getting Ash alone is impossible without an intervention. The five of us are all in the same classes and share our mealtimes, and his extracurriculars are at the same time as Avery's so there's never the chance to be alone together. He's always affectionate towards me, snarking and sarcasm included, but with his sister around I barely get more than a peck on the lips from him.

I feel so fucking guilty.

Blaise pins me to the bed most nights during our study sessions and Harley has been sleeping-over a few nights a week, kissing me senseless before the sun comes up and he has to leave for his swim practice, so it doesn't really seem fair.

I spend two weeks trying to carve out time for a private conversation with him, but nothing works. Avery starts to stare at me with suspicion and on the following Monday, when I ask her what her plans are for the third weekend in a row, she huffs at me in mock upset.

"Which one of them do you have a craving for? I guess I'll go find a park bench to sleep on for the night. Just don't fuck any of them in the kitchen, bathroom, or my bed. Or the couch. You know what, just stick to your bed and change the sheets *immediately* post-coitus."

I roll my eyes at her dramatics and usher her away from the breakfast dishes so I can do them instead. She moves to make us both coffees to-go and I could kiss her damn feet in gratitude.

There's no good way to tell her so I sigh, scrubbing the pans a little harder than necessary. "We promised not to lie to each other so… I'm not going to lie to you. I've found out that we're facing a new threat. It's not something you can help with right now so I don't want to tell you about it yet. You have enough going on with the cougar whore and keeping the sheep in line, and I'm already doing everything possible to neutralize the situation. If the situation changes, I will come to you and we will plan out a new course of action."

Avery hums under her breath softly. "You need some stress relief? Tell me which guy and I'll go sleep in their room. If it's Blaise I need to take my own sheets. I swear he doesn't ever wash his; I've trained the other two better than that."

I scoff at her and wipe my hands. "Actually, I need to talk to Ash. This isn't a... relationship thing. It's to do with the threat. I know you don't want to say anything that might push him when he's not ready to talk about the sheer fucked up levels of *bad* that your father is, but I need to know. The situation has forced my hand."

Avery stares at me for a second, then frowns and pulls out her phone. "I'll cancel tutoring with Blaise, tell him and Harley to stay away for the night, and Ash can skip track." She chews on her lip and then says, quietly, "I should stay, too. If it's... if it's a matter of safety I don't want him skipping things or trying to make it sound... less than what it is for your sake. He'll try to shield you from it all like he does with me. I mean, he shields Harley and Blaise from it, too."

My heart sinks all the way down to my stomach, but I nod.

Avery pre-warns Ash of the reason for our dinner so he arrives to our room in a vicious and argumentative mood. Avery puts up with it for about three minutes before she throws a towel at his head and tells him to go cool off in the shower. I make dinner and ignore them both because I'm smart enough to know that you shouldn't involve yourself in a fight between twins.

Avery dishes up our food and pours Ash a bourbon from her secret stash. I raise my brow at the pint-sized glass she fills because he'll be slurring his words in no time if he sculls that down. She shrugs and when the bathroom door opens she leans in to whisper, "There's no way he's going to talk about it without a little something to loosen his tongue."

Fuck.

I nod and take a seat. Ash hesitates for a second before taking the seat next to me, kissing the little wedge of skin that's exposed on my shoulder thanks to Blaise's oversized band tee I've, ahem, borrowed.

"Thanks for dinner. I've really missed the slum food since we got back to civilization," he murmurs and I roll my eyes at him while Avery kicks him under the table. I hold up a hand to stop the tirade that's about to spill out of Avery and she smirks at me.

"No amount of shitty attitude is going to stop this conversation. I realize this isn't something you want to do and I'm willing to offer you a trade; I'll tell you my shitty stuff if you tell me yours."

Avery's eyes flare before she can hide it. There's a whole list of things she is desperate to ask me and now I'm offering them to Ash as an incentive to talk. I'd thought a lot about it, but I'll do whatever it takes to keep us all safe.

"Questions, like you did with Harley? Or are you just going to tell me it all?" Ash says, his eyes icy as he glares at his drink. He hasn't picked up the glass yet.

"How about you tell me what you want to know? Because I need to know everything about your father. Why he's trying to kill you, what he's done in the past, why he favors Joey, and anything you know about who he chooses for his cleanup. I wouldn't be asking this of you if it wasn't absolutely necessary."

Ash picks up the glass and drinks half of it in two gulps. When he speaks, it's with clinical detachment and a steady tone. "My father is a sadist. He used my mother as a front for his standing in high society. He'd beat her, slap her around, 'punish' her, but he was never a monster to her. He saved that for the girls he'd buy at auctions. He enjoys hurting people. He prefers to fuck females, but it's the pain that gets him off and really, as long as the person is screaming, that's all he needs. The day my mother was killed, she had followed him through the manor to his private chambers. They always slept separately and she was never permitted to enter his rooms. He had a twenty-one year-old college student, who had been kidnapped and sold off to him, strapped to a table and he was carving his name into her skin with a scalpel, over and over again, while he jerked himself off over the open wounds."

Sweet lord fuck. Ash takes the glass again, a fine tremble in his fingers, and he finishes the bourbon. Avery looks like she's going to vomit, like knowing the facts and hearing them laid out right now with our dinner growing cold between us are two very different things.

Ash continues without so much as a grimace. "Joey found us in the kitchen as my mother was getting us out. She had known for years that he was a sociopath too; he'd already broken my arm twice. She had no intention of taking him with us and when he found us he called my father. He caught her by the chauffeured car and dragged her back to the house by her hair. He laid her out on the same table that girl had been strapped to, the blood was still warm, and he got Joey to help him. Then the two of them butchered her. When our nanny brought us down for dinner that night my father had Avery wait outside the formal dining room and he described to me exactly what they had done to her. He called one of his crooked higher-ups in the police department and my mother's death was ruled a suicide."

I swallow the bile in my throat and, very carefully, I reach out and cover his hand with mine. I hold back a sigh when he doesn't shake me off.

"What do you want to know? I'll tell you anything." I say, trying to offer him a break from his demons.

Ash shakes his head sharply and looks at Avery. "He told me that if I didn't 'show some promise soon' he'd be forced to do the same to me. He put Joey in charge of teaching me how to be a *real* man, not a fucking pansy that respects women. He can't stand that I love my sister, that I loved our mother. He just wants a legacy. He wants to die knowing his sons are continuing to torture, beat, rape, and destroy everyone and everything around them. He's insane, but he's also very smart. He looks handsome and put-together in a suit. Not a soul on this earth would believe the things he's done. The only thing reining the two of them in is our standing in high society. He gets away with everything because of who he is. If he were to be exposed, he'd be facing the death penalty in at least ten states and three countries."

I squeeze his fingers, but he ignores me. I'm starting to get a little worried that we've broken him. "So they've used Avery as the bargaining tool from the moment they killed our mother. I am to submit to everything Joey chooses to teach me, to do to me, or Avery ends up on that table. I've tested their resolve once, and Harley nearly went to juvie to get Avery to the hospital before she was gone forever, too."

Avery shivers and rubs her arms, trying to fight the memories from prickling at her skin.

Ash spins the glass on the table absently, still staring at Avery. "The clean-up is all done by officials. He has so many dirty pigs in his pockets that it would be harder to find someone *clean* then to find someone he owns. That's it, Mounty. That's everything."

I nod and clear my throat. "Do you know why he would contact someone else to kill you? To kill you both? If he's so… proficient and willing, why would he pay an obscene amount of money for someone else to do it?"

Avery frowns at me. "The threat is against us?"

I swallow roughly. "Yes. He's contacted a man about having you both killed. The guy is… actually pretty similar to your father, except everything he does is big and showy. I think he likes the attention of being so good at covering his own tracks that he's untouchable. It just doesn't make sense that your father would contract your murder out when it sounds like he would *enjoy* doing it himself."

Avery stares at me for a second and then her eyes flick to Ash. I wait for the planning to start. I wait for her phone to come out and her sharp, ruthless mind to get to work.

It doesn't happen.

She stands to grab the plate of dinner and shoves it, dish and all, into the garbage. I watch as she grabs everything from the table, all our plates and cutlery, cups and napkins, and shoves the whole lot in the garbage. The shatter of the glass breaking and ripping the garbage bag follows in her wake, but I let her go.

She has the exorcize the demons out of our space and she won't be able to rest until they're gone.

I sit in silence with Ash while Avery tears the kitchen apart. We're not going to have any utensils left by the time she's settled again, but who the fuck cares when I have a best friend losing her mind and a boyfriend who's just told me he's been the victim of *two* serial killers for the last decade? I certainly don't.

"What do you want to know? I promised you some truths." I whisper, careful not to touch him beyond the hands we have clasped together around his empty glass.

"Not tonight, Mounty. I'll take my payment some other time. Can I drink now? I don't want to become a sulking, morose fuck. We already have one of those in the family, no need for another." He says and I tug him to his feet gently, directing him over to my bed.

He frowns at me and says, "I'm not sleeping. I won't, and Avery is making enough noise that Harley and Morrison are going to hear it and come looking for our corpses. I need a drink to be able to deal with this."

My lips quirk, but I rest a palm on his chest. "Shh, Beaumont. We're not functioning tonight. You and me will be nothing in here together." His eyes stay fixed to my face and they don't soften at all so I shrug. "If that doesn't work, I'll come down to the track with you and sit on the grass while you run until you pass out, but we'll try this first. I don't want to have to call the cavalry to carry you back to the dorms because there's no way I can do it by myself."

I wait him out. Eventually, he slides between my sheets and I climb in next to him, flicking my lamp off so only the kitchen overhead lights are on. It kind of feels like mood lighting and I grimace at thinking such a thing while Ash is lying beside me with all of his internal damage on display. I'm surprised he hasn't hit anything yet. If someone challenges him to a fight tomorrow, I'll be calling a cleanup crew.

His story is on repeat in my brain and I start to think maybe alcohol isn't the worst idea. It's all just so fucking sick and twisted, and I'm no closer to figuring out what the fuck I can do to stop the Devil appearing on our doorstep. We're facing the most evil and well connected men in high society and the slums of Mounts Bay.

I really don't do easy, do I?

Ash moves to pull me into his arms, shifting me until my back is pressed to his chest and our legs are tangled together the way he likes, and when his fingers brush my thighs I shiver. His lips press into the soft skin of my shoulder.

"What do I have to do to tempt you into our room, Mounty? I've been very patient while Avery adjusts, but you really need to start sleeping in my bed," he mumbles into my skin and I wheeze a little as my chest tightens. The very thought of spending time in their room, choosing a bed for the night, being in their space—I need to get my head around it first. I need to figure out how to do that without dying of both lust and awkwardness.

There's something else I need to address first.

"You know I've killed people, right?" I whisper, brave now I'm not looking at him. It'll make it easier if he rejects me and walks out.

"So have I. I told you before Mounty, you're not going to scare me off."

I meet Harley and Blaise for breakfast in the dining hall the next morning. Avery didn't finish her room demolition until dawn, and now there's nothing left in the kitchen or bathroom that wasn't already nailed down. Ash decided he would skip class for the day to stay behind and coax her into sleeping. I brace myself for the questions the other two would inevitably have.

"She didn't take the news well then? She never does when Ash is involved." Harley says, stabbing at his eggs with the type of vehemence that has students giving our seats a wide berth.

"Well, he's always the one being fucking beaten and targeted so I don't blame her. Well, almost always," Blaise mutters, frowning down at his juice like he can magically spike it with a look.

I look between them both and ask, "Harley told you, then? I got the full, unedited family backstory to help us figure out what we can do to stop the hit, and afterwards Avery needed to scrub some demons out. Be extra nice to her for a while because she'll probably come back swinging."

They both stop and gape at me.

"He told you? He spoke to you about his father and Joey? Ash did? Alexander Asher William Beaumont, my best friend and total asshole extraordinaire, told you about what happens behind closed doors at the Beaumont Manor?" Blaise rambles and I frown at him.

"Yes. It was… really fucking bad, but now I have everything I need to know to navigate this mess we're in." I force confidence into my voice but, fuck, I'm not sure we're going to be navigating shit. It might be closer to blowing everything the fuck up and praying for the best.

They share a look but I ignore it. I push my empty plate away and gulp down the last of my iced coffee before we have to start moving off to our classes.

"Star, he hasn't even told us that stuff. Fuck, he really is serious about you," Blaise mumbles and my frown at him deepens.

"You thought he wasn't? Wow."

He cringes, cheeks flushing slightly, and Harley snorts at him before cutting in to save their asses. "Blaise and I both spend all of our spare time figuring out how to get you alone. Ash doesn't. This dick has been… *concerned* that Ash is having second thoughts because he's never really been the type to embrace celibacy."

Fucking idiot boys! I blush and clear my throat. "He told me last night he's waiting for Avery to stop being so defensive. He also told me I should start coming to your room."

At the predatory gleam in both their eyes, I hold up a hand. "I'm thinking about it. I'm not interested in hearing *more* gossip about how much of a raging whore I am. I'm pretty fucking close to snapping and stabbing some rich dickheads as it is. I don't need to test my patience much more."

Harley glares around the room with that fierce challenge of his and students start averting their eyes, turning their bodies away from his wrath. I'll say it again; I must be so freaking broken because that look is such a turn on. He turns back to me and smirks at my flushed cheeks. He cups my cheek gently, kissing me dirty, deep, and with entirely too much tongue for the audience we have. Blaise cackles at the looks we get from those brave enough to look as we break apart.

"I'll take care of them for you, babe," Harley murmurs and my blush deepens.

"Now who's flirting?"

All eyes follow us out of the room, especially when Blaise slings his arm over my shoulders, I hold my head high. Who the fuck cares what the rich assholes think? Not me.

Okay, I care a little.

Just enough to want them all to fuck off.

Chapter Ten

C

hoir is still my least favorite class.

Miss Umber smiles as Blaise and I walk in together and take our seats. She still insists we sit at the front so she can 'monitor us', which is her way of saying 'giggle and blush at Blaise'. I guess this is my life now, such a steep price to pay for the rock god in my bed.

Avery has transferred out of choir to take on extra dance classes and I have no one to share looks with at the lusty eyes Blaise has on him the second he starts singing. I mean, the ones other than mine.

"Okay, class! Time to start thinking about your performance for this year! You will already know from your syllabus that you're going to be working on your own original material to sing this year, an exciting challenge for some of you and a regular occurrence for others," Miss Umber says with a coy and completely inappropriate look at Blaise, who in return looks mildly uncomfortable.

I scoff at him and nudge him in the ribs. He's always been a shameless flirt and I have no desire for him to stop; he wouldn't be Blaise Morrison without it. He wiggles his eyebrows at me like an idiot.

"You'll be working in pairs, so choose wisely!" She turns to start writing on the board, detailing a list of requirements and resources for songwriting, and Blaise steals my pen from me when I start to take notes.

"I've already written our song," he whispers into my ear, and grins cockily when I shiver.

"I can't take credit for your work," I mumble but he just shrugs.

"Sing it with me, let me record it, and listen to it yourself. That's going to be the hardest work in the assignment and you'll be the only one who can do it."

Fuck.

He's not wrong about it being hard, but I desperately want to be able to do this. For myself and for him. Ash would also probably sell his soul for the song. I've had to ban him from playing the video Avery recorded of me singing around me because he listens to it so often.

"I don't know if I can. Listen to it, that is. I can… if you sing it for me I can copy you with the ear plugs in."

Blaise threads his fingers through mine. "We'll work on it together. We need to get you past this because I'm putting it on my next album. It'll be a single and on the radio and it's going to be huge. I want you to sing it onstage with me someday. We can't do any of that if you can't listen to it."

Holy fuck.

I suddenly feel too warm, too full, too *loved*. I don't know how to deal with it at all so I nod and squeeze his hand.

My good day comes to a screeching halt in our history class.

I look down at the paper in my hands and blink my eyes furiously like that'll somehow change the mark written in bold red ink.

B+

Before Hannaford, I'd never gotten lower than an A+. But here? I've never gotten a lower than an A. Never. Even when Harley beats me in our classes it's only by the smallest of margins and yet here I am staring down at a *B fucking plus*.

My head fills with a high pitch buzzing noise and my mind checks out entirely. Gone. Closed for some serious freaking maintenance. My breathing shallows into these weird little pants—I'm probably hyperventilating—and I vaguely feel a hand on my back, rubbing slow circles, while an argument starts around me. I can't seem to focus away from the panic that has broken my brain.

A chair scrapes back sharply, the warm caress of breath down my neck, and then the low rumbling voice as Ash whispers in my ear, "Avery will fix it, Mounty. Just breathe, for fuck's sake! No one is going to *die* over one crappy grade."

That's some perspective, right there. My chest eases enough for a deep, gulping breath. Just one, but it brings the room back into focus and I can hear the war waging around me.

"Mr. Beaumont, get back to your table! And *Miss* Beaumont, I will not be spoken to like that in my own classroom. If your little *friend* is unhappy with her mark, she will just need to work harder," Ms. Vivienne snaps out and, *hoo boy*, big mistake. My eyes finally unglue themselves from the mark and I look up at my best friend as her shoulders roll back and her chin lifts.

The room stops.

Stops talking, stops moving, stops *existing*.

Ms. Vivienne glances around, frowning and unsure of what the hell is going on, like the clueless fool she is.

Avery stands slowly, smoothing her skirt down with a steady hand. She's been teetering on the edge of bloodshed all week and this bitch just stepped into the ring. Ash leans back in his chair to survey the class, but there isn't a single student willing to meet his eye.

Sheep, the lot of them.

"If you think you can come to this school and play games with *my* family, then you're a stupid, desperate, old *cunt* that has a lot to learn. I've been lenient on you; observed the social niceties and played by the agreed set of rules, but now you're going to get the same as every other miserable whore that walks these halls. You have a single chance to give Lips the mark her paper deserves, right now, or you can continue down the path to your own destruction because I assure you, Ms. Turner, that *you* are not in the position of power here. I will wipe all traces of you from the face of the Earth."

Ms. Vivienne's cheeks flush and she flicks a look at where Harley's hand is still rubbing circles into my back. Her eyes narrow. The bitch is fucking deranged. If

Avery's icy speech didn't make her quake in her stupid whore heels then she's clearly got no survival instincts.

"Go straight to the principal's office, Miss Beaumont. I will meet you there after the bell and we will discuss your actions with Mr. Trevelen. He will find an appropriate punishment for your unacceptable behavior and threats."

Avery tips her head back and laughs, and even I shiver at the sound.

Harley starts packing his bag and when he sees I'm still struck dumb by the red ink he packs mine as well. Ms. Vivienne's eyes flash at him as her focus shifts away from Avery and to the only person she really seems to give a shit about. "Mr. Arbour, I have not dismissed you."

He snorts at her and stands, tugging me to my feet, and Ash and Blaise both get up as well, bags packed and slung over their shoulders. Harley even grabs Avery's bag so she's not weighed down during her rage-filled stomping to wherever-the-hell-it-is we're going.

"What the hell do you think you're doing?! All of you, sit down this instant! I will be calling your parents!" Ms. Vivienne screeches, but her eyes are still fixed on Harley. His hands clench into fists and Avery tucks her arm into his to prevent him from smacking the bitch out.

Ash gently pries my numb hands away from my bag and throws it over to Blaise, who swings it over his shoulder easily and walks out of the room with a cocky smirk at our gaping teacher, calling out to her, "Good luck with that!"

Avery stomps after him, tugging Harley with her while he fumes. Ash tucks me under his arm carefully and steers me out of the room, his grip so secure that even my numb legs can't trip us up.

"It's just a mark, Mounty, stop gasping like you're dying. Avery will have it fixed in under an hour," Ash says, and he leads me to the dining hall. None of the teachers we pass spare us a glance and Ash doesn't speak again until he has me settled in our usual seats at the long, empty table with a plate of pasta and an iced coffee in front of me.

He's too damn observant.

I *definitely* need to eat my feelings and the pasta here is unbeatable. I wait for a few minutes so my stomach settles and then I eat like it's my last meal on death row. Ash watches me carefully, like I'm about to break. Great. Now I'm a crazy liability; a shitty mark can set me off into an episode and I have to be coddled out of it. Perfect.

"Stop it!" Ash snaps and I shoot him a look.

"What?! I'm eating it, aren't I!" They've all become weird about my food.

"Stop thinking about whatever the hell is making you look so fucking miserable. It's one bullshit mark, given to you by a petty, jealous cunt. What does it matter?"

I put my fork down and glare at him when he scowls at me. I know compared to everything else we have going on it's nothing but, fuck. I wasn't ever expecting my grades to factor into this.

"It matters because my whole life, the only thing that was ever going to get me out of the shit-show I was born into was my grades. I've never had a B+. I've never *failed* because I can't afford to fail. I'm dead if my grades are anything less than perfect. I think I'm allowed to have a minute to freak out over that!"

Ash nods and crosses his arms, leaning back in his seat. I have a little moment of deja vu, having seen him do it a hundred times during our tutoring sessions. "Is Harley not worth the risk?"

I flinch back. "Don't be an asshole, of course he is."

He shrugs. "Then get over it. She did it because you have something she so desperately wants. Avery will fix it. We will fix *anything* that threatens you. This isn't going to work if you don't trust us to back you up. You're not the only one who can defend us."

My stomach turns. I'm panicking for a whole new reason. "I do trust you. I'm still learning how to do this... family thing."

Ash's mask is impenetrable and just this once I wish I could see through it. "I told you, I'll do whatever it takes to keep you. If you need that woman to disappear then she's going to disappear, Mounty, but we'll trust Avery to fix it for now."

I blush and look away. I need to get a hold of myself. Ash scoots across Avery's seat to tuck me into his side again, gently squeezing me until I feel my control slip back into place.

"Like I said last night, Mounty, come sleep in my bed and I'll make sure you're nice and relaxed by morning."

By the time we're all settled around the table back in our room that night, with takeout and assignments spread out around us, there's a mark change and formal apology in my inbox. It doesn't read as sincere at all, and when I show it to Avery she starts texting furiously.

"Don't worry about it, Aves. The mark is all I give a shit about," I mumble around my dumplings and she hums under her breath at me, distracted by the conversation she's having. I'm a little worried she's ordering a hit.

Her eyes snap up to mine. "How long are we going to be in the Bay? I'm making arrangements to meet up with someone."

Ash sets down his fork with a dark look. "Who?"

Oh dear.

At least we haven't replaced the fine china yet because Avery looks at Ash like she's going to throw a plate at his head. I slip my hand in hers because, well, ride or die. And by the looks Ash and Harley are throwing at us both there might be bloodshed. Harley's leg is tense against mine.

"None of your damn business," she snarls and I know *exactly* what that means.

It's Atticus Crawford.

Ash's eyes narrow and I cut in before our dinner is ruined. "Arrange to meet him for lunch or dinner at the hotel the first night we're there. That way if we have to get out of there after the meeting you won't have to blow him off."

Blaise smirks and I shoot him what I hope is a savage look. He doesn't give a shit. "Maybe *blowing him* is exactly what she wants to do, Star."

My quick thinking saves Blaise's life as I slide my ass into Harley's lap to stop him from getting up and throttling him. He grunts and grabs my hips to hold me still. I don't think about *why* because I don't need to be blushing like a damn fool right now. Ash is surprisingly more forgiving of Blaise's smart mouth and just shoots him a look.

"Right. Now that's sorted, let's discuss the party," I say and when I try to slide back to my seat Harley's hands stop me. Avery does not look happy. In fact, she looks like she's going to scratch his eyes out.

"I'm not allowed to go for dinner with an old friend, but you can grind on Lips at the dinner table? Get fucked, Arbour," Avery hisses, and I start to pray that I can eat my damn dumplings before she flips the fucking table at them. I pry Harley's fingers off of me and settle back into my seat. Everyone is throwing savage looks except me. Yay.

"I think I should go alone. Harley is being targeted by the Jackal, I don't want to paint targets on Ash and Blaise, and Avery wouldn't be safe there. Illi has offered to pick me up so I'm going to take him up on that."

All of the savage looks swing to focus on me.

For fuck's sake!

"Over my dead fucking body are you going to a party at the docks with *the Butcher* without me," Harley growls.

I grit my teeth. "It's not like I haven't been a million times before and Illi will watch my back. It's not somewhere I want to take you guys."

Blaise scowls, flicking his beer bottle cap at Harley. "Why? I mean, the Jackal could come to Hannaford and kill Harley whenever he wants to, the gossip site has announced our relationships to the world, and we always protect Avery. Why not take us so we can protect you too?"

I scrub a hand over my face. "You want to take Avery somewhere full of drugs, sex, murder, violence, girls being kidnapped, torture, rape, the list goes fucking on? You want that? Because I sure as hell don't."

I expect some sort of reaction from Blaise, but he just stares me down. Ash is the one to snarl, "Well, that settles it. We're all fucking going. End of discussion."

Chapter Eleven

It takes me weeks to find the things we need to attend the party.

Avery gives me a hard look when I ask her for everyone's measurements and I refuse to tell her why I need them. There is no way I'm telling any of them what the outfits are necessary, because fuck that. I don't need the headache any sooner than I have to have it.

I have the items ordered at one of the boutique stores in Haven and they arrive on the Thursday before fall break. I email all of my teachers to get out of class the following day and when I ask to borrow Harley's car to go pick them up he stares me down like I'm testing him. When he crawls into my bed after midnight, he informs me that he's escorting me to Haven in the morning.

I wake to Harley's hands cupping my ass and pulling me into his body.

I swear he was put on this Earth to tease me, to break all of my control and turn me into a desperate mess and, sweet fucking lord, he was fucking good at it. I keep my eyes closed as I reach out to find his face, drawing him into my lips for a kiss. I'm too content to deal with today, I don't want to leave the bed and let the outside world fuck with us. I need a break, dammit!

"We could stay here." I mumble and he groans into my mouth.

"Don't fucking tempt me, babe. You said we had to pick up the shit you ordered and it's already late. Ash and Blaise took Avery down to class hours ago."

I frown at him like a pissy toddler. "That's not helping. I don't want to leave this *warm bed* in my *empty room*."

Harley groans and pushes away from me, stumbling out of the bed and rearranging his dick in his shorts like that'll somehow help the raging hard-on he has. "If we don't leave now we can't stop for French toast at the coffee shop and we both know you'll lose your shit if you're hungry. If we leave now, we can get everything finished in time and I'll convince Avery to have a sleepover with Ash."

I shiver because, *fuck yes*. "Get dressed, Arbour. I need food."

We have to stop off at the guys room to grab Harley's spare set of keys after he turns the living room back at my room apart looking for his original set. I make a mental note to myself because I've been burned by missing keys before.

We take Harley's 'Stang to Haven and I get to admire the way he drives it like it's an extension of himself, effortless and smooth. I love watching his hands, big and rough and scarred, and then my lungs forget how to work as I remember what they feel like on my body. Fuck, I need to inhale my food and get this shopping over with.

Harley smirks at my flushed cheeks like a smug dick.

We park behind the cafe because it closes the earliest, and then I bite my lip as Harley refuses to let me pay for our food. I make a note to *never* tell him I've been the one giving him money since I inducted him. He might have a stroke.

We sit, side-by-side, in one of the corner booths at the back. The waitress keeps looking at Harley like she'd bend over any available surface for him and the haughty, disinterested look he gives her in return makes me concerned about eating the food she serves us, but it's worth it.

"How is Avery handling the news about Senior's plans to have them both killed?" Harley mumbles around his mouthful of eggs. It should be gross but the guy is so fucking hot he could get away with anything.

I shrug at him. "Our room has never been cleaner. Avery is pissed there's nothing she can do to help and now Ash is fucking livid that it'll all rest on my shoulders to get them out of this."

Harley scowls. "Well, of course he is. We all are. It's hard enough keeping you safe and alive as it is, we don't need some psycho coming to the Bay to join the mix."

I snort at him, ever the lady, and poke a fork in his direction. "I survived without you guys having my back for seventeen years. I'll be fine, it's all of you lot with your shitty families that are the concern."

Fuck. That reminds me… I clear my throat. "Look, the meeting isn't just about the Vulture's death. We're also going to go through the usual bullshit and I've put something big in motion. I've… fuck, okay… I've called in some favors to get you free and clear from your grandfather once and for all. You need to be prepared for that meeting. You need to stick to all of the rules I've told you and be on your best behavior because once we're through it, we'll have one less threat stalking us."

Harley chews slowly, frowning down at his plate. I wait him out, the last thing he needs is to be pushed about his issues.

Finally, he flicks his eyes up to mine. "Are you at risk? Is this putting you in more fucking danger?"

I shake my head and he sighs, scrubbing a hand over his face. "Okay. Okay, I'll play along. I don't want my grandfather coming after me and finding you, so if this gets him off my ass then I'll do it."

I lean over and try to kiss him sweetly, something I'm still unsure of because I don't know how the fuck to be *sweet*. He cups my cheek to hold me there so I think I succeed.

"Come on, let's get your shopping and go back so I can do more than just kiss you."

Harley carries all of the bags in one hand and threads his fingers through mine with the other. He swings our arms playfully as we head back to the alleyway we'd left the car in, so relaxed and unlike himself that I laugh like a besotted idiot at him in return. I guess that's exactly what I am.

The streets have cleared now that the sun is going down. Only the bar is still open, and it's on the other side of the sleepy town, so we're alone and happy to walk in silence, soaking up each other without the distraction of words.

We turn into the alleyway, and Harley gives my hand a little squeeze before letting go to fish his keys out of his jeans. My senses pick up the slight rasp of feet attempting to be silent behind us half a second before Harley realizes what's happening. My hand is already slipping into my pocket to grab my knife when the body slams into Harley from behind.

The bags all go flying into the air as Harley throws his arms out to break his fall.

I freeze for a second, assuming it's a rich asshole from Hannaford trying to eke out a revenge beating for a failed fight in the boys' dorms, and then I see the flash of light hitting the steel blade in the attacker's hand.

It's a hit.

Lips retreats back into the farthest reaches of my mind, where she's safe and protected, and leaves me with the Wolf.

Harley manages to dislodge the guy enough to roll over and I see first hand that he's a fucking good brawler; strong, fast, and willing to fight dirty. The problem is that Harley's only going to knock him the fuck out, and if we let him live it's a sign of weakness. Something that will eat away at the carefully constructed image I've built as the Wolf, and our lives all depend on that image. If we let him go alive, the Jackal will just keep sending guys until eventually one of them kills Harley.

I cannot let that happen.

Harley knocks the knife away and grabs him with one hand by the throat. I take my chance and use every ounce of strength I have to ram the blade of my knife through the base of his skull, the quickest and most effective way to kill someone. Harley's strong grip gives me just the right resistance to help push the blade through the spinal cord and it's lights out for the attacker.

He's dead instantly.

When the guy's arms drop and he slumps down, Harley's eyes flare and fix themselves onto my knife. I shove the limp body off of him before I yank the knife out because the last thing I need is for him to be covered in blood and have some sort of flashback to his dad's murder. Harley jumps up and stares down at the guy, then at me.

My hands are steady.

I stare at him blankly, waiting for him to start screaming, or hurling accusations, or for something else to happen, and when he takes a step towards me I move back instinctively.

He looks fucking devastated as he holds out a hand to coax me over to him. "Shh, babe. I just need to know you're okay."

I blink.

I blink again.

Nope, still no idea how the fuck he can be worried about me when I'm the one who's just killed a man. Shouldn't he be afraid of me? Shouldn't he be calling Avery and getting the family far, far away from me?

"Babe, please. Don't freak out," he pleads and I think the word 'please' eases the trance I'm in and I step into his arms. He holds me to his chest with the sort of ferocity that you can only feel when there's a leaking corpse at your feet.

He buries his face into my hair and says, "Tell me what you need me to do."

I think he means emotionally, but I lost the ability to feel anything about this sort of death years ago. I pull away and shove the guy onto his back with the toe of my boot to get a proper look at him. Great, I know him. He goes by Whip on the streets in Mounts Bay, fuck knows what his real name is. He's a scumbag, constantly hanging around the docks trying to get close to the Jackal's men. He thought being a gangster sounded cool.

It hasn't worked out for him.

I look back at Harley and he's watching me carefully, his eyes seeming to catalog every breath I'm taking. It's oddly reassuring.

"Call Avery. Tell her it's a 911 and ask her if there are any cameras in this alleyway, she needs to get them wiped immediately."

Harley nods and I stare down at Whip's vacant eyes. It's weird how quickly the life leaches out of them and leaves behind nothing, even though the eyes themselves haven't changed.

I shake myself to regain some focus.

Harley murmurs quietly enough that I can make my own call without moving away. I don't want to leave him here alone with the body. He has a rap sheet, a tattoo on his face, and a bad attitude towards authority and, well, anyone outside our family. If by some cruel twist of fate the cops showed up, he'd get himself shot in a heartbeat without supervision.

"Wolf." The Bear doesn't bother with pleasantries, thank fuck. I don't have it in me to fake it.

"I need a priority cleanup crew." I rattle off the address and I hear him directing people in the background. Harley hangs up and makes a series of complicated hand gestures that I assume mean there's no cameras around. I make a note to start teaching him and the others military hand signals in our oh-so-plentiful spare time.

"Two minutes away," the Bear says and I shift my focus back to him.

"Perfect. Payment?" I say, tone cool and calm. Harley scowls down at the body like he wants to revive the fuck and kill him himself. He's weirdly protective of my diamonds.

The Bear grunts, "It's nothing, kid. I have a job for you, a quick in-and-out you can do in an hour. So if you get it done while you're here for the meeting I'll take care of this and owe you another."

I tilt my head in consideration. I guess that's more than fair. I don't want to give up a diamond even though I have more from him than any other member. "It's a pleasure to work with you, Bear," I say, my tone still flat and he grunts out a laugh at me.

"See you in the Bay, kid."

Harley tells the others the finer details of what happened while I shower.

I'm still struggling with the detached feeling, and no matter how hard I try to slip back into Lips, when I dress and leave the bathroom I am still the Wolf.

They all look at me like I'm a ticking bomb.

I stare back blankly.

Avery is the one to try to approach me, to take my hand, and when Harley hisses out a warning she falters for a second. I don't move back because I trust her and the adrenaline isn't riding me hard anymore like it was when Harley first tried to touch me.

Avery sighs and goes to grab a tub of my cherry ice cream out of the freezer, jamming a spoon into it and then she holds it out to me like a peace offering. I look at it for a second, puzzled, and then take it. The tension in the room eases a little.

She gently guides me over to the couch and tucks a blanket around me. I'm not cold. I don't know why she does it, but it's easier to keep my mouth shut and let her go. She grabs her own tub of ice cream and settles at my side with her phone out, tucking her arm in mine. I eat in silence while the guys all move aimlessly around the room.

"I'm fine. It's not like I haven't done it countless times before," I murmur, and Avery nods without looking up from her phone. It's easier to talk without her eyes on me.

"I know, you're one of the strongest people I know. This is for me. I need to know that you're okay and being here with you is comforting to me. It's a part of being a family, Lips," she explains gently, with none of her usual fire.

I nod and relax back into the chair. I can do this for her. I'm not sure there's anything I couldn't do for her.

By the fourth spoonful my body relaxes. By the tenth I'm Lips again.

Hours of tense silence later, Ash and Blaise climb into my bed with me. Neither of them give me any space, Blaise's chest pressing my back into Ash, whose face is buried into the nape of my neck. They both touch me like they need reassurance that I'm still here, whole and unflinching.

Harley takes the couch because he knows he's not going to sleep.

He watches the door until dawn.

Chapter Twelve

Ash insists on chaperoning Avery's dinner date with Atticus when we arrive at the hotel and I think she only agrees because she's terrified it's not a real date.

It gives me some time to shower and shave, well, *everything* in preparation for the party. I still haven't told everyone that the dress code is strictly lingerie and briefs.

The Jackal is the host and he's trying to provoke Harley into taking a swing at him. My stomach feels like it's full of lead because he just might succeed.

I leave the bags of the guys' clothes in their rooms and lock myself in the bathroom at ten to start getting ready. Blaise offers to wash my hair for me, saying he'll even let Harley help him soap me up, and Harley cusses him out when I blanch like a virginal idiot. I'm so fucking tempted. Wet, naked, and pressed in between them.

Sweet merciful lord.

I'm standing in front of the mirror wrapped in a towel and putting on my makeup when Avery knocks at the door and joins me.

I raise an eyebrow at her and she blushes.

"I think he wanted it to be a real date. He stared at Ash like he wanted to break his arm when he walked down with me. I've just sat through their sniping for the last two hours."

"Why didn't you just tell Ash to leave? He would've." Maybe. Okay, doubtful.

Avery pulls off her stunning and elegant red silk dress that I'm sure Atticus took one look at and wished he'd be the one removing it. "Maybe I want to be chased. Maybe I think I deserve to have him work for me. I've been on a platter for him for years and he's turned me down."

No maybes about it; the guy can *grovel* for her. But if I've learned anything about girl talk, it's that you ask questions and offer to gut anyone who slights your bestie. "Did he ever say why he wasn't interested before? The age gap might have freaked him out. I mean, maybe he's been waiting for you to get a bit closer to eighteen so he didn't feel like a creep."

Avery hums and slips into the shower, scrubbing at her skin like she always does. I wince at how rough she is. "I tried to speak to him about that during freshman year. I told him I would wait if he was interested in something in the future. He told me he refused to tie me down. It was like a knife in my heart. That's when I started seeing Rory."

I pretend too gag. "Don't say his name! I was close to forgetting he exists. I wonder how he's doing these days?"

Avery smirks at me as she cuts the shower off. "Ash keeps an eye on him to make sure he's miserable and very far away from me. Apparently the spinal injury has affected more than just his ability to walk."

Ahh, perfect. Nothing the rapist deserves more.

I sigh happily and then again with less joy when I open the bags holding the lingerie I've bought for Avery and I to wear. She wraps herself in a towel and peers into the bag.

"You're joking, right?" she asks and when I shake my head she cackles. "Ash is going to be *pissed*." She gasps out as she laughs even harder.

I begin to wriggle my way into the stupid teddy-thing, but it's a struggle to get it on my body. It's made of lace and pure white, but with too many straps and a white choker. It looks like something an angel would wear if it gave bondage a whirl.

"I got us both the most coverage possible while sticking to the rules," I grumble, as I accidentally snap one of the many straps against my skin and curse viciously under my breath. It doesn't hurt, but I'm so fucking frustrated at this stupid thing. Avery giggles at me and takes pity, deftly fixing the mess I've made with it. She slips hers on with far more ease and I glare at her for being so graceful. And *bendy*.

"Do we have to wear the shoes? I'm not really a 'combat boot' sort of girl."

I roll my eyes at her. "Like I haven't noticed you'd rather break a fucking ankle than wear flats. The party is at the docks, in a warehouse, with probably a couple of thousand people attending. You'd die in heels and you'll be wearing *that* so you can't make Ash carry you. Imagine the therapy he'd need."

She snorts and frowns at me like the spoiled brat she really, really is. I grin at her with a little sarcastic edge. "You should be grateful, do you know how long it took me to find boots that were *completely* white? A long fucking time."

Avery sighs again, like I'm mortally wounding her, and there's a pissy thump at the bathroom door before Ash is growling, "This is a fucking joke, right? I'm not going to a party in fucking tightie-whities."

Her eyes turn into saucers. We both shove bathrobes on and then I fling open the door.

Ash is scowling at us both and he's dressed in the 'clothes' I left for him. They're definitely *not* tightie-whities, but they are underwear. He's standing there in a simple pair of white boxer briefs that I cannot help but look down at because *holy shit, there's his fabled giant dick*. Even without an erection it's huge. Fuck. Fuuuuuuuuuuuck.

I gulp.

"Are you *fucking kidding me*, Mounty?" Avery hisses, and then I remember that I'm literally just standing here staring at my hot ass boyfriend's dick while his sister watches my brain melt out of my ears.

I clear my throat and try to ignore my blush. "I told you I could go by myself. You all insisted on coming. This is what it takes to get in."

Ash snorts under his breath, and tugs me until I'm tucked under one of his arms. I start to sweat because I'm too close to his giant dick. He doesn't notice. "Like we'd let you traipse around in your fucking panties by yourself. How much therapy am I going to need when I see what you've put my sister in?"

Avery grabs her phone and then frowns when she realizes she doesn't have anywhere under the bathrobe to stash it. "I'm not sure we can afford the extent you'll require. We certainly can't afford the amount I now need."

I groan at them both when Blaise comes stumbling into the room in his own pair of white boxer briefs, laughing at Harley who is frowning and tugging at the waistband of his.

Avery mumbles under her breath and stomps over to her overnight bag, digging out one of her beautifully tailored coats. When she slips out of the bathrobe to pull it on Harley's frown turns into a snarl. "*What. The. Fuck. Mounty.*"

I sigh and hold a hand out, the other one keeping my own robe firmly closed. "Look. That is the most modest lingerie I could find her and she's covered more than when she's in a bikini! It has to be completely white. I did my fucking best and, *once again*, I said I'd go alone. At least it has a covered crotch."

Harley's eyes snap over to mine and away from the white, vinyl, halter-neck teddy that is showing a whole lot of Avery's cleavage and molds to her body like a second skin. There's a little chain holding the two strips of vinyl in place over her tits and it's looking a little strained. Every single male Mounty at the party may die tonight if that chain breaks.

"And what the fuck are you wearing to this shit-show?" Harley snaps, and I glare at him as I wrap the robe around myself even tighter.

"I'm not showing you until we get there. I'd rather drive there in peace and quiet."

He rolls his eyes at me and bends at the waist to shove his phone in his boot. Fuck me, that ass of his is *bitable*.

As a grumbling Ash helps Avery into her coat, his eyes fixed sullenly on the floor, Blaise pointedly keeps his own eyes on me and firmly away from her. He smirks and crowds me into the wall until his chest is pinning me and I can't breathe with him surrounding me. "Give me a peek, little Star. I won't tell the grumpy dicks."

Oh, the cheeky asshole is aiming for a punch to the kidneys. I scowl at him even as I hold the robe out for him to peer down.

The look in his eyes turns me into a fucking puddle.

He bites his lip and leans down to kiss me fucking senseless.

"Get the fuck off of her in my presence, Morrison! I know what she's just shown you and if you're now sporting a boner, I'll cut it the *fuck* off!"

We break away and Blaise smirks at me as I blush. He helps me into one of Avery's coats while shielding my outfit from the others, and then walks me down to his car. I sit in the back between Ash and Harley and I keep my eyes on the windshield so I don't ruin my lingerie. Well, anymore then Blaise's kiss has already.

I have to direct Blaise to the docks and the giant boat-shed where the Twelve park their cars. The security guard at the fence looks in and dips his head in respect when he sees me. Avery giggles about it, and Harley mutters, "I told you guys, it's fucking weird."

We park between a Rolls Royce I'd guess is the Lynx's and a Bentley that has to belong to the Crow. The guys eye them appreciatively as they all get out of the car. I give myself a minute to slow my heart rate and shake my nerves.

Harley leans against the open car door to wait for me, debating with the others about which car is nicer. I take advantage of their distraction and slide carefully out. With a deep breath, I take the coat off and drop it on the backseat. I push Harley gently out of way with a palm on his back to shut the car door and he turns to me to get an eyeful of the lingerie. His jaw drops, stunned, and then he's cursing viciously.

"Not a fan?" I gripe as he turns away from me.

"I'm walking around the fucking docks in the slums of the Bay, in nothing but boxers, and now I can't even enjoy seeing you in whatever the hell you call *that* because Avery will actually fucking castrate me if she sees how much of a *fan* I am."

Oh.

Right.

"Fuck," croaks Ash from behind us and I startle out of the daze Harley's words have put me in. Avery is smirking evilly with her hands on her hips, coat off and her phone in her hand. Ash's face settles into his cold mask as he takes a step backwards. "No. No, Avery, go on ahead." He snaps and Avery groans like she's being murdered.

Blaise roars with laughter, completely at ease with the whole situation. "Good, isn't it? Aves I don't mind you seeing what the Mounty does to my dick, we can walk together."

"Fuck. Off," she hisses at him, and grabs my arm. "You three can walk behind us until you learn to curb your fucking hormones. It's nothing you haven't seen before."

I smirk at them and turn to walk with Avery, flashing them the back of the teddy. I hear groans and give my ass a little wiggle for good measure.

"This way Aves, remember to let me do the talking."

The chump at the door stares at us all.

I don't know him, he's obviously new, and I do *not* like the way he's staring at Avery. I knew this would happen! I fucking warned them all and if he doesn't stop looking at her Ash is going to beat him then Harley will seal the deal and slit the fucker's throat all while Blaise watches them with glee.

"If you're trying to sneak into this party, you chose the wrong color. The Wolf doesn't bring friends. Ever."

Avery giggles mockingly, the sound like glass shards and open arteries. I smirk and take a step forward. "You should let us pass. You're going to regret it if you don't."

He looks over my shoulder at the guys and snorts. "I'm with the fucking Jackal. You think three pretty boys are going to scare me? You all reek of money, but cash ain't gonna get you in here."

He pauses again and gives Avery a slow sweep over with his eyes. He's so busy making an assessment of her that he doesn't notice the wall of muscle that appears behind him. Avery's body goes rigid as she takes the newcomer in, her only sign of fear, and the chump probably mistakes the reaction as a response to his assessment of her.

"Maybe I'll let you lot in, gimme that little rich cunt to break for the night and the rest of you can go through."

I lock eyes with Illi and say, "No one calls Avery a cunt, Illium. *No one.*"

The chump pisses himself when he turns to see the Butcher grinning at him, clad only in a pair of white boxer briefs and white combat boots. Well, he also has several knives, a gun, and his signature meat cleaver strapped to his body but personally, I know it's the grin that means danger.

He leans forward and reaches into the chump's pocket. Avery raises an eyebrow at me and my smile in return is smug as fuck.

"Y'know why your boss handed you this little torch?" Illi croons as he pulls said torch out and waves it in the guy's face. I laugh quietly under my breath.

Avery is going to lose her mind.

"It-it's to identify—" The guy fumbles his words so hard Illi pats him on the shoulder and interrupts him.

"Yeah. It's to find marks that don't show up otherwise. You used it tonight? You waved it at anyone or are you more of a big-man type? Ah, no, you like raping little girls. You like using your cheap little Jackal tramp-stamp to get you some unwilling pussy. I know *all* about your type."

Illi switches the torch on and aims it over his cheek.

The Wolf insignia glows.

I startle when I see it because I didn't mention it to him when I took him on. I didn't feel comfortable asking him to do it and now Harley's going to pitch a fit at me. *Fuck*.

The chump fumbles over his words again, pathetically, "I know y-you belong to th-the Wolf. Everyone does. B-b-but—"

Illi flicks the torch light over to me and Avery gasps as my skin begins to glow.

"Fuck!" The guy screeches and as he tries to scramble away Illi stabs him, right in the gut, and gives the knife a little turn for good measure. I didn't even see his hand move towards the knife; he's just that good.

I lift a brow at him as the guy squeals like the stuck pig he is.

"What? He'll live! You said no one insults your little bestie so I'm making sure it never happens again. You're *welcome*! I'd hug you but, honestly, seeing you in that thing is like seeing my sister naked. It's fucking disturbing and let's never do this again."

I laugh and grab Avery's hand, tugging her forward and glancing over my shoulder at the guys. They're all staring at Illi with a deep distrust, hatred, and just a little bit wary. I won't fault them; he did just stab a guy.

"So, this is Illi. He's a treasure."

Illi cackles and wiggles his fingers at the guys like he's an eighty-year-old woman trying to coax them into trying his cookies. Harley scowls at him, no longer looking nauseated around him which I'm taking as a win. Blaise shrugs and smiles at me, trusting me implicitly. Oh, my sweet naive rock god.

Then there's Ash.

He surveys Illi with a detached look and then looks at me. "This is the Butcher?"

I nod and wait him out.

"Anyone touches the Wolf or my sister while they're under your protection and I don't care what the fuck they call you, I'll be the one doing the butchering."

Harley looks at his cousin like he's lost his damn mind, but also like he's fucking *impressed*. I'm swooning a little because only Ash would threaten a man whose latest victim is still bleeding at our feet.

Illi smirks at him, his eyes twinkling like a proud fucking father. "I'd expect no different from the son of Joseph Beaumont."

The warehouse is writhing with people, the music is so loud it takes a second to learn how to breathe again, and Avery clutches at my hand as the bodies close in on us.

Illi leads the way and it's not until we hit the platform with the staircase that the black lights hit me, my tattoos instantly glowing, and the crowd parts like the Red Sea. Avery lifts our linked hands then stares down at my arm, turning it and marveling at the tattoos. It's too dark to read her face properly, but I know she's going to snark me out for this.

The second story is invite-only and safer than the bottom level. When I had told Illi that everyone was coming he'd arranged to have some guys keep an eye on Blaise, Ash, and Avery while we're in the meeting. I'm wary about it right up until we meet them at the bar and they dip their heads at me with that fear-drenched respect that can't be faked. Their eyes don't touch Avery at all and when Illi signs to them to guard her with their lives they agree willingly.

I make a note to ask Illi what they owe him for.

I kiss Avery's cheek and give her hand a reassuring squeeze which she returns easily. Ash and Blaise both do eyebrow acrobatics at Harley and then give me a quick peck on the lips as we move off. Harley wraps his arm around my waist and pulls me into his body. I let him, offering him that little reassurance I can before we hit the elevator.

There's only one way in and out of the room we're heading to, and that's the service elevator. The thug guarding it flinches when he sees Illi and fumbles over himself to get us in it. Illi grins and waves at him as the cage-like door shuts and we start to move, excruciatingly slowly.

I pull away from Harley's body but keep a hold of his hand, taking one last deep breath.

"Illi, we need a minute," I murmur, and the tattooed mass of muscle moves soundlessly to the corner, staring down at his shoes. I hate that Harley doesn't like him because he's actually the best guy, just a little fucked up and dangerous. Like me. He's going to be able to hear every damn word we say, but he's trying to give us some sort of space which is fucking decent of him.

Harley's hand tightens in mine. "I know the rules, I'm not going to lose my shit."

"He's going to try to provoke you. Look at what he has us wearing. Just ignore him and remember that I'm going home with you and sleeping in your bed tonight. I've made my choice, and he's not it."

Harley nods and presses his palm over my heart. "You got your knife on you? Or is Illi the only one who's going to be stabbing people tonight?"

He called him Illi, not the Butcher. I'm taking that as a good sign. Illi chuckles quietly and I scoff at them both. "I have one in my boot, but I trust Illi. I've seen him throw a cleaver before, he's got this under control."

Harley scowls and drops his hands from me. He looks over his shoulder at the Butcher and says, "Who the fuck did you throw a cleaver at in front of her? For fuck's sake."

Illi grins and steps back up, taking his place behind me right as the elevator grinds to a halt. "I threw it at the guy who held a knife to little Wolf's throat when we broke into the Vulture's den of evil to spring my wife. Caught him in the throat and the cunt squirted blood all the fuck over us like in the movies. Was so fucking cool, and little Wolfie made me promise her I'd show her how to do it. I did by the way, so don't piss her off in the kitchen."

The doors scrape open right as Harley nods at Illi and mutters, "Okay. You're a decent enough sort of guy."

Illi roars with laughter and we step into the meeting room together.
Holy fuck.
I hope I know what the hell I'm doing.

Chapter Thirteen

The table for the Twelve is round and I quickly choose my seat to be in-between the Coyote and the Bear. Before I sit down Illi snags a jacket from Luca, who is more than willing to help me cover myself thank fuck, and Harley helps me slide into it. He even zips it all the way to the top for me while his eyes twitch like he's trying not to glare at every guy in the room. I'm oddly proud of him for controlling his protective urges. Then my guys take up watch by the wall with the rest of the henchmen, flunkies, guards, and overprotective husbands.

Well, there's just the one over-protective husband and he's glaring at Harley like he thinks my boyfriend is going to try to jump the Lynx's bones. I frown, and then I see the woman herself is staring at Harley like she'd happily drop to her knees at his feet to worship his dick.

Fuck.

Just what I need.

I glance around and see we're still waiting on the Boar. The Jackal takes a seat directly across from me and I refuse to look in his direction at all. He's dressed impeccably in a three piece suit. Only the Fox and the Coyote are in the required underwear, everyone else has approached the Jackal for a pass to get themselves in without stripping.

I refused to speak to him after his spat in the car so lingerie it is. I quirk an eyebrow at the Coyote, the youngest member after me at twenty, and he smirks at me.

"Why the fuck not? I'm going pussy hunting after this, it's been a while since I left my dungeon."

I chuckle under my breath at him. He's the hacker of the group, there's no digital information in the world that's safe from this guy, and he's a certified genius with tech. Someday when I get a permanent residence I'm getting the fucker to set up my security system.

"Who's the hot piece you came in with? She a part of your crew?" the Coyote continues, and I give him a look.

"She's mine," I say with a flat tone and I meet the Crow's gaze across the table. My breath catches as the steel gray of his eyes cut me. He's as dangerous as the Jackal and I don't need any extra bullshit going on in our lives right now.

After a minute he dips his head to me and says, "Has my protection been sufficient?"

"Exemplary, as expected," I say and he nods, almost amicably.

The Boar finally arrives, clothed and with three giant bikers with big bushy beards and cuts with patches all over them. His crew is not one I'd be getting into a bar fight with willingly and I'm not exactly pleased when they stand next to Illi and Harley. Fuck.

The Jackal calls the meeting to a start and I'm forced to look at him. His gaze stays fixed on mine and he's not attempting to hide the possessive obsession from the others anymore. Just what I need. I stare him down because sending a guy to my school to kill Harley was the last fucking straw. I'm done trying to find a casualty-free way of fixing this.

I'm going to war.

The Jackal runs through some squabbles the bigger players are having with turf wars and cops getting involved and I keep my mouth firmly shut. No one cares about my opinion on these things and I don't care enough about it to offer them any advice. I just want to be left the fuck alone. It gets heated pretty fucking quickly and I sit back to enjoy watching the Crow shut the Jackal down at every pass. With their empires rivaling each other in size, the Crow is often the one to shut the Jackal down.

If only he weren't a terrifying, coldly-calculating man, I'd actually like the Crow.

Finally the Ox speaks and shuts the rest of them up, "Are we not going to talk about the fact that the Vulture is dead and his killer is standing here with us, protected by one of us?"

I don't freeze or flinch. I just stare them all down.

"Are you going to explain yourself, Wolf?" the Jackal taunts and I finally look up at him. He's smug and so fucking arrogant as he calls me out but fuck him.

"No. I'm not. Unless you have proof the Butcher did it, move on."

The Viper sneers at me, "He killed a member. If you're willing to look over that then you're spitting in the face of the institution of the Twelve. Maybe we need to dispose of you, too."

I hold my hand up because I know Illi is just about to start throwing knives and shooting people in my protection and I don't even want to know what's going through Harley's head. Fuck.

"I have known Illi a long time and we've been negotiating his induction for years. I believe him when he says he had nothing to do with the Vulture's death. If any of you have proof that he is guilty I will happily hand him over." Blatant fucking lie, I'd never sell him out and he knows it, but he's also sworn there's no evidence of his crime so it's a lie I'm willing to take the risk in telling.

"He's been telling people for years he'd kill the Vulture for what he did to that pathetic French slut, of course he fucking did it!" the Viper snaps and again I hold my hand up though I know it must be killing Illi to stay silent on this one.

"Exactly. If he's been saying it for years, why now? Why wait until the Vulture's business was bigger, his protection stronger, and thousands more girls have been sold? He wanted to kill him, but he didn't want to mess with the Twelve. Now the Vulture's death tipped in my favor and he's finally agreed to *my* terms to become one of mine. So, I'm not saying I'm happy the Vulture is dead but I'm very pleased with my outcome."

The Bear nods at me like my reasoning is sound and for a second I think I've won.

Nope.

Of course not, the Jackal would never let it go now I've openly defied him.

He smirks at me like this is his favorite game, cornering me and bending me hoping I'll break. I know for a fact it is. "I don't find that plausible at all. Majority rules, Wolf, and unless you're going to call in your favors you're not going to get the majority here."

My favors. He wants to force me into using them. Even he doesn't know how many I really have and, though I don't want to use any more than I have to tonight, I will. I only need six votes.

"Fuck the favors, the Wolf has my vote," the Boar grunts and the Jackal's head snaps over to him. I admit, I'm kind of shocked too. He's probably one of the last members I'd expect to back me.

He shrugs. "She's been nothing but true to the Twelve, and she's taken every job I've ever asked from her. If she wants him in her crew then so be it; it's her own back that will be knifed if he's not loyal."

The Jackal grits his teeth and says, "Any other votes in favor."

I hold my breath.

After a beat, the Bear, Fox, Coyote, and Lynx all make some noise or motion of voting yes. I only need one more and just as I open my mouth to call in a favor with the Ox, who owes me quite a few, the Crow says, "Aye. Majority wins, the Butcher is spared."

I glance over to him, but his eyes are on the Jackal. Their little rivalry has worked in my favor, *thank fuck*.

"Any other issues before we move onto the settling of the Vulture's business?" the Jackal snaps and I smile at him, giving him my best fuck-you impression of Avery. The girl is an ice queen after all. I've been planning this for months, knowing the Jackal expects the quiet, reserved Wolf he knows to be in this room and not the fierce, protective Wolf that's formed now I have a family behind me to guard. I throw myself in.

"Two things. Firstly; I would like to address some threats that have been made against my people. I would like to formally remind the Jackal that Harley Arbour is mine, and if he sends any more street rats to knife him in dark alleyways I will see it as an open act of betrayal against not only me, but the Twelve as a whole."

Silence.

I think I can hear the blood pumping furiously in the Jackal's veins from across the table and the slight flare of his eyes is the only sign I've just shocked him.

"Why would I have him killed?" he asks, carefully now the Crow and the Boar are watching him closely.

"Because you're pissed I turned you down. I may choose not to grow an empire but at this table, I am an equal to you. Send someone after my people again, and I won't have to call in favors to have you taken care of. The Twelve will have no choice, but to do it."

The Jackal doesn't try to argue or deny what he's done, he just stares at me like he wants to punish me the same way he's punished me for years, labeling it as training. Well, fuck him. I've learned a fuck ton in the two years I've been away from him and it's only made me more dangerous. Now I have people to protect.

"Jesus Christ, is your pussy gold plated or some shit?" the Coyote murmurs in my ear and I have to resist the urge to shove him the hell away from me.

"Either the institution stands, or it doesn't," I say and tension snaps through the table. The group behind us shifts on their feet, preparing to dive into the fight that we're edging our way closer to.

"The second thing, Wolf?" the Boar asks, clearly wanting to steer the conversation away from bloodshed and war within our own ranks.

I bend and retrieve the velvet bags I have stuffed in the tongue of one of my combat boots. I stand to place the pile in the center of the table. Ten bags, ten diamonds.

"You all know what I'm asking for."

The table all stare at the diamonds with ravenous hunger and I nod.

"Good. Now we can move on."

I'm forced to sit through an hour's worth of arguing about the skin trade and no resolution is found, just as I suspected. The Crow refuses to back down and at one point I think the Jackal starts to plan exactly how he's going to dismember him when the chance arises. Again, it works in my favor because the rest of the table sees it too.

The Jackal is unstable.

His time of being harmonious among us is counting down.

When the Jackal finally calls the meeting over no one stands to leave. He flicks his wrist at one of his men and the elevator starts up. The Twelve all slowly collect their diamonds and stash them away as we wait.

I take a deep breath.

This part is going to be immensely satisfying, but it's also the part I'm most worried about Harley seeing. I have thirty seconds of regret for not warning him, for not wanting him to argue with me about the price of his safety, before Liam and Domnall O'Cronin walk into the meeting room.

Neither of them notice Harley amongst the group of men, they both only have eyes for me as I stand. I'm so glad Illi got me the jacket as I place my palms on the table in front of me and lean forward to address the fucking scumbag mobsters.

"Thank you for joining us, Liam," I say in a dark tone, hatred and disgust clearly present. Domnall twitches at my complete dismissal of him and I mentally high-five myself for it.

Liam's lip curls. "Not like we had much fuckin' choice, ey? What's all this about? You've already stolen my heir, what more could you want from me?"

I ignore the disrespect he's showing me and smirk at him. "Oh, I didn't steal him. He sought me out. He decided that he wanted real loyalty, not the bullshit your family dishes out. But that's all beside the point. I've brought you here to inform you that your family is done. The Twelve are finished with the lot of you. You'll need to pack up and find a new state to live in. I hear Alabama is nice this time of year, try running your '*empire*' there."

Liam's face grows slack as he stares at me and then his eyes frantically dart around the table at the others. When no one speaks up to correct me his face slowly turns purple.

"Our family has lived and worked here for generations, you can't just fuckin' freeze us out!"

Again no one moves or speaks, exactly as I've instructed. I'm the one with power over the O'Cronin family now. My smirk only gets wider.

"I could be persuaded to let you stay. Maybe even keep your businesses running with us."

Domnall finally spots Harley and he freezes, his body locking up completely at the sight of his hulking, enraged, practically-naked nephew standing beside the Butcher, who I'm sure looks positively psychotic with the tats, and the grin, and arsenal of weapons strapped to him. Both of them clad in my color; both of them belonging to me.

Liam rolls his shoulders back, contempt deepening the curl in his lip. "What do I have to do to *persuade* you? If you want the boy that much then fuckin' keep him. If he's sold himself to you then he's as weak as his fuckin' da."

Fuck.

I hear Harley's first step and my breath catches in my throat.

Then silence, thank fuck. I lean forward again and stare Liam straight in the eye, unblinking.

"I want my money. I want the inheritance your grandson is due that you're hiding from him. I want every cent of it, transferred to my accounts, with interest. I'm guessing it's been making you a nice return? Well, that money is *mine*."

Domnall has lost the ability to school his features and he's openly glaring at me now. I arch an eyebrow at him and Illi takes a step forward. "Watch yourself, mobster. Only a stupid man would provoke the Wolf and I'm fucking *itching* to split you open for her."

I sit back down, smoothing my hands down the jacket as if it's a silk gown and I'm Avery Beaumont, all classy and shit. "I thought about buying a judge to retrieve the money. Easy, quick, simple. But I wanted the satisfaction of watching you realize that your little power moves didn't work. That money is mine and you're going to hand it over to me. If you don't, I will consider your refusal a declaration of *war*. I'll destroy every last O'Cronin in the state."

Liam does one last sweep of the table and then gives me a look that would boil the blood of a lesser man. Good thing I'm neither a man, or less than the deadly, calm Wolf. I nod at him like he's agreed with me. "If it's not in my account by Friday I'll be finding you, Liam. I'll be coming for you all. Maybe I'll start with your new heir, what's his name again? Oh, Aodhan? Maybe I'll come see if he wants to join me as well. I'll bring Illi to help sway him."

Domnall blanches at his son's name and I smirk. Hook, line, and sinker; they know they're fucked.

Liam spits out from his clenched teeth, "Deal."

The meeting room empties soon after the mobsters storm out. Illi and Harley step up immediately to join me and I avoid looking Harley in the eye. I don't want to see his reaction to my confrontation with his family while the Jackal is staring holes into us from the other side of the table.

The Crow takes his time getting up, and I know he's pushing every damn button on the Jackal he can when he gestures to the elevator and says, "Ladies first. I look forward to seeing you at the next meeting, Wolf."

I incline my head at him respectfully, and when I turn around to face Harley, he makes eye contact with the Jackal over my shoulder. I grab his hand gently, both to warn him and to tell him I'm fine, and he squeezes mine back. Illi snorts and crosses his arms next to him, obviously pissed off at the Jackal's actions and ready to throw down with him for Harley in a second. I'm so relieved they've found some sort of truce that I don't notice what the fuck Harley is doing as he maintains eye contact and—

And, fuck me with a cactus, he unzips the jacket, pushing it off my shoulders while running his hands all over me with such fucking possession my knees threaten to give out. I look up to find him *smirking* at the Jackal and then he kisses me like he's trying to fuck my mouth, my face cradled in his big hands.

Fuuuuuuuck.

Illi cackles and nudges Harley with an elbow. "Grab your girl. I need a drink and a fucking smoke after that. Let's go find the rest of our little motley crew."

Harley breaks away from my lips with another smirk, this one at me, then he just grabs my ass and hauls me into his arms, walking us over to the elevator.

"Did you just spend ten fucking diamonds on me?" he mutters against my neck, and of course that's his priority, even with the psycho behind us making eye contact with me. There's nothing but bloodshed and slaughter in the Jackal's eyes but I hold them, steady and calm. Harley steps into the cage and the door shuts.

"Did you just taunt the Jackal about being mine?" I retort, still a little gobsmacked.

"Fuck yes, I did. Fuck him, babe, you've just told them all about what he's doing. Besides, if he doesn't let you go we'll just get the Butcher to throw a meat cleaver at him."

Illi cackles and runs a finger down said cleaver lovingly. I laugh and wriggle out of Harley's arms to stand between them. I feel lighter, like I've taken the last step away from the Jackal and now I'm standing on my own two feet. It's fucking terrifying to feel so alone without his protection, and for a second it knocks the breath out of my lungs, but then Illi cracks some jokes and Harley grunts out a chuckle at them and I remember the family I'm carefully building is worth the risk.

Illi leads the way back over to the bar area where we find a fucking wasted Blaise, Avery holding a drink and staring down at her phone, and a very antsy looking Ash. When I point to Blaise with an eyebrow lift Ash rolls his eyes and points towards the other end of the bar, where there's a growing crowd of salivating Mounty girls, watching him like they want to eat him alive. Illi laughs when he sees them and wiggles his fingers at them, easily dispersing the crowd with one action.

I'm too hyped up to drink, but I need *something* to take the edge of my adrenaline off.

Ash watches me closely, then tugs on my hand and tilts his head towards the dance floor. Harley nods at him for me and I turn to gesture to Illi to get him to watch Blaise and Avery. Avery smirks at me with a little evil grin and lifts her cocktail at me in a salute. Okay, so tipsy Avery is much more agreeable to the guys turning me into the meat in a hot guy sandwich. Good to know.

As we move through the crowd, Harley presses me into Ash's back. The second story is safer, but still teeming with sweaty, intoxicated, writhing Mounties and without the black lights touching my skin none of them know who it is walking amongst them.

Ash leads us far enough away that Avery won't be able to see us clearly and that's my first clue that he's up to no good.

The second is the fucking panty-melting grin he gives me when he turns around to dance with me. Harley's chest rumbles with laughter against my back as Ash stoops down to kiss me, clutching my hips to move us both in a grinding sway with the music. He's not a natural at this style of dancing like Harley is but, fuck, the grind of his hips and the sweep of his tongue on mine render me incapable of doing much more than swaying. The other people dancing disappear completely as my world narrows down to the three of us and the touch of their skin on mine. Harley's mouth traces the tendons of my neck, nipping and sucking, and I know for sure that I'm not going to leave this party with my dignity.

It's fucking worth it.

Harley's hands slide up from where he was gripping my waist to slip underneath the lace of the teddy and roll my nipples until I'm grinding back on his dick and panting into Ash's mouth. Ash cups my soaking pussy through the lingerie and pauses for a second until I nod, breaking away from his lips to drop my head onto Harley's shoulder and moan like an utter slut. I fucking love it.

Harley bites down on my shoulder as his eyes glue themselves down my body to where Ash is tugging and shifting the teddy until he has room to touch me properly. The teddy has snaps along the crotch and I'm so fucking desperate I think about ripping it open, but I don't think either of them would be happy with me being bared to the whole dance floor like that. I don't think anyone has noticed us, there's a couple fucking on the bar so no one gives a fuck, but I know my guys.

It's like my nod to Ash unleashes the restraint he's been showing for weeks and he's merciless now that he has his hands on me. He slips a finger inside me and after a few quick pumps he adds another, raking them over my G spot sporadically like a fucking tease until I'm a babbling mess. I give him a stern look, but he's smirking at me like a smug dick and when his thumb brushes over my clit, in the lightest freaking touch, I want to cry.

The more he teases, the more I grind back on Harley's dick and his chest is heaving against my back. I can feel how much Ash is getting off at drawing this out, at driving me out of my mind, and when I'm about to shove him away and demand Harley finish the damn job he grinds his thumb into my clit and I break into a thousand jagged pieces. Only Harley's arms around me keep me upright as Ash strokes the orgasm out of me with nothing, but his demanding fingers.

When my brain comes back online, Ash slips his fingers out and stares at me, unblinking, as he pushes them into my mouth. Okay. Never tasted myself before but sweet lord *fuck*, that's hot. It only gets hotter when he leans forward to chase the taste with his own tongue and Harley's fingers slip down into the mess they've both made.

I gasp into Ash's mouth and when he breaks away I grab his biceps to steady my jelly-legs now Harley's steel grip has eased off. There's an odd pause where they both tense for a moment, and then Harley's fingers start to move against me.

He's obviously not trying to get me off, his fingers just playing in the come that's dripping its way down my thighs, and he presses his mouth to my ear to shout over the music.

"I'm cleaning this up, babe, I don't want you wasting it down your legs."

My brain short circuits a little because he's right, I don't want to go back to Avery with a soaked crotch, but there's no bathrooms here. I should have thought about that before I let them both distract me with their hotness and their hands.

I don't make any attempts to resist as they move me over to a small alcove-like area near one of the enormous speakers. I wait for Harley to give me some sort of idea of how he's going to make me presentable before we see Avery, but instead he swaps positions with Ash until he's standing before me and the look they share spells trouble. Deadly, sexy trouble.

I narrow my eyes at Harley but he ignores me, swooping down to kiss me, pressing me into Ash's chest as his arms band around my hips like steel. I have just enough room to wriggle between them, grinding against their dicks, torn between pushing forward or back. For the first time I think about having sex with more than one of them and I'm not scared. Jesus, what are they doing to me? I shiver and moan all over again, breaking the kiss with Harley.

Then he smirks at me and drops to his knees.

Oh.

Oh fuck.

My heart starts pounding. His hands skim up my thighs until he finds the opening at the crotch of the teddy and rips the snaps open, baring my pussy to him. Thank God I really did shave everything because I can feel his breath dancing over my skin as he leans in, and my eyes roll back in my head.

I'm trembling as I wait for his mouth to touch me. Then Ash's arms drop from my hips and he pushes me forward slightly as he leans down to hook his arms around my knees. He lifts me up and *open*, spreading me wide so my pussy is on full display for Harley. My cheeks burn, but before I can protest this *mortifying* position Harley sinks his teeth into my thigh sharply until I look down at him, and once he has my eyes glued to his he finally drops his mouth down to lick and suck at my pussy like he's been starving for this.

I can't keep my eyes open, not as his tongue swirls around my clit and toys with it until my thighs are trembling in Ash's hands, so I squeeze my eyes shut and drop my head back against Ash's shoulder. I want to wrap my legs around Harley's neck and grind on his face, but those hands are immovable even as I try to squirm. Instead, I wrap one hand around Ash's wrist to keep me stable and the other I twist into Harley's hair, pulling him closer and I feel his groan against my sensitive skin.

Holy fuck, if this is how I die then I accept.

I know if I look down at Harley I'm going to come straight away and I don't want him to stop the amazing torture. I can't think past what his mouth is doing to me and when he drops down to push his tongue inside me I cry out into the deafening noise of the party, no one any wiser of the dirty dreams Harley is fulfilling for me.

When I can't stand it any longer and his tongue is working my clit like he's trying to melt my brain, I open my eyes and the roaming lights of the warehouse hit Harley's face as he stares straight into my eyes. I come so fucking hard, my back arching to grind my pussy into his mouth even harder and Ash slackens his hold just enough to let my writhe my release out on his cousin's face.

When my head drops back onto Ash's shoulder again my gaze lands on the balcony above us, to find the Jackal is watching us, flanked by his men. He's gripping the railing and his back is so deadly straight I'm surprised he hasn't pulled his gun yet.

I stare up at him, defiance in every inch of my body, as it hits me Harley and Ash have known he was there watching all along. This was as much a claiming of me for them as a fun public fuck.

I can't see the Jackal's face clearly, but the lights keeping hitting us at random intervals and he's been able to see exactly what we've been doing.

Ash gently lowers my legs to the ground, kissing my neck possessively, and when he looks up at the Jackal I see the arrogant taunt; the challenge he's giving the sociopathic Jackal to come down and fight him for me. I suppose being raised by

Senior has made Ash a little reckless.

Harley tugs the crotch of my teddy back together, closing the snaps carefully to cover my pussy from view, before standing and turning away from me. I glance away from the Jackal to see the deadly glare he's throwing at the leader of a fucking huge criminal organization like the haughty golden god he is, and on impulse I lean forward to kiss the solid muscle of his back.

I will not submit to the Jackal's demands any longer.

Even if it costs me my life.

Chapter Fourteen

Avery is tipsy enough that she doesn't notice the state of my teddy or the wet spots on the guy's boxers, and I've never been so fucking grateful for margaritas in my life. Blaise has to be carried out and I tuck my arm into Avery's to keep her walking straight.

"Fuck guys, Lips. Just fuck them." She giggles, but tears shine in her eyes even as her giggles turn into a full belly laugh.

I *am* hoping to fuck three of them in particular, but I keep that little nugget of wisdom to myself. "What's happened? Atticus being a dick again?"

She tucks her face into my neck and I try not to breathe on her. The last thing in my mouth was Ash's fingers coated in my come so I really don't want her smelling it on my breath. I don't want to think about her reaction to that!

"I told him I was out on the town and he said I'm not the type of girl that should be out at parties. I didn't even tell him where I was! He thinks I'm some perfect china fucking doll, maybe that's why he won't fuck me."

My brain goes blank, and when Ash's head snaps around to look back at us he's all fury and rage. I shake my head at him with a *look*. Glass houses and all that.

"I'm confiscating your phone. We're making him come to you remember? If he wants to try to tell you what sort of girl you are instead of seeing it for himself then he's a dick. You'll feel better in the morning, and if he tries to make you feel bad about it, I'll stab him. Or we can ask Illi too, he loves that shit."

Avery laughs again and whispers, far too loudly so everyone hears her, "You didn't tell me Illi was so fucking hot! Do you think his dick is tattooed too?"

I see the tension form in Harley and Ash's shoulders as I giggle. I deliberate for a half a second but think, fuck it.

"Odie, his wife, told me he has her name tattooed down his dick because any girl that dares to go near it should be warned it belongs to her. I'm not sure if she was being serious, but I do know he has a piercing there. I haven't seen it! A few Mounty girls told me about fucking him. Before Odie, I mean."

Avery stumbles and my leg protests so fucking painfully as I hold her upright.

"A piercing?! Do you think he'd show it to me?"

"*Avery, shut the fuck up!*" Ash snaps and I snort with laughter at them both as we get to the car. Avery frowns at him, but at least the tears are gone from her eyes.

Harley drives us back. I sit in the back, with Blaise draped over my lap and Ash seethes about Avery's drunken ramblings next to us. I feel like warning him that she's just doing it to piss him off, but Avery needs to get her kicks somewhere, I guess.

When we get back to the hotel room, the guys drop Blaise on the couch and then Ash stomps after Avery to start an argument with her.

I wriggle my feet out of the boots, grabbing my knife to take with me to bed, and then move to follow the twins into our room. Harley catches me around the waist and drags me into his body.

"Did you forget something, babe? You're in my bed tonight. It's my reward for not mouthing off to that sick fuck."

Oh, right.

I turn in his arms, rubbing my face on his bare chest as I yawn, dead on my feet.

"I'm not sure you deserve it after your little private show for him."

Harley hoists my into his arms and carries me to his bed. "That's *exactly* why I deserve it, babe."

I'm woken by a text from Doc checking in to see if I still need to see him.

I flick him a quick text saying I'll be an hour and then I crawl out from underneath Harley and jump in the shower. I order an Uber as I throw some shorts and one of Harley's tees on, then shove my cherry Docs on at the door and swipe a room key from the side-table at the door.

"Where are you sneaking off to this early in the morning?" Ash whispers, and I jump about a mile in the air. Creepy fucker. He's standing there, already dressed and with a cup of delicious smelling coffee in his hands. I think about wrestling it off of him.

"I'm going to see Doc. I have an appointment," I whisper back, and try to ignore the blush that immediately starts.

Ash eyes my cheeks and quirks an eyebrow. "I'll drive you in. We can pick up breakfast on the way back."

Okay, that sounds amazing, but the chances of him waiting in the car while I'm in with Doc aren't great. He hands me his coffee while he grabs his shoes and I drink the rest of it in a giant gulp. "I need to speak to him about birth control and my period. I didn't think you'd want to sign up for a front row seat for that."

Ash smirks and grabs his keys. "I'm glad you're thinking about birth control, Mounty, and I'm not squeamish. Who the hell do you think helped Avery when she first got hers? I don't give a shit. Now, do you want to take the Maserati or the Mustang?"

Fuck.

I guess he's coming.

We take the Maserati because he has the keys for that already and I don't want this to end up a field trip to my uterus by asking Harley for the 'Stang keys.

It's strange to me that Ash has access to the largest amount of money and yet we're borrowing cars from the other two. When I mention it, he smirks at me. "I have a collection of cars and if I brought any of them to the slums of Mounts Bay, I would have to stab someone for breathing too closely to them. I leave them safely in the garage at Avery's horse ranch."

Huh.

Avery has a horse ranch?

Ash laughs at my expression. "She bought it freshman year and she's been renovating it since. She's been careful about keeping it a secret from Joey and Senior. She hates horses because she's a germaphobe, but the land is in a prime and secluded location. She built a garage for me and she's been renovating rooms for us all too. She'll start bugging you about moving into it during summer break soon."

Huh.

Maybe I do have a house I need to have secured by the Coyote? I make a note to ask Avery about it.

Ash is shockingly good with directions and remembers how to get to Doc's house without much prompting. The drive is clear of cars and he parks out front, unbuckling his seatbelt and pausing when I don't make a move. I don't like admitting when things hurt or are concerning me, I'd rather make a sarcastic joke, so I give myself a second to get my shit together.

He watches me fidget for a second, and then gives me a look. He says, with a surprisingly neutral but stern tone, "I'm coming in. I don't like him and if he has someone else in there I don't want you walking in alone."

I nod, but I don't move to get out.

"Is there something else?" he asks, and it's in that soft damn tone he uses at Avery. I cave.

"I get severe cramps. I've been getting the birth control injection from him for years to help lessen the pain but it's not working out, and being at Hannaford makes it hard to get them on time anyway. I'm asking for something else."

Ash frowns at me and shrugs as he opens the car door. "Stop worrying then. Let's get this over with so we can go get breakfast. I need another coffee."

Doc opens the door before we make it up the steps. "Hello, my girl! Brought a friend again, I see. I'm glad you're being a bit more social."

I can barely hear him over the noise of the kids running around the house and Ash is scowling around the room at them all. I wait until we're locked safely in the exam room before I quietly murmur to Doc, "This is Ash. He is the one who tried to help Maria."

Ash's eyes snap to mine. "What do you mean tried to? She got out, didn't she?"

Fuck. I grimace and Doc smiles wryly at Ash, clapping him on the shoulder. He doesn't act like a man deeply mourning, but I can see the strain in his face, the signs of his devastation there if you know him like I do.

Doc answers Ash for me while I'm still fumbling for the right words. "You did get her out and I cannot thank you enough. But she was a silly, love-sick girl and went back to Matteo. She's gone now. Those noisy little beasts out there are all I have left now."

The mask snaps back over Ash's features and I curse myself for not telling him earlier. Doc gives him another little pat then directs us to sit down.

"Here for a shot? You're late, my girl. I hope you're not here about babies."

I flush and grit my teeth at him. "No, Doc, I'm not here about babies. The shot isn't helping anymore and I want the rod. That's the next thing to try, right?"

He hums and starts rummaging around in his drawers. "Do you want babies? We could just cut it all out. That can be effective in stopping the pain. Not always, but it's an option."

Sweet mother of god.

Why did I bring Ash here again?

Fuck.

While I'm too busy freaking the fuck out about this, Ash snaps at Doc, "You're not cutting *anything* out."

Doc gives him a stern look. "Not your choice, boy."

Ash surveys the room with contempt. "If she wants anything cut out, I'll take her to a real hospital, with real doctors, so she doesn't bleed out at the hands of a second-rate hack in the slums."

I groan and bury my face in my hands. Is anyone safe from Ash's sharp tongue?

Doc looks at him for a moment and then laughs, thank fuck, pulling out the equipment to insert the rod in my arm. It takes under a minute and once he's finished sticking the band-aid over the wound he gives me a stern look. "Any changes from our last visit? Do you need me to test you? Boys lie about being safe and clean, you know, even rich ones."

I shake my head, still flushed, and Ash glares him down like he's going to stab him.

"Seven days until it's effective to stop babies."

I wish he would stop saying babies to me, fucking *lord*.

Ash slips his hand onto my thigh and sneers at Doc, "Are we done?"

We stop for waffles on the way back at Avery's request because she has a savage hangover and bad temper with it. Harley texts to say she's already kicked Blaise out of the room and bitched him out for his antics last night. All I can think is thank fuck she didn't know what I'd done with the other two.

Ash orders my coffee without asking what I like and when I raise a brow at him he smirks. One sip of the sweet nectar of the gods tells me the smug asshole has been watching me closer than I think.

He holds my hand the whole way back to the hotel, up the elevator, and down the hall to our rooms. I'm so happy I even hum a little under my breath, and he pulls me in closer to his body so he can hear it. I should know better than to let myself be happy.

There's a box waiting outside the door to our room.

There, in bold black letters, is my full name across the top. Middle name and all. My stomach drops instantly and Ash's hand tightens around mine. I wait for a second and then step up to open it.

"Mounty, you can't just fucking open it!" Ash hisses, and I ignore him.

I use my knife to slice it open. Ash snaps at me again and I cut him off, "Avery, Harley, and Blaise are in that room and there's no other way out. I have to see what it is."

I flick the box open and the smell hits me.

Fuck.

Fuuuuuuuuck.

It's a head.

There's a head in the box.

I flick it shut again and stand up abruptly. Ash steps forward, my body shielding the contents so he still has no idea of what's just been delivered to us. My face must look all sorts of fucked up as I try to figure out what the fuck is going on because his hand slips into mine again. I mean, it's not the first time I've seen a dismembered head, but I'd let my guard down again this morning. I'd let myself slip back into Lips and away from the Wolf.

"Is it dangerous?" Ash mutters. I shake my head, but when he moves to have a look for himself I tug him back.

"I need your phone. I left mine behind," I say calmly, and he hands his over without question.

"What's up, kid?" Illi answers, and I don't bother asking him how he knew it was me.

"Priority call, Illi. I need you to come to the hotel. We've had company this morning and they've left us a gift."

Illi snorts. "How kind. Gimme ten."

I gesture for Ash to get the door and then, grimacing, I pick up the box and carry it into the room.

Chapter Fifteen

The head in the box belongs to Lance, my stalker from last year.

Harley and Ash both refuse to wait for Illi and have a look, jaws clenched. Blaise gags at the smell but has a look too, and he's the first to figure out who it is. Avery doesn't look up from her phone and she demands that Ash puts her waffles in the fridge for later, when there's not stray body parts appearing out of nowhere.

Illi arrives and snaps on a pair of latex gloves before lifting it out. Avery gets one look at it and barely makes it to the bathroom sink before she vomits, then she refuses to leave until the head is back in the box. I don't blame her; she's hungover and it's not exactly *fresh*. She's going to clean every square inch of our room for hours when we get back to Hannaford. She'll probably have the guys' room gutted before the panic subsides.

Illi moves to empty out the rest of the contents of the box and finds nothing but the head and the plastic sheet lining the cardboard.

Nothing.

Fuck.

Illi stares at the box with a frown over his face. I don't like the look of that frown one bit because the same one is on my face. Fuck, he sees it too. He meets my eye and nods.

"I'll ask around a bit more. You might want to call the Crow, or even the Coyote, see if they know what the fuck this means."

I scowl and nod; we're going to need the extra help. Ash frowns at me and says, "This isn't the Jackal? It looks like a sick token of affection to me. Like he's proving his devotion to you. I'd assume after last night he was making a stand."

Blaise rolls bloodshot eyes around at us all. "What happened last night? Did Arbour piss him off in the meeting?"

I flush scarlet and desperately wish Illi wasn't so fucking perceptive as he grins at Blaise. Fuck, does he know what we'd done? I need some fucking whiskey.

Illi opens his mouth and I cut him off. "He saw Harley, Ash, and I dancing after the meeting. He was watching the three of us and I have no doubt he was planning out my punishment."

At that, the smirk melts off of Illi's face and he snaps his gloves off. "This isn't retaliation. This was done at least three days ago, and D'Ardo would leave a calling card. This isn't his style. Fuck knows *whose* style this is, but it's not his."

Harley groans and curses at the ceiling. "Mounty, is there any fucking chance you could stop attracting psychos and serial killers for five fucking minutes while we dig our way out of the mountain of shit we're already in?"

I shift my scowl over to him, sitting on the couch to rest my leg. "If I knew how I was doing it, clearly I would stop."

Illi snickers at us both and tucks the box under his arm without a care in the world of it's contents. "I'll deal with this. If the rest of it shows up we might have more of an idea of who's behind it. Stay safe, kids!"

He takes two steps towards the door and then swings back to smirk at me, his eyes fucking dancing around like he's never been happier. Fuck.

"If you decide to indulge in anymore *public frolicking*, please warn me. I've had a few threats neutralized already this morning, little Wolf."

I don't think it's possible to blush any freaking harder than I am as he laughs at me and walks out.

As the door clicks shut behind him, Avery comes out of the bathroom, her face still a little green, and slumps down next to me, eyeing the color on my cheeks critically. I tuck my arm into hers to distract her and she croaks out, "Fuck margaritas."

Blaise is still staring between us all like he's missing something big. I really hope that when he figures it out Avery and I aren't around.

"I don't like him." Ash snaps, and I glance up to find him staring at the door Illi just exited.

Harley shrugs nonchalantly. "He grows on you. Give him time to get under your skin."

Blaise laughs at them both quietly, like his head is still pounding and his usual raucous laughter wouldn't be worth the pain. "Well, I don't have a single fucking issue with the psycho. He doesn't look at Star's ass even in those booty shorts, he stabs people without her even having to ask him, and he gets rid of decomposing body parts with a smile. Don't be a jealous dick and just leave him alone."

Ash's eyes flare and he fixes them on me. Fuck, what next? "Oh, Mounty, how could I forget? Your name was on that box."

I tense up and throw him a stern look. His answering smile is a taunt. Fuck, I should've gone with a pleading look, but it's just not my style.

"Yes, Ash, we've just spent the last hour discussing her crazed stalker. Have you suffered some sort of brain damage I'm unaware of?" Avery hisses and he smirks at her.

"I was referring to Lips' middle name."

Fuck. I glare at him and Blaise bursts out laughing. Harley looks between them and then frowns at me like this is my fucking fault. Nope, I will not feel bad that he's practically pouting at me. No. Stay strong, Lips. *Fuck.*

"Ash, I would appreciate your discretion," I grit out, overly polite because I don't want to rage blackout and stab him for digging this hole for me. For the record, it would be justified.

"How does Blaise know it?" Avery asks sweetly, and it's a total ruse. She might slit my throat while I'm sleeping for not telling her.

"She loves me the most!" Blaise sings and shakes his ass as he heads towards the balcony for a smoke. I stare at his ass for a second too long but, *damn,* he can move those hips of his.

When I look back at the others Harley is staring at Blaise like he's planning exactly where he's going to stab the fucker. I hold out my hands as Avery scowls at me. "He found out while I was off my head on those pain pills you gave me. I made him swear not to tell anyone because it's fucking embarrassing and I'd rather die than ever hear it said out loud."

Avery rolls her eyes at my dramatics, but Ash stares at me for a second longer. Something in my eyes makes him shrug. "Fine, I'll keep it to myself."

Avery also shrugs and smiles at Harley. "Mounty will tell me when we get home. She loves *me* the most."

I squeeze my eyes shut so I don't have to see his reaction to potentially being the only one not knowing the damn name and snap, "It's Starbright, okay? My name is Eclipse *Starbright* Anderson. My mom was high and thought the moon was fucking cool and just ran with it. She didn't give a fuck about how it would affect me for the rest of my life. Fuck, she couldn't even stay sober long enough to get through her pregnancy or my birth, for fuck's sake. Okay? Cool. Glad everyone is on the same fucking page. Where's the fucking whiskey, I'm going to drink myself to death, or until I forget about it. Whichever happens first."

The Bear calls me with his job midway through the break and I instantly know it's going to be fucking messy.

He wasn't lying, it will be quick, but the chances of me getting it done without one of the guys or Avery finding out and throwing a fit is pretty slim.

The outfit requirement alone is going to piss them the fuck off. They're pretty twitchy about my ass in booty shorts, especially since all of the supervised eating has put a little meat on my bones. Harley in particular can't seem to keep his hands away from the curve and I find myself fantasizing about what it'll feel like to have his big hands spread me open.

I take a lot of cold showers.

After I get my brief from the Bear, I drag Avery into our shared bedroom at the hotel and give her a very basic and vague rundown of what I'm going to do. Naturally, the evil genius figures it out before I've even finished with the watered down sentence.

"So what you're trying *not* to say is you're going to assassinate the leader of a prominent illegal organization because he pissed the Bear off?"

Right. Well. I can't really argue with that assessment. "Yeah. I am. Is this going to be a problem?"

Avery switches her phone on silent, I trip over my own feet in shock, and then she props her chin up on her hands and watches while I throw together a good Mounty outfit. I need to blend in.

"No problem. How many times do I have to tell you, I'm on your side. I trust that you wouldn't be going and killing a decent person. Honestly, I don't think I would care even if he were decent. If he's in your way, take him out. Our family first; fuck everyone else," she says, taking in the tiny shorts and skintight razor tee.

Fuck, I really would kill and die for this girl.

I do a full face of make up, and then cover all my visible skin in the tinted moisturizer I use to cover the tattoos to get through clubs without notice. Avery helps out with the backs of my legs and when I grab my shoes she gets up and starts digging around in my bag. When she pulls out another pair of shorts and a Vanth tee Blaise gave me I raise my eyebrows at her.

"Don't be dense, Mounty. I'm coming with you and we'll tell the boys we're having some girl time. That way they won't try to jump in, as if you're some kind of damsel that needs saving, to mess this up for you, and I'll get to watch you work. There is nothing quite as satisfying as watching you destroy the male population one by one," she says and when she pulls my clothes on I nearly choke at her transformation into a Mounty girl. Sweet lord fuck, it's only a matter of time before some guy hits on her and I'll have to fucking kill him too.

Yep, just a regular girls night out in the Bay.

As predicted the guys all pitch a fit when they get an eyeful of Avery and figure out what we're doing, and she shoots them all down *beautifully*. She has an answer for everything and when Blaise tries to hand the keys for the Maserati over she smiles sweetly at him, waving her phone in his face.

"Mounties use Uber. I'm going to live like the locals for a night. I feel desperate already."

Ash snorts at her, pissed at the both of us, and I step away from them before I get caught in the crossfire.

Harley hooks an arm around my waist and pulls me into his body. When he whispers in my ear, I shiver. "Promise me you're not going somewhere dangerous, babe. Promise me it's just a girl's night."

Fuck. Avery shoots me a look and I fumble to talk my way around it without lying. "I'm taking Avery on a job with me. I wouldn't take her if I thought there was a chance it could get dangerous. Her safety is always a priority for me."

He nods and ducks down to kiss me, his hand trailing down my back to squeeze my ass in my shorts and I shiver. "Do you have any shorts that cover more of your ass?"

I pull away, scoffing at him even as I blush. "I have to blend in. Avery's wearing the longest ones I own, anyway, and on her long ass legs they still look indecent."

At this, Ash levels me with a look. I freeze for a second before snapping, "What the fuck have I done? I was going to go alone!"

He turns on his heel, stalking over to the bar to find the bourbon, and we take the opportunity to leave before he changes his mind and follows us both out.

Avery sits in the Uber like she's afraid she'll catch a venereal disease from the seats. I send a photo of her to the guys and she snarks at me like I'm a traitor to all womankind.

It only makes me laugh harder.

The bar we're heading to is seedy and dark, perfect to murder some asshole in.

I know the guy at the door, and a curt nod is all it takes before we're both in. I slip a little clip of cash into his pocket as we pass and then Avery's hand is tucked carefully into mine as we navigate our way through the room, blending seamlessly into the crowd of drunken locals.

Well, I blend in. Avery is shuddering a little too much to look local to the discerning eye, but no one here is sober enough to give her revulsion a second glance.

"That guy back there had cum stains on his shorts, Mounty." Avery hisses and I laugh at her, pulling her along until finally we reach the bar at the back.

Stephen is one of the bartenders on tonight.

Excellent.

I catch his eye and he smiles cheerfully at me, finishing up with his customer and making his way over to me before the busty blonde helping him can piss me off. The look she's giving Avery pisses me the fuck off before I realize she's glaring at the Vanth shirt. Right. A priceless collector's item.

"There's my favorite little ass shaker! Here to dance the night away or should I be worried? Picking things up or making a mess?" Stephen says and pours me a whiskey without asking. He tilts the bottle in Avery's direction and she nods, her eyes glued to the glaring blonde the same way you'd stare at a box of snakes.

"Making a mess, sorry. You'll have to call your boss," I murmur and he only smiles wider.

"Oh, he called and told me to expect you."

He hesitates for a second, wiping a glass with a rag I hope Avery isn't looking at, before gesturing at her. "A friend of yours?"

I nod and down my shot. "She's with me. I'm looking out for her."

"You know your friends are my friends, kid. I'll keep the hoards of ravenous cock in the bar away from her while you shake that ass of yours. Have fun!" he says with a wink and I laugh at him. He pours me another shot and walks back over to the crowd of people waiting to be served.

I survey the room and find the guy I'm looking for sitting in one of the booths with two other guys. They're talking, or more likely arguing as he shakes his head and sneers at them. I jerk my head at Stephen and he nods, grabbing a bottle of vodka and walking it over to the booth. I need the guy to pee.

"This is not what I expected. It's a lot more... open than I thought it would be," Avery murmurs and I shrug.

I smile at Stephen as he comes back over to the bar, the dirty rag slung over his shoulder like it's an everyday occurrence that he helps out with a hit. Belonging to the Bear, it may well be.

"Stephen belongs to the Bear. He owns this place and is kept safe by that loyalty so he's safe to talk to. He got the heads up and we drink for free. You'll always drink for free here now, by the way, not that you need the hand out."

Avery nods and downs the shot, pushing the glass away from herself to signal she's done for the night to the bartenders. Stephen grins and slides a bottle of water down the bar to her like the sweetheart he is.

While I wait for my mark to break the seal, we get approached by no less than five guys, each wanting to fuck us both. I shut the first guy down hard and Avery sends a blow-by-blow to the group message because she secretly hates me, I'm sure. I wait for her to jump in and destroy the Mounties but she just watches and assesses my words.

When my mark finally stands as the fifth guy approaches, Avery cuts him off before he can even open his mouth. I'm relieved until I see the evil little twinkle in her eye.

"She has three cocks waiting at home; she doesn't have anymore *vacancies* to fill."
Good lord.

The guy smirks at us both and reaches for my hand, "If you like groups, baby girl, my friends and I can show you a good time—"

I break his hand, then stomp on his foot with my good leg. The thick soles of my Docs make it hard to tell if I've broken his foot, but the squeal that comes out of him is disgraceful.

I lean forward to speak directly in his ear, "Leave while you still have hands for me to break because one more word and I'll cut them off, dickhead."

He scurries away and Avery gives me her best broken glass and bleeding hearts giggle. I make a note to never give her whiskey again. Apparently even in small amounts it turns her into a smug, shit-stirring siren.

I should get that on a shirt for her.

I wait until my mark moves towards the restroom by himself and I give Avery a stern look, motioning for her to stay put. I catch Stephen's eye, and then quickly duck behind the bar and into the store room. I've been here many times before and when I crouch down by the shelves, holding dusty boxes of red wine no one in the Bay will ever drink, I find my supply bag where I left it back in the summer break. There's nothing in the bag that could lead anyone back to me, but I've never worried about it. Stephen would never risk answering to the Twelve by moving it; he's just not that stupid. I make quick work of slipping my Docs off, wriggling my toes and centering myself. I don't have much time to waste, so one last deep breath in and I let the calm Wolf settle over me.

Time to work.

I grab the latex gloves and snap them into place. There's a plastic jumpsuit in there too, but it'll make too much noise.

If I need to go home bloody, I will.

I push the false back out of the shelf and squeeze through the small opening, checking to make sure no one is in the toilet cubicle on the other side before pulling myself the rest of the way into the restroom. Another sweep under the stall to make sure there are no witnesses, but the cash I parted with on the way in will keep the room clear.

The men's always stinks. It's fucking foul.

My mark is on the phone at the urinal, loud and brash down the line like he's invincible. I wait until he hangs up and his dick is safely tucked back into his pants before I step up behind him.

His eyes meet mine in the mirror and I see the exact moment he realizes he's dead.

The hot spray of his blood over the tiles just confirms it.

I can't get into an Uber stinking of blood.

The giant hoodie I had in my supply bag covers most of the damage and I'd scrubbed my legs clean before I'd left the restroom, but the tang of copper is overpowering where it's stuck to me.

I should have worn the plastic jumpsuit.

Avery is calm as we sit on a busy road in the slums, waiting for the guys to come pick us up. I let my mind wander as my eyes track the cars passing us, on guard as always in the Bay.

She breaks the silence first. "That was surprisingly easy."

It wasn't easy; it just ran smoothly. It's something I've done so many times, something I've studied and practiced and executed hundreds of times, so now it seems simple.

I'm too tired to explain it to her so I shrug, letting the silence fall over us again. Avery fidgets with her phone, distractedly. I watch her from the corner of my eye for a while before she scoffs at me, hesitating a little then slipping her hand in mine.

"I wore gloves, you're safe." I murmur, misreading her hesitance.

She shakes her head at me like I'm simple. "Harley told us about what happened after you… eliminated the threat in Haven. About how you didn't want to be touched. I don't want to push you if you're not ready."

I swallow, nodding my head. "It's getting easier. The lines between who I was and who I am now, they're blurring so much I think I'm just going to be the Wolf again."

Avery smiles at me and, *holy shit*, rests her head on my shoulder. I can't believe she's willing to get that close to all of the blood.

"You'll always be the Wolf. And we'll always be yours."

I rest my cheek on her hair and we fall quiet again, waiting to hear the roar of the 'Stang.

At peace with the family we've fought, bled, and killed for.

Chapter Sixteen

We don't talk about the smell of blood in the car, and the guys all pretend they didn't notice the piles of ruined clothes in the bathroom the next morning.

Blaise decides he'll singlehandedly clear the somber mood from the air and spends the rest of the fall break teasing Harley about being the last one to know my full name. I stay the *fuck* out of it because I don't need any extra drama in my life. It's only when Avery comes tearing into the bathroom the morning we're due back at school, screeching like a banshee about public sex acts, that I realize Harley finally snapped back.

Oh *joy*.

Which is how I find myself sitting in the Maserati with a whiny Blaise and a gloating Ash, while Harley is driving Avery back and listening to her tirade about *discretion* and *subtlety* and *keeping the details of our relationship the hell out of general conversation.*

I do not envy him.

"I can't believe you let Harley eat you out in *public* and I was too fucking wasted to watch. That's against the rules!" Blaise groans at me for the billionth time.

"What fucking rules, you insufferable dick?" Ash snarks from the backseat and I ignore them both, trying to focus on my reading for our literature class. I'm on the last book for the year and I'm determined to have it done before we arrive back at Hannaford.

Blaise fucking *pouts* like a brat at me, but I continue to ignore him. "I think there should be some rules and *that* is number one."

Ash scoffs and crosses his arms. "I should have ridden with the other two. I thought the Mounty would need help dealing with your attitude, but she can't even be bothered listening to you."

I turn the page, casually. "Oh, I'm listening. I'm just choosing to ignore you both because this topic is stupid."

Blaise snickers at me, aiming a sly look in my direction. "Wasn't he any good at it? Do you need me to come stay with you tonight and do it properly? Aves will be pissed but, now I know you *love* an audience, we can just ignore her yelling. Do you think Ash will hold you up for me too?"

I blush and then I decide that the cheeky fucker won't stop until I shut him down. I'm so fucking proud when my voice comes out strong and even. "I came so hard I creamed down his chin so no, it was better than good. Can you please shut up about it now?"

Blaise groans at me and he darts his eyes lustfully between the road and me. "Star, that was the hottest fucking thing I've ever heard come out of your mouth. Say something else! Wait, no, wait until we get back. Come whisper dirty things to me tonight. I promise I won't be a dick about it and I'll even make sure everyone is present. I'm a team player unlike the other two scheming assholes."

I try not to squirm in my seat and Ash smirks at us both, his eyes catching mine in the mirror. "Are you going to start sleeping in our room now, Mounty? Or are you still too scared?"

I give him a glare over my shoulder. "I'm not fucking scared, asshole. I just don't want to hear more gossip about myself."

Ash leans forward in his seat to kiss me, his hand gripping the back of my neck firmly, and I try to hold back a moan when he bites my lip.

He breaks away and speaks lowly, his voice annoyingly unaffected by the searing heat of the kiss, "I'll deal with the sheep. Prove to me that you're not being a scared little girl and come sleep in my bed."

He's baiting me, it's so fucking obvious he's using Beaumont Bullshit to get his way, but fuck it if it's not effective.

I lean in until my lips brush against his as I speak, "If I have to stab someone because of this, you're paying the cleanup fee."

Ash smirks and gives me one last peck, more teeth than sweet. "I think I can handle it."

Avery tucks her arm in mine as we make our way back up to the girls' dorms.

The guys head off to their room, still bickering and shoving each other like children, and I groan to Avery about Ash's demands to sleep in their room, wanting nothing more than a little vent. She, *of course*, wants to talk about it.

"Well, just go sleep there. *Are* you scared? Should I find you a therapist of some kind? I'm pretty sure sex therapists are just sex workers who charge more."

I blush and try to avoid her eye. "I'm not scared! I just… all three of them will be there. I've only been in their room once and… it's just a lot, okay?"

Avery snorts at me and unlocks our front door. "Is it more than having Harley perform oral sex in the middle of a crowded dance floor while my brother twiddled his thumbs and waited his turn?"

I flush scarlet and mumble, "It wasn't the *middle* of the dance floor, and *technically* Ash went first."

Avery shudders dramatically and pulls away from me, cackling when she sees the color of my cheeks. "Go there during the day while they're gone. Eat their food, smoke Blaise's stash, get comfortable in one of their beds. By the time they get home you'll be calm and less twitchy about it. I'll get you a key. It's only fair you have one since they all have copies of ours. If it turns into an orgy please put sheets down, because I do spend time over there. I don't need to find myself sitting in Morrison's DNA."

I elbow her gently while she laughs, and hum under my breath for a second while I think but it's a really great idea. She's a fucking genius, I almost feel bad for the sheep of the world. I'm also so glad we can ignore the weirdness of me being in a relationship with, you know, all three of her people.

When she's locked the door behind us, and I'm busy toeing off my shoes, Avery frowns and stoops down to pick up an envelope that's on our floor. It's been shoved under the door while we've been away. I never get mail so it barely registers with me.

I move away from her, already thinking about assignments and quiz notes, when I hear Avery's teeth grind together. Seriously, I'm kind of afraid they're going to crack under the pressure from her jaw.

"What now?" I sigh, rubbing a hand over my face. Avery watches me carefully, assessing me and cataloging every little sign my body is showing her. I probably look tired, grumpy, and a little hungry because when am I not up for food?

"Don't worry about it. I will deal with this," she finally says, eyes icy but firmly fixed on my face. I swallow because whatever the fuck it is must be bad for her to be looking at me like that.

I nod and let her. I have enough on my damn plate and she can hold her own.

I grab a tub of ice cream and spend the rest of the afternoon working on my studies while Avery deals with whatever was in the letter. By the time the sun is setting and I'm feeling a hell of a lot better about my studies, Avery is cooking enough food to feed an army and the sound of keys at the door tells me they've arrived.

I offer Avery help but she shoos me into the shower to clean up before dinner, snapping at Blaise when he once again offers his assistance. One day soon I think I'm going to take him up on his offer.

When I get out, rubbing my hair with a towel and my belly rumbling at the incredible smell of the food, Harley kisses me softly and directs me to sit next to him at the table. I usually sit between him and Avery so it's not an unusual thing to do but the way he's handling me sets off warning bells.

"What the fuck was in that letter?" I grumble, and Ash gives me a look, like he's already plotting the deaths of whoever sent it.

Avery rolls her shoulders back and starts to fix me a plate, her mothering only making me more concerned. "It's a notice. A warning that you'll be put on probation if you continue to behave in a manner unbecoming of a student at Hannaford."

I blanch and Harley grabs my hand under the table, threading him fingers through mine. He speaks softly, not to keep the others out of the conversation but to soften the blow of his words, "Someone got to the security video of us meeting Illi at the pool before Avery wiped it. He's not in the footage but we are. It hasn't been leaked but the principal and school board know it exists."

Unbecoming behavior. *Sweet lord fuck*, there's a video of Harley fingering me in the pool out there in the world. I think I want to die. I sure as fuck want *someone* to die.

"Mounty, Avery will deal with it. Don't panic," Ash says, and I snap back like a bitch for him assuming I'm breaking over this.

"I'm not fucking panicking. I'm *jumpy*, remember? Consider this me *jumping*! Avery, who the fuck am I stabbing? I'm stabbing someone!"

"Harley, for insisting on constantly putting his hands on you in public?" She snarks, but she tucks her arm into mine as she says it. "I've sorted it out with the school board and Trevelen. You'll have another formal apology by the morning because they can't punish you over a rumor of a video. I've put an official complaint in about Ms. *Vivienne* because this reeks of her."

I see red and clamp my eyes shut, counting backwards in French until I'm not likely to stomp my ass downstairs to hunt the cougar skank down.

I hear them all start to eat around me, ignoring my bloodthirsty rage in favor of the hot meal in front of them, and that cools the fire more than they could ever know.

By the time I start in on my food, Avery has finished hers and is teasing her brother about her admiration of Illi.

"He's the perfect man for me, Ash. I'm a little disappointed he's already married. All those muscles and the way he just stabbed that disgusting guy without Lips even telling him, too. He even wore gloves to handle the box!"

I cut in. "Do you have any idea how long it takes to get the smell of rotting human flesh off of your skin if you touch it bare-handed? No thanks! Odie would have shanked him if he went home stinking of corpses."

Avery gags and I rub her shoulder a little because I've got this best friend business down like a pro. Blaise swallows and turns a little green. When he notices the other two nod along he turns on Ash.

"What, you've handled *rotting human flesh* before?"

Ash stares at him for a second and Avery's shoulder tenses beneath my hand. Fuck. Finally he shrugs and nods. Blaise gapes and then mumbles under his breath, "What the fuck have I gotten myself into?"

"Second thoughts, Morrison?" Harley sneers, still pissy at him over the conversation in the car. Ash had, *so kindly*, told him the details.

Blaise glares at him. "No. It's just that every time I think I know just how fucked up we all are the bottom falls out and I find a whole new level of depravity. Ash; when, where, and why?"

Avery pulls a face and wriggles in her seat, looking down at her phone and effectively putting a barrier between herself and the conversation. I'm sure now that the death isn't what's bothering her; it's the *rotting* that turns her gut.

Ash stares at his glass and says, monotone and dry, "I had to help Joey dig up one of my father's toys. I think we washed more of her down the drain when we washed our hands afterwards than what was left of her on the bones when Senior finally fired up the incinerator."

Blaise swallows.

Harley nods, then grunts and pipes in, "One of my grandfather's lackeys was sunk in the bay, out past the docks. He'd been skimming, caught red-handed, and they chained him up and dropped him off a boat. He floated up a week later. I'll never forget the smell, Domnall made me help him scoop the gross fuck into a net and he paid some biker guy to dissolve what was left of him in acid."

I nod at him. "The Boar. You would have seen one of his guys. Pricey, but you're never going to get caught if he's the one getting rid of your problems."

Harley's eyes flash and he leans over to drape his arm around my shoulders. "He was the one that vouched for you and Illi, right?"

Avery's head jerks up. "That reminds me. We need to make a list of the members of the Twelve we like."

I groan and rub a hand over my face. "I'm not sure we *like* any of them. It's more like the ones who want us dead and the ones who could be persuaded to spare us."

Harley snorts. "There's also the ones who want to fuck you, babe."

Ash cuts me a glare. "Is that list longer than the Jackal?"

Harley's eyes only get more intense now he has backup in this brewing argument. "One of them asked if her pussy was gold plated."

Fucking rich, entitled, bratty boys.

Blaise snorts, enjoying this conversation a little too much at my expense, and I smile at Harley like I'm baring my teeth at the asshole. "Aves, we also need to add the Lynx to the list of cougars chasing Harley's dick."

Blaise's raucous laughter almost drowns out the frustrated groan Harley lets out.

I watch the cougar skank with rage in my blood and fire in my eyes. I watch her every move in my presence, cataloging her quirks and ticks, all the little mannerisms until I have a full picture of who Ms. *Vivienne* is.

She's a slut.

I know, I know, I've banned the word, but fuck if it isn't the right one for her. She doesn't just fawn over Harley. She touches every guy in our class and when I see her out in the dining hall she touches every being with a dick that crosses her path. I'm sure she must be hosting orgies in her room every night with the amount of winks and knowing looks she's getting.

Okay, glass houses and all that shit.

I'm not technically having any orgies, despite Avery's snarky comments. Also, how many people does there need to be involved before it's classed as an orgy? Fuck it, off topic.

I manage to keep my cool until classes finish for the day and then I drag Avery down to the gym for a training session, intent on sweating my rage out.

She's gotten pretty good at kicking my ass. I'm still going easy on her because I know she's a little hesitant about the knife, but I've found the best way to get her over that is to talk about what I've done in the past. She loves it when I walk her through scenarios, like she's learning a skill and piecing together more of my past. I think she wants to know everything that has ever happened to me, but there will always be things I'd rather never speak of again.

When my body hits the mat for the fifth time my fury has burned out enough to talk it out.

"Why Harley? Like, of all the dicks on this school she could climb, why him?" I'm totally fucking pouting. Thank fuck he isn't around to see it. His head would probably get so big it would explode.

Avery helps me off the floor and then hands me a bottle of water. "I've looked everywhere for a link to the Jackal and I can't find one. They've never crossed paths as far as I can see. I think she's just a desperate whore. A dirty, desperate whore who enjoys a challenge."

I nod and wipe my face with my shirt, ignoring the face Avery pulls over it. "He is fucking gorgeous, the bastard."

Avery shrugs. "There's plenty of gorgeous guys at Hannaford that she can have, you just don't notice them because you're too busy drooling over the three you're obsessed with."

"Rude," I grumble and Avery cocks an eyebrow at me, smirking at my attitude.

"It's an observation, not a judgment."

"Fine but you don't need to be so smug about it." God, I sound whiny. I need to harden the fuck up.

She scoffs at me and gets back into position. She changes the subject because she's a *saint*. "I spoke to Atticus again. He's pretty adamant I go to the Charity Gala this year, and he said he's going to dance with me there."

Fuck. I need to look this guy up, make sure he's not some rapist asshole. I make a note to talk to Ash and see why he hates him so much. I wonder if Harley likes him?

"Ash and I both have invitations with plus ones. I'll take Blaise and Ash will take you. Harley has a swim meet and now that he's taking his swimming more seriously he's going to go. He'll be pissy, but there's nothing I can do about it. Well, I could have the Gala date moved I guess. How badly do you want to see Harley in a three-piece suit?"

I try not to drool at the thought. She doesn't need any encouragement in her assessment of me. "It's fine. I'm sure being around you lot there will be other *Galas* to attend."

Avery laughs at my fake-ass airy tone and waves a hand at me. "Okay, no more distractions. Walk me through another. I think I'm almost ready to start stabbing my enemies myself."

I raise an eyebrow at her. "Any requests, Miss Bloodthirsty?"

She nods and hesitates for a second. I roll my eyes at her. "Just ask. I'm not going to lose my mind over it and if I don't want to do it I'll say no."

The door to the gym opens and I don't have to turn to see it's the guys. They're bickering and talking shit loud enough for Illi to hear it down in the Bay.

Avery lowers her voice. "I want to know how you won the Game. How you beat the last two men."

I stare at her for a second and then shrug. It's an old memory, not something I think too much about. Why not use it?

Blaise slips his arms around me and tugs me until I'm leaning back against his chest. I smirk at Avery and say, "Sure. We even have volunteers to be our victims."

Blaise cackles, squeezing me a little, and Harley swoops down to kiss my cheek, murmuring quietly, "I'll be your victim any day, babe."

I smirk at them all and pull away from Blaise, directing them all until they're where I need them to be. Ash stands with Avery, intent on learning everything I'm teaching her as well. It's a well calculated move from him; they all need to know how to read a situation and no one is better at it than Avery or me. If they're going up against the Jackal with me, they need to learn when to fight and when to manipulate.

I point at Blaise. "Do you want to be a loud idiotic beefcake or a silent, calculating sociopath?"

Harley cuts in before I finish the sentence. "He's the idiot. Where are we standing?"

Blaise scoff but nods along, "If anyone is the beefcake it's you, dickhead, you're going to fucking sink next time you get in the pool. Lay off the weights when you're frustrated at being stuck with the cougar, man, maybe have a wank instead."

He continues, but I zone out their bickering easier than I breathe air so I just direct them into their places and then I stand between the twins. Avery cools the arguing off with a single look and I'm a little jealous at her superpowers.

"Right, Blaise is Geordie. He's made it to the last three by sheer size so far. He's easily four times bigger than me, he sees me as a nothing job. He doesn't pay any attention to me at all."

Avery nods and tilts her head. "He's focused on the other male contender."

"Exactly. Harley is playing the part of Xavier. The best way to describe him is to say he was a sober Joey. All of the psychosis, none of the manic."

Avery shudders and I squeeze her hand. "Just watch and listen this time. Right,

Geordie lunges at Xavier. What's the plan, Aves? Ash?"

Ash waves a hand. "Let them fight. Then you only have one to take out, and hopefully whoever is left is injured."

I nod, oddly impressed that he's thinking it through. I shouldn't be; he's always been the level-headed one. Except for the entire year he insisted I was evil; that one time he was an emotional asshole.

Avery frowns. "You can't just watch them though, if Geordie lands even a single hit on Lips she could be out. You'd have to be watching for an opening to take him out."

Harley crosses his arms, watching me just a little too closely. "Xavier is the real danger. Joey sees fucking everything, even as high as he is. He picks up all the little shit that you guys do. If you're standing there watching, he'd be trying to find a way to throw Geordie at you."

Avery shrugs. "What did you do, Lips?"

I step up and slip the fake knife we practice with out of my pocket. Harley gets Blaise in a headlock at my directions and I stand behind him.

"I danced around them, never letting them get too close to me intentionally. I knew I had to wait for Xavier to be dealing the killing blow to Geordie. This was before my leg was destroyed and I was faster than any of them. Eventually, Xavier got impatient and stabbed Geordie, waiting long enough for blood loss to weaken him and then went about strangling him."

I press the knife into Harley's Achilles tendons and push him to kneel, dragging Blaise down with him, grunting in protest, but being a good sport overall. Fuck. I didn't think this one through at all.

I shoot Avery a look and she raises an eyebrow at me. "Remember you asked me to show you. This was your doing."

She frowns at me and Ash crosses his arms. "Well, hurry up then."

Ugh. I lean forward and whisper in Harley's ear, "Please don't be a dick about it, Avery will murder us both."

And that is the only warning I give him before putting him into a chokehold and using my free arms to grab a fist full of Blaise's hair to hold him still while I 'stab' him through the eye and 'kill' him. How did I have free arms to do this while strangling Harley, you may ask?

My thighs.

My *thighs* were wrapped around Harley's neck, ankles locked and squeezing just enough that he knows how fucked he really would be if I wanted to take him out.

"*Holy fucking shit, Star!*" Blaise sputters as he watches Harley very slowly, and I hope peacefully, grow weak from lack of oxygen. I let him go before he actually passes out and Ash gapes at me.

"Then once he's out I find a rock and smash his skull in. There was a crowd watching and I didn't want anyone watching thinking I was afraid to get my hands dirty. Half of the power of the Twelve is the rumors that precede us and as a starving teenage girl, I couldn't risk looking weak."

There's a sort of reverent, stunned silence for a second.

"Okay, teach me how to do that. Now, Mounty, I need to be able to do that. You looked like an assassin seductress, I'm *in*." Avery gushes, her eyes lit up like I've just handed her a box of blood diamonds.

"Fucking Christ, we're going to have two of them blood thirsty and trained."

Harley croaks and I lean down to kiss him sweetly in apology. He smirks into the kiss, fisting my hair in one hand and cupping my jaw in the other.

"I can think of worse ways of dying, babe. Your legs wrapped around my neck might just be my preferred way to go."

Avery snaps at us both and I pull away, ready to torture my boyfriends for a few hours while I arm Avery with enough knowledge to be a danger to society.

Well, *more* of a danger then she already is.

Chapter Seventeen

We fall back into a steady routine, the events of the party and our time away during fall break fading into the background with so much classwork to get done.

Harley is still barely around and I miss him so goddamn much it's like a hole in my chest. Ash is quieter and more reserved the longer we're back, but I decide to wait him out. There's no point pushing him, he'll only snark and hiss like the lovable asshole he is.

Blaise becomes so focused on his studies that I'm fucking impressed as shit at him. He refuses to fool around until his studies are done and we've worked on my vocal training. I'm usually so shaky after we're done that he won't do much more than kiss me, but fuck it feels good to finally hear myself sing without vomiting.

I think Blaise likes being able to help me, to teach me, and not always be the student. Plus I think he finds my voice a turn-on, more often than not he has to use his bag to cover himself when Avery gets back from ballet. There's nothing that girl likes more than threatening some dicks.

I start to relax a little., Just enough that I'm once again caught unaware by the next move on the board.

I'm sitting in choir with Blaise, trying to ignore the sick feeling of dread in my stomach as we warm up, when my phone starts vibrating insistently in my pocket. My rock god boyfriend raises his eyebrows at me and I shrug, knowing there's only one person outside of Hannaford who would be calling.

Well, two but I doubt I'm on the Jackal's speed dial these days.

When class finally comes to an end I check my phone and see Illi has called eight times and left three messages. I duck into a little alcove in the hallway to call him back, anxiety creeping up my spine. Blaise crowds into the little nook, his broad shoulders covering me from prying eyes and I lean my forehead onto his chest while I wait for Illi to answer.

"Is Odie okay?" I whisper the second I hear the phone pick up. Blaise wraps me into his arms at my quiet tone.

There's a beat of silence and then Illi sighs heavily down the phone. "You're too good for this fucked up world we're in. My girl is safe, kid. I'm calling to let you know I've just had to have a stern chat with three more guys sent by our friend." Translation: he's just killed three of the Jackal's men. He doesn't wait for me to comment, "They were sent up the coast, kid. They were sent after Iris, to finish what that dickhead Liam started."

I suck in a breath. Fuck. How the hell had I forgotten about Harley's mom? Of course the Jackal would go after her, she's a sitting fucking duck! Blaise runs a hand up and down my spine gently, resting his cheek on the top of my head.

"I'm only saying this in a phone call because I don't want to leave her. You might want to suggest to your little mobster that he send her somewhere a little more secure now he has the funds."

I finally find my voice again. "I'll sort it. Thank you, Illi. I don't know what we'd do without you."

He chuckles down the phone and says, "You have my back, kid, and you have from the first day we met. I'll have yours until I stop fucking breathing. Tell Arbour not to worry, I'll keep her safe until you can move her."

I end the call and let Blaise hold me until I can figure out my plan of action.

Avery is already handling Harley's fortune. The moment the money hit my accounts I had her move the money into investment accounts she had set up for him. It's a fuck-tonne of money, and he could easily pay for his mom to move to any facility in the world. Avery will know what to do.

The problem is I have to tell him first.

"Is his wife alive?" Blaise mumbles, and I shake myself out of my thoughts and pull away from him.

"She's fine. We need to go. We need to find the others, fuck," I mumble, and he tucks me under his arm.

"Avery's already texted to ask why we're late to lunch. Let's go eat and you can tell us what the hell is happening now."

I nod distractedly and let him guide me to the dining hall. The others have already gotten our lunches and are sitting in our usual seats. I'm relieved there's a little buffer of empty chairs around them and one look at the thunder on Ash's face tells me he's the reason.

"You okay?" Harley calls out as soon as Blaise has me in earshot and Blaise shrugs at him.

I step up to my usual seat next to Avery but I take a second to think before I sit down. Apparently that's the wrong thing to do because the tension at the table suddenly heightens until I'm choking on it.

"What the fuck has happened now?" Ash hisses, and I quickly drop to my seat.

"I'm trying to decide if I should say it here or drag Harley away so he doesn't rage out and flip the whole fucking table," I mumble and Ash's eyes narrow.

I sigh and turn to Harley before blurting it out. "The Jackal sent men after your mom."

His face shuts down, his body turning to stone and his cutlery drops to crash down on his plate. I reach over and grab his hand, squeezing until I know he's listening.

"Illi dealt with them. He called to let me know he's staying with her for now, but we need to move her somewhere more secure, somewhere far enough away that the Jackal forgets about her until we can... deal with him."

Avery immediately takes over. She's out of her seat and snapping orders down the phone as she moves to the door for privacy. We're too close to where the teachers are sitting for comfort. The Jackal has eyes in the school and we still don't know who they are.

"I'm sorry," I croak, and Harley's eyes flash up to meet mine.

"Don't apologize for that sick fuck; this is payback for us provoking him. Well, fuck him. I'm not giving you up." He says, his free hand closing over the little gold locket at his neck.

I feel like a monster.

All my bullshit is at our door.

Ash watches us both and then says, "Liam's been trying to kill her for years, Mounty. Adding the Jackal to the mix barely changes things. We all have demons stalking us, don't take it out on yourself."

My eyes flick over to him. "What's eating you today?"

His mask settles into place and he turns back to his food. "Joey."

I groan. Haven't we gotten away from that psycho? "What's the little fucker done now?"

Ash gives me a curt shake of his head that I interpret as *not here* but could be *fuck off* for all I know. Blaise snorts and starts on his lunch.

Harley turns his hand to lace his fingers through mine. "I guess I'm going to have to thank Illi now, aren't I?" he says, a little wryly.

I fight the smile threatening to break out over my face and say, "He loves a good muffin basket. Even better if there's blueberry."

By the end of the day Avery has Harley's mom transferred to a safe facility in Switzerland with a permanent armed guard. Illi stays with her until she's on the plane and, though he won't admit it, Harley is fucking relieved to have him there.

I still feel guilty.

I go through the motions for the rest of the day; dinner with Avery, studying with Blaise, then we work on my singing until Avery comes home. Blaise notices how crappy I'm feeling and slips me his iPod before he leaves, kissing me sweetly until Avery bitches him out on her way to the shower.

I climb straight into bed, messing around with the iPod to find a song that will help slow my brain down, when I hear the sound of keys in the door. I frown at the sound. It's barely ten, Harley never gets here before midnight.

Ash locks the door behind himself and stomps over to my bed, pulling the sweatshirt he's wearing off and climbing in wearing only his boxer shorts. He sighs and flings an arm over his eyes, channeling the drama of his morbid best friend, but the move only makes his chest look broader.

Oh fuck.

I try to focus on the blank mask over his features, because something has pushed him to come here, but he is something else to look at. A half-naked Ash Beaumont has angels freaking weeping at his feet.

I clear my throat twice while I attempt to focus on something other than his nipples but it's hard work. He snorts at me, rolling over to tug me into his arms, and the icy depths of his eyes cool me off a little.

"Has something happened?" I murmur, holding my breath as I wait for his answer because I have so many things on the planner I can't think about another one. I had pushed Joey out of my mind for now, Senior being the bigger threat.

"Are you planning on killing Joey?" Ash mumbles, his eyes screwing shut, and I grimace.

"I think I'm going to have to. He's going to force my hand and he's not someone we can neutralize long term. I have to figure Senior out first, because he's already made it clear that he'll kill you and Avery if anything happens to Joey but… yes. I'll take him out."

Any hesitance I had in telling Ash I'm planning on murdering his brother is obviously pointless because he just nods thoughtfully.

He strokes his long fingers over my face, brushing my hair back absently as he thinks. "The gossip site posted about our relationship and Joey messaged me to threaten you. He told Senior about you too. Mounty, I'm not going to let them get to you."

I swallow roughly at the emotion in his voice, something I'm not sure I ever thought would be aimed at me. "Don't think about it. The Crow will keep Senior away until we can deal with him properly. The only reason I haven't gone in to deal with him myself is because you and Avery are underage. Too many variables. Avery seems to think Atticus would step in for you both but—"

"Fuck Atticus. I'd rather live in the slums with you than owe that dickhead anything," Ash hisses. It's fucking hard work, but I contain my eye roll. How does he go from sweet to asshole in a flash?

I ignore his tantrum and say, "Like I said, too many variables. If we can keep him away from you, and somehow keep fucking *Morningstar* away, then we'll be able to wait until you're eighteen. Then I'll sneak into his bedroom and slit his throat while he sleeps. Or Illi can take a meat cleaver to his throat and then dismember him."

Ash mutters unhappily under his breath at the mention of Illi and I nudge him playfully. Avery exits the bathroom, quirking a brow at Ash's appearance but doesn't make a comment as she climbs into her own bed and cuts the lights. I hear her iPod start up and smile at her attempts to give us a little privacy.

I let my eyes drift shut, ready to sleep and forget about the sociopaths looming over us, watching our every freaking move. Ash presses his lips to mine and kisses me so sweetly I can't believe it's him. He usually kisses me with fire, with dominance, with that arrogance that only a Beaumont can have.

I tremble like a freaking wilting virgin in his arms.

When he breaks away to press his forehead against mine, he whispers, "If I lose you, then everything we've done has been for nothing. If he takes you away from me… I can't let that happen. Every time I close my eyes I see you strapped to that fucking table, bleeding out while they watch, and I won't live through that again. If there's a chance of that, then we need to kill them both. I almost wish you weren't so strong, that you'd dropped out freshman year, because even though I wouldn't have you, at least you'd be safe and far away from Senior."

I will not cry, I won't let myself, but fuck it's hard not to.

When I'm sure my voice won't betray me, I say, "If I had dropped out, I'd be the Jackal's personal whore by now. He would have chained me to his bed and fucked me until I was nothing but an empty, manipulatable shell. Then he would control two seats in the Twelve and be unstoppable. We'll get through this together, like we'll get through everything else life throws at us. As a family."

He nods against my neck, biting the skin softly until a shiver runs down my spine.

I don't know how long it takes me to fall asleep but I'm woken by the dip in the bed and smell of chlorine hits me before his voice does.

"What the fuck has happened now?" Harley whispers, pulling me back into his arms and Ash grunts unhappily in his sleep.

"Nothing. He just needed... me."

Harley nods and kisses my neck, right over the bruise Ash left behind. "We all need you, babe."

Chapter Eighteen

The only way to spend any time with Harley is to study down at the pool while he's at practice. It's stuffy from the water heaters and my notes somehow end up watermarked every time, but it's worth the trouble when Harley walks out in his swimsuit.

As my eyes trace the ridges and plains of his muscles, the Adonis belt I swear had to to be seen to be believed, I absently wonder if I'll ever be able to look at him without feeling lightheaded. It's not like he's some idealized dream; I've seen so many of his highs and lows already, I know he's human. I know he's not some perfect man. But, sweet lord, to look at him is like looking at the fucking sun; searingly hot and dangerous to your health.

I'm distracted from my lusty daydreaming by Ms. *fucking* Vivienne sitting her whorish ass next to me with a smirk.

"Stunning, isn't he?" she says, coquettish in her breathy tones.

I could rip her fucking head right off of her body.

"I would think a teacher in her, what, thirties would know better than commenting on the physical appearance of students," I snark, channeling Avery Beaumont at her scathing, polished best.

Ms. Vivienne just smiles at me. "Becoming a teacher didn't make me immune to the charms of the younger males. He's only a few months away from turning eighteen and then we'll be free to… explore the attraction we share."

I snort at her, shaking my head at the crazy that's spewing out of her mouth. Harley glances up at me and frowns when he sees the cougar bitch. I give him a sarcastic little wave and palm my knife. He notices and smirks at me, blowing me a kiss.

"Boys that look like him, they turn into men that won't settle for little girls like you. He needs someone with more experience, someone who is more worldly. He's not going to share you with his friends forever."

Huh.

She's just voiced my biggest fear about my guys, and yet the moment the words leave her mouth I know exactly how wrong she is. We're damaged, we're broken, we're desperate, but we're together and we're a family.

There was no jealousy or hesitation in Harley when he found Ash in my bed, only concern for what drove him there. Blaise only gets pissy about being left out of the group… activities, never about sharing. And Ash… Ash wants me safe and happy.

This bitch wouldn't know a fucking thing about what Harley needs, but I do.

"Keep pushing him, Ms. Turner. You'll learn that he's nothing like the pretty little boys you're used to playing with and I am *nothing* like the girls you've threatened away before."

Ms. Vivienne's spine snaps ramrod straight and the smile on her face now has a viciously sharp edge. "I was told you're a brilliant student, that your IQ is at genius levels, and yet you can't identify when you're outplayed."

"If I'm such a genius why am I not a part of your study group? Why isn't Ash? He's just as smart as Harley. You're a sexual predator and you belong behind bars. If you had any sort of intellect you'd leave Harley alone, because the path you're on leads to a six-foot deep hole."

She blinks at me, then turns on me with vicious intent only to falter as Blaise's says, "There you are, Star. I've been summoned to rescue you from the cougar. Harley's afraid you'll catch the clap from sitting too close to her."

His shadow hits me as I look up at his smirking face, every inch the spoiled rock god of my dreams in his leather jacket and ripped jeans. He winks at me playfully when he catches me giving him a lusty once-over. I might be horny, sue me.

The look on Ms. Vivienne's face… fucking priceless.

"How *dare you* speak to me like that!"

I scoff at her. If I were a nice person I'd warn her of Morrison's poison tongue but, y'know, fuck her.

"You're a desperate, panting whore who can't accept that you're over the hill so you fuck teenage boys to get validation."

She turns beet-red with outrage and I chuckle under my breath, stashing my books away. I don't need rescuing, but it's nice to sit back and watch Blaise destroy someone who's not me for once.

"Yes, I know, you're going to call my parents and go to the principal. Problem is, my parents don't give a fuck and Trevelen is under Beaumont's thumb so… maybe you should chase after someone else's cock and leave Arbour's alone. Also, if I ever see you so much as side-eye Star again I'll personally destroy you. Are you aware that my aunt is on the school board? Shriveled old hag, but she has a soft spot for me. How badly do you need this job? I think I'll start by taking it from you and working my way up from there."

Blaise's face only gets more vicious as the stunned silence drags out from the cougar and he holds a hand out to help me up. "Avery's waiting to have dinner with us in the dining hall before her ballet class. We shouldn't keep her waiting."

I tuck myself under his arm and don't spare the whore a backwards glance.

My phone wakes me the next morning and I don't recognize the number. Avery frowns over at me, unhappy at the early wake up call, and I force my tone to be even and cold.

When I hear the Coyote's voice I straighten.

"I'm not a fan of early mornings either, Wolf, but this is an emergency. I have some information for you and a job. I'm willing to hand over a favor if you're reluctant."

I bite my lip. "What is the information first?"

He huffs down the phone but I wouldn't say it's a particularly joyful sound. "You've royally pissed off the Jackal and now he's gone fucking insane. He's hitting back at the members who took your side in the vote. He's just popped by for a visit here but he seems to have forgotten that I live in a bunker and it could survive an atomic bomb blast."

I groan and rub my eyes. "I apologize that my… issues are now affecting you."

The Coyote laughs at me, still no joy to be found. "I don't regret voting for you. He'll have to try a bit fucking harder than this to push me into taking his side on anything. I'm just calling to let you know he's on the fucking rampage and no one is safe."

Avery gets up to make us both coffees and I switch the phone onto speaker so she can hear the conversation. "Right. Well, I appreciate the courtesy call. What's the job?"

There's a pause and then he murmurs, "You're in love with the mobster's kid, right? He's worth all of this?"

Avery hands me a cup of coffee and climbs into my bed, the side Harley crawled out of hours ago to head into swim practice. "I am. If I have to go to war for him then I will."

"The Jackal threatened my girl. I need you to get her to me and away from him before he gets his hands on her."

I shrug. "Easy. Name and location."

He hesitates and I cuss him out under my breath. "She knows she's your girl, right? I'm not kidnapping some girl you're cyberstalking, am I?"

"We've met."

Fuuuuuuck. Seriously?!

I sigh loudly at him, something I wouldn't do to any other member of the Twelve. "You want me to kidnap a girl you've met but aren't in a relationship with because the Jackal somehow knows you're into her and is threatening her. Does that about cover it?"

The Coyote laughs and says, "Yep. You in or not, kid?"

Avery cuts me a look, cold and calculating, with her phone in her palm ready to start work if I deem this a job we're taking. There's no way around it though, we need as many members of the Twelve on our side as we can manage.

"Sure, I'll do it for a favor. Send her details through to me and I'll have her to you by midnight tonight."

The Coyote chuckles at me. "Oh, I think you can have her here a little faster than that, kid. She sleeps down the hall from you."

Avery's eyebrows nearly hit her hairline and I'm sure mine are close too. The Coyote is stalking a Hannaford girl? For fuck's sake. "Who the fuck is she?"

The chuckles turn into a full fucking belly laugh. "Well, her dad's a senator and her mom's a news anchor so it may make some waves when she disappears."

Avery drops her phone. I have no idea of who this girl is but by the look on Avery's face I've just made a critical error. "Viola Ayres? You're cyberstalking Senator Peter Ayres' daughter?"

"Is that the hot girl you brought to the Lingerie Party? I never caught your name, hottie."

Avery sneers at the phone and I cut in, "Just answer the question, is Viola the girl you're stalking?"

"Yes and I'm not stalking her, I'm just *casually* keeping an eye on her from afar. I mean, I could hack her webcams and watch her sleep at night, but I *don't* because I'm not a pervert. Honestly, Wolf, it's like you don't trust me or something."

I don't trust him, or any other hacker on the planet. Which reminds me; my eyes narrow down at the phone as if he can see me. "I thought you wiped my middle name from existence? I keep getting packages with the name listed."

He scoffs. "I did. There's no way anyone has looked you up and found out your dirty little secret. Must be someone you know."

Fuck.

I can't think of anyone other than the Jackal who knows it.

Fuck.

I share a look with Avery. "I'll have her to you by midnight. Even if I have to gag 'er and drag 'er, she'll be in the bunker by midnight."

To say that I don't have time for Mr. Trevelen's bullshit is putting it fucking mildly.

Avery gave me the rundown on Viola Ayres while I forced myself to eat breakfast, my stomach roiling with nerves over the potential issues, and I try to scrape together a plan for how the hell I'm going to make this work. I sent word to Illi to do the drop off for me, he was far too cheery about it for my liking, and then all I have left to do is… kidnap the girl.

Fuck.

I'm busy trying to look calm around the guys so they don't get involved and complicate things when Trevelen pulls me out of math class. It's our first class for the day, and the second he calls out my name my stomach drops and I share a look with Avery.

Nothing good ever comes from being pulled out of classes.

I pack my bag, my face the picture of calm and stable, while Harley glares at Trevelen like he's seconds away from shanking him. I squeeze his arm gently, discreetly, then follow the principal down to his office.

A shiver runs down my spine as he directs me to sit. The last time I was in this room I was facing suspension and the Jackal got me out of it. I watch Trevelen attempt to pull himself into a power pose but he lacks the spine required to pull it off. I raise an eyebrow at him like a spoiled rich kid and he clears his throat.

"Miss Anderson, I'm going to get straight to the point. There have been… further accusations of unbecoming behavior against you put forward by an anonymous party. This time video evidence has been provided and the school board has made the decision to—"

The door slams open and an enraged Avery Beaumont stalks through, graceful even at her most furious. Not that you'd be able to tell from looking at her that she's pissed, it's more the air around her that gives it away; even the dust particles are running away from her.

My hands have a fine tremble in them, but I clench my fists and my jaw to ward them away.

"Mr. Trevelen—"

"Miss Beaumont," he interrupts and I tense. "There is no reason for you to be here. This issue is about Miss Anderson and her status as a scholarship student. It is none of your concern, no matter how much you wish it were so."

Fuck. Avery is going to destroy him.

Her eyes narrow and she leans forward in her chair, menacing and calm. I speak for her, just to make sure she has all the facts she needs to dig me out of this.

"Who was the anonymous source? I think I have the right to know who is trying to have me kicked out and defend myself."

Trevelen's eyes flash to mine and the regret that flashes there has nothing to do with me and everything to do with his own ass that is now firmly on the line.

He clears his throat again before saying, "She—the source has been granted anonymity by the school board to ensure there are no unjust repercussions. Your roommate has a... reputation for such things."

Avery smirks at him and I settle back in the chair, content to watch her work. I bleed people out for her and she does this stupid political crap for me.

It works.

"I have far more important and pressing issues to deal with than some desperate slut because we both know this reeks of jealous little whores. I'll have your job for this, Richard, we both know I own you. If you're lucky, we won't take your head with it."

"You can't just go around threatening people's lives, Miss Beaumont," He says but his forehead is covered with a thin sheen of sweat that belies the truth in his words.

Avery laughs at him, and I shiver at the sound.

Fuck, I love her.

"Oh, you're mistaking me! It's not a threat, it's a fact. If you fuck with my family, you bleed. Have you not met my father, Richard? The apple doesn't fall far from that tree, I assure you."

Trevelen is now moping his sweat up with a handkerchief, his fingers shaking. "Miss Beaumont, there is nothing I can do about it! The video has now been watched by the entire school board and the ethics committee will have my ass if I don't act upon in. Maybe Miss Anderson should have acted with—"

"Was Miss Anderson the only student in the video? Was she acting indecently by herself? No. This is all an attempt by Ms. Turner to separate Harley and Lips because she's a sexual predator. Are you aware she's fucking a fifteen-year-old student, Richard? How does your ethics board feel about that? Oh, I'm sure they're fine with it because she's fucking them too. I don't care what it takes, you will make this disappear. If you don't, I'll send my own anonymous letter out to the police and tell them exactly where you buried your first wife. Does Lucinda know the back porch she so dearly loves to sit on and enjoy is built on the unmarked grave you dug?"

Holy.

Fuck.

I did not see that coming.

Chapter Nineteen

Viola Ayres is *nothing* like I was expecting the daughter of a Senator to be.

She's a senior and has a private room so when we knock at her door, she frowns and ushers us in. She's taller than me, but that's not hard. Her hair is streaked with purple highlights and there's a stud in her nose so tiny you can barely see it flashing in the light. The teachers here would struggle to spot the dress code violation and I instantly like her more than any other girl I've come across. Well, other than Avery obviously.

The room only confirms she's a different breed. Everything is painted black, and there's whiteboards everywhere with physics equations and coding on them. She's a genius.

She's also fucking perfect for the Coyote.

"What exactly have I done to deserve a visit from the reigning Queen Bees of Hannaford?" She drawls, flicking a wrist between us.

I scoff at her. "I'm not a queen bee, that's more Avery's kind of thing."

Avery giggles at me, stroking my arm lovingly. "Lips doesn't like admitting she's alluring and powerful. She would rather enjoy lurking in the shadows and silently slitting throats."

Viola squints a little, glancing between us to try and spot the lie. "Right. Sure. What have I done?"

I rub the back of my neck a little sheepishly, not having thought this out much. I wasn't planning on liking the girl. I thought she'd be some rich bitch I'd just threaten and kidnap, but Viola is… kind of cool.

"Look, there's no easy way to say this so I'm just going to lay it out there," I start and Avery gives me a look.

"Let me, you're not very… diplomatic. Viola, are you currently dating? Or hoping to date someone?"

She scoffs at Avery and makes her way over to the kitchen. "I'm not chasing after your boys if that's what this is about. I don't need to be getting involved with taken guys."

That's it. I love her, too. Fuck the Coyote for making me kidnap her.

Avery smirks at the look I'm giving her. "No, someone else. Someone older, perhaps?"

Viola frowns as she pulls cups out of drawers and starts to make us all coffee. Another mark in her favor. Fuck, I should induct her and keep her safe myself.

"Maybe you should just let the Mounty be blunt about it, I'm not following you at all."

I take the coffee from her and sip. Not bad. "Do you know a guy, around twenty, who's tall as fuck, blond hair, brown eyes, good with a computer? Like, able to hack into the US Defense Force levels of good?"

Viola's eyebrows twitch, an easy tell to spot. "Jackson? Why do you need to know about him?"

Jackson.

I guess he kind of looks like a Jackson. I mean, it must be him. I can't imagine there would be that many guys who look like him and can do what he does in the state. Fuck, at least I hope not.

"Are you interested in him? Crush or something?"

Viola sets her cup down on her table, wrapping her arms around herself defensively. "Why are you asking this? If you're going to try and use me against him, you're out of luck. He's already told me he's not interested."

I groan without meaning too. I hate relationship drama and this reeks of it. "Look, I need to take you to go see him tonight. Something has come up, something life threatening, and you need to go see him. He's... a friend of mine."

Her eyes narrow at me when I pause. She hisses at me, voice scathing, "Are you fucking him too? Are the *three guys* crawling into your bed at all hours of the damn night not enough?"

Oh look, I found a nerve.

I raise a single hand up to stop Avery from pouncing on her, because I don't even have to look at her to know she's about to tear strips off of the girl. "I'm guessing you really like him and I assure you, whatever he said to you about not wanting you, he was fucking lying. I'll let him talk his way off of your shit list. For now, can you just come with me? I just want to get you to him safely so I can crawl into my bed with whichever guy deems it's his turn."

I even wink at her to try to soften her up a little. Avery looks pissed but stays quiet, letting my words sink into the girl's brain.

"Fine. He fucking owes me an explanation for this shit."

Yes, he does.

I convince Viola to pack a bag, then we walk her down to the staff parking lot where Illi is waiting for us standing beside the most beautiful muscle car I've ever seen. I sneakily take a photo for Harley to drool over later.

Viola takes one look at the Butcher of the Bay and freezes, planting her feet into the gravel. "I'm not getting in that car. He looks like a thug! Are you trying to extort my father for cash or something? I could have saved you the effort, you've picked the wrong kid. He prefers my younger sister."

I share a look with Avery, the quirk of her lip telling me she's just made note of that little gem. I'm not sure what we'll be extorting Senator Ayers for in the future but we have him if we need.

"His name is Illi and he's just driving you over there so stop looking worried. He's my... foster brother." I say, winking at Illi.

Technically, I did meet him in foster care, back when his name was still Johnny, his best friend was Matteo, and together they taught me the meaning of ride or die. Until one day they weren't. My heart feels sore in my chest just thinking about it.

"Come on, little girl, I'm glad to be of service." Illi does a ridiculous little bow and I snort with laughter watching it. He's too fucking huge to look anything but hulking and intimidating.

"I'm not stupid, there's no way I'm getting in that car," Viola snaps, and I decide I love her a little less.

I hold my hand up to stop her from running off, then pull out my phone. I hit dial on the Coyote's number.

"Trouble, Wolf?" he asks, smug and playful as always.

I smirk and I'm sure he can hear it in my voice. "Hello, *Jackson*. It's your dear friend Lips here. Viola is all packed up and ready to have a sleepover at your place though she's unhappy that our mutual friend Illi will be driving her over."

The Coyote groans. "Seriously? You're trying to get *him* to drive her?"

"You do understand I'm at school and have no car, right?" I snark and he laughs at me.

"C'mon *Lips*, we both know your little harem has plenty of vehicles for you to borrow. Alexander has eight Ferraris, for fuck's sake."

Eight?! Jesus.

"That's beside the point. Tell her to get in," I hiss, and hand Viola the phone.

She looks at it like I'm handing her a snake or some shit and I try to make my smile sweet. Avery cackles at me so I clearly fucking failed.

While she's busy arguing with her maybe boyfriend, I sidle up to Illi and bump my shoulder against him like we're close or some shit. "How's things?"

He smirks. "Great. I've killed eleven guys this week for our little crew. I took on a job up the coast while I was there with Iris too, so send me your bank details so I can tithe to you."

Tithe, the cheeky shithead. I snort at him. "Fuck off, I'm not taking your money. Consider it payment for running around after me."

He laughs. "Kid, I live for this shit. I even got to torture the last guy. I *julienned* him as if I were a sous chef and he was nothing but a fucking carrot. I'll send you the tape, looks fucking *sick*."

Avery gags dramatically from where she's eavesdropping and Illi roars with laughter at her. Their easy acceptance of each other is such a fucking gift to me, I wish the guys would take a leaf out of Aves' book and just welcome him into the fold. It's not like he wants to move in, he's got an amazing apartment overlooking the docks in a shady looking warehouse so he can... work from home if required. He does that a little less now Odie lives there too.

"I've moved Odie to a safe house, kid. Since the video of you getting freaky with the mob boy started circulating the lowlifes have been coming at us in droves."

I freeze. Video circulating? Illi notices and swears under his breath. "I thought you knew about it? Sorry. You got more enemies than the Jackal, I'm guessing?"

Avery snorts. "Lips collects them, like trinkets and pets. Nothing she loves more than pissing people off by living her very *best* life."

I groan at her. "I'm just trying to survive! Fuck. Okay, What do you need from me, Illi? Name it, it's yours."

He scoffs at me and bumps shoulders. "Whatever. I'm your *brother* remember? I'll drop the prissy girl off at the Coyote's bunker and then I'll go hunting. Maybe it's time to take the fight to D'Ardo. Stop defending and start attacking. Speaking of that, any of your boys good with a gun?"

I swallow. "Harley and Ash are. I'm not sure about Blaise. I'll check."

I wait until family dinner on Friday to bring up the gun question.

Avery cooks a stir fry and for once I take Ash up on his offer of whiskey to go with our meal. I feel like a nice buzz will help me with the headache this is going to cause me. I wait until the table is quiet, the guys all shoveling the food into their mouths like they're starved Mounty street girls, and then I ask Blaise.

The guys all pause their eating. Avery continues, unruffled and smug because she knew it was coming. There's nothing that girl loves more than to be in on the joke.

He blinks at me owlishly, and Harley swears viciously. "What the fuck has happened now? We aren't going to make it to fucking senior year at this rate."

Avery laughs, flicking her wrist at him the way a cat plays with it's prey. "We're doing a fine job. And you can't talk, it's your fan club that is causing all the issues. The video being leaked reeks of Annabelle. Or possibly Ms. Turner. They both stink of desperation so it can be hard to differentiate sometimes."

Blaise snickers at the dark look Harley gives her but she's right. I stay out of it, as always, and nudge Blaise with my foot under the table.

He gives me a little mocking smirk. "Footsies during dinner with Avery? Star, I would have never pegged you as the type to flirt with danger."

Ash chuckles at my withering look and Harley mutters, "She does more than fucking flirt with it."

I roll my eyes at them all. "Just answer the question, Morrison. Do you know how to use a gun? Properly, not just point and pull the trigger. I mean like, assemble, reload, clean, the whole fucking shebang."

He looks uneasy at me again. "I do. I'd rather not though. I'm more a beat-the-life-out-of-them kind of guy."

Ash flicks a sliver of carrot at him. "That isn't any better so don't think you have the moral high ground. You're saying you want to feel the life leave your victim rather than have the clinical, impersonal kill."

Blaise glares at him. "Oh, are we trading psychotic tendencies now? What's your preferred method of killing a man?"

Ash smirks and says, "Whatever is required to make sure they stay dead."

I should find this conversation unsettling.

Whelp, I don't. I'm suddenly squirming in my chair at the dark parts of them all.

I clear my throat twice, a sure giveaway of what is on my mind from the looks they all give me, and say, "I'm going to get everyone ghost guns. Completely untraceable. Just for emergencies now that the Jackal is being careless and sending guys out to catch us unaware."

The guys all share a look and something tightens in my chest. Avery slips her hand in mine, ready to take my side with whatever they're planning, and I'm so fucking glad she's with me.

Finally, Ash takes a sip of his bourbon and pegs me with a look. "We need to stop with this 'waiting around' bullshit and start being offensive. He's not going to stop until we take him out."

I try not to groan at him but it escapes me anyway. "Do you understand the risks of that? Really? Do you get how much blood will be on your hands, and the cleanup involved? I know we have the finances to back us but fuck, it's a lot. I've lived it. I woke up every day knowing I'm going to kill countless people and pray I'm not going to go down for it. Are you all prepared for that too? Because I've been working my ass off to keep you all out of it and… clean."

Harley cuts me a look, arrogant and haughty. "We're not clean though, are we? None of us are. Even Morrison has blood on him. We're going to figure this out and we're going to fucking kill the Jackal and every last one of his loyal followers. No more peaceful attempts at resolution."

I give Blaise a curious look, interested to know what blood he has on him. I know he's not afraid of a fight, and will jump in to defend his friends without a second thought, but I'd never guessed he'd done anything more than that.

They're all watching me, watching for an answer and I'm not sure I really have one but I squeeze Avery's hand anyway and say, "Okay. Offensive it is. We'll hunt the Jackal."

Chapter Twenty

Friday morning I find Blaise missing from our history class, and I can't concentrate on a thing the cougar whore says because I don't know where the fuck he is. When Harley notices me twitching and tells me he's gone to an appointment in Haven and I send the *utter* dickhead a pissy text about *security* and *threats* and *murderous sociopaths stalking us all.*

He ignores me.

Ash walks up to my room with me and collapses on the couch with a sigh, throwing his bag down and ripping his shoes off. Avery's mother hen act drops in an instant and she's snarling at him for messing shit up. I head to the coffee machine. Caffeine is necessary for my survival.

Blaise arrives to family dinner half an hour later covered in bandages and for a second my heart stops, then I see the easy grin on his face and I know he's fine. He winks at me and I blush when Avery cackles at the stupefied look I give him.

"I told you, I'm filling in the rest of my canvas, Star." He murmurs as he bundles me into his arms, kissing me chastely under Avery's watchful glare.

"Are you going to tell me what you got?" I grumble and he laughs at me.

"You'll have to wait and see. Or bribe me, I'm easily bought. Flash me some pink, Wolf."

I jab him in the stomach but his solid muscles only hurts my hand. Ash smirks at me and tugs me over to sit on his lap in front of the TV while we wait for dinner. Avery is on an Italian kick and refuses to let me help out now she's making pasta by hand.

She's the weirdest rich kid in the fucking building but god do I love her.

"Stop giving my sister lustful looks, Mounty," Ash snarks, and I elbow him.

"She's my favorite, I hope you know that," I snark back and he slips his hand down my waist until he gets to the hem of my shorts. My eyes flare and then narrow at him.

"I'm your favorite," he mumbles into the skin on my neck.

I shake my head, mostly to clear it. "Nope. Definitely Avery. You're my second favorite Beaumont though, so don't feel too bad about it."

His eyes fucking sparkle at me with evil intent and I gulp. I try to move out of his lap and his arms only tighten, trapping me.

"Don't run off. I'm fucking hungry, Mounty."

I blush. My heart stutters in my chest at the warm honey tone in his voice, something I've never heard from him before. Even when we had laid together in bed all those months ago in the Bay, his dirty talk had been whispered and decisive. Not this coaxing.

I can't fucking handle Ash Beaumont seduction if it's like this.

"Dinner's ready!" Avery calls out, and Ash huffs.

"I don't think I'm ever going to get my hands on you at this rate," he grouses, and I kiss him sweetly because I'm just as fucking frustrated.

We all take our usual seats at the table and Harley has already changed into his swim uniform to leave as soon as he's eaten something. The second I see it I remember the last time I saw him wearing it and heat floods my body until I'm blushing like an idiot.

I stare at my plate like it's the answer to all my damn problems because there's no way Avery won't notice the puddle I've turned into. Dammit, I'm drooling again.

Blaise unwraps one of his hands so he can handle his fork but I'm too busy trying not to ogle Harley to see the new ink.

"Did you get stars tattooed on you? You know that tattoos are the curse of relationships, the kiss of death," Avery says in a haughty tone, spinning her long strands of fettuccine perfectly between her fork and spoon.

Blaise gives me a look and I smile at him. I don't think tattoos are the kiss of death for fucking anything. I'm just not that superstitious.

His foot runs along mine under the table and my smile turns into a grin. His eyes fucking sparkle at me and I flush, looking back down at my food and refusing to look at him. Great. So only Ash is safe for now, because he's snarling at his sister.

"Why the fuck didn't you tell me Joey was coming to the Hannaford Family Dinner?"

Ugh. The stupid dinner all juniors and seniors have to attend, even if they're emancipated orphans, to sit and discuss their bright futures with their teachers and families. Fucking yay.

I glance up and see him glaring at Avery, all fire and rage that I don't usually see him aiming at his sister.

Oh fuck.

"You know as well as I do that Lips had Senior removed from the picture until graduation, so he's sending Joey in his stead. There's nothing I could do to stop it, but why would I tell you about it any sooner than I have to? Harley is already an insomniac, we don't need two sleep-deprived, grumpy assholes in the family."

Ash scoffs and downs the rest of his bourbon in one gulp.

What a lovely dinner we're having.

Blaise shoos Avery out of the door for her ballet class and flicks the lock with a little flourish.

"Oh, look. I find myself alone with my Star. Whatever shall I do?"

I smirk and point at our textbooks. "Studying is what you *shall do*."

He laughs at me and pulls his tie off, popping the first few buttons open on his shirt. Fuck. He's worked out that little trick too, the one where my brain melts the second any of my guys start showing extra skin.

I'm fucking doomed.

"You have three assignments due next week," I croak, so fucking ready to cave and he smirks at me.

"I'm just getting comfortable. Didn't you want to see my new tattoos?"

Right. Tattoos. Yes.

I nod and he peels the bandages, tape, and plastic away from the puffy, raw skin of his hands and neck. Avery was right, he's now covered in stars. There's even a little one inked behind his ear, right where he usually kisses me.

"You'll have to tape me up again. My hands are killing me," he grumbles, and I go to rummage around in the bathroom for the first aid kit. I'm especially good at taping hands back together with all of the practice I now get with Blaise and Harley's boxing, and Ash's fight club matches.

Once he's looking more bandaged than a mummy I try to get him to study but he's too damn jittery.

"I'd concentrate better if you were naked," he drawls, running a thumb over the swell of my chest. I bat his hand away.

"No you fucking wouldn't. If you fail this test I will be so pissed."

He shrugs. "I won't. I've been studying at night before bed too. I'm going to pass these classes and next year we'll take all the same classes again so I can keep an eye on you, and then we'll go on tour together before you run off to college to become a doctor or an astrophysicist or... whatever the fuck geniuses become."

I smile at him and close the textbook. "Why would I go on tour with you? Do you need a groupie on hand at all times or something?"

He leans back on the cushions, smug and relaxed. I bite my lip at the sight of him, all bandaged up, secretly marked with *me*. Maybe I hate my name a little less.

"I like the idea of you being there for my every need, but no. I meant because you're going to be singing with me. I'm going to release your song on the album... if I ever fucking release it." He sighs, and rubs his eyes.

"Why haven't you? I mean, the songs have been done for months."

Fuck it, I climb into his lap. He groans in frustration when he can barely hold me, but I do my best to avoid pressing on any raw patches.

"I'm thinking about leaving my label. Don't tell anyone that, not even Ash. He'll have a fucking aneurysm at me over it. But they keep interfering with the song writing and I'm just... I write and play to get shit out of my head. Because I love that I can turn the weird thoughts and pain into something I can hand to someone else. The band's agent wants me to clean up the lyrics and go more mainstream. He didn't like the new songs, he said they're too raw. Fuck him."

I frown at him and say, "They're amazing. They're the best songs you've written so far. I should know, I've heard them all."

He quirks an eyebrow at me, playful again. "You haven't though, have you? You never did open my present."

Fuck. I hadn't.

I shake my head and he smiles at me. He cups my face gently, pushing my hair away from my face and kissing me sweetly.

"I was so pissed that day. I'd put my fucking heart in that box and you wouldn't open it. I can't blame you, I'd been such a fucking dick to you, but I had put myself out there and hoped you'd see it... see me. It doesn't matter, Star, I have you now. My little muse. My sweet Nightingale, pretty and sings so sweet."

He starts to ramble, my crush only getting worse as he begins to describe all of his favorite parts of me, most of them naked body parts, but some of them immensely more intimate, like the scar the bullet from Diarmuid's gun left on my skin and the soft patch of skin on my shoulder they all seem to be obsessed with.

I wait until Avery heads to ballet the next afternoon and I dig out the package Blaise had sent me, untouched and hidden in my duffle bag under my bed. I'd been so tempted, so many times, over the summer break but it was like Schrodinger's box. What if I opened it and it was just candy, something small and meaningless? Or, more terrifyingly, what if it wasn't?

Now I know it's his heart, I have to see what it is.

I use my knife to slice the tape open and my hands shake as I lift the lid. I find a notebook and an iPod older than the one we now share.

I grab the notebook first and find poems, lyrics, stories, etchings in the margins and gold ink accents everywhere. The lyrics are all of his new songs, things he's written in the last two years, but they're all just a little different from the polished versions he's given me to listen to. I read the entire notebook, cover to cover, in disbelief.

It's about me.

The whole thing is a love story about me.

The drawings are of my hands, the scars on my leg, the dark shadows of my eyelashes on my cheeks.

The plump curve of my lips.

The songs have my name in them, over and over again, the longing and worship on Harley's face is reflected in the melodies of Blaise's songs. I can't breathe to read them, my lungs squeezing tight until I feel dizzy.

Thank fuck I didn't open it last year.

I would have had a stroke and died.

When I finally move away from the notebook, every word and image seared into my brain for all of time, I turn the iPod on to find it full of every single Vanth Falling song, even the covers Blaise recorded and released before he was famous. There are songs I hadn't ever heard him sing so I know they've never been made public because I followed his every move online back when I lived in the Bay.

Fuck.

It's every little piece of him I've always wanted, and I've been hiding it under my bed for months.

Chapter Twenty-One

Avery is fussing with her already perfect hair and I'm busy trying to figure out why the fuck we're being forced to a 'Formal Family Dinner' at Hannaford if none of us have family attending when a booming knock sounds at the door, like a giant's fist is trying to punch it's way through.

I frown, motioning for Avery to stay in the bathroom, and move to open it.

Illi and Odie grin down at me.

Holy sweet lord, this cannot end well.

"Le Loup, I am so happy to see you! When Johnny told me he was coming up to see you, I insisted on coming too! He said you're the top of all your classes, that's incredible! Oh, I've missed you." Odie gushes in French, wiping at her eyes delicately.

She smiles sheepishly at me and I sigh, holding my arms out so she can hug me. She doesn't realize I've had my family slowly teaching me to be normal, to tolerate all of the touches that happen between friends.

Avery eyes Odie critically for a second and then holds out her hand. *"Avery Beaumont, it's lovely to meet you."*

Odie grins at her, her eyes flaring in delighted surprise, and takes her hand to pull her gently in to kiss both her cheeks in a very European flourish. *"Odette Illium, but I prefer Odie. Your French is perfect! It is such a relief to meet more of le Loup's friends and be able to talk to you is wonderful. My English is still very poor."*

I shake my head at her. *"It's very good, you're just a perfectionist. What are you two doing here? I'm glad to see you but it's risky."*

Illi tucks Odie into his side and says, in English because his French is less than perfect, "The Crow has managed to keep Joseph Beaumont Sr. from coming to the family dinner, but I heard he's sent the little freak to take his place. Joey's been asking around about you and I think it's time to deal with him. I can make that as permanent as you want, kid."

I nod and cut Avery a look. She knows better than any of us what the repercussions of Joey's death will be.

"Senior will strike at us if anything happens to Joey. If Morningstar refuses to take the job then Senior will come and do it himself."

I cock my head at Illi. "What's your assessment of Senior?"

He eyes Avery for a second like he's worried about her reaction to his words, a very rare consideration from him, and says, "I think he's a fucking psycho and with the amount of money he's sitting on like a gargoyle we need to be very careful about how we get rid of him. We'll be better off taking him out and then the little freak."

I can't help smirking at his nickname for Joey. "Not a fan of Junior?"

Illi grins and kisses the top of Odie's head. "I'll skin the fucker alive for you, kid. I'll do it with pep in my fucking step. If he looks sideways at you or your girl tonight I'll gouge his eyes out."

I nod and turn to Avery. "You might want to warn him. Illi would do all of that for us and infinitely more for Odie."

And there's no man on the planet that wouldn't look lustfully at Odette Illium. She's everything the cougar whore is trying be; a sensual, blonde bombshell who oozes sex appeal. She looks delicate against the wall of muscle and violence that is Illi, but she's tall and curvy in all the right places.

The price she sold for at the skin markets was fucking *terrifying*.

Avery nods and pulls out her phone while I grab both of our blazers, a full uniform being a requirement to attend the dinner. Illi cracks another joke about the skirts and socks, and I shoot him a vicious look while Odie giggles at us both.

I open the door to leave and find the guys waiting for us. Harley smiles and kisses me, then does that weird, bro head dip at Illi who claps him on the back like they're best friends. Ash grimaces at them both, sidling past to get to Avery. Joey's attendance tonight is wound tight around his neck like a noose.

Blaise looks like he's going to vomit.

"What's wrong?" I murmur, and I step out of our room towards him.

Holy.

Fuck.

"Lips, these are my parents. Blaine and Casey Morrison. They've decided to attend tonight's dinner even after they disowned me and told me they no longer see me as their son," he says, his voice steady, but the look on his face makes me want to reach for my knife and start stabbing. His mother just stares at her feet like she'd rather be anywhere else but her son's school.

The look his father gives me would make me cringe with shame if I weren't the Wolf.

"I thought you said she was your girlfriend? Why is she kissing your friends?" he says, leering at the scant inches of my bared skin. I want to throat punch him so freaking bad.

Blaise ignores him and slings an arm around my waist, whispering so low I struggle to hear him, "Sorry, Star. They just showed up, I had no idea they were coming."

I nod and move away from the doorway so the others can get through. I glance up and see Illi's mischievous grin. Oh, fuck yes.

"Blaise, you remember my foster brother Illi? He's brought his wife to see me and they're both joining us for dinner. They're very excited to be here." I say, and Odie grins at Blaise with a sweet little, "*Bonjour.*"

Illi grins at Blaise, then turns that baring of teeth towards his parents. I swear I see Blaine Morrison shit his pants.

Perfect.

Blaise squeezes my side and Illi winks at us both.

One big, happy family.

The dining hall has been transformed into a luxurious looking restaurant, complete with Christmas decorations and waiters in three piece suits. Illi snorts at the entire thing and Odie giggles at him like she's the school girl here. I smile at the sound until my gaze hit Joey Beaumont and it slides right off my face again. Fuck, I hate that psycho.

"The seating is assigned. I made sure we'll be seated together," Avery whispers, her arm tucked in mine tense as she eyes both of her brothers.

Illi stares between them with the bloodthirsty glee that I usually see from Blaise, but he's still too worried about his own family's appearance to enjoy the bloodshed that's potentially about to happen.

Ash pulls out my chair for me while death glaring at his brother, ever the reckless asshole, and I sit between Illi and Avery. Joey takes Harley's seat across from me and I shake my head at him.

"Are you trying to provoke us? Because we're just here for the food," I say, more to remind Ash than Joey.

"My little Mounty. I really didn't think you'd make it at this school for so long! And without fucking anyone! I heard the bet was still ongoing. I'm starting to wonder if you're hiding a cock under that skirt and that's why you won't fuck anyone."

Odie makes a sound of disgust and turns to Ash. *"How is this disgusting man related to you and Avery? He shows none of your high breeding or decorum when he speaks."*

Joey smirks.

I learn that all three Beaumonts speak perfect French when he replies for Ash. *"I'm the better sibling. If you want to stop fucking gang bangers, I'll happily choke you with my cock."*

I count Illi's breaths as he slows them down, deep inhales and long exhales. I stare at Joey while I wait, crunching the numbers on how much a full cleanup will cost us if Illi slams his meat cleaver through Joey's throat and bleeds the fucker out.

Fuck I'd love to see that. I think I'd sleep better at night afterwards.

"I call dibs. I'll let Ash help but I'm skinning the fuck," he finally murmurs to me and I nod.

Odie looks down her nose at him, and then says in perfect English, loud enough for the Morrison's to hear, *"Mon monstre,* cut his heart out for me when you're done. I would like to eat it."

The people within earshot all freeze and turn to look at the stunning blonde, but she stares Joey down like there's nothing even slightly worrying about the psycho.

I guess if you share a bed with the Butcher you're immune to these things.

Illi raises her knuckles to his lips and kisses them like she's the very center of his world. My heart aches a little and I remind myself that if they can find each other and survive what they have together, then I can survive the threats we're facing, with my family intact.

After another minute of silence, I hear Blaise's dad start questioning him about his classes but he's too far away from me for me to chime in. I huff in annoyance but then Harley snaps, "He's in the top of his class in every subject and he's got a 3.5 GPA. *Fuck off.*"

The food had better be fucking amazing.

Ash stares Joey down, watching his every move while he grins at me. I ignore his eyes, focusing on his hands to gauge how doped up he really is. The tremble is there, enough to know he's recently gotten his high and he's still riding the effects. When the crash starts there's going to be bloodshed.

I can fucking taste it in the air.

The waiters all start to serve dinner and I stare down at the plate in front of me with disgust.

"What the *fuck* is this?" Illi says, and both Odie and Avery laugh at him, sharing a look that sets off warning bells in my head. Avery is the ice queen and, fuck, Odie is sultry fire. If they hit it off the whole country will fucking crumble. Sign me up for front row tickets. I meet Illi's gaze.

My sadistic glee at their camaraderie is written all over him as well.

The waiter fumbles over his words, intimidated by the fierce look on Illi's face and the manic bouncing of Joey's eyes. I wave him away before he pisses himself and Illi mutters at me, "What the *fuck* is a study of peas? They're vegetables, they can't go to fucking college!"

I nod, agreeing completely and craving some burgers. Avery and Odie both eat the blobs of colors delicately and I just swirl my spoon in it to make it look like I've eaten some of it.

There had better be a steak coming up next or Illi's going to riot.

"I heard you're fucking half my family now. What's my brother's dick got that mine hasn't? Other than the clap now he's wetting his dick in slum pussy," Joey says, ignoring his plate entirely. I watch from the corner of my eye as Ash carefully sets down his fork.

The hand around his knife only tightens.

I sigh, and make a big show of looking around at each member of my family, all of them glaring at Joey. I decide that if we're hunting the Jackal, then we're done dancing around Joey too. I can put him in his place without killing him… maybe.

I set my cutlery down and cross my arms, staring at the drugged fuck with unflinching rage. "You've made your decision to come here and start this fight with me. I've warned you, over and over again, that you have no idea who you're dealing with."

Joey laughs at me, too loud and with that crazed edge it always has. The Morrisons both angle away from us even though I know they'll hear every damn word. Good. I want them to know who they're pissing off every time they belittle and scorn their own damn son.

"I'm not afraid of some little slum whore who fucks thugs for protection."

I smirk at him. "Your siblings are under my protection and you can tell your father that. If either of you attempt to harm them in any way you answer to the Wolf of Mounts Bay."

Joey's eyes narrow, the knife in his hands still pointing in my direction. "Are you fucking him too?"

Illi snorts, "How the fuck are you still alive? Go back to the children's table, dickhead. The crack has set you back a few years if you can't figure it out."

Ash smirks at Illi. "He's alive because he hides behind his father. He's too fucking stupid to be a real danger. If we wipe him from the board we'll face Senior but we can take him on. I vote we kill him."

Avery sighs quietly, low enough that Joey won't hear it but I have. I slip my hand into hers under the table.

"Yes, well little brother, you should know by now that Father will kill the little slum cunt. And the pathetic bitch you shared a womb with. I'd personally like him to take the blonde slut too. She'd look perfect strapped on his table. All that blonde hair... just like Mom."

Harley manages to get an arm across Ash's chest before he flips the table but it's Avery I'm watching. I need to know if we're changing the plan because there are too many witnesses here.

Joey laughs, throwing his head back and sounding like a fucking loon. "You'll always be fucking weak if you're taking orders from pussy."

Ash smirks and points the knife at Joey. "That's your problem, Joey. You're too fucking stupid to notice when you're outmatched, and, brother, you're so far out of your league now you can't even see it."

The courses steadily get worse.

By the time dessert comes out, I won't even say what it is but I don't think Illi will ever hear the word 'foam' without feeling queasy and enraged again, Joey's hands have progressed from the fine tremble to full-blown shakes. Avery watches them as closely as I do, her appetite disappearing as it becomes clear he's going to rage out.

Joey takes a phone call and leaves the dining hall, blowing Odie a kiss because he must be the dumbest motherfucker on the planet, and some of the tension leaks out of Avery.

The waiters clear our plates and everyone stands to leave. Well, we stand to leave. The other students, parents, and teachers all start to mingle and network like this has been a lovely, productive dinner and I'd rather gouge my own eyeballs out than stay here.

"I'll hunt the little fuck down for you and finish him off," Illi murmurs, and I shake my head.

"Despite what Ash said, the plan is still to leave him for now."

Ash snorts and tucks me under his arm protectively. "I think we should contact Morningstar and give him a counter-offer. Whatever the fee is I'll pay it."

I groan at him but it's not the worst idea.

As we walk back towards the dorms, Blaise's dad starts to grill him about me.

Namely, why Ash is draped all over me if I'm Blaise's girlfriend. I pretend that I'm ignoring the dick but I hold my breath while I wait for the answer.

"We're in a poly relationship. It works," Blaise says, and Avery's eyes are *impressed* as they catch mine.

His father makes a noise of disgust and I tug out of Ash's arm, just enough to turn around and give the vile man my best impression of Avery's ball-shriveling glare.

"You seem to be having trouble getting it; no one here gives a fuck about you or your shitty opinions. If you want to keep breathing, you'll keep them to yourself," I say, low and even-toned. The color seeps out of his cheeks and he glances at his miserable son.

"What the fuck have you gotten yourself into now?" he mumbles, snapping his fingers at Blaise's mom and tearing off down the hall without even saying goodbye.

I take a deep breath to stop myself from chasing him and stabbing him through the eye, and Ash tugs me back into his side.

"Sorry, Star," Blaise murmurs and I shake my head at him.

It's been a clusterfuck sort of night.

Avery slips her arm through mine and frowns down at her phone as I help direct her. Illi grouches about the shitty dinner and Odie laughs at Harley's snarky comments. I enjoy it for about thirty seconds, then we round the corner and find Joey and two of Senior's bodyguards waiting for us at the bottom of the staircase. Great. Perfect.

I move to tuck Avery behind Blaise and he nods at me, understanding my silent instruction to protect her if this goes to shit. One of Joey's babysitters takes a step forward and then falters when he sees Harley, second only to Illi in sheer width of muscle. Harley is itching to make them all bleed. Now he knows the extent of what Senior and Joey have been doing to his cousins, he wants to bleed them all the fuck out. He was civil enough during dinner because of the witnesses but now we're alone, Joey is on thin ice.

I step forward, drawing his attention away from Ash. "You really are too stupid to survive, Joey."

He grins at me, the whites showing all the way around his eyes so he looks fucking deranged. "Father has told me to bring you home, Mounty. He's eager to meet the fabled Wolf of Mounts Bay."

Then he reaches out to grab my wrist, his fingers nearly brushing my skin, and Ash moves faster than I've ever seen a fucking human move. I swear right this second he's found his superpowers.

Joey is against the wall, pinned by his throat, before his bodyguards realize what's going on.

"Lay a hand on her again and I'll fucking bleed you out. I'm done with your games and your little lessons. I'm done toeing the line. Come after Lips or Avery and I'll destroy you both."

Joey's eyes dance around Ash's face, searching for some hesitance or faked bravado, but there's only the cold killer his father wishes he would embrace there.

Illi gently moves Odie so she's standing with Avery behind Blaise, then he flanks Harley with that little fucking grin of his slashed across his lips. His movement catches Joey's attention, but Illi only addresses the bodyguards, dismissing the psycho entirely.

"Do you two really want to die for this dickhead? Because this isn't going to be a beating; I don't do beatings. It's going to be your blood on my hands and your body melting away to nothing in a vat of acid. Is that how you were planning on spending your night?"

Joey's eyes flash back to Ash's face. "Do you really think some little gangster queen can keep you safe?"

Avery snorts at him, her tone as cold as ice as she says, "We've found bigger monsters than you to call our own. Run along to Senior and tell him that, too."

Ash chuckles and shakes his head. "He's not going to run anywhere. I've waited a long fucking time for this."

Harley doesn't peel him off of Joey until the little fuck is unconscious and unrecognizable.

Chapter Twenty-Two

For possibly the first time in my life I am excited for Christmas.

Well, not Christmas Day, I'm still trying to weasel my way out of that but the rest of winter break is going to be perfect. No plans or expectations, I'm going to eat my body weight in ice cream and figure out how the fuck we're going to hunt the Jackal without getting ourselves killed or found out by the Twelve.

Illi sends me a giant box of information he's been compiling, file after file of shady shit the Jackal is pulling on the other members of the Twelve, including putting a mole in the Boar's MC clubhouse. I know for a fact the giant biker will personally wage war with the Jackal if he finds out.

He's fucking touchy about his clubs.

The file about me curls my gut, but at least we now have a full list of the teachers on the Jackal's payroll. Ash is going to have to quit the track team until we can oust Mr. Embley from the coach's position and Mr. Trevelen is on borrowed time.

The guys move into our room and rotate between my bed and the pullout. Avery takes it all very well, happy we're all safe and in one spot, and the guys are all on their best behavior. Mostly.

Blaise makes it his mission to piss Harley off, over some spat I have no interest in taking sides over, and he starts to play his guitar and make up stupid songs at all hours of the day and night. Ash and I secretly love it. Avery puts in her headphones and ignores us all in favor of flirting with Atticus over text messages. It's messy and loud and fucking perfect.

I wake on Christmas morning to Avery's face hovering over mine. I startle, making Harley grunt and mumble in his sleep, and she motions for me to stay quiet and follow her to the kitchen. It feels like a trick, like she's using her Beaumont Bullshit to force me into accepting the day, but I smell the coffee she's brewing and decide to play along.

For now.

I sit at the table and Avery fusses over me until there's a perfectly made hot coffee and a plate of French toast in front of me and I'm a happy girl. Avery waits until I've eaten the whole plate before she speaks.

"Tell me why you hate Christmas," she says and I groan at her.

I take a deep, *deep* gulp of my coffee. "Did you know that even foster kids and kids in group homes get presents from Santa? Every kid on my street used to ask what

I'd done wrong every year when I had nothing. Once, when I was eight, I decided it had to be because we never had a tree. So I made one from shit in the backyard and decorated it with all the crap I'd made at school and put it all up in my room. I wrote a letter, asking for food because I didn't want a bike or a fucking doll or some other shit. I was hungry. I woke up to nothing, like always and sat there and wondered what the fuck I'd done to piss the fat man in the suit off. The next Christmas I was in the group home, and I puked when I saw my name on a present. I gave it to one of the other girls. I hate it. Last year, your present was the first one I've accepted. I fucking hate this day and I hate how fucking weak it makes me feel. Can I go back to bed now?"

Avery stares at me and I'm so freaking glad there's no pity on her face. I know she's feeling it, but she must know how badly I don't want to see it. All I can see in her eyes is the bloodthirsty Beaumont rage.

"Thank you for telling me. We should start working on our plans to hunt the Jackal soon. I'm not going to involve the guys in it. We'll make better plans without them getting all alpha-male over this."

I nod and sip my coffee. If there was any day I needed the caffeine to kick in and give me super powers, this would be it. Avery doesn't push me or ask any questions, so we sit in silence while we try to think of a way through this mess but no matter what angle I take, it all boils down to one thing.

"The problem is Luca," I say, frowning down at my now empty coffee cup.

"The hot guy that always kisses you in front of Harley? I thought you said he was nice."

I blow out a breath. "Yeah, he's nice but he's also loyal. I think he's so nice to me because he thinks I'm someday going to submit to the Jackal and become his boss too. He's always around and I haven't seen anyone get past him."

Avery taps her chin delicately. "You don't think you could get past him?"

"If they haven't switched up his security I could be in and out in under a minute and none of them would know the Jackal was dead until morning."

Avery nods. "But they would have changed everything since the meeting."

I hum under my breath and think it through. Should I go to him or draw him out? "I can't just send Illi in; I would never risk him like that and stealth will be our biggest asset. Plus, the other members can't find out what we're planning."

I need to take the guys to the gun range and see if any of them have some skills I'm unaware of. I know Harley has been trained by the O'Cronins and Diarmuid is the best sharpshooter I've ever seen. If Harley inherited those same family traits then maybe I can set him up on a roof to take the Jackal out that way.

"I need to meet with the Crow and discuss how we're going to handle the Jackal. He seems to be waiting for him to spiral and from what the Coyote said that's already happening."

Avery sighs and gets up, grabbing my plate for a second helping of breakfast. As she's piling on the toppings Harley groans and rolls out of my bed, rubbing his eyes like he needs another ten solid hours of sleep. I know the feeling well.

He kisses my cheek and then joins Avery in the kitchen to make himself a coffee.

"You forgot the sprinkles," Harley mumbles and starts rummaging through the kitchen cupboards until he finds them.

Avery arches an eyebrow at him and he scoffs at her. "It's Christmas morning, Lips deserves some fucking sprinkles on her breakfast."

I blush, swooning a little that he even remembers that, and Avery sighs at us both. "If the two of you can't contain your sickening love-struck selves I'm moving out."

I laugh at her, pissing her off until she drops a small perfectly wrapped box in front of me.

"You promised me no presents." I glare and Avery shrugs, smug-as-fuck.

"I already know you got us all gifts. You think I didn't search the entire room while you were in the shower last night? Please, I know you're not that dense. The boys even helped me."

I glare at Harley and he just shrugs sheepishly. Sighing, I shake my head. "There's no way you found the presents. I hid them too damn good from you."

Avery leans back against the table and smiles at me. "Sure I didn't."

Ugh. Fuck.

She has to be bluffing because there's *no way* she figured it out.

Avery laughs at the look on my face and flounced off to wake the other two guys up so we can start this awful day. Harley puts the plate of extra breakfast, complete with sprinkles, in front of me and kisses my cheek again.

"Thanks for joining us," he mumbles and moves to the couch.

Okay, maybe it's not completely awful.

I finish my toast and have a quick shower. Ash doesn't move until Avery wafts a coffee under his nose and Blaise bitches us all out for waking him. I end up on the floor in Blaise's lap by the time Avery wrangles everyone into exchanging gifts. She doesn't mention my sad little story this morning and I could fucking kiss her for it.

"I remembered that you didn't want things bought for you," Blaise mumbles into my shoulder, slipping our shared iPod into my hand. I smile, because a new playlist sounds *perfect*, and all that I really want. He smiles back at me like I'm the freaking sun, and my heart does this silly little backflip in my chest, then he turns the iPod on to show me the name of the song.

It's our song.

The one he wrote for us to sing together for choir. He's recorded it for me, somehow in secret because I know Ash still hasn't heard it yet. I furiously blink back tears. I will not cry in front of everyone, dammit!

Harley makes a pissy noise and I glance up to find him shaking his head at Blaise. "Of course you gave her a fucking song."

Blaise snickers under his breath and I elbow him. "What's wrong with a song? I love it."

"It's cheating because you're the hardest fucking person to buy for and Morrison has a secret fucking weapon," Harley mutters under his breath, but he hands me a small box with a card taped on top. I find a hot wiring kit and a promise to teach me to boost cars over the summer break. It's actually fucking perfect because when I am not wanting to learn more skills to keep me alive in the Bay?

I kiss him, with a little too much tongue for Avery's liking, and then Ash tugs me away from him and hands me a large black box, tied with luxurious black ribbons, and I start to panic a little that he's forgotten how weird I am about money and bought me something expensive.

"If that is sex toys or lingerie then please tell Lips now, I don't need to know the specifics of your relationship," Avery snipes, and Ash gives her a cool look as he hands her a much smaller box with a kiss to her cheek.

"I saved that one for later," he whispers into my ear and I shiver. I don't know if I want him to be joking or not.

I take a deep breath and open the box to find a bulletproof vest, brass knuckles, a tactical pen, and a belly holster for my new ghost gun.

"Ah, nothing says Christmas like weapons," Avery snarks, but I smile at Ash and give him a quick peck now Avery's pissy.

"Good call; I don't even care how much it all cost you. I love it, thanks."

Then I stand up and move the cabinet under the TV to the side until I can access the loose floorboard there that houses my safe this year. Avery groans and jabs Harley in the ribs. "I told you she'd hide the presents in there!"

I laugh at her and open the safe, slipping the little velvet bags out for each of them and handing them over.

They all look at the bags with varying degrees of curiosity and apprehension. And lust but, unsurprisingly, that comes from Avery.

"You're giving us favors for Christmas?" Ash asks.

I shake my head. "Just look in them, for fuck's sake."

Avery squeals when the deep blue diamond rolls out, caged in a delicate platinum sphere and hanging from a chain. Each of the guys have them as well, though the spheres look less *pretty*.

"Whose color is blue?" Blaise asks with a frown, and I smile at him.

"Mine. I don't give out favors, but if any of you need to I want you to have the diamonds ready. If something happens and I'm not there you can use that as currency."

Avery clears her throat and puts the necklace on, clutching at the diamond like it's the most precious thing she's ever held. "And how exactly did you pay for these? There's at least three million dollars worth of diamonds here."

I smirk at her. "I didn't pay for them. The Vulture did. The favors he owed died with him and I had eleven diamonds from him. More than enough to cover these."

Blaise grins at me and blows me a kiss, breaking the awed tension in the room. "Aw, you want to start your own gang. Do I have to start calling you boss?"

The next day, I wake up early feeling better now that Christmas is over with.

Avery refuses to take the day off from her rigorous training sessions for ballet, and I walk her down to the gym even though we're basically alone. She reads out her conversation with Atticus to me and I do my best to be supportive. It's fucking hard because I'm still firmly on Team Atticus-can-fucking-grovel but what Avery wants, Avery gets.

And Avery wants Atticus in the worst way.

When I've dropped her off at the gym and I'm sure there's no random spies hanging around, I head back to our room to wake the guys up and have breakfast. I want French toast again, because when don't I? Ooh and ice cream, and a giant mug of coffee. If Harley makes me breakfast I might kick the other two out to show him my, ahem, gratitude.

I'm still chuckling at my own hilarity when I unlock my door and step in, freezing as the door swings shut behind me.

Three sets of eyes take me in.

Harley is shirtless, holy hot *damn*, sitting on the couch holding a bottle of whiskey. Ash looks deliciously sleep-rumpled and he has shot glasses lined up on the coffee table in front of them both. Blaise looks tired and grumpy from where he's sprawled out on the floor.

"Wanna play a game, babe?" Harley says, waving the bottle at me as if that will entice me into playing along. I blush as I come out of my trance and I kick my shoes off, stalking over to slump down on the couch between the cousins.

"Can we just drink? I was also kinda hoping for breakfast," I grouse, but the second Harley slings an arm around my shoulders I'm in. Why does he smell so good?!

"I've got my truths up my sleeve. You owe me," Ash says, his tone like warm honey and it's almost enough to distract me from the words themselves.

Fuck.

I'd forgotten about that.

"Well, what do you want to know then?" I feign indifference but his smirk tells me I fail miserably.

Harley frowns at him and cracks the bottle of whiskey open, taking a swig and then handing it over to me. He hates not knowing shit about me, and Ash having the upper-hand will be grating on his nerves.

Ash keeps his eyes locked on mine as he swipes the bottle from me, laying out the shot glasses and filling them to the brim. "I'll be gentle, Mounty. We'll play by your rules and if you don't want to answer something just take the shot, and I'll wait until it's just the two of us to get the real answers."

I groan at him because nothing in this world will piss Harley off more. "I'll answer your questions. You guys can take shots if you don't want to. You go first, Ash, since I owe you."

He stares at me for a second and I almost think I see some regret on his face, but he asks the question anyway. "Why do you hate your birthday?"

I take the shot.

Harley curses under his breath, I think he's ready to argue with Ash for me, but I wave him off. "I can tell I need to be drunk for the rest of this conversation. I hate my birthday because my mom died on my birthday. Next question."

Blaise glares at Ash and tugs me until I end up in his lap. They've all taken to just picking me up and moving me where they want me and I'm still deciding if I like it or not.

I grab the bottle and start in on it. "C'mon, ask your questions. I'm giving you ten minutes and then I'll be fucking wasted and useless."

Ash opens his mouth but Harley cuts him off. "I thought you hated your mom. Why miss out on your birthday every year to mourn someone you hate?"

Another gulp, I'm not going to make it to ten minutes. "I'm not mourning her. I'm commemorating the day I got sent to a group home and met a boy there with big brown eyes and sweet words who told me he'd protect me and keep me safe. I'm commemorating the last time I blindly trusted someone and he turned out to be the biggest fucking monster under the bed. I'm mourning naive Lips Anderson who had no idea that boy had been watching her for months and sold her mom the dirty batch of heroin. I might have met him there but he'd been watching me for a while and my life ended the same day she died. Lips died too, the Wolf is all that's left. Next question?"

Harley takes a shot and then punches Ash in the arm so hard he winces. "Ask one of us one, babe. It's not just you playing."

Oh. That could be fun. I hand Harley to bottle and tap my chin with a finger dramatically. Blaise snorts with laughter at me, his chest pushing into me as he leans forward to grab a shot and down it.

Fuck it, I'll go for the throat. "Why don't you two get pissy that Harley always sleeps in my bed? Why is some shit harder to compromise on than others?"

Ash scowls at me, sighing and rolling his eyes. "You won't know this because Harley always sleeps well around you but outside of your bed he's an insomniac. Last year we had to drug him to get him to close his eyes for longer than twenty minutes at a time. I'm not going to get *pissy* over him finally having some sort of regular sleeping pattern. Would you say no to me sleeping in your bed while he's in there?"

I shake my head. It's a stupid question, I've had all three of them in there before.

"Well, there's your answer. Yes, I'd like you on my own occasionally but I knew what sharing you entailed when I agreed."

I look at Blaise and find him nodding. "I'm less... grumpy about it, I guess. I don't give a fuck who's in your bed or who you're fucking, Star. As long as I'm one of them."

I blush because that's sweet but also I feel a little like a skank for wanting them all. For enjoying the hell out of them sharing me. Ugh. I'm a total whore.

Harley brushes his knuckles over my cheek. "Stop over thinking things again, babe."

Blaise takes another shot and then moves me around in his arms like I weigh *nothing* which isn't fucking possible with the amount of ice cream I now get to eat every week.

He pouts at me and my eyes glue themselves to the inviting sight of his lip. "Why is this only truths? I want there to be dares as well. Kiss me, Star. I dare you to."

I laugh at him and squeeze his arms, the whiskey lighting my blood up until I'm all soft and pliable. "You don't have to dare me to kiss me."

He bites down on my shoulder and I have to consciously tell my hips not to rock forward into him. I glance back to find Harley and Ash are both watching us, not a shred of jealously in either of them, but I can taste the *want* in the air.

Fuck.

This is heady and overwhelming and fucking perfect.

Then keys slide into the lock and Blaise is cursing low and vicious under his breath and I'm the one pouting.

Firm hands band around my hips and Ash pulls me out of Blaise's lap. "Time's up, Mounty."

On the Sunday before classes go back Harley sends everyone else back to the boy's room while I'm in the shower getting ready for bed. When I step out and find him alone, perched on my bed in nothing but his boxers I gulp. Not in fear but in pure fucking lust.

"Uhm—"

He cuts me off. "I need another truth from you, babe."

I frown and step up until I'm standing between his legs, his big hands spanning my hips and drawing me in until he's taking up all of my senses. He raises his eyebrows at me and I nod.

"Avery went through my budgets with me when my inheritance came through and I told her to take out the exact amount I owed her. She was short and when I confronted her about it she told me you've been paying for my shit. Is that true?"

Fuck.

Avery hadn't warned me about this, dammit!

Harley nods like it's written all over my face even though I'm sure it's not. "So while I was being an asshole to you, you were paying for my tuition, my hotels, my fucking food. Everything."

I clear my throat. "Look, I had to. The Jackal was looking for any little opening to take you out and having you on the Beaumont payroll would have been the easiest opening for him. I was keeping you safe."

He shakes his head and lets his hands slide down until he's palming my ass, squeezing and kneading. "I'm not angry, babe. I'm hungry. I'm fucking starving and you're the only thing on the menu I want. One taste of what you've got and now I'm fucking addicted. Spread those legs for me."

Oh *God*. How the fuck did I end up with three Alpha males? And how the good *goddamn* did I find the only Alphas in the history of the Earth that are happy to share with each other? Sweet lord, I'm going to have a fucking heart attack.

Harley gets tired of waiting for me to come to my senses and do what he's asking, so he grabs the backs of my thighs to lift me and spread me out on the bed how he wants me. I'm only wearing my shirt and panties, and the tiny triangle of lace covering my pussy is torn from my body like it's a fucking insult to his very nature, and he groans like he really is a starved man.

"Take a deep breath and settle in, babe, because I'm not stopping until you've come on my tongue at least eleven times. One for every fucking diamond you've given for me."

I squirm and try to sit up, his hang ups on the favors and the money grating on me, but he flattens a big palm against my chest and pins me to the mattress. I want to say the dominant action pisses me off but the trickle of my wetness that lands on my sheets prove that's a lie.

"There is no way I can come eleven times," I croak and he scoffs at me.

"Start counting, baby."

By the fifth orgasm I'm nearly crying from the overstimulation but he's ruthless, driving me out of my mind with sensation until I'm a sobbing mess over the bed. Number eleven leaves me with numb fingers and toes, I'm fucking destroyed and he's the most smug asshole you've ever seen as he curls me onto his chest. I can feel his dick digging into my belly and I quickly decide that even Avery walking in here right now couldn't stop me from making him come too. I give myself thirty seconds to figure out how to work my limbs again and then I flip up to straddle his legs.

Harley's eyes flare but he gets on board with my plan pretty freaking quick, sitting up and pulling me until I'm right where he wants me.

"Get this fucking shirt off." He mumbles, and I laugh as he rips it off of me. My hips roll down on his, grinding away mindlessly and leaving a wet patch on his boxers. He groans like he's being murdered and I swear it's the hottest noise *ever*.

"Fuck babe, these tits." He bites his lip so hard I expect to see blood, and his eyes worship all of the newly exposed skin. His calloused hands are rough against my soft skin as he cups them, rolling my nipples like he had back at the docks.

"Do they feel fine?" I snark at him even though my breath hitches in my throat and I sound like a tramp. I'm still just a little pissed about his comment last year and fuck it if I'm not going to give him shit for saying it. He doesn't take any notice of me; all of his focus is centered on my boobs.

His hands squeeze and stroke, he mumbles, "Perfect," and then he ducks down to suck my nipple into his mouth. *Holy sweet lord fuck.* I'm dripping. When he moves over to the other nipple he catches my eye and, with a wink, he growls, "Taste perfect too, babe."

I moan and try to remember what the hell I'm doing. Right. I'm going to suck Harley's dick and I'm going to do it right. I pull his face back up so I can kiss him, pulling his hair to angle him just right. Fuck, he's like a drug.

"Why aren't you naked yet?" I mumble, biting at his lip.

He chuckles at me and then tugs at his boxers, lifting his hips and grinding into me as he gets them off, and then he's naked as well. Oh, Lordy.

He kisses me, deep and long and entirely too fucking hot, while he strokes himself. I whine into his lips and wrap my hand around his dick as well, craving the heat and the weight of it and needing a few seconds to figure this out. He grunts into my lips, moving my hand until I'm stroking him exactly how he likes it, firm and curling around the head.

Fuck him and his rational thought.

I wriggle down his body until I come face-to- well… dick. Harley's legs tense up. I glance back up at him and he's gritting his teeth like the sight of me face-down in his lap is all his dreams come true. Huh. Maybe it is. He moves his hand away from his dick as I lick my lips.

Good, I don't want him playing with what's mine right now.

I wonder if the guys would tattoo my name down their dicks, too?

I wrap my hand around the base and give it another tug, enjoying the heat and weight of him in my hand. Harley runs a gentle hand through my hair, his eyes soft on mine, but I don't want soft. I want him shaking with need like I am whenever he touches me.

"You've been tested lately, right? I refuse to swallow if you haven't," I say, arching an eyebrow at him even as my face flames.

He freezes for a second and then all of the gentle in him burns out, replaced by heady lust. "We all got tested when we agreed to share you. We're clean. Now make me come, babe. I want to taste myself on your lips."

I groan, my pussy waking up for round *twelve*, but there's no time for that now. I run my tongue up the length of him, swirling around the head like he's a spoonful of ice cream and I'm craving that sweet cherry on my tongue. Harley grunts when I do it again, slow and teasing, I want to push him like he pushes me.

When his jaw clenches I finally close my lips around him, taking as much of him in as I can, forgetting I need to breathe now I have him in my mouth. I pause for a second, just long enough to get my bearings and then I suck, pumping at the base with my hand because there's no way I can fit his whole dick in my mouth or my damn throat.

Fuck, I can't wait to feel him buried deep inside my pussy. I groan around him and the noise he makes has me humming to keep him on edge.

He starts to ramble on, mindless streams like he can't control his mouth. "Fuck.

Fuck, baby. Oh… that's my girl. How the fuck is this the first time you've done this, fuck me. You were made to take my cock, babe."

I know when he gets close because his hand threads into my hair and fists tight like he's going to pull me away but I've made up my mind. I'm going to swallow, at least this once. If it's gross I'll never do it again. He tugs a little and I only suck harder until he's coming down my throat.

It's not French toast and ice cream, but it's not terrible either.

Harley pulls me up and into his arms, moving me around until he can kiss me, slow and sweet. He's fucking perfect.

I could sleep for a week.

When I tell him that he tucks us both up in my bed, flicking the light off, and pulls his phone out. I assume it's to ask Avery to sleep in the guy's room but when he chuckles I suspect he's fucking bragging.

"What do you think you're doing?" I murmur and Harley pulls me onto his chest, cradling me gently against him.

"Just making sure Blaise knows I don't need any lessons on how to make you come, baby. The little fuck could learn from me."

I roll my eyes. "Of course you've made it a competition. Of course."

Harley drops a kiss on my head and murmurs, "It's not a competition. We both just want you. But if it were a competition, we both know I'd be winning it."

I bite him in retaliation and I fall asleep to the rumble in his chest under my ear.

Chapter Twenty-Three

Someone is breaking in.

I hear the window open and a body climb lithely in. It's too skilled to be a student, this is the efficient work of someone who breaks into places a lot and they're moving quietly enough that even Harley doesn't wake. I reach over and grip my knife as I hear the clinking noise of chains rattling on a pair of boots. *Great.* I know who those belong to; I've heard that noise too many times in the past before.

I slide a hand over Harley's mouth carefully and he wakes up instantly.

"You might want to get some bars on those windows, girlie."

Harley curses loud and vicious as he gets out of the bed. He pulls on boxers before he hits the lights. He grabs one of Blaise's shirts that's hanging on my bedpost to pull over my head, using his body as a shield so his uncle doesn't get an eyeful. Diarmuid watches us both with a cackling laugh.

"I thought you didn't mind sharing her, *buachaill beag*?"

One minute Harley is helping me lift the blankets and get out of the bed discreetly and the next he's landing a severe right hook into Diarmuid's cheek, knocking him to the ground. I scramble forward to grab Harley but he doesn't lay into him. He just stands over him with fire in his eyes and says, "If you imply she's a slut up for grabs again I'll fucking kill you."

Diarmuid rubs his jaw and stands, frowning. "Makes no fuckin' sense to me. I hear a rumor the girl you're in love with is out with both your best friends and I expect you to be dealing with it like a man would. Instead you're fuckin' sharing her?"

Harley shrugs. "I don't care if you get it. Is that all? See yourself out."

Then he turns his back and leans down to kiss my forehead gently, cupping my cheek sweetly until I'm a puddle on the floor.

"Right. Wolfie's off limits. I'm not here to talk about your love life anyway, I'm here because I'd like to join your merry little band."

I freeze and cut a look at him.

I do *not* trust Diarmuid. I don't trust him one fucking bit. Harley glares at him and then flicks his eyes over to me, his eyebrows doing a complicated dance I don't quite understand.

Fuck it. "Why?"

Diarmuid pulls out one of the chairs at the bench and slouches down into it, too casual for my liking. This is still my fucking room and I'm the Wolf of Mounts Bay, for fuck's sake.

"The Jackal wasn't very happy with me choosing your side in the car. He's making my life pretty fucking difficult so I need to swear allegiance somewhere. The Crow is a cock, no chance of me signing up under some suit pretending to be rough. I'm not a fucking biker, so the Boar's out."

I roll my eyes at him and cut him off. "Well, I don't take people in out of fucking pity so no. Try the Viper or the Fox."

Diarmuid grins at me and shrugs. "They've both sided with the Jackal. Besides, you took the Butcher in. He'd be dead without you. If my little nephew isn't sharing you with the sick fuck then what's he giving you? I'll pay double."

I use Harley's body as a shield to pull yoga pants on without flashing my ass at his uncle and then I stalk forward to stand in front of the Irish bastard.

"He gave me his loyalty, without question, like he always fucking has. You don't have a loyal bone in your body, O'Cronin. Fuck knows how Éibhear had it because the rest of you lot certainly don't," I snap, and hope that isn't crossing some line with Harley.

Diarmuid's eyes flick between us and the way his face sets I know Harley's backing me perfectly. Thank fuck.

"Right. You want loyalty, little girl? Name your price and I'll pay it. What's it going to take to prove my loyalty?"

Harley scoffs at him. "Maybe start with showing her some fucking respect."

Diarmuid's jaw clenches. "My apologies. Wolf, what can I do?"

I roll my shoulders back and stare at him while I think. I don't want to induct him, I don't want a fucking empire, but we could use another set of skilled hands while we're being hunted. Fuck it.

"The Jackal has put out a hit. I need every single man, woman, and child in the Bay to know that touching anyone under my protection is signing their own death warrant. The Butcher is aiming for subtlety at the moment so we don't rock the boat with the other members."

Diarmuid snorts. "The Jackal has flipped the fuckin' boat. The boat has sunk, litt- Wolf." He catches himself and shoots a look at Harley.

"Right. So I need you to be obvious about it. If you want to prove you're going to be loyal and one of mine I want the entire fucking state to know that they could catch a bullet between the eyes at any second from the best sniper in the country if they cross me."

Diarmuid's eyes narrow at me and I stare him down. Harley steps up until he's at my side and close enough that if his uncle tries something stupid, like pulling one of his guns on me, he can take him out before he can pull the trigger. I'm not worried. Diarmuid will never be a trusted member of our family, even if he does prove his 'loyalty'. He's only ever looked out for himself. He might be pissed about his father killing his brother but he didn't come looking for that revenge until Harley was old enough, and big enough, to do the dangerous work himself.

I don't trust this man.

"Fine. I'll start shooting every Tom, Dick, and fuckin' Harry that so much as whispers your name wrong. At what point does this get me in?" he asks, standing and straightening his jacket and running his fingers through his mussed, shoulder-length hair.

I shrug at him, nonchalant. "Impress me."

He snorts, then gives me a ridiculous and very obviously mocking bow, then leaves through the door. Harley watches his every step and doesn't relax until the door clicks shut behind him.

"He's not being inducted." He says, and I shake my head.

"No. He's not. But he can lighten Illi's workload for a while until we know if there's another reason he's coming to us."

I wait until family dinner before telling the rest of the guys about our midnight visitor.

Avery immediately gets on her phone and orders bars for the windows in both our rooms and I kick myself for not thinking about it sooner. Blaise gets on Harley's case about his fucked up family and Ash ends up snapping at them both to cut their shit out.

"The real problem here is what the hell is going on in the Bay," he says, and I nod.

"It's war. The Coyote warned us, and now more of the Twelve are choosing sides. We have the Crow, because he will never side with the Jackal so as long as we toe the line we have him. The Coyote and the Boar have both refused the Jackal. I need to find out where the others fall."

Ash snorts. "We're not toeing the line though, are we? Sending the O'Cronin dickhead after the Jackal's minions is a move against another member."

I smirk and shrug. "What the Crow doesn't know won't hurt him. Or us."

Avery sighs and stabs at her curry with extra force. "If we're turning this into a business meeting then I think you should all know that Annabelle is amping up her slander campaign and I'm having to clean up after the disgusting gold-digging whore. She's gone to every member of the school board about your relationship and said that she doesn't want Lips slandering the good name of Hannaford by... participating in orgies."

Blaise chuckles under his breath. "Are you three having orgies without me? I thought we discussed this, all for one and one for all."

I slap a hand over my face to try and hide my blush while Avery screeches like she's been stabbed.

"It's not fucking funny," Harley snaps, and Blaise flicks a pea from his curry at him.

"It's called lightening the mood, asshole. What can we do about Annabelle that Avery isn't already doing?"

Avery cuts through them both before they can start fighting again. "Kill her. I vote we just get rid of her."

I blanch and gape at her. I mean, I knew she was a bloodthirsty dictator but I kind of thought I'd have to convince her to let me kill Annabelle. Well, I assume I'm the one killing her. I doubt anyone else will put their hands up for the task.

"We talked about this. She's a dumb slut. We can't just run around killing dumb sluts," Harley says and takes a swig of his beer. I narrow my eyes at him and he grins sheepishly.

Ash looks between us both but I can tell he's uncomfortable. "I'm with Harley. If we kill her we're as bad as Joey and Senior."

I shrug and look at Avery, but she too busy rolling her eyes. "And of course Blaise will side with you and majority rules. I'll just keep running around after her when we have a permanent solution at hand that we ignore."

I bump her shoulder with mine. "I'll gut her for you the second she looks sideways at you. Or tries to touch one of the guys."

Avery huffs. "And what about you? I want her in the ground so she stops spreading bullshit about you."

I grin at her. "Aw. That's why you're my favorite."

When classes start after winter break, I bury myself in homework again. I finish all of the readings for our literature class, the workbooks for math, and I blitz past Harley in our history class. I even offer to do his half of the assignments so he has less on his plate and can spend more time with me.

The look he gives me would kill a lesser person.

I shrug at his pissy attitude and focus on Blaise's tutoring instead. I don't want to sound like a smug-ass-bitch but my smolderingly hot rock god is in the top half of all of our classes thanks to our study sessions. I stand firm on my rules, no fooling around until everything is done, and that motivates him like nothing else.

The nights we run out of time before Avery arrives home I go to bed cranky and frustrated. The only thing that helps is knowing Harley will climb in later with his wandering hands.

I wake on Friday to find him still fast asleep next to me. He always wakes before me, he has swim practice and never shirks any of his responsibilities. I frown and deliberate over waking him but the dark circles under his eyes worry me enough to leave him.

Avery makes us both coffees, moving as quietly as she can, and I shoot her an appreciative look. She shrugs and joins me in the bathroom as we get ready for classes.

"He needs to drop the study sessions. The cougar skank is working him too hard." She murmurs, and I try not to let the fury in my blood take over.

Working him hard.

I'll fucking stab the bitch.

Avery cackles at me, running her fingers through her hair even though it's already perfect. I scowl at her but with the toothbrush in my mouth I just look stupid.

The bathroom door opens and Harley blinks at us both, his eyes bloodshot and bleary.

"You could fucking *knock*, you Neanderthal," Avery snaps, but he just shrugs.

He kisses her cheek as he passes by her, then cups my cheeks as he kisses me. When he moves to the toilet I shove Avery out of the bathroom so he can get ready in peace. He's so fucking tired I might stab someone on his behalf today.

I hope Annabelle pisses me off and it's her blood on my knife.

Avery heads out for our classes but I wait for Harley to finish up. He takes twice as long in the shower and I make the decision that he's taking the day off. He can sleep in my bed all day.

He stumbles out of the bathroom in his uniform and I point at the bed with a stern look.

"In. Now. Don't argue with me, Arbour."

He smirks lecherously but the yawn that takes over his face destroys any chances of flirting his way out of this. He pulls his tie off, smirking again, then I watch and drool while he strips down to his boxers.

Fuck, temptation has a name and it's Harley fucking Arbour.

"I need to get to class but you're sleeping today. I'm not asking," I say, but the raspiness of my voice ruins the stern words. He walks over to me, his eyes burning my skin with the intensity of his gaze, and I gulp.

"I'm fine, babe. I wouldn't mind spending the day in bed with you though."

I gulp again and shove him into the bed, my hands lingering a little on him by accident. Totally an accident.

I tuck him in, ignoring the looks he gives me even as my cheeks flame, and I kiss him softly. "We need to sort Ms. Vivienne out next. I'm finishing the bitch and getting you back."

He smirks. "Whatever you do, make sure I'm there to see it."

Chapter Twenty-Four

The whispers that follow me only get worse now Annabelle is campaigning.

If I spot her in the hallways she scurries off like a fucking cockroach because she knows I'll break her in half if she so much as opens her mouth in front of me.

Avery watches her every move, waiting for an opening to destroy her. I try my best to forget about her. As long as she's not trying to touch one of the guys she's not my problem.

Weeks later, I wake to Blaise stroking my hair away from my face, whispering sweet words into my ear until I'm shivering and reaching for him.

"My brother was born this morning and my mom called me. She wants me to go see her, I think she's fighting with Dad over it. I'll be back in a few days, Star."

I blink up at him and then press my lips to his gently, a sweet kiss to say all the things I can't speak out loud to him; I'm sorry, I'm worried, I hope you're okay... I love you.

"It'll be fine, Star. I just didn't want to leave without saying goodbye. I'll text you when I land," he murmurs against my lips, his fingers still stroking away like he knows the anxiety that's curling in my gut.

I need to get past my worries about being away from them, but with the threats we have nipping at our heels I just want us all together and watching each other's backs.

"Come home the second it gets bad, Blaise," I whisper back, and he shrugs, nodding a fraction but in that distracted way that tells me he's already preparing to be in his father's presence again.

When Avery and I meet Ash and Harley for breakfast in the dining hall Ash is in a foul mood.

I quirk an eyebrow at Harley and he scoffs at me. "Isn't it obvious? His boyfriend is gone so he's pouting."

The look Ash gives him is so fucking cutting, I'm surprised Harley doesn't actually bleed from it.

"He's just gone home to meet his replacement sibling at his mother's demands but the woman is so fucking spineless that the second his father starts his bullshit she'll cave and send him away. Sorry for being concerned he's going to come home in a pine fucking box."

I swallow roughly and Avery sighs. "Can you not freak Lips out? She gets twitchy the second one of you are in trouble and I don't feel like making a cross-country trip on the fly. I never pack what I need under those sorts of pressures."

I try to focus in my classes but my mind keeps wandering away. I'm so far ahead it doesn't matter but I know it freaks Harley out when I space out. He keeps touching me, just little brushes of his fingers on mine, to try to pull me back into the real world but nothing works. Those three words keep circulating in my head: pine fucking box.

I decide it's an ice cream for dinner sort of day and Avery brews me a perfect cup of coffee, perching on the couch with me while she texts Atticus. Their flirting has been taken to the next level, constant and consuming. The little smiles and giggles she gives her phone make me so freaking happy but just as terrified.

What if he's a dick? Or a rapist too? What if he hates me and I have to pretend to like him? Ugh. When I say this to Avery she laughs at me.

"Don't be stupid, Lips. He has no choice but to love you. You're nonnegotiable."

I sip my coffee with a little smile as Ash stomps through the door and gives me a look that spells fucking trouble.

"What now?" I groan, and he grabs the remote and flicks through the channels until he lands on a news station.

There's Blaise standing outside a hospital in New York with his dad at a press conference. He looks fucking miserable and the smug satisfaction on his dad's face makes my jaw hurt from clenching so fucking hard.

"My son was born in the early hours of this morning. He's healthy and my wife is now resting in the capable hands of the hospital staff."

Even his voice pisses me off. I cut a look to Ash and he murmurs, "Wait, he's about to sign his own fucking death warrant."

My eyes snap back to the screen.

"Yes, we've made the decision to remove Blaise from the family business and trust. He is old enough now that he can make his own decisions on these matters. He has a... flourishing career ahead of him in the music industry and the Kora board has moved to sever all ties to him."

Sever all ties to him?

This dickhead has just publicly announced he's disowning his fucking kid?

"I'm going to gut that motherfucker," I snap and Ash nods at me.

"Only if you get to him first."

Blaise texts to say he has business meetings all week with his agent about the new album he's been putting off releasing. I tell him he has seven days to get his ass home before Ash and I charter a flight to come drag him ourselves. He sends me a bunch of hearts and laughing emojis.

I'm not joking. Ash texts him the same thing and I think he finally gets that we're dead fucking serious. Five days later, while I'm alone in my room after classes, a little lost without our tutoring sessions my door opens and Blaise stumbles in, drunk off of his ass. I groan under my breath as I move straight to him.

"I think I need a lie down, Star. Just give me a minute. I need—I need a minute." He slurs and I get him over to my bed.

A man walks in behind him, but I ignore him as I help Blaise strip down to his boxers then tuck him into my bed. I rummage around in the kitchen until I can find a bucket to leave on the floor for him. I pray he doesn't need it.

The man is so quiet I almost forget he's there until he says in a lecherous tone, "So you're the pussy he's tied himself to then? I was hoping it would be the little dark-haired one, the icy bitch. She would be fun to have on tour."

My spine snaps straight and I look over at the fucking perverted dickhead. "Excuse me?"

He smirks at me, stepping towards me with a swagger like he thinks I'm into forty-year-old guys with thinning hair and dopey, drugged up eyes.

"I heard you like to be passed around. I would've preferred the other pussy but I'll take yours."

I look down at Blaise but he's passed out. I'm guessing this is his agent, David Fyre. I don't want to fuck up his career by killing the dickhead but I'm never going to accept being spoken to like this. I also know for a fact Blaise would lose his fucking mind if he was sober enough to hear it.

I palm my knife. "I'm assuming you're the agent. You have ten seconds to get out of this room before I remove you myself. I'm only asking once."

The smirk on his disgusting face only gets bigger as he takes another step forward and the gods smile on me because the sound of the door unlocking stops him in his tracks.

Ash storms in and stops when he gets a look at the expression on my face and my hand in my pocket. His eyes cut to the agent and his lip curls.

"Fyre. You should leave," he says, cold and no-nonsense.

The fucker tips his head at him like they're such good friends and leaves with a little sleazy wave in my direction. Ash opens his mouth and I cut him *the fuck* off.

"I will never stand in the same room as that man again without stabbing him. I'm not going on tour with him. Firm pass. Avery is *never* allowed in his presence again. Nonnegotiable."

Blaise mumbles in his sleep and rolls, groaning. Ash throws a pillow at his head as he steps up to me. "What did he say to you? I'll go and deal with him now."

I shake my head. "Blaise can decide what to do with the sleazy pervert. Just leave it. Why are you in a shit mood?"

He grabs my wrist and tugs me until I'm in his arms, pressed against the hard lines of him. I tell my treacherous knees that they shouldn't be quivering now I've spent this much time around the asshole but he's too fucking hot to be real sometimes and the possessive way he just moves me where he wants me does something to my insides.

Also my panties fucking disintegrate but I swear I'm running out of them being around these guys.

"You're sleeping in my bed. Not tonight now that idiot is home and wasted, but tomorrow. I'm done waiting and if any little fuck starts talking about you being in there I'll gut them."

I wake the next morning to three large boxes at our door labeled, 'not heads' in Illi's scrawling handwriting.

I snort and text him to tell him he's an idiot.

I don't bother opening them, I already know exactly what they are. Blaise groans like he's being murdered and Avery snarks at him, though she's a little more gentle about it than she normally is. I make him coffee and nudge him towards the bathroom to get him moving. He's already missed a week of classes and I don't need him falling behind just because his father is a fucking asshole.

After classes, I drag everyone back to the room. I hand the boxes for the guys over and they open them to find Illi has decked them out for murder. Ghost guns, knives, holsters, and a promise to teach them all how to use them effectively over the summer break.

Blaise's eyes are still bloodshot and bleary as he mumbles, "Fuck. We are a gang now right? This definitely means we're a gang."

I consider stabbing him just a little. He cackles at me like he knows exactly what I'm thinking, the asshole.

Harley pulls a holster out of his box and adjusts it until it sits over his shoulders nicely, then he rolls his shoulders back like he's testing the feel of it. "These are good. Comfortable and lightweight. We should be able to wear them under a jacket without the sheep noticing."

I smile at him and knock his shoulder with mine, teasing him, "Are you good enough with a gun to be carrying all the time? Maybe you should wait for your lessons."

"Get me a rifle and a scope and I can hit a beer bottle lid a half mile away with wind resistance." Harley shrugs, and I gape at him.

That's pretty *fucking* good.

"Maybe we should be getting you to take the Jackal out from a distance. I feel like now we're building a fucking tactical team when I was supposed to be coming to school to get away from that life," I mumble, and Avery tilts her head at me.

"We don't live in a safe world, Lips. We don't live in the normal, blue collar world on the television. We'll always be chased by demons because we have power."

I nod and huff out a breath while I reevaluate my entire exit plan.

Finally, after stewing on it for five minutes, I get up to make another cup of coffee. "Do we have any ice cream left? I need the calories to plan this shit out."

Chapter Twenty-Five

With Ash's demand for me to go stay with him still ringing in my head I decide to just get the fuck over the whispers and the risks of the school board finding out and to stay there for a night.

I wait until Saturday when they're all busy; Ash is out for a run and the other two are at the gym for their usual afternoon of boxing. Blaise has a lot of rage to burn through these days thanks to his dickhead father and Harley is bearing the brunt of it in the ring. Good thing he's stacked and can take it.

I tell Avery my plans and she smirks at me as she hands over the key. When I blush she snarks at me, "I'll text them to be gentle with your sweet virgin body."

I think about killing her.

Okay, lie but I do think about messing with her scarves until she has to press and refold the whole damn box tower but the psycho would probably enjoy it.

I don't bother packing a bag because Avery has a drawer full of clothes over there and I'll steal a toothbrush from one of them if I have to. It's just me, my knife, and my newly cut key.

The boy's dorm is thankfully quiet.

I hold my breath until I'm safely inside with the door locked behind me. The room is different from last year and I toe my shoes off to walk around. Blaise's bed has been shoved in the corner to make room for a mountain of music equipment, speakers, and guitars in black cases. His bed is covered in lyric books and guitar picks, his acoustic guitar slung over his pillows like he set it aside seconds before leaving. His last album hasn't even been released yet so it makes no sense to me that he'd be working on new songs. Maybe it's all just stress relief.

Harley's bed is bare, his books still in boxes and the patchwork blanket missing. He's barely sleeping here anymore and with the extra study sessions with the cougar whore he hasn't even had a day off to unpack even though we've been back at school for months. I make a note to force him to have another day off.

Ash's space looks the most lived in and I instantly feel guilty as fuck over it. I know he's trying to be respectful, I know he's trying to make sure nothing gets broken by pissing Avery off, but fuck. I need him. I need his snarking and his asshole nature. I need his fierce loyalty and the ruthless way he defends what he loves.

I know that now includes me.

I text him to tell him I'm waiting in his bed, and seconds later he texts the group message to tell everyone to fuck off for the night. I blush and giggle like a freaking schoolgirl then I climb into his bed and bury my face into his pillow while I wait. My eyes drift shut and I fall asleep even as the excitement builds in my belly.

The dip in the bed doesn't worry me at first because I'm so used to waking up to one of the guys climbing in to join me. It's only when I hear the high-pitch and, definitely, female giggle that I bolt upright in the bed and snap the light on.

Annabelle *freaking* Summers has crawled into the fucking bed.

She stares at me in shock and then sneers, "You!"

I shove her off the bed with my foot, ignoring the shooting pain it causes me, and then I seriously fucking consider stomping on her face until she stops breathing.

"What the fuck are you doing in here?!" she screams and I gape at the bitch.

"Are you fucking kidding me, it's my boyfriend's bed! What the fuck are *you* doing in here? How the hell did you get in?" Fuck am I glad I fell asleep before I stripped off. I scramble out of the bed and grab my phone. I spot Harley's missing keys dangling from her fingers and see red.

Annabelle stands and looks down her perfect nose at me. "I'm not stupid, I know the boys will get sick of slumming it with your cheap, Mounty pussy. It's only a matter of time before they come back to me."

Yep. She's clearly fucking crazy and that's all I can take.

I take the keys from her and if I snap one of her fingers while I do it then the bitch deserves it. I ignore her screaming and cussing me out while I shove her out the door.

It's completely irrational but I get fucking livid and throw a little tantrum. If the psycho bitch goes to the school board again, I'll be expelled. I let Ash talk me into sleeping here and now I'm dealing with his *shared* psycho stalker ex. I call him ready to leave a scathing voice mail but he picks up.

"That impatient for me, Mounty? I'm already coming up the stairs."

I snort at him and snap, "Annabelle fucking Summers just climbed into your bed and woke me up from my nap. I've kicked her the fuck out and I'm going back to my own bed while I wait to see if this gets me expelled. Just a courtesy call." And then I hang the fuck up to the sounds of him cursing the whole damn universe out.

I lock the door and turn off my phone while I try to calm down.

It's only when I hear the door unlocking that I realize they all have *fucking* keys and can get the *fuck* in and I need some *fucking* space! I stomp to the bathroom and lock that door instead. They'd have to break the damn thing down to get to me and if they do that, well, I'll stab them.

I turn the shower on and then sit on the floor, doing some deep breathing to calm the fuck down. Like Marianas fucking Trench levels of deep.

The soft knock startles me and I frown. I can't imagine Ash knocking like that.

"It's me, Mounty. Ash called me to deal with Annabelle and I told him to deal with his own sloppy leftovers," Avery says, and I unlock the door for her, cutting the shower off now I know I don't have to pretend. I can't look her in the eye, I feel all raw and exposed at my little tantrum. Fuck, I'm being pathetic.

I say that to Avery and she breathes ice at me. "No judgment. *Fuck* them."

"I just—I knew it was a bad idea to go there. I knew it! I let him talk me into it and now I've been spotted in his bed by that bitch and for all I know she's managed to get a photo of me there. You're going to have to save me from being expelled again and the fucking whispers are only going to get worse!"

Avery nods and fluffs with her hair in that way she does when she's plotting and texting. I wait her out, pulling my socks off and starting to strip to have a shower for real. Avery always tells me hot water heals all.

When I step under the hot spray, Avery hums quietly under her breath and lifts her phone to her ear. I can't hear whoever is on the other end of the line but I watch instantly as a slow smirk slides across Avery's mouth.

"Oh, I'm sure it *is* a pleasure to hear from me, Summers. I have some news for you... I did warn you. If you piss me off again, I'll have your scholarship revoked... well, crawling into my brother's bed pisses me off... I can and I will... how about instead of slutting your way around my family you find another cock to worship... I hear Remy is desperate and he's due to come into a reasonable sum...you're not in a position to be picky Summers. Oh, and if you go to the school board about Lips again I won't put out a social hit. I'll end you."

She hangs up and smiles at me, genuinely sweet, as she leaves me to my shower. "I'll go make us a coffee. We can pull the drawers in front of the door so the idiots can't get in and then watch *Dirty Dancing* with ice cream."

I laugh at her enthusiasm for fucking with the guys and nod, lathering up and cleansing the shitty mood right out of my skin.

When I'm finished and wrapping myself in a big fluffy towel the front door bangs open and I stop breathing so I can hear who the fuck it is.

Avery snaps, "If you walk into that bathroom, she will tear your testicles clean off of your body, and I'll stand by and let her."

The bathroom door slams open and Ash storms in, kicking it shut behind him. I clutch my towel like he hasn't watched Harley eat me out in public and blush like an idiot.

"I have had the patience of a fucking saint," he says, and I gape at him.

"Do you want a fucking medal?" I sputter and he steps forward until he's crowding me back into the bathroom sink.

"No, I want you to trust me and trust that there's nothing that trashy whore could do that I couldn't fix for you. They want to kick you out? I'll fix it. They want to bad mouth you? I'll fix it. They want to hurt you in any way? *I'll fucking fix it.*"

His eyes are like the center of a flame, searingly hot blue that burns me until I'm panting up at him. I can't function or form a reply when he's looking at me like that.

I pull away and root around until I find a clean set of bra and panties, matching and chosen by Ash last year. I try not to blush and fumble as I slip them both on while his eyes roam over my skin possessively. When I reach for my shirt he grabs my hand and tugs me into his chest. Snapping the bathroom door open, he barks out, "Go away, Avery."

Avery startles from where she's sitting at the kitchen bench with her coffee texting, her eyes wide as she takes us both in.

I gape at Ash, and from the indignant noise his sister makes I know she's just as pissed about it. "This is my fucking room, asshole!"

He smirks at her and my heart stops. Oh fuck. "Well, I'm about to lay the Mounty out on the closest flat surface and spread-"

"DO NOT FINISH THAT *FUCKING SENTENCE!*" Avery screeches,

scrambling out of the chair and grabbing her ballet bag. Cursing him out, so fucking colorfully I can't believe it's her doing it, she storms out, slamming the door behind her.

I could die.

Ash only looks more determined once we have the room to ourselves.

"I'm still pissed off," I say, because a sweet little declaration hasn't changed my mood. Okay, it has changed it a little but I'm still practically vibrating with anger.

"Good. It'll only make you come harder."

Sweet merciful lord.

"Wait, you can't just—" He cuts me off with a blistering kiss and then I forget why the fuck I was arguing with him.

One of his hands wrap around my throat so his thumb fits under my chin, tipping my head back to where he wants it. It should *not* be a turn on, especially with his family's history, but I fucking *gush* at his firm grip.

He walks me backwards until I'm pinned against the table by his body, his dick pressing against my stomach and holy shit I forgot how big he is. I forget I'm kissing him, dazed and a little terrified, and he scoffs at me, tapping my hip until I hop up onto the table. When I move to wrap my legs around his hips he holds my legs down, spreading them wide. I frown at him, because I might be nervous but I don't want to stop, and the smirk on his face only gets wider.

"Lie back. I want to enjoy the lingerie I picked for you. I've spent a long fucking time thinking about how it would look on you."

I blush but do it, gasping as my back hits the cold table. The possessive look is back as he runs his hands down my chest, squeezing and teasing my tits, then sliding down until he can stroke back over the scrap of black lace between my thighs. I shiver, choking on the moan that claws it's way out of my throat when he rips the lace clear off of my body. The rumble deep in his chest lets me know what he thinks of the sight of my wet pussy spread wide for him.

"Avery will have an aneurysm if she finds out we did this on the table. She's been clear about her stance on the furniture," I choke out, and he drops to his knees.

"Don't tell her then, Mounty," he says, and any reply I could have come up with disappears the second his mouth touches me.

Holy. Fuck.

Holy Jesus *fuck*.

Okay, getting head is the best fucking thing and why did I wait so damn long to start dating? Stupid question, I was waiting until I found the three *hottest guys* who ever walked the Earth and then somehow managed to convince them all to share me. *Fuuuuuuuck*. As he teases at my clit my brain switches off and I start to grind against his mouth, chasing the sensation until I'm splintering apart at the fucking seams but he doesn't stop. He's fucking merciless as he pushes and pushes until I come again, gasping and crying out into the silence of the room.

Lord, he is good with his tongue.

When my thighs finally stop shaking, I sit up and tug at his shoulders until he stands, kissing me until we're just panting into each other's mouths, sharing the taste of my slick pussy between us.

I want him.

I don't think beyond that, sliding off of the table and onto my knees as I reach for his belt with steady fingers. He smirks at me and helps to undress. I swallow roughly at the sight of his chest, all the lean solid muscle of a runner. Only when he's kicked his pants and boxers off do I glance down but my eyes land on a smudge of ink right above his dick.

I can't even focus on anything but the tattoo.

"Are you serious right now?" I croak.

"Yes, I'm serious, that is my dick. I appreciate the awed tones though, Mounty," he drawls out, all fucking smug and I can't. I just fucking can't.

"No, I mean, do you seriously have the words 'you're welcome' tattooed above your dick? I changed my mind, I'm not doing this."

Ash chuckles at me as I move to stand up then he holds me down with a firm hand on my shoulder. Oh look, there's my damage again but sweet merciful lord if that doesn't make me gush all over again.

"It's Morrison's fault, get pissy at him, not me."

I scoff at him and then try to focus on his dick instead of the arrogant, smug, *totally-fucking-Beaumont* tattoo he has.

Sweet lord in heaven.

I forgot he was fucking huge. I gulp. There is no way that will fit in me. Not right now, and possibly not ever. I might dislocate my jaw doing this.

"You'll be fine, Mounty."

I punch him in the leg because I'm *excellent* at foreplay. He grunts at me, probably because the hit was a little too close to his monster cock for comfort, but when I wrap my hand around the base of his dick and pump he shuts up real fast.

He's right, I don't dislocate my jaw but fuck it if it isn't a stretch. He's less worried about hurting me than Harley is, his hands in my hair tugging and pulling while his hips jerk forward, but that only makes me moan louder. He doesn't warn me that he's going to come either, just grunts and shoots down the back of my throat. It's the soft touches afterwards that tell me how much I mean to him, and I love every fucking second of it. I could do that every day of my life and die a happy lady.

When he helps me up from the floor and kisses me, I can't stop myself from snarking at him. "You're going to have to make do with blowjobs for a while. That is not going to fit in me. I'm half the fucking size of you as is."

He laughs at me, completely unconcerned by my stern warnings, and walks over to climb into my bed. Fuck, his ass is all toned muscle. Perfect to sink your teeth into.

"Get in here. I need a nap."

Ugh, bossy asshole.

But I do exactly what he says.

The notification of my in-school suspension comes through as an email the next morning and I read it out to Ash while he sips at a coffee in bed, sleep mussed and fucking delicious looking after spending the whole night with me.

"I told you, Mounty. Trust me."

Chapter Twenty-Six

I refuse to let the house arrest stop me from doing whatever the hell I want, trusting in Ash and what he said to me.

Avery starts working her way through the teachers and students that have helped Ms. Vivienne and by the end of the week two teachers quit and eight students transfer out of Hannaford. There's nothing quite like Avery freaking Beaumont when she's on the social warpath.

On Sunday, after a long day of studying and trying to catch up on sleep, Ash texts me a demand to meet him in the boy's room and when I try to get him to come to my room instead he calls me a coward.

The manipulative asshole, except it's effective and I stomp over to rant at him in person.

When I unlock the door and fling it open the words die in my throat at the arrogant fucking smirk on his face and the fact that he's lounging on his bed in his fucking boxers. Dammit. His nipples are like my kryptonite and I think somehow he's figured it out!

"Do you want to argue, Mounty? I'd rather we go for round two but I'll fight if you need the foreplay."

I cut him a look but I lose the higher ground by drooling all over myself as I climb up onto his bed to get to him. "Shut up and kiss me, asshole."

Ash chuckles and nips at my lip, "Why, Mounty, I didn't think you'd be up for ass play just yet but if you ask nicely I could be persuaded."

Aaaaaaand now I kinda wanna die.

He doesn't let me pull away, his hand firm on the back of my neck as he strokes his tongue over mine until I forget why it was I was so embarrassed in the first place. I feel like a fumbling idiot as I clutch at his shoulders because his hands are steady and sure as he strips my shirt from me and with a quick flick of his fingers my bra is off and across the room.

I'm panting the second his hands cup my tits, kneading and toying with my nipples, and for a second I'm so distracted I don't feel the buzzing of my phone. It's only when Ash curses into the skin of my neck that I realize what's pissed him off.

911. Our room. Now.

I glance at the text from over Ash's shoulder as he works his way down my chest. I'm only checking it because I know it's Avery and my stomach fucking drops. I shove at his chest to move him and dial her number frantically.

"Atticus asked me on a date! A real one. He's going to come pick me up after my recital tomorrow night. We need to plan out everything, Lips. My outfit, my hair, my opening line, how I'm going to turn him down if he tries to kiss me because I want to string him along a bit. Stop sucking face with your man-meat and get over here."

I groan at her. "911 means life threatening, Aves, not help-I'm-freaking-out-over-a-guy! Fuck, I nearly shanked Ash to get to the phone."

Ash grunts, flopping over onto his back dramatically while I drool at the sight of him, and snaps, "I'm not giving Lips up just for your pathetic boy troubles. Which idiot did you snare this time? If you say Sebastien I will walk to his room right now and rip his fucking throat out."

I cringe and he eyes me for a second before it clicks.

He snatches the phone away from me and hisses, "You are not going on a date with that spineless fuck Atticus! Over my dead *fucking* body, Avery."

She screeches at him so ear-piercingly that I hear every word. "Well I guess you're dead then, asshole!"

I refuse to get involved in their little spats but I do leave Ash to go help Avery. He's fucking livid about it but I know it's about Atticus and not me leaving him. He even tries to talk me into helping him turn Avery against Atticus but I stand firm.

Avery deserves to be fucking happy and if Atticus is it, then he's it. I'm not questioning it.

She is standing in the living room in her skimpiest lingerie when I arrive and I decide that Atticus is a fucking lucky guy. She's a hot piece of ass and any guy would be fucking begging to have her.

"Would you go with the red or the black? Atticus always likes me in black," she says without looking back at me.

I kick my shoes off and join her. The dresses are both stunning and sexy without showing much skin. There's nothing Ash could possibly complain about when he sees her in them.

"Black with red lipstick. The dress and your hair will make it pop and he'll be falling over himself to kiss you. It'll make it that much better when you decline his advances."

Aves smirks and cuts me a little smug look. "This is why we're friends. How would you say no to kissing him?"

I snort out a laugh at her. "Well, I'm not a refined and graceful lady like you. I usually say no by breaking people's bones."

Avery hums and runs a hand down the black dress. "How did you say no to the guys while you were oblivious to them last year?"

I groan at her. "I didn't. I kissed them and then remembered I couldn't and told them that. Well, except that one time with Harley where he was the one who stopped us because I couldn't help myself."

Avery pretends to gag but she laughs while she does. "Was that before or after he got you drunk and found out you were a virgin?"

I head for the freezer. If I'm going under the Spanish freaking Inquisition then I need some cherry fucking ice cream. "I *am* a virgin, and it was before."

Avery hums and throws a robe on, grabbing a spoon to dig around in my tub of cherry goodness. "I would never have believed those three horn-bags would take this so slow. My screeching is working wonders."

I cackle at her. "And how much of your screeching is real discomfort?"

She shrugs. "I'm pretty sure you could fuck Morrison on the couch in my general vicinity and the only real concern I'd have would be the clean up required. Oh, and the fact I'd have to see his dick, ugh. But they don't need to know that."

I wait until Ash takes Avery down to the gym for her last ballet practice before her recital and I call Illi. There's no way I'm going to let Avery get involved with Atticus before I've done a full background check on the asshole. Rory had looked like the perfect gentleman on paper, great breeding and the poster boy for an all-American football player, and he'd tried to fucking rape her in a bathroom for dumping his cheating ass.

Blaise arrives as Illi picks up and I motion for him to stay quiet.

"What's up, kid? Who's dead now?" He laughs and I snort at him.

"You shouldn't joke like that when we're being fucking hunted like game. I need a full-scope background check. I'm going to call the Coyote also but I need your sources as well."

Illi grunts and I hear him moving around. The blaring horns and shouting tell me he's out on the Bay, probably chasing up the Jackal's hired muscle. "Who's it for?"

"Avery's new man. Don't ask, it's a potential shit-show waiting to happen. Ash is going to gut the fucker if he so much as side-eyes her."

Illi chuckles. "Good fucking luck to him. She might be prissy but the girl has claws and the grit to back it up."

That warms something in my belly. I love that he can see her worth just as much as I can. "She's fucking besotted so we need a full check. The last guy she got into… we had to deal with. Piece of shit. So, we're doing this right, Illi."

"Of course, kid. Gimme the dickhead's details and I'll rummage through his fucking sock drawer until we know he's clean."

"Thanks. I owe you."

"Shut it. Hey, what happened to the other guy? He still breathing?"

I grunt. "Unfortunately. Harley had him permanently taken out, and now he's in his own version of hell. A wheelchair and a non-functioning dick."

Illi roars with laughter. "That's fucking good. Send me his name too. Tell the Ice Queen it's an early birthday present from Odie and me."

I cackle and hang up, texting him through Atticus and Rory's details. I should just leave the rapist asshole to his own hell but fuck it. The world will be a better place without him around wasting oxygen.

Blaise sidles up behind me, resting his hands over my hips and kissing my neck. "Why are you telling Illi about Rory? I thought we were done with that dickhead."

I shiver and try not to melt into a puddle of goo at his feet. "I need to get Atticus checked out. What do you think of him? Besides hating him on principle for Ash's sake?"

Blaise huffs and his breath tickles at my neck. I have to take a step away from him so I don't embarrass myself. Well, more than usual.

"I think he's an arrogant dickhead but I also think he's kind of perfect for Avery. Don't tell Ash I said that, he'll fucking slit my throat in my sleep. He hates him. Actually he fucking despises him."

I frown and move to make us both coffee. Blaise doesn't drink coffee much but I refuse to let him drink beer while he studies so I'm slowly converting him.

"Why? Did something happen or does he hate him on principal?"

Blaise slumps down onto the floor in front of the TV in his usual spot. "Aves was fucking devastated when Atticus stopped talking to her. She holed herself up in her room and watched those stupid romance movies for weeks. It was pathetic. Nothing like she normally is. Harley ended up moving in here to make sure she didn't do something stupid and Ash went on the warpath. He nearly got kicked out for how often he was in the fight club fights. Avery eventually came around and dealt with the fall-out but Ash hates the idea of Atticus in her life again because he already knows the power he has over Avery."

I grimace and join him on the floor, smiling as he sips the coffee without pulling a face. I must be getting better at making his super sweet. I may like my sweets but my coffee needs to be as black as the stain on my heart to keep me going.

"I don't think it's worth getting into a relationship with someone if you feel anything less than that."

Blaise leans back and watches me carefully. "Less than what?"

I shrug. "Less than all in. That's how I feel about you. And Ash and Harley. It's how I know you guys are worth all of the danger and risks to keep alive. Why start something with anyone who doesn't hold that power?"

Blaise grins and when he glances down at his textbook there's color on his cheeks that squeezes my heart a little.

"Why the fuck are you blushing over that?" I laugh. Boys are fucking confusing.

He shrugs at me and flicks a pen in my direction. "I know you feel like that because you risk your neck for us all the time but you don't really say it. It's just fucking weird to hear you say it."

I huff at him. "I don't mess around, Blaise."

He shrugs again and I let it go, focusing on his assignments until I'm happy he's going to nail every last one of them.

When Avery gets back from dance, Blaise leaves with a lingering but sweet kiss and I ignore Avery's questioning look. I wait until she's showered and in bed before I tell her about my conversation with Illi.

"I don't need him to kill Rory. I'm comfortable with where he is."

I nod and switch the light off. "It's the principle of it. Illi doesn't ever let rapists live. What happened with Odie taught him that lesson the hardest way possible."

Ash and Avery leave for the recital early the next morning. I text Illi and he promises to follow them there, though he doesn't seem very happy about tagging along to high society functions. I think dinner at Hannaford has ruined the illusion that the higher societies have better things for us.

They certainly don't have better food.

I go to classes with Harley and Blaise, and we eat lunch in the dining hall. The whispers that follow me are even fucking worse now that I'm on my stupid school arrest but I grit my teeth and just fucking deal with it. Harley offers to start practicing with his new knives I got him for Christmas loud enough that the little freshmen assholes near us hear and scurry away.

I smile and say, "I can show you the best places to stab without making too much of a mess. DNA can be hard to completely clean off."

Harley smirks and shrugs at me. "Do tell, babe. I love hearing about your life skills. The Bay does teach girls valuable lessons."

I quirk an eyebrow at him and Blaise cackles at us both. "You two flirt like fucking serial killers, it's fucking hilarious. C'mon then, Star. Tell us where you'd stab…. that guy. The one who will die if he keeps staring at your tits like that."

The guy, who's sitting three chairs down, shits himself and darts off, leaving behind his bag, lunch, and dignity.

"I wouldn't stab him. I'd castrate him. Have you ever skinned someone before? If you do it right, it takes some time to work your way down to the layers of fat and muscle. You can technically peel a dick like a banana until there's nothing fucking left."

Blaise turns green and gags but Harley smirks, his eyes twinkling.

"Who taught you that, babe?"

I shrug. "Doc. I was thirteen and he taught me the birds and the bees. Then he rolled a corpse in and showed me all the best ways to hurt any guy who tried to touch me without consent."

Blaise nods but still looks green. He really does love his dick that much.

I finish my lunch in peace now we've subdued the sheep and Harley tucks me under his arm to walk us back to our classes. There's something about being pressed against his body, safely tucked into him, that slows my brain down and brings me some peace.

I only wish I could have it all the time.

Chapter Twenty-Seven

"What's this?" I wave at the board even though I can see exactly what it is. I'm more worried about why she has it.

Avery stops in front of it and props a hand on her hip, blowing on her coffee absently. "I feel like the best way to keep everyone on the same page about what we're dealing with is the board. I'll let the boys all know they can add to it if a new threat appears. We can't keep overlooking things because one person knows something the others don't. One board, total honesty, and fuck everyone who gets in our way."

I snort at her and take a gulp. "If a new threat appears we might need to move the boys, Diarmuid, Illi and Odie into our room. Stash them under the beds or something."

Avery grimaces. "I can't think of anything worse. Odie's fine and Illi's hot enough but Diarmuid sounds like a dick."

I smirk. "We could take bets on which guy snaps and kills him first?"

"I'd be the first. I'd pay Illi to do it for me," Avery snarks and sips at her drink.

I nod along. "I know how worried you've been about Harley. Inducting him is fucking risky and I'm still not sure how I can get out of it without making him our next threat. Snipers and sharpshooters are not people you want hunting you."

Avery squints at me, then sighs. "I want to take him out for what he said about you. What, you're the only one allowed to be protective? You're my Mounty, I'd stab anyone who implied you're a whore for loving those idiot boys. I'm still trying to figure out if I'm locking the doors and setting this place on fire after graduation or poisoning the water to take out all of the little jealous bitches here."

I blush and take another sip of my coffee. Changing the subject seems like the best idea. "What are we going to do about the Morrisons?"

She frowns. "I'm going to very slowly, and very carefully, destroy that man's business, family, and will to live. The Morrisons are clean but everyone has a price. I have some... feelers out."

Right. Feelers. Why does that make me feel fucking nervous? "Don't do anything to put yourself in danger, Aves. I can just climb through his window and slit his throat in his sleep."

Avery laughs at me, like it's all just a big joke. "I will say, getting Ash pissed off about everything that's going on was the best present you have ever given me. He's been very… motivated to help me."

Fuck, that makes me even more nervous. "What have you guys done?"

She lifts her coffee cup up for a sip. "You'll see, Mounty. You worry about your issues on the board, and I'll take care of mine."

Every time I take a breath at Hannaford and think my life is settling into a pattern something else happens to remind me that isn't my life.

We're in my least favorite class of the day when Ms. Vivienne decides to make the next move on the board in her attempts to pry Harley away from me.

She looks over the class with this smug little smirk that sets my teeth on edge and is my first warning that she's about to start her personal brand of bullshit.

"I've made some changes to the syllabus to reflect on the changes that have happened in our classroom."

What the actual fuck is she talking about?

I tense and Harley cuts me a look. He knows I've finished all of the damned assignments already and this just means more fucking work for me. This bitch. Ugh.

"We're going to discuss personal history, because that's what all of this is really about. Sometimes I think, as scholars, we can forget that in every battle and in every significant moment in history, it's all centered on people. Living breathing human beings. So, shall we discuss some of our own history?"

Fuck that with a cactus. I'm not discussing shit with her or any other rich kid in this class. A few hands raise and some girl starts spouting on about how her family got richer than god, a great opportunity for the narcissists to talk about how great they are.

I relax a little in my chair and let my mind mull over all of the plans I have going on.

"Miss Anderson, would you like to share with the class?"

I meet her eyes and the smug smile is fucking infuriating. "No, thank you."

The other students all giggle and whisper to eat other, like I'm some poor little Mounty girl to pity and poke fun at, but I ignore them all. The whispers will never end at Hannaford, no matter who my real family now is.

"I'm sorry, I worded that incorrectly. Miss Anderson, please share something about your own personal history."

I glare at her, flirting with danger because fuck it, and say, "My personal history is I grew up in Mounts Bay, worked my ass off to get a scholarship to come here, and now I'm at the top of every class because, again, I work my ass off."

She steps around her desk and stares at me, shaking her head. "That language shows your poor breeding. However I think it's commendable; most babies born addicted to heroin don't fare so well in the IQ lottery."

The breath leaks out of my lungs as the giggling starts up again.

This cunt—yeah I said it—this *fucking* cunt has looked up my medical history.

I'm proud of my steady tone when I reply, "What can I say, I'm a fucking lucky girl."

She smirks again. "You weren't so lucky when you broke your leg. How did that happen?"

I lean back in my seat and cross my arms. Harley finally snaps and says, "None of your fucking business."

Ms. Vivienne glances over at him, all doe-eyed again, and says, "Now, now, Mr Arbour. Don't let the crass language of the Mounts Bay local rub off on you."

He smirks at her. "Maybe while you were digging your fat nose into your student's private files you should've looked at mine as well. I grew up in the Bay with Lips. So *fuck off.*"

Avery giggles and the sound slices through the whispers happening around us. Ms. Vivienne looks ready to argue with us when Ash joins in the fray.

"If you don't stop, I'm going to bleed you out. Slowly."

Blaise snorts with laughter and calls out, "Shit, Beaumont never threatens pussy. You're really something *special*, Ms. Whore."

He looks back and winks at me. I'm still too stunned at Ash's words to react. Ms. Vivienne is about the same.

I watch as Ash pulls his phone out and hits play on a video he has recorded. The obscene sounds of moaning and grunting start playing.

"Oh, Ms. Vivienne, I don't see any of your high society breeding here while you're being fucked over a table by Mr. Trevelen. What does his wife think of this? The alive one I mean, not the one who's mysteriously 'disappeared'."

The whispers turn into giggling and catcalls. Ms. Vivienne's teeth clench and she takes a single step towards Ash before he stops her with a look.

He taps on the screen again and the moaning changes. "Does Trevelen know you're fucking Sebastien Steele? Does Sebastien know you're fucking his dad? And his uncle, both of whom are on the school board. Isn't that against the corruption clause? Something about keeping your dick out of school business? Hmm. Well. Maybe I should start sending these out."

"No—"

Every phone in the classroom buzzes. "Too fucking late."

Ms. Vivienne's eyes narrow at him but she keeps her head held high which is stupid. She's lost what little credibility she had in the classroom and now every student is sitting there whispering and giggling at her. Ash leans back in his chair, arms crossed and I know he's got his signature smug smirk across his mouth. Avery glances back at me and smiles, winking.

"Mr. Beaumont, that is a gross invasion—"

"So is looking up Lips' medical history and telling the whole class. So is stealing the recordings of two of your students going for a midnight swim. Fuck, I'd say nothing is as *invasive* as showing up to your study sessions with no panties and cum leaking down your legs but you didn't mind then."

My eyes flick back to Harley and he's watching Ms. Vivienne with that satisfaction that can only come from being pushed too fucking far. No panties. I could rip her fucking face off.

She dares to call my *breeding* poor?!

Her life is saved by a knock at the door and a red-faced Mr. Trevelen escorting a substitute teacher for the class.

My in-school suspension is lifted and we don't see Ms. Vivienne in our history class again.

After family dinner that Friday, I sit with Blaise while he strums our song out on his guitar. I hum softly under my breath, just enough that he can hear to tune and the smile on his face is only a little sad. I hate the miserable cloud that's hanging over him again but no playlist, make out session, or gallons of ice cream have managed to fix it yet.

"Ash told me my agent said something to you," he mumbles, and I shrug. I've been waiting for this conversation. I knew it would happen at some point.

"He's a pervert. I can't promise you I won't skin him if I see him again."

Blaise just nods and finishes off the song with a little flourish. "I'm going solo. It's just me and Finn who do everything anyway, and he's sick of Fyre trying to clean up our songs."

Finn Benson, the drummer. I try to keep my face blank like I haven't stalked the utter crap out of Blaise's career and know everything about the only other person in Blaise's life he trusts, but he smirks at me and it's clear I fail.

"You're not going to fangirl all over Finn, are you? I'll be hurt you've replaced me."

Avery scoffs at him. "No, you'll be jealous as hell because you enjoy being her idol. Besides, you can't go solo. Do you have any idea how much it would cost you to break your contract? Without your inheritance, you'll be bankrupt and begging on the streets. I think you're forgetting that you're a millionaire now, not a *billionaire*."

"I'll be fine," he says, nonchalantly shrugging and Avery's eyes narrow as she looks at her over her phone. She's been texting Atticus at all hours of the day and night, and I'm waiting for the engagement announcement. I'm sure it'll come any day and Ash will start flipping tables and stabbing people. I make a mental note to hide his weapons.

"You can't even wash dishes without guidance, Morrison, how the hell are you going to survive poverty?"

The bathroom door swings open and Ash strolls out, tucked neatly into his pajamas and I look the fuck away before I get caught drooling over him. I try to fix my eyes on my literature assignment, still spread out in front of me from where I was studying before Blaise distracted me, but Catcher in the Rye just can't compete with Ash Beaumont's nipples.

Blaise smirks at Avery and calls out to her twin, "I'm breaking my record contract and paying the company out. I'll be destitute."

Ash doesn't break his stride as he walks over to his drinks tray and pours himself a bourbon. "I'll sort out an allowance for you until you're back on your feet. It's for the Mounty, right? Harley will match it, for sure. What do your monthly expenses look like these days?"

Harley is down at the pool, putting in extra training sessions for his upcoming competition. Without Ms. Vivienne's bullshit study group he's thrown himself back into a rigorous training schedule, but he's so much fucking happier now.

Avery's scowl darkens, and when I open my mouth she shoots me a look. "You bled for your money, Lips, let the fucker *starve*. And, for that fact, Harley isn't paying *shit* after everything the Mounty did to get it back for him."

I join her on the couch and tuck my arm into hers. "His agent told me he'd enjoy his turn with me on tour. He was only disappointed it wasn't you getting passed around."

Blaise stiffens and looks up. Apparently knowing it happened and hearing the specifics are two very different things.

Avery gags dramatically. "Fine. Ash and I will pay an allowance but you better make your solo record the best damn thing anyone has ever heard."

Blaise is still looking pissed, and he only looks away from me when Ash hands him a beer. "It is. Star is going to sing on it too."

Ash sits next to me and slips a hand onto my thigh to trace little patterns while he drinks his bourbon. "And when do we get to hear this song?"

I clear my throat. "When I can sing it without puking."

Chapter Twenty-Eight

We fall into a new routine now that Harley's days aren't full of cougar flirting and bullshit study groups. Sundays become my favorite day of the week, waking up tangled up in boys and nothing on my schedule now that I've finished all of my assignments.

With Mr. Embley on the Jackal payroll and things getting worse in the Bay, Ash quits the track team and joins Harley and Blaise for their boxing sessions. He still runs but he does it in his own time.

When I try to apologize for my baggage ruining the sport for him he gives me a shitty look and snaps, "I don't give a fuck about team sports, Mounty. I was just doing it for the gym credit."

After a late breakfast, I walk Avery to her dance class and then head to the gym to meet the guys. I thank God, the universe, fate, and a million other things I don't believe in when I arrive to find all three of them stripped down to work out. *Hoo boy*, I have to talk my vagina down because I might just pass the fuck out at the sight of them.

They all snigger at me like smug fucking dicks, and I huff at them, stomping over to set up camp on the mats in front of the ring. I should have brought a coffee and ice cream because this is better than any TV show *ever*.

Harley swoops down to kiss me, dirty and raw like the urge to fight is thumping in his chest alongside his heart already, and I bite his lip in protest because I don't know what I want more; to watch him fight or to wrestle with him myself.

Oh, God.

Yes, please.

Ash smirks at my stupefied look and kisses me too, then joins Harley in the ring. He's wearing the tiny shorts again because apparently, he wants my brains to melt and leak out of my ears. They don't wait for a bell or one of us to call out or anything, they just throw themselves at each other, fists flying and grunting when they hit their mark. Watching them spar and grapple is just… porn. It's porn.

Blaise sprawls out next to me and roars with laughter when I get my phone out to record them. I ignore him because, well, a girl's gotta do.

The second Ash gets Harley on the mat I'm sweating and panting harder than they are. Harley rolls him off easily but his size isn't as much of an advantage as you'd think. Ash is fucking *quick* and brutal, completely unconcerned with the getting hurt.

I guess those're the real lessons Joey and Senior taught him. I shiver and try not to follow that thought. It'll just ruin the high of watching them.

Blaise grabs me around the waist and pulls me into his lap, one hand creeping under my oversized tee and grunting when he finds my hard nipples pushing against the thin lace of my bras.

"Are they turning you on, Star? We could fuck on the mats right here if you want to. I could eat that sweet pussy right here while you watch them," he whispers, then bites down on my shoulder as I groan.

"I've just had my suspension lifted, I can't get caught doing shit again," I mumble, and he hums against my skin as he marks me up until I squirm in his arms.

"Get off of her, dickhead. There are cameras in here," Harley calls out and Blaise curses, pulling away and glaring viciously at him. I slide out of his lap and away from his temptation. Harley shoves Ash out of the ring and glares at Blaise until he sighs, kissing me again before taking his turn.

Ash slumps down next to me; sweaty, bleeding a little, and looking fucking delicious. I hand him a bottle of water.

"We need to talk about Atticus," he says, and I groan at him.

"Why? His background check came back clean so he's Avery's business, not ours. Why are you so fucking against him? I know he's hurt Avery before but... I understand the why of it. He's clearly not a creepy pervert trying to touch fourteen-year-old girls. That's a mark in his favor and you know it."

Ash's jaw clenches. "His father buys girls like Senior does. They have similar tastes but Crawford doesn't murder his girls. Just breaks them and put them back in the auctions. I don't want someone like that around Avery."

I nod and watch Blaise and Harley jab at each other for a second. Sweet lord, it's a fucking sight to see.

I clear my throat. "I think we both know that having a piece of shit for a father doesn't automatically make you the same."

Ash shakes his head. "I don't like him. I don't trust him. You can decide for yourself at the Gala next week."

Fuck. I groan. "I forgot about that. For fuck's sake, what the hell do you think Avery is going to make me wear to a *Gala*?"

A slow smirk spreads across his face. "Oh, I'm sure I'll enjoy it."

The Gala is the same night as Harley's swimming competition and he's *pissed* he won't be coming back to the Bay with us. When he tries to convince Avery not to go she threatens him with her knife. I go take a shower to get the hell away from their spat.

I'd put money on Avery in that fight.

Once I'm dressed again, I lean on the I text Illi for back up because the thought of leaving Harley without someone to watch his back gives me hives. I might not throw a tantrum like Harley is but I'm just as pissed off.

I'll watch the little mobster. Have fun in your pouffy dresses and flower crowns. You know that's what they wear to those fancy parties, right?

I stare down at my phone in horror. Now, he could be fucking with me, but he's also lived in the Bay his whole life and there's every chance he's been to a Gala before.

He'd have been there to kill someone but he could've seen the dress code.

I feel sick.

I must look fucking bad when I step out of the bathroom because Avery stops mid-rant and says, "What's happened?"

I look up at her and croak, "What's the fucking dress code tomorrow night? I refuse to wear anything flowery or that a wouldn't look out of place on a Disney princess. Avery, I have a reputation to uphold."

She blinks at me like I've lost my mind. "I would never make you wear a flowery dress. I'll have to tell Morrison to stop planning your wedding though. I'm sure he's planning to get you into a full skirt."

She cackles like an evil witch at the face I pull but I let out the breath I was holding and send Illi a savage text back.

What a *dick*.

The next day, Harley kisses me at the Maserati, pressing me against the closed door like he wants to imprint himself on my skin and keep my safe.

"Promise me you won't go anywhere without Ash or Blaise. Promise me, babe," he murmurs against my lips, ignoring Avery cussing him out from the front seat.

"I will. I promise. You need to be careful as well, Annabelle has signed up to help with the time trials so she'll be stalking your ass the entire time you're away."

He smirks and sucks on my bottom lip, rolling it with his teeth gently like he's trying to stop himself from eating me. "You own my ass, babe, she can't have it. Send me photos of the dress and tell Morrison if he tries to fuck you at the buffet to outdo me, I'll skin him."

I blush and nudge him away, glaring at him while he opens the car door and tucks me in like he's a chivalrous gentleman. Dread pools in my gut but I don't know what it is that's freaking me out so much, we've been separated before and there haven't been any new threats.

I wave at him as we take off, Blaise blasting some techno crap just to get a rise out of Avery, but I can't look away from Harley's slowly shrinking form.

"What's wrong?" Ash whispers, but I shake my head.

I'm being stupid. But I also trust my gut.

I flick a text to Illi to tell him we've left and then I try to focus on the conversation happening around me.

I hope I'm wrong, but that feeling tells me something fucking bad is going to happen.

That feeling says I won't see Harley again.

Chapter Twenty-Nine

The dress Avery puts me in is fucking ridiculous.

There's so much delicate lace covering my arms and my shoulders that I feel like a fraud. I'm not a lace person, I wear booty shorts and band tees for fuck's sake! Avery clucks at me like I'm an unruly child and I sulk a little because why the fuck not. The slit up the skirt is a plus though, all the way up one thigh, making it impossible to wear underwear without revealing it. I quirk an eyebrow at Avery and she shrugs, smug as fuck.

One look at Ash's eyes when I walk out and I remember why Avery is *the* evil dictator in power.

Blaise smirks at him, muttering about drooling, before kissing my cheek sweetly and holding an arm out for Avery to take. He looks sharp in the suit, the new ink on his hands and neck a statement to the crowd of higher society we're about the walk into.

I'm so fucking proud of him.

Ash waits until Blaise and Avery move to the door before stalking over to me, his icy blue eyes stripping me, layer by layer, until I feel like he's exposed my soul.

"Fuck the Gala. We're staying here," he snaps, and Avery snarls from the door at him.

"Keep it in your *fucking* pants! I'm here for Atticus and you *promised* me you'd be on your best behavior."

His eyes squeeze shut like Avery is sucking the life out of him and I scoff at him. "We can go down for an hour and then come back up. Blaise will probably drink like a fish and watch out for her."

He glares at me for taking Avery's side but tucks me under his arm anyway. Blaise shoots me these lusty looks over his shoulder and I know he's doing it to piss Ash off, the little fucker. When we get to the elevator and step in he says, "I'm not drinking tonight, Star. Atticus is a dickhead but he's also a fucking pussy for Avery so we can leave her with him. I'm pulling that dress off of you."

I glare at him but Avery takes his comments a little harder than I do and stomps on his foot with her stiletto heel. He grunts and cuts her a look that has me cringing. She's going to stab him. Or choke him out now I've taught her the best ways to do it.

"I'm taking you down, I'm bringing you back, you're sleeping in my bed," Ash says, breaking their intense face-off, his voice steely, and Blaise breaks eye contact to glare at him too. Ash nods like he's won and the elevator door slides open, his hand curved possessively over my hip.

I feel a little like I'm walking on stilts and, although I'm not totally happy with the caveman glares Ash is throwing at Blaise right now, I'm grateful he's holding me because I'm sure I'd be on my ass by now without him.

Avery smirks at the sheep as we pass. It doesn't matter that they're all twenty-plus years older than us, they all stare at her like she has an executioner's order with their name on it.

I fucking love it.

It's nice to see those looks directed at someone else and to know that I'm not alone in my infamy. Avery Beaumont has already carved a place for herself in high society as a force to be feared *and* reckoned with.

"I'm going to find Atticus. Blaise, you may as well stay here and dance with your girlfriend because I won't tolerate your moping," Avery says, smiling sweetly at me and then sashays towards the bar. They serve her, knowing full well she's only seventeen, and Blaise trails after her.

"Do you want a drink, Mounty?" Ash murmurs in my ear, and I shiver at the warmth of his breath dancing down my neck.

I clear my throat. "Why not, I'll have a whiskey."

Ash jerks his head at Blaise and then he walks me over to one of the sitting areas. The plush lounge feels expensive and I'm instantly uncomfortable perched on it. What if I spill something on it and it's worth thousands? Rich people are stupid.

"Stop frowning at everything," Ash says, as his fingers dance along the slit in my dress. He murmurs happily when he finds my skin and then groans when he realizes I'm *only* wearing the dress.

"Are you trying to fucking kill me? The crowd here is a little less oblivious to public sex acts but I'm sure we could find a bathroom somewhere. I'll even let the brat join in this time," he snaps right as Blaise walks up with our drinks.

"How fucking *kind* of you. Here's your bourbon, asshole, next time get your own," he snarls and then drops down on my other side until I'm wedged between them both. I sip the whiskey quietly, trying not to get involved in their drama.

Everyone around us is wearing hundreds of thousands of dollars worth of clothing and I don't want to think about where the decimal point would land on the jewelry. The women all float around like this is the highlight of their year and the men all eye them predatorily. This party is the same as the ones in the Bay, just better dressed and less open. I'm positive there are drugs being used, crime being organized, and if there isn't some dirty fucking going on secretly somewhere then I'll be damned.

I let my gaze continue their path around the room when I spot Avery and the man with his arms around her waist, holding her against his chest.

My heart stops.

I scramble to grab Ash's arm, tugging to get his attention, and he frowns when he sees my face.

"Who is that with Avery?" I croak and he jerks to look in the same direction I am.

"That's Atticus. Fuck, Mounty, you scared me. I thought she was being fucking attacked by the look on your face," he snaps, and I glance away from the horror in front of me.

"Blaise, go get her. Now. Go get her and meet us back at the room. Don't be obvious about it, say I'm sick or something. Just get her," I ramble, and Blaise nods, moving quickly away.

Ash's face turns thunderous and I tug him off of our seat. I get us both moving out of the room as quickly as I can in these stupid fucking heels.

"What the fuck is going on, Mounty?" He growls and I shake my head, moving as quickly as I can. We get to the elevator at the same time Blaise pulls an enraged Avery along behind him. When she looks up and sees me she freezes.

"You don't look sick but you don't look okay, what's happened?" Avery says softly, tucking her arm into mine.

The elevator door opens and I pull her in, jabbing at our floor number violently as if that will make the thing move faster. As the doors slowly shut behind us I glance up and make eye contact with Atticus Crawford.

The Crow of Mounts Bay.

"I am not leaving this elevator until you tell me what the fuck is going on, Lips," Avery says, and although her words are sure, her voice shakes.

She's guessed what the problem is.

"I know Atticus. I know how he makes his money, I know why he wouldn't let you intern with him, I know *everything* about the world he lives in, Avery, and I need to get you out of here."

Avery's eyes well up but she doesn't let the tears fall as she gives me a curt nod, stalking down the hall the second the elevator doors open. Ash grabs my elbow and pulls me into his body sharply.

"Who *the fuck* is he, Lips? Tell me right now."

"I'm not telling you before I tell her, now let me go. We need to get her out of here," I snap back and jerk my arm away from him. He shouldn't be arguing with me, he *knows* I always put her safety first.

Once we're back in the hotel room, I snatch my shoes off of my feet and try to herd Avery towards our room. "You need to pack. We have to leave now, he saw me. He knows that I know."

Avery nods but she stays put, her face calm and blank now she's had a second to compose herself. "Who is he? I have to know."

I glance back to find Blaise and Ash standing in front of the door like they're waiting for someone to break it down. With the empire, Atticus controls he fucking could.

"He's the Crow. He's a member of the Twelve. He's more powerful than any person in our world, except for the Jackal, but even they are equal. He's the one I called the favor in with to keep Senior away from you because I knew he had ties in the upper class."

Avery's lip quivers just a little but her eyes stay dry and unwavering on my face. "What does he do? Why are you so afraid of him? You said the Crow deals in information, why does that mean we have to leave?"

I open my mouth to answer her when my phone begins to buzz on the coffee table. Dread trickles down my spine and I move to answer it.

I know it's him before I pick it up.

"Which room are you in? We need to talk."

I squeeze my eyes shut but my voice is steady. "We're leaving. We're going back to Hannaford. Avery is under my protection and if you want to discuss the parameters of that protection with me, we can do it at the next meeting."

He sighs down the phone. "Open the door, Wolf."

The smiling man that was holding Avery gently against his chest is not the man we open the hotel door to. This man is purely the Crow.

Avery is sitting, rigid and scowling, on the plush living room chair and I position myself a few feet in front of her, the guys flanking me. Ash is trembling with rage and blood lust, ready to just kill the Crow and be done with it. He never trusted him in the first place. Blaise takes one look at Ash and rocks back on his heels, ready to throw down the second this all turns to shit.

The Crow steps forward and inclines his head to me respectfully but the cold, cutting edge of his gray eyes rake over me like he's planning on bleeding me out for this. Fuck. Has Avery just been some pawn in his game for power? A Beaumont on his arm and in his bed?

Joke's on him. He picked the wrong girl, in the wrong family.

"I already told you we're leaving," I say, my voice pitched low and even.

His gaze stays fixed on mine as he kicks the door shut, and even though he's moving smoothly I can see the tension in him. My mind runs through every little scrap of information Avery has ever told me about her crush, the man who has become her obsession.

I wonder what his father would think if he knew the power his son had amassed. The conversation I'd had with Ash earlier flashes back to me. He's probably just like his disgusting father.

"I'm not leaving here without her. Name your price," the Crow says, and fuck if that isn't the worst thing to say.

"*She's not for fucking sale!*" Ash hisses and there it is; the ruthless, killer Beaumont blood. Threaten Avery and you'll push Ash right into the dark place that exists in his soul. The darkness that lives in him and burns in his eyes when his mask slips. The same fire his father and brother both use to destroy women, Ash uses to protect Avery.

I know I'm pushing my luck when I hold up my hand to stop him. His eyes break away from the Crow for a second to aim that fire at me. Blaise stiffens next to me and I can practically feel the heat of his glare swing around to narrow in on Ash, not liking the shitty attitude one bit.

This is big. This moment could change everything between us all. Ash is holding a grenade and toying with the pin if he doesn't trust me now then this relationship, and I suspect our family, are going to be blown to pieces. I hold his gaze and I *pray*.

His eyes don't lower. He doesn't back down at all.

A tiny crack starts on my heart and then he crosses his arms and swings back to face the Crow. I don't know if he's chosen to trust me or not but I have to follow through. I have to make sure we're all safe. I glance back at Avery and I see it in her eyes that she knows. She trusts me to get us all out of this safely.

"How much? How much is she worth to you?" I say coolly.

The Crow's eye never leave mine. He doesn't so much as glance at her. Another black mark against him. "Three favors."

Fuck.

Fuck.

This man never gives out favors. I've had three favors from him already but those were torn from him in moments of true desperation, for things only I could do for him. For him to offer me three for Avery alone... *fuck.*

I shake my head at him and he grits his teeth.

"Six but I'll have your word that you will never tell the Jackal about her."

I freeze.

The Crow *never* breaks the rules of the Twelve and that's pretty fucking close to crossing a line. That's not what I'm expecting at all. Granted we all keep our cards pretty close to our chests but it's the unwritten law that we never conspire and scheme against each other. I know he's been biding his time, waiting to take the Jackal out, but he's *always* played by the rules. Even now the Jackal's gone fucking rogue. What the hell is he playing at?

I look at him then, a proper once over without the rage clouding my eyes.

His face is blank and unreadable but his body speaks loud enough. His fists are clenched, his shoulders stiff, and his elbows are bent slightly like he's poised ready to attack. He's not the Crow, here to buy some skin for the night like his father would or a pawn in the game we're all playing. He's Atticus and he's waging a war for Avery. The feelings he's had for her are real, real enough that he's here for her, risking the wrath of the Twelve and losing the empire he's built.

I take a step forward and when his chin lifts I narrow my eyes at him, the tension in the room crackling like electricity.

"You're in love with her, aren't you, Atticus?" His eyes narrow to slits at the sound of his real name. I've broken protocol but I don't give a fuck. He's going to have to come clean if he wants to leave this room with any sort of a relationship with Avery.

Or his life, because Ash is fucking teetering.

"I told you, I'll—" he starts but I cut him off.

"She's not for sale. Not to you, not to Matteo, not to anyone. Either admit you're here because you have real, genuine feelings for her or leave. And to be perfectly clear, there is *nothing* I wouldn't do to keep her safe. I'll risk the Twelve if I have to."

His eyes finally leave mine and swing down to land on Avery. I see it then, the feeling in my gut is right, he looks at her like she's the center of his world. He looks at her with longing and sweetness and worship. He's here to *save her from me.*

His eyes only get more vicious when they cut back in my direction but he softens at the sound of Avery's voice, "The Wolf is my family, Atticus. I'm not leaving with you."

Some of the tension in Ash eases a little like he was afraid Avery would skip off into the sunset with this guy and he'd lose her forever. I make a note to talk to him *again* about letting her make her own fucking choices.

The Crow slips away, something I've never seen another member of the Twelve do, and it's Atticus standing there with us again.

"You can't let Matteo know about her, or what she means to me. He'll fucking destroy her. It's bad enough she's with you." He sinks down in the armchair and rubs his hands over his face. The room seems to take a deep breath.

"You don't need to explain to me what that man does to innocent girls when he has an agenda," I whisper, and regret flashes on his face so quickly I think I might have imagined it.

He chuckles darkly, "I guess I should remember that better than anyone. I was there when he snapped your leg with his bare hands. What were you, twelve years old?"

Blaise's hand runs down the inside of my arm until he threads his fingers through mine, tugging me back until I'm back at his side. I don't want to look at any of them while we talk about the damage done to me. "Thirteen. I was thirteen and I had just won the Game. He told me he wanted to teach me how to deal with pain but really he was trying to break me in. Nothing he hates more than a female he can't break."

"Well, he didn't break you, did he? Here you stand with two Beaumonts and the richest kid in the country. You've inducted the heir to the O'Cronin family into your fold and let's not forget the Butcher. I'd wager *this* wasn't Matteo's plan."

I chuckle, a little shocked that I have it in me to do so, and then I sit on the couch, tugging Blaise down with me. Avery moves to sit with us, perching on the arm of the couch stiffly, and then, slowly, Ash joins us. When he slips his hand to rest on my thigh my shoulders finally relax. Atticus watches us all carefully.

"I was under the impression you were with the O'Cronin kid? That's what Matteo thinks anyway. I heard a rumor of… more but I thought that was just his delusions."

I feel a blush start and Avery scoffs at me. "Seriously? We're in a life-threatening situation and you're getting all shy about your harem of obsessed boys?"

Blaise nudges Avery's leg with his shoulder and cackles at her. "Leave her alone, she's used to being a badass under pressure."

Atticus watches her the exact way that Harley watched me during our sophomore year, back when I was oblivious to want it meant. God, I was so fucking blind. "This isn't a life-threatening situation, Avery. As long as you are safe, I'm not going to do anything. The last time I saw the Wolf I knew things had changed between her and the Jackal but I couldn't risk being wrong. I couldn't leave your fate up to chance because the Jackal would do things to you that I've spent *years* making sure your father didn't fucking do."

Atticus's voice is kind and gentle. It's fucking weird. I've only been around him a handful of times and he's always a cold, ruthless dick. Probably because I was always with Matteo.

Avery stares over at him like he's a stranger to her and if I didn't hate his guts for lying to her, I'd feel sorry for him.

She is ride or die, and I think Atticus is now firmly on her shit list.

"It's Lips, and I'm not Matteo's protégé or girlfriend or whatever it is that the Twelve think. He sponsored me for the Game and he's helped me out but he's also done things to me that I can't ever forgive or forget. I went to Hannaford to figure a way out. That's what we're doing, we're finding a way out of all of this."

Atticus nods and rubs his chin. He looks older than twenty-two but then he's the leader of one of the largest criminal organizations in the state, possibly the country. Rivaled only by the Jackal's numbers. I had never thought to approach him for help in getting away from Matteo, his cold manner making me wary. I'm starting to see that was a mistake.

Avery hesitates for a moment and then asks with a surprisingly strong voice, "You were at the meeting with Lips and Harley, do you think the Jackal is going to continue to send people to kill him?"

Classic Avery; she's just found out the guy she's been in love with for half her life has been lying to her and she's instantly thinking about what information she can mine for the protection of her family. I both love her and want to shake her. She should be chewing this fucker out.

"He's in less danger now he's under her protection. He was on very limited time with his grandfather before then, despite my efforts. Matteo can't just kill him, he has to find some sort of betrayal or dishonesty to be able to take him out. He doesn't just answer to the Wolf if he does, he answers to the Twelve. He's a big player but he's not the biggest and definitely not bigger than us all."

"And what if he continues to try to kill him stealthily?" Avery continues. "I'm sure you're aware he's spiraling and recruiting."

Atticus grins and cocks an eyebrow at me. Again, I blush which is fucking ridiculous.

"Oh, after the Wolf's declaration at the meeting the Jackal has been served a severe warning about touching her toys. The rest of the Twelve are much more aware of his… instability now. Those who have chosen his side are in as much danger as he is."

I ignore the look Atticus is giving me, and lean forward in my chair. "If I induct these three as well, would you be willing to back me up in the meetings if Matteo starts with his shit?"

Ash's leg tenses against mine. I haven't spoken to him about this but I know how badly Avery wants it. It's a move on the board against their father. He could no longer threaten them without risking the wrath of the lower criminal organizations. Lower in social standing but certainly dangerous to him and his business.

Atticus stands and runs a hand down the front of his suit jacket. A slow smile forms on his lips and he suddenly looks closer to his age. "If you cut yourself off from the Jackal and start calling *me* when you need help instead of him, then I will take him on with you. Induct them, keep Avery safe from the Jackal and her father, and I will offer my help with *anything* from this moment onwards. Whatever the cost."

That's *exactly* what we need.

I glance up at Avery. This is her choice, if she doesn't want to trust this guy ever again then we'll figure something else out. If I decide for her then I'm just as terrible as everyone else in her life.

She's staring at Atticus, her eyes guarded and her mouth turned down a little. I'm not sure he'll ever be able to repair the damage this has done to her trust of him. She sighs and gives me a little nod. I look at Blaise and he leans in to kiss me under the ear, sweet and sure. Then I take a deep breath and turn to Ash. He's looking at my thigh, where his fingers are drawing lazy circles on the skin exposed by the deep slit in the dress. I wait him out, this isn't something I'd ever rush. This is lifelong. As long as I breathe, I am the Wolf. If he chooses this then he will be tied to me forever. His fingers still and then he gives me the smallest squeeze.

"Done," I say to Atticus, and he shoots a resigned smile at Avery, who stares back at him like she's plotting his death, before turning to the door.

He hesitates for a second and then turns back to me. "Don't ever let her wear red again. She wears your color or mine."

And then he's gone.

Blaise gets up and locks the door behind him and Avery slides down to take his seat, her hand finding mine.

"His color is black. Mine is white," I murmur and she nods.

"I'm guessing the Jackal's is red from that little display. I'll burn it all. What does induction look like? If you tell me I have to be naked or bleed I'm pulling out. My brother too, I'm not having him frolicking around the city in the nude."

"Should have told him that earlier," Blaise murmurs and then laughs at the glare he gets from Ash.

"It's done. I told the Crow, he passes it on. It's weird but, yeah, it's that simple."

Chapter Thirty

My phone wakes me at three.

I have to struggle my way out from under Ash to reach it, and when I see it's Harley I answer immediately.

"What's happened?" I whisper, not wanting to wake Ash if it's nothing serious.

The line stays quiet, I can hear a rhythmic rustling, a sort of swishing noise, but nothing to tell me what the hell is going on. I sit and just listen for a second, and realize his phone is in his pocket and the noise is the sound of his pants as he walks.

I'm on edge immediately.

Why is he walking around at this time? Why has he called me only to put his phone in his pocket? Butt dialing isn't really a thing anymore, is it? Is he in danger?

What the fuck has happened in the last three hours?

I keep the phone to my ear and climb over Ash, who's the deepest sleeper out of all of us and barely mumbles as my weight hits his chest. I grab his phone and then use his finger to unlock it, like some creepy stalker girlfriend but fuck it, this feels like an emergency.

I fucking hope it's not an emergency.

I dial Illi's number with my heart in my throat.

"What's happened?" he answers, an echo of my own worry.

"Do you still have eyes on Arbour? Something is wrong."

Illi grunts and starts to move. The swishing noise in the other phone stops, and a door opens and then shuts.

He swears low and colorful under his breath. "He's just taken a girl into his room, kid. Fuck. He's clearly fucking wasted, she's practically holding him up, but cheating's fucking cheating. I didn't fucking see him doing this, he's so fucking taken with you. Fuck. You need me to kill him? I can do it with a bullet, nice and quick if you feel squeamish about it," Illi says, gentle in a way I didn't know he had in him.

But fuck that.

I know Harley and I fucking trust him.

"No killing, no matter what. Go and get a look at what the fuck is happening in that room."

Ash grunts and his eyes open, an arm winding around my waist before his eyes even open. He blinks up at me and frowns when he sees his phone at my ear. I cut him a look and, thankfully, he keeps his mouth shut.

"Right. I'm outside the room and - *FUCK!*"

502

The booming sound of a door being kicked in startles Ash and he sits up, his arm keeping me stable on top of him.

"What the fuck?" he mouths at me and I swallow roughly.

"Harley," I croak, my eyes welling up, and Ash can't contain the vicious curses that spill out of his mouth.

He sets me down on the bed and starts pulling his clothes on, yelling for Blaise and Avery. I can't move. I can't do anything until I know Harley is alive and safe. Whatever the fuck has happened I'm frozen until I know he's okay.

But the second I know he is, someone is going to fucking *bleed* tonight.

Through Harley's phone, I can hear screaming and sobbing. I recognize it immediately and look up to find the others, dressed and ready, waiting for me to tell them what the fuck is going on.

"Annabelle *fucking* Summers. I don't know what's happened but Illi's there and she's sobbing," I croak and Avery collapses on the bed next to me. Her eyes are wide and when she tucks her arm into mine I can feel the tremble running through her.

"Call 911, you dumb fucking slut!" Illi roars, and Harley's phone makes a scratching noise before the line goes dead.

Holy fucking shit.

Avery's shoulders shake and Ash yanks her up off the bed as Blaise pulls me to stand. I protest, I don't want to hang up, but he maneuvers me into a pair of yoga pants. Then he hoists me into his arms and carries me like I weigh nothing.

"We're going to him. Tell me once you know where the ambulance is taking him."

I nod and he sets me back onto my feet in the elevator. Avery is taking deep, shuddering breaths, and Ash is scowling, his hands clenching.

It takes us over an hour to get to the hospital, even though Blaise drives like a fucking maniac the entire way. I can't think, or breathe, or function. My mind just keeps playing Illi's voice over and over again, the urgency when he screamed for Annabelle to call 911. The dread in my gut has grown, spread down through my limbs until I walk into the hospital lobby on numb legs. Only Blaise's strong arm banded around my waist keeps me upright.

Avery snarls at the reception staff until they tell us Harley is in emergency room. My brain sort of shut off after that, like a rage blackout except I can see Avery nodding and taking in all the information for me while I freak the fuck out. Then we're directed to the waiting room.

Illi is already there, vomit and blood covering his clothes.

I could fucking pass out.

He looks at me with such fucking sorrow for a second I want to punch him. He nods at me. "This way kid. I've got what you need in here."

I stupidly think he's taking me to see Harley but no. He directs me over to a supply cupboard and jiggles the door until the lock pops. Inside, Annabelle goddamn Summer's is hogtied. All trussed up like a turkey at Thanksgiving, and what good luck because I'm going to fucking carve her up.

Illi motions me in and then I block everything out, every sound, sight, and smell while I stare down the pathetic *whore* who's tried to take Harley from me. If he dies…

no. I can't even think about it. He's going to live. He has to.

I step forward and yank the gag out of her mouth, watching with grim satisfaction as she tries to swallow and winces.

"What the fuck did you do to him?" There's nothing human left in my voice.

She whimpers pathetically.

"Tell me," I say, and she sneers at me, all the fake simpering vanishing like the manipulative skank she is.

Eclipse Starbright Anderson ceases to exist. I don't know who takes her place because the Wolf has *nothing* on the deadly rage that takes over me. I stay completely aware as I pin Annabelle to the wall by her throat. I watch with a detached sort of fascination when her eyes light up with terror and, as my hands tighten around her neck, her face darkens until she looks almost purple.

I only squeeze harder.

I don't notice the argument happening behind me until a large, colorful hand wraps around my wrist and a broken voice croons softly in my ear, "Let go, Star."

I shake my head. I'll never fucking let her go again.

She dies *today*.

"She can't speak if she's dead," he says calmly, and my grip loosens a fraction. I must have spoken that thought out loud.

Her eyes are still bulging as she sucks in air, and she fixes her gaze over my shoulder like she always fucking does. No one else matters to this fucking despicable, money-hungry whore but the guys she's fixated on. My *fucking* guys.

"Blaise, please—" She gurgles and he cuts her off.

"Just get the facts out of her so we can get back to Arbour. That's where we need to be, babe."

Babe. Only Harley ever calls me that. My lip threatens to wobble but it's like my emotions are just out of reach. Annabelle's eyes stay glued to Blaise like I'm not even there, pinning her to the wall by her throat. I can't get what I need like this. She won't look at me with Blaise in the room.

"I'll get the truth. You should go."

Blaise moves his hand from my wrist to my hip, covering my body with his own until I'm surrounded by him. "I'm not leaving you with this cunt. I don't care what you do to her; I'm with you."

Annabelle starts fucking crying and I can't contain my snarl at her. "She won't focus with you in the room. She'll just spout her usual fucking lies."

Blaise grunts and shifts on his feet like he's going to put up a fight. Illi speaks up from the doorway. "Go on, kid. I'll watch your girl and you can go help the other one watch over the Crow's little ice queen. Nothing will touch her with me around, I'll see to it."

When the door clicks shut Illi speaks, "The doctors said he was dosed with ketamine. A dirty batch."

This fucking *cunt.*

I stare her down but there's no remorse in her. "So you were going to rape him?"

She scoffs at me. "Girls can't rape guys! I just needed him to forget about *you* and your fucking *magical slum pussy* for an hour and then we could be together again. Everything was finally working out; he has his money and we could be together without the other two. How the fuck was I supposed to know the pills would do this?"

She's dead.

The second I have the story out of her, I'm gutting her. Nice and slow. Clean up will be a bitch but, fuck it, I'll call in a favor and the Bear can pin it on some underling of his. While I'm plotting her disembowelment she continues on her little rant until something she says pings in my memory.

"What dealer?"

She sputters to a stop. "What? Some guy. What does it matter? He was from the slums like you and gave me the pill in a little bag."

Slums.

The Bay.

My voice shakes. "Show me."

"What?"

"*Show me the fucking bag!*" I hiss at her.

She fumbles around in her pocket before dropping the little clear bag on my palm. I know it's the Jackal's before I turn it over and see his insignia. Even with Illi taking out the stream of underlings the Jackal hired he's still found a crack in our defense.

I stare at her, long enough that it finally dawns on her that she's utterly defenseless, hogtied in a closet with a murderous girl and her thug-looking mountain of a friend.

She's fucked.

"Look, I didn't fucking know it would do this to him! I just wanted him back!" She sobs, and I feel fucking nothing but icy bloodlust pumping through my veins. I drop my hands away from her and start to look for my knife. Blaise had grabbed it and stashed it in his pocket for me while I'd been frozen in fear, waiting with my phone pressed against my ear. Illi steps up and takes my arm, pulling me out of the room and into the hallway, pushing me until I find myself wrapped in Blaise's arms.

"I'll sort this for you, kid. It's my job and my fucking pleasure to take care of this for you."

I stare at him, cold and detached. He nods at me like he knows how blank I am inside.

"She fucked with the wrong family. I'll treat her with the same *patience* and *understanding* as you did with the guy who bid on Odie. Stay with your mobster kid. I'll check on you guys when it's done."

He ushers us back out to the waiting room and at the last moment, he grabs Ash's arm. Ash stares at him with the rage that's filling every fiber of his being. If anyone else did that Illi would thumb their eyes out, but he just nods at him with respect. "Welcome to the family. We're going to burn this place to the fucking ground."

And then he leaves with a deftness no man his size should have.

Ten minutes later, we're all still sitting in the waiting room when Diarmuid shows up. He takes one look at me and collapses on a chair across from us.

"Liam?" He snarls.

I shake my head. "Matteo."

He nods and unsheathes his favorite knife. Blaise tenses for a second but the Irish bastard pulls out a whetstone and begins to sharpen the blade. It's an old habit, something he does when he's plotting. I don't know how we're going to do it, but the Jackal just signed his own death warrant.

505

Five hours later they finally let us in to see him.

The overpowering smell of the disinfectant burns my nostrils and my chest tightens instantly. The beeping of the machines monitoring him just makes me want to scream and fucking chase Annabelle down, slamming a knife through her gut before Illi gets the chance. He would have already taken care of it but fuck, I wish I would have fought a little harder to make the kill myself.

Blaise helps me climb onto the bed next to Harley as Ash lifts wires and tubes out of my way without unplugging anything. It's a tight fit with how big he is but I make it work. Avery sits in the chair by the window and watches me with vacant eyes.

It's not until I cry that her soul seems to come back to her body. The tears start as silent streams of salty liquid, leaving tracks down my face. Then comes the sniffling until finally, my whole body is trembling at the force of the sobs I'm desperately keeping in.

I'm taking today.

I'm giving myself today to lay here with him and touch him and know that he's alive. Tomorrow I'm going to start a war, I'll call in every last favor until the blood pours like fucking rivers through the streets of Mounts Bay and every damn man, woman, and child knows to stay the fuck away from my family. But today is for Harley.

Hours pass like that, me crying into his chest, while the others all try to find some comfort on the cheap, spindly plastic chairs. Blaise eventually passes out on the floor, his jacket balled up under his head, and Ash sprawls out over four chairs with his head in Avery's lap.

I am nothing but blind rage and gut-wrenching fear.

"I've never seen you cry before." Avery looks absently out the window and strokes at Ash's hair. I don't speak, I can't open my mouth without the sobs coming out messily, so she continues. "I've always known you liked them. I mean, you protect them all so fucking fiercely, it's obvious it's not just for my sake. I just... I didn't realize you loved him like this."

I take a minute to wipe my eyes and collect myself. It takes every last ounce of my strength I have left.

"I've never given anyone the power to break me. Harley is... on paper, he's the worst choice for me. He's a mobster's son. He's from the Bay. He's lived in the world that has tried to kill me every fucking day of my life. He's a killer, he has that darkness in him that every single man in my life so far has used to hurt me. Trying to get away from that life means he's the *worst* option. But he's... a part of me. It goes so far beyond having my heart. Hearts can be broken, torn out, fucking burned. Harley owns a part of my soul and, if he wanted to, he could destroy me in ways Matteo never fucking could. They all do, Aves. It's why I couldn't fucking choose in that bathroom back when you asked me because how do I choose between the parts of my soul?"

I lift my eyes to her and I feel the calm settle back over me. "Avery, I'm not going to take careful steps anymore. I'm going to wipe the fucking board clean until there isn't a threat left. I'm going to take out the Jackal, the O'Cronins, Senior, fucking *Morningstar himself* if I have to. Every single one of them will die before I let this happen again."

Avery's eyes stay fixed on mine, unblinking and unflinching in her resolve. "I would watch the whole world burn to keep our family safe, Lips. I'm calling Atticus.

I don't forgive him and I don't want him anymore, but I'll use him until every last threat is gone. We're done playing it safe and keeping the body count low. Whatever it takes, to the end."

Chapter Thirty-One

Harley doesn't wake up for two awful, gut-wrenching, devastating days.

I don't leave his side, only getting out of the bed when the nurses need me to, and Avery works her magic to have supplies brought to us.

Ash takes up watch by the door like he thinks the Jackal is going to come down here personally to finish Harley off. I think he's actually hoping the fucking sociopath will. We all want him dead in the worst way for this.

Blaise only lasts a few hours before he rigs up a stereo and starts singing the most ridiculous songs. When Avery snaps at him he shrugs and says, "Quickest way to wake him up is to piss him off, and nothing pisses him off like my taste in music."

I could cry all over again but my tears have all dried up.

Now there's nothing but rage left in me. Rage at the Jackal, rage at Annabelle, rage I didn't kill her myself. Rage that he won't wake up. I need him, dammit. I fucking need him.

When he finally opens his eyes Avery is busy fussing with his blankets while I'm cuddled up on his chest, making sure his damn heart is still beating.

"Fuck, Harley! Lips, he's awake!" Avery shrieks, and my neck damn near breaks as I snap upright to get a look at his bleary eyes, doped up and fussy.

He's never looked fucking better in his whole life.

Avery jabs at the call button for the nurse as I lay there just staring at him like an idiot because I can't fucking move or think now he's awake.

"What's wrong, babe?" he mumbles, slurring a little, and I kiss him gently.

"Nothing. Everything is going to be fine. Just rest," I whisper against his cheek, and he nods.

The nurse bustles in and Avery starts to snap out orders at her, ever the dictator. The nurses all tiptoe around her, having learned on day one of our stay not to piss her off. Ash helps me off of the bed so the nurse can check Harley's vital signs and reflexes now he's awake.

I stand by the bed, ready to stab the bitch if she so much as flinches in his direction because now I'm convinced everyone is a fucking Jackal spy. Avery does the same, even though she liased with Atticus to have the hospital swept clean before the surgery was even over.

When the nurse mumbles she's happy with his reactions, she starts to mess around with his IVs and Diarmuid walks in, Illi on his heels looking pissed the fuck off.

Diarmuid gives a wry smile when he sees Harley's eyes open and reaches out to sling an arm around me. I flinch away from him, I don't want to be touched by anyone but my family and I don't trust this asshole. Not one bit.

"*Don't fucking touch her.*" Ash hisses and Diarmuid snaps away from me.

"Right. I'm just here to check if my nephew is okay. Now I can see he's awake I'll leave you all to it. Call me if you need help making this right, Wolfie."

I shake my head at him and he leaves, Illi glaring at his retreating back. Once he's out of sight I share a look with Illi. He doesn't trust him either.

"How your boy, kid?" he murmurs, and I nod.

"He's awake and he's going to be fine. I need you to clear your calendar for the summer. We're going hunting."

A week later, we travel back to Hannaford in the Maserati and I clutch Harley's hand in my own like he'll somehow slip away without my touch. Ash notices my anxiety and slips his hand around my thigh, what little weight I was managing to keep now gone so there's not much for him to get a hold of.

Blaise drives much steadier and slower than normal, and Avery stays glued to her phone the entire time. When I'd told Harley the truth of who the Crow really is he'd snarled at Avery to ditch him. It's a testament to how worried we've all been about him that she let him go with nothing but a kiss on the cheek for his troubles.

It's mid-afternoon on a Tuesday, so when we pull up there isn't a person in sight.

Harley is grouchy as fuck, irritated to be fussed over and when Blaise offers to carry him back up to our rooms he snarls and takes a swing at him.

Blaise just laughs because everyone is fucking relieved to be out of that fucking hospital room.

Avery and I are a little more discreet in our fussing, but we're still fucking fussing. Avery's fingers fly over the screen on her phone as she covers for our absences and plots out our next move. I watch Harley's every step as if he's going to drop dead any second and when we get to the stairs right as classes let out for the day, I death glare every single student who dares come near us.

I can't trust that the Jackal hasn't sent someone else to finish the job.

The whispers follow us; about Annabelle's absence, the takedown of Ms. Vivienne, why we've been gone. I try my best not to roll my eyes at them but Ash is openly smirking like a smug dick about it all. When I jab him in the ribs he shrugs, "I'm just enjoying the theories of the sheep. Imagine their faces if they knew the truth."

He's not wrong.

Blaise and Ash go back to their room and I coax Harley back to our room with the promise of ice cream and coffee. He doesn't give a shit about either of them, I start to suspect he's just humoring me. It's only after dinner I find out his real plan.

"Over my dead fucking body are you going to swim training. I will knock your ass out."

He frowns at me, cutting a look at Avery like she'll help him but she's firmly Team Sit-The-Fuck-Down. "I'm going fucking insane, babe. You gotta ease up."

There's no way I can let him out of my sight without the panic clawing at me.

Instead of admitting any of that I glare at him and point to the couch. "Sit your ass down and don't move. Your doctor said no swimming for another week, *so no fucking swimming for another week.*"

He growls at the two of us, like that will scare us into submission, and Avery laughs in his face. He cusses the two of us out to hell and back, and I ignore him on my way to the shower. When I'm done and brushing my teeth, Harley calls out to grab my attention.

My heart skips a beat, as I scramble but I find him on the couch where I left him only now Avery's joined him and Harlow Roqueford's face is on national TV, with an Amber Alert out on her. Her father stands at a press conference, blotting at his eyes, and listing all of her saint like qualities.

"What school did she end up at?" I ask, and Avery answers without looking up.

"Huxerly Prep in Boston. Her father has business associates there to keep an eye on her. She did her stint in rehab, too. She's probably just fallen off of the wagon. I'll make some calls and make sure she hasn't run back to find Joey."

I nod, but there's something not right about this.

The sound of the door unlocking breaks through our thoughtful silence but we don't look up, confident only Blaise and Ash can get in here, and it's Blaise's voice that calls out.

"Star. You have another package."

The difference between finding Lance's head and finding Harlow's is fucking huge.

Avery starts to collect every frame of footage taken at Hannaford for the entire day while I call Illi, staring into the box at Harlow's vacant eyes. He picks up immediately.

"Don't fucking tell me. You have another package."

I curse under my breath. "How did you guess? What the fuck is going on?"

He groans at me. "Because a headless corpse just got found at the docks, strung up like a fucking crucifix. It's a girl, fake tits on her and nails like a fucking housewife. Who is it?"

I rub a hand over my face. "Oh, you know, only the oil magnate's beloved daughter who's got every fucking cop in the country on the lookout for her."

"Okay, kid. We need to have a chat about who the fuck is stalking you."

I snort at him. "No shit. Can you make it up here to get the package? I can call the Bear if it's too much."

"We can't be trusting any member of the Twelve right now. Leave it with me, I'll be there as soon as I can sort... the rest of it out."

He hangs up and I tell Avery what he said. She stares at me for a long time, silent and calculating.

She shakes her head. "It doesn't make sense. It can't be the Jackal. Senior doesn't play these sorts of games. Who else would be this invested?"

I shrug at her. "Whoever it is, they're not killing people I like. They're killing people who've threatened me... or our family."

We've managed to attract some sort of sick, twisted guardian angel.

Fuck. Me.

Chapter Thirty-Two

Harley goes back to school on Monday and I continue to watch his every move, waiting for something to happen and for him to drop dead. I've never been this fucking paranoid before but his hospital stay has fucking broken something in me.

He deals with my over protectiveness for exactly three classes and then finally he snaps and tells me to get the fuck over it.

I just nod along; it's easier to agree with him and then do whatever the fuck I like.

We eat dinner in the dining hall because Avery has an extra dance practice and none of us feel like cooking. Ash leaves for a run straight after, kissing me far too possessively for public consumption, but after Annabelle's disappearance the other students are now silent in our presence. No whispers follow me and even the clueless freshmen give me a wide berth.

The rumor is I ran her off.

The truth is worse.

Harley tells Blaise to go ahead and start studying back in my room, and I give him a curious look. He shrugs, "I want you to myself for an hour after your freak out all *fucking* day."

"I can't help it. You *died*."

He nods and tucks me under his arm, walking me back up to his room. None of the guys in the hall dare to look at me and I can't say I'm unhappy about it.

Harley kicks his shoes off at the door and waits for me to do the same, then he grabs my ass and lifts me into his arms, burying his face into my neck. I wind my arms around his neck and thread my fingers through his hair, sighing.

What the fuck would I have done if he'd died?

"Stop fucking thinking about it," he mumbles into my skin, and I shiver uncontrollably.

I shake my head at him. "I can't help it. I haven't ever had someone to lose before and now I have four people I can't live without. Six if you count Illi and Odie, and I do. Fuck. I don't think I'm cut out for... loving people. I can't fucking breathe when I think-"

"Well, stop fucking thinking then," he growls and kisses me, effectively turning my brain off the way only he can.

I groan and kiss him back, pushing and desperate because how fucking dare he nearly die on me? After everything I've done to keep him breathing, dammit!

He grunts and walks us over to his bed, falling until he's on top of me, catching himself with one hand so he doesn't crush me. He feels fucking perfect on top of me. I wriggle until the heavy weight of his hard dick rubs against my clit through our uniforms.

I definitely want to suck him off. I want to taste him and remind myself he's okay, he's here, he's mine.

When I tell him that, he grunts and kisses his way down my neck. His hand slides underneath the tiny triangle of lace between my thighs and two of his fingers ease into me, my pussy already wet and aching for him. "You first, babe I need you first."

I think about arguing with him but I swear his mouth is magic and the second his lips and tongue touch me all rational thought just leaks out of my brain until I'm writhing underneath him. When his mouth closes around my clit and he groans, the vibrations tip me over the edge until I'm screaming and thrashing, clenching down on his fingers, held down by his firm grip on my hips.

He chuckles under his breath at me, all satisfied alpha male at making me lose my damn mind, and I yank at his hair until he crawls but up my body.

When he kisses me, I groan at the taste of myself on his lips and decide that this isn't enough. I can't wait any longer, we've been slow enough. I need every fucking inch of him.

"I need you. I'm on birth control, and I know we're both clean so I need you inside me right now," I whisper against his lips. He groans and pulls away, his hips jerking to rub his dick against the soft skin of my belly. He opens his mouth and I cut him off.

"I know what I'm doing. Okay, I don't know exactly what I'm doing but I know that I want you so don't argue with me."

He scoffs and laughs at me then slides his hand back down my stomach until two fingers slip back inside me. I frown at him, ready to chew him out for trying to distract me, when he adds a third and my heart stutters in my chest at the stretch.

Oh.

Right.

I scramble until I get my shirt and bra off, my skirt and panties are a little more tricky because Harley refuses to stop kissing and touching me, even for a second, but I manage it somehow. I feel a little frantic as I yank his shirt off, my legs starting to shake as he crooks his fingers inside me and rubs my G spot mercilessly. I gasp out his name as I come again, and my hands become useless. I swear I must black out a little because then next thing I know he's gone, standing to take the rest of his clothes off, thank *fuck*.

He's fucking perfection, and I can't breathe when I look at him. How is that still possible, after months of kisses and touches, orgasms and blowjobs, how can I still feel lightheaded just looking at him?

He smiles at me, slow and so fucking adoringly I want to *die*, and then he settles back on top of me again, kissing me until I'm panting.

"You sure?" Harley mumbles against my lips, and I bite his lip until he grunts back at me and shifts his hips, lining himself up and pushing in.

The stretch is uncomfortable, just this side of pain, but I'm no stranger to things that hurt and he kisses me to distract me. I'm so fucking full of him, I can't breathe but I don't even want the air in my lungs anymore if it means we have to stop.

"Babe, fuck, babe…" he mumbles into my skin and I nod, tugging and pulling until finally he moves, rolling his hips and *holy fuck* this is it. This is how I want to die. Impaled by Harley's fucking dick, stretching and filling me until I'm his.

He catches my lips with his in another blistering kiss and rocks slowly inside of me until I can't take the easy pace anymore, desperate for *more*, and I bite his lip again.

His control snaps and the next stroke is harder, building and building until he's slamming into me, and fuck if that isn't exactly what I need. I hold onto his shoulders, his neck, fucking *anything* I can and he doesn't stop.

It's fucking perfect.

He shifts to hold himself on one arm and slips his hand between our bodies and the second his fingers touch my clit, I'm gone. All I see is white light and pure fucking bliss. I hear him grunt my name and his hips stutter to a stop, grinding rather than pounding.

When I blink up at him, trying to get my eyes working again, he grins down at me like I'm the most perfect thing he's ever seen. Like I'm his soul, his reason for being.

I have to duck my head and blink rapidly because I will not be that pathetic girl who cries after her first time, and he scoffs at me, pulling out to go clean up and I kind of think he's giving me a second to pull myself together. It's sweet.

Harley cleans me up too because apparently he's a gentleman, then he climbs back into bed and bundles me into his arms. I rest my head on his chest, secure in his arms, listening to his heartbeat like I had for days in the hospital. His mom's heart locket catches in the light as he catches his breath.

"How did Joey get a hold of the locket? You said you'd been trying to get it back for years."

He grunts and shifts so he can thread his fingers through my hair, stroking my back until I'm a boneless mess.

"The first time I went to juvie was also the first time Avery and Ash even knew I existed. Senior wouldn't let Alice and my mom see each other. Used to fucking kill Ma, they were as close as Ash and Avery were as kids. So they didn't know about me until Social Services knocked on the big, ugly fucking door at Beaumont Manor and Senior had his staff turn them away. But the kids all heard my name, heard how I was related and Avery started to pull strings until I got out. She got me into boarding school with them, got me away from my grandfather. I was too fucking scared to wear the locket in middle school. Scared I'd lose it, scared I'd break it. It was like a fucking night light, I'd go to sleep with it in my hand. Joey found out and broke into my room and stole it. I raged out destroyed the whole room, went after Joey, the only reason I didn't kill him was because Ash and Blaise stopped me. I fucking hated Ash for stopping me. I didn't know… I didn't know what was going on. I thought he was picking that psycho over me. Avery had to do a fuck load of mediation to get us through that. Now I feel like a dick. He was being fucking tortured and protecting us all and there I was being pissy at him for it."

I blink away tears and clear my throat. "He doesn't blame you. He only blames Senior and Joey. He's just as fierce as Aves with his love. He's just a dick about it."

Harley chuckles, the rumble loud and warm against my ear. "I don't regret anything, babe. It got us here. I'd do it all again, and Ash and Morrison would too."

Chapter Thirty-Three

Harley tells me not to make plans for my Saturday.

When I ask him why, he gives me a smug, haughty smile. I'd be pissed about it but all three of my guys keep sharing these little secretive looks and eventually I give up and just go with it. I'm stupid enough to ask Avery if she knows what going on and she gives me her own smug fucking smile.

"Why don't you ask your *lover?*"

I could die.

She screeches with laughter at my blush. "I'm so glad to know that having sex hasn't stopped you from blushing like an eighteenth-century contessa on her wedding night."

So that's the end of my inquiries.

I wake to pancakes and coffee for breakfast and then Harley drives us all into Haven in the Maserati. Apparently he won a bet about Avery but I'm too afraid to ask what the hell it was. Blaise sulks in the back with me, dicking around to piss Harley off but my golden god is above the petty bullshit today. I finally break and ask him why he's so happy and he gives me a smug look in the mirror.

"We're getting tattoos. Do you have any idea how long I've waited to get your insignia on me? I fucking hate that Illi's had it all this time and I haven't."

I blanch, fucking shocked that *that's* what's going on. "You don't have to. None of you do."

He gives me a look in the mirror. "I only waited because the others hadn't been inducted. I'm not waiting anymore."

Avery rolls her eyes at him, then smiles at me. "We are all doing this. As a family, even if there are *needles* and *bodily fluids* involved."

Blaise roars with laughter at her. "How's Atticus faring with your hatred of bodily fluids? Does he know he's going to have to wear a hazmat suit to fuck you?"

I groan as Ash turns to stone next to me but Avery snarks back before he can come to her defense.

"I don't want *his* fluids or any other fucking piece of shit man that walks this Earth. I'm taking a vow of celibacy because you're *all* fucked," she says through clenched teeth and my stomach drops. Fucking Atticus.

I sigh, and wonder how the fuck I'm going to help her with this now we've agreed to work with him. That's a fucking headache to think about later. I lace my fingers into Ash's.

"Do you know where you're getting yours?" I murmur, trying to distract him from the conversation happening around us. If I didn't already know, his clenched jaw would tell me everything I need to know about his feelings towards Atticus.

He stares out the window, a frown over his brow and replies, "We discussed it after the Lingerie Party, we're all getting the same thing. Well, not Avery. I'm sure you'll find it suitable, Mounty."

I nod and rub my thumb along the back of his hand.

Harley parks behind the tattoo parlor and as we all pile out of the car I rub my arms, the chill in the air biting at me. Ash tucks me under his arm and leads me in.

The guy sitting behind the reception desk nods at Blaise and they start talking shit about how his last tattoos turned out. One of the tattoo artists looks Avery up and down dismissively, obviously used to Hannaford girls and their rich bitch attitudes, and she stares him down like he's a steaming pile of shit.

Then his eyes flick over to me and he frowns. Ash cuts in front of me and snarls at him, "What the fuck is your problem?"

The guy raises his hands in submission, "Nothing man. She just looks familiar, that's all. I thought I recognized her."

Blaise starts to snicker under his breath and I sigh.

"Any chance you're from Mounts Bay?" Avery says, sickly sweet, like poison.

He nods and pulls his chair up, ready to draw up the design they want. A group of high school girls come in for piercings and I start getting twitchy at the looks my guys get. Avery rolls her eyes at me but joins me in glaring at them.

When Harley tells the guy they all want the same thing he cracks a lame joke about boy bands and Ash looks ready to gut him.

Then Harley gets a UV torch out of his pocket and shines it on my face.

The tattoo artist shits his fucking pants.

Oh, *goodie*.

"You get that it takes a week to heal, right? You can't go to classes with that on your face!" Avery hisses, but they all ignore her completely.

I sit in the corner in a state of shock.

The tattoo artist from the Bay took a good ten minutes to calm down enough to trace the image out nicely, but the tremor in his fingers is finally gone. I try to look friendly and approachable but I think that only freaks him out more. Something about me being an assassin and renowned killer has him freaked out. Who knew?

Then he hands it off to the second guy and we're in business.

Harley and Blaise go first, unflinching and completely at ease as the needle drags through their cheeks. The jaw bones and sharp teeth only make them look hotter, the assholes, and the giggling girls in the corner refuse to leave after their belly button piercings are finished. Finally, after one of them tries to talk to Harley, the receptionist kicks them out. The blonde gets snooty and tries to play the rich daddy card but Avery only laughs at her, the cruel edge cutting.

"These are gang tattoos, you dense bitch. Do you want to risk a bullet by fucking the boss's boy?"

They scurry out quickly after that. I glare at Avery and she shrugs, smug as always.

It takes an hour and Ash smirks at Harley when he gets taped up, puffy and grumpy at the inconvenience. Avery cringes the second the gel hits her skin to transfer her little wolf onto her wrist but she doesn't flinch at the needle piercing her skin. Hers only takes ten minutes, being so small, and I make my decision to cement myself in the family with them.

I catch the tattoo guy's eye and ask him to tattoo me as well. He blanches for a second and them recovers nicely, nodding and clearing his throat.

When I point out Harley's tattoo he agrees quickly but when I move to take my pants off all hell breaks loose.

"What the fuck are you doing?!" Harley hisses, and Avery giggles at him.

I glare back at him, and then over his shoulder at Blaise. "I'm getting a tattoo as well. Go wait with Avery, it'll only take a few minutes."

Harley plants his ass in the seat next to the tattooing table and refuses to move like the stubborn asshole he is and Blaise takes up watch by the door. I roll my eyes and try to ignore them as best I can. By chance I'm wearing my most modest panties but, given that Ash picks them out for me, they're still fairly sheer. Harley glares at the tattoo artist like it's his damn fault.

"I want it on my panty line, where my hip meets my thigh, because it's fucking personal and the only people I want seeing it are you three dickheads so lay off," I snap, and he calms down a little.

Then I zone the fuck out while the family creed is inked into my skin, a permanent reminder that I belong to them just as much as they belong to me.

I couldn't be fucking happier with it.

We take the next week off while the tattoos heal and spend it in the boy's room watching trashy thriller movies Blaise loves and drinking too much whiskey. Avery continues to go to classes and tells the teachers we've caught mono, something they all accept without question because who in their right mind argues with a Beaumont?

Blaise and I mess around with songs for our playlists, him playing the guitar and me sweating as I sing without my earplugs in but fuck, we sound perfect together. Ash bans us from singing around Avery because the second we start he ends up hard as stone and drooling for me. It's a nice fucking compliment, better than any stupid roses he could ever give me.

Harley cooks me French toast and insists I eat it in bed, sulking when I refuse to do it naked. I'm positive it would quickly turn into an orgy if I did and I'm not quite sure I'm ready for that. There's an unspoken agreement amongst the boys not to talk about my new non-virginal status, thank *fuck*.

On the Sunday before classes go back I step into the shower, getting ready for bed and pouting that my week off has come to an end, when Harley ducks in behind me. I give him stern look that quickly melts away because sweet lord *fuck*, he is glorious to look at.

His personality ain't bad either.

"You're going to flit back to your room tomorrow and I'll have to make do with the smell of you on my sheets. You've turned me into some pathetic sap, it's fucking sad."

I snort at him, blushing wildly, and then I grab the soap to wash him, any excuse to run my hands over the solid plains of muscle on his chest.

"You'll just come sleep in my bed anyways. I'll try to sleep here a bit more. We can work something out. What are we going to do after summer break when we're all used to being in the same bed all of the time?"

Harley groans and rubs his dick against my belly. "You're going to move in here next year. Fuck it, Avery can get the room next door and we can live together. We all know she could make it happen."

My teasing dries up in my throat because, fuck, that sounds perfect.

Chapter Thirty-Four

The school staff decide that the students need motivation going into the last few weeks of classes before exams so the class rankings are posted on every door. Our first class for the day is history, and I do a double-take when I see that the second spot, under me, is Ash. Not Harley.

Oh fuck.

"Are you *fucking* kidding me?" Harley snarls, and the look Ash gives him is total arrogant asshole.

Do I stand between them or just let them fight it out? Stupid question, I get the fuck out of there and zone them the fuck out. When Harley finally takes his seat, I smile at him only to have him glare back at me.

Fuck.

"Maybe if you hadn't spent half the year with the cougar and a little more time studying with the Mounty you'd be getting those marks too," Ash says from his seat in front of us, and the smug tone only makes Harley's rage spread.

I decide to walk away and let them battle it out amongst themselves.

Harley spends the rest of the class furiously writing notes and snarling questions at our teacher like that alone will raise his mark the fraction it needs to reclaim the second spot. We make it through history in one piece only to find that Ash has beaten Harley by the tiniest of margins in every. Damn. Class.

Harley wouldn't take the news well at the best of times but Ash makes it his personal mission to mock his cousin mercilessly until I'm sure I'm going to be helping Avery clean intestines off of the walls by dinnertime.

Blaise enjoys the show just a little *too* much. He's practically bouncing with glee when we get back to our room and when I drop onto the couch next to him he pulls me into his lap.

"Wanna fuck on the couch and see if that distracts them?" he murmurs, but it's loud enough that Avery hears him and throws a dirty look at him.

"No fucking on the furniture, Morrison, or I'll burn all of your guitars."

He pouts at her and she snarls at him as she shoves Harley towards the bathroom to cool off. I abandon Blaise and his wandering fingers, too much of a temptation, and I convince Ash to walk me through my share portfolio. I hope it'll distract him enough to leave Harley alone.

He relents, but only if I'll sit in his lap. Avery side-eyes the fuck out of him but

I don't care. It's easy enough to learn and seeing my profits makes me wriggle in his lap with excitement.

"Now, now, Mounty. Avery's already on the warpath. I don't need to die just because you got over excited over your money and want to fuck me at the table," he says and I blush furiously.

"Who said I want to fuck you?" I whisper, eyeing Avery's back as she stirs the curry she's cooking. Her new obsession is cooking her way through cookbooks and I for one am not complaining.

"Other than your hard nipples, and your thighs? If I touched you right now I think I'd find you dripping."

Oh, Lord have mercy on my poor soul.

Yes, yes he would find me dripping. Even more so now he's whispering dirty things to me again. I try to move away from his lap but he slaps my thigh and tells me to focus on the laptop screen or he'll have to spank me, loud enough that the entire damn room hears him.

Avery's death glare at him only makes my blush worse.

I would have never thought I'd be up for being spanked but holy god damn. I think I could be convinced.

We're all seated in chemistry together when there's a bang outside and the building rumbles.

A few girls squeal and dive under their desks, but the teacher stands and locks the classroom door, calling for us all to stay calm.

My phone buzzes in my pocket at the same time Harley's does. He gives me a look and Avery turns in her chair with an eyebrow raised. Great. Another mass text, what the fuck now?

Every damn student forgets about the lockdown and checks their phones to see what the hell has just been sent out.

It's a video from Joey.

My heart stutters in my chest for a second when I see the entrance of Hannaford on Harley's phone screen but then it video pans down to the staff parking lot and the cars there.

Harley's Mustang and Blaise's Maserati.

I start to pray he trashes the fucking Maserati and leaves the 'Stang the fuck alone. Blaise could not give less of a fuck about his car but I can't bear for Harley seeing another version of his dad's car destroyed.

Joey doesn't just trash the 'Stang.

He fucking *blows it up*.

I should've known by all the noise but I'm still shocked to see the video. Ash groans and Blaise starts cursing Joey out in new and thought-provoking ways. Harley doesn't say a word, he just stops the video and slides his phone back into his pocket, before getting back to his chemistry notes. I chew my lip for a second and then grab his hand under the desk, rubbing his knuckles with my thumb like he does for me when my world starts to fucking break. He nods at me without looking up and something in me breaks a little.

I meet Ash's eyes over his shoulder and nod. Joey is escalating and I vote we kill the psycho fucker now too.

When the school admin finally lets us out and cancels classes for the rest of the day while the police and fire department clean up the mess, we all go back to our room so Avery can rage clean and drown herself in coffee.

I keep a hold of Harley's hand the whole way up there, trying to ignore the fearful stares from the other students. Everyone knows whose car just got bombed.

"He's fucking pathetic. He knows he can't take any of us in a fair fight so he's going after shit he thinks will hurt. Well, fuck him. The car is important to me, but it's just a fucking car. Ash and Avery mean more to me. He's just proving how fucking weak he is," he murmurs, and I wonder if he's explaining it to me or trying to convince himself.

I squeeze his hand and smile up at him, trying to lighten the mood. "Remember you're fucking loaded now and you can get it fixed. Or buy a new one."

He scoffs at me. "I don't want a new one. Morrison bought me this one, and it doesn't matter that I've paid him back; he did it because he's family and we do that shit for each other. Fuck Joey and his pissy attitude."

Be still my fucking heart.

Blaise turns and bats his eyelashes at us both to be a dick and Harley snarks back at him. I can take a deep breath again but my chest still fucking hurts.

Joey knows that the only way to truly hurt his siblings is to hurt our family and that makes him a fucking danger.

When he gets back into our room my phone buzzes again and I find a text from Diarmuid.

I can hunt the Beaumont down for you. Will that prove my loyalty? He'll be dead by sunrise.

I show Avery and she stares at me for a second, running the risk analysis in her head for the hundredth time. Finally, she sighs and shakes her head.

Joey lives to die by my hand another day.

Chapter Thirty-Five

Much like last year, I feel fucking sick to my stomach the morning of our choir performance.

Harley wakes me with kisses and soft touches, stroking my face and neck possessively, and I enjoy it for about three seconds before I remember what I have to do in a few hours and then I'm shaking again.

Avery cooks me French toast and I choke down a single piece, my stomach revolting the entire time.

She hides the coffee from me.

I've never been so fucking angry at her, not even when she was trying to destroy me in freshman year. When I snap that at her she just nods and smiles in this infuriatingly kind way that sets my teeth on edge.

When I snarl at Harley to piss off and let me shower by myself she laughs at his kicked puppy expression. "She's not going to be our Lips today until she gets this over with, Arbour. Just leave her to wallow Morrison-style."

When I get out of the shower, stomping and throwing myself around, I find the whole family out in our room waiting for me, staring with various levels of sympathy and glee.

Ash can't contain his *fucking* glee.

"I've been waiting all year to hear this, Mounty, Morrison's being fucking shifty about it. He never records songs without letting me listen to them, I've been feeling put out," he says as he tucks me under his arm. I can't do much more than nod and grimace.

We walk down to the chapel and I sulk the whole way. They all ignore me, which is usually what I want but just this once I'd like Avery to save me from this fucking assignment. I don't feel ready to sing yet. I don't feel ready to listen to myself do it but I've promised Blaise and... fuck. I love him.

I fucking love that asshole.

I sigh and pull myself together. We leave the others on their claimed bench in the front row. Avery squeezes my hand as we walk past and I attempt some sort of smile at her. I can't look at the other two, afraid they'll try to kiss me and I'll puke on them.

Blaise sweet talks Miss Umber and gets us the first slot so I only have to wait five minutes while they set the piano up. Then we're being introduced and the squealing of the freshman girls at the front has a little of my usual fire returning.

Blaise roars with laughter.

"There you are, Star. I was afraid I'd lost you," he teases and laces his fingers through mine.

"I fucking hate this, you're lucky I love you," I mumble and his hand jerks in mine. I frown and glance up at his shocked face. He swallows roughly but I'm too busy freaking out to realize it's the first time I've told the idiot I love him.

We walk out on the stage and Blaise grins easily, waving and bowing like the natural performer he is. I stomp out like I want to commit mass murder on every fucker in the damn room. Well, everyone but my family.

I sit on the piano bench, away from the crowd so I can hide behind Blaise's broad form. He smiles and bumps my shoulder as he rolls his own back, loosening up before his fingers rest on the keys.

"Ready?" he murmurs and I give him the slightest nod. I swear I'm going to puke.

His fingers start to dance over the keys in a somber, lilting dance and my heart finally slows down until it's following the beats of the music.

My mind turns off, my eyes drifting closed, and I let myself fall into the song.

I hit every note and my voice doesn't falter.

I'm so glad Blaise's chest is shielding my face from the audience because the second his voice joins mine in the first chorus tears prick at the back of my eyes. We sound fucking perfect together.

I sneak a peek at him and find him staring down at me, ignoring his music sheets and playing the song by heart. He's practiced for this moment for hundreds of hours all year.

We've fucking smashed it.

I feel more powerful than I've ever felt before. Better than standing across from the Jackal drawing lines in the sand.

I've reclaimed my voice for myself and I'll never let anyone take it again.

We're going to war and for the first time, I feel confident that we're going to fucking win.

As Blaise finishes the notes there's a stunned silence like the whole room is holding it's breath and then the applause is deafening. I can hear Avery screaming again, exactly like she did last year, but I can't look over. I'm still trying to pull myself together.

Blaise grins out at the chapel and gives a little wave, before turning back to me and wiping my cheeks with one of his big, colorful hands even though they're dry.

The microphone is still on so he can't speak without the whole room hearing, so he quirks his eyebrows at me until I nod, I'm okay. I'm not broken. I'm just so fucking relieved to be healing finally.

He stands, making sure he's still blocking me from the crowd, and then tucks me into his side to walk us both off of the stage. Miss Umber catches his arm at the bottom of the stairs to gush but I don't want to look at her while I'm still so raw.

Ash pries me out of Blaise's arms and wedges me between him and Avery. I take a shuddering breath and Avery slips her hand into mine.

"That was fucking incredible, Mounty. I have goosebumps," she whispers, and I nod. I swallow and smile at her, my eyes still a little watery.

Snickering comes from behind us and the look Harley serves the freshmen there would shrivel the balls of any gangster in the Bay.

I try to find my voice so they don't think I'm going fucking crazy. "I'm fine. It's just—"

"I know," Avery cuts me off, running a soothing hand down my arm. "You're slowly being put back together."

This girl. Where the fuck would I be now without her?

Blaise takes his seat next to Ash and we sit through the rest of the performances, none as breathtaking as ours had been. My hands stop shaking, and by the last song, I can hum along under my breath.

The grin Ash gives me when he hears me is worth all the fucking tears I've ever spilled.

The chapel empties out and we wait until the crowd disperses. I look like I've spent a week in bed moping like some pathetic heartbroken teen and I don't want photos of that shit on the gossip site for the Jackal to see.

He'd probably enjoy them too much.

"Right. Dinner? I think we should order in, I feel like sushi," Avery says, and everyone agrees though I just want coffee and ice cream after my stressful day.

We stand and start towards the door only to be stopped by an unfamiliar voice.

"Blaise," a woman's voice calls out and I frown when he freezes, then jerks his head around to follow the sound.

It's his mother.

Harley curses viciously under his breath and moves in front of me while Avery and Ash both stare over at her like they're hoping she'll drop dead.

I try to stay calm.

"What are you doing here?" Blaise croaks, and my heart breaks a little more at the haunted tone in his voice.

Casey Morrison steps forward and wrings her hands nervously, clutching at the - *holy fuck* - baby strapped to her chest. "I wanted to see you. Your agent called me about your contract, I know how hard you worked for it and I can't believe you'd throw that away for... for a girl."

Oh.

Hell.

No.

I step around Harley and cross my arms, pegging this weak and fucking gutless excuse for a mother with a look that rivals the Beaumont's in ice. She winces and gives me a watery smile.

"I didn't mean it like... no, I did but that was before I heard the song. It was beautiful. You both sound so lovely together."

I try to ease my glare up a little but it's impossible to shift. Blaise shakes his head at her but his eyes are glued to his little brother.

"So you've seen I'm fine and now you're going to, what, leave? Scurry back to Dad? Fuck, I can't call him that anymore, can I? Go back to your husband, Mrs. Morrison. I'm fine, my girlfriend is none of your concern, and my choices are no longer yours to help shape."

Casey takes another step forward and looks around at the other parents here, at the teachers all watching their little reunion with badly veiled interest. Being the wife of a billionaire in this level of society must be like living under a microscope.

"I am still your mom and now I've left your father. He... he's left me with nothing and our pre-nup has protected his right to do that but I can't live without you in my life. I thought... I thought I could but I was wrong."

Ash snorts and steps up to Blaise, angling his chest until he's covering his best friend from the prying eyes, the same way Blaise had just done for me.

He looks at her like she's *nothing*, and says in a low voice, "If you had ever given a fuck about your son you would've stood up for him against that miserable, egotistical excuse of a man years ago. Choke on your apology. Come on, Morrison. We have a *family* dinner to get to."

Then he stalks off. Avery shares a look with me and then follows. Harley tugs at my hand and I nod, shooing him away after his cousins until I'm left standing there with broken mother and faltering son.

Blaise sighs. "Give me your number. I'll call you later and we can... figure something out."

Casey smiles and I try not to stare at how much she looks like Blaise when she does. It must be all the fucking sadness in her eyes but I'm not letting her off the hook. Not at all.

Blaise takes the baby from her while she fumbles around for her phone. He smiles down at his little brother and my heart clenches in my chest at the look of wonder.

Lord help me.

"Isn't he cute?" he mumbles at me while he pulls faces and I clear my throat.

"He looks like you, so yeah he's cute."

Blaise grins and tries to hand me the baby.

No.

No, thank you. I do not hold small humans. Not ever.

Blaise cackles at the terrified expression on my face, snapping a photo on his phone because apparently, he can just ninja the baby around in his arms like a freaking wizard without dropping it. I feel a little lightheaded and kinda wish I'd left with everyone else.

"Calm down, I'm good with kids. I'm surprised you're not," he says and I roll my eyes at him.

"I have enough on my plate keeping you lot alive, I don't have time to... hold those things."

Avery will not stop laughing over the photo.

"I'm framing it and hanging it above your bed, so you remember even during coitus that you shouldn't ever get pregnant."

I side-eye her but nod, because I should never, ever have a baby.

Ash scoffs at her. "I was told very sternly by her doctor that those decisions are hers alone, Avery."

Avery hands him a glass of bourbon and says, sickly sweet, "I have far more say in it than you ever will. Besides, how would that even work? Would you guys draw names out of a hat to see who gets to pass their DNA on?"

Fuck this.

I join Harley on the couch to hide from their snarking and he folds me into his chest easily. Blaise is distracted, tapping away on his phone to his mom and I chew my lip as I watch him.

"We'll be on suicide watch by the end of the week," Harley whispers.

I wince but I think he's right. "He can sleep here tonight. I'll see if I can talk him into keeping his expectations low."

"Good fucking luck."

After dinner has finished, and Harley and Ash have gone back to their room, I cuddle into Blaise's chest and sigh. He rubs his cheek against my hair and whispers, "I promise I'll be okay, Star. I'm not going to let her drag me under again."

I wish I could believe him.

Chapter Thirty-Six

My phone pings after midnight and I have to wriggle out from under Blaise to reach it, my rock god boyfriend wrapped around me like a second skin. He doesn't falter in his faint snores and Avery's headphones are in her ears blaring still so neither of them have woken at the sound.

The dining hall. Now. Don't bring your little friends unless you want me to slit their throats while you watch.

I stare down at the Jackal's text and a cold wave of dread takes over me for a second. Then I get angry.

Really fucking angry.

I slip out of the bed and into one of Harley's hoodies and some yoga pants because I'll be damned if I let that psychopath see me in booty shorts ever a-fucking-gain. My knife gets slipped into my pocket and, after a moment of hesitation, I slip my gun into the waistband of my yoga pants.

Then I stand over Avery for three minutes, my heart in my throat, debating telling her but, fuck, she might follow me down there or call for back up and that's a bad situation looking to turn nuclear.

When I'm out of the room, door locked firmly behind me, I text Illi.

The Jackal is here. I'm going to meet him. If you don't hear from me in thirty minutes call Diarmuid for backup. Tell the boys I love them and Avery she's the best fucking thing that ever happened to me.

It's sappy as fuck, and Illi will give me so much shit for it, but I need them to know how much they mean to me if I'm… dead. Fuck, I hope I'll be dead and not taken.

But I'm done bowing down to this man's whims.

I walk slowly, calmly, down the silent halls of Hannaford as if I'm not heading into the very hell I enrolled here to escape. Luca is waiting outside the dining hall doors with three other flunkies. I dip my head and for once Luca doesn't grin and flirt.

"He's not very happy with you, princess."

No shit. "He doesn't have to be happy with me. He's forgotten he's an equal to me in our world." I'm proud of how strong my voice sounds.

Luca just looks at me for a second longer, his eyes searching mine, and then nods.

I give him a nod back like I'm not concerned in the least, and he opens the door for me. I keep my eye on Luca and not the man dressed in a sharp suit, sinfully handsome and utterly soulless. He ushers me in with a firm hand at the small of my back I try not to flinch away from and helps me to my seat across from the outwardly calm Jackal.

He's sitting in Harley's seat.

He knows everything that happens in this school.

I meet his gaze and, fuck it if he doesn't look menacing in his suit. I suppress the shiver that tries to take over my body. He looks calm, with his hands on his knees below the tables, but that only intensifies the dread clawing at me.

"Good evening, little Starbright. I hope I didn't wake you?"

I raise my brows at him. "Don't you know? I assumed you'd have found a way to get a camera in my room by now."

He smirks at me and tips his head. "But of course. I have to say, I'm not a fan of watching those boys defile you."

I fucking refuse to blush or think about him watching us, watching *me* during my most intimate moments. He could be bluffing. He's probably not but I hold onto that hope for now. "What would you like, Jackal? What are you really here for? Because I'm not going to leave with you. I'm content here and who shares my bed every night is no concern of yours."

He twitches. His little tick when he's trying not to attack someone coming out in full force. I've watched him torture, maim, humiliate, pulverize, and destroy a thousand times before and I know his every tick.

He wants to break me.

"You will leave here with me tonight. I've grown tired of our little game, Starbright. I was hoping to wait for you to be a little older, a little wiser, before I claimed you but you've pushed my hand."

I cross my arms. "Claim me? What are you, a fucking caveman? I'm not yours."

He leans forward, the gentleman mask melting away and leaving nothing but the sociopath behind. "You are mine. You've been mine from the second I saw you. I've fixed every single problem you've ever had. You owe me and there's no way I'm going to let some little rich cunts take what's mine."

I laugh at him, so clearly I've gone insane, but the haughty, arrogance of the boys fills me. I've had a steady diet of it for months and now I can breathe that same fire, even if it gets me killed. "You killed my mom. You destroyed my leg. You took my voice away. You murdered any person, man or woman, that tried to be my friend. You did everything you could to cut me off from any help that may have been offered to me. You're not a good man, Matteo. You never have been."

He laughs back at me, flicking a hand at me dismissively. "And you think Johnny is? He's far crueler than I am with his kills. He taught me half of his tricks, back before the French slut ruined everything."

I grit my teeth. "That's your problem; you don't want friends. You want to own people, and Illi and I have never been the type to bow down to your rules."

He drums his fingers against the table, glaring over at me and then nods at me like I've agreed with something he's said. "I can see you've been tainted here. I think your time at Hannaford is over, little Wolf. We need to go home and wipe you clean of all of these new ideas. Rich people can have dreams, and love, and free will. But we are not rich people. We are the lurking shadows."

I grip my knife and his eyes track the movement. I don't care that he knows, that he's watched me just as closely as I've watched him. I'm not going with him without a fight.

"You're a rich man now, Matteo. You may still stand in the shadows but you're richer and more powerful than God. Just not to me."

He stands, revealing the gun in his hand. He's had it pointed at me the whole time. I knew it but seeing it pisses me off. Fine. We'll play this his way for a little longer. I just need to be patient.

"Let's go, Starbright. I'm looking forward to wiping you clean from all that this school has done to you."

I stand and keep my hand around my knife. He smirks at me and puts his gun away, motioning for Luca to get my arm. I force myself not to tense as his fingers wrap around my elbow but he's gentle enough with me that it's not so hard.

The moment the Jackal is no longer watching me, Luca drops his hand away and when I glance up at him he gives me a stern look. I frown.

The Jackal walks ahead of us, lazy and confident in his stride and he never sees it coming.

Luca wraps an arm around his neck and squeezes.

Holy fuck.

Holy. *Fuck.*

I stand there like an idiot as the Jackal scrambles against his most trusted and loyal supporter, a man who's been with him since the very beginning, but Luca is bigger and stronger than Matteo and holds firm, even when his arms begin to bleed from the deep gouges Matteo leaves.

The door to the dining hall bursts open and Ash storms through, gun drawn and wild looking, with Harley on his heels. I stare at them both, at the blood on Harley's hands, and then back to Luca who is now laying an unconscious Jackal down on the floor.

He's not dead, not yet.

"WHAT THE FUCK MOUNTY?!" Harley roars, and I blink at him.

I think my brain is a little broken.

Luca gives me a wry smirk and then shocks the shit out of me. "I've been waiting to do that to him for years, princess. It felt as good as I thought it would."

I turn to look at him but I can't get my head around his words. He's never been anything but loyal to the Jackal and now he's standing over his prone body. I just... I can't figure this out.

He chuckles at me and I glance out the now open doors at the other flunkies but they're all on the floor, bleeding and groaning. Fuck, I forgot how good Harley and Ash are.

The sound of feet slapping on the wood floors has us all tense and then Blaise and Avery bolt through the door, looking frazzled and desperate.

"Good fucking use you two are!" Ash snarls at them both, but Avery ignores him, stumbling over to me and wrapping her arms around my waist. I've never seen her so shaken.

Luca plants a foot over the Jackal's throat in case he wakes up and says, "Atticus sends you his *personal* regards and would like you to know he's been watching you for a long time. Now he is sure Miss Beaumont is guarded by such a capable and competent friend he would like to assure you he will not hesitate to offer you any help necessary. That includes me."

Holy.

Sweet.

Lord.

He's a double agent. A spy. A fucking made man in the Jackal's den, spying on the psycho's every move, and I never would have guessed it. The Jackal clearly hasn't either. Luca has been trusted with *everything* since the very beginning of the Jackal's reign of terror in the Bay. Fuck.

Atticus is *good*.

"I guess he'll know now that you're a spy," I say, breaking the silence.

We all stare down at the Jackal and Luca shrugs. "Don't worry about it. I'll drop him home and head back to the Crow. I'm sick of watching the sick fuck hurt people anyway."

I nod and then pull away from Avery to hold my hand out to him. "Thanks for breaking your cover for me. I hope it was worth it."

He grins at me and tugs me into a hug. "Like I'd let him kill you, princess. Even if I wasn't on orders from the boss, I'd have figured a way out for you. It's time for me to go home, it's been too long."

Ash finally lowers his gun but he's still staring at Luca like he wants to shoot him. Harley shakes himself out of his stupor and stalks over to me, so fast I don't realize he's moving until he's pulling me away from Luca's arms and running his hands over me to check for blood and bruises.

"Are you okay? Did he touch you? Tell me he didn't touch you, babe. What the fuck were you thinking?!" he says, voice hoarse and panicked. I catch his wrists in my hands and pull away.

"I was thinking he wasn't leaving without seeing me and I needed to face him. He would've killed you if I had brought you guys. It's fine, I told Illi—"

"We know what you told Illi, who the fuck do you think called us?" Ash snaps, and I glance up to see him staring down at the Jackal, his eyes like black voids. Luca steps in front of the Jackal's prone form.

"You can't kill him. The Twelve will come after the Wolf if you do. There's a process that needs to be followed," he says, hands out placatingly.

Ash's gaze doesn't waver from his perusal of the Jackal. "The Twelve are choosing sides as we speak and we have Atticus, don't we? Without this dickhead, we'll be able to take on the rest."

Luca shakes his head. "He's been recruiting. There are other members who have sided with him. They don't like the Crow cleaning things up. There's a lot of talk about the Vulture's business being disbanded. They're criminals for a reason, they don't have morals. Even the Bear isn't happy with the skin markets being gone. He used to sell in them as punishments to his followers. We have to let him go and do this the right way."

Ash sneers at him and I sigh, stepping in. "He's right. The Crow can't defend against nine other members."

Luca shrugs. "Five. The Jackal has five that have followed him. He's working on the Boar but he's very reluctant to side with him over you."

I startle. "Over me? Why the fuck would he side with me?"

Luca shrugs again, grabbing his phone and tapping out a text. "We can't figure that out either. The Jackal is going fucking insane over it, but the Crow can't find a reason why either. He just says it's a blood thing. Whatever the fuck that means. Bikers are a strange breed."

I groan. Will anything ever be straightforward and simple?!

"Fine. Take him and drop him off. I'll call the Crow later and we can… discuss plans."

Luca nods and grins at me again, swooping down to kiss my cheek and making Harley growl at him like a rabid fucking dog.

"I guess I'll have to carry him out myself now you've incapacitated my men, O'Cronin," Luca jokes and Harley snaps at him, "It's Arbour, dickhead."

We head back to the room for a debrief and Avery's hand shakes in mine the whole walk back. I feel awful for not warning her and also a little shocked at how badly this has affected her. I mean, I've known all along we're family now but to know just how much she cares is still jarring.

Harley won't stop touching me, clutching at my hand if I move away from his arms, and I think I made a mistake in going down without telling them.

Avery makes us all tea, even though we all said no when she offered to make them, and I clear my throat in an attempt to move the lump in my throat. "I'm sorry I didn't wake anyone. I didn't know Luca was a plant. I thought I'd have a better chance getting him out of here if I wasn't worried about him killing one of you."

Blaise nods but he's staring at his feet, refusing to meet my eyes. Fuck.

Ash takes the cup Avery hands him but doesn't sip it. "There were a lot of options you had, Mounty. This won't work if you don't trust us. Not just the relationship, the whole fucking family won't work if you run off towards the threat to sacrifice yourself at every sign of danger."

I wince but nod. "I know that. I just… I don't want him touching any of you."

Harley's fingers flex in mine, a reminder of how close we got to losing him only weeks ago at the hands of the Jackal. Avery gives me a soft look, knowing exactly what I'm thinking.

"Don't be so harsh. Annabelle drugging Harley did a lot of damage. Lips is barely sleeping now, and she can't make perfect decisions every time something happens," she says and Ash snorts at her.

"I'm not asking for perfect, I'm asking for trust. We all trust you, Mounty. With our lives. Why can't you trust us with the same?"

Tears prick my eyes but I refuse to cry. "And if he'd killed you, Ash? What would I do with myself then? Knowing that he did it for me. He thinks I belong to him, even with me telling him it'll never happen, he doesn't give a fuck about what I want."

Ash slams the coffee cup on the table and stalks into the bathroom, closing the door quietly, though it sounds like a deafening bang in the silence of the room.

Harley squeezes my fingers again. "Just tell someone next time. I thought you were dead at the look on Ash's face when Illi called."

My gut squeezes again and I pull away, ready to grovel at the bathroom door until Ash forgives me.

The Jackal poisons fucking everything.

Harley stops me and directs me back to bed, undressing me and tucking me in as if I can't do it myself. It's only when I end up jammed between Harley and Blaise that I notice how badly I'm shaking. Maybe I wouldn't have managed undressing.

Avery climbs into her bed but the glow of her phone confirms she's not planning on getting any rest. We're all stuck in the limbo of what-ifs.

What if Luca wasn't a plant?

What if I had woken them up?

What if I died?

I startle awake hours later, having not even realized I'd fallen asleep, to Ash sleeping across the bottom of the bed. I'm penned in completely.

"I think he's worried you'll run off on him. He's asked me to put a GPS tracker on your phone," Avery murmurs, making me jump again.

I look over and find her tapping away on her phone again. "I think I fucked up, Aves. I'm really fucking sorry."

She nods and smiles at me. "I get it. I don't like it, but I get it. Ash will too, he's just… worried."

I fight back tears again and nod. When I'm sure I won't cry, I carefully pull out from between the bodies and crawl over to Ash, curling myself around him. His eyes fly open the second I touch him but he relaxes back once I'm plastered to him, his arms wrapping me up tight as he kisses the top of my head.

"I'd rather you hate me for going alone than being dead. I'm sorry I worried you but I'm not sure I'll make a different decision next time. In my mind, I will always be expendable because… I've survived it all before. I can survive it again. I can't face that stuff happening to you and he wouldn't torture you. He'd slit your throat and bleed you out in front of me. He told me that when he called me down to meet him."

Ash nods but doesn't speak. I don't think he's forgiven me, not even close, but I know we'll be okay. At least until something else happens.

"Sorry to interrupt your little make-up session, but Atticus just informed me that we've been summoned by Senior. He's told Atticus he knows about his… plans to keep us separated and he wants to meet with the Wolf." whispers Avery and I groan.

There are too many threats in our lives.

I need a week off.

Chapter Thirty-Seven

Exams consume our every waking moment for two weeks.

It's a blessing really because no one has the chance to panic or argue about the Jackal's impromptu visit and Avery is so consumed by her studies that she trusts Atticus to put protective measures in place for our meeting with Senior, despite her rage at his deception.

Harley and Ash become so competitive that I ban them from talking about classwork around me. I can't cope with the snarking and arguing at all, especially not with Blaise looking green the second they start quoting random lines from our literature readings to out do each other.

I just need to get him through the exams.

He's ready. I know he is. We've worked too fucking hard this year, around all the fucking bullshit trying to kill us all, for him not to pass his exams now.

Avery refuses to let any of the guys sleep in our room for the week, claiming they're a distraction for me and bad for my sleep, and I don't have the heart to tell her I sleep better when I know they're all around me. I'm plagued by constant dreams of Jackal, and what would have happened if I hadn't snuck off by myself.

On the last day of exams, I am the first to finish our history exam and I spend ten minutes rereading my answers even though I know they're perfect. The teacher, still the substitute, takes a call and then gestures me to the front. Ash glares as his eyes follow me and I shrug at him.

"You've been called to the principal's office, Miss Anderson. If you're finished, you need to head there now."

What the actual fuck? Mr. Trevelen must be losing his damn mind.

I collect my bag from the front of the class, away from where we could sneak looks at our notes, and make my way to the office.

Something is up.

I slip my knife into my blazer pocket in case it's Joey or Senior, and I prepare my defense in my head if it's some skank running her mouth about me and the guys again to get me kicked out. I mean, Annabelle is taken care of and the cougar was fired so I should be finished with that bullshit but Hannaford knows how to test my very will to fucking live sometimes.

I'm rehearsing the exact way I'll tell Mr. Trevelen to *fuck off* as I arrive to the office. The receptionist is missing and I frown, weaving my way through the partitions until I get to the principal's office, the door open for me.

I walk in only to find a gun aimed at my chest.

Ms. Vivienne looks fucking deranged as she holds the piece in her shaking hands. I stare at her, unblinking and unafraid. Well, I'm a little worried she's taking the safety off and she's going to shoot me by accident with all of the trembling she has going on, but one look into those big doe eyes of her tells me she has no real spine for murder.

"You just couldn't let him go, could you?" She hisses and I struggle to keep myself from rolling my eyes. Really, bitch? *Seriously*?!

"You're going to go to prison for killing me just so you have a chance at climbing on Harley's dick? I mean, he's good but is any dick really worth that?" I say, calmly. I'm waiting for the perfect opening to break the slut's arm. There, I said it; she's a dumb slut and I'm a hypocrite. Sue me.

"Like I give a fuck about that mobster's dick. I don't want to fuck him. I want him fucking dead. I want to deliver you to my love so we can be happy together finally. He can't focus now you've betrayed him. He's fucking gutted you've left the fold."

She continues rambling, on and fucking on, and it takes me a second to process her word.

The Jackal.

The fucking slut was sent here to kill Harley by the fucking Jackal.

I snap. My patience and her fucking arm. She screams so loudly the whole school will have heard it during the exams and fuck it if I care.

I hope Avery can clean it up for me. When I have her on the ground, her unbroken arm pinned behind her back with my knee and her own gun pressed against her skull, I lean down to question her.

"Are you so stupid that you believe Matteo's lies? What did he tell you, that I'm a defector? That I belong to him?"

She sobs and whimpers, not planning on answering, so I grab a fistful of her hair and yank until her neck bows beautifully. "Answer me. I'm not a patient person."

"He loves me. He just needs you out of the way so we can be together. He found me, he saved me from my husband. Why wouldn't I help him catch you after what you've done?"

I shake my head and fish out my phone. I hesitate for a second and then text the group number. I have to trust them this time and contact them before I call Illi.

I fucking hope it's the right thing to do.

Ash texts back immediately. *On my way.*

I don't want him to see the mess I've made of Ms. Vivienne, I don't want to risk it triggering some deep dark memory, but I have no way of cleaning her up a bit.

Fuck it.

When the door eases open and Ash steps through, barely three minutes later so he must've fucking ran here, the look on his face when he sees the gun is *bad*.

"That's not yours, is it?" he snaps, and I shake my head.

"I've just been chatting with the lovely cougar. It turns out we have a mutual friend. Would you like to tell Ash who it is you love so much that you were trying to kill Harley for him?"

She laughs, spitting blood on the floor from where I've broken her nose. "He'd be fucking dead if you hadn't sent the Butcher in. That dirty roofie would've done the job perfectly."

I freeze and Ash's eye flare.

"You gave Annabelle the roofie?" I ask, my hand steady as I press the gun into the base on her neck.

The slut chokes on her own blood a little more as she gurgles out, "I drove her down to the Bay myself. We had struck up a lovely friendship before you ran her off. Now I have to answer to her parents, they blame me for not knowing where the fuck she went."

The door slips open again and my other two guys walk in. Blaise frowns at me for a second and then leans back against the door like he's holding it shut. I doubt anyone will disturb us if the scream hadn't sent them running but I guess I should've locked it by now.

Harley pulls up a chair and then helps me off of Ms. Vivienne, before peeling her off of the floor and dropping her into the chair. I can't look at him right now because all I'll see is the thick tube down his throat and black circles under his eyes that had been permanent while he was in the hospital.

Ms. Vivienne is going to die.

She's going to die bloody.

"How about we call your little friend, hmm? How about we ring him and see if he wants to collect you?" I say handing Harley the gun and directing the guys until Ash is guarding the door, Blaise is covering the cougar's mouth, and Harley's finger is steady on the trigger.

I lean forward until I'm right in her face. "I didn't defect from him. I'm the *fucking* Wolf of Mounts Bay, and that sadistic fuck sent you here against the Twelve to die for him."

She shakes her head, sobbing behind Blaise's hand and I hit dial.

I hear him breathing as he answers but he doesn't say a word.

"Your little girlfriend is dead."

Her eyes widen at me and she tries to shake free from Blaise but his hand is steady. I'm glad it's him holding her. His trust in me is so complete that he's willing to get blood on his hands because he knows I'll clean it up.

The Jackal's voice is the same one he uses when he's trying to sweet talk me. "Like I give a fuck about some cougar pussy. I wouldn't put someone in that building with you, little Wolf, unless they were disposable to me and we both know every pussy I've ever had is disposable. Yours is the one I want to keep."

Pathetically, tears fill her eyes. I cannot understand what these women see in Matteo. How can they look at him and not see the monster under his skin?

"I told you I'm not interested."

"And I told you, you're *mine*. I'll kill every fucking man that touches you. You think the Butcher can keep them safe? The Crow and his *fucking* spies? Little girl, I was born in hell and I fought my way to the throne. If I want you, I'll fucking have you."

I stare over Ms. Vivienne's head to my guys and say, "Enjoy the throne for now. It'll be mine before this is all over."

I hang up to the sound of him laughing.

Ms. Vivienne is sobbing behind Blaise's hand now, big heaving gasps like she's heartbroken. I can't stand the sound of it. She's just as fucking weak as the rest of the rich skanks at this school, only she thought she could win over the Jackal.

He doesn't have a soul to win.

My phone pings and I jerk my head for Ash to answer the door, murmuring quietly with Avery until she hands my bag over. He shuts the door and drops the bag at my feet. Ms. Vivienne's eyes land on the bag and the sobs dry up in her throat.

"Let her go, Blaise. Go wait outside, all of you." I say, and I unzip the bag slowly, enjoying the way her eyes track that movement. I'm not a sociopath but fuck it if it doesn't feel satisfying to finally get rid of this bitch.

I dig around for the plastic sheeting, spreading it out with steady hands. It's much easier to be patient and prepared than to be rash and attempt to clean up evidence later.

Ms. Vivienne watches while I prepare for her death and the sobbing starts up again until she's fucking hysterical. Ash grimaces and grabs Blaise's arm, pulling him out the door until I'm left with Harley. I sigh at him which he totally ignores.

"Do you ever listen to me? I'm not trying to hide this from you, I just don't think you should have to watch it." I grumble, tugging my uniform off and then slipping the plastic jumpsuit over my lacy lingerie. I'll have to get Ash to pick me out some more.

Harley's eyes don't falter from where he's watching Ms. Vivienne. One wrong move and I think he'll break her neck. "Blaise is green and Ash has a history that makes killing women hard for him, even when they're treacherous sluts. I don't give a fuck. She pulled a gun on you, she's gotta go."

I grab her by the hair and lean down until I'm at eye level with her. The tears don't work on me, not at all. The second she told me she gave the dirty pills to Annabelle she'd sealed her fate.

"The second you climbed into bed with the Jackal you killed yourself. If I delivered you back to him, he'd cut you into pieces first just to hear you scream. I don't get off on that shit so I'll kill you first even though you deserve all the pain in the fucking world for what you've done. *You're welcome.*"

Then I get to work.

Chapter Thirty-Eight

It takes five hours to deal with the problem.

Once she's dead and her heart stops pumping I'm able to do what I need to with minimal mess. I send Blaise to go pick up a couple of black tubs while Avery runs interference so no one stumbles on us while I work. Harley and I argue when he tries to help and eventually he agrees to sit on a chair by the door and just watch. He niggles at me until I explain what I'm doing, and why I'm doing it, teaching him the optimal way to dismember a corpse for transportation and an easier cleanup.

There's still a fuck ton of blood.

The smell is fucking vile and once the body, plastic sheeting, and my suit are all sealed in the tubs we open all the windows and I scrub the floor with bleach, killing the smell and any leftover DNA that might have spilled over. Once that's over with Harley cracks the door and snaps at Blaise to grab a tub while he grabs the other one. Ash takes both of my bags and slings them over his shoulders. We head down to the staff carpark together to stash the tubs until we can hand them off to Illi in the morning.

"What the hell is in this thing to make it so fucking heavy?" Blaise grouses, and Harley shakes his head at him.

Ash snarks, "I've seen your exam marks, so I know you're not that fucking stupid."

Blaise blinks at him and then at me. I sigh. "We have to get rid of the… problem somehow. Rolling her up in a rug would have us all in juvie in a second."

He scoffs. "Avery would never let that happen… fuck, is the cougar in here? Disgusting! How the fuck did you bend her into it?"

Harley bursts out laughing but it's more of an are-you-fucking-kidding-me sort of sound. "She didn't bend her. She hacked the cunt into pieces. You wanna fuck a member of the Twelve then you should know your girlfriend isn't scared of getting her hands dirty."

Blaise blinks. Then again. Then finally he looks are me and says, "With that tiny knife? Fuck, that seems like a lot of hard work."

Fuck me.

Is he for real?

"I have a bone saw. Can we just move this shit quietly and get this over with? Avery is going to have a fucking fit if we're not back soon," I say and they all grunt in agreement.

My leg is aching by the time we have both of the tubs loaded into the Maserati. It's a tight fit and when Harley starts bitching about the lack of space Blaise snaps back, "Well, I didn't pick it for its trunk size! How the fuck was I supposed to know we'd be moving… this shit. I'll buy a fucking truck for next year."

I groan. "I don't want to think about next year. Let's just get back to Avery."

Ash stops me and then slowly checks every inch of my skin for signs of the work I've just done. I'm thorough, so I'm not worried, but he turns me and pulls at my clothes until he's sure I'm blood-free.

I crack a joke in an attempt to lighten the mood. "I could just blame my period if I've missed a spot."

He glares at me and then slings his arm around my waist, helping me to walk with my sore leg. "You're so fucking strange, Mounty."

I scoff at him. "So the joke is strange but the work isn't? You're just as twisted as I am, Beaumont."

Avery is twitchy when we arrive in the dining hall for dinner. She scans my body, much like her brother had until she's satisfied I'm unharmed. I smile at her a little crookedly but I'm still mostly human. The new and improved Lips, the one who wears the skin of the Wolf even while I'm at school, she doesn't need to be coddled. She isn't wary of touch anymore.

I'm so fucking glad I have my family.

Blaise pulls a face when Ash asks him what he wants for dinner and I ignore their snarking. I can't eat now, not until tomorrow at least and for once they don't push me.

Harley eats just fine.

Blaise gags at the sight and I can't help but laugh at him, his moral lines as fucking blurred as the rest of us despite his dramatics.

When I go to bed that night, tucked between Harley and Ash and listening to Blaise soft snore from the couch, I sleep like a fucking baby.

No one goes after my family and survives.

The end of year assembly is subdued this year compared to the last few years.

I'm not worried about anything and even the whispers have completely stopped around me. Every student at Hannaford has noticed the disappearance of anyone who crosses me and my little family.

They're all terrified.

I get the top of the class in every subject except choir, which Blaise wins by the smallest of margins. No hard feelings and the smug look on his face makes my chest hurt in the best way. Harley and Ash come second, Harley in more subjects than Ash which I'm sure he'll crow about until classes start up again next year. I'm honestly a little terrified about it.

We spend two days packing our rooms and when it's time to leave Blaise is grumbling and pissy over how bad the smell in the Maserati will be thanks to the tubs being left in them for days. He's shocked to find them missing and I laugh at him.

"Did you really think I'd leave them laying around? Illi picked them up for us."

Blaise frowns and pops the trunk to sling our bags in. "How the fuck did he get into the car? The alarms on this thing are insane."

Harley chuckles at him. "The key. I gave him my set when he called. Why are you being so fucking precious over this thing? At least it's still in one piece."

Blaise cringes and nods. No one likes to bring up the 'Stang.

I give Avery the front seat even though Blaise pouts about it and we head back to the Bay together. Avery starts telling us all about the renovations to her ranch and I make another mental note to call the Coyote for a security system upgrade. There's no way I'm calling the Crow, if Ash lays eyes on him he'll fucking skin him and the only help in that situation will be Harley holding the fuck down.

We stay at the same hotel, stupidly I should know better than to stick to a routine.

I walk with Avery, our arms tucked together as the boys trail behind us, bickering and arguing like idiots. Avery freezes at the door and I glance up to find a well-dressed thug in the hotel room.

I dart around her, shielding her even as Ash does the same, but his eyes don't look shocked. They look wary, knowing. Fuck, that's not a good sign.

"Your father has invited you to dinner. You will not be late. You will not decline. You will not invite any further guests. The Wolf and the Crow will both attend. If you know what is good for you, you'll track your brother down and bring him as well. Nine sharp."

Then his lists off the name of a place I've never even driven past, it's so far uptown and walks out. Avery groans and slumps down, resting her forehead on my shoulder.

"I need a week off," she mumbles and I sigh. Don't we all.

Ash stalks to the bar, foregoing the glass entirely and taking deep swigs straight from the bottle. Blaise waves a blunt at him and they disappear out to the balcony. I narrow my eyes at them but Avery stomps over, cussing them out.

"There's hours left. He won't go down there without a clear head," Harley murmurs behind me and I nod. I don't like it but it's not my choice.

Hours of stewing on the couch in silence later, I climb into the shower and pray the hot water will give me the fucking answers on how to get through tonight without losing one of our family.

Avery sits on the bathroom counter, wearing only a silk robe, and pouts. "I don't want to see Atticus. I'm so angry at him, I'm not sure I ever want to see him again."

I scrub at my hair and shrug. "Why? I mean, I know he didn't tell you who he was but... you know the real him."

She narrows her eyes at me. "Are you defending him? Ash will spit it at you."

I snort at her, such a lady. "No, I'm asking my best friend what the exact problem is so when this entire night goes to hell in a handbasket I know enough to pick the right battles."

Her eyes soften and she sighs, leaning back to bump her head against the mirror gently like she trying to knock some sense back into her brain. "He still sees me as some precious little girl that needs to be protected. I'm not angry he didn't tell me he's a member of the Twelve, I'm angry he came up to buy me from you like I'm... an object. That's exactly what Rory thought of me too, but Rory was a distraction not... Atticus."

There are tears rimming her eyes but the look on her face is fucking fierce. Oh boy, he's fucked up. He's fucked up so bad he may never dig himself out of this bullshit he's buried himself in.

"Well, maybe it's time we reminded him that you're Avery fucking Beaumont and you might have shown him your soft side because he meant something to you but that doesn't make you any less of a ruthless, cutthroat dictator. Beat him in his own game because Aves, he has no fucking clue who he's really dealing with."

She smiles at me and hands me a towel. "None of these stupid boys do."

Chapter Thirty-Nine

I hate the dress Avery has put me in but I have to admit, she knows her shit. I fit right in. The restaurant is flashy, overdone, and intimidating to stand in. If I didn't already know half the waiters I'd be uncomfortable as fuck, but Joseph Beaumont has underestimated my reach.

I nod at the maître d> and he tips his head at me respectfully. Ash scoffs at me. "Is there anyone you don't know in the Bay?"

I shrug and wait for him to take us to our seats. The Crow is already waiting for us in the lounge, sipping a malt whiskey, with Luca flanking him in a sharp suit. I sigh as Harley's fists clench at his sides.

"Wolf."

I shake my head at him and say, "Are we the Twelve today, or are we friends? I don't make my friends call me the Wolf."

Harley glares at Atticus like he wants to beat him bloody for everything that has ever happened to Ash and Avery while this man stood by and let it, and I grab his wrist gently to try to remind him of our conversation.

We win nothing here by being obvious in our dislike of this man.

"Forgive me, I'm not accustomed to seeing you as anything but the Wolf." Atticus's eyes flick over to Avery and the slow perusal of her outfit is the last straw for Harley.

"I'm going to bathe in your blood, you manipulative, spineless *cunt*," he hisses and Blaise barely manages to grab him before he chokes the fucker out.

"*Ha!* There it is! There's the impulsive Irishman in the kid. Can't say I blame him, I'd slit your throat any day of the week for the shit you've pulled on *our* family," says Illi, sauntering in behind us, looking as dangerous as ever in his suit.

I gape a little and then snap a photo on my phone, giggling at him like a little schoolgirl. I don't even care about the danger we're all facing in that second. Because Illi. In. A. Suit.

He smirks at me and shrugs. "You can't get in here without one and I didn't want to make a scene."

Ash quirks an eyebrow at me and I laugh, "He didn't even wear a suit to his wedding! It's ridiculous to see him in one now. What the fuck did Odie say when she saw it?"

Illi cackles and when he steps up alongside Ash, I'm shocked to see them exchange a knowing, and respectful, nod. They stand like a wall between Avery and Atticus like they've become best friends without me noticing. When the fuck did that happen?

Atticus looks straight through them, unconcerned with their clear threat. "Avery-"

Her voice is glacial. "No, thank you. I'm quite fine where I am. Lips, I'm happy to wait for our table here with Illi."

That's my girl. I smirk and Illi catches on quickly, slinging himself in the chair next to her and slinging an arm over the back of her chair.

Neither Ash or Harley tense up in any way but Atticus stares down at the Butcher of the Bay like he's planning on ripping that arm right the fuck off of him.

Illi winks at Atticus. "Odie has decided to embrace the polygamous lifestyle of our little club and she *loves* the little Ice Queen."

Blaise snickers under his breath. Harley elbows him in the ribs but the smirk on his face gives him away.

I wait, fully prepared to dive into the fray to get Avery out safely if Atticus loses his damn head. Illi's arms are loose and casual but I know he could tear Atticus in half in a split second without breaking a sweat.

The silence stretches on until finally, a waiter comes to direct us to our private table in the back. Illi jumps up and helps Avery to her feet like the perfect gentleman, guiding her over to walk with Ash behind me. Then he takes up the rear, watching everyone and ready to start swinging his cleaver the second things go south.

As we weave our way through the tables to the private area I glance back to Ash and raise an eyebrow at him. He knows what I'm asking and rolls his eyes at me.

"The night he called me to go find you, even after you told him not to, I decided he's not so bad."

I shake my head. "Not so bad?"

Blaise laughs, his fingers dancing along my arm. "Star, he's a part of our family now too. Maybe not our *immediate* family, but he's like a distant cousin we hang out with at family reunions because everyone else sucks ass."

Illi cackles at me, listen to our every word. "See kid? I'm the cool cousin you can't wait to drink with."

Harley snorts. "The cousin we call when we need a body to disappear. How useful."

Avery giggles and says, "I'm just glad Ash approves. It's nice that he's no longer snarling at my choice in men."

Atticus's shoulders tense so badly even his expensive suit can't hide it. To think I've been so wary of this man from the moment I met him and all along his weakness has been my dictator best friend with an icy gaze and a heart too fucking big for those she loves.

No matter what happens between them, I'll back her.

Even if we have to add him to the list of people hunting us.

The waiter ushers us into the back room where Joseph Beaumont Senior is already seated at the table waiting for us.

"Who would have thought a slum slut from Mounts Bay could look so good in a dress? From Joey's descriptions, I thought you must be hideous but I can see the appeal."

His voice makes my skin crawl.

How the fuck did he convince a young Alice Arbour that he was human? He sounds like a fucking monster.

Atticus steps up next to me and pulls out a chair, gesturing for me to sit. Harley cuts him a look, then takes a seat to my right and Avery sits to my left. One by one, everyone sits on my side of the table, except Illi who takes up watch by the door, a knife dancing back and forth between his hands.

I'm tempted to get him to throw the fucking thing right into Senior's throat.

"I don't appreciate being summoned," says Atticus, taking a napkin and laying it across his lap like he's actually preparing to eat. There is no way I can stomach food right now. No fucking way.

"And why would I give a fuck what the useless third son of Crawford should want? Ah. But you've gone out and made a new name for yourself, haven't you? The peasants of Mounts Bay don't impress me and neither do their kings."

I keep my mouth shut while I watch him.

Ash is right, he and Avery get their looks from this vile man. I suppose this is what Ash will look like in thirty years, but only if all of the humanity has been squeezed out of him. The difference between Ash and Senior is his soul, the same one he shares with Avery. I look at Senior and see nothing of his children in him. Not the twins anyway.

I see far too much of Joey.

I glance around, but the psycho fuck isn't anywhere to be seen. I glance at Avery and she gives me the slightest shake of her head. Fuck.

"I'm not here to speak to *the Crow*. I want to talk to the little girl who thinks she can take my children from me."

I glance back to Senior and stare him down, my gaze and my breathing as steady as always. He's a monster, but he's not the worst I've ever faced.

"I don't think I can take them, I *have* taken them. I'm only here so you know for sure that they're mine now. We can discuss terms, but nothing changes that fact."

Senior's eyes flick across my face and neck, the same way Joey's do like he's looking for my weak point. I don't rise to the bait.

He leans back in his chair, flicking a wrist to summon himself a drink. "And what are you going to do if I don't agree to your terms? I have plans for them both."

I make a big show of staring down each of his bodyguards, all eight of them. "I'd put money on my men over yours. Honestly? I'd put money on the Butcher taking care of the whole lot of them without any help."

Senior raises his glass to his lips and smiles at me, chilling my blood with the cruel twist to his lips. "I own everyone. I own the police who will arrest you and the judge at your trial. I own the prison officers who will tuck you into bed every night and fondle you in the showers. I own your teachers and taxi drivers, and I own your friends. I think you're underestimating me, little girl."

I don't let the trickle of fear running down my spine show. He may have reach, it might be widespread and tangled up in our lives, but I know he isn't as powerful as he's making out. Why else would he try to deal with the Devil?

My voice doesn't waiver as I reply, "And I *know* you're underestimating me."

He lifts a shoulder at me and then fixes his gaze on Ash. The sadistic gleam to his eyes lights something in my blood and I damn near climb over the table and slit his throat myself.

"Where is your brother? I told you to bring him with you."

I mentally call dibs on killing him.

Ash stares at him, unflinching, and my heart nearly bursts with pride. "How should I know? He's not my responsibility."

Senior's eyes narrow a fraction. "Your time fucking slum pussy has made you forget yourself, boy."

Avery's leg tenses against mine and I tuck my hand in hers under the table.

"I will never set foot in your house again. I will never live by your rules again. I will never babysit Joey and cover for his deranged games again," Ash hisses, leaning forward slightly. Illi rumbles happily under his breath by the door, reminding us all that he's watching and prepared to spill blood.

Hmm, more than prepared. Itching to bleed them all out.

The anger leaks out of Senior's face as he replies, "You could be so much more than your brother. I look at you and see every inch of myself, all the bloodlust and rage. If only you weren't corrupted by the little cunt in the womb, maybe then you'd be a man."

I roll my eyes and clasp my hands in front of myself on the table, drawing his gaze back to me. I'm done with this little show of power. I want to go home and plan how I'm going to climb the walls of Beaumont Manor and gut this fuck in his sleep, nice and quietly, where none of his bought police force can save him.

"I'm leaving now. I was hoping for a more productive dinner meeting but if all we're going to do is boast about whose dick does more damage then I'm leaving."

Senior flicks his wrist again and the waiters start to bring out the first course of dinner. "You can leave if you want, little girl, but Avery isn't going anywhere. I've secured a buyer for her and the exchange is being made on her birthday."

Buyer?

Exchange?!

Over my dead fucking body.

I open my mouth to tell the sadistic fuck that when the waiter moves to place my plate in front of me. Only it's not a plate.

It's a cardboard box.

With my full name on it.

No one at the table speaks. Harley hasn't noticed the box, he's too busy trying to contain the rage pumping through his bloodstream and clouding his brain. Avery's skin is beyond white, a thin sheen of sweat covering her forehead, but she's now looking at the box.

Why would Senior be giving me this?

Has he been sending the heads all along? Why? I look up at him but he's staring at the box with the smallest of lines between his brow. So not from him. Fuck.

The Crow doesn't look away from Senior either.

I pick up the steak knife and slit the box open. The smell is less putrid, the head clearly a far more recent kill than the last two.

I lift the flaps and find that for the first time there's a note sitting on top of the head. I grab it first, stupidly because I should grab gloves from Illi first in case we can lift some prints, but my brain isn't working properly at all. The words are written in large cursive letters and a chill races down my spine.

No one touches my blood.

Fuck. Who the hell else have I pissed off?! I think back over the people I've taken out but there's been too many to narrow it down at all. Fuck.

Avery stops breathing next to me, her lungs just ceasing to work.

I look down and my heart jumps into my throat as I stare down into the vacant, lifeless eyes of Joseph Beaumont Jr.

Joey is dead.

Fuck.

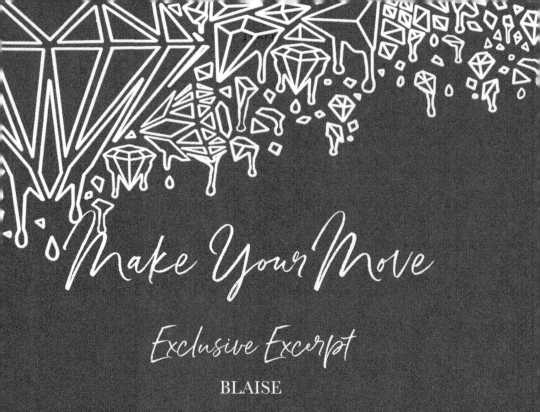

Make Your Move

Exclusive Excerpt

BLAISE

"I need to pee but I can't move but I don't want to pee myself."

Fuck, keeping a straight face is almost impossible but I don't want to piss her off or get stabbed for laughing at her while she's this… vulnerable. "It's okay, Mounty. I'll help you over to the bathroom."

I hoist her up into my arms and laugh at the way she kind of flails about before she gets comfortable, her arms looping around my neck. Her mouth starts running about how much ice cream Avery has been feeding her and I have to shut that shit down fast. She weighs practically nothing and I'm all for the extra roundness her ass has these days.

"Calm down, there's no way I'm dropping you. I'll get you on the toilet."

The gasp out of her is hilarious. "You are not watching me pee, Morrison. Nope. That's- nope."

I scoff at her, gently lowering her to the ground in the bathroom. There's nothing for her to hold onto but she frowns at me when I try to help her out.

"I can shut my eyes if you're that worried, Star."

The nickname slips out but she doesn't notice it yet.

She pouts. "There's absolutely no fucking way, Morrison."

I leave her to it, laughing at her talking to herself and then when I hear the flush and the scuffing sounds of her hobbling around again I step back in.

"Oh. He's still here."

I chuckle and brace her hips as she washes her hands. "I'm not going anywhere, Star. You're stuck with me now."

Her leg starts to wobble again and I lift her up a little to get her weight off of it.

"What the hell does that even mean? I've ruined everything."

This again. I could fucking kill Arbour for how he reacted this morning, the dick. I try not to sounds pissed though, I don't think she could take it with the way her mouth is running right now. "You haven't, Star. Look, we all agreed to share you. That means you're not getting away from us that easy. What ever it takes, we're keeping you."

I see her brain melt a little more and I swing her back up into my arms, walking back over to the bed and sitting down with her in my lap. She hums happily under her breath, wriggling and rocking her hips until I grab them to steady her.

The dopey, loved-up grin on her face is adorable. Fuck, I never thought I'd be calling the Mounty adorable but here we are. She starts stroking my chest, and I'm struggling not to get hard at the grinding she's absently doing on my dick.

I'm not a total asshole, I'm not going to fuck her while she's high like this but fuck is she tempting.

I try to distract myself by recording her and sending it to Harley, a little payback for his fuck up this morning, but she's too fucking hot. The rocking has me as hard as a fucking stone underneath that ass of hers.

"If both of his hands are on my hips then that hand must belong to me."

I try not to burst out laughing at her. "Yes, that's your hand."

Her eyes widen and I see the hazy sort of panic take over her. Fuck, after everything we've said to her for the last two years no wonder she's freaked out about touching me.

Fuck, I want her touching me.

I lean forward to whisper against her lips, "You can touch me wherever you want, little Star."

I swear I see her brain break.

I'm about to just say fuck it and spread her out on the sheets, strip her naked and taste every fucking inch of her skin when the door flings open and Harley storms into the room. Great.

He's pissed the fuck off for something different.

"Morrison, if I find out you've laid a single fucking finger on her while she's been high, I'll gut you."

To The End

Hannaford Prep Year Four

Prologue

BLAISE

Star looks down at the box and I don't have to be psychic to know whose head is in the fucking thing. She looks like it's the worst possible choice and her face is blank before her eyes flick back up to the deranged serial killer at the table.

Joey is dead.

I can't say I'm sorry to see that psychotic fuck go but as Senior's eyes bore into my girl I kinda wish Joey was still breathing. How the fuck do we get out of this?

Harley knocks my leg under the table and I dip my chin a fraction so he knows he's got my attention. He traces an 'A' on the table in front of him, an old signal we've used a million times before.

He's telling me to get Avery the hell out of here and for the first time I'm torn. She's not cut out for when shit goes south like this, not physically at least. Someday that girl is going to dance on a big stage and have pompous rich dickheads falling at her feet. She can't afford to be injured.

More than that, we can't afford for Ash to see his sister hurt.

I'm fairly certain Ash is more dangerous than Senior, one-on-one. It's the damn statement about the cops that has me worried. What the fuck is Star going to do?

It's only that I'm watching her so closely that I see her pass her phone to Avery under the table, and Floss' face stays carefully blank and her fingers move swiftly across the screen by memory alone.

"How much do you owe your buyer? Now that you can't deliver?" Lips says, her voice so fucking flat and bored I'm impressed.

The serial killer just ignores her, cutting his steak up into tiny pieces with surgeon-like precision. He takes his time, waiting until he has a piece speared on his fork before answering her. "What's in the box, little girl? Who is delivering parcels to you during my time?"

She leans back in her chair, cool and calm. "Answer my question, Beaumont. The box is none of your concern."

He doesn't like that. Not one fucking bit.

His lip curls at her, slowly shifting into a cruel smirk that makes him look

deranged. "He was very interested in her, I don't think even the *Wolf of Mounts Bay* could convince the Devil not to take what is his. Run along, go hide her. He'll only enjoy the chase."

The Devil.

Harley's fingers twitch and I bump his leg with mine, reminding him that we'll be fucking fine.

We've survived the kinds of hell people couldn't even dream.

Why not add *the Devil* to the mix?

Lips stands, smoothing her dress down like Avery does, and we all stand with her. Even that stupid fuck Atticus.

"I'd thank you for the meal, but your company has been… lacking." Lips says, tucking her hand into Harley's and tugging him away from the table. Avery looks up at me and I give her a curt nod.

Senior watches Lips' back like he's imagining all of the things he's going to carve into her skin and get off to and I can't fucking take it.

Apparently, neither can Ash.

"Here. Just so you know we did our best to get him here. He seems to be… otherwise occupied." Ash sneers, and pushes the box until Joey's head rolls out.

I could fucking vomit.

I hold it in, because no one else looks sick and I'll be fucked if I'm the only one puking over this shit, and I tug Avery away from the table.

Two of Senior's bodyguards jolt away from the far wall, ready to throw themselves at Ash and Lips, and I hesitate for a second.

I shouldn't bother.

Illi palms two meat cleavers and *throws them across the room.*

Avery makes a little noise in the back of her throat and I decide pretty fucking quick that I need to keep her walking. We stalk through the restaurant at a slow enough pace that no one notices us but still cutting through the building pretty fucking quick.

She hums under her breath, completely distracted by whatever-the-fuck-it-is she's piecing together in that evil genius brain of hers. I'm too busy trying to look out for more of Senior's men to question her.

When we get to the exit, there are cop cars everywhere and I curse viciously under my breath, but there's also more than a hundred motorbikes with scary-ass bikers on them, starting fights with the pigs and smashing up the cars.

Right.

Lips called in a favor.

There's a biker leaning against the wall of the restaurant, watching us both intensely. He's wearing a president patch so I figure out pretty quickly he's the Boar.

Avery stares right back at him, cataloging every fucking inch of the man until I bump her shoulder with mine to distract her. I don't need her accidentally starting shit with a member of the fucking Twelve while Star isn't here.

"Does he look familiar to you?" she murmurs, and I shake my head.

"I don't exactly spend much time with dirty bikers, Floss."

She purses her lips at me, something she does when she thinks I'm being particularly stupid. I fucking hate it.

"I need to speak to Atticus. I need to look into Lips' background. We know nothing about who her family really is. Or her father."

I blink at her.

What the *fuck*?

Chapter One

Standing in the forest at the edge of the city limits in Mounts Bay feels different this time around.

The last time I stood here it was to compete in the Game myself. I killed two men, stabbed one through the eye and bashed the others skull in with a large rock after I'd knocked him, but it's more than just that. Last time I was here, I was desperate right down to my core. Desperate to eat, to live, to survive this hellhole.

Now I have something to lose.

Avery has her hand tucked in mine and her phone is, for once, switched off and left behind in Blaise's Maserati. There's a strict ban on electronics during the Game and nothing that will happen here tonight is worth the risk of being caught with a smartphone. Illi stands on her other side, arms crossed and the signature Butcher scowl on his features, looking every inch the nightmare that he's known to be on the streets in the Bay. Harley and Blaise stand a step behind us, muttering quietly together at the show of masculine strength before us.

Ash shifts from where he stands beside me, a sneer on his face as he stares the O'Cronin family down. I ignore them completely, pissed they're trying to get the upper hand on me like this. Liam and Domhnall keep making remarks that would get them gutted if we weren't here and doing this. But, fuck my life, we are and I have to keep my mouth shut until we know who's won.

Every member of the Twelve are present, as required, and there's a huge crowd of loyal men watching. Everyone here wears the colors they've been inducted into, everyone here belongs to someone.

The Jackal stands on the other side of the clearing. His eyes haven't left me, not even once. I know this for sure even though I haven't so much as glanced at him, because Avery's hand is tense in mine. She's watching him.

The Crow is watching the Jackal too, careful never to let his eyes land on Avery.

What a fucking mess.

The gurgling sound of the idiot on the ground draws me back to what we're doing. The Vulture needs replacing and the only way to replace the repulsive cretin is to hold the Game.

I have to attend every damn trial and watch as men, boys, and a few young girls all brutally beat and slaughter each other. It's enough to turn a strong stomach and I'm oddly proud of Avery for refusing to stay back at the ranch she's got us holed up in, safe and secure now the Coyote has installed his security over every inch of the place.

There's shouting from the crowd and I let my gaze wander over the bodies to assess where we're at in terms of numbers. A lot of red and black. Too close to tell who has brought more muscle along.

The Coyote shifts and walks over to stand at my side. Ash glares at him, enough that I grit my teeth but the asshole could not give less of a fuck about protocol. The Coyote, thankfully, doesn't seem to care.

"Which one are you hoping wins? I like the kid," he murmurs, leaning into me.

I can smell Viola Ayres' perfume on him and smirk at him. She's not here. He's smart enough to leave his little captured rich girl at home in his bunker where the Jackal can't kill her stealthily.

"The kid will cause me issues if he wins, but I don't really care either way." I murmur back, lying through my teeth.

Anyone but the kid, fuck, anyone but the kid.

The Coyote's eyes flick behind us to Harley and he smirks. "Sure. I thought we were friends now, Lips?"

The fucker is playing with fire. The Crow hears his use of my name and shoots him a glare. I ignore him.

I no longer fear that man. Not when Avery holds his balls in the palm of her perfectly manicured hand.

Ok, I don't think a man like Atticus Crawford will ever be truly whipped but I know when it comes down to it, he's not going to hurt her and threatening me would truly hurt my ice queen bestie.

"How is Viola doing?" Avery murmurs, and the Coyote grimaces.

"She'd like to go home and see her sister, but the little love-spat the Wolf has going on is ruining that for her."

I cringe and Ash gives the Coyote a look that could kill, hissing at him, "It's not a love anything. He's fucking deranged."

The Coyote laughs dismissively. "You'd know all about deranged, wouldn't you Beaumont? Where is your brother these days? Viola has told me all about your family."

I keep my face carefully blank. No one here needs to know about Joey's death. Avery's eyes flick away from the Jackal for the first time to land on the Boar.

He's watching us all.

I make a note to ask her what the hell she's planning later. She's become weirdly interested in bikers lately.

I'm starting to think she's going to great lengths to get over her infatuation with Atticus and I'm so not interested in dragging her off of the back of some dirty biker's hog.

The sickening crunch of bones breaking signifies the fight is over. With my heart in my throat, I stare down at the victor who is panting and sweating but wholly unharmed, and fuck, we have a problem.

Aodhan O'Cronin has won.

There's an O'Cronin in the Twelve.

The Crow steps forward, cutting the Jackal a look when he attempts to step forward as well. Oh yay, a pissing contest. Harley shifts behind me, the sounds of his body moving something my entire body is now in-tuned with.

"You've won, welcome to the Twelve. You're replacing the Vulture. Who do you choose to be?" The Crow says, and Aodhan smirks. Fuck, he looks way too much like Diarmuid when he does that.

"The Stag."

How fitting for the Irish mobster. I'm sure he's going to be a whole new pain in my ass. When he glances my way, I tip my head to him respectfully. I'm not having the little fuck try to use the bad blood between us as an excuse to stick a knife in me.

Liam and Domhnall start to whoop and cheer like fucking children, and I forced myself not to roll my eyes. Avery drops my hand and steps back, preparing for whatever violence is about to come thanks to their antics, because the look Ash gives them is pretty fucking telling.

The dinner meeting with his father seems to have burned away what little restraint he had and now he's eager for blood.

I don't want to wait around to see how far he wants to take it, so I catch his eye and tilt my head until he gives me a curt nod. The groups splits off and Harley carefully directs me away, making sure to act as though he's shielding me and being a bodyguard rather than what he's really doing, which is pushing me around to get me the fuck away from his family before Liam or Domhnall try to knife me.

Of course the mobster fuck can't just let me leave without starting shit.

"Wolf."

Harley freezes and shifts until he's blocking me from his cousin completely. I give him a look and duck around him, ignoring the vicious curse he murmurs under his breath. Illi takes my side immediately and Ash steps up to my other side, his icy stare sending little shivers down my spine.

Fuck, he's hot when he goes all Beaumont-killer on someone for me.

Aodhan ignores the wall of muscular threat and meets my eyes, unflinching. "I don't want to start my time amongst the Twelve with conflict."

I barely contain the snort at him words and my gaze flicks to his father. Domhnall smirks at me and I quirk an eyebrow at him. "There's more conflict amongst the Twelve than there has ever been before. Your family's issues are small in comparison."

The other members of the Twelve have all stopped to watch us. I feel the unease settle in my gut at having another fucking threat to worry about.

Aodhan's eyes trail over Harley, taking in his size and the vicious look on his face and the tattoo Domhnall and Liam forced on him as a kid. He glances back at me and flicks out a hand as if he's cutting through the bullshit surrounding us. "As I said, I don't want any of the conflict to be about me. What is it going to take for you to let go of what my family has done to... yours."

He's damned fucking right that Harley's my family, my boyfriend, mine.

I cross my arms. "While your father and grandfather breathe, I will never let it go. Your uncles too. Every last O'Cronin involved with what happened to Iris. Loyalty is highly valued in the Twelve and what they did to one of their own, it just doesn't sit right with me."

The loyalty isn't the half of it. What they did to Iris, when they killed Éibhear in front of Harley, they put themselves on this path. I've tied their hands for now but someday, when we have less on our plates, I'll give them exactly what they deserve.

Aodhan glances back to Harley and my golden god smirks at him, saying in a low tone, "You're not going to give the Wolf that, are you? You're not so fucking desperate for friends within the Twelve that you'd get rid of the spineless, manipulative cunts."

Aodhan smirks and shrugs. "You underestimate me, cousin."

Then he reaches back to palm his gun from the holster at the base of his spine and—

And fucking shoots his father. Right between the eyes.

Liam O'Cronin gasps, his eyes peeled back and a stupid look of disbelief on his face, and then a second bullet comes out of Aodhan's gun and lands in his temple. There's brain matter fucking everywhere and I wince when Avery takes a large step away from the mess. Blaise moves with her, still covering her, and for the first time the Crow's eyes flick over to the object of his infatuation.

The Jackal is still watching me.

Fuck me, this situation couldn't get any worse.

As if to prove me wrong, Ash and Illi both draw their weapons of choice, and I grab Ash's wrist to stop him from actually shooting Aodhan.

I wait until everyone has taken a breath, and then I raise an eyebrow.

Aodhan looks at me and the shift starts to take place in his eyes. The shifting from who he was, into who he is now amongst the Twelve. The Stag is born here in the blood-soaked dirt the same way the Wolf was.

He smiles at me, a baring of teeth that isn't all that threatening. Not to me. "Are you satisfied, Wolf, or should I send you the heads of all of my uncles? Say the word and I'll do it."

My blood turns to ice and Ash's eyes narrow.

It has to be a coincidence. It's a turn of phrase, right?! I glance over my shoulder to find Avery staring at the Boar again and, fuck me, I need to ask her what the hell is going on there.

"If you think killing them buys you my friendship, you're wrong. I'm not entirely sure why you want it so badly in the first place. Finding your feet and building up your name takes time, and connections. You should be cozying up to the Jackal or the Crow," I say, and I keep my voice calm and level.

There's no warning the guy away from the Jackal, the sadistic fuck would use that against us, but I can't have him trying to fucking bond with me. Harley would lose his fucking shit over it.

"I don't want to be friends. I want to know that you're not going to climb in my bedroom window and slit my throat while I sleep. I also want to know that my cousin is going to stay the fuck out of the family and leave it all to me. Keeping you alive and happy will get me both of those things."

Harley snorts and says, "I don't want your pathetic excuse of a family or business. Stay the fuck away from us and I'll do my best to forget you exist."

I nod. "That's a fair trade. Harley has already dropped the name, he isn't looking to take over... whatever the fuck it is you lot do now."

Aodhan smirks at me and nods. "We have a wide skill set, Wolf. And despite your reluctance to be around me, I'm happy to help out if your... situation doesn't clear itself up soon."

Fuck.

Right.

I stare him down until he finally nods and leaves, without so much as a glance at his father or grandfather's dead bodies. I wait until the mobsters that are still breathing leave the clearing before we start to move again. I want a shower, ice cream, and several great big orgasms to get over the events of tonight. Maybe even ten of the suckers. I give Ash a sly little look until my lashes, all coy as if I know how the hell to flirt, and he smirks back at me.

Yay.

As he opens the car door for me and just as I grab his arm to climb in he stiffens and curses under his breath.

"Should I expect to see Luca with you at your next meeting? Have you added him to the rotation of men you're spreading your legs for?" the Jackal says, and I take a deep breath.

When I turn to face him it's as if the whole clearing pauses in fear. I don't recognize any of the guys he has with him tonight. He's probably killed everyone I've ever met in the inner circle of his crew after Luca's betrayal.

I'd be dead if the Crow hadn't planted him within the ranks of the Jackal's men, and it's clear the Jackal still hasn't figured out he was a spy to begin with.

I raise an eyebrow at the Jackal and say, "Whoever spends time between my legs is none of your concern. I'll see you at the meeting, Jackal."

Then I turn my back on him and slide into the car.

After a moment, Ash slides in after me and the smug look on his face makes my chest tighten. We will not bow down to any of our demons. Not anymore.

Chapter Two

Avery's ranch is exactly what you would imagine a Beaumont's ranch to look like. It's over the top, looks like a fucking palace, and I'm kind of afraid to touch anything. Blaise laughs at the faces I pull every time I bump into the furniture, but I mean, is there anything in the damn place that doesn't cost the same amount as a small country's tax assessment? Jesus.

The part that makes it a home, a real one, is the photos that line the walls of the staircase. The freezer full of cherry ice cream and the garage with millions of dollars worth of cars Ash protects like they're his children. The recording studio in the pool house and the boxing ring in the gym. Yeah, this place has a freaking pool house and a gym.

It's set up perfectly for the whole lot of us and the look of pure satisfaction on Avery's face when she sees us all around her dining table every night makes my chest ache in the best possible way.

I kind of assumed we'd be playing musical beds every night but Avery hadn't lied to me when she said she was custom ordering me an orgy-sized bed. I blushed like an idiot but after the mess our dinner with Senior had been it's a relief to go to bed every night knowing they're all safe, and breathing, with me.

I still wake up shaking with dreams of Harley dying because of Annabelle's obsession.

Doesn't matter that Illi handed me a jar with one of her hands in it. He's a sick and twisted man, but I love him like a brother and I'll take that fucking jar with me everywhere I go until I get over the damage of nearly losing Harley.

The night before the next meeting, I wake up in a cold sweat and shaking. Ash is curved around me and the second I open my eyes I find Harley still asleep beside me, looking peaceful and unaware of the random bouts of panic his near-death is still fucking causing me. What an asshole.

I look around and Blaise is nowhere to be found. A quick glance at the clock shows it's four in the morning and not a normal hour for him to be awake yet. He's more of a late afternoon riser.

I wriggle out of the bed, careful not to wake the other two, and creep around the house until I find him smoking a blunt out by the pool. I watch him for a second and take in the lines between his eyes, the dark circles and the way his mouth is turning down at the corners, and I sigh. There's only one person left in contact with him that has this effect on him.

His fucking mother.

I walk over to take the seat next to him and he murmurs happily at me, the smile he gives me a little forced and a whole lot morose. I can feel the pity party brewing already. Great.

"What are you doing out here?" I murmur, and he flicks the ash from his blunt. I try not to let the smell bother me but he gives me another sad smile and puts it out on the ashtray.

"Sorry, Star. I can't sleep."

Fuck.

We're a bunch of fucking insomniacs.

I shift to curl myself into his lap, enjoying the little grunts he lets out as my ass wiggles against his *very* interested dick. It's been a while since I've had any of them alone and I'm not quite ready to use the orgy-sized bed for the exact purpose I'm sure Avery got it for, so this little moment to ourselves is not only perfect but it's like a drug to me. Yes, fucking *please*. I give myself a second to clear the hormones out of my brain.

"Has something happened?" I mumble into his chest.

He sighs, tangling his hands into my hair, scratching at my scalp in a way that has my toes curling. "My mom wants me to go see her and Blaire. I'm not sure it's a good idea. I'm not exactly a safe person to be around anymore but... I miss her."

I nod and press my forehead against his chest. I still don't like the woman but fuck, she's his mom. I guess as long as she's not trying to kill him I have to deal with whatever he wants to do.

Blaise tugs at my hair until I look up at him and see the lecherous smirk he's giving me. "Wanna suck me off to help me get back to sleep?"

I snort at him but, uh, *yeah*. That's exactly what I want.

"Maybe if you're good I will. If you're *extra* good I might even swallow."

The smirk on his face triples in size and he leans down to whisper in my ear, "You love my come, Star. You're greedy for it, you'd never spit me out."

I mumble about *arrogant, smug assholes* as he stands, still pressing me into his chest, and walks us both back into the house. He doesn't stop until we get to his room and he kicks the door shut, way too loud and I'm cringing at the thought of it waking Avery. The last thing I need is for her to come looking for blood and finding me blowing Blaise.

We might both get stabbed.

Blaise lowers me to the ground and chuckles at me. "Stop looking so fucking scared, Avery is on the other side of the building and if the other two hear us the worst that will happen is they'll come find us. We're very good at sharing you, Star."

I glare at him but the little shiver that runs through me only has him laughing harder. I shove at his chest a little but that only distracts me more. The ink running up his neck has been added to and now there are little stars curling behind his ears and a few little ones on his temples. It's fucking hot, and completely unfair because now there's zero chances of me looking at him without ruining my panties.

"Fuck, *that's* how I want you looking at me. I want you looking at me like you're fucking desperate, Star," he drawls, tugging me over to his bed and I straddle his lap again.

If I were any good at flirting or foreplay I'd give him sultry look and use a coy voice to say "I am," but that's just not something I have in me, so I kiss him instead.

It doesn't matter how long we've been doing this, making out and grinding all over each other, Blaise still kisses me with his whole damn body. He curls around me, covers me, and groans into my lips until I forget myself.

I pull his shirt off and yank my own off so I can press myself against him, rubbing at his chest and arms like a freaking cat in heat. He grins at me and flips me over so I'm underneath him on the bed. The second his dick rubs against my clit through my panties I realize three vital things: we're alone, we're horny, and I'm no longer a scared virgin.

I grab the waistband of his boxers and yank them down, far enough that I can stroke his dick and, fuck yes, this is want I want. Blaise groans into my lips and breaks away, panting and thrusting his hips up into my grip.

"Do you want a blow job, or do you want to have sex? Both?" I whisper, blushing so fucking hard but whatever. I manage to say the words so it's a win.

Blaise freezes, then props himself up to look down at me with a smirk. "I knew it. It was Harley, right? He fucked you first? Ash would've broken you."

Well, *fuck*, why is *this* a conversation he's insisting on having? And right now, of all fucking times!

I clear my throat. "Why the hell are we talking about this? You already know it was Harley. He wouldn't have lied and Avery wasn't exactly quiet about it."

He scoffs at me and moves to kiss down my throat. "Other than gloating about the party at the docks, Harley doesn't talk about what you guys get up to. He did suddenly become less of a grumpy dick so I guessed."

I squirm, more at his words than his tongue, and try once again to get him to *shut the hell up*. "Does it matter? Can we go back to the orgasms now? I'd really like to cuddle and nap afterwards."

He licks a stripe down my belly until he gets to my panties and then blows on my skin. Fucking seductive, evil dick. I bite back a moan.

He peels my panties off and whispers against my pussy as he begins to lick and suck at me, "It matters, Star. I've changed my mind, I don't want you to swallow my come. I want to see it dripping down your legs."

Holy.

Merciful.

Lord.

"I don't ever want to know where you learned to talk like that," I gasp out as he sucks at my clit and hums under his breath. I can feel how wet I am, I can feel I'm coating his face, and I groan when he slips two fingers into me.

"I'm naturally talented, Star. I thought you'd know that by now," he says, and he pumps his fingers into me mercilessly and I come with a tiny little scream I hope no one else hears.

I need a second to coax my soul back into my body, but when I can move again Blaise climbs up to sit against the headboard and pulls me back into his lap. I bite his lip while he moves me, lining up and lowering me down slowly until I'm impaled on his dick. It knocks the breath out of me, he's still too fucking big and even though I've had sex with Harley a few times I'm still fairly new at this. His eyes stay focused on mine until they roll back in my head. Fuck, I love this.

Blaise doesn't treat me like glass. He doesn't wait before he's grabbing my hips and moving me up and down his cock until both our legs are shaking, a stream of encouragements and filthy words falling out of his mouth faster than I can make sense of. "Fuck, yes. Move your hips, Star, fuck, *yes*. Just like that. Perfect, a fucking perfect pussy for my cock."

I can feel the orgasm building in me again, and my movements grow desperate. Blaise grunts and slams his hips up into me, his head rolling back, and I kiss and lick my way up his throat, sucking on every star he's itched into his skin for me. I come again, clenching around him and biting his shoulder so I don't wake the whole fucking house up, and he grunts, slamming his hips up into me as he comes, too.

When I climb off of his lap, his come does run down my legs.

I fucking love it.

My brains must be completely fried, because when he snaps a photo I don't even care, I just preen under the possessive look in his eyes. Once I've caught my breath, I clean up in the bathroom and then settle into his arms in the bed.

"I'm never letting you go, Star. You're mine." He whispers against my hair in a sleep-soaked voice.

I yawn and press a kiss to his chest. I don't want to think about anything that might ruin my sleep. I don't want to think about how he might not have a choice.

The demons stalking us might take me out.

The final Twelve meeting for the summer is being held on neutral ground.

Well, it's technically neutral because the Vulture is dead but taking Illi back to the place where he watched his future wife get sold to her rapist isn't going to be pleasant, and I find myself getting wound up over it. I hate the auctions. The entire building stinks of death, despair, and perverted men. Even after months of disuse I'm sure it'll still fucking *reek*.

I must wear my unease like a neon sign because everyone stays three feet away from me all day, the guys all going down to the gym to work out and Avery sitting in front of the TV with her phone for hours.

When I finally come out of my fog and join her, I cringe at the movie that's playing.

Dirty Dancing.

Fuck.

"Men are swine," Avery says around a mouthful of pancakes, more chocolate syrup and whipped cream than anything else. Right. Best friend duty is calling but how the fuck do I fix this?!

"What's he done? I can lightly stab him. Nothing permanent but enough to ruin his day."

Avery sighs and cocks her head, tucking her arm in mine. "You're the best. We're still… *communicating* daily, but I'm keeping it all strictly business. He's just told me I'm forbidden to come to the meeting tonight. Forbidden. Like I'm a fucking child, or a puppy, or… something else pathetic."

Atticus Crawford, the Crow of Mounts Bay, is a fucking dumbass.

"So stabbing? Because that sounds like he needs to shed a little blood and gain a little perspective. I could hold him down while you bleed him? Well, Blaise and I could. I wouldn't trust the other two. They'd make it permanent."

She smiles and shakes her head. "I'm not a pathetic girl. I don't mope and moon or boys."

I nod, except I'm also very aware that that's exactly what she's doing. However, I'm not a dumbass so no amount of torture could get me to utter those words out loud.

"I'm coming tonight," she says, her tone firm and I nod again.

"There was never a doubt in my mind. Someday he'll figure it out, Aves."

She sniffs just a tiny bit and says, "I'll be gone by then. I'm not waiting for him to figure out I'm not a child. I'm not the little girl in the pretty dresses he used to like."

I steal a forkful of pancakes and say, "You should throw a knife at his head, like Illi taught you. That'll teach him."

The lessons Illi had been teaching all of my family were fucking amazing to watch. He's not exactly a natural teacher, but the guys all respond well to his arrogant ribbing and he treats Avery with the same level of respectful patience as I imagine he had back when he'd first taught me. She was a quick study, and now she's a danger with a knife. Atticus better watch out.

She scoffs at me and I see my cold, cruel, perfect Beaumont back in her eyes again. "Why are you so intent on hurting him? Should I be worried about the first argument you get into with those stupid boys?"

I scoff at her and steal more food. All of my stewing has brewed up an appetite. "I don't know what the hell you're talking about, I fight with them all the time."

The front door opens and the guys all walk through, bickering and snarking at each other like they always do. I turn back to the TV, intent on ignoring them but Avery's eyes narrow dangerously.

"Do the three of you ever do anything *productive*, or are you just going to spend the summer beating each other up and glaring at crime lords so Lips has to go into damage control to save your miserable asses?"

Ash scoffs at her and sits on the couch with us, sliding his palm along my thigh in a cruel and calculated move. Cruel to me, because I can't control my reactions, and calculated towards his sister, because I think he's done with her moping. It works like a fucking charm.

Avery's eyes drop down to glare at his hand and when she looks back up at him I almost cringe at the look of pure disgust.

Ash smirks at her. "Maybe you should stop moping about that spineless fuck Atticus Crow and find someone worth your time?"

I move to get up, and away from their war, and they both hold me in place. Well, *fuck*.

"And who exactly do you suggest I date then, Ash? Who would meet your impossible standards?"

Blaise sprawls out on the floor in front of us and winks at me as he says, "Maybe you should date girls instead? Ash probably won't give a fuck about a girl getting up in your pussy."

Avery arches a brow at him and says, "If I were going to fuck a girl, it would be Lips. Don't tempt me, she would drop you idiots for me in a second."

I bite my lip to stop myself from smiling but the girl has a point. Blaise doesn't seem to agree. "Star loves my dick Aves, she'd never give it up for you."

I blush and stand, brushing off Ash's hand and grabbing the empty plate. "That's more than enough bullshit for me for one day. How about we get ready for the meeting? I don't need you guys getting pissy right before we leave. We'll already have Illi to deal with."

I sigh, thinking again about what the fuck to do about the Butcher's reactions to being back at the auctions. I know the Jackal has picked that building on purpose to torture his old friend because he's a fucking sadistic dick like that.

The retaliation I have planned for him will be enough to keep Illi level.

I hope.

Chapter Three

Blaise drives us down to the auctions in his new Cadillac, and I sit in the back between Ash and Harley. It's quiet in the car, everyone is a little on edge, but I enjoy the time to think and plan and prepare.

When we pull up to the warehouse I direct Blaise on where to park and we find Illi waiting for us, leaning against his own Camaro. Harley mumbles under his breath in appreciation and Ash scoffs at him, the tense air broken by a freaking car of all things. I slip out behind Ash, a hand in his because he's pretending to be a gentleman for the night, then I tuck my arm into Avery's in a show of support.

The Crow will already be here, in the building checking the Jackal hasn't planted explosives I'd guess, and I don't want Avery feeling anxious about it. I'm not sure this girl can actually feel such a thing but Atticus is fucking ruining her.

"Can we get this bullshit fucking over with? I have other things to do." Illi snaps, and takes the lead. That's breaking protocol and something I'd bitched the boys out for at dinner to remind them. Harley raises an eyebrow at me and I shake my head.

This place is fucking evil.

We walk after him, up to the door where one of the Jackal's men is standing watch. Illi sneers at him and I gently nudge Avery behind me.

It's about to get bloody.

"The Jackal has put a limit on how many men go in tonight. Pick one, the rest can stay out here," the chump says and I stare him down.

My voice is cold and flat as I reply, "The Jackal doesn't tell me what to do. Move or die."

The chump startles, and looks between the Butcher and I with panicked eyes. "You can't kill me, I'm with the Jackal! He gave me an order, I can't—"

"Die it is." says Illi, and he swipes one of his cleavers from its sheath. The chump shits himself and scrambles back, slapping a hand onto a hidden earpiece and shouting about being murdered.

It's not murder, it's taking out the fucking trash.

Avery winces and turns around at the sight of blood, but the boys all watch with varying levels of interest as Illi shows them exactly how he got his name. The chump screams through the first arm but is out for his leg. There's blood fucking everywhere, and it feels like it's coating the inside of my nose by the time he stands again.

"Fuck that egotistical, sadistic, spoiled fucking sociopath," Illi snaps, and I nod my head.

"Well, if that isn't a statement, I don't know what is."

Ash rolls his shoulders back and flicks a hand at the mess. "Is that not going to get you into trouble? And here I am being on my best behavior."

Illi wipes his hands on his shirt, a pointless move because there isn't much of him that isn't covered in the gore, and snaps, "If that fuck D'Ardo has a thing to say about it I'll fucking gut him as well. Fuck playing nice, kid, let's get this over with."

I shake my head at him, hesitating before grabbing his hand and giving it a squeeze. "You can wait outside if you want. Or head home. I've got this under control."

He scoffs at me and drops my hand. "Like fuck."

Great.

It's going to be one of those sorts of nights.

We walk in and the smell is as bad as I'd thought it was going to be. The cages are all still hanging everywhere and the seating still looks like someone's taken a cum-bath on them. When Avery gags and covers her nose, Ash tucks her under his arm.

The meeting is held on the fucking auction stage because the Jackal really is a sadistic fuck.

We're the last ones to arrive. Harley pulls my chair out for me, and kisses my neck right before I take my seat because he can't help but push things. Fuck it, this night is already going to be a shit-show, why not fuck with the Jackal a little more?

I ignore the scoff out of the Coyote and when I turn to give him a look I catch Viola's eye. He's brought her with him.

Fuck.

She walks over to stand with my family and they accept her without question. Good. The Coyote may not have an army but he comes in handy and I already have a great deal of work I need him to do. The less diamond I have to part with the better.

"She wants to talk to you before you leave tonight." he murmurs into my ear and I nod, meeting the Crow's eye across the table and giving him a nod, nice and big where the whole fucking table can see it and see the lines being drawn.

"Shall we begin? I'm sure we all have better things to do than sit around here gossiping." The Crow says, arrogant and cold, and the Jackal sneers at him.

"I think we should begin by asking the Wolf how exactly she thinks she's going to get away with killing off my men?"

I laugh.

Fuck it, I'm so over this man's bullshit.

"Did you ask everyone else to enter this building with only one man? Did you choose this building to piss anyone else off? Have you been sending men after any other members of the Twelve? Have you pulled a gun on any other members?"

The mood in the room sours even more. The Boar's eyes bounce between us both and then settle on the Jackal, cold and fucking dangerous in a way I've rarely seen from this man.

From the corner of my eye I catch Avery watching him, shifting on her feet. The others don't notice except for Blaise, who looks so uncomfortable and I cannot for the life of me figure it out.

Right.

I'm asking her the second we get in the car what the fuck is going on with her and the Boar. She would tell me if she knew him, I'm sure she would, so there's something going on with her and I'm not sure how Atticus is involved but it's clear he's thinking the same as she is. He's watching the Boar with more than his usual cold calculation.

Fuck it.

"If you're going to start an inquisition over things we are and aren't allowed to do, then I have my own topics to bring up."

The Bear scoffs. "Yes, we all know you want him to stop chasing your pussy. We get it."

I level him with a look too because fuck caution. "I was talking about all of the spies he has on the other members of the Twelve."

Well, I have their full attention now.

The Jackal stares at me, unflinching, and leans back in his chair like it doesn't matter to him and I'm sure it doesn't. Whatever he has on the Bear and the Lynx won't be affected by me revealing he's got spies in their houses. The Lynx wouldn't even kill the man watching her; her son is a spoiled fucking brat.

"Name the spy in my house, Wolf, and he'll be dead by sunrise," the Fox says, the quick smiles and playful winks absent.

Good. Fuck him.

"I'll name them all. I think it's time the Jackal toes the line. He's gotten too big-headed. I wouldn't want him setting a bad example for the Stag."

The Stag stares around the table and I'm weirdly proud of the guy for being so unaffected by our squabbling. Only a few years older than me, the Stag growing up in the Bay means the people at this table would be terrifying to him.

The Jackal leans forward in his chair again, smiling at me like he's baring his teeth. "Tell them anything you want, Wolf. It makes no difference to me, or how this is all going to end."

Game on.

I tilt my head at him, with a little fuck-you smile on my face. "Do you think it would make a *difference* to everyone to know you invited the Devil to Mounts Bay?"

I think a bomb detonating under the table would have had less reaction.

"The Devil?! What the fuck is wrong with you?" snaps the Bear, and the Lynx does the sign of the cross as if that'll fucking help her.

I stare at the Jackal across the table as the exclamations and shouting only gets louder. He watches me and there must be some serious issues in the man's brain because he only looks more obsessed with me. Like I'm impressing him by selling him out. I need a little less psycho in my life.

The meeting is fucking pointless.

It's supposed to be an induction of sorts for the Stag but all he learns is that the Jackal is a power-hungry psycho and the Crow isn't up for playing his twisted games.

I don't speak again, I keep my mouth firmly shut even when I'd love to chip in, and I watch them rest of them carefully to not only see who is siding with the Jackal, but *why*.

The Fox is being blackmailed. The twitchy looks make that clear. The Lynx is hungry for power and she doesn't care who she gets it from. The Bear is harder to read, but I'm guessing he's just thinking about what is best for his business, and the Jackal needs his services on an hourly basis. I'm not sure if the Crow has such a blood-soaked legacy.

The Tiger is hating every second of this.

I'm not sure he has much use in this war of ours, but he's very useful to me in my plans with Senior so I'm fucking praying he lands with the Crow.

The Crow calls the meeting to an end and then stands to wait for everyone to leave. I move slowly, hoping to catch the Tiger, but he bolts like one of his twitchy clients. Fuck.

I nod at the Crow again, being so respectful is hard work, and I start to leave when the Lynx sidles up beside me. I give her a look but she just gestures for me to lead the way. Right. That's weird. The Coyote and Viola Ayres follow us out.

Once we're out by our cars I turn back to face her with a raised eyebrow. I don't like this woman, and I really fucking hate the smug look.

"I could be persuaded to join your side," she says, and the look she gives Harley says everything. Just this once, I wish he were a little less fucking gorgeous, because if I'm a magnet for fucked up killers and psycho rapists, then he's cougar bait.

"He's not for sale," I reply, my tone icy enough to give Avery's a run for its money.

She smirks at me. "I admire you, little Wolf. Forcing all of these alpha males to share you. If you're not willing to lose a little pride and give him to me for a night or two, then why should I join your side?"

I take a deep breath and I don't know what the hell is in the air around here but the words that come out of my mouth are almost entirely *Beaumont*. "What little assistance a washed up, old Mafia queen could give me isn't worth an ounce of my pride or a second in Harley's company. Maybe you should find some real skills or assets to offer me and then we'll talk."

And then I turn on my heel and slide into the Cadillac before I slit the bitch's throat. Tonight isn't the time for it, but I will kill her.

I'll enjoy every second of it, too.

There's a gentle tap on my shoulder and I glance up to find Viola Ayres.

"Slide along. I need to talk."

I shake my head at her but I move anyway. Avery takes the front seat and the guys wait outside the car. The Coyote starts making terrible jokes and Viola shuts the door to block them out.

"When can I go home?" Viola says, staring at her chipped nails. She looks thinner than when we bundled her off to the Coyote's safe house. I hope he's treating her right. She doesn't look abused but she's clearly miserable.

I share a look with Avery. "Is there something going on with the Coy- Jackson? You don't have to stay with him, we can find somewhere else for you to be."

She snorts at me. "Jackson isn't the problem. The problem is that my father is dirty, bought and paid for by a certain billionaire you may know, and now my sister is in danger, too. The Jackal is in contact with your dad, Avery, and it's only getting worse for us all."

I groan and slam my head back into the seat. Avery snorts at me and snaps at Viola, "You didn't think to call a little sooner? Knowing this before we came to the meeting would have been helpful."

Viola shrugs. "I thought you and Atticus were close? Jackson called him with the information. I assumed you both knew this."

Fucking *Atticus*.

Avery turns to stone in the front seat and I'm pretty sure the Crow has just tipped her over the edge. Her phone is in her hand, switched on and with her fingers flying across the screen frantically, in seconds.

I sigh and Viola snorts. "So, Jackson told me you bashed some guy's head in to become the Wolf. That's pretty fucking dark. What do you do in the Twelve?"

I roll my eyes at her. "I kill people. Ask Jackson when you can meet his mother, I'm not the only murderer you know."

I lock myself in my bathroom when we get back to Avery's ranch.

The mood in the car back was a little better than the way there. The guys all seem to think we've won something, that the information I've handed over has pushed the Twelve into taking our side. It's not that easy, and only Avery seems to know that.

The guys all grab their drinks of choice, and head to the pool to drink. Avery waits for five minutes before picking the lock to the bathroom door and joins me with a smirk. Evil dictator, but she's not the person I'm worried about hearing this conversation.

I can't put it off for any longer. My hands shake as I hit dial on my phone, turning the speakerphone on so Avery can listen in.

"Morningstar Enterprises, may I ask who's calling?" It's a woman's sultry tone so I'm pretty sure it's not Morningstar himself.

"The Wolf of Mounts Bay."

There's a pause and then she replies, "Please hold."

Avery gives me a look and I shrug. I had no idea contacting this guy would be so fucking formal but here we are.

"Wolf."

I shiver. Ok, yep, he sounds positively fucking terrifying with one damn word. Avery's face pales but her eyes stay fixed on the screen like she's memorizing everything that's going on.

"I've heard you were the buyer for Miss Beaumont. Her father was out of line. She's not for sale, and I'd like to discuss rectifying this… miscommunication." My voice is flat and steady, thank the sweet lord.

He hums under his breath, then says, "I could be persuaded to let her go. Is she yours?"

"Yes. She's one of mine. Whatever the cost, I will pay it."

Avery threads her fingers through mine and I squeeze her hand.

Morningstar replies, "I have some business in the Bay to attend to. I will contact you for a formal meeting then."

He hangs up and I don't feel any better; my stomach is heavy like I swallowed a pound of lead.

Why did that feel too easy for me?

I always trust my gut. I've honed my instincts for years, growing up the way I did I already could read situations other kids just couldn't process and once I joined the Twelve it was those instincts that have kept me alive. Retrieving information and removing people from the board is only possible because my gut is always right. Even when it doesn't make sense and, after that call, I'm sure of two things; Morningstar is planning something, and we have too much on our plates to take him on as well.

Avery clears her throat and says, "There's something else we need to talk about, Lips. What do you know about your father?"

I startle out of my deep thought and look up at her. I don't like the look on her face, not one freaking bit.

"Nothing. I've never met him. My mom told me he was locked up for drug trafficking and I've just... never really thought about him. I have too much other bullshit to deal with."

Avery nods and cringes just a little. "Is there anyone who would know about him? I checked your birth certificate and the person your mom put on it... doesn't exist."

I frown at her. "What do you mean he doesn't exist?"

She sighs at me and taps away on her phone before handing it to me. I find a file compiled by one of her many, *many* contacts, and see that every attempt to track down the man my mom listed on my birth certificate has come up with nothing.

For fuck's sake.

"Why is this relevant? Does it matter who he is? If he's just some drug addict I'd rather not have another one of those in my life. My mom was bad enough," I say, but I can't let go of the phone. Why would she lie? I can feel a headache coming on.

"I hope you're not angry at me for looking into this, it's just... the note in the box with Joey's head, it said blood. The people being targeted are people who have wronged you in some way and the note sounded... protective. The person sending them is protecting you in a really disturbing way."

Huh.

Ok, maybe my gut isn't that great.

I've been so caught up on the fact that I kill people for money that it never occurred that maybe someone would kill for me. Outside of my family. I already know the guys would all kill for me, or at the very least severely maim.

"Ok. There's a few things we could try." I say, hating the very fucking thought of those things but dealing with the heads could be a quick and easy fix, and once less thing to think of.

Avery smiles at me and says, "I have a guess. It's a good one, but we'll see what your... *things* tell us."

I stare at her for a second and then it falls together in my brain. I shake my head at her. "The Boar is not my father. There's no fucking way. For starters, he only moved to the state, like, ten years ago. He's never given a shit about me."

Avery smirks at me and stands up, smoothing a hand down her dress and looking freaking perfect in a way I'm still green with envy over. "He said he wouldn't join the Jackal. He said it was a blood thing. Exact same wording Lips, that's not a coincidence."

Fuck.

Chapter Four

The spy in the Crow's organization had disappeared before the meeting was over. I knew there were a few of the plants that were flight risks and the Crow had called me the second he found out the guy was gone.

What a fun conversation that was.

"Avery isn't answering my calls," he says, his voice monotone and cold. Months ago, what felt like a freaking lifetime, that would have sent a shiver down my spine but, fuck, a lot has changed. I'm not afraid of this dick anymore, only slightly wary.

I make my voice sound as bored as freaking possible as I reply, "I'm not her keeper, if she doesn't want to speak to you then she doesn't have to. What do you need?"

The distinct sound of his teeth grinding together echoes over the line and I grin at myself like a smug-ass bitch. Grovel, Crawford, *grovel*.

"The plant knows about Avery. Knows our connection. I don't know why he hasn't said anything yet, but if it gets back to the Jackal—"

I cut him off. "You think I didn't know already? You think I didn't have a plan in place for that guy? Come on, Crow. I didn't become the Wolf because I'm some naive piece of ass, twirling my hair and hoping for the best."

He sighs at me. "I think I liked it better when you were afraid of me."

I snort at him. "That was before I knew you're just like every other dick out there: arrogant and self-serving. The guy will be dead by dawn. Pleasure doing business with you."

I hang up before he gets the chance to reply. Blaise raises an eyebrow at me from the driver's seat of his newest toy and I shrug at him. When picking out the new car, purely for shits and giggles because the Maserati is still in perfect condition, he chose possibly the flashiest car possible. The Cadillac is white and I swear to God, it has diamonds in the dashboard. When I raise an eyebrow at him, he smirks and pets it lovingly.

"I thought the theme of our little family was diamonds? I love nothing more than matching shit."

The snark in his tone is at a whole new high, and I settle back in my seat to ignore his bullshit. "How can you afford this now? Did you lie to Ash about what your expenses are? Avery will make you wish you were dead if she finds out."

He shrugs and smirks at me. "After I bought out my contract, I released my new album. I thought you would have heard it by now. Ash asked me about it over dinner the other night, didn't you hear him?"

I stare at him, then pull out my phone to look it up. I've been listening to the songs on repeat for over a year so it's not like it'll be anything new for me, but I feel like this is something I should have known. Plus I'd like to see how well it's doing.

Blaise chuckles at the look on my face. "Star, I'm not pissy you didn't know, you've been a little busy keeping us all alive. Besides, I'm taking this as proof you're definitely not stalking me. It's been out for *weeks*."

I still feel bad but I try to joke my way out of the feeling. "I have it on tap now, I don't need to keep up with what you're doing."

His chuckle turns into a laugh and he runs a colorful hand through his hair, tugging on it a little. Fuck, it looks like he's been rolling around in his sheets for a few hours, not driving me to the middle of fucking no where with a gagged man in the back.

Yeah.

I wasn't lying to the Crow; the plant disappeared because I made him disappear. I've had too many close calls involving Avery lately so there was no way I was leaving her fate in Atticus Crawford's fumbling hands. Although now he knows I'm out of the house and dealing with his problem, I'm sure he'll be at the ranch to try to force Avery to talk to him. Ash and Harley had happily stayed behind, having a knife throwing lesson from Illi, so if he does show up he'll be lucky to leave with his jugular in tact.

Which is how I have the rock god to myself... well, kind of. If you ignore the grunting and groaning in the back every time Blaise hits a pothole.

"Now you've asked I'll let you know; the record is doing well. I got rid of most of the band, they were all brought in by the label, so it's just me and Finn now. You'll have to meet him soon. Once this fucking *war* is over, I mean. He's probably a little too delicate for this kind of thing."

I hum under my breath at him, and grab his hand. He's probably a little too delicate for this too, a little too naive and green, but he loves his family. He's utterly unflinching when shit hits the fan. He belongs with us.

"Take the next left, then follow the road to the end," I murmur, and Blaise pulls off of the highway. We're a good three hours away from the ranch now, out in the backwoods of Cali, but the little cabin is well known to me and has everything I'll need for the job ahead of me.

I leave nothing behind.

"Is there anything left behind after you melt the bodies? Anything that could identify the dead guy?" Blaise murmurs.

I shrug. "No. The acid breaks down everything, but the Bear is the one with the access to the acid, and he's chosen the Jackal so we're not using acid today."

The guy in the back makes a sort of gurgling, squealing sound and I snort at him. "If you're lucky, I'll kill you before I throw you in the pens."

Blaise's hands spasm on the steering wheel. "Pens? Fuck, Star, where the hell are you taking me?"

I smirk at him. "Worried, Morrison? I'll keep you safe from the little piggies, don't worry."

Blaise scowls at me. "Pigs? What the fuck?"

"They leave nothing behind. I know the guy who owns the place, he owes me *quite* a few favors."

Blaise gives me a sidelong look. "Is there anyone in Mounts Bay who doesn't owe you favors?"

I shrug. "Clean people don't, but they're few and far between in my world."

One of the perks of having the guys around while I'm on a job is that I no longer have to lug around dead bodies or writhing victims, and my bad leg has never gone this long without a flare up before.

Once Blaise has the guy out of the trunk and slumped in one of the empty pig pens, I nod at Brian to get him to leave. He clicks his tongue and jeers at the pigs as he walks away, happy enough to turn a blind eye and owe me one less favor.

Blaise wipes his forehead with the back of his hand and grunts at me, "How the fuck do you normally move them? You're fucking tiny."

I scoff at him and shrug. "Perseverance. You might want to go back to the car for this, it's not going to be pretty."

The guy starts grunting and squealing behind the gag again but we ignore him completely.

"I told you I'd come to work with you today, I'm prepared to get my hands dirty, Star," Blaise says, and rocks back on his heels a little. He watches me carefully but I just shrug. If he's really that keen on it then I guess we're doing this.

I slide my knife out of my pocket and cut the guys gag off. He dry retches as he spits it out and coughs before a stream of begging starts up. "Don't kill me! I'm useful to you, I can tell you things! I know about the Jackal's plans. I know who the other spies are, just don't fucking kill me."

I crouch down into his face, trying not to grimace at the stink of him. Fear turns sweat into a foul smelling thing and he's dripping with it under the hot summer sun. I tilt my head and look at him assentingly. "Convince me. Tell me something that makes it worth my while to keep you breathing. I mean, I've already driven all the way out here, I may as well finish the job."

His eyes dart up to Blaise then back to me as he gulps, his voice shaking as he replies, "The Jackal is putting spies in your school. He's cleared the board and put in his own men to get close to you. He still wants you bad, kid, and he's desperate to kill your men and get you back. He's fucking crazy, I took the spy position to get away from him. Look, I don't want to go back to him. I'll patch over! I'll join the Crow, just don't kill me."

I hum at him. "Anything else? Because I already knew all of that."

His voice raises and he practically squeals, more shrill than the pigs themselves. "He's looking into the O'Cronins. Trying to find something about them, something to catch the kid out. Morrisons, too. He's working with Beaumont, but I think he's planning on killing him, too."

Nothing new or useful.

And fuck, I wish it were going to be that easy. I wish I could just sit back and wait for them to kill each other. "I knew all of that, too. I've gotta tell you, you're not making a good case for yourself."

"He has a meeting with the Devil! He's meeting with Morningstar about you and your people. He'll be out of the state for a few weeks, he's gone to plead his case. The Devil said no to killing the O'Cronin boy but the Jackal now wants him to come kill all of the other members of the Twelve who've sided with you."

Ok. That's new.

I don't let that show on my face though, and when I raise an eyebrow the guy starts sobbing and wailing. That's all he's got and I'm still going to take him out.

Letting people live nearly cost me Harley last year.

I'll never make that mistake again.

I grab my bag and start to dig around for my plastic jumpsuit. I don't really want to strip down to my underwear and slitting throats is messy work. Blaise watches me grab it out and sighs, tugging at my elbow until I step away.

I misread him completely.

"It's the way things work in the Bay, just go back to the car and forget we were ever here," I mumble, but he grabs the ghost gun Illi got him last year and rummages around in my bag until he finds my silencer.

How the hell he knew I have one in there is beyond me because I'm too damn busy gaping at him as he screws it on.

"You're going to shoot him? I didn't think—"

He cuts me off. "I told you, I'm all in. You're mine; my girlfriend and my family, so this is our *gang life*, or whatever. Consider this my blood in."

Then he shoots the guy, his hand steady and effective as it only takes one bullet. I'm fucking *impressed*.

I don't wait around to talk about it, I just flick the gates open and let the pigs in to start their work. Blaise grimaces and climbs the fence to get away from them and I laugh at him. Happy to shoot a guy but a total fucking wuss about farm animals? He's as bad as Avery.

I scramble over the fence and he helps me down on the other side, mindful of my leg. I smile up at him, completely unaffected by the crunching and munching going on behind us.

Why the hell should I care about a spy meeting his fate?

Blaise tucks me under his arm and tips his head at Brian as we get back to the Cadillac. The cheeky fucker helps me climb up into the car and snarks something about getting me a step ladder. I do my best to ignore his jabs out because I'm not about to let him rile me up.

Once we're back on the highway he slips a hand between my thighs and strokes my pussy through my booty shorts. My thighs tense and trap his hand there, the little grin he shoots me is nothing short of devious.

"Want to fuck in the car on the way back?"

Uh, yeah. I do.

Chapter Five

On the morning we're due to head back to Hannaford, I startle awake in our bed. The room is still dark and it takes my mind a second to catch up to my body, because Harley's dick is rock hard between my thighs and one of his hands is clamped over my mouth while the other toying with my pussy. I choke back the moan clawing up my throat because I can hear Blaise's soft snores and the small sliver of light from the morning sun is bright across Ash's sleeping back.

Harley kisses my throat, whispering against my skin, "I'm being selfish this morning. I need you for myself, babe, just for now."

I shiver and nod, all-fucking-in.

I'm not sure how the fuck he's planning on doing this without waking the others but his fingers are magic and my eyes slip shut as he works me over. I've been sleeping in panties, more from habit than anything else, but the lace Ash picks out always errs on the scandalous side and Harley rips the crotch out without any real effort then he plunges his fingers into my pussy, grinding the heel of his palm into my clit until I'm struggling to stay silent even with his hand still firmly covering my mouth.

He waits until I'm right on the edge of coming before he pulls away, tugging my leg up and back until it's resting on his and he has a little room. Then he lines his dick up, rubbing it against my wet pussy lips, and bites my shoulder as he pushes in. I definitely make some fucking noise at that.

His hips pump into me, a slow and smooth rocking motion that winds me the hell up until I'm shaking. His hand manages to smother the sobs wrenching out of my chest a little so they sound like little gasps instead but I feel desperate and mindless.

"Shh, if you're too loud I'll have to share you," Harley murmurs into my skin, but I'm too far gone to listen and his dick feels that fucking good buried inside me.

It's too much for me to take and my heart stutters in my chest as I come. Ash's eyes snap open as the last little gasp wrenches out of my throat, and I moan softly behind Harley's hand. He doesn't seem to notice Ash has woken up and his hips are relentless as he pumps into me.

My body stokes higher and higher until I think I'm going to come again when Ash slides closer and tugs my shirt out of the way so he can pinch one of my nipples. I try to hold Ash's eyes with my own as I come again, clenching around Harley until he grunts and moves to hold both of my hips. I lean forward to give him some room to move and Ash catches my chin in his hand, kissing me firmly until I'm moaning into his lips

I break away to try to catch my breath and Ash slides a hand around my throat until his thumb can trace over my pulse. I stare into his eyes and the look he gives me is pure, dark lust. Watching Harley fuck me has once again snapped the tight hold he has on himself around me.

He squeezes at my throat, just enough that I have to tip my head back to breathe. "Turn over."

Harley huffs and grumbles under his breath but he helps move me around until I'm facing him, holding my hip with one hand as he pushes back in. He cups my cheek with his free hand and kisses me, dragging his teeth over my bottom lip until I'm boneless. He knows just how to touch me to make me feel both *owned* and fucking *worshiped*.

I'm lost in Harley's lips so I miss when Ash shifts closer and palms my ass, kneading my curves and spreading them until I gasp into Harley's kiss. He bites my lip and then moves to lick and suck his way down my throat, marking me up so there isn't going to be a single doubt in the other students minds of what we've spent the summer doing together when we get back to school. Ash tugs at my hair to pull my head back and sticks two fingers in my mouth. I suck on them and wish it was his dick. I'm not ashamed to say I whine a little when he pulls them out.

Just as Harley's kisses get to my collarbone and nips me there, Ash's finger presses against my ass and I just about *die*.

"Tell me to stop, Mounty," Ash murmurs, but I can't. I physically cannot force the words out of myself and he kisses the back of my neck sweetly, whispering, "Good girl."

Then he pushes his finger into my ass and *sweet merciful lord* I did not expect to like it *this* much. A gasp rips out of my throat and I clutch at Harley's shoulders while my brain whites out a little.

Ash huffs out a laugh and bites down on my shoulder again, adding another finger and alternating the pumps with the drag of Harley's dick inside me until I'm always filled with one of them. Ok, maybe his dick would be fucking amazing. Maybe being truly shared will be the best fucking feeling and I'll refuse to leave this bed.

It takes *seconds* before I'm coming again, a freaking record, and Harley groans as he comes too. I'm too blissed out to get pissy at Ash's smug laugh. He pulls his fingers out and then rubs his dick between my ass cheeks. My eyes might go a little crazy at that. It feels amazing, much better than I ever thought it would, but there's no fucking way he's going to stick his monster cock up my ass.

Harley grunts when I clench around his softening dick, pulling out and snapping at Ash, "You stick anything else in her, you fucking better have lube."

He kisses me sweetly and rolls out of the bed for the shower. I pout for a half second and then Ash turns me around, stripping my shirt off and shoving his boxers down his legs.

"Feeling brave yet, Mounty?" He smirks, and I scoff at him.

"Wasn't that brave enough for you?" My voice sounds weirdly breathless.

He nods and takes my hand, wrapping it the thick length of him. "You're right, that was very brave. If you'd given me a little warning I would have had lube and we could have both fucked you at the same time."

I get a full-body shiver at that and his eyes go all molten. What the fuck are these guys doing to me? I've gone from terrified of their dicks to fucking melting at the thoughts of gangbangs. Jesus take the wheel.

Then I remember I have a handful of Ash's dick and wriggle down the bed to suck him off because that's something I can get behind. Yes fucking *please*.

Ash insists on joining me for a shower afterwards and I struggle so freaking bad to focus on washing myself with him naked around me. I wonder idly if this feeling will ever wear off but I kind of enjoy how much they affect me. It's also nice to know they're just as affected by me.

When we're done, I throw on some yoga pants and one of Ash's v neck shirts, the perks of having boyfriends is having full access to their clothes in my humble opinion, and then head back into our room to pack the last of my bags. Blaise is awake finally, rubbing the sleep from his eyes and frowning around the room.

"Why does it smell like sex in here? What the *fuck* did I miss now?" he snarls, and I pretend I don't hear him as I start shoving the last of my clothes back into my duffle bag.

Ash saunters out of the bathroom with a towel wrapped around his waist, smug-as-fuck, and says, "Maybe you should drink and smoke a little less before bed so when Arbour decides to wake the Mounty up with his dick you can join in, too."

Blaise's arm drops and he levels a vicious glare at his best friend. "What. The. Fuck?! I thought we agreed to *not* be exclusionary dicks about this?"

Ash shrugs and drops his towel. I look back at my clothes because we have no time for round two... or three, whatever, who's counting?

"So don't be a dick. I wasn't an asshole about you guys fucking in the Cadillac without me even after I had to get in there and smell it right after."

Fuck. I'd forgotten about that.

We'd gotten back only to find Avery had a craving for Pizza. Ash and Blaise jumped straight back into the Cadillac to drive into the closest town, mostly because Ash and Avery were still at each other's throats over Atticus.

I try to ignore my blush and snap, "Can we just get a move on? We have to stop off in the actual slums before we head back to Hannaford and I'd rather we get it over with."

That gets them to shut up and start moving. None of us want to go back to my old house. I don't want to take them there and they don't want to face the reality of where I came from. It's easier to think of it all as some sad story, something that wasn't so fucking desperately dangerous.

I manage to finish up my packing without falling into a complete sulk. I meet Avery at the car and when she hands me a coffee I attempt a smile at her.

"If there was any other way I wouldn't ask you to do this," she murmurs and I nod.

"It doesn't matter. It's over with now. We'll just get in and get out."

When the car is finally packed and we're all strapped in, I try not to stare wistfully out of the window at the ranch. I fucking love the place and going back to the snake pits of Hannaford has never been so fucking devastating. My mood only gets worse the closer we get to the Bay. The car is silent as we drive, moving through the 'burbs and the commercial districts until we're driving through the very worst parts of the city.

It doesn't matter that it's nearly been a whole fucking decade since I was last here, the only things that have changed is everything has gotten more run-down and derelict. I hate it, I hate being here and I hate my whole damn family being here, too. The shame and embarrassment crawls over my skin until I become a snarling asshole myself.

"Stop here. This is it," I snap, and I swallow the bile creeping up my throat as I look out the window at the tiny shed-like structure I once lived in with my mom.

No one says a word as we pile out of the car and Avery hesitates for a half second before tucking her arm in mine. "I don't give a fuck about this place, Lips. I just need to check if there's anything here that can tell us about your birth father."

I nod and swallow again, trying to keep my voice civil as I say, "You guys should just stay in the car. The place isn't exactly big enough to have us all in there at once."

Ash eyes me and then nods, leaning back against the car casually as Blaise pulls out a blunt for them both. They're both armed and I give them a quick nod, my eyebrows hopefully conveying the motto 'shoot first, ask questions later' because this is possibly the worst area to be standing next to a fucking Cadillac with diamonds in the freaking dashboard. I'm kind of expecting to come back and find them being held up by rough and tumble eleven year-olds. I'd also be tempted to put money on the Mounty kids in that situation.

Harley tucks his hand in mine, ignoring my glare, and jerks his head towards the house. "Let's get this over with. I want to get back to school in time to talk to the coach about the swim trials."

Avery scoffs at him and I pull away from them both to jiggle the door open. It never did lock properly.

I guess we should have been at least a little concerned about squatters or a new drug-addicted family living here but honestly, I'm not sure there was anyone out there desperate enough to move in to the absolute stinking shithole.

Avery tries her best to be polite but gags anyway. Disuse and being sealed has only made the damp, moldy, *death* smell a million times worse.

"C'mon, I know where she used to hide her stash. I'd guess that's the best place to start looking for clues."

None of the rooms have doors, just curtains that are so old and moth eaten they've mostly fallen down and turned to dust. Harley doesn't gag or pull faces, he just takes everything in. I hate it. I feel like something vital is being exposed right now that shouldn't ever be fucking seen, like my kidneys have been carved out and put on display.

There's still a few bags of cocaine in my mom's old stash hole, and I pocket them. They're stamped with the Jackal's insignia and I know they're the dirty batch he sold her. Might come in handy to have some dirty drugs, fuck knows what we're going to need this year.

When there's nothing out in the open, I rummage around until I find an old crowbar and start ripping up floorboards. Harley grunts at me and takes over like I've insulted him by doing it myself.

"Why the fuck did you have a crow bar but no fucking doors?" he asks, but the boards all lift easily. The wood is rotting away.

"I don't know. Well, I know we had the crowbar to use on people trying to break in for drugs. I once watched my mom break a guy's leg with it. But the missing doors don't make any sense. I guess they'd been gone long before mom started squatting here."

Avery ducks down and grabs a handful of papers from the floor cavity. "I think they're just newspapers but we should take everything just in case. I'll go grab a box, I told Ash to bring some."

I nod, and start flipping through the papers anyway. Nothing I can see, nothing until I find a photo stashed amongst them. It's of my mom, long before she had me. She looks so fucking young and healthy. It must have been before drugs, before the fire, before everything went wrong. Strangely, my heart sort of spasms in my chest and I feel the need to keep the photo. Fucking weird.

"She looks nothing like you," Harley murmurs, and I startle. I didn't hear him stop and come over.

I nod and clear my throat. "Yeah, we were polar opposites. This was before her life went to shit, back when she was still happy. Fuck this place, I hate it so much."

He nods and grabs my hand again. "I know, babe, but I'd rather be here and have you face this than have your past bite us in the ass."

I nod again, I get it. Doesn't mean I have to like it.

Chapter Six

We pick up one of Ash's Ferraris, one with a tiny back seat with zero leg space, and I ride the rest of the way to Hannaford in it with the twins, and Harley rides in Blaise's Cadillac with him. I spend the entire trip listening to them both snark each other out and doing my best at avoiding being dragged into their arguments.

"The Mounty is moving into our room this year. If you haven't figured something out to get us a little closer to you then we'll just have a rotation to keep someone in your room each night. It'll be like freshman year all over again, Floss," Ash says, changing gears and then tracing patterns against my thigh.

Avery scoffs from the backseat, extra pissy after our search of my old house came up with nothing. "Lips is as loyal as they come. She would never turn her back on the bonds of our sisterhood; she'll move in with me and then spend the whole year being woken up by one of you climbing in to drool over her."

I turn the page of my book without a word. Apparently that's the wrong thing to do, on both sides of this argument, because they both hiss at me.

"Lips, tell him you love me more—"

"Mounty, you know where you'd rather be—"

I move the book to cover my face. "I'll set up a roster and move between the two rooms. My shit is going in my room with Aves but it's a win for everyone."

Neither of them like that for an answer but at least it gets them to drop the subject. I can't say I'm not relieved when we pull into the staff parking lot and I scramble out of the car to get away from the animosity. Harley raises his eyebrows at me but Avery's snarling starts up again and he smirks.

"Picked the wrong car, babe?"

Smug dick. "Oh, I'm sure you and Blaise would have just started the same crap at me, too."

Blaise decides to be his own personal brand of helpful and jumps into the ring with Ash, snarking at Avery, "Why are you defending Atticus again? I thought you'd given up on your little crush."

I tuck myself under Harley's arm and drag him away from the spectacle. I know we only have to find a crowd for them to quit their shit, nothing is more important in this place than a united front. When we finally get past the statues and immaculate landscaping, and into the building the looks we get from the other students… pure, unadulterated terror.

Well, That's nice.

Harley pulls me in closer to his body, kissing the crown of my head and whispering into my hair, "The sheep have finally figured out a Wolf hunts among them."

I roll my eyes. "You're so fucking funny, babe. So funny."

His eyes flare when I use his pet name for me and the smirk only gets bigger. "It's true. There's a whole bunch of wolves here now. Best fucking tattoo I've got."

I squeeze his waist and tuck my face into his chest. "Maybe we should keep that under wraps for a little longer. We don't need to be dealing with any Hannaford snake pit drama this year."

He chuckles under his breath. "Well, I'm not putting up with some cougar cunt trying to fuck me this year. We're firmly a stab-first family going forward. Apparently you have the perfect farm animal disposal system."

Ugh. Gossiping freaking boys!

Avery takes the lead and we head straight up to the boys' dorms. I follow without question, because Avery Beaumont knows her shit, but Blaise isn't quite so trusting.

"I want Star in with us, not you as well. I'm not getting fucking bitched out for not washing my sheets daily or making a fucking sandwich when I'm hungry."

Avery doesn't break her stride but the look she gives him should best be described as *ball-shriveling*.

"Maybe if you didn't constantly have questionable stains on your sheets I wouldn't have to bitch you out and three in the morning is not the time to be fucking around in the kitchen," she snarks at him.

Blaise shrugs at her. "We can't all sleep like Beaumonts. Some of us actually feel things and it keeps us up at night. Harley never fucking shut his eyes before Star, you never bitch him out for it."

Avery stops at a door at the end of the hall in the boys' dorm and pulls out a key. Her tone is icy as she says, "When your sleep issues stop being about the amount of blunts you smoke, and shift to being flashbacks to your loving father being murdered, then I'll change my stance. Now stop whining, you petulant brat."

She shoves open the door and we find a double room, slightly smaller than our room last year in the girls' dorm but with more couches and a bigger TV.

"Dibs not sharing the fucking bed. I get we'll be in rotation but, fuck, can't we at least have our own bed when we *are* here?" Blaise grumbles, and Ash snorts at him.

"Did you pack seventy-eight boxes? This is Avery's shit. She's moving in here with Mounty."

I cut Avery a look and she smiles sweetly at me. "Hannaford is having renovations this year and they've had to reshuffle where students are being housed. The boys' room is next door. I hope the walls are thick enough that I won't hear the orgies but at least I won't have to see them."

I blush and clear my throat, and for once it's not in embarrassment over her use of the word *orgies*. I was starting to feel antsy about being away from the guys at night, too much can happen in this place, and being away from *any* of our family was going to be fucking hard. "Thanks."

She shrugs. "I can't have you turning into an insomniac either. This way we're all in one spot if something happens. I was thinking about having a door cut into the wall between the rooms for easier access but, really, the ones in the hall should be enough."

I kick my shoes off and sling my bag onto the bed, pulling out my safe and tapping my feet on the floorboards as I walk around the room, looking for the perfect hiding spot. Ash watches me carefully as he kisses the top of Avery's head. He looks the most relieved about our room change. Being away from Avery is hard for him at the best of times, but with the war brewing in the Bay, it's only made it more dangerous.

"I'll make burgers for dinner. Did you order shit in, Floss?" Harley says, opening the fridge and grinning when he finds it full. He grabs a beer and throws one at Blaise. Ash starts rummaging around for the hard liquor and I roll my eyes at them all. Starting senior year with a hangover sounds fucking awful but I grab one of my emergency whiskey bottles out and offer it to him anyway. He grimaces.

Avery scoffs, carrying the first of many, many boxes labelled 'bathroom' to start unpacking, and snaps, "The bourbon is in your room, go unpack your own crap."

Harley starts pulling out pans and says, "I'm fucking starving and Lips skipped breakfast because of our stop-off in the slums so we're having family dinner. We'll help you unpack, Floss."

She scoffs at him and I continue my hunt for the perfect hiding spot. When I find it, Blaise grabs his own knife out and helps pry the floorboard up. The diamond I gave him for Christmas catches in the light and I grin at him, my stomach fluttering with happiness. Maybe this year won't be so fucking terrible. Maybe Hannaford is the perfect place for us to get some space from the Bay.

I barely manage to get the thought out before Ash's vicious cursing interrupts us.

"Mounty. It's happened again."

I glance over my shoulder to the front door, held open by Ash, to find what's caught his ire. I hear Avery dart out of the bathroom and join Ash in cursing.

Fuck. It's a fucking box.

"Who the fuck could be in it this time?" Harley growls from the kitchen, and I shrug, totally resigned to this bullshit following us everywhere.

"Fuck knows. Grab it and get it out of people's sight, Ash. I'll call Illi for a pick up."

It's the first head that isn't immediately obvious why the person is dead.

I call Illi for the pick up and he doesn't bother to comment, and then we open it to find my third-grade teacher's head inside. When I tell the others who it is Blaise groans and slumps back on my bed.

"I fucking hate riddles! Why would anyone give a fuck about your grade school teachers? Do you? This is fucking stupid!"

Ash watches Avery as she stares at the head with a hand clamped firmly over her mouth to try to keep the smell and potential airborne germs away from herself. I mentally make note that we need to get her a face mask or, fuck it, a hazmat suit to deal with this shit in the future.

Harley watches me.

"Any ideas?" Avery asks and I shrug.

"Plenty. If we're still going on the assumption that the killer is taking out people who've wronged me then this woman was an absolute fucking bitch to me. She hated the entire class, hated her life, and she especially hated me. I was smart. She didn't like the idea of one of us making it out of the Bay and my brains are my ticket out."

Avery sighs and then startles when my phone pings. I give her a little smile and then move to let Illi in.

"Who the fuck is it this time? Tell me it's Matteo, or Senior, I'd fucking love it if it were one of them," he says as he gives me a quick squeeze. None of my guys bat an eyelash, completely accepting of Illi now he's apparently paid his dues into the family.

"It's Ms. Rickard. Did you ever have her as a teacher?" I say, and Illi frowns, rubbing his face with one of his massive scarred hands.

He steps up, giving Ash a bro nod of his head and slapping Harley on the shoulder.

"Kid. This is not a good sign. This is actually a really fucking bad one," he says as he snaps on a pair of gloves.

I groan, "Tell me something I don't know."

He rolls the head around looking for some clue, some little thing that will tell us why the fuck this is happening. "You get why it's her, right?"

I frown at him and step back up beside him to stare at the head. "She was a bitch to me. They're all people who've wronged me."

He sighs and gently lifts the head back into the box, closing it up and snapping the gloves back off. Avery immediately moves to grab a bottle of bleach and start scrubbing.

"She put you in detention. She put you there and that's where you very first met Matteo. You probably don't even remember him being there, you didn't speak to each other, but that is where he first saw you and that's where his obsession with you started."

I blink at him.

What the fuck?

"Some kid shoved you and you stabbed him with a pair of scissors or something."

I tip my head back and groan at the ceiling. "Seriously? My whole fucking life changed course because I stabbed Cory Ryan? Fuck, I might hunt him down and stab him again for that shit."

Illi laughs at me and tucks the box under his arm. "Fucking weird I remember that so clearly but yeah, that's when it started. Then he dosed your mom, got you into foster care with him, and taught you how to aim for places that kill instead of just hurting like a bitch."

I smirk despite how fucking angry this is making me, "And you taught me how to do both. I guess I'll let Cory live, the fucking dickhead that he is."

Illi shrugs. "He's dead kid. You forget how many people don't make it to twenty-one in the Bay. He started running with the Bear's crew and they paid him a lot of money to do some time for something he didn't do and then he got shanked in prison. He owed me a lot of money, I'm still fucking pissed about it."

Then he gives us one last wave and leaves to dispose of the head.

We all watch Avery as she scrubs furiously at the coffee table, the only surface we were willing to put the head on, and after a second I catch her arm.

"Let's go over to the guys' room for dinner and sleep there tonight. Go have a shower and we'll get rid of the coffee table. We don't need it, we'll just throw the fucker out."

She hums under her breath and then shoots a quick look at Ash, nodding when he gives her a tight smile. Well, it's more of a grimace but he's trying.

Harley gets rid of the coffee table and after everyone has scrubbed their skin raw in the shower we sit down in the guys room to eat. Blaise looks a little put off but after his fourth beer he mellows out enough to go for seconds.

When we've all piled into bed that night, Avery in Ash's bed and me jammed between Blaise and Ash in Blaise's bed, I take forever to fall asleep. We just have to survive the year. Everything will be over by the end of senior year.

Or at least I hope it will.

Chapter Seven

It becomes very clear on the first day back at class that Atticus Crawford is not taking any chances this year with our safety while we're attending school. Mr. Trevelen has been replaced by a stern-faced woman who takes the time to personally introduce herself to Avery and me before our first class. She seems proficient enough, and when we pass her in the hallways on our way to classes, her eyes barely touch the guys.

Fucking perfect.

Avery cackles at me and tucks her arm in mine. "Are you going to stab any girls that look at Harley from now on? Just shed blood from the get-go? I feel like Illi is going to spend the year disposing of corpses for you."

I tilt my head as if I'm thinking about it but, ah, yeah. That's exactly what I'm going to do. Ash seems to scare girls off with his cold demeanor and asshole-ish nature and Blaise's rock god status makes him unapproachable to most of the girls at Hannaford.

Harley is fucking rape-bait, I'm sure of it.

When I'm stupid enough to say this over lunch he stares at me like I've greatly insulted him and Blaise roars with laughter. I feel kind of bad but I mean, *really*, he's the one that nearly died on me so he can put up with my weirdly overprotective response to that.

"Says the girl with every fucking deranged psycho in the fucking state chasing after her. Fuck, you get your enemies delivered on a platter by one of them. I'd put money on that guy wanting a taste of you," Harley snaps, and Ash gives him a look.

"Don't ruin my fucking appetite, now I'm being reminded of Joey and I need to fucking vomit."

I cringe. "Can't get his head out of… your head?"

He looks at me like I'm dense. "I was talking about him trying to rape you, I could not give less of a shit about him being dead. I'm relieved. I only wish I'd taken a photo of his decapitated, vacant face before we left the restaurant."

Avery sighs at him. "Can we not talk about dead bodies while I'm trying to eat please? I have three hours of dance recital prep this afternoon and I need my carbs."

Ash rolls his eyes at her and changes the topic. "So how are we all faring in our classes so far? Harley? Are you managing to keep up?"

Harley's face goes from grumpy to fucking thunderous, and I abandon all pretenses of eating and grab a book.

It's going to be a long-ass year.

We're all sharing the same classes again, except for choir and the gym classes, and the rivalry between Ash and Harley has picked up from last year as if we hadn't even gone on break. The usual pop quizzes had been sprung on us, a way for our teachers to weed out the students who slacked off over the summer break, and they were neck-and-neck for taking out second spot. I've beaten them in everything so far, having actually read through all of our syllabi and started on the assignments already.

Blaise spent the summer doing the reading for our AP lit class and I'm secretly confident he's going to be more on top of things this year. Avery also spent a few nights studying with me, but she's more worried about our 'extracurriculars' getting in the way of her college applications.

She doesn't have to worry about our safety at Hannaford. There isn't a single teacher, other than poor Ms Umber, that hasn't been replaced by Atticus is his efforts to keep her safe. It's frustrating from a workload perspective, I knew what the others expected, but I do breathe a little easier and Ash is much less of a dick once he's back on the track team.

We just have to survive the year.

One day at a time.

On Friday, after classes are finished and Avery is at her ballet training, I head to the library to get some studying done. I need to get ahead early on, like I did last year and it's too tempting to get distracted by one of the guys if I stay in our rooms. Blaise and Ash have joined the basketball team again now the Jackal's men have been ousted and Harley is spending all his spare time in the pool again, so there's not much of a chance at getting a few hours alone with them again but I'm weak. I might fucking beg for the distraction from the workload the AP classes have given me.

I get a solid hour in before my coffee is finished and my skin is crawling from the eyes on me. I do my best to ignore it but fuck, they're all fucking pathetic.

I sigh and start to pack up, my mind firmly in my reading for my AP lit class, when Lauren takes the seat across from me.

I startle and then give her a little smile. She hasn't tried to speak to me since I became friends with Avery back in our sophomore year but we smile and wave in the hallways often enough that her opening words catch me off-guard.

"I was moved into the boys' dorms because of the renovations as well, I'm two doors down from you guys. I noticed a weird guy leaving a package at your door, I was going to call the admin staff but I looked in the box first. What the hell is going on, Lips?"

I force my face to be a blank mask, the shadow of my smile still lingering. "I have no idea what you're talking about. The only boxes we've had delivered have had Avery's mountains of crap in them. If you found her stash of sex toys then I'd suggest you keep that information to yourself. She doesn't really like gossip."

Lauren bites her lip, rolling it between her teeth nervously. "Look, my dad's the Police Chief in the Bay. I know exactly what the Beaumonts are like. I know what Avery does for her brothers. If you want to get away from all that, away from the Bay, then you need to get away from her. Ditch Ash and Harley, and run away with Blaise. Otherwise it'll be your head in the box."

My spine snaps straight and my eyes narrow. Big mistake. Fucking huge.

No one insults Avery on my watch.

No one gets away with trying to split me and the boys up. I learnt that lesson well last year. No exceptions, no leeway, I'll start gutting people without question this time around.

"Watch your fucking mouth. You think you've seen something? Maybe you should get your eyes checked because there's no heads being stored in my room. My family is none of your concern."

Lauren rocks back in her chair at my tone, her face screwed up in confusion. "I saw the Butcher come get the box, how the hell does Avery know him? He came to the dinner last year for her, I mean, seriously Lips, get out of there before they take you down, too."

I shove my books in my bag and stand. She stands with me and crosses her arms like she's trying to hug herself. "Being popular isn't worth dying for Lips. It's really not."

I laugh at her, just straight up lose it right in her face. When I can finally breathe again I lean in to whisper to her, "Avery knows the Butcher because I introduced them. Maybe you didn't read the name on the box but it came to me. Stay the fuck away from me, my family, and our business. Don't turn into Annabelle Summers, Lauren. Just don't."

Then I turn on my heel and get the fuck out of the library. I'm fuming, furious that Lauren's added herself to the list of people I have to look out for.

I make it back to the rooms before anyone else and I let myself into the boys' room. I need a shower, a dozen shots of whiskey, and like seven or eight orgasms to calm myself down.

I flick Avery a text before I climb into the shower, letting her know we need to discuss the conversation and then I scrub at my skin like a psycho. I use a little of everything and the smell of all of my guys slowly mellows me out a little.

I've dried and dressed myself in one of Harley's sweatshirts by the time I hear the front door open. I scrub my teeth and fling the door open, expecting Avery but finding Harley. His eyes take in my bare legs and his chest rumbles in appreciation until he sees the scowl on my face.

He waits until I'm done with my teeth before cradling my head in his hands, staring into my eyes and murmuring, "Who am I beating for you, babe?"

I swallow. "When is shit going to settle down enough that I can just enjoy having you? When are we ever going to be left alone?"

He kisses me softly and tugs me until I'm pressed against his chest. "We're going to figure this out. Now, stop trying to distract me. It's been too long since I've been in a fight, I'll send the text and fix it tonight."

I shiver and meet his eyes again. A fight club fight? That sounds like the perfect way to spend a Friday night at Hannaford but he can't challenge Lauren.

Before I can answer him the door opens again and Avery, Ash, and Blaise walk in. Avery doesn't make any comments about Harley being wrapped around me, she only stomps over to the coffee machine and turns it on before rummaging in the freezer for ice cream.

I pull away from Harley and peg Ash with a look. "Where's the whiskey? We need to do serious damage control and I need something to take the edge off."

Ash's eyes narrow but he goes to the bar he's set up and pours us both drinks.

Blaise makes a stupid joke and Harley scoffs at him while he grabs them both beers. I try to soak it all up to calm a little more of the rage in me.

Once we're all seated and there's a giant tub of cherry ice cream in front of me I finally speak. "Lauren saw the head in the box. Her dad is the Police Chief back at the Bay and she said that she knows all about Senior."

Avery frowns and starts to tap on her phone. I already know that there's a good chance she's talking to Atticus for information and I grab my own to ask Illi for his own assessment. They get their information from very different channels. I consider it for about a half a second before sending the same request to the Coyote. Fuck it, all hands on deck.

Blaise takes a swig of his beer and says, "What are we going to do if she won't let this go?"

I cringe and take a huge mouthful of ice cream, not keen on discussing that avenue. I'll take her out if I have to but I'm also pissy she's forcing my hand. Ash watches me for a second and then pries the spoon out of my hand.

"I'm not watching you tongue-fuck the spoon tonight, Mounty. Her dad belongs to Senior. The problem is if she speaks to him about the box. He might come to investigate it to try to impress the Senior. The only reason he can afford to send his kids here is because of the dirty money Senior and his friends give him."

His eyes flick to Avery's and I can see his brain working. She can too.

"Yes, I'm well aware the Crawfords pay him too. I'm also very aware that Atticus has nothing to do with them anymore," she says, her tone is just a little too civil to be genuine.

Harley scoffs at them both. "If we walk down the hall and kill her now there'll be a fucking mass exodus. The students here are already twitchy as fuck about Annabelle and Harlow disappearing. Word's out that Joey's dead. It's pretty fucking obvious it all leads back to us. If we start killing students off then we'll have the fucking FBI showing up. Senior got any of them in his pocket?"

Ash flicks a wrist at him dismissively. "Of course he does. He has fucking senators and governors on his payroll, for fuck's sake. FBI agents are nothing in comparison."

I snatch my spoon back off of him and tap on the table idly as I think. Avery watches me carefully. I meet her gaze and she nods. "I agree."

Harley huffs at us. "Wanna let the rest of us in on your telepathy? I fucking hate it when you both pull this shit."

Avery smirks at him and sets her phone down on the table. "We need to start building our own network. We need to have legitimate people on our payroll as well as Lips'… connections. I have some but we need more. We need people that Senior hasn't already gotten to, or people that want protection from him."

Blaise blows out a breath and rubs the back of his neck. "I have a whole fucking list of people for you then."

There's a sort of stunned silence and then we all turn to look at him. He rolls his eyes at us. "Seriously? I've been dragged to the Kora headquarters in New York every fucking year by my parents, you think I don't listen to the shit going on around me? My parents sent me to Hannaford to stop me from falling in with the wrong crowd. Half the board of Kora is owned by someone. My dad has spent a lot of time and energy keeping himself away from corrupt political influence and he only deals with other people that are the same. So I can give you a whole list of people who are clean."

Avery leans forward onto her elbows and pegs him with a vicious look. "Why the fuck didn't you tell me this earlier? I could have had them in our pockets months ago."

Blaise shrugs. "You banned me from talking about my dad and Kora. I could probably get my mom to help with the list. She could tell us who's most likely to break and what pressures are best… applied."

I can't think of anything worse than involving the woman currently holed up in an exclusive five star resort being paid for entirely by the son she's spent eighteen years treating like utter shit but I keep my mouth shut about it.

For now.

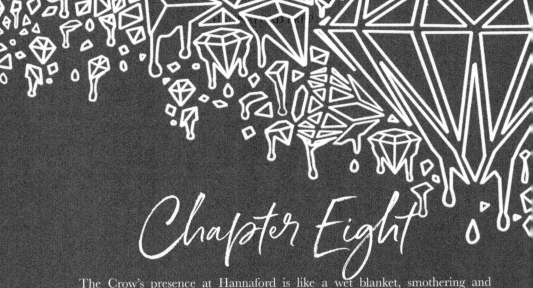

The Crow's presence at Hannaford is like a wet blanket, smothering and uncomfortable. The riots in Mounts Bay are on the TV everyday, and the violence is only getting worse. The entire student body at Hannaford is edgy. I steer clear of Lauren, because I'm pretty sure I'll be tempted to stab my way out of that conversation, and focus on my studies instead. It's easy enough to do because she avoids me as well.

I start to notice that the fear in the other students' eyes only gets worse as the weeks go on. I hate it but it's a fuck-load better than the whispers I've dealt with before. Harley fucking *preens* over it, smirking in every class as we sit together. I should have known he'd enjoy being infamous for deadly reasons.

One the the perks of having the Crow's men as our teachers is that I no longer have to even pretend to be discreet when my phone buzzes in my pocket. Harley's eyes stay glued to his notes but he raises an eyebrow at me. He's intent on beating Ash but he's also super freaking nosy and overprotective of me, even when it's only Illi messaging.

Stay at school. Things are getting worse here. I'll check in with you tomorrow.

I sigh and flick the screen to Harley, and then to Avery when she turns in her seat to see what we've been distracted by. Her lips press into a firm line and she doesn't pay the teacher another second of attention, her hands flying over her phone screen in her lap.

I shift my focus back to my classwork and try not to think about the potential dangers Illi is facing. Luckily our AP classes come with more than enough assignments to keep my mind busy. For a month or two at least.

I start up study sessions in the evenings again and this time around the whole family joins in. Harley goes to swim practice first and Ash always goes for a run, but by the time Avery has cooked some massive, complicated gourmet meal we're all back and ready to tackle our classwork.

Harley and Blaise take three weeks to come to an agreement of who can sit next to me because Avery claims best friend rights and has a permanent seat next to me. Harley argues that we have too many joint assignments, while Blaise still needs more help than the others.

I consider chiming in but Ash gives me a sly look and says, "They're probably going to fight it out, Mounty. I know how much you enjoy that."

Avery makes a disgusted noise when I get goosebumps but I shrug her off. She's been extra pissy and touchy since we got back to school. I make a mental note to aim for the most painful points if I ever go hand-to-hand with the Crow. I think I can punch him hard enough in the dick that he'll piss blood for a month.

When we've eaten and everyone has survived the Beaumont Bullshit I immediately jump into my studies. Ash snarks at me for how far ahead I already am. I ignore him, my greatest skill, and completely focus on Blaise's homework. Possibly the only downside to our family group sessions is that Blaise struggles to focus with so many people around. The margins of his pages are full of little drawings, stars and roses, and I place my hand over his to stop him. He scrunches his nose up at me but not without looking.

"I'm not gonna survive this year," he mumbles.

I shrug at him and squeeze his hand. "You can always move to the lower classes. I mean you're not planning on going into business, you don't need to know complex algebraic equations to play guitar."

Harley smirks and says, "He's not in the classes for the education. He's just being a brat and doesn't want to sit by himself."

Blaze flicks a beer cap at him. "Maybe I'm just worried about ending up singled out like you were last year. The principal looks a little too buttoned up for my liking, that usually means she's a closet freak. You should watch yourself, rape-bait."

Harley's eyes narrow dangerously and Avery gives Blaise a severe look. "Atticus would not put anyone in this building unless he were sure they're clean."

I hum under my breath and do my best not to make eye contact with her. I don't want her to see what I think about her assessment of Atticus and his business, but of course she notices straight away and calls me on it.

"Do you have concerns about the Crow's men?"

Ash bristles at her tone but I don't care. "I don't think that he would send anyone unless he was sure, but the Bay has taught me that you can never really be sure. I mean, I'm sure about you guys and I'm sure about Illi and Odie. I highly doubt Atticus has such a close relationship with any of these men and women. They're not family."

Avery's anger simmers down just a little and she tucks her hand into mine under the table, her own little version of an apology.

Ash stares at her for a second, and then snaps, "Crawford isn't family either. We don't trust him or his people. That's the quickest way to fucking die."

I sigh and settle back in my seat as the fighting starts up again around me. This is going to be my whole fucking year. Beaumont Bullshit over Atticus fucking Crawford.

I could stab the dick for that alone.

Ash decides that Saturday mornings are his time to spend alone with me, kicking everyone else out of my room and settling me into his lap to eat breakfast in front of the TV. He always comes with a giant mug of coffee for me so I don't really ask questions.

Avery is in the shower washing her hair, something that usually takes at least forty-five minutes, and so Ash is taking advantage of the time by feeding me French toast and kissing down my neck, grunting when I squirm and grind against his very interested dick.

Fuck, I'm addicted to him.

I'm glancing at the clock and doing quick math to figure out if we have time to get off before Avery catches us when the front door unlocks and the other two stalk in. I don't really look away from the shitty cartoons, I'm not worried that they're walking in on us, but when Ash grabs my hips to stop me moving I frown and turn to them. Harley looks thunderous, fucking enraged, and I slide out of Ash's lap.

"What? Fuck, what now?" I say, and Blaise grabs the remote to fumble around the channels until he lands on a news station.

Senator Ayres is dead.

I sit and soak in the report, my hands shaking. Ash takes the plate from me and sets it down on the coffee table where my rage won't break the damn thing. The reporter is standing in front of a large, luxury looking office building and she's surrounded by flashing lights and uniform officers.

"Senator Ayres murder is said to be gang-related, with reports of gang activity across the state only getting worse. When interviewed, Senator Ayres' widow, Hannah Ayres, pleaded with her daughter Viola to come home. Reports say the teenager dropped out of school to run away with an older lover. Police have not yet confirmed if there is any connection between the young girl's disappearance and her father's murder."

The image shifts to the crime scene and, sweet lord *fuck*, the Jackal has lost his damn mind.

Written in blood across the wallpaper in the senator's office is a message. For the Coyote, the Crow, and, probably most of all, for me.

The Jackal sends his regards.

Well, fuck.

"I have other news," says Avery.

She comes to sit down next to her dressed in her workout gear. I wrench my eyes away from the TV and give her a side look.

"Lauren's dad is *owned* by Senior. I know that we already knew that but the list of things that man has done that Senior can hold over his head... it's a lot. More extensive than I thought. We need to do what we can to stay out of that man's way."

Harley scoffs and snags a piece of French toast off of my plate. "It's not like we didn't already know that. One of us just needs to go down the hall and put the fear of fucking god in that girl."

Ash's fingers drift back to my thighs, tracing his little patterns there, something he does when he's thinking. For once I don't have to fight a shiver; I'm too busy hating myself. The TV flicks through other scenes in Mounts Bay, of the unrest and riots starting up everywhere. I frown at the screen as I see a familiar building, it's on fire and hard to see but something is so damn familiar.

My phone buzzes and I grab it answering without even bothering to look, I know at this point it's going to be Illi. I'm hoping he has a lead or a plan or *something*. We need to retaliate, the Jackal can't be left unanswered.

"Have you seen it?" His voice is all fucked up. I lurch forward, my spine snapping straight. Harley's gaze flashes to mine and Ash's fingers still on my leg. I try to ignore them both and find my voice but there's something so fucking *raw* about Illi that I struggle.

My brain fills it in for me as the pictures on the screen change. The building is burning but everyone in it are already dead. Bullet's in their brains. It's Illi's safe house.

Odie.

"Kid. She's in that fucking building. She's... *fuck*. FUCK!"

I can't breathe.

I can't move or think of fucking breathe. Ash jumps off of the couch and starts yelling at Blaise to grab his keys because they're heading out and Harley snarls at Avery when she tells them they can't.

That there's no point.

I can't breathe.

Harley's phone rings in his pocket and that triggers something in the back of my mind. Who would be calling him?

"I'm fucking busy," he snaps and then his entire body freezes, his eyes jerking to mine. I stare at him and I fucking *pray*. He stays silent for a second and the whole room goes quiet, then he says, "How?"

Everyone turns to face him and Illi snarls from the phone, loud enough that we can all hear it, "*What the fuck is going on?!*"

Harley switches his phone to speakerphone and Diarmuid speaks, "I'm assuming you've seen the news, Wolfie."

"Don't fuck with me, O'Cronin. Why are you calling?" I say, and then I hear the best fucking sound on the planet.

Odie starts cussing him out in colorful and vicious French. Illi obviously manages to catch this down his line and snarls, "*Where is she?*"

Diarmuid laughs. "I told the Wolf I'd prove my loyalty. I heard talk of one of your informants flipping and siding with the Jackal, I knew that would leave your girl open to his rage and I've been watching your safe house. You might need a new one. Oh, and you all owe me big time. She's kicked me in the dick so many times my balls have climbed up the back of my fuckin' throat."

I lean back on the couch and squeeze my eyes shut, trying desperately not to cry but the adrenaline in riding me hard. Harley snarls at Diarmuid until he gives up his location to Illi and my old friend hangs up to find his girl. I sigh, resigned to what I have to do.

Harley's jaw clenches but when I raise an eyebrow at him, he nods. I have no real choice here, we've strung him along for long enough and saving Odie is fucking huge. Avery sits down next to me and Blaise gives me a little relieved smile, I'm not sure he's on board completely but it's enough. I glance over to Ash and even he gives me a curt nod.

"O'Cronin, you're in. Get a tattoo, put the word out, and start paying your dues. I'll call you when I need you." I say, and Avery slips her hand into mine.

Fuck, I hope I don't regret this.

Chapter Nine

Ash sleeps like the dead.

It's good for nights like this, nights where I have to sneak out and take care of business, but when I'm dressed for business and ready to leave I look back over at him and all I feel is dread.

How much more would I damage him, and us, if I leave without telling him?

I blow out a breath and pray I'm not going soft. Well, not *soft*, I just hope I'm compromising on the shit that matters in a relationship without losing the edge that keeps me alive.

Sliding my hand around his neck and into his hair, I give it a little tug as I kiss him sweetly on the lips. He groans a little, never happy to be woken, and I try my best to smother the sound so Avery doesn't wake up and turn this whole thing into a field trip.

I wait until his eyes open before I speak. "I need to go take care of something. It'll keep our family safe."

He swallows and frowns at me. "Why didn't you wake me earlier? I'm coming with you."

I sigh and nod, motioning for him to hurry up. I don't want to lose my window of opportunity. He pulls on jeans and a black tee, then one of Blaise's black leather jackets to cover his gun and holster. I bite my lip at the sight of him in the leather; it's completely un-fucking-fair that he can look so sinfully good in a suit *and* leathers. I wonder if I can convince him to wear leather pants for me? Hoo boy.

We arm the security alarm and I shoot a text to Harley and Blaise to tell them we're heading out.

They're not happy but we can't leave Avery alone. She will always be our biggest target and to lose her would fucking break our family. When I say this to Ash, more as a random thought than anything else, he scoffs at me. "Don't be dense, Mounty. There isn't anyone in the family that wouldn't break us to lose. I won't choose between the two of you. Not now, not ever."

I try not to blush and he scoffs at me again, opening the car door for me like a gentleman and then sliding in behind the wheel.

Ash drives the Ferrari with such fucking *passion*, it's obscene. He drives it like the polished steel and soft leather is in his blood. He's not assured like Harley, or reckless like Blaise. He moves like he never wants to get out of the car. I love it and struggle not to tell him to pull over to let off some steam. Fuck, focus Lips!

I keep my eyes firmly away from him and settle back into my seat for the drive to the Bay. I direct him to the right house in the slums. He sneers at the neighborhood and I sigh.

"You didn't have to come," I say, and he shakes his head at me like I'm so freaking dumb.

"You should have told me we were coming *here*. I would've brought the Cadillac instead."

I snort at his shitty attitude and check through my stash of supplies. His eyes follow my every move, his eyebrow arching. "So it's a hit? Not a little visit to warn the idiot of who he's crossing?"

I meet his eye as I say, "He knew who he was betraying. He knew the risks. I have to do this."

He grabs the back of my neck and hauls me forward until he can whisper against my lips, his thumb sliding over the pulse in my throat, "Show me how you work, Mounty. Show me how you keep us safe."

Ash is shockingly good at moving silently.

I make a mental note to ask him where he picked it up, I'm assuming it'll go back to his 'training' with Joey, but I can't imagine that deranged psycho ever being any good at subtlety.

I use my lock picking kit to get us through the front door. Ash watches my every move, from the angle I hold the two tools to the sound of the click when the lock finally releases, and I recognize the look on his face now. He's soaking everything in and he'll have the basics down now. Good. I'm sure that will come in handy later.

We step into the house and notice two things immediately; there's music on loud enough to drown out pretty much anything and the smell of drugs is heavy in the air. A flutter panic start in my chest but I push the feeling down, roll my shoulders back, and force myself to be empty. I fucking hate the smell of that shit.

I have to glance back over my shoulder to make sure Ash is following me. His feet are as silent as mine, and I'm seriously impressed. We move through the empty kitchen, and when we walk past the lounge we find a group of Mounties enjoying their high. Some of them are unconscious, some of them are fucking, and some of them are ranting at each other, at themselves, at the ceiling.

Our mark isn't in the room.

We move past them, they don't even notice us, and we head up the stairs. The music playing downstairs is a low thrum, and it's easy to move without being detected. The first room we come to has a closed door but I can hear voices behind it. I motion for Ash to follow me. The next door slightly ajar and I move until I can see the bed. Lying across the bed, sprawled across it, is our mark. He's out like a freaking light, flat on his back and snoring like a freight train.

We walk into the room together and Ash shuts the door behind us silently. I do a quick check to make sure there's no one else in the room, no girlfriend hiding under the bed, and then I grab my device to make sure there's no extra eyes in the room. Once we are clear, I pull out my knife.

Ash grabs my arm and holds up his gun. His silencer is already in place and I give him a tight smile. I do not understand why these boys keep attempting to stop me from being the one killing people, it makes no sense. I'm the Wolf of Mounts Bay, what does one more life matter when I've killed hundreds before?

I'm not sure I can get my eyebrows to tell him that this has to be done by a knife.

It's my signature kill, and we're not just here to take out a mark. We're here to send a message.

He watches me carefully and then unscrews the silencer and re-holsters his gun. When I move towards the bed he stops me again and tries to take the knife from me. I roll my eyes at him and wave him away.

I do a quick check of the window and find it open already, thank fuck. I quickly slip my hoodie and my yoga pants off and hand them to Ash as he watches me with pissy eyes.

And then I slash the guy's throat.

If he hadn't been laying on his back I would have stabbed him through the base of his neck. This is a much messier way to go, there's blood on the fucking ceiling, but I guess it sends the right sort of message.

Ash watches with a blank sort of interest. He catalogs everything, from the gurgling sound the guy makes as he chokes on his blood, to the jerking his arms and legs are making as the life slowly slips out of him. I don't bother watching the scene, not the way he is, I just make sure the guy doesn't roll off the bed and pump around.

The second he loses consciousness, not quite dead but safe to turn away from, I wipe my knife, tuck it back into my waist holster.

I slip my clothing on over the gore I'm covered in and when I move to the window Ash grabs my arm to stop me. I glance at the door, worried that someone is about to walk through, but Ash snaps on a pair of gloves and coats his hands in the blood. He finds an empty patch of wall, and leaves his own message for the Jackal.

No one touches the Wolf.

It shows just how much I trust Ash when I startle back into myself as we pull into the driveway at Avery's ranch. I hadn't noticed we were heading here at all, too lost in my own head. Ash's hands are still gripping the wheel with white knuckles but his face is less guarded. He parks and gets out without a word.

"Why are we here?" I ask but I follow his lead and get out of the car.

"I can't take you back to Avery covered in blood and if we go back to my room I'll have to share you," he replies as he unlocks the front door and disarms the code. I get an immediate text from Avery asking what we're doing at the ranch.

Your brother insists on pretending that my work isn't bloody and that you'll break if you realize it is.

I pocket my phone and head to our bathroom. I've left enough of my clothes that I can leave this set here. Yep, that's right, I have so many clothes now I can leave them places. Avery has forced me to buy more because she *cannot* wrap her head around the fact that I only need two pairs of jeans.

Ash follows me and then leans against the bathroom counter on his phone while I undress and get into the shower. His eyes keep flicking over to me, like he can't help but watch as I scrub away the death from my skin, and once the blood is down the drain he sets his phone down and starts to strip.

Hoo boy.

There's nothing quite like a naked Ash Beaumont. He smirks at me when he gets to his jeans, arrogant as ever, and I try my best not to drool at the sight of him. I think he's brainwashed me into loving that giant dick of his, even if I am still a little gun-shy at actually having sex with him, because the second I see it I want it in my mouth. Clearly it's written all over my face.

"Don't worry. I'll let you swallow, Mounty," he says as he steps in behind me. I shiver and try to turn around but his hands grip my hips and force me to stay still.

His tone is haughty as he whispers into my ear, "I'm enjoying the view."

Then he slaps my ass and I clamp my teeth together to stop myself from moaning. He grabs the soap and starts to wash my back. Ok, he's groping my ass and legs but he pretends to care about swiping the soap over my back as well for about a second. It's like he's drugging me with his soft touches, so unlike him but it feels amazing.

I start to wonder if maybe I should get over myself and just have sex with him. Maybe his dick really is magic and I'll crave the stretch just as much as I crave the taste of him.

"Why are you mumbling about my magic dick?" he snarks at me and I snap my mouth shut. Ugh. His stupid hands!

"Are you going to let me blow you or not? A girl has needs," I snap back and he laughs at me, the utter dick.

He bites my ear and then whispers, "I'll never stop you from swallowing my dick and I'll kill anyone who tries."

I shiver, hello damage, and I shut the water off, soap be damned. "Liar. Your sister tries all the damn time."

He laughs at me again, far too happy for a recent accomplice to a murder. It doesn't matter to me, I've killed so many it's all the same.

How many people has he killed?

Maybe not the best time to ask as he grabs a towel and wraps me up. I try not to look too desperate as I quickly dry myself and then head back to my giant bed but the snort Ash gives me says I fail. Fuck it, he knows how much I love him.

Oh.

Oh, *fuck*.

I can't think about that right now either. We don't do mushy, not when we're facing each other and the lights are on, and certainly not when we're naked.

He gives me a look. "Why do you suddenly look like you're about to jump out of the window?"

I swallow, and again, then I snap, "*You'll* be the one to jump out of the window if I say it. Can we just do this?"

He shakes his head at me, God do I feel dumb when he does that, and shoves me back onto the bed, covering my body with his and kissing me like he's trying to crawl inside my skin. I'd let him. I'd let him do anything to me. Jesus. Ok, I need to figure this shit out.

"There's lube somewhere around here, right?" I break away to mumble and he bites the spot where my shoulder and my neck meet.

"I stocked up after Harley put group sex on the table. Are you feeling brave now, Mounty?" He slowly works his way down my body, biting as he goes and my toes curl as I moan.

"Fuck. Fuck, stop, I'm trying to think," I croak, and he smirks at me.

"I don't want you to think. Tell me you're being brave and I'll let you have my cock."

He bites the inside of my thigh and I swear I see stars. Jesus fucking wept, how is that possible? He refuses to touch my pussy until I answer. When I can't form the words he teases me by blowing air onto my clit in the most torturous imitation of a touch and I groan at him.

"Fuck, *yes*. I'm being brave and I want your dick. If you break me I swear to God I'll fucking stab you."

He laughs at me and then fucking buries his face into my pussy like a champ. Ugh, maybe I could convince him to set up camp and live down there because it's so *fucking* good.

I come twice before he moves back up to kiss me, his face and lips still wet, and I moan into his mouth. He rolls away from me to grab lube and I almost think we don't need it. I'm dripping on the sheets. But then I glance back down at his *perfect* fucking monster dick and yeah, maybe we *will* need it.

"Stop freaking out. You know you're not the first—"

"Do *not* finish that sentence if you want to fuck me tonight, Beaumont. I'll fucking *end* you."

He smirks at me. "Jealous? Since when do you care about our histories?"

I think about punching the fucker but I don't want to ruin the mood so I take a deep breath instead. "I care. I'm just not hung up on it. Ok, that's a lie but I try not to think about it so it doesn't ruin my fucking day."

Ash nods almost absently, and slicks his dick up, giving it a few firm pumps that distract me. I'm almost jealous of him touching himself.

What the fuck has he done to me?

He stares down at me, his eyes so icy and intense that my breath catches in my chest, and he wraps a hand around my throat. My body stills, and then I turn liquid for him. I trust this asshole that fucking much.

"I've never wanted to keep someone before. I've never wanted someone like I want you. I get it, I don't want to think about someone else touching you either, but you're mine. I promise you no one else will ever fucking touch me again."

Then he lines up and pushes in, firmly and without stopping until he's all-the-fucking-way in. Even without the squeeze of his hand I wouldn't be able to breath. It's too much, too full, too big, and I fucking *love* it. He smirks at the slack look on my face, the way my entire body just goes boneless for him, and then he starts to pump into me in long, unforgiving strokes.

I swear, I fucking *purr* for him.

The hand around my throat doesn't budge, and his fingers flex as he moves. There's too much sensation for me to focus on anything except the feel of him and my own desperate need for oxygen. Fuck it, if I had to choose I'll die right freaking here because there's no way I'm asking him to stop.

And then he fucking stops.

The snarl of frustration I let out has him chuckling, and he tugs me to the edge of the bed, flipping me over so I'm on my hands and knees and he can push back in. I can't catch my breath and I scramble at the sheets to try to keep myself upright but he holds my hip in one hand and grabs a fistful of hair with the other. I moan so fucking loud when he tugs until I'm kneeling, pressed flush against him and panting as he rocks his hips into me.

"Did you really think I'd stop? Did you think after waiting this fucking long to get inside you I'd stop? I'm going to fuck you *raw*." He bites down on my shoulder until I gasp and then he slaps my ass, the cracking of his palm drowned out by my moan as I come so hard he has to hold me up.

His hips slow to a grind until my vision clears and I can see past the stars, and then he runs a palm down my spine like he's soothing me. I shiver as he traces the scars, the bullet hole, the crisscrosses of blade marks, the burns on my lower back, and the sharp sting of the slap on my ass takes me by surprise this time. I clench around him without meaning to, a startled reaction, and he grunts, bending me down until I'm facedown on the bed again, pinning one arm behind my back.

When his hips move again they're relentless, pounding into me as he holds me down and I have no choice but to take it.

As I come again, I clench around him again so hard he grunts and slams into me harder, snapping his hips until he comes with a low groan. When he finally stops moving he pulls out, stroking my ass in a soft caress, his fingers playing in the mess he's made of me. It's like he's rubbing it in and I scoff at him.

"I told you, it's mine." He chuckles at me, stalking into the bathroom to clean up and find his phone.

I take a minute or twenty to figure out how to stand before I go clean up then I burrow into the blankets on the bed, sore and used and fucking blissful. When Ash has finished his call to the others, to tell them we're alive and safe, he digs around in the bed until he finds me, moving until he has me tucked into his chest where he wants me.

"We have to get back. It's not safe to be separated and Avery will lose her fucking mind if we don't get back soon," I mumble, but I don't move away from him. My eyelids are too fucking heavy, I could pass out for a month.

Ash kisses that little patch of my shoulder he loves so much and whispers back, "I'll wake you up before dawn, Mounty. Get some sleep."

I think I try to argue with him but before the words fully form, I'm out.

Chapter Ten

I avoid Avery when we get back to Hannaford. I don't know how she found out about my other experiences, but I'm certain she doesn't know exactly what went down at the Ranch overnight. Harley, on the other hand, realizes the second he looks at me.

He tucks me under his arm to walk me down to the dining hall for breakfast, Blaise messing around on his phone trailing behind us. Ash took an extra long run this morning and Avery had stayed behind to walk down with him later.

It's ridiculous but I blush at Harley's questioning look. He scoffs at me and says, "You might want to put something on that bite mark to cover it up unless you want the whole school talking."

Dear lord, no thank you.

I elbow him and ignore his snickering while Blaise roars with laughter behind us. When I shoot him a dark look he grins at me and says, "We're just happy Ash can stop being a snarling, jealous, blue-balled asshole now."

Nope.

I pull away from Harley, ignoring his grunt of annoyance at me and stalk off towards food. Their legs are ten miles longer than mine and they keep up with me easily, damn them, and by the time we get to the dining hall Harley manages to corral me so I'm back under his arm.

Harley grabs us a tray and picks out our food without any need for input from me, even somehow managing to get sprinkles on my French toast. I grin at my toes while they laugh at my enthusiasm for my food, Harley even getting a good squeeze of my ass in, then we make our way over to our usual seats.

We haven't spent much time eating in the dining hall this year but no matter how busy it is, our seats are always empty. Infamy does have some perks.

The boys wedge me between them, spreading out so their legs are touching mine and their arms taking over my space as they set out our food. It should be annoying but it just makes me feel more fucking cherished than anything else.

Maybe I'm turning into a fucking sap after all?

"If the other two don't get down here soon they're going to be late for class. There's no way Ash will get a higher score than me in calculus if he's late," Harley gloats, and Blaise groans under his breath.

"Can the two of you lay off a bit? Who the fuck cares who gets second? The last thing the rest of us want to listen to is your bitching and snarling."

Harley stabs at his eggs and I nudge him gently, trying to stop the shitty mood from starting, "Maybe he'll be a little less focussed on his studies since… Well, you know."

Blaise snickers, "You mean he's going to stop studying at the time because he's finally getting laid? Yeah, he'll probably need your tutoring again."

Harley tips his head back and roars with laughter, so light and happy again that my chest aches to look at him. My phone buzzes in my pocket and I grab it, my heart dropping at Avery's text.

911. Boys room. Senior called Ash.

I drop my cutlery and pass the message on, bolting up and out of the room without looking back. 911 means bad, life threatening. What if he's here? What if he's come to Hannaford to pick Avery up and take her? I need to call in for backup now if he is.

I call Avery as I hit the first staircase, my leg screaming at me even as I ignore it completely.

"Is he here?" I ask the second she picks up, and she whispers a quiet 'no.' He's still talking to Ash in the background, I don't know what the hell they could possibly have to chat about.

I can't hear it well enough to stay on the phone and listen in so I hang up, grit my teeth, and sprint the rest of the way back. I get a few mildly curious looks but mostly the other students all dive out of my way, as if being in my path is truly life threatening. Well, Good for them.

I make it to our rooms and manage to get the key in on my first try. The door swings open right as Senior says, "When I'm done getting rid of her, I'll come find your pretty little girlfriend. I think she would look rather stunning strapped against my table. Have you fuck her like that yet, son? Have you laid her out and forced her to take you, bleeding and screaming? There's nothing quite like it. I think I'll enjoy watching the slum cunt bleed all over my cock."

I try to control my breathing as I roll my eyes and step in, toeing out of my shoes to try to stop my leg from hurting quite so badly, and then I stalk over to the phone. I'm going to hang up on the useless stream of bullshit but Ash stops me. His fingers are cold as he wraps them around my wrist, stopping me from grabbing the phone and ending this stream of fucking bullshit. I give him a hard look but he shakes his head, even as a tremble of contained rage runs down his arm. He's close to the edge, right at his breaking point, but there's something he needs.

"What the fuck are you doing working with the Jackal? Lowering yourself to common criminals? You won't be able to hide behind high society if you're too busy hiding behind the Jackal's skirts like a terrified child."

Avery stares down at the phone like she can somehow force her father to reveal all of his secrets and his plans, just by directing her loathing there, but Ash watches me.

Senior laughs and I try not to cringe away from the sound. "You've forgotten your lessons, boy. The cattle in the working class do the work, that's what they're bred for, why should I go looking for your little slum queen when I can get someone else to do it for me? You spent too long fawning after your sister, I've been too lenient. It's time you remember who you belong to."

The phone beeps as Senior hangs up and my eyes stay glued to Ash's.

And then all of hell breaks loose.

Ash loses his *goddamn* mind.

I've seen him get pissy before, I've seen him be overprotective and beat men until they have to be scraped off of the floor, but I've never seen the tornado that is a truly *enraged* Ash.

Avery watches, with a passive stance but calculating eyes as he destroys the boys' room. I stand next to her, leaning against the far wall where we're out of his destructive path, as the two of us watch him smash the furniture to pieces as if they were nothing. I'm kinda glad classes are on and there's no way he can get into a fight; pretty sure whoever he went up against right now would die. He's now leaving blood on everything he touches from the steady stream coming out of his knuckles.

As the damage bill slowly gets higher and higher I lean in to murmur to Avery, the disgust dripping in my voice, "It's pretty clear to me that money means absolutely fucking *nothing* to you people."

Avery rolls her eyes at me. "Lips, I don't think you've grasped just how much money you now have either. Between the dirty money we first invested, your earnings from the bet, and Harley paying you back with interest you probably don't need to work a day in your life either. You certainly won't need to at the rate that you spend money."

I narrow my eyes at her, no longer concerned with the bloody state of Ash's hands. "What the hell do you mean he paid me back *with interest*? What the fuck are you doing letting him pay me back at all, let alone with fucking *interest*?"

Avery shrugs as she tries to smother a smile. "You know I'm not getting involved in your *relationship issues* and I'm definitely counting this as a relationship issue. Take it up with him."

I scoff at her but any witty remark I could come up with is interrupted by the door opening and Harley and Blaise walking in. Harley has my abandoned breakfast tucked under his arm but I don't have it in me to feel warm and fuzzy about him caring for me like that. I'm too worried about the state Ash is in.

"Fuck me. What's your dad done now?" asks Blaise, and Avery gives him a look that would strip the skin off a grown man.

"You know better than to call that man my *dad*. Senior called, he wanted to discuss my sale. He made it clear to Ash that he intends on doing whatever necessary to hand me over to Morningstar. He also threatened Lips, so naturally the best course of action is to give this disgusting pit of a room a fresh start. A completely *rational* reaction."

I raise an eyebrow at her, assuming she's being sarcastic and, well, glass houses, but then I realize she's being deadly fucking serious. Right. I had always thought her cleaning after shit goes down was a germaphobe thing not a Beaumont Bullshit thing. I stare at her for another second and then turn back to the mess that Ash is in. We all watch him in silence for another minute, then Harley and Blaise share a look, nodding at each other.

"Grab him, I'll grab the bourbon to mellow him the fuck out," Harley says, and Blaise grunts at him.

"Star can grab the bourbon, you grab his other arm. I'm not getting knocked out before we even get in the ring," he argues, and I head for the bar, skirting around the mess, because I'm absolutely onboard with the plan to get Ash drunk.

I'm pretty sure if we don't get him wasted before we put him in the ring he will kill someone. If only he were climbing in there with one of our many enemies and not the members of our family.

Blaise and Harley tackle Ash and get him sort of under control, though he cusses them both out viciously. I hear a few pained grunts. Avery announces she'll stay put, telling us she will clean it up and meet us down there later. I nod as I follow the boys out the door, knowing already that she wouldn't want to watch Ash beat the rage out of his system.

Harley and Blaise manage to drag him down towards the gym without too much trouble, probably because classes are in and there are no other students walking the halls, because I'm fairly certain if we had bumped into anyone and they so much has looked at Ash he would have beaten the life out of them.

When we get to the gym the guys finally let him go and he turns to me to grab the bottle of bourbon. His eyes still look crazed but I'm relieved to see he still looks human. I'm not sure what I would do if they were empty like Joey's always were, even before he was a head in a box.

He cracks the bottle open and takes deep gulps straight from it. Harley winces, and then tries to wrestle it off of him before he drowns himself.

"You can't get in the ring if you can't fucking stand."

Ash levels his icy eyes on Harley and says, "And you won't walk out of the ring if I haven't had something to drink."

Fuck.

I moved to stand between them and I press the palm to each of their chests but they just keep glaring at each other over my head. I'm going to have to pull out the big guns to distract them.

"Maybe I should get in the ring with Ash. Just until he calms down enough."

All three of them look at me like I've lost my fucking mind. Fuck that.

I cross my arms and peg Ash with a look. "I hate to say it, but you won't be the most dangerous thing I've ever faced. Get in the ring and I'll teach you some shit."

He shakes his head at me, and strips out of his clothes. I'm about to snap at him for trying to use a secret weapon against me when I noticed that Blaise has their training bag slung over his shoulder and yeah, maybe it would be for the best if Ash isn't wearing his uniform for this. I don't look back at him until he has the obscenely short shorts on and he's winding the tape onto his hands.

Harley looks relieved that Ash seems to be in a clear enough state of mind to go through these motions. I think we would be in a lot more danger if he had just thrown himself into the ring. The room takes a breath.

The other two change into their sparring clothes as well and I do my best not to drool now that the pressing danger has passed. Blaise throws himself down on the mat and tugs me until I'm in his lap. Just as Ash and Harley step up the door to the gym opens and three of the Crow's men walk in.

Oh fuck.

Ash turns and takes the sight of them in. Blaise groans under his breath and presses his lips behind my ear as he whispers, "That's it, someone's gonna die today."

I struggle out of his lap and stand to face the men. The smiles slowly slide off of their faces and their heads dip at me with respect. I hope Ash is paying attention and decides to let this go.

"We were just coming down here to train, we could join you if you want some fresh blood?" the bigger of the three guys says.

I open my mouth but, of course, Ash interrupts me. "Get in then, dickhead."

Harley huffs but he steps out without a word and the bigger of the three men strips out of his shirt. I keep my eyes on them all, not trusting them one fucking bit.

Blaise twirls a strand of my hair around his finger and I glance over my shoulder at him to find him and Harley flanking me the way they do at the meetings. They both look ready to pounce, whether in my defense or for their own need for blood I don't think they care.

I wonder if they'll ever grow out of this?

The guy looks at me before he steps up and I jerk my head in the direction of the ring, giving him my approval. He nods and grabs the tape from Harley's outstretched hand, the two of the staring each other down. It's hard not to roll my eyes. I shouldn't, the guys are behaving exactly as the Wolf's men should, but I know this is about their protective natures about me and about Avery, not about their positions in my... fuck, my *gang*.

I take a seat on the mats again, giving Blaise a curt shake of my head when he tries to pull me back into his lap. Harley takes a seat next to us both and watches the Crow's men carefully.

"First blood?" the guy asks, and Ash smirks at him with the absolute arrogance of a rich kid that knows how to kill.

"Tap out or knock out, nothing less."

Oh fuck.

I don't expect it to last long, and it doesn't. Ash is ruthless, deadly, and fucking insane. It takes me a second to recognize what it is that I'm watching but then it clicks in my brain; Ash has no fear. He's not afraid of taking a hit or the pain that comes with it. He moves as if death means *nothing* to him.

Senior and Joey really have broken something in him.

Harley jumps up to pull Ash off of the guy once it's clear he's out, and the other two guys scrape their friend up and throw him down next to us on the mats.

The larger of the two left takes his turn and the last guy starts to pour water on the unconscious guy's head.

"He's good. Where'd a little rich boy learn to fight like that?"

I ignore the question, I don't need friends, but Harley scoffs at him. "You wouldn't survive what he has, dickhead."

The guy shrugs. "Just trying to be friendly. We're all on the same side, why not try to get along?"

Blaise strokes a hand down my leg in an obviously suggestive way. I sigh at him but let him go. He has to shit stir, it's in his fucking blood to do it, so why not let him have his fun.

"Is the Crow your family? You fucking him? Do you make him scream your name, does he have you on your knees for him? We're not on the same anything. You're owned. You signed away your life to a fucking crime lord just so you can, what, wear cheap suits and carry guns? You're nothing."

The guy bristles, wincing a little as Ash gets his friend on the ground and just starts whaling in on him. "You think you're better than me because you're fucking the Wolf? When she's done with you she'll just slit your throats and be done with it. I know better than to climb into bed with a member of the Twelve."

Harley smirks and pushes my hair off of my shoulder, rubbing at the little patch of skin peeking out from my button-up shirt. I smile at him and then speak, fuck the consequences, "I get it. You needed to eat so you sold your soul and now you're expendable, replaceable, nameless, and nothing. That's what you made yourself when you became one of the Crow's men. I could have done the same with the Jackal a lifetime ago but instead I crawled my way out of hell. So shut your fucking mouth and get ready to be beaten down because Ash Beaumont is going to own your fucking ass."

Chapter Eleven

The Crow stands at our bedroom door, two of his men standing behind him, scowling at us all like we're disobedient children.

Ash ignores him entirely but he holds the ice to his hands after Avery snarls at him for attempting to move it. Harley stands a step in front of them both, as if his body is a shield and he can protect them both from this man and his influence of them, and Blaise lounges on the bed as if there's nothing to worry about.

I sip my coffee at the table and do my best to ignore them all. Ok, not ignore them, but I pretend I'm not listening to the whole episode because it's not strictly Twelve business so it's none of my concern. Avery will tell me if she needs backup.

"If you're going to put my men out of commission could you at least call me before? I could have sent in expendable suits," Atticus says, and Ash scoffs at him.

"We're going back to escorting Avery everywhere if that's the protection you're offering us. Not a single one of those *men* lasted longer than a minute in the ring. If Jackal comes down here himself we're fucked."

It's a very good point and I tilt my head as I sip at my coffee again.

Atticus doesn't rise to the bait, his anger at Ash's words tightly contained. "They all know not to harm you, they wouldn't walk into the ring with any real intentions of bringing you harm."

Oh dear.

I turn to watch them and sure enough, Ash's shoulders are so rigid I can see the fine tremble. I give Blaise a look and he huffs at me.

"Are you fucking serious? I didn't beat them because they *let* me, I took them out because they're fucking *weak*," he hisses, and Blaise finally stands and walks over to him. He leans against the table and offers him backup. I'm hoping he'd also jump in between them if Ash dives at him.

Atticus rolls his eyes and stares at Avery. "Is there any real concern for your safety? Has anything happened?"

I'm so fucking proud of her, just bursting with it, when she turns to face him with cold eyes and her perfectly frigid tone. "My safety is no longer of your concern. You can discuss it with the Wolf, not me."

He grinds his teeth at her and then stalks forward, ignoring the daggers the boys all glare at him with. He gestures at the chair across from me and I nod at him. Once he's seated he folds himself into what looks like the signature Avery Beaumont power pose. Hm.

When he speaks, his voice is tightly-controlled and formal. "The Viper has left the Jackal's side. He has requested a meeting but I'm unable to attend. Is it possible for you to go?"

I sigh and give him a stern look, pulling myself into my own version of the power pose until I'm mirroring him. "I'm supposed to stay at school, you know. Some of us want to be more than just a crime lord. What's the meeting for and why can't you go?"

His eyes flick to Avery as she takes the seat next to mine. She ignores him but I slip my hand into hers under the table anyway.

"I have to take a meeting with my father about… the sales of girls. He's still purchasing despite my efforts to get rid of the auctions. I can't move the meeting and the Viper needs to speak to one of us as soon as possible so he doesn't get spooked and go crawling back."

Avery hums under her breath but doesn't speak. I'm sure she has plenty to say but I stick to the topic. "Where and when. I'll see what I can do."

His eyes flick around to the guys and then he speaks slowly, like he's choosing his words even more carefully. "Take the Butcher with you and leave everyone else here for the night."

My spine snaps straight, and Harley snarls at him, "You don't get make those fucking decisions; where she goes, we go."

Atticus rolls his eyes, and doesn't bother to look at the three enraged guys plotting his death. "The Viper wants to meet at the Dive. You have to put a body in the cage to get in, you're better off taking the Butcher with you because that's his idea of a fun Friday night."

The scheming *bastard*. I somehow manage to keep my face impassive as I shrug. "I'll go. The details are none of your concern."

He isn't as good as I am at keeping his tells in lockdown, not when it comes to Avery, and his jaw ticks as he grits out from between his clenched teeth, "Avery *cannot* go. The Dive is too dangerous, what the hell is the point of keeping her away from her father if you're just going to take her with you to the pits of fucking hell in Mounts Bay? This isn't a sightseeing exhibition, it's not the place for some naive girl rebelling from her privileged life."

I suck in a breath and mentally start planning how *the fuck* we're going to end this war without the Crow because Avery is going to slit his throat.

She doesn't.

Instead she tilts her head at him and breathes pure ice his way. "You're not my fucking keeper. You're not even my friend, you are a means to an end." She stares him down and then flicks her hand at him dismissively, "If you're done with your power display, I'd like to get back to our family dinner."

Atticus stares at her again, his eyes cataloging everything about her, from the color of her nails to the faint, dark smudges under her eyes that a damn near permanent now. She's not sleeping well. She's barely eating. Even her dance classes have started to slip now she's working so hard on gathering the information we need.

As if reading my mind, Atticus pulls an envelope out of his jacket pocket. "There's not much, but I know who you can speak to about Lips' father."

The detached, cold look slips on Avery's face a fraction as she takes the envelope. I can't look at it or touch it, so fucking terrified of what's in it. Atticus looks between the two of us and then says, "You need to call the Boar. Everything leads back to him."

Fuck.

God-fucking-dammit.

Avery Beaumont looks fucking devastating in a pair of leather pants, a ripped band tee, and the all-white combat boots I'd gotten for the lingerie party last year. Her winged eyeliner is sharp enough to kill a man and her mood could do even fucking worse.

I choose a pair of ripped jeans that have half my ass peeking out and a razorback tee. I put my hair up and let Avery do my makeup, mostly to try to improve her mood before she guts someone. She's now carrying her knife everywhere we go and, fuck if she isn't good with it too now that Illi's gotten some training sessions in as well.

When we head down to the cars I grab Ash's hand and squeeze it a little, still nervous as hell over how our night is going to go. He ignores it, and me, until we get to the cars and everyone else piles into Blaise's Cadillac. When I move to climb into the back with Harley he tugs me back, plastering me against the side of the car with his body and shoving his leg between mine. I shiver as he kisses me, rough and fucking dark, biting my lip hard enough to draw blood.

"You better not be doubting me, Mounty," he whispers against my lips, and I grab a fistful of the buttery-soft shirt he's got on.

"Nope. I'm just preparing myself for the entire night. I've got to be the Wolf, and you've got to focus on your fight, which means I'll watch your back. If the Jackal shows up, if he has men there, you'll be a prime target. I'm going to keep you safe while you do this for us. That's family."

He smirks at me and tugs me until he can kiss me again. We get a little too carried away and Avery snarls out of her open window, "For fuck's sake, can we get this night over with already?"

Ash's eyes narrow at her but I shift away from him and back into the car, ignoring Blaise's snickering and the eye roll Harley gives my flushed cheeks. Ash is less than impressed with their attitudes and tucks his hand onto my thigh before staring out of the window, ignoring everyone for the rest of the drive.

I direct Blaise to the edge of the city, right where the air changes from smog and people, to salty air and stinking docks, and we park outside the most disgusting building on the street. Rundown doesn't even begin to describe the place.

The Dive is exactly that, a fucking dive.

The doorman tips his head at me in respect but he's not a guy I know. I try to stay away from this place if I can help it, and I know there's going to be more than a few men here waiting for their opportunity to shed some blood, whether mine or my family's, they don't really give a fuck.

I grab Avery's hand and weave through the crowd, heading to the private section at the back of the room. There's a viewing platform to watch the cage fights and a private bar, though the bar is a plank of wood on old barrels and a bartender too fucking high to mix any drinks. Did I mention I fucking hate this place?

The crowd doesn't part for us even though they all know who I am, and the guys all press in around us protectively. I start to worry Ash won't be the only one fighting tonight as Harley snaps at a group of bikers that look even more rowdy than the last.

We make it to the private section and I keep Avery close as we approach the table set up for our meeting. There's two spare seats and we sit down, Avery grimacing at the state of the cushions.

The Viper is already seated.

He flicks his fingers at me, the light catching on the diamond encrusted rings he wears. The man wears an obscene amount of diamonds, he's fucking dripping in them, and even sitting here in the dirtiest, most fucking filthy pit in all of Mounts Bay he's not worried about being mugged. He's that confident in his boys, and his own fighting prowess, that he wears his wealth with unaffected ease.

It's gross.

"I thought you'd leave your pretty little girlfriend at home for this one, Wolf. She doesn't have the stomach for this kind of thing. I supposed she's a good lay for you, to make up for these things," he says, but his eyes stay locked on the cage.

There's two of the Jackal's men fighting already, I know them both well enough to know exactly how it's going to end. The Viper does too so I know he's choosing not to look at me on purpose.

"You're putting one of your pretty boys in the cage? I thought you'd bring the Butcher."

I shrug and motion at one of his men to bring me a drink. They move without complaint, which is a nice change. "The Butcher is busy taking care of… other tasks for me tonight. Beaumont is going to fight, I'll sure you'll get your money's worth."

The Viper turns at eyes Ash. "Beaumont? Jesus. Has he ever even left his castle before? I'm not going to give him an out, not even for you, Wolf."

I side-eye the fuck out of him. "Even for me? You've never given me anything easy. You're only here talking to me because the Jackal has you running scared. What did he say to you? What's he holding over your head that it worries you this much?"

The Viper grimaces, and waves his men away. I sip at my whiskey, slowly because I need my head.

"I have a kid. I keep her out of this life, but somehow the Jackal found out. Probably his fucking spy, the gutless fuck, but now he knows. I've sent her to go live in another state but that hasn't kept his men from turning up at her fucking house. I need the Crow to take her in. His place is the safest. He gave you permission to speak on his behalf or what?"

All this war has done is reveal everyone's weak spots, the little snippets of secrets they've guarded carefully but not quite well enough. The Coyote and his girl, now the Viper and his daughter. I wonder how much more will come out before the Jackal has been taken out. I refuse to think about the chances that we don't win. I can't.

I give the Viper a curt nod, and the bell rings out over the cage. I'm not sure the body they drag out is still alive but it'll only make it easier for me if there's one less of the Jackal's men out there.

The Viper jerks his head at Ash and he stalks down to the cage, Harley following to watch his back. Blaise stays with us, leaning against the railing and looking out over the voracious crowd as the jeering and shouting starts up. I watch as Ash strips down to his training shorts and I take a second to remember he's fucking good in the ring. He's the best option. When he straightens up and I see him in his full, almost-naked glory I take a deep breath and try to focus on my conversation with the Viper but it's a freaking challenge.

I'm sort of glad there aren't many women in this place.

"We'll take the girl. We'll have her as insurance so you don't change sides," I murmur, and the Viper shrugs.

"I chose the Jackal because I don't need some fucking suit coming down here and cleaning the place up. I like my fights. I like the gambling , booze and the easy women. Not everything in life is clean and I don't need The Crow's black and white fucking moral system spilling over into my world. He needs to remember who the fuck he is."

He gulps down his own murky glass and lifts the empty glass for a refill, then turns to look at me again. "I thought that school had changed you. I was wrong, I'll admit that. You can take Mira and keep her in that showy fucking castle of the Crow's, you can call me for anything, but he can keep his nose out of my business. I'm not cleaning this place up and I'm not going to stop sending my men after dickheads that don't pay their debts. If you're with me on that, then I'm with you on everything else."

Another of the Jackal's men climbs into the cage with Ash, and I try to contain the icy dread in my gut. I know Ash is good. I know he's fast. It doesn't matter that the guy is older, brawnier, more street smart. Ash Beaumont has survived hell. He can survive this too.

"Your boy wins this, maybe he should come here more often," the Viper murmurs, and I cock my head at him. The Viper never extends invitations; this is a fucking big deal and tells me more about his loyalties than any other part of our conversation so far.

"He'd probably be up for that. He's not as clean-cut as he looks. If you have money on this fight I hope it's on him," I mutter back, and the Viper grins at me, his gold tooth shining at me.

"Sounds perfect for you kid. Sounds like he's just what you need."

The noise from the crowd gets louder, amping up for the fight and the room becomes predatory. There isn't a whole heap of faith for the stunning and very obviously rich guy in the ring but I wasn't expecting any different. There's a reason Ash is the one fighting and not the lost O'Cronin heir.

Someone calls out, "Ten grand on the pretty boy. It's a night for gambling." and Blaise startles, his face all fucked up. He turns back to us and his face is pale as fuck. I frown at him as he rubs his eyes, but he only gives me one of his lopsided grins.

"I think I fucking smoked too much before we came. Usually I'm better about it. I could fucking swear I just… never mind. Too fucking high for my own good."

Avery sighs and stares at him like he's the densest man on Earth and I nudge her leg with mine under the table. He's only watching over us for show, I can take care of anything that goes down by myself.

The bell rings and my attention snaps back to the ring. The Jackal's guy lunges at Ash, big mistake, and Ash darts out of his path, swinging as he moves and smashing his fist into the guy's skull. Ouch.

Avery's gaze drops down to her hands, but there's no other signs that she's hating this. She never could stand to watch her brother fight and, after years of being forced to watch him endure Joey's torture without being able to fight back, I don't blame her.

I, however, am enjoying the ever-loving shit out of it.

The room slowly grows quiet as Ash efficiently, and fucking brutally, beats the shit out of the Jackal's guy. It's probably because the Jackal's mark is in the center of the guy's chest, like a badge of honor, and Ash is taking all of his rage out on him.

He gets him on the ground and just whales on him, the guy never stood a chance.

"Yeah, he can come back here any time," the Viper says, and I do my best not to smirk like a smug-ass bitch but fuck it if I'm not one.

The sound of the guy's cheekbone breaking as Ash knocks him out is loud enough that Avery hears it and flinches, then the bell is ringing and Harley steps in to try to get his cousin to stop pounding the guy. Blaise roars with laughter, and the Viper's men eye him with a faint sort of respect. Clearly the lesson of underestimation has been learned.

I signal for a refill, more to keep my hands busy than anything else, when Avery's leg tenses against mine. I glance up to find another of the Jackal's men approaching our table. I give her the tiniest shakes of my head; we're fine. I know Cole and he's not someone I'm particularly worried about. Blaise scowls at him but doesn't say a word. He'll have no idea who he belongs to and he's a hell of a lot less cautious than Avery is.

Cole stops in front of us, crossing his arms and speaking to the Viper as if I'm not even here, "I spoke to the boss about you being here with her. He's not happy."

I narrow my eyes. He always was a spineless fuck but I didn't realize he was this stupid either. Avery stares at him with her icy eyes and every last one of the Viper's men turn to face Cole until he's the center of attention. He starts to sweat a little but I'm sure he's more afraid of the Jackal than he is of me.

That's his first mistake.

The Viper turns to me, jerking his head at Cole, and snaps, "Division breeds disrespect. This is why we need this over with *now*."

I squeeze Avery's hand under the table in warning, then I say, "We'll have to make an example of this sort of thing, make sure the others know to stay in their fucking lane."

Then I move.

Cole doesn't see it coming, none of the men do, only Avery and the Viper are unruffled as I shoot up from my seat, grab a fistful of Cole's hair and slam him face-first into the table. Blaise lurches forward but stops when I shoot him a look. He gets it, he understands from that one look what's going on, so I know he can't be that high.

Cole knows how to take a beating and fuck, he's here to get in the cage and earn some green, but he's so sure his place with the Jackal will keep him breathing tonight.

That's mistake number two.

I lean forward and whisper in his ear, "Thank you for sending this message to your boss. I think he needs the reminder."

"Whatever it is, I'll pass it on," he mumbles, and I chuckle at him.

"Yes, you will."

The flash of white as his eyes widen is the last sign of life from him before I stab him in the base of his skull, conscious of the fact I didn't pack a spare change of clothes. My hands and forearms end up covered in blood but it's less intense than an arterial bleed. I let go of his hair and let his body slip to the ground. The Viper grunts at his men and a couple them move quickly to dispose of the body.

"Make sure he gets back to his boss safely. No point drawing lines unless the psycho fuck gets the message," he says, and his men all make noises of agreement.

Once they've moved out the Viper holds his drink up in a salute to me and says, "Your boy is good. Bring him back sometime soon and we'll headline him. Good money in it."

I keep my mouth shut about how very little we need the cash, and instead I take my own shot. I hold my hand out for him to shake and he doesn't hesitate. "I'll send Mira to the Crow in the morning. I look forward to being on your side, Wolf. I look forward to seeing what you'll do to him."

I nod and help Avery to her feet, moving away from the private table and down to meet with Ash. His fists are a bloodied mess and his cheek and lip are both busted but there's a dark glee lighting up his eyes.

"How was that?" he snarks, and I smirk at him.

"Decent. We could make a lot of money here together, if you're ever in need."

He scoffs and slides his leather jacket back on without his shirt. He's pulled his jeans back on and in one word, he looks fucking *edible*.

Avery elbows me. "You're drooling, Mounty."

I blush a little but shoot her a grin. "Can't help it. Nothing better than a little blood."

She finally cracks a smile, shaking her head at me entirely. I tuck my arm in hers and frown at the guys, all of them gravitating towards the bar. "If you want a drink then we can go someplace else. I have a friend with a bar that's less... Jackal-filled."

They nod and we head out.

Chapter Twelve

Ash and Blaise get fucking hammered.

We go to an old favorite of mine on the other side of the docks, where Illi has friends and I know we'll instantly have backup if we need it. Harley slowly drinks his beers but he's experienced enough that they barely take off the edge, and Avery sips at a margarita for an hour before declaring herself done. I have another whiskey and then stick to planning quietly in the corner booth with her. When the bartender comes over to ask if we need him to extend his hours for the night I wave him off and collect my wasted family. Harley grabs Ash, leaving Blaise to Avery and I.

Once we're out in the cold night air, he tucks his face into my throat and breathes me in. I huff at him and he starts to ramble mindlessly, "You're so perfect Star. You're everything."

Avery rolls her eyes and ducks under his other arm, propping him up and helping take the weight of him off of my bad leg. "You're so fucking wasted you wouldn't know who you were professing your undying love to. You were just telling Ash you'd be lost without him."

Blaise looks over at her with a frown. "I don't love anyone else, Star is fucking it for me. She's everything. I see her face every-fucking-where I go. Why do you have to be such a bitch about it? I'm with Ash; we should fucking gut Atticus for being such a miserable cock to you. Maybe you should fuck him and see if that cheers you up."

He's not even making any sense, just blurting out random crap, but Avery is not in a forgiving mood. "Why are you all so fucking hung up on who's in my bed? I kept my mouth shut about the revolving fucking door during freshman year."

Aaaaand now I wanna puke.

Blaise frowns at me and gives me his most morose eyes. "I'm sorry Star."

I shake my head and smile at him. "I know. It doesn't matter. Let's just get you back before you need to puke."

He groans and mumbles sweet nothings at me until we get to the car. Harley eases Ash in with a surprising amount of care, but Avery just drops Blaise entirely. He stumbles and body checks me into the side of the car. Harley growls at him, and Avery, but I'm barely winded. It's fine. Totally fine.

Avery shoots me an apologetic look and huffs, slipping into the front seat and crossing her arms. I slide in and wait for Blaise to collapse in behind me. I get the seatbelts on Ash and myself, then lean forward to Avery and whisper, "You should tell Atticus we had a great night. Tell him Ash won his fight, the Viper is on our side, and we had a great night drinking with Illi's friends."

The corners of her lips tip up, but she still doesn't look like my badass best friend. Fucking Atticus.

The drive is quiet, thank fuck, and Harley drives much less erratically than Blaise. When we get back to Hannaford, Harley manages to carry Ash back to the rooms on his own, and Avery and I stumble underneath the weight of Blaise once again. When I wince as we finally make it up to the top of the staircase Harley snarls about the drunken brat and I give him a wry smile.

Avery has mellowed out enough to laugh and joke with us, even going as far to offer to babysit the unconscious idiots for us to have the night to ourselves. The grin I give her is bright and relieved and lasts about three seconds before I see the box waiting for us at the door.

I've had another head delivered.

Whoever is sending these boxes was at the Dive tonight with us.

I stare at the Jackal's man with my phone wedged between my ear and my shoulder, keeping my hands free as I write lists from memory of who the hell was there tonight. None of my options make sense.

"Kid, you should have called me for backup," Illi grumbles, and I try to ignore the guilt starting up in my gut.

"We had it under control, and Odie needs you. Do you have time for a pickup?"

He grunts out a yes and I hear his car start before he hangs up. I drop the phone and look back at my list. It's not really anything.

Harley comes over and hands me a beer, knocking back his own as he catches my hand in his. "You forgot something. There were bikers there. If we listen to what the Crow says then maybe the Boar is protecting you. Maybe he is your dad."

I shudder at the thought. "Well, this isn't making my life better, it's making shit harder. If he feels guilty for not being around then he should man up and come fucking talk to me."

Avery calls out from the kitchen, where she refuses to leave while the head is present, "Actually it makes me think he really is your father. He'd have to admit he was wrong about lying to your mother and men usually have the emotional range of a *fork*."

Even Harley nods at that little nugget of wisdom.

When Illi finally arrives, Avery has gone back to our room to scrub the night from her body and pass out, leaving Harley and I in the boys' room by ourselves with the head.

Illi ignores the head, completely disinterested in it now we have some semblance of a lead. "Bikers? You didn't catch their names? Did you at least see a patch? There's at least three clubs that frequent that place."

I groan and shake my head. "I know pretty much nothing about how MC's work, Illi. Is there anyone you can ask?"

He nods and looks around. "Where's Beaumont? I was going to congratulate him on his fight. I've already heard it was brutal."

Harley smirks and shrugs. "He celebrated a little too hard. He's sleeping it off with Avery and the other dickhead."

Illi chuckles and tugs at his leather jacket. "It's good, he's broken the assumption that the Wolf chose you guys because you're pretty, not because you're good backup. There's a lot of the Jackal's men who are now hesitating about coming after you."

I let out a breath and roll my shoulders back like a weight I didn't know I was carrying has lifted. "Thanks Illi. Thanks for coming out here."

He smirks. "No worries kid. I guess this is my way of paying my dues. I heard O'Cronin isn't too happy about handing over his."

Fuck. No, he isn't. He tried to get out of it and it was only after I called him to tell him I'd be sending the Butcher in after him that he paid up. I don't think any of the members of the Twelve really give a fuck anymore about the way things are supposed to be, not with the war that's brewing, but we can't afford to take on anymore bullshit than what we already have.

"I'll let you know when I have a lead on the bikers. Any chances this is your daddy's work?" Illi asks with a chuckle as he grabs the box. I try not to gag at the thought.

Harley gives him a warning look but Illi only laughs harder.

Once the door is shut and locked behind him, Harley tugs me into the bathroom, stripping us both off and climbing into the shower behind me. I sigh under the hot stream of water and lean back into his arms.

"I don't need a father," I mumble, and Harley kisses my neck.

"At least he'd be better than the other two. Killing your enemies is a sweet gesture, helpful and just psycho enough for us to be sure you're actually related."

I snort at him and let him soap me up, his hands wandering over all his favorite places and lingering long enough that I'm panting by the time he shuts the water off. He is less impatient, wrapping me in one of his huge towels and drying me off. I'm shivering and trembling, desperate and needy, but he looks almost unaffected.

I mutter this at him and he scoffs at me.

"Can't I just take care of you sometimes? I hate hearing about this guy that might be your dad, makes me pissed and fucking twitchy. I'm distracting myself so I don't drive down to the Bay and beat the fucker."

I think about the Boar and how fucking massive his men are, and yet I'd put money of Harley in that fight. I think half the Mounties in the Bay would back my guys now too.

Harley chuckles at me. "You're thinking about the fight again, aren't you? Your eyes do this glazed over thing that would make me jealous as all fuck if I didn't see them doing it about me all the fucking time too."

I roll my eyes at him. "Yes, I get it; I'm fucking damaged. But I love that you all can hold your own. I love that you can fight and hurt and kill when you need to. It makes me feel less... alone. And it's hot as fuck."

His chest rumbles and he picks me up by my thighs, carrying me back into the bedroom buck-ass naked and I swear to God, I fucking giggle. Ugh. He cackles at the sound I make and throws me onto the bed.

"Guess I'll need to take good care of you tonight then, babe."

I guess he does.

We go down to the dining hall the next morning for breakfast because Avery and

Ash are still arguing. Ash and Blaise both eat the greasiest foods they can find on the menu, hungover and grouchy as fuck, and Harley enjoying talking shit at them.

I take the list of people who were at the Dive with us down and read it over and over again as if the answer to the boxes will jump out at me. I zone the conversations out completely and it's only when Harley nudges my foot with his that I startle to find them all staring at me.

"How do you survive in the Bay if you're so unaware of shit?" Blaise grumbles under his breath, and I cut him a glare.

"I'm not unaware when I'm there. I trust you guys enough to block you out when you're talking shit. What's up?"

Avery sighs and slides her phone over to me. Atticus has sent more information about my ghost of a father and instructions to attend a meeting during the fall break. Great. Just what I fucking need. No wonder Ash looks like he's going to start stabbing people in the eye with his fucking fork.

"You don't have to come. I can take Illi and one of the guys, leave you and the other two back at the ranch," I murmur, and she shakes her head.

"Ash just needs to get the fuck over himself and stop doubting me. I'm not a fucking child," she replies, just loud enough for everyone to hear and the bullshit to start up again.

I dig back into my granola. I hate it but I'm trying to make better food choices because I'm starting to get worried I won't fit into my booty shorts for much longer. I made the stupid mistake of mentioning it to Harley and he snarled at me. Apparently my ass looks great with the steady diet of ice cream and French toast. Who'd have thought it?

We finish up and head back to our rooms, everyone blowing off their extracurriculars to catch up on homework and sleep off their hangovers. Blaise slings an arm over my shoulder and rubs his cheek on the top of my head. I smile like a crazy woman and just enjoy the feel of him, even if he does still kind of smell like stale beer and whiskey. It's not so bad.

Avery and Ash don't stop snarling at each other the whole way back. Harley eventually shoves his way in-between them and becomes like a freaking brick wall. Avery rolls her eyes but cuts her shit out. Ash is harder to deter but Harley just gives him a haughty look, the asshole golden god himself.

When we get back I move straight to our room, ready for the boys to go back to their room and give me some study time but they all tag along. Blaise grumbles at me when I tug away from him and head straight to my bed where all of my homework has been spread out for me to look at. The stack of information from the Crow is sitting there too, haphazardly piled and rifled through.

"Where did all of this come from?" Harley murmurs as he shifts the pages around. I shrug, because the Crow always did have thousands of informants, but Avery gets this twitchy look on her face that sets Ash off.

"What the fuck has he done now?" he snaps, and I'm seriously about to walk out. I'll just grab my homework and head to the library, fuck this shit.

Avery crosses her arms and gives me a look. "Luca. The Jackal had been looking into your background and digging through everything to do with you. This is everything he has on you, Luca contacted one of his guys who's still on the inside and got it sent through."

I nod, impressed with Luca but also sick to my fucking stomach at being reminded once again at just how badly the Jackal is obsessed with me. I swallow and get back to reading. It's not that much really, except there's a whole fucking dossier about the 'training' I had been put through that I'd literally rather stab my own eyes out than read. Or, fuck, let anyone else read. When I move to stash it Blaise frowns at me.

"What the fuck is that?" he snaps, and I look down at the photo on the front.

Me. Fourteen, covered in bruises, booty shorts and a bralette that covered what little tits I had back then. The scars on my back still taped up and a blank sort of look is on my face. I look like a trauma victim and, yup, that's exactly what I was. That's exactly what... I am.

"Just leave it. You don't need to read it, none of you do." I say, but of course that's not good enough. None of them like secrets.

It takes me a second to decide what I'm going to do, lie or talk about it. I choose the third option; run.

When Harley comes over to stand behind Blaise and glare I shove the file at them and stalk off to the shower. I hesitate at the door and then speak without looking back at them, "I'm not talking about it. Any of it. Just read it and then keep your mouths *shut*."

I don't lock the door, too flustered and angry, and I strip off to climb into the shower, shoving my head under the hot water. If I could drown myself here I probably fucking would, just to get away from having to face everyone knowing all of the little broken parts of me. Having the general and vague details aired was bad enough, having the torture logs written out by the Jackal is just fucking *bad*.

After I've finally found enough energy to wash my hair and I'm rinsing it out, the bathroom door opens and I try not to sigh. I expect it to be Avery or Harley, maybe Ash if he's angry enough at what he's found, but instead Blaise hops up to sit on the bathroom countertop, his phone in one hand and our shared iPod in the other.

I raise an eyebrow at him and he grins at me lasciviously. "Harley and Ash have gone down to the gym to beat on each other. Avery needs a break from us all so she decided to go to her dance class after all."

I snort at him and shut the water off, grabbing my towel and stepping out. His eyes drop down to my wet naked body and I roll my eyes at him. "So the file scared them all off? Why aren't you running away from my damage?"

He tugs the towel away from me, stopping me from drying off, and then grabs my hips to pull me to his chest. "They're not scared. They're trying to distract themselves from running down to the Bay and killing the Jackal today, now, for what he's done. You never told me it was that bad, Star. You never told me he was torturing you."

His voice is steady enough but the look in his eyes makes me want to die. Even my nakedness can't distract him.

"And why aren't you trying to go avenge me then?"

He strokes my hair back with his colorful hands, the stars moving and flexing on his fingers like they're alive. "I don't need to avenge you. I need to follow you down to the Jackal's fucked up den then watch you slit his throat until he chokes to death on his own blood. I need to watch you get your justice, and your freedom, because it's not mine to take away from you."

My heart flutters in my chest. "What if I don't want to kill him? What if... I can't?"

His smirk is like a knife's edge. "Then I'll love every second of doing it for you, Star. I've never slit a man's throat before, I'd be pretty fucking happy with him being my first."

We enjoy the room to ourselves for the rest of the day.

Blaise bitches me out for being so far ahead in our classwork but still being so fucking terrified of being left behind. I bitch him out for slacking when really, he's been doing fucking amazingly. We talk about his mother, just a little, and I try my best to not get all stabby about it.

He rolls his eyes at the faces I pull. "At least she's left the dickhead. If she really didn't care about me then she would have just fucking stayed with him and I'd never have met Blaire."

I swallow the giant gulp of coffee I take to try to stop myself from having to answer but he just raises an eyebrow at me like a dick.

"She's a shit mother. If she cared, she would have left him the second she realized he didn't really love you, just the idea of a son to follow in his footsteps," I mumble, shifting the pages around on my bed again and avoiding his eyes. Fuck me, I hate all of this emotional talk and who the hell was I to give my opinions on mothers? I mean, mine didn't give a fuck about me my entire fucking life.

I guess that made me an expert on shit mothering.

"I don't care about me. I care about my brother. She got him out, she got him away. That's what Alice and Iris were both trying to do for the others, they were good moms."

Fuck.

We're so fucked that our only yardstick for good parenting are the two women who are now gone. Killed or broken to pieces by fucking psychopaths. I feel like that doesn't bode well.

"Well, I care about you and what your mother does to you. I care a whole fucking lot," I mutter, still looking at the pages and trying desperately to get the fuck off of this topic.

Blaise snatches the page away from me and grins when I glare at him. "Star, you fucking love me. You told me months ago. You're in love with me and my dick."

Sweet merciful lord.

"I'm too emotionally damaged to comment on that. If you're not going to fucking help me with the information then you need to quit talking," I snap, blushing and fumbling over my words like an idiot.

He grins at me. "You've already told me; no taking that back now, Star."

By the time the others arrive back for dinner, Ash and Harley have beaten each other to a bloody pulp and Avery is wincing as she moves, having pushed herself too hard and too far.

I feel just a little fucking guilty but I'm smart enough not to try to apologize. There's only so many times I can get snapped at by my family before I learn my lesson.

I fall asleep in Blaise's arms and wake later to Harley climbing in, grumpy and huffing from attempting to sleep alone. I lay there, listening to the all too familiar sounds of my guys sleeping, and I thank the fucking stars I have them.

And I obsessively plan how I'm going to keep my family safe.

No matter the cost.

Chapter Thirteen

My phone wakes me with a text message, which is never a good sign.

Harley wakes as well, grunting and pulling me into his body tighter until Blaise groans in his sleep and rolls away from us both. He's always been the precious one about sleep and I huff at him.

I climb over Harley to grab my phone, my gut clenching when I see the Jackal's number and photos waiting for me. Harley sits up and moves me to sit in his lap, then I click on the photos.

Fuck.

"Aves. We have a problem," I croak, and she startles awake.

She sits up and flicks the light on, straight into cleanup mode. We all ignore Blaise's complaints and I send her a copy of the photos. The photos of tongues impaled on the ornate spikes of Hannaford's wrought iron fence.

There's at least eighty.

"What the fuck is he playing at? The cops are going to be crawling up our asses in no time and that's not good for any of us, for fuck's sake," Harley snaps, and I get up to start pulling clothes on. I flick a text to Ash, the only person in the other room because he's a grumpy shit, and then I slip my knife into my pocket. Harley starts to rummage around for clothes as well, no chance of me doing this alone.

I find my Docs and shove my feet in them as Blaise sits up, rubbing his eyes and glaring at us all. I ignore him and say to Avery, "Can you keep the administration away for long enough that I can clean up the... evidence? I'll call Illi for a pick up and we can figure out what to do about this."

She nods, her eyes never leaving her phone as her fingers fly across the screen, and then curses under her breath. Her eyes flash as she looks up at me. "Someone has already called the cops. They're down at the fence already. The Jackal must have waited for them to come in before sending you the photos."

I groan as the door unlocks and Ash comes storming in, dressed and deliciously sleep rumpled. He makes a beeline to the coffee machine without acknowledging any of us and I feel the same damn way. Gimme some caffeine to deal with this bullshit.

"Why the fuck would he call the cops? Surely someone has to notice a hundred guys walking around with no tongues. Or a hundred dead bodies," Harley snarls.

I shrug. "He has the Bear on his side. He can dispose of that many bodies all at once easily so there won't be any evidence for the cops to find. The problem is that they're going to be hanging around here, questioning everyone, and we don't know how many of them are dirty and in Senior's pocket. The two threats are fucking blending together, just like they want them to."

Avery nods but doesn't look up from her phone. "Call Illi. Tell him, and I'll speak to Atticus. We'll make sure we're protected before the cops get here."

I step into the bathroom to call Illi so I can hear him over Harley's bitching. I glance at the clock to find it's only five in the morning. Fuck this.

"Kid, just because you don't sleep, doesn't mean the rest of us don't need our eight hours," he snarks and I snort at him.

"Eight? Fuck, I wish I got eight. We've had a visit from our friend. He's cleaned house to make sure he doesn't have any more snitches, then called it in with the pigs. We're going to be put into lockdown, possible interference from the serial killer. Just another day at Hannaford Prep."

Illi groans and I hear the rustling of him sitting up in bed, Odie's murmuring low and soft. My heart does this weird clench thing in my chest at just how freaking close we got to losing her. Again.

Fuck.

"Right. Get the ice queen to wipe your phones and I'll come have a chat with some old friends I have in the force. Everything will be fine, kid. Just keep your family safe," he says, and I listen to the rustling sound of him pulling on clothes.

I sigh and rub a hand over my face. "Yeah, I know we'll get through this but fuck, I'm tired and Illi I'm… I'm worried about who he's going to go after next. Get Odie somewhere safe, ok?"

Illi grunts down the phone at me. "Look. No one is touching her. No one is touching you or the rest of the family. We're fine, stop getting the fucking jitters because he's going fucking psycho, that's what he does. We knew it would get bad and his temper tantrums aren't going to stop us from taking him out. Now hang up and clear your phones. I'll be there in under an hour."

I hang up and shove my phone in my pocket, glancing up to find Ash in the doorway with a scowl on his face.

"Did you just get a pep talk from the Butcher? Fuck, we are in trouble," he sneers, and I roll my eyes at him.

"I'm allowed to feel shitty about this whole… thing, you know. Don't take your issues out on me, talk to your sister and actually fucking listen to her for once."

He narrows his eyes at me and grinds his teeth. "Atticus Crawford is a fucking cancer and we need to cut him out now before he gets Avery killed."

I blow out a breath at him, grabbing a fistful of his shirt to pull him all the way into the bathroom and pushing the door shut behind him.

"Nothing is going to happen to Avery. Not ever, I won't let my world or yours hurt her but if you don't pull your fucking head out of your ass she's going to walk the hell away from you. That's where this shitty attitude leads, Ash," I whisper, trying to keep my tone civil but I don't think I succeed.

He gives me a dark look, one I haven't seen aimed my way since sophomore year. "She's not going to walk away, the only way I'm going to lose her is if she's dead which is exactly where this is going. Atticus is a selfish fucking dickhead, he's always thought he's better than what he really is, and if she goes along with him, he'll get her killed."

I stare at him for a second and then nod slowly. "Ok. Ok, I'll do what I can. Just ease up and I'll do what I can."

I fucking hate politics.
Especially the family kind.

Avery has all of our phones wiped before I make it out of the shower. I'd dragged Ash in with me to try to get him in a better mood but by breakfast they're back at each other's throats. I go back to my default and ignore them completely, and Harley and Blaise seem to be happy enough to do the same.

There are extra men in suits lining the halls and when we walk to our classes we find pigs trawling through the school grounds, taking photos and questioning the Crow's men. One of them tries to stop Avery to speak to her and at the mere uttering of her name they scatter like mice. I share a look with her; they'll all be in Senior's pocket for sure but how much of this little stunt has he hand a hand in?

In our first class of the day we're told by our teacher to go about our lessons as if there hasn't been dead body parts left on campus. Half the students in the class look like they're about to jump out of their seats and run screaming from the room but it's the other half, the bored half, that holds my interest.

What's happened in their lives that spiked tongues don't bother them?

Avery follows my gaze and starts to take note, this could be useful for us and I have no doubt she'll have a whole new list of filthy rich families under her thumb by the end of the week.

I find myself unable to concentrate for the entire freaking day. Something nags at me and I can't let it go. Something pulling at the back of my memory, and my mind worries over it like an obsessed child until it works it out. It's so frustrating I can't even focus on my classes. Harley notices, he watches me too closely to miss fucking *anything*, and finally at lunchtime when were in the dining hall together with our family, he snaps.

"What the fuck is going on in your head today? You're a twitchy mess."

The whole lot of them stop eating to eye me, Avery frowning and slipping her phone out of her pocket like she's ready to wage war the second I tell her who's pissing me off. It's sweet, a better gesture than any other she could offer me.

I roll my eyes at Harley because I haven't been *that* bad. "How did the Jackal know someone had snitched? I can't let it go. The only people we spoke to about it were the Crow and Illi. Illi would never betray us, *never*, we're family and he's all fucking in. But… I don't think the Crow would either. We have a leak and we need to plug it before it gets someone killed."

Avery's eyes drop down to her phone. My stomach drops, I don't want to have to tell her she can't message Atticus and ask him about this, but then she places the phone on the table where we can all see it. Harley's shoulders relax just a little at the show of loyalty to us, her real family.

She ignores him, giving me a curt nod and says, "It has to be one of his men. Atticus wouldn't play these games or go back on his word. That's not who he is, even Ash would agree."

Ash doesn't notice *any* part of the conversation except the bit where Avery is defending Atticus and now he looks about ready to murder someone. It's plain to see that the possible question of his loyalty makes Ash positively giddy with murderous intent. "We didn't know he was the Crow, Floss, what makes you think we know enough about him to say whether or not he would betray us?"

I sigh at him and knock his foot with mine under the table. It's a little hard considering I've got to go around Avery but I make it work. I'm pretty impressed with Avery because she manages to control her own murderous intent, everything except her hand tightening around the handle of her knife. "I know you hate him. He's not my favorite either right now. But can you honestly tell me you think that he would do this?"

Harley cuts in before this turns into a full-blown Beaumont Bullshit session, "I agree with the girls, it's gotta be one of the men. The real problem here is we didn't discuss with the Crow what had happened."

And then it hits me like a baseball bat to the back of the head. I stand abruptly and curse viciously under my breath. Everyone else goes on high alert and Avery snatches her phone back into her hand ready to run after me or call for backup.

"Someone's bugged our fucking room," I grit it out between my clenched teeth. That gets a reaction.

Avery snatches her phone back off the table and stands, walking away from the busy table. Ash snarls and takes off after her, cursing Atticus's name six ways to freaking Sunday until every eye in the room follows him out the door.

Harley shoves my plate back at me and gives me a glare. "Avery can sort it out, finish your fucking food."

I glare at him, my food situation isn't an issue anymore, but Blaise crosses his arms and joins the fight. Fuck's sake.

I sit and shove a forkful into my mouth, chewing without tasting a goddamn thing. "I need to call the Coyote, he needs to come and upgrade every-fucking-thing. We need our own surveillance in the room too."

A slow smirk spreads across Blaise's face and a blush starts creeping across mine. I know that smirk. I fucking love it when he gives it to me, but only when we're alone and certainly not when we're surrounded by students.

"We should probably make sure Avery isn't the one monitoring it. She wouldn't be too happy to find out I bent you over her bed while she was at ballet."

Fuck.

I do not need to be reminded of that particular memory, not right the fuck here, and not while Harley is sitting there with raised eyebrows and a fucking smirk that mirrors Blaise's.

"And here I was thinking Avery's shit was off limits," he drawsl, and I steel myself against the shiver that tries to work its way up my spine.

"It is. Blaise just… caught me off guard for a second there. Can we stick to the topic? We have shit going on."

Blaise shrugs at me, sharing a look with Harley. "There's always going to be something going on, Star. I'd rather talk about all of the sex tapes we're about to be making. Can you ask the Coyote to make it a live feed straight to our phones, too? That way I can keep tabs and make sure Harley isn't being a selfish *dick*."

Harley scoffs at him and shrugs. "You'll learn some valuable fucking lessons on how to keep our Mounty satisfied."

Fuck.

I'm out. I don't need the two of them to turn this into a competition in the freaking dining hall of all places. I stand and stalk away listening to them both roar with laughter as they follow me out.

Today has been a fucking *day*.

After classes end for the day, we head straight to the chapel for the assembly that was called to deal with the aftermath of the Jackal's visit to Hannaford. There's an air of sheer, blinding terror amongst the students as we walk into the room together, and there's a small bubble around us, as if the other students are afraid of bumping into us and losing their heads. Good. Fucking great.

Avery frowns down at her phone and when I move to direct us to our usual seats at the front she stops us, tugging me by our joined arms to one of the bench seats at the back of the room. Harley mumbles something under his breath at her but she ignores him until we're seated. Ash takes his seat next to me with Blaise on his other side and Harley next to Avery. When Avery cuts me a look my stomach drops.

"Ash, don't make a scene but Senior is here," she murmurs, and Blaise groans when Ash turns to freaking stone between us.

I grab his hand and give it a squeeze, leaning in to whisper in his ear, "We're safe. He can't get close to us and I'll gut him before I let him touch Avery."

He gives me a look like I'm crazy or fucking stupid but I only smile in return.

Then the door on the far side of the room opens and Senior stalks in looking clean cut and disturbingly handsome in his suit. His eyes cast around the room until he finds Ash and then he fixes his stare on his son, the obsession and loathing a potent mix of crazy I haven't seen since Joey's head ended up in that fucking cardboard box. A man I've never seen before follows behind him closely, looking sweaty and uncomfortable as he tugs on his tie. Definitely not one of his paid bodyguards, he's far too fucking twitchy.

"Who the hell is that?" I murmur, and Avery's arm tightens where it's tucked into mine.

"That's George Drummond, the Chief of Police. Lauren's father."

I survey the room to look out for any extra threats we might have missed on the way in and I make eye contact with one of the Crow's men. His face is carefully blank but his hands are clenched into fists at his side. The room is uneasy, the students all sensing something is fucking wrong in this room.

Any room with Senior in it would feel this way.

Drummond steps up to the microphone and clears his throat. His voice is clear enough but there's a fine tremble to it if you listen hard enough. "Good evening, students. I am sorry to have to be here today but as you know there has been a crime here at your fine school and we must address that."

The whispers start up around us but Avery shuts them up with a single look.

"We are aware that your parents may have concerns about your safety due to the rise in gang activity. We are here to assure them, and you, that we are doing everything in our power to keep you safe. There are a number of people of interest, those with ties to the criminal underworld, that we are currently investigating and will move in on. We are confident that this will put an end to the current rise in crime. We have assured your parents that the... evidence that appeared here this morning will be handled with the utmost care, however we are confident that they are not from any students or faculty, past or present."

Senior's gaze is like a freaking laser, incinerating and destructive, but Ash just stares him down like the reckless asshole I know he is and fucking love. The corners of my mouth tug into a smirk that is entirely Beaumont, because fuck this man. Fuck him for ruining his kids and trying to tear us all to fucking pieces.

When Drummond finally stops talking about how fucking important we all are, and protecting us is their top priority, Senior steps up to the microphone. Drummond falters as he steps away, swiping at his forehead like it'll somehow stop him from looking terrified and wet.

Senior's voice still gives me the chills. "As you may all be aware my son, Joseph Beaumont Junior is currently missing. If any of you have information regarding his whereabouts or anyone who may have had a grudge with him, I am offering a large reward. I just want my beloved son home safe."

Every damn eye in the room turns to fix on Avery and Ash. At least that's what it feels like. Even the Crow's men all glance their way.

I want to start swinging, but the cleanup would be fucking colossal and we can't afford any extra work on our plates to I school my face into an innocently blank look and pray Ash is doing the same.

Chapter Fourteen

Fall break arrives and we're all set for the drive down to Avery's ranch. Harley slings my bag over his shoulder along with his and Blaise tucks me under his arm to walk down to the Cadillac. Avery had gotten up early with a phone call and I don't have a freaking clue of where Ash disappeared to, but I'm buzzing with excitement about leaving Hannaford for a week.

We come to a stop on the bottom floor while Harley texts his cousins and tries to figure out what the fuck is going on. I tell the nerves fluttering in my guts to calm the hell down, everything is going to be fine. Ash is probably just chasing Avery around to piss her off because he lives for that shit at the moment.

"Are you excited at getting back to having your own room again, Star?" Blaise mumbles into my hair. I elbow him but he ignores it. "Looking forward to your orgy-sized bed? Maybe we should put it to good use."

Fuck.

I shiver and pull away a little to scowl up at him, trying to ignore just how turned on I am at the thought. "When are you guys going to learn to stop talking about our private shit out in the halls when we're surrounded by the fucking snake pits of Hannaford?"

Blaise gives me a smug look. "When are you going to stop caring what they all think?"

I sigh at him as Avery rounds the corner, marching towards us like a woman on a mission, students scattering out of her way. "If the roles were reversed, you'd by getting high-fived for having three girlfriends, not glared at and whispered about. I don't really care, I'd just rather not hear the gossip about it later."

He frowns at me, and Harley steps up closer to us both with a vicious look when Avery finally makes it to us and interrupts them both, thank fuck.

"We need to talk. Now." Avery says, tugging me away from the guys and along the hall until we're standing outside the principal's office. I give her a look which she ignores, knocking sharply while her foot taps impatiently.

I don't really want to be in the room again, the last time I'd stood here I'd had to hack Ms. Cougar Whore to pieces, but there's no sign of the carnage left here when the principal opens the door, ushering us in.

"Atticus has already had this room swept. I've arranged to have our rooms done again and the Coyote has already called about upgrading the security system. We should have had him do it in the first place."

I nod and try not to think about just how fucked we are if he double crosses us. This is the fucking problem with the Jackal crossing the line and starting a war; there's no longer any sort of honor amongst the Twelve.

Avery flicks her wrist at the principal and she nods respectfully, exiting the office and leaving us to speak privately. Even knowing she belongs to the Crow, it's fucking weird to see, even more so when Avery perches on the desk and crosses her arms at me. I take a seat and steel myself to whatever the fuck has happened now. If we're all alive it can't be that bad, right?

"I used Blaise's list to start recruiting our list of contacts and it's paid off. I have big intel from the raids on Senior and his pocket pigs."

I snort at her use of Illi's term for the men Senior owns, in her cultured tones it's something else. "Yeah? Are we about to have our doors beaten down?"

Avery smirks. "No. But last night the Bear's doors were blown wide open."

I freeze. "The Bear?"

Avery nods, tapping away at her phone and then handing it over to me to show me the file. Every last one of the Bear's businesses, the legit ones and the fronts, have been raided. Millions of dollars in drugs, stolen cars, weapons, and illegal chemicals have been seized.

An entire empire taken down in one day.

"Fuck. Me," I gasp, and Avery nods.

"Either the Bear tried to switch sides and the Jackal found out, or Senior sold him out to prove a point." She says, taking the phone back and tapping away at the screen.

Fuck. Me.

I blow out a breath and stare at the ceiling for a second, mulling over the price of the Jackal's insane and traitorous ways. No fucking honor in the man. I mean, I know we're all criminals, I kill people for fuck's sake, but there's always been a code we live by. Without it… anarchy. Chaos. Bedlam in the streets of Mounts Bay.

We're all fucked because he doesn't know how to be rejected.

"No word on who got the bug into our room. It's definitely one of the Jackal's men though, the Coyote traced it back to him. Jackson isn't so bad I guess, once you look past his smart mouth and atrocious fashion sense," Avery mutters, and I raise an eyebrow at her.

"Not into baggy jeans and band tees? He looks like every guy I ever went to school with, you're lucky you were born richer than god."

She shudders. "It's disturbing that someone of Viola's pedigree has fallen for him. I thought she was just trying to piss her parents off but Jackson made a comment to me last night and I thought she was going to reach through the screen and choke me out for it. I don't know why, he was the one saying it."

He always was a flirty dickhead. Viola should know better than to listen to a word that comes out of his mouth by now.

"Right. So we go back to the ranch, unpack, have a shower, then head into the meeting. Atticus has said the entire of the Twelve are attending thanks to the Jackal's stunt. Well, obviously he's not going. I don't even think they're counting him as a member anymore. Is there some sort of process you go through to kick him out?"

I stand and tuck my arm into hers.

"We kill him."

Ash reappears and we head down to the Bay piled into Blaise's Cadillac, though Avery packs so much that we really should have brought both cars. Ash is still feeling pretty pissy about his Ferrari being put in any danger and no one seems to be able to get the steaming pile of wreckage out of their mind, all that was left of Harley's Mustang after Joey had gotten to it, so we're stuck with bags on our laps and under our feet.

I don't mind but Harley looks ready to kill.

The ride is reasonably quiet, mostly because Ash and Avery are no longer speaking to each other, and I do my best to zone out and ignore the tension in the air around us. I haven't had the chance to ask Ash where the hell he'd disappeared to, instead burying my nose into the last of my literature books that I need to read for class for the year. Harley reads over my shoulder, which sounds sickeningly cute and romantic except he reads much slower than I do and I find myself getting bored in between page turns.

After a quick stop off at the ranch, we head straight to the meeting. The Crow lives in an honest-to-god fortress on the rich side of town. I've been there a few times, long before I knew his name was Atticus Crawford and he was in love with my best friend, but I've never been further than the reception room. Yup, the place has a reception room. Fucking rich people.

When we arrive at the large stone walls and electric gate Blaise puts down his window and makes eye contact with one of the Crow's men. The guy nods at him and, I kid you not, he speaks into a microphone lapel, as if he is protecting the President of the United fucking States and not a well-connected crime lord. When I murmur this to Ash it barely gets a reaction out of him. I sigh and roll my eyes at his pissy nature. I can't fucking wait for this whole bullshit to be over with.

"If he did all of this to protect you then I'd be worried, Aves. Pretty sure this place has a fucking sex dungeon or some shit," says Blaise, smirking at her as she sits with a rigid back in the front seat.

You'd think just this once he'd let it go and not make some dumb comment but no, that's just not his style. For once Avery has no snappy comeback, she just sits there and glares out at everything.

Blaise parks next to Illi's car where the Butcher and his stunning wife are waiting for us. I give Odie a quick hug and she kisses Avery's cheek sweetly, murmuring pleasantries in French. Then we walk into the fortress.

The Crow is waiting for us in the reception room, the place still as cold and bleak as ever. Harley looks around curiously but Avery keeps her eyes ahead, barely even acknowledging the Crow's existence. I give him a respectful nod, which he returns and then leads us further into the cavernous building.

"It's like a castle that some doomsday prepper lives in but with like… weird-ass paintings in it," Illi fake-whispers at me, and Harley and Blaise both snicker at him like children.

To be fair, he's not wrong.

The Crow casts a disapproving eye at us all over his shoulder. "The first year of being the Crow, the Jackal attempted to kill me seventeen times. This building was built like this for a reason."

Avery's mouth turns down like she's taken a hit. "That painting is a Delacroix.

It's a classic."

Odie nods and says, "My father had some in his collection too, but he could not afford one of this size. It's very impressive."

I keep my mouth shut because I know exactly nothing about old French paintings. Ash rolls his shoulders back like he's preparing to take a swing, then he shocks the hell out of us all by stepping up to Avery and tucking her under his arm, something he hasn't done in months.

"Let's get this meeting over with. We have other… commitments to get back to," he says, squeezing Avery's shoulders and she waits until the Crow turns his back before giving him a cold look. He doesn't react, only walks with her into the large meeting room the Crow is leading us to.

We're the last ones to arrive.

I keep the surprise from my face as I take in the room. Every member of the Twelve, except the Jackal, is present, with a whole heap of their flunkies and followers jammed in as well. I'd been expecting the Bear, he'd lost everything, but to see the Fox and the Tiger here is shocking. The Tiger has been too afraid to turn his back on the Jackal, and the Fox's businesses are so intertwined I really thought he'd stay with him until the end. The Lynx is a devious bitch so I'm less surprised there.

There's quiet chatter, murmuring amongst the flunkies, as I take a seat and my family all spread out around me. Harley helps me into my chair and then takes up watch by the wall with Blaise. Ash helps Avery into the seat next to mine and then takes my other side, a cold and detached look on his face. His hand keeps drifting to his pocket like he's checking his phone is still in there. Fuck.

Once the Crow sits at the head of the table with his sharply dressed men, the room falls quiet without any instruction needed.

"I think it's best if we keep this meeting short and to the point—" the Crow starts, only to be interrupted.

"I think it's pretty fucking clear; the Jackal is out. What's the plan for killing the backstabbing fuck?" the Bear snarls, and I do my best not to roll my eyes at him. It's hard. It's fucking hard.

"How about you shut your fucking mouth and let the adults talk? You're only sitting here because you're broke and about to do life in federal prison because you picked the wrong fucking side," Illi drawls, and I bite my lip to stop the smile from spreading across my face. Fuck, I was not expecting this meeting to challenge me so much.

"Why the fuck is the Butcher talking for you, Wolf? Is he crawling into your bed as well?" the Bear snaps, gesturing between my family with a leering look. "You guys take turns or fuck her all at once?"

I can see the effort it takes the Crow to not roll his eyes as the room explodes around us. The rest of the Twelve either laugh or make some noise of disgust. Harley's tattoo flexes as he grinds his teeth to stop himself from unleashing on the dickhead but he's the only one trying to show restraint.

From the corner of my eye, I catch Blaise cross his arms with a scoff, a lazy grin on his face that doesn't hide the danger flashing in his eyes. "I know this must be hard for you, knowing a teenage girl is getting way more ass than you, but if you stopped stinking like rotting corpses and that cheap cologne then maybe you could find someone who'd look past how fucking ugly you are. I can't give you any tips for your micro-dick, sorry. Not something I've had to deal with."

Avery lets out her sweetly murderous giggle and Illi's hand drops to his side to stroke lovingly at his meat cleaver that's strapped to his thigh. The Bear watches that hand like he'd stand some sort of chance if he could see the moment Illi chooses to kill him.

He wouldn't.

The Bear opens his mouth to snarl a comeback to Blaise and two very different but equally startling things stop him: the Crow interrupts him with a snarled, "Can we stay on topic so we can get the situation under control? Preferably by killing the psycho fuck?"

I'm not expecting the ever-proper and rule following Crow to just come out and say we're here planning to take out a fellow crime lord.

The Bear is stunned, shocked enough that he doesn't see Ash move until there's the barrel of a gun pressed to his temple. That shuts him up real fucking quick. The whole room goes silent again until you could hear a freaking pin drop.

"Let me make this crystal clear to every last person in this room; insult the Wolf and I'll personally end your life. Piss me off enough and I'll let the Butcher join in, make a real mess of the job."

The Bear's jaw clenches but he dips his head. He has no choice but to agree; he's here alone, all of his men are in lockup, and here I am with the only guys in the room that don't look worried. It's a weird position to be in, to watch this empire fall right as my own is slowly, hesitantly, building.

Ash finally lowers his gun again and the Crow takes over. He details a very specific, and very discreet, plan to take the Jackal out. I don't agree with the plan at all, but I choose to keep my mouth shut. It doesn't affect me, I'm not involved, all this meeting has told me is that I won't be hunted for taking out the Jackal myself when the time is right.

Avery is not so easy to accept the shitty plan.

"Shouldn't we be sending in a team, not just a single shooter? The Jackal is not someone who is easy to sneak up on and since the defection of Luca—"

"Less is more." The Crow cuts her off. Fuck me.

Avery finally looks at him and raises an eyebrow. "True, less is more… unless we're talking about dick. Maybe you should stop acting like one."

Illi chuckles and slings his arm over the back of her chair to pull my Ice Queen bestie into a sort of side hug. Odie snuggles into his other side, a self-satisfied smirk across her stunning face. They look like a very happy, if psychotic, threesome. That's fucking weird to think about, but I enjoy the look on Atticus's face all the same.

Ash develops a fucking eye twitch, but he manages to hold it together. Harley smirks at the look Atticus gives Illi and Blaise outright fucking roars with laughter, throwing his head back and just fucking shaking with glee.

I slip my hand into Avery's and give it a little squeeze, the smirk on my own face directed at the Bear. "I don't see why we've sat around waiting for the intel, only to send a single guy in. If we're going to do that, I'll just go in myself."

Three sets of eyes glare daggers at me but I keep my attention focused on the Crow. He smooths a hand down the front of his jacket, something rich people must do a lot because I always catch Avery and Ash doing it, and then he leans back in his chair.

"The Jackal is on high alert. He has thousands of loyal men and every last one of them will be on the lookout for you. Your trip to the Dive to see the Viper was a fluke;

there's a bounty on your head and every last one of the Jackal's followers want it. You cannot go after him. We are outnumbered, unless I call in all of my own men which I won't do. Therefore, we send in one shooter. Take him out quickly and quietly, then clean up the mess his organization is in."

It's not going to work. "I'm the best there is. No one else will come close."

Avery catches my eye. "You would have been better off getting Luca to kill him, then plead your case with the Twelve."

Atticus shakes his head at us both. "Anarchy is what has gotten us into this mess."

I huff out a breath and shut my mouth again. No point trying to argue with the holier-than-thou, pretentious, arrogant fuck. He might have struck a nerve with me. Just fucking maybe.

When the meeting is finally over, shitty plan and all, Avery stands before anyone else and moves to the door. Ash stays in his chair, his eyes glued to the Crow, so I wave the others out and stay with him. If he needs to have a showdown to get this out of his system then fuck it, we're having a showdown.

Lord fucking help us.

"Anything else?" the Bear snarls, and the Crow shakes his head at him, dismissive as though the Bear is a disobedient child. It's funny as fuck to see and my little dark stained heart soaks it the hell up. They all stand and make their way to the doors.

Atticus gives us a hard look, but his steely gaze means nothing to Ash. "Is there something else you need?"

Ash reaches into his pocket and pulls out a scrap of fabric, soaked in blood, and he throws it down on the table in front of the Crow. I stare at it and try not to let the shock show on my face. What the ever-loving fuck is that?

"You might want to vet your men a little better from now on, Crawford. It wasn't that hard for me to find the Jackal's mark. You're really not doing a good job of proving me wrong. You'll never be worthy of Avery. Never."

Atticus unwraps the fabric and sure enough, there's a piece of skin with the Jackal's insignia on it. Holy freaking shit.

I stand before all of the words streaming through my head burst out of my mouth and I pull Ash up with me. His hand is steady in mine as we leave the Crow behind, pausing by the door when he calls out to us.

"The Coyote needs to do another sweep of Avery's ranch. You should all stay here tonight to ensure it's safe. I've had rooms set aside for you all," he says in a blank tone, and I nod.

No matter how much I'd like to tell him to shove it up his ass we have a job to take care of. "Thank you, we will stay but we only need one room."

Then we head back towards the reception room to find the others.

"Where the hell is he? What if someone finds the body?" I hiss at Ash the second I'm sure we're alone. Fuck me.

He tugs me into an alcove by the painting Illi hated, his eyes like icy blue pits. "Obviously I didn't leave anything behind. I'm not fucking braindead, Mounty."

I give him a hard look and his mood sours even more. "I called Illi to get rid of the body and my clothes, then I had a fucking bleach bath. I'm a little fucking insulted you think I can't do this."

My eyes dart over his face, taking in his ire and his fierce protective look. "I'm not doubting you. I'm not good at letting you guys take the lead. You know that already. I can't handle something fucking happening to one of you."

His hand wraps around my throat and squeezes until my head tips back and our lips meet, rough and desperate. Fuck, the taste of him is addictive and fucking poison.

He breaks the kiss and whispers to me, his lips brushing against mine, "Illi asked me why I was calling, not you, and I told him that when I said I was all in, I meant it. That means if someone is threatening you or our family, I'll fucking deal with it."

I stare up at him with a whole new level of respect and adoration. Fuck me.

He leans forward and pins me to the wall, covering me entirely with the hard lines of his body. Sweet merciful lord, I do not need to turn into a puddle here and have the fucking Crow find me looking weak and pathetic.

"Knowing I can use all of the twisted, fucked up shit my family has taught me to keep you safe… well, I feel a little less fucked up because of it. Knowing that it turns you on is just icing on the fucking cake."

Chapter Fifteen

I wait until Avery is asleep before I decide I need some answers. I've never felt so watched as I do inside the Crow's fortress. I don't call it that lightly, it's a fucking stronghold and I know I'm going to go to sleep tonight without the slightest fear of having one of the Jackal's men climb through my window.

The room we're put in has no windows.

Blaise and Harley steal a mattress from one of the neighboring rooms and Blaise locks himself in the bathroom to get high enough to sleep soundly. Avery bitches him out but she's asleep before he's finished. Ash takes up watch by the door, one of his guns resting in his lap while he cleans the other. Harley snickers under his breath in pure delight at the whole thing.

I find it less amusing.

At some point, this is going to blow up and I need to make sure Avery isn't going to be kidnapped or some shit. I manage to convince Ash to stay behind and drag Harley back downstairs to hunt for the Crow. We need to have it out and draw some fucking lines.

He can't keep dismissing her ideas, just to 'keep her safe'.

The moment we find him in the formal sitting area, Atticus tips his head towards the bar and I nod. Yeah, his fortress has a fucking bar, complete with staff and bowls of nuts.

Fucking rich people.

I take a seat at the booth and Harley slides in next to me, keeping himself firmly between the Crow and me. It's sweet and entirely unnecessary, but I let it go.

"We need to discuss Avery," the Crow says, the member of the Twelve slowly slipping away until we're staring at Atticus Crawford.

He flicks a hand at the bartender and we're served our drinks of choice, only I never told them what I wanted. Harley's beer is even his preferred brand. I raise an eyebrow at Atticus and he flicks a dismissive hand at me.

"It's my livelihood to know everything about everyone."

I decide that if he's going to be himself then I'm going to drop all of the formalities as well and tell the fucker some hard truths. "Well, you're failing. For someone who's known Aves her whole life you fucking suck at really knowing her. You keep cutting that girl so deep she's never going to forgive you."

He sips his bourbon. He has it the same way Ash does, so it must be the preferred drink for all pompous assholes.

He sets the glass back down on the table and says, "Everything I've done is to keep her alive. I couldn't always keep her safe, not completely, but I did what I could to keep her breathing long enough that I could get her out."

My eyes narrow. "Oh yeah? How have you done that? Built yourself an empire, trade in information, but how has that done anything for her? Because I've gotten her out and safe. I'm guarding her, I've killed and bled and tortured for her. What have you done?"

His lip curls into a snarl at me and Harley palms a knife. Illi taught him well and Atticus could be bleeding out in a fucking second if Harley doesn't keep his cool.

"Her father has already sold her twice. The buyers are both dead, because I took care of it. Her father was going to split the twins up, he was going to send her to finishing school across the country where he could have her killed without Ash's protection, I stopped that. I walked into the fucking slums of Mounts Bay and became the Crow for her. If I took her away then I would have had to leave Ash behind. I think you're underestimating Joseph Beaumont's reach. Everything you do for Avery only happens because I take care of the officials. I'm running out of information and bribes to keep her safe. I'm doing everything I fucking can to keep her and Ash safe. I know he hates me, I know that he won't ever trust me, but I'm trying to get him out too."

Fuck.

Dammit. I like him, and from the look on Harley's face he does too. Jesus, what a mess.

"Alright. I'll help. We can work together."

Atticus snorts at me. "I know exactly how loyal you are, Wolf. It's why I didn't put a bullet between your eyes when I found out you'd become friends with her."

Harley's eyes narrow again and I give Atticus a stern look. "Maybe not the best idea to threaten me while you're asking for my help."

Atticus shakes his head. "I'm not threatening you and I'm not asking for your help. I know you won't do anything for me without speaking to Avery about it. Like I said, you're loyal. I'm only telling you what she won't listen to, which is that I'm trying to get her out of this alive and sometimes that means I have to treat her like she's made of glass. I ask her not to come to meetings because I can't keep my fucking eyes off of her and the Jackal will notice. He was looking for my weaknesses to exploit and I've aggressively kept her away from me and the Bay for that exact reason. I had to weigh up the benefits of having her inducted to you very carefully. The Jackal knows about her now but she's a little bit safer from her father. It's a fucking constant battle, walking through landmines and praying I'm not mis-stepping and losing the only fucking reason I have for living. So don't underestimate me, I know exactly who Avery Beaumont is. I know how strong she is. I'm willing to have her hate me if it means I can get her out of this mess alive. I'd rather have her alive and happy with someone else, than selfishly keep her only to have her die because of it."

I finish my whiskey in two gulps and say, "Right. So, what threats are you dealing with for her and what do you need me to do? I'll take care of anything."

"I told you, I don't need your help. If I did, I'd ask," he says in the sulkiest, asshole tone but little does he know I'm fucking immune to it.

I do spend a fuck-load of time with my guys and they're the kings of this shit.

"Explain exactly how you managed to have one of the Jackal's men get through your security then? I thought you'd vetted everyone you put into the school?"

His jaw clenches and he gives me the slightest nod, like he's conceding the point or some shit. "I've pulled everyone from Hannaford. There's a whole new batch of my men, and every last one of them has been personally vetted by me. I've called in an old friend; he's going to stay on top of things. I will find out how the spy got through, then I will deal with it."

Atticus finishes his drink and straightens his lapels uselessly. "She'll forgive me. Someday she will understand the depths I've reached to keep her safe."

I hum under my breath, as Harley flexes his hands, probably to rein in his temper. "She will. But first you have to stop treating her like a delicate princess and remember she's been waging her own war for years. She can handle your empire, better even than you can, if you'd just cut your shit out."

He shakes his head at me like I'm dense. "It's not about handling it. It's about surviving it. What kind of a monster would I be if I asked an eighteen-year-old girl to step into a criminal empire?"

I give him an ice-cold look. "One that recognizes she was born into a den of monsters and survived it."

I stand up to leave before he says something else that makes me want to rip his arrogant face right the fuck off, and Harley takes my arm to help me out of the booth. A server comes over to refill Atticus's drink and clear our empty glasses. I run through his story in my head again, and sigh.

"Atticus?"

He glances up and, without the mask of the Crow he looks fucking miserable.

I blow out a long breath. "You have my vote. We don't work on a hierarchy or whatever, we vote on shit like a family. If it comes down to it, I'll vote in your favor."

His eyes flash and when he looks at Harley they harden. My golden god shrugs with a haughty smirk. "Two votes to three still means you're fucked, Crawford."

Atticus grits his teeth then relaxes, lifting his glass to his lips again. "What will your vote cost me, Arbour? I'll pay it."

Harley tips his head back and roars with laughter. "You've already got it, dickhead. Avery never backs down, though, and she's going to hold out on you until the bitter end just to prove a fucking point. Ash fucking loathes you, and Blaise always votes with Ash. On everything, except Lips, so you're fucked."

I shrug and smile. "Illi and Odie might decide to vote, you'll have to make a plea to the Butcher. Good luck with that, he's very fond of our Ice Queen."

Atticus gives me a disgusted look but nods. Harley tucks me under his arm and walks us both out of the bar, up the stairs and into our room.

Avery is tucked into the bed, her cheeks red like she's been scrubbing at them the whole time we've been downstairs. Ash is sitting in the armchair, watching her with a dark look and my gut clenches.

There's no way he's going to let Atticus in.

There's nothing quite like getting back to the mundane normality of Hannaford after the break.

We get in late, shuffling upstairs and passing out wherever the fuck we land. When my alarm sounds in the morning I kind of want to smash it to pieces but mostly I just want to cry.

Avery gives me a knowing look and declares, "French toast in the dining hall sounds perfect, Mounty."

Fuck yes, it does. "Avery Aspen Waverly Beaumont, marry me."

She startles and then cackles like a witch, happy in a way she hasn't been for months. "How the hell did you know my full name? Harley's going to be heartbroken you chose me over him, you know."

I slip my arm into her and ignore the grumbling bullshit around us. "Chicks before dicks, Aves."

Blaise gets me the biggest plate of breakfast I've ever seen and I'm sure I'll puke if I eat the whole thing but fuck it, I'm always up for a challenge. Ash is softer with his sister again, carrying her tray and helping her into her chair.

I ignore the chatter around us like I always do, trusting Avery and the guys to tell me if I need to take more notice, so I don't notice the excitement until Harley glances up and snarls, "What the fuck?"

The chair next to mine scrapes back and Luca folds himself into it, swooping in to kiss my cheek. "Morning, princess! Missed me?"

A grin bursts across my face, I'm sure I look like a psychotic toddler. "I kinda did. How's things? You enjoying being out of the Jackal's den of evil?"

He cackles at me, ignoring the looks of loathing my guys give him. All three of them. Fuck my life. "It's been quiet, that's for sure. I've been working on a new project for our mutual friend... the non-psychotic one. Apparently, someone is getting gifts from a secret admirer?"

Ugh. "Have you had any luck in your search?"

He shrugs and winks at me, tipping his head back to drink his iced coffee and I think a few of the freshman girls around us swoon. Huh, ok maybe that's why Harley is looking so... snarly.

"There's been a few leads. Whoever is sending them is good... like, fucking good at this. I'd be worried except they're obviously obsessed with you. Thinking about adding to your little harem, princess?" he asks with a little sly smile. Ok, bordering on flirty but that's just how he is. It doesn't mean shit.

"You're going to stand the fuck up and walk away. Right now, before I drag your ass across this table and beat the life out of you," Harley snarls, and for once, Blaise doesn't make a joke. He just nods along like it's the acceptable thing to do.

Avery rolls her eyes. "Just leave him. They're friends, it's the same as Illi and you don't go all Neanderthal on him."

Harley cuts her a look. "Illi is family. This dick might be a Crow spy but he lived with the Jackal for too long for me to trust him."

Luca leans back in his chair, nonchalant but he doesn't quite pull it off like Illi does. "I saved your girl's ass last year. Isn't that enough for you to cut me some slack? The Crow is your ally."

Ash snorts and stands, tugging Avery out of her seat and then he grabs my arm to haul me up too. Jesus fucking wept. He gives Luca his most vicious glare and says, "Were you there when the Jackal was torturing the Wolf? Did you stand by and watch it all, collecting your information and telling yourself that absolves you from taking responsibility for that?"

Luca smiles at him, shaking his head. "You only care because you're in love with her. Any other girl and you wouldn't give a fuck. How many girls have you buried for your father?"

Ash leans forward until he can whisper in Luca's ear, just loud enough that I hear him. "Enough to know you're doing a shitty job of protecting the Wolf, and my sister, and you're not fucking welcome here."

And then he drags us to our classes for the day.

Fuck me.

After our classes let out for the day, Avery heads straight to her dance class for the evening to put in some extra hours to work on a new routine and I head back to the guys' room on my own. I'm meeting Blaise for our usual study session and it's easier to get ready there than run between the rooms. I'm halfway through my shower when Ash stalks in, a broody look on his face as he stops in front of the sink and stares at me.

He crosses his arms and just stands there for a second until I get self-conscious and snap, "What? You coming in or not?"

He raises an eyebrow at me. "Not. Hurry up, I've got you to myself for the night and I've made plans."

Plans? I rinse the soap from my body quickly. "Are we going somewhere? Have you decided to kill Atticus because I should warn you I've promised Avery I'd try to stop you from doing that."

He scoffs at me, grabbing a towel and flinging the shower door open. "Don't talk about him, he has nothing to do with my plans and I don't want him ruining my mood."

I step into the towel as he holds it open, a little weirded out by how he's acting. "Are you going to tell me what we're going to be doing then?"

When I reach for my pajamas he grabs my hand, tugging me out the door. "My plan is you naked in my bed for the whole night to myself. I don't want to talk about my sister or that dickhead Crawford."

Oh. That sounds… perfect and not at all what I thought was happening. I let him tug the towel away from my now dry body and he leads me over to his bed. I climb up and wait while he strips off to join me. He's not in any rush, he folds each item and leaves in on the chair by his bed, and I find myself happy enough to just watch him.

When he lays down I tuck myself in against his chest, my head over his heart and one leg sliding over his. It's the fucking perfect way to spend the night together.

We're both silent and still for a minute, soaking each other in, and then his hands slowly start to move. They're sinful as they stroke over my body, like he's got all the time in the world to touch me. He focuses on sweeping up and down my back, a soothing gesture and nothing sexual about it, but then his fingers start slipping and brushing over the slight swell of my boobs from where I'm pressed up against him, or slipping between my thighs when he curves his palm over my ass. Never enough to properly arouse me, just the little light petting that keeps me on edge.

He's a fucking tease.

When he pulls his knee up, splitting my legs open just enough that the tip of his finger can brush though the lips of my pussy then he moves away again, I snarl at him.

"Either touch me or don't, quit teasing."

He smirks at me. "It's never enough, is it Mounty? You always want more."

My cheeks heat and I huff at him but he chuckles at me, finally plunging two fingers deep into my pussy and murmuring praises when I instinctively clench around them. "Good girl, you keep that up and I might let you come."

The flush on my cheeks deepens, there's something about him praising me like he owns me that sets my blood on fire. I hum as I lean up, kissing him as I roll my hips against his hand, desperate for a little more friction.

"I want some truths, Mounty. If you're good and give them to me without fussing, I'll play with this wet pussy and make you come so hard we'll have to change the sheets afterwards. If you give me all of the details, even the ones you would normally hide, I'll let you ride my cock. You can be on top and take it however you want."

Huh.

Ash is usually the most demanding of my guys in bed, never relinquishing the control or letting me call the shots. It might make it worth whatever the fuck he's going to ask. He moves so his fingers start to slip out of me and I scowl at him.

"Yes, ok, fine. Whatever, ask me. I owe you from last year anyway."

He makes these little appreciative noises under his breath, that type that have me secretly preening for him, and his fingers press up firmly back inside me again. A little gasp tears out of my throat and he looks at me with hooded eyes, his lip almost curling into a lusty snarl.

"Tell me where the Jackal lives."

I groan at him. If I hadn't been preparing myself for the worst that would have probably killed the mood but he knows exactly how I like to be touched, where to sweep his fingers and just how far he can push me.

"The old bank in the slums. It was built in the 1860s and there's a warren of underground vaults. The walls down there are reinforced steel and concrete so it's strong enough to hold off an army of bombs and bullets. He sleeps in one of the biggest vaults and he modified it so the door locks from the inside as well as the outside."

He purrs at me, his other hand stroking over my cheek lovingly. "How do you get in? If he's in there and it's locked, how do you get in?"

Fuck. It sounds suspiciously like he's making plans to go find the Jackal himself, but I let it go for now. "You unlock it. It's old and impossible to change the combination but the Jackal never told anyone what it is. Ever."

He hums under his breath, and curves his hand so his palm can brush against my clit, just a little and then he pulls away. My jaw snaps shut and I try to chase his palm but he stops me.

"How do you get in there then, Mounty? You have to know a way."

I blink a little, try to clear my head but it's so hard when he's touching me like this. He clicks his tongue at me like I'm disappointing him, goddammit, and I pull myself together.

"I watched him open it. I watched enough times that I know the combination. He doesn't know that I know, I'm sure of it, otherwise he would've switched vaults. It's long but I remember it. I remember fucking everything from my time there."

He presses up into my clit a little harder, enough that I actually shiver and shake. His hands should be fucking illegal.

"How do I get down there? If I needed to find this vault, how do I know which one it is?"

I groan and bury my face into his chest. I just want to come, for fuck's sake! "It's the biggest vault, he does his torture and maiming there too. It's on the bottom level, the only one down there and it has a secret set of stairs, right at the end of the hall."

"Good girl." He whispers, and finally, finally, he lets me come, three fingers pressing deep into me and his palm grind against me as I ride the waves of pleasure out.

When I finally stop shaking, I sit up and run a hand through my hair. I feel wrecked, like I always do, and I rock forward onto my hands to try to find my brains. Why the hell does he want to know that? He can't go down to the Bay by himself, this was a terrible fucking idea! He chuckles at me and I glance over my shoulder at the sound.

He's leaning against the pillows in a sort of recline but halfway to sitting up. He looks like a spoiled prince, like he's the black-souled prince of hell and here I am to serve him.

Well.

That kind of sounds perfect.

All of my reservations go out the freaking window. He gets tired of waiting for my brains to stop leaking out of my head at the mere sight of him and cracks his palm cracks against my ass. "Well, get up here then, Mounty. You earned it."

He sounds a little less smug when I slide down his cock in one go, the stretch still taking me a second to breathe past but, fuck me, he's worth every inch. His hips roll up to meet mine and I tsk under my breath at him.

"You're supposed to be laying back and taking it, Beaumont," I gasp, aiming for stern but falling flat as he spreads one hand between my tits, inching up towards my throat, and the other grips my hip.

"No, I said you could take it however you want. If you want to be on top then I'll fuck you like that. What the hell have those lazy fucks been teaching you?"

I grind my hips down into him, gasping and groaning, and he finally slides his palm around my throat, his fingers firmly finding their place and tugging me forward into his lips for another kiss.

When I try to move my hips again he tightens his hold, keeping me still so he can pump his hips up, driving his dick into my wet pussy like he was made to fuck me so good. I moan like a wanton Mounty slut, and just take it, take every fucking inch and pump of his hips until I'm clenching around him like a vise, coming so hard I black out a little.

He grunts and shoves my hips back down, slamming me onto his cock as he comes, his teeth sinking into the hollow of my throat and his arms wrap around me until I'm surrounded by him.

I take a second to find myself, find my brains and my dignity, and then I snap at him, "If I have to go down to the Jackal's lair to find you because you've taken off down there by yourself, Beaumont, I'm going to tear fucking *strips* off of you. You'll wish you'd never been born."

Chapter Sixteen

I throw myself back into studying, college scholarships still my top priority. What is the use of being this smart if I can't get someone else to pay for my education?

I pick Avery up from her dance class to walk back to our rooms for dinner. The guys are all running late from their sessions at the gym and after a full day of studying I'm antsy to move around.

Avery tucks her arms into mine, flicking her hair over her shoulder like a pro, and says, "It's much nicer having you come get me, Ash has turned into a snarling dick again. I knew his change of heart was too good to be true."

I groan. "Maybe you two need to sit down and sort... everything out. Stop being at each other's throats for a while. I know we'd all appreciate some calm."

She smooths a hand down the front of her shirt, pristine even though she's just spent two hours sweating and dancing her ass off. Fuck, still jealous. "I've tried. This is clearly one of his nonnegotiable issues from our childhood. Atticus wasn't even... that bad. I think now Joey's gone, he's found someone else to loathe being around me."

I nod, it makes sense. "And how are you feeling about Crawford?"

Ice. Pure fucking ice in her tone and she snaps, "He's not worth my time."

Yeah. I'm not sure I believe her and, fuck, I don't think she believes herself but if I've learned nothing else about her, Avery Beaumont is not fucking rational around the Crow. Their story is as dark and twisted as mine and I'm not going to judge them.

Ok, lie. I'm not going to judge Avery. I'm going to judge Crawford a whole freaking lot.

We round the corner to the main staircase and find the way blocked by a crowd of students. It's not until Avery's arm tenses in mine that I spot Lauren standing with a girl that has to be related to Viola Ayres, they look so similar. Well, this girl is the preppy version of Viola. No badass streaks and piercings in sight.

"There they are! The former reigning Queens of Hannaford, we've been waiting for you to arrive."

Avery's eyes narrow at the word former. "Imogen, get the hell out of our way before I destroy your will to live. I've been bored lately, I need a new pet project."

A total lie, she barely sleeps with the workload we're now under, but she would never show the sheep that weakness.

Grief flashes over Imogen's face and I try to remember that this kid has just lost a parent. We should give her just a little bit of leeway. Lauren looks uncomfortable but she doesn't move away. I give her what I hope is a disappointed look but the flinch she gives me says it's probably just a little too murderous.

"Just tell me where my sister's body is. My mom needs the closure."

Avery's shoulders roll back, her arm in mine meaning my shoulders do too. "Your sister isn't dead. She's run off with her boyfriend, that's none of our concern. Move."

Imogen crosses her arms, pulling herself up and stares down her nose at us. Insolent little fuck, isn't she? The guys in the room grin and shift their weight on their feet like they're eager to tear us to pieces and I subtly shift myself in front of Avery.

If I have to kill them all then I will, fuck the cleanup.

"I know you guys are new around here, but you really don't want to do this with me," I say, and I catch Lauren's eyes. She shifts again, leaning in to whisper to Imogen but the girl just shakes her head.

Fuck it.

The guy closest to us takes a swing and I shove Avery back, ducking so he lurches forward from the momentum. Avery gasps, stumbling, but she doesn't hit the ground. I don't even notice why she hasn't hit the ground until the next guy reaches forward to grab me. My knife is in my hand, ready to stab him and end this shit now, when Harley grabs his fist midair and breaks his arm, the crack of his bones deafening.

Harley's big hands clamp over my hips and gently shoves me behind himself like I'm a delicate princess, not a crime lord with a deadly knife clenched in my hands ready to spill some blood. The guy with the broken arm is screaming and dry retching on the ground, and although the others look a little more wary, they haven't backed down. Fucking idiots.

"Well, come on then. If you're big enough to ambush my girl, you'd better hope you're big enough to take on me as well," he snaps, stripping his blazer off.

That gets some attention.

He's wearing his guns, the two of them strapped into his shoulder holsters and I know for a fact they're clean and loaded. If he wanted to, the whole fucking lot of them would be dead in minutes. I kind of wish Hannaford operated on the same rules as the Bay because fuck these rich little bitches. They have no fucking clue.

"Fucking mobster trash," Imogen spits, and Harley smirks.

"Yep, I'm the mobster trash that's going to bleed every last one of you gutless fucks out."

Avery steps up beside me and gives me a look. Right. We can't let him kill these guys, no matter how much they deserve it, because we have enough heat on us as is. Fuck.

I catch his wrist and Avery snaps, "Looks like we'll see you boys tonight at the fight club. I haven't attended in years, what are you sluts wearing to those things these days?"

One of the guys steps forward and Harley rolls his eyes at him. "Really, Kettering? You wanna bleed that badly you can't wait for tonight?"

Kettering sneers, "You'll show up with your friends and fight dirty. I'd rather finish it here."

I snort at the fucking dickhead. "So, you'd rather your six to one instead of six to three? Good to know that you're aware of exactly how pathetic you lot are."

Harley chuckles at my smug tone. "I don't need backup, dickhead."

Avery arches a brow until they all start moving away. Lauren tries to flee but I grab her arm and wrench her into me until she has no choice but to look at me. Imogen stops and eyes Harley warily as he stands over us both, watching my back.

"I can't believe the girl who tried to befriend me in freshman year would be here today organizing a lynching," I say, my tone even but my face must be all sorts of fucked up. I don't give a fuck, she needs to know just how fucking badly she's misread this situation.

You'd think the head in the box and the Butcher would have been a big enough warning.

"She's scared for her sister! Her dad has just been murdered!" Lauren shrieks, and I roll my eyes at her. Everyone else has moved away now, leaving her with no protection so she's back to being a terrified little girl, hiding behind her 'good intentions'. Fucking spare me the bullshit.

I grab my phone out and hit dial on Viola's number, switching it to speaker. She answers almost instantly, grumpy as hell.

"Who the fuck is dead now? Jackson is already speaking to Crawford—"

I interrupt her before Lauren gets anything important out of her. "You sister just tried to jump Avery and me. I chose not to kill the little bitch, so you owe me one."

She swears viciously, snapping, "She never did have any fucking sense! I'll call her now."

Imogen's eyes flare and I smirk at her. "She's right here if you'd like to tear strips for her. I wouldn't mind hearing that."

Before Viola can speak Imogen cries out, "Well, if you didn't run off with some guy then maybe Dad would still be here! Why are you siding with trash from the Bay?"

Viola hangs up, then Imogen's phone rings. Fine. I guess they have their own conversation to have but Lauren isn't being let off so easily. I grab her by the arm and pull her into the alcove, where there's no chance anyone passing by will be able to hear our conversation.

"Your dad is a dirty cop. He's bought and paid for, and he's chosen the wrong side. Senator Ayres death lands at his feet. Get your fucking head around that, then make the smart choice and stay the fuck away from my family. You shouldn't be warning me away, the person who needs to run is you."

"I still don't understand why you didn't just kill them there and get it over with," Blaise drawls, lounging in front of the TV in our room like a freaking cat. Avery's already snarked at him for lying around in his underwear but the snark just bounces off of him.

I ignore the comment and shovel the pizza Avery handmade into my mouth like I'm a starved Mounty kid. I mean, I'm totally not one these days but old habits die hard.

"Maybe because I'm currently averaging three hours of sleep a night as it is, Morrison! I can't clean up anything else for you guys, I'm at my fucking limit!" Avery snarls, and I get a bad case of the guilts.

"What else can I do, Aves?"

She gives me a look. "Nothing. You do more than enough. Maybe if the guys all stopped, I don't know, running off to hack bodies to pieces without telling us, my job would be a little easier."

Blaise pulls a face. "I had nothing to do with that. I just helped keep Star busy, you can't put that shit on me. Besides, you're just pissed Ash got to call your boyfriend out for being sloppy. If he says this place is clean, he should be fucking sure it is."

I narrow my eyes at him and he gives me an unrepentant look, the dick. Avery goes back to scrubbing at the dishes in the sink like a crazy woman and I keep my mouth shut. I'm not stupid, poking at a cleaning Beaumont is not a smart move.

Harley arrives back from his swim practice, his hair still wet and the smell of chlorine clinging to him. He grabs a slice of pizza from my plate and kisses my head before eating half of it in a single bite. "What's the problem now? You guys don't have to come tonight if you're busy. Ash will watch my back."

Like fuck am I missing out on this. I don't have to say a word, Harley reads it on my face. "Just saying, babe. I know how badly you're freaking out about not being finished with your assignments yet... you fucking *freak*."

I smirk at him. "Jealous, much? There's no way you're talking your way out of it; I'm watching you and I'm going to enjoy the hell out of it."

Avery pulls a face. "Stop flirting. I don't need to hear about your weird kinks, Mounty. I can't think of anything worse than watching Harley pummel some guy, ugh. Have we decided what the dress code is yet? Are we going there as a gang, matching leather jackets? We should get patches or something. I feel like we all look great in black."

We'd have to wear white, and it's not exactly a subtle color, but I keep that to myself, rolling my eyes instead. "Just throw something on! It's not a charity gala, Aves."

She gives me a look. "Mounty, I don't throw things on. We can't all look stunning in ripped jeans and band shirts."

Liar, she's freaking *devastating* in everything, even dressed up like a Mounty, but I give her a look until she grabs one of her perfectly tailored coats and slides it on. "Where the hell is Ash? We're going to be late!"

Harley huffs at her and grabs another slice. "There's no such thing as late to fight club, Floss. You show up when you're ready and then wipe the floor with the posing dickheads."

She rolls her eyes in return, smiling when he kisses her cheek sweetly. "I'd rather we get this over and done with. Now, stop avoiding my question; where's Ash?"

Harley grimaces. "He's already down there, he went straight from track."

I jump up from my chair, Avery cackling at the look on my face. If I've missed out on Ash fighting, I'm gonna be *pissed*. "Morrison, throw some pants on; we gotta go."

He huffs at me, like it's such an inconvenience, but he pulls on a pair of ripped jeans and throws his leather jacket over his tank. I shove my feet into my cherry Docs and we're out the door. I tuck myself under Harley's arm and Blaise grabs my hand, laughing and messing around with Harley as we make our way down to the chapel. Avery trails behind us, her phone out and her lip between her teeth. Fuck. I need to figure out how to clear the board for her, take out just enough of her problems that I get my ice queen bestie back.

Blaise drops my hand to answer a text right as we get to the chapel, and the guy at the door startles when he sees us all walking up together, his eyes wide and panicked. "Arbour! I wasn't expecting you to show. This isn't really your scene anymore, is it?"

Harley's arm drops away from my shoulder to grab my hand, his fingers threading through mine. "Shut your mouth, Smith, before it gets you in the shit."

The guy's eyes flick down to me. "Uh, girls aren't supposed to come in man, you know that."

I smirk at him, dark and deadly. "You gonna keep me out, Smith?"

Maybe he has some survival instincts after all because he gulps and steps away from the door, ushering us in with his eyes fixed firmly to the ground.

There has to be at least fifty guys bare chested and grunting, and another hundred standing around taking bets.

The room stinks of sweaty boys, blood, and desperation. Not something that's the norm for my time at Hannaford but Mounts Bay has made me immune. Avery scrunches her nose up and I laugh at her.

"Gross, right? I thought rich people would sweat some ritzy cologne or some shit," I murmur, and she snorts at me as she tucks her arm into mine.

"I wish. I've spent most of my life surrounded by those idiot boys and they've never smelt that good."

That's a freaking lie, my three smell amazing. I have no clue what she's talking about but that's beside the point. Harley leads us over to take a seat in the same place I sat last time, when he'd beaten Hillsong for smacking me around back when I had no clue he liked me. He winks at me, probably thinking the same thing, and I blush like a swooning fucking virgin.

Lord help me.

Then he strips down to his shorts, the tiny ones he wears to boxing, and cups my jaw, kissing me dirty and raw.

The first guy to step up to the challenge is unconscious in under a minute. Fucking *pathetic*. I lose interest pretty fucking fast and search around the room until I find the other idiot down here looking for blood. He has his back to us, he probably hasn't even seen we're here yet, and he's straddling some guy as he lays into him. It's a fucking sight to see.

Ash finally stops smashing his fist into the guys face, sweat dripping down his chest, and sweet baby Jesus, I kinda wanna lick him. He glances up and notices we've arrived, smirking like the cocky dick he is.

"Give me a freaking break." Avery mumbles under her breath at me, her eyes rolling but the tiniest of smiles on her face. I give her a sheepish smile and she giggles. It's a fucking magical sound.

Ash gets up and saunters over to us, wiping his face on his shirt. His knuckles are bloody and raw but the energy around him is buzzing with the kind of exhilaration you can only get from the high of winning a fight. The flutters start in my stomach and I'm kind of tempted to challenge someone to a fight myself.

Blaise cracks a joke and strips out of his jacket to give to Ash, who takes it and pulls it on, a wide grin on his face. I decide right here and now that when all of the bullshit with the Jackal is over, we're going to make nights down at the cage fights in the Bay a regular thing. If this is what it takes to get the tension and bloodlust to a manageable level in Ash then we'll buy fucking stocks in the Dive.

Avery catches my eye and grins with me, totally unconcerned about the fighting happening around us. She's that happy that her brother has mellowed out. Good. Life is returning to normal, thank fuck.

Harley finishes off the second guy, barely even panting, and motions for the next one. At this rate we'll be out of here in under an hour. Not such a bad thing.

I'm definitely sleeping in the guys' room tonight.

Chapter Seventeen

I'm proud to say we make it back to the guys room before I rip Ash's pants off and swallow him whole. It's fucking hard, damn near impossible, but I manage to contain myself.

Blaise complains the entire way back, outvoted and sleeping in my bed alone tonight, but for once Avery is giggling and snarking at him with us.

"Isn't there a camera in that room? Just this once, I'll let you jerk off in the shower, Morrison." She laughs, unlocking the door and winking at me. I blush just a little from where I'm sandwiched between Ash and Harley, but I give her a little wave too, barely managing to contain a squeak when Harley palms my ass and squeezes.

I fumble with the keys on the way in but no one notices, Ash is too busy snarking at Harley about sharing while my golden god kisses his way down my neck in the most distracting way.

I stumble into the room and out of Harley's arms, catching my breath for a second and he rips his shirt over his head, pausing when he sees all of the blood covering him in sweaty streaks.

"I'm going to wash this off first." He grimaces, stomping off. Well, fuck.

Ash chuckles at me, my eyes snapping back over to find him standing in his boxers by his bed. Fuck, that was quick. "Come on, Mounty. I'll keep you entertained while he's off being a gentleman."

Lord knows what gets into me, but I stare him straight in the eye as I strip off slowly, not making a show of it but just slowly revealing myself to him. It doesn't matter that he's seen it all before, that he's fucked me three times this week, he stares at every inch of my skin as it's revealed like he's never seen it before, like he can't get enough of me.

Like he's as desperate as I am, always, never-ending, fucking out of his mind for me.

"Get that ass on this bed now, Mounty, before I come down there and get you."

I shiver at his tone and hesitate just a little. I might like the punishment he gives me, I fucking bet I will, but I'm too fucking desperate for him tonight to wait. Maybe next time.

The second my knee hits the mattress Ash yanks me down and into his arms until we're tangled together, limbs everywhere in the fucking best way. I love this relaxed side of him, the smug grins and dark chuckles, it's fucking perfect. His hands are possessive as he strokes over my body, squeezing and pinching, even throwing the odd slap in, and, fuck me, I'm owned by this man. *Owned*. I could lay here and make out with him all fucking night, but he has different plans for our evening.

I'm completely distracted by the feel of him on top of me because the next thing I know, there's lubed up fingers in my ass and he's caught me the fuck off guard.

Ash laughs as I gasp into our kiss, the whole thing turning into a moan. I sound fucking obscene, my cheeks are on fire and I kind of hope Harley doesn't come out and add to my shame by seeing me writhing on the bed.

I give the smug dick a half-hearted glare. "Why, exactly, are you so obsessed with my ass? Your dick is never going in my ass. Never. Get rid of that idea now, Beaumont."

The slow smirk he gives me has me dripping for him in the *worst* way. "I thought you were brave, Mounty? Sounds like you're back to being *jumpy* to me."

Fuck him.

He's trying to goad me into saying yes and the worst part is the asshole is succeeding. Ugh. He grins at me like I've already agreed to it so I kiss him again, biting his lip and pull his hair just a bit to get even.

It only makes him more frantic.

I swear, I've been fucking brainwashed by his dick or something because I'm all in. Fuck it, what's the worst that could happen? I'm dumb enough to say this to him, and he rolls his freaking eyes at my dramatics.

"You need to spend less time with Morrison, he's rubbing off on you."

Well, yeah, that's kind of the point. I look over my shoulder to quirk an eyebrow at him and he slaps my ass. "Have I ever fucked you without you coming over and over again?"

I gulp. "No."

"Well, ass up then, Mounty."

He manhandles me around until I'm face down on the bed. When I grunt in protest at him, he bites my shoulder, licking and sucking at the spot until I'm sure the mark will be visible a freaking mile away. He shoves a pillow under my hips and pours even more lube on my ass, stroking a firm hand down my spine as if he's settling me but also reminding me that I'm *his*.

As if he's worried I'll tap out, he doesn't waste any time lining up, pushing in slowly but not stopping until he bottoms out. There's a burn but it's not so bad. Then he moves and, fuck *yes*, that's what I need.

The sound I make isn't quite human.

He chuckles at me, though he's breathless and gasping a little. His hips start to move, I'm gushing fucking *everywhere*, and he drops down to hold himself over me, fisting his hand in my hair to jerk my head back and kiss me like he's trying to crawl up inside me.

I could die a happy fucking Mounty right now.

Ash grabs my arm and rolls us both until I find myself staring at Harley, naked and dripping wet from the shower. His eyes are like a searing brand on my skin as he takes in my flushed cheeks, trembling thighs, and my dripping pussy.

"How did I know you were going to be the one to talk her into this?" he mumbles, and Ash laughs as he hooks his arm around my leg and spreads me wide open.

"Don't make me say it," he grunts back, biting down on my shoulder and I don't know what the fuck they're talking about, words are too fucking hard to process right now. All I know is I want *more*.

I don't even realize I've said it out loud until Harley joins us on the bed and catches my face in his hands. "Whatever you want, babe."

Then he kisses me, his tongue a slow but demanding stroke against mine, and two of his fingers push inside me until I gasp. His palm grinds down on my clit and I fucking *break*.

A strangled sound comes out of me as I see stars, my body clenching down around Ash and Harley's fingers, and Ash groans as he comes with me, his hips jerking and grinding into my ass.

Harley gives me just long enough to catch my breath, and for Ash to pull out and head to the bathroom to clean up, before he has me on my back, thighs spread, his forehead pressed against mine as he lines up and pushes in.

"You have no idea how fucking hot you are when you come, do you?" He grunts, kissing me with more teeth than tongue.

He doesn't ease into it, just fucks me hard and desperate until my back is arching off of the bed and I'm screaming again, so loud I'm sure the entire boys' dorm is getting a show, but I come so hard I don't give a fuck.

Ash cleans me up and Harley carries me to his bed, ever the gentleman, because the wet spot is more of a puddle and none of us can be fucked changing the sheets. Once I'm firmly pinned between the two of them Ash hits the lights and I try to focus on sleep, not the delicious soreness that's taken over my body.

I'm still shaking, just a little, when Harley's and Ash's phones both buzz. Harley snickers like a dick as he shows me the text from Blaise.

I fucking hate you both.

Avery declares she needs me to herself on Sunday and the guys all disappear to beat each other up or drink themselves to death or something. I didn't pay enough attention to the details, clearly.

We spread out college brochures and scholarship applications out on the table in our room and then spend a couple of hours going over our options. I feel kind of bleak about the whole thing, like it could all slip through our fingers at any fucking second because of the war and Senior's psychosis, but Avery refuses to leave anything up to chance.

We can't decide on a school.

"I just think we need to stick to an Ivy League school, Lips. They got to be where they are through their exemplary standards for education."

I groan at her. "Or, they enjoy pretending they offer something more than state schools do so they can triple their prices. I just don't see it. If I don't get a scholarship, I'm not going there."

Avery huffs out a breath at me. "Mounty, you're rich enough to pay for it. *I* will pay for it. God, Ash and Harley will probably duel it out over which one of them is allowed to pay for it for you. Money isn't something we're concerned about, you need to adjust your thinking."

I take a deep, deep breath. "I've been too poor in the past to *ever* stop worrying about money. I could have a billion in the bank, I'm still not going to want to spend it. I've gone hungry too many times to forget that feeling."

She rolls her eyes at me again and starts to sort through the papers, making little piles which I'm sure are cataloged perfectly in her head. She seems happier today, less bogged down, and I decide to bite the fucking bullet and just ask. "So, have you heard from Atticus lately? Is he the reason you're smiling like a freaking siren today?"

She cringes and shoots me a worried look. Fuck.

I groan and slap a head over my face. "Seriously? What now?"

Avery fidgets with her pencil and I do my best not to cringe at her. She has such tight control of her body language the majority of the time, I know when she's fussing it must be fucking hell inside her head. "The attempt on the Jackal's life was unsuccessful."

I blink at her. "Uhm, yeah. I knew it would be. Why is that freaking you out so much? We always knew it would come down to us."

She bites her lip. "I might have... called Atticus and gloated a little. In a more... official way. The Coyote and the Tiger both heard it and have assumed there's tension between you two."

I roll my eyes. "And you're worried because you think I'll be angry? Aves, the whole fucking world is going to shit. I'm sure the Boar called and said the same damn thing to him. I don't give a fuck what you say to him, he already knows where I stand."

Her shoulders roll back. "What? Where do you stand?"

My eyes flick to the door as if Ash will have some sort of psychic premonition that I'm about to talk in Atticus's favor and storm in here to climb up my ass... in a not fun and sexy way. "I told him he has my vote. If you two sort out your issues, then I vote him into the family. Harley did the same."

The coffee cup in her hands slips to splash coffee on the college brochures in front of her but she barely notices. What the fuck is going on in her head today? "Harley did the same? Harley Arbour gave Atticus his vote? My cousin, Harley?"

I stand to grab a towel and mop up. She just stares at me blankly until I sigh and answer her. "Uh yeah, the only Harley we both know. Atticus explained himself and we both... like him. Kind of. I mean, I don't want to kill him anymore so that counts as liking him, right?"

Avery grabs a handful of ruined brochures and shoves them into the bin, grabbing her cleaning supplies and getting to work on the mess she's made. I watch her for a minute, moving my books out of her way and saving what I can from her destructive cleaning wrath.

"I just feel like there's this... gap between us now. Like, the guy I've been waiting around for, hoping he'd notice me, he's gone. He never even existed. I don't know what to do with that," she mumbles, and I nod.

"I kind of think this one is better though, Aves. The guy you were thinking of, the clean-cut gentleman, our world would have eaten him alive. He spoke to me about you and, honestly, the guy is crazy for you. I'm not saying you forgive him, fuck that, I'm just saying maybe you should stop being so angry at yourself for still wanting him. Or even wanting him more now. Just think about it."

She scrubs at the table a little harder but I let it drop. Maybe I've gotten through to her, maybe not. I'm sure she'll work this all out at some point.

Maybe.

Chapter Eighteen

We arrive at the ranch on Christmas Eve and I head straight to bed, ready to hate every fucking second of the day but fully aware that I'm not going to be left alone for a single second of it.

Sometime after midnight, I come awake to the feel of Harley's fingers brushing my hair away from the nape of my neck, dropping gentle kisses there as he goes. When I wriggle in place he whispers, "Shh," into my ear and slips a necklace around my neck.

My eyes pop open but the room is too dark to see anything.

Blaise's arms tighten around me, pulling me in and pressing me close, and I let myself fall back asleep.

I'm woken again hours later to the smell of coffee being wafted under my nose and I smile before my eyes even open. Avery grins down at me, barely batting an eyelid at the jumble of naked limbs I'm cocooned in.

I smile at her like she's my freaking soulmate, because coffee, and she continues to grin down at me, happier than I've seen her in weeks. I scramble out of the bed, carefully so I don't wake Harley because he's the only one who couldn't sleep through an earthquake, and I slip a shirt on, whichever one is closest. When I step out of the room, trailing behind Avery I feel the weight of the necklace Harley had slipped on me and pull it out from my shirt to look at.

I try not to get choked up but, seriously, is he trying to break my heart here?!

Sitting in my palm is a tiny heart locket, identical to his mother's, so similar it's only when I turn the locket over to read the inscription that I know he's gotten me one of my own.

Mine.

To the end.

I almost turn on my heel to go and jump on him but Avery snorts at my lovestruck face and I remember that we have plans.

French-toast-with-sprinkles plans.

We share the kitchen while I cook. I'm not great at French toast but this morning is for the two of us so I can't drag Harley over to do it for me. Avery grins and chatters away, totally content in her new Christmas morning routine.

I love it.

When we have food and, most importantly, more coffee, we sit and solve all our problems, theoretically.

"I still think if we go after the Jackal ourselves it should be in small teams. I know you say you could slip in and out easier without us but… you can't go alone. Take Illi at least," Avery argues. It's an old argument, one we have every single planning session, so it almost feels like it's a part of the routine.

"I'll get distracted if I have to watch Illi as well. It's better if I go alone."

She shakes her head. "If we really are a democracy like you say, you will be outvoted seven-to-one every time. Or, well, maybe Diarmuid will side with you, he seems like the ass-kissing type. He'd probably do it just to try to drive a wedge between you and Illi."

I snort. "There is no driving a wedge between us, we're as close as two people in a non-sexual relationship are. I'd kill and die for that man… I mean, I have. repeatedly."

Avery hums as she takes a sip. "You never have told me the full story of Odie's… sale."

I shudder. "And I won't. It's too fucking… *bad*. Let's just say the fact she can smile and laugh is a fucking miracle to me every damn time I see it. She's… she's a good person. One of the best."

Avery nods. "I agree. We've kept in touch, she worries about you a lot. I thought she might be jealous of how close you and Illi are, especially with how much we've needed him lately, but she always asks about you first."

I see the pleased look on her face. "That gets her in your good books, doesn't it?"

She rolls her eyes at me. "Well, obviously! You need more people looking out for you, lord knows you don't care about yourself enough."

I scoff at her and wipe my mouth, sure I've dripped my syrupy goodness everywhere. "I care about myself! Everything I've done has been to get myself out, that kind of means I look out for myself a lot."

She smooths a hand down the front of her robe. "And yet the second you inducted Harley, you threw yourself in front of him at every chance. You risk yourself without thought the second one of us is in danger, so yes, I'm very happy there's someone else out there who would attempt to rein you in a bit."

I roll my eyes but the sound of doors closing, feet stomping, and, well, bitching lets me know our planning session is over.

It's time to endure Christmas.

Avery grabs my hand and squeezes. "It's like all of my hard work just gets wiped out. All of the joy and life sucked out of you in a split second."

I shrug and give her a wry grin. "Sorry. I just hate this fucking day. It's getting easier but I still fucking loathe it."

Harley rounds the corner and grins when he sees me. He kisses Avery's cheek sweetly before grabbing my face and drawing me in for a blisteringly hot kiss. She snorts at us both and gets up to organize food for the guys. Harley only lets me go when Blaise punches his arm, snarking each other out.

"It's Christmas, stop fighting over Lips like she's a joint gift, it's gross," Avery snaps, and I laugh at the looks they give her.

I kiss Blaise with the same fire I'd given Harley, it's only fair, and he groans into the kiss, pulling me into his body to grind on me right here in the freaking dining room. I'm dumb enough to let him.

"Avery will cancel Christmas if you fuck the Mounty on the table, Morrison. I'm sure Lips is secretly hoping for that so fight your urges," Ash drawls, and I break away from Blaise to grin at him, twisting in Blaise's arms. He doesn't care, only rubs his morning wood against my ass instead.

"Bah humbug."

Ash smirks at me and draws me in for his Christmas morning kiss, leaning in so I'm squished between them both. Yum.

"Your Christmas present is on our bed. I didn't think Avery would want to watch you open it," he says as he nibbles his way down my neck, more bites than kisses. I can't freaking breathe when he does that.

Blaise grunts when I arch into him. "Mine's up there too, but for less pervy reasons."

Nope, still can't think like this. Harley comes out of the kitchen with a plate piled high, and snaps, "Don't fucking ruin Christmas by setting Floss off. Get off her."

I shoot him a look and he only quirks an eyebrow at me, waving a tub of cherry ice cream at me like it'll make up for the whole day.

I mean, it will, but he doesn't need to know that.

We enjoy breakfast together. I enjoy the pure, unadulterated satisfaction on Avery's face as she fusses over the guys, handing out presents and pouring coffee. She loves every freaking second of the day and that alone makes it worth getting up for.

Sometime after lunch, a full spread with turkey and all the trimmings because Avery is nothing but a perfectionist, I'm lying half on the couch in the reception room and half on Harley when a car pulls up. I groan, sure it's Illi and Odie here to celebrate this godawful day, but Harley tenses as he cranes his head up to check the car out.

"Who the fuck is that?" he growls, sliding out from under me and stalking over to the door.

"Oh, for fuck's sake!" he snaps and opens the door to the Stag.

I sit up as they stare at each other, Harley looking like he wants to rip the Stag's face off. Avery scoffs from the armchair she's perched in. Ash and Blaise are watching shitty Christmas movies and getting wasted in the theatre room.

"Merry Christmas, cousin. I was hoping we could have a chat, nothing too serious."

I shoot Avery a look. What the fuck is going on now?

Harley holds the door, his arm is blocking the Stag's path, and looks over his shoulder at me. I shrug. What can it hurt?

"You know it's polite to call ahead," Avery says in her sweetly poisonous voice, and he gives her the famous charming O'Cronin grin. It's a sight to see and Avery jerks back in her seat. Huh.

"I knew Harley would tell me to fuck off if I tried, better to come in person so he can tell I'm sincere."

Avery quirks an eyebrow. "And are you sincere? I thought the last O'Cronin with a soul died in front of his son years ago."

The Stag grimaces, rubbing the back of his neck sheepishly. "Look, I know you all think we're shit. I'll take that, Liam and the rest were shit. But I'm not. There's a lot of us who live by a very different code and now that I've taken over, the code is going to be the family way."

Harley sits next to me again, rubbing the soft organic, fair-trade cotton of my new yoga pants Avery bought me, because nothing makes that girl happier than spending too much fucking money on clothes for me.

The Stag watches this interaction with shrewd eyes. "This is a family conversation, not business. Can we do this alone?"

Harley shakes his head. "Lips and Avery are family, Stag."

I sigh. "We can go."

Harley's hand clamps down. "No."

The Stag, Aodhan, shrugs. "I'd always heard you were difficult, Wolf. Too hard to speak to, guarded by the Jackal, bloodthirsty and cold. I thought my cousin was insane for leaving the family for you but now I see the charm."

I roll my eyes because I know exactly how that is going to go down with Harley.

He reaches over to grab me by the hips and he lifts me easily from the couch and into his lap. His hands stay firmly fixed to my hips, like a brand, and his voice is dripping with poison when he says, "Are you here to try to fuck my girlfriend? I've killed people for less, cousin."

Aodhan scoffs at the way Harley spits the word cousin at him and I ready myself for the fight that's inevitably going to happen.

Instead, he leans back in the chair and shrugs. "I get it, she's your girl and our family history says I'm the biggest fucking danger in the room to her. That's why I'm here. You haven't taken up my offer of help and I want to clear some shit up so you know where we stand."

Hm. I slide off of Harley's lap and I'm a little shocked when he doesn't argue with me over it. His eyes are intense on Aodhan, even as he threads his fingers through mine.

Avery's phone rings and she steps out. Some of the tension in Aodhan eases.

"You have three minutes to convince me."

Aodhan's eyes grow intense. "Your ma isn't the only woman who has been hurt by the family. I would have left years ago but I have younger siblings. I decided that instead of abandoning them, I'd fucking fix it for them. Our family is supposed to be strong, rich, unshakable but under Liam's guidance it's just a fucking mess. I've cleaned house."

He rubs a hand over the back of his neck and blows out a breath. "Look, all of our uncles have been dealt with. Most of our aunts were already dead, there's only two left. I'm doing my fucking best. I don't want you coming back and taking over because the family needs direction and trust, you don't have that for any of us. I'm here because I need the Wolf to vouch for me with the Boar so I can get the businesses back on track. None of us can go legit, it's not in our blood. Being the Stag means I can get us back to where we're not worried about putting food on the tables again. If you don't want to help me, that's fine. I just thought I'd make you aware of what's really going on here."

Fuck.

Harley stares at him for a second, his eyes intense, and then he looks at me. "What happens if you vouch for him and he fucks us over?"

I shrug. "I can handle it. I have more than enough favors to get us through… pretty much anything."

His jaw clenches like it always does when I mention the favors but he nods. "What work are you going to do? Have you inducted the whole family already?"

Aodhan blows out a breath. "I've got the entire family inducted, and there's eight of us old enough to work. I was a bit worried that wouldn't be enough but I guess the Wolf has proven you can do it alone and still make it, as long as you have enough connections."

He leans forward in his seat, and I finally see some sort of resemblance between the cousins, the fierce determination they both have. "I'm not asking for a handout. I'm telling you I'm going to do whatever it takes to make things right and keep my family safe. Part of that is fixing things with Harley. If you offered to vouch for me in exchange for me never speaking to him again, I wouldn't take it. I couldn't help him when we were kids, but I can now and I'm going to."

I hold his eyes with mine for a second longer and then I nod. "If Harley wants me to, I'll speak to the Boar for you."

Harley squints at his cousin for a second longer. "You kill them all yourself? All of the uncles?"

Aodhan grimaces and shrugs. "Jack helped. They did the same to his girl as they did to your ma, he hasn't been right since. I'm trying to keep him stable but... he might not make it through this."

Harley winces. "Amara? They took her?"

Aodhan nods. "Killed herself before Jack could get to her. Liam decided he was getting weak about her because he'd taken on a legitimate job to get an apartment for her."

He moves to stare at his toes for a second then he grits out between his teeth, "She was pregnant. Jack was just trying to keep her safe from our family and the Bay. She lost the baby when they attacked her. Jack's not right."

I don't know who Jack is to Harley, where on the family tree he lies, but the wheeze that comes out of Harley makes my chest hurt. I slip my hand onto his knee and squeeze, trying to offer him some sort of reassurance though I know it all feels so fucking trivial.

"Liam deserved a much more painful death," he finally mutters, and Aodhan nods.

"He did but I had to get him out of the way before he did something to you. He was already in talks with the Jackal over the entire thing."

Fucking Liam O'Cronin. "Do you know where the treacherous fuck is buried? I feel the need to dig him up and piss on him."

Harley roars with laughter, pulling me into his side and kissing the top of my head. "You wouldn't. You bitch me out for taking my morning piss while you're in the shower."

I blush, goddammit. "Fine, I'll get Blaise to do it for me. He'd fucking love that shit."

I'm trying to enjoy my last night at the ranch, half-naked making out with Harley in my giant bed, when the car pulls up outside. When the crunching noise of tires on the gravel driveway reaches us, we both freeze. Then the front door opens and slams, and I scramble out of Harley's lap to find out who the fuck is interrupting our break now.

I don't get to the window before the yelling starts.

"If you think you can just show up here and demand to see her, you're more of a fucking idiot than I thought." roars Ash, and it's pretty clear who it is.

Harley groans behind me. "Why the fuck is that dickhead here? Has he got a fucking brain?"

There's a quiet knock and then Avery breezes into my room, scoffing at Harley's shirtless state. I'm wearing it, so she can't see whether or not I'm wearing underwear, thank fuck.

"I need you to get Ash back in here so I can talk to Atticus by myself. He has... that information I told you about."

Ugh.

Right.

The information about the Boar and his dirty biker world, to see if there's a chance that's where my DNA has come from. Harley's eyes narrow at us both, unhappy we're keeping secrets, but I just nod at her.

"I mean, I'll try to get him back inside but you know as well as I do Ash Beaumont kinda does whatever the hell he wants, consequences be fucked," I say, and she arches an eyebrow at me.

"Just text him for a booty call. I'm sure Harley will take one for the team and step out while you keep him busy."

I blush so bad and Harley must be in a mood about being interrupted because he snarks back at her, "What's the point in the orgy-sized bed if we don't use it for one? You can't be that naive about what happens in here, Floss."

Kill me now.

I give him a glare and grab Avery's arm to pull her out of the room and downstairs before she guts her cousin. I'm too freaking tempted to let her.

I forget I have no pants on until we're both out the door and Atticus raises his eyebrows at the sight of me. Ash's head whips around to see who's interrupting their screaming match and his eyes darken as they take in my obviously tousled state.

"For fuck's sake," he snaps and stalks over, covering me from Atticus's view and I roll my eyes at him.

"Please, he's so fucking obsessed with Aves he wouldn't give a shit about my ugly legs," I mumble when he glares at me and nudges me back into the house.

"A fucking monk would be tempted by your legs. Now get the fuck back upstairs and let me deal with that asshole."

I grab his arm and tug him through the door with me, shooting Avery a look. "She's a big girl, she can fight her own battles."

Ash sneers at me but I just roll my eyes at him. Fucking arrogant assholes.

I get him back up to our room, snarling and pissy, and he joins Harley by the window.

"I called Morrison. He's down there in case Atticus tries anything," Harley says, pulling a shirt back over his head. I roll my eyes at them both and then, fuck it, I join them.

Avery's back is so goddamn straight Atticus must be saying some bullshit to her.

"Can I shoot him? I feel like I should shoot the dick," Harley mutters, and Ash snorts.

"Do us all a favor and shoot him in the dick. That will solve everything."

I roll my eyes at them again. "She's stronger than us all, she's got this under control."

Atticus takes a step forward and Ash tenses, probably fucking planning on jumping out the window to her rescue, but then Atticus holds out a manilla file and a small, beautifully wrapped box.

"The fuck is that?" Harley snaps, and I swear I'm going to strain my fucking eyeballs at this rate.

"Clearly it's a freaking Christmas present. It's not big enough for a pair of shoes so clearly he missed that memo."

Harley is relaxed enough to chuckle but Ash acts like he hasn't heard me, glaring down at Atticus with all the rage and fire he used to throw at his brother. Avery is right, he's just found a new target for all that loathing.

Atticus turns on his heel and gets back into his Bentley. Avery opens the box and stares into it for a second. When she turns and stalks back into the house there are tears in her eyes.

"I'll gut that worthless fuck," Ash snarls, and I know things are only going to get worse before they get better.

Chapter Nineteen

I'm beyond angry at myself for taking so long, but two days before the Hannaford family dinner I finally finish all of the assignments and workbooks for my classes. I climb into my bed that night with the feeling like I have one less thing stalking me. Maybe I should start on Avery's homework and lighten her load a bit? She'd probably be happier with that, than anything else I could do to help.

Harley climbs into bed with me after his swim practice, risking Avery's wrath by touching me until I'm shaking and desperate for his dick. I do my best to not do anything with the guys in our room but his hands are intoxicating and I end up spread out on my bed in no time.

He stays the night, ignoring Avery's scathing tirade about the sex stench in the room, and I walk down to breakfast the next morning tucked under his arm grinning like an freaking idiot.

"The two of you are sickening, try and contain your hormones so I can eat." Avery hisses, and Harley scoffs at her as he grabs a tray and starts organizing our food. I don't have to say a word, he knows exactly what I want.

"I'm just in a good mood, sorry you picked the wrong guy to get infatuated with. You never did say what the asshole got you for Christmas," Harley says, and Avery levels a glare at him.

"And I never will," she snaps. I link our arms and give hers a little squeeze in solidarity.

"Want to plan how we're going to take over the world over eggs? That always cheers you up."

She lets out a little giggle, just enough to show she appreciates my efforts, and I grab her an iced coffee.

We sit together, Ash and Blaise already there and eating, and Harley dishes out our food. "Well, what about the information he gave you? Is there anything we can use?"

Avery gives him a look, and then turns to speak to me. "There's nothing concrete but everything still vaguely points to the Boar. The drug running that was happening in the Bay at the time was controlled by the Chaos Demons MC."

I frown. "The Boar's MC is the Unseen."

Avery nods. "Yeah, it is now. He was with the Chaos Demons. He patched his entire club over a few years after you were born. There was a lot of conflict at the time, maybe that's why he's kept you out of it."

Ash scoffs. "That doesn't explain why he didn't say something when he met Lips. He would have seen her at the Game and known."

Harley shakes his head. "Lips doesn't look a fucking thing like her mom. How would he know? You ever spoken to him about your mom?"

I grimace. "I don't talk to anyone about my mom. I've only ever spoken to the Boar when I've taken jobs from him. I was shocked when he sided with me at the meeting remember?"

Harley grunts and shovels more eggs into his mouth with a frown. Ash rolls his eyes at us all. "So why would he suddenly care? What's changed?"

Avery leans back in her chair, her fingers tapping against the table. She's barely touched her food, too caught up in her thoughts. "The heads started appearing after the Jackal and Lips declared war right?"

I shake my head. "No, it was after the meeting but the Jackal was still pretending to follow the rules. Something had changed in the dynamics but it wasn't war."

Avery frowns. "It has to be him, though. We should have just spoken to him at the meeting."

"Too many people around." I say, but really, I was too fucking nervous. I don't need a father. I don't need the extra responsibility of family. I have everyone I need in my life right the fuck now.

Ash checks his watch and starts to bully Avery into finishing her food. I shove the last piece of toast into my mouth and stand up, needing another coffee on the way to get through class. Blaise comes with me, twisting his fingers into mine and rambling happily about his new song.

He'd given me his newest lyric book for Christmas and I'm freaking obsessed with the thing. Now that he knows how much I love his artwork, the little scratched pictures in the margins, he's taken to filling entire pages with portraits of the entire family. The ones of the guys are usually unflattering caricatures that make me snort with laughter, but there's one of Harley in the boxing ring that makes my heart squeeze in my chest. The one of Ash grinning with Avery nearly fucking kills me, especially when they're at each other's throats.

"I'm organizing a tour. Nothing big, more like gigs at bars and maybe a festival or two. The festivals would be good because I want to see you running around in those little fucking bodysuit things that girls wear to them. Fucking hot, Star."

I blush and elbow him. "I wouldn't wear one. I'd wear one of your shirts and be a smug bitch when everyone sees me in it."

He grins down at me. "Promise me you'll sing with me for our song and it's a deal."

I groan as we arrive at our first class for the day. "No way, I'll puke and ruin my reputation."

He roars with laughter at me, dropping me off at my desk and giving Harley a weird bro-nod thing as he walks in that has me shaking my head at him.

Harley sits down and kisses my cheek. "You can't sing on stage anyway, babe. Ash would end up fucking you wherever you stood and Avery would skin him alive."

I ignore his comment, unpacking my bag and smiling at Avery as the twins finally arrive. Ash pulls her chair out for her and when she smiles up at him it's genuine, thank the sweet lord. Maybe they'll stop their shit.

The class starts and I let my mind wander now that I've finished up. Harley scoffs at me as he starts taking his perfectly legible notes. I just don't get how his handwriting can be that fucking perfect. It's unnatural.

I'm startled from my daydreaming, and planning, by a sharp knock.

I glance up to find two cops standing in the doorway.

Fuck.

I shoot Avery a look and she gives me a tiny shake of her head. So not something she knows about, which means it's not something the Crow has planned or is even aware of. Fuck.

The female cop looks around the room until her eyes fall on our table. Harley tenses and his hand clamps over my knee under the desk. I catch his wrist and squeeze. I'll be fine. Whatever it is, I'll survive their questioning and be out by dinner time. The Tiger owes me.

"Harley O'Cronin? We have some questions for you. You'll need to join us down at the station."

My breath catches in my throat. Nope. I can handle it being me, fuck, I was hoping it was me. I can't handle it being one of my family members.

My face must say everything because Harley kisses my cheek sweetly, whispering, "Don't freak out, babe. Avery will have me out, I'll be fine until then."

But that's not true. He'll be alone, he'll be in lock down, and when one of the cops step forward I notice the district badge on his chest. Mounts Bay. Fuck.

I refuse to leave until they let me in to see him. The lady at the reception knows exactly who I am and each time she has to tell me no, I swear I see her age ten years. Finally, there's a shift change with the officers and she ushers me in.

Harley isn't really in the mood to talk, he just sits and seethes as he stares at his own reflection in the mirrored wall. I don't look at the mirror at all, entirely uncomfortable with the idea of Senior's pocket-pigs watching us here. Any one of them could take us out right now and there's nothing I could do about it. I fucking hate it.

When the door opens we both look up to find the Tiger in the doorway, a little pale and shaky under the terrible fluorescent lights. Atticus escorts him with a firm hand wrapped around his elbow and gives him no choice but to take a seat at the tiny table with us.

I give Atticus a nod, my mouth a firm line across my face, and try to be civil as I say, "Is the room clean?"

He nods and turns his attention to Harley. "There's been a lot of talk about your missing family members."

Harley scoffs at him. "No shit, dickhead, and we all know exactly what happened to them. We were all there that night."

The Tiger tugs at the neck of his collared shirt as he sweats. "Yes, well, I can't exactly get the Stag to come in here and confess. We're better off getting you the best plea deal possible and then working out compensation from the Stag for taking the fall for him. These things happen amongst our organizations all the time. No different."

Nope.

I've been pushed too far today, way too fucking far, and my mind just snaps.

I don't even realize I've moved until I'm staring down at the back of the Tiger's neck, my hand clenched in his expensive haircut and pressing his now bleeding nose into the table. He doesn't make a sound. I forget sometimes that he had to shed some blood to get into the Twelve. The suit and the arrogant attitude can make him seem clean.

"If I find out you've switched sides and you're getting Harley out of the way for the Jackal I won't just kill you, I'll climb in your fucking window and gut your entire family."

Blatant lie, but the trail of headless corpses that now follow me have made me look a hell of a lot more callous and bloodthirsty than I really am. I'm going to use it to my advantage.

"Harley leaves here with me today and whatever it takes, he does not see the inside of a cell again. I don't care what it costs you, I have a fucking diamond and you owe me, Tiger."

He gives me the barest nod and I ease up, sitting back in my chair. The Crow gives me a disapproving look but Harley slips his hand into mine under the table. I try not to think about the cold steel handcuffs tethering him to the floor.

"I wouldn't have brought him here if I didn't trust he was on our side," Atticus says, and I shrug without glancing at him.

I keep my eyes glued to the Tiger as I snap, "I don't trust people outside of my family. Keeping my mouth shut in the Twelve meetings and taking jobs from you all seems to have given you the impression that I'm easy to influence and manipulate. I'm not. You'll do as I say or you'll die."

Atticus huffs at me but the Tiger nods. "I know. I chose this side because this is the sane side." He huffs out a laugh at himself, "How crazy is that? The side that just threatened to butcher my kids in their beds is the sane one. But it's true. If I'm honest I'd rather it be you climbing in my window than the Jackal and his men. I just needed to make sure you're aware that this is not going to be easy or cheap. The police chief is dirty."

I roll my eyes. "I'm well aware thank you. Find me a judge who's also dirty, but happy to be out of Joseph Beaumont's clutches. I'll pay, in cash or blood."

Harley's hand does a funny little twitch in mine and I squeeze his fingers. Whatever it takes. I really don't give a fuck what it costs.

The Tiger nods and leaves the room, his phone to his ear. I stare at Atticus and try to arrange my face into something a little less hostile but, fuck, I'm not in the best of moods.

"I'll pay for this." he says.

Harley scoffs, leaning back in his chair, and replies, "I have the cash. I'd rather you take care of the blood if it comes to that."

I give him a look but Atticus nods. "If it's something I can take care of, I will. You have my word."

I try to ignore the swirling discomfort in my gut but it bubbles out of me. "You can't buy our friendship. We already said you have our vote. Maybe you should wait until Ash or Blaise need the bail and give them the same offer."

Atticus's eyes narrow at me, like cold steel, and Harley snarls at him for it. Atticus ignores it and says, "You said you work as a family? Well, that's what I do for my family. I told you back at the Gala, if you keep Avery safe then I will back you on everything, regardless of whether or not she forgives me."

Dammit, he just keeps making it harder for me to hate him. "If it's blood I'll take care of it. Illi has been enjoying the… workload that being mine entails."

Atticus scoffs. "He's just as deranged as Matteo. You need to watch him carefully."

Ok, that helps me hate him again. My stomach fills with butterflies when Harley snaps, "He's family too, dickhead. He got my vote long before you did, and I'll side with him over you to the fucking end."

That's the real family line. We don't have to get along all of the time but once you're in, you're fucking in. Unfortunately for Atticus, two votes don't make you family.

Atticus shakes his head at us both. "You grew up in the Bay, how can you not see who he really is?"

Harley smirks at him, cold and arrogant. "Did you know Illi has Ash's vote too? It was unanimous. Just because you see him at his day job means nothing. Fuck, we've all shed some blood at this point, who the fuck cares how much he enjoys it? Don't get pissy just because he likes playing you. He does that because he's all in and Avery loves it. He makes her feel important just because she's a tyrant and he respects the hell out of her for it."

Atticus stares us both down and then shrugs. "If he touches a hair on her head, I'll walk into that school and drag her back home with me. Then I'll deal with him."

I smirk and Harley makes a big show of dragging his eyes up and down Atticus's carefully styled appearance, all pressed lines and cashmere suits, and says, "My money is on Illi but feel free to give us a good show."

Chapter Twenty

"Do I need to drive down to the Bay and gut an O'Cronin? Because that sounds like the exact way I'd like to spend my evening."

To his credit, the Stag doesn't bitch me out or try to make excuses, he just listens to the fucking venom I breathe down the phone at him and takes it like a champ.

It had taken another three hours for Harley to be released, the Tiger and the Crow pulling some freaking strings to get him out, but the only way to get the case dropped is for the witness to retract or die.

The witness is going to fucking die.

"The Crow has already called, it wasn't a member of my family."

I scoff. "I have the Coyote hacking into the police record system, you better fucking hope it's not one of yours."

He sighs at me, and the call of gulls in the background tells me where he likely is. He's down at the docks, probably on his first job now that I've vouched for him with the Boar. Fuck. "If it's a member of my family, who would be working on their own, I will deliver them to you myself. It won't be."

I hang up on him, pissed off and feeling kinda stabby, like someone needs to pay for this and nothing but my knife buried deep in their neck will be good enough.

Harley changes gears in the Cadillac, the one I'd borrowed to come after him, and gives me a side-eye. "You think it was really one of my family?"

"I'm your family. Avery and Ash and Blaise are your family. Illi and Odie, and that's fucking it. I don't trust the Stag. He's a whole lot of talk at the moment, I want to see some action to back it up."

Harley nods and slows the car as we pull into Hannaford, the gates opening automatically for us. My phone starts to ring.

"Why hello there, my good friend Lips," says the Coyote, and I roll my eyes. He must be with the Crow, he lives for pissing that man off.

"I'm not in a fun-and-games mood, Coyote. What have you found?"

He coos at me, "Aw, did your little friend have a bad time in lockup? I hear your first time can be rough."

I take a deep, deep fucking breath. "Jackson. It wasn't his first time in lockup, you already know this, why are you being a dick? Just tell me."

He grunts and Viola snaps at him in the background. "Ow, fine, yes, I knew that. Did you know he got more time for fighting while he was in juvie? Fucking brutal, you're in bed with a beast. I heard about the other one fighting with the Viper's guy, too. You got a thing for blood or something? I always knew you were a kinky fuck. I could just tell."

I squeeze my eyes shut. "Are you high? Put Viola on the phone."

He cackles and then Viola speaks, "We were out having dinner when Atticus called, sorry."

Harley parks the car and quirks an eyebrow at me. I shrug. "It's fine, it's just fucking weird to hear him like that. Did he find the rat?"

She scoffs. "He couldn't find his own dick right now. I found the rat, some guy called Michael Byrne."

No idea who that is but Harley curses under his breath. "Thanks. Can you send through his info? I'll deal with it tonight."

Viola makes a choking noise. "Ok, it's still so weird to me how casual you are about this... stuff. Gross."

I hang up and Harley's hand tighten on the wheel even though the car isn't running. "He's related by marriage. His daughter married one of my uncles, I think she's still a part of the family."

I nod and call the Stag back. "Michael Byrne is dead. If you have to make arrangements to contain the fallout in your family, do it now."

He curses. "Fucking scum. You don't have to worry about Deirdre, she's fucking delirious with happiness now her husband is gone. He was beating her and the kids, if her own family is pissed about the changes in my family well then he deserves a cold hole in the ground."

Hm. Ok, maybe he isn't so bad. I guess it's just ingrained in me to hate anyone with the name O'Cronin.

Harley helps me out of the car and kisses the top of my head as he tucks me under his arm. We head back to our room to shower and grab supplies. I'm doing this the right way and I'm doing it tonight.

An hour later, we take Blaise's Cadillac and leave Avery safely stashed at Hannaford with Illi and Odie, watching a movie together in our room. Ash insists on driving and I sit in the back with Harley to try to get myself in the right headspace for what the night is going to bring us. The car is quiet, only the sound of the engine revving as Ash changes gears. My bag with all my supplies is on the floor at my feet, re-stocked and ready to go, and I know without a doubt that all three of my guys have the holsters and weapons strapped to them. I have no intention of letting them be involved at all, but it's good to know I'll have the backup if I need it.

"You're not fucking going on your own, so don't even try to start with that shit," says Harley, drumming his fingers against his knee.

I roll my eyes. This is a simple fucking job, there's nothing for him to worry about.

"I told you guys I could do this by myself. I need to send the Jackal, and anyone who makes the stupid decision to work with him, a message. You heard the Crow, half of this fight is dealing with his numbers," I murmur. Harley mumbles something under his breath but I ignore it. He just can't let go of his protective nature, it's something I love about him, but in this situation it's not needed.

I'm not scared of the fucking Jackal. Not anymore. I'm wary, sure, anyone who has ever met him would be wary, but I'm not afraid of him.

I use the rest of the drive to look over the information Viola gave me even though I've already committed it to memory. I always was an obsessive over-planner, but I'd rather put the work in and get it right.

When we finally arrive, I make Ash stop the car at the end of the road. He's not happy about it but I need him to stay put. He's pissed about *that* but he also knows Harley and Blaise won't let anything happen to me. He insisted on being the driver because he's less reckless at it than Blaise and Harley had bitched him out when he tried to get him to drive instead. Apparently they're taking turns in coming with me on jobs.

I slip on my tiny black ballet slippers. Harley looks at them and then down at his own shoes. I lift a shoulder at him in a half shrug.

"As long as you're quiet and it'll be fine. Occasionally my Docs make a squeaking noise and it's just not worth the risk."

He nods and gives Morrison a look. "And what about him? Those boots aren't exactly discreet."

Blaise sneers at him. "I can take them off if I fucking have to."

Deep breath. I really don't want to deal with their snarking, not after the day I've had. "He's gonna be the lookout from downstairs. The info pack Viola gave me said that it's just Byrne and his wife here. The kids are all grown up and married off. He doesn't have any men for a security detail, he's just got the system, so Blaise will watch the door and Harley can come with me because I'm sure he'll insist."

Harley smirks. "You bet your ass I insist."

The walk to the house is quiet, no one else on the street and none of the houses show any life. This is one of the best areas in Mounts Bay. The house is close to a mansion, nothing like the Beaumont manor but still pretty fucking pricey.

When we arrive at the Byrne's place, and it looks as though he's compensating for something, all grandeur and over-the-top details. I bite my lip trying to keep that joke in but Blaise wiggles his eyebrows at me to tell me he's thinking the same fucking thing. Harley rolls his eyes at us both.

I disable the security alarm, too fucking easy to do thanks again to Viola, and we step into the house. Marble floors, Persian rugs, paintings that would easily cost six figures, it's the biggest show of wealth for a guy who isn't really that rich. He's got money, but he ain't a Beaumont. I motion for Blaise to stay put and he nods, leaning against a wall and frowning around the room like the shadows might come to life.

Our feet are silent as we make our way through the house. I wait until we get to the top of the grand staircase before I slip my hand into my bag. I'd rearranged it and left it unzipped in the car so that there was no noise involved. Harley watches me as I carefully pull out a hypodermic needle and a small vial, something Doc had given me years ago and replaces every time my supplies get low.

I lift a finger to my lips to remind him to stay silent. It's not like I think he actually needs the reminder, but I do it anyway. He nods silently, taking the bag from me, and follows me to the bedroom.

Mr. and Mrs. Michael Brynes sleep in the most ridiculous fucking bed, I barely contain my sounds of disgust. Not really, but fuck man, it's something else. It's the type of bed I would've imagined Avery sleeping in, back when I thought that she was a pampered princess. This man must think so fucking highly of himself, it only makes the kill sweeter.

I make my way over to the bed. Byrne is a handsome enough sort of man, if you're into middle-aged Irishmen. He's sleeping on his back, his snores louder than Blaise's and way more fucking irritating.

The bed is a Cal King and there's a huge divide between him and his wife. The universe must be working in my favor today because his wife has an eye-mask and earplugs in. The snoring coming out of Byrne's mouth isn't actually that bad but apparently it's unbearable for his wife.

I fill the needle with the liquid in the vial, silent because I've done this so many times I can't even count, and then I slip the empty vial into my pocket.

I have one chance to get the needle into his neck and the liquid in his system without waking his wife. I don't have any plans to kill her, I'm sure with the way this man treats his daughter that his wife is just as badly mistreated, but if she wakes during this it will force my hand.

I motion for Harley and he gets into position. I slow my breathing down so I am completely ready and then I slap my hand over his mouth and punch the needle into his neck at the same time, shooting the drug straight into his bloodstream. Harley grabs both of his arms and holds him to the bed.

His eyes open but the drug is faster.

GHB is a magical thing. While it takes 10 seconds for the entire body to grow slack, it only takes three seconds for his arms to stop struggling. There is nothing he can do.

Once I know it's taken enough of an effect, that he's awake and aware and *completely* unable to fight back, I move my hand away from his face. Harley lets go and takes a step back as well.

I stare down into his eyes so he can see his own death in them, then I lean forward until my lips are an inch away from his ear.

"No one touches the Wolf."

And then I slit his throat.

Harley texts Ash to drive past and grab us.

I could have made the kill cleaner, less of a total bloodbath, but now I'm playing tit-for-tat with the Jackal, every blood soaked crime scene counts. Blaise climbs into the front and Harley shepherds me into the back, then climbs in after me.

Thank fuck the Cadillac has leather seats.

Ash meets my eyes in the mirror and I give him a calm nod, trying to push down the adrenaline of the kill. Everything went well, I'm a fucking professional after all, and then he pulls the car back onto the road. I look down at myself and sigh. I guess Avery is going to have fun replacing more of my wardrobe.

I peel my shirt from my body, more gore than material.

Harley pulls his shirt off and hands it to me to wipe some of the blood from my face. I try to swallow, my mouth dry as fuck at the sight of his bare chest, and croak out a, "Thank you."

Between rumble of the engine under my thighs, the warm leather caressing my back, and the dark stain in Harley's eyes as he searches every inch of my skin for damage, my chest starts to heave and fuck, I want him. I want to fuck him so bad, the adrenaline of the kill riding me hard, pushing me to fuck or fight.

"How long until we get back to school?" I ask, the need for sex drenching my tone. Ash glances over his shoulder and whatever he sees in his eyes makes his own flare.

"An hour, Mounty. You'll have to wait."

I whimper.

I honest-to-fucking-god whimper.

The sound decimates Harley's control.

"Fuck that." He snarls, and tears his seat belt off, hauling me into his lap and crushing our lips together.

My hands tangle in his hair, smearing a trail of bright red wherever my skin brushes his, and I bite his lip, desperate and raw. Harley grunts and pulls my hips in until he can grind his dick into me. But I don't want a mindless grinding induced orgasm in the back of a speeding car.

I want to fuck him until I can't breathe. I want desperate and rough and hard, and I want it the fuck now. Harley grunts into the kiss when my hands start to tug and pull at his jeans, desperate and empty without him.

I glance over my shoulder at Blaise and he gets on board with my plan real fucking quick. It's a tight squeeze for him to fit between the seats but what he lacks in space he makes up for in enthusiasm.

"Try not to come on my seats, Arbour." Blaise drawls, but it's a heady sound and I shiver. I've gotten blood all over them, isn't that worse? Harley smirks at me, loving every inch of my damage lighting up my skin until I'm on fire from his touch.

"I'll pay for a cleanup, fuck it, I'll get it reupholstered. Get a new one, set this one on fire, just fucking bill me for it," Harley grunts as I get his pants down enough to free his dick and then I stare down at my booty shorts with utter contempt. How the actual fuck am I going to get them off without kicking someone in the dick?

Blaise laughs at me, reaching over and hooking his fingers into the fabric of the crotch and tugging until it splits. Harley groans and does the same to the delicate lace, and then I slam myself down onto his dick, filling myself up and losing myself in the stretch.

Fuck.

Yes.

Harley grunts and fists my hair, tugging me into a blistering kiss. The noise that I make is fucking embarrassing but these guys have seen me at my worst, at my writhing, shaking, screaming worst, so having them know just how much I fucking worship their dicks is nothing really. I get a few good strokes in before Blaise gets impatient and needy. He tugs at my hair to turn my head into his kiss but the angle is wrong and I'm going to break my neck if we keep going like this.

I wriggle around, ignoring Harley's grumpy grunts and snarling at Blaise, until I'm riding him reverse cowgirl. We barely fucking fit in the backseat together, a tangled pile of limbs, but I'm filled to the brim with Harley's perfect dick and Blaise is right there in arms reach so all is right with the world.

I lean forward, bracing myself on his legs to get leverage, and Blaise groans at the sight of my bare and bloody chest.

Ash swears viciously, and our eyes meet in the mirror. "Fuck this, I'm pulling over."

Harley groans as I start to move, managing to snap at his cousin even though it's more gasps than fire, "She's covered in evidence, do you really want to have one of Senior's dirty cops find us on the side of the highway?"

My hips just keep moving, grinding down onto his dick.

"I fucking hate all of you," Ash snarls back, but the car doesn't slow down.

Harley's hand clamps over my hips, moving me faster and harder, and Blaise fists one hand in my hair to keep my mouth locked onto his and his other hand strokes down my chest and stomach until he gets to my clit, circling and pressing until I'm screaming into his lips. Harley grunts and shoves me back down onto his dick as he comes with me, the clenching of my pussy around him sending him over the edge.

Blaise grunts and mutters about the lack of space as he shoves his pants down his thighs and I climb off of Harley's lap and into his. Harley's eyes are less frantic as he rearranges his pants but he keeps them locked on my body as I reach down and impale myself on Blaise's dick. His hips roll up to meet me and I lace my arms around his neck, all of the urgency still thrumming through my blood even though I've already come once.

My legs are shaking, still fucking buzzing, and Blaise holds me still so he can thrust up into me instead. When he bites his lip I groan at the sight and kiss him, then he bites my lip and I want to die. I come again, gasping and shaking, but he doesn't stop moving, he just fucks me through it until I'm groaning and panting into his kiss. He loves kissing me through my orgasms, like he can taste the feeling on my tongue.

Ash takes some corners too fucking fast but by the time we roll back into the staff parking Blaise has his pants back on and I... still look like a fucking mess. There's a beat of silence and then Ash tears out of his seat, yanking the door open and pulling me into his arms. My legs are like jelly so I'm fucking grateful he's intent on doing the caveman thing.

Harley growls at him, but Ash snaps, "Fuck. Off."

He waits until the other two walk off, back up the grounds and into the building. I shiver in his arms and wait until he's ready to speak. He ignores me, glancing around like he's trying to find the cameras.

"Sorry about the blood." I murmur, and he lowers me back onto the ground.

"Fuck the blood, Mounty." Then he bends me over the back of the car and fucks me until I see stars.

Chapter Twenty-One

Avery wakes up in a bloodthirsty mood.

I don't question it, I know just how much this is all grating on her, and although I've taken the rat out and retaliated she's still out for blood.

We go with the guys down to the dining hall for breakfast and the looks Harley gets from other students set my teeth on edge. We're standing in line, all arguing about colleges choices which is my least favorite topic, when Imogen fucking Ayres steps up behind us.

"I heard you killed your mom, Arbour, good thing the Mounty trash fucked a decent lawyer for you. You're way too pretty for juvie."

Nope.

No.

Not dealing with shit today, or any other day here at the snake pit that is our fucked up school. Imogen lifts a perfectly manicured hand up to cover her mouth as she giggles and I grab her by the wrist, twisting her arm behind her back and slamming her face-first into the drinks table.

Her squeal is magical, and the whole damn dining hall falls silent to watch us. Like I give a fuck at their attention, no one is going to step in for this spoiled bitch.

I lean down to whisper in her ear and press her further into the table until she whimpers. "Being Viola's sister only gets you so much leeway, Ayres."

She grunts at me. "I don't care who you think you are, you're nothing but a gangster slut from the slums gang-banging your way to an easier life. You may have scared my sister into submission but I know you're nothing, Mounty."

I break her arm.

Oops.

I'm sure Viola will be pissed at me but, fuck, I've dealt with worse. I'm sure the Coyote will understand, if he's ever met this prissy little bitch he'll probably thank me. I let her fall to the ground as she sobs and cradles the break to her chest. I stare down at her, my whole family does, and I'm fucking proud that none of them flinch. Even Avery stands tall, the fire in her eyes kicked up ten fucking notches because today is not the day to fuck with my family.

"Does anyone else have something to add?" Blaise drawls, his hands in his pockets and a cocky smirk on his face as he looks around the silent room. Nothing. No one tries to come and save Imogen, even Lauren just stares at us all with terrified eyes. Pathetic.

Imogen stumbles to her feet and gives me a glare through her tears, stalking out of the room clutching at her arm as she sobs. I feel nothing but satisfaction.

The room seems to take a breath, but no one is whispering about us anymore.

Avery links my arm in hers as we pick out what food we want for the boys to grab. Blaise also picks shit out and Harley snarls at him but he grabs it for the idiot anyway.

"You know Senior was the one to orchestrate Harley's arrest, the Jackal only helped him find a willing witness," Avery murmurs quietly in my ear while the guys all snark at each other.

I give a curt nod. It hadn't been a huge leap to figure that out. "What do you want to do about it?"

Avery tugs me away from the line and towards the long table. "I'm waiting to hear back about some details. I should have confirmation soon."

I nod. I trust her implicitly, if she says she's got it under control then you bet your ass it's under control.

We sit at the table and Avery ignores us all while she taps away on her phone. I dig into my food and read over my notes for my AP History test. Just because I've finished the assignments, doesn't mean I can slack off. The pop quizzes and tests are still challenging. Ash tries to read my notes and sneers at my shitty handwriting.

"Don't you have your own? Fuck man, you're in trouble if you don't." Harley sounds like a smug asshole as he shovels his omelette into his mouth. Ash opens his mouth to snap out a scathing retort when Avery interrupts.

"He doesn't need them, we aren't going to class today."

My head snaps up and away from my notes. "What?"

Avery slips her phone into my hand and I look down at her deviousness. Holy shit. Holy fucking shit.

This girl is going to rule the freaking world.

The press conference is held outside of the police station in Mounts Bay, though I can happily say I feel a helluva lot better about being here today. Ash escorts her into the building and then a short time later joins me and the others behind the crowd of journalists, reporters, and camera men.

It only takes another minute before she walks out with the Crow and some guy. The crowd quietens down. We all stand and stare at her like she's the center of our fucking universe because, right at this moment, she is.

The Fed smooths a hand down his tie in a carefully controlled way that suits the stern look on his face. A savage, proud, fucking elated grin bursts across my face when he glances over his shoulder and nods respectfully at Avery.

He belongs to my ice queen bestie now.

Fuck. Yes.

"Thank you for coming today, I have a lot to cover so leave all questions until after my statement." He says in a clear and commanding voice. The press don't make a freaking peep, just stand there with their voice recorders, cameras, and even some old fashioned paper.

The Fed goes on and on about some bullshit policy and it takes me a second to catch on. "Corruption of law enforcement and political parties is not only illegal, but it demeans our great country. It has become clear that there are individuals using money, blackmail, and threats against lives to control vital members of our police force, both on the streets and in management positions."

Harley leans into me and whispers, "What a fucking hypocrite."

I shrug. "As long as it gets us what we want, who gives a fuck? This is the way of the world."

Ash threads his fingers through mine and takes the blunt Blaise offers him. "The world will be a better place without Senior in it, and if that means Avery has the entire fucking country in her pocket than fuck it. Hail Hydra or whatever."

I roll my eyes at him. "You're such a freaking nerd. To think, everyone thinks you're this cool and unaffected asshole badass and you're out here quoting Marvel movies like a fanboy. You're a fucking disgrace, Beaumont."

Harley and Blaise both snicker at him like children but the glare Ash gives me promises a spanking later and, uhm, sign me the fuck up.

The Fed rambles on for even longer until I start to get antsy, ready to get the fuck out of this city and back to Hannaford, and then he clears his throat, looking for the first time just a little bit nervous. I know before he speaks that this is the real move on the board, this is Avery's giant FUCK YOU to Senior.

She doesn't disappoint.

"And finally I have new information on an on-going investigation into the disappearance of the German socialite Lena Müller. As you all know, she was last seen in the Mounts Bay area four years ago and despite extensive canvassing the MBPD was unable to find her. We had an anonymous tip and based on that information we have been able to find and identify the remains of Miss Müller yesterday. We have already been in contact with her family and we ask that you all respect their privacy during this difficult time."

Ash's whole body tenses and I squeeze his hand, whether to comfort him or to try to stop him from flipping his shit I don't know, but he barely seems to notice.

The Fed takes another deep breath. "Further investigation of the burial site is still underway, but it has become clear that Lena's death was at the hands of a depraved serial killer. Eleven bodies have since been recovered and we are working hard at securing positive ID's on these women. The MBPD and the FBI are now working together to catch the person responsible and we will pursue them with the full force of the law."

"Holy fuck. Did you know about this?" Harley asks, and I shake my head.

"Aves told me she had Senior sorted, I didn't realize she was going to ass fuck him like this," I murmur.

Ash takes a last lungful of musky smoke and then crushes the blunt under his boot. "Senior started it. He sold people out, Floss is just leveling the playing field. What do you think his chances of staying out of prison are?"

I hum under my breath, watching as Avery and Atticus step away from the media circus now the questions have started flying. There's no reason for them to stick around now the gauntlet has been thrown.

"You said something about Senior's crimes in other countries? Maybe an anonymous call should go out to them as well. Twist some arms and all that."

Ash grins for a second, staring down at me like a weight has been lifted from him and I smile back up at him like a pathetic, love-sick puppy. I mean, I'm a total fucking sap for him. Ugh.

"Nothing would make me happier than Senior in a Columbian prison being made into some guy's bitch."

Huh. You know what, I feel the same way.

I meet Avery for dinner that night and leave the boys in their room watching some stupid movie.

Avery cooks us some over the top Italian dish I can't pronounce the name of but there's pasta and sauce and I'm always down for that. She preens like a happy housewife at the look of appreciation I give her when she settles a plate in front of me. I grin back at her, totally fucking elated after the day we've had.

"Is there a reason you're wining and dining me? Or is this just because you love me the most?" I say, trying not to moan at the taste of the food.

She settles in her chair and fusses with her cutlery until it's all perfectly straight. I know exactly what that means; I'm fluent in Avery Beaumont's body language.

"Just spit it out, Aves. You know you can say anything to me."

She sighs dramatically. "I think it's time. I think it's time for you to go and confront the Boar."

I stare at her for a second as I wind the pasta onto my fork. It's not like I haven't been expecting this, it's not like I haven't been expecting her to call me out on my own bullshit, but I guess I've just been waiting for the shove in the back to actually go do it. I normally confront everything headfirst no matter how much pain it will cause me. But there's something about this, there's something about the idea of having a dad, that terrifies me.

My mom dying was the best and worst day of my life. Not having her poison was such a relief but it also delivered me into the hands of the Jackal, creating the mess I'm in right the fuck now.

What will my dad give me? What bullshit am I going to have to face for sharing DNA with this guy?

I shove more food into my mouth like a sullen child, chewing and swallowing it without really tasting the deliciousness anymore. "Yeah, I know. I guess I have to bite the bullet and just go fucking do it."

Avery nods and we both eat for a moment in silence as we think over what exactly this is going to entail.

"I'm going by myself. I don't want the boys starting their bullshit. Ash is likely to stick a bullet between his eyes the second he tells me he's my dad just because he doesn't trust fathers, not that we can blame him for that. Harley will want to have an argument with him over the whole fucking thing in my defense, and Blaise… Blaise will crack some joke about our relationship and I don't know what sort of father the Boar might be but I don't need that shit in my life. Fuck that."

Avery smirks at me. "I think if he had a problem with it he would've said something by now. If it is him sending the boxes of heads, don't you think one of the boys would've shown up in there by now if he didn't approve of your relationships?"

A full body shudder takes over me. I cannot imagine the feeling of opening one of those fucking boxes to find one of my guys in there.

Avery grimaces at the look I give her. "Sorry, I didn't even think before I spoke.

669

Do you think it's him sending them?"

I poke at my dinner. "I guess if this is a blood thing. It just freaks me out to think how much of my life he must know about if he's the one sending them. I mean, my full name is just the tip of that fucked up iceberg."

She nods. "To know that much about your life and to not have helped you this far is disgusting. Sending you the heads of your enemies now is too little too late. Are you going to tell him that?"

I shrugged. "I have to be careful about what I say. Clearly sending the heads of enemies means he's a little bit fucking deranged. What if I reject him and his attempts at forming a relationship and he goes psychotic on us? We already have enough of that going on with the Jackal and Senior. The boxes are inconvenient but they're not currently a danger to us. I think I'll play it by ear, see how the conversation goes, and if he wants to keep in touch in a permanent, fatherly way I guess I can pick a phone up every now and then, even if I don't fucking want to."

Avery hums. "Phone calls are easy. It's just if he wants to join us for family dinner, then we'll have a problem. I don't think we can contain the guys from being absolute dickheads to him over a nice meal. What do bikers even eat?"

I laugh at the look on her face and her use of the word dickhead. It's still funny to hear the girl curse.

We fall into our usual topic of choice these days, college because fuck my life, and it's not until we're starting in on dessert and coffee that she brings up the other taboo topic, the one we can't talk about around the guys.

"Explain to me the Crow's empire," she says, sipping at her coffee delicately but I know it's an act. She wants to look like she's completely in control, even as her whole world is kind of crumbling away at the thought of the guy. Ugh, I hate it.

"Like I said before, it's all information and money. A bit of influence too. He does a lot of what you do."

She nods and drums her fingers against the countertop. "Explain the difference between his information and Illi's. And the Coyote, you always call the three of them."

I hum under my breath, searching for the right way to explain something that's now so ingrained in me that I don't even have to think about it. "Illi is the man to go to for the word on the street. Like, stuff that isn't written down, stuff no one is willing to pass on with their name attached to it. The Coyote is all hacking and data. He doesn't give a fuck about anything except the numbers and the inboxes he digs into."

I take another deep sip. "Atticus deals in the type of information that can bring down businessmen, politicians, and entire countries. The stuff that happens in soundproof conference rooms and in the back of chauffeur-driven Rolls Royces. Now we have access to all three sources there should be less gaps in our information. We won't have the same problems we did with Atticus in the first place."

Avery hums under her breath. "So his information is like mine. I guess I knew that, but he seems to know everything before me so I did wonder who his sources were. Do you have any names?"

I shake my head. "To be honest, before I knew who he was I stayed the fuck away from him. He's kind of… infamous."

Avery arches an eyebrow. "For information? Were you afraid he'd dig up your middle name?"

I groan at her, ignoring the cackle that tears out of her, except that I freaking love the sound. "No. He and the Jackal… they came in a tie. They won the same year, two members were killed in the same incident. The Jackal fucking hates that he didn't come out on top of the Game. No one else even remembers it but I guess he's always been deranged."

Avery's head tilts. "So this rivalry comes from the Jackal not wanting a joint win? Jesus H. Christ."

I nod. "Yep. He thinks it makes a difference even though it really doesn't. He's been after the Crow from day one, it's why their empires are always about the same size, if the Jackal gets bigger than the Crow he'll be more likely to take him out."

Avery's fingers drum out a pattern on the countertop again, the sound soothing to her. "That's all the more reason to take the psycho out then, isn't it?"

Chapter Twenty-Two

I step into the Boar's clubhouse and do my best not to let the disgust show on my face. The whole place smells like cigarettes, cheap whiskey, and gun powder, with the underlying smell of sex covering every flat surface. Fucking gross.

A lot of eyes track me as I make my way up to the bar. I ignore them, totally unconcerned with their interest and secure in my status as the Wolf of Mounts Bay. They all know what I can do.

"You lost, little girl?" Someone calls out, and I slide onto one of the bar stools.

"I need to speak to the Boar," I say to the bartender, a biker bitch with a low cut tank barely covering her chest. Fuck, I think I can see the tops of her freaking nipples which was not on my plans for tonight.

She nods at me, sliding a glass of whiskey my way and jerking her head to one of the other girls. "Just excuse the boys, your type don't come in here much and they're not really used to acting like gentlemen."

My type? Fuck me, I'm wearing booty shorts and a Vanth tee not a Chanel fucking dress.

I'm saved from saying any of this by the Boar arriving, a deep frown on his face. The bartender grimaces and steps away as if being next to me is going to make her guilty of something.

"Wolf. I wasn't expecting you."

I shrug. "I was in the neighborhood. Thought I should pop in for a chat."

He stares at me for a second, then gestures at me to follow him. I leave the glass of whiskey, happy to see more of this place. I like to know my way around places, just in case. If the Boar isn't my dad, maybe someday I'll need to get in here and take him out. Fuck, even if we are related I might slit the fucker's throat someday.

It's not like he's given a shit about me so far.

He leads me to a large meeting room with a huge table and at least fifty chairs, all hand carved out of a deep rich wood. Someone around here has some serious talent. The Boar dismisses two of his bikers and shuts the door behind them until we're alone.

"This is where we hold church; never been a woman in here for anything except cleaning. Some of the boys might take offense to that."

I roll my eyes. "They are welcome to come and voice their concerns with me. I'm not as selective with who I kill for insulting me."

He huffs out a laugh and takes a seat across from me, leaning back in the chair like he's on a fucking beach somewhere and this is all so relaxing. I'm sitting like I have an iron rod rammed up my ass, I'm that freaking tense.

We stare at each other for a moment, the silence thick but not exactly uncomfortable.

There's no point in beating around the bush, I cut straight to the point. "I want to know why you sided with the Crow."

There's a pause for a second while he eyes me like he's trying to decide if I'm worthy enough for a real answer. I try not to let my irritation show.

"You're a smart kid, what's the going theory?" he asks and I study him to try and find some sort of tell, some resemblance I've missed before but there's nothing.

I ignore his question. "Why did you say no to the Jackal?"

He grunts and scratches at his beard. "Because he's a fuckin' psycho. Something just not right in that kid's head."

I nod and say, "Why did you tell him it was a blood thing?"

He grimaces and cuts me a look, finally dropping his bullshit. "I've heard about the Crow sniffing around my bloodlines, kid, I ain't your daddy."

I should feel relief but, fuck, now we have to start at square one again. "I didn't say you were. I just don't understand why blood comes into it and I'm kind of on a time crunch here."

He frowns and turns in his chair, placing the bottle of beer down to focus entirely on me. "Why? Someone bothering you?"

I snort. "Uh, yeah. Lots of people are bothering me. The Jackal is only about a third of my overall problems, believe it or not."

"And why is asking me about blood going to help you with the rest?"

Fuck, I hate the secrecy bullshit. I hate the half-truths and twisting of words. Answering questions by asking another. I should've asked Avery to come here and do it for me.

I pull myself into the Avery Beaumont Power Pose, hoping it'll help me keep my damn head, and I make sure my voice is level as I reply, "Someone is killing people who have wronged me. Sending me their heads in fucking boxes. There's only ever been one note and it mentioned blood, the same way you did."

The Boar blinks at me.

Then he swears viciously under his breath. It's pretty clear this motherfucker knows who it is. Maybe the trip wasn't completely wasted after all.

He scrubs a hand over his face. "Look, I ain't your daddy but I know who is. He's a miserable excuse of a human and I wish to God I'd killed him when I had the chance long before you were born. He ain't the one sending you the boxes, he doesn't give a shit about any of the poor bastards he's fathered, but I know who's sending them. I'll... stop it from happening."

Two very important things stand out to me from his little speech; my father is definitely scum, and I have siblings. The Boar knows about my siblings.

I manage to find my voice, but it's no longer calm and even. I rasp out, "Don't. Just tell me who it is and give me my father's real name. Please. I'll call in a favor if I have to."

He shakes his head at me and grabs the beer bottle, draining the last of the liquid in one go. "No favors, kid. Your father is my older half-brother. He's the President of the Chaos Demons MC up in Indiana, and he's a piece of fucking shit. Don't go looking for him, he'll only find a way to break you open and sell you for parts. You have two brothers in the MC and five other bastard siblings around the country because your pop doesn't like wrapping up. He tells women a fake name so they can't come knocking for child support. I took one look at you when you showed up at the Game as a scrawny little kid and knew you were one of his. You look just fucking like... never mind. Just don't go looking. I'll back you in this fight, and any others you might have because of blood."

Seven fucking siblings?!

I need to sit down before I pass the fuck out. Wait, my ass is already planted. Sweet lord, how the fuck am I going to track them all down? Do I want to? Fuck!

The Boar gives me a wry grin. "The boys in the MC are good enough, but they're under your pop's thumb so don't bother going looking for them. Three of the bastard kids are fine. Grown up with decent moms, going to college, living white collar lives."

I clear my throat but it doesn't help. "And the other two?"

The smirk turns into a grimace. "I watch out for them, like I do for you. I do what I can."

I don't see how he's watched out for me, not really, and I scrub my face with a palm, groaning. "Why? If you hate him so much then why bother?"

The Boar leans back in his seat and glances around the room, rubbing his jaw. I study him but I still can't find any resemblance. Fuck, he's my uncle. Today couldn't get any fucking weirder.

He glances back. "I went to visit your pops years ago for something. Don't matter what it was for, but when I got there two of his biker sluts were there too, dragging kids behind them. I looked at them and... it wasn't good kid. Bad situation. But I did nothing. Not my business, not my problem. I was a stupid fucking kid myself. Three days later one of the kids was dead, the other was... worse than dead. Your pops doesn't give a shit, but I'm not that fucking evil. You look... just like our mom. She was a biker slut, switched up MCs when she'd pissed off enough of the brothers, but she was a good woman. I can't look at you and not try to fucking help."

I nod, but it's weird to hear this sort of family history. My own mom was bad enough, but to hear that my father was worse? Jesus, could I be more cliche? The kid from the slums with a million fucking siblings. I need a drink. I need a whole fucking bottle of whiskey and maybe some tequila. Fuck it, being angry and drunk is where I need to be.

"Thank you for telling me. Once I've dealt with this mess I'd like to meet... some of my siblings. Whichever ones you think I should." I say as I stand, and he nods his head while he stares at the empty bottle on the table.

"I could use your help with one of them. I think you might be able to if... yeah. I need your help too, kid."

I nod because apparently I also would do anything for blood, imagine fucking that?!

I make it to the door before I turn back to him and say, "What's your real name? What's my father's real last name?"

I can give it to Avery and she can work her magic, give me a whole fucking file on this family of mine so we will never be caught unaware again.

He scoffs at me. "Breaking all the rules tonight, little Wolf? Daniel Durack. Your pops is a Graves."

Eclipse Starbright Graves.

Nope.

Don't like that at all.

Is the whole fucking universe playing a joke on me? I'm sticking with Anderson, even if it is a fake name from a fucking asshole. Ugh.

I turn back to the door to walk out and find two of his biker men, brothers, whatever they call them, are standing in the hall and their eyes are on me.

Do they know about my blood?

"I need some fucking whiskey," I croak, and the Boar lets out a wry chuckle behind me.

"That's a blood thing too, kid. Call me if you need anything."

Nope.

I don't like that either. I bolt out of the door and into the cool Mounts Bay night air.

I drive the entire way back to Hannaford with a head full of clouds and air.

What the actual fuck has happened to my perfectly empty life? I mean, I'm happy with the family I've made, I don't need anymore showing up. This is bad, this is really fucking bad.

I park, make my way up the stairs and into my room only to find my bed full of Harley, Ash lounging on Avery's bed, and Blaise sprawled out on the floor. I think about bitching them out for taking over my space but I decide to leave that for later, when I don't feel like my whole fucking life has been a lie. Oh, there it is; the Blaise Morrison Pity Party has just taken ahold of me and I'm going to need to start drinking before I throw a freaking tantrum.

"I need whiskey. I'm freaking the fuck out and I need to drink my body weight in, like, an expensive aged whiskey that will get me wasted super fucking quick," I say, and they all look up at me.

Avery stands from where she was sitting at the table doing homework and comes over to me, but it's Blaise who speaks first.

"So, do we have to explain ourselves to your daddy? Tell him about our intentions?"

Sweet merciful lord.

I could fucking swoon at the thought of any of them speaking to my biker pops.

"Alcohol, Avery. Non-negotiable. 911. We have entered an emergency state." I could go on but she grabs my wrist and looks at me, all concerned and shit, and I feel light-headed.

"You need to breathe, whatever you found out can't be that bad. Do you want ice cream too?"

"Fuck ice cream."

Avery's eyes widen as she nods and she cuts Blaise a severe look. "No more jokes."

He grumbles at her but he's sitting up to get a better look at me and frowning. I stumble over to my bed and half collapse on it, my skin crawling with extra energy like I need to run a fucking marathon to get it out.

Harley gets up and snags some whiskey from fuck-knows-where and I crack it open to take long, deep gulps straight from the bottle.

I know I'm panicking for no real reason but I've been alone for so long. No family, no one who gives a shit, I've only had myself to deal with. Now I have my family, my real family, and it's hard fucking work keeping us all happy and alive. To find out I have siblings is too much. A father. A fucking uncle who's been looking out for me... though I don't know what the hell he's been doing for me. It's not like he got me away from the Jackal.

"Can you tell me anything before you drink yourself into an oblivion?" Avery murmurs, and sits down next to me on the bed. I can't look at her, or the guys, and the whiskey is already heading straight to my brain. Fuck it.

"My dad's a piece of shit. I have seven brothers and sisters. The Boar is my uncle. He knows who's sending the boxes and said he'd get it to stop. My family is as trailer trash as fucking possible and now I have a whole list of people I'm related to and responsible for and I need another fucking drink, Aves. I can't. I just fucking can't."

There's a minute of stunned silence and then Ash grabs the bottle from me. "Let's get you a glass so we do this properly. Morrison, find me the bourbon, Mounty can't drink alone. That's just pathetic."

Everyday life at Hannaford starts to become suffocating.

My skin is already crawling with the news of my biker dad, but with the extra men the Crow stations at the school, there isn't a second of the day that doesn't have the oppressive feel that his fortress does and I can't fucking stand it. My entire life I have survived by being unseen, by being the underestimated unnoticed little girl in the room, and now there isn't a person in the entire fucking building who isn't aware of me. It goes beyond my earlier years as the Mounty scholarship student. It goes so far beyond the fucking bet when everyone wanted a piece of me. The students all watch me with fear. The Crow's men all watch me with calculating eyes.

Harley sits beside me at breakfast and hooks an ankle around mine under the table as we eat. His phone buzzes and he checks it with a grimace. "That's Aodhan, he's fucking persistent. He's keeping me updated on what's going on in the Bay. The streets are so fucking bad now that even the locals won't go out at night."

I grimace. "The Coyote has sent me some footage. The Jackal has gone fucking insane."

Harley nods, and glances around the room. We've come down to breakfast by ourselves, the others still tucked up in their beds this early on a Sunday morning. Harley had gotten up early for his swim practice and I'd texted him to meet up for food once it had finished. I didn't want to wake Avery by fixing something to eat after the week she's had, and it's nice to get some one-on-one time with my golden god of a boyfriend.

"We've gotta do something about him. We can't let this go on forever," Harley grumbles, stabbing at his eggs viciously.

I shrug. "It's not like we can do anything about it right now. Illi is already on top of everything and we're no good to him right now. We have to finish school, we have to keep up the pretense of being normal teenagers, especially now Senior has the pigs interfering with our lives. The Jackal is keeping his head down for now so we will too."

Harley grumps. "Why can't we just send my uncle in to shoot the psycho fucker?"

I snort. "Well, if I thought that would work I would have sent him in. The problem is the Jackal is smart enough to know Diarmuid is on our side now, so he's smart enough to know not to put himself out in public without the right sort of protection. None of his plans will be documented, no one will know anything about his movements, he'll have a full security detail, the whole fucking nine yards. I'm not going to underestimate him. The Crow might be cocky enough to give it a try, he might think that they can send in a spy to end this, but I know it isn't gonna work."

Harley quirks an eyebrow at me. "He got Luca in, didn't he?"

My eyes drift over to the man in question. He's just arrived at the dining hall, wearing workout shorts and a black tank so looking nothing like a teacher should, and he's filling a plate up. My mouth automatically quirks into a smile but I smother that shit so fucking quick when Harley gives me a foul lock.

"What? I can't help it. We've been friends for too long."

He nudges me gently with an elbow. "Friends? He calls you 'Princess' and talks about your ass a little bit too much to be a friend."

I roll my eyes at him. "You used to talk about my tits!"

Harley wipes his mouth with a napkin and throws it down onto his plate, a freaking sexy smirk on his face. "Yeah and I wanted to own every fucking inch of you. You're not helping your argument here, babe."

I roll my eyes again. "Just because you're obsessed with my ass doesn't mean everyone else is. I mean it's not that great. Fuck, can we stick to the topic? We're supposed to be talking about how Mounts Bay has gone to fucking shit, which is saying something considering it was already pretty fucking bad in the first place."

Harley slings an arm over the back of my chair and pulls me in as close as he can. Luca walks past us and gives me a cheeky grin, dipping his head in my direction in a respectful nature. Harley growls under his breath and I do my best to look innocent as I nod back at him.

"Fucking flirting babe."

Chapter Twenty-Three

By Monday morning the school is writhing with gossip again and, while I don't pay much attention to that shit unless it's about my family, Avery is buzzing with excitement over it by the time we make it to our first class.

She leans against my desk with a grin. "Imogen was expelled. She went to Luca about you breaking her arm and he expelled her for bullying. Oh, and lying about you hurting her. He told her mom to seek therapy for her compulsive need to lie."

She's loud enough that the students around us all hear it and see it as the warning it is; we're untouchable, don't fuck with our family.

The grin I give back to her must look deranged but fuck if I care. Harley smirks and slings a casual arm across the back of my chair, looking around the classroom like a haughty asshole. I love it.

We get through our classes for the day which are mostly pop quizzes and tests so Blaise is a freaking morose dick and the other two are at each other's throats with their competitive bullshit. Avery floats around the school like she's the fucking Queen and I love it.

I study with Blaise while everyone else is at their extracurriculars. We spread out on the floor in front of the TV on cushions with pizza, like the first time we'd studied alone.

Blaise smirks at the little happy grins I give him. "You're such a fucking sap, Star. You're so in fucking love with me."

Dammit. "Like you're not over your fucking heels for me too. Stop trying to distract me, we're finishing this assignment tonight so we can take the weekend off."

Blaise rolls his eyes and tugs me into his lap, rocking his hips into mine until I can't focus on any-damn-thing. "Say it, Star. Tell me you love me."

I feel so fucking weird about it, the words so raw and revealing coming out of me at him. "Ugh. Fine. I love you, Blaise Morrison."

He gives me a look and I sigh at him. "Fine. I fell for the idea of you when I was listening to your lyrics while I was going through hell. Then I met you and found out the real you was even fucking better. I don't say it easily but… I do love you."

He grins at me. "I know you do, Star, you prove it every fucking day you protect us all. It's just nice to hear it sometimes too."

Ugh, why is he being so sweet today? I wrap my arms around his neck and draw him into a kiss, fuck the assignment. He groans and nips at my lips, his hands trailing up my ribs and under my shirt until he's palming my tits.

"You've been fucking teasing me all night with these, not wearing a bra. I knew all I had to do was get you in my lap and then I'd get to spread you out on this floor and fuck you until you're screaming for me."

Whelp. Yes please. I rock my hips and grind down onto his dick. "Maybe we should go to your room, so Avery doesn't get back and stab you for this."

He bites my shoulder. "Maybe we should defile her bed again."

My hips falter and I give him a glare. "What the fuck is with you and her bed?"

He laughs and pushes me up so he can stand and haul me into his arms again. "Well, when she's bitching me out for shit it's nice to remember how tight your pussy was around my dick when I fucked you on her bed."

Ok, we did not fuck on her bed. My hands might have been braced against it, but at no point did our naked bodies touch it. I feel a little woozy at the very thought of Avery finding out about it.

"Take me to your room and fuck me. We can do it on Harley's bed if you're so set on pissing someone off tonight."

He laughs and walks us out into the hall and through to the guys' room. I tuck my head into his neck so I don't have to see any of the other students who may be lurking but Blaise doesn't even bother to look.

He kicks the door shut behind us and flicks the lock, holding me tight against his body with one arm under my ass.

"I'm glad all my extra food hasn't stopped you from being able to haul me around everywhere," I murmur at him, wriggling a little against his chest.

"You're fucking tiny, Star. If anything, we should feed you more. Fuck, your tits are amazing as it is, if they get any bigger I'm going to give up on school and music, just stay locked up at the ranch titty fucking you at all hours of the day."

That doesn't make any damn sense. "Just shut up and stick your dick in me, Morrison. You've officially fucking lost your damn mind."

He cackles at me and slings me down on Harley's bed, the dick. Then I watch as he strips off. Fuck, the sight of him still has me drooling, all colorful ink and long, muscular limbs. Ugh. It's just unfair for him to be so hot, like how am I supposed to be a functioning human when he looks at me like that with that face on that body? Rude. Just plain rude.

"Well? Are you going to stare, Star, or are you going to get your fucking clothes off?"

I throw my panties at his face, laughing when he catches them and throws them on his bed. "Don't fucking steal them! I barely have enough as it is!"

He crawls up my body, kissing and running his tongue along my skin as he goes. "You better not have some guy stealing them again. I'll be the first to kill him for you."

I snort but it comes out all weird and moan-like. "Yeah, the guys stealing it are you and Ash. Is it some fucking kink I should know about?"

He drops down so he's covering me, his dick rubbing against my thigh and I wriggle until he's lined up with my pussy. I'm not like clawing-at-his-back desperate yet but it won't take much to get me there.

He grins down at me, kissing me slow and deep, like there's no rush at all. I mean, there's not but I'd kind of like his dick in me now. Like now.

The fucker laughs at me. "I love that you never get sick of this, you're always fucking desperate for me."

I grunt at him. "What part of 'stick your dick in me' has you confused, Morrison?"

He smirks at me, all dark and devilish, and slides two fingers in me, hooking them and rubbing at my G spot. He rolls until we're on our sides and he has both hands free.

He hooks his hand behind my leg and yanks it up over his hip for better access and then pulls his fingers out to run them through my dripping pussy, spreading my arousal around until he can slip a finger into my ass.

I grunt, because these guys keep catching me unaware with their wandering fingers, but I don't say a goddamn word. Ash has well and truly taught me that I love this.

Blaise smirks at me, all cocky pride, and I try not to blush and snark back at him. "Ash told me all about your night, Star. Did you love it as much as he said you did? Did you love Ash's dick filling you up here and Harley's fingers in this pussy? Maybe I should call one of them, get them to come help keep you nice and full."

I gasp out moaning and rocking against him, his dick sliding against my soaking pussy and rubbing on my clit. I can't think straight. I don't even fucking want to anymore, I'd rather stay in this hazing, lusty state where none of our problems matter anymore.

The door unlocks but I'm so fucking lost in Blaise's lips I barely acknowledge the sound. I don't know if it's Ash or Harley, but we're past the point of me caring. I know they all want me, I know none of them care about sharing, and Blaise's words have sunk into my brain now.

I want them to fill me up.

"Fuck Mounty, I'm glad I left training early," Ash drawls, and I shiver.

I moan into Blaise's lips and he breaks away. "I was just about to call you, man. Get the fuck over here."

Then he kisses me again, his hand sliding into my hair and fisting so I can't move away. I want to watch Ash strip, there's nothing fucking better than seeing them get naked for me, but the firm dominance of Blaise's grip is such a fucking turn-on. I get so lost in his kiss that I startle when Ash presses in behind me, like a fucking wall of turned on Beaumont. Ugh. So freaking hot.

Ash bites my shoulder and runs his hands down my back unit he gets to my ass, spreading my cheeks wide. I break away from Blaise's kiss to glance back at him, his eyes glued to where Blaise's fingers are pumping in at out of my ass.

Ash smirks at me. "Turn over, Mounty, looks like Morrison has staked his claim."

Blaise laughs and helps move me around, reaching back to grab lube. "I've definitely called dibs. No more waiting until I pass out for the group sex, Star."

Ash doesn't snark along with him, his eyes are fixed on my tits as I get an eyeful of him as well. He's all flushed and clean from his shower after his track practice. I don't know how the fuck he looks so good right after he's run for miles, it's like he's fucking blessed or something. Inhuman. A fucking god.

They both also work together a little too well, stroking and touching me, and the cogs start turning in my brain.

"Have you done this before?" I don't want to know, not really, but the curiosity claws at my gut.

Ash's hand slides up to my throat as he kisses me. "Not like this. I've never wanted to like this."

"And now?" I whisper, out of breath entirely.

"I want everything with you."

He pulls away from me and slides down my body, biting my hips until I gasp. Blaise chuckles in my ear, pushing me until I'm flat on my back and Ash is flicking my clit with his tongue, then moving down to slide his tongue inside me. Holy fuck, I'll never get used to this feeling.

"This will be easier if you've already come, Star," he murmurs against my neck, sucking and kissing me there so I'll be marked up for the whole damn world to see. Fuck, I can't find it in myself to give a damn.

He sucks at my nipples, biting softly and groaning when I gasp, but I can't figure out where to focus my attention when Ash is eating me out like I'm his last freaking meal on Earth. I'm shaking and crying out, nearly fucking screaming when I finally come, grinding on his face like somehow I'll be able to get closer to him. His eyes are dark and hooded as he pushes up to kiss me, sharing the taste of me between our lips. Blaise grabs my chin and turns me so he can chase the taste. My whole body shudders.

Ash rolls and pulls me onto his chest, grunting as I slide myself down onto his fucking perfect cock, letting him fill me up. I give myself a second to breathe before I lean down and kiss him, rocking my hips to meet his own thrusts.

I feel Blaise kneel on the bed behind me, his hand running over my ass as he slicks his dick up with the lube. The synthetic smell of cherries hits me, the smug dickhead, but before I can think of something to snap at him he pushes in.

Well, holy sweet lord fuck.

Just. Seriously. Fuck.

"Look at that face. Mounty, have you died and gone to heaven? I can feel you dripping down my cock, you fucking love it," Ash drawls out, and Blaise's hips begin to move and fuck yes, I have gone to heaven. I can't think, they're touching every single part of me, rubbing and grinding and pushing, and my body just fucking overloads with lust. It's fucking perfect.

Ash catches my throat with his hand and pulls me down to a biting kiss, his other hand gripping my hip and grinds his dick into me. Blaise has a little more movement and he holds my other hip, pumping away like he has something to prove.

I gasp and clench down on them both as I come again, screaming against Ash's lips as he tries to swallow the sound. He's trying to fucking consume me.

Blaise's hips stutter to a halt as he groans, long and low, and pulls out to come all over my ass.

The second Blaise pulls away Ash flips me over onto my back, hooking my knees up and spreading me open to him, pounding into me until I think we're going to break the damn bed but it feels fucking incredible and I'm gasping as my body slams into another orgasm. I think I must blackout for a second because the next thing I know Ash is grunting and biting my lips as he comes, absolute fucking perfection.

These boys are going to fucking kill me but I'd die every damn day with a smile for them.

Ash drags me into the shower with him, holding me up when my jello legs try to give out. He's full of slow touches and murmured praises, and I just soak it the fuck up.

I jump out and leave him in there to finish up, he's been too focussed on me to clean himself off, when my phone rings. I frown and fumble around to answer it, pulling a sports bra over my head.

"I'm outside your door, come open up for me," Illi grumbles and I frown at the weird tone he's using.

I throw a shirt and yoga pants on, ignoring Ash's pissy comments about our shower being interrupted. "Why didn't you just knock? Blaise is here too, he'd let you in."

He grunts and gasps a little. "Ok, fuck, don't freak out but I've been... stabbed a little."

I blanch, and scramble to get to the door, flinging it open without really considering if that's a good idea. It's not, because Illi was leaning on it and he falls forward. As soon as his weight hits me my bad leg buckles and we both go over.

Blaise shouts loud enough as he lurches towards us that Ash hears him and comes running out of the bathroom, a towel clutched around his waist. He curses viciously at Illi until I manage to roll the Butcher off of me and he catches sight of all of the blood.

"What the fuck happened?" he snarls, and I frantically start searching Illi for exactly where he's been stabbed.

He barely has the energy to reply to Ash, and his voice is thready when he says, "Let the record show, I can take on fourteen of Matteo's best men and walk out alive. That psycho fuck needs to train his people better. It was like fighting drunk toddlers. One of them got lucky, it was a cheap shot that somehow managed to land."

I scoff at him, and rip my shirt off to pack into his wound. I speak without thinking, "What the fuck did they stab you with, a fucking sword? It looks like they twisted it."

Avery bursts through the door. She gets one look at Illi and chokes on her gag reflex, but her voice is strong down the phone as she calls for a doctor. I'm so fucking glad she's here; I need someone who's got contacts and a clear head because all I can think about is the fact I can see Illi's intestines. Fuck.

"Why didn't you go to Doc? I could've come down and had your back, fuck school," I croak and when he chuckles it's all gurgling and wet sounding.

"Doc's dead kid. The Jackal is cleaning house. Everyone who likes you is out, and Doc fucking loved you. There aren't gonna be friendly faces left in the Bay for us soon."

Tears start but I ignore them. They won't help hold Illi's guts in.

"It's not that bad, babe," I startle, and Harley's big hands gently pry mine away, taking their place. "Go wash up, Avery's doctor isn't too far away. We'll get him fixed."

I stare at him for a second and then nod. It's going to be fine.

It fucking has to be.

Avery's doctor arrives before I leave to wash the blood away from my hands. I only go because Ash and Harley insist, and Blaise comes with me to force me back into the shower. The sports bra and yoga pants are ruined, I had no idea I was so completely covered in Illi's blood.

Fuck.

It must have been fucking close to hitting something life threatening. I try not to panic as I scrub. Everything is fine. Maybe if I keep saying it to myself, it'll come true.

Six hours and one very competent but nervous doctor later, Illi is tucked into the roll out bed and snarling about taking the pain meds. He'd refused to be knocked out while he'd been sewn back together, but thankfully he'd passed out a few times. It made the whole thing much more bearable for me.

Once the doctor has been paid, from my pocket much to Avery and Ash's annoyance, and escorted out, Illi tries to get out of the bed and I prepare myself for a fight. I don't want to have to fight him while he's injured like that but I will.

"Odie's at a safe house but I'm not fucking leaving her there after Matteo's shown just how far he's willing to go to take us out," he snarls at me, and I plant my feet, hands on my hips, and stare the fucker down. He's not fucking moving.

Ash snaps at him, clearly pissy at the tone Illi's using, "Where is she? I'll bring her here. No one will get past us all."

Illi grunts and seals his mouth shut until I think about upper-cutting him. Stubborn dick. Finally, after they've glared at each other for a good minute, Illi grunts an address at him then snaps, "If you let anything fucking touch her—"

Ash cuts him off. "I'm not going to promise you anything, I'm going to state a fucking fact. She will be here in under an hour, untouched and only worrying about you. While I'm gone, refrain from speaking to Lips like you just did or I'll choke the fucking life out of you."

Then he grabs his car keys, jerks his head at Blaise, and they walk out together. I'm kind of a puddle but I manage to contain my swooning. Illi's eyes stay glued to the door for a second then he grunts at me, "He's a good kid. Make sure you keep that one."

Harley grunts at him from where he's helping Avery mop up the gore from the floor and walls. "She's keeping us all, this isn't a fucking competition. It's not a trial to see which one of us is the best fit."

I scoff at them both and say, "They're all a good fit. I'll have them until they're sick of me."

Illi grunts and grinds his teeth as he settles back in the bed to get comfortable. "I look forward to being the joint best man at your weird-ass wedding."

Chapter Twenty-Four

A blood-soaked crime scene makes the news.

Avery pulls faces the entire way through but watches the coverage with eagle eyes, scouring it for clues and tip-offs. I watch just enough to know that Illi isn't going to be hauled in for questioning and then I get my focus back on my old friend. He's a grumpy fuck when he's injured and worried about Odie.

My phone rings while I'm trying to talk him into taking the drugs Avery's doctor left behind.

"Is it possible for your deranged friend to keep a low profile? We already have enough work on our hands now the Jackal and Senior have made this a media play-off."

I grit my teeth at the Crow's tone. "Why are you trying to get on my shit list, Atticus?"

Avery's head snaps around and her eyes flare as they catch mine.

"His DNA was everywhere. The Coyote will be up for days wiping it all from the police files."

I roll my eyes. "Tell Jackson I'll triple his fee as an apology. Tell him I'll use one of my favors."

I hear his teeth grind. "Wolf, there's a protocol—"

I cut him the fuck off. "No, there's no fucking protocol left because the Twelve is in a fucking mess. You should have killed him when you had the chance! Now he's just had Illi gutted. Yep, I just had to help hold my brother's fucking guts in until the doctor got here! Oh, and we had to call someone new because our usual doc is dead, killed by the Jackal for being my friend. No. No, I'm done with the protocol of the Twelve. Either you're my family or you're not. That's the fucking line."

I hang up on him.

My hands have a fine tremble to them, I mean, I've just cussed out our biggest ally and someone who is probably in the top ten most powerful men in the country but fuck, I'm so fucking done.

Avery gives me a tiny smile, full of worry and respect, and my phone buzzes again. I take a deep breath before I look down.

Ignore the cold-hearted asshole. You're right. Can me and Vi be part of your fambam?

Lord help me.

I'll take it to the vote. You might want to quit calling Avery the hottie though, Ash will beat the life right out of you.

I tuck the phone back into my pocket as Harley walks over to me with a coffee, catching my fingers in his and tugging me over to the couch. I take the coffee, gulping it down to get me through this all-nighter. Harley slumps down next to me, tucking me under his arm and kissing the top of my head.

"Did you just tell Atticus to go fuck himself?" he murmurs into my hair, and I nod.

"Jackson and Viola want in, too. We need to vote about it once the others are back and Illi is… conscious," I say, and the stubborn dick himself scoffs at me.

"I'm not fucking sleeping until Odie is here," he rasps, and I wince. He sounds fucking awful.

Then, thank the fucking universe, the sound of the door unlocking is as loud as a gunshot through the silence of the room. Odie bursts in, frantic and terrified, and the stream of French pouring out of her is almost too rapid for me to pick up, and I've been fluent for years. The grimace on Illi's face is a sure sign she's tearing him a new asshole for getting hurt. Good. I don't want to think about how badly he was injured, I'll never freaking sleep again.

"I'm fine, baby girl, I'm fine," he says, holding a hand out to her and the glare she gives him would melt skin off of most men.

"You are very fucking clearly not fine, *mon monstre*! Ash said you needed surgery, that's not fine!" Her voice gets higher and higher as she goes on, pouring salt on all of his wounds.

Blaise slumps down on the cushions on the floor and Ash sits with Avery, rubbing a hand over his face.

"Did you have to tell her about the surgery?" Illi grunts out, talking over Odie who is cussing him out something fierce as she looks at his bandages.

Ash's hand drops and he gives Illi a savage, poisonous smile. "Payback. Don't ever be a dick to Lips again. You're lucky you've lost too much blood or I'd wipe the floor with you."

Illi huffs and tries to coax Odie onto the pullout with him but she's pissed, all the fear and terror solidifying into pure rage at her husband for daring to be stabbed.

It's fairly amusing.

"I'm glad you didn't cuss me out like that for nearly dying." Harley says, his eyes on the spectacle.

I snort. "I would've if you'd been awake when I got to you. Your extended nap saved your ass."

I wait until the next afternoon, after we all survive our classes without sleep, before I pull Odie aside and tell her they should stay until Illi has healed up enough to pee standing without passing out. She agrees completely and then spends the rest of the night arguing with Illi over it.

We all eat dinner together and watch it unfold.

"They must have the best angry, hate sex," Avery says, and Ash cuts her a dirty look.

Blaise roars with laughter, as much as he can when he looks so fucking exhausted that he might drop dead at any second. The poor little rich kid. "She's a fucking badass for climbing into bed with the Butcher as it is, throwing hate sex in there means she's got balls of steel."

Harley scoffs and knocks back a beer. "I wouldn't be talking about her balls within Illi's earshot. He's not going to be an invalid for long."

After dinner, we all split up between the rooms for the night and I sleep like the dead tucked between Harley and Blaise in the boy's room, lulled to a dreamless sleep by the sounds of my family surrounding me.

I wake to Avery next door in our room making French toast, pancakes, oatmeal, piles of bacon and eggs, enough food to feed an army of teenage boys, not just the three we have taking up space around us. I flick the coffee machine on and fix us both a cup each without saying a word. If Avery needs to cook out her feelings, then who am I to judge?

"You're right, none of this would have happened if we'd have killed the Jackal when he came to Hannaford last year," she murmurs, and I shrug.

"We didn't have enough people on our side at that point. I was just saying that to him because I'm angry about it all and I hate how much shit Illi gets. He's a good guy."

Avery nods and sips her coffee, stirring at a mountain of eggs like this is all completely normal. "He's the best. I don't need to know the whole story to agree with you, your word is enough for me. Plus, he's done everything for our family. I'm glad you told Atticus to fuck off."

She still looks conflicted, so I start moving the food to the table for her. "So what's eating you? He's alive, we're all safe enough here, we're... closer to having a plan for the Jackal."

She chews her lip and fusses with the plates as I grab them. Her eyes flit over to Ash's sleeping form, tucked up in my bed alone, and she says, "I'm just having an off day."

Fucking Atticus Crawford.

After a raucous and filling breakfast Harley and I help Odie force some painkillers into Illi and he passes out again. His wound looks good, not inflamed or weeping, so I start to think maybe we're out of danger with it. The thought of how many infections he could have caught between the alleyway in the Bay and the boys' room here at Hannaford is fucking mind-numbingly terrifying. Obviously, the antibiotics Avery's doctor has mainlined into him is doing wonders.

It's a Saturday morning, so Harley and Ash head out to their extracurriculars and Blaise skips out on boxing so he can sprawl out in front of the TV with his lyric book and guitar. I stay at the dining room table to help Avery with her homework because I don't need Odie seeing me turn into a puddle over his music.

Odie joins us, flicking through the textbooks and murmuring in French about the shortcomings of the education system here. I smile at her, used to her ramblings and grumpy attitude. There's never a time where she's mellow about shit when her husband is injured.

"I'm bored," she says with a sigh.

Avery's eyes flick up from her phone and she shrugs. "How are you at planning world domination? That's what Lips and I usually do when we're bored. I'm sure you'll have some insight, what with your upbringing and your life with the Butcher."

I flinch. Odie hates Illi's nickname just as much as I do, we both see the man behind the reputation, and when we're not around other people she refuses to acknowledge that name for him. I sigh in relief when she doesn't react to it at all.

Instead, Odie smiles sweetly, always a sign of her devious mind at work.

"World domination should always start by taking out the weak men and finding a strong one to stand by your side. Or three if you are le Loup."

Avery smirks, then her eyes flick to where Blaise is sprawled out in front of the TV. He's messing around on his guitar, not taking notice of us at all, but Avery doesn't ever talk about guys in front of… the guys.

Odie's eyes follow Avery's and she switches to French. "Are you in love with this man, the Crow?"

Blaise glances up at us with a frown, but I just smile sweetly at him. He frowns harder because, seriously, when do I ever smile sweetly?

Avery pulls a face. "I was in love with a man who doesn't exist, I was in love with the idea of who I thought Atticus Crawford was. Lips and I have gone through this so many times. I think I should just stay away from men."

I sit back in my chair to watch them both go through this. I feel like I'm about to get a master class at girl talk, because Odie and Avery are so much better at this than I will ever be.

Odie shrugs. "What are the differences between the man you thought he was and the man that he is, are they so different that you do not love him anymore?"

Avery sighs and flicks the page in her own copy of Vogue. "The Crow is much better suited to me. It's the lying I can't get past. It doesn't matter that he was doing it for me, it matters that he was doing it in the first place."

Odie nods. "I get that. How do you know he's not going to lie again?"

"Exactly. If he was willing to do this and tell himself it was for my own good what's to stop him from doing worse? The world we live in is never going to be safe. I can't be questioning whether or not he's lying to me every time something happens."

Ouch. Sucks to be the Crow today. I ask, "So you're voting no? Because I was only voting yes for you."

Avery rolls her eyes. "Why do we have to vote right now? Can't we leave it open until I figure out what the hell I'm going to do?"

Odie leans back in her chair. "So there's a chance that you'll change your mind? There's a chance he can prove himself to you?"

Avery groans and covers her face with her hands. "I hate how pathetic he makes me feel. I would skin any other man for treating me like this and making me feel like some pathetic little girl. I fucking hate it."

Even in French the swearing sounds weird coming out of her mouth. "We don't have to decide now. We do need to vote about Jackson and Viola though."

Odie points out an outfit to Avery and I watch as they giggle over it together. "We need to get you out and about on dates as soon as this war is over. Johnny has quite a few friends I could set you up with."

I shake my head vehemently. "I've met his friends and there is no fucking chance she is dating any of them."

Odie giggles. "Now now le Loup, you can't judge a man by the worst thing he's done."

I pull a face at her. "Yes, I can."

She giggles and shrugs, and we all fall silent again for a few minutes. I get back to critiquing Avery's history assignment while they flip through their magazines.

"I love him," Avery whispers, Odie nods with a little smile.

"I know. Let's get it out and in the air. Talk it out so we can figure out how to get him under your thumb. Men can be stupid sometimes."

I blink. Avery just let it out there without any extra prodding, Odie is a freaking wizard. Fuck, maybe I should take notes?

"I don't take failure well. I don't like things being out of place." Avery stops and takes a deep breath, her eyes catching mine before she continues, "My father used to beat Ash if I failed at things. I get the sense of death in the air when things don't follow my plan. Atticus has always followed his own path, but I always thought I could trust him. Him lying to me about being the Crow… it was too much. I've always trusted him and told him everything. He's lied to me from the very beginning. I can't help but be angry at him."

Odie shrugs. "That's fair. He deserves some hell for that. Do you understand why he's doing it though?"

Avery rolls her eyes. "I have eyes, I know he's doing it to protect me. The problem is… this is our world. This is how we live, and that is never going to change. Even after we kill the Jackal and Senior, someone else will take their place. Either he trusts me to be strong enough to deal with this or he doesn't. We're doomed."

My chest aches at the tone she's using. She sounds so fucking… resigned. Bleak. Unlike herself, that I want to change my fucking vote.

She's right though, there's never going to be a time in our lives where we're not being stalked by monsters. I'm always going to be the Wolf, he'll always be the Crow, and she will always be a Beaumont.

We can't change that.

"Maybe you need to take a step back. Let le Loup take care of the Crow, let her take the weight of his anger and misguided care."

I nod. "I can do that, Aves. We can do that. Just give yourself some time to figure out how you're going to get him on his knees for you."

A week later, Illi finally wins the argument and they both pack up to leave. I secured a safe house for them that was picked out by Avery, security set up and monitored by the Coyote, and only members of our family know where it is.

We voted Jackson and Viola in, unanimous though Illi is still a little pissy about it. The Crow is still out.

"Thanks for letting us crash here kid," Illi says, flinging his arm around my shoulders and squeezing me in a weird side hug.

I shrug. "Anytime."

Ash rolls out of my bed and stalks past us, stealing my cup of coffee on the way through. "She says anytime but what she really means is upgrade your security so we never have to do this again. Being jammed in here all together like this has given me hives."

I roll my eyes at him. Jammed in? There's three times the amount of space in one of these rooms as what our group home had and we shared with eleven other kids.

Fucking rich kids.

Odie smiles at Ash like he's her best friend, and my heart does this weird little clench over it. Everything that is happening is bringing us closer together as a family, so as long as we survive it, it's all worth it. I will tell myself that every damn day until this war is over.

Illi grunts at him, throwing an arm around Odie's shoulders and tucking her firmly into his side. "Alright, you grumpy asshole, we'll get out of your hair before your blue balls fucking kill you. Horny teenage boys; I don't know how you fucking keep up with them, kid."

I will not blush. I'm a killer, *dammit.* "It's not so bad. One of them is usually a grumpy dick and tantruming so it makes it a little easier on the… scheduling."

Illi roars with laughter, fucking quakes with it, and whispers loudly into Odie's ear, "Three guesses which one is the grumpy dick, baby girl."

Chapter Twenty-Five

After Illi's stabbing we decide to stay at Hannaford for spring break where the Crow's men will be walking the grounds and watching the security cameras around the clock.

I spend the time pouring over the plans I've drawn up of the Jackal's fortress, talking Avery through the best ways in and out, provided he hasn't taken a fucking jackhammer to the walls in an effort to keep me out. Now that Illi has had to slow down his protection of us until his guts are less… perforated, the death toll in the Bay is only getting worse.

Avery stays true to her word and stops speaking to Atticus, leaving all of the planning and liaising to me. I quickly decide that I owe that girl another blood diamond because within days I'm ready to smash my phone and never replace the fucking thing.

I also grit my teeth the second I see Atticus' phone number because it's always him calling.

"You can't induct another member of the Twelve. That's not how the institution works," he snaps, and I seriously consider stabbing my fork into my own eyeballs to get out of this conversation. Ash steals my coffee, the dick, and slips his hand onto my thigh, his fingers stroking and petting.

"Yeah, I know. I'm not inducting him, he just joined the family. It means he's one of us."

Atticus huffs down the line at me and I start to count in French to stay calm. "He's just gotten a Wolf insignia tattoo. Viola got one too. They both wear your mark now and that's not how things are done, Wolf."

Well, fuck. "I didn't ask him to do that. If you have a problem with it, talk to him. Just know, if you start shit with Jackson, we side with him."

He hangs up on me. Grumpy fuck.

Ash squeezes my thigh. "We should go take a shower."

Harley huffs and rolls his eyes from where he's sitting at the other end of the table. "Avery will stab you for trying."

I glance over my shoulder to where Avery is doing yoga in front of the TV. It's been a part of her detox and she's trying to focus on her dance more, to find her joy or some shit. I dunno, I just want her to be happy so I'm all about it.

"Good thing you're going to stay here and keep her nice and distracted for us."

Harley quirks an eyebrow. "And why the fuck would I do that?"

Ash smirks at him as his fingers drifts up until they're stroking me through my shorts. I flush and Harley's eyes flare.

"You keep Avery busy and I'll sleep in here with her tonight so you can have our room to yourself. I'll even talk Morrison into sleeping here as well, I'll suffer through some bullshit movie for you."

His fingers are fucking sinful. Without meaning to, my hips start to rock against them but I catch myself and snap my legs shut, glancing back at Avery who hasn't noticed, thank fuck.

Harley stares at me for a second longer, then he stands to stalk into the kitchen for beer and snacks. "Fine. But you better get Morrison on board."

Ash drags me into the bathroom with him and I follow him like a lost fucking puppy. He strips me off, biting his lip at the tiny scraps of lace covering me, a set he'd given me for Christmas that I haven't worn for him yet. I fucking preen under his gaze.

He tears his own clothes off without a care and I drop to my knees the second his pants hit the floor. I lick my way up his dick, slowly sucking on the head and looking up at Ash in a way I know sends him insane, and he doesn't disappoint.

"You look so fucking good down there, Mounty." He groans, fisting his hand in my hair to hold me still so he can fuck my mouth. It's taken me a minute to work up to this but now I can swallow around his dick like it's my favorite fucking treat at the drop of a hat.

You'd think this was degrading, him using me like this, but the adoration in his eyes as he watches me is the best compliment and, when he pulls out to tug me to my feet, his kiss is intoxicating, his own type of worship that's so different to the other two but just as fucking complete.

The bathroom door opens and Blaise stomps in, looking grumpy and tired. I glance over at him and Ash runs a hand down my spine, cupping my ass possessively.

"You getting in or not?" he grunts at Blaise, flicking open the shower door and lifting me in. I get my hand around his dick and slowly pump, hating that he's stopped me from making him come. I'm sure he has other plans but fuck it, I'm pouting.

Blaise watches us both as he strips off, his eyes flaring as Ash positions me exactly how he wants me, tugging at my body and slapping my ass once I arch my back for him.

He slides in and I could die, it feels that good. My skin heats as Blaise's eyes stay fixed on me, watching my body move as Ash's hips start to grind against my ass, like he doesn't really want to pull away. I moan, low and throaty, as he gets his phone out and takes a photo. I should snap at him, be fucking pissed off he's leaving evidence someone like the Coyote could easily find, but right now I think I'd let him do anything just so long as he keeps watching me.

He hops up on the bathroom counter and fists his own dick, pumping it and groaning. Oh sweet merciful lord, I could die.

The bathroom door bangs loudly on the wall as Harley stomps in, dragging Blaise off of the sink and shoving him out of the room, nakedness be damned.

"What the fuck——"

"You know what, dickhead. Go walk Avery to ballet."

Then Harley throws a pile of clothes at him and slams the door, ignoring the vicious curses my rock god throws at him and the equally enraged snarling from

Avery.

Ash scoffs against the skin of my neck, his hips still pumping into me, so full I can't fucking breathe. I didn't think it was possible to feel more than what I am with Ash buried inside me, but when he pushes me forward, bending me so my hands are braced against the glass and he can hold my hips to move faster, I watch Harley slowly strip off and the fierce need in his eyes sets my body alight until I'm coming, squeezing like a vice on Ash's fucking huge cock.

Ash grunts like he's dying, and says, "Get the fuck in here before she makes me blow too fast. I want to watch her take us both."

I shiver all over, the aftershocks of the orgasm rippling through me are nothing compared to the excitement of having them both at once.

Harley's eyes track the shiver, the goosebumps, the gushing between my legs and around Ash's cock, and the fire in his eyes only burns hotter. He steps into the shower and grips the back of my neck with one big hand to pull my face up to meet his kiss. Ash releases his death-grip on my hips and pulls out, while I whimper pathetically at the loss of his perfect cock.

"Shh, babe, we'll fix it. We'll give you what you need," Harley breathes in between his long and lingering kisses, deep and consuming.

He turns me around, shifting and lifting and tugging, until I'm held between them both, Ash plunging back into my pussy while Harley is lining up to take my ass. I let my head drop back onto Harley's shoulder, the way it always does, and I stare into Ash's eyes as Harley pushes in. The last thing I see before my eyes roll back into my head is the smug look on his face as they both take me apart. Pushing and pulling, groping and squeezing, the rough strokes of their hands all over me, a girl can only handle so much before I die.

Ash's hand slides back up over my chest to my throat to tug my lips back to his. "Come around my cock for me, I want to watch you go over the edge with both of us inside you."

My breathing stutters to a stop even before his fingers tighten, and Harley's hand slides down over my hip to my clit, licking and sucking at my neck as he strokes and I'm a squirming mess between them. I can feel myself dripping around Ash as I come, shouting out so loud I pray Blaise and Avery have left for her dance class already. Ash grunts as he comes with me, his hips pumping as he strokes out his orgasm inside me. Harley groans slowly under his breath as Ash pulls out, dropping my legs down and bending me over until I'm back to where I started; braced against the glass door as he fucks me from behind. His fingers tighten on my hips when he lets out his own shout, coming so hard it joins Ash's mess dripping down my legs.

I take a second to remember how the fuck to breathe.

Harley washes me off, his fingers gentle but firm, and my legs shake so much I have to hold his shoulders to stay upright. When his fingers slide over my raw and deliciously abused pussy I jerk away and he scoffs at me.

"You're a fucking skittish thing."

I'd poke him or something if he wasn't holding me up. "Sorry, my brain is leaking out of my ears right now. Stop looking so freaking smug!'

He laughs at me. "I'm allowed to be smug for making you come so hard, babe. Come on, let's get you into bed before Morrison gets back and throws his fucking tantrum."

I stay in my room for the night because I have breakfast plans with Avery in the morning and don't want to deal with pissy boys if she marches into their room at seven to get my ass up. Harley keeps his dibs on being with me for the night, leaving the other two snarking at each other as they go back over to their room, neither of them wanting to take the couch for the night.

Harley and I eat leftover pizza in bed with a movie playing on Harley's beat-up laptop because finally having access to his inheritance hasn't changed him one freaking bit.

When I mention this to him he quirks an eyebrow at me. "I dunno, I'm looking up what it's going to cost to put my 'Stang back together and I think I'm going to fucking pay it. It'll triple the cost of the thing but… I think it's worth it."

I nod and put my coffee back on my side table, leaning back into his chest. "I think it's worth it, too. It'll still be less than what Avery spends on hair care for the year."

His chuckle is a rumble under my cheek and I let my focus slide back to the laptop. The movie is an old action flick, something I've never seen before but Harley knows all of the words and pokes me when something important is about to happen to make sure I'm watching. It's cute but I can barely keep my eyes open, being here, warm and safe and wrapped up in his arms, it's my happy place.

The door unlocks and Avery stomps through it like the devil in on her ass. "Lips, there's another box. Lips, it's—I can't! I'm sorry!"

I jump up and off of the bed, Harley cursing up a storm behind me as he scrambles up. "It's okay. I'll get it. Go to the bathroom, or the boy's room! I'll sort it out."

She clamps a hand over her mouth. "This one is different, Lips. I could smell it."

Ah fuck. "Bathroom, Aves. I promise you, I'll sort it out and have the smell gone before you're out of the shower."

Blaise stalks in after her, the box in his hands but held as far away from his body as possible. "It fucking reeks! This one isn't fresh. I need to go burn my clothes and sit in a fucking bleach bath."

I grimace as the smell finally hits me and, yep, this one has been dead for a few days. Fuck, depending on how much the skin has slipped we might not even be able to tell who the fuck it is. That adds a whole new layer of headache to this fucking situation! I'll have to call the Crow and see if we can run the DNA through the police and FBI databases. Fuck, I'm also going to have to call the Boar and tell him he fucking sucks at sorting this shit out!

While I'm planning and raging in my head Blaise moves towards the coffee table to set the box down and out of his hands.

"Wait! I'll get some plastic sheeting from Lips' kit, don't put it down until I do," Harley snaps, and I wait until it's all set up before I go over. Blaise tears out of the room and back over to his room, I'm assuming to burn everything he owns, and I snap on gloves before I slice through the packaging tape holding the box together. Ah, fuck. It's leaking. Greeeeeat, dead head juice all over the fucking room to clean up. Avery's going to have a freaking aneurysm.

The head is way too far gone to tell who it is. The bloating and the blood pooling makes it impossible to even guess an ethnicity. Long dark hair though, and it was once curled, so I'm going to assume it's a woman for now. I reach in to move it in the box a little, just sort of shifting it for clues. I don't want to lift it up in case the slipping skin... well, slips right the hell off.

That's when I see the tattoo.

The fucking tattoo.

Fuck.

Holy fuck.

"Okay, we have a serious fucking problem. Avery, call Atticus and get him here now. 911, state of emergency, whatever it takes. Harley, call Illi and get him here too. We need the security surveillance and we're officially on fucking lockdown," I ramble, hoping I have all of our bases covered but holy fuck, this is a whole new level of bad.

"Who is it, Mounty?" Harley says, and I turn to see them both watching me. Avery is hovering in the bathroom doorjamb, but she and Harley both have their phones to their ears. Their eyes are glued to me, my face must be all sorts of fucked up.

"It's the fucking Lynx."

Chapter Twenty-Six

The entire school goes into lockdown.

Everyone is told that there's been a bomb threat and Luca takes up watch at our front door. I invite him in, there's no point in him sitting out there, but he shakes his head, all of his usual charm and smiles wiped clean.

Illi arrives, looking far more alive than the last time I saw him, thank fuck. He's moving better, and the grins and cheeky jokes are back. He talks shit with Harley and Blaise as they start strapping their weapons to their body.

Ash leans against the bathroom door, already armed to the freakin hilt, and tries to talk Avery down from the ledge. She's so freaked out by the smell and… fluids, she's already had two showers. Her skin must be scrubbed raw by now, if she climbs in again she's going to be shredded to pieces.

"You can swap rooms. You can have our room, and we'll all stay over there until we're sure this mess is dealt with." His voice is coaxing and her answering snort makes it through loud and clear.

"So my choices are rotting brain matter or slipping in Morrison's DNA matter? Fuck this, I'm dropping out!"

I slip my knife into the pocket of my ripped jeans and pull one of Avery's cashmere cardigans over the soft v neck shirt I've permanently borrowed from Ash. I like that Harley's necklace sits between my boobs and only the chain can be seen when I'm wearing this shirt. It feels like our own little secret, something between the four of us, like my creed tattoo.

I lean against the door with Ash. "Aves, I'm going to deal with this and then I'm going to spend the rest of the night bleaching the entire room. You can stay over in the guy's room until I'm done, Blaise will change all of the sheets. You and Ash can do a total renovation if you want. How about you get rid of all of their china and start again. That usually cheers you up."

There's a pause and then she says, "I am getting sick of the blue. I was thinking about a deep, forest green. Not olive."

I pull a face because I have no fucking clue of what she's rambling about. "Of course not, fuck olive. Do you think you can leave the bathroom now?"

She retches. "Not until the head is gone. And the smell, too."

I sigh and turn to Ash who's glaring at the box. Guilt pools in my stomach and I lean against him, my forehead pressing into his chest, and I mumble. "I'm sorry. My shit is haunting us again."

He scoffs at me. "Your shit is just messing with our shit. She's like this because of Joey and Senior, and technically your shit has dealt with one of those issues already. I don't want her going down to the meeting with us while she's rattled. She works well under pressure but not rotting-head-in-her-space pressure."

I sigh again and he lets me lean on him for another minute.

Fuck, to think just a few hours ago I was being held up in that shower by him and Harley having the time of my fucking life, and now the real world has come back to slap me in the damn face again.

"Stop thinking about it. If Avery finds out we'll have to burn the entire school down for her and start again. Huxerly is a shit hole, I don't want to graduate there," he murmurs, and my head jerks up to meet his eyes.

He traces his finger over my cheeks. "Pretty fucking obvious with this blush what you're thinking about, Mounty."

Well, fuck.

There's a knock at the door and Harley opens it allowing the Crow to step in with a frown as he takes in the room. I frown right back at him as the Boar follows behind him with his usual crowd of surly bikers with him.

Fuck. I was not expecting a fucking family reunion in my room while I'm draped over one of my three boyfriends. Jesus fucking wept.

"Wolf," the Boar grunts, and Harley's eyes narrow to slits at him.

Ugh. "Boar. I thought the meeting was in the dining hall? We were just about to head down."

Blaise gives me a look, smirking even as he still looks a little green. I sigh at his twisted freaking humor and Ash huffs at him as well.

The Boar looks at each of the guys in my room and then stalks over to the box, a couple of his bikers moving with him. "I'm here for the box. My boys will get it out of here before the Lynx's family comes looking."

I swallow as he looks inside it. "They know she's dead?"

He grunts. "Yeah, her body was left for them to find."

The Crow gives him a sharp look. "What was left of it, he means. She was mutilated."

I hear Avery start to shuffle around in the bathroom, getting dressed and prepared for the meeting finally. "You gonna give me this guy's name so I can have a chat with him?"

The Boar's eyes snap over to the Crow, who's standing rigid by the door, his eyes as cold as ever. "Not in mixed company, kid. I was waiting to do it in person but I'll put in a call, speed things up a bit. We're due for a meeting anyway."

The Boar tucks the box under his arm like the leaking doesn't bother him, fucking gross, and leaves with his men. There's a second of silence before Ash starts up.

"What the fuck are you even doing here?" Ash snarls, and Avery sighs loud enough it travels through the door.

Atticus turns his trademark cold, calculating looks to Ash and he tenses against me, rage slowly seeping into every fiber of his being. "I needed to check if Avery was okay."

Harley groans as Ash stalks forward, two of the Crow's men stepping up and between them. Avery comes out of the bathroom, looking perfectly put together and hugging the far wall to stay as far away from the mess as possible.

Atticus continues, "I've called the meeting so I can question the Boar. We need to know who is sending the boxes. Killing the Lynx was not really in Lips' best interest and what's to stop this deranged stalker from taking you out for being around her? What about Avery, what if he comes for her next?"

Ash's eyes narrow. "We'll protect Avery like we always have."

Atticus's eyes flick over Ash's face and then he opens his stupid mouth and starts a whole new fucking war for me do have to deal with. "Great job you've done so far, when is the Devil due to collect his property?"

Ash is easily the quickest human on the fucking planet and Atticus's men have no chance of stopping him from taking their boss down.

It takes Illi and Harley to peel him off. Blaise refuses to help, he just stands in front of Avery and smirks when Ash's fists come back bloody. I stay out of the way because all hell would break loose if I got caught in the crossfire. Harley would pull his gun and we'd all be fucked once the Crow's brains were in pieces on the freaking floor.

Harley grabs Atticus by his neatly pressed shirt and hauls him back onto his feet, shoving him towards the door. "You never fucking learn, do you? You just gotta start shit."

Atticus' nose is pouring blood but he barely seems to notice it, other than pressing his pocket square against it. Knowing that rich asshole that thing probably cost more than my entire wardrobe did.

Ugh.

"The others are on their way here. Try to remember that they're all the leaders of large criminal organizations and keep your smart mouths shut before you get us all killed," he snaps and walks out.

I slip my arm into Avery's as we walk, wincing at her flinch. Her hands are a mess from all of the scrubbing, her body must also be a freaking mess. Ash watches her obsessively, as if looking away from her will have her whisked out from under his nose. Blaise walks with him, watching them both with that look on his face, the one where he's getting himself ready to defend and destroy for his family.

Illi leads the way with Harley, the two of them talking about the car parts Harley is looking for. We're not exactly being quiet and yet not a single door opens to see what the noise is about on the way down to the dining hall. The other students are that terrified of us, of the whole fucking world going to shit around them, that they stay in their own lanes.

Smart move.

When we get to the dining hall, half the members still aren't here yet but there's coffee being served.

Coffee.

Illi quirks an eyebrow at me. "Quickest way to take someone out is giving them a dirty batch of their drug of choice."

I huff at him but really I'm crying on the inside; I'm supposed to be asleep in Harley's arms right now not dealing with this bullshit. "I know. I won't touch it."

The Crow overhears us and snaps, "I'm not going to poison my allies, I'm not the fucking Jackal."

Illi smirks over his shoulder at him. "Nah, you're something else entirely."

Great. Wonderful. Fucking perfect. "I shouldn't have caffeine this late on a school night anyway."

Avery giggles at me, her first real sign of life since the box showed up, and I laugh with her. The Crow has rearranged the seating plan and we find seats where I can keep an eye on the doors, not trusting the Jackal or, fuck, the Lynx's family to not show up and kill us all while we're busy having a chat about sweet fuck all. Avery takes the seat next to me and Ash hesitates for a second before sitting on my other side.

Illi, Harley, and Blaise all lean against the dining table behind us, murmuring quietly to each other as more members arrive with their usual groups of followers, flunkies, and paid men.

"This place is fucking swanky," the Coyote says, walking into the room like he's casing the place for a heist later. He probably fucking is, though he definitely doesn't need the money.

Viola rolls her eyes at him but it's affectionate and he blows her a kiss in return. It's fucking weird to see him like that, he's usually such a playful flirt. When he catches my incredulous look he winks at me, ignoring the scolding look from the Crow.

He sits next to Avery and Viola sits on his other side, giving Avery a halfhearted smile. "Thanks for not killing my sister. Sorry she's been a fucking nightmare."

Avery shrugs. "I hope she's enjoying her new school, hopefully there's less gang members there."

The Coyote rolls his eyes, slinging his arm around Viola. "She's already fucking half the school there, I think she's enjoying being the new girl."

Viola elbows him in the gut so hard he does this little wheeze thing and I grin at her. He needs someone to keep him in line.

The Stag arrives with another O'Cronin, a little older than him and a little more… haggard-looking. He nods respectfully at the Crow, then the Boar, then he sits next to Ash and does the same to the Coyote and me. He glances over his shoulder and I don't see what Harley does but he gives him a nod too. Well, well. Aren't we a cozy fucking bunch?

When the Tiger finally arrives, frazzled and alone, the Crow takes his seat. The rest all spread out, the room falling silent as the severity of the situation sinks in.

"Another member has been taken out, the Lynx's head was delivered to the Wolf tonight."

The Tiger starts to sweat, I'm half-afraid the fucker is going to keel over of a heart attack. The Bear, looking thinner and frazzled now he has nothing left, just stares at the floor like nothing matters anymore. His defeatist posture pisses me off. How fucking pathetic.

"So the Jackal has decided enough is enough and he's going to start killing us all for the Wolf? Maybe it's time we got her out. Maybe it's time we all stop paying the price for her being a cocktease," the Fox snaps, and the Crow holds a hand up before one of my guys starts swinging.

"This was not the Jackal. This was someone else who is… working on their own but killing anyone who crosses the Wolf."

"I thought you were going to deal with this?" Avery says to the Boar with an arched eyebrow and a fucking fierce look on her face, and I narrow my eyes at the looks of shock the other members give us.

Avery fucking Beaumont would tear any-freaking-one of them to pieces if given the chance and I'll be fucked if she has to show them respect now the whole institution of the Twelve has gone to hell in a hand basket. Plus, she needs a little pep in her step after the box and nothing makes her happier than tearing down powerful men.

The Boar's eyes drop down to where my hand is tucked in Avery's and then he answers her plainly, no censure or ego in him at all. "The Lynx went back to the Jackal. She decided she didn't want to risk her rat of a son after all, so I think the Wolf's... ally made the right call."

The Crow frowns at him. "This... ally is unknown to the Wolf, that makes him a wildcard. The Lynx should have been dealt with by the Twelve, not taken out by some outsider. How do we know this ally won't turn on the rest of us?"

The Boar crosses his arms and leans forward in his chair. He looks every inch the cold-hearted biker lord I've always known he is. "It's pretty fucking simple; don't hurt the Wolf, don't threaten her, don't stalk her, don't piss her off, and don't ever conspire to fucking kill her. Stay on her good side and you'll live."

What. The. Actual. Fuck?

Harley raises his eyebrows at me and I shrug. I'm officially out of ideas on what the fuck is going on.

"Good thing we're team Wolf," the Coyote says to Viola, loud and brash as he tucks her hair back from her face. I see the Wolf insignia tattooed to the back of his hand and I raise my brow at him. He grins and blows me a kiss like a dick, like he's impersonating Illi's roguish charms and not quite hitting the mark.

Illi himself stares at the other members of the Twelve, one by one, like he's sizing them up. The Crow takes it without so much as an eyebrow lift, but the Viper rises to his bait.

"Just because the Wolf has decided to put up with your shitty attitude doesn't mean the rest of us have to. Remember that you have no power in this room except maybe having the ear of the girl you sold your soul to."

Illi shrugs. "I don't give a shit about the opinions of some gambling man. Things are changing. My loyalty stays with the Wolf, but the institution of the Twelve is going to go through some big fucking changes now the Jackal has lost his head."

The Ox crosses his arms and huffs at him. "Talking like that will get you and the Wolf in deep shit, Butcher. The type of shit you don't walk away from."

The Boar leans forward in his seat, his face a vicious mask that lets you know the biker shit draped all over him isn't a persona he's a fucking killer, through and through. "Did I not just tell you to keep your fucking mouth shut about her?"

The room bursts into argument, the Ox and the Viper cussing the Boar out, but the biker doesn't look at all phased by it. His eyes are on the Crow, sizing him up.

Ash does his own assessment of the shit-fight before us, looking the Boar up and down. Then he waits until the room quietens down to say to me in a not-so-subtle whisper, "You look nothing like him."

Fuck. I cut him a look as half the fucking room turns to look at us. "Can we stick to the topic on hand? Another member is dead. What are we going to do about that?"

There's silence for a second and then, surprisingly, the Fox says, "What we always do. Split the empire, run the Game, and keep the streets of the Bay under our control."

Chapter Twenty-Seven

The Boar leaves the meeting before I can speak to him, snapping at his guys and stalking out like his ass is on fire. I let it go, only because I'm still fucking worried about Avery and we've got to deal with the mess in our room before we can pass out. The Coyote bumps knuckles with Illi, fucking weird, and then leaves with the Crow. I'm sure they'll still be trying to dig up every last clue into who the hell the killer is.

It takes four hours to get the smell of rotting flesh out of our room and to bleach every surface. We lose more furniture because Avery goes on a rampage but it's not like she can't afford it. Once we've finally gotten rid of all evidence we all go to bed in the guys' room, just to let the bleach scent air out a bit more.

We're woken by the sharp rap of knuckles on the door at dawn, less than an hour of sleep for us all.

I lurch up and out of bed before Avery manages to hit the light, and Harley snarls at me to wait for him but I ignore him. This isn't going to be good.

Luca is dressed and armed to the hilt, sour-faced and grim-toned as he says, "The Boar's MC was hit last night while the meeting was on. The Jackal took out the entire fucking building, only the guys at the docks and those who came with him survived. Things are about to get much, much worse. Just letting you know, Wolf."

Wolf.

He never calls me that unless we're around the other members of the Twelve, fuck.

I nod and close the door, rubbing my hand over my face. Was the bartender there as well? Did the Jackal kill her just for being there? It's a stupid thing to ask myself, of course she was and of course he did. Women mean nothing to him.

Not even me.

Harley kisses my forehead and heads to the shower to get ready for his swim training. I feel exhausted just thinking about the hard work he's about to put his body through but I know it's his coping mechanism. Ash will probably head out for a run soon and Blaise will… well, he'll be a morose fuck and write a song or drink or something.

I climb into Ash's bed with Avery and stare at the ceiling with her for a minute, neither of us speaking while we sort through the mess in our heads.

"We need to kill him. He's working his way through the Twelve, picking off the bigger members so we have less numbers. The Ox will be next, I bet," Avery murmurs, and I nod.

"He's probably working on the Crow's numbers too, we just haven't heard about it from the secretive dick."

She snorts at me and her hand finds mine under the blankets. "Sorry I freaked out. I feel like a pansy."

I shake my head. "Don't be stupid, you know I don't care about that shit. I'm sorry, hacked up body parts keep following me, no matter where the hell I am."

She giggles and squeezes my hand. "I think it's kind of sweet. Whoever it is must care a whole lot about you. The Boar made him sound fierce. Maybe it is your dad, maybe he just doesn't know how to speak to you after he… you know, abandoned you."

I groan. "I don't think he even knows I exist. The Boar didn't, not until the Game. What would you do, Aves? Would you go find him and have it out with the guy?"

Harley gets out of the shower and interrupts us, kissing me again on his way out. The other two are still out, Blaise snoring and Ash so deeply asleep like always that there's no chance of waking him with our whispers.

Avery hums under her breath. "I guess I'd want to know. I'd have to. It was the same with Harley, as soon as I knew he existed I had to know him. Once I realized he was another good family member, someone worth having in our lives, then I did everything I could to keep him. Would you keep your father? How the hell are you going to explain the guys to him?"

I shudder. "I don't need a father. Besides, the way the Boar spoke… I just don't see us ever having any sort of a relationship. It's the… brothers I want to meet. The Boar said they were 'good enough', whatever the fuck that means. I know we won't have what you and Ash do but it'd be nice to know them, I guess."

Avery squeezes my hand again. "So we kill the Jackal, deal with Senior, then we meet your brothers and pray they're nothing like Joey. Brothers can be deranged serial killers you know."

I roll my eyes. "Yeah, you kind of ended up on both ends of the spectrum there didn't you? The perfect brother and the fucking psycho brother. Let's pray these ones are closer to Ash."

She sighs and nods, getting up and heading to the kitchen to start on breakfast. When I see the cookbook out, I know she's over the panic and we're back to our regular programing of being her human lab rats at meal times.

The school stays in lockdown, only our family still coming and going as they please because we're not dumb enough to post shit on the internet about the school or try to sneak out to get high in the groundskeeper's cottage. Ash goes for a run after breakfast and I snark at Blaise until he finally relents and works on his homework with me. It's peaceful and soothing for Avery and she only scrubs the bathroom out twice. I'm taking it as a win.

Illi calls me later that day.

"The streets are lined with bodies. There isn't a man, woman, or child in the Bay who isn't aware that the Jackal has lost his shit. The MC was bad, kid. Some of his most blood-soaked work. The pigs are everywhere trying to figure it out but he's got enough of them in his pocket now Beaumont is working with him that they're getting nowhere."

Holy shit. I knew it was going to get bad, I knew he would come after me and my family, but somehow I didn't think his crazy would take over the whole fucking city.

"What's the plan, kid? What are we going to do to fix this?"

I sigh. "I can't leave this up to the Crow anymore. He might know state secrets, he might know about business, but he knows sweet fuck all about dealing with Matteo."

"He's like a fucking cockroach, kid. He'll survive anything."

I duck into the bathroom so I don't disturb Blaise and Avery from where they're still studying together. Avery gives me a look but I smile at her, I'll catch her up on the important shit later. Harley stalks in after me, not trusting me to keep him fully in the loop too. I roll my eyes at him.

"It's not going to happen with one of the Crow's attempts. It's going to take you and I going down there and dealing with it ourselves," I murmur into my phone. I scrub a palm over my face and Harley pulls me into his arms, running a soothing hand down my back.

Illi scoffs at me. "Yeah, no shit. None of these guys know how Matteo thinks. Crawford keeps expecting him to act like any other guy but he's not, he's a fucking psychopath. It takes a lot to get into that sort of mindset. Crawford's too clean-cut for that shit."

I chuckle at him. "Yeah well, neither of us need any help thinking like a psycho. You're the Butcher and I'm the Wolf. That kind of explains everything."

Harley chuckles under his breath at me and I glance back up to meet his eyes. He looks particularly panty-meltingly hot when he's gloating over my fucked-up mind.

"You're making eyes at one of your boys right now, aren't you? I can tell by the way your breathing. It's alright, it's not like I was hoping for your full attention or anything, kid." Illi teases, and goddamnit a blush creeps over my cheeks.

"Like you can talk! I've sat through so many nights in bars with you draped all over Odie and me trying not to puke at the cheesy lines you give her," I snap.

He cackles at me and hangs up.

Classes resume the next day and I find myself... bored.

I'm itching to head down to the Bay and deal with the Jackal myself. Knowing that he's gone full-blown bloodthirsty killer has only made me more sure of our plans to take him out. There's no chance of redemption. There's no tortured hero buried underneath the controlling obsessive psycho, there's just an egotistical maniac who is throwing a temper tantrum over not getting his own way. He's lost the backing of the Twelve so now he's going to make the entire city pay.

Harley deals with my twitchy attitude all day like a saint but by dinner I think he's ready to either fuck or fight it out of me. Avery glares over her pasta at him, reading him like an open freaking book, and he snarks at her.

"This is my room. If I want to fuck my girlfriend in my own room, then I fucking will."

I roll my eyes at him. "Don't be a dick, she's working her way up to being okay in our room again."

Avery's eyes sparkle with sadistic glee and she uses her sweetest voice to say, "Keep up with that attitude, Harls, and I'll gut you in your sleep. Illi showed me how to do it to a big guy like you, you won't stand a chance."

Harley grumbles under his breath about not teaching Avery any other techniques until she stops being quite so bloodthirsty, then he tugs me to my feet. "Let's go to the pool. We can go for a swim to get some of this energy out of you."

I shrug and get up to grab a bathing suit, ducking into the bathroom to get changed and ignoring Avery's snarky comments about never using the pool again because of Harley's jizz floating around because just nope, no thanks. I don't need to be a part of that conversation at all. Avery takes way too much pleasure in embarrassing the absolute shit out of me.

We get out the door and halfway to the stairs when we find Blaise, all sweaty and flushed from the gym. My knees go all weak at him and he turns on his heel to come with us to the pool.

"Pretty sure I didn't invite you," Harley snarks, and Blaise scoffs back at him.

"Pretty sure I don't need an invitation. Besides, I was there when Star's bathing suit arrived, I'm not missing this."

Oh. Right. My bathing suit.

I'd stupidly told Avery she could pick one out for me so I didn't have to steal hers any more. I'd felt guilty for my last encounter in the pool with Harley, especially when the video got out and she'd thrown the last one out. I'm assuming it was at least a thousand dollars, because all of her shit is at bare minimum a ridiculous price.

So the bathing suit is just barely a one piece because there is a piece of string connecting them. It's fucking obscene but I guess I should get over being shy about this shit considering they've both fucked me until I was screaming. Ash and Harley even fucked me at the same damn time. Jesus. I need to get a hold of myself.

Blaise threads his fingers through mine, smirking at my blush. "I hope you never lose that, Star. It would make fucking with you less fun."

Harley joins him in laughing, the traitorous asshole.

The pool is empty, thank fuck, and Harley immediately strips off, diving into the water in an elegant arc. He looks like a freaking god as he moves through the water.

"You're drooling, Star," Blaise drawls, and I elbow him in the ribs.

"Don't get pissy, I drool at you all the damn time."

He nods and pulls at my shirt, peeking down the back. "Show me what you're hiding under here. Arbour is an idiot for jumping in and missing the show."

There isn't going to be a show. I pull my jacket off and unbutton my jeans when he interrupts me. "Do it slower, Mounty, it doesn't feel like a strip tease if you rush it."

I roll my eyes at him. "You've seen it all before, what the hell does it matter?"

He tilts his head back, his eyes hooded and dark, and my mouth suddenly gets dry. "Because when you strip slowly, I get to think about all of my favorite parts of you. All of the parts I want so desperately to see and you make me wait. Then I get pissed off at waiting and tear the whole thing off of you and fuck you on the edge of the pool while Harley does laps."

I gulp.

He makes a great case.

I drag the zipper of my jeans down a little slower, feeling just a little bit stupid as I slowly push them down my legs. When I bend over to grab them from around my ankles he says, "Turn around if you're going to bend over, Star."

I do it, snarking at him, "How many strip teases have you had? Fuck, don't answer that."

He laughs at me, which I do not take as a good sign, and I spin back around to slowly strip my shirt off. I still feel like an idiot but when he bites his lip that eases a little.

Him palming his dick through his shorts, already hard for me, helps too.

Harley's phone buzzes but we ignore it, he's busy doing laps and then only people we give a shit about know where to find us. But then Blaise's phone buzzes too. Fuck.

He huffs, frustrated as fuck at being interrupted. "What, asshole I'm kind of busy… no, you said you were taking her down… no, she's definitely not here… Lips and Harley are both here, there's no one else… *Fuck*!"

He doesn't have to say another word, my spiraling mind already knows exactly what's happened.

Avery is gone.

Chapter Twenty-Eight

I'm on the phone to the Crow before Harley is even out of the pool, cursing up a storm as he snatches his clothes and shoves them on. We all scramble for the door, the pain in my leg be damned.

"Who the fuck was watching her?" Atticus snarls at me and nope, not today, motherfucker.

"She was in our room which is guarded by your fucking men, so this lands with you. You had better fucking find her right the fuck now."

There's a pause and then I hear Jackson say, "Ash goes in and then fucking nothing. I don't see how she's not still in that room."

"Well she's not hiding under the fucking bed!" I snap and Atticus snaps back, "I thought Ash could take care of her? He has no issues throwing it in my face that he guards her better than I do."

"You fucking survive what he has and then we can talk about whether or not he's allowed a shitty attitude," I hiss back at him, and Harley's phone rings. He frowns at his phone for a second and then answers. His eyebrows shoot up.

I grab his arm to get his attention.

"We've got her."

I ignore Atticus's enraged snarl as I hang up on him and Harley hands his phone to me.

"Looks like my family has fucked Harley over again, Wolf," says Aodhan, and I could fucking scream.

Diarmuid.

That piece of fucking shit Irishman.

"Tell me everything right now, we're on our way," I say, attempting to stay calm but calm went out the window the second Blaise answered Ash's call. Fuck, Ash must be losing his damn mind right now.

"I'm following them now. He drove through the docks with her, he hasn't been down here since you inducted him, so I knew something was up."

Fuck me, the traitorous piece of shit must have driven like a psycho to get her down there that fast. He knows if I catch him he's fucking dead and he's right, my fingers are itching to slit him open. Slowly, and with great fucking glee.

Aodhan continues, the sounds of cars hooting and shouting coming through the phone loud and clear. "I saw him sling her over his shoulder to switch cars... Wolf, he got in with the Jackal. They're heading for his territory, I'd say they're going back to his vaults. I'll go in after her, you have my word."

He hangs up on me just as we arrive back at our room. I fling the door open, ready for the chaos and carnage Ash must have unleashed when he'd gotten out of the shower to find her gone.

Ash hasn't destroyed the room.

He's standing by the kitchen, staring at the photo Lance had taken of us all together that Avery loves so much. He doesn't move when we come in, like he's saying some prayer over her photo.

"We know where she is. Diarmuid took her, Aodhan is following them," I say, and Harley starts throwing shit around as he grabs his guns and a leather jacket, suiting up for blood. The Crow tries calling me and I ignore it. There's nothing he can do for me now.

Ash doesn't speak, he just moves to strap his body with every single weapon Illi delivered to him, and then he perches on his bed with blank eyes. He watches me with the sort of intensity that chokes me up but I ignore all of that as I pull my clothes on.

I've been here before. I've lost someone like this before. I can get her back.

I just can't think about what exactly might be happening to her right now. I can't think about whether the Jackal has gotten his hands on her already because that'll only make me reckless and I can't be that right now.

I need to be as calm as Ash is. As sure as he is that we're going to fucking fix this.

Blaise finishes up strapping his knives on and then he perches next to his best friend without a word, just a silent show of support. All in, ride or die. We're going to do whatever it takes to get her

My phone starts buzzing again and I finally look at the fucking thing, only really to turn it off. The Boar's phone number flashes at me. Fuck it, I pick it up.

"The Crow called so I heard you've lost your friend, kid. I've got info on her, a couple of guys heading over there to take stock, they were with the Stag when the Irish cock went past. The Crow is heading over here now, so stay calm and just head over—" I cut him the fuck off even as my vision goes fucking blood red in my rage at his nonchalant tone.

"Don't fucking tell me to stay calm, my fucking sister has been taken. That's what she is, she's more to me than blood!" I scream down the phone, and the Boar just fucking lets me.

"I've sent someone else to watch her. There is nothing that could happen to her with him there. Nothing, Wolf," he says, calm as anything and I try not to fucking scream at him again but, sweet lord fuck, it's hard.

"I'm not really up for trusting anyone right now, Boar. The last person I trusted is the dead man walking who took her."

The Boar grunts a little and I can hear him walking. He's somewhere in the Bay, I hear a door swing shut behind him and the noise of the street turns into the raucous sounds of bikers. "The guy watching her is the guy who's been sending you those packages. He walked into Beaumont manor and cut little Joey Beaumont's head off while fifty or so of his father's men were downstairs keeping watch. Did the same thing at the Lynx's estate. You telling me you don't think he can handle O'Cronin and D'Ardo? I promise you, he won't let anything happen to your girl. Fuck, if I thought you were one to sit around I'd just get him to bring her home but we both know you're already halfway out the door to her."

I groan and let my head drop back against the wall. "Tell me who the fuck he is."

He sighs and I hear him swallow. I know it'll be whiskey and that makes something kind of break in my chest. "I think it's better if you meet him. You two can talk things through after we get your girl back."

He hangs up and then my phone lights up with a text from the Crow.

The Boar's MC clubhouse. Now. We're going in together. Be ready to end this, whatever it takes.

I argue with Harley about going to the clubhouse the entire way out to the car.

I get it, I want to head in there for her right the hell now but the Jackal knows we're coming. Illi is going to meet us there, having been away at the safe house with Odie, and we can't show up without the cavalry; we'd be dead and gone in under a fucking minute. Surprisingly, it's Ash who agrees with me.

"We can't save Avery if we're dead. Just get in the fucking car."

The rest of the trip is silent.

We arrive at the MC clubhouse and before I get out of the car Harley grabs my hand. I glance up to find him mulling over something in his head, a deep frown over his face.

"Everything is going to be fine. We are going to find Avery, we are going to find your uncle, and we are going to fix everything." My voice sounds so sure and fuck I wish I felt that sure.

He nods and says, "Diarmuid's death is mine. Avery took me in after my parents died and she's helped me with fucking everything, no questions asked. The O'Cronins only ever wanted a fucking puppet. An empty heir they could mold into the perfect leader they wanted. It doesn't fucking matter that he left them, Diarmuid's the exact same. He wanted me to prove a point and now that Liam's dead, he just wants the fucking bounty taking Avery in will get him. Fuck the O'Cronins, I'm taking him out myself for touching her."

I squeeze his hand back. "I would never take that right from you, but you'll have to work it out with Ash. He's going to need blood for this and I will also say, the Stag is turning out to be a decent enough kind of guy. Maybe the next generation won't be so fucking bad."

Harley grunts, not exactly agreeing with me. I slide out of the car and meet up with Ash and Blaise, who are both staring at the clubhouse like they're about to raid it.

There is nothing human left on Ash's face. I thought that would remind me of his father, or his brother, but it doesn't. All it does is remind me that we are perfect for each other because we won't let anything happen to Avery. We will get her out because how the fuck can we not?

The biker at the door nods at me respectfully and lets us pass. I was expecting the place to be empty after the Jackal attacked but the walls are bursting with brawny bikers.

"There's our fucking backup," Blaise mutters, looking around like he's afraid to catch a disease just from standing in the room.

I shrug. "As long as they know how to shoot, I don't care what they look like."

Harley rolls his shoulders back. "The fuck are we waiting for? Where's that dickhead Crawford?"

As if summoned, he stalks out of the hallway the Boar had taken me down for our meeting, looking… well, like a pile of shit. Okay, so he's still dressed in his usual suit and his hair still looks all perfectly trimmed but his face is all sorts of fucked up.

I feel a little less like gutting him.

The Boar walks over to him to take his side and face the room. The chatter dies down instantly, the respect for their Prez is a palpable thing. They start giving out the orders for how the night is going to go down, who is moving in where. None of it matters to me, I just need them in there shooting at the Jackal's guys enough to slip past them all and find Aves.

Illi stalks in behind us, quietly clapping Ash on the back. Ash ignores it, doesn't even acknowledge Illi is there but the Butcher doesn't take offense. He just gives me a grimace.

"Sorry it took me so long."

Harley shrugs. "We've just been standing around with our thumbs up our asses anyway, no big fucking deal."

I roll my eyes and Blaise crosses his arms, staring the Crow down like he's planning on killing him for Ash. Fuck, I forget sometimes just how loyal he is. I need to get this over with before the whole lot of them start throwing themselves into danger to get her back.

If anyone is doing that, it's me.

Illi starts huffing and grunting under his breath, entirely unimpressed with the plan of action. I am too but I trust my family to get the job done.

When he huffs again, loud enough that bikers around us turn to give him a look. I elbow him and whisper. "How obvious is it that he wasn't made for blood?"

Illi's dark chuckle is soft but I hear his answer well enough. "Good thing we were."

No truer words spoken in this shit-fest of a night.

I finally decide I cannot take any more and I grab Ash's arm, tugging him out and back into the night air. I can't stand to listen to anymore of the bullshit. The Crow finishes up as we leave, solidifying his bullshit plan. They aren't going to be able to find the Jackal. None of them have been in there before except Luca, and I haven't seen him anywhere so far.

It's going to come down to me.

Illi takes his own car and we all pile back into the Cadillac. The drive is short enough, the MC might be out of the slums but it's still straddling the line between there and the docks.

Blaise parks the car and we all step out, silent and fucking ready to face whatever the fuck is happening in that building. The roar of the motorcycles is deafening as dozens of men ride in, then the sleek black town cars of the Crow's men park around us. I don't bother paying any of them attention. I'm too busy looking at the mess the Jackal has made of this place.

There's blood and bodies everywhere.

None of them are men.

For fuck's sake.

"He always was a fucking psycho," Illi murmurs, lighting up a cigarette as he walks over to me.

"Odie safe?" I ask, and he nods.

"Left her over at the Crow's place. I hate the cockhead but his place is secure enough, and she's got her GPS tracker if shit goes wrong. I did have to threaten that little creepy fuck about touching her though."

I frown. "Jackson? He's a flirt but he's not going to touch her. He's in love with Viola."

Illi pulls a face. "I don't like him. I don't trust any man that spends all his days playing on his computer and jerking off over porn. He needs to get out a bit more."

I roll my eyes. The conversation is good for distracting me at least, I'm thinking a little less about Avery and what is happening to her right now. I just... I can't think about it until I have her safe, then I can lose my fucking mind over it.

I'm also trying not to think about how many of these dead girls I know, how many of them lived near me in the slums, went to school with me, danced at the same parties as I did back when my life revolved around the sick games the Jackal likes to play.

Stepping back into the Jackal's territory is a jarring, fucked-up experience now that I'm away from him. My life has never felt so different as it does right now staring at these corpses. Illi steps up to my side, grimacing as he glances around at the gore still left on the streets.

"You going to be okay, kid?"

Fuck. I don't know. I roll my shoulders back. "Of course. Let's get this over and done with."

I pull the bandana tied around my neck up and over my nose. Illi pulls his up as well and I roll my eyes when I see what it has on it. The guys' face tattoo, the snarling jaws of the Wolf, stares back at me in white. The cocky bastards.

"Where the hell did you get that?" I say, glancing back to see they all have them.

Blaise shrugs. "Avery got them. Apparently, being a part of a gang means we have to coordinate this shit."

My chest hurts at the mention of her name. I let myself feel it for a second longer and then I empty myself of all of the pain, the feeling, the wishing. Once I'm nothing but a cold void, I nod to Illi.

Let's fucking end this.

Chapter Twenty-Nine

The Crow and the Boar send their men in through the front entrance of the vaults.

On paper, this is the only way into the dilapidated bank the Jackal has made his headquarters. It's wide open and easier to defend against a hoard of bikers, so a smart defense move on the Jackal's part.

I know better than to use this entrance.

"He'll know we're coming that way, kid," Illi murmurs as I move away, and I shrug.

"It's still the best option. We take out the guard and then we're further into the building than the rest of the men. I know I'm going to face him, I know he's going to be counting on that."

Illi palms his cleaver in one hand and squeezes my arm gently in the other. "We're in and out like old times. The plan is go in through the back, find the vault keys, go to the basement, then get out, killing anyone in our way, cool? We care about nothing else going on except getting our girl and killing that fuck D'Ardo."

I nod sharply. "The Stag too. He went in after Avery so we're here for him as well."

Harley grunts under his breath and when I look at him he shrugs. "You forgot Diarmuid. He's dead too, no matter what it takes I'm killing that fuck."

The sounds of gunfire that starts up all around us gets us moving and I take the lead because I know where to go and I need Illi taking up the rear to watch our backs. The alleyway is disgusting, full of trash and reeking of piss like the whole damn street uses it as a toilet. I mean, they probably do. The Jackal would encourage it to keep unsuspecting Mounty kids the hell away from here.

"Once this is over with, we are never coming to the slums again," Blaise says as he gags at the smell. There's filth everywhere so I don't exactly blame him, I'm just used to looking around it all, ignoring the signs of how bad this place actually is.

Harley scoffs at him. "You wouldn't have fucking survived growing up here, Morrison. Maybe you should wait in the car, leave this to those of us who aren't spoiled pussies."

I sigh. "We're trying to be stealthy here guys. Do you not see the guys on the roof with guns ready to be aimed at us the second we're in range?"

Though none of the Jackal's guys have Diarmuid's level of skills and I know O'Cronin won't be up there, he's probably not even here anymore but I don't tell

Harley that. He's not one to stick around after he's been paid.

I know all of his little hiding places anyway; we can track him later.

Ash pulls his gun out. "Like Illi said, the Jackal knows we're coming and how we're getting in there so who the fuck cares if they hear us coming."

And then he shoots at the roof of the building. He has a silencer on, thank God or my eardrums would've been blown out at this close range, and it takes a second for the body to fall off of the roof and land at our feet.

Well.

"That was a great fucking shot," Illi says, kicking the corpse as we pass it.

Ash shrugs. "We've been training for this day for months. You don't think Harley's taught us some extra tricks?"

I know the guy on the ground, I don't look at him because I don't need to think about what a shitty person he was right now. I need to focus on getting us in there without catching a bullet between the eyes. "There's two others, you think you guys can get them too? Illi and I will take the door."

They still can't see the door from where it's obscured but their trust in me is rock solid. Harley and Ash both pause and aim at the roof, while Blaise stays close behind me, his own gun drawn and held in his hands with the sort of confidence that comes from extensive training. I knew they'd all been working with Illi while I'd focused on planning and homework with Avery but I didn't realize just how much they'd grown into exactly what I need.

Confident, assured killers.

Fuck.

"Blaise, when this is over remind me to apologize to you for making you a killer," I murmur, and he scoffs at me.

"Ash did that a long time ago, Star. No regrets. Now tell me what I'm shooting, because at the moment I kind of think I'm just going to be used as a human shield if someone aims something at you."

I roll my eyes and make a mental note to ask him for that story. How do I keep forgetting to ask?

"Kick it in? The vests should be enough, the fuckers the Jackal has working for him aren't exactly professionals," Illi murmurs, and I hear two more bodies hit the cement behind us.

"Shoot it out first, let's not start the night filling up on lead." I say, and Illi raises his gun, shooting at the hole in the brick wall that's covered by a large sheet of steel. It looks like nothing from here, there's plenty of other places that have old signs propped up or slabs of wood, which is why it's the perfect escape route.

The Jackal had used it once while I was working with him. There had been a party here and some flunky got drunk and set the place on fire. The Jackal had dragged me through here to get away from the smoke and once the fire was out he'd executed half the men here. He'd rambled and seethed about it for weeks, sure that it was an assassination attempt, not a stupid mistake by some guy who couldn't hold his beer.

"On three——" Illi says, and Ash stalks up behind him.

"Three." He snaps, and he shoves past us, ripping the sheet off of the wall like it's nothing and letting it crash to the ground. He keeps his body away from the hole and thank God he does because a shot rings out from the blackness of the hole. There's shouting, a few of the Jackal's guys still standing, and Blaise shoves me behind him as

Illi and Harley deal with them.

"I'm fine." I snap, but Blaise holds me there with one arm easy enough. He doesn't let me go until Illi calls out it's safe.

"You know I'm also wearing Kevlar, right? I'm just as covered as you are," I snap at him, and he steps back behind me as we catch up with the others. I feel irritated that he'd cover me, that he thinks I not only need his protection like that but that I'd be able to live with myself if the fucker took a bullet for me. Nope, couldn't do it.

"You're also nearly two fucking feet shorter than us all and your head is an open target so yeah, you can stand the fuck behind one of us. Get over it," Harley snarks back, and for the record I'm not *that* much shorter than these overprotective assholes.

We step over a dozen dead guys, the Jackal clearly wants a few of us taken out before we get to him. He's underestimating my guys. I hold tightly onto the Wolf as I walk through the blood and gore, ignoring the crunching underneath my boots every so often as I stand in bone fragments. You shoot a guy in the head, you better believe you'll be stepping in pieces of his skull.

The hallway leads into the center of the dilapidated building. There are old beams strewn across the cracked and scorched marble floor, giving you the feel that the ceiling might cave in on you at any freaking point. Well... more of the ceiling, there's already sections that have come down.

"If he's that rich, why does he live in a shit hole?" Blaise mutters, and I shrug.

"He lives in the vaults. It's... different there. This is where the parties happen, and some of the killing," I say, and Harley's gaze meet mine as he takes the area in.

The gunfire and shouting echoes through the building and the fighting has already made its way inside. We hug the outer wall as we work our way through, staying unseen but seeing exactly what's going down.

There's a whole fucking lot of blood and death.

I start to wonder how it is the Crow is going to wipe this night from the legal history of the Bay. Does he have enough police and governors on his payroll to do it? I wonder if Avery does? How does the city explain a hundred men suddenly disappearing? Fuck, I need to keep my head in this and stop worrying.

"I'll clear the way, you lot get the keys for the vault doors. It'll be with the dope, always was," Illi says, and I nod. It'll be much easier getting down to the Jackal with them. He disappears through the dark hallway, silent and deadly.

He kills two cowering guys and stalks off as we get to the back rooms, full of drugs and cash and dead girls chained to the wall, and I grit my teeth as I take it all in. I hate this fucking place. We need to set it on fire as we leave.

Harley grimaces as he looks around. Blaise keeps his eyes on me and Ash is a blank fucking void still, cold and uncaring about anything except the job.

Harley huffs and starts to rummage around, looking for keys or something else that might come in handy, but when he opens the only other door in the room his whole body jolts and he snaps it shut again. I raise an eyebrow and he shakes his head at me.

"Whichever flunky or biker did that needs fucking therapy. He's made the Butcher look mentally balanced."

Illi rounds the corner and grins at Harley. "Aww, sweet of you to say! I've just hacked a man to pieces for saying he couldn't wait to watch the Jackal fuck my wife once I was dead so my night is going fan-fucking-tastical. Next level amazing. I'm practically jizzing myself with joy."

Ah hell. "Big pieces or did you really get down to business on him? I feel like no piece of him should be bigger than a quarter."

Blaise pretends to gag, but the little psycho frown Illi has between his eyes eases off a little. "I guess I've been a bit slack. Wanna stomp on his skull with me?"

Fuck, the pretend gag turns into a real one as Blaise's skin takes on a green-y tinge. He turns on his heel and starts pawing through the drugs as he helps Harley look. Nothing.

"Stop fucking wasting time. Get over here and look," Ash snaps at Illi, and he grimaces at him.

I start tapping my way around the room, nothing the Jackal loves more than a loose floorboard to hide shit in, and Illi checks the doorframes and window sills. Harley gets frustrated and kicks the chair, flipping it. Yup, there it is.

I duck down to grab the key from where it's taped on the chair.

Harley rolls his eyes. "Are you fucking kidding me? This feels like amateur hour."

I shrug. "The Crow is the one with all the high-tech shit. Sometimes simple works in your favor, but not today."

I try to ignore the feeling that this *is* all a little too easy. It feels like the Jackal is playing with us, that he's doing all of this for us, and us alone.

There's nothing I can do but play his little game. Illi opens the door that leads to the staircase, flinging it wide and waiting for any gunshots or shouting. When there's nothing he stalks through, gun first, then motions us forward when it's all clear. The staircase down to the vaults feels like it never ends, like you're heading to the center of the Earth itself as we step over the rotted-out holes every so often. Harley grabs my hand to steady me, like he knows my leg will get sore from all of the stairs, and I do my best to be gracious about it.

When we finally get to the bottom of the stairs, guns drawn, there's already people fighting down here but it's too fucking dark to see much. We have no choice but to push on slowly, steady and careful.

The guys on our side made it through the Jackal's flunkies while we were finding the key and we're forced to duck behind one of the open vault doors for cover until the gunfire moves away from us, echoing down the dark, cavernous hall.

Then we move. It's dark down here, but I could walk through it with my eyes closed if I had to and the layout hasn't changed a bit since I was last here. I try to keep my eyes off of the damage being done, of all of the men currently being torn apart by bullets and bikers and men dressed in black. I keep my feet moving. I don't owe loyalty to any of these men but the level of carnage around us makes this place look like a war zone. Even for me it's unsettling.

I just need to make it to the stairs because Avery will be in the basement. She's going to be as close to the Jackal's vault as possible.

"We heading straight to hell, kid?" says Illi.

Ash gives him a look. "Do I even fucking want to know what that is?"

I shrug. "It's where he does all of his evil, and it's in the fucking basement. Pretty self-explanatory."

Illi shrugs. "Every man, or woman if she's like the Wolf, should have a room to work in. The Jackal's is just extra fucking bad because he's a dick."

Harley scoffs. "What's yours called then? The shop?"

Illi smirks. "I work in a fridge. Slanting floor with a drain to clear the blood. Lots of knives. You should come check it out when this is over."

I roll my eyes and hiss quietly at them, "What part of this being a stealthy operation is escaping you guys? Talk shop later."

I'm not used to all of this chatter while I work and it's getting on my nerves pretty damn quick. Illi shrugs and lets it go, and my guys all fall silent.

I motion the guys forward and we do our best to stay out of the bikers' way. They are here to get rid of the Jackal's henchmen. My job is to find the Jackal himself.

I choose not to tell my guys that I'm planning on doing it myself, no matter what it takes. I let them think that we're here to get Avery back, just to retrieve her and let the others take down this empire, but I doubt the Crow is going to focus his energy personally on finding the Jackal. I can't leave here tonight without knowing he's out of our lives permanently.

Illi gives me a side eye. "I know exactly what you're thinking, kid. I can take care of it."

Harley cuts us both a look and I do my best not to glare back at him. "Like you're gonna be any better facing him. He loves nothing more than playing with your head, Illi. He's been in yours as much as he's been in mine. I'm sure he has big plans for us both."

Illi strokes a hand down his cleaver. "That's a shame for him because my plans include pulling his intestines out and strangling him with them. Doubt he's factored that in."

Blaise snorts. "Are we sure you're not the deranged one? That's not even physically possible, is it?"

It is.

Illi just gives him a slap on the back, smirking and shaking his head, and we creep forward. The sounds of fighting and gunfire gets louder and louder as we move but the echoing from being underground makes it impossible to figure out exactly how close we are or where it's coming from. At every corner we have to stop and scout it out, usually Illi checking it out while I pray he doesn't catch a bullet between the eyes.

When we finally get close to the vaults we need, I know for sure that the Jackal has been waiting for us. It all works out too perfectly to have been a coincidence.

There's a loud crash, the snapping and cracking of the slabs of stone that make up the walls breaking apart and smashing on the ground, and Illi shoves the guys to the side, slinging an arm around me and slamming me to the ground as he shields me from the falling stone and the shower of bullets that come through once the wall is down. I don't have time to protect my face on the way down and pain bursts through my nose as I slam into the ground. Fuck. It's probably broken.

Illi's body is at least three times bigger than mine. He's fucking huge, a wall of muscle and untapped fury waiting for release, and he curves himself around me protectively. I flatten myself to the dirty stone floor so Illi isn't a bigger target, he's already huge so he doesn't need to stick out any further.

I hear the rough shouting and growling of the bikers, and the slang the Jackal's guys all use, and I lay there and pray they all get taken out and that my guys are all safe. I pray that they're all out here and none of them are in torturing Avery, that she's tied to a chair somewhere being pissed off at the fucking audacity of these people, daring to kidnap Avery fucking Beaumont. Don't they know she's an evil queen, a dictator that breathes fire and can eviscerate a grown man with a single look?

That's what I lay here and pray.

There's more grunting and the wall next to us starts to break apart as well. Illi shoves me again as he lurches the other way and the skin on my hands and legs get torn up by the rubble on the ground as I move, the wall crashing down where we were. If he hadn't been so fast we'd have been crushed, except now I'm all alone with a pile of stones and concrete rubble separating me from the boys. The icy fingers of dread creep up my spine. Too fucking convenient.

Then a hand wraps around my mouth.

Chapter Thirty

There's no point struggling.

He's much bigger than me, like most guys are, and his arms are like iron bands around my waist. He wouldn't hesitate to break my arm, smash my other leg and destroy my life, none of these things are even close to too far for this man.

So I wait.

He drags me into his vault, into the room Illi called hell, and I start to take note of everything. Avery isn't here, thank fuck, but there's blood everywhere. It's not hers. I won't believe it's hers, not for a second, because grief only blinds you. I need to be wide awake to deal with this man.

My old friend.

If you could ever have called him that.

He slams me back into the only chair in the room. There's straps and chains hanging off it, a dozen different ways to keep a man sitting still for all of the torture the Jackal wants to put him through, and I force my face to stay blank as he straps me in.

The things I've seen him do to men in this chair, well, let's just say I'm not fucking happy sitting in it, even if it's only going to last for a little while.

The Jackal smiles down at me, stroking my cheek and spreading the blood from my nose around like the image of me covered in my own blood is the best fucking thing he's ever seen. "Did you like my little treasure hunt for you, Starbright? I left you clues in all your favorite places. All the places only you would know, all the things only you could do."

I grimace at him, baring my bloodied teeth and wishing I could stick my knife through his throat. As if reading my mind, he slips it out of my pocket and throws it behind himself like it's nothing.

"Me and Johnny. The best friend you betrayed because you're not loyal or trustworthy or worthy of love. Johnny knows every last thing about you, and he'll be here for you soon."

He tsks at me. "They left you behind, Starbright. After I took you they just kept moving."

His tone is coaxing, like he thinks he can sway me. That my mind is so weak willed I'll crumble at his feet at knowing they stayed the course. He doesn't get it, he doesn't get me and my family at all. It doesn't matter to me that they went after Avery, that's exactly what I wanted them to do. They could leave here with her now and I'd be fucking thrilled about it.

I also know they won't leave me.

He turns his back on me as he sets out his tools, confident the thin straps around my thighs will be enough to keep me secure without my knife to help me get free. He's right; without my beloved Matriarch, the knife that had been with me for years and hundred of kills, it would be impossible to get out.

The razorblade in my sleeve will get me out.

Avery's Matriarch in my boot will be perfectly adequate to kill him.

"I see it. I see you defying me, you think they love you. Ah, my Wolf, they don't. They weren't here for you, Starbright. They don't know all of your secrets, they don't know about the monster inside you. Only I can be that person for you, I need to remind you of that, so we can be together. You need to remember that you're mine." He's still using that voice, the one he uses to fool women into thinking he's human. The one he used on me as a child, to get me to follow him around in the group home, the one he used to teach me how to kill a man.

I don't believe it anymore.

His mouth sets into a dark slash across his face, the fury and loathing seeping into every fiber of his being. He doesn't like it when I say no. I never was allowed to say no to him.

He stares into my eyes as he slides his knife into my gut.

Sweat breaks out over my forehead but I don't scream or cry or *plead* with him to stop.

"I'm picking all my favorite places, Starbright. All of the sections I can slide right into without hitting something vital. Should we do this all day? Should we spend the day like our good old times, finding all the ways I can make you scream?"

I will not scream.

I will not utter a fucking sound, even if it makes my death excruciating.

I let my head roll back on my shoulders and I stare up at the inky black ceiling. Countdown in French. The best way to deal with this is to breathe through it. Empty my mind, nothing, counting, don't think, don't think about-

He grabs a fistful of my hair and rips my head back down until I'm staring at him. "Don't hide from me, you'll take this and you'll do what you're told. I'll keep going until *my* Wolf is back."

There's no holding it back. I laugh in his face, savage and wild and *fuck him*. Fuck him for being evil, for not being the guy I wanted him to be. Fuck him for being evil, manipulative, and not really giving a fuck about who I really am. I let every last one of these things show in my expression because I'm not afraid of him anymore.

He grabs my face, squeezing until my cheeks and my bleeding nose scream at me, my head going a little fuzzy. "You know better, Wolf. I taught you better than this."

He lets my face go, his fingernails dragging down my cheeks, to turn away from me again. He grabs the blowtorch, one of those little ones that chefs use, and fuck no, I'm not getting burned today. That's not fucking happening.

I flex my wrist until my sleeve rides up, something Illi taught me to do, and the razor blade is easy enough to slice through the leather. The fucker should have used the chains but, as he keeps on pointing out, I know him so fucking well.

He likes the indents the leather leaves in skin when his victims struggle.

I move quickly while his back is still turned. He's an arrogant fuck, and he's so fixated as he lifts the brand up to the blowtorch flame. There's no fucking way I'm leaving here with his insignia burned into my skin.

No fucking way.

The straps are sliced and off my thighs, Avery's knife clutched in my hands as he turns and I stab him in the side, right where one of his kidneys is. Fuck, I hope I've hit it.

He grunts and shoves me away, grabbing Avery's knife out and getting a hand around my throat. I kick a leg out and hit the torch, still burning away on the ground where he's dropped it and his grip loosens off a little as the flame hits his ankle, a vicious stream of cursing streaming from him.

He slams my head back against the wall and I feel as though my brain rattles around in my skull, stars bursting across my eyes. While my vision is still patchy, he slams Avery's knife into my stomach again, pressing in close to whisper in my ear. "That was very stupid, Starbright. Now you don't have any chances to get away from me."

My voice comes out all gurgling and slurred. "I don't need to get away from you. I need to keep you focused on me."

He chuckles, his breath fanning down my neck until I want to peel the skin off just to get any trace of him off of my body. "You need to stop thinking about them, my little Wolf. They won't get here in time. I timed everything perfectly, so I could have you here and keep them out until I made you mine. You think I had all of my men out there dealing with that cock Crow? No, I have them here. Keeping us safe and away from those arrogant, entitled soon-to-be-dead boys you gave yourself away to."

I snarl at him and he strokes my face again, petting me like I'm someone important to him. "Shh, it's okay. You'll be on the end of my cock by the time they get through all of my men, as much as I'm enjoying this foreplay. One look at you and they'll leave you behind."

My blood coats the inside of my mouth and dribbles out of the corner as I reply, "They'll be here. Even if your pathetic little army holds them off and you manage to rape me, it makes no difference. They'll kill you and I'll still go home with them."

He laughs at me, brushing my hair away from my face as he twists the blade slowly. The sadistic fuck, my vision whites out a little but, fuck me, I hold onto reality by a thread.

"You're a toy to them, something fun and cheap to play with for now. The second they see I've had you they won't want you anymore and then all I'll have to do is show them the door and you'll be mine. Oh, I'll kill them. I would never let them live for touching what's mine, but they won't try to fight for you, Starbright. You'll be used-up slum pussy; broken and *worthless*."

I open my mouth to answer him but the words get caught in my throat. I shut my eyes so the Jackal doesn't see it reflected it them, the relief and fucking love, and turn around.

Whether it was watching Illi and I or something his fucking father taught him, Ash Beaumont makes zero sound as he walks into the Jackal's vault.

He remembered.

He remembered the story I'd told him, all of the details and the combination, and how to find this place. He remembered the plans Illi and I had drummed into them all, of where things are kept, of where the Jackal like to work. Every last second of training that Illi had done with him has been leading to this.

Most importantly, if he's able to creep in here like this without the rage taking over... Avery must be alive.

"Given up, Wolf? I'll have to tell your little friends that you caved to me so fucking fast, you've been gagging for me," the Jackal says, his tone cruel and smug.

"The only person gagging is me over your fucking egotistical dribble. Honestly, who the fuck would be desperate for you? Isn't that why you built this empire, so you could tempt pussy into your bed willingly? Pathetic," Ash drawls, and I open my eyes again to see the Jackal's eyes widen a fraction as the barrel of a gun is pressed to the base of his spine.

He really did think an entire fortress of men could stop my guys from finding me.

"If you pull the trigger, the bullet will go straight through," he snaps, and Ash chuckles at him.

"Good thing I'm angling the bullet so it'll go straight into that petty brain of yours then, isn't it? The real question is, do you want to die now by bullet, or do you want to step away from the Wolf and have a chance at fighting me and getting out of here alive? I've been dreaming about tearing you apart for a long time. I'd rather do it properly, with my hands."

I frown, but I keep my eyes on the Jackal. Ash should just shoot him and get this over with.

The Jackal drops his hands away from the handle of the knife right as the door to the vault opens, this time loud enough for us all to hear. I stiffen, ready to have to fight off the Jackal's men if I have to, but Harley and Illi walk through, bloody and covered in gore. Blaise steps through after them, his eyes blank until they spot me and then he's full of heartbreak. Fuck, I must look *bad*.

"Fuck. Is that a knife in her gut? You miserable fucking *cunt*," Harley snarls, and I stagger away from the wall towards him. I don't know whether I'm trying to calm him down or get help from him but I'm happy enough to leave Ash with the Jackal's death at the moment which kind of tells me the blood loss is getting bad. *Fuck*, I stumble and the pain is unreal. I'm so woozy from the wounds, this is not good.

"I heard you were so fucking pathetic at finding us and taking us out that you went to my father for help, is that true?" Ash says, moving the Jackal until he's sitting in the chair he'd strapped me to.

"Interesting man. He's got a whole fucking collection of pigs in his pocket, how are you going to deal with him when you walk out of this building? You know I've called him, right? I never start a fight without a Plan B," the Jackal says, his voice mocking and I give a hacking chuckle at him.

Harley and Blaise start to quietly snark at each other on how best to deal with my knife situation and I ignore them both as I stare down at the man I once thought of as my friend. A long ass time ago.

"You're blind, Matteo. You think Senior is the danger and, yeah, he's fucking psycho, but he's not the only person with connections."

He laughs and spits at Ash's feet, spraying his shoes. I make a conscious decision not to look down to see which ridiculously expensive shoes have just been ruined because it's an irrelevant thing I should not care about and yet here I am, giving a shit. Ash doesn't flinch, he just stares down at the Jackal like he's *nothing*.

Fuck.

Ash could give his father a run for his money, the dark void of his eyes pulling you in until you're empty too. I don't find it terrifying, I feel safe and fucking adored when

I see him like that because he only gets like that for family.

Illi hands me my knife from where he's snagged it on the Jackal's workbench, pulling his shirt off to stabilize the knife and staunch the wound at once. This ain't his first rodeo with knives in guts so I guess it'll be staying in there until we find a doctor. Ash's eyes glance down at the knife still clearly inside me and then back to my knife in my hand.

I give it to him.

If he's doing it for me, and the woozy feeling in my head tells me it isn't going to be me doing it, then it needs to be my knife.

"Oh, D'Ardo, I've been counting down the days for this," Illi crows, unstrapping one of his cleavers and rolling his shoulders back.

The Jackal shrugs, a smirk on his face like he's not afraid to die. "If you think I'm going to beg you, you've got another thing coming. I would never beg some pussy-whipped thug, you became pathetic the day you left with her."

Illi slides away from me, leaving me with Harley and Blaise, and turning to where Ash has the Jackal. "Your men are all dead. Your empire is gone. We've got both of our girls back. You're a dead man, Matteo, and worse than that… you're a forgotten man too."

Ash's eyes flick to Harley. "You got her?"

Harley cradles my face in his big palms. "Always."

Ash smirks and lowers the gun. I see the little gleam in the Jackal's eyes, like he thinks this is his chance, only Ash doesn't give him the chance to do a goddamn thing.

He shoots him in the knee.

A scream rips out of the Jackal's chest, and he collapses onto the floor. I see the blowtorch at the same time Illi does and he swoops down to grab it.

Ash ignores us all, his eyes locked onto the Jackal. "I read her file, you know. I read every last thing you did to her while you were trying to break her into something you could say was yours. I know every last thing you did and you are going to feel them all. Every last one of them."

Ash drops the gun and pounces on Matteo, snapping his leg with the heel of his boot. I watch on as he slowly, meticulously, tears him apart, piece by blood-soaked piece. Every last scar on my body now a wound on his and when finally I think he's dead, Illi hacks his head off just to be sure.

He gives me a look, his words making their way into my brain even as I start to finally pass out in Harley's arms. "We'll all sleep better knowing there's no way he could survive it."

Chapter Thirty-One

I come to when Harley carries me out of the vaults.

There's blood and gore everywhere, Illi and Ash are covered in it, and the smell is fucking foul. I groan and try to wiggle out but he snarls at me, "The knife is still in you just stay fucking still."

I stay fucking still.

Right up until we hit the cold early morning air. The sun hasn't quite risen yet but there's that cold, fresh, new feeling in the air that promises the sun is on its way. Every inch of my body hurts, from my broken nose to the raw skin on my hands to the fucking knife still in my gut. It all hurts but nothing hurts more than my freaking chest when I see the dark halo of curls, waiting with Luca and the Crow, tears streaming down her face as she reams them both a new asshole.

"Well, where the *fuck* are they then? If the entire place is clear then they should be here, I'm not *fucking* leaving until I see them."

Ash looks down at his arms and grimaces, there's no hiding what he's done. I don't think he should worry so much, Avery will not care.

As if I said her name her head snaps up and she sees me.

"*Lips!*" She screeches and rips herself out of the Crow's hands. I notice her bare feet, fucking weird, but then she's wrapped awkwardly around me and Harley as she trembles.

I refuse to tell her to stop, even if it does hurt like hell, but my guys aren't so forgiving.

"Do you not see the blood and the wounds and the fucking knife, Floss? I need to get her to the car, we can hug and shit at the hospital." Harley snaps, and I elbow him weakly.

Avery looks down and a shrill noise comes out of her that I've never heard before. "What the *fuck* happened?"

Ash hovers away from her, probably desperate to hug her and comfort her but he won't touch her while he's covered in blood, no matter how well she seems to be taking all of this. "She had her showdown with the Jackal. He got a few hits in before he got what he deserved."

Avery finally notices the blood. "That's his?"

When Ash nods her mouth curves into a little smirk. "Perfect, and Blaise? What happened to you?" She says, and I quickly look over to where he's bleeding from a gunshot wound to his arm. When I scowl at him and the sight of his blood he shrugs me off, scowling fiercely.

"It's a graze, doesn't even hurt."

What the fuck? "Who the hell shot you? They had better be dead."

Illi outright fucking roars with laughter at me. "Really, kid? And you wonder why you have admirers everywhere. How about you let your boys take you in and get the stomach dealt with, then we can start hunting for the dickhead who dared to scratch your singer."

I roll my eyes at him and turn back to Avery. "What happened to you? Are you okay? Where the hell is Diarmuid, who killed the fucker?"

Her lip wobbles but she holds it in, crossing her arms and glancing around us at the Crow's men still milling around. "I was stupid. I opened the door when I saw it was him to tell him you weren't here and he should call ahead. I didn't have my knife close and he grabbed me so quick I couldn't call out for Ash. He dropped me off and left, no one has seen him."

"It's my fault, I'm the one that inducted him. It lands with me, I'll do whatever it takes to make it right, Aves, but all that matters to me right now is that you're okay. Did he do anything?" I croak back at her, speaking around the lump in my throat. A tremble takes over her and my stomach drops.

"He… burned me a little. It's fine, I'm fine. He slapped me around a bit too when I didn't scream. I don't know how you do it Lips, I thought I was going to pass the hell out. If it wasn't for Aodhan… I don't know what would've happened."

Ash curses under his breath and, blood be damned, he crushes her into a hug.

"Get off of me, you're gross and I'm fine!" she says weakly, her voice trembling as the tears she was holding back finally fall and her arms clutch at him desperately.

She makes that little gasping noise in the back of her throat and I try not to lose my shit at the sound of it. Harley finally decides enough is enough and snaps, "We're going to the fucking hospital *now*, no more talking about shit that can fucking wait."

No one argues with him.

He carries me the whole way over to the parking lot as if I weigh *nothing* and bundles me into Illi's car, the both of us in the backseat and Illi's shirt still firmly against the bleeding mess my stomach is in.

I glance up to see who is following us and find Avery back in Atticus's arms, trembling and his head bent low as he whispers in her ear. Ash and Blaise are both watching her like they're about to rip them apart.

"Fuck. Maybe Morrison should come with us instead, kid," Illi grunts as he starts the engine, and Harley scoffs.

"No fucking way, they're dragging Avery away from that dickhead and following us."

The doors behind my family swing open again and out hobbles Aodhan, propped up by the same guy he'd brought to the meeting at Hannaford, and Avery rips herself out of Atticus's arms to throw herself at the injured Irishman.

"Well, fuck." I gasp, and Harley grimaces.

Aodhan grips her back just as firmly, even as he wobbles on his feet. The O'Cronin hovers by them both and his eyes look clearer than they had been when I first met him. Ash watches them and I don't know if it's the fact he's covered in blood or not but he looks kind of like a serial killer himself. Jesus.

"Just what we fucking need," Harley mutters, and Illi pulls the car away, driving as smoothly as the shitty, pothole filled roads in the slums will allow.

"He saved her. She told us herself, the Jackal didn't have time to do much more to her because of what Aodhan did," I murmur back, and he kisses my forehead.

"I know. I... I think I trust him now. I think Ash likes him a helluva lot more than he likes Crawford too."

I nod and let my eyes slip shut for the rest of the trip. Every inch of my body hurts but it's a great distraction for the mess that my head was in.

Once I have my stitches in, a bottle of pain meds I refuse to take in my pocket, and a fresh set of clothes on I sign myself out of the hospital. I fucking hate them after spending the week sleeping in it when Harley was drugged, and I completely ignore my family when they all bitch me out over it. I don't care, I'll survive. I've survived bullet wounds and stabbings with nothing but dirty needles and a bottle of whiskey before so I'm good. I'd rather be in agony at home than drugged in that fucking place.

Ash drives the Cadillac back to Hannaford, snapping at Blaise about his rough driving, and Harley stretches out on the backseat with me tucked into his lap. Avery laces her fingers through mine and glares out of the car window like she's hating the whole fucking world. I get it, I get how bad being tortured by that man is, I get how terrifying a shower of bullets and gunfire is when you have no weapon of your own, I get how scary it must have been to see me covered in all of that blood. I never want to put her through this again and yet this is our fucking life. There's no way I can protect her from it forever.

The stairs are fucking impossible.

I try to walk it but the first one nearly knocks me the fuck out, so I relent and let Harley carry me. Classes are in, so thankfully there's no students around to see it, because I don't even have the strength to hold onto him properly, his hands have to hold my legs in place around his waist. Avery stays tucked under Ash's arm and keeps making all of these weird gasping noises but my own head is too full of *pain* and *hurt* and *stop* to be able to concentrate on it and question her.

When we get back to our room, I insist on a shower even though I'm in absolute agony. I can't stand the smell of the hospital on me and I need to get comfortable so I can pass out for three days. Avery starts on dinner, scrubbing at every pot and pan before she cooks, and I'm positive we're going to be ordering a whole new freaking kitchen by morning. Even that isn't enough to get through to me that she's not okay, my brain is fucking scrambled.

Harley directs me into the bathroom and strips me off carefully, his frown getting darker every time I gasp or wince. When I nearly blackout at lifting my arms over my head Ash cusses us all out and grabs scissors to cut it off of me.

Thank fuck it's not one my Vanth shirts.

Then Ash rolls his sleeves up to hold me up while I shower. I'm so fucking weak I can't do much more than stand there so Blaise strips off and climbs in with me, soaping and scrubbing gently until I smell like me again. When they turn me so they can wash out the blood from my hair something breaks in me and I finally cry.

Deep gulping sobs.

I can't fucking help it. I hate the Jackal. Hated him and wanted him dead. I needed to get my family clear of his poison.

But for over half my life he's been my shadow. Not a good one but he also never let anyone else hurt me without consequence. It's not a good thing, it's not okay, but my brain is fucked up on drugs and blood loss and I'm too fucking overwhelmed with relief that he's gone to hold the tears in. I'm a fucking mess.

"I'm sorry," I croak, and Blaise pulls me into his chest, resting his cheek on my wet hair.

"You're allowed to feel shit about it, Star. It's… fucking confusing but I'm sure this is all hard for you."

I try to gulp down the sobs but it only makes them worse. "I hate him. I hate him so fucking much and I'm glad he's gone but I still feel like I've lost something. I feel like that part of me is over with and I'm fucking scared without it."

He cradles my cheeks and gives me a little peck on the lips. "It's okay. It's okay to feel like that. Let's get you dry and into bed. Sleep will help fix… this."

I stay in his arms under the warm stream of water until my tears dry up, and his hands never stop stroking and soothing my skin. I tell myself the second I get out of the shower, I will never think about that man again. He isn't ever worth mourning or remembering, that part of my life really is over.

When I have my head together I glance up to find Harley gone and Ash leaning against the bathroom sink, watching us intently. I expect him to be pissed at me, but his face is calm and blank, and when Blaise hands me over to him, his hands are gentle as he carefully dries me off. I get choked up all over again at the intensity of his love for me.

I refuse to put clothes back on, it hurt too much getting them off in the first place and everyone here has seen me naked anyway. I try not to cry as I get into my bed and Harley climbs in with me, refusing to eat or talk or do fucking anything aside from stroking one of his big palms down my spine. It hurts to breathe, it hurts to exist, but somehow I still manage to fall asleep like that.

I don't wake up for two days.

When I finally come back to the land of the living, Avery is a freaking mess.

I wake in-between Blaise and Harley, and I feel like a stinking wreck. Covered in sweat, my eyes still gritty with sleep, I need to pee so bad I think I might actually piss myself on the way to the toilet but I just barely hobble there in time.

I take a shower and though it still fucking stings like a *bitch*, I no longer think I'm going to pass out in pain. The chair someone has left for me in there helps. When I get out, I find Avery standing in the kitchen in her Chanel bathrobe, bags under her eyes, whisking eggs in a bowl. I ease myself into a chair and then curse at myself for not making a coffee before I sat down.

"Don't be fucking dense, Mounty. I can get you a coffee," Ash snaps, because apparently he can interpret my huffing and groaning, and steps up behind me to kiss the little patch of skin of my neck he loves so much.

Avery startles and glances back over at us like she had no idea we were even in the room.

"Lips! *Fuck.* Never do that to me again. No more being stabbed and checking out for days, I can't do this on my own," she hisses, looking a little fucking crazy and I give her a lopsided grin, pretending it's not agony to breathe and getting worse every second I'm sitting upright.

"I'll be fine, Aves. Everything is fine." I aim for a soothing tone, but my voice sounds fucking terrible after two days of sleep. Also, I'm kinda starving.

Ash sets a cup of coffee in front of me and I gulp it down in one go. Gimme the fucking caffeine, maybe the fine tremble in my hands is just withdrawals. He waits patiently for me to finish and then refills because he is the single best human being on the planet. I'm dumb enough to say this out loud.

"*Lies.* I am. I've been covering for you for days, I also had all of the finals moved back for you, which wasn't easy at all but I love you so I made it work," Avery snaps, still grumpy as fuck.

She places a plate in front of me, full of eggs and bacon and mushrooms, and I could cry. I mumble a thanks under my breath as I get to work, refueling being more important to me right now than anything else and Avery takes a seat next to me.

"You know I cooked French toast the last two days, hoping the smell would wake you? Figures that the morning I let the idiot boys bully me into something else you'd wake up," she snipes, sipping her own coffee and moving the eggs around on her plate.

I pause in my inhalation of the food and give her a proper once over. "What's going on? Why are you so worried about me? I know I slept but that's what I needed to do to heal."

She bites her lip. "I can't sleep. I keep dreaming about the Jackal and... what he did to me. I know that's pathetic—"

Ash and I both cut her off.

"It's not fucking pathetic."

"Don't start that shit again, Floss."

Her lip trembles but she holds it together. "Lips, you had to be stitched back together. You have internal *and* external stitches, your face looks like you just climbed out of a freaking boxing ring, and you had to kill people. You slept like the dead! I only got roughed up and yet here I am being unable to shut my fucking eyes without blinding terror. It *is* pathetic."

I shrug at her and get back to my food. "I'm pretty sure the blood loss helped me out. I'm feeling the repercussions too, Aves. My body is just taking what it needs first. You'll be ok. I can sleep in your bed with you tonight if you need."

Ash scoffs at me. "Not with all of her thrashing around you won't. I'll stay in her bed until the nightmares ease up, it's fine."

I'm not ok with this, not at all, but I keep my mouth shut and just keep chewing. I need another week to heal up, then I'll be able to fix Avery and deal with whatever she needs to have her usual fire back.

Avery's alarm goes off and Harley and Blaise both cuss it to high fucking heaven, only stopping when they realize I'm up and about. Harley lurches over to me, cupping my face and pressing his forehead against mine as he breathes me in. I'm glad I had the shower.

"You fucking scared me, babe," he murmurs, and I clutch at my necklace. It hurts too much to lift my arms around his neck, but his eyes flare when he sees the golden heart in my hand.

When he takes a seat, Blaise drops a kiss on my forehead and slumps into a seat across from me, looking like he's either hungover or halfway to the freaking flu. He gives me a slow smile. "It's been hell without you, Star. Maybe now everyone can stop being such morbid fucks now you're back."

Chapter Thirty-Two

Avery managed to push the exams back a week, thank fuck, so I have a few extra days to lie in bed and feel shitty about my wounds. I turn into a grouchy bitch but the real cause for my angst isn't the pain I'm in, it's watching Avery slowly lose her shine as her nightmares get worse and worse.

If I could go back, I'd have killed the Jackal myself and made it ten times worse than Ash and Illi did. I'd have killed myself trying but *fuck* would it have been worth it.

Ash sleeps in her bed every night and we're all woken by her thrashing around. I think about finding her some type of therapist or something, but when I ask her about it she arches an eyebrow at me and snarks, "You first, Mounty."

No fucking thank you.

When I'm finally forced to get dressed in my uniform and leave our rooms, I sit through my exams in absolute agony. I guess I've always done my best work under extreme pressure so it's not like I'm worried about my marks, but every breath feels like I'm being stabbed all over again and the walk between classrooms has my vision blurring around the edges.

Harley is a snarling, enraged asshole to everyone, and I have to remind him that he needs to do well in these exams too. It doesn't mellow him out at all and I make a note to get Avery to check his scores before they post.

There's no way I'm dealing with his sulky ass if he gets shitty scores, I'd rather we change them.

I sit for lunch and do my best to eat at least half of my plate. It's hard to do, I can't take full breaths, only shallow panting, and when he notices Ash shoves some aspirin in my hand.

"That won't get you high but at least it'll be something in your system."

I grimace but take it, it really does hurt that much.

"Shouldn't it be healing by now? This feels like it's taking for-fucking-ever," Blaise mutters, and Avery shoots him a glacial look.

"It's been a week. How about you stop acting like a spoiled toddler and join the real world. She has three stab wounds, a broken nose, and gravel burn. I think she's allowed to be in pain, asshole."

Blaise's eyes turn to slits and I nudge his foot with mine under the table to remind him to keep his cool. The dark circles under Avery's eyes are so pronounced that even her massive amount of beauty supplies can't hide them. She looks tired, brittle, sort of fragile in a way she never has before, and if he snaps at her I'll be *pissed*.

Even if she is being a little harsh.

"I'm worried about her, Floss. I'm worried she has an infection or something that's slowing down the healing. I'm worried about her, not myself," he grits out as gently as you can when you're talking between your teeth.

Avery's eyes snap to mine. "Is it red? Puffy? Do you have a fever? Why does Morrison think it's infected? Ash, we're taking her into the hospital, grab the car."

I grab her hand under the table and give it a squeeze. "It's fine. You're all just on edge because something extra shitty happened. I'm fine. Just stop getting on each other about me, wait until I'm back at a hundred percent before you start your snarking."

Harley snorts at me, filling my juice up and sniffing the glass a little before handing it over because we're all paranoid like that now. "You need to be at a hundred percent to ignore us all over lunch like you normally do, babe?"

I grin. "Yeah, takes a whole lotta energy to block you lot out."

Ash tucks Avery under his arm and murmurs in her ear when her eyes stay glued on me, assessing and critical, "I checked her out in the shower this morning, I promise you they're fine."

Avery shoves him away. "Gross. Harley was in there with her, I don't need to hear about your group sex. In fact, I'm banning you all from showering together in my bathroom the second Lips can stand in there on her own."

I squeeze my eyes shut the second I see the smug grin start on all three of my guys' faces because nope, I'm too *wounded* to deal with this. That's my excuse and I'm sticking to it.

After our finals are over for the day I tuck my arm into Avery's as we head back to our room together, slowly and steady in our steps. When we get back, Avery triple checks all of the locks are in place and then gets me set up on the couch, fussing over me like I'm the freaking queen and not just her injured friend.

I feel guilty as fuck.

She ignores me when I say that to her, just grabs us both ice cream and turns the TV on. I nudge her gently and she shakes her head at me.

"I was the one who let our family down, Lips. I knew you didn't fully trust him, I knew he forced your hand. It's my own fault I was taken and it's my fault you're hobbling around with *fucking* stab wounds."

Ok, Avery swearing still sounds so freaking wrong. I shut my mouth but only until she takes a deep, shuddering breath.

"I'm only going to say this once Aves, so listen up. You did nothing wrong. Yeah, we now know that we need to have better plans in place for this shit, but you were supposed to be safe here. Atticus has a hundred men watching this school and yet Diarmuid walked right in. I was supposed to make sure only people we trust are allowed to get close to us and yet I let him manipulate his way into our family. I can't change that, no matter how shitty I feel about it, but I'm not going to let it eat me up either. We've had a bad year. We've still got a ways to go before we're out from under it all. But we're doing it together and without any useless guilt because I swear to you Aves, not for one second have any of us blamed you for being snatched. Not for a single second. You're my sister, closer than blood, and I won't hear a word against you. Not even from you."

From the corner of my eye, I see a single tear roll down her face and she hastily wipes it away. I don't comment on it, we're not the type to cry about shit and I know how exposed you feel when the tears fucking happen. I just sit there, eating my ice cream and watching some stupid reality TV show with her as we both haven't gone through hell.

Avery sleeps eight hours straight that night.

Seniors at Hannaford get a week off after our finals.

I take this time to catch up on sleep because my body just can't get enough at the moment. Avery decides that a spring cleaning of both of our rooms is required and when Blaise tries to bitch her out about it she tells him she'll burn all of his guitars if he doesn't help.

I stay in bed.

After three days of this my skin is itching with the irritation of being stuck in one place with nothing to do, so I drag everyone into an emergency college meeting because we all seem to have forgotten we're supposed to be going to freaking college next year.

I get the sweats thinking we've missed all of the cut off dates to apply.

Avery sets a plate of freshly baked cookies on the table and rolls her eyes at me. She's going through a 'homemaking' phase as Harley and I are very secretly calling it and I swear to god I'm going to triple my weight by the time she's done with it. These cookies are to freaking die for.

She smooths down her skirt as she sits so everything is *just* so. "Whatever college you want to go to Lips, they'll take you. Between your GPA and finals scores, and the cash we'll throw at them, we're in anywhere. Just pick and I'll make some phone calls."

Blaise pops the cap off of his beer and clears his throat. "Can we talk about taking a gap year? I've been talking to Finn about doing a tour and now that Lips is insisting I actually go to college with you lot… it'll clash. Plus I think we need to take some time and actually breathe for a minute now we're not being… you know, actively hunted like deer or whatever."

It's the weirdest little speech but I also feel like a tight fist in my chest loosens off a bit. Like maybe we do need a minute. Maybe I need a minute.

Harley watches my face closely and then nods to Blaise. "Yeah, that's what we're doing. She needs this."

I snag another cookie and shove half of it straight into my mouth, talking around it like a savage, "We're going to live at the ranch, right? Like tour on a bus or whatever but our home is the ranch still? I want to unpack my bags and know that they're staying like that for… a while."

Avery clears her throat and pegs me with a gentle but stern look. "Wherever I live, you live, Lips. Us leaving Hannaford doesn't mean you need to get your own place… or decide how the hell the four of you are going to go about a plural relationship outside of school. You live with me until you want to live somewhere else. That's how we work."

Harley groans. "Are you going to get jumpy and weird about this shit now because school is ending? Can we just have fucking *normal* for five minutes?"

I honestly don't know how to do normal, but I nod my head anyway, just to keep him happy.

And we do get normal for a little while. We go back to Avery dancing and snarking us all out when she can. We get Blaise drinking a little too much at all times and singing at random times to piss Harley off. Harley goes to swim practice and the gym everyday and kisses me sweetly overnight when he crawls into my bed to hold me desperately like he can still see the blood on me when he closes his eyes.

Ash acts as though he didn't tear a man apart with his bare hands and a few small swipes of my knife. He spends a lot of time either at the gym with Harley or out picking fights in the halls with unsuspecting students. He sleeps in Avery's bed every night, even though her nightmares have stopped, because she's better but she's still not okay.

We let ourselves forget that the Jackal was only a third of our issues, right up until our week off comes to an abrupt end.

I'm sitting on the couch in Ash's lap when he gets the message.

We're watching some shitty thriller movie with the family, Blaise sprawled out on the floor and Avery tucked into Harley's side, helping him find parts online for his 'Stang. I feel the phone buzz in Ash's pocket but I ignore it, content to just soak Ash in. I miss waking up with him, not that I'd ever say that to anyone because the twins need each other right now, but I'm enjoying this while I have it.

Ash stares down at his phone, his body rigid under mine and I curse viciously under my breath. "What now?"

He stares at me for a second and then hits play on a voicemail and Senior's void-like drawl fills the room. I get freaking chills from the sound of it.

"I've spent the evening looking over your work on the Jackal. I had an old friend send me through the files on it. Well done, son. I thought I'd lost all chances of having a legacy when your slut killed Junior. I've decided to take matters into my own hands and I'm calling you home to me. Something has gone wrong in your upbringing, that you can only torture men, but now that Morningstar has arrived to take your sister, we can get you back on the right track. Say your good-byes now, Alexander. Your pathetic little family will be taken care of, your sister will be owned by the Devil and you… you're coming home."

Morningstar has gone back on his word.

Fuck.

Sweet merciful lord, *fuck.*

He never did call me back; whatever Senior has offered him must be big. My eyes snap shut and I take a second to breathe. Can't I catch a fucking break? I just wanted my family safe and left the hell alone and now this.

"We've survived the Jackal, only to be taken out by some dickhead called the *Devil?* Fuck this," Blaise snaps, stomping off to the fridge to find the beer.

Avery's hands have a fine tremble in them as she picks up her phone. "Should I call Atticus? Do we call the Boar? I need you to tell me what to do, Lips."

I know what we need to do, and none of them will like it. "Don't worry about it, Aves. Let's just get through graduation on Monday and then I'll deal with it. I've already made some calls, I have some things in place. Don't think about it until then."

Harley eyes me, aware of just how bad Morningstar really is, but I keep my face so fucking blank he'll never see through it. Finally he nods, and I don't let my relief show either.

I know then that there's nothing I can do to stop Senior, without driving myself up to the manor and killing him myself. I don't even really know if that will stop

Morningstar from finding us, but it'll get one thing off of our plate. All of our caution and careful planning goes out the fucking window because I'm not letting Avery get hurt again. I'm not letting anything happen to Ash, I'm not having Harley lose more family or Blaise lose his best friends. It's just not fucking happening. Maybe the Jackal hit something vital but not life threatening inside me when he stabbed me because I feel reckless but also I'm just fucking *done*.

I'm not in a state to go, not at all, but there's no way I can take the guys with me and Illi is still dealing with the fallout of the Jackal. The streets of the Bay have never been so dangerous, so chaotic and lawless. Now is the best time to go and deal with this man by myself.

Blaise and Harley sleep in my bed, and the twins sleep together in Avery's bed like they have every other night since Avery was taken. I lay there, silent and still, until I'm sure they're all asleep. Then I lay there a little longer just to be sure.

I slip out of bed, extra quiet, the way I had last year when the Jackal summoned me downstairs. I stare down at Ash for a second and I know, deep in my twisted and crookedly healed bones, that not only do I love him, but I'd die for him. Happily, and with such fucking conviction. He'll hate me, he'll fucking loathe me for leaving him again, but I have to. He can find someone else to love, they all can.

I could never live without them now.

I make it downstairs without any interruptions, then I boost the Cadillac exactly how Harley showed me. I hate driving, it's not something I'm particularly good at, but I get onto the highway and start the journey to the end.

Whether it's the end of Senior and the demons hunting us, or the end of me I don't know.

But it's the end.

I wait until there's some distance between the school and me before I make the call.

The Boar picks up on the first ring, like he's never too busy for little old me. It's fucking weird. He's obviously at his clubhouse, the noise is unmistakable and earsplitting.

"I need you to do something for me," I say, and he growls out orders for silence. The din quiets and I go on. "I need you to approach my family if… if what I'm about to do kills me. I need my diamonds to go to my sister. You said shit was hard for her? I want her to be set up, to get out of whatever life her junkie mom has left her in. I have close to thirty million dollars worth. Put it in a trust or something so she's taken care of. The combination to my safe is Harley's birthday, get it off of him. Avery will square it with him."

The Boar grunts at me again and growls, "Kid, where the fuck are you? Tell me so I can at least try to help. I have… someone nearby. Just tell me where you are."

I laugh, a hollow sound but fuck it, I've always had a dark sense of humor. "I'm about to go have dinner with a serial killer. My life is crazy bad, but it's all been worth it."

Ok, so I'm being a little dramatic but fuck it, I kind of think I'll be dead before help arrives so I think I should be given a pass.

Chapter Thirty-Three

I park the Cadillac up the street from the Beaumont Manor. I get out immediately and grab my bag, slinging it over my shoulder gingerly. My wounds are better but still not fully healed. I'd taken some painkillers, nothing too strong, just to help me move for a few hours. Hopefully that's all I'll need.

My phone buzzes as I start to walk.

There's no one on the streets, it's the middle of the fucking night, so I don't hesitate in answering it. If I'm going to be yelled at by one of the guys I need to give myself the time to clear my head before I go in.

What's the chances that Senior will be asleep and I can gut him quietly?

Probably not great.

"Where the fuck are you?" Ash's voice doesn't sound like his usual ice, it's fifty degrees colder than sub zero.

"I'm fixing the problem. Go back to bed," I whisper but I can hear them all moving and slamming doors in the background.

"You promised me. You promised me last year you wouldn't pull this shit again. Are you there already? Are you at his house?" Ash hisses, and I give myself thirty seconds to be weak and girlie and tear up. Then I'll be hollow and carved out and nothing but the Wolf.

"I told you I wouldn't choose," Ash says in a flat, cold voice when I don't answer. He knows where I am.

I wince but I can't back out now. I look up at the Beaumont Manor, clutching the wound at my side. The drugs are only making it bearable to move, but by no means am I pain-free.

"I'm not making you choose, I've made the decision for us all. I'm the expendable one. I'm the one that can do this. I swear to you, Ash, he's not getting out of tonight alive. No matter the cost, you and Avery will be safe. I've done this before, I can do it tonight."

I hear car doors and yelling. I have two hours to get this done before they get here. It's doable.

A car engine roars to life and Ash snarls at me, "You aren't fucking expendable. You're nonnegotiable. You're everything I've ever fucking wanted and needed, and you're trying to get yourself killed."

I swipe my cheeks and clear my throat. "I love you, Ash. I love you and I won't ever let this man touch you again. That's the line I'm drawing. I can do this."

He groans, then snaps, "I'm not saying it over the phone. You'll stay alive so I can say it to your face."

Arrogant until the end, but I hope he's right.

"Tell Harley and Blaise I'm sorry too. Tell them I love them and tell Avery I love her too, that she's the best fucking thing that ever happened to me. That being her friend has been the greatest fucking honor and if I die, she's worth it. You all made this entire fucked up life of mine... worth it." I rip the phone away from my ear before I can hear his reply, ending the call and shoving it in my pocket before I break down completely.

The first step is the hardest to take, but the second I do my feet don't stop.

It ends tonight.

I'm expecting to have to take out a whole hoard of Senior's thugs to find the serial killer himself but the closer I get to the house, the more I realize how alone I really am here. It's as if he's cleared the whole place out for me but I didn't exactly call ahead and tell him I was on my way. The psycho probably thinks he's enough to take me on by himself and, fuck, he might be. With the stitches still fresh in my gut, he just fucking might be.

My original plan is to scale the outer wall and catch the psycho fuck by surprise but the closer to the monstrosity that is the Beaumont Manor I get, the more I know that something is not right here.

I get a bad fucking feeling about walking into this place tonight.

Then I see the blood.

I tighten my grip on the strap of my bag as I walk up the steps of the manor, through the river of blood streaming down them. It looks like a fucking horror movie, nothing like the refined facade I was expecting to walk in to, and I pull my knife out of my pocket as I step through the already open doors.

Holy. Fuck.

Senior's gone off the fucking rails and killed all of his own men.

There's pieces of them everywhere, blood and bone and innards spread around like they're fucking nothing. Jesus H. Christ, an arm here and a leg hanging there... I take it all in for just a second, long enough to scout out for danger or clues, and then I ignore it all and stalk through the gore.

I need to replace these shoes the second I make it out of here alive. Just burn them and my clothes because there's no amount of scrubbing that will wash this scene away from them.

There's no sounds of fighting or dying men, the whole place is as silent as the grave and it's eerie as fuck. I try not to let shivers take over my body but something here feels fucking wrong. More than just Senior, something truly fucking bad is going on here.

I give myself a shake as I move silently through the house. My plan has gone out the freaking window, I'd guessed at this time the psycho would be asleep, but every light is the place is on and there isn't a single room without a dead body in it.

The fuck is going on?

I climb the stairs and head for Senior's private rooms. I know he has his own wing and that all of his evil happens there, but I guess tonight his evil happens every-fucking-where. I have to make it past Avery's and Ash's rooms to get there and, oh look, dead guys are piled in their rooms too.

I make a note to burn this place to the ground before Avery ever has to see it.

The Jackal has done enough damage to my Ice Queen, I don't need this serial killer doing anything else to her to her head.

The hallway that leads to Senior's rooms is dark and gloomy but there's less death up here. The plush carpet doesn't squish under my feet like the one downstairs. The only fucked up thing up here seems to be the paintings of the Beaumont's ancestors on the walls and, fuck, that's because they all look a little deranged. I make a note to ask Avery if there's any fucking normal in their bloodlines, on their father's side at least. Their mom sounded nice enough, just had shit taste in men.

The painting of Joey makes my skin crawl.

I'm busy trying not to tear the thing off the wall and shred it with my knife when the door at the end opens and Senior himself steps out. He's wearing a suit and looks as unruffled as the day I met him at that fucking dinner. There's a gun in his hand, not pointing at me yet but the threat is still clear. I slow my steps and he smirks at me.

"You've caught me at a bad time, Wolf, but I suppose I can make an exception for the little slut that stole my son."

Well, here we fucking go.

I shrug. "I've been looking forward to finally dealing with you so I'm sorry but it can't wait."

The smirk only grows and he gestures for me to enter his rooms. "Ladies first."

Like fuck. "As I'm sure you'll love to point out to me, there are no ladies here. After you, Beaumont."

It feels weird calling him that, something I usually reserve for Ash when he's being an arrogant dick, but calling him Senior seems wrong as well. He turns his back on me, like there's no chance I'd be able to stab him or slit his throat from behind, and I try not to get pissy about it. I need a clear head.

He leads me through three very luxurious rooms until we get to what is obviously his killing room. The only luxury in this room is the single plush seat sitting next to a small, fully stocked bar. I imagine this is where he watches the girls he's torturing scream and writhe in pain, sipping a fucking bourbon and enjoying the show.

Fucking gross.

The table that Ash described to me is sitting in the center of the room, all of the lights on the ceiling pointing towards it so it's the centerpiece of this sick spectacle. The bench he has with all of his carefully cleaned tools is pretty standard, nothing unexpected on it. There's a security camera setup and as the views flick through the screen I doubt there's a single inch of this property that doesn't have surveillance. Jesus, Alice never stood a chance against this fucking psycho.

He notices my eyes and walks over to the screens, again giving me his back. I slide my bag down to the ground, it was only ever here to take him out if he was asleep, and I make sure my knife is open and ready in my pocket.

Senior looks up from the security camera. "It seems my guest is making a mess of the place. I suppose this is what happens when you invite the lower classes over to play. He showed such promise, I really thought he might be able to reach Alexander but he's turned out to be such a disappointment."

So Senior isn't killing all of his own men? There's another psycho on the loose. Ah, *fuck*. It's fucking Morningstar.

"Does it matter? We should get this over with," I murmur, and he nods slowly.

He turns back around to face me, his hand sliding into his pocket casually. The smirk is back and I grit my teeth so I don't snap at him. That's what he wants, he wants me brash and reckless. I've got to keep my head.

"I think I'll have a taste of that cunt, the one that bewitches all of the men who meet you. You're pretty enough, for a piece of slum ass, but I don't feel the pull. You're already too broken for my tastes."

I ignore his words, watching only his hands. If he goes for any of the weapons on the bench, I'll see it and make my move.

"How sweet it must be to trap both my sons. The Jackal. Morningstar, himself."

I startle but my eyes stay fixed on his hands. "Oh you didn't know that? Didn't know that he was invited to come kill you and take my useless daughter? He had a good look into your life. Saw something he liked and now he's at my mansion, killing my men and making a *fucking* mess. I guess killing the Jackal hasn't stopped you from being stalked. I wonder if my son would be willing to share you with him too? Not that we'll find out. I need him home with me, my legacy where it belongs. I'll have to break him myself."

He's just trying to get a rise out of me. It all means nothing, if he gets into my head then he wins, so I ignore him and keep my focus true.

A sensor pings and Senior huffs under his breath. "More unwanted guests. The gall of you people."

Fuck. There's no way it can be Ash and the others, no fucking way. I do the math in my head twice before I take a breath. Even at the Ferrari's top speed the entire trip I still have an hour. Ash is fast and arrogant but he's still subject to the same laws of physics that the rest of us are.

Senior takes a step forward and I take a step back, watching as he shakes his head at me, his finger tracing down the length of the scalpel on his workbench. "If you came all the way here and didn't want to work with me then you're in for a rude shock, slut. Either you get on the table yourself and we do this the right way or... you displease me. That will not be satisfying for either of us."

He's talking like I'm going to enjoy being carved to pieces and killed, like this is an erotic game for the two of us.

No wonder Joey was fucked in the head.

"Apparently you didn't get the message. I live for displeasing men."

He raises the gun in my direction for the first time. "On the table now. I'd like to enjoy you without interruption."

I move slowly enough that he doesn't see my knife in my pocket, I just need to get close enough to him to use it before he sees it coming.

I don't want to touch the table at all but I slide my ass onto it without a flinch, even as the bare skin on my thighs touch it. I pray Avery got her cleanliness from him and this thing was bleached after the last time he used it.

If I'm sitting in a puddle of blood and his semen I'll lose my fucking shit at him. After he's dead.

"Lie back, I need to get you strapped in."

Ugh.

I pivot so my legs are on the table as well, ignoring the dull pain in my stomach as I slowly lower myself. The sadistic twinkle is back in his eyes and the bloodlust starts to take him over. Good. I need him all worked up.

He walks over to grab my ankle to strap it down and I take one last deep breath. Now or fucking never.

I kick my foot out and slam it into his wrist, knocking the gun out of his hand. He snarls at me but I'm faster than him, grabbing my knife and swinging it at him. He turns at the last second and it sinks into his shoulder, not his throat where I was aiming.

Fuck.

He grabs a fistful of my throat, roaring in my face and lifting me from the table. My feet don't even touch the ground as he slams me into the wall.

"You stupid whore! All of this is your fucking doing, I've lost my sons because of some worthless slum slut who thinks she can climb out of the hell she belongs in, on the shoulders of my bloodline. You are nothing. *Nothing.*" he hisses, and I focus on staying calm, slowing my pulse so I can stay conscious for longer. Passing out now means death, and when I'm done with him I still have to get out of here without the Devil finding me.

He leans his torso into me, my arms pinned, and he starts to really fucking rant about me and my dumb, slutty pussy. Men are fucking pathetic sometimes. He gets himself all worked up, badly enough that I manage to hook my ankle around his leg without him taking notice until I break his choking hold, ducking out from under his thumbs and taking his leg out on the way down. I lurch towards the workbench at the same time as he roars at me, all of his refined gentleman exterior gone.

Senior shoots towards me, but I'm prepared for how fast he's going to be. I snatch the knife and slam it into his throat. The triumph I should feel is cut out of me as the searing pain of my own knife in his hand slicing through my gut hits. Fuck.

What the hell is with these assholes stabbing me in the stomach? I'll be fucking lucky not to lose a fucking kidney or some shit at this point.

He gets his hand around my throat again and it tightens just a little before finally he lurches back, slumping down to the ground, grabbing at his throat uselessly. I'm freaking covered in his blood but I barely notice.

I slide to the ground, hacking and choking on my own blood as my mouth fills with it. He's hit something important, fuck knows what.

The bubbling finally stops and the rattle in his chest dies down to nothing.

He's dead.

Thank fuck.

The only problem is that I think I am, too.

I sprawl out onto my back, my head lolling about uselessly, and suddenly I see my own eyes staring down at me like I'm having some sort of fucking out of body experience. Fuck. They look angry, fierce, fucking furious and yeah, I guess I am pretty pissed that after everything I've done, now I'm fucking dead.

Fuck this, and then I pass out into nothingness.

Chapter Thirty-Four

The next time I open my eyes I come face-to-face with the Devil.

I mean, I've always assumed I'd be going to Hell for everything I've done, even if it's all been self-preservation, but seeing the man who is freaking legendary in the underworld for what he can do to a person is actually worse than waking up in the flames for one very vital and terrifying reason.

He looks eerily like me.

Our eyes are exactly the same, the shape, the color, everything.

He stares at me and leans back in his chair. "You can imagine my own surprise, when Joseph Beaumont invited me to Mounts Bay to play with his children, to find another little lost sister down here."

I actually feel it click together in my sluggish brain, the drugs slowing me down some. My mouth is as dry as the Sahara and hurts when I swallow. "You were sending me the heads."

He nods again, but his eyes move to the door like he's waiting for someone to show up and try to kill me. The air around him is protective, I know it well now. The guys are all the same way with me. It's… fucking jarring.

"We only have one other sister. I have no time for our brothers but Poe is… everything. You two could pass as twins. We all look like the cunt who fathered us, but you two are so similar."

I struggle to sit up but, fuck me, the stab wounds in my gut hurt like a bitch. "So, I look like our sister and that makes you feel protective of me? I don't need a bodyguard."

I've clearly lost too much blood and gone insane, because not only am I talking to the Devil himself like this but he's also just saved my damn life. That kind of proves I might need some help, just a little.

He shrugs and still doesn't look at me. "I was formally diagnosed as a sociopath at eight."

A shiver runs down my spine. Fuck. Maybe this is the part where he paints my innards all over the walls.

"I don't feel things. I don't feel happy or good about people. I enjoy cutting them to pieces. I enjoy blood on my hands. I didn't question the diagnosis."

I discreetly try to find a weapon or the nurse call button or something to get me out of this situation. He notices and looks back over at me, pinning me to the bed with a single look.

"When I was seventeen I went looking for our father. I decided it was time to end him, to destroy him for his many sins, so I rented an apartment next to his clubhouse. I watched it for weeks, and then one night I was woken up by a knock at the door. I opened it up to find a little girl, a little sister, and my heart beat for the first time. I looked down at that girl and knew that I'd kill anyone for her."

Right.

Ok, so he's got some deep-seated issues but that's noble enough and we're fucking related. I relax just a little and stop looking for weapons to just listen to him.

"Her mom is a junkie. She went back to our father to get a hit and he told her to earn it. No one in the MC wanted to touch her so she sold her daughter off instead. Our sister was six."

Fuck. I can see why the Boar said not to go looking for that man. I feel my fingers twitching to go hunting. Morningstar, the Devil, *my brother*, turns back to watch the door.

"The first biker to climb into her bed was drunk. Made him slow, easier to fight off. Poe managed to get out from under him and climb out the window. She ran to the closest house, but no one would answer her knocking. The only people desperate enough to live that close to the MC were junkies and whores. I was the only person to open the door for her. She still had blood running down her legs. I looked down at her and knew I'd never let anything hurt her again."

I find my voice again, and years of being the Wolf means it's clear as I say, "That was the MC you tore apart. How is our father still breathing?"

He shrugs. "I got her cleaned up. Got the whole story out of her. The biker managed to get his fingers inside her but nothing else, so I didn't have to take her to the hospital. I didn't know how to take care of people. I called our uncle to come get her but when he arrived she wouldn't leave with him. She only wanted me. So I told her what I was going to do and she told me she would be a good girl and keep her eyes shut. Her mother had taught her how to do that when she got high and fucked men for drugs. The junkie cunt had already left by then, didn't care that her kid was gone. Our father had left for a run so I sent him a message. I heard about his reactions to it a few weeks later and I've found I like the idea of him watching over his shoulder, living in that state of fear, while he waits for me to come find him. Someday I will."

A fight breaks out outside the room and I look up to find Harley screaming at Illi. My oldest friend, the only one left, tries to keep Harley from bursting in the room but my boyfriend is having none of that. Illi has to use every muscle, every ounce of strength in him, to keep Harley out.

If Blaise and Ash show up, it's game over.

"If you don't want to speak to me, you don't have to; I know my reputation precedes me. I'll leave you with my contact details and you can call if things go bad again. I would have been here sooner, but Poe had… an incident I had to take care of."

I look away from the brawl. "What's your name? It's not Morningstar, is it?"

He shakes his head. "Nathaniel. Poe calls me Nate. Morningstar is my middle name, my own addict mother thought it would suit me, seeing who our father is."

I take a breath and reach out to touch his hand. He's my blood and he's saved my ass. The least I can do is try. "I'd like to know you. I just don't understand why you'd want to know me. Just because I look like our sister doesn't mean you owe me something."

He looks down at my hand and I think about taking it back, but then looks back up at me and says, "One look at you and I knew I'd kill for you too. You're different to Poe, more guarded and cynical, but if anything, that proves you're my blood."

Huh.

Holy fuck. Ok.

I nod at him and squeeze his hand before letting go. "I'd like to have a brother. And I'd love to meet Poe. I'd... love for you to meet my family too."

His eyes flick out to the raging screaming match happening outside the room. Ash and Blaise arrive as we look up and Illi glances over at us. Nate stares him down.

"The Butcher is a good addition. The Beaumont kid seem to be proficient, and the mobster is decent enough. Not sure why the singer is hanging around," he says, and I gulp. I've never had to tell a brother anything, let alone about my complicated, messy, fucking perfect relationships.

"I'm dating him. And the other two, not the Butcher. I'm... with three guys."

The Devil, shit... Nate nods and says, "I know. I was planning on killing them too until I saw how they are with you. I don't give a shit who you're with, as long as it's what you want and you're not being hurt."

I look up at Illi and jerk my head to tell him to let them in before Harley hulks out and beats his face in. Ash shoves him away from the door so hard he bounces and Blaise completely ignores Nate to bundle me gently into his arms.

Harley and Ash both know exactly who is sitting by my bed.

Nate doesn't speak to them, doesn't acknowledge them at all, he just watches the door. I tuck my face into Blaise's neck for a second and then let him go when Harley yanks him off to get a good look at me.

"What the fuck happened to trusting us and not running off on your own? You could have fucking died, babe."

"She did die," says Illi from the doorway, a frown pulling the corners of his lips down. I grimace and try to smile at him.

"Sorry. Thanks for coming for me."

He scoffs at me and waves a hand at Nate. "You're lucky your brother was stalking you. He found you first, staunched the bleeding, then did CPR while I drove you both in. You'd be dead in that fucking mausoleum if it weren't for him."

I don't point out that Nate made it there first, that I'd interrupted him taking care of Senior for me. I don't think the guys will take that very well.

"Brother?!" splutters Blaise, and Avery stalks through the door with Atticus hot on her eight-inch heels.

She arches a brow at my rock god. "Isn't that obvious? You only need eyes to see it."

I swallow and stare at her for half a second before my eyes think about leaking. We made it. We're alive, the demons stalking us are dead, or I guess related, we're going to be ok. She smiles at me then frowns.

"I'm angry at you, Lips. We're having our first official spat as friends. Ash, you and Illi are on my side. Lips can have the other two idiots."

I smile at her but Ash snorts, and snaps, "Not fucking happening. I'm not on your side after the year we've had and I'll never side with Atticus fucking Crawford." Ash sneers, and I hold my hand out to him. He stares at it for a second and then takes it.

"I'm angry at you too, Mounty, but I'll wait for you to heal before I spank you."

Avery makes a disgusted sound and elbows her way over to me. "You haven't even introduced yourself to your girlfriend's brother and you're talking about spanking? Jesus H. Christ, Ash. Anyone would think you were raised by wolves."

She stops and gets this weird look on her face. We stare at each other for a second and then burst out laughing until my stitches hurt. I'm not sure if the tears streaming down my face are from joy, hysterics, or pain, but fuck it, I feel alive.

"Well, guys, this is Nate. He's my sociopath half-brother and we've decided to keep in touch. He also approves of our relationship."

Nate speaks without looking at any of us, "I didn't say I approved. I said I don't care, and as long as you're happy I won't kill them."

Avery swipes a hand over her own wet cheeks and shrugs at him. "It's a start. Avery Beaumont, lovely to meet you. Thank you for saving Lips. Losing her would have been unbearable."

Nate nods. I don't understand what the threat is that he's staring at the door so obsessively, but I decide to let it go. He's here, and he cares enough to kill for me and watch my back while I'm down.

It's more than my parents ever gave me.

Nate doesn't move from his chair for hours.

The guys all take it in turns sitting in my bed with me, forcing me to eat jello and snarling at the nurses to give me more drugs when I start wincing. Avery sits at my bedside and has a death grip on my hand at all times, like if she lets go I'll disappear again.

It's fucking perfect.

Atticus sits in the corner on his phone, completely ignoring us all, and Ash keeps watching him like he's going to knife him in the kidneys the second Avery isn't paying attention. I raise an eyebrow at him but it only makes him smirk back at me.

"Maybe wait until the drugs wear off before trying to look stern, Mounty. You look like a pouting toddler."

Well, fuck.

Illi brings Odie in to see me with pizza for lunch, which the guys inhale like it's their last meal on death row, and Avery refuses to touch it. She's looking exhausted, and I kick Blaise out of my bed to bully her into it for a nap. She's out like a freaking light the second her head touches the pillow.

Nate watches her for a second and then says, "I didn't think such a spoiled princess could be as tough as her. She'll be a good influence for Poe."

Atticus glances away from his phone for the first time and, hoo boy, I'd put money on Nate skinning him alive for the look he gives him. "She's not spoiled, she's just from a different class than your sisters. Anyone who isn't a biker brat would look like a princess to you."

Nate's head tilts. "Last person who called my sister a biker brat ended up being put through a wood chipper. The noises he made were the sweetest sounds."

Atticus holds his eyes for another second and then flicks his attention back to me. "Your friendship with the Butcher makes more sense to me now, knowing that 'deranged psychotic killer' is in your blood."

I smile at him, more teeth than sweet. "I'm taking that as a compliment, Crawford. The best people I know are all a little psycho. Avery included."

He huffs at me, and we're interrupted by a knock at the door. It swings open as the Boar steps in. Nate's eyes turn glacial and he turns to look out the window. Right, so their relationship isn't all that great after all.

The Boar doesn't acknowledge anyone, just pegs Nate with his own glacial look and says, "I've just gotten done cleaning the mess you made down at that billionaire's mansion. Thanks for that, by the way. You could've done it clean, just this fuckin' once."

Nate doesn't move or look away from the spot he's fixed his eyes to. "They deserved to die screaming, I wasn't going to give them anything less."

A shiver runs down my spine but I don't let it show.

The Boar huffs. "Well, your sister is here, Nate. Some of my boys brought her in so she can meet the Wolf."

Nate shows the first sign of life, his eyes narrow at our uncle's words. "Your boys? If he's touched her—"

"He hasn't. He's a good man, wouldn't trust him with her if he wasn't. Besides, Thorn came up with them," the Boar says flippantly, and I decide here and now that I'm *firmly* Team Morningstar.

I've been thinking about Poe all day, from the second Nate told me her story. I'm weirdly protective of her already and I haven't even met the kid yet. Fuck, how old is she? Nate looks young, is she still in grade school? Christ. I'm not good with kids.

Nate stands and presses his back against the wall where he won't be seen by anyone looking in. I arch an eyebrow at him.

"It's best if they don't know Poe's my sister. Makes her a target."

I nod. Smart. I'm starting to really like him.

"The bathroom might be a better choice, we can watch out for Lips," Avery murmurs from where she's woken up, meeting Nate's eyes like a badass bitch. I'm freaking proud of her.

He stares at her for a second and then back at me. I don't know what the look means but I jerk my head towards the bathroom with a smile. Aves knows her shit.

He closes the door behind him and Avery leans into me to whisper, "He's fucking terrifying, Lips. Honestly, I feel like he really is the devil incarnate."

I nod, and clear my throat, scared of what they all think about keeping him around.

Harley reaches over to grab my hand and says, "Family is family. He saved Lips; he's in."

Avery opens her mouth and Ash cuts her off, severely, "He's done more than that dumb fuck you're still mooning over. He's in."

She ignores his comment entirely and slides out of the bed, yawning and stretching. Odie murmurs softly in French to her, passing a fresh cup of coffee and sitting with her on the plush chairs against the wall. I must be in some ritzy hospital because every other hospital I've been in had those cheap plastic chairs.

My mind goes off on that tangent for a minute and then the door opens again and in walks a girl who has to be my sister. Holy *shit*. Poe is not a kid. She's a teenager, younger than me but not by that much. She's... gorgeous. She looks like me but without any of the demons, the dark stain nowhere to be seen. I could fucking cry all over again and it just confirms once again that I'm with Nate.

I'll fucking gut anyone who tries to take that sunshine away from her.

"Holy shit, we look exactly the same!" She squeals and bounces into the room. A dirty-blond biker steps in behind her and tips his head at Nate, who steps back out of the bathroom now it's clear Poe hasn't come up with a hoard of bikers.

"Morningstar."

"Thorn." He replies, and Poe rolls her eyes as she climbs up onto the bed next to me, careful about the wires and tubes.

"Brothers are dumb. Hi. I'm Posey, but everyone calls me Poe because Posey is a stupid-ass name."

Her southern accent is freaking adorable, especially with the curse words, and I fall hard. I glance at Avery and see the same thing on her face, even as guarded as she is. Looks like our family really is growing again.

"My name is Eclipse, but I go by Lips because Eclipse is a stupid-ass name too." I say, and Poe giggles.

"Do you think our dickhead father can only get it up for junkies with shitty taste in names?"

Blaise cackles beside me and I grin so fucking wide my cheeks protest.

Thorn kisses Poe's head and walks out. Poe calls out to him, "Don't wait up!"

I have no idea what to say to her as she glances around the room. "So, ah, who the hell are all these people? Are we planning a heist? I always thought I'd end up in a life of crime. No one tell Thorn I just said that, he'd fuckin' skin me alive."

Nate gives her a dark look. "What's he said to you?"

She rolls her eyes and grins at me. "Nate doesn't get expressions. Like, because he does skin people alive, he doesn't get that I'm not being serious. Thorn would be pissed off, is what I'm saying. He said he's putting me on the path to a blue-collar life or some shit. There's no way."

I look her over. "Is he also your brother? I'm guessing I'm not related to him, though apparently I have about a billion siblings."

Poe cackles. "Nah, Thorn and I have the same mom. He shares custody of me with Nate because Nate doesn't want his annoying kid sister cramping his serial killer style or some shit."

Illi fucking loses it, just roars with laughter until tears stream down his cheeks. "You've got a way with words, kid. How old are you?"

Poe grins. "Fourteen! Fifteen in the fall, which means I'm so fuckin' close to freedom. Nate said I had to be sixteen before he'd let me live with him and... I mean, I think I still wanna live with him. I think."

Nate's jaw clenches and I try to steer us to a safer area of conversation though I have no idea what the deal is there. I introduce Poe to the rest of the room, stumbling like an idiot over my guys and how exactly I'm supposed to explain them to her. She laughs at me, like I'm a fucking comedian. It's fucking perfect.

The Crow leaves shortly after Poe arrives and Illi takes Odie home for the night, confident that I'm safe with my guys and Nate watching over me. We order in Chinese for dinner and Poe takes a seat between Harley and Ash to eat. They all treat her like she's not just my little sister, she's theirs too. My chest aches over it all.

Nate gets a phone call and steps into the hallway to take it privately while also still guarding the room. He hasn't eaten a thing.

"Oh, whose car is that!" Poe says, peering over Harley's shoulder and he tenses a little.

"It was mine. I'm fixing it at the moment, it doesn't look like that at all anymore because someone blew it up." He mumbles, still torn up about the 'Stang.

"Who the hell would do that to such a beauty? I hope you beat the fucker." She says, prying the phone out of his hands and staring at the car lovingly.

Ash stares at her for a second and then shrugs, "Your brother cut his head off."

I shoot Ash a look, because I know she's just been joking about that shit but I'm not sure how much she really knows and let's not fucking break the kid, but Poe just laughs like a freaking witch.

"Good. Fucker deserved it. You shouldn't pay that for the muffler by the way, the guy is ripping you off," she says around her mouthful of fried rice.

Harley frowns at her curiously as he swipes his phone out of her hands. "What do you know about cars?"

She shrugs and clicks her tongue. "I build 'em with my pops. I hate school but I've never met a car I couldn't fix. I wanna drop out and work at the garage with him but I think that's the one fucking thing Thorn and Nate agree on and… never mind. Everyone agrees."

There's a hint of color on her cheeks and, *sweet merciful lord*, that's my blush. The one I get about the guys, the one that let every-fucking-one know I wanted them.

Who the hell does my sister have a crush on and how quickly can I kill him?!

Harley's eyes narrow and I know he's onboard with the killing. "Who else agrees? No lies in this family, kid."

She grins at him, so happy at being his family, and fidgets a little. "It's nothing. He's too old for me. We're just friends, he would never… I'm not someone he'd ever want."

Too old? Fuck, I need to nip this in the freaking bud.

"Just forget about guys for now, Poe. Focus on fun shit before boys tie you down." Lame, so freaking lame, but whatever. Avery scoffs at me and I shoot her a look. She should be helping me!

"You'd know, you've got three of 'em." Poe says, all sly and coy, then she scrunches her nose up at us and shrugs. "Rue's not going to be interested in some dumb kid. We're friends. I help him with cars and he beats up guys who ask me out because he thinks he's my protector like that. It doesn't matter."

"What kind of a name is Rue?" Blaise jokes.

Poe grins, "The type of name a Prez's son has. The type a future Prez has. His name is Ruin, but there ain't a biker out there without a nickname."

Fuck.

He's a dirty biker and my sister is crushing hard.

"Which MC would that be?" Avery says sweetly, like she's taking a passing interest when really she's digging for enough information to do a background check. Good. I say we shank the dickhead.

"The Unseen, back in Mississippi. When I moved in with Thorn, Rue lived next door with his uncle while his dad was in lock up."

The door opens and Nate steps back in. Poe shovels another forkful into her mouth until there's no way she could say another word and we all follow her lead.

Clearly Nate isn't big on that sister having a love life.

Good.

Chapter Thirty-Fives

Avery works her magic and by the early evening there's extra beds in the room for everyone to sleep in. I wake up to the sounds of Poe teasing Nate and his gruff replies. I rub my face against Harley's chest, wriggle a little against the hard lines of him, and he grumbles under his breath at me.

"It's fucking weird enough having your brother in the room, babe, don't make it any worse."

I blink at him. "What exactly have I done wrong? I was getting comfortable."

He gently eases me off of his chest and grumbles under his breath at me again, something about me being a drug-induced temptress, but it still doesn't make much sense to me. I must look like a freaking mess so it's not like I was trying to tease.

Nate doesn't say a word about it, or anything else, he just comes over to my bed and says, "I need to take care of something else here at the hospital. Is Poe ok with you for an hour or two? I won't be far, she's got my number."

I nod and he gives each of my guys a fierce look before heading out. I have no idea what the fuck is going on there but Poe is still laughing and full of jokes so I let it go.

Atticus arrives and I find myself wondering why the hell he's sticking around. He brings Avery and I coffee though, the real stuff not the shitty sludge the hospital has, and I think a little more favorably of him.

When he steps out to take a call Poe jerks her thumb at the seat he's just left empty. "So, who's the fuckin' suit? He some sort of dirty cop or somethin'? He looks fuckin' pissed."

I cringe. Avery rolls her eyes when Ash starts glaring at the doorway Atticus just walked out of.

She turns to Poe and speaks in her sweetest, most dangerous tone. "He's an old friend of mine. We're having a little bit of a disagreement at the moment, so Ash has decided that Atticus is the number one enemy of our family now that the others have been taken care of."

I scoff and Ash gives me a foul look, like it's all my damn fault.

"Isn't that the point of brothers? To hate any guy who comes within spitting distance?" Poe says, that sly little grin on her face, and Avery narrows her eyes at her even though it's so fucking clear she's being charmed so freaking hard by the kid.

"Is it? What do your brothers think of Rue?"

Poe cringes, her eyes darting around at us all and blushing a little under the intensity of our eyes. Or maybe just at the boys who are all now glaring just a little at the talk of this biker. "Well, Nate doesn't know I'm sweet on him because if he did, Rue would already be nothing but DNA matter. And Thorn... Thorn knows I have some feelings and he's told me if my panties come off at any point before I turn eighteen he'll tell Nate and that'll be the end of that. I think he's bluffin' but I ain't risking it. Nate's fuckin' fierce when he needs to be, and I don't want Rue dying over some stupid... crush I have."

She sounds so miserable as she trails off and, fuck it, now I want to hug her or something. I clear my throat. "I agree with Thorn about the... panties thing but once you're... ready or whatever, I'll help you tell Nate. We'll tell him together and before you start anything so he has time to adjust to the idea of his baby sister being with a... dirty, fifty-seven year-old biker named *Ruin*."

Poe smiles again, giggling and rolling her eyes at me. "He's twenty, so he'll only be a dirty, twenty-four year old biker when we have to tell Nate about him. That is, if he hasn't shacked up with some stripper or biker slut before then."

I swear to fucking God, my eye twitches and if we keep talking about this it'll be a full-blown tick.

I do my best to stay awake with them all, but I find myself randomly falling asleep while I listen to them all shoot the shit together. I wake up later in the afternoon with Poe tucked up next to me, tapping away on her phone sending a text to someone named Trink on her phone.

"She's my best friend back home. She's pissed I got out of school to come see you, there's been tests and shit all week and here I am hanging out in the party capital of the country."

I roll my eyes. "I'm never letting you come to a party here, Poe. Not ever. I'd spend the whole night gutting guys for looking sideways at you."

She giggles and wriggles down in the bed. "Do you gut them for looking at you too? Or do you just collect the hottest ones?"

I give her a side eye and she cackles right back at me. "I'm going to pretend you didn't just say that, Harley looks like he's about to have an aneurysm over there."

Poe glances over and freaking loses it at the look he gives her. "My bad, no more teasing your man meat, sis."

Man meat.

Jesus fucking Christ.

"Hand me the brain bleach, this is as bad as that one time Lips told me how much Harley would go for on the blackmarket. I could fucking gag." Avery snarls, and I join Poe in laughing, even if it does hurt like a motherfucker.

There's a knock at the door and Nate glares out the window at whoever it is that's there. Harley waits until he jerks his head before he opens the door to... fuck, I guess he's our uncle.

The Boar looks over at us all, Poe tucked up in my bed with me and Nate obsessively watching our every move, and there's a ghost of a smile on his face.

"Good to see you kids together. I'm glad you made it out alive, Wolf, I didn't get the chance to say that yesterday."

Nate's eyes flick up at him and, sweet lord *fuck*, there's his inner psycho right there. "No thanks to you. None of this would have happened if you had told me about her sooner."

The Boar shrugs. "She was happy. Doing fine. She didn't need a big brother, and when she did need you, you were here."

I cringe because I know what's about to happen before Harley even opens his mouth, and he doesn't hesitate in snapping, "She was starving, you utter *fucking* dickhead. She was starving and being stalked by a rapist psycho who thought he owned her. She's had years of abuse and because she never talked about it to you, a fellow member of the fucking Twelve, you think she was fine. Fuck. You."

Posey does this sort of gasp thing that makes my heart hurt and I hold her hand tighter. "I'm fine. It's all over and done with, I'm fine."

But her eyes stay glued to her brother.

Nate is no longer with us, that man is nothing but the Devil.

I wince as I lean forward and grab him by the arm. He doesn't tense or anything at my touch but he's so far on edge I think it'd be impossible for him to get any more agitated.

"Nate, listen to me. I don't need any vengeance for that part of my life. I'm here today because of what happened, and I would do it all over again. Don't go looking for blood on my behalf, not for this. You've got my back for the future shit, that's all I need from my brother," I murmur, and he doesn't move an inch. I don't take it personally or anything, I still don't know how to talk to him yet, and I consider how else to calm the rage in his blood.

His eyes finally flick to mine and then down to Poe. "This is why we only trust each other. Anyone else is a liability."

Fuck. I'm saved from answering him by Poe snorting and saying in her teasing tone, "Well, I have a whole fuckin' heap of people I trust so maybe you need to rethink that line."

Nate turns his back on the Boar dismissively and I nod to… our uncle. Fuck, that's still weird to think.

The Boar doesn't seem to care, he just turns back to Poe with a wry smile. "Thorn and the boys are downstairs, kiddo. They're here to take you back to the clubhouse for the night then you'll ride back tomorrow."

Poe pulls a face and wraps an arm around my shoulders. "If I could, I'd stay. If Thorn would let me but he's already told Nate I could only stay the night here. Promise me you'll call though. Promise?"

I swallow the lump in my throat. "Of course I will. You have my number, and everyone else's so if you need anything, Poe, anything at all, you just call. Any of us."

She smiles and hugs me again, her chin wobbling a little. "You too. Not that I'm much help, though I did totally save Harley a couple of grand on that muffler."

He smirks at her. "We'll come see you when I have the rest of the parts, kid. You can help me put it back together."

The grin that lights up her face is fucking unreal. I love it. Harley catches my eye and I give him a nod.

"I'll walk you down. Too much bad shit has happened lately, I'm not letting anything happen to the baby of the family," he says, and Poe grins so fucking wide my heart clenches. This kid needs a family. She needs people loving her. Well, I'm up for it.

I watch them both walk out and then I heave myself up so I can peer out of the window to look out over the car park. There's a heap of motorcycles and bikers loitering, but I make an educated guess at which one this Rue guy is. He's pacing, twitchy and pissed off, and that makes me twitchy and pissed off.

He looks like a fully grown man, and my baby sister is in love with the fucker.

"I say we gut him. Too late to take care of Atticus, but let's not ever let that happen again," Ash murmurs in my ear, and I shiver.

"Agreed. I don't like him."

Blaise snorts at the two of us from the chair he's still firmly planted in, though he does stare at the pacing biker with as much interest as we have. "You haven't even met him yet. She's not going to be happy about you guys even lightly maiming the guys she's sweet on."

I grit my teeth. "Fine. All we need to do is tell Nate about him and then we're golden. Job done."

I glance back to the carpark. Harley has an arm slung over Posey's shoulders as they come out of the hospital and into our view. My heart clenches, I'm so fucking happy they get along, and then I see exactly what he's doing when Rue's pacing slams to a holt, his spine snapping straight as he gets an eyeful of my golden god cuddling up with my baby sister.

It's fucking perfect.

Blaise freaking cackles and hoots like an idiot, but Ash just glares down at the biker like he's planning on dismembering him before Nate gets the chance to.

Not long after Poe leaves, I decide I can't fucking stand being in the hospital for a second longer. I tell Ash I want to leave and there's something in my voice that lets him know I mean business.

We're being discharged thirty minutes later.

Nate watches me emerge from the bathroom wrapped firmly in Harley's arms and I do my best not to blush like an idiot. I clear my throat and Harley, noticing all of the attention we're getting, props me up against the bed and takes a step back to let Nate say whatever it is he needs to say.

"I'll head out to keep an eye on you and Poe tonight. Call me, Wolf. I'll come whenever you need. I mean it, you *will* call me from here out."

I nod and feel freaking emotional as hell at him leaving. He watches me closely and then holds out his arms. Holy shit, he wants a hug?

"Poe taught me sisters need hugs," he grumbles, and I step into his arms.

"Maybe normal sisters do, but I'm fucking broken," I say, but I enjoy the hug anyway. How different would my life have been if he'd have found me a little sooner? Before Matteo became the Jackal, before the war in Mounts Bay started?

No. I would never have met my guys. Ash and Avery would be dead at Senior's hands. Harley would be killed by the O'Cronins. Blaise would be... dead too, suicide or alcohol probably. No. If everything I've been through, fought, and conquered got us here then it's worth it. And now if anything happens again, well.

We have the Devil on our side.

"You know you can call me too, right? If you need anything, or Poe, just call and I'll be there."

He gives me a look, like I'm a mystery or something. "You don't owe me anything, Lips. You don't have to pay me back for protecting you."

I shake my head at him. "Well, here's another lesson for you from a sister; family means ride or die. You're not only my blood, you've been voted into my family, my inner circle. That means call me, anywhere, anytime, for anything, and I won't be the only one to show up. My whole fucking family will."

Nate nods and pauses for a second before saying, "Posey tell you about the biker she's been making eyes at?"

Ah fuck. Apparently, Poe hasn't done such a great job of hiding her feelings for Rue after all. I nod hesitantly.

"He makes a move on her before she's eighteen and he's dead. You with me on that?"

I sigh. "Yeah, I am but I should warn you that I promised her I'd help her to convince you not to kill him when the time comes."

Nate nods and looks over my shoulder at the guys. "Once she's old enough I don't care. I'm not her fuckin' jailer. Though, bikers are known for being whoring, abusive, spineless cunts so if he so much as looks sideways at her I'm going to blood-eagle him and enjoy every fucking second of it."

Blood-eagle?

I'm not sure I even want to know what that is, but I nod. "I'll help you if that happens. Whatever it is, I'll help just so long as it's for the right reasons. I don't want to push Poe away by trying to be too overprotective. The girl needs to live."

And I'll keep telling myself that until it sticks, because I'm still firmly in favor of killing Rue right *the fuck* now. Avery smiles at me like she knows the words nearly fucking killed me to get out and Ash looks at me like I've betrayed him, *goddammit*.

We all walk down together and then Nate leaves in a car that has Harley fucking drooling. I have no clue what type it is but apparently it's fucking good.

I leave the hospital in one of Ash's Ferraris so doped up on pain meds I ramble and cackle like a fucking loon. It would be way more embarrassing if Ash wasn't shooting me all of these little looks and biting his lip like I'm fucking delicious or something.

"You are delicious. I'm going to get you home and spread you out. It's been way too fucking long since I've tasted that pussy."

Avery gags in the backseat.

Right.

I forgot she was in the car as well.

"Oh, I know you've forgotten all about me, Mounty. I'll forgive you because of the blood loss. Just this once."

I fucking love her.

"I love you too, Mounty."

Chapter Thirty-Six

The ranch feels different now we're not just hiding out here.

It still feels like home, but it's not the secretive hiding place it was before. I take a few weeks to heal up in bed and it's fucking amazing to do that without worrying about being attacked. We get a lot of takeout delivered. Illi and Odie come over for dinner a few nights a week, and when Jackson and Viola find out about it, they tag along too. I unpack my bags and find places for my things to live in. I get the overwhelming sense of belonging here and it takes me a week or two to come to terms with that.

I still sleep with my knife but it's not the first thing I grab when I wake up in the middle of the night anymore.

Avery still isn't sleeping. She's still my perfectly snarky, evil genius best friend but there's shadows in her now that weren't there before. I hate it, I hate that she still doesn't want to talk about what happened in that room with the Jackal, but I don't push her. I just spend a shit-load of time with her and guard her fiercely.

It's why her announcement at family dinner shocks the shit out of me.

Illi, Jackson, and my guys are talking about car parts, and Odie has roped me into a conversation about college I'm still not ready to have while Viola smirks, when Avery clears her throat delicately.

The talking stops instantly.

"I know Morrison has been talking about doing a tour and the assumption is that I'll be tagging along. I just wanted to let you all know that I'll be staying here. I have some remodels being done on the ranch that I need to be here for." She says, and then she takes a sip of her wine like she hasn't just ruined dinner.

Ash's eyes narrow at her. "Why would you need to stay behind? You've had the rest of the place done while we were at school."

Avery's back straightens. Good lord, here we go. "I don't have to ask your permission, Ash, I'm not going. This place is secure, Senior and the Jackal are dead, Illi is here if anything happens. I'll be perfectly fine."

Harley and I share a look while Ash grips his knife like a psycho. I hold up a hand. "She's right, she'll be safe here and she's been forced into a constant security detail for years. I'll miss the absolute hell out of you, Aves, but I also get it."

Illi tips his head at me like I've made the right call and I grin at him. "You'll call if you need me to come home."

He laughs. "Kid, you won't have to come home because if anyone gets close to her, I'll sell their body parts on the black market. I hear kidneys are going for a good price these days."

Jackson and Harley both snicker at the look Viola gives Illi but nothing can distract Ash from his temper tantrum.

"You've never cared about being stuck with us before, you've always preferred to have us all together. You bought this fucking house to fit us all in comfortably. You're already talking about where you're going to put Posey's room for when she comes to stay. Fuck, you've been looking into how the fuck we can adopt her. What's the real fucking reason Avery?" he hisses, and I slip my hand into hers under the table. I fucking hate it when they fight and doing it now, in front of everyone, is only going to end in blood.

"I'm not leaving him," she snaps back, and there it is; the same fight I've been listening to for the entire freaking year.

Ash throws his cutlery down onto the table and leans forward in his chair. "You are not staying behind with that gutless fuck Crawford and—"

Avery interrupts. "I'm not talking about Atticus, I'm not leaving Aodhan."

Well, fuck me.

Fuck me sideways and eight times on a Sunday, what the hell does that mean?

The whole table just kind of sits there in silence while we figure out what the actual fuck to say to that. Harley recovers first.

"He's fine, Floss. I spoke to him this morning, he's alive and getting back into the swing of things."

She nods. "I know. I'm going to visit him tomorrow, we've been talking. I would just rather not leave him right now while we're both still… recovering."

Right, what the actual fuck happened in that room? What the hell is going on, I need some fucking answers. I give her hand a little squeeze and she smiles at me but it's a little forced.

Now I don't want to go on tour either.

Illi and Blaise manage to steer the conversation back to safer topics and we get through the rest of dinner. Avery insists on scrubbing all of the dishes herself by hand, fuck the two dishwashers her kitchen has apparently, and I walk everyone out.

Illi and Odie are busy telling Viola a long-winded story when Jackson stops by the door with me. I tense, waiting for his usual snarky teasing bullshit but he gives me a wry grin instead.

"So… the Devil is in your pocket now too? You're a very popular young lady. Must be all the self-sacrifice. You're pretty fucking quick to throw yourself in front of bullets for people."

I give him a look. No one outside of the hospital room has been told about Nate, I was fucking clear with my family, so unless Atticus has told him… how the fuck does he know?

He grins at me. "I told you, I wiped your name from existence. He had to get it from someone who already knew it."

My mind blanks out with rage and I just stare at the fucker for a second.

"You knew? You gave it to him?" I snap when I finally remember how to speak, and Jackson rolls his eyes at me.

"Look, if the Devil shows up at my door, you'd best fucking believe I'm going to tell that motherfucker whatever the *fuck* he wants to know. Besides, he's your brother right? He was helping you out by killing people for you? I thought you'd forgive me for telling him your name. You're welcome, *Starbright*."

I don't even think about it, my knife is just suddenly in my hand and I flick it open and press it to his femoral artery because it's the closest and the one all guys freak about. "Don't. You. Ever. Fucking. Call. Me. That."

Jackson swallows, his eyes wide as he slowly nods his head.

I press just a little harder for a second and then calmly say, "You're lucky you're family and that the Devil is my blood, otherwise I'd kill you. To be clear, you ever rat me or any other member of our family out again and you'll beg for me to kill you once I'm through with you."

He nods again, a little jerk of his head, and says, "You know, I really do see the family resemblance."

I slip the knife back into my pocket and bare my teeth at him in a savage grin. "You have no idea."

Avery won't talk to me about what's going on with her.

She tells me she's not ready yet, that she has to figure it all out in her own head first before we can talk about it, but it's all slowly eating me up inside. I have to bite my cheek and remind myself that this isn't about me, it's about her and if she needs time then fuck it, I need to give her time.

Even if it's killing me.

I make it down to the sitting room in time to see her and Harley off as they leave to go see Aodhan. If I weren't completely certain she still loves Atticus I'd think she was dressing up for Harley's cousin because she looks fucking devastating in her long Chanel coat. You can't tell if she's wearing a dress or not underneath and the long stretch of her legs will probably cause Harley all sorts of trouble for the night because men are going to come running. She's wearing one of her new pairs of Louboutins, the ones Blaise had gotten her for Christmas, and the slash of red lipstick and perfectly styled curls completes the look and tells me for sure that this girl is on the warpath of some kind. Whether she's dressing to impress or she's just trying to get some of herself back, I don't know but I love it.

"Harley's going to take me to visit Aodhan and Jack, and I think Illi will meet us there too. He said he has business there tonight but I'm sure he's just playing mother hen for you," she murmurs as I very carefully hug her, I don't want to ruin all of her hard work or pull at my newly healed skin.

"I'm a little jumpy about you heading back into the Bay. I'm actually surprised Ash didn't insist on going as well."

She leans back so I can see the eye roll. "He did. I told him to fuck off."

I wince. It's never a good thing when Avery drops the F-bomb and I feel like it's all I hear out of her these days. "I'll try to keep him busy so he doesn't text you the whole time. Call me if you need anything."

She smirks at me as Harley jogs down the steps looking fucking edible in a pair of jeans and a tight white tee. Yum.

"You should fuck him, might cheer the arrogant dick up a bit. You've probably healed up enough to do it if you take it easy," Avery snarks, and I choke on my own damn tongue.

"Since when do you wanna weigh in on our sex lives? Especially Ash's?" Harley asks, eyebrows nearly in his damn hairline.

Avery tucks her arm in his and slides her phone into her pocket delicately. "Lips and I talk about it all the time, we just choose to do it away from you idiots. Besides, Lips loves me and wants me to be happy. Ash mellowing out a bit would make me very happy. Fuck him for me, Mounty."

I turn on my heel and leave them to it. I'm not exactly embarrassed but yeah, I totally don't need to be thinking about Ash's dick and drooling in front of his twin freaking sister, especially after the few weeks I've gone without sex on doctors orders to heal up. Avery and Harley both laugh at me as they leave but, fuck it, that's not unusual and I'm glad Avery sounds happy for once. This year has been fucking hell on that girl.

I wander around the ranch looking for Ash but the asshole must be hiding. I find Blaise swimming in the pool so I sit on the edge and dangle my legs in, my toes skimming the heated water.

"You should hop in," Blaise drawls, looking like a fucking dream with the water sliding down his chest in tiny rivulets.

I shake my head. "I don't want to tire myself out, I'm just barely getting around as it is. I'd rather just watch you."

He smirks and swims over to me, his arms arching through the air and, lord help me, there's something about the colors and patterns of his tattoos that pull me in.

"You look lost, Star."

I shiver. "I can't find Ash. Do you know where he's hiding?"

He pulls himself out of the water using only the strength in his arms and my panties just fucking combust for him. He grins at me like he knows all about the inner workings of my brain and I pull a face back at him.

"He's hiding on the balcony in our room, smoking a joint and being a morbid dick. What do you need him for?"

I wrinkle my nose. "I'm supposed to be finding and fucking him for Avery."

Blaise tips his head back and roars with laughter. "That lucky dick, using his sister to get laid. If I start pouting and throwing tantrums will you fuck me too, Star?"

I groan at him and he pulls me up and into his arms, sitting on one of the poolside lounge chairs, ignoring the fact that he's getting me wet and I don't see a freaking towel anywhere. I'm pretty sure this chair is the same one we kissed on, right before he carried me to his room and fucked me for the first time.

I hum under my breath happily at the memory.

We lay there quietly and I let my eyes slip shut, content to just be there with him, relaxing and carefree as if we're just normal eighteen year olds who haven't just been through hell together.

"Well isn't this just fucking cozy."

I glance up to find Ash scowling and broody, a glass of bourbon dangling from one hand. He looks like the spoiled rich asshole I truly thought he was when I first laid eyes on him. Okay, he kinda is exactly that, but he's also mine.

"Your sister is trying to get you laid. I'm calling that a party foul and against the rules," Blaise snarks, and I groan at him. He laughs and folds me into his chest.

Ash stretches out on the chair next to ours and when he puts his glass back down on the ground after taking a sip, I thread our fingers together.

"Does that mean the dry spell is over and you feel up to it, Mounty?" he drawls, and I curse the stupid flush my cheeks get.

"I'm not sure you have gentle sex in you, Ash. You might have to wait another week or two."

He chuckles at me, a possessive twinkle in his eye, and then he and Blaise start bickering over pointless shit and I zone them out. With a sigh, I press my head down onto Blaise's chest and look up at the stars, Ash's thumb running over my knuckles as he talks.

I know we're not completely safe, I know there's more than enough monsters hiding in the shadows for us, but right at this second I *feel* safe and loved and like the whole thing, all of the blood and death, pain and heartache, the whole lot was worth it.

My family was worth it all.

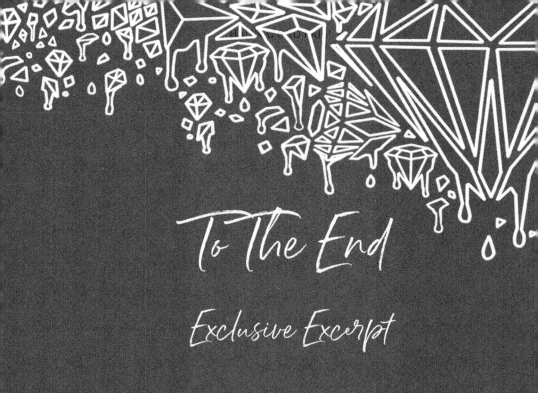

To The End

Exclusive Excerpt

ILLI

There's blood *everywhere*.

It means fucking nothing to me usually but my gut curls at the sight of it. I haven't prayed for anything since Odie was taken from me, not since the safe house at least, but I find myself fucking begging that Lips is okay.

Fuck, don't let it be the kid. Let it all belong to Beaumont and his army of bodyguards, let it not be her.

I take the stairs three at a time, barely registering any of my surrounding except that the bodies are all definitely male so far. They've been hacked to pieces, strewn around, blood spatters everywhere. Fuck. There's only one person that could be responsible for this type of death.

I make it to the top flight of stairs and start searching the fucking dozens of rooms to find her. It's pretty fucking clear that this place will never come clean from this mess. We'll have to burn it to the ground once I have the kid.

Fuck.

Please let her be alive.

Nothing. She's not fucking here. I run past the ugly as fuck portraits and make it through the far set of doors, down a dark corridor and find myself in a serial killers play room.

Joseph Beaumont Senior is dead.

Bled out on the ground like a pig.

I'd be fucking thrilled at the sight except the kid is splayed out next to him, the Devil himself rummaging around in her guts like a fucking psycho and something snaps inside me.

"Get the fuck away from her, you fucking piece of shit."

He doesn't react, his head doesn't lift up towards me at all, but my blood turns to ice at the sound of his voice.

"I'm assuming you brought a car, go get it started. She needs a hospital."

I take two steps forward before his words register. "What the fuck did you just say?"

He looks up at me and holy fucking shit.

Holy.

Fucking.

Shit.

"She needs a hospital so get your fucking car started before I skin you alive myself for the keys." He says, every word out of his mouth a promise he could keep without breaking a sweat.

My eyes flick down to where he's packed her wounds. Fuck me.

"You got her or am I carrying her down? My car is still running, let's fucking do this."

He ignores me, lifting the kid up and cradling her in his arms with such care I could fucking keel over in shock.

The Devil.

The kid.

Related.

Fuck my actual life, why hadn't I seen it before?

"If she dies, I'm killing you and every last one of her friends for letting her come here alone."

He moves fucking quick, my own legs taking a second to come good underneath me. "No fucking problem there, if she dies her guys will self-destruct."

Acknowledgements

To Greg: Thank you for believing in me and this lifelong dream of mine. Thank you for the writing weekends away, for hanging out on the couch by yourself all night while I tap away at the keyboard, thank you for telling everyone you know about my dream and how proud of me you are.

To my Mum and Dad: Thank you for everything you have done for me. For making me who I am today, for endless babysitting and support, for cheering me on, for always being a phone call away. Thank you for living across the road and popping over at the drop of a hat. Thank you for all the coffee, cake, and therapy.

To my sister: Thank you for cheering me on and helping out whenever you can. Thank you for loving my kids like they're your own and thank you for letting me do the same with yours. Thank you for listening to me ramble endlessly about things you don't know or care about with a smile on your face.

To Laura, my ride or die. You're perfect and our friendship the best thing this little series of mine has given me. Thank you for everything you have done for me and my family, and for this book and the little community of readers we've found. You're my favourite weirdo.

To Katy, thank you from the bottom of my heart for all of your support, encouragement, love, understanding, and dick gifs. Thank you for always being there for me when things go south with my story, which is too often.

To Sloane, thank you for all of your support and encouragement, for being available at the drop of a hat to help with my melt-downs and flailing. Thank you for all of the sprints that helped me get this book finished when I thought it might never come together how I wanted it too.

To everyone in my Facebook group, you all give me life and make this whole journey so much fun. Thank you from the bottom of my black stained heart.

And thank you to my amazing readers who gave Hannaford Prep a chance.

Printed in Great Britain
by Amazon

42194265R00423